VORTEX CHRONICLES

THE COMPLETE SERIES

VORTEX CHRONICLES

THE COMPLETE SERIES

ELISE KOVA

Silver Wing Press

Published by Silver Wing Press
Copyright © 2020 by Elise Kova

Cover Artwork by Livia Prima
Editing by Rebecca Faith Editorial
Proofreading by Kate Anderson

eISBN: 978-1-949694-20-8
ISBN (paperback): 978-1-949694-21-5
ISBN (hardcover): 978-1-949694-22-2

Books in the Air Awakens Universe

AIR AWAKENS SERIES
Air Awakens
Fire Falling
Earth's End
Water's Wrath
Crystal Crowned

GOLDEN GUARD TRILOGY
The Crown's Dog
The Prince's Rogue
The Farmer's War

VORTEX CHRONICLES
Vortex Visions
Chosen Champion
Failed Future
Sovereign Sacrifice
Crystal Caged

A TRIAL OF SORCERERS
A Trial of Sorcerers
A Hunt of Shadows
A Tournament of Crowns
An Heir of Frost

Also by Elise Kova

MARRIED TO MAGIC
A Deal with the Elf King
A Dance with the Fae Prince
A Duel with the Vampire Lord
A Duet with the Siren Duke

LOOM SAGA
The Alchemists of Loom
The Dragons of Nova
The Rebels of Gold

See all books and learn more at:
http://www.EliseKova.com

CONTENTS

APPENDIX

About the world of Vortex Chronicles

Head to the Appendix at the back of the book,
page 985, for maps, pronounciation guides,
and more about the book.

"You did well, but things are only beginning now.
The vortex still spins."

— *CRYSTAL CROWNED (Air Awakens, #5)*

VORTEX VISIONS

VORTEX CHRONICLES

BOOK ONE

for the dreamers who never woke up
and the doers who never gave up

I N THE DARKNESS, A bitter smile crossed her lips.

It's just a candle, Vi told herself. One single candle in the holder at the edge of her bedside table. Vi took a deep breath, trying to quell her nerves. It was ridiculous, laughable even; she was a *Solaris* for the Mother's sake. Yet she was more daunted by this one candle than she would have been facing down a beast in the jungle.

Most Firebearers could light it with a thought. She should have been able to do the same. Vi's hands balled into fists, clutching her bed sheets over her knees. Deep within her was an insurmountable wall. She was on one side, barely able to do more than dredge up a spark of magic. On the other was the power of her forefathers.

Her fingers relaxed, and she reached out. The burnt wick drew a dark line of soot across her hands, nearly invisible in the night.

"It's just a candle," Vi repeated aloud, searching for a sliver of magic. "A tiny spark, that's it."

White lightning flashed in the darkness between her fingers. The wick caught the heat, ignited, and she breathed a sigh of relief. For a brief second, Vi watched the fire dance around her fingertips and imagined the stable little flame was her own.

Vi pulled her hand away quickly, pushing aside the thinly woven blanket covering her bed along with the thought.

She didn't have time to spend on fantasies. There were things she wanted to do and not much time to do it. Her obligations as the Crown Princess would begin all too early.

The air was heavy with the aroma of fresh wood, sap, and the damp tang of morning. Vi had smelled this perfume her whole life. Her chambers were cut into the trunk of one of the massive trees of Soricium—capital of the North. The wooden walls of her room were sleek, polished. They contrasted with the gnarled ceiling of decorative roots and branches that spilled down, weaving into each of the four corners of her bed, all crafted by the magic hand of a Groundbreaker.

As she moved beyond the foot of her bed, the halo of light from her candle glinted off gilded frames lined on the dresser opposite. There were several, but they all contained carefully painted portraits of the same three people—her mother, father, and brother.

The family she should have been reunited with three years ago. The family that lived far to the south in the Empire's capital, Solarin. The family that had traded her away in a political deal.

"Another year," she murmured to the pictures. Her eyes landed on the flaxen tresses of her brother—a direct contrast to her own dark locks. No one would guess they were twins by looking at them. Vi tried to swallow the lump that grew larger in her throat the longer she looked at the portrait. "Happy birthday to you, too, brother."

Vi turned away from the painted, staring eyes of her family and toward the small pile of supplies stacked in the corner between the dresser and her window.

Everything was as she'd left it the night before, and the night before that. Her quiver hung on its peg, bow attached, the fletching of half a dozen arrows peeking out from the top. A metallic sun—the Solaris sigil—glinted as the candlelight moved over it before illuminating the clothing she'd neatly folded on a chair underneath the quiver.

She would only be gone for three days. Not much was needed. But Vi took stock of every article of clothing and ration as though her life depended on it.

Three precious days of freedom were all she got every year.

It was the best thing her birthday had ever brought her.

"One more thing and I should be set," Vi muttered to herself, straightening away from her packing. Grabbing her candle, she strode out of her bedroom.

The living space of her quarters held a table and two couches for her use—though Vi rarely used them when she was alone.

Which meant she rarely used them at all.

The main entry had four doors; the bedroom Vi just left was one. Clockwise, the next door led to her personal study, after that was her classroom, and then the main door which led to an outer balcony that connected to the rest of Soricium's fortress by rope bridges and wide branches alike.

She'd always thought of her chambers like a daisy. The sitting room was its yellow center and everything else spun out around it like petals in the trunk of a giant tree.

Vi ventured to her study.

In the daytime, the room would be illuminated by the window above the drafting table sandwiched between the bookshelves that lined the walls. Now, her candlelight fell on every hanging map and book spine. But it also revealed something that shouldn't be there.

Candle wax dribbled over the edge of the holder and onto her fingers, but Vi didn't notice. Her breath caught in her throat as she engaged in a staring contest with five foreign objects. It wasn't the first time presents had been left for her, but it caught her off guard every year.

Some wicked little corner of her mind would always tell her that *this* would be the year her family would give up on her. That they had never wanted her to come home to begin with—never wanted *her* to begin with. The doubts would compound into stories about how her parents had been eager to make the deal with Sehra, now Chieftain of the North. That the peace assured by Vi spending her first fourteen years of life as a ward was only a fringe benefit, and not the main goal.

She knew better. The deal had been struck well before Vi was conceived. Before her parents were even wed. Had it not been for it, she may not even exist, as her father was originally betrothed to Sehra… But every time her birthday approached, Vi seemed subconsciously keen to avoid logic, and the doubts grew louder.

And every time she saw the stack of presents, the doubts were silenced for a blissful second. Vi crossed the room, resting her fingers lightly on the ribbon of one of the packages.

"When did he stash you in here?"

Setting her candle down, Vi gravitated to a suspiciously cylindrical present wrapped in Solaris blue and Imperial gold. She recognized her brother's script on the card.

The Senate had never let her brother come north to visit. They'd argued that having both heirs in the hands of former enemies of the Empire was far too great a risk, making a huge deal of it every time it was brought up. So while her mother and father had visited, Vi only knew her twin through letters and portraits.

Vi unwrapped the delicately embossed paper, exposing the contents within. As expected, it was a document tube. Even on her most bitter day of the year, Vi found a smile. Only a map from her brother could do that.

Carefully sliding out the parchment, she unfurled the delicate blueprint.

"The Solaris Castle—Rose Garden," Vi read aloud, then set about finding an open spot on her shelves to pin the sketch among the others her brother had sent her of the castle in Solarin.

The bookcases were so cramped that not even shadows could squeeze between the spines—packed to the brim with manuscripts of all shapes and sizes, scrolls, and stacks of papers. Pinned on the outward facing edge of the shelves were maps, some created by professionals, others drawn entirely by or embellished with her own hand. In the swirling lines of ink and charcoal were countless stories of places she'd never get to see, and yet, felt like she somehow knew.

Places that she longed to someday visit… if she only ever had the chance.

Vi found a relatively open spot, tacking the blueprint in place by its top corners so she could lift it to still access the shelves behind. Her fingers trailed the lines of the architect's skilled hand, and she silently thanked whatever nameless artist her brother had found this time.

Returning to her table, Vi skimmed over the gifts from her parents, Aunt Elecia, and Uncle Jax. They were of predictable shapes, mostly books. It made a singular, strange-looking parcel stand out all the more.

It was wrapped in black silk and nearly feather-light. A small black envelope had been slid under the black ribbon, fastening it together. Vi undid the knot at the top, lifting the letter and affirming her suspicions.

Black was a peculiar color in the Empire. No one wanted to associate with it… unless they were a Sorcerer.

On the back of the envelope was a silver seal: a dragon curling in on itself made a perfect circle, split in two and off-set. It was called the Broken Moon, and it was the symbol of the Tower of Sorcerers.

She slid her finger underneath, gently tearing open the letter.

Dear Vi,

Forgive my informality in addressing you, but you will always be a dear child to me as I have been by your mother's side since long before you were born. I was there waiting as she delivered you and your brother. I held you when you were a babe. And your mother is still one of my dearest friends in the world, confiding in me all the pains she feels at your absence.

I have only ever known and loved you as Vi, nothing more or less.

When your mother was seventeen, she began to manifest and was Awoken to her powers with the help of your father. She has consulted me with her worries surrounding the fact that your powers have yet to Awaken. I have told her not to fret, and will pass on the same advice to you. I believe in you, Vi.

That statement was nearly enough to make her stop reading and throw the letter in the trash.

Not to worry, that was easy to say by someone across the world who knew nothing of her. What could this man possibly understand about her struggles with her magic? Vi doubted he had been born into a long line of illustrious Firebearers, only to have his magic be nothing more than a cheap parlor trick.

Still, curious about the package, and already halfway through, Vi kept reading despite herself.

I would like to offer this token to remind you that magic has an odd way of finding us when we need it most.

It has been in my possession since before you were born. Many years ago... When the world was at its darkest, and hope seemed all but lost, your mother found the strength to overcome overwhelming odds and be reunited with her power, thanks to this. I've held onto it for years as a reminder to never give up, no matter how impossible a situation I may find myself in.

Now, I think you may need it more than me. Perhaps it will help you find your magic, as it helped rekindle your mother's after her channel was forcibly closed.

Your friend who cannot wait to meet and teach you,

Fritznangle Chareem, Minister of Sorcerery

Her eyes lingered on the word "teach." There was nothing to teach. He'd said it himself, didn't he? That he understood her magic had yet to fully Awaken?

Still curious, Vi looked to the parcel, unwrapping the silken scarf to reveal a small, silver necklace.

"A locket?" Vi lifted it, squinting at the chain. She couldn't place where she'd seen the links before, but was certain she had. There was an undeniable familiarity about it. The chain fastened around a loop at the top of the locket where there was a small button she depressed. She stared at the plain face—white with black numerals. "A watch." Vi continued to stare at the hands, but they were still. "A... *broken* watch?"

It was certainly an unexpected gift. Her father had been known for his love of watch-making, a fascinating art that was said to have originated in Norin. Perhaps this had once been a gift from him to her mother?

Vi snapped the cover closed. In the motion, her spark leapt from her fingers unbidden. The arc of white-hot lightning crackled around the watch, engulfing it, and for a brief second, there was something there… but her attention was immediately stolen by the second arc of flame—which landed on her drafting table.

"No!" Vi reached out her hand as the papers—all her work—caught the fire. She'd never seen parchment go up in smoke so fast.

Control it, Vi willed mentally. She tried to envision her magic extending out from her, engulfing the flames, gaining command over them. But they wriggled and writhed, slippery and shifting; she couldn't get a grab on it and before she knew it, her whole precious study would be gone. Her only connection with the home she was supposed to have would be ash. She would be—

The flames blinked out of existence without warning.

Vi stared, wide-eyed, at the blackened edge of her desk. In the moment, the fire had burned for what seemed like forever. Like a whole inferno had surrounded her. In reality, it had been a scorch and mere seconds.

But had she really… Vi brought her hand to her face, staring at her palm in wonder.

"Don't get too excited."

Vi's back went rigid and she turned slowly to the source of the voice. Jax leaned in the door frame, arms crossed over his chest. His long black hair, the same color and nearly the same length as Vi's, was tied in a messy knot at the top of his head. Half of it was spilling down his shoulders.

"It was you, wasn't it?"

"You'd know if it was you," he replied, painfully simple. Sure, she'd know if she suddenly had control over her magic. Just like she'd know if she was fully Awoken to it and not just peering through the crack in the wall between her and her power. "I see you found your presents."

The change in topic was welcome. She'd postpone thinking about magic for as long as possible.

"Thank you for dropping them off. It was a nice surprise." She knew the presents had been sent ahead months ago. But Jax always kept them hidden, waiting for her birthday. She knew he did it to try to cheer her up on the day and Vi never had the heart to tell him it made no difference in her overall mood.

"You get anything good? Or just more boring books and maps?"

"Books and maps are *not* boring." Vi knew he was trying to get a rise from her and she didn't want to give him the satisfaction. "Maybe if you'd tried reading one once in a while, you wouldn't be such an uncultured vagrant."

"That's *Lord* Uncultured Vagrant, thank you very much." Vi gave a snort of laughter at the remark. "What's that?" He motioned to the watch in her hand.

Vi stared at it, forgetting she'd been holding it at all. The metal was warm under her skin, almost too warm. She'd melt the delicate gears inside if she wasn't careful. Luckily it'd been broken before her spark had decided to dance around it.

"The Minister of Sorcery—"

"You can just say Fritz." Jax chuckled.

"Fritz, right… Well he sent this for me." Vi fastened the watch around her neck.

"It suits you," her uncle appraised. His eyes lingered, as though he too found it oddly familiar. It seemed his mind went in a similar direction as hers initially. "Did your father make it?"

"He didn't say." Vi shrugged. "Just said it was my mother's." And that alone was reason enough for Vi to keep it close to her heart.

"You'll have time to go through the rest of the gifts later." Jax looked to one of the windows of her study. The dark morning was finally giving way to the first hazy colors of dawn. "We should get down to the pits."

"Do I have to?" Vi dared to ask, knowing better. "It's my birthday." She may hate the day, but she'd gladly use it as an excuse.

"Yes."

"You are truly heartless." Her words had no bite and Jax's grin assured her he didn't take them personally.

"One of my many positive traits."

"Let's get this over with." Vi rolled her eyes dramatically as she started for the door.

The rules of her life were simple, structured, and painfully clear.

If she followed them to the letter, remained the model future Empress, her reward would be reuniting with her family. She would be liberated from her beautiful, comfortable prison.

In *theory*.

In practice, she was supposed to have been returned when she turned fourteen. But three long years had dragged on, and here she was on her seventeenth birthday. Still in the North. Still a ward confined to Soricium—the fortress, specifically, for her "safety." Still stuck feeling trapped, repetition defining her days as she continued to try to jump through political hoops so high and obscure, she barely knew where she was half the time.

There had been delay after delay, issue after issue, preventing her from heading south. The years had slipped by until, at seventeen, growing bitterness had all but replaced waning hope.

Every effort she had ever expended toward this one goal seemed more futile by the day, and now she headed for the most futile effort of all: sorcery training.

THE SKY WAS BARELY orange, and she was already drenched in sweat. It rolled down her neck and was caught by the collar of her shirt, pressed slick to her back. It stuck to her just like every couple labored breaths stuck in her throat.

There was nothing enjoyable about trying to wrench her magic to the surface. Her shoulders sagged and her whole body ached. She'd only left her bed a few hours ago and Vi already felt like she needed a good night's rest.

"You look like you're about ready to try again..." Jax said from across the fighting pit. He'd sat on the steps while she caught her breath after the exertion—and frustration—of her last failure.

"This will be, what, the seventeen-thousandth attempt to Awaken my magic?"

"I hear seventeen-thousand-and-one is a lucky number."

"You're such a liar," Vi muttered. "How is it that you, of all people, ended up the guardian of the Crown Princess?" The question was a running joke between them. She'd long known the answer.

Jax, not her uncle by blood, was an old friend of her parents. After the fall of the Mad King Victor, he was even hand-selected to rebuild an illustrious fighting force—the Golden Guard. But he'd chosen to come North with Vi after she was born, giving it all up to look after her.

Guardian might be his official title, but for Vi, Jax was the closest thing she had to an in-person father figure.

"Right now it's because I seem to be the only one who can put up with her ill-tempered moods in the morning."

"If I'm ill tempered then you only have yourself to blame. You could make more of an effort when you are in the presence of your Crown Princess." Vi made an attempt to put on a regal air, fighting a grin.

"Not when I wiped that princess's arse when she was in nappies."

"Your service to the crown is much appreciated." She gave a bow, making a point to stick out her bottom for emphasis.

"Is it? Your family has an odd way of showing appreciation. Shite from you, shite from your parents." If anyone else had said those words, Vi would've risen to anger in defense of her family. But she knew better with Jax.

Jax could say whatever he wanted. Vi knew he would die for her and her family.

"Well now you're getting shite for magic from Solaris's latest installment."

"Your magic is stubborn, not shite." He gave her a tired smile. "You will open your magic fully soon, I can feel it."

"What if I don't?" Vi said softly, confessing one of her greatest fears. "It's already been two years since I manifested... What if I've already Awoken and this is all I have?"

"You don't believe that." Jax stood. "You've told me of the spark you feel within you. That chasm of light you can peer into but not reach."

"Perhaps that's something else?" Though she didn't know what it would be.

"Or perhaps we simply need to keep trying."

"How about, instead, we take a break today and I focus on something actually attainable? I could prepare for my lessons, work on my maps, read the books my parents sent..."

"I think if you spent as much mental energy on your magic as you did your maps, you would've long since opened your channel and we'd no longer be standing out here."

That was the last thing she wanted to do. Vi looked up at the treetops dizzyingly high above her. The fortress of Soricium was built in and around them. A noble house beginning to wake—which gave her an idea.

"Aren't you hungry? We could go inside and have the nice big skillet cake Renna makes for me on my birthday. The ones she drizzles syrup over with pats of butter and fresh berries and candied nuts? Maybe some of the rum whipped cream you enjoy so much?" Her mouth was already watering, stomach grumbling to match.

"And think of how much sweeter it will be when you've properly tasted your power."

"It's hard to learn magic when your stomach is eating itself." Vi plastered a hopeful—but knowingly futile—smile across her lips. "I leave for my birthday hunt tomorrow morning; surely I should maintain my strength today."

"You're not going to win me over with the promise of food... no matter how delicious Renna's skillet cakes are." She opened her mouth to object again, but he continued before she could. "Try once more, Vi—a good showing of it—and then I'll let you go."

Vi knew his acquiescence was a victory, but it didn't feel like one. Her cheeks burned and she didn't know who she was more frustrated with: Jax for not giving in, or herself for being such a coward and a weakling about her magic.

Two heavy hands fell on her shoulders, holding them tightly, giving her a light shake. Vi looked up at Jax, his dark eyes set against tan skin. "You know you must."

"I know." Vi sighed heavily. "The Senate expects me to learn magic. The Tower will want to see it. I have a lineage to uphold..."

"More than any of that, the longer you go without being fully Awoken, the more likely it is that the eventual, *inevitable* release will be violent." His voice had a deathly seriousness to it. "You already have enough strikes against your future rule, Vi. Having grown up here. Being a sorceress at all. Don't add a magical incident to their fodder. Awaken here, where it's safe."

Every action had an equal reaction with the nobility of the South. Romulin made them out to sound like vipers, waiting for her to fail. Delighting in her every mistake. Never in public, of course, but behind closed doors.

She was the one forced to stand in the sun while they lobbed their volleys at her from the shadows.

"So, one more time?" Jax persisted. "Give it a good effort?"

"One more time, and then you promise that's it for today?"

"I promise."

"Fine." Vi lifted her hand, reluctantly obliging. One more attempt at magic for the day. *What could it hurt?*

"Remember, when opening your channel, it helps to articulate a physical action."

"Let's not put the cart before the horse. I'm not opening any channel until I've Awakened my powers."

"It's important to start building good habits from the beginning," he insisted. "Maybe it'll help draw out the power."

"I've tried just about every physical action imaginable."

"Then try something you can't imagine."

"I think I'll stick with knuckle cracking," Vi muttered.

"Suit yourself." He shrugged and Vi saw how little faith he had in her.

Believe in me, she wanted to say. If she had one person believe in her when it came to her magic, then maybe it'd be enough. But how could she ask that of Jax when Vi didn't believe in herself?

Fritz's letter appeared in her mind once more.

I believe in you, Vi... magic has an odd way of finding us when we need it most.

Her hand rose to the watch around her neck. Vi closed her eyes, holding it tightly. Maybe it would bring out her spark a second time.

"Find me," she whispered.

Vi didn't know if it was a prayer to the Mother above, or just a plea to whoever might be listening. But the words were the first thing all morning to feel right. If Jax heard them, he made no indication.

Watch in one hand, the other outstretched, Vi dug deep within herself. She tried to coax the power upward, feeling it crackle under her flesh before it crept through the pores around her wrists and hands as shimmering heat that finally ignited into fire.

This pathetic flame was the best she could muster while maintaining any control over it. Daughter of Emperor Aldrik Solaris, regarded as one of the most powerful Firebearers alive. Granddaughter of the late Empress Fiera Ci'Dan Solaris, also regarded as one of the most powerful Firebearers in the world before her son. And now... all eyes were on Vi.

"More," Jax encouraged.

"There is no more." Vi pressed her lips into a thin line, trying to tame her frustration. Her uncle had heard it all already.

"There is."

"There isn't." She looked from the fire to him.

Jax's eyes were alight with the orange hues of her blaze. It lit up the stone walls of the pit, winning against the yellows of dawn. He had a hard expression that she already didn't like.

"More, Vi."

Vi shifted her feet out slightly on the barren ground, getting a better stance. She tried to push the other thoughts from her mind, focusing only on her magic. Her muscles tensed as she urged more power into the flames around her fingers. The moment the ball grew past three times the size of her hand, the fire became wild, barely tamed. Her magic would only extend so far while staying under her command.

"Now, protect yourself with it."

"*What?*" Vi looked out to him. This was not part of their normal training regimen.

"Use the fire to push against mine, like a shield. Protect yourself."

"I don't think that's—"

She didn't have a chance to finish her thought before a wall of flame hurled toward her.

The fire passed over her, nothing more than a whisper.

Fire—naturally occurring or their own—could not hurt a Firebearer. The only fire that could singe a Firebearer's skin was one created by another sorcerer—a more powerful sorcerer. So Vi would be fine... as long as Jax didn't really levy his full strength against her.

"Protect yourself, Vi," he repeated, lifting a hand. Flames crackled, rising up through thin air, binding together into another wall that he pushed toward her. These flames had a tickle to them. Nothing dangerous or uncomfortable, but more powerful than the last.

"I can't!" Vi called back to him. But he was already moving his hand again. Another wall of flame; Vi staggered.

What was he doing? Her heart was racing. If he kept this up he would actually harm her. *Would* he actually harm her? Vi thought she knew the answer, but he was making a dangerous case for proving her wrong.

"Yes you can!" He was already readying another pulse of flame.

Vi gritted her teeth, clenching them so tightly her jaw popped. She dropped her eyes to her own flame and willed it to grow.

The fire swirled, condensing into a column, slowly growing in height. Vi began to sweat yet again from the mental and magical exertion. Even if she couldn't feel heat from fire as a Firebearer, the humidity of the northern jungles did her no favors.

Like a wave crashing against her, another wall of Jax's fire hit. Vi stumbled, knees hitting the dusty ground. The fire she had been working on completely vanished.

"I—"

"Again!" Jax shouted at her.

Why was he doing this? He had never been like this in any of their lessons before. Vi stared at him, anger singeing her chest. It made the watch feel unnaturally cool against her skin as she struggled back to her feet.

The moment she was upright, another wall knocked her back over. Vi balled her hands into fists, knuckles pushing on the rough ground. *She couldn't give up like this.*

She lifted her hand, readying herself, but the next wall never came. Instead, fingers closed around her forearm, hoisting her back up. Vi swayed slightly, looking up at Jax.

"That's enough for the day, I think," he said gently. "Sorry for pushing you so hard. I thought it might help jostle something."

"I… it's fine," Vi mumbled, looking aside. Shame took over her for every nasty thought she'd had. "I know you were only trying to help me."

"Yes, well, I think it's time we get that skillet cake." Jax gave her a pat on the back and they started for the stairs.

"You go on ahead." Vi lingered, sinking onto the bottom step.

"Vi…"

"I'm fine, uncle. Just a bit tired. Just want to catch my breath is all." Vi twisted, looking up at him and forcing the biggest smile she could. "More like, I'm trying to sneak away to look at maps instead of skillet cakes."

"It's always a ploy for maps." He started up. "You should consider joining me for breakfast, Vi. As you said, you should keep up your strength."

"We'll see," Vi called back. But he was already gone.

With a soft sigh, Vi leaned against the stone, closing her eyes. *Why?* Why couldn't she manage anything? Her hand closed around the watch at her neck.

So much for magic coming when she needed it. The bitter thought was the ignition strike. Her eyes shot open.

"One more time," she whispered, knowing that it wouldn't yield anything but hoping against hope it did.

The spark deep within her was ablaze, bright and hot. Rage fueled it—from her birthday and its reminder of how she was stuck in the North, from the leftover feelings of anger at her uncle's test—rage at her magic itself for betraying her as it had.

Fire exploded around her hands.

Hotter, brighter—she pushed her magic as though Jax was still levying walls of flame against her. But instead of attempting to shield herself with it, Vi poured all her energy into the tiny ball in her palms. Every ounce of frustration was set ablaze, brighter than she'd ever seen her flames before.

The scales tipped without warning and magic flooded her system. Its white-hot flames roared like an unruly beast. Vi gasped as magic poured from her faster than she could find air.

Without warning, the wall had been broken down within her. This was the power she'd longed for, and now that she had it, she didn't know what to do with it. It was as though sunlight itself had turned molten and was now pouring from her.

She stared into the bright, shifting light, her eyes blown wide, and in it, she saw a figure come into clarity. Suddenly the world she knew was gone, and something new clicked into focus.

She was no longer in Soricium, but in a stone passageway she'd never seen before.

It was akin to what she'd imagined the dungeons of Solaris to look like—damp, dark, unembellished, rough stone. But there were no cells, just a long tunnel that continued stretching into the darkness in both directions. She turned to face the source of light at her left.

Vi blinked, disoriented.

Waiting with a small ball of flame hovering over her shoulder was… herself. At least, Vi thought it was her. It looked like her, the resemblance as uncanny as looking into a mirror. But there were notable differences. The woman across from her looked hardened, far more toned, and the natural tan hue of Vi's skin was deepened even further on her cheeks. The large cowl hood that covered the majority of her head cast further shadow.

The woman's clothes were drab and threadbare. Her hands were wrapped up to her elbows, like bandages, or the wrapped knuckles of a brawler. She stared into the darkness, watching, waiting.

Vi didn't have to find out what she was waiting for.

Soon, another light appeared far in the distance. As it grew, it illuminated a man.

He had a tousled mess of black hair cut at odd angles that ultimately ended at his shoulders. *No…* not quite black. It was another hue—a deep plum color off-set just slightly by the light.

A wicked, sickle-shaped scar ran down his left cheek and beneath the high collar of his intricately embroidered jacket. It brought her attention to a pair of piercing green eyes. He stared from underneath long lashes, fixated on the woman.

The mirror of herself spoke, but there was no sound. It was then that Vi realized she hadn't heard the dripping of water off the dank walls and ceiling, or the crackle of the fire over the woman's shoulder.

The whole world was muffled. She could see, but not hear or touch.

Can you see me? Vi tried to ask, though she already knew the answer. They couldn't. Their focus was entirely on each other. Tension filled the air nearly to the point of sparking into magic.

The man spoke and again she heard no sound. But Vi could tell by his expression that, whatever he said, it was serious.

When the woman replied, her free hand rose to her chest, touching her cowl lightly.

Vi's hand reached upward in tandem, her fingers falling on the watch Fritz had given her.

Looking down, she saw a shimmering glyph hovering above it—weak, frail, and flickering. As soon as her eyes landed on it, the symbols shifted and changed, spiraling in concentric circles. Sounds filled her mind suddenly. It was a maddening cacophony she couldn't understand, but desperately wanted to.

She hadn't quite *heard* the symbols, nor had she read them. It was as though the word—words?—had vibrated in the very core of her being. Vi looked back up from the watch around her neck, but the two people had gone blurry and over-saturated. They were fading into white light.

Vi blinked, swaying.

The world came into focus once more, light vanishing from around her. *No, it hadn't been light, it had been flames, hadn't it?*

She slumped against the wall, struggling to breathe. Ash coated her hands up to her elbows, coated her lungs as though she had been breathing fire instead of air. Her head spun.

Vi had wanted magic. Begged for it. She'd anticipated flames like her uncle's, like those of her forefathers.

She'd never expected to see the future.

3

THE WATER POOLED AROUND her feet, black with soot. It clung to the ceramic tiles and hung in the grooves between them that surrounded her rectangular, wooden bath. It lingered bucket after bucket, its granules impossible to wash away from the inside of the tub.

Her eyes looked at it unseeing, focused instead on the vision.

Shaking, Vi continued to scrub.

She'd wanted magic. Future sight hadn't been in the plans. Vi looked at the murky water as it slipped between her tan fingers.

That's what it was, wasn't it? It had to be, based on everything she'd read. But if she had future sight, why had she never received a vision when she looked into flames before?

There were four affinities that commanded the four elements: Windwalkers for air, Firebearers for fire, Groundbreakers for earth, and Waterrunners for water. Yet each of those four affinities could, sometimes, tap into a deeper, more mysterious magic called an affinity of the self.

For Firebearers, that was future sight.

"Do you need more water, your highness?" A servant called from outside the door to the bathing room.

"I'm fine," she lied.

The water was tepid and like ice on her skin. But she relished every raised goose bump that now lined her arms. Smoldering embers had taken up residence in her stomach. White-hot lightning arced between them. It escaped, wrapping around her fingers if she moved them too quickly.

She was Awoken now, there was little doubt of that. Her uncle had said it would result in her being able to truly command her magic. But this did not feel like control.

The Crown Princess felt as if she was one breath away from burning alive.

As if she was one breath away from burning *them all* alive.

"Can I get you anything else, your highness?" The woman asked. Vi knew to read between the lines and understood she needed to get moving, go about her day. But how could she act as if nothing had happened?

"I'm done." Vi stood, wrapping her arms around herself, shivering. But she didn't know what from—the cold, or feeling the rising tide of the magic within her. What a fitting tone for her birthday.

The servant came in, head bowed, towel in outstretched hands. Vi allowed herself to be attended to and was ushered out into the narrow dressing area that attached her closet, bath, and toilet with her bedroom. She was silent as the servant moved hastily around her, placing her mind as far from her body as possible.

She was no longer Vi the sorceress, but Vi the princess.

Princesses did not object. Princesses did not attempt to dry or perfume themselves. They didn't choose their outfits or decide what powders to put on their cheeks.

Yet when the woman's hands moved to plunge themselves into Vi's hair, she raised a hand.

"I can plait it myself."

"Are you certain?" It was the usual question, even though whoever was attending her among Vi's rotation of servants already knew the answer.

"I'm certain. You can go now."

The moment the servant was gone, Vi's fingers were in her hair, weaving the braids her mother had taught her were fashionable in the South. They shouldn't allow her this. But they did.

She carefully twisted the braids, stretching them back, pinning them in place, repeating the process time and again.

By the time Vi was done, she felt some sliver of emotion trying to work its way out from underneath the ash that still coated her soul. Between the strands of hair, she'd almost completely woven the morning out of her narrative. If she tried, she could convince herself to pretend this was like any other morning before her classes.

To sell herself on the fiction, Vi wandered from her bathing and dressing rooms to her study, as she would on any normal day.

Hair still wet and dripping from the ends of her braids, Vi pulled it over her shoulder and tucked it carefully under the collar of her shirt so it didn't get water on any of her most prized possessions. She closed the door tightly behind her and shut out the world.

What should she do?

Write down her vision? Ignore it entirely? Vi's eyes fell on her drafting table. The burnt spot stared at her like a bad omen. Could she trust herself with her magic feeling so unstable around her books?

Vi crossed to the table, sitting heavily. She tilted her head back, eyes wandering the maps lazily. They landed on the blueprint her brother had sent her of the rose garden.

"How about you, Father?" she asked the parchment. "Did you ever see the future?"

How nice it would be if she could actually ask her parents. It was a fantasy Vi pushed away as she shifted back toward the desk.

Her hand moved slowly, reaching for a quill and parchment. Every move was drawn out, intentional, no unnecessary energy expended so no magic would spark from her fingers again. A blank sheet in front of her, Vi drew the first line of ink across its surface.

She'd intended to write down her vision. But her hand seemed to move of its own accord, darting across the page while her mind lingered on nothing.

Swirling circles, connected by symbols Vi didn't understand. Dots, lines, smaller circles, they all wrapped together. As Vi drew, the sensation of rightness swelled in her, just as it had in her vision.

Why did something that seemed like it made so much sense also terrify her in equal measure?

Her quill stopped, and Vi looked down at the drawing. It was the same symbol she'd seen hovering over the watch around her neck, drawn with what Vi was certain was uncanny precision. Her heart began to race, staring at it. If she looked at it long enough then she may just—

The door opened behind her and Vi jumped, startled.

The paper in her hand incinerated in a bright *pop* of fire. The room filled with the scent of smoke and ash covered her fingertips yet again. She stared at the servant from earlier who stared back with equally wide eyes and an unsettling skepticism Vi had never seen before.

"Forgive my interruption." She gave a small bow, saying nothing of the magic she'd witnessed. "A courier has arrived."

"Jayme," Vi breathed in relief. Perhaps this birthday wouldn't be a complete waste. "Thank you, please excuse me." She pushed past the woman, starting out the door, only to be stopped again by a man who was heading into her classroom.

"Princess, where do you think you're going?" Martis questioned.

"Jayme has arrived."

"And you still have your lesson as normal, even when your courier arrives," he said hastily, trying to stop her with words alone. "You're about to have three days off, now is not the time to be skipping."

"We're about to get a whole fresh batch of news from Jayme's delivery to debate during our lessons. Don't you think it's worth postponing things a little?" Vi braced herself for another rejection. But it seemed Martis would be softer on her than Jax had been.

"Very well, go on." He shook his head and started into her study. "But hurry back. I expect at least a half lesson from you, princess. You're not to get out of this entirely."

"Understood," Vi called over her shoulder and was off before he even had time to set down his folio on one of the two desks they used in her classroom.

Out the main door was a serpentine walkway, wrapping around the tree, tunneling back into the trunk as it spiraled down. Two different rope bridges connected across to other structures, and walkways that were really massive limbs with railings or twisting stone bridges. High above her, the buildings stretched into the leafy embrace of the most ancient trees in the world. Far below her, the buildings grew up from the ground to make a living fortress that looked like more of a magical treehouse than the strict definitions of castles and fortresses she'd seen in the architectural books she'd studied.

The rope bridge leading away from her room creaked loudly, swaying under her feet as she darted across it. From the platform on the far side, Vi could get a much better look of the main entry of the fortress. Sure enough, if she squinted, she could make out golden embellishments glinting off the standard saddle for an Imperial courier. Two people stood by the mount; one had dark hair like Vi's, the other brown—like her mother's.

But unusually, there was a second mount, and a man with bright blond hair.

Vi gripped the railing beside her so tightly the rough edges of the weather-worn rope splintered into her palms. She leaned over, bending at the waist, trying to get a better look without falling.

She couldn't breathe.

From here, the man looked like he could be... might be... *was it Romulin?* Her heart nearly exploded from her chest with hope.

"Ellene!" Vi called upward. She took the curving steps that wound around the large tree trunk two, even three at a time, her long legs making quick work of the stairs. "Ellene! Jayme's here and someone's with her!"

"Princess." A green-eyed maid gave a small nod, her hands laden with fresh linens. "The chieftain's daughter has gone down to the stables."

"Of course she has," Vi muttered. Ellene and Vi had an unspoken race for who would be the first to greet their friend, and she was currently in second place. "Thank you!" she called as she began running back down the stairs.

Vi spiraled down, in and out of hollowed tree trunks that held the living quarters of the fortress of Soricium. She dashed across bridges of rope and stone, through sitting areas, gaming parlors, libraries, and more. She knew every shortcut, every back-door that led to a tree-limb that ran parallel with another where nimble, confident feet could jump.

In mere minutes, she was breathlessly emerging into the sunlight on the ground below, catching deep inhales of the dust cloud that perpetually lingered in the stretch of dirt that ran the length of the stables. At her left were smaller stables where horses were kept. At her right was a massive pen that contained five large noru cats, lounging about. Vi ignored both feline and equine alike, focusing on the small group collected around the courier she'd seen from above.

"Jayme!" Vi called over as she quickly approached.

"Don't you have a lesson to be attending right now?" Jax turned quickly, giving her a stern look.

Vi stopped mid-step, freezing in place. The severity of his tone hardly fit him. It was the tone he usually used when they weren't among friends.

"Martis agreed to a half lesson so that we could properly account for new news from the capital." Vi's eyes drifted from Jayme to Jax, and finally to the man still seated high on his horse—the new presence and undeniable source of the tension.

He had cerulean eyes, a square-cut jaw lined with pale stubble, and a mess of wavy golden hair. Vi supposed most women would find him handsome. She also supposed she wasn't like most women... because his appeal did little to interest her.

She only cared about one thing: he was certainly *not* her brother. Vi knew it from the portraits of Romulin she'd been sent and she knew it from the way he looked at her—eyes shifting, constant glances askance—awkward. Nothing like what she would expect of her brother's gaze.

"Greetings, your highness." He finally swung one dusty trouser leg over the saddle, dismounting and dipping into a low bow with the same motion. "Allow me to introduce myself. I am Lord Andru Rarren, son to Head of Senate, Lord Tomson

Rarren."

Son to Head of Senate… Vi merely blinked at the man for a long minute as the words sank in. She took long enough that her uncle elbowed her side. Vi coughed softly, trying to ignore her lapse in etiquette.

"It is a pleasure to meet you, Lord Andru." Vi held out her hand expectantly.

Andru stared at it for a long moment as if confused. Long enough that Vi wondered if somehow she was remembering what her tutors had told her about Southern introductions incorrectly. But he finally, almost too hastily, grabbed her palm and brought the back of her hand to his lips for a light kiss.

"And you as well, your highness. I've heard much about you. Your brother talks much of you. It's good to finally put a face to a name." He straightened and Vi shifted, drawing her height as well. They were nearly the same measurement and she relished the fact. She was tall for a woman and would leverage her height as often as possible against men who thought they could look down on her by stature alone.

"I believe there have been portrait artists sent before to capture my likeness. Have you not seen their renditions?" Vi asked, part coy, part cautious.

"There is nothing like laying eyes on you in the flesh. The artists do not do you justice."

"Indeed, they are far too generous," Vi remarked dryly. "Why have you come, Lord Andru?" Vi folded her hands before her. "I know it is not to merely set eyes on me. Otherwise you came very far, for very little."

She could feel her uncle shift uncomfortably next to her. He wanted to scold her for her boldness. But Vi didn't feel the least bit sorry for her remarks. The Senate had done her no favors in life and she had no interest in bowing before them or their appointed messenger.

"You are correct, princess. This is not a mere social call. I am here to assess you."

"*Assess me?*" Vi repeated, shock seeping into the question. He would seek to assess her? More than her tutors already had? More than her parents every time they came? Every inch of her had been inspected and measured since birth. What more was there to assess?

"Yes, on behalf of the Senate."

"What does the Senate want to assess me on?" Vi asked cautiously. More like, what did they think they had the *right* to assess her on? At least her tutors and parents had ground to stand on for placing her under scrutiny. The Senate was an extension of the people, but far below the crown.

"Your fitness to rule." He had the audacity to smile as he said it. "The people and Senate question if one raised in the arms of our enemies could be fit to be a leader of *all* the Empire's peoples. Especially before she returns home next spring."

Vi didn't know where to start. Correcting the idea that she had been raised in the arms of enemies? The notion that she needed to be tested at all? Ruling was her birthright—the one unquestioned element of her life.

Or perhaps she should start with the last and most important thing of all…

The fact that she would *finally* head South in the spring.

*H*OME, A PLACE SHE never thought she'd see. A place she had given up on ever finding. Now dangled before her by the words of a stranger.

"Can you say that again?" Her voice had fallen to a whisper. She didn't think she could muster anything louder if she tried. Everything felt fragile, as though the world itself might shatter if she spoke too loudly. The world likely wouldn't, but the thin veneer of hope that now coated her heart certainly would.

"Come spring, or as soon as the passes thaw enough to get the military parade through, the Senate has declared for you to be returned to Solarin."

It couldn't be real. It wasn't real. Without warning, suddenly, she would be reunited with her family.

"I…" Words completely failed her. Thoughts failed her. She'd fantasized so often about this moment that she should know exactly what her reaction was, and yet Vi froze completely.

Andru's mouth quirked up into a smile that Vi couldn't quite read. It was self-satisfied certainly, bordering on arrogant, slightly condescending perhaps. He must be relishing in rendering the princess speechless. Somehow, though, his blue eyes were kind. Leaving her conflicted about how she should react.

"Yes, princess?" Jax brought her back to the present.

"I am glad to be returning to the home of my forefathers at long last." Vi turned to Jayme, and then Ellene. Her two friends and confidants had been oddly silent. She needed time to process everything that was happening, and she couldn't rightly do that standing in the middle of the stable grounds. "Jayme, you have letters for me, I believe?"

"I do." Jayme gave a bow of her head then turned, reaching for a familiar box at the top of the small pile that had been unloaded from the over-sized saddle bags of her mount. "This is for you, princess… And for you, Lord Wendyll… And I have a satchel for your tutors and staff."

Vi gave a small noise of agreement and focused mostly on the small, lacquered white box. On its top was the imperial seal. Inside, packed between folds of blue velvet, were a series of small envelopes and parcels from her family.

"Let us head to my chambers, Jayme and Ellene. Martis should still be there; you can deliver the letters directly to him." Vi took care to properly enunciate her words for Andru's benefit, drawing each one out, as was customary for nobility—especially Southern nobility. "Uncle, can you kindly work with the staff and see that Andru is settled in to suitable chambers for the duration of his stay?"

"It seems Andru is not the only one who will need chambers for a longer stay." Jax lowered a letter he'd been skimming; Vi recognized her mother's script. His eyes went directly to Jayme. "You have had a promotion."

Jayme folded her hands before her, head bowed slightly. It was a position Vi had seen often. Spending time in the company of the Crown Princess could be difficult for a woman who didn't really enjoy being the center of attention.

"What is this?" Ellene finally spoke up. It was unusual for the girl to be so quiet, and the fact only emphasized how much Andru's sheer presence could change their dynamic. "A promotion?"

"I've been appointed as a royal guard." She raised her head, looking directly at Vi. "*Your* royal guard, to be specific. I will oversee your protection and guard detail, if you'll have it."

Vi could practically explode with excitement and she struggled to keep her face passive and manicured, especially in front of Andru. "Of course I'll have it. You have been a loyal courier of mine for years; we all know that you can gracefully endure my various quirks."

"You're too hard on yourself." Jayme gave a small smile.

"No, that's about right," Ellene muttered, finally breaking from decorum. Vi successfully fought a grin.

"You will be staying as well then? You will not be going home this winter?"

She shook her head. "I'll be here until the Imperial parade comes to collect you this spring... and then after that also, naturally."

Imperial Parade comes to collect you this spring. The words rang in Vi's ears. She'd never heard something so wonderful and yet so hard to comprehend. There was some kind of disconnect. A wave of familiarity came over her, as though she was living a moment she'd dreamed thousands of times.

Likely, because she was.

Vi felt dizzy all over again. She shifted the grip on her box. It only contained letters but they were as heavy as a powder keg. Depending on what was written in them, it might be just as explosive. Vi could only imagine what her brother had to say about the newest development Andru revealed.

"I will be assessing Jayme as well." There was that terrible word again from Andru's lips. *Assessing.* "It's quite a strange affair to see a common-born courier appointed to soldier so young. By the Empress Vhalla Solaris herself, no less."

"Jayme is no mere courier," Vi said defensively.

"She must not be, given the circumstances." Andru looked away and then dragged his eyes back to Vi. She fought the urge to squirm under his gaze. The man made her downright uncomfortable. "The Senate wants to make sure you are properly protected, your highness."

"I have the utmost faith in Jayme." Vi left no room for debate in the statement.

She didn't like people questioning the merits of her friends—Vi had few enough, and she wanted to keep the ones she did have. "If she feels fit for the job, then I'm certain she is."

I'm. Vi caught her slip too late. *I am.* Judging from the slight widening of Andru's eyes, he hadn't missed it. She hastily continued speaking, as if that could cover it.

"Now, if you will please excuse us. Jayme has letters to deliver to Martis."

"Yes, of course." Andru gave another bow of his head. "I shall find my quarters and then yours."

"Pardon?" Vi stopped mid step, half turned away. "A little bold, is it not? Inviting yourself to the Crown Princess's chambers?"

"For your lessons," he clarified.

"Of course…" Vi gave him one last, long look, trying to uncover whatever secrets he was hiding. But the man was a closed book.

It was a good thing books of all kinds were Vi's specialty.

The moment the door to her bedroom closed and they were alone, Vi put the box on her bedside table and threw her arms tightly around Jayme's shoulders.

"You are the best birthday present a girl could ask for."

"It's good to see you too." Jayme gave Vi a small pat on the back. "While it wasn't intended, I'm glad I could make it by your birthday. Honestly, I didn't know if I was going to make it at all before the new year."

"Really?" Vi pulled away, looking into the familiar set of hazel eyes she hadn't seen for over two months. "The passages are that bad this year?"

"Worse than ever." Jayme gave a small nod and paused to give Ellene a tight hug next. "Winter came early, and in a bad way. The passes are becoming too treacherous for even the largest warstriders trained in ice and snow."

"Well, I'm glad you made it safely."

"I always do my best to deliver you a taste of home."

"Yes, speaking of…" Vi looked from the box to her friend. Her head was spinning. Vi pulled her hair over her shoulder and fussed with the ends of her braids, giving her fingers something to do.

"What's happening there? An Imperial Parade? Spring? Andru?" Ellene asked in Vi's stead, as if sensing her tension.

"There's a lot going on at the capital," Jayme affirmed. "I'm sure your letters detail it better than I could."

"Give me the quick summary. I may not have time to read them all before my lesson," Vi urged, impatient. "You always have the best pieces of news that no one else writes about." No one but her brother. Romulin rarely spared details, one of many reasons why she went for his letters first.

"You've heard the quick summary already…" Jayme ultimately obliged her. "The Senate is determined to bring you back South, no more delays or excuses."

Finally. "What made them suddenly demand it?"

"A number of things, based on what I heard. But remember, I was only there for a week or so to deliver and collect replies. I'm hardly embroiled in it." Jayme began to pace as she spoke.

"I know your usual disclaimers." Vi sat on the bed, pulling her legs up to sit in a crossed position. "I want to hear what you saw, what you think. I value your counsel."

Jayme stopped, gave Vi a small smile, and then began pacing once more. The tiny expression of gratitude at Vi's flattery instantly faded away as Jayme's tone became serious. "The White Death has become much, *much* worse—that's a good place to start."

"The plague? There hasn't been a single case of it here in Soricium still." Which was on the list of the many reasons why it had been argued that Vi should stay in the North.

"Soricium no, but—"

"It's in Shaldan now—to the southwest border," Ellene finished for Jayme.

"Why didn't you tell me?" Vi looked to Ellene.

"My mother only told me recently... and you know I don't like speaking about the White Death."

The last Chieftain of the North, Ellene's grandmother, had died not more than three years ago of the White Death, after heading West to Norin at the request of the Empress and Lady of the West. She'd gone to see if the strange yet powerful magic of Yargen could be of any help to the efforts to find a cure.

"Not to linger..." Jayme continued with an apologetic look toward Ellene. "But with the knowledge of the disease being here, the argument of keeping you here to protect you has vanished. In addition, your father set out shortly before I did for the Crescent Continent. I think the Senate wants to see you back with your father gone. I think they may feel nervous having neither the Emperor nor heir near them."

"What?" Vi breathed. "My father left?"

"I'm certain he wrote about it." Jayme stopped her pacing. "They say a cure for the plague may be found there."

"So they still are at a loss for how to treat it," Vi muttered. She turned to her box, plucking it off her nightstand. "Thank you, Jayme. I want to catch up further, but I think you were right and I should read my letters."

"Don't be too shocked that I was right," Jayme remarked dryly.

Vi gave a snort of amusement, eyes flicking up. "How I've missed that wit of yours."

"Careful, you may get more than—" before Jayme could say anything further, her head jerked toward the heavy wooden door. Vi's followed as the sounds of movement and muffled voices grew on the other side.

"That must be Andru arriving with your tutors," Jayme whispered.

"Aren't they noisy?" Ellene frowned. "He comes in here like he owns the place."

"He has that air about him. Well, I don't know... Something is off..." Jayme's frown deepened. She sat quickly on the edge of Vi's bed, leaning in. There was a tension that hadn't been in her actions before, not even when she was talking about the plague. "Listen, Vi. You need to be careful about him. I was with him for over two weeks on the road and have barely learned more than his pedigree. But I can tell you this: the Head of Senate, Lord Tomson, will do you no favors. Tomson is vocal about his concern for you taking the throne, and in the wake of the White Death worsening, the people are getting desperate... desperate enough to listen."

"What are you saying?" Vi whispered back. Her mind had already connected the dots, but she didn't want to see the words the lines spelled out. She'd do anything to ignore them.

"I'm saying that some say the crown may no longer be needed. That the Senate can represent the people alone."

"What?" Vi hissed. "They have no right."

"They don't. They don't, *alone*. But if they make the people believe the future of the crown is unstable—if *you* are unstable—then..." Jayme paused, letting the rest go unsaid. "The people are a powerful force if they unite behind a banner, and getting Andru on your side may be the only thing that could prevent such a tide from rising."

"I don't..." She didn't understand? No, that wasn't it. Vi understood perfectly, so perfectly that it was agonizing. She didn't *want* to understand.

"Read your letters, and look for any advice on the political climate. There won't be mention of Andru in there; the Senate practically ambushed me with him at the last minute after the letters were written. I'm going off the rumors of the people, which are always to be taken with a grain of salt. You may be able to derive better insights than I. But I do know that nothing good will come if you lead Andru to believe you're anything other than the perfect princess the Senate wants."

Perfect princesses didn't speak back to their tutors, or fantasize about running off at the first possible opportunity. Nor did they debate strong opinions about the senate as Vi so often had. Every one of her teachers had been hand-appointed by the Senate. How could she have been so reckless as to feel comfortable?

A cold chill tingled down Vi's spine. She felt as though she was about to be sick.

Unfortunately for Vi, she'd have to shove aside the queasy feeling, as a knock on the door brought their conversation to a close.

"Princess?" Martis asked through the door.

"Enter." Vi stood, in the same motion opening her box and selecting a letter at random. The seal was broken and parchment unfurled by the moment the door was opened in full, revealing her tutors—Martis, Callope, Fredrik—along with Jax and Andru. Jayme was off the bed, standing two steps away, rigid. Ellene leaned against the wall by the bathroom door.

"I do believe it's time for your lesson. We have much to go over," Martis said.

"Yes, of course." Vi made a show of rolling up the parchment as though she'd been engrossed in its contents. "I was trying to get a head start on reading through my correspondence."

"There will be plenty of time for that." Andru's eyes met hers. Ice blue, Vi decided, his eyes were ice blue and void of all warmth. "You shall have all winter, before the Imperial Parade arrives, and there will be no more letters in or out until then."

No more letters meant that whatever information her box, and Jayme, contained was all Vi had to work with. She would get no advice from her brother, and no insights from her parents. Vi pressed her lips into a thin smile, trying to use the expression to conceal the pain that heavy stone was still inflicting in her stomach.

"You are very right." Vi closed her box, standing as straight as possible. Panicking didn't change her situation. She would keep herself together, and learn all she could. Vi had been groomed from birth to play the games of nobility. She smiled at each of them, the expression of a perfect princess, even when worry threatened to burn her alive. "Well then, shall we begin?"

5

Vi EASED HERSELF DOWN into the chair behind her desk as though it were a throne. As though she wasn't completely surrounded by the men and woman who sought to pass judgment on her. Her eyes fluttered closed and she took a small, stabilizing breath.

She needed to keep her head about her. Her magic seemed erratic—more so than normal today—and the last thing she wanted was it running away on a rogue emotion and causing a mishap in front of Andru. She needed to be a perfect princess, just as Jayme had said.

Vi opened her eyes once more. They had all been waiting for her to speak as the highest rank among them. *Silence can be control*, her father had told her once. This was the first time she felt she truly exercised it.

"Let us start from the beginning. I would rather not have the details, and thus my understanding, be in pieces." Vi looked to Andru, folding her hands on the desk.

"Yes, your highness." Andru gave a small bow of his head and took the floor. He produced a small folded envelope, a broken seal bearing the blue signet of the Senate. Handing it to Vi, he paraphrased: "Your upbringing has been unconventional. As a result, many are concerned if you will truly rule with the Empire's best interests in mind.

"Since the Senate helps bridge the people and the crown, I have been sent to compose an assessment of what you have learned and your overall demeanor. This will help the Senate give you their vote of confidence immediately on returning home."

Vi had a few things she could think of that the Senate should be doing rather than assessing her—chief among them was not meddling with her family. Her rule did not have to be complicated and she had no idea why the Senate was making it out to be.

"Why the urgency?" Vi asked, already suspecting the answer based on her discussion with Jayme. "The Senate can assess me in full when I return home in the spring. I will not sit the throne for many years, so even the people will have a chance to come to know me when I am no longer bound to Shaldan."

"As you may have read in your letters, your father has left the capital, and soon the continent. We wish to account for contingencies."

A nice way of saying, "in case he dies," and they all knew it. It was the way of royalty; Romulin was the contingency plan for her, she was the contingency plan for her father, alongside her mother.

"Or perhaps you could consider me collateral." Andru shifted his weight from side to side, glancing askance. "To ensure that Chieftain Sehra will not do anything to try to keep you. The Imperial parade will come to collect me as the son of Head of Senate, ensuring your return as well."

Her own lips turned into a bitter smile. He wasn't nearly as valuable as she was. If the Senate changed their mind on making the trip for her, then the trip wouldn't be made, regardless of who else was stuck with her.

"Yes, well, it is not as if I can send you away, even if I wanted to." Jayme said the passages were too perilous now for safe travel. They were trapped together, for better or worse, for a winter. "So how will your assessment work?"

"I will sit in on all your lessons." He lifted a folio off the desk her tutors usually used. "I have notes from the Senate of things they wish to see, certain subjects they want reported on. As you might imagine, princess, they are keen to learn more of your politics."

Vi gripped her hands tighter still. Now she was to be graded like a child. They didn't respect her, or her authority.

She took a calming breath, squelching her eager spark to show them all why they should heed her. If this was what she must do, then she would do it gracefully.

"I fear you shall be bored, but do as you like." Nothing in Vi's words betrayed the swirling emotion within her.

"Well then, now that we are all acquainted, I would like to begin that half lesson you promised me, princess," Martis interjected.

"Yes, certainly, I am ready when you are."

Martis moved behind the desk. Andru moved for a chair in the back corner of the room. Something about having him sit off to her side and behind her right shoulder had Vi uneasy. But there was little she could do other than sit straighter and try to ignore him entirely.

"Since I am still going through my letters, let us resume with our discussion from two days ago, if you please."

She didn't please, if Vi was being honest.

More than anything she wanted a few solid hours with herself to regain her mental footing. Her eyes drifted to Jax for support, but he was already leaving the room.

Outwardly, she'd be the princess, while inwardly she'd boil from her magic super-heating her nerves.

"Yes, Martis, where shall we resume the discussions?" Vi said as the door closed behind her last tutor, leaving her alone with Martis and Andru.

"We had been talking about the nature of the Senate." What an apt thing to be discussing now with Andru in the room. "Our last lesson had ended before you could answer my question."

"Please refresh my memory." Vi remembered perfectly, she just hoped to look for an opening to change the topic.

It didn't work, and Vi settled in for several long hours of tutelage.

She had never been so exhausted at the end of a day of lessons. It felt like an entire lifetime had transpired. She'd woken up before dawn and now emerged from her classroom after the sun had set.

But her back was still rigid, a relaxed expression turned into a small smile as she thanked her final tutor and sent him away. Andru was close behind but he paused in the doorway.

"Thank you for allowing me to sit in on your lessons."

"You're welcome." He was as welcome as a viper in her bed. Vi wanted him gone. She wanted him gone as badly as she wanted out of her formal clothes, which at that moment was *very* badly.

"I look forward to the next time we have lessons together. But I hear that will be in a few days' time, as you are going on a hunt."

"Yes, I am quite excited." What Vi really wanted to say was that if he tried to do something to take her hunt from her, she'd burn him to ash where he stood. "Leaving Soricium is a gift from Sehra. She gives her blessing for it every year."

"Her blessing? Prince Romulin has said that you, as the Crown Princess, can do as you please."

Vi couldn't ever do as she pleased *because* she was the Crown Princess.

"Even a Crown Princess can show respect toward her host." The quick response seemed to satisfy him. "Now, if you will excuse me, I am quite exhausted from the events of the day and I can only imagine you are as well, since you've been traveling for some time."

"I am tired." Andru looked out the door. But instead of leaving, he slowly closed it.

"Lord Andru, I am not sure what you think you are doing, but I do not think it is appropriate for you to be in my chambers, unescorted, at this hour." Perhaps it was a test, Vi reasoned. Perhaps he was trying to see if she would object or if he could uncover some deeply romantic corner of her, looking for a moonlight tryst. If that were the case, he was about to be sorely disappointed.

"I realize. Forgive me, princess." Andru took a step inside, and then another. There was something she disliked about how unhurried his movements were, combined with that shifty look of his. "But there is something I must tell you, alone."

Vi stood her ground, straightening. She wasn't going to take one step back. If this was an intimidation tactic, it wouldn't work.

"We are alone. Tell me and then leave."

"No, no, it's not *tell* you." He shook his head and finally stopped. One more step and he might have had his nose singed. "Give you." Andru reached into the breast pocket of his coat.

Vi watched, admittedly curious, as he produced a rumpled envelope. It was worse for wear, but the seal—the Solaris seal—was still intact. Only four people in the world were permitted to seal their envelopes with that mark.

"It is from your brother," he said stiffly, holding it out.

Vi looked between the letter and the man, trying to choose her next words carefully. "Why did it not arrive with Jayme?"

"The decision for me to come North was rather… last minute. There was not time for more letters to be added to Jayme's satchel."

The story linked up, but Vi still regarded the envelope with suspicion. Even so, she took it. Regardless of how he got it, the contents were from one of her family members, and that was worth more than gold.

"Thank you for bringing it." Vi held it in both hands, flipping it over. There was no writing on the outside. Andru continued to hover. Her eyes flicked up to his and neither moved for a long second. "Is there anything else?"

"No, well, I—"

"You are dismissed, then." Vi gave him a smile, trying to ease away the harshness from the statement. "As you agreed, it is improper for you to be here."

"Yes… of course." Andru took a step away and Vi felt like she could breathe that much easier. Andru paused one final time, door halfway open. Over his shoulder, he gave her a small smile, the long bangs of his otherwise short blond hair tossed to one side. "Do enjoy your hunt tomorrow, and be careful—we wouldn't want anything to happen to you."

Before she could respond, the door closed.

"*Finally.*" Vi all but ran into her bedroom. She pulled at the lacing of her dress, slipping it off and donning a simple nightgown.

Vi sunk onto the thinly woven blanket that covered her bed.

"Now, let's see what's really going on," she mumbled, placing the white box next to her on the feather mattress. Opening the top, Vi fished out the envelope marked with a golden seal of a blazing sun—the imperial signet—and her brother's handwriting in the corner marking "from Romulin."

She glanced at the letter Andru had given her, but decided to start with her box first, and save that for last.

Dearest Sister,

I'm sure much of what I'm about to tell you is repetitive to mother and father's letters and Jayme's reports to you. If you find it annoying, I'd like to remind you of your previous request for me to tell you of everything in my own words.

A small smile crossed her lips. Her brother's handwriting was not the tight, slanted script of her father's, nor was it the wider loops of her mother's, but somewhere in-between. Every time she read his letters, she tried to imagine a new voice for Romulin. It was a game she'd started playing as a child, and intentionally never asked anyone who knew her brother what he sounded like so that it would be a surprise when she did finally meet him.

The Senate has decided that you are to come home, that they can wait no longer, regardless of the plague and its spread. I think the final straw was word that there was evidence of it in the North. Or perhaps it was father's departure and the feeling that they are in dire straits without their C. Princess here in their sights.

Regardless of the reason, Mother could not be more excited to see you again, even though she just left you a few months ago. Which, speaking of, thank you for the cookies you sent. Even though they were crushed somewhat in travel (despite

Mother's best efforts), they were quite curious indeed.

Vi closed her eyes, savoring the memory of her mother's visit the past summer. It had been postponed later than usual due to winter lingering in the mountains. But that meant her mother stayed later, and Vi remembered every tangle and curl of her mother's hair, the soft smell of fresh eucalyptus in the perfumes she wore.

When Vi reopened her eyes, they fell back to the words *father's departure*, and prompted Vi to keep reading.

Mother was rather a force in demanding that the entire family be permitted to come and get you. It seems she's finally had enough of "the Senate insisting on our separation"—her words, not mine. Though, I whole-heartedly endorse her on this. She all but made an Imperial decree on the matter. She wanted to come and get you sooner with a small contingent that could navigate the icy passes, but the Senate insisted on a full military parade—no doubt to show the North its might. They also reasoned the protection was necessary if I was to come as well. So concessions were made.

Sister, I advise you to steal the ear of the Chieftain sometime soon and warn her of this. Help her set her people's expectations for when the army arrives. The Senate sees this as a display of strength and a necessary level of protection for the royal family being all in one place, but I worry it could strain relations.

There is enough political uncertainty right now around the White Death. The people are afraid, and a populous living in fear is an unstable one. You are possibly the singular thing that can unite the Empire, but you'll need to play your cards right...

Vi read on, gaining as much insight as her brother could give her on the dance of politics. Several passages she had to read twice. The whole letter was nearly four pages, but not a single mention of Andru.

... and, with that, I leave you for now. This may be the last letter I ever write, since Jayme will be staying up there with you and the passages will be too frozen for safe travel in short order. No more letters will have a chance to go through before the passes thaw, and when they do I will be on them, heading to you.

Can you believe it? The last letter I will ever write you. I have only known you through the tip of a pen... and soon, I will speak to you. I imagine what you will sound like, what our conversations will be in person. I cannot wait to hear about how your birthday hunt went this year, or what mayhem you and Ellene made at the winter solstice festival.

Everything feels as though it is happening so fast, yet I cannot wait. Somehow, I already know you feel the same, my twin.

Until we meet, dear sister.
Romulin

At least it seemed fast for him. For Vi, she had lived her entire life waiting. She folded the letter and sought out her mother's next, hoping for a little brightness.

Vi was not disappointed. Much like Romulin said, the missive contained words of love, excitement, and encouragement. Only Vhalla Solaris could pen a letter that was equally beautiful and sorrowful. She clutched the letter to her chest, as if it could ease the dull ache there.

One more important letter remained: her father's.

Both Romulin and Vhalla had mentioned her father's departure, along with Jayme and Andru, and now Vi hoped that his own words would give more clarity on such a critical decision. Yet she found the letter painfully lacking. Judging from his penmanship, he'd clearly scribbled it in haste.

My darling daughter,

I did not want to miss the opportunity to both send you an almost ceremonial final letter in this last batch, as well as my apologies with it.

There is reason for me to believe that a cure for the plague sweeping across our lands is on the Crescent Continent. I must go and meet with their leaders, inquire as to this potential cure myself. It is imperative for our family, for our future together.

The leaders on the Crescent Continent refused to discuss it with anyone else and our situation—our personal need of it—has become dire. Please understand, had this not been the case, nothing would've taken me from this land so close to bringing you home.

Please forgive your father for not taking the time to come north and visit you before leaving. The urgency surrounding these matters cannot be expressed in a mere letter. But the sooner I depart from Norin, the sooner I can return and make everything clear.

I promise you, I shall be there with your mother and brother when the time comes to collect you. We will be one family soon enough.

With love,

Your father

"I understand, father," Vi said with a thick throat. She'd spent her life being groomed to take his seat and assume the throne following him. Yet Vi couldn't imagine what it was like to be an Emperor or Empress. To be simultaneously responsible for all the good and bad of the Empire.

To think that was a job some imagined the Senate to take from them, Vi thought bitterly. The more power they attempted to chip away from the crown, the greater their own responsibility. She'd heard it said that a heavy crown made a good ruler, but from where Vi sat, the Senate seemed to have necks far too thin to wear the sun crown—even if it were split among them.

Rubbing her eyes, making sure no rogue tears slipped from them as they were wont to do whenever she received her box of letters, Vi returned the envelope to sit with the rest. There were others among them, their wax seals telling Vi who was vying for the eyes of the Crown Princess. She recognized a few crests of court members; one senatorial seal was possibly noteworthy, but likely just another noble attempting to get in the good graces of the future Empress.

She placed the box on her bedside table and picked up the final letter she'd read for the night. Vi slid her finger under the seal and lifted. The flap opened and, just as Andru had said it would, her brother's script greeted her.

V—

Forgive my brevity. I'm sure you'll understand. I had to send something ahead and there's no time.

Andru is more important than you could possibly know. Please, be on your best behavior.

R.

Vi flipped over the letter, looking for more, but there wasn't any.

"What does that even mean?" she groaned, flopping back onto the bed. Vi gripped her pillow, rolling onto her side, clutching it.

Be on her best behavior. Be the perfect princess. Manage her magic that just so happened to show her strange visions of the future now, when normalcy was the watch-word.

She pressed her eyes closed and took a breath, stopping the spark before it set her bed sheets ablaze.

The only thing Vi wanted to think about was the freedom tomorrow would bring. One more sleep and then she'd be on the hunt—far away from everything—and would hopefully have a moment to herself to think.

Hopefully.

"WAKE UP, SLEEPY PRINCESS!" Ellene declared, barging into Vi's room. She didn't remember falling asleep and her letters were still strewn about her on top of the covers.

"Shouldn't you knock?" Vi groaned.

"Not when the day is getting away from us." Ellene threw open the window shutters and Vi yanked the covers over her head. "Come on, up, it's time to go!"

"I need to check my pack a final time." What Vi really wanted to say was that she needed five more minutes of sleep. She'd been up before dawn yesterday and was now up with the dawn today. Vi was not a morning person and this was testing her limits.

"I figured as much." Ellene grinned. "It's why I took the liberty of checking and packing it for you."

Vi sat up at that, rubbing sleep from her eyes. "I don't know if I should be grateful or frightened that you were in here rummaging around in my things while I slept."

"It's your fault for being such a heavy sleeper." Ellene put her hands on her hips. "And I can't tell if you're offending my person or packing skills by that remark."

"Both?"

"You wound me!" Ellene launched herself onto the bed, flopping heavily with a dramatic sigh. This was the Ellene Vi knew—someone caught somewhere between girl and woman still, and had all the best parts of both. Not the quiet observer she'd seen before Andru.

"Given that the last time we went hunting, I believe you forgot your bedroll…" Vi poked the girl's nose.

"You like snuggling with me." Ellene cuddled up to her for emphasis. "How could I deprive you of that joy?"

"The time before that, I believe you forgot rations." Vi struggled to keep her face serious—it was a losing battle.

"You're a good hunter. I was giving you incentive." Ellene grinned.

"What about forgetting your—"

"You could just say thank you." Ellene threw her hands in the air, raised up her legs, and half-jumped off the bed as quickly as she came.

Vi was quickly out of bed after her and throwing her arms around Ellene's shoulders, hugging her tightly from behind. "Thanks."

"You're welcome, sister." Ellene squeezed her forearm before Vi let go. "I'm glad you're still going out, given Andru and all the weirdness of yesterday—" Ellene still didn't know the half of it, Vi realized. "I think you could use the distraction."

"I really could."

"That's the spirit."

"I want to grab one more thing…" Vi started for the door to her study. She realized her presents had distracted her from grabbing her journal yesterday morning.

"I already grabbed your journal. It's at the top of your pack."

"What?" Vi stopped in her tracks.

"See, now who's not forgetful?" Ellene asked over her shoulder with a satisfied smirk.

"You're tolerating my map-making? Is it my birthday?"

"I think it is, actually. Or, was." Ellene paused in her doorway. Vi was briefly reminded of Andru and the thought woke her spark. She fought to keep it suppressed, not allowing it to run wild. She would not allow it to ruin this hunt with any outbursts or visions. "Now, get dressed and meet me down."

Today was not the day for dresses or finery. Vi picked her softest leather leggings, pairing them with a fitted shirt that wouldn't impede her movements. She dressed quickly and made her way down the wooden stairs and winding arches of the fortress.

Vi emerged from the main entrance to find Jayme and Ellene waiting with Jax, Sehra, and… unfortunately… Andru.

He'd said he wasn't coming the night before. Vi balled her hands into fists, hoping he hadn't been lying to her. He'd better hope he hadn't been lying… The sight of only three packs—one at Ellene's feet and one at Jayme's, and the third having her bow attached, put the fear to rest.

Vi's eyes drifted upward, landing at Jayme's hip. There was something new strapped there—a sword. The hilt was done in gold and made to look like wheat. A properly Eastern design, seeing as they were the bread basket of the Empire.

"You really look like a proper soldier," Vi said to Jayme, motioning toward the sword.

"Thank you." Jayme gave the scabbard a pat.

"Hopefully she functions as a proper soldier, too," Andru remarked.

Vi's gaze turned to him with slightly narrowed eyes. But Jayme beat her to the retort.

"I have practiced with it all my life. It's been in my hands every time I return home and in the training grounds with the other soldiers when I'm in Solarin. I am more than confident."

"And you were born to wear that blade." Jax wore a small, tender smile as he looked between the sword and the woman who wore it. Whatever he was seeing, it wasn't the rising tensions. Vi almost wanted to ask, but kept silent. Now wasn't the time, and she was still guarding secrets from him.

"Born or not, she is to be your sole guard for this adventure," Andru continued. "A curious choice."

"Do you have something you would like to say about it?" Vi couldn't stop herself from asking. The question was a little too direct, said too quickly. But she didn't regret the words even after they'd left her.

"Certainly not. I am here to observe, note, and report. Nothing more. I leave any decision-making or judgment-passing to my betters in the Senate." He smiled his full-lipped, toothy smile.

"You three need to take note not to go too far." Sehra was the one to get the conversation back on track. "Lord Andru has stated truth; Jayme will be your sole guard for this excursion."

"You're actually letting us go unattended?" Vi asked skeptically. What kind of a test was this? They'd never been permitted to go on a hunt without at least one of the Chieftain's warriors in tow—usually four or five.

"First, you are not unattended, you have the new captain of your personal royal guard," Jax said sternly. "Second, do not make us regret this. If there is any danger, shoot fire into the sky."

Vi gave a small nod. She hoped it wouldn't come to that. The last thing she wanted was to be around fire.

"Stay close enough that our watchers can see that alarm," Sehra continued, oblivious to the sub-context of Vi's magic lesson the day before. "And do not be gone for more than four days or we will use the noru to track you down."

"Yes, mum."

"Understood." Jayme brought a fist to her chest in salute.

"We will be exceptionally careful. Thank you again, Chieftain, for permitting us to hunt. I am particularly grateful this year." Vi lowered her eyes, dipping her head slightly.

"You are welcome." Her green eyes had turned hard, cold even in the early heat of the morning. "Perhaps you may practice your magic in the forests? I hear from Jax you've made progress lately. I would like to see it when you return."

"Perhaps…" The last thing Vi wanted to do was practice her magic. "Though I think I am looking forward to a vacation from my lessons."

"Are they too rigorous for you?" Andru asked.

Vi bit the insides of her cheeks. The sooner she left, the better. Or she may show Sehra her magic a little too soon.

"I find the wealth of knowledge my tutors give me settles in best when I have fresh air and time to process. I come back with the best questions."

"I look forward to hearing them during our next lessons, then."

With that, she put Andru mentally behind her, eager to find physical distance as well. Vi adjusted her pack, looking to her friends. "Ready?"

The two girls nodded.

"Stay safe," Sehra said as she leaned in to plant a kiss on her daughter's forehead.

"You're the oldest, Jayme, be sure to keep them in line," Jax gave one final command.

"I'll do my best, sir!"

The three started away from the towering trees of the castle and into the wooded city of Soricium. The trees were smaller, but still large enough to fit whole homes within and, thanks to the magic of the Groundbreakers, the people of Shaldan did just that.

Soricium, overall, was much like the fortress. It was a mix of stone and foliage. Groundbreakers bent earth and plant alike to make dwellings that came alive right alongside their residents. Doors appeared from solid walls and branches arced over the streets to create pathways for the confident footfalls of the magically inclined. Rooftops were covered in mosses that kept the houses cool in summer, warm in winter, and flowered in springtime.

"We're not going to stay even remotely close to the city, are we?" Ellene dared to ask when they were well out of earshot.

"Oh, not at all. I wasn't lying when I said I needed distance. As much as we can manage in the time we're allowed."

"What?" Jayme looked between them. "I just got done promising I would—"

"How many times have you come here, Jayme?" Vi interrupted.

"Given that I've been your courier for four years now and make a trip almost every month, that'd be…"

"At least forty-eight times." Ellene jumped in. "Well, almost every month, so at least forty."

"At least forty times and you've never even seen the Northern coast." Vi gasped loudly, drawing even more attention than the two heirs and their guard already were, walking through the shaded city. Medallions of sunlight danced on the road ahead, striking beams like the footprints of mythical fairy folk the elders spoke of around campfires.

"Can you keep it down?" Jayme looked around, uncomfortable.

"I just think that's something we need to fix."

"The coast is a little far," Ellene said uncertainly. "Why don't we—"

"No, we're going to the coast," Vi insisted. "We can dip our toes in the water before it's too cold."

"Yes, this has everything to do with water and nothing to do with the news that the fishing town has moved." Ellene easily called out Vi's true intentions.

"They always change the landscape. I must update my maps!" The fishing town was a nomadic ground that traveled along the coast. They used their abilities as Groundbreakers to terraform the land for better fishing. Living in a region full of those with the power to manipulate the earth itself was both a delight and nightmare, for a hobby cartographer like herself. "Besides, you knew this was going to happen, or you wouldn't have put my journal in my pack. You practically ensured it."

"Did you really?" Jayme looked to Ellene, but the girl looked anywhere else.

"She's an enabler." Vi laughed, hooking her arm with Jayme's. "Now, it's just us and we have a long hike ahead. Tell us all about the news of the South?"

Luckily, Jayme had no shortage of stories this time, for she talked as they left the city proper and the trees became free of dwellings. Her stories continued as they traversed the burnt stretch of earth that ringed Soricium—a holdover from the Empire's siege during the war well before Vi's birth.

On the second day, Vi and Ellene caught Jayme up on their adventures since the last time Jayme had been in the North—much less to talk about. Which was good, because by the late afternoon they had reached the sea, and Vi had all but forgotten the storm of power that loomed within her, threatening to break free.

FROM THIS HIGH IN the treetops, there was only wind.

A vine as thick as Vi's bicep was wrapped around her waist and the bark of the tree curved upward to cradle her feet and give her a comfortable stance. She squinted into the sunlight, trying to make out the exact curve of the land around the waves—nearly impossible with the midday glare off the sea.

Her journal was propped against her upper abdomen, held by her left hand. In her right was a stick of charcoal she was using to make hasty sketches—desperately trying, and failing, not to smudge. Every now and then, Vi lifted her eyes toward the horizon, checking her rendering.

It was close, not exact, but coming along. Vi stared again, this time in sheer wonder at how much the land seemed to have changed from the maps pinned back in her quarters. She'd stared at them for hours on end, committing their wiggling lines to memory. To think that some could make such a difference on the earth itself. Vi couldn't help but wonder what it was like to control power like that.

To have full control of magic at all.

"Are you quite done?" Ellene called up to her. The girl was stripped to her underclothes and dripping wet.

"Are you?" Vi shouted back. "You two look like you're enjoying the water a lot for people who didn't want to go this far."

"You should enjoy it too. Rather than spending the *entire* time perched in that tree."

"She'll just spend *most* of the time perched," Jayme chimed in.

"All right, all right, I'm basically done. I'll come down." Vi returned her charcoal to behind the front flap of her journal, quickly lacing the tie closed.

Ellene raised a hand and the tree shuddered and came to life. The vine around Vi adjusted its grip before hoisting her into the air. Her stomach rose to meet her jaw as she descended from the canopy. She'd been so high up that the wind in her ears grew to a whistle well before she neared the ground.

With a twist of her wrist, Ellene brought Vi to the earth gently. Her feet touching down on the soft carpet of small grasses that quickly became white sand. With a snap of her fingers, the vine uncurled and hung limply behind Vi.

"Was the snap really necessary?" Vi asked, kicking off her shoes and putting them with the other pairs.

"Everyone likes a bit of drama."

"Who did you hear that from?" Vi knew neither of Ellene's mothers would say such a thing. She was fairly certain she'd heard them espousing the opposite.

"Darrus," Ellene answered simply, quickly, as though she could sweep the name away. It didn't work.

"Who's this Darrus I keep hearing of?" Jayme asked from where she sat, legs stretched into the sea foam.

"Don't get her started," Vi cautioned, pulling up her leggings to step into the warm waters of the northern sea. If she didn't know better—didn't know that to the northwest, just over the horizon, there was a whole series of tiny islands separating the Main and Crescent Continents—she'd think she stood at the edge of the world itself.

"Darrus is just a boy." Ellene huffed, sitting back down where she'd been before.

"Wait, it's not *that* Darrus, is it? From the spring dances?"

"The same," Vi affirmed. The last time Jayme likely heard about Darrus would've been months ago. Which was the last time he was anything to Ellene.

"I thought we weren't speaking of him any longer? How did you word it?" Jayme made a show of thinking, but there was no way she'd forgotten Ellene's emotional tirade. "He was 'dead to us'?"

"Apparently asking Ellene to dance at the winter solstice can bring a man back to life." Vi grinned.

"So this is still about dances?" Jayme's eye roll conveyed exactly what she thought about that.

"Can we please change the topic?" Ellene begged.

"Sure, how about Lukke?" Vi recounted the last suitor before Darrus. Ellene had quite a few. But it was hardly surprising. She was smart, fierce, beautiful, enjoyed the chase, and most importantly—had the time to deal with boys.

"Another boy?"

"You two are the worst!" Ellene laid back into the sand with a huff.

Vi and Jayme both shared a small laugh at her expense, but allowed the teasing to subside.

"What about you, princess? Any suitors catching your eye?" Jayme turned the tables.

"You know the answer is no. If it wasn't no, you'd already be aware from the gossip that would be flying around the Capital." There was one thing Romulin had always been quite clear on—that regardless of where she was in the world, any romantic involvement on her part would have the gossip mongers of the Capital talking. She was the heir to the Empire, and just about everyone seemed to want to have a hand in her match... except for her.

It wasn't that Vi didn't care. She hoped that she'd find love, or love would find her someday. But she'd just never felt that way about anyone, not like the storybooks made it out to be, all butterflies and stardust. Certainly not the instant attraction that had Ellene swooning over someone new each of the three springs since she turned twelve. Vi counted her blessings for the fact, since it made following Romulin's sound advice to avoid romance entirely even easier.

"Plus, I have too much to worry about. I don't have time to add a boy to the mix."

"The Senate might disagree with that when you get back," Jayme muttered.

"Yes, the crusty old men and women who want to take my crown also want to decide my romantic fate." She'd never be so bold in front of anyone other than Ellene and Jayme. Her directness had them both laughing, and Vi spared a small smile on the outside. She knew it was no laughing matter though. Eventually, she would have to marry—and it would no doubt be a politically arranged union.

"And what about you? You're doing an awfully good job at pointing fingers at Ellene and me."

"What time would I possibly have to find a suitor?" Jayme shook her head. "Last I heard, most suitors like their other half at least relatively present, and I'm traveling across the continent every few weeks."

"Well, you won't be now." Vi sat down between them, not caring about her clothes getting soaked in the process. She didn't know when she'd feel the water again. "Sounds like you'll be stuck with me now."

"Lucky me," Jayme said, deadpan.

Vi roared with laughter. "I'm *the worst*, aren't I?"

"You have no idea."

Even Ellene snorted with amusement at that.

"Perhaps you found love already in the man you're traveling with?" Vi suggested, not entirely sincerely.

"How dare you!" Jayme gasped and Vi couldn't tell how much was for show. "Andru is awful."

"He's as bad as he seems?" Ellene asked.

Jayme sighed heavily. Her brow softened and she shook her head—a slight reversal on her earlier position. "I don't know. Perhaps I've been unfair to him. He's just so uncomfortable to be around, with that shifting gaze and those fidgeting hands. I assumed—"

"Don't go sympathizing with him," Vi cautioned. "You're *my* ally." Romulin had said Andru was more important than she could realize. Vi needed her friends on her side to help navigate whatever *that* meant.

Jayme just shrugged. She was never one for hesitating when it came to contesting Vi, at least in private. Vi appreciated the woman all the more for it.

"Either way, he's not a love interest. Certainly not for me."

"Then maybe we'll both find love when we get back to the capital?" Vi suggested.

Jayme just shrugged, seizing the opportunity to shift the topic. "Speaking of Solarin... Can you really leave all this? For the capital and all its snow and ice? It seems like paradise here."

"Everywhere is paradise, just a different kind." Her maps told her that much. The world was wide and diverse; there were highlands and lowlands, frigid mountains and tropical jungles. Who was to say which was better than the other?

"Spoken like an Empress," Jayme groaned.

"What's wrong with that?"

"Because it's such a cliché answer."

Vi shrugged. "It's the truth."

"I don't even want to leave this spot right now." Jayme looked out over the waves, toward the horizon. "Everything seems so… simple here. Being with you two, like this. It's almost like I can believe the three of us are just girls relaxing. Nothing more complex than that. I can almost tell myself that time may not come for us, and we could be forever this way."

Vi studied Jayme's face. There was something distant and sad about it. It was almost the same expression Jayme got whenever she spoke of her family—her father specifically. But before Vi could really put her finger on it, Jayme stood and shook the emotion from her with the sand clinging to her legs.

"Speaking of leaving, though. We likely should. If we're going to lie about how far we went we need to make sure we're back in four days."

"Our guard hath spoken," Ellene said to Vi.

"Right!" Vi jumped up, giving Jayme a salute.

"Don't mock me." The soldier rolled her eyes. "Some of us have to work for our positions in life, you know, we're not just born with them."

"We're not mocking you, we're very proud of you for your hard work," Vi said with genuine sincerity that she hoped shined through. "If it weren't for you, I wouldn't have had half the connection with my family I did."

Jayme glanced askance, clearly uncertain about the praise. True to form, she pushed past it. "We should also likely hunt something. It'll be even more believable we were on a hunt if we come back with a kill."

"Don't look at me, that's Vi's area of expertise." Ellene tugged on her tunic and the shorts she wore underneath. The girl often went barefoot, claiming it was a Groundbreaker tactic to feel the earth better.

"Do you mind? Seeing as I doubt I'll be killing anything in this jungle with a sword." Jayme strapped the weapon in question back to her waist.

"No, I can hunt something on the way, I'm sure." Vi detached her bow and quiver from her pack, handing the pack itself to Ellene. The girl already had a system for managing both. But before she could sling it on her back, Jayme took it and had it over her shoulder.

"If I can't help with the hunt, the least I can do is carry supplies," Jayme insisted.

"But—"

"Let her, Ellene. You may be able to help me with your magic like you did the last time," Vi thought aloud.

They were a good twenty paces into the forest when Jayme dared to ask the question Vi could only assume had been burning her up since the mere mention of magic. "What about *your* magic, Vi? The Chieftain said—"

"I've no idea what Sehra was talking about. The last thing any of us want, myself included, is for me to use my magic," she said quickly, sternly. Her friends shared a startled look at Vi's tone. "Sorry… It's been… strange lately, is all."

"Strange how?" Ellene asked.

"I think I'm Awoken now," Vi confessed.

"Why didn't you tell us sooner? That's excellent news!" Her friend hopped from foot to foot. She'd never really understood Vi's plight. Ellene had manifested early, was Awoken quickly, and moreover had an ancient power in her that was said to have descended right from the Goddess herself. The Northerners called her a Child of Yargen.

"Like I said, it's been weird and I'd rather not test it," Vi said firmly. But, unsurprisingly, Ellene missed it.

"Why? You should—"

"If you think it's for the best," Jayme interrupted Ellene.

"The best would be for us to move more quietly so we don't scare away any jungle fowl."

At the suggestion, they moved through the forest silently and Vi appreciated that her play for a reprieve from the conversation worked.

Ellene made almost no noise, the ground curling around her feet with pulses of power to muffle her steps. Vi was the next most quiet, her steps in the jungle confident from a lifetime of venturing through it. Jayme... she tried her best. But she clearly wasn't accustomed to the shrub brushes, dangling vines, or gnarled roots that reached up to trip an unwary traveler.

The first day yielded nothing. They broke for camp, and all agreed that the next morning they'd find their luck. After a few hours of walking, their optimism was rewarded. Vi held up her hand, stopping her companions.

Movement in the distance caught her eye. Vi squinted, looking through the shifting shafts of light that were determined to make their path through the thick canopy. She crouched low, hearing the others following her lead.

There was another flash of green, the light hitting a rainbow of colored feathers. Vi slowly pointed, making sure they both saw it. She brought her finger to each of them, pointed at the ground, and then mouthed the words, *"You stay here."*

Ellene and Jayme nodded. Ellene soundlessly ascended into the trees above and Vi began her slow crawl through the brush. She pushed aside large fronds, using them to half-keep her concealed as she approached the unsuspecting beast. Vi ignored the branches sticking to the messy braids of her hair as she found a good vantage.

Slowly, she slid an arrow from her quiver, notching it and drawing back. Sweat cut through the grime that coated her like a second skin after spending days in the jungle, raining into her eyes off her brow. It stung, but she ignored the haze of dirt and salt just as she ignored the ache in her legs from pressing into the roots and rock underneath her.

There was nothing in the world beyond the sound of her heart, and the tall-necked and long-legged bird that pecked the ground before her.

Vi took in a deep breath through her nose, holding it as she stretched every last bit of tension from her bow. The creature raised its head suddenly, looking through the forest. Whatever had startled it, Vi couldn't sense.

This was it. One clean shot.

The bird swiveled its head back around. The feathers of its flightless wings puffed outward. Vi could see it squat slightly, loading power in its nimble legs before it would bolt once more into the dense underbelly of the jungle. Her eyes widened slightly and fingers relaxed.

Vi's arrow shot straight, narrowly missing its mark. It whizzed past the head of the bird, her prediction of its movements off by a mere hair.

"Ellene!" Vi leapt from her vantage, sliding down the leafy forest floor. She would give chase, wouldn't let this one go.

Above her, trees groaned and shifted. Their canopies arced and swayed in unnatural ways. She heard the crackling and groaning of wood as branches and vines alike came to life at the behest of her magical friend sprinting across them.

"Head left!" Ellene shouted above.

Just as she finished speaking, a wall of stone jutted from the earth, causing the sprinting bird to track left. Vi notched another arrow, drew, took a breath, loosed. Once more, it whizzed past, missing by the smallest of margins.

"Again!" Vi shouted, pumping her legs against the forest floor, struggling to keep her balance and keep up with the creature. She was determined. This wouldn't get the best of her. She wouldn't let it win.

"Right!" Another curved wall of stone; the bird course corrected.

With flaps of its tiny wings, it launched itself up in a long leap onto a low branch. Every feather stood on end, tail upright and fanned like a rainbow as the bird gave an indignant squawk at her.

Vi was breathless, but from running, not from fear. If it tried to attack her with its long claws, it'd be dead. Either by her arrow, or Ellene's magic dropping a tree branch or rock on it. She was hunting for sport. But all sport would be gone if it actually became a threat to her.

She watched its motions, calming her breathing as much as possible as her legs continued to propel her forward. Her arm strained from holding her bow drawn as she made her calculations. It would try to use the height to its advantage and leap to attack. But that also made its movements relatively predictable, as its options were severely limited.

Wanting to keep her advantage, Vi dashed forward, forcing the creature to act. She tracked the tip of her arrow over the face of the animal as she watched its eyes— almost in slow motion—shifting to the left. *There, it would go there*, everything in Vi's body screamed.

Pushing her heels into the ground, Vi skidded, leaning back to get a better angle and bracing herself to come to a stop as her feet would eventually catch rock or root. The bird leaped just as she'd predicted. Her heart raced right before the kill.

"Vi, look out!" Ellene's shrill cry barely registered.

Where she'd expected her feet to meet something solid, there was only air. Her stomach shot up and out through her mouth in a scream, as the world was plunged into darkness.

8

S HE WAS FALLING.

The arrow she'd notched flew in a strange arc as she let it go in surprise. Vi watched it whiz past the jungle fowl harmlessly, missing by a large margin, and the creature continued its escape. That was the last thing she saw as the light of the jungle quickly faded.

Ditching her bow, Vi's hands moved on instinct to try to brace her. Vi saw only stars as her body struck against a tall, wide stone. Her bow clattered, finally hitting the ground. She tried to calculate how far down it must be, but there was just pain and tension as her body rolled down the stone. When her body met the ground, Vi flopped onto her back and wheezed.

She could breathe. That much was good, at least.

But she couldn't use the word "good" for the rest of her situation. Vi stared up, blinking at the circle of light above her. It was a green oculus to the jungle she'd fallen from. Vines swayed down into the cavern she now found herself in, dirt padded the ground under her, and the creeping plants that had masked the hole she'd fallen into were torn to leafy bits and cast about like confetti.

Groaning, Vi wiggled her fingers and toes, then moved her elbows and knees. She stretched her arms above her head, slowly, feeling the muscles in her chest expand over her ribs. Nearly every corner of her body hurt, but the stone pillar that stretched at a diagonal through the cavern had broken her fall enough that nothing seemed worse than bruises.

Pillar.

Vi rolled onto her side and pushed herself up from her elbow. Blood trickled across her skin, and she felt the same warmth rolling down her temple. Bruises and scrapes weren't so bad, all things considered, and Vi had more important things to focus on—like where she was.

The cavern was dark, the only source of light from the hole she'd fallen through. It cast long shadows on the ominous, gray underground she now sat in. But what fascinated her the most was how those shadows clung to sculptures carved into the far walls, barely filling their cracks and carvings enough for her to make them out. Her eyes darted from pillar to pillar, to the domed ceiling above her.

It was a ceiling. Not a naturally formed cave someone had decorated—which would still be incredible—but a man-made structure.

There were stretches of stone beam with small, black, shining bits of glass or stone placed between them, like dark stars glittering on a gray sky. There were supports around the edge of the room. And an archway, half collapsed, that led further into the mysterious darkness.

She tried to force her mind to ignore the pain and think. Had she seen ruins on her maps in this area? Vi couldn't recall, but likely not. She trusted her memory of her maps more than their accuracy, especially when it came to Northern ruins. No one seemed to think them important enough to mark. Or, if they were known, they were taboo—either too sacred or too cursed to traverse. The two facts combined resulted in precious little information on them.

"Vi!" Ellene's face appeared in the hole above. "Oh thank Yargen." Worry melted instantly into relief. "Are you all right?"

"I'm fine." Vi finally stood, fighting a small wince. Her left elbow ached the worst. It was her non-dominant arm, but also the one she used to hold her bow. "Bruised and scraped is all."

"I'm sending down a vine."

"No, wait." Vi took a step forward. "This is some kind of ruin."

"So?"

"None of my maps have ruins anywhere near this area."

"Vi, *really?*" Ellene groaned. "Forget about your maps this one time and come back up."

"Don't you want to know what this is?" Vi looked up at the girl. "It looks like it's from the early days of Shaldan."

"I'm sure it's old if it's completely buried and unmarked. Do you ever consider that maybe there's a reason for that? Some things are best left uncharted and undisturbed."

"I don't know if that's true…" Vi turned her eyes back toward the archway, peering into the darkness beyond. It was utterly impenetrable from where she stood. There would be only one way to know what lurked in that blackness. "I'll be back in a minute."

"Vi, no, please," Ellene whined softly. "Don't go exploring, come back up. We need to get going."

"I'm sure Jayme isn't far behind." Holding all the packs likely slowed her down. "I'll only be a minute and I'll be back before she gets here. It won't slow us down and then I can mark my maps."

"It looks dangerous," Ellene said, even though she could barely see the whole of it.

"It's been standing for a while like this. I think it can stand a little longer." Vi took a step forward, toward the edge of the circle of light the hole cast on the floor.

"Vi—"

"I'll only be a minute," Vi said firmly, looking back up at her friend. "Just wait there."

Ignoring the soft whimper from above that was equal parts worry and frustration, Vi stepped into the shadow.

Her eyes quickly adjusted to the dim light as she stepped over rubble, heading first toward the carvings on the walls. There were men and women, standing among trees, carving the land and building civilization. Always among them was the single figure of a woman, an axe in hand.

She paused at the threshold of the arch, taking Ellene's concerns to heart. Half of it had collapsed, a giant tree root stretching through the holes it'd punched in the stone. But that same tree root seemed to be helping support the ceiling of the narrow tunnel that led farther underground.

Even with her eyes continuing to fight to adjust to the dim light, it became harder and harder to see. The room opened up again; Vi felt it more than saw it. For now there were only the ghosts of light catching on the outlines of stone before her. The still, dank air felt expansive around her and Vi had the sensation as though she'd stepped into the mouth of a slumbering beast.

Taking a breath, and raising a slightly quivering hand, Vi carefully brought her spark to the surface. It shot up her forearm, running along the tendons under her skin. Vi focused on condensing the sparks into a single flame as they arced between her fingers and palm like tiny bolts of lightning. It was barely more than a candle, yet against the darkness that had rested undisturbed for countless years, it may as well have been a torch.

Before her was an expansive hall. Rows of columns at least three stories tall sloped down and away from her. Vi couldn't tell if the room had always sloped, or if it was the weight of the jungle above it, pressing down for years on this forgotten place.

The damp aroma of water filled the air. But it wasn't stale or moldy smelling. Instead, it was bright, fresh, as if fed by an underground spring. She'd heard of such underground channels feeding the jungles of the North from a great reservoir, but Vi had never seen one with her own eyes.

Vi moved her hand to get a better look at one of the carvings on the walls and her eyes were drawn to the flame. Suddenly, it was as if invisible fingers had grabbed her face and were stretching her lids upward and downward at the same time, holding her head in place. She felt the spark creeping up her neck, magic rattling in her skull. The flame brightened, going white hot.

No! Vi struggled against the sensation. She didn't want a vision here and now. But all her muscles were rigid and locked, her mental resistance quickly thwarted. The fire was all she saw as it quickly consumed her senses.

All at once, Vi was no longer standing in that dark underground ruin, but in a city she'd never seen before.

The day felt sickly hot, and the aroma of death clung to the square where she stood. Her eyes darted from the sun-shades that looked more like sails extending up from the white-washed stones of the walls. Orange and red roof tiles dipped into gutters made of steel, embellished with faces that had wide open mouths to pour rain from.

To her left was a row of chairs, a throne in its center. A woman, dressed in whole bolts of draped silk, sat with an ornate crown of gold on her head. At its peak was a sunburst, pillars supporting it. Vi squinted, trying to make out the face hidden underneath the long veil attached to the base of the crown. It looked almost like the sun crown of the Empire, yet not… Vi was certain it wasn't her mother sitting before her.

Flanking the queen were men and women, all dressed in finery with badges pinned over their left breasts. They each stared down a few short steps to the center of the square. There, kneeling before them, was a man Vi recognized.

"*Father!*" she called out. Her voice was muffled, smothered by the whole atmosphere of this strange place. It was then that she noticed there was no sound at all. She could hear nothing, despite seeing it with nearly perfect clarity.

Aldrik wore clothing she'd never seen him in before. It was embellished in patterns from his heels up to the long panels of the coat fastened with silver closures up to the neck. The sleeves were tucked into gloves, billowing at his elbows. She couldn't recognize where such a cut would hail from.

Where was he? And who would the Emperor Solaris kneel to? He alone was the ruler of all civilization.

The queen spoke, her words silent, and waved her hand. Aldrik stood, looking behind him at double doors pulled open by men posted to either side. Vi squinted; the vision was growing hazy.

A burly man—no, a *monster*—emerged. While he walked on two legs, and had two thick arms attached to broad shoulders with a single head between them, the similarities with "human" ended there.

He had a snout much like a lizard, and his skin was armored with plate-like scales that seemed to grow naturally underneath his flesh. They extended up in small horns along his snout, running along his brow. They also extended in the opposite direction, down his long tail. When he spoke, two rows of razor-sharp teeth glinted in the light.

Vi could not hear the words, the silence suddenly suffocating.

He pushed forward a cage and within it was an even more horrifying sight. A man was slamming his head against the bars, white oozing from the splits in his skin. His eyes had gone milky, streaked with pulsating red veins of unnatural magic that bulged from his skin and ran down his cheeks like tears.

She could not hear every sickening thud of the diseased man's body as he slammed it against the bars, but she could see her father's wince. She could see his hands clench at his side as he no doubt fought to stand rigidly still. The vision continued to fade, the details blurring, slowly blotting out as though it were overexposed—burned away.

In a blink, Vi was back in her body.

She landed hard on her knees, hands digging into the slightly moist stones beneath her. Vi gasped for air. Her equilibrium reeled. What was real? *What was that?*

"It's you." The words were smooth and rich, and colored by a soft lilt. The voice's timbre was deeper than the lowest string of a cello, more resonant than a war drum.

Vi slowly rose her head toward the sound of the voice.

When she had fallen, her flame had extinguished—thankfully. But the room was now lit up by the man himself standing before her. Concentric circles of light spun slowly around his feet, raising up to his knees before fading into the darkness; every few moments a new one repeated the cycle. He gave off his own illumination, and every movement seemed to trail sparks of magic through the dark air.

She recognized him from the first vision—dark purple hair, nearly black; his green eyes, the overall litheness about him. The Vi of the future had been on some clandestine meeting with this strange man who now stood before her.

"It's you," Vi whispered back, certain now that she'd hit her head and this must be a dream.

The man moved slowly. Every wisp of light caught along his hair and trailed off of him as he knelt before her. Eyes at her level, he stared at her, through her, with irises that glowed with their own strikingly green inner light. He looked at something in her that Vi wasn't sure if she'd ever even seen.

"You… you are the champion?" He continued to stare at her. Vi slid back slightly, trying to put more distance between them. Her elbow ached from the fall, but the only thing she paid attention to was the man before her.

"Champion?" Vi shook her head. "I'm the Crown Princess of the Solaris Empire." She'd look a lot more the part if she picked herself off the ground. But her muscles wouldn't obey her commands. She felt frozen under his gaze.

"Solaris…" He scrunched his nose with what Vi would dare say was disgust. He looked her up and down one final time. Vi knew when she was being sized up, and this was certainly one of those times. She also knew when she didn't measure up. "Why would she choose one of the Dark Isle as her champion?"

"I have no idea who you are or what you're talking about. I'm not the person you think I am. What I'd like to know is—"

"I know who you are," he said quickly, sharply. His accent had a harshness when whispered that silenced her immediately. "You are the one who has tortured me, year over year."

"You have the wrong girl." Vi stressed every word, as if that would somehow get it through his thick skull. "Who are you?"

"I am the voice." A frown crossed over his lips. "You do not know who I am. You don't know who you are. Do you even know you stand at an apex?"

"Do I dare ask a question or are you just going to berate me and not answer it anyway?" Vi asked with a frown. Frustration and anger were beginning to win out over the wonder and fear at the mysterious visitor. He wasn't answering her questions. She doubted he was even listening to them.

Vi thought she saw a small smirk cross his lips, but she couldn't be sure, for it was gone as quickly as it came.

"You're useless to me as you are now and time is running short." He stood, taking a step backward.

"Useless? Excuse me?" Vi tried to push herself off the ground. Her whole body felt heavy. "How da—"

He lifted a hand. Magic spiraled out from his palm, a swirling glyph similar to the one around his feet—similar to what had glowed before her watch. "*Samasha*," he whispered.

The word struck her like a punch to the gut. It knocked the wind from her, leaving Vi gasping and doubled over once more. She squinted up at the man, fighting for words. But behind her eyes were explosions of light that rippled across her skin, leaving goosebumps in their wake.

"Wh-what did you do to me?" she forced out the words. Her whole body rattled, her flesh searing hot against the ice-cold air of the underground.

She was going to be incinerated from the inside out. Her magic was going to break free of its tethers and, somehow, she would be burned by it. Firebearers could only be burned by the flames of stronger Firebearers, levied with the intent to harm. It should be impossible, but every searing nerve ending screaming in pain told her otherwise.

"Find the apexes. Seek me out." The man vanished, taking his unnatural light with him, leaving Vi gasping, struggling for consciousness against the bone-rattling tremors that shook through her, alone in the darkness of what she hoped would not be her tomb.

9

I T COULD'VE BEEN SECONDS, or hours.

But eventually, the shakes faded. Her jaw had been locked, preventing her from making any noise greater than a whimper in the darkness—forcing her to suffer quietly. Yet when those bolts of agony finally vanished, Vi felt better. Great, almost.

She pushed herself away from the ground, straightening. Behind her, the hall stretched onward, but she'd had enough exploring for one day and didn't exactly feel like going for a swim in the dark. She wanted to put it all behind her, for now, and return to the world above where things made sense. Where she knew what was up, and down, and most importantly… what was *real*.

"… maybe five minutes now?" Ellene's voice echoed back to Vi as she emerged from the collapsed archway.

Five minutes? Had it really just been five minutes? She felt as though she'd lived an entire lifetime, died, and been reborn in that cavern.

"That's it, I'm going down there," Jayme declared.

"There's no need for that." Vi stepped back into the circle of sunlight, looking up at her friends. "I'm right here."

"What happened to you?" Jayme gasped.

Well, if that wasn't a question with an answer worthy of a thousand gold. Vi didn't really know where to begin. But she knew Jayme was focused on the bruises, scrapes, and blood still rolling down her knees from where the wounds had been ripped open again.

"I fell into a hole." Vi shrugged. Her friends wouldn't understand—or believe her—if she'd told them what she'd seen. Frankly, Vi didn't believe herself. Standing in the sunlight, it all truly felt like a dream… more like a nightmare. "I got banged up a bit, but I'm fine. Ellene, can you help me out of here?"

"Gladly."

A vine slithered down into the hole, bending itself unnaturally into a U shape. Vi grabbed her bow and sat on it like she would a swing. Holding on to both sides, the vine lifted her up and out, depositing her on solid ground next to both of her friends before falling limply behind her.

"Are you sure you're all right?" Jayme asked, looking her up and down.

"It's not as bad as it looks. It's all superficial—bruises and cuts—nothing serious," Vi assured them. "I just may be a little slow getting back."

"I can still carry your pack," Jayme said, even though it was already slung across her back.

"I can manage." Vi held out her hand. "I'm certainly not going to be attempting to hunt anymore."

Jayme just shrugged, starting into the forest, Vi's pack still over her shoulder. Ellene and Vi shared a look, a non-verbal agreement that sometimes it was best not to even attempt argument when Jayme had made up her mind. Ellene started first behind their friend, and Vi followed.

"At least now we have a good excuse for why we're taking the whole four days," Ellene mused, clearly trying to gild the tension with a silver lining.

"I'm sure they expected us to take the whole time regardless." Jayme glanced over her shoulder, as if making sure they were still following. "You two will always run to the end of whatever leash you're given."

"I think I should take offense to that." Ellene's tone clearly conveyed she didn't.

The two continued on talking, but Vi stayed focused on her feet and the ground below her.

What had happened in those ruins?

Small tremors still shook her hands, and she wished Jayme had let her carry her pack so she'd have something to hold on to. Instead, she balled them into fists, trying to use the tension to still the shaking. The embers within her were now an outright blaze.

She stared down at her fists as if waiting for them to ignite with the raw power that was steadily filling her. *Fists.* It reminded her of her father's motion in her vision.

"What is it, Ellene?" Jayme had stopped walking. Vi had been so lost in her thoughts that she almost went face-first into Ellene's back, who had also stopped dead in her tracks.

"What's wrong?" Vi rested her hand on Ellene's shoulder to jolt her from her thoughts.

Ellene gazed eastward, the same direction the bird had when it'd been initially spooked. The movement was so similar, so instinctual, that Vi knew instantly the correlation was not by chance. Whatever the animal had sensed then, Ellene sensed now.

"What is it?"

"Something big." Ellene crouched down, digging her fingers into the earth. She closed her eyes. There was a quiet pulsing of magic rippling out from her. "It's odd…"

"What is?"

She seemed startled, as if she'd somehow not realized she'd spoken aloud. "There's an odd feeling in the trees around us, all of them."

"Odd *how*?"

"As though the earth itself is shuddering."

"How can the earth shudder?" Jayme asked

"I don't know." Ellene's tone matched Vi's thoughts. A flight of birds took to the skies in the distance, punching through the canopy of trees with chaotic squawking. The branches of the trees swayed and Vi wondered if the rumbling she felt was only in her mind, brought on by Ellene's words.

"What do you think it is?" Vi was almost afraid to ask.

"Nothing good." Ellene went from perfect stillness to motion. She sprinted past them, calling over her shoulder. "We need to go, now!"

They didn't question, running immediately behind her.

A rustling in the distance grew to a cacophony of snapping tree branches and crunching undergrowth. With a roar, a hulking noru cat burst into view. Vi turned, and froze with a mixture of fear, fascination, and stomach-churning recognition.

The beast oozed white globs from open sores that *plopped* sickly to the ground. It was as if every drop of blood in its veins had been replaced by the grotesque liquid. Its eyes were glossed over and pale, with familiar red streaks bulging in them. In fact, the magic-filled veins pulsed upward from its fur across its body, casting an ominous glow on the tree bark around it.

"The White Death," Jayme uttered from behind her.

It suddenly made sense. What Vi had seen in her vision, what she was confronted with now. They'd said the plague was in the North. But it hadn't seemed real until the moment she stared it in its unnatural, white eyes.

"Grandmother," Ellene whimpered, her voice nearly as frozen with fear as Vi's feet.

The beast slammed into a tree, as though it were drunk. A new wound burst open in the center of its head, as though its skin had gone brittle; chunks fell off like chips from a sculptor's chisel. It shook its head, swayed, and picked itself back up slowly.

"Ellene," Jayme whispered. "Can you take us up to the treetops? It hasn't seen us yet, maybe we can avoid it entirely."

Its hulking head turned slowly. Two orbs, like polished stone, stared right at Vi. A shot of energy ran straight up her spine.

"It saw me," she breathed, panic flooding her.

"How do you—" Jayme never finished her thought. The beast turned, charging right for them. "Ellene, we have to go!"

Jayme lunged for Ellene in an attempt to get her moving. Vi watched as the girl buried her hands in her hair. She knew what was coming next—Ellene's magic would act on instinct to protect her. A stone shell, like a turtle's carapace, shot up from the ground around her. Jayme was close enough that she was encased in it as well.

But Vi... she'd been two steps too far away, and now she was alone with the charging Noru.

"Let me out!" Jayme's muffled shouts could be heard.

"Mother, mother," Ellene cried. If it were possible, the rock seemed to thicken. The voices vanished entirely.

Vi's eyes turned back to the still charging Noru.

This was how she was going to die. That was the prevailing thought that ran through Vi's brain, muffling everything else except for her heartbeat. Why was her heartbeat so loud? She couldn't hear the snapping of wood or the snarls of the beast. All she could hear was the sound of her own vital signs. Well, at least as long as she heard that, she knew she was alive.

And if she was alive, she'd do everything in her power to stay that way.

Turning, Vi began to run. There was no way she could outpace a noru, so she'd have to try to outsmart it. Vi slid, gripping a tree root to swing into a shaded alcove at the base of the tree. She pressed her back into it, hoping to confuse the maddened animal and hide from it.

The tree rumbled, bark snapping, as the beast ran head-first into its trunk. Vi bit back a scream. The noru roared. Vi curled her legs, digging the balls of her feet into the earth, seeking some purchase underneath the thick covering of leaves. Her toes slammed into a root and her thighs wrapped under her chest, exploding with power as she began running again.

Fire. She had to make fire. Surely they were close enough now for the watchers to see a warning.

Her side burned from her heavy breathing; her knees ached. The only thing keeping her moving was the knowledge that if she stopped she would be a snack for the giant cat trying to kill her. Darting between the trees, trying to out-nimble the large beast, Vi swung in a wide arc, trying to dredge up her spark in the process.

A paw, twice her size, came out of nowhere. Vi dodged inward, narrowly avoiding the claws, but was batted across the jungle like a toy. Her body slammed into another tree and stars exploded behind her eyes for the second time in one day. Vi fell limply to the ground, trying to push herself up as the creature stalked closer.

Get up. She had to get up. She was the daughter of Aldrik and Vhalla Solaris—cut from a cloth that couldn't be sheared so easily. Even if the giant saber-sized claws were about to prove her wrong.

"Get up!" Vi cried. Tears were streaming down her cheeks. She would die before ever having the chance to live with her family—without ever finding her true home.

The noru's breath was hot on her face as it leaned down. A row of razor-sharp teeth glinted. The cat reared back, and dove in to eat her whole.

Vi screamed, and fire exploded from her.

Like a sailor watching a lifeline slip over the deck-rail, Vi watched as her control over the magic escaped her hands. Just as Ellene's magic had sprung forth to craft a shell to protect her, so did Vi's. Except hers was an inferno. Flames spread across the ground, fed by her magic and uncontrolled.

Too much. She had to get control of it. Her mind was frozen, unable to do anything but look on in horror as her magic took over.

She felt like she could burn the world down if she wasn't careful.

Vi continued to fight to stand, the ground beneath her ash and barren already. Her clothes had burned off entirely, as they had the last time, and the only thing she saw was white-hot flames.

Withdraw, withdraw, her mind urged in panic, mirroring her uncle's words. She would hurt her friends if she didn't. But the fire was too big. It had spread too far, too fast, and was beyond her control now. There was too much magic.

There were screams—distinctly animal. Hopefully Ellene's rocky shield protected her from the blaze. Vi curled into a ball, holding herself, trying to make herself as small as possible.

Find the void. *Find the void*, she chanted in her mind. Vi closed her eyes, but there was no darkness. Instead there was only light, and the unstoppable tide of her magic.

She felt every expanse of flame, as though it was a part of her. It filled her lungs and seared in her ears, as though trying to lick her mind itself.

The screams cut through to her. How was the animal still alive? Or was it perhaps Ellene and Jayme?

Vi's head jerked up and she looked around frantically. But it was the same as behind her eyes. It was as though she had been dropped into the sun itself.

Her friends, confidants, the two true allies she had. She would kill them with her own hands. Vi looked down, already seeing their invisible blood staining her skin.

What Vi had always seen as fire was replaced by strands of magic peeling off her flesh. They unfurled as though spinning from a spool of magic within her. Vi watched as they stretched off her, flowed into the air, and knotted into tendrils of pure fire.

What was this power? It wasn't anything like she'd ever witnessed before. Yet it was as if she'd known it all along.

Samasha.

The word echoed through her like the peel of a bell, bringing crystalline clarity to the chaos roaring around her. All at once, Vi realized she'd never truly seen her magic before. This was not future sight. This was not fire magic at all.

Her power was light itself, and all the possibilities of the world stretched within it—the code of the universe writ large. Just like the glyphs she'd seen winding around the man, and around her watch—*this* was her magic. Vi took a breath and slowly brought her hands together, pressing her fingertips to make a cage. Narrowing her eyes, Vi focused on channeling the wild tendrils of light and fire to condense, to form a knotted ball of those same incomprehensible glyphs underneath her palms.

The fire subsided, her magic focused on one place. When it was squarely under her control, Vi merely pulled a string in her mind, and watched it all harmlessly unravel. Just like that, the flames vanished.

Vi blinked into the black, barren, smoking field, her eyes adjusting. They barely had a moment to come into focus on the charred bones of the noru, all flesh burned away, before darting to where Ellene's protective cocoon of rock pulled up from the earth.

It had been split open, and Vi let out a scream of anguish—a sound unlike any she had made ever before.

10

SHE HAD KILLED HER friends.

Her magic had broken free and unleashed its true nature—whatever that thread-like power had been—and it had been deadly to the two people who had been closer to her than any others in the world.

Vi buried her face in her hands, wishing she had been the one to burn instead. She stayed curled up on the barren field, naked and uncaring in her grief. The Empire would carry on just fine without her. She'd served her purpose as a ward in the North to keep peace. Romulin could take the throne and her parents—

"Vi!" Jax's voice broke through her thoughts.

Vi lifted her head, turning. Off to the side, at the edge of the burnt ring, a group stood. Her eyes widened as she looked past the noru—the non-diseased kind—past the two warriors who were still mounted, and landed on Sehra clutching tightly to Ellene, with Jayme standing awkwardly off to the side.

Sehra was saying things Vi couldn't hear from this distance. Her green eyes, on occasion, would flick Vi's way. But neither woman made any motion to bridge the gap between them.

Better Ellene angry with her than dead.

"Vi," Jax repeated, panting as he came to a stop before her. He stood bare-chested, eyes turned up toward the sky. His tunic was clenched in his palm. "Here."

Vi looked from him to the article of clothing he'd removed to give her. Vi took his shirt and hastily slid it over her shoulders. He waited an extra second with his eyes averted, then looked back. She could see the relief that flooded his expression.

"By the Mother." He dropped to his knees before her, wrapping his arms tightly around her shoulders. Vi winced slightly from all the cuts and bruises, but his embrace was welcome support. "What in gods' names happened?"

Where should she begin?

She'd banged herself up falling down a hole. Had an out-of-body experience tangling with the future, *again*, and then met a man who'd seemed to be more light than matter. She'd been chased and nearly eaten by a diseased noru. And then saw a magic she didn't even know how to describe unraveling from her.

If she'd been tasked with imagining the strangest, most exhausting day possible, Vi wouldn't have been able to come up with half of it.

"There was a noru that had the White Death and—"

"The White Death?" She hadn't thought his tone could get more serious, but he proved her wrong. "You're sure?"

"I'm sure," Vi affirmed without doubt.

"How do you know?"

"Jayme saw it," Vi explained, avoiding mention of the vision of her father and the caged man. She'd tell her uncle eventually. But right now, her head was already swimming and there was only so much she could process at once. "She said she knew its signs from the capital. But even without her account, I had no doubt as to what it was."

"This close to Soricium..." he muttered. Jax's dark stubble folded in around his mouth as he pressed it into a thin line. "Let's head back. We can discuss this with Sehra."

He brought his fingers to his lips, letting out a shrill whistle. Gormon, the noru Sehra had gifted Vi a few years ago, came padding over. Vi watched it come close, swallowing hard. She'd had enough noru for one day. But she also knew when she was being ridiculous; Gormon was a loyal beast.

Crown princesses did not have the luxury of clinging to past emotional distresses.

She'd already learned that the hard way, multiple times. Whatever trauma life threw at her, she had to bury it, push forward, and move on, or else risk being suffocated by her own self-doubt. No one would understand, or have any sympathy, if she complained.

"Come on, up with you." Jax held out his hands. "Can you stand?"

"I think so." Vi took his hands, trying to pull herself to her feet. She let out a yelp of pain in the process and her left knee folded. Her uncle quickly caught her, using his strength to support her so Vi didn't have to put her weight on what now seemed likely to be broken. "Or, not."

"First, cleric. Then we speak with Sehra."

Vi gripped him tightly, looking back to Sehra at the mention of the woman. The scolding would be well deserved, but Vi wasn't looking forward to it.

"Are Ellene and Jayme truly all right?" she whispered.

"Shaken up a bit, but Ellene's magic protected her, barely. If you hadn't stopped the fire when you did, this might have been a very different day."

"A day I don't want to think about."

"But you did have control at the end, didn't you?" Jax murmured. "The fire stopped before we reached it."

"I don't know how," she confessed. "My magic seemed... strange."

"I'm not surprised. Given that display, Vi... You're Awoken." It seemed much more than that to her. "We'll discuss it when we're back. Let me help you up." Jax laced his fingers and held them down, granting her some relief and not pressing further about her obvious hesitation. "I know you're more confident riding these things than I am. But that's usually without a bad leg."

Vi hesitated, staring at the animal, balancing as best she could on her good leg.

Gormon turned his furry head toward her, and Vi saw the dead eyes of the noru layered atop his bright, clear ones. She flinched.

"He's the same Gormon you've always ridden," Jax said encouragingly, soothingly, as if reading her mind.

"I know." Vi tried to roll her eyes as she placed a hand on the beast's dense fur. "I'm not afraid of him."

"Of course you're not."

"I'm merely debating if I can endure your help mounting. But I suppose I shall this one time." Vi made an attempt at the dramatic for a laugh and her uncle indulged her. Together, it distracted her from the pain as she got astride the animal. Her leg screamed in protest, but could still be moved—marginally—so perhaps it wasn't entirely broken.

"You settled?" Jax asked with a grunt, mounting behind her.

"Yes, and more than ready to get this mended."

The cat sprang to life and they bounded back in the direction of the capital of the North. Uncle Jax muttered to himself the whole time.

"It's a miracle you're all right. Thank the Mother. I couldn't have imagined what might have happened if something befell you or Ellene. We should've never let you go. *I* should've never let you go. The Senate advised against these hunts of yours as you got older and there was less supervision. I should've listened. Mother knows what that boy is going to write in his reports of his.

"But… to think, your magic is Awoken and you're already learning to control fires of that power and size. We may be able to work with this before you return south…"

The words blurred like the trees passing to either side. Vi stared at nothing, letting her eyes glaze over. She could see her father, kneeling before a foreign queen in strange clothing. He had to be on the Crescent Continent in her vision… so how far in the future was that? Tomorrow? A month? A year? She wasn't sure how long ago his farewell letter had been written.

Then there was her other vision… and that man. The voice, he'd called himself. He'd done something to her and then left with nothing more than a command to find him again.

Vi didn't know where to start—the fact that he would command her… or the fact that even if she wanted to summon him, she had no idea how.

Soricium emerged before them. The buildings with bases of stone and second stories of wood blurred past them as the noru bounded down the main streets of the city, heading to the large castle-like fortress at its center. The street forced the noru closer together, close enough that Vi could speak with Jayme and Ellene.

"I'm sorry," Vi called over. They both turned, startled. "I didn't mean—"

"What're you sorry for?" Ellene shook her head. "We're glad you're all right!"

"Likewise." Vi breathed a sigh of relief, knowing there were no hard feelings between them.

The noru came to a stop and Jax immediately swung his legs over, reaching up to help her off. Vi allowed herself the assistance once more. She was far too tired and in too much pain to object. His hands fell on her waist and he eased her down. Vi put all of her weight on her right foot, allowing him to shift an arm around her back to help support her.

"Call for Ginger," he shouted, loud enough that Vi was certain half the castle heard. "The Crown Princess is injured."

"You don't need to make such a fuss. I can manage," Vi muttered, hobbling alongside him. She hadn't even crossed halfway to the castle when said cleric ran out.

"Princess, what has happened?" The blue-eyed woman fussed, eyes immediately drawn across the constellation of bruises and scrapes across her body, then to her leg. "Goodness, just what have you gotten yourself into this time? The older you get, the worse shape you're in when you return from these hunts of yours." She dropped to her knees, setting her basket down, and began rummaging through it. She continued muttering as she worked. "Hunts, why do we even still call them that? We all know they're just excuses for you to have a few days out exploring."

Could she be blamed for it? Everyone had their limits in captivity. But Vi held her tongue. She'd caused more than enough trouble for one day.

Ginger, a Waterrunner, had been sent from the South with Vi from the very beginning. Waterruners made some of the best clerics due to their abilities to manipulate the water in the body as well as change the properties of salve. She'd been the best cleric Vi could ask for—overall focusing mostly on mending her after she fell, or reviving her when she was ill, rather than the recklessness that usually brought those things about.

"When we saw the flame, I prepared. I just knew you'd come back worse for wear." Ginger paused, hands sticky with salve. "It was you, the fire, wasn't it?"

Vi quickly tried to weigh the scales of answers in her head. As trusted as Ginger was, she was also a Southerner with deep ties to the capital. However, any word she could send back wouldn't make it before Vi was headed back as well, which meant she and Romulin could thwart any nefarious uses for information.

Then again, who else could've started and stopped a fire like that?

"It was me behind the fire. There was a threat to my person and the Chieftain's daughter," Vi answered ambiguously. If there was one thing Romulin had stressed, it was that she owed no one more explanation than she wanted to give.

"A threat? Goodness, of what kind?" Ginger paused. "But that also means you've finally Awoken, princess. How exciting!"

"Thank you, Ginger," Sehra interrupted, as if somehow sensing it had crossed into sensitive territory. Vi hadn't even noticed her walking over. "When you are finished seeing to the Crown Princess, would you mind tending to my daughter and Jayme?"

"Not at all." Ginger gave a smile and a small nod. Of all of Vi's staff and tutors, Ginger had integrated the easiest. Perhaps it was her clerical demeanor—that she saw all people as patients, nothing more or less. Or perhaps Ginger was a better soul. Either way, Vi trusted her more for it. "Just one more second and I'll have finished sorting the worst of it."

Vi closed her eyes, feeling the thick salve Ginger had coated her swollen leg with chill to a temperature that was almost ice-like. As it warmed back up in the heat of the air, the pain was significantly reduced, swelling gone. Vi placed her weight on the leg delicately. There was stiffness, some stinging, but, as Ginger put, the worst of it seemed sorted. Luckily the injury hadn't been too severe.

"It may feel better, princess, but it is still mending so do take care. No running, jumping, riding, fighting, or whatever it is that you find yourself inclined to, cleric's orders."

"Yes." Vi gave a nod to the mostly white-haired woman. She was one of the few who had never seen an issue ordering Vi around, despite their difference in status.

Ginger gave a nod, stood, and departed, leaving Vi with Jax and Sehra.

"I apologize for not checking on you more promptly, princess," Sehra began and Vi couldn't tell if she meant it, or was merely saying what would be expected in such a situation.

"It's I who should apologize to you." Vi turned to face the woman. "Know I would not have endangered Ellene with my fledgling magic if were it not for the noru afflicted with the White Death. Our lives were at stake."

"An infected noru? The plague has spread to animals?" Sehra turned from Vi to Jax.

"I was already planning to send word of it to Lady Elecia in the West. She may be able to help get a message to the capital." Jax never failed to jump at an excuse to reach out to Elecia. The two of them were in a hopeless orbit around each other. But Vi couldn't read too much into this particular suggestion, given the circumstances.

"I think her mother, Ambassador Ioine, is still in the southwest region of Shaldan. I can send couriers there."

"Certainly. I'll draft a letter."

A thought crossed Vi's mind, briefly, that perhaps her uncle would leave her when they arrived south. She would no longer need a guardian and Jax would be far happier with Elecia, Vi would bet. It settled an ache in her that she was ready to ignore the moment Sehra spoke again.

"Thank you for handling it." Her uncle gave a small bow of his head. Sehra turned to face her, and her alone. "More pressing, for now… Go clean yourself up, and meet me in my throne room."

Vi kept her face passive, keeping her worry at whatever punishment would be levied against her locked within. "Understood, Chieftain."

The stronghold of Soricium could be maze-like for the uninitiated. She'd heard of the castles in the south being rather twisting as well… but it was hard to think they could twist a person more backwards than branches that became bridges that connected to wide platforms before disappearing into the trees themselves in a series of hollowed out tunnels.

It could easily set a person on the wrong course. That is, if they weren't like Vi, and hadn't grown up among them. So she had no excuse for any delays other than purely dragging her feet.

Now, Vi stood before an intricately carved door at the end of a long stone bridge, set against the trunk of the center-most tree in the fortress. This was the oldest tree in the world—so the wrinkled men who sat around fires said—and they called it the Mother Tree. It was this tree that was said to have caught a falling star—a shard of the Mother's light—in its branches. By the time the star finally reached the ground, it had absorbed life from the tree and became a woman. The same woman cut civilization from the boughs of the Mother Tree, forming all of Shaldan.

Briefly, the ruins she'd landed in appeared in her mind. But Vi pushed them from her thoughts. She had more important things to focus on now.

Lifting a fist, Vi gave a few raps of her knuckles against the wood. The doors peeled apart, opening inward by a magic force. Inside, the hollowed center of the tree arched above in a dome. Flowers and vines hung from the ceiling, giving off a cloyingly sweet smell that hung in the room despite half of it being open completely to a wide balcony.

"Come in, Vi." Sehra was standing several paces in front of her throne, right at the edge of where the tree-trunk vanished and the balcony extended, uncovered, underneath the open sky.

Vi swallowed, accepted her fate, and stepped inside. The doors closed behind her, leaving Vi little option but to cross over to the Chieftain of the North—the woman whose protection Vi had been destined to rely on before she was even born.

"Are you wondering why I summoned you?"

"I honestly find it quite clear." Vi stepped beside the woman, looking out into the expansive archways and paths of the fortress before them. "You showed me kindness, allowing me to leave. And when you did, I abused it, going farther than I should have. In the process, I endangered your daughter."

"You went farther than you were supposed to?" Sehra interrupted her list of transgressions with a look of genuine surprise.

"I figured Ellene would've told you." Vi cursed her luck. The girl used to tell her mother everything. But it seemed, with age, she was learning how to keep a secret.

"I expected it, as did Jax."

"Yes, well..." Vi tried to find her previous thought. "Even still, I endangered Ellene and Jayme with my outburst. I should have stayed here, and trained more after being so recently Awoken."

Sehra looked straight ahead, out over the treetops of the fortress. She was rigid, regal, everything Vi hoped she could be someday; she had a long way to go.

"I am not going to punish you."

"I may be the Crown Princess, but I should not be above punishment." She didn't particularly enjoy reprimands. But getting off, free and clear, felt wrong.

"There's no time now for punishments," Sehra said ominously. "We have too much work to do, you and I."

"Work?" Vi repeated, glancing from the corners of her eyes at the woman. She had yet to move. She was hardly even breathing.

"Yes, I was waiting for today to begin. I was waiting to be certain, beyond all doubt, for the knowledge I will impart to you has never been heard by ears outside my lineage." Vi had no idea what Sehra was talking about. "Why do you think it is that you have struggled so much with your flames?"

"I... I don't know. Everyone always said I was a late bloomer, like my mother. But I have Awoken. And managed to find control in the jungle. My magic..."

The man in the cavern flashed through her mind, his glowing emerald eyes, the singular word he'd uttered. Something had changed with that man, that word. What had he done to her? What was that word that had echoed in her the next time her magic was unleashed?

"And?" Sehra pressed, reminding Vi she had stopped talking.

"And I think I have a better understanding of my magic. I think Uncle Jax will be able to teach me now and—"

"Jax can teach you nothing."

"What?" Vi turned to face the Chieftain, anger bringing her spark to the surface faster than talking about it had.

"He will teach you as a Firebearer."

"That's—"

"That is not what you are. You are not a Firebearer, Vi. Not at your core. Certainly, you are able to create and manipulate flames, but this is a manifestation of your expectations for your own magic and the expectations of those around you.

"Like nature versus nurture. You have been nurtured by Firebearers, so you and everyone else believes that is what you are. But that is not your nature. That is not your magic."

"I'm certainly not a sorcerer of any of the other affinities." Something about this conversation felt like being backed against a cliff ledge, knowing she was about to be pushed over. Everything was about to change.

"No, you're not. You are like me, like Ellene. You can control an element, but it is merely a fraction of your true power."

"What?" Vi whispered. She knew what Sehra was alluding to before she said it, but it didn't make sense. It was so jarring that her brain only interpreted the logical conclusion as confusion. Even when Sehra said the words, they sounded like a lie.

"You, Vi Solaris, are a Child of Yargen."

11

A CHILD OF YARGEN, LIKE Ellene and Sehra. One who could harness a strange and mysterious power. A power very few possessed—a gift rarer even than Windwalkers like Vi's mother. But there was just one problem with Sehra's claim...

"All of the Children of Yargen are in your lineage." Vi shook her head. "Ellene is like a sister to me, but I don't think that's close enough to count."

"Perhaps it is." Sehra shrugged, an action that seemed far too light-hearted for the seriousness of her words. "We know that while certain lineages have similar magic, magic is not in the blood. Two commons can give birth to a sorcerer. Why not two who have no relationship to Yargen giving birth to a Child of Yargen?"

"Because it's *never* happened," Vi challenged. It was bold. Sehra certainly knew the history of her land and people far better than Vi did. But Vi knew this much. She'd talked with Ellene about it to the point of circles countless times before. All swirling around questions like, why didn't the Tower of Sorcerers in the South recognize the magic of Yargen? Or, what really *was* the magic of Yargen?

"You are a special case," Sehra agreed, as though such a simple explanation could put her concerns to rest. "But we always knew you would be. We planned for this."

"We?" Vi repeated. "Who's 'we'?"

Sehra began to walk over to the far side of the room. "Your mother, father, and me."

Everything went from not making sense to being downright impossible. "Let's say I believe you, that I'm a Child of Yargen—which is an incredible amount to believe at face value, just as an aside. How would my mother know? Or my father? Or you? Why keep this information from me all this time?"

Sehra paused, looking back. Conflict was written over her face at what her next words should be. She placed a palm on the wall before her, and the wood folded like an accordion, revealing a small sunlit study Vi had never seen before and certainly had never known was there.

"Perhaps it would be best if I started at the beginning... Come."

Vi didn't want to. She wanted to stand and demand answers, order them as the

Crown Princess if that's what it took. Yet she couldn't seem to find words. Her arms hung limply at her sides and her spark seemed dull and quiet, even without her forcing it to calm.

Her parents had known?

Was this insane belief what had kept her trapped in the North for so long? That question alone, the need for the truth, was ultimately what drove her to follow Sehra.

The study was narrow, similar to Vi's own, wrapping around the circumference of the tree. Windows, no bigger than archer's slits, let in the midday sun through a lattice of woodwork. It reflected off bookcases filled with scrolls and manuscripts alike. It sparked off motes of dust, as though magic filled the air itself.

"When I was a girl, younger than you, even, I was engaged to be wed to your father…"

Vi knew the story. Shaldan was the last nation to fall to the Empire's armies, becoming the Solaris Empire's "North." Vi's grandfather, the late Emperor Tiberius Solaris, sought to tie subservience with blood and engaged her father—Aldrik—to Sehra. But when the Mad King Victor murdered the Emperor and stole power, the engagement was called off. In its place was the wardship Vi had lived for the past seventeen years.

"… it was just before the uprising of the Mad King. When the last Emperor Solaris was still alive and I was engaged," Sehra continued the story, nearing the end, "I was visited by a traveler.

"She possessed the magic of Yargen, unequivocally, and knew the words of the Goddess, drawing the future from them. She told me of the Emperor's impending downfall, the violation of the caverns, and the rise of the Mad King. She also told me that Vhalla Yarl must wed Aldrik Solaris, for they would give birth to two children. One would bear his forefather's position in the capital of the Empire. But the other, the first to be born, would be a girl, a Child of Yargen—a daughter imperative for the future of our world."

This was insane.

It was more than insane.

"She… This visitor… you said she could see the future? She was a Firebearer?" Vi swallowed, staying focused even as dizziness spun the room.

"No. I saw in her the power of Yargen and it was a magic that was far beyond even mine. She used it to tap into Yargen's plan for us all." Sehra motioned to two small chairs seated on either side of a circular table at the end of the bookshelves in the far back of the room. "Sit, you look weak in the knees."

"No," Vi whispered. "I—I don't want to move until I know the truth."

"Which is what I'm telling you."

That was not the truth she wanted to know. They were not the words Vi wanted to hear. The truth she was after was far more personal than prophecies or mysterious visitors.

"Is this why I have been kept in the North all this time? I was supposed to go home at fourteen. All those times it wasn't the logistics of travel, the timing being wrong, or the plague. It was stalling because of something a traveler said to you?"

Sehra paused, shifting slightly to face Vi directly. She didn't back away or hesitate. It would be admirable, if her words didn't suddenly feel like they carried the weight of Vi's collapsing world.

"Yes."

She couldn't breathe. The air in the room was gone. It was only the spark in her lungs, rattling around them. She would spit fire if she wasn't careful.

"I was *trapped here* for seventeen years because of what some woman said?" Her voice was rising with her anger.

"She was not just 'some woman,' she was a Child of—"

"I don't give a damn what she was!" Vi seethed. The thin veneer of royal decorum had cracked and fallen away. All that was left was a frustrated, utterly unapologetic, and extremely tired young woman standing among its pieces. Meanwhile, Sehra calmly folded her hands before her, unflinching, taking Vi's searing verbal blows. "She—I could've had a life with my family. I could've known my brother. I would've had a home rather than being the Empire's latest territory to lay claim to!

"I am too Northern to be Southern. I am too Southern to be Northern. Eastern to be Western. Western to be Eastern. I belong *nowhere*, and to no one, and it's all because of some stupid magic and the words of one person—whose name you don't even know." Vi guessed on that last point, and assumed she was right when Sehra didn't correct her.

Sehra's eyes narrowed slightly. Her voice was still calm, level. "Heavy is your burden, isn't it, your highness?"

Vi stilled. The rigidness in her spine relaxed and every vertebra rattled until she slumped. She gripped the bookshelf for support and left black singe marks in the shape of her fingerprints.

She pressed her eyes closed, stopping the burning there so the books didn't catch. Even emotional, she managed some form of control. Her spark was burning her once again. But this time it was slow. She would die raked over coals rather than in a blazing inferno. She would keep it wound tightly in the spool that was her channel.

"You belong nowhere, because you belong to the goddess herself. You are her chosen child, more than even I or Ellene, as you were hand-picked outside her lineage."

"I don't want this." Vi opened her eyes narrowly, looking up at Sehra through her top lashes. The woman still hadn't moved.

"No child chooses the circumstances of their birth. Rich parents, poor parents, high and low. We are all handed the starting point. What you make of every step thereafter is what defines your life." The woman's eyes were as hard as the green stone they mirrored. "What do you choose, Vi Solaris?"

Vi pushed away from the bookcase, swaying slightly, and forced the jelly from her knees by tensing her muscles. The leg wounded by the Noru attack still ached, but the pain was a welcome momentary distraction. She took a deep breath, trying to find a corner of her mind that was cool and collected for her to curl up in. She wished she could throw her whole body into the void right now.

"You said my parents know this?"

"They do. They knew they could not teach you on their own. I am the only woman on this continent who knows anything about the power of Yargen, and it is my destiny to teach you."

Betrayal was dripping from her pores. Even when the logical side of Vi's mind tried to rationalize through it, all she could think was that thanks to some stupid traveler, she had been trapped away from her family—away from the place that should've been her home—for her whole life.

"I want…" Vi's shoulders sagged. She turned her head up toward the ceiling to keep the moisture welling on her bottom lids contained.

She didn't even know why she was crying. Perhaps it was the fact that the veil of the unknown had finally been ripped off. Or perhaps it was the agony of knowing what could've been if it were not for some woman. If Vi should ever meet that traveler, then she too would know the full extent of Vi's agony.

"I want to handle this with grace, Chieftain. I want to remain poised and listen. But how can I? How am I supposed to trust you after you've kept this impossible secret from me?"

"Because it was impossible," Sehra said simply when Vi's eyes fell back to her. "When I saw the flames today—white, not orange—saw how they rippled outward like strands of Yargen's pure light—when I felt them… I was given my proof and I knew that the time had finally come." Vi remembered how the magic had been spinning out from her skin like burning threads. "And you saw the light too, didn't you?"

"I don't know what I saw." It was a lie and Vi knew it. But she didn't want to admit to this impossible truth.

"Yet the fact remains that you saw enough for what I am saying to seem believable to you. Before today, if I had told you I had met a traveler who foretold your birth—you, a Child of Yargen, despite one *never* being born outside of my lineage—and it was my destiny from the goddess herself to teach that child… would you have believed me?"

"I hardly believe you now," Vi muttered. Then, she let out a heavy sigh. What was the point of continuing to fight this? "You truly believe it's your destiny to teach me the magic of Yargen?" Sehra nodded. "So much that you gave up your engagement to my father, the potential to sit as the Empress?"

"Having an heir to the throne sympathetic to my people from growing up in my care was a fringe benefit," Sehra remarked almost a little too coolly.

"You have to understand, this is all very hard to believe."

"And you must understand that, thanks to the endless impatience of the Senate and your delay in Awakening, we have less time than I would've wanted for the actual teaching, so I cannot afford you the luxury of processing this slowly. Your mother and I could only stall them for so long. That was the one thing the traveler got wrong; you were supposed to show signs of this magic much younger."

"Why not just teach me earlier?"

"As I said, and as you already know, because this knowledge is sacred. Ellene won't even learn it for a few years yet—when she is mature enough to handle it. You shall be the first outside my family to know it. I had to be sure." One thing was becoming painfully clear. Sehra had never done anything she didn't want to. Vi had always thought her engagement to Aldrik at thirteen had been cruel. Now, she wouldn't be surprised if Sehra was the one to have suggested it.

"Will you truly let me go in the spring?"

"Only if I have fulfilled the destiny set out for me by Yargen. Only if I have fulfilled the promise to your mother and taught you what she entrusted you to me to learn."

Vi took a deep breath through her nose, letting her eyes flutter closed, and exhaled through her mouth. She didn't want to hear one more mention of her parents from Sehra's lips. Every word she spoke of them made Vi's stomach churn and the last thing she wanted was tension from the first moment her mother arrived in the North.

If learning this magic was what it took to return home smoothly—for Sehra to let her go, for her powers to remain under control, for her parents to be pleased, then Vi would do it.

"All right then, where do we begin?"

12

"WOULD YOU CARE TO sit first?" Sehra asked, motioning to the chair once more.

"Very well." Vi finally acquiesced, crossing over and sinking into the plush chair. She rested her elbows on the armrests, watching Sehra as she went to skim the shelves, her many braids swaying back and forth between her shoulders. The gold beads woven throughout clinked together softly.

"First, you must learn about the world. Nothing will make sense about the power of Yargen until you do." Sehra pulled a heavy tome from the shelf, set it on the table between them, and then started back to the shelves to retrieve something else.

Despite Vi's outbursts, the Chieftain's demeanor hadn't changed. Vi had always thought Sehra was fond of her, given her calm and congenial nature around her. Now, after endangering Ellene, after all but yelling at her, Vi was beginning to think that Sehra's tranquility was merely the woman's fundamental nature. It was as though a veil was being lifted from her eyes and she was seeing the world as it truly had been all along.

She wondered if Sehra had ever felt any genuine fondness for her.

Likely not, Vi decided, still bitter. She was a means to an end for Sehra—whether that meant fulfilling her supposed destiny or seeing a sympathetic ruler sit the throne. Vi suspected that even her hunts were somehow a ploy for her to find her magic. For all she knew, Sehra's traveler and the mysterious dark purple-haired man were in cahoots.

"I know a fair bit about the world," Vi forced her voice to stay level. She would have no more outbursts. She couldn't afford them. She was not a child and she needed her full mental faculties to think through her new situation logically.

"You do have an understanding of *this* world—our small corner of it." Sehra walked back over with a dusty scroll in hand. "Which, as you'll see, is quite different from *the* world."

"What're you—" Vi was cut short as she unrolled the scroll before her. "What is this?" she whispered.

"Aires. The world, as it's known beyond our lands."

Even her maps would betray her today, it seemed.

Before her was a world unlike anything Vi had ever seen. It was like looking into a mirror and seeing a person she'd never met before. There was the great crescent-shaped body of land that she'd always known as the Crescent Continent. But it had never appeared in any of the Empire's maps as more than a speck creeping in on the northernmost tip of the Main Continent, so Vi had always been left to believe it was relatively insignificant.

Yet on this map, the Crescent Continent—Meru, as it was labeled—was over four times the size of the Main Continent.

It was so large that there was a smaller island nestled in its watery eye. The barrier isles—called the Shattered Isles on this map—were far more detailed and expansive than she'd ever seen them. Trailing up farther northwest was a large body of land, almost the size of the Main Continent.

To the southeast was yet *another* continent, with more islands surrounding it. More islands stretched out southwest from the Crescent Continent, or perhaps they were continents in their own right, with land in the bottom left corner only peeking on the map.

"Is this to scale?" she whispered. By her count, if it was, there were at least five continents, if the Main Continent was still even considered one.

"Roughly." Sehra nodded; her tone had become more serious, heavy even. "Close enough for what you're asking."

Vi ran her fingers over the map, her eyes scanning the names and her nails brushing over the ink strokes that designated islands and mountains, forests and valleys, that she'd never known existed.

"The Dark Isle—Solaris?" That was how the Main Continent was marked. The man had said something about the Dark Isle as well. "Is this some kind of joke?"

"The Dark Isle is what the rest of the world calls us."

How could a man from off the continent be communicating with her? Nothing was adding up and all Vi wanted to do was curl back up in her library where things made sense.

"I don't understand… If this is real, why have I never seen it? Why have I never heard of it before?" Questions swirled in her mind, all beginning with *why*.

"Only those of royal blood, and the lords or ladies that oversee each of the Empire's parts, know this truth. You would have found out eventually, before you took your throne, but it is now relevant to everything you must learn."

"Not why haven't *I* learned of it…" Vi shook her head, trying to rephrase her question. "Why is this not taught to everyone? Why isn't it common knowledge?"

"Many reasons, but two reign among them. The first is that Meru seeks to keep us cut off from the world. They govern trade and travel with an iron fist, and should any vessels from our lands stray too close to them without proper approval, they're immediately sunk without question. Some say they even employ the pirates that terrorize the Shattered—Barrier—Isles."

"And the other reason?" Vi barely glanced up from the map, already trying to memorize it.

Now that the initial shock, and irrational feelings of betrayal toward an inanimate object, had begun to fade, fascination was taking over. She needed a distraction, and her mood could rarely stay sour around a new map. Every curve of the cartographer's brush left Vi wondering. Wondering what was there, what stories were out there to unfold... and why she felt like even though this was certainly the first time she'd learned of the greater world, she could already count every island in the Shattered Isles with her eyes closed.

"Power." How many times in history had that been the reason for doing or not doing something? "As far as the people of the Solaris Empire know, the 'Main Continent' is the world—the only one that matters, at least. I'm sure you've heard the rumors that the Crescent Continent is filled with nothing but dangerous and barbaric peoples and things?"

"But it's not... is it?" Vi whispered, her vision coming back to her of the queen draped in silks, and the courtyard that looked like it belonged in her dreamscape of the Southern castle, not on a land declared by the Empire to lack civilization. Of course there was more to it. Her father had set out to meet with their leaders about a cure. That didn't seem like something he would do if the Crescent Continent was nothing more than roving bands of disorganized peoples.

"It's not. As you can see, we are a very, very small portion of the world. But by giving the people of the Solaris Empire pride—pride in seeing themselves as the pinnacle of the world—they strive to fight harder, to follow the rules, and to oblige their Empire."

"Doesn't it seem... dishonest?" Vi frowned, looking up from the map. All her life she'd been complicit in the greatest lie of them all without even knowing it.

"Perhaps, but then we return to reason one—the world is, overall, hostile toward us. Keeping the people here is for their own safety as well."

Passing judgment that would affect people she'd never met, but declaring her actions were for their best interest. If that wasn't the burden of royalty, Vi didn't know what was. It's what her parents had done with her, wasn't it? Made a decision that impacted Vi's whole life before she was even born and declaring it in her best interest.

"Why are they so dangerous?" Vi chose to ignore, for now, the reasons behind the rest of the world's dislike for them. She found hatred rarely had good reasons.

"Because of the magic they possess... The same magic you and I possess—the magic of Yargen."

"What *is* the magic of Yargen?" Vi finally asked. "All I've seen is... light? Light that you seem to be able to do almost anything with."

"It's a fairly apt description, in all honesty." Sehra sat in the chair across from Vi, the small table between them. "The rest of the world has a magic far more complete than ours. What we know as magic being elemental affinities, is merely a mutilated fraction of the true power—the power the goddess herself bestowed on mortals that we here on the Dark Isle have lost control of."

"You're saying that sorcerers on the Crescent Continent—Meru—all have the power of Yargen?" That could certainly be an explanation for her mysterious visitor.

"That is what I have been led to believe," Sehra affirmed. "Naturally, I have not stepped foot off this continent... nor have I met with anyone from Meru."

"The traveler you met... she wasn't from Meru?"

Sehra paused at that question for what felt like a long time. The silence stretched and Vi leaned forward, the anticipation helping the earlier frustrations fade away.

She hung on Sehra's next words, but Vi didn't know why. Perhaps she just wanted to hunt the woman down and find justice for what she'd done to her.

"I could not tell. She truly seemed a woman of the world—ageless, nameless, one who had seen many things."

That was utterly unhelpful. Vi relinquished herself to the fact that finding information about a woman who approached Sehra mysteriously years before her birth would be hard to track down. "If you've never met anyone from Meru, how do you know all this?"

"Because of this." Sehra rested her hand on the book she'd retrieved. "It has been passed down in my family for generations and is the only primer I have on Yargen's magic from the rest of the world."

"It came from Meru?"

"I don't know where it came from, but I assume so."

Vi bit back asking what Sehra *did* know. Little and less, it seemed, the more questions she asked.

"All right, let's go back to the power of Yargen itself," Vi suggested. Asking about the history of it was getting them nowhere. "It's a magic not based on elements?"

"Indeed. Think of it as all the elements combined—a pure form of power that can be manipulated by the will of those who wield it."

"I don't understand…" Vi shook her head, rubbing her eyes tiredly. Sorcery wasn't overly common in the Empire. One in ten people, likely less, possessed some kind of magic. And those magics were directly linked to a single element. Firebearers could do nothing but manipulate fire—even the affinity of the self required fire to stare into to see the future.

"It will become clearer as you learn, as you master these powers for yourself. We will begin tomorrow afternoon, following your regular lessons." Sehra stood and Vi followed suit, deeming the conversation finished. "For now, you've had a long day. So rest, recover, and we shall start tomorrow."

"I take it these lessons will be a regular occurrence for us henceforth?"

"Yes, we have already lost enough time. From now until the time you leave, you will spend the hours you would have been training with Jax—those hours, and then some—with me, learning the magic of Yargen." Sehra paused, looking down at the book that still sat out between the two chairs. "We have lost enough time, indeed," she whispered, mostly to herself. Then, as she lifted the small tome, handing it to Vi: "I shall lend this copy to you. Perhaps you can get a head start tonight reading what you can of the magic."

Vi accepted the book mutely, running her fingers along the spine. She was forced to admit that there was something reassuring about having a book involved. For now, she could trust that all her answers were somewhere between the front and back cover. They stepped out onto Sehra's balcony and the accordion entry to her study folded back in place, melding seamlessly with the wood of the trunk.

"I shall see you tomorrow, princess." Sehra raised a hand and the doors of the throne room opened.

"Until then." Vi gave a bow of her head and departed.

She should apologize for her outbursts; her feet almost faltered as she considered doing just that. But they carried her out of the room, and the closing of the heavy doors marked the end of her window of opportunity—for now.

Vi wandered back to her room. She was exhausted and worn down to the bone. So tired that she couldn't tell if the exhaustion in her eyes was from the strain of keeping them open for so many hours in a row, or if it was the raw emotions still were churning through her, mingling with her spark.

The fatigue kept her silent as the servants attended her. Faceless hands placed themselves on her body, scrubbing everywhere, checking on her leg. Vi allowed herself to be moved along mindlessly until they left her alone in the dark room.

She should sleep.

But her eyes were wide open.

Vi stared at the ceiling, frozen in place, as if the whole day had perched itself on her chest. The visions… her magic… the noru. She squeezed her eyes closed to block them out, but the darkness there was no more forgiving.

No, if she could focus on all of that instead, it would be a blessing. What was really keeping her awake was the lingering feeling of betrayal. When had Sehra told her mother the truth? How long had they kept her here needlessly? Mother above— did Romulin know?

The questions swirled in her mind until Vi was forced to scare them away by lighting the candle at her bedside.

Vi looked to her letter box, slowly opening the top. The book Sehra had given her just barely fit within. She stared at it, competing feelings of contempt, anger, hurt, and… admittedly, curiosity.

"I should hate you," she whispered. She should hate it for all it represented. It was what had kept her from her family, from her home.

Yet she reached out and took the book into her lap, opening it to the first page.

"'Words of the Goddess…'" Vi softly read aloud. Her eyes devoured the forward at the beginning of the book. It spoke of the basic principles of words of power. That the goddess—Yargen—had bestowed magic on man through giving the words of divinity to mortals.

By invoking these words, by her holy light, a mortal hand can do her will.

Vi's eyes lingered on the last line of the page. The whole thing read more like a religious text than a magical one. Sehra had said it was from Meru; perhaps there they had different opinions on magic. Vastly different… given magic in Solaris was feared by the average person.

She flipped the page and let out a soft gasp.

At the top was a glyph.

It was the same sensation Vi had felt when she had first witnessed the shining symbol above her watch during her first vision. Then, it had been a litany of noises she could hear but barely make sense of. This time, the chorus of sound sang in perfect harmony.

She heard the word, felt it in her bones. It was not a language Vi had ever seen— if it was a language at all. The symbol imbued her with a deep understanding that surpassed reading and made sense of the sounds it invoked within her.

"*Durroe,*" Vi whispered. The word tingled across her skin, as though she was sinking into a warm bath, or lying underneath a hot sun after spending an hour rummaging through the ice house.

She quickly flipped the pages. More symbols were scribed in the chapter for *durroe* and more sounds filled her mind as she skimmed the glyphs. Her hands stopped at the next chapter.

The symbol here was carefully drawn in red ink. Circles within circles, lines connecting between them, carefully drawn symbols encased among them. The moment her eyes lingered, she was met with the same sensation and then, clarity.

Halleth, to heal.

The lines on the page almost seemed to move, to come to life. It was as if they were begging for her to recreate them—though Vi didn't know how.

No... that wasn't quite true. Her breath was loud as she remembered being in her study after her first vision. She'd meant to write down what she'd seen in the flames, but she had drawn one of these symbols instead.

"Which one was it?" The pages slipped through her fingers as she searched, almost frantically.

The symbol above her watch during the first vision was the same that had appeared after the second. It was the same symbol she had sketched on the paper in her study, perfectly from memory—the very same glyph she'd seen swirl around that man.

Her fingers stopped.

"*Narro*, acts of the mind." She stared at the glyph for several long breaths. No, she'd been wrong. It wasn't identical... there was another layer to it. Something wasn't quite right. Vi flipped the page. "*Haath*, communication."

Vi flipped back and forth several times. The two symbols blurred together, overlapping until something audibly *clicked* in her mind.

"*Narro haath*," Vi whispered aloud again.

The spark surged up her throat to form the words. Magic radiated out from her flesh—not as fire, but as thin, shimmering strands of light. They swirled before her, not quite taking shape.

Warmth rippled across her with the vibration of a voice that she felt as much as heard.

"You again?"

"WHAT?" VI LOOKED AROUND quickly, trying to locate the source of the voice. Aptly, the disembodied words were undoubtedly from the same man who had called himself "the voice."

"How…" He started a question but quickly abandoned it, as if trying to cover his own confusion. "This is different than before." There was a heavy note to the statement, one Vi couldn't read. "What magic is this?"

"Wouldn't I love to know!" Vi wrapped her arms around herself. Every time he spoke it sent tiny ripples across her skin, prickling it into gooseflesh. "You told me to seek you out. Well, I did." *Apparently.* She hadn't exactly planned on this. "So, give me some answers."

Vi hoped that, whatever connection this was, he couldn't feel her emotions. Then he'd know that the demand was said with far more confidence than she felt. Outside, she could present all the confidence of the Crown Princess. Inside… Vi felt like a very tired and confused seventeen-year-old girl. But she really did not need anyone else to know that.

"You are not at an apex of fate?"

"I don't think so. Not unless my bed has become one."

"Unlikely…" There was a long stretch of silence and Vi seized the opportunity. "What are the apexes of fate?"

"Places the world changed, or places where it still could be changed. They're locations where fate was malleable and the future was—is—yet undecided." His matter-of-factness surprised her. She'd been made aware of so many secrets in the past day, that to find someone willing to tell her the simple, unvarnished truth felt oddly foreign.

"Yes, my bed definitely isn't one," Vi muttered. She hadn't intended him to hear, but a chuckle radiated through to her. So he could hear everything, no matter how softly she said it—a good mental note. Vi cleared her throat, trying to ignore the fact that she was still radiating light and talking to a man in her head. "Why can I only see you at the apexes of fate?"

"Since I am the voice, and you the champion, we are intrinsically linked with the fate of this world. In those places, the distance between us is greatly shortened."

"Then why can I talk to you here?"

"That same link between us, I would assume," he said simply.

Vi resisted calling him out on the fact that he sounded as unsure as she felt. She also ignored the voice and champion bit, for now. He hadn't really answered when she asked in the ruins. So, instead, she asked, "What is your name?"

"My name?"

"Yes, your name. You know mine from the last time we spoke... and, well, seeing as I'm talking to you from my personal quarters in the middle of the night, I think it's owed."

He scoffed. "I owe you nothing."

"Just tell me." Vi sighed, pinching the bridge of her nose.

"Taavin."

Taavin. It was certainly a name she'd never heard before. Vi swallowed hard, looking down at her hands and watching the light trailing off her skin and disappearing into the darkness like the streaks of fireflies.

This was impossible to comprehend. Less than a week ago, Vi didn't think she had any magic at all—or at least very little. Now, she wanted a whole lot less magic in her life.

"Do I dare ask if you're real?"

"I am quite obviously real." The offense in his voice brought a small smile to her lips. "I should be the one asking you that," he murmured.

"I'm real too." Vi sank back into her pillows. *Really tired*, more like. She stared up at the threads of light that unfurled from her. They looked thinner than they had before. "What's happening to me, Taavin?"

"That is a question that will take a lifetime to answer."

"This magic..." Vi paused and he didn't fill the space with words. Silence stretched as her magic continued to fade. Vi looked down at her hand, nestled in the folds of her blanket. There were only a few threads of light clinging to her.

First, she had made fire. Then light that became fire. Now... this.

"This magic," Vi continued, stronger. "Is it truly that of Yargen?"

"Yes," he said solemnly. "When I used the word *samasha*, you were gifted the ability to understand Yargen's gifts."

The word washed over her, and with it the last threads of light left Vi's body. Taavin sounded as if he had been about to say something, but Vi could no longer sustain the connection; for now, at least, his words would have to remain a mystery. The sounds of night flooded her ears; she hadn't even realized they'd been muffled. Sehra had been right. The traveler had known Vi would have this power...

There were easily a hundred questions buzzing through Vi's mind in that moment. But she found herself too exhausted to keep her eyes open a moment longer, let alone consider their answers.

The moment Vi knocked on the doors and stepped inside Sehra's throne room, she heard an immediate, "You're late."

"I'm sorry." Vi tried to avoid making excuses. "I slept late, so my lessons started late and I've been behind ever since."

"Do make an effort to start on time, princess, because we have much ground to cover." Sehra stood from her wood-and-leaf throne, starting over to the secret door that led to the study. "Come, we'll work in here."

"I slept late because I was up late reading your book." Vi held up the small tome as she sat down in the same chair she'd been in yesterday.

"Were you?" Sehra sat as well. "Then perhaps you can give me a short summary on the magic of Yargen."

"It is a magic the rest of the world has, that also extends beyond the elements. It's somehow…all elements at once. The magic of Yargen is invoked with words of power."

"A good, concise summary." Sehra held out her hand and Vi passed her the book. "We'll begin with the word I learned first."

Sehra opened the book, holding it between them. To Vi's immense relief, the page was not *narro*. She had no interest in confronting her mysterious friend in front of Sehra.

"*Durroe*," Vi read aloud, eyes on the page.

"What?" Sehra looked up at her quickly. "What did you say?"

"*Durroe*?" she repeated, the word less certain. "I'm sure my pronunciation is off…"

"I've never heard it said that way. I pronounced it the way my mother did, and she pronounced it the way her mother did as well."

"How do you pronounce it?" Vi was forced to ask.

"*Darol*." Vi watched as Sehra's mouth formed the word, making sure that she was hearing exactly what the woman was saying. It was an odd disconnect, because everything she saw in the woman's moving lips was nothing like what was written on the page.

"*Darol*," Vi tried to repeat it, but the word felt clumsy, awkward even. There was no magic hum to it.

"What made you say *durroe*?" Sehra asked, somewhat cautiously. Much like how Vi felt when she tried to mimic Sehra's pronunciation, the Chieftain looked strange recreating hers—and slightly missed the mark to Vi's ears.

"That's what's written." Vi motioned to the page.

"You can read these symbols?"

"Yes…" Vi said cautiously. Sehra leaned back in her chair. The Chieftain's eyes ran over her, cool and calculating. Vi shifted in her seat, crossing her leg and folding her hands. She waited as long as she could, but at a point was forced to ask, "Can't you read it?"

"No." The answer rung in Vi's ears.

"But… how do you know what it says? Surely you must be able to read it?" Vi looked back to the book. Sure enough, *durroe* was still quite clearly written on the page to Vi's eyes. She didn't see how the symbols could be read as anything else.

"I told you, I learned from my mother, and she from hers. But what I did not tell you was that none of us could read these strange glyphs."

"You do see the circles and lines, then?" Vi asked cautiously.

"I do." Sehra thought a moment. "How did you come up with the word?"

"I don't know," Vi confessed, hoping Sehra believed that she wasn't attempting to dodge the question—which, for once, she wasn't. "I see it and I... I hear sounds? I see words? No, not quite... It's as though the shape moves before my eyes and by the time it's finished, it looks nothing like what I saw at first but somewhere in its shifting I see the meaning and know how it should be said."

Sehra tapped the armrest of her chair, thrumming her fingers along its edge in quick succession. "I have no such sensation," she said finally.

"I'm not lying," Vi said hastily.

"I know you're not."

"How?"

"Grandmother said that her great grandmother could derive meaning from these symbols. But I never believed it, nor did my mother, for all we saw were the strange circles and spirals. But you... You can read it?"

"I... I think I can? I can't say for sure I'm right..." Vi looked back to the page and then, as slowly as she dragged her eyes away from it, looked to Sehra. "What does it mean, that I can read it?" *Read* still seemed a generous term for the sensations Vi experienced when looking at the page. Perhaps it had something to do with Taavin's word giving her an "understanding."

"I cannot say yet. But I do think it will expedite your studies."

"Good... because all I care about is controlling my magic and keeping it hidden," Vi emphasized. There couldn't be any incidents like the one in the jungle with her fire getting away from her... or randomly glowing. Sehra gave her a hard look. "I mean no offense," Vi added hastily. "I don't want to keep it hidden because of..."

"I know what they will say of 'magic from the North' in that city of ice." Sehra gave her a thin smile.

"Truly, the most important thing is for me to control it. If I go back to the capital and start an inferno—"

"We will see that you establish control. That was my task in all of this, what the traveler told me; I am to teach you all I know about the magic of Yargen. Now, *durroe*... I recommend holding out your hand." Sehra held her palm up to the ceiling, her long fingers outstretched. Vi mimicked the motion. "I imagine this as a platform for my magic. On this platform, I will build *durroe*."

"Build it?"

Sehra outlined the glyph in the book with her finger. Then, she did the same about an inch off her palm. Her movements were precise, and shaped out *durroe* exactly as it was in the book. The ghostly outline of the glyph appeared, hovering midair above Sehra's skin; above the glyph was a round orb of light.

"You're not... glowing." Vi remembered the threads of light radiating from her body the night before.

"No." Sehra looked at her strangely. "I envision the illusion I wish to make—the orb of light. Nothing else would be glowing."

"Of course not," Vi murmured. Sehra continued to stare. Well, if she was raising suspicion, she may as well go all the way. "Have you ever heard voices from the magic?"

"Voices? Of what kind?" If Sehra had to ask, then she most certainly hadn't.

"Nothing." Vi shook her head. "I had a strange dream last night, that's all." She knew better. Nothing about that had been a dream. She could still feel Taavin's words washing over her, rippling through her veins. Vi worked to push it from her mind and quickly mirrored Sehra's motions. "So I hold my palm out like this?"

"Yes." If Sehra was suspicious still, she gave no indication. "Now, you will attempt to conjure the essence of *durroe* above your palm. Try drawing it first—that was how my mother taught me."

Vi closed her eyes, summoning the symbol of *durroe* to the forefront of her mind. Lifting her other hand, she made an attempt at tracing the glyph in the air. At first, her skin, and the space above it, remained dark.

But Vi tried a second time. A third. And on the fourth, trails of light lifted from her skin, beginning to take shape before fading away frustratingly quickly.

She stared in wonder where the glyph had begun to form.

"Again, princess."

Vi took a slow breath, held out her hand again. By the time she completed drawing the symbol, the initial lines faded and there was no illusion—no orb of light, no strands peeling off her skin to hover in the air.

"What am I doing wrong?"

"Nothing, you merely need practice," Sehra assured her. "Try again." The Chieftain settled back in her chair, plucking a book off a nearby shelf. She flipped through it nonchalantly, clearly settling in for what she assumed was going to be hours of work.

Vi pressed her lips together in a firm line. Sehra may not know what she was doing wrong, but Vi would bet she knew someone who did. Taavin—a voice, a man linked with fate, and most importantly, someone who was from a region of the world that supposedly had intimate knowledge of this magic.

She'd summon him again tonight, and Vi wouldn't take no for an answer when she asked for his tutelage.

VI'S HAND RESTED ON her drafting table, turned upward.

Everyone else in the fortress was no doubt tucked safely in their beds at such a late hour. But she had stayed up, waiting and listening for quiet to take over the air and assure her that it was safe to slip into her study. She could've summoned him in her bedroom. But that had made her feel slightly... vulnerable last time. This was going to be a business transaction, and Vi wouldn't start it on weak footing.

She allowed magic to trickle across her skin. Sparks crackled between her fingertips and condensed into a flame in her palm—small and harmless. It was the same action she'd performed since she'd first manifested her magic. But now the flame didn't jump, or leap, or singe the desk as it had a mere week ago. The tiny fire was a mirror of what burned on the wicks of her candles and nothing more.

After a day of practicing with Sehra and making minimal strides, she needed this.

This was the reminder that, for the first time in her life, her magic was beginning to flow easily. Even if this wasn't the glyphs or magic of light. This much she could now do without fear, and that was progress.

Vi closed her fist, snuffing the fire.

Enough dreaming of things being simple. There was work to be done.

Taking a deep breath, Vi allowed the air to fill her lungs and feed the spark that she associated with the brilliant magic within her. She didn't bother with Sehra's instructions. So far, Vi had found the most success on her own, summoning the glyph and her mysterious contact in her own way.

"*Narro hath*," she whispered. Just like before, light danced on her skin, and Vi felt the connection nearly instantly. "Hello again."

There was a long pause that drew a smirk across her lips. She would bet Taavin didn't expect her to be the first to speak between them, and Vi was glad she'd seized the opportunity.

"I see you decided to contact me again." He made it sound as if he'd been waiting on her. As if she'd been inconveniencing him in some way.

"You don't sound surprised."

"I'm not."

"Why?" Vi asked.

"Because you need me." His words were arrogant, yet they smoothed across her skin like sunbeams.

"I don—"

"And because I need you." That stilled her. There was a begrudging reluctance about the sentiment, and an undeniable sincerity. Vi stared up at the ceiling, looking at the intricately curved wood, waiting for what he'd say next. Fortunately, he didn't make her ask. "We need to find the apexes." He paused. "*You* need to find them."

"Excuse me? I'm not your errand girl." She'd contacted him to demand help and now he was trying to turn the tables on her.

"This is far greater than your ego," he said sternly. Vi wished she had a face to look at. Though, perhaps it was better. As a disembodied voice, he couldn't see the expression she was making at his words right now.

"Why are they so important?"

"In all the recordings by the voices through the ages, they have mentioned apexes of fate as the places where Yargen's will is at work. You, as the champion, and me as her current voice, must go there and learn of her wisdom."

"Her wisdom." Vi snorted. "All I've seen at one of these apexes is a vision of my father and you."

"A vision of your father?" Taavin's voice rose with obvious interest. "Tell me of it."

"Maybe…" Vi didn't want to share her family with this disembodied man. That was a subject far too precious and personal. But… as he needed her, so she needed him. Which gave her an idea. "What do I get in return?"

"You're withholding the visions of Yargen from me?" He sounded positively aghast. Vi grinned wider.

"I need a teacher, to make sense of this magic I have." The sooner she did, the sooner she could put all worry about returning to Soricium to bed and merely be excited about being reunited with her family.

"I am not some lowly tutor. I am the voice," he said haughtily.

"And I am the champion—" Whatever that meant. "So unless you want to find these apexes on your own, I suggest you work with me."

There was another long pause. If it weren't for the magic radiating off her skin, Vi would've thought he had disappeared entirely. But he was still with her. She could almost feel his breathing.

"Very well. You find the apexes based on my direction and tell me your visions there… And I shall endure the questions of a resident of the Dark Isle about Lightspinning."

Vi remembered Sehra's map. *The Dark Isle…* that was how the rest of the world had labeled the Solaris Empire. This confirmed for her beyond all doubt that wherever Taavin was, he wasn't in the Empire. Which meant he really did need her to find these apexes. Vi could work with that leverage.

"You have a deal, Taavin. I'll find your apexes in the Solaris Empire and you teach me… Lightspinning." It was an apt name for the magic, she supposed, thinking about the swirling glyphs she'd seen surrounding him and what Sehra had conjured.

"Now, tell me of your first vision."

Vi obliged him, recounting what she had seen in the ruins. She spared him her emotions at seeing her father, and stuck to the facts. Taavin stayed oddly quiet throughout, not even a hum of affirmation that he had heard her.

"I see... Then, the next apex you should seek will be in a tomb marked by Yargen. I would suggest—"

Vi interrupted him before he could finish. "Wait a minute, I told you my vision, now it's time for you to tell me how to make use of this light."

There was an audible sigh.

"My teacher here, she can draw these glyphs in the air to use the magic." Vi barreled ahead before he could make any kind of objection again. "All I can do is make it radiate off my skin like tiny threads."

"You're not focusing it carefully enough, then," he said, after what seemed like forever.

"That doesn't help me." She pursed her lips together. "'Focusing' is too vague."

"You said you have a teacher there, on the Dark Isle?" She couldn't tell if he was impressed or horrified by the fact. "Why not consult with her? She'll be able to help you far more than I can, being physically present."

"Because I'm asking you, remember? You need me." *And because Sehra doesn't know very much*, Vi refrained from saying. She'd allow the other noblewoman some pride. "She draws the glyphs with her fingers in the air, but I—"

"No, physically drawing them is a fool's endeavor."

"Then what do you suggest?" Vi tried and failed not to take offense at his tone. She suddenly felt very silly trying to doodle in the air with her index finger for hours.

"Yargen's words are too complex for a mortal hand to draw efficiently—maybe it's possible to achieve *something* in that way, clearly your teacher manages. But that seems an utterly ineffective means to harness her power...You must, instead, understand the glyphs beyond all doubt. Know them in your soul—more than your eyes and ears can tell you. Know how the words resonate with your will. Only then can you gain mastery of them."

Intent was what this magic seemed to boil down to. Not unlike the elemental magicks of the Solaris Empire, she supposed. Vi flipped open Sehra's book, looking thoughtfully at the random page she opened to.

"When you say words... you mean the glyphs?"

"Yes, we aren't equipped to fully capture the language of the gods with mortal means. The best we can do is through the markings—glyphs, as you call them," he said, matter-of-fact. *A godly language*, that would explain why she saw them come to life on the page and resonate sound in her mind. Though if Vi hadn't had the week she'd been having, she would've scoffed at the notion of these words of power entirely.

"So you're saying I just need to memorize them more?"

"Yes and no. When you say the word, you will not draw the glyph with your hands, or ink, or by any other means. But with your mind. You must know it there. Like a musician knows his pieces, inside and out, well enough to know how it must be played in his own style."

"Yes, intent... That should be doable," she mumbled. If there was one thing Vi could do, it was amassing useless knowledge derived from books.

"It's not as easy as your tone tells me you think it is." He chuckled.

"Don't underestimate me." She hated how condescending he sounded. No stranger would speak to the Crown Princess that way, voice or no voice.

"Don't underestimate Lightspinning," Taavin fired back. "After all, if it were easy, you wouldn't be asking me for help."

Vi chewed the insides of her cheeks. He had a point. She'd spent hours with Sehra today and hadn't made much progress. But those had been hours working in the wrong direction; now she had a headway.

"All right," she started with renewed determination. "I'll begin really committing them to memory."

"With what?" His question reminded her that he couldn't see the book she was looking at.

"My teacher has a tome with a great number of these glyphs."

"Interesting…" Taavin's voice went low. "You know that's contraband to have on the Dark Isle. The person who delivered it could be put to death under the Queen's law."

"I'm the Crown Princess. All knowledge in Solaris is open to me." Vi wasn't sure if it was a lie or not. The map of the world—the true map—had been kept from her until recently. What other falsehoods of her world did she unquestioningly accept as fact?

"And that distinction means so very little to the rest of the world." The statement stilled her. His words weren't harsh or cruel. It was simple, factual. He wasn't trying to tear her down, merely state truth.

"Regardless, it is what it is. I have it, and I will make progress," she vowed.

"And while you make that progress, you shall seek out the next apex—a tomb marked by Yargen."

"Yes, I remember our deal." As if she could've forgotten so quickly. "Until next time."

Before he could get another word in, Vi released the magic and took a moment to breathe. That had gone well. She'd accomplished her goal, at the very least.

Leaning forward, Vi began to pour over the glyphs and symbols in the book before her. *Memorize them.* She'd look over every line and circle, feel the words they invoked, until she dreamt about them.

She'd prove to Sehra and to him that this wasn't something she was going to be daunted by. But, more importantly, she'd master the only thing standing between her and going home. Vi flipped the page and took a breath.

"*Durroe*," she repeated, time and again. Vi didn't have her hand outstretched— she wasn't even trying to conjure the orb of light. She merely said the word and allowed her ears to become accustomed to the syllables as her eyes ran over the glyph that came to life on the page before her.

She said the word fast, slow, soft, and as loudly as she dared. With every utterance, Vi seemed to notice something new about the symbol in the book. There was a line she hadn't understood before or a juncture she'd overlooked.

Snatching up paper from the side of her desk, Vi began drawing on it as she repeated the word. Just like after her first vision, her hand seemed possessed. It moved flawlessly over the page and crafted lines that were at first clumsy and smudged, but became flawless with practice and cemented in her memory.

By the time Vi finally leaned back in her chair, papers scattered the floor, *durroe* drawn across them. Her voice was horse from countless repetitions, her eyes bleary. Dawn streaked the sky, competing with the fading candlelight that now burned low. She needed to go to bed—if she was up much longer, she'd risk running into a servant coming to attend her and arouse suspicion.

"But first..." Vi lifted her hand tiredly, palm flat. The open air was now her parchment, her words the ink; her mind and will together formed her pen. With a word, she combined them all, and willed the illusion to take shape. "*Durroe*."

The tiniest of threads lifted off her hand, coalescing into lines that Vi knew inside and out. For one brief second, the symbol flickered faintly above her hand, an orb like Sehra's atop. As quickly as it came, it disappeared.

A small blurt of sheer joy rolled into laugher as Vi's hand went limp at her side. She stared at the ceiling, the back of her head against her chair. Slowly, Vi turned her head, looking at the sketch of the rose garden Romulin had sent her.

"One word closer to mastery... only a dozen more to go," she whispered to the blueprint tacked up against her shelves. "I'll get this, I promise. Then, I'm coming home to all of you."

S HE WAS GOING TO summon him again tonight, Vi decided.

It had been two days since her first lesson with Sehra. Two days, two more lessons later, and Vi's progress had been minimal—but it had been there. Her glyph was becoming stronger, slightly more stable, but it seemed to unravel all too quickly as if there was some knot she needed to tie in the light that she couldn't find.

Summoning balls of light was still proving difficult, but she knew she could summon a voice in her head. So that was where she'd return to. As mysterious as that man was, he knew about the magic and his help last time had been invaluable. This time she'd insist he tell her some way to expedite—

A shadow blocked out the sun as Martis's back-lit silhouette moved in front of her line of sight. Vi sat straighter, called to attention. But before she could mutter an apology for the distraction, he started in on her.

"Princess, please pay attention." Martis tapped the desk in front of her with the pointed end of the long stick he favored. She wondered if it made him feel authoritative to hold a mini scepter before the Crown Princess. In a way, he had more command over her life than she did.

The scratching of a pen from behind her brought Vi's mind fully back to the present. She glanced over her shoulder at Andru, who sat in the corner. He glanced back at her, as if sensing her attention. Vi swept her hair over her shoulder as she turned forward, fussing with the ends of her braids.

She couldn't be as relaxed as she used to be anymore. Whatever rapport, however small, she had built with her tutors was gone now. She was under the watchful eyes of the Senate. After her magic got out of hand, she shouldn't take any more risks. Especially not before she had her new powers sorted.

Vi could imagine what the Senate and Southern nobility would say if she was discovered to have a rare magic only passed down in Sehra's bloodline. They would make her out to be so Northern that even the magic had worn off on her. Claim that Sehra had adopted her outright and she was no longer heir to her birthright. No, on second thought, they'd likely invent far worse lies than that.

"Yes, Martis. I am sorry. While it is no excuse, this past week merely has my mind preoccupied." She made an effort to enunciate her words properly, draw them out even though she was so tired from days of double lessons. "I shall endeavor to be a better student."

"You had four days off from your tutelage. You have six months—at most, likely less—until the parade arrives for you, and you are expected to return South with full and proper knowledge of your station. Now is not the time to add delays by daydreaming, however tempting it is to preoccupy your mind with all that has yet to pass."

"I understand." Vi folded her fingers, avoiding doing anything that could land her in further trouble.

"And you are by no stretch a bad student," he mumbled softly. "In any case, perhaps a change of topic would refresh your energy for what remaining time we have."

Martis crossed over to the desk opposite Vi's. He shuffled through his papers, selecting a letter.

"Ah, yes, let us discuss the War in the North."

"Did we not cover that last year?" Vi hoped she came off as curious rather than obstinate.

"Every year you can learn something more, because you are older, wiser, and more mature."

"Right, of course." Vi picked up her quill and promptly put it down. If she was holding any kind of writing utensil, she'd be at risk of scribbling cartography lines or magic circles on her page, either of which Martis certainly wouldn't appreciate. "So what are we going to begin covering this year about the War in the North?"

"How the War in the North was a precursor to the rise of the Mad King Victor. So we are, in effect, drawing new connections between the two topics we have previously discussed."

Vi tilted her head to the side. "The connection is plain, is it not? The War in the North directly preceded the uprising. It was the last war of Emperor Tiberius Solaris."

"More than that. For it was an article collected by your mother during the War of the North that enabled Mad King Victor's rise to power."

"What?" He had her attention now. "But, the Mad King... he tried to slay my mother and father. My mother would not have helped him."

Vi had seen the raised and angry scar that ran from her mother's shoulder to the center of her breast. Vhalla had let her run her fingers over it as a curious child, and said a wicked man had given it to her, but never elaborated further. When Vi finally had a name for the "wicked man," she never asked again.

The scar was not unlike the one on Taavin's face, Vi realized. Then instantly shook it from her thoughts. She had to remain focused or Martis's limited patience for her would run out.

"He did. But *how* he did it is of great import, for it was the start of the end of the Crystal Caverns."

"So, how did he do it?"

"Do you remember the lore of the crystal weapons?"

Vi nodded. Long ago there were said to be four crystal weapons, one in possession of each of the unique geographical regions of the Main Continent. They seemed to be things relegated only to tall tales... yet two of those crystal weapons surfaced, marking the rise of the Mad King. But that was all Vi knew. As she conveyed the fact to Martis, it suddenly seemed a glaring deficit in her education.

"Just so," he affirmed. "One of those weapons the Mad King Victor used was a crown that had been in your family's possession for centuries." Vi wasn't sure how a crown could be a weapon, but she did know that crystals were strange, powerful, and extremely dangerous. "The other was an axe that was retrieved from the North."

"An axe?" Vi repeated, her mind spinning, trying to recall every fireside story she'd been privy to and every mention of lore from Ellene. "Like the axe Dia, the fallen star, used to carve civilization from the boughs of the Mother Tree?"

"If you believe these Northern stories." Martis's sniff clearly conveyed that he didn't.

Vi bit back a retort asking why it was so unreasonable to believe Southern histories of crystal weapons and a power that could turn men into monsters... but similar Northern oral histories were mere "stories" to be dismissed. Even if she felt in the right, arguing with Martis would get her nowhere. Vi had long since learned that some minds, once made up, could not be changed.

"I think, perhaps, it is more than just coincidence that an axe shows up in their stories and our history."

"Yes, well, I am not here to speak about that. I am here to speak about what your mother has passed on to me in her letters." Martis tapped a series of papers on the desk. What Vi wouldn't give to leaf through it. But her parents' correspondence with her tutors was as private as their correspondence with her. "She would have me tell you of when she retrieved this weapon with the intent to benefit the South, and protect it from falling into the wrong hands. But all she did was foolishly—her words, and I think them far too harsh—think that she could make the axe safer than its own people had by placing it in a Northern tomb.

Tomb. Vi sat a little straighter. She'd heard the word before, and recently. Perhaps too recently to be a mere coincidence.

"She was here during the encampment, and on the edge of the city..."

Ellene and Jayme were waiting when Vi finished with Martis. Seeing people occupying her sitting room was truly a welcome anomaly.

Jayme had made the long table in Vi's sitting area her weapon smithy. She currently had a whetstone atop layers of rags; the sound of the metal sliding over stone made a soft yet sharp *shhing* noise that had the hair on Vi's arms standing near immediately.

The young heir to the Northern throne was lounging on a sofa, clearly much less bothered by the noise as she hummed to herself a tune that was scribbled out on a sheet of paper. Vi vaguely recognized it as something she'd heard being sung recently among the city commoners. But she didn't recognize the words.

Both perked up immediately on seeing her.

"You're done for the day now, right?" Ellene asked eagerly.

"Not quite." Vi hated to see her friend deflate, but there was nothing she could do. "I promised your mother I would work with her on something."

"On what?"

What, indeed... Vi had been half hoping Sehra would've told her daughter something to explain their new tutoring arrangement, and spare Vi the lie she'd now be forced to think up on the spot. "Going over details for when my family comes to collect me."

"That sounds tiring." Ellene flopped back onto the cushions.

"But necessary," Martis interjected from the doorway, pausing briefly to give Vi a bow. "Thank you for your work today, princess."

"Yours as well."

"I look forward to continuing our discussions. Hopefully, next time, they will not be so one-sided." He gave a thin smile, and left.

"Rude," Ellene muttered. "Is he allowed to talk to you like that?"

"Given all that I've put Martis through over the years, I'm going to say yes." Vi ran a hand through her hair, sorting the carefully plaited braids.

"Careful, you give that kind of leeway to the Southern court and they'll walk all over you," Jayme said without looking up from her work. It sounded like something Romulin would say.

"I'll deal with the Southern Court when I have to." Romulin's letters had painted the court as a garden of roses—fresh smelling, beautiful at a glance, but with thorns attached and filled with vipers at the root.

"An apt advisement, I'm certain Prince Romulin would say much the same," Andru interjected, as though he could read her mind. Vi nearly jumped out of her skin. The man had an innate and unnerving quality to go unnoticed—which was unusual for a man as equal parts handsome and awkward as he was. "They can be quite brutal."

"More or less brutal than the Senate?" The question left Vi's lips before she had time to even think.

"That depends on who you ask." Andru did not look at her when he spoke. He was so transfixed on the other corner of the room that it drew Vi's attention as well. But there was nothing there, and when her eyes swung back, his attention was solely on her.

"Senates and courts, boring and far away." Ellene shifted to the edge of her seat. "Can you go over things with my mother later, Vi? The Winter Solstice market is beginning to set up and we're going to see this year's layout."

"Given our incident in the jungle, I'm not going to push my luck." Plus, the sooner she got these lessons out of the way, the better. Vi needed to master her magic and be done with all of this Yargen business.

"I could go with you," Andru said suddenly. All three sets of eyes were on him. "I would be happy to see the market."

Vi stared at him. Just what was he trying to do? She didn't think for a moment he was genuinely interested in the market.

"It's a girls-only trip." Ellene spared Jayme and Vi having to turn him down.

"Any particular reason?" Andru was back to looking in the other corner of the room. But he quickly brought his eyes back to Ellene.

"You don't ask girls what they're doing during girls-only time." Ellene laughed.

"Is there anything else we can do for you?" Vi asked, trying to give Andru a graceful out.

Luckily, he took it. "No, I shall be off."

With that, he all but bolted for the door, head held high. The momentary discomfort Vi had observed was gone entirely.

"Goodness, he's strange…" Ellene murmured. "Did they send him to try to make you so uncomfortable you'll heed the Senate's every word just to get rid of him?"

"You could be nicer," Jayme chided.

"You said yourself he was unbearable on the road," Vi pointed out. Jayme merely shrugged.

"Anyway! Back to the market." Ellene was like a dog with a bone. It was times like this that Vi recognized she was just toeing the line between girl and woman, not decidedly one or the other. "Jayme is going to meet Darrus for the first time."

"I met Darrus in the spring." Jayme stole the words from Vi's mouth.

"Briefly. And he's changed so much since then. He's *grown,*" Ellene said with a somewhat dreamy look, clutching the sheet music to her chest. That motion alone made Vi suspect that the song had something to do with the young man.

He hasn't, Vi mouthed to Jayme while Ellene wasn't looking.

Jayme hid a snort of laughter with a particularly swift movement of her blade over the stone. "It's hardly been seven months."

"Practically a year."

"Seven months is more like half a year." Jayme rolled her eyes and began to pack up her things. She paused, looking to Vi. "Should I go with you?"

"Go with me? Why?"

"I am your sworn guard." Jayme had a small smile, one Vi hoped was from pride at the fact.

"I'm staying in the fortress. You go make sure this one's feet stay on the ground so she doesn't fly away with that boy." Vi pointed to Ellene.

"Hey!"

"Understood." Jayme gave a mock-serious salute.

"I'll catch up with you two later."

"Don't be too long!" Ellene was off the couch, pulling Vi in for a quick squeeze. "If you're quick, you can join us. But we'll be happy to go again later, too."

They were out the door in a blink. Vi wasn't long behind them. One more set of lessons with Sehra… and then the real work would begin when she summoned Taavin.

16

VI TAPPED HER FINGERS along her drafting table, debating with herself. Martis's words about the tomb still lingered in her mind from the morning. Compounding with that was some genuine progress made with Sehra, assuring her that another night of Taavin's tutelage wasn't essential for her at this moment.

She had promised him she'd hold up her end of the deal.

"Oh, fine, let's get this over with then." Vi threw up her arms and uttered, "*Narro hath.*"

She felt the connection thrum between them. It came to life with vivid sensations that culminated in an awareness of Taavin's existence somewhere across the world. But, for this brief moment, that distance didn't seem so impossibly large.

"You again?"

"Hello to you too." Vi huffed at the curt introduction.

"Back for more elementary explanations on Lightspinning?"

"No," she said firmly to the disembodied voice. "I think I know where this tomb of yours is located."

Silence. Stillness. And then, with a nearly quivering eagerness, "You do?"

"Yes. I think so, at least… How will I know?"

"When you arrive, merely repeat the process of the last apex and receive the vision. If it truly is a place where fate was malleable, that should be all you need."

"That's a bit vague, don't you think?" Vi mumbled.

"I think it's perfectly clear."

He would. He wasn't the one having to conceive a way to get to these apexes. "After I do this for you, we need to discuss how to stabilize these glyphs. I keep losing them too quickly."

"The fate of our world hangs in the balance and you're focused on Lightspinning technique?" His voice went low, almost growl-like.

"The fate of *my* world counts on me learning this," Vi insisted. She'd keep up her end of the deal, but she needed him to know that she wasn't going to be distracted from his in the process.

"I think you need to—" Taavin never got the chance to finish.

A knock on the door startled Vi to the point of nearly jumping out of her seat.

"Vi, may I come in?" Ellene called through the door.

Vi looked at her skin. It was back to normal. The startle must've jostled whatever connection had been there. Given how he'd begun his final statement, the productive part of the conversation had ended anyway.

"Yes, come in," Vi called back, lifting her quill in an attempt to look as though she'd been pouring over her maps.

The door of her library cracked open, and Ellene peeked her head in before emerging the rest of the way. "Maps? Is that seriously what's kept you this whole time?" Vi couldn't tell if she was frustrated or pleasantly amused.

"Yeah, I realized I hadn't had a chance to incorporate my sketches from the hunt onto my main maps." Vi felt bad for lying to Ellene. But she was in so far over her head when it came to this mysterious power that she didn't even know where to begin.

Ellene crossed over to her desk, looking down. She dragged her fingertip along the winding lines that Vi had sketched weeks ago, the dry ink staying securely in place. "You really do have a knack for this."

Vi glanced up, her pen stilling from the three strokes it'd made on the page. There was a softness to Ellene's voice that Vi was unaccustomed to hearing. If she had to attach a label, she'd call it sadness, and that fact wrenched a corner of her, twisting to the point of pain. But the reason for Ellene's sorrow or her own was unclear until her friend gave it words.

"Soon, you'll finally see some of these places with your own two eyes." Ellene's finger tapped on the Crossroads in the Western Waste before trailing down to the southern capital. "It isn't long now, until you leave."

"We have a whole winter." Vi caught her hand, giving it a squeeze.

"Don't spend it here cooped in your room alone with your maps," Ellene whispered. "Don't let the idea of places you want to see, that you'll see soon enough, take you from me in these final weeks that I have you."

"I won't." It sounded like a promise, but Vi didn't know if such a promise was fair to make. She could never control what consumed her attentions. And it seemed, now, that learning the magic of the world beyond was going to quickly absorb all free thought if she wasn't careful. Could she go that quickly from merely wanting control of her powers to wanting to excel in them?

"Promise?" Ellene must've heard the reservation, too.

"I promise."

Ellene was right; soon enough she would be taken away. Then, she would have a whole lifetime to spend in the South, years as an Empress going on tours across her territories to attach visuals of locations to the names on her map. She could find tutors for the magic that was already intriguing her, bring them from the Crescent Continent, if she must. She would have far more clout as Empress than Sehra had as Chieftain; she might have better luck as a result.

"Good. I'm going to hold you to it." Her voice was much brighter, a smile sneaking on her lips.

"You already have something in mind." Why was she not surprised?

"Well, you missed the market today with Jayme, Darrus, and I, *and* dinner. You owe us."

Vi gave a snort of laughter and decided to play along. She owed everyone something right now it would seem. "Okay, I owe you... how can I repay my debt?"

"Tomorrow, after your lessons, come out with Jayme and me. We can walk through the market—show you what you missed—on the way to the outer ring." The outer ring was the burnt stretch that still remained like a scar on the earth from the Empire's occupation during the War in the North.

"And what are we doing in the outer ring?"

"Noru races!"

She suppressed a shiver at the mere mention of noru. After the incident in the jungle, Vi was quite content not interacting with the beasts again for a while. But she already promised Ellene...

"They're the preliminary races for the winter solstice festivals," Ellene continued. "Darrus asked me today to join the first heat with him. But, of course, I played coy and told him that I'd have to see if you were planning on joining. Since you're the Crown Princess, I had to be deferent to you and all." Vi snorted at the idea of Ellene showing her proper etiquette. Ellene clearly had the same idea as she giggled with laughter. "I was thinking we could take Gormon out—he's faster than mine. Mother still insists I ride the old slow Stanos for safety or some such."

"Some safety may be good for us," Vi muttered.

"Vi, don't take their side."

"Okay, okay, continue this plan of yours," she conceded.

"So, we'll say you race, and we take out your noru. Then, when we get there, I'll let Darrus be disappointed that I'm not riding with him because you wanted to. And you can say that you won't ride because... Well, I don't know. You can decide that there. You're sick or something." Ellene giggled. *Sick of noru, more like*, Vi thought flatly. "Think of how surprised he'll be when I'm astride. How impressed he'll be when I come in first on your noru." Ellene clasped her hands over Vi's hand. "He'll fall in love with me then and there, Vi, and we'll live together happily for forever."

"How can I argue with true love?"

"So you're saying you'll do it?" Ellene squeezed tighter.

"There's not much I need to be 'doing.' More what I need to make sure I'm not doing." Vi chuckled. "Yes, I'll do it. I'll tell the servants first thing in the morning to saddle Gormon—full Imperial leathers. Just think how impressive that will look for Darrus."

"I knew I could count on you!" Ellene clapped her hands. "I'll let Jayme know in the morning that you agreed to the plan."

"Not tonight?" It wasn't like Ellene not to immediately rush off and tell everyone involved of her latest schemes.

"She wasn't feeling too well after dinner. Said she might have ate something her stomach wasn't familiar with in the market." Ellene shook her head. "You know her, no matter how many times she's been to Soricium, her stomach just refuses to agree with something at some point."

"I'll send Ginger."

"I already offered to get a cleric." Ellene raised her hands and shoulders in a dismissive motion. "She said she needs to sleep it off and that she doesn't need help."

"Well, we'll see how she feels in the morning, and if we have to we can force some clerical help on her." Vi gave Ellene a wink that was returned with a laugh.

"You can do that. I'm not going to be the one to test Jayme. She can be scary when pushed!" Ellene paused in the door frame. "Thanks again, Vi, for helping me. It'd be nice to have a friend in Darrus, at least, after you leave."

Before Vi could comment on the sentiment, Ellene was gone.

She stood at her desk, tapping her fingertips on it thoughtfully. *Darrus, at least.* That was one more thing she needed to keep an eye on before leaving—how Ellene would handle it all. She didn't want to see the girl running into a relationship purely to fill a void of companionship brought on by Vi leaving.

Then again, Sehra would be certain to ward against that as well. She would not allow her daughter to fall into despair, or resort to less-than-wholesome means to fill the gap.

Vi stood, extinguishing the candles in her study and starting for her bedroom.

It was then, in the silvery moonlight streaming through the windows, that Vi's eyes landed on the outer edge of Soricium. All Vi wanted was a good night's rest. But it seemed that would elude her yet again.

V I CLUNG TO THE walls and interior passages of the fortress as much as possible. Some were usually reserved for servants only, but they were vacant at this time of night. If she did run into someone and kept her head down, no one would suspect her to be here.

She hoped.

Because if she was conspicuous... anyone in the fortress would stop her. That person would take her to Jax, and there was no way she could explain what she was doing. Or, perhaps, she could *maybe* get them to take her to Jayme, who would either not believe her or insist on coming as well—and this was something Vi felt certain she needed to do alone.

She'd never attempted to sneak out before. It was all very cloak and dagger—quite literally. She wore her darkest and heaviest cloak, hood pulled high and tight.

Yet despite all her worries, Vi stepped out of a back door at the end of a long stairwell and vanished into the city proper without issue. She glanced back, looking at the fortress in relief.

Her feet slowed and she stared up at the silent giants that extended their leafy arms to the heavens. All her life, she'd stayed put, exactly as intended. Never questioning, never wondering what would happen if she did venture beyond the confines set out for her.

Some part of her felt silly for not doing this sooner. It was so easy to slip out unattended. Likely because she had never really attempted it. There was no guard posted at her door or individual on duty watching her room at all hours of the day.

A smile crossed her mouth, an expression that quickly vanished when two small glints of reddish light flashed into view.

It was only a glimpse, and yet it felt as though someone was staring down at her. Vi scanned the bridges and walkways of the fortress, stretching upward with the trees to merge with the dark sky above. There was no indication of anyone watching, no other bright red spots, and yet she had the distinct, sinister sensation of being observed.

She was imagining it, surely. Maybe she'd never snuck out before because she didn't have the proper constitution for espionage. Paranoia was her just reward.

Turning quickly, Vi crossed through alleyways and wove around small trees that curved to support signs and rooftops. Vi kept her face down, hood up, and hunched slightly. She'd braided her hair and tucked it away. No one should be able to recognize her... Unless they recognized the cloak itself. But outside of the fortress, no one knew Vi well enough that they'd know her by that alone.

Several times, she could've sworn she heard footsteps behind her. But when Vi stopped, so too did the sound, forcing her to believe her mind was just getting the better of her. Still, one time, she called out softly, "Jayme?" thinking that perhaps her friend had sneaked out behind her in an effort to keep her safe.

A response from behind her nearly had Vi jumping from her skin.

"Princess, is that you?"

Her eyes landed on a robed man. Long sleeves were tucked into heavy gloves that went to his elbows. On his face was a pointed mask, crafted in heavy leather, extending like a long beak away from his mouth. The inset glass goggles shone in the darkness, like some kind of terrifying monster.

She took a step back. The voice hadn't been hostile, yet given the strange garb the man wore...

"I'm sorry, I didn't mean to startle you." The man quickly pulled off his mask, revealing a handsome face Vi instantly recognized.

"Darrus?" Vi blinked from the mask, to the heavy gloves, to his face—indents of the inside of the mask lingering on his flawless skin. "What are you wearing?"

"You haven't seen one yet?" He lifted the mask slightly. "I would've thought..."

"There's been much going on of late," Vi answered cautiously.

"Oh right, Ellene mentioned, you're going back to your home soon."

Vi resisted correcting him that she'd never actually lived there. The North could be as much her home as the South... if she had ever been fully accepted.

"What is it?" She pointed to the mask, reverting the topic back to safer territory.

"They call it a plague mask. There are medical screens the clerics have made on the inside of the beak to help filter out the White Death. We don't know if it's effective yet... but it feels a lot better wearing one than not when you're around the infected."

"White Death..." Vi swallowed hard, remembering all the words of panic her tutors had used when her travels were first starting to be delayed due to the plague. She couldn't get sick, the Empire needed her. "Why are you wearing one? Is someone in your family ill?"

"Thankfully no... I'm helping the clerics. We set up a building for the ailing over there." He pointed up to the outer ridge of Soricium. Vi couldn't see the building from where she stood, but she gladly took his word for it. That was one area that, for all her curiosity, she knew better than to explore.

"Are there that many ailing?" Vi asked. She didn't want the answer, but she owed it to her people to pursue it.

"Again, thankfully no..." He paused, cleaning one of the lenses on his mask. "There might be, though. They expect it to get worse with time. They're already talking about if we have to move it—the infirmary, that's what they're calling it— where the next, or new one, will be.

"But we think we have a handle on the spread. Giving the infected a place to go and be treated, keeping them sequestered from the masses seems to have stinted the spread."

"What can I do?" Vi asked.

"Unfortunately, nothing."

"I'm the Crown Princess," Vi needlessly reminded him for the sake of emphasis. "I have resources, I can get you what you need."

"I misspoke." He gave her a tired smile. "There's nothing anyone can do. The clerics have no idea what's causing the plague, how it spreads, who it chooses. It's seemingly random... as if people's bodies just... give up and die."

"That's... terrifying," Vi whispered.

"It is." Much like in Ellene, Vi saw two different forces existing in Darrus. There was the terror of the boy she'd seen dancing with Ellene in the spring. But there were also the makings of a man who had the bravery to face his fears. Perhaps Ellene was right, and he had actually grown some.

They fell silent, Darrus looking from his mask to her. Then, as if remembering what he'd stopped her for initially, he asked, "What are you doing out so late? Is everything all right?"

"Yes, just... I needed some air."

"I see." He did not sound convinced in the slightest and his blatant disbelief made her feel awkward. His emerald eyes set on dark skin were striking, and they reminded her of a similar set she dared hope to see again.

"Please, don't tell," she whispered. "Not even Ellene." Her and Darrus had never been particularly close. But she could only hope the man had enough favor for her as a friend of Ellene, or enough fear of her as the Crown Princess, to oblige.

"Should I come with you? Is everything truly all right?"

"I have to do this alone. It's important. It's for the crown."

He gave a small nod, clearly still unsure. "Well, I need to get back to my work. I'm the lowest rung, so that means I'm stuck taking the late shifts. They're expecting me."

"I didn't know you were so interested in being a cleric," Vi said thoughtfully. She'd only seen Darrus through the context of Ellene's gaze—a handsome man who was a good dancer and charming to no end. The fact that she'd never invested more time in learning his true nature, his hopes and dreams, when her friend was so invested, made Vi's insides tighten slightly with guilt.

"I'm not sure if I am, to be honest."

"This must be a bit of trial by fire."

He chuckled. "Spoken like a Firebearer." Vi's mouth quirked into a small smile. If only he knew how wrong he was on that. They both knew precious little about each other, and were now unlikely conspirators in Vi's nighttime jaunt. "But yes, these are rather hard conditions to learn under. I'm not sure if I'm cut for it, but I do want to help people and it seems to me that this is the best way to do so presently."

The words he spoke now were in stark contrast to the free-spirited boy she'd seen originally become the target of Ellene's girl-like crushes. Darrus was fast becoming someone Vi could respect. Perhaps, if this gentle and heartfelt manner was Darrus's true nature, she should be less worried about the idea of Ellene drifting even closer to him after Vi left.

"Thank you, on behalf of the crown." Vi hoped he took both her meanings:

gratitude for his work in dealing with the steadily spreading White Death, and for his silence on her being out long after dark.

"Yes, your highness." He paused, right before putting his mask back over his face. "Perhaps you can return the favor by putting in a good word with Ellene to dance with me at the winter solstice? She still has yet to give me a response." There was the boyish grin she remembered.

"Consider it done." He turned to leave and Vi stopped him. "And Darrus, don't worry so much about Ellene. She's crazy about you." They shared a small smile.

"That's good to hear." Just as Vi turned to leave, he caught her by her shoulder. "One last thing…" His voice had dropped low and was tense.

"What?" Vi whispered in reply.

"I could've sworn I saw someone following you. I thought it may have been Jayme but…"

"I'm alone," Vi insisted. She wasn't sure if she was informing him, or saying it out of hope that the fact remained true.

"Keep your hood up, and be careful, okay?"

"I will."

They parted ways, then, and she slipped into the night on her hasty path.

At the edge of the city was a ruin so ancient it was nearly taboo. Everyone had always been hushed about the worn and ominous structure. But with Martis's lesson, Vi now knew why. If she was right, and this was the place her mother had retrieved an axe that had changed the course of history… then she could understand why it was willingly being expunged from memory. *Expunged*, just like her parents had decreed the dangerous Crystal Caverns following the Mad King's uprising.

She scrambled up a hill and into the trees that surrounded the city. A shadow began to loom against the starlight winking through the leafy canopy. Vi paused to look up at the tall, pyramid-like ruins that towered above her. She didn't know if it could be called a tomb, but she would say based on the embellishments that it was made by the same people who had crafted the underground ruins she'd discovered— just far worse for wear, having been exposed to the elements.

It couldn't be coincidence that Taavin had used the word *tomb*, then Martis, and it all added up to this particular place. Looking around for any who might be watching, and finding none, Vi dared to hold out her hand.

"Repeat the process," she whispered. Only one way to find out if this was her next apex of fate…

Fire ignited in her hand. Vi stared, and waited for the sensations of future sight to overtake her.

N O VISIONS CAME.

"Why?" Vi whispered, as though the fire would answer. It didn't, and she extinguished it, looking around. "This has to be the place…" She looked up at the ruins, hoping they would give her the answer, and was surprisingly rewarded.

"Repeat the process—I have to be inside," Vi mumbled. Of course it wouldn't be as easy as standing at its base. She had to be inside the last set of ruins and assumed this to be the same. "Now… how to get in?"

Vi took a lap around the structure, then doubled back to where the remnants of an old cave-in could be found. Time had taken its toll on the collapsed rubble, as with the rest of the weather-worn ruins. Roots and vines pulled it apart, creating an opening barely large enough for her to wiggle through.

Taking a deep breath, Vi debated if she was extremely brave or stupid to go into something so dangerous-looking, and began to clamor over the rubble anyway. Just as she suspected, it was barely large enough for her to fit through. A narrower portion dug into her wide hips and made her twist and contort her legs to get her thighs through. But get through they did, and with a small tumble she landed in a hollowed alcove eerily similar to what she'd seen in the jungle.

Shards of what looked like obsidian scattered around her, leaving Vi to pick a few from indents in her hands with small winces. Miraculously, they did not draw blood. She stared at the glass-like stones, lifting up a larger piece for inspection.

Martis had said that following the fall of the Mad King Victor, the blight of the Crystal Caverns had been put to an end, once and for all, on the Main Continent. According to his telling, the crystals, once illuminated with their strange and twisted magic, had gone dark, fractured, and broken.

"This will work," Vi whispered into the darkness, letting the shard fall from her hands.

Readying herself once more, she held out her hand. Already, the atmosphere around her felt vastly different than it had outside. The feeling of sinking into the flame, of being consumed by it, of not being able to tear her eyes away even if she tried, was already on the edge of her consciousness.

As if drawn from her by an invisible string, her spark rushed forth the moment Vi allowed it freedom. It hazed into the air over her palm, condensing into an open flame. When Vi looked at it, the world went white; like last time, she was quickly overcome.

Shapes were slowly drawn into existence.

While white threads of magic continued to blur at the edges of her vision, the scene she was presented with was one of night.

A man stood atop a dais, a curving silver blade with runes etched along its flat side was gripped in a fist. In the other he held a hand up to the full moon overhead, blood streaming down his palm. It mingled with blood from a secondary source—on an altar behind him was a figure, distinctly human and wrapped in what looked like burlap, whose blood was soaking through the fabrics covering them and dripping into a channel that ran down to a symbol painted on the ground.

She tried to make out who the sacrificial person on the altar could be. But they were wrapped tightly and immobile. Dead, more likely, given that she couldn't see them breathing. For some reason, Vi couldn't move; she was positioned in one location in the vision and no matter how she tried, she couldn't change her vantage.

Ignoring the body, altar, and bleeding man, Vi followed the channel of blood that was flowing down to a symbol Vi recognized near instantly.

It was a dragon, curled in on itself to form a perfect circle. A line had been drawn through the middle, cleaving it in two, off-setting the halves. It was the broken moon of the Tower of Sorcerers. But Vi had never heard of a place like this in any sorcerer lore she knew. She certainly knew there were no sacrificial rituals codified at the Tower.

Men and women were bowed around the outer edge of the glyph. They rose in unison, slowly, chanting under their breath in time with the louder calls of the man bleeding at the dais. At least, what she assumed were louder calls, based on the red of his face and the gulping breaths he took before opening his lips wide for each chant. To her, the world was silent, just like the last time; she could observe only but not interact further.

She couldn't gasp in her bodiless state. But Vi felt the shock ripple through her as she saw more clearly the faces of the men and women beneath the large black hoods. Most possessed sharply angular features—not unlike the queen she had seen in her last vision—but their skin was ghostly pale and they had bright red eyes that glowed in the darkness.

Whatever they were, Vi had the distinct feeling it was not human.

There were some who had snouts like a lizard—identical to the man she had seen carrying the cage before her father. More, still, looked like normal humans, but with no eyebrows. Instead, glowing dots lined their foreheads.

It was a mix of races Vi had never seen before—never even imagined—and only further cemented that what she was looking at couldn't be some secret Tower ritual in the South. This felt like a different world entirely.

They turned their eyes skyward, lifting their arms up. The man slowly descended from the dais, his unnaturally glowing crimson eyes gaining in brightness till they were nearly white. The moment he reached the center of the symbol, everything reached a crescendo in a bolt of blood-red lightning.

It struck the man, sparking off and sending the other men and women around him flying back. Their bodies, dead, littered the ground. Magic arced through the air like the rebirth of a cosmos, all condensing on a glowing figure slowly rising from where the leader of this dark ritual had once stood.

It was the same man, but changed. He wore the red light as a second skin, seeming to grow in size before Vi's eyes. She knew she was witnessing true, but Vi couldn't fashion words or sounds. He turned; Vi could all but feel his sightless white eyes on her. They were like the noru. They were worse than death.

A scream—her scream—broke the trance of the vision.

Vi collapsed back, scrambling away, as though there was something physical she could distance herself from. She pressed her eyes closed, but all she saw were the scattered bodies, and the nightmarish figure emerging from the collection of their sacrificial essence. Vi shook her head, as though she could dispel the images.

She let out another yelp of startled surprise when a hand landed on hers.

Opening her eyes, Vi locked gazes with Taavin. He was there, closer, sharper. His hand was on hers with a warmth that was not quite real—as if he was touching her soul, housed under her skin, more than the skin itself.

"You actually found it... So you're not totally worthless like most on the Dark Isle." Suddenly, as if realizing he'd reached for her, his hand lifted and the sensation of the ghostly touch vanished.

"Is that supposed to be a compliment?" Vi muttered. There was another retort in her mind, but it vanished when his other hand rose, hovering just above her face, as though he was about to tuck a stray piece of hair behind her ear. Vi quickly did it herself, and he ignored the motion entirely.

"Are you all right?"

The question was surprisingly sincere. Vi blinked at him, swallowing, and gave a nod. The vision still lingered on her, uncomfortably heavy. Was she all right? Likely not. Her world had been shaking at its foundations for weeks now. But the only option was to press forward. She was in too deep.

"Tell me what you saw."

"A ritual, men and women with red eyes, a sacrifice, a man made of lightning... I think he saw me." Vi shook her head, trying to rattle her thoughts back into place, trying to make her words make sense. But there was no sense to be found. The whole thing felt impossible and she felt insane the second she vocalized it. Despite the fact, she tried to recall as much detail as she could for him.

"Elfin'ra." The man cursed when she'd finished her more detailed recounting, and shook his head.

"What are elfin'ra?"

"Those men and women you saw with red eyes worshipping the evil god Raspian. They should be sealed away, but with the barrier that had been holding Raspian broken..." He cursed softly under his breath again, this time in a language Vi didn't recognize. As Taavin shook his head, his hair shifted, and Vi noticed something she hadn't before.

She shifted back involuntary. "You... are you one of them?"

"Do I look like one of them?"

"You have pointed ears like they did." Sure enough, the pointed tips of his ears extended out from the waves of his hair. How had she never noticed it before? Likely because there were about a thousand things she needed to focus on and she'd only seen him twice... but still...

"But do I have pale skin and red eyes?" Taavin asked dumbly.

"Well, no, but—"

He explained as though she were a child. "I am elfin. They are elfin'ra."

"And that means nothing to me," Vi stated, deadpan. She was pleased that, despite his general look of frustration and tedium, a small smile graced his lips at the remark. But it was quickly abandoned.

"The elfin'ra are a splinter of elfin... their worship of Raspian has twisted them, changed their magic, their bodies. For it, they were banished to Salvidia over a thousand years ago."

"Salvidia..." Vi repeated. Her mind instantly summoned the map Sehra had shown her. "An island, far off to the south?"

"I'm impressed you know that, being on the—"

"Dark Isle. Yes, I get it. I'm very impressive for an uncultured swine," Vi said hastily, trying to keep them on track. "This ritual they are performing... what is it?"

"To give their god a mortal casing, and bring about the end of the world when he walks among us once more."

All she had wanted was a little bit of magic, and a little bit of control over it. She had wanted that magic to ensure that she could be reunited with her family without issue. Simple, clean, easy.

Yet, somehow, she was facing a man with glowing green eyes, in the middle of ruins, discussing the end of the world.

"Do you understand the severity of what's at stake now?" Vi studied his face. His frown caused the crescent-shaped scar that ran along his cheek to shift. His eyes were serious, tired, more tired than she had last seen him. "Will you help me find the apexes without question? I need your visions to know what path we're on, and what the future will hold, so I can prevent the elfin'ra from achieving their dark goals."

"The deal still stands," Vi whispered softly. "Help me learn how to control my magic, and I'll find your apexes." She didn't want a place in all of this. She just wanted to be reunited with her family.

"Yes, you have your deal." He gave a small nod. "Because you will need the full power of Yargen as her champion when the end of the world comes."

19

I T WAS ALMOST AS if the Mother herself had conspired with Ellene the night before, for Vi couldn't imagine a more perfect day for preliminary noru races leading up to the winter solstice. The weather was good enough that Vi didn't even feel exhausted waking early with very little sleep.

The North was always so warm that, even in winter, the trees never lost their evergreen leafy boughs. But the heat did relent, some. The nearly perpetual stickiness of the air vanished, and there was almost something that Vi would dare call cool on the front end of every breeze.

The changing seasons—fall to winter—brought out new smells and animals. Birds that migrated up from the south flitted between the railings of the walkways Vi traversed as she headed down to the stables. There was the usual fresh scent of greenery, mingling with the earthy aromas of wood, but as new flowers bloomed, so too did they give up their perfumes to the bouquet of the atmosphere.

Vi worked to put her lessons and magic behind her. She'd promised Ellene she'd be present in the moment during their final weeks together, and Vi would do her best to honor that promise despite all that was going on. She also, admittedly, needed a break after the night she'd had. While there had been no issue sneaking back into the fortress, her vision and encounter with Taavin had left its mental mark on her already exhausted mind.

"Why are you following me?" Vi asked dryly. Andru hastily caught up with her.

"It is my job to observe you."

"In my lessons."

"In general."

Vi sighed heavily. "I am too tired to argue with you today."

"Are we arguing?"

"Banter, then." Stupid semantics.

"That's what Romulin would've called it," he said mostly to himself with a soft chuckle. "I hear you are going to partake in noru races this afternoon." Andru took a step behind her, allowing Vi to lead them down one of the spiraling wooden stairwells as she made her way to the stables.

"Where did you hear that from?" Vi glanced over her shoulder.

"I have my ways." He looked out the windows as they strolled.

She was too tired to pry. Even though she'd made haste after her lessons, she was still the last one to arrive at the stables.

"Sorry, I tried to get out as fast as I could," Vi called over to her friends the moment her feet met the packed earth.

"Apparently you still have yet to escape." Ellene shot Andru a look.

Vi fought a smirk and failed. But she made sure it was off her cheeks when he could see her face.

"Escape? Am I truly so terrible?" He looked to each of them.

"Of course not. We'd merely planned this to be a girls' outing."

"Oh, like last time." He smiled, once again ignorant of the dismissal.

"How are you feeling?" Vi asked Jayme quickly, eager to change the topic. Her friend looked as she always did—brown hair tied back in a bun, straight posture, sword on her hip, usual Eastern golden-tan skin, nothing betraying any cause for concern on her face.

"Much better." Jayme gave a small nod, recognizing the source of Vi's concerns. "I don't know what did me in, but I'm pleased to report that it will not keep me from performing my duty as your guard today."

The formality brought laughter to Vi's lips, amusement that was mirrored by a quirk of Jayme's own. "I am lucky to have one so loyal in my service."

"Now, ladies, you both know the plan for today." Ellene clapped her hands and brought them to task.

They both gave a nod, leaving Andru in the dark.

"One small deviation," Jayme started hesitantly. "After the position it put me in yesterday… I have no interest in returning to the market." She turned to the saddled noru. "And while this beast is nimble, perhaps not nimble enough to go through the market. So I'm thinking that I'll take it out on the main road, and meet you both on the outer circle."

"We can go with you," Vi offered.

"Don't you want to see the market?" Ellene linked her arm with Vi's. "A caravan arrived from the West two days ago. All the way from Norin, so there's a whole host of unique goods to peruse."

That thought hadn't crossed Vi's mind. Just because it was near impossible to get in and out of the southern capital didn't mean the rest of the world was shut off.

"Just agree." Jayme tried to fight a laugh and failed. "We all know how much you love Western spices."

"Fine, fine." Vi held up her hands in agreement. "You two know me far too well and I concede." She looked to Jayme. "You're sure you don't mind? And that you can handle Gormon? A noru is a lot different than a horse."

"I think I'll be fine. Yours is far better trained than the one we met in the jungle." That much was certainly true. Jayme turned to Ellene. "I'll help build suspense for you. Talk about what a shame it is that you decided not to race this year, to allow our Crown Princess to shine."

"You're the best." Ellene threw her arms around Jayme's neck. "We'll see you out there soon."

Jayme left first, noru reins in hand. Gormon was a fairly gentle beast, so Vi didn't worry too much for her handling him. Ellene was right: he was faster than her noru, but only because he was younger. Vi watched as his long tail swayed back and forth with the sort of prowling sashay that marked all noru.

She looked away quickly, reminded of the last time she found herself on the receiving end of one of the beast's paws.

"Well, it is a good thing I'm here then," Andru reminded them of his presence.

"How are you so quiet?" Ellene nearly jumped out of her skin. "I'd forgotten you were there at all."

"I am not sure if I should take offense to that," he muttered, then continued, louder, "You two will need an escort through the market, now that your guard is gone."

"We could easily get a warrior."

"Do not be silly. It is no trouble." Andru smiled.

"Thank you," Vi said, earning a look from Ellene. "That is kind of you."

"Is it?" Ellene murmured under her breath.

It was Vi's turn to give the girl a pointed look. She hadn't received Romulin's missive about the importance of Andru. Vi hastily returned her attention to the man in question, hoping he missed the nonverbal layers of communication. Fortunately, he was staring off at the noru in their pen.

"You have yet to properly see the city, right?" Vi dared to ask.

"I have been out a few times."

"Well, allow us to show it to you from our point of view." She didn't know when, exactly, he'd been out.

"Is it very different? Your point of view?"

Did he want to come or not? Vi plastered on a wider smile. "I shall let you reach that conclusion on your own."

With that, they started off with Andru in tow into the city proper.

They wound around the many unorthodox structures of Soricium. Some short, some as tall as trees. Some made of masonry, others of carved woods, and most magicked into existence with the help of Groundbreakers. Vi did her best to point out things along the way to Andru. In the back of her mind was her brother's letter—he was important, and she had to be on her best behavior. She'd done an admittedly poor job of it so far, so perhaps she could recover some ground today.

There was an amphitheater to the north of town where most of the performances and lectures for the solstice would take place. The area around it was mostly residential, unused for most of the year, but built with wide roads and space to accommodate the city converging on the spot for those special times. That made it a logical place to pop up the market for the solstice.

"It's even larger than last year," Vi appraised.

"Mother says it's the biggest year yet. The merchants filled all the open space here, they're overflowing—some are even forced to stay back by the main road. I can't imagine how full the city will feel when others come in for it." Many of the smaller towns and cities in Shaldan poured into Soricium for the solstice events.

"What do you think?" Vi asked Andru as they started down the makeshift market stalls.

"It is very different, indeed."

"Different... in a good way?" She tried to lead him along.

"I think so. It is a shame your brother will not arrive before this festival is over. I do think he would enjoy seeing the collection of so many cultural notes."

Vi folded her hands before her thoughtfully. She'd never thought of what her brother would think of the market—of anything in the North, really. It had always been such an impossibility for him to be present that she never even considered what he'd enjoy about the life she'd lived.

"Does my brother enjoy learning of different cultures?" Vi knew the answer already, but she was curious what Andru would say. How closely had he positioned himself to the royal family?

"Oh, incredibly so. He practically bounces off the wall when a new batch of texts arrives from the library in Norin, Hastan, or sent from you. Especially if it's sent from you." As Andru spoke, he looked nowhere in particular, eyes darting from stall to stall. His words were fond, but his eyes were distant.

Did he care for her family or not? Vi couldn't put her finger on the answer.

"Do you spend—"

"Oh, look at that," Andru interrupted her. More like, hadn't even realized she'd started speaking. "Now *that* is something Prince Romulin would find fascinating."

Andru wandered off toward a leatherworker's wares. Vi started in his direction but was stopped by a hand on her sleeve.

"There's a Western spice seller." Ellene pointed in the opposite direction. Vi looked between the two locations. "Unless you'd rather go with him?"

She was curious what Andru thought her brother would find so fascinating. There was an uneasy feeling about the notion that Andru might know things about Romulin she didn't, merely by virtue of his usual proximity to her brother. That fact soured her stomach.

"No, no… he'll be fine on his own for a moment. Besides, I want to get Uncle Jax something."

"I thought you might." Ellene hooked her arm with Vi's leading her toward the stall.

A woman sat in a folding chair, surrounded by baskets that Vi recognized as Northern make, but filled with the bright colors and smells of the West. There was a pile of what looked like sand, next to small hard black nuts. Vi didn't know what half of it was for, but she did know that Jax loved almost all of it; whenever he prepared food with these spices, it had the most magical taste.

"Hello, young princesses."

"I'm not a princess," Ellene insisted. "I'm a future Chieftain."

"Good day." Vi gave a small nod of acknowledgment, ignoring how, exactly, the woman had identified her as a princess. She wasn't wearing any sort of circlet or other royal regalia, though perhaps proximity to Ellene was enough. "May I have a scoop of this one?" Vi pointed to what appeared to be a coarse-ground, reddish spice blend.

"Do you have your own bag, or will you need one?"

"I shall need one."

The woman took a metal scoop from a small bucket at her side and filled a tightly woven satchel with Vi's selection. The bag plumped and their nostrils were assaulted with the tangy aroma. She tied it off at the top with a short length of twine.

"How much?" Vi fished out a few coins from the pouch at her side.

"For the Crown Princess, nothing." The woman handed her the bag and sat back in her chair, a thin smile on her weathered lips.

Vi continued to ignore the slightly unnerving feeling she was getting from the merchant, focusing instead on extending out a thin silver coin. "I can't possibly take something without payment."

"Seeing you is payment enough." The woman's beady black eyes looked her over from top to toes. Vi's arm went slack. "I heard the stories, but had to see it with my own two eyes. You really do look just like her, our dear, late princess Fiera."

"My grandmother?"

The woman nodded. "You have her hair, her voice, her blood, and her fire, too, from what I hear."

Vi bit back a correction. One of the reasons she needed to learn the magic of light from Sehra and Taavin was to keep that illusion alive—that she was a Firebearer like her predecessors. It gained her far too much favor in the West to allow the perception to slip.

Still holding out the coin, Vi tightened her elbow and extended it further. "Truly, I insist."

"Very well. I shall consider it a boon from our princess returned." The woman leaned forward and took the coin from between her fingers. "Do you have her tastes as well? Do you like Western spices?"

"I enjoy cuisine from all across the Empire." Romulin would be proud of that response, Vi decided. She'd have to tell him about it in her next letter—but no, there would not be a next letter. She would merely tell him in person. An odd rush overtook her.

The woman hummed and Vi got the distinct feeling that she saw the response for the politically approved statement that it was. "Well, perhaps when you are in the West enjoying our cuisine, you will enjoy other aspects of our culture."

"I am sure I will." Vi made a motion to leave.

"Perhaps a curiosity shop."

"A what?" It was Ellene who paused now, clearly intrigued.

"A curiosity shop," the woman repeated, answering Ellene but continuing to stare directly at Vi. Her eyes felt like they would never leave her for the rest of her days. "In the West, the Firebearers among us with the power to peer among the Mother's lines of fate and look into the future will sell this ability to those who seek them out. The places they use their future sight for profit are called curiosity shops."

"Can you see the future?" Ellene asked eagerly.

"We should go. Darrus is waiting." Vi stopped the conversation there. She'd had enough talk about future sight. She still hadn't told her friends, or Uncle Jax, about her visions. Vi was juggling too many things—too many secrets—for her taste, and didn't want to stand here and be reminded of them.

"Right, right." Ellene gave a small wave to the elderly woman, clearly not as unnerved as Vi was. "Thank you."

"You're very welcome." Her black eyes stayed stuck on Vi. "Should you ever decide to go West, seek me out at my curiosity shop in the Crossroads. It has been passed down in my caravan for generations, the key to it said to have been gifted from Lady Fiera herself. You may find it enlightening, princess. The lines of fate are wound so tightly around you that they could strangle you if you're not careful." Her voice had dropped to a whisper, but Vi heard perfectly. The day suddenly felt far, far colder.

"What is it, Vi?"

"Nothing." If she insisted it firmly enough to Ellene, perhaps she'd believe it as well. Vi plastered a smile on her face. "Nothing at all. Let's get to the noru races. We don't want to keep them waiting, and there's only so much talking up Jayme can do."

Just as they were leaving the stall, so too was Andru leaving his. He also had a small satchel in his hands, though it was canvas, not leather. Whatever he had purchased was concealed within.

"What did you buy?" he asked.

"Some spices for Jax. What about you?"

"A little gift as well, for when I return home." *A gift for whom?* Vi wondered, but didn't get the chance to ask. "Shall we continue to these races?"

Without another word on fate, future seers, or gifts, they did.

20

EXPECTEDLY, THEY WERE THE last to arrive at the noru races, and Ellene seemed to relish in it because it meant all eyes were on her for her grand entrance.

"I wasn't sure if you were really going to come." Darrus wasted no time in crossing over to them.

"I would never abandon you," Ellene said smoothly.

His emerald eyes drifted over to Vi. She braced herself, remembering him in his mask from the night before. Would he out her now? A tiny, knowing smile crossed his lips, and then he carried on as though nothing was out of the ordinary. "I heard you were racing?"

"Well, I'd fully planned on it." Vi rested a hand on her stomach, hunching slightly. "But I think I ate something in the market that didn't agree with me. It's coming on quickly."

"What, no!" Ellene gasped, bringing her hands to Vi's cheeks.

Jayme rushed over to Vi's side, resting a hand on her back. "The same thing happened to me last night. Was it something from the cheese stall? The wheel with all the bright colors marbled underneath the wax?"

"Yes, that one!" Vi leaned into her friend.

"I do not remember you stopping at a cheese stall," Andru murmured.

"We must have gone when you were distracted," Ellene said with a glare.

"I only remember the spice stall." He shrugged.

Vi gave a loud groan of mock pain, trying to bring the attention back to her. "And after I've saddled my noru and everything."

Did this sound as fake to everyone else? Vi couldn't help but wonder. It was a good thing they were all born nobility or in service to nobility, for none of them were about to win any acting awards. Even still, Darrus seemed to be believing it, and that was all that mattered. Then again, he hadn't taken his eyes off Ellene for more than a minute and the two gravitated closer together with every second.

"Should we get a cleric for you?" Darrus asked, concern coating his words. "I may have some potions on hand. One of my friends is a Groundbreaker with a gift for healing and I think they—"

"No, no. I'm fine, or I will be." Vi made a show of wincing.

"It passed quickly for me as well," Jayme affirmed. "But, as your sworn guard, and in the interest of your safety, I must insist you do not race. Doing so could agitate things, and the unsightliness of being sick astride a noru…"

"But Jayme, my noru is all saddled and ready to ride." As Vi finished, she glanced at Ellene from the corners of her eyes, waiting for the girl to jump in and be the hero she wanted to be… *any second*… But Ellene was too busy making looks of adoration at Darrus. Looks he was returning, so at least he didn't consciously hear the conversation running head-first past awkward. "If only someone could—"

"I could ride the noru for you!" Ellene returned to the realm of the present at the last possible moment. "If you do not mind, that is, princess."

Vi fought a blurt of laughter at Ellene's display. "Are you certain you don't mind?"

"Princess, for you, anything." Ellene gave a low bow.

"Are you sure you don't want to try?" Andru asked.

Vi looked at him sideways. They'd all but settled the matter. This was overkill even by the most histrionic standards. Unless he was that dense and hadn't figured out what they were doing?

"No, I think it is best I don't." Vi straightened, trying to make sure she still looked appropriately ill in the process, as though standing tall was a struggle she was willing to endure for the sake of her station.

"But you have given your word, princess," Andru continued to press. "Prince Romulin has said that a royal should always keep to their word."

"It is very unfortunate, yes," Vi ground out. "But I think I must sit out."

"But—"

Vi outright interrupted him this time. "Ellene, if you are to race for me, then I must command you to win."

"It would be my honor." She turned to Darrus. "If this last-minute substitution is accepted…"

"Of course it would be." Darrus didn't miss the chance to take Ellene's hands. Vi couldn't fight a smile—a smile that quickly vanished when she remembered Taavin's nearly identical motions the night before. As though he too hadn't wanted to miss a chance to… *Focus*. Vi forced her mind only on the present. "For the Chieftain's daughter, for you, anything."

"Thank you, Darrus. I really don't know what I'd do without you…" Ellene was saying, as the two walked off toward the noru along a starting line drawn with gravel in the barren dirt.

"They are so cute, it is a little disgusting, is it not?" Vi murmured.

"He is certainly cute," Andru said so softly under his breath that Vi wasn't certain she'd heard it. She looked in his direction, but her thoughts were near instantly diverted when Jayme let out a large snort.

"We'll see if it lasts a season this time."

"Must you be so cynical?" Vi laughed at Jayme's remark. "Let the girl have her romance."

"I'm being reasonable. Is he of a good family? Will her mother approve? What marriage must she make for the sake of alliances?"

"The North is not as concerned with such things as the South," Vi reminded her. Jayme might look Eastern, but she'd grown up in the South. Her concerns and sensibilities were distinctly Southern as a result.

"They must not be," she murmured.

"Are you concerned with such things?" Andru asked.

"I know that when it comes to my romantic life, it is best if I am not concerned. My opinion of my match will be the lowest rung on the ladder of considerations when the time comes."

"Spoken like Prince Romulin," he said softly. Vi turned, catching his icy blue eyes. It was spoken like her brother, because he was the one to have given her those words. "Do you find your brother's counsel wise, princess?"

"More than any other's."

"He would make a fine ruler, had he been born first." The words were said like agreement... but there was something that felt akin to a knife twisting in her.

A similar sensation to the one in the market returned, sweeping across new corners of her. Andru clearly thought Romulin was more fit to lead. He knew Romulin better— the whole of the South would. Romulin was their darling child and she was...

Vi swallowed.

She was the faraway heir no one knew anything about and likely no one wanted. Vi opened her mouth to speak again, though she didn't know what she wanted to say. Did she want to confront him about the sentiment surrounding her and her brother? Did she want to somehow try to see if the Senate was keeping tabs on Romulin as they were her? Was the Senate trying to pit them against each other?

Whatever she might have asked was cut short by a man walking along the center line. He stared up at the different noru, all shoulder to shoulder.

"This preliminary heat will be one lap around the outer circle," the man boomed. "The first two will advance to the finals to be held during the winter solstice festivities. There is no attacking, or intentionally bumping into other noru. Claws to anything but the ground equals immediate disqualification. Are there any questions?"

The riders shook their heads.

"Good luck, Ellene!" Vi cupped her hands around her mouth and called.

"You're sick, remember?" Jayme mumbled.

"I'm sick, not mute." Vi rolled her eyes.

Ellene gave them a small wave, then settled further into her saddle. She looked like a proper racer. Everything Vi would expect for someone who'd grown up in the North. It was almost comical to imagine her sitting on a saddle even half as confidently.

"Get ready." The man who had outlined the rules lifted a small green flag. "Mark... Go!"

He dropped the flag, and they all moved at once.

There was a unified rallying cry from all the riders. Some yelled the word "go" at their massive cats. Others cried out their own, unique words. Most said nothing at all, a wordless shout that could easily be interpreted as a mix of excitement and exhilaration filling the air.

The noru lunged forward; dust kicked up off their hind legs, pluming in the air like smoke. They charged forward, alight with the crackle of magic. Vi realized, then, that the leader had never specified any rules about magic for the race.

Beneath Gormon's feet, two large pillars of stone emerged at a forward angle. Vi was forced to give all the credit to the animal that he was not unnerved by it, and merely adapted to the new terrain. Gormon crouched, and the noru leapt forward, capitalizing on the momentum Ellene's magic had bought him.

He soared through the air in a massive leap, gaining a lead on the pack quickly.

"Go, go!" Vi couldn't help but cheer, even though Ellene likely couldn't hear.

Ellene was making headway, a solid lead. Perhaps Gormon was faster than Vi had given him credit for and she just didn't know how best to ride the animal. But he was pulling ahead with nothing but open track before him.

Vi began to run alongside, hoping for a vantage to see the finish.

"You're supposed to be sick!" Jayme repeated.

"I want a better view!" Vi retorted.

"Do you think you can keep up with the noru?" The question was a half laugh as Jayme was already running behind her.

Vi knew she couldn't. The track was long, and she could only see the noru for just a bit longer, even with the time running would buy her. But she wanted to see Ellene for as long as she could.

And see she did, as the straps on Gormon's saddle broke all at once; as the leathers flapped limply in the wind; as the small silhouette of her friend was airborne. Time seemed to suspend. Leather and girl alike hovered mid-air.

If Vi had been a Windwalker like her mother, she could've caught Ellene before she even neared the ground. But she was useless as a Firebearer and as a Lightspinner. All Vi could do was watch in horror as Ellene's body met the ground with a sickening bounce.

"Get up!" Vi screamed. "Ellene!" Excitement turned to panic. "Stop, stop!" The other noru were coming in fast. Surely they'd seen what had happened? Surely they'd see Ellene on the ground through the dust cloud?

The riders were struggling to swerve. The heat had too many noru, and the pack was confused between riders who saw and those who didn't, bunched together with shoulders bumping—no one could coordinate who was going left and who was going right.

Ellene was going to be trampled.

Vi lifted a hand, debating with the precious few seconds she had. Did she try to make a fire and spook the giant cats, divert them into the woods? Could she trust herself not to burn Ellene and everyone else alive? She hadn't learned enough of Yargen's magic yet to use that confidently.

At the last second, Ellene raised her head.

There was a scream before Ellene curled in on herself, face to the ground, hands over her head; once again, her magic reacted on instinct. Large curls of stone rose from the ground, creating a cocoon of rock around Ellene.

The other noru bounded over top of it. Vi watched as they leapt off of it, continuing forward until their momentum was spent and the riders could get a better handle on the beasts. Vi ran, crossing the distance.

"Ellene! Ellene!" Vi cried out, even though she knew, logically, that her friend was all right. If she could survive the inferno Vi had made in the jungle, her rocks could hold up against some noru weight.

The rocks retreated, like an egg cracking, revealing the precious girl within. Vi only ran faster toward her dazed friend as Ellene straightened. She slid to a stop, wrapping her arms around the girl's shoulders.

"Ellene, are you all right?" Vi held her fiercely.

"I'm fine…" she muttered. "Not so loud… I think I hit a rock… or something. My head feels funny."

Vi straightened away. Sure enough, a river of blood ran down the side of Ellene's face. Vi looked over her shoulder in a panic. Jayme was on her way, but slower in her military garb. She turned in the opposite direction, to the riders that stared on in shock and horror.

"Darrus!" Vi stood and called. He was there in a second. "Take Ellene back to the stronghold. Summon Sehra and Ginger. And try not to jostle her too much."

"I'm fine, I'm fine…" Ellene's mutterings faded when she was solidly in Darrus's arms.

"She's not. Don't let her say otherwise and avoid being checked out," Vi commanded.

"Yes, princess." There was not one mention of the mysterious disappearance of Vi's aforementioned sickness. Darrus shifted his weight in his saddle, making sure Ellene was situated. In a tone that he clearly only meant for the girl to hear, he whispered, "I'll take care of you, I swear."

With that, the noru was off.

"What, what happened?" Jayme panted.

"I sent Ellene back." Vi turned to Gormon. He was off walking as though nothing had happened. Then, she looked down to the saddle. "What in the Mother's name happened here?"

"A terrible or brilliant stroke of luck." Jayme frowned at it. "If you had been on that saddle, as we'd said was the intent… then you would've been the one trampled."

It was true.

If the riders couldn't stop for the daughter of the Chieftain, Vi didn't think they could've for her. Even if Vi technically outranked Ellene, in the eyes of most Northerners, she was merely the daughter of the man and woman who had brought them to heel. *Disliked in the North, disliked in the South,* the day's realizations compounded. Knowledge she'd always had, on some level, of her position made real.

No… if she'd been astride Gormon when the saddle straps broke, her only hope would have been for Ellene to have made a shell to protect her.

But Vi had seen what had happened with the other noru bounding above the stone with such ferocity that the ground itself rumbled. And she knew Ellene's control of her magic was not mature enough to be relied on beyond the instinct of her own self-preservation.

"We'll see if it's brilliant luck… if Ellene is all right," Vi muttered, picking up the saddle. "Now, to bring this back and have a word with the leather master… let him know there's something faulty in his design." Jayme's expression darkened as she stared at the saddle. "What?"

Jayme crossed over, holding up the girth. Right where the leather curved into the buckle was a straight line—impossible to see once the saddle was in place, but now undeniably sinister. Vi stared at it, knowing what she was seeing. But she couldn't process it. It didn't make any sense. It *couldn't* make sense.

"Someone, I think was hoping you were on that saddle…" Jayme said. "Because this has been cut nearly all the way through."

"What?" Vi whispered. But what she really meant was *why*?

"Someone wants you dead, princess."

O N SOME LEVEL, VI had always known she'd lived a sheltered life.
When she was less than a year old, she'd been transported to the North and placed under the care of Sehra's mother. When that Chieftain died, Vi's protection fell to Sehra herself, the same woman who had struck the deal for her life. While both relationships had never been particularly warm and the people's opinion overall reflected their leader's, Vi had always felt *safe*.

Now, staring at the tampered saddle leather, she wasn't so sure. Yet another time in a terribly short period, her world felt different, inexorably *shifted*. Vi swallowed hard. Staring at the saddle would do her no good. There were no more answers to be had here, for now, and staring at them would only rouse suspicion from the others.

"We'll bring it up with Jax when we get back. Tell no one else."

"Understood." Jayme slung the saddle over her shoulder. The cut pieces swung harmlessly, no doubt unassuming to anyone who didn't know to look for the betrayal. Her eyes drifted over to Andru, who was still staring at the tree line. "Not even him?"

"Not even him."

"Is the Chieftain's daughter all right?" The man who had gone over the rules finally ran over. The racers still perched on their noru were finally becoming brave enough to venture forward as well.

"Ellene was dazed, but she seems all right, thank the Mother. I sent her to be looked over by Chieftain Sehra and my personal cleric," Vi reported, putting on an air of authority.

Suddenly, everyone looked suspicious through Vi's eyes. Every eye trained on her was one looking for her death. She forced herself to quell the feeling; these were the men and women she'd grown up alongside. She couldn't see them as lurking enemies now... But she also couldn't stop herself from wondering how many had access to the castle, to her noru?

The old wars had left deep scars, even on the children of those who had fought. How many of them would want her dead for the crimes her parents committed against theirs? How many knew she was supposed to be the one in the race?

Vi glanced back to Andru. He had known she was intended to ride... and he had pressed for it.

"Praise Yargen." The man gave a small bow. "And thanks to her that it wasn't you on that saddle."

"Yes, well... If you'll excuse us, I'm going to return and check on your future Chieftain."

"Take care, your highness."

Vi gave a small nod, and began to lead the way back toward the main road. She gave a shrill whistle and Gormon trotted over, falling into step behind them. Lumbering along, getting distracted by the birds flitting in the trees, he seemed a gentle giant; Vi felt silly for ever being nervous around him. Especially when she had something far more tangible to worry about.

"Who do you think it could be?" Jayme asked only when they were far out of earshot of anyone else.

"I don't know."

"Truly?"

"Why does that surprise you?"

Jayme paused, thinking to herself. "You're in the North, the granddaughter of the man who conquered this land and put it under the heel of the Empire. There are many, I'm sure, who remember seeing their loved ones die at the hands of a man bearing your name. I would have thought someone might have been exceptionally cruel, enough to be a suspect, at some point."

"The North has been good to me," Vi defended. She didn't know why, however. Hadn't she followed the same line of thinking in her own mind? But she still wanted to reject the notion that she'd been sleeping alongside enemies all along.

"Certainly... But the North is wide, and full of people. Sehra has been good to you, surprisingly so, all things considered. Ellene is like your sister. And that goes far with many. But..." Jayme paused, picking at the saddle straps. "There are many who cannot forgive the sins of the father. Some would argue that perhaps those sins shouldn't be forgiven until justice is exacted... regardless if that justice falls to the children to bear."

Jayme's voice took on a hard, protective edge—one that nearly surprised Vi. She glanced over, but decided it best to leave the woman to her thoughts for a moment.

"It's impossible to say for certain it's a Northerner." Vi remembered keenly the old, Western woman in the market. "The solstice has brought a flood of strangers to the North."

"But the East and West see you as their own, given your parents."

Vi couldn't argue that. Her mother was born and bred Eastern. Her father was the grandson of the last great king in the West. And given how the woman in the market had claimed she'd come all this way just to lay eyes on Vi...

She shook her head and heaved a heavy sigh. "I don't know. Everyone seems as likely and unlikely as the next. Perhaps we're making something from nothing and it was an accident?"

"This—" Jayme held up the straps again. "—is *not* an accident. Not knowing who to suspect is one thing. But don't be ignorant, princess. Someone is out to get you— someone with access to the fortress. I'm going to find out who."

As if on cue, Andru strolled over to them. He had a small frown on his face, but his overall lack of urgency made any concern he laid on seem insincere.

"Is everything all right?"

"Everything is fine," Vi answered quickly.

"Those beasts, the riders could not even get them to stop for their future chieftain." Andru looked back at Gormon. "Wild things." Vi wanted to argue and explain that it was a deadly combination of momentum, the shroud of a dust cloud, and the overall excitement of the race. But he continued before she could. "If you had been on that saddle, you would have been dead."

"Yes, I am aware."

The road dipped down, heading back into the city proper.

They came up to the stables and Vi directed her noru into the pen. Gormon leapt over the fence, heading to a back corner of sun, and stretched out with a massive yawn. He rolled half on his side and promptly forgot about Vi's existence, distracted by a low-hanging branch he batted at like a kitten with a ball of yarn.

"Vi, thank goodness you're all right." Jax's voice cut through the heavy silence that had been hanging over them like a cloud. He crossed over quickly, resting his hands on her shoulders.

"We can agree on that." Vi turned to Andru. "If you will excuse us now, please. I would like a word alone with Lord Jax."

"Yes, of course." Andru gave a small bow of his head, starting in for the fortress. *Now he takes the hint*. They all watched him go. When he was far enough out of hearing range, Jax turned back to her, a frown on his face.

"What's wrong? What's happened? I can see it on your faces."

Jayme held up the saddle straps. Jax walked over and, judging from his deepening scowl, saw what Jayme had before she spoke. "They were cut."

Jax held out his hands and Jayme passed him the saddle. He flipped it over, placing it on the ground, and knelt to get a better look. Vi wasn't surprised when his investigation didn't yield more than theirs had. There weren't really clues to speak of.

"I'll have a word with the stable master," he said grimly, standing. "Find out who has access to this area."

"Do you think there's any way it could've been an accident?" Vi asked, ignoring the look from Jayme. So she was hopeful that someone wasn't trying to kill her—that should hardly be surprising.

"I pray it is. But I'm forced to act like it's not. You are not to leave the fortress again, even with guards, until we get to the bottom of this."

She felt as though the remark should upset her, but Vi was too focused on the notion that someone was trying to kill her. She'd never had that much freedom to begin with, and she was leaving the North soon enough. The idea of further confinement was more palatable than Vi thought it should be. If anything, it felt normal.

"Are you going to raise an alarm?"

"Not yet. Whoever did this, I want them to think they got away with something. Perhaps that way, we can catch them in the act."

Vi gave a small nod, ignoring the feeling that she was so much bait on a hook.

"How is Ellene?" Jayme asked, unintentionally making Vi feel terrible for not asking sooner.

"She's fine, up and about. It was just a small bump, a bit of daze, a potion to help clear her head and a salve to mend the spot. But you did right sending her back."

They both gave a small nod.

"Now, try to put this from your mind and allow me and Sehra to worry about it. Focus on your studies and stay in the fortress. You'll be safe so long as you stay here and take no unnecessary risks."

Vi felt odd about the notion that someone was lurking in the shadows, searching for a chance to kill her, and she was doing nothing about it. But for now, Jax was right. With no leads, it was all she could do. She had to wait until they made their next move... And hope it wasn't the move that killed her.

"I'm going to return to my quarters."

"Jayme, would you stay and help me investigate?" Jax asked her friend.

"Yes, sir. It's my duty as guard."

Vi gave them a wave goodbye and headed in.

She had just started up the stairs when she realized she wasn't alone. Slowly, Vi turned, seeing Andru standing two steps behind her where he previously hadn't been. There were no alcoves he could've hidden in, or doorways to emerge from. That meant he had to have come up from the first landing area. But she hadn't seen him there either.

It was like the man appeared in mid-air.

"What is it now?" Vi asked, ignoring the tingling feeling creeping up her spine.

"I wanted to stress caution to you, princess."

"I think I have had that stressed to me enough." It was all she'd heard for the majority of her life. Be careful. Stay in line. Don't venture too far.

"I know Prince Romulin has stressed it to you, but I am not convinced his warnings were heeded."

"And why is that?" There was something about his whole demeanor that had her hair standing on end. Vi shifted her feet on the step, trying not to let her discomfort show.

"Someone who fully understands the danger they could be in would not go wandering at night."

Her blood ran cold. Vi suppressed a shiver. He'd known she'd been out.

"Was it you?" Vi whispered, remembering the feeling of someone following her. Darrus mentioning possibly seeing someone on her tail. Andru had a knack for fading away even when he was in plain sight. What could he accomplish if he *tried* to sneak?

Andru started up the stairs and Vi took a step back. He paused, one foot on the step she was on, the other below. Vi leaned away, trying to put as much space between them as possible.

"Be careful. You never know who might take advantage of your carelessness."

"Is that a threat?" Her racing heart nearly drowned out her words.

"Merely fact." He studied her face. "Remember why I am here—because people do not have faith in you." There was the dagger again, the one only he could twist in her stomach. Had those words ever been said so directly? Vi was grateful for the cool wood of the wall at her back supporting her. "As far as many are concerned, there is another heir, nearly equal in birthright, only minutes behind you. Some would argue your brother was meant to sit the throne."

"Are you sure this is not a threat?" Vi's hand balled into a fist. She allowed her spark to crackle around her knuckles. If he made a motion, she would be faster. He wouldn't know what hit him.

"Again, merely stating facts." Andru straightened away, starting upward. "Watch yourself, your highness."

Vi watched him leave, letting any possible argument go with him. This was one conversation she didn't want to pursue. Not right now. Not when she had so recently stared her own mortality in the face.

Andru had said he was loyal to the Empire above the Senate or crown.

Vi had written it off at the time as hyperbole. But what if he'd been speaking the Mother's honest truth? And if he had been... What did that mean he'd do if *he* suddenly thought she wasn't good for the Empire? What if the Senate had already made up their mind that she wasn't the best heir for the throne?

Would he go so far as to remove her himself?

JAYME AND VI JOINED Ellene in her room in the evening.

Vi shared with them her interaction with Andru, effectively moving him up to "suspicious person number one" on their list. Even Jayme, who didn't want to jump to conclusions, admitted his actions were questionable. She was already working with Jax to seek out any suspicious persons and volunteered to keep a close eye on Andru without raising any undue alarm.

During her lessons, Vi tried to do the same as well. But it was as if the incident in the staircase had never happened. Andru said less and less each day, focusing mostly on scribbling away during her lessons and leaving promptly at their conclusion. He wasn't even trying to linger anymore when Jayme and Ellene lounged in Vi's room after.

A week passed.

Seven days of relative calm. A deceptive normalcy Vi tried to lose herself in by day, because by night her dreams were torturous, filled with men who had white glass orbs in place of their eyes, or horrors rising from sacrifices and red lightning. It was as if the sight had been imprinted on her soul, so much that she was even incapable of losing herself in her lessons.

As a result, she refrained from contacting Taavin. She didn't want to think about her visions and he would, no doubt, force the subject. He'd given her enough of a starting point, and there were plenty of words for her to pour over in Sehra's book. Vi dedicated hours on hours trying to get lost in mindless memorization at night, avoiding sleep, avoiding thinking of anything at all.

"You're distracted today," Sehra appraised. "Your magic looks like it did the first week we began this process… not the progress you've made so far."

"I am distracted, I'm sorry." Vi shook her head and rubbed her eyes. The faint orb of light that had been hovering in her palm vanished. *Durroe* was undoubtedly becoming easier, even if she couldn't seem to keep the magic steady for long periods of time. "I've been having trouble falling asleep lately. And if I do, I have strange nightmares."

"Nightmares?" Sehra repeated.

"Why do you sound surprised?"

"I'd heard word from your tutors that you had been distracted lately, more tired than usual. The winter solstice tends to be a special time for men and women your age… I thought perhaps a suitor had finally caught your eye."

Vi blurted out laughter. "Excuse me," she said hastily, realizing how rude she'd been. "I'm just a little too busy and too confined to find a suitor right now."

She barely had enough time to spend with her friends, and she couldn't remember the last time she'd sat down with Jax for dinner. Guilt collected in a haze around her. She had to be better for the ones she loved… but with what time? How did she even begin to prioritize with all that was going on? Her mind wandered down a brief tangent, wondering if this was how her parents felt between caring for her and Romulin, and their Empire.

"Very true." Vi appreciated that Sehra took her words at face value, rather than pressing further. "The dreams… are they of any specific variety?" Sehra asked, likely an innocent question. But it put Vi on edge.

"Not particularly. Just run-of-the-mill nightmares," she lied. The smothering cloud of guilt grew thicker. Vi didn't appreciate lying outright; at the worst she much preferred a half-truth or deflection. Not that those were any better in practice, and she knew it, but they *felt* better. A blatant lie had her sitting so uneasily that she crossed and uncrossed her legs.

"I can't say I'm surprised." Sehra sighed heavily, leaning back in her chair as well. Her shoulders sagged slightly, and there was a bit of a slouch to her. Vi had never seen the sturdy woman look so worn. It seemed as if all at once the weight of the Chieftain's position had come down on her shoulders. "Given everything that's going on, I'm having a hard time sleeping myself. The White Death is coming, I can feel it in my bones. I merely hope we can last out the winter solstice and give the people one more celebration."

Vi remembered Darrus's talk of the infirmary. It seemed forever ago now. Had it truly only been a week since that night?

"I'm sorry. Taking time out for lessons with me must not be helping."

"Well, our lessons may be severely cut back soon enough," Sehra said gravely.

"What? Why?" Vi leaned forward in her chair. Sehra had seemed so determined to teach her at the start. Now, only a few months in, she was already cutting back their lessons?

"Between the solstice and the construction of the infirmary, along with the spread of the White Death, my attentions are needed elsewhere." Sehra ran her fingers along her lips thoughtfully, as if debating her next words. "No… not merely that. I am already seeing you progress beyond what I can teach, princess."

"That's not true," Vi whispered. "I still have so much to learn."

"But I only have so much I can teach."

"You told me you would help me control my magic." Her voice rose slightly.

"Foremost, I told you I would teach you all I know of the power of Yargen… which I have. Between the fundamentals and the tome you have been pouring over, you know as much as I do. No, more than I, for you can read the glyphs and I cannot."

Vi swallowed air down a dry throat. This couldn't be right. There was so much more to this magic, so much she didn't understand.

"But… my fire, at the capital they will expect… I need to masquerade as a

Firebearer."

"Do you think you cannot control your magic?"

"I…" She thought of the small motes of flame she had conjured from time to time, reminding herself that she was gaining more control. "Not well enough."

"I doubt that." Sehra stood. "Come."

Vi couldn't do anything but follow. Leaving everything behind, they walked down to the back edge of the castle. Vi hadn't ventured down this way since her lessons with Jax had ended in favor of her tutelage under Sehra.

"Leave," Sehra commanded. The warriors heeded their Chieftain, but Vi heard them grumbling. Sehra must have as well, but she led by example in ignoring them, moving once they had the area to themselves. She pointed to the nearest stone pit. "Vi, down you go."

As Vi descended, Sehra stood on the upper edge of the ring, held out her palm, and the nearest tree branch arched unnaturally down, as if trying to shake her hand. Vi watched as the Chieftain broke off a few smaller sticks and sent the branch back on its way. She tossed one nonchalantly into the pit. The stick landed unassumingly in a small puff of dirt.

"Set it on fire with *juth*."

"*Juth*." As Vi repeated the word, the symbol appeared to her with perfect clarity, her hours pouring over the tome paying off. After practicing so much with *durroe* and the subtle vibrations that word left behind, this was like the crackling of a coming storm just beneath her skin. Vi had ignored it from the start; this was the one word she didn't want to embrace. "To destroy. I think that's the last thing I need. All I want is to make sure my fire *doesn't* destroy things."

"Perhaps the best way to ensure that you do not reap destruction accidentally is by learning how to destroy things intentionally?"

Vi stared at the stick. She'd never felt so daunted by something so harmless as a twig.

"If you wanted a simple fire, I could summon one." Before Sehra could speak, a thought occurred to her. Vi's head jerked upright. "How can I make fire without words?"

"It is what I explained to you foremost… Your first relationship with your magic was with the understanding of a Firebearer. On some level, we learn magic the way we learn anything else—by imitation. Everyone expected you to be a Firebearer, demonstrated it for you…so your malleable magic did its best to imitate what it saw.

"For small feats, it is only natural that you can channel the magic to use it in that way," Sehra said in a manner that assured Vi she spoke from experience—though with Groundbreaking, Vi would assume. "But could you create an illusion as a Firebearer?"

"No Firebearer can." That was squarely a Waterrunner skill.

"Do you feel confident creating a large fire you could control with those methods you use to make a spark?"

"No…" The small sparks in her palms were one thing. But the only way she managed to control any large amount of magic—like the fire against the diseased noru—was by looking at her magic as light.

"Then destroy it with *juth*."

Vi stared at the stick, sliding out her feet to hip-width as though she was facing off against an invisible opponent. Lifting one hand in the air, the symbols attached to *juth* were already swirling in her mind.

She allowed the glyph to encompass all her thoughts. It pushed aside Jax's former tutelage—the instincts she'd had drilled into her for years about how to summon fire. She was not making fire—she was making a channel of light that would *become* fire.

Vi's eyes dipped closed as she tried to imagine the power seeping forth from her fingers, spinning from a white-hot invisible spool deep within her. It didn't radiate off her skin without focus. It was like a candle-wick, ready to burn.

"*Juth.*" Vi's voice went low with dangerous intent.

She knew this glyph—inside and out. Her upbringing as a Firebearer gave her an additional lens to understand it that Vi did not have with *durroe*. Fire was something she understood or, at the least, had ample practice with.

Just like Taavin had said... The words were not just words. They weren't mere sounds or symbols. They were meaning combined with understanding brought to life with intent. It was greater than the sum of any individual part.

Woven lines and circles appeared above her hand, streaking through the air in bright beams of magic. It carved the pure essence of destruction itself. Vi may not understand everything yet, when it came to being a Lightspinner.

But she understood how to make something burn.

Power sparked up her chest, little crackles like tiny fireworks exploding behind her ribs. It was as though they were rushing along her arm in a race where the finish line was somewhere behind her fingertips. A similar glyph appeared surrounding the twig. Her magic had never looked so bright—so confident.

As quickly as it came, it went, snuffed out with an almost audible *crack*. The scent of smoke filled the air and there was a small pile of blackened ash where the twig once was. Vi turned up toward Sehra, balling her hand into a fist.

"On your first attempt... Just like I said, princess, you will soon surpass all I can teach."

Back in her room, sweating and exhausted, Vi locked her door. She'd sent all her servants away—reassuring them several times over that she could, indeed, bathe and dress for bed on her own. It was early for her to be secluding herself for the night, so they gave her strange looks, but eventually agreed.

Let them gossip to Andru about the strange princess, Vi thought bitterly. He may well be trying to kill her anyway. Did it really matter what he thought?

There was something she wanted to try without an audience.

Something had changed in her, in that fighting pit. There was a different feeling about her—her magic specifically. A feeling of control, of a deep understanding she'd never quite mastered before.

Taking a deep breath, Vi held out her hand and let her magic lift off her skin. It hovered in the air, almost gracefully, tiny wisps of bright white light woven into threads that only she could command. For the first time in her life, Vi thought there might be something beautiful to magic. Not just any magic, but *her* magic.

"*Narro hath*," she uttered, and willed the symbol to take shape just as it had with *juth* in the pit. She knew the words. She knew her intent. And, most importantly it seemed, she now understood how to draw out her power in a stable way.

The two magic words left her mouth, but all Vi thought was, *show me*. She wanted more than a disembodied voice. She wanted a stable connection—an opportunity to truly talk to Taavin face to face as she did at the apexes.

This time, when she summoned Taavin, Vi made it clear to her magic exactly what she was expecting.

The glyph lifted off her hand. For a brief moment, Vi worried she was losing control. But the supreme sense of rightness surrounding the words *narro hath* continued to fill her and Vi trusted in her act. She trusted in her magic.

Starting near the ceiling, the magic circles spiraled downward. They gave off strands of magic that took form. And in the next moment, Vi's black eyes met a pair of bright green ones.

"H OW… WHAT…?" HE STOLE the words from her lips as he looked around her room, shock on his face. "How did you—?"

"I did what you said to—"

But before she could finish, the magic sputtered. The symbol unraveled and vanished from her grasp like a line cast out to sea, slipping through her fingers as it caught on a tide. She stared at his eyes as they widened by a fraction, and then he was gone. The light vanished.

Vi widened her stance some. She wasn't about to give up that easily. Not after she'd come so far. She raised her hand and repeated the process. "*Narro hath.*"

The light spun out, and she watched him appear once more. So she could confidently make the glyphs now—brighter and more complete than before. But she still couldn't seem to sustain them.

"Anchor it," Taavin said quickly, as if reading her mind. "Keep the circle around you, connected to you. Yes, closer to your hand, don't project it out so much. It'll be more stable that way."

Vi took a deep breath, focusing more on the magic pouring from her fingertips than on the man himself. She tried to imagine it winding around each finger, tying it there like a kite string. Only when it seemed secure did she dare shift her gaze to him.

Taavin was focused on her arm. He was still cast in light, mostly transparent, shifting between there and not. It was less than the connection they seemed to have at the apexes, but far more than what she'd managed thus far.

"How are you doing this?" he whispered after a long moment. His eyes trailed up her arm and to her face, searching. Vi dared to meet them, searching back.

"The same way I have been talking to you until now—*narro hath.* I've just managed to actually make a glyph this time rather than the haphazard approach I've been doing until now." Vi spoke slowly, trying to keep as much focus as possible on keeping her power stable. "I'm getting better at it."

"No, that's not how this works… this type of connection…" His gaze shifted from her hand to her chest. Vi followed it, looking down. There, just like during her very first vision, like the ruins, was a faded symbol shimmering over her watch. "You have an imprinted token of mine."

"A what?" Vi's free hand rose to the watch. The magic stuttered with the motion and Vi fought to keep it.

"To communicate with *narro hath* requires an imprinted token of the other person." He took a step forward, looking down at her over the narrow bridge of his nose. Vi studied his features—they were sharp, not unlike hers, but with a distinctly inhuman edge to them. "I had thought our communications were merely a result of our relationship as the voice and champion. But now I know this whole time it's been *narro*... How do you have a token of mine?"

"I don't know," Vi answered honestly.

"Is it because of this you were able to torture me all these years?" His voice deepened, becoming deathly serious all at once.

"Torture you?" she whispered in shock. "I wouldn't—"

"Your voice haunts me." The solemn statement stilled her. His eyes searched hers, as though he'd find answers there. "I know your face better than my own mother's. You've reaped destruction on my mind with the mere sound of your voice. I lose days behind my eyelids and wake, only remembering your form." His eyes fell back to the watch. "Why? Is it because of this? Or because you are the champion?"

He wasn't lying. There was too much pain there for him to be lying. This wasn't some joke or test. It was real suffering he had endured. Suffering, apparently, *she* was responsible for. How had she not seen it until now? Why hadn't he told her from the start?

Vi was overwhelmed with the sudden urge to help him, but she didn't know where to begin.

"I'm sorry... But I don't know." She held the watch tighter. "This was a gift. It was my mother's—not even mine until months ago."

He looked away, toward her window. Vi wondered if he could see her room. For her, it was only him. Wherever he was remained hidden.

"Maybe she found it somewhere?" Vi suggested, taking a step forward. The light around her hand flickered again and his form almost blinked from existence.

"That would be quite impossible, as I have not stepped foot beyond Risen since I was a child." There was a note to the longing in his voice that resonated with her own. She knew well what it was like to be trapped somewhere, tortured by things she could read and see through her maps but never reach.

"Where is Risen?" she asked softly.

"Meru. You know it as the Crescent Continent." He turned back to her and once more Vi found herself transfixed by his ears.

"Are the elfin common on Meru?" Vi asked.

"You could say that."

"How about vague answers? Are those common?" Vi frowned in frustration.

"That may only be me."

The magic flickered once more. He blinked out of existence and Vi stretched her arm further, as if she could push more magic out that way. Taavin re-solidified, looking back to her hand.

"You're losing strength."

"I can manage," Vi insisted. There was so much more she wanted to talk with him about.

"You're lying."

"And you're a little annoying." Vi didn't expect him to smile at that, but he did. The shortest upturn of his mouth.

"Rest, Vi. If you've managed this connection now, it will be there still for you to continue bothering me with when you've replenished your energy."

"I haven't done anything to you—" Vi paused, then quickly corrected herself, "—until recently."

He looked at her for a long moment. The argument Vi expected never came.

"You're not what I expected you'd be," he said softly, thoughtfully. His gaze was almost… tender. How could the same person look at her with equal measures compassion, skepticism, and pain? It was a mix of contrasts that shouldn't fit together.

"I suppose it's mutual," Vi whispered in reply. "I didn't expect you at all."

They simply stood, staring, for a long moment. In him, Vi saw a portal to a world she'd barely imagined. She saw truth, and secrets of the universe she hadn't fathomed weeks ago. And she couldn't help but wonder what he saw in her.

"Does our deal still stand?" Vi asked finally. "Even though I have this supposed token of yours… will you teach me how to use this magic if I find the apexes for you?"

He paused for a long moment. Briefly, her heart raced in fear that he was going to say no. But then…

"Yes, it still stands. If anything it'll be more effective now that you've mastered this much." He looked away again. "Besides, it's not as if we have any choice. We have roles to play, you and I."

That sense of duty was one Vi knew better than any other. "Taavin, I—"

"Rest now, Vi. Summon me again when you have the strength."

It was as if her magic had been waiting for his permission. The threads, worn down like her energy, snapped, and the light disappeared into the darkness. Vi staggered back, collapsing on the bed and staring at where he had been—staring at her hand and what she'd done.

She summoned him the next day.

Immediately after her lessons, Vi feigned a stomach ache and had a simple dinner sent to her room. On hearing she was supposedly ill, Ginger tittered about, but Vi finally sent her away too. She waited for a good hour before holding out her hand and uttering the words.

The light appeared before her, flickering at first and becoming stable. Vi remained focused on every line, ensuring that the slowly swirling circles around her fingers stayed in place—close to her skin, just as he'd instructed. Only when she felt the magic stabilize did she look to her visitor.

"You seem more confident with that."

"Me? Confident with magic? You have the wrong girl."

"I'm just as surprised as you, to see one of the Dark Isle using Lightspinning. Though I must remind myself you have your contraband book that should've never made it across the Shattered Isles."

"If my book upsets you so much, why don't you come and get it back?" Vi retorted. The jab hit harder than she'd intended.

"If only I could."

Taavin looked away and Vi studied his profile. Other than the scar that ran from his left eye, down his cheek, his face was as polished as a sculpture. Though she was certain the light that constantly outlined him contributed to the ethereal illusion.

"Why can't you?" she dared to ask. He'd said he'd never left his city the last time they spoke and Vi had heard volumes lingering under the statement. Until now, however, they'd only ever spoken of practical things—magic and visions. This was the first time she was making an intentional effort to venture beyond the basic framework that had brought them together.

"You wouldn't understand."

"Try me." Her lips curled up into a smile, hopefully encouraging and not mocking.

"My position, as the Voice of Yargen, means I am to remain by the flame at all times. I couldn't leave if I wanted." *And he did want to.* Of that Vi was certain.

"Trapped by your position…" Vi looked at the swirling magic around her fingertips. "That's one thing I think I understand better than most."

For the first time in her life, Vi shared the sentiment with someone and did not have them immediately disagree. He didn't try to point out all she had in the power of her station. Nor did he chastise her for the feeling of entrapment. He merely stood in quiet camaraderie.

"What does the Voice of Yargen do?" Vi asked. "Keep this flame burning?"

Taavin took a small step back, as if surprised by the question. She watched as his guards slid back into place—mentally battening the hatches against her once more.

"No… the flame of Yargen has been burning since the goddess last left this world. It is a remnant of the goddess herself—and her power. Through it, her chosen voice hears the words of power Lightspinners use, as well as her guidance for the mortal realm she created." He sighed, running a hand through his hair. "At least, that is what I am supposed to do."

"I see…" Vi murmured. He couldn't hear the goddess through this flame. Vi knew it by his expression and reaction alone. But something prevented her from saying so outright. Perhaps what stopped her was the keen knowledge that pointing it out would only bring him extra pain. She didn't want to be torture to him, intentionally or otherwise. So Vi shifted the topic slightly. "What about the champion? You always bring up the voice and the champion together."

"Because the champion is Yargen's other chosen mortal. Though… there has not been one since the last time Raspian walked this earth."

Vi suppressed a shudder at what she knew now was the name of the dark god she'd seen the zealots worshiping in her last vision. "Why do you think I am the champion?"

"Because a traveler told me of our meeting."

Traveler. Vi stilled at the word. It couldn't possibly be… "This traveler, was it a man or a woman?"

"A woman."

There was no way it was the same traveler who had spoken to Sehra. No possible way. That meeting had to have been more than twenty years ago. Yet was it truly just chance she'd heard of two different mysterious travelers with knowledge of Yargen so close together?

"What did she tell you?" Vi dared to ask.

"That my visions would reveal the locations of the apexes of fate—landmarks on the path of a dying world where my destiny overlaps with the champion's. That the champion holds the key to fueling the flame once more, and making sense of Yargen's will." Vi snorted, then laughter exploded from her mouth. Taavin blinked out of sight for a second and she quickly re-drew the glyphs for *narro* and *hath* in her mind, securing them back around her hand. A frown crossed his mouth. "Just what is so amusing?"

"I can see why you hate me so much. I haunt your dreams and then, when you finally meet me, I'm absolutely useless." Vi gave another self-deprecating laugh. When it came to magic, it seemed nothing she did would ever be enough, in any direction. There would always be someone she was letting down.

Her laughter subsided as she became keenly aware of Taavin's stare. Vi turned up her face to look at him, waiting for his retort. The silence stretched on, and his eyes traced her features what must have been a thousand times.

Vi forced a smile and ignored the tension. She didn't want it to be there. There wasn't time for it. But before she could think of another substitution for discussion, he spoke.

"I never said you were useless."

Vi swallowed. His words tightened her chest and stomach. Some kind of relief punched her in the gut, leaving her breathless and stinging in a way that was foreign to her. Was she really so desperate for affirmation that she was doing all right?

"Well, perhaps I can continue to prove I'm not by helping you find the next apex? Do you have any ideas from your visions?" She resisted asking if she was present in these visions.

"I'm still working to discern their meaning."

"What do you have so far?"

"It makes little sense…" he murmured, pacing back and forth twice.

"You have someone to be a sounding board off of," Vi reminded him. Given how he acted, and all he'd said, Vi suspected it was a relatively new development for Taavin.

"I doubt it'll be much clearer for you."

"Will you just let me help?" She threw her hands up in the air and the magic disappeared. "Oh, by the Mother," Vi muttered, holding out her hand again. She took a breath, finishing a string of curses, and then uttered, "*Narro hath.*" Taavin reappeared. "Sorry about that."

"You're persistent, aren't you?" He tilted his head slightly. When he did so, the bottom of his hair nearly touched his shoulder.

"I've been told I can be when something piques my interest."

"I'm glad the end of the world has inspired your curiosity." Vi opened her mouth to say that *he* was the one who had, but before she could, Taavin saved her from herself.

"I have seen a room, dark, two women standing before a single flame. Roses and wheat…"

"Not enough to go off of," Vi reluctantly agreed with his earlier sentiment. "At least for that one. Any others?"

"In my dreams I have also witnessed a throne room—covered in the crystallized fragments of Yargen's magic. A dying man who was tainted by touching godly power with mortal hands."

Vi sighed softly, wishing it were a clearer lead. "That sounds like something more on the Crescent Continent than here."

"It is unlike any throne room I've ever seen on Meru."

"Is that all?"

"Do you know anywhere called Eye-owe?"

"Eye-owe," Vi repeated, then shook her head. "It doesn't ring a bell. What's it like?"

"Something about a temple, perhaps?"

Vi thought back to all her maps. She certainly didn't recall any temples named Eye-owe. But, given the North's opinions toward marking their ruins, she couldn't exactly rule it out.

"One more has been clear and reoccurring," he continued when it was clear she had nothing more to add. "Though I doubt it'll be any clearer for you. I see two women by a statue. I see a tall tree, towering above them."

"That statue…" Vi shifted to the edge of her bed, an idea dawning on her. "What does it look like?" She knew what he was about to say before he said it. Vi could already see it with perfect clarity.

"One woman standing, the other kneeling, holding—"

"An axe," Vi finished for him.

"What?"

She pushed off the bed, starting for the door. "See? It was a good thing you told me. Because I know exactly where that last apex is."

23

THE MOTHER TREE, OLDEST of all the trees in the North, was at the center of the fortress. It was into this tree that Dia—a star from the gods—had fallen. On her descent, she had become mortal. Under its leafy boughs was where the Mother was said to have gifted her the axe.

This had to be the location of the next apex.

It was easy to identify it by its height and overall grandeur. But it was harder than one would think to get to. She had to spiral around smaller—but by no means small—trees, go up to go down, and spend nearly a half hour getting to the end of what should've been a five-minute walk, had she been able to go straight to the center. It was made worse by sneaking around in the dead of night, constantly looking over her shoulder to ensure she was alone.

But she saw no one and now the final barrier to her goal was before her. Vi was almost breathless from her haste. She stood on the other side of a living wall. Groundbreakers had woven saplings together to make a beautiful fence. Beautiful... and without any sort of clear entrance unless one had the magic to manipulate the trees to unweave themselves.

Vi looked up and around cautiously. The sensation of someone watching her was back. But Vi was certain it was nothing more than paranoia. She'd heard no footsteps and had seen no eyes peering at her through the darkness.

She stared through the woven barrier to the base of the Mother Tree. Shaded in an alcove was a ceremonial room that Vi had only been in a handful of times. Once for the blessings of Yargen to be placed on Ellene shortly after her birth, then twice every year since, for solstice rituals. The Mother Tree was a highly sacred place; Vi didn't blame them for keeping people, or wandering princesses, out most other days of the year.

The bark of the natural barrier bit into her palms as she gripped it tighter. The room would be opened soon for the upcoming solstice; she could wait and not risk discovery now. But Vi doubted she could find a time to confidently come alone during the handful of days it was open to all in the fortress. Now she was certain to have time alone to see her vision, and speak with the man who came after.

Furthermore, Vi continued to try to rationalize her decision, she was a Child of

Yargen too, wasn't she? That meant it would be acceptable for her to trespass on the most sacred space in the North. *Not trespass,* she couldn't trespass as a child of Yargen, right? Vi quickly tried to tally up the pros and cons in her head, before pushing the thoughts away. Rationalized or not, her path ahead was clear. She wasn't going to back away now, not when she was this close.

"You understand, right?" Vi whispered to the Mother above, looking up toward the heavens. Nothing changed and Vi took that as tacit permission to begin climbing the woven barrier.

Luckily, its lace-like weave made plenty of gaps and spaces for hand- and footholds as she climbed. From the ground, it looked much shorter than at its top, and Vi employed great care in swinging her legs over and starting down the other side. Thankfully, she'd spent a lifetime trying to keep up with Groundbreakers in the jungles. Tree climbing was easily a strong-suit of hers, and Vi moved with swift confidence.

Feet back on the ground, Vi raced underneath the arch that led to the hallowed room that very much mirrored Sehra's throne room. Except in place of a throne at the center, a barely-visible sculpture of two women stood. One was kneeling, her long braids nearly touching the ground—Dia, the forest star—and the other was said to be the Mother, imparting an axe upon her to carve out a new civilization from the raw earth she'd created for all mankind.

"A giant tree, a statue of a woman holding an axe." This had to be the apex Taavin had seen.

Vi held out her hand and readied herself. Whatever the vision showed her this time, she would be ready. She could handle it. At the very least, she wouldn't shout in horror and alert everyone to her presence. Good or bad, she was trained to be an Empress, and should not startle so easily.

Her eyes were wide. She could not look away if she tried. Yet the vision that possessed her was different from all the others. It was clearer, sharper. Now it was as if time itself flowed through her, posing her at its edge to peer through its secrets.

The world around her shifted. Days turned to nights. Stars spun across the sky. Flowers blossomed, saplings grew into trees, and vines knotted further over the remains of a civilization progressing quickly toward decay.

The fortress around her took shape and quickly changed, time and again. The city of Soricium grew and retreated with the seasons becoming more and more scarce—fading into a grayish stasis—as the trees withered, decayed, and exposed a sky larger than any Vi had ever seen, unbroken by treetops, to Shaldan's barren earth.

Finally, the spinning top of the progression of time stopped on a desolate landscape.

Vi looked out over a barren field. Rubble lay like tombstones around the rough stumps of trees that looked as though they had been shredded to toothpicks. The great giants of Shaldan—trees that had stood from the dawn of time—lay on the ground in charred husks.

The Mother Tree was little more than sawdust.

She could almost taste the ash in her mouth, bitter and still smoldering from what looked like the aftermath of a battle that far exceeded even the horrific stories of the siege on Soricium during the War for the North. The smell of rot somehow reached her and brought Vi to gagging, as the remnants of what could be called men and women had been left as carrion for the birds.

Each corpse was contorted into angles of agony. They twisted with open mouths, locked in an eternal scream. Their eyes were wide and absent of all color—gone completely white and glossy. Deep trenches cut into their skin from where they had clawed at the white and rocky parts that coated their bodies between veins of still-glowing red.

Without having ever seen it, Vi knew that this was the ultimate end of the White Death: a stony, cold agony that kept one trapped for eternity in its suffering.

Vi half-wheezed, half-retched, gasping desperately for a breath of fresh air—for sound, liberating sound from the deadly silence that surrounded her. There was nothing but silence and death. It was then that her eyes turned skyward.

The heavens had been broken.

An all-black sky, void of stars, was ripped apart by a bloody slash trimmed at the edges with white. Drifting through the bleeding fragments of a broken cosmos was the form of a serpentine, winged monster, wide talons dipping to tear off pieces of the world below. Red lightning cracked around its body, as if charged by the ripping of reality itself.

Vaguely, the terrifying imagery registered to her through the words of crones and soothsayers. They had spoken of an apocalypse, of a reckoning where all souls would be summoned to the Father's realms—a day where the sky itself would shatter and the world as they all knew it would come to an end. But Vi had never heard the tales spoken in this much horrifying detail.

The dragon roared and the world shuddered, vibrating with a sound that she couldn't hear. Vi may have screamed, but there was still no sound in her ears. The monster turned its gaze toward her and she was filled with the same sensation she'd felt the moment the diseased noru and the lightning man in her vision had looked to her.

It saw her and it wanted her.

She raised her hands on instinct to shield herself, to make herself small. She wanted it to end, to be free of the horrific images she was being inundated with. No vision until now had been this horribly vivid and she would not be able to endure should it continue.

"Make it stop!" The sound of her own voice broke the trance.

Darkness, the blissful darkness of the backs of her eyelids, filled her sight, and when Vi opened her eyes again, the world was as she knew it. She staggered and sank, her trembling knees no longer able to bear her weight. Gasping through fingers holding in silent screams at the horror she'd witnessed, Vi continued to stare wide-eyed at where her fire had been. Surely, surely, there was some mistake.

That wasn't their future. It couldn't be.

Gasping, Vi relished in the sound of her voice and the familiar cool darkness of the North in winter. A pair of boots, illuminated by hazy glyphs, appeared in her field of vision. Vi followed them up to the intricately embroidered coat Taavin always wore, along the scar on his cheek, and to his eyes.

"What did you see?" he asked grimly.

"The end of the world." The words didn't sound like her own. They were detached, removed, split from her body. What she now could never unsee would forever change her.

"Tell me everything."

Vi recounted the vision in as much detail as she could bear. For as difficult as it was, doing so gave her some clarity. It removed the initial shock and horror and turned the sights into something to be analyzed.

When Vi had finished, she asked, "This dark god you speak of—Raspian—and his followers... the White Death... they're all linked, aren't they?"

She didn't want him to nod. This was the one time in her life where Vi desperately wanted to be wrong.

"They are."

Vi let out a string of curses that would make her tutors blush. Taavin stayed silent, allowing her to reach the end of her list before speaking again. Curses were cathartic, but they weren't going to help them get anywhere. Vi tried to remember everything he had told her following her last vision.

"The elfin'ra, you said they were sealed away on Salvidia?"

"They were."

Past tense. "What changed? Why is all this happening now?"

"Raspian and his followers were sealed away by the goddess in their last, ancient struggle for power over this realm... but nineteen years ago, that seal was broken. Since then, his evil, his pure chaotic energy, has been seeping into the world—twisting it. And his followers, who were also set free with it, now seek a way to bring his full return."

If everything he said was true, it meant there was no cure for the White Death. Her father had left for nothing. Her people sought a cure that could never be found.

No one on Solaris knew how desperate their situation was, but her.

"Taavin, these visions I see at the apexes... are they what *will* be, or what *may* be?"

"What will be, should the world progress without any changes in course."

"So, then, the course can be changed?"

"Perhaps."

Vi breathed a sigh of relief, even though a corner of her mind still refused to believe it. Normal future sight—by a Firebearer—was generally regarded as absolute truth. But Vi wasn't exactly a Firebearer. So she'd have to take Taavin's word for it.

"How do we make sure?"

"Just as there have been apexes of fate in the past, there will be apexes in the future. Places where—"

"—the world changed or places where it could still be changed," she finished for him, remembering what he had said when she first asked. Vi finally pulled herself off the ground, feeling stronger. "So we need to find future apexes, and make sure we shift fate there." Simple logic, but Vi expected it to be much more difficult in practice. "How do we find them?"

"I will need to study... and record your vision to compare against my notes on my own dreams as I look for the next apex for you."

She wanted to go now. She wanted him to have the answers immediately, and Vi shifted from foot to foot in an effort to let out some of the restless energy. Vi let out a deep sigh, trying to let go of the strange tremors rippling through her.

"Are you afraid?" Taavin cut through her racing thoughts.

"What? No." Vi folded her hands before her to keep them still.

"You should be. Only a fool wouldn't be."

"I—"

"Go and rest now, Vi. I have work to do." He vanished.

Vi stared at where Taavin had just stood. "Are you happy to have the last word?" Vi mumbled at the thin air, before turning and leaving.

Dark gods, plagues, fate… Vi was wrapped up in her thoughts as she slowly made her way back through the fortress. For the first time in her life, Vi felt small.

There was a red flash in the darkness, nearly identical to what she had seen the night she'd snuck out. Vi looked up, pulled back to reality, and squinted into the dark. Her exhaustion had vanished entirely, heart racing.

Her feet stopped halfway across the walkway she'd been traversing. She was frozen still by the silhouette of a figure blocking the path forward.

Vi narrowed her eyes, trying to figure out if the person was male or female. Male… probably, she decided, based on the broadness in his shoulders. The wind rustled the trees above her, the light catching on his eyes again, and Vi's breath caught in her throat with a strangled choke.

Distinctly red eyes set on ghostly pale skin were narrowed directly at her.

He had a similar jaw line to Taavin's, a narrow bridge to his nose, and Vi knew if she peeled back the man's hood she'd see pointed ears. She'd seen creatures of this type before, recently, even. But never standing in the present.

Her whole body went icy.

"Wh-who are you?" Vi whispered, struggling to keep her voice level. She hated the weak quiver that caught the beginning of the first word.

The man unsheathed a narrow dagger. It had the same markings on the side as the one the leader of the acolytes had held in her vision—the elfin'ra. It further contributed to the surreal nature of everything happening around her. Those creatures were on another land, far away. They weren't *here*.

Vi took a step back, glancing over her shoulder. Her room was still three stories up. This was the most direct route… but there was an alternate if she took a shortcut through a storage hall.

"What do you want with me?" Vi whispered, debating when she needed to make her break for it.

"The champion's blood for Lord Raspian." The words slithered from his mouth, curling through the air with pure malice, curdling in her ears.

The man lunged for her. Vi had barely a second to react. Her hand lifted, palm outstretched between them.

"*Juth!*" she cried. The symbol exploded from her palm, imperfect and half-formed in her haste. It shattered under the weight of its own power mid-air, casting sparks down on either side of the walkway like the embers of a firework. But Vi didn't have time to appreciate them.

She was already running.

Vi dashed back into the tree behind her. The elfin'ra's footsteps were close behind. Vi made a hard left, turning for a cramped passage that led to a narrow stair. At least here there was no way he could flank her.

There was a grunt behind her right as she jumped for the stairs. Vi turned just in time to see the flash of the dagger in the dim moonlight. It narrowly missed the back of her heel. If he'd sliced the tendon, it would've been the end of her.

"*Juth!*" Vi attempted a second time.

But as she raised her hand, the elfin'ra was already speaking, preempting her motions. "*Juth mariy*," he snarled.

Vi's magic fizzled beneath her palm. In her shock, she stumbled at the top of the stair, half rolling down the narrow hall. The horrifying creature stalked closer, his red eyes piercing the darkness as easily as it pierced her soul.

"*You* are the champion?" The question was a cross between shock and condescending amusement. "I am to believe you are Yargen's chosen?"

Vi glanced to her right, where a towering shelf stood freely alongside where the man was approaching, dagger still in hand. At least, she hoped it stood freely.

"*Juth.*" Vi tried again. This time, she did not telegraph her attempt with a movement of her hand, nor did she direct it at the man. Instead, the front legs of the shelf burned away in a white-hot burst of fire.

Off-balance, it was sent toppling over, and Vi scrambled to her feet, running again.

One more flight of stairs; she didn't look back. Across one more rope bridge and she'd be at her room and there… there she would… *what?*

Her room had always been her haven. Her safe place. But now it would be a secluded area for her to die. There was nothing there that could protect her any more than where she now stood.

Vi looked around frantically, her head spinning with every sway of the rope bridge beneath her feet. There had to be a warrior patrolling somewhere who could help her. Her eyes scanned every passage and walkway, seeing no one. It was as if she were the only one left alive in the whole fortress.

A cry for help rose in her throat, stopping as she turned toward the sudden creaking on the bridge behind her. The man was mid-lunge. His ominously glowing dagger was tracked over her chest.

He was going to kill her.

Vi looked down at her feet. If she was going to die, she'd take him with her.

"*Juth,*" she said, one last time, watching as his eyes went wide and the bridge exploded into flames beneath their feet.

THE NIGHT RUSHED AROUND her.

    She'd known the sky trees were tall, but Vi had never really heeded Jax's warnings when it came to *how* tall. It seemed she would fall forever. Every second seemed longer than a hundred years and yet she knew it would be over all too soon.

    Vi reached upward on instinct, flailing through the air, looking for a branch or walkway. But she couldn't find a hold. Surely, there was a window she could grab onto? Somewhere? Her nails ripped back, the pads of her fingers scraped off against rough bark.

    There was a flash of red light—the elfin'ra was performing some kind of magic. Vi braced herself. She could almost feel the magic spinning at the man's whim—a twisted distortion of the power she knew, yet so similar it was painful.

    All she could do was wait for it to strike her and then she'd be—

    Two hands closed around her sides. She slipped through their grasp. They dug into her shoulders, friction ripping through her clothes. The fingertips pressed further into the meat of her arms. They gripped and didn't let go.

    Vi heard a shout, but it was cut off abruptly as she swung face first into the tree she'd been trying to catch herself on.

    Everything went dark.

She was falling.

    Above her were the trees of Shaldan, shadowed and faded like ghosted sentries peering down at her through a hole that became smaller and smaller the longer she fell. The ruins she'd explored in the jungle passed her. Countless eyes, peering through the darkness, stared only at her, waiting.

    What were they waiting for?

    Why did they look at her as if they knew her?

    Her questions went unanswered. She didn't scream. The wind whizzed around her; she must be falling fast, but her stomach was settled. Vi felt calm. She was sinking into something familiar, warm. She accepted the waiting darkness beyond the reality she knew and the worlds she'd only begun to explore.

Perhaps this was how Dia felt when she fell from the sky. Fearless. Not knowing what awaited her at the bottom but knowing it wouldn't harm her. Knowing that wherever she landed, was where she was meant to be.

Taavin was there.

That was the first cohesive thought that registered on the edge of Vi's mind. There was his familiar shape, pressed against her, clutching her, supporting her. He was warm like sunlight, as though all the brightness in the world was contained within him.

Familiar shape?

Her mind was at war with itself. She didn't know him, not really. They were unlikely allies and she'd certainly never made physical contact with him in any of their meetings. Yet there was a distinct sense of rightness about him. Merely knowing of his existence put a label to something that Vi had never quite paid attention to or understood, something that inexplicably filled her with joy and excitement.

"What happened to you?" His words were muffled and distant, even here when he felt so close. Would he forever be just out of her reach? When had that even become a concern for her? "Is this the real you? Or just another night?"

She wasn't quite sure what happened to her, so she didn't answer. Everything was murky. All she knew for certain was relief that he was here now. That with him by her side she could endure the long night ahead.

"You're too far from me." That, they could agree on. "I can't help you."

Just having you here helps, Vi thought, and the words sounded as though they had passed through her lips. His ethereal presence shifted, slightly, as though his chest rose and fell with a sigh.

"Will you ever free me from this torture?" he lamented softly. Vi felt it as though he'd whispered it right into her ear.

The words rumbled through her. They were deep, contemplative. Full of a profound emotion Vi wasn't even sure she could name. She wanted to twist, to see him, to hold him, to touch him. She would burn away his sorrows and reveal the brightness that only he contained.

But he wasn't truly there. There was only darkness surrounding her; every passing moment had him drifting further away from her. He was always fading in and out of her life, like a weak pulse that vanished the moment she put her finger on it.

He may have never been there to begin with. Yet she could still feel his skin on hers. She could still feel the rough embroidery of his coat under her hands. There was a phantom memory of feeling things she'd never touched, so perfect she wasn't even sure what was real anymore.

Vi opened her eyes slowly, blinking into the light.

It was dawn. When had night become day? She turned her head, feeling soft hands pressing into something uncomfortably squishy.

The someone pressing was Ginger, and the uncomfortably squishy was a section of her body that was where her ribs *should* be.

"Oh, Mother, princess, that's the second time you've scared me half to death!" Ginger nearly jumped out of her skin the second she saw Vi's open eyes.

Vi continued to look around. Her hands rested on her quilt; the feather mattress she'd always laid in was soft underneath her. The portraits of her family stood on the dresser, and her box of letters was on her bedside table... This was undeniably her room.

"Do you feel pain?" Ginger asked again. At least, Vi thought it was again. Her mind was still sluggish.

"No, I don't," she wheezed. "Discomfort, but no pain." Why did her voice sound that way? Vi pressed her eyes shut and in the darkness behind them saw the glowing eyes of the man at the other end of the bridge. "We're not safe."

"Princess, *no*, I must insist, you cannot sit right now." Ginger pushed her back toward the bed. "You're young, and you received treatment promptly... You'll be back up and about in no time flat. Even your face will get back to normal. But, Mother, child, give it at least a day. I'm a cleric, not a goddess."

Vi allowed herself to sink back into her pillows. The haze was beginning to lift. A dullness still lingered on the edge of her mind, but Vi blamed it on whatever potion Ginger had forced down her throat when she was out.

If she was lying in bed, it meant she hadn't died—simple deductions first. That meant, somehow, she was saved... The arms. Her face meeting the tree. Vi winced, raising a hand to her bandaged head, the echo of a terrible crunch in her ears.

She was alive. That also meant the red-eyed man hadn't come back to finish the job. Like the saddle, he'd done his work in the shroud of night when he thought himself most likely to elude capture, vanishing in time to fade into suspicious coincidence by morning.

"How bad is it?" Vi asked, watching Ginger rub salve over her abdomen.

"As bad as you'd expect. But a whole lot better than dead. Which, were it not for Andru, you would've been."

"Andru?" Vi wheezed, barely moving her lips.

"He was out, he saw you fall. The man nearly fell out of the window himself catching you. Popped both his shoulders pretty badly, too," Ginger said, as though she could read her mind. "Promise me the rest of the day in bed, no unnecessary ventures, bathroom only. You can take dinner here. I'll check you in the morning and hopefully give you the all-clear to begin moving, at least around your quarters. In the meantime, don't hesitate to summon me should you ever need, princess."

"I will, Ginger, thank you."

Her cleric hovered, clearly debating something. Then a small, almost conspiratorial smile crossed her lips. "Princess, if I may, who is Taavin?"

"How do you know that name?" Vi tried to ask calmly, so as not to give away the instant feeling of protectiveness. She didn't even want to share the mere thought of Taavin with anyone.

Taavin. Just the thought of his name, the way it settled with her, told her she'd dreamed about him. But the details of that dream had vanished on waking. Vi couldn't recall anything.

"You were murmuring it in your sleep over and over."

Vi felt a heat rise to her cheeks that had nothing to do with her spark.

"It's normal for girls your age to begin feeling things," Ginger started. Vi could tell from her tone that she *really* didn't want to have this conversation. First Sehra, now Ginger. "Even your tutors have noticed that perhaps someone may have caught your eye, given your distractions lately. You've been taking more lunches and dinners in your room and, well… They'd suggested that I perhaps speak with you on the—" she cleared her throat "—*logistics*, of men and women."

Vi went from merely "not wanting to have this conversation" to being willing to do just about anything but. "I appreciate all you do for me, but I don't think this is the time."

"Of course, princess. I understand. Merely consider me a resource for whenever you're ready to discuss such things. For a lady of your status it is imperative to be careful, and your parents have entrusted me to cover such matters with you as is needed." Ginger tucked one foot behind the other, dipping into a curtsy. She started for the door, but never got the chance to turn the lever.

The door opened from the other side, revealing Jax—Vi thanked every scrap of luck he had not entered moments earlier and been privy to the mention of Taavin. The moment he laid eyes on her, his whole expression crumpled into relief. She'd never seen such tenderness line his brow before.

"Thank the Mother," he whispered. He turned to Ginger. "How is she?"

"The bones and organs are on the mend. We're lucky it's not more serious. Her face should mend up just fine, the nose should set right if she keeps still. And I've told her to stay in bed," Ginger said pointedly, looking back to her.

"I'm not fighting you this time."

"Good." She turned back to Jax. "I'll take care of the rest of the bruising in the morning."

"Thank you for everything." Jax clasped Ginger's hand, sending her out the door in the same motion. He quickly closed it behind her, giving them privacy.

They had a small staring contest, but Vi was the first to avert her eyes. She didn't know why she felt guilty for making him worry. What had happened certainly wasn't her fault. Perhaps it was her regal training—that all fault ended with her. "I'm sorry, uncle."

"Sorry?" He crossed quickly to the chair at her bedside that Ginger had just vacated. "Vi, I'm uttering prayers of thanks with my every breath that you're alive."

"Someone attacked me." Vi reached for him and her uncle's hand was there to grasp hers right when she needed him. "There was a man and—"

"I know." He squeezed her hand tightly. "There were remnants of the struggle in the halls. After the cut girth… I should've expanded my investigation further, faster. The leather-smith claimed that, perhaps, when he was making some last-minute trimmings to account for some weight loss in Gormon, he dug too deeply on the tail of the straps. When I could find no other leads, the trail went cold and I stalled. Forgive me, Vi."

Vi shook her head, the horrifying ordeal playing out in her mind. The elfin'ra had powers like her—like Sehra—but twisted by that same red lightning she'd seen in her visions. This was unlike anything Jax could fathom going against.

"Whoever this person is," Vi began slowly. "I think they're well trained in the art of stealth and subterfuge."

"Clearly."

"Did you find their body below where the bridge collapsed?" Vi thought back to the bridge. There was no way the elfin'ra could've avoided plummeting to his death.

"Body, no…" Horror crept across Jax's face. No body meant no confirmed kill—the elfin'ra was still alive. "Tell me of your attacker," he demanded. "I'll oversee the warriors personally and we shall hunt them down."

Vi searched his determined expression. How could she hope to explain what her attacker looked like? What he was?

The memories of the visions returned to her—men and women decaying alongside the world at its end. Her uncle was in knots over the mere idea of something happening to her. How could she explain they were all sprinting head-first toward the end of days and red-eyed elfin'ra were seeking her blood as Yargen's champion to expedite the process?

She couldn't explain it all. So she didn't even try. She couldn't subject him to that.

"It was dark… I couldn't make out much."

"Tell me what you can."

"Skin as white as a ghost and red, glowing eyes."

"Red eyes? Like a Firebearer who has freshly seen the future?" Jax asked.

"I suppose…" Vi murmured, now wondering if her eyes glowed red after her visions. She'd never been around a mirror for one.

"Can you tell me anything else?"

"He was hooded." Vi shook her head. "I'm sorry. I know saying a pale skinned and red-eyed man attacked me seems difficult to believe."

Jax leaned forward, tugging on her hand gently. He tilted his head up, staring in her eyes. Vi searched her uncle's weathered face. Lines were drawn across his brow and hung in arcs underneath his eyes. He was only slightly older than her father but worry made him look nearly ancient.

"I will always believe you," he vowed softly. She nearly told him in that second of her visions. But the moment passed as quickly as it came. "I'll speak with Andru, see if he has any other details to contribute."

Vi nodded. Ache seeped into her bones and Vi gently pulled his hand toward her. She brought it to her cheek, holding it there gently. It was the closest thing to a hug she could manage in her present condition.

"Thank you, uncle," she whispered.

He said nothing more, shifting his palm to her forehead. Vi's eyes fluttered closed for several moments as he gently stroked her hair. In a different world, the touch would be her father's. But in this world, Jax was the closest thing she had.

"You should rest," he said, soft enough that he clearly thought she was halfway to sleep. "I will position extra security at your room at all times."

Vi appreciated the sentiment, even if she didn't think the elfin'ra would be caught or stopped by any normal means. Her eyes fluttered open.

"Can you please send Andru to me?"

"He's recovering as well, like you should be."

"It won't be long. I'd like to thank him," she said trying to prop herself up a little more on the pillows so she didn't actually fall asleep. "He saved my life. I promise I'll be a good patient the rest of the day. Just ten minutes?"

"Very well." Jax gave her a tender smile. She should have near-death experiences more often. It clearly softened him. "Never claim I don't spoil you."

"Thank you," Vi called after him.

In a few minutes, Andru arrived. Vi watched as he slipped through the door, moving stiffly.

"Close it behind you," Vi requested softly.

He did as instructed but continued to hover. His icy blue eyes stared down at her and Vi looked back at him. Neither of them said anything for several long moments.

"I thought you were trying to kill me," Vi blurted.

"What?" He blinked, startled. "Is that really what you summoned me here to say?"

"No. Well, it was one of the things I wanted to say…" Vi admitted.

"Why did you think I was trying to kill you?" he asked skeptically.

"Because you showed up and suddenly strange things started happening." A lot of strange things, but none of them could be blamed on Andru, it seemed. "You said you followed me into the city—"

"Because I wanted to protect you." His eyes darted around the room, shifty. *No, they weren't shifty*. She'd only thought they were. He was simply… awkward. "I can see the door to your room from my bedroom. I had been having trouble sleeping with all the forest noises and was up." It was then that Vi realized she didn't even know where they had put him up in the fortress. "I saw you going out, alone, looking very much like you were sneaking about. There was someone else following behind you, too, but they were gone when I went to approach them."

"What did they look like?" Vi asked eagerly.

"I did not get a good look." He walked slowly over to the chair Ginger had been using. "May I sit?" Andru rubbed his midsection and Vi remembered what Ginger had said. She gave a small nod. "What else did I do that made you think I wanted to kill you?"

"You wanted me to ride the noru with the broken saddle—"

"I thought you were going out because you *wanted* to ride the noru."

Vi stared at him, dissecting the words. They sounded truthful to her ears, which meant… "You really are dense."

"What?"

Vi laughed at his expression, her whole body aching as a result. "That was all a ploy for Ellene and Darrus."

"Oh. *Oh.*" She watched as comprehension lit up his face.

"And then everything about my being fit to rule, and maybe my brother should… you haven't exactly been friendly with me."

"What? I tried to be." Andru leaned back in his chair, folding his hands in his lap. He looked at them, speaking more to his fingers than her. "I am not the best at making friends. I think." His head slowly rose and he stared at her for a long moment. Then said, simply, "I am sorry, your highness."

"May I speak plainly?" Vi asked thoughtfully.

"I should be asking that of you."

She took his statement as a yes and let out a small sigh as the last of the tension that had wound between her shoulders was unleashed. When she spoke again, it was no longer in the drawn out way of nobility, but the simple phrasing she'd use for Jax, Ellene, or Jayme.

"I think I have as much to apologize for as you do. I could've—should've—been nicer to you from the start." Vi gave a small huff of laughter, mostly at herself. "You know my brother even told me you were important, and I think that, with all I've had going on, I botched it."

"I wouldn't say that..." Andru said slowly. His eyes drifted to her letter box. "Romulin said I was important?"

"'More important than I could imagine'," Vi answered delicately. She studied his face, trying to read the expression that lingered there.

"Did he ever write anything else about me?" Andru asked in a small voice. He'd never spoken so plainly around her. Perhaps having a shared near-death experience was what they both needed.

"No..." He hadn't. Vi blinked slowly, realization dawning on her. "He never really wrote about any of his friends."

Andru seemed just as shocked as she was. "What did he write about then?"

"Books he was reading, mother and father, the court, news of the South, advice for how to manage things..."

"All very useful nuggets of information. Romulin's terribly savvy." Andru smiled.

Vi tried to smile back, but her mind was preoccupied for the moment by musings of a similar vein to what she'd thought around Andru before. How much did she really know about her brother? Vi had always imagined they were close... but what sort of music did her brother enjoy? What hobbies filled his days when he wasn't in his lessons? She was certain she'd written about those things.

"Your brother was actually the one who encouraged me to take this post," Andru continued, oblivious to her moment of turmoil.

"He was?" Vi tried to shake her discomfort. She was merely overreacting due to exhaustion, seeing things that weren't there.

"Romulin wanted me to help prepare you, and I don't think I've done that at all."

"You saved my life, surely that counts for something?" She gave him a small smile and his eyes darted away.

"At least I did that... Otherwise I might be in trouble."

"Why?"

"I don't know if I'm doing my job well." He folded and unfolded his fingers, eyes darting back and forth, not quite making eye contact with her. "I *need* to do my job well."

"Isn't your father head of Senate? Aren't you basically set for life?"

He laughed bitterly, a sound Vi recognized because she'd made it herself.

"Wouldn't that be nice?" Andru shook his head slowly. "My father is more of an ass than a donkey, and far more stubborn. You're not the only one he has high expectations for."

"At least you're not an ass, then." Vi sunk farther back into her pillows, ignoring the ache in her jaw from speaking so much.

"You don't think so?"

"Not at all."

"Well, that's a relief." He let out an audible sigh, bringing his gaze back to her. Perhaps it was all in her mind, but Vi would swear he was beginning to look her in the eye more.

"There's something else I wanted to ask you..." Vi hadn't been planning on the conversation taking this tone when she first summoned him, and though she was glad it did, she needed to find out the truth.

"Which is?"

"On the bridge… did you see him?"

Andru went very still. He said nothing, hardly breathing.

"You did." Vi let out a sigh of relief. She didn't expect having someone who knew even part of her secrets to be so relieving. Nor did she expect that someone, out of everyone, to be Andru.

"I don't know what I saw." He shook his head. "It was… It was like—"

"A monster?" An apt description, all things considered. "A man with glowing red eyes, not quite human?"

"And a magic to match," he affirmed. "I thought… when I woke up, I thought I'd dreamed it but…"

"It was real," Vi assured him. "What, exactly, did you see?"

"The sounds of your struggle woke me… But I only saw you on the bridge. I saw you both fall and as I reached out to catch you, a cage of lightning surrounded the man. By the time I had you in my arms, pulled in from the window, he had disappeared with nothing more than a flash."

"I see…" Vi murmured. At least that explained, somewhat, why there was no body. She'd have to ask Taavin about the magic of the elfin'ra—learn what she was up against.

"What was that thing?" he whispered.

"A creature from very far away." She didn't bother launching into a description of a dark god and his acolytes. That was far more than would be useful for Andru in this moment. "Uncle says he's going to investigate, but I doubt he'll find anything… What I want to know is how he got here."

"When you say very far away…"

"Farther than the Crescent Continent."

"But there is nothing beyond the Crescent." How wrong he was. But Vi didn't see the point in correcting him. She never expected to pass up the opportunity to educate someone on geography, but today was turning into a banner one for firsts.

"You say there is nothing. But there are monsters. Trust me on this," Vi half begged, half commanded. "As your sovereign and your new friend."

"I do… I have no other choice after what I saw." He shook his head. "Had I not, I would've had a much harder time believing it."

"I'm glad you can affirm I'm not crazy, then." On the list of possibly insane things to have happened to her, this wasn't even at the top.

"It's just that no one should be coming from the Crescent Continent. Trade was shut down due to the White Death."

"Which is why I want to know who is getting in and out." She would be certain to ask Taavin too, at the next possible opportunity. But first, exhaustion was beginning to catch up with her.

"I'll see what I can find."

"That's all I ask." Vi shifted slowly. Her whole body ached, and her torso felt more jelly-like than she remembered. Every shift and smile hurt her face. But she grabbed his hands with hers. Andru jumped, startled at the touch. His eyes drifted up to hers and they stared questioningly. "Thank you, truly."

"For Romulin's sister, I'd do anything."

Vi hoped it was true. Because she had the distinct feeling that she would be asking more of him in the coming days.

THE HOURS AND HER consciousness slipped between her fingers like unformed strands of magic for the rest of the day.

Jayme and Ellene stopped in at some point—either the first or second day, Vi couldn't quite remember. The conversation was kept light, mostly her friends expressing relief that she was all right. Vi could sense some tension from Jayme, mostly stemming from guilt over not being the one to protect her. But, to her credit, the woman knew it wasn't the time to dig into Vi about it. After spending so long speaking with Andru, Vi didn't want to rehash everything. She needed a day to think and the quiet space to do it in.

On the morning of the third day, Vi created that space thanks to Ginger. She told the cleric that she wanted a day to rest and the woman became her sworn guard. Since breakfast, not even one servant had come in. Vi waited until Ginger returned to deliver lunch, knowing she should have a few more hours of uninterrupted time afterward.

Vi sat upright in her bed, as tall as she could manage. The room was cool; winter had finally taken hold in the North. A light breeze tickled between her fingers before the heat of her magic flowing freely replaced the sensation.

"*Narro hath,*" she whispered.

The light was thinner than normal, faint and flickering like a candle burning the bottom of the wick. But it was enough to carve a hazy outline. Her glyphs hadn't been this weak since she first began.

Taavin stared at her for a long moment, hovering at the foot of her bed. His emerald eyes looked her up and down. Concern darkened his features.

"I'm fine," Vi said before he could speak.

"You don't look fine." He crossed to her bedside, shifting strands of magic unraveling and then re-condensing until he solidified at her left elbow. It was as if he was sitting on the mattress, half leaning over her. Vi stared up at him; pressed back against her pillows, there was nowhere she could go. She was pinned beneath his gaze. Instead of focusing on his eyes darting all over her, she focused on keeping her magic wrapped tightly around her fingers. *Should she have dressed in more than a simple sleeping gown before summoning him?* When had summoning him in her bedroom, rather than her study, become more natural? "What happened to your face?"

"Is it that bad?" She smiled tiredly. Ginger had removed the majority of the bandages that morning. "I haven't had the strength to look in a mirror yet."

"You're still beautiful, if that's what you're asking," he whispered.

A spark crackled in her chest and her magic seemed to feed on it. He grew brighter, more solid. For a brief moment, Vi could almost ignore the glyph swirling around her hand and focus solely on him.

"I bet you say that to all the princesses you have clandestine meetings with." She should've just said thank you. But Vi had to reach for the joke. If she didn't, that meant acknowledging the feeling that had flooded her whole body at his flattery.

"I'm afraid you're the only princess I meet with…" Taavin looked out the window. "The only person, really."

"Where are you, Taavin?" Vi looked at his hand on the bed, light dancing where there should be contact. If she tried to touch him, what would it feel like? Would he be warm like sunlight? Or icy, like the misty illusions Waterrunners made? Would he feel like anything at all? Fear of the last answer being no was what kept her from reaching out.

"I told you, I am in Risen."

"No, I don't mean that." Vi slowly shook her head. "Where are you? Where do you live? Is it hot or cold there? What do you see out your window?"

"*Ah.*" He made the sound of understanding, but said nothing for a long minute. Taavin stood, strolling over to the window—though Vi still wasn't sure if he could see through it. When he spoke, he didn't look at her. "I live at the top of the Archives of Yargen."

"Is that a place where they keep the history of the goddess?"

"All the history of this mortal realm." Taavin looked back to her. "Every record of the world's knowledge is kept here… Well, what can be found, at least."

"That sounds…" Her heart raced with excitement at the mere thought of it. "Beautiful."

"I've only seen it from the outside twice."

"Why?" Vi asked delicately.

"Why do you care?"

"I want to know you," she said simply, honestly. Since when had baring herself become natural around him? Perhaps it was her wounds making her too tired to care about pretense. "I want to know what your days are like. What you eat. What you see when you look out your window."

"I see… I see a view not unlike yours, actually," he said softly. "A city sprawling beneath me. Far enough away that it looks more like a painting than an actual home for living, breathing elfin. I see the terracotta spires of the gilded palace adjacent to the archives. I can see the harbor where Risen nearly runs into the sea… I can see the worn whitewashing of buildings hiding behind slatted wooden shutters that hang on rusty, weeping hinges."

"The way you describe it makes me feel like I can see it too," Vi whispered. She could envision those narrow cobblestone streets. The buildings packed too tightly together, like crooked teeth. But in her vision, her breath fogged the air, and snow lined the edges of walkways.

In her visions, it was Solarin she saw.

"I've spent a lifetime looking out that large window."

"So have I." Vi wished she could leave her bed and stand with him. She wished she'd summoned him not in her room, just once, so he could see the world beyond through her eyes... what little she had to show of it.

"You don't seem quite so trapped." He crossed back over, perching himself on the edge of her bed again.

"Then appearances are deceiving. I spend most of my days in these quarters... maybe out in the fortress to join Ellene for dinner. If I am on top of my studies and in everyone's general good graces, I may walk the city below. But never freely, never without an escort. That's the extent of my leash."

His gaze was hard, closed off. For the first time, she wished desperately to know what he was thinking—but lacked the bravery to ask.

"If you are so sequestered... how did you obtain such injuries?"

Vi swallowed. This was the real reason she'd summoned him. It wasn't to talk about windows or the worlds beyond. It wasn't to lay eyes on his tanned skin and emerald eyes.

"Someone tried to kill me. An *elfin'ra* tried to kill me," Vi hastily clarified before he could get a word in.

Taavin went very still. When he spoke, a protective edge limned his voice that Vi hadn't heard before. "Tell me." Vi obliged him—what little information there was. "They're moving quickly..." he murmured when she finished.

"He used *juth*..." Vi started and then abandoned the question. Luckily, Taavin picked up her meaning.

"As I said before, the elfin'ra are splintered from the elfin. They know Yargen's words, but twist them with Raspian's power—as well as use words of Raspian's own making."

"Lovely," Vi muttered. That explained the lightning Andru spoke of seeing before the man vanished. "There's something else."

"What?"

"He said he wanted 'the champion's blood for Lord Raspian.' What does that mean?"

Taavin stood and began to pace. The magic trailed through the air behind him, as though his very essence was unraveling. Vi's technique had improved with his tutelage, but she was struggling to catch up.

"Can you hold more still, please?" she asked. He stopped abruptly but did not face her. "Taavin, I need to know what I'm up against."

"The ritual you saw, with the man of red lightning, do you remember?"

How could she forget? "Yes."

"To perform that ritual, to bring back Lord Raspian to walk along this mortal plane, they need a sacrifice of Yargen."

"How do they get the sacrifice of a goddess?" Vi asked slowly. Suspicions were dawning on her even as she asked, but she wanted to leave no room for error.

"Ashes, from the flame if it is snuffed. The blood of the voice... or the champion." His eyes fell heavily on her. Vi swallowed hard. It was as if his words alone reignited pain in her ailing body.

"That's why, in my vision… the body on the altar in the bag…"

It was one of them. One of them had been gutted, bagged, and laid across an altar to resurrect an ancient evil.

"You must be careful, more than ever, Vi. Yes, in the vision there was a whole body and that would be the most… effective way." He grimaced at the word *effective*. "But given the strength they're already displaying, I have no doubt that all they need is blood from one of us to pull off the ritual."

"Should I start telling Ginger to burn my clerical rags?" Vi didn't want to begin keeping track of everywhere she spilled a drop of blood.

"No… It needs to be fresh blood spilled at the sacred site. Or blood captured by one of their ritual daggers so that it is kept in a specific stasis to be brought back for their ritual."

"That explains the dagger he was holding," Vi murmured, remembering the strange-looking weapon the man kept slashing at her with.

"They shouldn't even be able to create those weapons. It takes great power to craft them, ready them for collection of blood, and then keep the blood viable for ritual." Taavin shook his head grimly. "Yet another sign of how Raspian's power is growing while Yargen's dims."

"Dimming… The traveler said the flame will be fueled again, didn't she? That the champion holds the key." Taavin gave a small nod. "Taavin… I don't know anything about your flame. Even if I wanted to rekindle it… I wouldn't know where to begin."

"And that is what I hope the apexes of fate will show us."

"Do you have any new leads?"

"None that I haven't already told you." He sighed.

"The throne room… the dark room… and a temple with eye-owe?" Vi recalled.

"Just so. Do you have any new leads on them?" he asked hopefully.

"Unfortunately not…" Vi admitted. "Eye-owe keeps sticking with me, but I haven't been able to place it. I'm sorry. I'll do my best to find it, though."

Vi looked down at her hands: one rested in her lap, supporting the glyph, and the other rested at her side. A shimmering hand interrupted her thoughts. Delicate fingers rested on hers. Vi couldn't tell if her mind filled in the sensation she expected, or if he truly felt warm.

"You must be careful in your search, Vi. More than ever. The elfin'ra and their dark arts were locked away, but the barrier keeping them in exile vanished when the seal on Raspian's tomb was broken." Her eyes drifted up the embroidered sleeve of his coat to his face. "I am protected in Risen. I am the most guarded man on Meru in a city surrounded by a barrier of its own that's directly connected to the flame itself." Taavin leaned forward slightly, and Vi wondered if she just imagined it. His voice was deep, pained. "But you are an easy target—and they will continue to come for you."

Vi felt fear rising within her but forced herself to swallow it down. Jax had always told her she would be a target for enemies of Solaris. This was no different. She had been raised for this.

"Teach me how to protect myself," Vi demanded. "Teach me beyond anchoring the glyphs and basic principles. I want to use Lightspinning to fight." For a brief second, she was afraid he would reject her.

"I shall do my best to make myself available at every moment to be your tutor."

Vi let out a small sigh of relief, leaning back into her pillows but making no motion to pull her hands from under his silhouette of light. "Thank you."

"You're welcome." He glanced sideways. Then, speaking mostly to himself, said, "Here I am, willingly seeking you out after you've haunted me my whole life... I feel I should hate you for entrapping me once more."

"Do you?"

"No... The only scrap of hatred I can find in me now is for the elfin'ra who harmed you."

"Then what *do* you feel about me?" The question brought his eyes back to her. Taavin stared for a long moment and Vi held his gaze. Whatever he said would be fine. Her chest tightened. Whatever he said next wouldn't change anything for her— not their pursuit of the apexes, not his tutelage, not her heart.

"I don't know," he whispered.

"Good." Vi's voice had gone equally soft. "That makes two of us then."

He finally pulled his gaze from hers and Vi felt like a trance had been broken. Taavin looked down at the magic spinning around her fingers. She'd all but forgotten she was maintaining *narro hath* still. Now she stared into it, watching it curve and double-back on itself before spinning outward again.

"You should let the magic go, so you can recover."

"Or you can keep me company until I fall asleep." Vi shifted farther back into her pillows. The magic had been thin to begin with. Now it was nearly exhausted. It wouldn't be long until he was pulled from her again.

"That, I suppose I can do. I'm beginning to enjoy having some company in my solitary life. Even if it comes from the woman I can't escape."

"Maybe..." Vi whispered, "I'm glad you can't escape me."

Taavin gave her a small smile, one Vi returned. They stayed just as they were, his ghostly hand on hers. Looking at nothing, looking at everything, until Vi could no longer sustain the magic and she drifted quietly off into sleep.

EVEN THOUGH VI WAS only in bed on cleric's orders for three days, her tutors decided they did not want to "push her" right away.

A part of her was offended at the notion, but a larger part was relieved.

There was work to do.

"The more words you add, the more detailed the spell and its outcome," Taavin explained, perched on what had become his spot at the edge of her bed.

"The book outlines two words—the main and subordinate." Vi had one of the drawers of her dresser opened. Sehra's book was perched inside, the inner lip of the drawer holding open the page so her hands were free. "That's how it breaks up the chapters at least... So there's *narro*, and then *hath* is a sub-word underneath it."

"Yes, that's correct. There's a structure to the chants... The first word of every chant is the high-level discipline you're invoking." Taavin held up a finger.

"Such as healing, or deception, or destruction..." Vi said, to make sure she was following along.

"Just so. The second word is the classification within that discipline." He held up two fingers now. "Most chants will have at least two words. But sometimes there's a third—the clarification."

Vi lifted the book, flipping through the pages. She was becoming more familiar with the glyphs, her mind more accustomed to reading them. "I don't see—"

"They're there, likely not marked. Let me see." Taavin stood and looked down over her shoulder. "Go to *narro*... flip the page, again, again—no wait, you've gone too far, back one." Sometimes, it was a pain to be his hands in the physical world. "There—*loreth*."

"*Loreth*," Vi repeated, allowing the new word to settle on her. "To imprint a communication mark."

"Like this." Taavin pointed to the watch around her neck. Vi looked down. She was so familiar now with the hazy mark that hovered above it whenever she spoke to him that it barely registered any longer. "That was created with *loreth*; it is my unique communication mark."

"So that's why I can summon you, but you can't summon me."

"Unless you're at an apex." He took a step away and Vi fought a chill. She was growing familiar with how his magic registered as warmth. Especially when he was near.

"Right…" Their means of communication remained a noru in the room. Neither of them could offer an acceptable explanation for how she came to be in possession of his token. To some extent, Vi didn't want to try to figure it out. As curious as she was, doing so would remove the mystery—the magic—of it all.

"So you have your first high-level discipline word, then the secondary, then the clarification," Taavin continued.

"Would you ever have two clarifications?"

He shook his head. "At that point, the magic is shaped by intent. Take *halleth*, for example." *Halleth, to heal*, Vi filled in mentally. "*Ruta* is the sub-discipline of *halleth* for mending the flesh. But then there are clarifications beyond that—*sot* for inner wounds, and *toff* for outer. Let's say I were to heal that crooked bit in your nose that hasn't quite set right."

"There is no crooked bit in my nose." Vi's hand flew up to her face, gently feeling the bridge of her nose.

"Don't be self-conscious, I think it suits you." She narrowed her eyes at him, and Taavin had the audacity to have a laugh at her expense before continuing. "So if I wanted to heal that, I would use *halleth ruta sot*—" Taavin's voice had a soothing quality to it, his accent running words together in a way that was smoother than silk. "—and make sure my glyphs were crafted with the intent of repairing the tissue in that location."

"Understood—three words, and then intent beyond that." Just as she'd originally suspected. Lightspinning was not so different from the principles of elemental magic she'd been taught her whole life.

"Sometimes there's a fourth word."

"You're just making this difficult now." His mouth quirked up just slightly, as though he was not only amused by, but satisfied with, her accusation.

"It's the last word, I promise—even more rare than the clarification."

"Which is?"

"If you are particularly blessed, you'll be told a word from the Goddess—a word only for you that will give you the opportunity to enhance your spells, somehow. Again, it's different for every person, but individuals with a goddess-word know how to wield it."

"Have you received a word?" Vi asked delicately, hoping he'd answer.

"I've received multiple."

"Then you can hear the goddess through the flame?" Taavin's gaze went hard. Vi's heart raced. Perhaps she'd been wrong and even though the flame was weak, he could hear *something*?

"I am the voice. It is my duty to hear her and guide the people with her words."

"Yes, but—"

A knock interrupted them.

"Your highness?" Andru asked through the door.

Was it dinnertime already? She could hardly believe they'd been working that long.

Vi's eyes darted to Taavin and he gave a small nod. Vi stretched out her fingers and felt the tethers she'd summoned Taavin with unwind. Once she closed Sehra's book and slipped her dresser drawer closed, it was like he hadn't been there at all.

"Yes, Andru—" Vi opened the door and was assaulted with the aroma of steaming food "—thank you for joining me for dinner."

"Thank you for having me."

The servants were finishing setting the table in her main room. When she was no longer on bed rest, it became inappropriate for him to sit alone with her in her bedroom, so they had to find other means of communicating privately. Dinner seemed to be the easiest excuse. Jax had even praised her for making an effort to "win Andru over" while warning her to be careful in the same breath.

Vi had to fight back laughter the whole time during that conversation.

Navigating merely meeting with Andru made Vi appreciate her easy relationship with Taavin all the more… and underscore how necessary it was for her to keep him a secret. She couldn't imagine the look on her tutors' faces if they discovered she could summon a man to her room on a whim. Though thinking about it had her fighting a grin.

"How are you feeling?" he asked as the servants left.

"Better. I ache all over still." Vi rolled her shoulders as she crossed to the table. She couldn't help but notice a little bit of oil staining the wood where Jayme usually tended to her blade.

"Likewise." Andru hurried over despite the ache, to pull out her chair for her. Vi eased herself down, feeling the seat hit the back of her knees and assure her she wasn't going to land on the floor.

"Are your shoulders still giving you trouble?" Vi asked as he took up the seat to her right.

"They're much better. Ginger does good work."

"Doesn't she?" Vi helped herself to one of the large leaf pouches on a platter in the center of the table. When she opened it to reveal the rice and poultry mixture inside, a billow of steam hit her face and went right to her stomach, reminding her that she was actually quite hungry. "Speaking of work…"

"Yes, I've been doing my best to secure and review trade notices and communications." Andru followed Vi's lead, though he struggled more unwrapping the leaf pouch. "Which hasn't been entirely easy given my position here. But emissaries are arriving from the West for the solstice and I have found some information."

Vi ate quietly, listening intently as he continued.

"It seems there are rumors that goods are still being bought and traded from the Crescent Continent."

"Despite the trade ban?" Vi asked after washing down a particularly hasty bite with a gulp of water.

"Likely because of the trade ban. Nothing drives prices like scarcity and perceived rarity. It's making tokens from the Crescent Continent even more valuable in the West, according to one trader I spoke to." He paused, taking a sip from his own goblet. "Poor man, thought I was going to arrest him for selling illegal goods."

"Did you?"

"What? No." Andru looked at her, looked away, then looked back. "Even if I had the authority, do I strike you as someone who could apprehend anyone?"

Vi laughed at his apt self-assessment. "No, you don't..." And she liked him more for the fact. "So how are these goods getting here?"

"That's the question I had the hardest time answering. What we know is that it must be a network—people meeting on both sides, likely in neutral territories in the barrier islands. Nimble, well-guarded ships. Ever since official trade stopped, the barrier islands have become rife with pirate activity."

"Do we know who might be leading these networks?" She could already speculate that the elfin'ra may have smuggled himself on one of these illegal trading vessels. Perhaps he had allies Vi could uncover. Or, at the very least, she'd know how the red-eyed monsters were moving to report to Taavin.

"Forgive me, all I know is hearsay, suspicions, and rumors." He sighed, looking at his lap.

"Tell me," Vi commanded gently.

"Perhaps... the Le'Dans." Andru looked back up to her, gauging her reaction.

If he had been expecting her to be upset or offended by the notion, he was wrong. "It'd hardly surprise me."

The Le'Dans were one of the oldest families of the West, only rivaled by Vi's own lineage through her grandmother—the Ci'Dan family. They had warred across the ages in feuds that read as everything from thrilling adventures to tragic romances. But in modern times, the Le'Dans had become essential to the crown, holding the purse strings of the West through their jewelry empire and being an essential voice of confidence in the remnants of the Western Court.

Despite all that—no, *because* of it—Vi knew exactly what the Le'Dan family was: shrewd business people who never found themselves on the wrong end of a deal.

"There are rumors they're still getting fresh stock. They claim any Crescent jewels entering the market are from their vaults, but in reality... well..."

"People aren't convinced," Vi finished for him. He seemed uncomfortable at the notion of accusing one of the most powerful families in the Solaris Empire of illicit deeds. Vi couldn't exactly blame him.

"My father included."

"Oh?"

"He had me look into some things while I was in the Crossroads on the way here. Jayme and I stopped there as a halfway resting point." The Crossroads was at the center of the Solaris Empire—a large city housing the intersection of the two major roads that connected the major capitals of each of the Empire's four regions. "It was Romulin's idea that I should start with the Le'Dans, given their clout. So I went to investigate one of the Le'Dan stores for myself."

Andru had stopped looking at her as he spoke. The casual, calm nature he'd had when he'd first arrived vanished completely. This was the shifty-eyed man she'd met at the stables weeks ago. What she'd taken then as suspicious behavior, she now recognized as extreme discomfort.

"What is it?"

"I found nothing there." But he radiated too much anxiety for that to be true.

"There's more…" Vi pressed as gently as possible.

Andru looked at her through his upper lashes. She leveled her gaze at him. For as friendly as they were becoming, he was not exempt from her command, and she wasn't afraid to pull rank if necessary. She just hoped he'd tell her of his own volition instead.

"Your highness—"

"Let's not go back to formalities, Andru. At least not in private."

"Vi…" He was practically squirming with discomfort. She would have spared pity for him if she didn't so desperately want to know what he was hiding. "Does Jayme know the Le'Dan family?"

Vi sat a little straighter in her chair. "Why?"

"Well, when I went to investigate… I found her already there. I… I'm sorry. But I followed her."

"Go on." Her food was entirely forgotten.

"She went around back. There was someone from the store there, unloading boxes off a cart—a Southern woman, by the looks of her long blonde hair. They exchanged some words. Jayme handed something to her. The woman handed her a small satchel in return. And then they parted."

"Did you hear what they said?"

"No… I didn't want to get that close."

"Understandable. Thank you for telling me. I'm sure it was just a friend of hers." Vi smiled, hoping to put the matter, and Andru's clear worry, to rest.

Jayme had never spoken of the Le'Dan family. But Vi had never asked, either. In fact, she'd never inquired much about Jayme's journeys from south to north and back. It wasn't unreasonable to suspect she'd made some friends along the way—companions to share a table with in the Crossroads to make her travels less lonely.

"Well, I think that—"

The door burst open, interrupting her thought.

"Vi Solaris!" Ellene exclaimed, barging in without so much as a knock. "We have not seen you in—"

When Ellene and Jayme actually saw her, they froze mid-step. Both women looked from Vi to Andru, to the meal laid between them. Jayme, to her usual credit, kept her composure. Ellene, however, looked utterly shocked.

"We're not interrupting something, are we?" Jayme asked slowly.

Vi could practically see the incorrect assumptions tallying up in their minds and she burst out laughing. "No, no you're not."

Andru sat rigidly in his seat, looking between Vi and her friends, and then focusing on anything else in the room

"Are you sure? Because we could come back." A fox-like grin was creeping across Ellene's lips.

"Andru and I are not having some sort of clandestine affair under your noses." Vi snorted again with laughter at the notion. "Not in the slightest."

"Wait... *What?*" It seemed to have dawned on him all at once what the two were hinting at. "No. No we are not. Her highness is right. This was just dinner to... to go over things."

"And what were you 'going over'?" Ellene waggled her eyebrows as she sauntered over to the table and helped herself to one of the leaf-wrapped pouches.

Jayme continued to hover, looking between Vi and Andru. For one brief second, Vi was worried she'd somehow heard them discussing her. But she followed shortly behind Ellene, sitting at Vi's left and picking at some of the skewers from a nearby platter.

"Something I need to go over with both of you, so I'm glad you're here." Vi leaned back in her chair, food forgotten for now. "Someone is trying to kill me."

"More than the saddle?" Ellene asked through her food.

"Yes." Jayme was the one to answer.

"How do *you* know?" Ellene asked with a mix of shock and hurt.

"Jax told me, as part of the investigation, since I'm Vi's guard. He swore me and the other warriors to secrecy over it... He doesn't want word spreading that the Crown Princess could be in danger."

"You could've told me at least." Ellene huffed and pressed her back into her chair. "You know I wouldn't have told."

"She was just trying to do her job," Vi spoke for Jayme, hoping Ellene would listen. "It's a recent posting and all."

"Yes, yes, I get it." Despite what she said, Ellene still folded her arms over her chest, clearly frustrated. "Though, that explains why there were so many warriors around the bridge and halls leading to it... To think, I believed them that they were merely looking for any other structural weaknesses!" Ellene turned to Vi, the full depth of the situation dawning on her. "Are you all right?"

"I'm still here," Vi said gratefully.

"Speaking of being here..." Jayme turned to Andru. "You know something. That's what this dinner is about, isn't it?"

He gave a small nod, looking anywhere but the guard staring him down. "Yes... I saw him. The attacker."

"Tell me what happened," Jayme demanded. "I'm clearly missing something that wasn't imparted to Jax."

"I told Jax the truth," Vi insisted.

"Just not the whole truth." Her friend knew her too well.

"The man we're fighting isn't entirely... human."

"What is he then?" Ellene was a mix of horrified and excited. The latter worried Vi slightly.

"He's a monster, from far away—across the sea."

"Like the Crescent Continent?" Ellene asked.

"Like that... Yes." It was a miracle Andru had believed her. Vi didn't want to push her luck with her friends by going too far into the details. *How could she tell them the world was ending?* "Andru is helping me investigate how such a creature may have arrived."

"I'll ask my mother, see if she knows anything," Ellene offered. Vi was certain Sehra had already been consulted. But she knew her friend merely wanted to be of help. "And Darrus, he may have heard something in the city."

"Don't spread word of our investigation too far," Vi cautioned, thrumming her fingers on the table. "We don't want to alert my attacker to our movements… or Jax or my tutors—they'll tell us not to worry over such things and put me under even tighter scrutiny for fear I'll be reckless."

"But you *are* reckless," Jayme muttered.

Andru gave a snort of amusement at her final sentiment. Jayme and Ellene both turned their heads in shock at the noise. He coughed, looking away.

"That sounded like something Romulin would say, is all…" he mumbled.

"So we're all in on this, then," Jayme said finally, slowly, her eyes on Andru.

"Yes. All of us," Vi affirmed. They would see Andru was a friend soon enough. She had to have faith in that. "Thank you all for it."

"It's what we're here for." Ellene squeezed her hand. "And in the meantime, when we need a break, we can focus on winter solstice activities!"

Vi gave a small nod and smile. She felt marginally better getting everyone on the same page. Even if they might not be able to do much, having some path forward was enough, for now.

Tomorrow, and every day between now and the solstice, she would be working with Taavin.

If she was truly going to survive the threat of an elfin'ra, he would be the one to equip her with the knowledge on how to do it.

V I WAS WITH TAAVIN whenever she could find a moment alone, which was more often than she would have expected.

They spent time working on her technique. He guided her through finger placement, and how he formed the glyphs in his mind. Vi watched his hands, skilled and effortless, as they moved through the air. She listened to his words so carefully that they resonated in her sleep.

For the first time, it was as if she had a real magic tutor who knew what to do with her.

When Vi wasn't with Taavin, she spent the hours scouring her maps and notes for the location of "Eye-owe." And when that ultimately yielded no results, she sought out Andru, Ellene, Jayme, or all three. The ladies still expressed skepticism about Andru in private, but they made a good-faith effort to give him a decent chance. Vi took it as a good sign when Ellene felt comfortable enough to open up about the fact that she had *finally* agreed to dance with Darrus.

On the morning of the winter solstice, Vi woke early.

It was still dark when she got out of bed. The world had become chilly in the mornings and the floor was icy on her feet. But she knew it would warm significantly as soon as the sun crested the horizon.

Vi dressed in the clothes the tailors had made special for the occasion. Her Southern tailors had insisted that she should be in a dress befitting the Crown Princess on a ceremonial occasion. Vi knew she had to look the part, but she also enjoyed the winter solstice and wanted to be able to participate in the festivities. She'd won everyone over by pointing out that while it was important to pay homage to her Southern roots, she should also show respect to her Northern hosts.

What was crafted was a compromise of the two fashion sensibilities.

On top, she wore a golden shirt fitted to her torso with a tall, wide neck. The shirt split at her hips into a front and back piece that draped down to below her knees, reminiscent of the tabbards the Northern warriors wore. A tightly fitted white undershirt had long sleeves that reached a point over her hands, hooked to her middle fingers with small rings. Her legs were covered with a patchwork of lynx leather, tucked into knee-high boots.

Underneath it all, the watch was warm against her skin. She'd grown so accustomed to its weight that the idea of removing it now seemed virtually impossible. In her mind, it had become synonymous with the newfound confidence she was still working on building in her magic.

Around her wrist was a glowing glyph. Vi had learned how to make and sustain *narro hath* so well that she could now slide it from her fingers to her wrist like a bracelet, that way she could move her hand with it staying in place. Which was good for a morning like this, when she couldn't lose time.

"*Juth*," Taavin said from over her shoulder.

Vi paused, closing her eyes. She summoned the symbol in her mind, drawing every line with precision. When she opened them again, her hands continued to move through her hair, carefully weaving braids.

"*Calt*."

She repeated the process, summoning a new symbol to her mind. Taavin had stressed how summoning the glyphs needed to be second nature. Not only did she need to know them as they appeared in her book. But she needed to know how they changed, slightly, to adapt to her own internal voice—that was where mastery came from. Or so he claimed.

"*Mysst*," Taavin said from over her shoulder.

Vi paused, watching as circles formed and lines intersected them behind her eyelids. *Mysst, to craft.*

"That one you'll find useful…" Her eyes flicked up, looking at him in the mirror. He hovered in his otherworldly way, not quite solid, not quite ghostly, right at the edge of her closet. "We should focus there more. You can use it to make shields and weapons of light. Now that you have a better handle on *juth*, it's a logical progression."

"In theory," she corrected for him. Taavin arched his eyebrows. "I have a better handle on *juth in theory*. We haven't been able to do much practice…"

"Yes, well, you said you'd find a training ground for that soon."

"I'm trying," Vi mumbled, tying off a braid. Luckily he didn't press. Vi had a suspicion that Taavin didn't doubt how hard it was for her to concoct reasons to do anything in her structured life.

"What is it you're getting ready for?" Taavin's voice audibly shifted when he was no longer asking as her tutor but her friend.

"Today is the winter solstice. It's a big holiday here in Shaldan."

"What do you do?" He walked over to her side.

"It starts with a ritual to Yargen at dawn… then merriment—singing, dancing, performances, shopping—until the final ritual of the day at dusk."

"That sounds like heaven." Taavin's eyes fluttered closed as he spoke.

Vi's hands stilled, falling from her hair. She turned to look at him. The room was dim, a few candles her only light to see by. He radiated light that couldn't seem to touch her world. It didn't reflect off her mirror or the shine of her wooden walls.

It was as though he only existed in her mind.

"Do you like to dance?" he asked, opening his eyes again.

Vi looked quickly back to her mirror, pretending she hadn't been inspecting him in his moment of thoughtful longing. "I like it well enough, I suppose."

"Is it difficult?"

"You don't know how?" She turned back to him, surprised.

"I've never had a partner."

"You don't need a partner to dance." Vi laughed softly. "You can do it alone."

"No one has ever taught me." He shrugged.

"You've never felt so merry at the sound of music that your feet just moved on their own?" She was hardly one to talk. Vi was not one to be swept away by a beat. But it had happened once or twice.

"I have not had many reasons—until lately—to feel merry, Vi."

Until lately. The words stuck with her, shining like the light that surrounded him. Vi swallowed, facing him. They talked so much now, but it felt like even more was going unsaid. There was no logical explanation for the feeling, but it put a lump in her throat.

"Perhaps I can teach you some time?"

The tiniest of smiles crossed his mouth. His eyes were soft, tender almost. A welcome change from the hard-as-gemstones man she'd first met.

"I'd like that." There was a soft knock on her bedroom door. Vi looked between Taavin and the source of the noise. "You should go."

She should. But all she wanted to do was stay and teach a man made of light how to dance.

"I'll summon you tonight. It's quiet after the festivities. We can go over *mysst*," she whispered hastily.

"I'll be waiting."

Vi kept her eyes on his face as it disappeared. She felt the strands of light release from her fingers, knots of tension in her magic relaxing. He was gone, as though he'd never been there at all. And it was that impermanence that put an ache in her chest.

"Come in," Vi called, finishing up her braids as she emerged back into her bedroom. She was finding it easier and easier to switch back and forth from talking with Taavin to engaging with the rest of the world. It was a necessary skill to ensure he remained her secret.

"You look beautiful," Jax said from the doorway.

"Good thing my face healed, right?" Vi remarked, pausing to rub the bridge of her nose lightly. She wondered if it had set correctly.

Jax laughed, then had the decency to look guilty for it. "I meant your clothing, not your face."

"I told you I wasn't insane for wanting to go a little untraditional."

"By all standards… it's certainly something no one would dare call traditional," he appraised. "But it's a very nice merger of North and South." The statement was punctuated with a yawn.

"Too early for you?" Vi grinned. "It's not much earlier than we used to get up for our magic lessons."

"Yes, well, we haven't had those in some time thanks to Sehra stealing you from me for lessons." Jax glanced at the window. "Speaking of Sehra, I believe I saw her headed down."

"Is it that late already?" Vi jumped from her seat.

"Not late, perfectly on time."

They walked down together through the tree fortress, across the same pathways and passages Vi had traversed more than a week ago to get to the Mother Tree. The barrier she had to scale was completely gone. In its place were pathways of fresh grass lined by woven roots, and patches of flowers nursed to bloom by the tender hands of a Groundbreaker. As far as Vi could tell, there was no sign or suspicion of her earlier trespass.

Jayme was waiting for them on the outer edge.

"Good morning, princess." She gave a small bow of her head. Even in her nicest dress clothes, attending a sacred event, her sword was still strapped to her hip.

"Good morning." Vi ignored decorum and pulled her in for a close hug. "And happy solstice." She felt the woman relax in her arms.

"Happy solstice to you as well." Jayme gave her a pat on the back.

"This is your first time, right?" Vi linked arms with her friend, walking toward the tree.

"Yes, I usually stay in the capital or go home over winters."

"How is your father doing?" Vi asked delicately. The opportunity to broach the topic of Jayme's family wasn't frequently afforded; speaking about them upset Jayme terribly, and while Vi had no desire to trouble her, she wanted to make plain that she cared. "Have you heard word since arriving?"

"Mother says he's well."

"I'm glad to hear it." Over the years, it had come out that Jayme's father was ailing... some constant, chronic problem. But Vi didn't know any further details. The only solace Vi took was that he had grown sick long before the White Death made landfall. So there was no suspicion of the deadly plague being the cause of his illness.

Her father's sickness... Friends made on the road... Her ambition to become a guard... It suddenly struck Vi just how little she actually knew about her friend. There was the same sickening feeling that accompanied the realization about Andru's knowledge of Romulin.

"Happy solstice!" Ellene ran over from her mother's side, throwing her arms around them both and interrupting Vi's thoughts before they could run away from her. They echoed the sentiment back. "I thought you were going to be so late you'd miss it."

"The sky is barely turning colors."

"Yes well, we need to—"

"Ellene, your place," Sehra called over to her daughter.

With that, the rest of the room fell into their places as well.

Sehra and her wife, Za, stood before the statue of Dia and the Mother, Ellene sandwiched between them. There was a ring of men and women around them, and Vi stood with them. She recognized some of the others in her circle like dignitaries, nobles, and even a Crone of the Sun. Vi tried to peer under the woman's over-sized cowl, but could only see the lower half of her face, as was customary. It was rare to see crones in the North... perhaps she'd come with the same caravan as the old woman in the market.

Behind them, around the edge of the room, was everyone else. Still a small group, so mostly important people in Northern society and to Sehra. Of them, Vi only recognized three—Jax, Jayme, and Andru. Quite a few leaders from the outer townships of Shaldan had come to Soricium this year, it seemed, so the usual attendees from the fortress had been edged out.

Clearing her throat, Ellene stepped forward.

"The world was young," she began, her voice wavering initially before she caught her stride. "Young enough that only the Mother Tree which stands here now, oldest in the land, is the only one who can recall the hours. This land was dark, absent of the sun's light.

"Then, a star fell.

"The star was caught in the boughs of the Mother Tree. As the branches swayed and shook, the star was jostled, collecting the tree's life energy on the way down to earth. This energy—part godly, part mortal—became the young Dia when it reached the earth. Her skin was made of the bark of the tree and her hair shone with the stardust she brought with her from the heavens.

"The Mother saw this falling star, and the holy light that radiated in her, and said, 'Take this axe, my child, and by its blade, carve a new society in my name. Teach its people the ways long forgotten in this land of night. Use the magic within it to guard and guide them.'"

Ellene stepped back, and Sehra stepped forward.

"Dia did as the mother asked," the Chieftain continued. "She guarded and guided the people to prosperity. And when the end of her life drew near, she returned to the Tree and asked the Mother for one more gift—an heir.

"Yargen told Dia that the power lived in her. So Dia cleaved a seed from the Mother Tree and consumed it. In nine months' time, she gave birth to an heir that carried on a part of her light."

Vi's eyes drifted to Ellene as Sehra spoke. She'd heard the story many times before. But every time, at this part, Vi couldn't help but wonder as to the exact logistics—a mystery she'd likely never have the answer to.

But she believed it. Because she also had powers supposedly from the Mother, was visited by a man made of light, and was hunted by a red-eyed assassin who worshiped the godly incarnation of evil itself. Was it really so hard to believe that a woman could get pregnant by a magic tree?

"We, descendants of Dia, remain steadfast in our mission to protect our people.

"We honor the old ways.

"And we still have not lost the command of her light to guide us through dark times."

Sehra raised her hand and Vi watched closely. Every time she'd seen this ritual before, she'd missed it. A small sigh escaped Sehra's lips, one Vi knew to be the sound "*durroe.*"

It was true what Sehra had said, that in time she had learned the words to the point of hardly needing to speak them. It was an illusion, nothing more, but the usual *oohs* and *ahhs* from those gathered showed that they saw it as the Mother's pure blessings.

The ball of light Vi had stared at for hours on end filled Sehra's palm. Sehra turned to the statue, and placed it in the Mother's outstretched hand. It stayed there after she took her hand away, and Vi knew it would remain for the better part of the day before fading with sunset.

When she was younger, she too thought it was the Mother's blessings fueling the orb. Now, she knew it was nothing more than a spell and the Chieftain's own power.

Vi honestly couldn't decide which was more impressive.

"On this day, as we prepare to endure the longest night of the year, and go the longest stretch without seeing the Mother sun, Yargen's visible force on our world, we pray she will watch over us from her heavenly throne." Vi could've sworn she saw Sehra's eyes flick in her direction. "We are those who keep Dia's light alive."

28

V I HAD A MUG of steaming cider and couldn't feel more content. She'd needed a day of merriment and relaxation, and that's precisely what the solstice provided.

Music lofted through the air near midday. The bands had been playing non-stop after the noru races had concluded in the morning, immediately following the rituals. The solstice festivities were so large this year that the dancing alone had sprawled across three separate clearings in the city—one Vi suspected was made by some determined Groundbreakers to have their own dance floor when everything else was full.

Everything muddled together like the spices in her drink. It was impossible to focus on any one singular thing—but she didn't want to anyway. The sum of all the parts was too wonderful to try to separate them. Vi wanted to take in everything, as much as she could. This would be her last solstice to enjoy in the North and she was awash with nostalgia, and regret over the worry that she had never really spent long enough enjoying it before.

"How long does this go on?" Jayme asked from her side. They sat on a raised platform of stairs with Andru, others escaping the dancing, and those merely enjoying the merriment. Though none sat too closely. It was the invisible force field of nobility keeping others at bay. With an elfin'ra on the loose, for once Vi wasn't irritated by the imposed isolation.

"They celebrate as long as the sun is in the sky, so the Mother can see joyous appreciation for her goodness before she settles in for her long sleep. When the sun is gone, there will be one more ritual and then everyone braces for the long night."

"Braces? Braces for what? Is there some kind of ritual combat in honor of the Father?"

"No. Braces as in goes to sleep." Vi laughed.

"You could've just said that, you know." Jayme shook her head, exasperated, but a smile spread across her cheeks. "The drama of the ritual from earlier has you swept up."

"Perhaps." Vi took another sip of her drink, savoring the way the flavors drifted over her tongue before burning down her throat due to heat in both temperature and spice. There was a lot of drama Vi was wrapped up in, way more than Jayme would likely ever understand. "Isn't that part of the enjoyment, though? Getting lost in something that seems as if it should be impossible?"

Impossible... like a man made of light. A smile fought its way onto Vi's face at the thought.

"Well, if that isn't a *romantic* notion." Jayme gave her a sidelong look, one Vi ignored. The last thing she wanted to do was give Jayme any suspicions about Taavin.

"She certainly seems lost in romance," Andru said from their side, nodding at Ellene and Darrus as he sipped from his mug.

"That's the truth. This whole place could burn down and I don't think she'd see anyone but him."

Jayme snorted in amusement. "Us, maybe? She might try to save us from the fire."

"*Maybe.*" Vi stressed the word to the point they broke into laughter. She turned to Andru. Something about the time that had passed bringing them closer, the cool day clearing her head, or the warm cider sitting in her belly, had made her comfortable enough to dare asking a personal question. "Has a lady caught your eye back home, Andru?"

He sputtered and coughed, cider going everywhere at the question. Vi and Jayme fought laughter at his expense as he set his mug aside, trying to wipe it off the front of his shirt.

"Me? A lady? No..." he mumbled, glancing at them, then back to his shirt. Vi tilted her head slightly, trying to see his face. There was something there... something she couldn't quite put her finger on.

"But—"

"My father is adamant that I make a good match." He grew still, maybe preternaturally so. Vi had lost count of the times Andru's demeanor brought to mind helpless prey caught in the crosshairs of a predator. She couldn't hear the words that echoed in his mind, but she could see his eyes were no longer fixated on the present. He'd said his father was an ass, so Vi could only imagine how *that* conversation went.

She reached out a hand, resting it lightly on his. Andru stiffened at the touch, and they made eye contact. She held it for a long moment.

"I'm sure I'll be the same," Vi whispered softly. "I'll have a good match made for me, too." A match she'd have little say in.

"Your parents certainly defied those expectations," Jayme mumbled. Vi opened her mouth to reply, but it was Andru who beat her to the words.

"Prince Romulin has said that's precisely why they—Vi especially—are expected to make smart matches. A commoner rising to marry the Crown Prince as Empress Vhalla did is not something we can come to expect often."

"And here I thought they'd set a precedent." Jayme took a sip of her cider.

"They had unusual circumstances leading to their being crowned." Vi sighed softly. There had been the assassination of her grandfather, the uprising of the Mad King, the final war of the Crystal Caverns before the caverns went dormant—.

The Crystal Caverns going dormant. Vi sat straighter. Taavin had said the barriers on Raspian and his followers had been broken about eighteen years ago, which corresponded with the end of the Mad King's rule and his use of the power from the caverns. Could that have been the barrier?

Vi fought the urge to race back to her room and summon him, instead taking another lingering sip of her drink.

"Romulin says much the same," Andru said, ignorant to Vi's thoughts. "He thinks Vi will be married to a prince of the East and he a princess of the West."

"Don't you mean, *Prince* Romulin?" Jayme leaned forward slightly. "You're always going on about what the prince does and doesn't say. Are you sure you report to the Senate and not to him?"

Andru turned scarlet. "I-I am merely fortunate enough to know his highness and think he is very wise."

"I agree with you, Andru," Vi said over the top of her mug. Jayme had connected something she'd overlooked. Something Vi was now incredibly curious about. But much like her other revelation about the caverns, this was neither the time nor place. "He gives me excellent counsel, and I am looking forward to getting such wisdom in person when I go home." Along with knowing him better in every other way.

"Home..." Jayme repeated thoughtfully. "Vi, may I ask you something?"

"You know you can ask me anything."

"Do you really want to go south?" Vi frowned, turning to face her friend. Jayme took a sip, clearly mulling over her words with the cider. "You did say I could ask anything."

"It's fine you asked." Vi didn't want Jayme to feel like she couldn't be honest. "I'm merely wondering where that question comes from... Have I done something to make it seem like I don't appreciate the South?"

She glanced over at Andru. Even if he'd become her ally... did she have to worry about matters like this being repeated to his father? Jayme clearly didn't think so, as she continued the line of questioning.

"Nothing of the sort. But if I'm honest, you haven't done anything to make me think you have a deep love for it, either. You've lived here your whole life, you know this as home... do you really want to leave it?"

"I expected this sort of questioning from Southerners, but not from you." Vi had been bracing herself for it, preparing herself, but she hadn't thought it'd come so soon.

"A good thing to expect," Andru murmured.

"I'm just curious, princess," Jayme insisted. "I didn't mean any offense."

"I know, I know. I'm sorry if I sounded curt." Vi sighed.

"Answer honestly now, princess," Andru advised. "You may not have a chance when we return home." He *was* on her side—she was sure of it.

Vi searched for an answer to the question—an *honest* answer. Everything she could think of to say sounded as though she was channeling her best public princess face. But they were right. This might be the only opportunity she had to answer as just Vi—not the princess, not the heir, but Vi Solaris.

"Home is a funny thing..." she said, finally. "I don't really know where home is or what it will look like. I have dreams, ideas, but nothing concrete."

"But it's not here?"

"Sehra has been... kind, most of the other Northerners as well... All right, hit or miss sometimes with them—not that I blame them, given how recently the war was, all things considered... But overall, yes, they've been kind. And Ellene is like the sister I never had." Vi's eyes landed on the girl in question. She was laughing, full-bellied and head tilted back, as Darrus spun her in time to the music. "But Ellene is the only one who could make this feel like home. Everyone else has always maintained a level of distance; they see me as Southern. I don't look like them, or talk like them, and trying to would be nothing short of offensive. I know that without my tutors telling me as much.

"But I know the South won't feel like home either, if I'm honest. I think it'll be the closest thing—because my real family is there. I'll finally live with them, come to truly know them, for better or worse. And if family isn't home, then what is?"

"You're right, family is important," Jayme said. There was something almost wistful in her tone. "Perhaps the *only* thing that's important."

"Agreed." Vi stood, ending the conversation. She didn't want to talk about their families, or philosophical homes, or worry about what it would be like when she returned south. She wanted to try to enjoy what little time she had left. Her life was already changing faster than she could fully comprehend. There was work to be done tomorrow, but today she could just enjoy herself. "Want to dance, or mill about the market stalls? Or are you still too sensitive after your last cheese failure?"

Jayme chuckled and took a long drink of her cider, downing what remained in one gulp. "I think my constitution has improved enough. Walking a bit sounds lovely."

"Are you coming, Andru?" Vi asked.

"I think I'll stay here, just watch. I like being out of the crowds."

"Sure thing. We'll get you another cider before we come back." Vi gave him a smile, one that was returned, before walking away.

Just as they started down the wide steps toward the ground together, a scream shattered the festivities.

29

A MAN RAN INTO THE square, crazed and wailing. Behind him raced three others in the same terrifying, long-beaked masks Vi had seen Darrus wearing the night she'd escaped to the ruins.

The diseased man's head drifted back and forth, mouth slightly parted. It had that same sickening sway that the sick noru had possessed, as though the tendons in his neck had gone slack and the pain of the awkward movement wasn't even registering to him. His eyes were glossed over, completely white, shining red lines pulsing outward from their centers. His skin around the angry veins of magic had turned hard and glossy, almost like a pale stone was protruding from his dark flesh. The outline of the diseased tissue was straining against the healthy skin, cracking and opening into sores that oozed globs of white.

"No one touch him!" one of the men wearing the plague masks commanded.

The oozing man looked around, ready to dart again. Sehra stepped forward from the crowd. With a raise of her hand, four walls of stone bars imprisoned him. He immediately darted against them, straining madly against his prison.

Vi swallowed hard, trying to push back the first vision of her father and the man in the cage. For all she wanted to look away, this was not another vision. This was not her father in a distant land before a foreign queen. This was not an end of days, dangerously removed from her here and now.

These were the people she was responsible for and the disease that was killing them slowly.

"There's another round of outbreaks flaring up!" one of the women lifted her plague mask to shout. "Should anyone feel ill or notice any strange sores, please immediately report to the clerics at the infirmary."

"I would like to recommend everyone return home and regroup with their families," Sehra announced. "In the interest of public health, we will end the festivities early. Please listen to all instructions from the clerics and thoroughly check yourselves for any signs of the disease."

There was murmuring and for a brief moment it sounded as if there was going to be dissent at the idea. Then, a scream. All eyes jerked in the direction of a woman.

She held out her arm, scratching at something. Scratching to the point of drawing blood. From where Vi stood, she could only see healthy skin. But perhaps there was something there. Or perhaps panic made people mad.

"I think I have it. I think I have it!" she wailed.

Then, someone else. "Wait, is this one? My skin feels tough here... I think I have it too!"

The man in the stone cage gave a guttural growl, gripping the bars and snarling like an animal. Vi knew what he was going to do next, but that didn't stop the horror at seeing him pull his head back and smash it into the stone. It was the same as the noru, the same as the sick man the queen of the Crescent Continent had shown her father.

"We should go back to the fortress." Jayme was close now, a hand on the hilt of her sword. Vi realized that chaos was beginning to break out.

"You're right, let's get Ellene." They began trying to weave through the crowd as quickly as possible.

"Please stay calm and return to your homes," Sehra was shouting. "The clerics can see you all individually there."

"You!" A man Vi had never seen before darted in front of her. His face was twisted in rage, spittle flying from his lips. "Crown Princess Solaris," he sneered.

"I would advise you to step back, sir," Jayme cautioned, taking a small step forward. She didn't have her sword drawn, but her grip had certainly tightened on its hilt.

"What are *you* doing?" The man ignored Jayme and kept his eyes on Vi. His shouting was starting to gain attention.

"I—"

He wasn't interested in whatever answer she could come up with. "You came, destroyed our home, dragged us through the mud, then told us our lives would be better. But all the Empire has brought Shaldan is disease and heartbreak."

Vi opened her mouth to speak, but no words came out. What should she say? What *could* she say? She certainly hadn't done anything to try to stop the White Death or its spread. Even if she had wanted to, she wasn't Darrus. She couldn't go and work in the infirmary... she had a role to fill as the heir.

And for the very first time, Vi wondered if that was the role she *should* fill. If her mission was to do what was best for her Empire, then she should let nothing, not even her throne, get in the way of that... right? It was an answer she didn't have time to come up with as the brief moment of introspection was quickly interrupted.

"What will Solaris do?" he demanded again. "All I see are *our* clerics, *our* blood on the ground, *our* people in danger. Is Solaris just leaving us to die?"

"Is help coming from the Empire? Or are we alone?" Another woman stepped forward, emboldened by the man's tirade.

"The White Death is affecting everyone—the South, East, West, and North. It is a plague on us all. My father has already left for the Crescent Continent," Vi said quickly. She cleared her throat, trying to dictate her words as her tutors had instructed, putting on her best Empress voice. "He has gone in search of a cure that—"

"They say the disease itself comes from the Crescent Continent," another woman spoke. Vi turned, surprised to see the old Western woman she had purchased spices from. Her beady black eyes bored into Vi's soul. "He will meet his demise on that foreign land. If he has gone into those pirate-infested waters, into the territory of Adela, she will kill him as she killed his grandfather before him. The Emperor Solaris is already dead."

"Hold your tongue," Vi whispered. There was a dangerous note to her voice, one she had never heard herself make before. "Careful, lest someone hear your words for the treason they are."

"We ask questions and it's treason?" The first man balked, talking even louder. "This is how Solaris treats us!"

"No, that's not what I—" Vi tried to say quickly but was interrupted.

"That's enough," Sehra said quietly. She didn't shout, didn't need to. "Focus on the wounds yet bleeding before you go looking for old scars to tear open." She narrowed her eyes at the man. Vi watched how, with a look, Sehra suddenly made herself seem twice her size and the man half of his.

"Chieftain, I meant no disrespect." He lowered his eyes, shoulders curling forward slightly.

"Is that so? Certainly an odd way of showing it. You disrespect me, as I told everyone to leave, and you disrespect my honored guest, the Crown Princess." Sehra's eyes swung to them as the others scattered. Vi looked for the Western woman, but she was already gone. All of the transgressions against her family tonight would have to be forgiven, it seemed. Forgiven, maybe, but not forgotten. "I told everyone to leave, and that includes you three."

Vi was suddenly aware Andru had materialized at her left. For all his awkwardness, he was proving himself a true friend time and again.

"We're gathering Ellene and then going back to the fortress," Jayme reported stiffly.

Sehra gave a small nod of approval. "No more distractions."

This time, no one stopped them getting to Ellene. She was engaged in a heated conversation with Darrus, arms flailing, voice strained to a barely audible pitch.

"Ellene, we need go back." Vi grabbed the girl's elbow.

Ellene jerked away without even looking at them, focusing on the man she'd been dancing with all night. "Not without Darrus, he's not talking sense."

"I have to go to the infirmary, Elle," he said gently.

"This is getting serious!" Ellene grabbed his hands, tears welling in her eyes. Vi resisted the urge to correct her that it had been serious for some time. Darrus was the only one among them who had really done something. "Come, stay in the fortress— it's safer there, with us. Let other clerics do the work, they don't need you. You're not even fully trained yet."

"Ellene, I can't." Darrus pulled her in tightly. "I have to help our people. New clerics just arrived with medicine from the West today. They have more insights. We're going to beat this."

Vi found herself admiring Darrus once more. He was composed and certain of himself when she could barely fend off the panicked ravings of one of her subjects. He continued to fearlessly step up, putting his life in danger, for the sake of his people—her people, her Empire.

What kind of a leader did that make her if she needed others to stand in for her at every turn? What could she be doing for her people?

Finding the apexes of fate was a way to stop this. If they held the knowledge of how to stop Raspian, it would stop the White Death, too.

"Don't... Please, don't..." Ellene gripped at him so tightly that Vi was certain she left bruises. He lightly kissed the top of her head through the young woman's spiral curls, then looked to Jayme and Vi.

"Take her and keep her safe. Do *not* let her come after me."

Vi gave a short nod, overlooked the fact that a commoner had technically just issued an order to her—sometimes etiquette was best ignored, particularly in the face of what was very obviously young love—and pulled Ellene into her arms. "We have to go now."

"No, don't take me!" Ellene twisted. "I'm going with him."

"Your mother asked us to take you." Jayme got a grip on Ellene's other arm.

"*Ellene.*" Za's voice was a sharp and searing blade to the heart of her daughter's contention. "Back to the fortress. Now."

Ellene slumped against Vi and let herself be shepherded away.

More and more people were beginning to panic. There was wailing, crying, shouting, and accusations thrown their way whenever someone bold enough got a good look at Vi walking in their midst.

The four of them navigated through it, hastening back to the fortress to wait out what already truly felt like the longest night of the year.

30

THEY SAT AROUND A small table in the back corner of one of the kitchens. Between each of their hands was a mug of warm tea; a plate of food steamed in front of them, but none of them could muster the will to eat.

After the events of the day, Vi certainly wasn't hungry.

"He's going to die," Ellene mumbled grimly.

"You don't know that."

"He's going to get sick with the White Death, and die."

"No one knows how it's transferred," Jayme started.

"Part of what makes it so terrifying," Andru interjected under his breath.

Vi was silent. The old Western woman was still in her mind. She'd said the White Death came from the Crescent Continent. If Vi's theories on the crystal caverns were true, then the plague's origins were far more homegrown.

But the solution might lie across the sea, nonetheless... with a man she knew through strands of light. What would she ask Taavin first? She worked to sift through the chaos of the day to find an answer.

"I saw houses in the capital, families who lived together in one room—five people—poor folk who couldn't afford any clerical help." Jayme continued to try to cheer up Ellene. "Mostly left to fend for themselves... One fell ill, but the other four survived. I'm no cleric myself, but I don't think it's transferred by mere proximity, like autumn fever."

"He'll catch it. If anyone will catch it from proximity, it'll be him." Ellene wasn't hearing them. She wasn't seeing them either. She stared off at nothing, wallowing in her own doubt.

Vi wrested herself from her thoughts and rested a hand on her friend's shoulder. "Listen to Jayme."

"He's going to be taken by the illness just like my grandmother!" Ellene pushed her hand aside and crumpled into tears. Jayme and Vi shared a look.

The death of the last chieftain had been particularly hard for the North. A people who were still relatively new to the Empire, still stinging from the loss of their sovereignty, had their leader called to a foreign land to see if her rare magic could assist in finding a cure for the White Death. Sehra's mother, Ellene's grandmother, had never returned from that journey. She'd succumbed to the disease and her body was burned in Norin, her last rites given by foreign people in a foreign land.

"Darrus is strong," Vi attempted. "He's much younger than—"

"My grandmother was not that old." Ellene's head jerked up, tears streaming down her cheeks. "And she was one of the strongest chieftains to ever live."

"You poor lot, stuck in here on the night of solstice." Renna made a clicking noise with her tongue as she shook her head in disapproval. "You should've been dancing the dusk away, filling your stomachs with good food, filling your souls with the final rites of the evening, and then drifting to sleep as the wonders of the day filled your mind."

"Unfortunately a plague doesn't wait for festivities to be over." Vi sighed, still rubbing Ellene's back with an open palm as the girl sniffed softly.

"It does not. But at the very least, would you three like a story? Seems a shame to head to bed without even hearing one of the old tales around a fire. What good is the solstice if you don't?"

"I wouldn't mind." Jayme was the first to seize the opportunity.

Vi recognized as well what Renna was trying to do for Ellene. The kitchens were large, but Renna had been in ear-shot since the moment they'd sat down. Moreover, there wasn't much activity at this time of night, so there hadn't been much noise to drown out their words.

"I'd like that as well. I don't think you've told us stories since we were kids, sneaking in for whatever cookies or cakes you had baked for the day."

"Well, speaking of…" Renna glanced over her shoulder. "We made a whole batch of candied nut rolls for the festival that no one has touched thanks to all this madness. If you finish your dinners, I could cut you each a hefty slice and I'll tell you one story before bed." She looked right to Ellene. "Would you like that?"

Ellene gave a small sniff and, for a brief second, Vi was afraid she would protest that she was far too old for sweets and fireside stories before bed. They all were. But for one night, retreating into the comforting ignorance of childhood wouldn't harm any of them.

"I think I would," Ellene said finally.

"Then finish your meals and I'll have warm sticky sweets ready when you're done."

"Sticky sweets for finishing a meal; I feel like a child again," Andru murmured.

"There are worse feelings," Vi said quickly, with a small nod toward Ellene. Understanding dawned on Andru's face, and something like gratitude. Vi was starting to understand how this shy, awkward man's mind worked—and how often it missed what seemed like obvious social cues. Renna was just trying to help, and one slice of nut roll would not turn any of them into a toddler again. And, if Vi was honest with herself, her mouth was already watering at the thought.

Renna was good to her word. The wiry woman had a plate waiting for each of them when they arranged themselves around the giant stone hearth of the kitchen. In proper fashion, they each sat on the floor, the woman easing herself into a stool she'd pulled over.

"When was the last time we did this?" Vi asked with a small laugh and nudge to Ellene's shoulder. "Seven? Ten?"

"It's been so long I can't remember." She stared at her nut roll and inhaled through her nose. "It smells just like I remember, though."

"Sounds like you had a nice childhood," Jayme said softly.

Vi resisted the debate that would follow any kind of correction. Her childhood hadn't been bad... but nice? Nice was living with your family, knowing your sibling, and not growing up as the Empire's trading chip.

But there were layers to Jayme's statement, ones Vi may not have considered before Andru revealed her clandestine meeting in the Crossroads. What had her childhood been like? She knew Jayme had become the official courier almost immediately after enlisting. How did a fourteen-year-old manage that? It was something Vi hadn't really considered, but the older she got, the more she wondered at the logistics that had lined up to make such a prestigious honor of delivering Imperial letters fall on a young girl's shoulders.

Just how well did she really know her friend?

"What story would you like to hear?" Renna asked.

"I have no preference," Jayme said, louder, as if to speak over the echo of the words she'd uttered under her breath. "They'll all be new to me."

"Something romantic," Ellene eagerly chirped. Vi didn't know if returning her mind to romance was the best course.

"Something happy," Vi suggested hastily.

"Something romantic and happy..." Renna leaned back in her chair. "How about the creation of the reservoir?"

The reservoir was a large freshwater lake to the south east of Soricium. It was said that its underground tunnels fed most of the springs throughout the jungles. And, if that were true, it made it not only the largest source of freshwater on the continent, but also the primary water source for the people of Shaldan.

"The one with Dia and Holin?" Ellene asked eagerly. "Yes, that one, tell that one!"

Renna chuckled. "Very well, if my little chieftain-to-be commands it...

"Long ago, as Shaldan and its people grew under the care of Dia, so too did their needs. No longer could they collect water from when the skies opened, or rely on small trickles through the jungles. Something far more substantial was needed.

"'Cut a layer beneath the earth,' a young man suggest—"

"Holin!" Ellene said through a particularly large bite of her sweet roll.

"Yes, Holin." Renna smiled brightly at Ellene's ever improving mood. "He suggested such to Dia—that if she could use her axe to cut not just the earth above the ground as trees, and plants, but the earth below, that water would gather there in a mighty basin for all to utilize..."

Vi hadn't heard the tale in some time, and she found herself as entranced as her friends by Renna's storytelling. Andru seemed to be getting particularly into the way the weathered woman spun the tale as he inched forward, hanging on every word, nut roll forgotten.

It was a story of love being enough of a reason to master a power none had seen before, a story of triumph, full of such fantastical embellishments that even though Renna presented it all as fact, Vi was certain very little was actually true.

"... and while it was aptly called the reservoir, even then, a new name was eventually given—Lake Io, named after Dia and Holin's first daughter. Some even still call it that name, in honor of our first chieftain."

"What?" Vi sat straighter. "What did you just say it was called?"

"You've heard it before." Ellene tilted her head, clearly not understanding what had Vi so worked up.

"I know, I must've... But on all my maps... It's just 'the reservoir'..."

"Perhaps because your maps have been made by the South." There was a cool edge to Renna's tone. One Vi chose to ignore. "Lake Io is how most of the old folk will refer to it."

"How is it spelled?"

"I-O."

Vi had seen it before on her maps.

But she had always thought it was intended to be some kind of acronym, one she'd never understood—one she'd always assumed meant *reservoir* in the old language of the North. If she had tried to pronounce it as a word, it was always I-*ooh* in her mind, nothing like how Renna or Ellene said it.

Io.

Pronounced *eye-owe*.

Just as Taavin had said—Lake Io was an apex of fate.

Vi shot upright. She had to tell him she'd pieced together his clues. "I have to go."

"What's wrong?" Jayme asked.

"Have I done something to offend?" Renna was visibly nervous as Vi passed.

"No, no," Vi said hastily. She gave the woman a small nod—a huge sign of Imperial deference, as far as etiquette was concerned. "You've done me a great service. I need to consult my maps. They're not marked properly and I must go fix that."

"Don't try to think through it," Ellene said through a mouth of food to Renna. She'd cleaned her plate, so Vi could only assume she was starting in on her half-finished roll. At least someone would eat it. "She gets like this about her maps sometimes. I'm sure she needs to correctly label every one."

Vi let them think what they wanted; all she needed was to get back to her room.

Her uncle appeared in the doorway, stopping her in her tracks. He had a serious look about him, the look that usually heralded a scolding. But he said nothing, simply stared.

"Excuse me, uncle, I need to go do something." Vi stepped around him, and he just watched her go, shoulders sagging. There was a glint to his eyes, a shining wetness that was strange to see. He wasn't one for emotion, but after helping Sehra with the outbreak, Vi couldn't blame him for reaching a deeper-than-usual level of physical and mental exhaustion. Her heart had contorted as well for those suffering.

"I need to speak with you, Vi." He cleared his throat, forcing out the words.

"Not now, uncle." Vi was starting up the stairs, taking them with her long legs two at a time.

"Vi..."

"This is important," she called over her shoulder. He still hadn't moved from that partly hunched, limp-armed position. "Tell me tomorrow morning!"

He opened his mouth, but no sound came out, and Vi rushed off. She wondered briefly just what he needed to say, and what had him in such a state. But whatever it was could keep.

Right now, she had to get back to her room, chart the best course to get to Lake Io, and tell Taavin of her discovery.

31

V I WAS BREATHLESS BY the time she ran into her chambers.

"Okay, Lake Io…" Vi mumbled as her fingers traced her shelves. She knew she had an atlas exclusively for maps of the North. One book that would be perfect for… "There you are."

Lifting it from the shelf, Vi placed the over-sized tome on her drafting table and began flipping through it. She looked over to one of the unlit candles on the wall and lit it with a thought.

By candlelight, Vi selected a map detailing Soricium and the surrounding area. The edge of the map bled over onto the next page, where the topmost corner of Lake Io could be seen at the edge of the vast and mostly uninhabited jungle. Reaching into her drawer, Vi resisted the urge to grab for her pen and add "Lake Io" under "Reservoir." Instead, she grabbed her trusty caliper—a metal tool composed of two straight edges screwed together at the top to precisely tune the width between their points.

She rested the tool on the page over the scale marker, reducing the width to match. She began to chart out her course. No map was perfect… but Vi needed to know about how long this trip might take, so she could formulate an appropriate story to secure permission to go on it. That particular logistical nightmare was one she'd reckon with in short order.

Pulling out a spare sheet of paper and a pen, Vi began to jot down notes on distance, time, and terrain. She couldn't have been working too long, because there wasn't that much to do, but a knock on her door frame jostled her from her thoughts.

"Ellene, hello, what…" Vi tried to shuffle the paper without looking suspicious, which was utterly futile and only succeeded in smearing ink across her hand. "What're you doing here?"

"I need to talk to you, Vi," she said gently. Tears were still streaming down her cheeks.

Vi looked down at her maps, then back to her friend. She'd promised Ellene she'd try to be present in their final weeks together. But this was an apex of fate! Their world depended on Vi's "distraction" more than Ellene understood.

"Give me ten—twenty more minutes and then you'll have my undivided attention."

"Vi... you, you really should talk to me now. I want to... I'm trying to help, as your friend."

"I'll be done in just a moment, I promise." Vi forced a smile. "If you tell me now, I'm just going to be distracted with my maps anyway. Wait a just a minute or two and—"

"This is more important," Ellene insisted.

Vi bit back a sigh and looked to the girl again, ready with a retort. She hadn't known what she was going to say next, but whatever dismissal she'd have attempted died on her lips. Ellene stood with her hands knotted in her shirt, balled so tightly they were trembling. Her eyes continued to overflow with tears, spilling onto an expression of absolute torture.

"Is it Darrus?" she asked softly. There was no way he'd contracted the disease that fast. Even knowing nothing about the White Death, Vi knew that was impossible.

Ellene shook her head. "I—I wanted to tell you, but I..." Ellene sniffled loudly. She looked off to the right, just beyond the door frame. "I can't," she whispered weakly. "I'm sorry, I tried. I thought I could."

In stepped Jax.

"What's going on?" The weight of the situation was finally beginning to catch up with her. The whole atmosphere had gone heavy. Ellene continued to hang in limbo and her uncle's expression had darkened further from the last time she'd seen it. "What is this?"

Vi closed her maps, slowly sliding the paper she was working on into one of her drawers. They were acting like she was about to bolt, or do something uncharacteristic, like attack them.

"I—" Jax's words choked in his throat, escaping as a croak. He swallowed hard and Vi watched the knot in his neck bob once, twice, three times. "There were messengers from the West. They arrived this morning, right as the festivities were beginning. That's why it took so long for their missive to get here. We weren't in the fortress, so it took time, then with another outbreak, things were chaotic..."

"Is everything all right with Aunt Elecia?" Vi asked hastily. Messengers from the West, her uncle's state—that was the only thing Vi could think of that would have him so distraught. Elecia and Jax had never been anything official, yet everyone with eyes knew there was more than a little bit of something there. Since Norin, the city Elecia ruled, was the first city outside the South with the White Death... "Is she sick?"

"No."

"Oh, thank the Mother." Vi gave a huge sigh of relief. "Then what is it?"

The relief she felt quickly abandoned her. Her uncle's face twisted further. She could almost feel the tension in his muscles, as though he was forcibly trying to hold himself together.

"Uncle... if it's a message... I can read it myself," Vi offered in the hopes that would alleviate some of his struggle. Still, Jax persisted with another shake of his head. "Then I could—"

"Your father is dead."

What?

She hadn't heard him right.

Vi's ears rang. There was a buzzing, like bees had begun to occupy them. She couldn't hear anything correctly anymore. She certainly didn't hear those four words said so plainly... so heartlessly... that her own heart fractured instantly, trying to break apart, to fill the void between each word with emotion.

"What?" It was barely a word. More of a blurt of sound that was half a laugh of disbelief and half the start of tears.

"We received word with the messengers." He sniffled loudly. "Emperor Aldrik Solaris has perished at sea."

"W-what?" Vi stuttered. That was the only word that would make sense, because nothing else did. The words her ears were telling her she heard, and the truth Vi felt within herself, were diametrically opposed.

Her father couldn't be dead. He was coming with her family to finally, *finally* retrieve her. He had promised he would be back from the Crescent Continent in time. *He had promised.*

"The Imperial Vessel, the *Dawn Strider*, was to send back word when she docked at the Crescent Continent. Nothing was heard for some time... longer than it should have taken them to reach their destination."

How long ago had her father left? Vi tried to run the math in her head. She'd received his letter when Jayme arrived months ago—two months? It was the end of fall. It must've been two, almost three months. It was already almost the new year. It was impossible for Vi to add anything up—nothing was adding up.

He'd said he was leaving then. He must've left around the same time as Jayme, or just before, to escape the passages freezing over.

That meant he had to go north to the Crossroads, then west out to Norin. From Norin he would've boarded the ship... how long did it take to prepare a ship? Vi's head was swimming in questions that came so fast she would drown in them.

Nothing made sense.

This wasn't real.

Her toes had gone numb.

"They sent out search parties throughout the barrier islands," Jax continued, as if trying to preempt her likely questions. "There has been talk of increased pirate activity lately—stories of ghost ships and mysteriously vanishing vessels." Jax stopped again, swallowing, collecting his thoughts. The seconds he took to do it were both too long and too short. Long enough that Vi's mind ran wild with possibilities of what he'd say next. But short enough that by the time he continued, she wasn't ready for it. "Those search parties found debris, along with the bodies of the crew of the *Dawn Strider* in the waters, washed ashore on the beaches of Diamond Sand Island."

"My father?" Vi whispered in a voice so tiny she couldn't believe it came from her.

"They have yet to recover his body... The search efforts will continue, however. At least for a time."

"If they didn't find his body, then—"

"Aldrik was not a Waterrunner." Jax hung his head. "He was strong and powerful. But against whatever storm or pirates befell the *Dawn Strider*, his magic wouldn't have been enough. There have been no survivors."

"You don't know that."

"Vi—"

"He could be out there, still! If we haven't found his body, then, then..."

"Then it could be at the bottom of the ocean or torn apart or turned to dust!" Jax snapped. Hurt raised the volume of his voice, making his words sting her ears. They stung worse than the tears prickling her eyes. "You don't think I thought of all that? Elecia thought?"

"I... But..." Her chest heaved with soundless sobs. A pain so agonizing ripped through her that all she could do was breathe.

He couldn't be dead. Her father couldn't be dead. Everything she'd done had been for her family—a complete family—for her father. Vi's mind was beginning to fracture, her thoughts not quite adding up.

"Elecia has been scouring the seas for weeks now. She, nor the Senate, no one, wanted to declare your father dead, especially prematurely. She's seen vessels going as far as they are allowed in the waters beyond the Main Continent before the armadas of the Crescent Continent strike them down as part of their mad travel and trade restrictions... the bunch of brutes."

"One of them could've found him," Vi thought aloud, hopefully. She moved for her uncle, grabbing his hands. She didn't know if she was trying to support him, or seek support for herself. Either way, it felt right. "He's the Emperor Solaris, you said it yourself, and my father was powerful. He could be on one of the Crescent Continent ships and they took him back and—"

"Do you think if your father was alive he would not return home? He would not even write?"

"Perhaps they're holding him hostage?" Vi countered frantically. She felt like she was the *Dawn Strider*, holes being punched through the hull of her arguments. She was sinking further into that rising tide that had been taking the air from her lungs and reducing her to frantic whispers and thin words since the start.

"They invited him to begin with. And if their plan from the start was to take an Imperial hostage, why would they be silent about it now?"

"I..." She didn't know, and was running out of counter-arguments. Her arms went slack, falling limply at her sides. Her eyes were burning now, and not from her spark but from the tears streaming down her cheeks. "I know he's alive. I just know it. He—he *promised me!* He would be home. He would come with Romulin and Mother. He would be here and we would be a family—together—once and for all. He promised me and this is the one thing I have ever wanted. He won't deny me it!"

She'd hunched in on herself as she spoke, holding her chest, trying to breathe. When had breathing become so difficult?

"I'm so sorry, Vi..." Her uncle shook his head, pulling her to him. Vi's eyes pressed closed and the tears spilled over uncontrollably. She didn't want to give into them, or the tremors in her shoulders. But the grief was too much. The world she'd always been promised was no more, before she could even step foot in it. Everything she had lived for and waited for was suddenly pulled out from under her feet.

"He—He's not dead," she insisted again through tears. Jax held her tighter. Vi shook her head, her nose grinding lines of snot across his shirt. "He can't be dead."

"He's—"

"Don't say it again." She tried to pull herself away enough to look the man in his eyes. The moment there was a gap, Vi instantly missed their embrace. She wasn't even sure if she could stand on her own right now without him. Yet she also didn't want him to touch her. Everything had been disconnected all at once in her now fragile form. "Don't say he's dead. He's not dead! He can't be dead!"

"Vi—" Ellene started weakly. Vi had forgotten entirely she'd been standing in the doorway. The girl ran over in a sprint the moment Vi's eyes landed on her. She wrapped her arms awkwardly around Vi's waist, so she was now held in two places by two people. "I'm so sorry. I'll be here. And you still have us, you still have your mother and—"

"Stop, stop!" Vi practically screamed, forcing them both away. She bumped against her desk, nearly falling on top of it. She'd jump on top of the thing to get away from them and the horrible words they were trying to pass off as truth. "He's *not* dead. My father is alive."

"I know this is hard for you… Take your time."

"Don't speak to me like a child!" Vi shouted at her uncle. "I know he's alive."

"How?" His voice had hardened once more. She knew he was bracing himself for the tough love he thought she needed. Good, he should brace himself; Vi wasn't going to give up this fight easily. The spark lived in her and she'd unleash it on them all if she had to, if that's what it took to get them to stop saying her father was dead. "How do you know, sitting here in the North, far from everything, what has happened in the barrier islands? How do you know more than Elecia and her search parties?"

Her uncle had intended the questions to be rhetorical. Of that, Vi was certain. But he'd asked the right thing to give her an answer.

She knew how her father was alive.

"You said he died on the barrier islands?" Vi whispered. This time, it was not grief, but a delicate, quivering hope silencing her words.

"Yes."

"On the way *to* the Crescent Continent, *not* back from? He never made it there?" she emphasized.

"Yes. He was to make it to the Crescent Continent and send back word. There has been no word, and the *Dawn Strider* was sunk on the way."

Her whole body was trembling now. She knew her father was alive. For she had seen a vision of him on the Crescent Continent, kneeling before a queen in clothes similar to Taavin's, in a city that mirrored what he'd described.

If she'd seen the future with her sight, and saw her father there, that meant her father had somehow made it. Vi remembered her conversation with Taavin. Her visions were of things that would happen if the world remained unchanged. Had the world changed already? Changed enough, and in the specific ways that would have altered that scene?

There was only one way to be even remotely certain—she had to somehow trigger another vision of her father. If she could see him again, she could squelch the doubt that even now threatened to smother her. But the only places Vi had ever received her visions were the apexes of fate.

In one frantic motion, Vi snatched up the sheet she'd been working on, turned, and ran.

32

"Vi, WAIT!" ELLENE CALLED after her.

Her father wasn't dead.

"What the—" Jayme and Andru were standing right outside of her main door, though Vi blew right past them.

Her father wasn't dead.

"Jayme, Ellene, keep an eye on her," her uncle called after sadly. Three sets of footsteps took up chase behind her.

He couldn't be. There was no way he was. *Her father wasn't dead!*

The words resounded in her, bouncing back and forth around her ribcage, puncturing her heart and healing it in the same action. The world could think he was dead. But she knew better. She'd seen it. She would be the one flame of belief protesting against their bleak darkness that could be a lighthouse to guide him home.

All she needed now was proof.

"Vi, wait!" Ellene tried again.

Vi didn't even slow down to respond. She sprinted down the curving passageways and bridges of the fortress. Her feet knew the way in and around the trees, down a pathway she'd run countless times in her life to greet Jayme, her mother, and her father at the stables.

Rubbing her eyes with her palms, Vi forced her lungs to burn only from the exertion and not from sobs. She wouldn't mourn her father until she knew he was dead. She would mourn when she had proof of that. Not before. Never before.

At the hard-packed earth of the stables, Vi made a hard right toward the noru pen. Her hand met the top of the fence and Vi hoisted herself over, landed hard, and was off again. She brought her hands to her mouth and let out a shrill whistle.

Gormon's ears perked up and his head turned. On her command, he came plodding over.

"What do you think you're doing?" Jayme shouted between labored breaths. "Let us help you, Vi!"

"I have to go." Vi hoisted herself up onto Gormon with giant fistfuls of fur. There wasn't time for him to be saddled. If she asked for a saddle it would delay things, and someone would stop her.

"Leave? And go where?" Andru asked.

"There's someone out there trying to kill you!" Jayme motioned to the road that led from the fortress. "Now isn't the best time."

Vi looked down at them from Gormon's back. Every moment she wasted was another moment she could be making headway to Lake Io. Another precious second that she could turn into finding information about her father before anyone else could reach her.

"You guys can come with me, or stay here. Andru can ride with me, Jayme behind Ellene on her noru. But I have to go *now*." She gripped Gormon's sleek fur tighter, trying to make sure she wasn't hurting the beast. They all stood, staring at her in shock. Vi let out a curse under her breath and jumped the fence.

"Wait!" Andru, of all of them, was the one to speak up. Vi didn't know who looked more surprised by the fact—her or him. "I'm coming."

"Well if he's going, I am," Ellene declared, quickly summoning her own noru.

"Jax told me to keep an eye on you, so it's not like I have a choice!" Jayme mounted, somewhat awkwardly, behind Ellene. Though Vi only saw it for a moment. She was already turning forward, looking at the long road out of Soricum.

Down the road, past the burnt outer ring, turn hard south, and ride into the dawn. The map spun in her head, confirming the path forward as Vi sprung Gormon into motion.

"Can you hold me less tightly?" Vi finally asked, slowing Gormon from an all-out run. She would continue bounding through the jungle if his sides weren't heaving. They'd made enough headway… she hoped.

"Is it over?" Andru slowly released his arms. Vi glanced over her shoulders to see his eyes slowly opening. "I feel sick."

"Mother, of course you do. Don't ride with your eyes closed on a noru." She shook her head and looked forward again, setting Gormon into a good trot.

"I've never ridden one of these before," Andru muttered as Ellene and Jayme came alongside them. Vi glanced over long enough to see Jayme's face set in a scowl.

"Just what is going on?" she half-seethed, half demanded.

Vi took a deep breath, enjoying feeling her lungs fully expand without Andru's death grip. She looked forward as she spoke, making sure they kept their headway. Not once had she checked the paper in her pocket.

"My father isn't dead." They may never believe her. But she needed their help now, more than ever, regardless of what they believed. They'd elected to come this far with her and she couldn't let them turn back now and give away her plan.

"What?" Andru asked from behind her.

"Denial won't help. I learned that with my own father," Jayme lamented bitterly. "Denying the truth is only going to lead you down the path toward even more hardship later… Especially after this stunt."

"It's not denial."

"Vi… Jayme's right," Ellene said softly. "Take your time processing, but pretending it isn't real isn't going to help."

Where did Vi begin when it came to telling them the truth? How much truth could she tell them? After keeping her magic secret for so long, Vi wasn't even sure if she knew the way to honesty.

"I have future sight, and have had a vision of my father on the Crescent Continent," she said succinctly. Ripping off the bandage seemed like the most efficient approach.

"What?" Ellene gasped. Jayme was silent.

"There's no record of you having future sight," Andru said cautiously.

"Are you shocked that it would be kept off the record, given how the South feels about sorcerers?" Vi looked over her shoulder at him. He shook his head and glanced away. "More than that… it only just happened, the morning you arrived, actually."

"Of your father?" Jayme asked slowly, no doubt piecing it all together.

"Not… that time." Vi hadn't given the vision with Taavin much thought since it first happened. There had been so much since to focus on. But now, knowing who he was, that he was on the Crescent Continent… She would find a way there. Her father *must* be there. Unless Taavin would come to her… All the possibilities of future sight made her head hurt. "But I did see my father in a later vision."

"What did you see?" Ellene whispered in awe.

"I saw my father, before the Queen of Mer—the Crescent Continent," Vi corrected quickly. "Which means he *must* make it to the Crescent Continent. If I saw him there, he's alive, he didn't go down with his ship. He survived, somehow."

Jayme and Ellene shared a long look with each other. It was as if they were having a silent conversation that ended in a debate of who would speak first.

"Are you sure these are visions of the future?" Jayme challenged. "Not just dreams or wishes?"

"I know what I saw," Vi insisted.

"But what if you were wrong?" her friend persisted.

What if she was… That was the solitary wound that had been struck deep within her, a gaping hole she refused to acknowledge. What if her father was actually dead and this was all false hope? What if the events that needed to come to pass to see him on the Crescent Continent hadn't happened or wouldn't happen?

There was still only one way to find out. Vi kept her eyes forward. The trees blurred around them and Vi cast her doubts aside, letting them fall under Gormon's large paws and be left behind.

"I'm not," Vi lied to them and herself. "I know it."

"How?"

"I don't know!" Vi shook her head. Tears stung her eyes again and she swallowed them down, setting her mouth into a hard line. She struggled to keep her composure. "You're right, I don't know. But I can find out. The answer is at Lake Io."

"Lake Io?" Ellene repeated with surprise.

"I can only have my visions at certain places… and the next one is at Lake Io."

"Is this why you're so obsessed with maps?" Andru asked. It wasn't. But by the Mother was that a convenient excuse. So Vi ran with it and gave him a small nod over her shoulder. "Why not just ask Jax for permission if he knows all this?"

Because he doesn't know all this. "With the assassin still out there, and the outbreak, there's no way he'd let me go. All my life, I have played by their rules. I've done what they wanted of me. I've sat and prepared and repeated and studied unquestioningly. I did it because that was the deal—if I played my part, I would someday be reunited with my family.

"Now, fate is trying to take that from me, and I'm not going to let it." Vi stared ahead, waiting for the break in the trees that would show the water she'd hung her hopes on. "I'm not going to sit quietly by. I'm not going to be the perfect princess if breaking the rules will help me save my father. My family is the one thing I've wanted, the one thing I've been working toward. I can't give up on it now."

The conversation died with that.

Vi didn't know if they believed her or not, but they'd stopped objecting, and that was the best she could hope for. At the end of it all, they didn't need to believe her. She merely had to save her father.

"I think it's admirable," Andru whispered softly from behind her. Vi could barely hear him over the rustle of trees and snapping of foliage underneath Gormon's paws. She glanced over her shoulder, hoping Ellene and Jayme hadn't noticed. "Looking out for your family with such fervor when you don't even know them."

Vi swallowed. "My parents have come and visited me, when they were able. I exchanged letters."

There was a long pause.

"I'm in love with your brother… and he's in love with me."

Vi's hands tightened around Gormon's fur. She didn't look at the man behind her—the man who had been sent to *assess* her. She thought of his nerves around her, nerves she'd misread. She thought about how he mentioned her brother with such reverence at every possible turn. Andru's slip-ups in saying Romulin's name without "prince" before it. The letter about Andru's importance written in Romulin's own hand.

"I know," Vi whispered. And her brother—her twin!—hadn't trusted her with the fact.

"Don't be upset with—"

"I'm not," Vi interrupted sharply. Then, much more softly. "I'm not upset with him… Or you. I'm sure you both had your reasons to keep it from me—from everyone. But I don't want to discuss this now. If I'm going to know, I want him to tell me on his own. He deserves that… I love Romulin, too. He's my twin. Of my essence. The one I've known longer than any other. And I want him to tell me. It's his truth to say."

Andru was silent for a long moment and for once Vi felt as awkward as him. Vi released Gormon's fur and patted the back of his hand lightly where it rested around her waist. She hoped he understood.

"Please don't misunderstand me. Romulin can love who he loves," she whispered. "I couldn't be happier for both of you… But I want him to tell me all his secrets, in person, when we're together for the first time—with *both* our parents— come spring."

THEY'D MADE GOOD TIME.

The sun was setting over Lake Io when they first laid eyes on it.

Out of nowhere, a lake larger than any Vi had ever seen—so large she couldn't even see the other side—appeared like magic in the center of the jungle. Trees ran right up to the water's edge, their gnarled roots draped lazily over giant rocks to lap up the deep blue waters. Even in the fading light, the foliage was bright and verdant. The greens were more vivid—almost neon—the flowers boasted full rainbows of color in nearly iridescent petals. Vines created extensive spider-like webs, folding over each other, curled anchors holding them together.

"It's beautiful," Jayme whispered softly.

"Isn't it?" Ellene said proudly. "I don't come here enough…"

"Why don't others?" Jayme asked, dismounting. "Surely, there would be more buildings, towns, along the water?"

"Sometimes there are… some of the traveling clans will set up camps here. But this is a sacred place. It was made by Dia herself and said to give us all life-sustaining, fresh water. It's more of a place of pilgrimage than of residence or industry."

"Is it all right that we're here?" Andru asked, dismounting stiffly.

"If anyone is permitted, I would think it's the future Chieftain, future Empress Solaris, and their sworn guard," Ellene said with a note of pride. Then, hastily added, "And a future Senator, son of a Senator, Southern Court… man."

"I think my title was somewhere in there." Andru gave her a sly grin.

"Even still… we don't exactly have time to linger." Jayme reminded them. "I'm surprised they didn't send a search party immediately after us."

"For all we know, they did, and we're just ahead of them," Vi admitted. "I was hoping I'd get enough of a head start to throw them off our trail…"

"But mother has trackers too good for that," Ellene finished Vi's thought. She gave her friend a nod.

"Which is why we need to get you your vision and return." Jayme folded her arms over her chest.

"Do you need something special?" Ellene asked, turning to Vi. "Is here good enough?"

"I don't know," she admitted. "One way to find out."

Vi took a few steps back from the water. They'd been surveying the lake on one of the large boulders protruding from the earth. It was a good vantage to see from. But not the best place for a vision—just in case she collapsed in shock, or fear, or exhaustion after. The last thing Vi wanted was to go into the water head first and unconscious.

Holding out her hand, Vi summoned her flame, stared at it, waited...

And waited.

"What do you see?" Ellene asked with a whisper. Her face was alight with awe, as though she was witnessing something mysterious and sacred. Vi hated to be the one to burst her bubble.

"Nothing." She closed her fist, looking across the lake.

"Could we be in the wrong place?" Ellene looked back the way they'd came.

"Perhaps it wasn't Lake Io?" Jayme mused.

Vi shook her head. "No, it's here... But Ellene may be right. This spot, right here, may not be the right place."

"How so?" Andru asked.

"All the other places I've received my visions were remnants from the start of Shaldan. There were the underground ruins, the ruins at the edge of the city..." *Ruins.* That's what it was, Vi realized. Taavin had said something about a temple of the sacred family.

"So you're saying we need to find ruins?" Jayme followed Vi's logic. "Or some other remnant of old Shaldan?"

"There must be some near the lake, somewhere." Vi looked to Ellene. "Do you know of any? Specifically related to Dia and her family?"

Ellene shook her head.

"That's a lot of ground to cover." Jayme looked out over the water.

"Perhaps there's a faster way," Ellene mused, wiggling her toes.

"What're you thinking?" Andru glanced between Ellene and her feet.

"I could feel out the earth. If there are ruins underground, or an odd shape of stone, it should feel different to me than normal earth."

"If this is really supplying the water for all of Shaldan, there must be countless passages underground..." Vi murmured, trying not to dash their hopes.

"I can try," Ellene insisted. "I'll try to feel for smooth rock, something finished."

"It can't hurt if you can do it while we walk." Jayme was already moving around the lake's outer edge, starting off in a somewhat arbitrary direction.

"I should be able to."

"If it goes too slowly, we can always jump back on the noru," Andru suggested.

Vi gave him a nod and they started along the water.

She felt small pulses emitting from underneath Ellene's feet with every step. The girl's eyes closed from time to time, but she never ran into a single tree or bush. Even with her eyes closed, her magic mapped the forest for her into a sight beyond sight.

Once in a while, she'd touch a tree, and Vi felt the same pulses vanish into the bark, down into the roots, and then fade past the realm of her perception.

"Wait, stop." Ellene turned, looking to their right. She lifted a hand, pointing. "There's something over there."

"You're sure?" Yet even as Jayme was asking, Vi could make out the outline of a shadow in-between the trees that she would've missed if not for Ellene.

"One way to find out." Vi led the charge, away from the lake itself and back into the jungle.

Sure enough, not far from the water, stood a ruin. It was completely unmarked on any of her maps—like most were, but Vi couldn't believe no one knew of its existence. It seemed too magnificent to leave lost to time.

"It looks almost like another fortress," Ellene whispered.

"It does," Vi agreed, her voice falling to a hush as well.

Large archways supported crumbling stone pathways between trees, draped with vines and moss. The skeletons of long-dead trees rotted in the shadow of the ruins, feeding newer life that would someday grow tall enough that their mighty roots would crack even more of the crumbling foundation.

It wasn't as pristine as the first ruins Vi had discovered. But it was far more intact than those around Soricium. Perhaps this site was more removed, protected from anyone bothering it throughout the ages. Or perhaps it had once been so large, that even what was left after time had taken its toll still maintained breathtaking grandeur.

"Have you ever seen anything like it?" Vi asked Ellene.

She shook her head. "Not outside of Soricium. It… I can't describe it. It doesn't look like the other cities in Shaldan." She must've been truly confused, because she returned to her earlier sentiment. "It looks like the fortress—or an early version of it."

"It's incredible, whatever it is," Andru whispered in awe. "This must be the place, right?"

"I think so." Perhaps there were hundreds of ruins dotting the shore of the massive lake. But Vi didn't think there were any that would look so grand. If any place was going to be an apex of fate, this would be it. "Let's go in."

"In?" Jayme caught her hand. "That's a crumbling death trap."

"Everywhere else, I've had to go in. I've had to stand right at the heart of it. There's no time to waste debating this. You can wait out here if you'd like."

"If you're going in, then so are we," Ellene declared. "We've come this far together. Besides, you have a Groundbreaker on your side. I'll fix any cracking bits and keep us safe."

"We won't abandon you now," Andru agreed.

"Fine. Even if I'm not completely thrilled by the idea…" Jayme looked uneasily up at the ruins.

Vi stared at her friends in wonder. Standing in front of ancient ruins that could well lead to their deaths, she felt the first cornerstone of something she could call "home" fall into place.

"Let's go, then. Fate is waiting."

34

THEY SCRAMBLED OVER LARGE stones and other rubble as they neared the heart of the ruins.

Half perched in a tree, half supported by the stone that extended unnaturally from the earth, was a structure that looked more like the cathedrals to the Mother Vi had seen in her architecture books than anything Northern. It had pointed spires and more soaring archways to support its large columns.

"Where to from here?" Jayme asked as they climbed up a broken stairway to a wide platform.

"In there, I think." Vi pointed across a crumbling bridge. "That looks like the center of it all."

"Leave it to me." Ellene stepped forward ahead of them. She swept her palm out and across her chest. Before their eyes, old cracks were smoothed, large chunks of stone settled back into place, and the vines tightened, lending further natural supports.

Yet, despite all this, Jayme and Andru seemed skeptical.

"Are you sure it's safe?" Jayme asked.

"We're pretty high up…" Andru glanced over his shoulder, panting softly at the exertion of their climb.

"I may not be a builder, but I know how to use my magic to manipulate the earth enough to make a secure path," Ellene insisted.

"I have faith in Ellene." Vi started forward.

"As if I don't." Jayme rolled her eyes, taking a wide step, determined to be the second on the bridge.

Once across, the four stepped into the smothering darkness of the heart of the ruins. The shifting moonlight of the jungle already hadn't been enough to see by. The small flame that magically hovered over Vi's shoulder, guiding them, had provided just barely enough light.

Here, however, the darkness seemed to have that same impenetrable quality as the first set of ruins Vi had stumbled on. It clung to every corner of the cavernous inner space, darkening relief sculptures and collapsed columns alike. Her friends huddled closer, staying in the halo of light from her flame.

"This feels like the right place," Vi whispered.

"How so?" Jayme's voice had dropped to a whisper as well. Something about the atmosphere was making them all tense. Perhaps it was they couldn't see the far walls or ceiling. The only source of pale moonlight was the archway they'd entered from.

"I can't describe it..." Vi shook her head. "A place with purpose? Something important happened here." Vi wondered if she truly felt that way, or if Taavin's words were merely inspiring the feeling.

"I can only imagine." Ellene's voice echoed off the high ceiling. Whatever the girl could imagine, it wasn't the need that Vi felt to remain as quiet as possible. "What's over there?"

With a flick of her fingers, Vi sent the small flame ahead of them. They hustled to keep up, none seeming to want to linger in the darkness for too long. The pale outline of two figures were highlighted in orange, slick with damp that dripped softly from the tall ceiling. One figure held an axe and knelt before the other. It was almost an exact replica of the statue in the Mother Tree... save for a few key differences.

"Is that... a man?" Jayme squinted. Time and age had taken its toll on the statue and it was impossible to tell. "Wearing a crown?"

"I think so?" Vi tilted her head, trying to imagine what the statue might have looked like when it was first made. There was something masculine about the figure... yet it also had a litheness that read as feminine. Androgynous, would be a better term. "Wearing a crown? I didn't think chieftains wore crowns?"

"We don't." Ellene frowned slightly. She seemed disturbed by the sculpture. "And what's he holding in his other hand?"

"Some kind of blade?" Vi wondered aloud. It was curved but half-broken. She couldn't tell from the blunted end alone what it may have been originally.

"He has a sword on his hip, though," Jayme pointed out.

"Maybe he was some kind of warrior?"

"Dia would kneel to no warrior," Ellene insisted. "She would only kneel to the Mother."

"Perhaps it's not Dia," Vi suggested, more out of kindness. The woman was holding an axe, and nearly in the same pose as the sculpture of Dia in Soricium. It seemed too similar to be mere chance.

"Maybe not..." Ellene was seeing what she wanted to see. But there was no use in pointing that out.

"Perhaps he's a warrior for whoever this is..." Andru's focus had wandered to the wall behind the statue. Whatever he saw had him entranced enough that he'd wandered away from the halo of light.

Vi, Ellene, and Jayme joined him. With a mental command, Vi had the fire lift above her head, illuminating another relief on the wall.

It was massive in scale, the figures easily four times life-sized. A man and a woman were locked in combat. The woman had a blazing sun behind her and she pointed a staff at the man. The man was angular and sharp-looking, wings of lightning crackled behind him. Soundless cries of battle had been cast on their stone faces, resisting the wear of time in an impossible way.

"I would think it's the Mother and Father but..." Andru trailed off.

But they're fighting, Vi finished mentally. The Mother and Father were said to be in an eternal dance, hand in hand, forever with each other throughout the ages as one watched over day and the other night. The crones of the Empire said they were lovers, not enemies… And that's what Vi would've believed before Taavin had told her his truths. Now, she saw it and knew she was laying eyes on a great battle.

This was the truth of their world. An ancient good—Yargen—pitted against an ancient evil—Raspian. They were all mortal pawns laid between them, cast in stone at the gods' feet.

The Solaris Empire and its people had been so far removed from this great struggle that they didn't even see its impact on their lives.

"It's likely also something else." Vi shrugged. She might know better, but her friends didn't and there was no way she could explain otherwise. Just looking at the image was making her uncomfortable. It was as if she was looking at something she was never meant to see. "Who knows what this place really was, or who even built it."

"Maybe your vision will give us insight?" Ellene suggested.

"Right. I'll need to use my flame for it… if it goes out when I'm finished, it may be dark for a moment."

"I think we can survive the dark." Jayme readjusted her stance, stalwart as usual.

"All right, then." Vi closed her eyes and held out her hand. Like a bird, her flame perched in her palm. She felt as much as saw the orb of light moving on the other side of her eyelids. When Vi opened her eyes, she prepared herself to be thrown into the vision.

This time, she wasn't disappointed.

Once more, the world was over-saturated with white. Slowly, by the brush of an invisible artist, color returned, filling in shapes and lines that were as foreign as the last time. As she was coming to learn was normal, there was no sound filling the cavernous room she stood in.

Taavin knelt before her in stunning clarity.

For a brief moment, Vi merely studied his face: immobile, focused, sharp. Sharper than she'd ever seen it before. He looked real, almost like something she could reach out and touch…

Her hands were frozen in place, and Vi was forced to be nothing more than the observer she'd always been during her visions.

His expression was somber. He stared forward, seeing through her, but Vi felt as if he could actually *see* her. His shaggy hair had been pushed back from his face and set. It was the first time she'd seen it not spilling over his brow, curling around the pointed tips of elongated ears.

The light of a fire blazing behind her, glowing through her disembodied spirit, cast his cheeks in oranges and yellows. His mouth was moving quickly, though the words were lost on her deaf ears, and Vi got the distinct feeling that she was watching another ritual unfold. Light peeled off his skin, spinning around his form, condensing over his hands as he continued to chant.

Taavin's hands were folded together, holding something. A silver chain looped around them, dangling and catching the firelight. She could recognize those links anywhere. They were identical to the chain she wore around her neck.

A shadow moved in the background.

Inexplicable dread filled her and Vi fought the urge to shut her eyes. *She didn't want to see this*. Somehow, she knew what was coming with a sickening certainty.

No, don't do this.

The words drifted through her, soft as a whisper, heartbreaking as a scream.

The man continued to chant, continued to stare at the flame at her back that Vi couldn't see. All she wanted to focus on was him and the steadily intensifying light peeling off his flesh. The world was reduced to his magic as it mingled with the bright white power that always hovered at the edges of her visions.

In the background, there was more movement. Vi squinted. She could see a figure nearing, but the darkness of the room had become so intense that it was impossible for her to make out who the person was.

A pair of feminine hands rested themselves on his shoulders. Light wrapping around them as well. The glyphs of the two sorcerers bounced and sparked off each other in the air before they merged. One spell, two casters; without even seeing the person's face, Vi knew the stranger was reciting the chant in unison with Taavin. Just as she knew that soon, it would all be over.

The glyphs brightened and spun to their breaking point, shattering in a blaze. She watched Taavin's head tilt back, mouth open in a soundless scream, as fire arced forward—through Vi herself—and onto him. He was immolated as the glyphs brightened to strands of pure light that wrapped tightly around him.

Vi bit back a cry of anguish as the world turned white. She kept her eyes on his face for as long as possible, watching as flames cracked through his skin, charring it instantly to ash. It was a horror she did not want to see, but she refused to turn away. She would see every detail up until the end.

She hadn't made a sound this time when her vision ended, it seemed, nor had she fallen. Vi spun in place, looking for her mysterious ally. Panic set her heart to racing, as if somehow he could've already been lost to her.

What did she say to him? How could she tell him? Panic rose in her. *She had to protect him.*

"*Hoolo!*" Taavin's voice rang through the darkness, ceasing all thoughts with the single word. It curled between her ears, taking residence in her mind with all the rightness of the world. "Vi, Yargen has spoken! She's given you a word!"

Vi turned, looking for Taavin. But she did not find him. Instead, she saw a pair of glowing red eyes cutting through the darkness.

"**Y**OU SEE HER VISIONS. One of the Dark Isle is truly Yargen's champion," the man with the red eyes spoke. "How the mighty fall…"

"Stay back," Vi commanded, scrambling to her feet. She held out her hand, fire igniting across her fingers. "Or I'll—"

She never had the chance to finish her threat.

The man moved so quickly that he became one with the shadows themselves. He was in one place, and then in a blink he was before her. Red magic sparked off his shoulders, casting the relief sculpture on the wall of the battle between the gods in a bloody glow. He held up a hand, a red circle forming around his palms, and brought it down to her.

"No!" Ellene cried.

Suddenly a column of stone emerged from the ground at Vi's feet. The side of her foot caught its edge and was pushed upward. As she slid off, she lost her balance, staggering and hopping from foot to foot. Her fire was extinguished and the only light was from the man's red irises.

"This doesn't concern you, child," he growled from the other side of the column. Vi was quickly scrambling to her feet, heading opposite of where Ellene stood; she had to draw his attention away from her friends. "But that won't stop me from killing you."

Vi held out her hand. Strands of magic were already collecting, illuminating the room.

"*Juth!*"

Vi felt her magic split and the glyph took shape. The swirling circles curled around him, a smaller replica before her palm. It happened in a single breath, but Vi felt every shift and change in her powers. She had never been so utterly confident wielding magic before. There was not an ounce of fear at losing control; every inch of her will was woven into the carefully crafted glyph.

The only person that should be afraid was the man she was levying it against.

The elfin'ra spun, raising his hands upward, as though her circle had become ropes around his arms that he was breaking with muscle alone. But this wasn't a physical resistance. His magic pushed against Vi's, and they shattered together in an explosion of flame and red lightning.

Fearlessly, Jayme dove in with a shout.

She leapt through the fire and sparking magic, sword in hand, elbows tight to her, point tracked over the man's chest. She lunged, and the sword point almost hit. But the man, or whatever he was, was too fast and well trained. He brought up a hand, as if batting the sword away with a shield. The magic that arced from his middle finger to twist around his pinkie to form the half-shield was hotter than any blacksmith's tool.

It seared off the edge of Jayme's blade and cast the woman off-balance. Vi could see her eyes, bulging in shock, outlined by the glowing red stump of her sword.

"You think that could harm me?" The man laughed. "You worthless girl, you do not even have magic, not even an element of Yargen's precious, splintered boon on this Dark Isle."

Luckily, Ellene was not so distracted. A box of stone rose up around the man. It stretched in a blink up to the ceiling, trapping him in a column of rock.

"Let's go, now!" Ellene shouted.

Jayme had recovered and was on her feet, sheathing her now useless sword. Vi started to move, but then looked around. *Where had Andru gone in all the chaos?*

Her eyes landed on him, huddled in the corner by the statue, looking between Vi and the stone box trapping the elfin'ra in. Vi sprinted over and linked her arms around him. "We have to go."

"What's going on?" He jerked away, eyes wide. They were fearful... of her. These were the eyes she'd expected from the Southerners. *So why did they hurt?*

"We have to go!" Vi ignored the sensation. "Get to the noru, get away." She ran around behind him, pushing the small of his back. Andru finally spurred into motion and Vi wasted no more time behind him.

A surge of magic had her skidding to a stop.

"Vi, come on!" Ellene shouted.

He was about to break free. She could feel it before she saw the red cracks in the stone or felt the rumbling. Even if they ran, they wouldn't get very far. The elfin'ra was faster than lightning and more powerful than all three of them combined. They had to fight here, or they would die running.

Her mind cycled through all the words she knew. She repeated everything Taavin had ever told her on how to string them together. Every lesson they had stolen with each other would have to pay off now.

"You three go ahead."

"I'm not leaving you. I am your guard and—" Jayme started an objection that Vi would have none of.

"That is an order from your Crown Princess!" Vi shouted. Jayme stared at her, shocked. "I know what I'm doing." *She hoped.*

"Fine. Andru, Ellene—"

"No, we're fighting with Vi," Ellene insisted. Andru looked less than certain at the notion, but said nothing.

"You three need to go now!" Vi looked between them and the column of stone frantically.

"She seems to have a handle on this." Jayme pushed on Andru and yanked on

Ellene.

"I don't—" Ellene never finished. Vi watched as Jayme hoisted the girl into her arms. Her powerful legs bulged against her trousers, arms shifting the bundle of weight. Ellene stared in anger, already beginning to thrash. "I'm not going!"

Vi was distracted with them; Jayme was distracted with Ellene and Ellene with her. Andru used his long legs to get several steps ahead. Her friends were almost out and that meant—

They'd all taken their eyes off the column for far too long.

It exploded outward with molten stone and interconnecting cracks of red lightning.

"*Mysst xieh*!" Vi screamed, raising her arms. A glyph appeared before her, hasty and half-formed. It withstood the brunt of the blast, but fractured with every bolder and stone that pelted against it. When the shield broke, Vi was cast backward, confetti of rubble pelting her body.

She groaned, rolling onto her stomach. She didn't want to see the state of her friends... but she had to. Vi heard the scream before she lifted her eyes.

Ellene was on the ground, rolling several feet away from where Jayme lay. Stones scattered off of her shoulders, and small fires that ignited from the molten rock coming into contact with her clothes were snuffed. Vi's mouth dropped open, trying to find a word. Not a word of power. Not a word to summon her magic.

A word to call out to her chillingly immobile friend.

Jayme was on her side. There was a giant, steaming gash in her back, where a stone had pummeled her spine. Blood poured out from her. Vi had seen hunters bleeding kills... but those were animals. She never thought a person would have so much blood in them.

"No," Vi whispered.

"Jayme!" Tears were already streaming down Ellene's cheeks as she half-crawled, half-ran toward their friend. "You idiot!"

"There is no escaping," the man with the red eyes spoke. "Champion of Yargen, this is your fate."

"What?" Andru groaned, sitting up as well.

"Return with me to Salvidia, a willing sacrifice, and I will allow your friends to live."

The body on the altar in her vision. Was this how she got there?

"If you were letting us live you wouldn't have... you... you wouldn't have!" Ellene sobbed over Jayme. Her magic was moving on instinct, vines and mosses curling around the prone woman. Vi made note of it. If there was one thing she could—and would need to—count on, it was Ellene's powers having a mind of their own in times of stress.

"Andru, get to Ellene and Jayme." Vi pushed herself to her feet, ignoring every fiery pain in her limbs. She didn't care if the man heard her plot to keep her friends safe. He'd made it clear she was his quarry. But she also didn't believe for a single moment that he'd let her friends go if she offered herself up as a sacrificial lamb.

"Last chance." The man unsheathed his dagger once more—no doubt a vessel of sorts to bring her blood back if he could not acquire her whole body.

"Ellene, protect yourself," Vi ordered simply.

Vi lifted her arm slowly as she heard the groans of stone lifting upward into what she hoped was a protective shell over Ellene, Andru, and Jayme.

She dipped into the well of power that had always lived in her. It had been her enigma, her bane, as she'd struggled to control it and make sense of it. But now, however limited her knowledge still was, she had the circular pathways to channel it through. She had the words she'd read over and over in Sehra's book, locked in her mind.

She had the knowledge Taavin had imparted to her.

"Do you think you can burn me with your pathetic flames?" he sneered.

"I am Vi Solaris. Anything burns if I will it."

"You are—"

"*Juth starys hoolo.*" It was the perfect combination. The perfect pronunciation. The words resonated with her magic in a way Vi had never imagined possible and clicked together to form a glyph unlike any she had made before.

The circles spun wider, consuming the whole room. They ran over Ellene's cocoon of stone and lapped against the walls, white hot, leaving singe marks in their wake. The second the final word finished echoing through the space, her power exploded.

Destruction. Destroy it all. Burn everything and let nothing remain.

Those were the singular thoughts in her mind as Vi watched the world erupt into white flames. Red lightning arced through it, pushing against her power. But unlike every other time she'd evoked *juth*, the circles did not disappear after the initial explosion. They sustained, burning brighter and hotter with each passing second.

Magic poured from her, filling every nook and cranny of the room with fire. From the outside, the ruins must have looked like a furnace, filled to the brim with coal and burning out of every orifice.

Juth—destruction.

Starys—incinerate.

Hoolo… to hold.

The word had not been in Sehra's book. Taavin had not had a chance to explain it, yet she knew what it was down to her very core. He'd armed her with the ability to hold, to maintain, to keep her fire burning as long as she needed until everything finally went dark.

It didn't feel as though the power was even coming from her. This unstoppable magic was pouring from a source Vi had never seen from her own eyes. These flames were not her own, but something far greater.

When the light and fire of *juth* dimmed, the elfin'ra was gone, and she was left to hope that it was because she had burned him alive.

She'd burned a man alive. Vi stared at her palm. Warriors had spoke of the disgust that flooded a person after such an act. Of the horror of committing such an atrocity. Of the ways in which you were fundamentally changed by such an act.

But Vi felt no different. If she was honest, she didn't even feel guilty. Perhaps it was because the man was a monster… or, more likely, because she had other concerns.

"Ellene!" Vi called, staggering over to the cocoon of rock. Her fire had heated all the stone to the point of glowing. The soles of her shoes had burned off. But at least she'd mastered enough control of her magic not to allow it to burn her clothes during the act. "Ellene! Jayme! Andru!"

The rocks half melted, half crumbled away, revealing her friends. Sweat ran down Ellene's temples, whereas Vi's brow was still dry. But she otherwise looked fine.

Andru was in a similar state. Jayme was not so lucky.

"Is he…"

"I killed him," Vi declared, still hoping it was true. She knelt down at Jayme's side. "I can cauterize some of the bleeding."

"Don't." Ellene stopped her. "The plants are medicinal for clotting, healing, sleep… I'm trying to keep her in stasis."

"How long can you hold it?"

"I don't know." Ellene looked at her with fear in her eyes. "She's bad, Vi. I don't know…"

"Stay here. Keep her alive… I'll go back and get help."

"Vi, I—"

"She's still breathing. The best thing to do is not move her." Vi clamped a hand over Ellene's shoulder. "You can do this."

"Don't leave," Ellene whispered softly, grabbing Vi's hand.

"Be brave." None of them had any other choice. "We both have to be brave for Jayme, because she was brave for us. Andru will stay with you."

Andru slid a little closer to Ellene, avoiding eye contact with Vi. He'd known she was a sorcerer… No, this was the trauma of the day, nothing more.

Ellene sniffled and then her face hardened. She gave a stiff nod. "Be hasty."

"I will."

Even though she was sill exhausted and every limb felt like lead, Vi left at a jog. The singe marks from her flame extended halfway across the bridge Ellene had made between the platform they'd ascended and the heart of the ruins. Vi didn't even glance over her shoulder, immediately clamoring down the worn stairs and large boulders toward the ground far below.

She started into the woods, raising her fingers to her lips and letting out a shrill whistle. Jayme was dying. She had been wounded because of Vi, and if Vi couldn't save her now, she would never forgive herself. That would be the death that would linger with her. Not the elfin'ra. But Jayme, her friend, her first sworn guard.

Gormon came bounding through the trees, skidding to a stop before her. Vi worked to mount him. Her muscles ached, spasming with every thrum of his large paws on the ground.

She would make it, she had to. There was no reality Vi would entertain where she didn't save Jayme. She gripped Gormon's fur tighter, spurring him onward.

V I FELT EVERY INCH of her bruised, battered body. Every rock that had pelted her was making its ghostly presence known as she rode Gormon deeper into the jungle. The rush of the fight was fading and, in its wake, pain bloomed. But Vi rode onward.

There would be time to rest soon enough. Jayme was hanging on by a thread—*her friend was counting on her*. Vi swallowed down panic and focused on moving with the animal beneath her so she wasn't unseated. She couldn't let her emotions get the better of her; there would be time for that later as well.

Dawn was breaking when Vi saw a rustling in the jungle in the distance. She sat straighter, a cry for help stuck in her throat. She didn't know if she had the strength to fight off another diseased noru.

The beast came into view—normal fur and eyes. On its back were two of Sehra's warriors. Vi didn't recognize their faces, but she recognized the special tabbards they wore. Then, another noru emerged... and a third behind it, bearing Jax.

"Here!" Vi shouted. Clearing the thickness of her throat and adjusting her grip on Gormon, she raised a hand and waved, shouting again. "Over here!"

The ears of the noru swiveled toward her and they were bounding over a second before even their riders had fully registered her presence. Vi slowed Gormon to a stop, allowing herself to be circled. Jax was the last to arrive, his face was a twisted mess of anger and unshed tears of relief.

"I—"

"What in the Mother's name were you thinking?"

"Uncle—"

"Running off like that. I thought you knew better than—"

"Jayme is dying!" Vi shouted, fearing he would go off on one of his usual tirades where she couldn't get a word in. Jax was startled into silence. "Jayme is dying, please, help her." Her hands were shaking, clutching Gormon's fur for support. Had she ever been so tired?

"Where?" The anger melted to serious concern.

"I'll show you the way. Is there a cleric among you?" Vi asked the warriors.

"I know some basic salves and procedures for the field."

Vi gave a small nod to the man who spoke. "You, come ahead with me." She turned to the other noru with two mounted warriors. "You two head back to the fortress and get Ginger. Tell her to bring her box. We'll meet you here or closer to the fortress, if Jayme can be moved." Vi finished giving her order, but then added at the end, hastily. "Also, Ellene is fine. She's mostly unscathed and is keeping Jayme stable."

"Yargen bless." The warriors gave a small bow of their heads before turning the noru and bounding back into the jungle.

"This way." Vi shifted in her seat, guiding Gormon with her knees and thighs. She spurred him into motion, leaving the rest to catch up with her.

"As soon as we arrive you should go back to the fortress as well!" Jax shouted, riding up next to her.

"No, I'm seeing this through, uncle. It's my fault she got hurt." Vi shot him a glare. "If not for me, she wouldn't have come—she didn't want to come."

"She was always the one who had the most sense! You should try listening to her some time," Jax grumbled.

"I know. I'm sorry. But don't send me back, yet." Vi knew the decision had been made, given that she was riding in the opposite direction of the fortress. "Let me see Jayme well. And then I'll take responsibility for my actions and whatever punishment comes with it."

The wind rushed in her ears, and Vi strained her tired eyes to make out the initial outlines of the ruins. She had thought the matter closed. But Jax was apparently not yet finished. When Vi saw him open his mouth again, she braced for whatever tirade he was about to unleash.

"There will be punishment." It was a promise that prickled up Vi's spine like a threat. "But seeing you take charge and responsibility just now... Perhaps it may not be as bad of a punishment as you think."

"All I care about right now, uncle, is making sure my friend is all right."

Vi could tell by the movements of Ginger's hands alone that the cleric was tired. Not that she could blame her. The woman had been woken up at an ungodly hour, dragged out across the jungle, saved a life, and then came back to attend Ellene, Andru, and now Vi.

"Sorry for the trouble," Vi murmured as she finished her tally of what she'd put Ginger through.

"Princess, you really are always trouble." Ginger sighed. Then paused, glancing up from her work on Vi's legs. "Sorry for my loose and tired tongue."

Vi gave a soft laugh. "I think I deserved that."

Her eyes drifted away from Ginger to the window of her room. The sun streamed though it as normal, as though it were any other day. It felt like anything but.

"I'm sorry for your father," Ginger said softly. "I don't think any of us really blames you for running off. Grief can take up residence where our better judgment resides."

Father... There was a dull ache in Vi's chest. She had gone out and risked her friend's lives to get a vision of him. While she'd failed in that, she had seen the end of another man's life.

"I realize you likely only think of me as a cleric who mends bones and cuts," Ginger continued. "But, princess, some of the most important—and difficult— healing work is done on the mind. Please reach out if you need. There are many around you who care."

"Thank you, Ginger," Vi said softly. "I'm very lucky to have your support."

"Any time, princess. I've looked after you your whole life and have no intention of stopping now." Ginger finished up her work and tiredly packed her box. "I'm going to tell Jax that you need some rest before he storms in here scolding. Try and close your eyes for a bit, princess. If you have trouble sleeping, let me know and I can give you a tipple for deep sleep."

"I'll be fine, thank you." Vi gave the woman a nod and watched her leave.

Letting out a sigh, Vi sank back into her pillows. Her whole body ached and felt exhausted. Could she even manage to spin the light right now?

She looked down at her hand. It wasn't as if she had a choice. She needed Taavin right now. She needed to tell him what she'd seen, and about her father… More than anything, she needed Taavin's ear, his support.

"*Narro hath hoolo,*" Vi uttered.

Light blossomed above her chest. A magic circle more complete than she'd ever seen before hovered at her watch, expanding outward. It floated before her, spinning parallel to the floor. Slowly, the magic lowered, unfurling like the spool on a spinner's wheel. The strands that hovered in the air took a new shape, a new outline.

Just like every time previously, Taavin came into sight. Color filled in and the light settled around him before disappearing entirely. There was no glyph swirling around his feet, no tendrils of light wafting off of him. It was just a man, standing at the side of her bed, looking around in wonder. He looked even sharper, more solid, almost like she could…

Vi's hand moved, drawn on instinct. It rose, reaching out to what had been thin air moments before. But her fingers landed on him, feather-light. She pressed further, her fingers stretching up his forearm. They spread across the fabric of his coat, feeling every bump and groove of the intricate embroidery.

He was there. It was not pulsing magic, or warmth, or light. It was a man she could see and touch.

Taavin said nothing. He looked down at her through half-lidded eyes with an inscrutable expression. His attention alternated between her face and her rogue hand, staring at the place where it rested on him.

In his expression was knowing. Sorrow. Determination. Everything she'd seen of him from the start and then some. Neither of them said anything, and she would've been content to let the peaceful silence of simply being in his presence for the first time drag on for eternity.

Were it anyone else and any other situation, Vi may have felt embarrassment at her actions. But all she could feel was him. All she knew was the outline of his form—knew she was even now committing it to memory.

"I can touch you," she whispered up at him.

"I can feel you," he said in reply. "It must be the word Yargen gave you. This was why she bestowed it on me." Taavin sat on her bedside. The feather mattress didn't sink or sigh. *So he was real to her, but to nothing else.* He wasn't actually with her, it only seemed to her he was. "You're all right?"

Vi gave a small nod. "Bruises and scrapes mostly… But Jayme, she—" Something caught in Vi's throat and the words stuck. She swallowed, once, twice, but couldn't dislodge it. Her eyes burned, and Vi knew if she dared speak again, emotion would spill from them.

"Is she alive?"

"Yes." Vi forced out the word, closing her eyes. When she felt more stable, she said, "Thank the Mother, yes."

"Yargen's blessings." Even though he'd never met Jayme, Taavin breathed a sigh of relief. His other hand closed over hers. Vi hadn't even realized she'd still been clutching his sleeve. "I saw you and the elfin'ra. Did he…"

"I killed him. He didn't get my blood."

"*You* killed him?"

"Don't act so shocked," Vi gave a small laugh. "Isn't that what you were teaching me? To protect myself?"

"Yes but…" He squeezed her fingers. "It's a relief to know you can."

"The word you gave me helped, if I'm honest."

Taavin gave her a small smile, one that quickly vanished. "What were you out there for anyway? I thought I told you not to be so reckless."

"What are you, my keeper?" Vi gave a small grin.

"This is the second time you've scared me." Taavin leaned forward slightly. She wondered if he realized he'd tensed his grip on her hand. "I don't know what I would do if something happened to you."

The world stilled. Everything hung on her shallow breaths. Vi searched his shimmering emerald eyes and the sentiment in them suddenly sparked fear.

"You're going to die," she blurted.

To his credit, he didn't even flinch.

"Death comes for us all," he said softly. "Your vision… Tell me what you saw."

"Taavin, you don't understand." Vi straightened away from the pillows. Her other hand reached over, sandwiching his. She clung to him, relishing in finally *feeling* him. "Someone is coming to kill you and I don't know why, and you're far, and I can't help you, and—"

"You can help me by telling me what you saw." Vi shook her head and he freed his arm. She looked away, realizing how forward she'd been, only to feel his hand land on her cheek, gently guiding her face back to his. "Take a breath and tell me, Vi." His voice was firm, stabilizing, as though cementing her mind back into place from whirling doubt.

Vi recounted the broad strokes of the vision for him. "… but what you were holding, it looked like this." Vi pointed to her watch.

"You said I was kneeling before a fire?" Taavin asked and Vi nodded. His eyes dropped to the watch around her neck. "It must be…"

"Didn't you hear me?" Vi shook his hand lightly. "Someone is out to kill you."

"Do not worry so much for me," Taavin mumbled, still clearly lost in thought.

Vi balled her hands into fists. The spark roared to a blaze in her. The marrow of her bones was replaced by molten rock. She rose from the bed and stomped over to him.

"Firstly, don't you presume to tell me what I can and cannot do." Vi held a finger in front of his handsome face. "Secondly… You are the only person who knows what in the Mother's name is going on with me. So you can bet that I worry 'so much' for you."

Her two fingers hovered in the air between them. He looked down past them, to her. A small smile snaked across his lips.

"Good to know your compassion is purely a result of pragmatism."

"You didn't let me finish." A third finger lifted. "And... third... I-I care about you, Taavin," she said softly. His eyes widened a fraction. "You are the only person I've ever spoken to that I feel both listens and somehow fully understands what I say. I don't want anything to happen to you." Vi hung her head. "I may have lost my father," she finally said aloud. "I don't want to lose you, too."

"Your father?"

"They've declared him dead. Killed by pirates between here and Meru." Vi shook her head. "I saw the vision of him with the queen, but what if the world has changed? What if *I* did something that led to my father's death?"

She looked up at him, searching, though she didn't know what for. Their hands shifted once more, curling around each other in a new way. It was as though, regardless of how they moved, neither wanted to relinquish their hold on the other. They had finally found this connection... what if they never had it again?

"I will look for information on your father. And we will seek out more apexes of fate—perhaps you will see him again. Do not despair yet."

She swallowed, giving a nod. As long as there was hope her father was alive, she would be strong. She would not believe he was dead until she laid eyes on his body, or the person who claimed to have killed him.

"I can find more apexes here. I'll be headed south in a few months... Surely there will be some along the way. Maybe I can make sense of the two I don't yet know."

He paused, eyes darting over her face. Vi knew the look of a person who was hesitating. She leaned forward slightly, hanging on his next words.

"We need more than that. Your latest vision... I believe the key to saving this world lies in the watch around your neck."

"What?" Vi freed a hand, grabbing it protectively. Taavin's glyph shimmered over and through her fingers.

"I need you to bring it to me."

"I can't just leave... It doesn't work that way," Vi whispered, knowing he was all but trapped in the Archives of Yargen on Meru. "I have a duty to my people. And my family, they're here, on this continent."

"If Raspian goes unchecked, your people and your family are forfeit. If you remain there, the elfin'ra will hunt you until they have you. Vi, come to Meru." Taavin stared down at her with his impossibly brilliant eyes. "We will find the truth of your father along the way. You will learn full mastery of your Lightspinning. And, together, we may find a way to seal away Raspian once more, and put an end to the plague that heralds the coming end of days."

Vi swallowed, trying to clear her throat. She wanted to sound braver than she felt, ignore the odd nerves firing within her and setting her to quivering. Champion of Yargen, Lightspinner, heir to the Solaris Empire... Vi did not speak on behalf of any of her titles.

She spoke for herself and herself alone when she whispered a simple, "Yes."

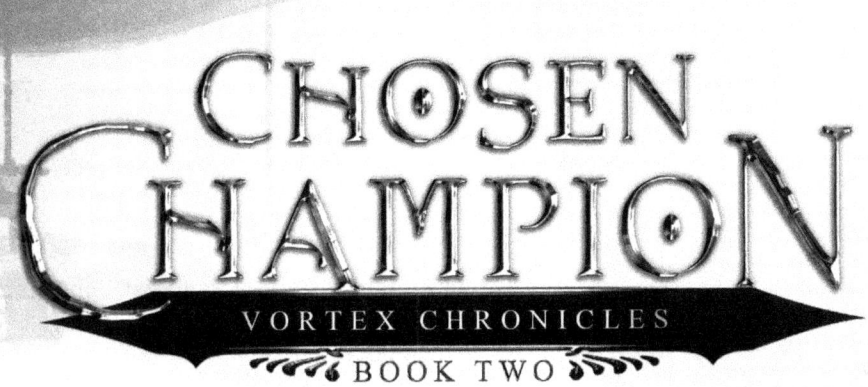

CHOSEN CHAMPION

VORTEX CHRONICLES

BOOK TWO

for my author community

1

Her hands moved through the dark night, leaving strands of light in their wake.

Vi Solaris was illuminated by the lingering remnants of fading spells and bright sparks of sorcery that caught on the rough-hewn walls of the sparring pit. The lines cut against the darkness in brilliant streaks—concentric circles, triangles, and dots that all spun together. Every mark had meaning, crafted by her knowledge and will, and brought to life with the utterance of intricate sounds.

"*Juth starys.*" As she spoke, her right hand lifted. The left was balled at her side, rigid, an anchored glyph circling her wrist. It held a completely different spell in place.

"*Juth mariy,*" the man opposite her quickly called back, impossibly fast. Symbols flashed into existence around him, hovering before her. The glyph was the embodiment of the words he'd spoken—words of the Goddess Yargen. It crashed against her own forming glyph, snuffing it instantly. "Don't lift your hand. You're telegraphing your movements."

"My mother had a problem with that, you know."

"Not surprised, then." Taavin lunged for her. "*Mysst siti larrk!*" The light sparked, running down his outstretched forearm as he moved. It condensed before his open palm, shooting out and away from him to form a short sword.

"*Mysst xieh,*" Vi said hastily, dodging even faster. His sword bounced off the glyph she used as a shield.

Taavin uncurled his fingers, allowing the sword to fly from his hand at the momentum. When it left his palm, it looked just as any other normal sword would. But before it could hit the ground, the weapon unraveled into thousands of threads of light and vanished. Around his other hand, fresh magic was already gathering.

She could almost see the meaning in it before he even spoke the words. She had been studying the glyphs for months now. Training with their shape and words. Vi knew what he was about to levy as the magic collected.

But she saw it too late.

"*Loft dorh.*"

"*Jut—*" Vi began to say. But his glyph had formed before she could complete the two words that, when combined, meant to destroy magic.

Her body went rigid and all movement vanished. *Loft*, the high-level magic to incapacitate. *Dorh*, the secondary for immobilization. Vi fought against the invisible chains holding her, but they were too strong. No matter how hard she struggled, she couldn't even move an inch. Even her mouth was frozen open, mid-*juth*.

Taavin stared at her. The glyph still surrounded his fingertips. His magic was elegant, carefully crafted, and twice as bright as Vi's. She admired it, just as she admired the way its glow highlighted the deep purple of his hair and cut of his jaw; there wasn't much else for her to do in her present state.

Finally, he lowered his hand. The moment the glyph vanished, Vi could move once more. She stumbled, found her footing, and turned to face him.

"How do I fight against that?"

"You were right to go for *juth mariy*. You just weren't fast enough." Taavin ran a hand through his messy hair. When he pulled it back his pointed ears were visible. Whenever she saw them, it was a reminder that for the easy closeness she had found with the man, there was nothing physically close about him. He was elfin, a race that didn't exist as far as the Solaris Empire was concerned, and he lived across the sea in Risen on the continent of Meru—a distance Vi could barely comprehend and hadn't even known existed until a few months ago.

A distance she'd have to find a way to traverse to get to him.

Her magic tutor, her friend and confidant, wasn't *actually* there at all. She could see, hear, and feel him, but he only existed for her. The magic Vi had anchored to her left wrist had summoned him, and would keep him with her as long as she willed without sapping her magic, thanks to the word of power the goddess had bestowed on her at an apex of fate.

"So if I can't cancel the immobilization, I'm trapped?" It seemed a vastly unfair spell.

"As long as the caster holds the glyph."

"Someone could keep me trapped forever?" Not that she wasn't already trapped, in a way. Vi hadn't left the fortress for weeks now—not since the latest and worst outbreak of the White Death had taken hold of Soricium.

"No one could hold the word forever. *Loft* takes a great deal of energy because a whole person is very difficult to keep completely still. The second the caster's magic or attention wavers, you'd break free."

Vi looked him over skeptically. He'd shed his usual heavy, embroidered coat for their practice. Now he wore a tight-fitting, long-sleeved shirt that hid little of his lean chest and was tucked beneath a wide pair of trousers. Not one area of fabric clung with sweat.

"You don't look like you expended a great deal of energy."

"Looks can be deceiving." A small grin quirked the corners of his lips. "And I am the Voice."

Yargen's Voice. It was a title Vi still couldn't fully comprehend. She knew it meant Taavin was important, that he held vigil over an eternal flame said to be the last remnant of the goddess's power on earth... And that he had been kept sequestered all his life above the city of Risen, under lock and key.

It was a situation all too similar to Vi's.

"A similar form of incapacitation you may want to begin with is *loft not*—to sleep. It's not as effective, because anything could wake the person and the spell would be broken. But it's easier to cast and maintain. You could actually move while holding it."

"Well, *I'm* the Champion… so I should be able to make *loft dorh* look just as easy in time." She hoped, at least. But the only thing Vi knew less about than being Yargen's Voice, was being the godddess's Champion. "Speaking of our supposed titles… Any progress on the Apexes of Fate?"

Vi started up the stairs to the pit, Taavin following dutifully behind. She glanced over her shoulder at him, pausing when the silence continued to stretch on. His brilliant emerald eyes were fixated across the pit, avoiding hers.

"That's a yes." Vi slipped her long braid over her shoulder, running her fingertips along its end. "What is it?"

"I'm not sure, entirely." Rather than pestering, she waited for him to find the words. "The vision of the room keeps appearing."

"Room…" Vi thought back to the last time he'd listed possible locations for apexes. "The throne room? Or the one you mentioned with the two women?"

"The latter."

"Have you seen anything different?"

"That's the thing: every time I see it, it's different." He looked up to her. "All glimpses… sometimes focused on shelves crammed with jars of various objects— bits and baubles stacked around them to the point of chaos. Sometimes there are people, sometimes not. Tapestries darkened with soot hanging over a fire. I see them holding things, and—"

"Casting them into the flame?" Vi finished for him. Taavin's lips hung, slightly parted, the words he'd been forming never leaving. Instead, they closed briefly, and a new statement was put together.

"How did you know that?"

"It sounds like a curiosity shop." Vi glanced over the top of the training pit, looking for the horizon line—or as close to it as she could see in the jungles. The sky was still dark, which meant she didn't have to be rushing back to her room. This was a conversation that Vi didn't want to cut short. "I've never seen one, of course…" She had spent her life in this fortress, confined to the city and at most its immediate surrounding area. All of that would change soon. "But that sounds like the descriptions I've read in books—the variety of objects to burn, people there sometimes and not at a later date. It all seems to add up."

"It can't be a curiosity shop, then." Taavin shook his head, his tousled hair getting further out of place in the process. For one brief second, Vi wondered if it was as soft as it looked. But she fought off the need to tuck a stray strand behind his pointed ear.

"Why?"

"Because in the last dream I had…" His voice disappeared, and with it his attention on her once more.

"You… what?" Vi shuffled on the step. There wasn't much room, and she couldn't catch his eyes without all but stepping into him.

"I thought I saw *you* looking into the flame." Was that a blush on his cheeks, or a trick of the magical light that lingered on him? "I think it was likely just a run-of-the-mill dream—not tied to fate or us or the apexes."

He'd "run of the mill" dreamt about her? Vi swallowed down her heart so it wouldn't beat so loudly in her ears. She was being ridiculous. He'd said she'd tortured him in dreams all his life.

But wouldn't those be related to the Apexes of Fate?

Did he dream of her differently now than he had before?

"Why—" Vi cleared her throat. "Why couldn't it be me?"

"You see the future at the apexes, but my visions and dreams seem to look to the past—places where fate *was* changed, not will be."

"Well, then I suppose it couldn't be me, given that I've always been cooped up here." Vi shrugged and started up the stairs again, ignoring the opportunity to follow up on the implication that she'd been appearing in his dreams. If she acknowledged that, then she'd have to admit he'd begun to do the same for her and that—

A new thought stopped her dead in her tracks at the top of the pit. Taavin's hand rested lightly on her back as he rounded her side.

"What is it?" he asked, gravely serious the moment he saw the expression on her face.

"Unless it was me, but wasn't me," Vi whispered, looking through him, back to a strange interaction with a Western woman in the winter solstice market.

"How is that possible?"

"If you dream of the past, where the lines of fate twist and align, then perhaps I've never been the one torturing you."

"I've seen you." He took a small step closer. "I'd know your face of any in the world."

"Perhaps... Unless my face isn't my own, but that of a princess reborn," Vi whispered.

"What?"

Vi glanced once more to the horizon. She should have time still. If she hurried, she should have time.

"Vi, rebirth isn't—"

"How clear of a look did you get?" Vi turned to him, scooping up his hands. They were warm under her palms, as though he eternally lounged in sunlight. "Are you *certain* it was me? Beyond all doubt?"

"I can't say beyond all doubt about anything." He sighed heavily. "My dreams don't come with instructions."

"Good, because I think I know who it was—who it might have been all along." Vi started off over the hard-packed earth that lined the fighting pits.

The fortress of Soricium, built directly into the towering trees that were hundreds of stories high, had many entrances from the fighting pits. There was the walkway that arched over the center of the fortress, up to a balcony that connected to the tree that housed the nobility. There was a gaping entrance in a trunk that ultimately led up to where Chieftain Sehra's warriors resided—not far from the new wall that now surrounded the whole fortress.

But Vi headed for a staircase off to the side that wrapped around a smaller tree.

"Not that I can't keep up." Taavin matched pace at her side. Vi wondered if he had to exert energy to traverse her world with her or if it happened by sheer will of magic. "But I don't know if you really want to bring me into the fortress." He pointed to the glyph around her arm. "Just in case someone sees..."

"Right." Vi held up her left hand, looking at the magic she'd anchored there hours ago, about which she'd all but forgotten. What would it be like if his presence wasn't solely determined by a set of words? His fingers closed around hers, as if he could sense the thought, and her eyes jerked to his.

"Before you do, tell me what you've managed to piece together?"

"Curiosity shops are a distinctly Western trade. My family has roots in the West." She could see as he began to connect the dots she'd already joined to form a clear picture in her mind. "Months ago, during the winter solstice, there was a Western woman who mentioned curiosity shops—that her caravan was said to be in possession of one bestowed on them by my grandmother."

"Your grandmother?"

"Princess Fiera, the last princess of the West." Her insides wriggled in excitement. Vi's fingers closed tighter around Taavin's and they were drawn closer together, by just a fraction. "The woman said she came to see me, because in the West they say I am her, reborn. That I look *just like* my grandmother."

"The grandmother of the Champion... a curiosity shop designed for peering along the destiny Yargen has laid for us..." Taavin's grip tightened to match. "That sounds like it could well be an apex. You are brilliant," he whispered.

"No, I'm not. I'm just doing what any good Champion should and helping find a way to save our world." There was a small, determined smile on her lips. She wanted to joke and be jovial. But she couldn't. She had seen the end of the world in all its horrifying detail. The only thing standing between her and the ultimate death of everyone she loved was finding the apexes, seeing the futures there, and helping Taavin use those visions to stop the destruction the freed dark god Raspian wrought—or would, if they didn't find a way to thwart him from gaining a physical form once more.

"Don't be afflicted by a false sense of modesty. You can be both brilliant and a good Champion." His mouth quirked into a similar grin. Then it fell from his face as his eyes drifted back down to her wrist. "You should go," he said softly.

"I don't have much time," she agreed. Yet their fingers lingered, entwined. "I'll summon you again when I'm able."

"Please do. It's much less lonely with you."

What were his days like? The question lingered in the forefront of her mind. It was obvious Taavin didn't like talking about himself. But at some point he had to—at some point she needed to know, if for no other reason than to get to him when she finally made it to Meru.

"Keep your fingers crossed for me." Vi released him. "Hopefully, we're on our way to another apex."

Taavin gave a nod as she let go of their communication. Vi watched, staring through the spot he'd once stood. The man seemed so real to her. She could feel him, touch him, smell him as though he stood before her. But when she let go of the magic strung between them, there was nothing—a sobering reminder that Taavin was, in true flesh, across the world.

Pushing it from her mind, Vi sprinted up through the fortress, taking the stairs two at a time to hasten toward the unorthodox jail of Soricium.

2

ON THE FAR edge of the fortress were the holding cages. Getting to them was no easy task—a feat Vi shouldn't be able to perform.

After the first stairwell, Vi headed to a second via a long walkway supported by a branch already several stories up. She crossed to a third that wound around the outside of the tree. From time to time, she would look down for the sole purpose of continuing to acclimate to the dizzying height.

She couldn't falter when the time came.

Her legs were aching and sore by the time she reached the top of the stairs. But her journey wasn't nearly over yet. She stood on a wide landing that stretched outward toward another landing on a tree opposite. This tree was unique from all the others in the fortress for two reasons: the first was the wooden and stone cages that hung off its tall canopy; the second was that it had no permanent connection with any other tree.

To gain access, a Groundbreaker, a sorcerer with earth magic, would stretch a branch from the canopy of the tree she now stood within over to the far tree. But Vi wasn't a Groundbreaker. The magic she practiced didn't belong to any elemental affinity—it was an ancient sorcery known as Lightspinning.

Vi inched her way to the edge of the wide platform. The ground was so far below her now, the details blurred. She leaned over slightly, swallowing air down a completely dry throat.

"I hope this works…" Vi muttered.

Mysst, to craft.

Xieh, shield.

The two words together saved her life once when she'd fought against an elfin'ra—an agent of the dark god Raspian. Together, they formed a shield of magic that guarded against any form of physical or magic attacks. But Vi had a theory about it, one she'd been testing in her room out of curiosity.

If the shield could block physical things, it could also support them. With that logic, she'd balanced books on the magical discus *mysst xieh* formed. But she was a lot heavier than a stack of books.

"*Mysst xieh.*" Vi raised her right hand, pointing it before her. The glyph appeared at her command, hovering above the balcony's edge.

Timidly, Vi lifted her foot, resting it on the spinning light. It was firm, yet there was some give to it—as though she was sinking through a layer of magic to a solid base. She imagined this must be what snow felt like, based on what Uncle Jax had described—but thankfully, the magic was much less cold. Placing her weight on her leg, Vi lifted her other foot onto the disk.

It held, and she let out an audible sigh of relief.

"Now, for the second." Lifting her left hand, Vi pointed before her. "*Mysst xieh.*"

A step away from the first, a nearly identical glyph formed. This one, however, hovered over the open air. There was no safety net of the balcony beneath her. If her magic failed her… she'd be dead.

Vi had fallen from these trees only once, when she was attacked in the night. She had no intention of doing it a second time. Steeling her resolve, Vi took a step forward, leaving doubts behind her.

Her right foot landed on the second glyph, followed by her left. She could see the ground underneath her through the shimmering rings of magic. Her stomach soured. Lifting her eyes, Vi looked across to the other tree.

Had it always been that far? Closing her right hand into a fist, the first glyph disappeared. She stood on the second with both feet as she pointed her right hand just ahead of her.

"M-*Mysst xieh.*" The light flowed together, failed to link up, flickered and vanished. Vi swallowed hard. She had to keep herself together or her magic would fall apart.

"*Mysst xieh.*" Vi's confidence was rewarded when the third, much more stable shield formed. She quickly balled her hand into a fist, holding it in place as though she were gripping a lifeline in open, shark-infested water. Her nails dug into her palms as Vi stepped from the second shield to the third.

When all her weight was balanced, she released her grip on the second glyph and moved to make the fourth.

Like stepping stones, Vi made her own bridge of light across to the other tree. Every howling gust of winter wind swept up her long braid, catching it like a whip, trying to yank her over. Vi crouched, keeping her center of balance low, her magic focused.

Around halfway, Vi noticed the glyphs began to diminish in size. She had to conserve her magic, otherwise she'd risk them breaking under her weight. But if she made them too small, there may not be enough room for her feet at all. By the time she made it across, they were barely larger than her shoe.

"By the Mother." Vi doubled over as her feet landed on the balcony at the other side. She grabbed her knees and breathed for a moment. Her whole body quaked with nerves she'd refused to acknowledge moments ago. "That actually worked," she whispered in wonder. If she'd been a Firebearer like her father and grandmother, there would've been no way to cross.

Father. Vi stood straighter. Finding the apexes wasn't just to prevent the end of the world—though the apocalypse was a pretty good motivator. It was also for him, to see him again, to confirm he had not died a watery death.

His body still had yet to be recovered.

Turning, Vi started into the tree trunk and up a final set of stairs. She reached the top of the trees as the sun crested the horizon. Vi blinked into the light as it broke. There wasn't much time; the stewards and attendants would come soon, and if they didn't find her in bed it'd arouse suspicion.

Around this walkway, the cages she'd seen from before drifted back and forth in the wind. Vines as big as her thigh held them in place, securing together a birdcage of rock and branches. Most were empty—Soricium had a city jail for drunkards and cutpurses. These pens were for the exclusive use of the Chieftain.

The people held here were the worst of the worst.

At least… that was how it was supposed to be.

"You're new." A man in the cage opposite her as she rounded the tree trunk slowly raised his head. Vi could barely make out his words over the creaks of the swaying branches in the wind.

He was curled in a ball, knees to his chest, arms around them. His shoulder-length dark hair was stringy. The man's clothes were dingy and his lips were chapped from exposure to the elements.

His eyes narrowed slightly as Vi approached the edge of the walkway.

"You're not one of them."

She assumed "them" to mean Sehra's warriors—the guards of the fortress. "I'm not."

"To what do I owe the honor of the crown princess of the Solaris Empire coming to see me?" he finally asked after a minute's staring.

"How did you know I was the crown princess?" It was time to test her theory on familial similarity.

"You have her likeness."

"How would you know what my grandmother looked like?" she asked, venturing her guess at his meaning. "You don't look much older than I."

"Princess Fiera is legendary. Any Westerner who grew up with sand between his toes knows her face." A small smile cut his lips, the white of his teeth a shocking contrast to the deep tan of his skin. "And looks can be deceiving, princess."

"That they can." Vi glanced over at the other cages. Three others were occupied. "Where's the rest of your caravan?"

"Why?" The smile fell from his face. "Are you asking as a Westerner, to help your kin by blood? Or as a Northerner, to help the kin who raised you?"

Vi knew why they were here, so she knew why he inquired.

Jax had been livid the night Sehra's warriors had rounded up the remnants of the remaining Western caravans from the winter solstice festivities two weeks ago. After the outbreak of the White Death, the Northern capital was thrown into chaos. The people looked for a scapegoat, feet at which to lay their blame, grief, and anger.

The Western caravans fit the bill neatly.

"Neither," Vi confessed. The man didn't want to hear how Sehra's imprisonment of them was as much for their own safety—to prevent the city from tearing them apart—as it was to keep some illusion of peace. At least, so she claimed. "I came to ask a question."

"And why should I help you with your questions?"

"Because I am the granddaughter of the late Empress Fiera."

He snorted. "I am not a Knight of Jadar. While I do see her likeness in you, I do not see you as her reborn, come again to liberate the West."

Vi folded her hands in front of her. The Knights of Jadar were a small group of nationalistic antagonizers. Little else. She stayed focused; he would not distract her.

"Because I can put in a good word for you with Sehra."

That gave him pause. "Truly?"

"Help me, and I'll beseech her for leniency." The night of Jax's rage, Vi had overheard Sehra telling her uncle she had no intention of finding the imprisoned men and women guilty of bringing the White Death to the North. How could she? No one rightfully knew how the plague spread.

But this man didn't need to know that now.

"What is it you seek?"

"I'm looking for a woman. I don't know which caravan she belonged to… she was selling spices during the solstice. I had—"

"Bought some from her," he finished. "Yes. Grendla. I know her."

"You do?" Vi inched forward, but there wasn't much farther to go.

"She wouldn't silence herself after you bought the spices. Kept going on about the honor of your patronage."

"Where is she now? Was she captured?"

"I'm sure she's dead." The man shrugged as though he hadn't just dashed Vi's hopes.

"Dead?" Vi whispered. "Why?" Sehra had intervened before tensions between the residents of Soricium and the solstice guests had erupted into violence.

"Why else? The White Death claimed her. Last I saw she was being taken to that useless clinic of theirs to die far from the Western sun." The man shifted, looking out at the breaking dawn. "Not sure who was the luckier one between us," he whispered.

Her insides tightened at the sentiment. Even if Sehra intended to set them free, even if this was a show to keep peace… These were men and women whose mental and physical wellbeing were being used like tokens on a carcivi board.

And Vi couldn't do a thing about it.

Her hands were tied, especially while she worked toward something far greater. If she helped put an end to the White Death, then she'd help them all. Her father had told her once to always keep her eyes on her greater goal; *never risk losing the war to win a battle.* That was their burden as rulers—a burden Vi still wasn't entirely sure she was ready for, or worthy of.

"Thank you." Vi stepped away from the edge of the walkway.

"Wait," he called after her, all but lunging for the other side of the bars. Vi paused, staring back at him. "If you… if you find her… tell her we're all alive. The ones who got taken at least. Most were with her…"

"I will." Vi gave a small nod. Her eyes stayed locked with his. They were black as well, a hallmark of Western blood. She swallowed. "And I'm sorry. Stay strong, you'll be free soon."

"Will I?" he shouted over the wind as she walked away. "Don't forget, princess— you said you would put in a good word with the Chieftain. You said you would help us!"

Vi didn't look back.

She kept her eyes forward as she stepped into the darkness of the hollowed tree trunk once more. She stayed focused and silent as she made her way back across her stepping stones of light. Not once, all the way back to her room, did she look back in the direction of the cages.

But the whole way, his words stayed with her.

You said you would help us.

Vi laid down in her bed, the plush feather mattress almost too soft underneath her. What did it feel like to sleep in a cage? Did the prisoners manage to sleep at all? This luxury was all she'd ever known and yet somehow it was swiftly becoming uncomfortable.

Did she even deserve it?

"I'm trying to help," she vowed to the air between her and the gnarled wooden ceiling above her four-poster bed. She was helping in the only way she could—by trying to put an end to the source of the plague killing her world. But no one around her was likely to understand that.

Just like they wouldn't understand when she finally slipped away, likely in the dead of night, leaving her crown and duty behind to make for Meru.

She would leave them all, for them all.

But first, she had to find a way to sneak into the deadliest place in Soricium: the clinic.

S HE WAS ONE more droning minute of Martis's lesson away from needing
to physically hold open her eyelids.

"Yes, princess?" He paused, catching Vi at the start of a yawn. "Is there
something you'd like to say?" Martis's eyes darted to the man at the back of room.

Andru sat over Vi's shoulder. Now and then he'd glance up through his blond
locks and long lashes before looking back to his paper—scribbling away. He was
the one the Senate had sent to assess her, to make sure she would be a "princess for
all" and not just the North, despite where she grew up. He was the son of the Head
of Senate, the same Head of Senate who questioned the crown's authority in broad
strokes.

By all counts, Andru should be her enemy. Dislike for the crown should have
been bred into him. With one stroke of his pen, he could write the words that she was
unfit to lead and throw her birthright into question, possibly even pen fodder for the
Empire to question her whole family's rule and allow the Senate to consolidate even
more power.

So she knew what Martis was doing. He was giving her an opportunity to save
face for yawning and possibly being perceived as a poor student. He was trying to
protect her, however misguided that was.

"I was going to say that I agree with your assessment on the grain stores in the
southern capital. It sounds as though with every year, winter gets worse in the South
and the harvest from the East grows thinner." *As though the land itself were going
barren.* Vi briefly spared a thought for whether this was yet another symptom of
Raspain's return; the end of the world had been bleak in her vision. She pushed the
thought away, focusing on the task at hand for now. "It's essential for us to prepare
the populous for the worst."

"Just so." Martis smiled, glanced once more at Andru, and continued on.

Martis was none the wiser that Vi had transformed the person who should've been
her enemy into a dear friend. Her tutor had no idea that the awkward man sitting
behind her was an ally. Or that Andru was the secret lover of her brother.

Vi spared one more glance over her shoulder. Her eyes caught Andru's and she saw
the tiniest movement on his face—a smile shared only with her as Martis prattled on.

"That lesson lasted forever," Vi grumbled, well after the main door to her quarters had closed behind her tutor.

"It was the normal time." Andru slipped his paper into his folio and left it on Martis's desk before starting out the door. Vi followed behind him, pausing at the edge of the desk.

"What is it you write?" She rested her fingertips on the folio.

"You can read it, if you'd like. If you're worried." He paused in the door frame, hands in his pockets, eyes on the folder.

"No, I'm not accusing you of anything. I know you're not out to harm me." She trusted her friend and needed him to know that. "Merely curious."

"It'd likely bore you anyway." Andru gave a small shrug. "It's not too exciting. Father provided me a fairly strict format."

"He's trying to give a rigid framework so there's no room for shades of gray—trying to make me look bad by forcing me into black or white."

"Romulin said much the same." Andru rarely missed an opportunity to mention her brother, or his wisdoms. "Which is why he told me to be vague—honest, but stick only to answering the question and nothing more."

"I would've thought the opposite, actually," Vi mused. "The more the better. If things are left open-ended, I find people assume the worst." Quotes and quick notes were easy to take out of context when not given proper framework around them.

"He said the more I offer, the more likely they are to take that as absolute truth. Offer a little and they're forced to ask me to elaborate. It also means less put in writing."

"Makes sense. Leave it to Romulin to figure out the best way to navigate a political minefield."

"He can turn even the worst losing position into a winning one," Andru said, full of admiration.

Vi stretched her arms over her head and started for the door, leaving the folio behind her. She could admit she wanted to see what Andru had written. But the papers had always been there for her to leaf through at night... and she had yet to. She trusted Andru enough to respect his privacy, and whatever he wrote didn't really matter.

The Senate would have a grand old time spinning stories when the news broke that she had run away.

"What is it?" Andru asked as they left her room, stepping out onto the wide balcony and starting across the creaking rope bridge that connected her quarters to the platform across.

"Hmm?"

"You look somber." His eyes bounced back and forth from being focused on her to looking anywhere else. Andru's hands fidgeted briefly before him before he quickly pocketed them. Vi gave a small smile at his quirks—a smile that fell as her mind returned down the wandering path of her upcoming escape.

Just when she would finally be with her family, she would leave them. Guilt was growing at the thought and if she wasn't careful, it might prevent her from doing what ultimately needed to be done. Then again... it wasn't really "with her family" as she'd always dreamed if her father wasn't there, too.

"The Senate isn't exactly a joyful topic for me." Vi shrugged. "No offense."

"None taken." He took a half-step closer and their shoulders brushed. For him, it was a fairly prominent sign of affection and support. "It's not my favorite topic of conversation, either. But we'll manage it together, Romulin, you, and me."

"We will." Vi forced a smile as she lied through her teeth.

They worked their way down the fortress, spiraling down staircases, crossing studies and kitchens. They took a shortcut through a butler's pantry and a servants' branch walkway. Most of the staff paid them no mind. They were accustomed to the paths the princess took to get where she needed to go.

Eventually, they descended to ground level, to a plot of hard-packed earth. To her right was the noru pen, her left the equine stables, and before her… was a manned gate.

All around the fortress was a large stone wall that had been constructed with Groundbreaker magic. It was tall and perfectly smooth. Sehra's warriors walked along its top edge, patrolling at semi-regular intervals. She'd heard that a wall even greater than this had been constructed during the siege of Soricium. But Vi had never seen anything like it.

In her lifetime, the fortress had always been open to the people. Most respected the boundaries of the sacred trees, choosing to enter through the main inroad of the fortress—and only if they had business. But in theory, it had been accessible to all.

Now, the people were kept away. And, for the first time in her life, Vi's beautiful prison actually looked like one.

"You two finally came," Ellene shouted from the other side of the Noru pens. "All the food has nearly gone cold."

"Sorry, I'm dragging today." Vi climbed the simple fence, jumping down on the other side. The fence was more for display than anything else. Any of the large noru cats that lounged in the patchy shade of the giant trees above them could be halfway across Soricium in a moment if they felt like bolting. But most were more occupied with getting in their fourth nap of the day. *Lucky beasts*, thought Vi.

"You look utterly exhausted," Jayme observed from where she sat at the edge of a picnic blanket.

"I am." Vi rubbed a hand over her face. "I didn't sleep well last night." More like, she didn't sleep at all.

"More nightmares?" Ellene asked softly.

"Yeah, you could say that."

"You always seem tired around this time of the week… almost like clockwork," Jayme observed. Vi knew the look she was giving her—one of pure suspicion. "Any particular reason why?"

"Vi can't control when she gets good sleep and when she doesn't. It's not scheduled in advance." Ellene huffed, sitting on the other side of the blanket. The young woman began rummaging through the basket set out in the center of them as Vi and Andru sat down.

"Are you sure it's nothing?" Jayme persisted, locking eyes with Vi.

"It's nothing," she insisted. She'd have to change her training time; Jayme was a little too suspicious. It was already hard enough to sneak past all the warriors at their new postings ever since Sehra had tightened security after Vi had run away.

"You'll feel better with some food in you." Ellene handed over a long skewer, filled with fire-roasted meats and vegetables.

"I'm sure I will." Vi smiled and made quick work of eating, busying her mouth long enough that the conversation shifted.

"So what did we miss while Martis was wrapping up?" Andru asked, selecting his own skewer. He stared into the basket. "Other than you two completely consuming every last morsel."

"Clearly not every last morsel. Otherwise, what are you eating now?" Jayme rolled her eyes.

"We were dying." Ellene flopped back, tousling her mass of dark curls. "Dying!"

"Dying?" Vi quickly swallowed a half-chewed mass of food to ask.

"Yes, dying," Ellene groaned. "We have, what, a week or two left before your mother is supposed to arrive? I did not intend on us spending it like this." She sighed heavily. "There's nothing to do. We're cooped up here all day, every day... I've forgotten what the sky looks like out from under these trees. And if any of you dare suggest carcivi or balls and mallets again, I will pommel you with said mallet."

Vi looked over her shoulder and back toward the wall that surrounded them once more. She wasn't the only one who was feeling far more trapped.

"It's to keep us safe." Andru rested the end of his half-eaten skewer on his knee. Vi didn't feel as hungry anymore either. "And carcivi is fun."

"That's because you always win," Ellene muttered.

"We're safe, while everyone else is out there dying. It's worth it." Jayme rested her palms on the ground behind her, leaning back. The movement was nonchalant for such a grim statement.

"No talk of dying." Ellene glared at her. "That's the rule as long as Darrus is out there, remember?"

"Sorry," Jayme mumbled.

"He's still working for the clinic then?" Vi asked nonchalantly—at least, she hoped it sounded that way. The topic had come up naturally and she couldn't have hoped for a better opportunity.

"He won't listen to a word I say on the matter. There's no way, he says, that he'll accept my offer for him and his family to stay in the fortress," Ellene said softly. Usually, she'd rise to anger. Vi braced herself for whatever was the source of the introspection—she already knew she wouldn't like it. "Especially not after his cousin was taken to the clinic."

Vi fought a wince and failed.

"Not surprised he won't," Jayme said softly.

"Oh?" Andru finally placed his half-eaten skewer back into the basket. Vi took the last bite of hers and did the same.

"Common folk have solidarity. We're not used to special treatment... so when we get it, it feels... wrong. Unfair. As though we're turning our back on our kin," Jayme elaborated.

"I invited his kin." Ellene propped herself up on her elbows.

"I mean the greater kin of us poor folk against you nobles."

"Against?" Andru hung on the word, but Vi focused on something else.

"You don't feel like we're kin?" Vi asked, shocked.

Jayme gave a small laugh. "I'm not the best example. Half of my life has been spent around you two and your families."

"Regardless of why, Darrus won't. That's all that matters," Ellene grumbled, keeping them on the topic of conversation—her suitor. "I just wish that if he was going to stay out there, he wouldn't take unnecessary risks and work at the clinic."

"It may not be an unnecessary risk," Andru mused hopefully. "We *still* don't know how it spreads, right? Maybe it has nothing to do with proximity."

"And he's working to figure out how it spreads," Jayme offered hopefully. "He'll know first, so he'll know how to protect himself."

"Or he'll be exposed first." Ellene was inconsolable on this matter.

"When does he work with the clerics?" Vi worked to stay focused, to guide the conversation in the direction she needed it to go. Perhaps she could have Ellene summon him the next time he was free. Then Vi could try to get a message to the Western woman through him... or, at the least, find out if she was even still alive.

"Nights, sometimes late afternoons."

Vi could work with that. "Maybe, perhaps, we could steal him away one afternoon, keep him from exposing himself further? Maybe convince him to take one night off, even. If he won't stay here permanently, we could at least lessen the risk some?"

"That's not a terrible idea..." Ellene sat back upright, crossing her legs. "It's been a while since we—"

"Open the gates!" The shout of a warrior patrolling the wall interrupted Ellene. All four of their heads jerked in the direction of the manned stone gate. The two warriors were moving forward, sweeping their hands up and then down, magically lowering the stone pillars that blocked the main path. "Imperial rider!"

Vi rose to her feet slowly, vaguely aware of the others doing the same.

Imperial rider. Squinting, she could make out a horse in the distance. The details of its leathers were impossible to decipher, but Vi already knew what they looked like. She knew they had the emblazoned suns of Solaris stretching across them just like Jayme's did when she was out for deliveries.

"Vi—"

She didn't know who called after her, but Vi was running. She was over the fence and on the other side, starting toward the gate. She knew it wouldn't be her mother or brother. And yet... this person was from them. Her heart was still racing at the thought of how close her family was.

The horse sped through the open gate and the two warriors on either side raised the pillars once more. The woman slowed the speckled stallion down, her feet pressing forward as her body leaned back slightly in the saddle.

Without a second thought, Vi walked right up to her.

"Report," Vi commanded. There were warriors coming from the wall. She had no doubt Sehra and Jax were on their way from within the fortress. But her attention was solely on the blonde-haired woman hastily dismounting before her.

"I have a message for the chieftain, please excuse me." The rider handed Vi the reins.

Vi blinked at them, glancing down at herself. Well, she wasn't exactly dressed like a princess today. Though the overall finery in fabric and make should've given something away. *The Westerners had known who she was at a mere glance.* A Southerner clearly had no idea.

"I believe it is information I am privy to." Vi dropped the reins and stepped in front of the woman.

Her blue eyes narrowed slightly as her face twisted into an indigent look. "I was told to deliver my message to the chieftain, not a stable hand. Now, see my horse is fed and brushed while I carry out Imperial business."

A tiny smile crossed Vi's lips. She had a lot of options on where to go from here, and all were appealing.

"That is no stable hand." Her friends had joined her, and Jayme was the one to speak up on Vi's behalf. "I believe it is customary to bow before your crown princess."

The woman looked back to Vi, and Vi saw the moment realization dawned on her. She did more than bow. The woman practically fell to her knee.

"Forgive me, your highness. I did not—"

Vi held up her hand. She didn't care right now about appearances, even though she could practically hear Martis's voice in her head droning on about how she should. This was the moment the true judgment of the South began. With this woman's first impression, rumors would spread. And she had been plain enough to be mistaken for a stable hand—not the most ideal start.

Perhaps it was for the best she had already intended on running away.

"Tell me news of my mother," Vi demanded.

"The Imperial parade is approximately three days from Soricium." The woman raised her eyes. "I was sent ahead so your preparations could begin."

Vi's heart skipped a beat. In fact, it skipped several. She struggled to find air while keeping her face regal and passive.

"Three days, that's much earlier than expected," Ellene murmured.

It was, and that meant she didn't have time to wait and find an excuse for Darrus to be sent to the fortress.

She had to go to him herself.

4

"*N*ARRO HATH HOOLO.*" As Vi spoke the words, light spun Taavin into existence. Vi pulled the magic back from her fingertips, drawing it tightly around her wrist, imagining it as though it were a rope knotting in place.

"I'm surprised you're not asleep yet." He looked toward the window. "You usually don't summon me after we're up all night."

"Tonight isn't going to be any normal evening."

"I'm not going to like this, am I?" A frown crossed his lips as he looked her up and down. "You're dressed to go out."

Vi pulled at the hem of her cloak. He must've remembered it from when she had last sneaked out into Soricium. That was when she still questioned the necessity of finding the apexes—before she had seen the end of the world. Before she had become invested in *him*.

"I am." Vi crossed to the window, putting her back to him. She didn't want him to see her face because she still had yet to train an expression onto it when talking about her family. "I received word today that my mother will be here in roughly three days' time."

Taavin made no sound when he moved. *He's not actually here*, she reminded herself time and again. Every instance was harder. Because she wanted him to be. She wanted his feet to actually touch the floor, his body to move the air around him as he stepped.

Yet, even though he wasn't, Vi felt him as though he was. She felt his essence near as he crossed the room to stand behind her. He could make not a single sound or footfall, and she'd know exactly where he was.

She waited for him to say something. Curiously, he didn't. Taavin was oddly quiet, as if waiting.

So Vi filled the silence.

"They've been preparing me all day for it. Tailors measured me and sketched 'options' as each of my tutors reviewed things. I took dinner with Sehra to discuss logistics… the White Death has really pared back the plans for the arrival.

"The whole Imperial parade was supposed to come into the city with all its fanfare and might. But now they don't want to subject the military—or my mother and brother—to the illness that's ravaging Soricium.

"Likely for the best. I can't imagine the older residents of Soricium being particularly pleased about the Imperial militia in their city again, even briefly. Sehra agreed with me on that much."

"How are you handling it all?" Taavin stopped her nervous rambling with a gentle hand on her elbow. The touch nearly made Vi jump from her skin, and she turned in place.

"What?" Vi's voice had dropped to a whisper, though she didn't know why. Perhaps it was because the question was so confusing. Or perhaps she had been wrong about knowing *exactly* where he was. Taavin was far closer than she expected. "What does that even mean?"

His emerald eyes searched her face. "It seems a lot all at once."

"I can handle it." She looked back toward the window.

"I never said you couldn't."

"It sounded like you implied it." Vi still wasn't looking at him, so she only heard the soft sound of his laughter.

"Inquiring after your emotional state suggests your ineptitude?"

"If you're worried about my emotional state, you must think it's unraveling. You must think that I can't, or I won't—"

"Or I merely care for you." Her eyes flicked to him at that, and then promptly away. There was a raw emotion on his face that she didn't want to investigate right now. Perhaps he was right to ask about her emotional state. Because merely seeing him look at her that way knotted her insides. "Does anyone around you see how *you* are—the woman—not the princess, during all this?"

"Of course not. And why would they?" Vi added hastily. "This is what I've always wanted." Now she didn't know if she was speaking more to him, or to herself.

"Sometimes, getting what you've always wanted is the hardest part," he murmured.

"What do you mean?" Vi turned in place to face him outright, rather than look out the window. Their chests were nearly brushing. Had he taken a step closer without her realizing?

Magic radiated off of him in warm, invisible waves. He was close enough that she could almost smell him, though Vi was certain she was merely imagining the soft aroma of lilies, cedar, and the fresh, clean air of spring.

"I've always wanted to leave this place, to see the world—to merely see Risen from beyond my tower and not through the curling smoke of Yargen's flame. But I have no idea what I would feel, or do, if I had such freedom."

"This is different," she whispered. *Was it?* She was staring down the eve of her freedom, the day she would leave Soricium and finally see the wide world that had been confined to the four corners of her maps until now.

"I always wanted to understand *you*," he continued, ignoring her insistence. The statement stalled any further objection. Vi was vaguely aware of his hands scooping up hers. She had never recalled someone being as forward with her as he had become—all she knew was that she liked it. But Vi couldn't recall much right now; the world started and ended for a few all too brief breaths with his shockingly green eyes. "The visions I had of you... relentless. I prayed to Yargen time and again to make sense of them, for the chance to understand them. I had all but given up hope in my confinement. And then, miraculously, you came to me. I got what I wanted and now…"

His voice faded away. Vi leaned in slightly, hanging on the absence of the rest of his thought.

"Now?" she barely breathed the word of encouragement.

"Now I don't know what to do with you in my reach." His gaze dropped to their hands and Vi's did as well.

Their fingers wrapped and unwrapped, slowly shifting like the lines of a magic glyph, changing and taking new shapes as they knotted together in different ways. Much like a glyph, there was power in his hold, and a hidden meaning. Ever since she'd reached for him after the first time she was attacked by the assassin, it had become more natural, easier. There always seemed to be an excuse—at the very least the need for reassurance—for them to reach out and touch each other. But it was undeniable they made use of every opportunity.

Maybe now, they did it without an excuse at all.

"I'm not really in your reach," she whispered, reclaiming his gaze. "Not yet." Vi pulled her hands away, drawing her cloak tighter around her. "I have to get to Meru first."

"And you require something out there to accomplish that feat." Taavin gave a nod to the window. "That's why you're leaving, isn't it?"

"The woman I went in search of is in the clinic." A frown crossed Taavin's lips. "I must go and find her. That place, she said it's in the Crossroads. The Imperial party is heading through there. It's where I'll need to break away and head to Norin. I can find an Apex on my way to you."

"You won't make it to me if you're afflicted with the White Death."

"How does it spread?" It was meant to be a mere question, but it came out as more of a demand. Somehow, she was confident he knew. He had to.

"I don't know how Raspain's tainted magic works." Taavin shook his head.

"You must have a sound guess at least."

He sighed at her. "I suspect it started with sorcerers on the Dark Isle, because they have a fragment of Yargen's magic—an inroad for Raspian to take root in their souls. Non-sorcerers may not be as susceptible, but even their bodies, as creations of Yargen, will eventually break down when confronted with Raspian's evil."

"It's as though the world is rotting from the inside out." Vi remembered her earlier lesson with Martis. Would the White Death have a chance to ravage the population, or would famine do the work of it on the dark god's behalf?

"An apt description." Taavin took a small step closer. Their toes were nearly touching and Vi tilted her head to look up at him. His hands rested on her upper arms, holding them gently. "I don't know if you will be in less danger, having Yargen's full power. The White Death is only just beginning to appear on Meru. It is possible that since this land is still touched by Yargen's unfractured magic, the White Death has been warded off… but even her magic is becoming too weak to stop it entirely. So it may have just prolonged the inevitable."

"Or it's possible I'll be in more danger—that I'll somehow be targeted by Raspian's power because I'm a shining beacon for Yargen." Vi reached the logical conclusion of his thought. Taavin gave a small nod. "I don't have a choice though."

"You can't possibly find every Apex—"

"It's not just about the Apexes." She gripped his forearms in a sudden burst of energy. Vi leaned forward slightly, beseeching him. Their noses nearly touched. "It's about my father, too." Taavin stilled. "There's no word of him here—no word there, either?" He gave a small shake of his head. "Then I… What if fate changed from my first vision? What if he will not make it to Meru? What if he perished at sea?"

Vi hung her head, taking a slow breath. She didn't know if Taavin understood or not. He'd never said anything about his family.

"If I go to the Apexes, maybe I'll see him again."

Taavin released her. Vi continued to avoid his gaze, hastily working to compose herself. She didn't like how quickly her emotions ran away from her when it came to the mere mention of her father.

His index finger hooked under her jaw. A shiver shot straight down her spine as he gently tilted her face upward. The pad of Taavin's thumb rested lightly on her chin. She'd never been so keenly aware of such a small touch.

"I understand…" He swallowed, as if choking on the words. "This is our fate."

"Help me?" Vi whispered.

"Anything."

"I need a new face to sneak out with."

His mouth tipped up into a small, sly smile. "I thought I told you not to worry about that crook in your nose from where it smashed into the tree."

Vi took a step away, her hand flying up to her face. She felt the ridge of her nose—reaffirming for the dozenth time that there was, indeed, no crook. Her eyes narrowed, and just like that, whatever trance they had been falling under was broken.

"There is no crook. And it's not about that," she hastily continued before Taavin could get them off track again. "It's about *durroe*."

"Yes?"

"I've been trying to make an illusion to mask myself… but I can't seem to get it to sit right."

"Show me."

"*Durroe watt ivin*." Vi held up her free hand, raising it to the top of her head. She closed her fingers as she chanted, imagining she was puling an invisible mask over her face. Light shone under her fingertips as they trailed over her eyes.

The world was hazy, softly illuminated. Vi crossed the room to her dressing area, standing before the mirror. Sure enough, a face that wasn't hers looked back at her. But it seemed to ripple and shift, like condensed smoke lit by candles, and it certainly wasn't about to fool anyone.

"See, it doesn't sit right."

"How are you constructing it?" Taavin made a quick circle around her, inspecting the edges of her magic.

"Trying to think of how my face could change and tweaking that—maybe like a mask of a modified version of myself."

He hummed at that. "I admit, I've never tried this before… It's a curious application for *durroe*."

"Does that mean you can't help?" Vi's heart sunk. He always had an answer.

"I will always help you," Taavin said, mumbling through his thoughts. "*Durroe watt ivin* is much easier if you try to think of it as creating something new, rather than modifying something that's there. I would try changing your whole appearance. Don't even imagine yourself inside. You are vanishing, and the new form is appearing."

Vi let go of the magic and made a second attempt. "*Durroe watt ivin*." A shifting outline overtook her, still not completely whole.

"Who are you trying to replicate?"

"No one, just reinventing some things."

"Well, that could be another part of the problem. Start with something simpler. Instead of trying to invent every last detail of someone who doesn't exist, or tweak yourself in ways you have to struggle to imagine and keep straight in your mind. Start by turning yourself into someone who already exists. Someone you know well."

Vi looked to the mirror, seeing her own dark eyes reflected back. She hadn't considered that… *Who should she pick?*

It would have to be someone who wouldn't raise suspicion going in or out of the fortress. Someone the warriors would open the gates for, but wouldn't care about leaving. Someone whose every detail she knew as well as she knew herself.

Sehra, Jax, or Ellene would be too noteworthy. Andru never left and never expressed any interest in doing so.

"*Durroe watt ivin.*"

Vi and Taavin both stared in the mirror for several seconds, looking at her handiwork. It was a near spitting image, down to every last brown wave of hair.

"That'll do, I think." Taavin patted her on the shoulder. His hand went through the illusion, landing oddly underneath as though plummeting through a smoke screen.

It reminded Vi of how Waterrunners could manipulate water vapor in the air to shift the light and make illusions. For the first time, she wondered just how the elemental magicks of the Solaris Empire were connected to the power of Yargen the rest of the world possessed. Taavin had said the sorcerers in the Empire possessed *fractured* magic…

But that was a line of questioning for a different time.

Right now, the moon was already up, and this was going to be her only chance to get the information she needed.

5

V I SLIPPED OUT of her room and into the welcoming embrace of darkness. Patrols had increased throughout the fortress following the attack on her and the rise of the White Death. But they were still relatively scarce this high up—especially after the wall was erected. It seemed most still believed that if they stopped people from entering the fortress at the ground level, they didn't have to worry too much about the upper levels.

She kept her hood up and face down, taking an alternate route than the one she normally wound down. Vi paused in a shadowed stair, right before the final main bridge that led out of the section of the fortress that housed nobility. A guard was always positioned here now, and this would be her first test.

"*Durroe watt ivin,*" she whispered under her breath. It was as if she were stepping into a second skin. The light wove around her, clinging to her as she pressed onward. Vi's vision was hazy, illuminated by the shifting power at its edges. But she could see in her periphery that her hand had changed.

Gone was the cloak, and in its place was a simple jerkin.

Vi strode forward. The warrior glanced over her shoulder as she neared and Vi gave a small nod. She held her breath and prayed that the woman guarding the path had no interest in small talk. All remained silent, the warrior made no move to stop her, and Vi slipped further into the night.

Her heart was racing, waiting for the guard to rush after her. Waiting for some kind of alarm to be called as her guise was up. But Taavin's quick instruction held as firm as Vi's white-knuckled grip around the glyph that surrounded her right fist.

As Vi stepped out onto the barren earth of the stables, she raised her left hand to her lips. If she could make it through this, then she could masquerade as anyone.

"*Durroe sallvas.*"

Durroe, to deceive.

Sallvas, create sound.

Her lips tingled. Vi could practically taste the magic as it wrapped around her tongue. She could imagine with startling clarity the symbol that had taken residence over her voice box.

"Open the gate," Vi said in Jayme's voice.

"Ma'am?" One of the warriors asked.

"Imperial business." Less was more. She got away with that as the princess, could she do the same pretending to be Jayme acting on her behalf?

The two guards shared a look and then one lifted his hand. A portion of the gate lowered in response to the magical command. Vi merely stared at the rocky ground that the stone had retreated into.

Was it really going to be that easy?

"Thank you. I will be back in—" Her voice cracked. Vi could hear the octave raise slightly, breaking into her natural cadence of speech. The magic unraveled.

"Jayme, are you well?" One of the men stepped forward. Vi had never seen his face before and she had no idea who he was. But Jayme might, and that was something she wasn't prepared to try to cover.

Quickly raising her left hand to her lips, Vi made a show of coughing. In-between forced coughs, she hastened a mumbled, "*Durroe sallvas.*" The man made no indication of hearing.

"Something in my throat," Vi said softly, trying not to break the magic by speaking too quickly. Her right fist felt warm, as though her illusion was struggling to get away from her. Navigating both disguises at the same time without flaw was proving difficult. "I shall return."

With that, Vi hastened away.

If the guard was suspicious, he wasn't suspicious enough to run after her. Vi continued on the main road, forcing her pace to be as slow as she could bear, before dipping into a side alley between two large tree trunks. Glancing around and seeing no one, Vi let out a sigh and felt the magic unravel.

Exhaustion soaked into her bones. Wearing someone else's face was no easy task. But she'd pulled it off. Vi stared down at her hands in marvel and horror. To think, a few mere months ago she could barely make an orb of light with Sehra—could barely muster magic at all. Now she was deceiving people with light and sound.

If she managed to truly gain mastery of the illusions and sound manipulation... If she could hold it—*hold it! Hoolo!* Vi smacked herself lightly in the forehead.

"I'm an idiot." She gave a soft laugh at herself, one that quickly vanished as she looked back to her hands.

Hoolo. It was her personal word of power—to hold, to sustain—given to her by the goddess herself, through Taavin.

Whenever Vi added the word *hoolo* to her spells, her magic wasn't depleted. Vi didn't know where the power was drawn from, perhaps the goddess herself... but the how didn't matter so long as it worked. Vi made a note to see if the word had any limitations; if it worked the same with every combination of words, then the depth of *hoolo*'s power was unfathomable.

Could she use *hoolo* on two spells at once? Or would it lose its effectiveness? It was something she'd have to try, and pick Taavin's brain over.

With *hoolo* and confidence in her Lightspinning abilities, she could be anyone. She could wear any face, have any voice. Her hand balled into a fist. That also meant anyone else gifted with Lightspinning likely could too, maybe just for a shorter period of time.

She had to be careful. Enemies could be lurking in plain sight.

Vi treaded lightly as she continued into the sleeping city. She glanced over her shoulder, making note of every other lone wanderer in the midnight hours. Even at this time, it seemed unnaturally quiet.

A city overtaken by the shroud of death.

It took her two wrong turns before she finally found Darrus's family home. She'd only been there twice before with Ellene. So while her map-inclined memory of the city had not failed her, her recollection of where he lived had. The house was expectedly dark, not a soul stirring. Vi looped around the back, crouching below shuttered windows, glancing through the cracks.

The first room she peered into at the front was what appeared to be a family area. The back half of the house was occupied by a larger room that had a wide bed with two sleeping figures in it. Off the main road, a stairway wound around the tree the home was built into—leading up to more homes stacked on top of each other in the hollowed out trunk.

Setting her feet down softly, Vi made her way up the stair toward an upper window. She pulled it back slightly, hoping the hinges didn't squeal. They didn't. Inside the room was a single bed, and in it, Darrus asleep.

This was the last moment she had to turn back. But Vi ignored it, instead whispering a hushed, "Darrus... Darrus!"

It took four tries for him to stir, each louder than the last. She was at the point of crawling through the window when the man groaned. He twisted from one side of the bed to the other, and then finally sat upright, rubbing his eyes with the back of his hand.

"Darrus," Vi hissed again. She saw his eyes come into focus, landing on her. His hands dropped slowly to his lap as he blinked at her.

"P-Princess?" He rubbed his eyes again quickly. "Am I dreaming?"

"No, you're not. Be quiet and come here," Vi commanded sternly. The last thing she wanted was his surprise to rouse his sleeping parents below.

Darrus slipped out of bed, looking uncertain, and crossed the room to her. Halfway, the air must've hit his bare chest and caught up to his sleep-hazy mind, because he looked down and hastened over to a short dresser. Vi resisted the urge to roll her eyes; it was hardly the first man's chest she'd seen. But she allowed him his modesty as it only took him a second to pull on the knit sweater and make his way to her.

"What're you doing here?" He eased open the shutter the rest of the way and leaned out, looking around.

"I'm alone." Vi suspected he was looking for Ellene and Jayme.

"Just what're you getting up to in the city alone? *Again*." While Darrus had never mentioned it to anyone, he clearly had not forgotten the first time they ran into each other.

"I need to get to the clinic." Vi didn't mince words.

"*What?*"

"I need you to help me get into the clinic."

"No, no, no."

"I have to."

"If you want to get in there, seek out another cleric." Darrus leaned away from the window, folding his arms over his chest. "I'm still an apprentice. They'd cut my lessons entirely if I took, of all people, the crown princess in there."

"Or I could command them to cut your lessons entirely if you don't." Vi lowered her voice, giving him a hard stare.

His arms fell to his sides. "You wouldn't."

"You have no idea what I will and won't do." Vi was still learning herself. "One is a possibility, if we get caught. The other is far more certain."

"Why me?"

"Because I know you can keep a secret." That was an honest answer. "No one can know I was there."

"Why do you want to go?" The question was skeptical, uncertain, but wasn't as firm as his first objection.

Vi had anticipated the query, and thought of a number of angles from which to answer it. There was doubling down on her threat. Commanding him outright. Telling him some part of the truth of her visions. Or... a lie that may hit a little too close to home after what Ellene had told her.

"It's..." She forced her voice to go soft, looking away from him. The guilt for the lie wasn't as overwhelming then as when she looked him in the eye. "It's personal."

"What is it, princess?" He leaned forward once more. Oh, Darrus did love a good damsel to save. She'd seen Ellene tap into the fact countless times.

"There's a woman there—she came with one of the caravans. I was talking with my uncle and he said that she... that she may be related to my father's family, through my grandmother." Vi buried her face in her hands. "I never knew my family, and now my father, he's—" She didn't have to fabricate the choke in her throat. "—he's gone. I feel like I'm losing everyone before I even knew them."

She pulled her face away from her palms and looked up to him. Darrus sighed, his whole demeanor softening. Guilt began to rise; Vi hastened to close her mental floodgates, blocking it from pouring out.

This was for the best. What she was doing was for everyone—for the whole world. She'd do whatever it took to find the apexes. Every action she took toward that goal steeled her further.

"I understand." Darrus rested a hand on her shoulder.

"You do?" she asked, making her voice thin and frail, as if she teetered on the edge of tears.

"I do."

"I just want a few moments alone with the woman... Can you help me? No one else will. You're the only chance I have."

He sighed, and Vi knew what he'd say before he said it. "All right. But we're in and out quickly. If anyone finds I took you there, I'll be in a kind of trouble I don't even want to imagine."

"I don't want to get you in trouble," Vi reassured him. "We'll be fast, and I'll stay hidden under one of the plague masks."

He nodded, starting back in his room. Vi watched as he went and gathered his own heavy clothes, gloves, and mask, which he settled on the top of his head. Darrus crossed back over and Vi straightened from her crouch, taking a few steps down the stairs so he could crawl through the window. She suspected this was not the first time he'd snuck out in the night; she wondered if Ellene had ever been involved.

Giving him a nod, Vi started down the stairs. But she paused when she didn't hear him following her. Darrus stared down at her, unmoving, and for a brief moment she was worried he'd reconsider.

"Princess," he whispered. "The clinic... it's a hard place to be. Once you go there, well, you'll see things that you can never unsee."

Vi fought a bitter smile. She knew he meant well, just as she knew there was no way he knew of all the things she'd already borne witness to that she couldn't unsee. Her dreams were becoming more torturous as the weeks and months progressed, the remnants of seeing the end of the world impossible to escape.

How much worse could it get?

6

S HE FOLLOWED DARRUS through the back alleyways and suspended bridges of the city, crossing into the still-lit parts of town. No one paid them any mind. No one expected to see the crown princess walking in their midst, and certainly not toward the clinic.

Moreover, the plague mask, even propped on her forehead, covered and shadowed the majority of her face.

Finally, they ended up on a single road stretching away from the city. Vi could see the mark of Groundbreaker's work, practically feel the magic still lingering in the air. There were no more houses here; even the trees seemed shrunken without all the additions of living quarters, walkways, and balconies. She'd thought the city had been quiet, but it was nothing compared to the heavy stillness of the first few steps into the vacant space between the city's edge and the clinic.

Then, she heard the first shouts of the diseased.

It was a soft rumbling, a litany of moans and groans, punctuated by shrill screams and cries. Vi drew her cloak more tightly around her, staring up at the dark shadow of the stone building before her. The trees around it had been stripped back and the moon stared down, as if watching. She looked up at the celestial body.

Perhaps the dark god himself was watching.

"Here." Darrus tapped the mask on her head. "Put it on now."

"What about you?" Vi grabbed for it, her hand lingering.

"I'll say I lost mine and get another when we get inside. But we can't have them noticing you before then." He gave a nod toward the entrance and it was then that Vi noticed two people positioned on either side. "And you should have the protection from here out."

Two more warriors were at the front corners of the building, and she'd bet two more were at the back. They were bulky, tall, and wielded bows, spears, and swords. Vi had no doubt they were Sehra's best. Just as she had no doubt that their guard was not to keep people away from the clinic—no one in their right mind would enter here willingly, Vi excluded.

No… These warriors were to keep people *in*. To ensure that the only way someone left the clinic, other than the clerics, was as ashes.

"Are you sure?" Vi asked softly, still holding the mask. What she wanted to ask was if he was certain he wanted to take the risk of going in unprotected. Luckily, it seems he heard the unspoken question.

"They still don't know how it spreads. The masks may not help at all." He shrugged. Vi knew the bravery was a front. "I'll get one in short order, so don't worry about me."

"I do, because Ellene will slay me if anything happens to you because of me."

"Not that she'd know," he muttered. "Come dawn, we weren't here at all."

He stepped into the moonlight, and Vi wondered when he'd become so brave. Staring down your own mortality daily could do that—change a person fundamentally. Hadn't it done the same to her? If she had never seen the visions she'd witnessed, would she have the ability to be here now, risking his life and hers?

Pushing the thoughts from her mind, Vi stepped into the moonlight and followed closely behind toward the boxy stone building.

"Halt," one of the guards said, stepping forward. "No one without a mask is permitted within." He paused, his head turned to Darrus, moonlight flashing on the glassy orbs of the mask that covered the warrior's eyes. "You shouldn't even risk being this close without a mask."

"Mine broke," Darrus lied. "I need to get another."

"I see," the guard said, somewhat skeptical.

"Come on, I'm doing a double tomorrow starting at dawn and Romou will kill me if I'm late for it." Darrus put his hand on his hip.

"What happened?"

"I was putting my mask away and it fell, shattered the eyes. I didn't want to deal with this in the morning so I came now." Darrus motioned to her. "I brought a friend so I don't even have to go in without a mask. She can go in and grab me one and bring it back. Does that work?"

The warrior turned to Vi. She stared at him through the haze of the glass that covered her eyes. Her breath was hot on her face, nerves turning the inside of her mask into a sauna. Thankfully, her cloak hid her swiftly rising and falling chest just as the mask hid her face.

"Yeah, fine." The warrior shrugged and returned to his post. "Do what you need to."

Darrus turned to her. "Get me one of the flatter ones—I don't want one of the beaked ones," he instructed slowly. "I'll need a larger one. They keep that style on the top shelf of the storeroom to the right."

Storeroom to the right.

"Flat one, got it," Vi mumbled. Her voice was utterly unrecognizable when muffled by the long beak of Darrus's mask and all the filters it contained, no magic required.

Trying to seem as though she'd entered the clinic a hundred times, Vi pushed open the doors. Neither of the warriors so much as glanced at her as she slipped into the building.

The immediate entry was a wide room with absolutely nothing in it. Stone walls, stone ceiling, no windows. Only a few flame bulbs positioned in the corners illuminated the ominously dark room. The rock was so thick that the sounds of wailing had vanished and a heavy silence settled on her.

"To the right..." There were two doors on the right wall. Vi walked over to the closer one first. She had a fifty-fifty shot.

Opening the heavy door, Vi was greeted by a room filled with various tools. Shackles and chains hung on the wall at her left. A wide, flat, disturbingly stained table sat in the center. A wall of shelves contained jars with all manner of grotesquely severed parts suspended in a clear liquid.

What was this place?

She stepped into the room, uncomfortably curious. It was a question she didn't think she wanted the answer to, yet wondered all the same. Scalpels and saws were hung along the back wall. A table underneath had all manner of wickedly gleaming instruments.

Vi turned away from them, to the second door at her right. Behind that heavy door was a small closet-like room. Shelves lined every wall, filled with heavy gloves, thick coats, and masks. Luckily, she was tall and only had to step up using the bottom shelf. If she'd been shorter like Ellene, she would've had to scale half the shelves to reach what Darrus needed.

Quickly closing the doors behind her, Vi returned to the main entrance.

"Thanks," Darrus said, stepping forward to take the mask. Without another word from the warriors on either side, he followed her within.

"What are these rooms?" Vi whispered, though she didn't know why. There was no one around and the guard certainly couldn't hear them through the heavy doors.

"Triage... more or less," Darrus answered grimly. "We keep it empty so the diseased have nothing to attack us with."

"Do they attack you?"

"Often... either they don't have their wits about them any longer, they're more animal than human." As he spoke, Vi remembered the crazed man from the winter solstice, and the man in the cage from her vision of her father on Meru. "Or... they are still in denial. Some, I think, truly want to fight for their freedom. They see this for the death sentence that it is. Others are hoping that maybe one of us will make a mistake and kill them as we try to subdue them."

"Have you killed anyone?" Vi whispered.

"Not personally." He took a step forward, pointing at the doors as he walked. There was a mechanical quality to him now. Vi couldn't tell if it was a wall, guarding the more tender man she'd seen with Ellene, or a complete switch in personality—a new side of him born of necessity. She wished she could see his face, the mask only further added to the unnerving quality of his current nature.

"That door—" he pointed to the one she'd found the storeroom through "—is for those already dead, or one breath away, when they're brought here. The master clerics dissect them, trying to find out a root cause for the disease." He pointed to the left. "That one is for those still in the early stages. Ahead is for those who are far along, but not quite dead yet."

"And this one?" she asked as his hand landed on the second door to the right.

"Clerics only," he answered as they stepped into a small sitting area.

There were two tables, some low benches in a corner, what could only be described as a small kitchen on either side of a hearth—though Vi couldn't imagine who found their appetite in a place like this. Two clerics lifted their masked faces toward them. They raised a hand by way of greeting, and Darrus did the same—but that was all the attention they paid them, as they quickly returned to their hushed conversation.

Vi strained to listen as she followed Darrus behind them. But the words were impossible to make out underneath the heavy mask that covered her head. Neither of the clerics said anything as her and Darrus slipped out a back door and into a narrow hall.

"We're going up to the walk," he said softly, glancing over his shoulder. "Mentally ready yourself."

Vi didn't dare ask what he meant. Her heart inched up her throat with every beat, a rising apprehension at the sheer unknown she'd find at the top of the stairwell. There was a landing, another door, and then on the other side, death.

They stepped onto a narrow walkway, guarded by stone bars on their left, that overlooked a great pit to their right. It was then that Vi figured out the layout of the clinic. The front third were the rooms Darrus had talked about—the ones she'd walked through. The back two thirds were split like two rectangles set long-ways against each other. The far rectangle was covered—Vi could only assume more rooms and better accommodations for those less progressed. The final third that she now laid eyes on was open to the sky, and packed to the brim with people.

This was where the wailing she'd heard originated from.

Vi watched as men and women in tattered clothing, some completely naked, drifted from place to place. Some howled and wailed. Some had enough sense to weep white, sticky tears across bulging red veins from milky eyes. Vi watched in horror as one man ran into the wall, head first, again and again. She didn't know how long she watched... but it was long enough that he fell a final time and did not get up.

"Vi." Darrus rested his hand lightly on her arm and her head jerked toward his. How she wished she could see his face in that moment—see another human's face, not diseased. It was the first time he had referred to her without the title of "princess" and Vi didn't even remark on it. In fact, it was welcome.

Standing before one's own mortality, titles meant nothing.

"Can we do anything more for them?" she asked weakly, clearing her throat, trying to find strength and authority. But there was none.

"We do all we can. We're not prepared for an outbreak of this size... But at least, by the time we lead them here, they can't seem to feel pain."

Vi looked back to the pit. They were doing their best. *This* was their best. It was horrific and inhumane—Vi could see that. What she couldn't see was another solution. Her mind had gone as blank as the milky eyes of the nearly deceased.

"I didn't want to upset you."

"I know." She swallowed hard. "I'm not upset." It sounded like a lie. She didn't rightly know what it was. She didn't even know how she felt.

"Well, I brought you here first to see if you saw your kin... if she's already in the pit, there's no way we can get to her," he said solemnly.

I have a job to do. Vi put the words on repeat in her mind. She couldn't balk now. She balled her hands into fists to keep them from trembling.

"Let me look." Vi began to walk the length of the pit, looking at the men and women of all shapes and sizes. Luckily, it was a full moon, so she could make out most of them. The majority were Northern, making the few Westerners and one or two Easterners easier to pick out. Finally, Vi shook her head. "I don't see her."

"Then you may be in luck. If she's not out here, she has some of her mind left." Darrus started back toward the door.

Vi reached out, grabbing his sleeve at the elbow. "Can nothing more truly be done for them?"

"Do you have an idea? Because the clerics have come up with nothing." The question sounded genuine, as though he'd take any answer she could offer. When she said nothing, he spoke again. "Some have suggested mercy kills... But we're clerics. We want to heal. Not slay. And if there's a chance to find a cure—a chance for just one person to be saved—we want them alive to see the next dawn."

Vi gave a small nod. "I understand."

"You do?"

"I do." The lie was said with confidence. She said it because she knew that he needed to hear it. But in truth, she had no idea what her stance was on the matter. "You're doing all you can... and I thank you for it. So let's move on."

They retraced their steps to the entry, then across and through the door that had been on her left when she entered. The two clerics she'd seen were busy mixing some salve in a large vat in the corner of a completely new room. Vi could smell their potions through the filters of her mask. Both looked up as they entered.

"We'll do a round," Darrus announced. The two gave nods, then ignored them as Darrus led her into a secondary hall.

The echoes of soft moans and groans filled her ears. Unlike the guttural, almost beast-like noises of the pit, these sounds still seemed distinctly human. They were aware of pain still, Vi realized, thinking back to what Darrus had told her.

"Go ahead and look," Darrus instructed quietly. "I'll stand guard by the door and stall if those two get suspicious. Be as quick as you can."

"Thank you."

Vi slipped off down the hall, looking at the cells on either side. At first, they all contained multiple people who looked relatively normal; they raised their heads, weak and listless, as she passed. But the further she walked, the fewer people were housed together, until ultimately the sickest among them were contained in isolation.

It was there, almost all the way in the back, that Vi found the spice seller Grendla.

She was slumped in the back corner, a curtain of black hair covering her face. Her hands were at her sides, upturned, legs straight out, as though she was bearing the ravages of the disease on her body for all to see. She looked as limp and lifeless as a doll.

Vi crouched and then, as if sensing her, Grendla's face jerked up.

"Who?" she hissed slowly, her all-white eyes unseeing.

"The crown princess, Vi Solaris," Vi announced softly. Let the woman tell the clerics the princess came to visit. Vi doubted she'd be believed.

The woman smiled. It stretched between two gnarly red veins on either side of her cheeks. For a brief second, Vi was reminded of the crescent scar that ran along Taavin's face.

"You came. I knew you'd come."

"I have to ask—"

"But you're too late... too late. I don't have it."

"The key?"

"It's with my things, in the caravan. But it is yours. Your fate is there, in the main market of the Crossroads, on the way to your throne, just as you left it, Princess Ci'Dan." The woman's head lobbed back and forth, her jaw slack.

"Princess Solaris."

"You are she come again." She was delirious in her disease. "It is yours. The place. The main market. Given for you."

"How do I find the key?"

"Too late, too late. It's hidden with the rest. Back of the tome, the records I kept. Too late…" Grendla repeated the words again and again, white spittle dripping down her chin and onto her lap.

"Did you ever see any visions about me?" Vi dared to ask. "You were a future seer in the Crossroads, right? Did you—"

"Too late… too late…"

Vi straightened, looking down at the woman. Maybe a day more, and she would be in the pit with the rest of them. But she'd secured enough information for now—a headway.

Now, to find the remnants of the caravan, and some kind of record book.

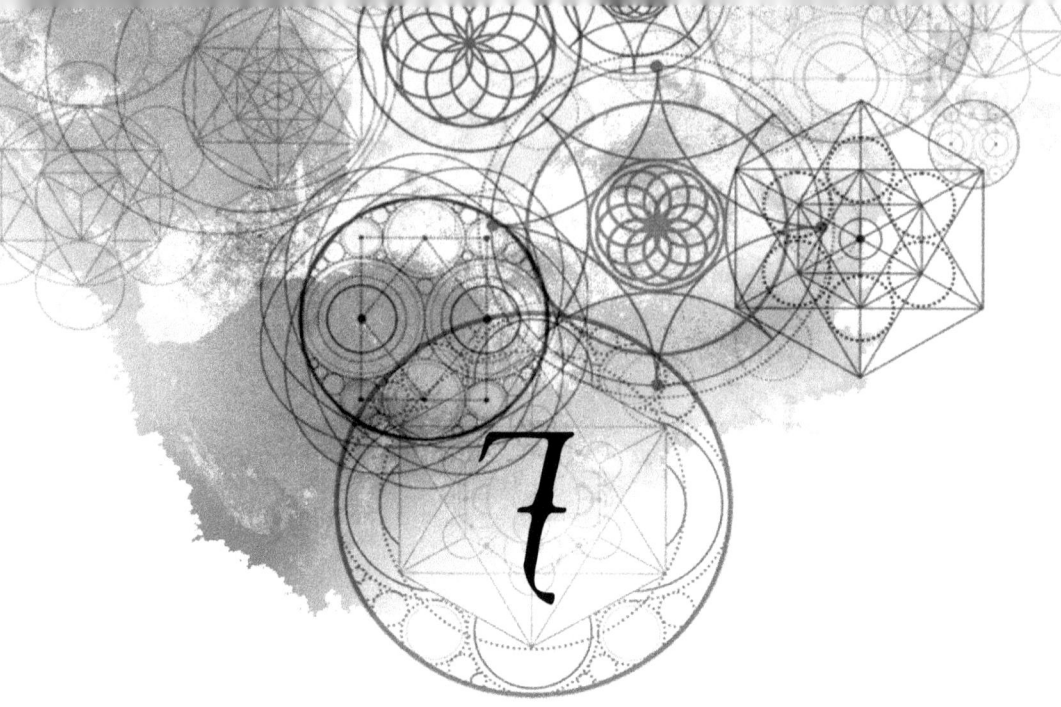

T HEY WERE SILENT walking back from the clinic. It wasn't until they were halfway back to his home that Darrus finally removed his mask.

"Did you get what you needed?" he asked, not looking at her.

"I did… I know I've already asked too much of you." He snorted at that, but Vi ignored it. "Do you know where the Western Caravans were set up?"

"Other side of the amphitheater," he answered. "But there's not much left there, now. They were ransacked, you know?"

She didn't. "I still have to look. There may be some of her things there—family heirlooms."

"Do you need me to come with you?" His body language and tone made clear he didn't want to.

"No," Vi said softly. "You've done enough for me for one night." She pulled off her mask, handing it back to him. "Thank you, though. You don't know how much you've helped."

"Helped by showing you death?" He stared into the goggles of the mask, as if asking it the question more than her.

"Yes," she answered firmly. "My kin aside… I needed to see the White Death with my own two eyes. Solaris needs a ruler who has seen it, who knows it and doesn't hide behind castle walls." She'd make every effort to stress as much to Romulin.

"It does indeed." Darrus looked over her shoulder in the direction of the amphitheater. "Go safely, princess."

"You too." With that, they headed their separate ways. She was halfway to the remnants of the caravan when she realized that was likely the last time she'd ever see Darrus. Vi turned in place, even though there was no possible way to catch him still. He was long gone.

She pushed onward.

The remnants of the winter solstice were still visible in the city and it filled her with an uncomfortable sense of dread. There were clearings that had been made for dancing surrounded by the empty stands Vi had sat on with her friends in the final moments before the outbreak. Whole sections of abandoned markets looked like remnants of a battlefield that no one had the energy to clean.

Vi couldn't blame them. The stink of death was heavy in the city. Now that she had seen the White Death with her own eyes, she could see its mark everywhere. In some cases, literal marks: white exes painted on doors.

Her eyes were bleary, heavy, but Vi forced herself to stay alert. The last time she'd been wandering at night, an assassin was lurking. The elfin'ra could come at any time.

"Where would you be?" she murmured as she rounded behind the amphitheater.

There was an open stretch of land that had some makeshift stables—empty. The grass was condensed, showing where wagons and carts had stood for days, but the carts themselves were gone. The remnants of a caravan were all there... except for the caravan itself.

"Mother," Vi cursed softly, walking through the empty field. Her eyes caught a pale streak of orange. Kneeling down, she pressed her fingers into the fine powder that was slowly seeping into the earth. Raising her hand to her face, she inhaled. "Spices..."

They had been here, certainly. But where were their things? Darrus had said they'd been ransacked, but she'd expected there'd still be remnants—like sun-bleached bones picked clean by birds.

But there was nothing here. If not for the imprints on the grass and having been told, she would've never thought the caravan had been there at all.

Vi rubbed her eyes, forcing herself to think. The prisoner, the woman, and now the trail went cold. She let out a groan of frustration and lapped the clearing, searching for someone who might know. But she was just as alone as when she'd first set out.

Alone and frustrated was ultimately how she returned to the fortress.

The sky was bleeding red as Vi made her way upward through the tree trunks and stairwells back to her room. No one stopped her, no one paid her any mind. She didn't even need to say a word. Which was good, because she was so exhausted she didn't even know if she could manage to conceal her voice. Maintaining Jayme's face to get in and up was almost too much.

A few steps from her room, tucked away in a blind spot, Vi let go of her guise with a sigh. Another night of no sleep behind her, likely another ahead, too. She had to figure out where the key had gone before she left the North.

Vi opened the door to her room and stopped dead in her tracks.

She wasn't alone.

A pair of brown eyes—identical to the ones she'd just worn—stared at her, narrowed, waiting. Jayme had positioned one of the chairs from Vi's table to face the door. Her fingers thrummed along the armrest impatiently.

"Close the door," she said softly. "I don't think you want anyone overhearing this conversation."

Vi did as she was told. She was too tired to argue and Jayme looked as though she'd tolerate none of it.

"I think you know why I'm here."

"Do I?" Vi leaned against the door.

Jayme sighed, shook her head, steepled her fingers, and then went back to gripping the armrests. She clearly couldn't make up her mind as to what emotion she wanted to portray.

"How did you do it?" Jayme pushed away from the chair, beginning to pace. "I expected you to come in with make up, and masks, something more than... you."

"How did you find out?" Vi asked instead, hoping Jayme wouldn't notice she hadn't answered the question.

"Imagine my surprise when, on my way to my morning rounds, I was stopped by Parn and asked when I *returned*. I didn't recall leaving."

"Did you tell him that?"

"Of course not." Jayme paused, looking to Vi. "I know when you're up to something, even if I don't know the details of how or why." The statement was definitely angry, but maybe a little proud too. Vi fought a smile. "So I came right here, confirmed my suspicion, and waited. Now, tell what you did." Jayme folded her arms over her chest, turning to face her, legs wide, as if ready for a battle.

"I can't—"

"Do not give me that, Vi Solaris." Jayme pointed at her. "I am expected to be your guard. How in the Mother's name am I supposed to do that if you're continually running off, going gods know where, in the middle of the night without me?"

"Trust me when I say it's for the good of the Empire." And the world.

"Trust me when I say I believe you." Jayme sighed and shook her head. "Vi, I'm not Jax, your mother, or father. Frankly, I couldn't find any way to care less about discipline or making sure you 'act a princess.' That's not my place. The only thing I want to do is protect you. So please, for that sake alone, tell me what's going on?"

Vi looked to the window. The sky was turning orange and that meant servants would be coming soon. She did a quick mental tally. Perhaps Jayme was right. She wouldn't betray her confidence and run to Jax or her mother. It could benefit her to have an ally...

"Remember how I said I saw visions at special places?"

"Is that what this is about? Another vision?"

"More or less." Vi held up her hand, showing was easier than telling. "*Durroe watt ivin.*" Vi stepped forward into the illusion.

Jayme's eyes widened to a third of the size of her face. She took a step forward, then back. "H-how? What magic is this?"

"It's complicated." Vi let go of the glyph and with it the guise of being Jayme's twin. "I have a rare magic..." Rare in the Solaris Empire, at least. "And part of learning it is rooted in my visions."

"That's why you're so adamant..."

"And... I want to see my father," Vi confessed, looking at her toes. "I'm still hopeful."

After a moment, Jayme crossed over to her. Her toes appeared in Vi's field of vision and Vi felt the weight of her hand clasping over her shoulder. She looked up, meeting Jayme's soft brown eyes.

"I don't blame you for that. But from now on, let me help you. You can trust me—I'm supposed to keep you safe. After we leave the North, it's going to be you and me." She had a point. Vi's circle of friends wasn't exactly large, and it was about to shrink by a fourth.

"I will keep you in the know," Vi promised, hoping she could keep it.

"Good. Did you get everything you needed tonight?"

"Unfortunately not." Vi started for her room, talking as she went. They were running out of time, and she needed to be in bed. "I made progress... but I needed to get to the Western Caravan and that ended up being impossible, so my lurking is on hold for now."

"Western Caravan?"

"The one that had the spices... they have an heirloom of my family and I think it may literally be the key to the next vision." Vi stepped into her dressing room, quickly donning her sleeping shift. "But they were completely gone, so—"

"Yes, Sehra had us confiscate all their goods right when she caught wind of possible looting."

"What?" Vi froze.

"When she arrested the Westerners and had them rounded up, she also had us collect their things in the night—that way they wouldn't be raided, stolen, or destroyed... More destroyed than they were in the initial rage."

Sehra was brilliant. It wasn't the first time Vi stood in awe of her tactical mind and foresight.

"Where is it? Here in the fortress?" Vi asked eagerly.

"I believe so." Jayme looked to the door, her mind no doubt going to the same place Vi's was. Any second, a servant would walk in. "Let me look into it and I—"

"I have to get to it before we go south." Vi grabbed Jayme's wrist. "Please."

"I'm going to look into it today." Jayme pulled free her hand. "Trust me, Vi. I'm here to help."

"I know." Vi scooped her up into a hug, feeling the woman stiffen as she usually did. "Thank you."

"Don't thank me yet... wait until I actually have answers for you."

"Just being willing to help is enough," Vi assured her.

Jayme gave a small smile, then looked to the window. "Catch an hour of sleep, if you can. I'll come back tonight after dinner and report."

"Thank you," Vi called after her as she pulled back her bed linens.

"Don't thank me yet!" Jayme repeated. Vi felt an answering smile spread across her lips.

The door closed behind her friend and Vi settled into the plush of her mattress. She listened as the outer door closed as well, her eyes drifting shut with it. For a few blissful moments, there was silence. Vi thought briefly about summoning Taavin again to give a report of her own. But Jayme was right: if she could catch just an hour of sleep, it'd be enough to get through the day.

But that was too much to hope for, as the door to her main room was opened with such vigor that it thumped against the wall.

"Princess!"

Vi pressed her eyes closed, and braced herself for the unrelenting chaos that was about to descend on her.

8

V I WAS ON a pedestal, quite literally.

"I cannot believe they're making you ride out." Holina, Vi's tailor, tittered over the pins that lined her mouth.

"It cannot be helped," Martis reminded Holina. "With the way the White Death is now, there is no reason to subject the Empress Regent or Prince Romulin to the city."

They talked about the White Death so casually, as though it were a rainstorm or unfinished stretch of road—inconvenient for their purposes, but otherwise unimportant. The clinic she had seen with Darrus was seared in her mind. The disease was far more serious than they gave it credit for. But Vi kept her mouth shut. She was far too tired today.

"Still, I would like to see her fitted in a more proper gown for the reception. Riding—what am I supposed to do with that?" Holina shook her head and put a few pins in the asymmetrical hem that extended down to the floor behind her, and to her mid-thigh in the front. She'd sewn wonders in just one night. "And considering her highness will not ride side-saddle…"

"It's utterly impractical." Vi stood her ground. "And I have never once seen my mother ride in any way but astride."

"Your mother has her habits from when she was younger," Holina murmured.

"Excuse me?" Vi looked down to the woman. Her mother may have been common born, but she had now been Empress for over twenty years. And now she was Empress Regent. With the declaration of her father's death, Vi's mother was no longer the Empress; she was merely holding Vi's seat until she was crowned. That didn't mean Vi would tolerate anything intended to be disparaging against her family.

"Let's remain focused," Martis said hastily, tapping his papers spread out on Vi's table across the room. "There will be an imperial contingent that will—"

"I've come with lunch!" Jax announced, opening the door to her common area. Martis groaned at the continual interruptions.

"Thank the mother." Vi's stomach growled in anticipation. They'd been fussing over her since dawn.

"No eating for you yet, princess." Holina had a death-grip on her hem. "I need you in place if I'm to finish this in the next day."

Jax attempted to come to her defense, but Holina stopped him with a hand.

"She can eat when I'm off stitching."

Vi stared down at the bolts of golden fabric wrapped around her body. Cut, hemmed, and trimmed to the most flattering shapes on her. She was never one to put much stock in fashion, but in the wake of everything she now knew about their world and its state, it seemed even more pointless.

She would ride in finery, putting on a strong mask, as there was a pit full of the dying a stone's throw from her.

Vi took dinner alone.

After being poked and prodded all day, and every person in her employ coming to instruct her about something, she was well and truly done with people. She knew she should've gone and had dinner with Sehra and her family—for Ellene's sake, if nothing else. But Vi was far too tired.

Instead, food was sent to her and she ate it with gusto before picking at the scraps as she inspected the aftermath of all the activity that had taken place in her room. Vi trailed her fingers along the couches and table; the objects she'd always known and used would not be coming with her on this journey. Books were the only exception.

Romulin could enjoy them after she left.

Vi stood in the doorway of her study. The world outside had gone dark, and the room was now lit by flickering candles on either side of her drafting table. All her maps had been removed and carefully rolled before being placed into tubes. Most of her books were packed into trunks, but a few still lined the shelves, waiting to be collected.

The door to her room opened, stealing her attention. Vi's eyes met Jayme's and they stared at each other for a long moment.

"I found it," Jayme announced, stepping in. She had her sword strapped to her hip. Even though Vi sincerely hoped they wouldn't need it, she was glad to see the smith had finished repairing it before they had to leave. "The remnants of the caravan—their goods. It's all here in the fortress."

"That makes it easier. Where are they?"

"In the storerooms by the warriors' barracks."

"Are they guarded?"

"Not exactly, but the entrance is where warriors walk frequently." Jayme's tone was uncertain, less than thrilled, but not totally dejected. Which told Vi there was a chance to get in.

"Thank you. I can take it from here."

Jayme caught her wrist as Vi started for the door. The woman's grip was much stronger than it looked—and Jayme already looked strong. "Not so fast. You agreed to let me help protect you."

"You said it was in the fortress. I'm not venturing beyond protection this time."

"Firstly, *this time* matters as much as the next. I want you to be in a habit of including me." Jayme held her grip firm. "Secondly, I can help you."

"You saw my magic…" Vi didn't think she'd need to remind Jayme after the woman's reaction the night before. "I can be well hidden."

"Does your magic tell you the warriors' rounds also? Does it tell you when they'll be coming and going, or up on the wall? Does your magic keep watch for you? Can it offer a convenient excuse if you're caught?" Jayme slowly released her grip on Vi. "There's no shame in having some help," Jayme said softly.

"All right," Vi reluctantly agreed. She'd always had either Jayme or Ellene by her side. Just because the stakes had changed didn't mean she had to let go of her friends entirely. "Let's go."

"Not yet." Jayme looked to the clock that hung on Vi's wall. "Wait an hour, then we'll go."

They didn't talk much while they waited. Vi had half expected Jayme to probe her for information about her magic. To ask about her visions… search for reasons as to why she felt so strongly about getting to the Apexes.

But when they did talk, their subject was much the same as all her other conversations for the day: departing the North. As exhausted as Vi was about that topic, she appreciated that Jayme wasn't digging too deep. Perhaps the woman had been completely honest about wanting nothing more than to ensure Vi's safety. Throughout her whole life, Jayme had been nothing but helpful, always on Vi's side.

When the clock struck ten, they ventured outward.

"The guards are on rotation right now," Jayme murmured as they wound down. "By the time we get there, they'll be settled in positions. We should have a blind spot of about ten minutes before anyone has a chance to notice us at the store room."

"That should be enough time." At least, she hoped it would be.

They passed by the guard positioned at the entrance to the royal quarters. The woman gave a nod to them both, settled her eyes on Jayme, and didn't ask any questions. Otherwise, they only ran into two other servants on their way down to the pits.

The storeroom was just as Jayme had said, adjacent to the warrior barracks and back by the wall. There was one door that led in and out of it, a lantern blazing over top, and a heavy padlock hanging from the handle that seemed to grow larger as they approached. Vi stared at it, running through the words of power in her mind. She could destroy it clean off with *juth,* but that would likely arouse suspicion, prompting a search. Perhaps there was something with *mysst,* fashion a key of some sort? Though Vi didn't know of—

"Stand there." Jayme pointed to a spot just before the door, by the padlock. "And keep an eye out."

"What?"

Jayme was already crouching. She unrolled a small kit, tools lining various pockets. Vi stared at the silver that flashed in the lamplight as Jayme selected her first picks and began to insert them into the lock.

"How did you…?"

"You pick things up on the road." Jayme shrugged. She situated one of the tools and held it in place, beginning to fidget with a second at the bottom of the lock. "I want to do the best I can for you and your protection, princess. That means learning as many skills as I can."

"I don't know how many guards learn lock-picking to protect nobility." Vi swept her eyes across the pits and bridge-ways, but saw no one.

"Well, don't you think my eagerness to account for every possibility makes me even more valuable?" There was a metallic click, and Vi heard the shank of the padlock slide from its place. She turned, shocked at Jayme's speed. By the time her eyes landed on on the lock again, Jayme had already hung the lock on the door, her tools collected. "After you, princess." Vi continued to stare dumbly, struggling to process what she had just witnessed. "Ten minutes, remember? We need to keep moving."

"Right," Vi mumbled, slipping past her and into the darkness.

Just how much about her friend did she not know? How many skills did she possess that Vi would never suspect? Who had she learned them from? Vi glanced back at Jayme, who closed the door nearly all the way, leaving just a crack to peer through.

Questions for another time, Right now Vi had to—

Her mind went blank as she stared at the sheer amount of goods stacked up. Boxes were piled high, making small mountains out of the tarps that covered them. Baskets lined the floor, making it difficult to walk. Everything was sealed and packed away.

Where should she even begin?

"What're you looking for?" Jayme asked, glancing at her.

"A key."

"A key in a haystack." Jayme looked back out. "If I can help, let me know… but I want to keep an eye out for any rogue warriors who happen to wander by and notice the lock dangling open on the door."

Vi shifted all of her focus on the goods before her. She began peeling back canvases and taking a quick loop of the room, trying to see what was there. She was looking for something familiar—something that would remind her of Grendla—though there was nothing in the illogical piles to suggest that any one person's goods were still together.

Closing her eyes, Vi took a deep breath and followed her nose. It led her to the back corner, where six familiar-looking baskets stood next to each other. Pulling off the tops, Vi affirmed they were the same the woman had in the market.

"Then… where's the rest of your things?" Vi mumbled. She began pulling back all of the tarps in the area, looking for something—anything that seemed like it would belong to that woman.

"Any luck?" Jayme called back. "We should move soon, the patrol up on the wall will be crossing shortly."

"Do you really think they'd notice?" Vi had only just begun sifting through everything. She'd barely made a dent. If she had more time in the North, she could come back and slowly sort through methodically. But this would be her only shot.

"Trust me, they'll notice," Jayme said gravely. "Sehra's training for the warriors is second to none and you saw how big that lock was. The Mother herself sees it from the sky."

Vi cursed under her breath. There was nothing she could do but continue looking and hope she'd be lucky. With far less care, she opened up trunks of textiles, more spices, tools of a leather worker. But nothing that even remotely resembled a key.

"I think I see them coming."

"Mother—" Vi's tirade was cut short. A small piece of fabric, nearly completely hidden by the others she'd been sorting through, caught her eye. Stepping over two baskets and sitting on a trunk, Vi hastily opened a small box.

She recognized the dress as the same the woman had worn in the market that day. There were other clothes, simple and finely spun. Beneath them was a bag of jewelry Vi pulled into her lap. If she was going to hide a precious heirloom key, she would do it with her other valuables. But there was nothing beyond bangles and gold.

"Vi—"

"Just one more minute."

"That's all you have," Jayme said firmly.

Vi pulled out the blanket underneath the jewelry. Some other personal effects. And then a series of book spines were at the bottom. All of them had markings in the language of old Mhashan—words Vi couldn't read without putting in some careful thought first—but it was the blank one that caught her eye.

It's hidden with the rest. Back of the tome, the records I kept. The woman's delirious words echoed in her mind. Perhaps she'd been answering Vi's question after all.

Sliding out the tome, Vi opened it, flipping right to the back. It was more writing in the old language. For a brief second, Vi thought about taking the whole thing with her. Were they just records of sales? Or something more?

Her debate was cut short when the pages stopped flipping, revealing a section in the back that had been glued together and was hollowed out in the center. All sorts of markings were on the pages around it, made in dark red ink. But Vi focused on the iron key nestled in the secret compartment, a rose carved into one end, and skeleton teeth on the other.

"Vi!"

"I found it!" Vi grabbed the key and quickly snapped the book shut. It was only as she was halfway to filling back up the woman's trunk that she realized she'd even thought about taking the tome with her to translate later. Vi paused, staring. Did she dig it up again? Did she care if the warriors knew someone had been shifting through the goods?

"Vi, we have to—"

"I'm coming." Vi sprinted over, key in hand. On her way she threw a few of the tarps back into place, trying to make it look less like someone had been nibbing through things. By the time anyone found out, she'd be long gone.

Jayme opened the door, quickly locking it behind them. They stepped out of the lantern's orb of light and into the shadow of darkness behind the tree trunk right as the warrior was rounding the wall. The two young women crouched down, holding their breath and waiting before slipping into the night the second the coast was clear.

9

AFTER A GOOD night's sleep, relatively speaking, she should feel much better. But a rock had taken up residence where Vi's stomach used to be, her eyes burned, and her hands wouldn't stop shaking. She occupied them with the key she'd retrieved the night before, turning it over time and again as she sat on the windowsill of her bedroom for what would be the last time.

The linens had been stripped that morning, still warm from the night's sleep. Every worldly possession she owned—and some she didn't even remember she owned—had been packed into several trunks, now loaded into a cart far beneath her. If Vi strained, she could barely see it. But she didn't look down; she looked out across the treetops that had been the only home she'd ever known.

Vi closed her eyes, taking a deep breath to try to settle her stomach, and then, "*Narro hath hoolo.*"

Taavin appeared at her side. Vi barely looked at him, her eyes still turned outward. He sat slowly on the opposite side of the window sill from her—she more sensed the movement than saw it. Vi slowly brought her eyes to him and he held her with his thoughtful stare.

"Is today the day?" he asked, finally. All she could do was nod. He turned, looking out over the trees, and Vi did the same. The early morning wind picked up, tousling her hair and leaving his untouched. "How do you feel?"

"I don't know. Much the same, I suppose," she said. "Though today it's far more real. This room... it's been all I've ever known." She looked at the gnarled ceiling, polished wood, the heavy scent of sap that always clung to the air like a persistent child at his mother's leg. "It's odd to think I'll never be here again."

"And when you leave, you'll be on the long road to Meru."

The mention of her forthcoming journey returned Vi's attention to the key in her hands. She held it up in her palm, showing him. Taavin leaned forward, inspecting it.

"Does it mean anything to you?" she asked.

He shook his head. "I haven't seen any keys in my dreams. But that doesn't mean it's not significant."

"It is... I'm sure of it," Vi insisted. Perhaps it was just hopeful thinking that her efforts hadn't been for naught.

"We will find out." Taavin placed his hands on either side of hers. The motion drew her attention back to his face. Without either of them realizing it, they had leaned forward, the distance between them shrunken to almost nothing. "I admire what you're doing and wish I could do the same. You're one of the bravest people I've met."

"You're just saying that." Even if he was, it made the rock that was her stomach soften some, the weight within her lessen. If he could believe she was brave, then maybe she could trust him enough to believe it herself.

"I'm not. I've never said anything to you I don't mean." His voice was soft and soothing. The warmth of his hands was melting into her, soothing her trembles. In moments like this, Vi forgot his corporeal form was halfway across the world.

"Don't abandon me on this journey," Vi whispered. "If I'm to walk out that door today and put on my bravest of faces, it will be because I know you will be with me." *Was that true?* Vi hardly had time to think before the words were out. She certainly hadn't planned on saying anything of the like.

"I will be with you until the end of time." The words illuminated her brighter than the glyph slowly rotating around her wrist. They were said in the common tongue, but they were three times as powerful as any of the words of Yargen.

"Do you mean it?" she breathed.

"So much it frightens me…" The sentence trailed off. Vi could feel that there was more unsaid. More that he thought but couldn't bring himself to say.

Or perhaps she was merely imposing her own feelings onto him.

"Taavin, I—"

There was a knock on the door. She looked to it, and then back to him. There was a brief, pained expression on his face. She didn't want to let him go yet. There was more to say. But she didn't quite know what, yet. And that meant it couldn't be said now.

His expression softened and, as if reading her mind, Taavin gave a small nod.

"Come in," Vi called, pocketing the key and releasing the glyph that brought Taavin into her world.

The door opened and Ellene poked her nose in. Her eyes were already red and shining. Vi swallowed hard, forcing her own not to match.

"How weird…" Ellene murmured, looking at the empty bed. Her eyes swept across the room. "I always thought you didn't have very much by way of personal items… but now I realize there was a lot more than I ever noticed because it feels so empty in here now."

Vi couldn't argue. She felt it too. Her presence had already been scrubbed from these chambers.

"Sit with me?" Vi directed the young woman's attention to where Taavin had just been.

Ellene wasted no time. In one fluid movement she crossed the room, sat on the other edge of the ledge, and scooped up Vi's hands in a bone-crushing grip—a grip Vi was certain she returned. "I will come to you the first moment I can. Even if it's in winter."

Vi was forced to look away. Her gut twisted. There would be no chance to visit, in winter or otherwise, and Ellene would find out that fact through the words of someone else. Her secrecy would betray their friendship and all the trust Ellene had ever placed in her.

Yet a secret her plans must remain. She couldn't risk it. So, instead, when words weren't enough, actions would shine far brighter.

She pulled Ellene's hands toward her, and with them the girl herself. Vi loosened her grip in time to catch her before they both tumbled out the window. Ellene's arms were around her waist, Vi's around her shoulders. Her dark corkscrew hair tickled Vi's nose.

"I will miss you more than you know," Vi whispered.

"And I you." Ellene's words were muffled, spoken into Vi's chest. "Mother told me that I must be strong. She told me not to be sad, because your fate is far greater than even ours."

Vi squeezed her tighter, closing her eyes. Despite everything she had just said to Taavin, despite her resolve, despite her lifelong dream to be reunited with her family... some small part of her wished to stay. What would her life have been like if she could run the jungles with Ellene for the rest of her days? She could settle with a kind and handsome man like Darrus, and they would live comfortably.

There was happiness she could stumble on, here.

Slowly, Vi's eyes opened, turning toward the brutal dawn. The statement brought another brief wondering. How much did Sehra know? How much of her fate had the mysterious traveler revealed? Had she always somehow known Vi was the Champion?

It didn't matter much now, she supposed.

"We will write our own fate," she whispered. That was why she must leave—to stop the White Death and do what she could to prevent the end of the world she'd witnessed. Her visions were still malleable. "In a few years' time, Ellene... your mother will teach you about the magic of Yargen."

"Yargen's magic?" Ellene straightened, rubbing her eyes. "What does that have to do with anything?"

"It's hard to explain now." Vi gave her a tired smile. "But when that time comes, ask your mother about people who could read them."

"Read... *them*?"

"Yes. It'll make sense to both you and her then, I promise." Vi rested a hand on her friend's shoulder.

"I don't understand."

"I know."

"Can't you tell me?" she pleaded, and Vi nearly gave in.

"No, not yet. Eventually though."

"Swear to me."

"I swear." Go to Meru. Put an end to the White Death. Find her father. Reunite her family. And *then* tell Ellene everything. It was a long list of things that had to come first, but Vi would do them all. She had no other choice.

Another soft knock stole their attention. Jax stood in the halfway open doorway. His expression was closed and difficult to read.

"It's time," he said, and Vi didn't know where his solemn tone came from. What did he feel? Joy, surely? This had never been his home. He must be far more eager to be liberated of it.

Ellene gripped Vi's hand again, as though she could stop her from leaving.

"I'll give you two a moment to finish up." Jax stepped out of the room.

"Vi... please don't go." Ellene's voice cracked. "What am I to do without you?"

"The same things you do with me." Vi forced a smile. Crown princesses did not fall apart outwardly. Any crumbling would be hidden from the world. For Ellene's sake, right now, if nothing else. "You will get into trouble. You will race noru, and go on hunts, and learn how to be a good and just chieftain from your mother. And at—" Her throat went thick, choking on her lie. "—at the first possible opportunity before the roads close in winter, you'll come visit and I'll hear all about what trouble you're making."

Ellene nodded, once, twice, several times. As though she could convince herself if she jostled Vi's words around in her mind enough. Her fingers squeezed once around Vi's, so hard her knuckles popped. She opened her mouth, closed it, opened it again, and closed it once more when no words came.

Slowly, the girl lifted her hands, releasing Vi's. She undid the clasp on the bracelet she always wore during ceremonial events—a simple leather wrap with a single wooden bead carved from the bark of the Mother Tree.

"I want you to have this."

"Ellene, I cannot." But even as Vi spoke her objection, the girl was tying her treasure around Vi's outstretched wrist. "This is—"

"I will live under the shade of the Mother Tree for the rest of my days. I don't need its bark protecting me. You need this more than I do." Her dark fingers wrapped around the bracelet, holding it against Vi's skin. It was a comfortable warmth, like a security blanket. "If nothing else, it will be something for you to remember me by."

All objections dropped with her stomach. A sorrow unlike anything Vi had ever felt before flooded in, filling the space, rising through her chest and pouring from her eyes and onto her cheeks before she even had a chance to stop it. She pulled her wrist from Ellene's grasp and threw her arms around the girl, her friend—her sister of another's blood. Vi tightened her grip and Ellene held her just as fiercely. Crushed against each other, they could each feel the quivering breaths, the shaking shoulders of the other that meant the tears finally won.

The two sat, quietly crying, holding each other, airing their grief in private, so that they would each be prepared to wear the faces of royalty when the world needed to witness them separate for good.

When Vi descended, it was with a stoic Ellene at her side. Jax and Jayme were behind them, Andru and her tutors behind even them. Not one more word was said among any of them the entire way through the fortress.

The horses were already saddled, carts strapped to bigger stallions who could bear the loads. At the front was a massive warstrider—black, said to have descended from the same lineage of equestrians as her father's favored mount.

Sehra and Za were waiting for them, and Vi said her goodbyes and final thank-yous in a blur. She wanted to ask if the traveler had said anything else. If Sehra had secretly known about the visions, or somehow had some of her own. But nothing mattered now other than the road ahead.

Nothing could change the path she was on—the path that led to her mother, brother, father, and a man far across the sea.

Ellene stayed at her mothers' sides as Vi continued on alone. The jungle had never felt so cold, though Vi was dressed in more layers than she usually sported. Her hair was carefully done, the riding clothes that had been made for her impeccably stitched.

She was the image of perfection, molded in every way.

Perfect… so long as no one looked past the facade to the nearly crippling worry and doubt that festered within.

Vi mounted and two servants helped adjust the elongated train Holina had stitched over her mount's haunches. Vi took up the white leather reins and spared a moment to admire the gilded buckles and embellishments glinting in the sunlight. She suppressed a snort at the notion that she and her mount were similarly bedazzled, the golden circlet she wore heavy on her brow. "Are you ready?" Jax asked softly.

"I am." Vi did not take her eyes off the road ahead. A princess did not waver or hesitate. And she was not going to smear her makeup a second time with doubt or fear. The colors on her face were now her mask and her warpaint, protecting and strengthening her.

"Keep your head high."

"I know." She turned slowly to him, her back rigid in the saddle. "They will see my strength."

Jax stared at her for a long moment, and Vi didn't know what he saw. "When you're ready, your highness."

The gate was open before them. Warriors lined the way, halfway down the road. A contingent of Southern soldiers in gleaming plate surrounded her, more at the end of her parade. Four held pennons, the Solaris sun emblazoned on white.

"Onward," Vi commanded loudly.

"Onward!" Jayme repeated.

The soldiers spurred their horses to movement.

She passed the stables for the last time. Vi took one last inhale of straw and noru feed. The wall was behind them, warriors saluting as they passed.

Some of the citizenry had come out to witness them. They stood in eerie silence. There were no cheers or shouts of farewell. No well wishes were lauded on her.

Vi didn't blame them for it. She was the representation of the Empire that had brought them to heel. The same Empire they now blamed for the disease tearing apart their families.

In a blur, she thought she saw Darrus. But Vi didn't dare turn her head. She had to stay focused, or the careful balance of her charade may come toppling down. They continued to speed away from everything she'd ever known, to the fate that awaited her.

The party went through the trees, past the barren ring outside of Soricium, further down the North West Way. They rode for what seemed like forever—though Vi knew it was merely minutes, not even hours. Further down the road, her eyes landed on two mounts—the same size as hers—waiting in the center.

On one dark brown horse was a woman, a crown extending from her brow. On the white horse beside her sat a blond haired man. Surrounding them, stretching back into the trees on mount and foot, were soldiers at attention to receive them.

As they neared, Vi felt moisture on her cheeks, and she worked to hastily wipe it away as inconspicuously as possible. Princesses didn't cry in front of their army, and this was the second time in one day her emotions had betrayed her. It was already less of a reception than the Senate had intended, thanks to the White Death, so Vi didn't want to do anything that could force further deviation from formality, from their plans.

But laying eyes on her brother—her twin—for the first time was almost more emotion than she could bear.

10

S HE WANTED TO leap from her horse and onto his.

The world had stopped existing around her—shifting of plate armor and stomping of horses was muffled and gone. The only other person was Romulin. His sky blue eyes stared at her on a canvas of Southern pale skin—only lightly kissed from the sun on their long journey. Like day and night, brother and sister couldn't look more different.

But in his eyes, Vi saw her mother and father. Where the rest of the world saw differences between them, she saw an undeniable kinship that may well only be recognizable to her…and hopefully to him.

"Greetings, my daughter." It seemed Vi wasn't the only one fighting tears. "It is good to see you again."

"And you as well, mother." Vi lowered her head slightly.

"We are enthusiastic to receive you, and to take you home."

"I am enthusiastic to return to the lands of my forefathers." All eyes were on them. Every ear in the clearing was attuned to their conversation. Her tutors had gone over this exchange in particular over and over again, drilling in the words Vi needed to say. "And I am both honored and humbled by this display of the might of Solaris on my behalf." Vi lifted her arm and swept it across her body, gesturing to the soldiers.

"We would traverse the world to collect the heir to the Solaris throne."

Vi certainly hoped not.

"Shall we begin our journey?" Vi proposed.

Her mother bowed her head, and Romulin mirrored the action. With a gentle tug of their reins they maneuvered their horses to the sides of the road, leaving a clear path for Vi between them. She, not her mother, was to head the army.

They all believed her father was dead. Which meant they saw her as their ruler. Her coronation was perceived as a mere formality, an eventuality.

In the eyes of all those surrounding her—in the eyes of the world—she was now the head of the Solaris Empire.

And she would ride forth to prove them all wrong.

Vi gave her mount a gentle nudge and the beast moved forward. Her mother fell into place just behind and to the right, Romulin on the left. One by one the rank and file moved behind her as they began their long march south.

Her emotions were ready to burst by the time they stopped their march for the day. Vi was eager to be off her horse. But she waited to receive directions as they broke for camp.

"Your highness." Jayme rode up swiftly as Vi had just turned her mount to speak with Romulin. "Please, come this way. I shall show you to your tent."

Vi looked to her brother and mother.

"When you are both settled," Vhalla said, looking at both her children in turn, "come to my tent and we shall have dinner together."

"Yes, mother," Romulin said with a nod—though his attention was on Vi, as hers was on him. "Shall I come and collect you, sister?"

His voice was smooth, soft, not unlike Taavin's in those respects. But where Taavin's accent made his words more lyrical and overall lighter, Romulin's quiet words were weighty with the natural bass of his voice. It wasn't how Vi had imagined he'd sound, and Vi found herself oddly pleased about the fact.

"I would like that." She gave a small nod.

"Excellent, I'll be with you shortly. If you'll excuse me for now." Her mother followed behind him, leaving Vi and Jayme alone.

"If you'll follow me." Jayme dismounted, handing her horse to a waiting soldier.

Vi did the same, silently grateful her stiff legs did not give out. Riding for hours on end wasn't something she was accustomed to and she'd have to develop stamina fast. Ignoring the aches and needles sinking into her muscles with every movement, Vi walked tall.

"It is a wonder how you take steps at all after your long rides," Vi mumbled under her breath for Jayme alone as the other soldier walked away with their horses. From the corners of her eyes, she could've sworn she saw the woman fighting a smirk.

"You'll get used to it."

"I hope so, otherwise I'll be landing on my bum tomorrow when my legs give up on me."

They walked through camp. Vi was keenly aware of the feeling of all eyes on her. She always thought she garnered attention everywhere she went in Soricium, but now she realized the city was largely accustomed to the crown princess in their midst. These soldiers looked at her as though she was the Mother given flesh.

Vi tried to ignore them. Her tutors had said that the worst thing that could happen was to stare back and acknowledge them. She had to hold herself apart—regal—and hope they grew bored of her soon enough.

Jayme led her toward a tall, six-sided tent. It had one flap opening with a canopy suspended above. The pointed roof was supported by a single post inside. Soldiers were going in and out, carrying items and finishing tying off the last of the tent supports.

"This will be your home on the road," Jayme said, pausing in the opening.

Vi stared, attempting to rectify the disconnect between what she was seeing and what her expectations for travel were. There was a proper bed, and a small sitting area of wooden folding chairs adorned with pillows and gathered around an iron brazier. There was even a table at naval height, the perfect place to stand and think and work.

"This seems excessive…" Vi pitied the poor souls who had to set up and break down this behemoth every day. "Where are you staying?"

"I have my own lodging to set up." Jayme gave her a small grin, her demeanor relaxed in the semi-privacy of Vi's abode. "I assure you it's nothing to be jealous over."

"You could stay here with me. Mother knows, I have the room." Vi motioned around her.

"And then some," Jayme muttered. "But no one would want me underfoot here."

"Underfoot? You could never be."

"I'm not anyone important, and you'll be discussing sensitive matters of state here."

"*I* value your opinion. I want you here."

Jayme fought a small laugh, glancing outside. "Despite what they tell you, yours isn't the only opinion that matters. You have to keep what others will think or feel in mind."

"But you—"

"It's fine, Vi." Jayme turned to leave and Vi knew the woman wouldn't hear any more of it. No matter how hard Vi tried, Jayme would always see herself as the odd woman out in a world of royals.

"Stay a while. Just a little. Surely that's all right." Being alone with her thoughts and emotions was the last thing Vi wanted. The day was both joyous and sorrowful at the same time and she didn't know which emotion would win. Perhaps they'd just split her right down the middle, tearing her apart from the inside out.

"I need to set up my own tent." Jayme stepped out under the canopy that stretched in front of the opening to Vi's tent and started off to the right. "I figure you'll want some time with your brother, in any case."

"I will, but when he gets here." Vi followed behind, rounding the corner of one of the tent's six sides. "Perhaps I can help set up your tent?"

"I'm fine, Vi, really. I'm setting up right here by you. So if I really need help I'll ask someone else… and *then* the crown princess." Vi didn't even bother hiding a grin at that particular smart remark. "Go get off your feet, you said they were hurting."

"You're so stubborn."

"I have to be to contend with such a stubborn princess," Jayme said, deadpan. Vi fought a snort at the quiet words. Jayme looked around; luckily none of the other soldiers had been listening in on their conversations. It reminded Vi they were in public once more. "I'll catch up with you soon, Vi. I'll be posted out front as your guard most of the time—you're not going to escape me."

"All right," Vi relented, and rounded the corner of her tent to leave Jayme to her work. She was right: Romulin would be there soon enough and then—

She stopped the moment she lifted her tent flap.

An unfamiliar man stood inside.

He was stocky, biceps as big as her thighs. Usually, Vi could look a man that large in the eye and match his height. But this man was so tall she had to crane her neck to look up at him. A mess of shaggy, ruddy hair was cut just above his shoulders. He stood at her table, a box of her things before him, a journal in his hands—the journal into which Vi had copied Sehra's words of power.

"May I help you?" Vi asked coolly. A smug smile pushed his stubble—a brighter red than his hair—across his cheeks.

"Merely unloading your things." He set the journal down, slowly reaching for another. He was wearing the tabard of a foot soldier... but there was something markedly different from the other head-down soldiers she'd seen during the day. They'd looked at her through stolen glances and from the corners of their eyes. This man stared at her outright.

Like a challenge.

"I can do it, thank you." Vi stepped to the side. The canvas flap closed behind her, casting the tent in twilight. She lifted her hand, motioning toward it. "You are dismissed."

"Are you certain, princess?" The man lifted another book. "I am here to serve."

"You may serve me by leaving me."

"Very well." He shrugged and started for the door. The ground seemed to rumble under his massive, booted feet.

She shouldn't let him leave... yet. "What's your name?"

He stopped, turned, looked down at her. The man had a massive nose, almost beak-like, and thick black eyebrows that looked painted on. In fact, she was fairly sure they *were*, and they were in unnatural contrast to the brown-red of his hair.

Where was shaving and painting one's eyebrows considered fashionable?

"Fallor."

"Fallor..." Vi repeated, trying to mimic the hard way his tongue landed on the O. "Where are you from?"

"I doubt you've ever heard of it." He smiled wider.

"Try me. I am a hobbiest cartographer."

"It's not a place you can draw on maps." The man folded his arms over his chest, looking down at her with eyes that were such an icy blue-grey, they looked nearly purple.

"What does that mean?" Vi's voice dropped lower.

"That—"

"Sister?" The tent post by the flap rattled as Romulin knocked from the other side.

"Excuse me, princess." Fallor ducked his head and stepped out, giving a nod to Romulin as he passed. "Your highness."

"Who was that?" Romulin asked, seeing her on the other side of the tent flap and stepping inside. Vi was more focused on the soldier leaving.

"I don't rightly know. He called himself Fallor." Vi walked over to the table, picking up the journal Fallor had been holding. Copying Sehra's book on Lightspinning had been a liability—how had she not seen that before now? "I was hoping you might have seen him around before."

"There are so many soldiers, my head would explode if I tried to remember them all." The tent flap closed behind Romulin, casting the space in deeper darkness. Vi lit the brazier in the center of the room with a thought. Night was falling, and the heavy canopies of the jungle made it dark on the forest floors below.

She walked over to the brazier, casting the book in the flame. Just because she'd made the mistake didn't mean she had to live with it.

"You're burning it?" He balked.

"I don't make a habit of burning tomes." She knew where his mind was without him having to say anything. "But it was a journal. The words within it are more of a liability than anything else."

"If you insist…" Romulin looked from the fire to her. "So it is true, then. Your magic has Awoken."

"It has."

"I'm so happy for you, sister!" Without warning he threw his arms around her, pulling her in for a tight embrace. Her brother was wider than the portrait artists had portrayed him, but Vi enjoyed the feeling of how stable he was in her arms.

They pulled apart, before going back in once more for another long hug.

"How I longed to see you," he whispered in what sounded like relief. "*Finally.*"

"I know." Vi finally pulled back, to better take in her brother from head to toe. Even though he was younger by mere minutes, something about his shorter stature made her feel like a true elder, protective to boot. They continued staring for another few long minutes, before Vi broke the silence with a laugh. "I've replayed this meeting in my mind so many times, and now that it's here I don't know what to say."

"Thank the Mother I'm not alone in that." He chuckled and then motioned to her sitting area. "Shall we sit?"

"Yes, that sounds like a good place to start." She was ready to settle into a long conversation with him, but as Vi went to sit down, her legs screamed in protest and she fell ungracefully onto her bottom.

"Are you all right?" Romulin hastened to her side.

"Yes." Vi gave a small laugh directed at herself. "The saddle—"

"—is brutal," he finished for her. Without even trying, their minds already seemed to be working in tandem. She wasn't surprised, but it still pleased her immensely. "I know, it took me the first week to work out the stiffness coming up here."

"I hope it doesn't take that long," Vi mumbled, bending at her waist, trying to stretch. "Push on my back, will you?"

"Sure." He eased off her shoulders as quickly as he applied pressure when she hissed in pain.

"No, good pain, do it again," Vi said quickly. Romulin pushed back to the point and held her there for several long breaths before letting her up. Vi closed her eyes, moving her leg around its socket.

"Better?"

"Marginally."

Romulin finally sat across from her. "I have another stretch, if you'd like?"

"Since when have I ever said no to your counsel?" Vi smiled.

"Do as I do." He patted the spot next to him and laid back. Vi stretched out next to him, copying his movements. "Now, put your heel there, against your knee. And reach through, grab your shin. No, there. Yes. Now pull and you should feel it—" She interrupted him with a sharp inhale as her whole hip seemed to tense and then blissfully relax all at once. "—there it is. Sounds like you got it."

Vi repeated on the other side before dropping her legs. "I got something, all right…" She turned her head, looking at her flaxen-haired brother. "How'd you learn that?"

"Master of Horse in the palace. When I first started learning to ride, I had the same problem. Couldn't find a comfortable seat for years. I'd have all kinds of pain after. It still haunts me from time to time. Like when I have to travel across the world to collect my sister." They shared a grin. He paused before something else seemed to strike him. "Pain in your lower back?"

"No… Or should I say not yet?"

"Hopefully it stays that way."

Vi pulled herself into a seated position, arms wrapped around bent knees. "Thanks for that."

"Any time." He smiled. Somehow, they had found an easy cadence near-immediately. "How was the trip north?"

"Tedious, but worthwhile, because you were at the end of it." That had her beaming from ear to ear.

"Thank you for coming."

"There's no way I wouldn't have—so long as the Senate allowed." He reached over, grabbing her hand lightly. Sorrow filled her brother's eyes all at once. He took in a breath that hitched halfway through, but his words were level, not betraying the emotions Vi could palpably feel. "I'm sorry Father isn't here."

It was then that she realized her last letter to him had been sent before her visions. He hadn't even known she was Awoken. There was so much she had to catch him up on.

"Brother, I need your counsel on that."

"I know, there's much that needs to be done. Your coronation—"

"No, listen," Vi interrupted. He looked mildly offended, but she spoke too quickly for him to say or do anything about it. "Father's alive."

"What?" Romulin took a sharp inhale of air.

"Father is alive," she repeated.

"How?"

"I had a vision of him."

"A vision?" he asked, clearly skeptical.

Vi wasn't sure where to begin, so she started all the way back to her training with Jax. She summed up her months working in the pits to the eventual Awakening of her magic. She told him of her visions, and even training with Sehra on the magic of Yargen—complete with a small demonstration of *durroe*. The only thing Vi didn't mention was Taavin. He was the one secret she couldn't seem to share with anyone and the fact filled her with a mild twinge of guilt as it brought her mind briefly to Andru.

When she finished, he was silent, looking down at his hands folded in his lap. Eventually, Romulin shook his head, ran a hand through his short-cut hair—shorter than she remembered from her portraits—and stood, beginning to pace.

"I've read about Firebearers, and their sight."

"But I'm not—"

"Yes, you have this other magic, Lightweaving."

"Lightspinning," she corrected.

"And I don't know about the visions that come with that…" he mumbled.

"I know this is hard to believe." Vi stood as well. "But you must."

"Why do you?" Romulin stopped suddenly, looking back to her. "Didn't you say you rode off in pursuit of your last vision because you were worried that fate had changed? Why do you believe father is alive?"

Getting called out on illogical jumps by her brother in person was far worse in person than in letters.

"I just feel that… he is…" The small kernel of doubt in herself sprouted a small seedling that poked through her confidence.

"How?" Romulin shook his head. "And even if he was… Why would he not come back to us? Why not send word?"

"I don't know," Vi muttered. "Perhaps he can't? Perhaps he was captured, or gravely injured, and that's why."

"What is more likely, Vi? He's alive and none of our ships or search parties have found him. By some miracle he survived the pirate attack and now he merely hasn't sent back word, even though he's totally fine?"

"Pirate attack? I thought it wasn't certain what—"

"The public reports leave room for doubt." Romulin preempted her question with grave severity. "But a small vessel was cornered by one of the search parties. Most of the sailors aboard put themselves to their own swords—" Vi grimaced at the words. "—but one was taken alive. He bore the mark of Adela and swore he had information on Father."

"Which was?" Vi asked eagerly. Romulin sadly shook his head at her. "The man was stark mad, Vi. He spoke of an island of ice and a ship of mist. He said Adela herself still sailed the waters."

"But you said he had Adela's mark…"

"That's just a tattoo of a trident—anyone could get one, and most pirates do to strike fear in their enemies." Romulin shook his head solemnly. "There's no way Adela still lives. Stories of her date back to our great grandfather's time."

Vi sighed heavily.

"I was hopeful too…" He rested a heavy palm on her knee. "But the man was clearly saying whatever he could to try to save his skin. It was likely pirates—given that the Crescent Continent has abandoned patrolling those waters and has pulled in their military vessels. But ships of mist and infamous pirate queens? Father's—" Romulin choked on the next word "—death can more likely be attributed to run-of-the-mill cutthroats."

Vi watched as he stood, beginning to pace. The conversation made him understandably unsettled. She hardly enjoyed it. But it was a conversation that must be had.

In the silence, something else struck her—he spoke of Meru like he knew it. He hadn't even batted an eyelash when she brought it up during her recount of the past few months. *He'd already known*; he'd found out before her. Vi tried not to be upset, but something about it—about the whole conversation—was beginning to hurt in a way her current mental state wasn't prepared to handle.

He had known things and hadn't told her. When had he learned these truths? For how long had he let her stay in the dark?

How many things had he kept from her when she had told him everything?

"I want to believe you." Romulin's voice was pleading, but Vi didn't know what he was pleading for—her forgiveness, or for himself to believe her. "But it's difficult, Vi."

"He may still be alive, we can't be sure. One person claimed he was and he may have a cure, Romulin. Maybe that's why he hasn't returned to us and—"

"Forget the fool's hope of a cure!" Romulin's voice rose slightly. Vi stared, stunned, trying to piece together why such a suggestion would make him so upset. He mumbled a soft apology as he recomposed himself. "You have more important work to do, now. If father is alive, he'll find his way back to us."

"More important work?" Vi rose to her feet and took a step toward her brother. "More important work than reuniting our family and healing our Empire?" Vi balked. As if he couldn't look at her any longer, he turned, walking back toward the tent opening. "Don't you even want a cure? Don't you even want to find him? You grew up with him—*you had him*. How could you not want him now?"

It was unfathomable to her. Shouldn't the absence of their father hurt him even more than it did her? After all, he knew what it was like to have a present father and she didn't. He knew what the loss felt like more profoundly. Or, he should.

Romulin paused, looking in a distant corner of the room. "Our family has never been whole, and will never be."

"What?" Vi whispered.

"First you were gone, then father left, and now—" Romulin stopped himself short.

"I can find father, and I can bring him back."

"Are you insane?" Her brother threw his hands in the air. "Find him? What can you do from the throne?"

"I—"

"And even if you found him and brought him back, we still wouldn't be a complete family. You'd be too late."

"Too late for what?" Vi wasn't sure if she even wanted to know the answer. Romulin looked at her with a mixture of hurt and anger—a raw expression she'd never wanted to see from her brother.

"Just focus on becoming the Empress, Vi." There was a broken quality to his words. A bitter resignation that now laced every sound his mouth made. "I will be with you... even after everyone else is gone. Even when we're forced into bitter political arrangements. You'll have me in your corner."

"Will I? Because you seem to have no problem abandoning family." Vi regretted the words the moment she said them.

Hurt painted his expression, then anger, then the same resignation she'd seen before, as her brother stormed out and brought an abrupt end to their first real meeting. Their first real argument, too.

Vi's hands trembled. She stood, staring, until her legs gave out. Vi grabbed for one of the pillows and buried her face into it, screaming out her frustration silently, so none could hear.

11

THE STRUCTURE OF the imperial parade relaxed after the first day.
Vi and her family were still spearheading with soldiers and guards surrounding them. But there was less of a strict structure and more of a mass slowly marching along the seemingly endless road. The vast majority of the soldiers were on foot, making their pace almost painfully slow.

Vi glanced at Romulin from the corners of her eyes. He was talking quietly with Jax, but the words were lost entirely on Vi's ears.

"So," her mother started from her right. "Tell me what happened."

"What?" Vi's head swung over.

"Tell me what happened," her mother repeated gently. There was no urgency to the words, no strict demands. Just a calmness that Vi had always seen her mother portray. "It was clear at dinner last night that something has already transpired between you two."

"I see…" Vi knotted the reins around her fingers and relaxed them before they became tight enough to pull on the bridle. With a soft sigh, she relented. There wasn't much that she hadn't shared with her mother over the years during her visits to the North. "I suppose… it was just a difference of opinion."

Vi looked over to her brother to find him staring back at her. Romulin looked away quickly, turning to Jax once more. She briefly wondered if Vhalla and Jax had coordinated for this investigation. Perhaps her uncle was asking her brother the same set of questions right now.

She wouldn't put it past them.

"Over what?"

That gave Vi pause. Did she tell her mother of her visions? Surely her mother would want to know. But there were too many ears too close by now for her to divulge that particular secret yet. After Romulin's reaction, she didn't know how her mother would handle it, and putting her on the spot in the public eye seemed a poor choice.

"Our family," Vi said simply.

Vhalla sighed and the sun glinted off her crown with the small motion. It was far more ornate than Vi's and looked impossibly heavy.

"You know, we never *wanted* to send you away…" Vhalla said softly. "It was simply how fate had aligned. There was little else we could do at the time. We desperately needed to know the North wouldn't flank us at the first opportunity when we were weak from the Mad King."

"I know, you've said time and again." Vi wished they weren't on horseback and she could reach out to her mother. She'd have to make due by injecting as much tenderness as possible in her voice. "I don't blame you." Vi dropped her words to a hush. "Sehra told me everything, mother."

"Did she?" Vhalla's brown eyes, flecked with gold, looked at her in surprise. *"Everything?"*

"I believe so." Vi gave a firm nod. "She taught me a good deal about my magic, and the world."

"Thank the Mother," Vhalla whispered in relief. "I was unsure if she ever would."

The reaction affirmed everything Sehra said as truth. Her parents had known of this supposed mysterious traveler. They had known of the premonition of her Lightspinning, and had kept it all from her. Vi wanted to feel hurt by it… but the hurt was gone.

She merely felt tired. Tired of secrets and half-truths. Which was ironic, given the fact that she currently bore the burden of the greatest ones.

A full day of marching later, they finally broke for camp.

Vi spent most of it wallowing in silence and guilt. She wanted to reach out to Romulin, but didn't know where to begin and knew the road wasn't the place for the talk that needed to happen between them. Her conversation with her mother had continued, but about simple topics and matters of state. Merely speaking with her mother should've brought her joy, but it didn't, and that was yet another thing Vi felt guilty for.

As soon as they came to a stop, Vi was eager to dismount. She hunted out Jayme, looking for the familiar tent structure she'd stayed in the night before. As expected, Vi found her friend helping delegate tasks.

"Your highness," Jayme said with a bow of her head as Vi approached. "One more moment and we shall have everything ready for you."

"May I assist at all?"

"That is most generous, but we would not want to burden you," Jayme said loudly, clearly for the benefit of the soldiers in earshot.

"You didn't mind burdening me with your pack for a good hour on our last hunting trip," Vi said under her breath, barely moving her lips.

"Really? You're hung up on an hour?" Jayme was clearly fighting rolling her eyes, and Vi was fighting laughter. "After I carried your pack for how long because you were allegedly 'hunting'?"

"I was hunting."

"Until you fell in a hole."

Vi turned her eyes from Jayme, knowing she was at risk of cracking a smile that would be far too wide. Her gaze landed on the man from the day before—Fallor, he'd said his name was. He was carrying the same crate with her personal effects and Vi was all the more relieved she'd thought to burn the journal. Just the sight of his hands on her things, especially something that precious, made her skin crawl.

"Jayme," Vi said softly, keeping her eyes on him.

"Yes?" Her friend clearly heard the shift in Vi's tone.

"I don't want him carrying my personal effects any longer."

"Who?" Jayme looked to her tent and the soldiers hastily working around it.

"Wait, he's inside... there, *him*, the man who just left, the big one, he calls himself Fallor. Do you know him?"

Jayme stared at the man for a long moment—long enough that his eyes flicked in her direction. The two stared at each other for half a breath and then Jayme looked back to her. "I do not." She paused, folding her arms over her chest in thought. "But I can see how he'd make you uneasy. He's a small giant."

"I'm glad I'm not alone," Vi mumbled. "I don't like him, Jayme. He rubs me wrong."

"You really shouldn't go around demoting people from their jobs just because they 'rub you wrong.'" Jayme sighed softly. She was ever the challenge and counterweight to Vi's authority. "I'm sure he's just a common man trying to make a living. It's a high honor to carry the princess's luggage, you know. You nor I should try to remove him from the post for no good reason."

"I hope it's as simple as you say." She sincerely did. Vi had too much to worry about already; she had no interest in adding a nosy soldier to her list. "Still, I think he was going through my things when I wasn't in my tent."

"Now, that'd be an offense to the crown. Do you have proof of it?"

"I don't... Just a feeling, given how he was unloading them." Vi rubbed the back of her neck, trying to smooth down the hair that stood on end there from the mere sight of Fallor. "You're right, I know you are. It's likely nothing and I'm jumping at shadows."

Vi didn't want to abuse her power. Even if she was going to leave, she didn't want rumors of her being a harsh ruler flying around with the rest. It would be a mark against her family, if nothing else.

"You have a lot on your plate right now," Jayme said softly, the tone of the friend Vi knew slipping in. "Stress gets to everyone."

"Still, do you mind indulging me?" Jayme looked to her and Vi added hastily. "Please? As my friend? Keep an eye on him when you're not stuck at your post outside my tent, that's all. You don't have to go digging or let him know he's being investigated. For my peace of mind?"

"Of course I will." Jayme gave a small nod. "If I find anything I'll be certain to let you know. But try to not let worry over nothing consume you."

"Thank you." As if somehow the soldiers had been waiting on their conversation ending, the tent finished going up in that moment. "Would you like to stay for dinner tonight?" Vi offered, already knowing Jayme would, yet again, find some excuse to excuse herself.

"I can't find information on this Fallor if I do." Jayme shook her head. "And I should stay close to the soldiers, make sure I can be your ear on the inside."

"Right," Vi begrudgingly agreed. "Thank you for all you do."

"I'm here for you, you know that. I'll be back to take up my post right after I grab some food." Jayme gave her a fond smile and quickly departed for the ration line.

Vi entered her tent alone, waving at the brazier to light it. Before her hand fell, she whispered the incantation to bring forth Taavin, anchoring the light around her wrist.

"This is different…" Taavin looked around her tent. "You're on the road now?"

"Only a few days until we reach the northern edge of the Western Waste, then it's a straight shot down to the Crossroads."

"Where you'll make your break for it?"

"That's the plan," Vi muttered, her thoughts still swirling around Romulin, feeling distant from Jayme, and the knowledge of Fallor touching her things. It was all a heavy burden, and that was ignoring the fact that she still had to think of the right moment to slip away.

"What is it?" Taavin shifted, his attention solely on her.

"Nothing." Vi wanted to look anywhere but at him. If she gave him her eyes, then he would see everything—all her insecurities, fears, and worries. Of that, Vi was certain. The last thing she wanted to do was look weak before him of all people.

"I know it's not nothing."

"You don't know anything." She wrapped her arms around herself protectively. Even though she could send him away if she wanted, she didn't.

Everything about him was a conflicting feeling. Yet she loved it all. She needed him close; even when she wanted to be alone, she still wanted *him*. She wanted to be alone with him.

"I know you."

"No, you don't."

"I do." Taavin took a step toward her. "Well, I'm still learning, yes… But I know a good deal, and I want to know more."

"No, you don't," she repeated, softer.

"Yes, I am quite certain that I do." His hands lifted, as though he was going to reach for her. Then, thinking better of it, they fell back to his sides. Which made it all the more notable when a single finger found itself under her chin, directing her eyes to his. "I want to know everything about you."

"For your visions?" Vi asked softly. Part of her screamed, *let it be for that*. Because if that's all it was, she could ignore the fire that had begun to smolder between them both, smoking out feelings she didn't want to address.

"For *you*." His eyes searched her face. "I want to know every nook and cranny of your mind. I want to know how your thoughts work. I want to know your heart, your will, your wants."

"Why?"

"Because I'm afraid if I don't, I may go mad."

They both took a soft inhale of air, and for a moment it felt like they shared breath. Shock was on his face and Vi could only imagine much the same was on hers. What was he really saying?

Taavin swallowed hard, the lump in his throat bobbing. But his voice was still thick when he spoke again. "Now, tell me, what's happened to bring such conflict to your brow?"

"It's a lot…"

"I have time."

"But I'm not sure if I want to talk about it. I wanted to see you, to forget about the world beyond here… To be with you, because you calm me just by being near." So it was her turn to have words fall from her lips that she hadn't quite intended to say.

"I see," he said finally. "If that is your wish, then let's distract you with Lightspinning?"

"I'd like that." Vi breathed a sigh of relief that almost turned into a soft groan of frustration when his hand left her face. She wanted both. She wanted to be emotionally bare before him so that his words could smooth over every rough insecurity and worry. But she also wanted to think of nothing, and simply enjoy his presence.

Simplicity was best, for now. She'd have time to explore whatever these feelings were later… Whenever that was.

"Thank you," Vi breathed in relief.

"I've been thinking of something worthwhile to teach you next… I was thinking of your adventure sneaking out and how *radia* would be a good word for you to master."

"*Radia*," Vi repeated, letting the word slither over her tongue. It begged to be whispered, barely said, clinging to the last breath. It glided over the air and then vanished before it could be fully realized. "To hide?"

"Yes, *radia* is a sub-clarification of *watt*, underneath *durroe*."

"So it would be *durroe watt radia*?" First in Lightspinning was always the overarching discipline. Then the sub-discipline, then any clarifications, with personal words of power at the end.

"Just so." Taavin moved around her. She watched him from the corners of her eyes. His profile was sharp enough to cut glass and his overall elegance was completely out of place in the tent. "Let's use one of these." He gestured to a pillow in the makeshift seating area beside them.

"All right." Vi sat with one.

"Place it in front of you." She did as he instructed. "Now, you're going to make it disappear from sight. Whereas *durroe watt* or *durroe watt ivin* is to create an illusion, for *radia*, you need to know the area around the item—in the physical world—that you want to vanish."

"Around it?"

"Yes, you want people to *see through* the item. To look at it and see the ground below—see past it. *Radia* is an illusion to trick the eyes and mind into missing what's before them."

"So wouldn't it then be under *narro*—acts of the mind?"

"It's deceiving the mind through the eyes. It's firmly under *durroe*," Taavin insisted.

"What if I said it under *narro*? *Narro watt radia*?"

"Do you presume to know better than the Goddess about her words?"

"I meant no offense, I just—" Vi said hastily, realizing that she'd just likely offended him as the keeper of the Goddess's flame. He grinned, and burst out laughing.

"I didn't take it offensively." Taavin's laughter settled into a warm smile that had her stomach simmering with happy bubbles. "I don't think you could offend me."

"If I recall correctly, you found me quite offensive when we first met." Vi remembered back to his initial gruffness toward her—when he thought she was just another iteration of torturous visions.

"Well, then, I don't think you could offend me *again*."

She settled her palm behind her, leaning back. It was astounding just how quickly they fell into an easy cadence, as though nothing had happened at all. The flames that had been flaring between them were relegated to a smolder once more. "Should I try? Is that a challenge?"

"Oh, certainly not, I'd fear seeing what you'd come up with to rise to that challenge." He leaned back on his palm as well. Their fingers were nearly touching. His posture was angled slightly toward her.

"I'm not one to back down." Her voice had gone breathy, and when Taavin spoke, his matched.

"No, you're certainly not."

Was he leaning closer to her? Or was it her imagination? Vi took a slow inhale that got stuck halfway down her throat. The world seemed to slow, silence overwhelming them. Such a heavy silence, it was making her dizzy.

Vi stared up into his eyes. Taavin loomed there, close enough to touch, yet far enough that the world was still between them. She searched his face, looking for secrets and truths alike and landed on his lips—as though that was the place they were all hidden.

Those feelings she'd wanted to ignore were back, with a ruthless urgency she could no longer ignore. The more she saw him, the less they could be denied. *No, oh no*—her mind screamed warnings through her haze as she focused on the delicate curve of his mouth.

This was a terrible idea; she was headed down a road with this man that she never even realized she'd gotten on. How had she let this happen?

She was the crown princess. She was the one who would live out her days in a political arrangement beneficial for her family and Empire. She didn't care about things like feelings... or love... she couldn't. It was the one luxury a princess didn't have. Heartache was the only thing that awaited if she did.

"But," Taavin started slowly, as if trying to find his momentum, too. He continued to hover there, his own eyes embarking on an exploratory mission over her face as if he were looking at her for the first time. "I suppose it's only natural, isn't it?"

"What is?" Her hand shifted slightly; the side of one fingertip touched his, lightning up her side just as his touch had earlier. *What was she doing?*

"Oh—" Taavin cleared his throat and shook his head, as if emerging from a haze. Vi watched as he straightened away, looking at his hands instead of her. "It's a natural question to ask—about *narro* and *durroe*. I think many others have, and you raise a good point. But I think you answered your question by saying it aloud. Did you feel anything?"

He spoke so fast it took her brain a good three seconds after he finished to process the words. She'd never seen someone try so hard to be nonchalant and it made the weight of the moment all the more glaring. Vi swallowed, giving her head a shake of its own. If he was ignoring it, then so should she.

It was for the best, and they both knew it.

"No, I didn't feel anything with them. None of the usual sparks... no glyphs coming to mind."

"Exactly. That illuminates why it's important to remember that the words we know are merely an interpretation of the Goddess's. It is the way our mortal minds can understand a language far beyond our own. Her power is multi-faceted and there are many ways for us to tap into it. Moreover, there may be layers that we do not—and could never—understand."

"When you say many layers..." Another thought occurred to Vi. One that was hazy, but slowly coming into focus. "Are the elemental magicks of Solaris merely layers of this greater power? You've called the elemental magicks 'fractured powers' before—and that the rest of the world merely possesses a more general magic."

Taavin made a low humming noise. "It's something I would certainly like the opportunity to study more. Magic *should* merely be magic—any discipline being a way to focus the channel to achieve a goal.

"But, according to lore and passed-down stories, the magic of the Dark Isle is fractured—a whole power broken into its base elements. Thus, the sorcerers there cannot explore whatever discipline they please to see what they take to. They're relegated to one element."

"So you're saying my power isn't broken like everyone else's in the Empire?"

"Likely because you are her champion." He nodded.

"Then… Could I possibly someday learn how to control the other elements as well?" Vi asked eagerly, imagining a time when she would control the currents of air alongside her mother.

"I believe it should be possible. In fact, I imagine I—or anyone else on Meru— could do the same. But the question is how much effort would it be worth when you've so clearly taken to Lightspinning?"

"Right…" Vi looked down at the pillow she was supposed to be making disappear. It was a delightful hypothetical. But she had far too much to worry about right in front of her to explore too many tangents. "So I'll stick with Lightspinning for now. Specifically, *durroe watt radia*."

"For the best… Like I said, when you say it, imagine you are seeing through the item. Project the glyphs onto it."

Vi raised a hand, trying to keep it still. Her heart was still racing around him. "*Durroe watt radia.*"

Light peeled off her fingertips, spinning through the air. This was far more delicate than any glyph she had constructed with her magic until then. The strands holding together the shifting lines and circles were tenuous at best. Vi tried to imagine it slowly building around the pillow.

"It's very faint… Is it working?"

"It's hazy… you'll need to work on your construction more for this one. Here—" Taavin reached over, resting one hand on her wrist, the other on her palm. He lightly adjusted her hand position with his fingertips. Vi's spine had never been locked so straight. "This hand position may help. It's a softer glyph for sure… it needs a delicate hand. Not your *juth* rigidness."

He smiled at her, and Vi forced a smile back. Inside, she was melting before the heat from the fire that was burning between them anew. Her mind was consumed with the fact that she had to navigate her family, her visions, running away… and now, worst of all… the budding feeling of *something more* with Taavin that she never asked for.

He paused, his expression falling, lips parting softly. She shouldn't have looked him in the eye. She knew he'd see right through her from the start.

Quickly, he pulled away. A smile had returned to his lips, but it read as fake. "Let's give it another try, shall we?"

She had never wanted to do anything more and less at the same time.

12

THE TREES WERE shrinking.

The sky-reaching sentries Vi had grown up playing and living in, the behemoths that had been at once a prison and playground and home, were slowly vanishing. It took Vi longer than she wanted to admit to notice, but when she did, it was all she could obsess over.

First, the canopy thinned, admitting sunlight to warm her cheeks. The feeling struck her oddly, but she didn't make much of it. But then that same canopy looked as though it would come down right on her head—the trees shorter than she'd ever seen them. Finally, they disappeared altogether.

The North ended, and the West began.

Back during the War of the North, Western Firebearers had maintained the border actively. Now, just like the ring around Soricium, those scars left by man remained etched in nature, where jungle met desert.

Vi blinked into the oppressive sunlight, raising a hand off her reins and shielding her eyes.

"Welcome to the Western Waste," Andru said from her right. He hadn't said much since he'd ridden up in the morning, but Vi had appreciated the quiet companionship of her steady friend.

"I don't think I've ever seen so much sky."

"Just wait until you see the view from the pinnacle of the palace in Solarin. The way the mountains carve a jagged line is stunning."

"I think this sky is impressive because it's *not* chopped up." Vi swept her gaze across the desert. Like an alabaster snake, the Great Southern road wound through the dunes and cut across the sand, giving a solid path for their horses and boots in an ocean of gold.

"I can see how that would be a change for you." Andru shifted in his saddle, avoiding her gaze. "But I assure you, you're in for something magnificent this winter. When the mountains are covered in snow, they mirror the clouds in the sky and it's like a never-ending horizon."

"I'm sure you're right," Vi said softly, hoping he didn't notice the sorrow that had crept into her voice. She would never see that winter.

"Speaking of returning home, princess…" he continued, blessedly oblivious to her struggle. She'd been waiting for this. Vi knew what was coming before he said it. In fact, she was surprised there was still a good hour before they broke for camp for the day—he'd worked up the nerve in record time, knowing him. "I think you should make up with your brother before we arrive."

Vi sighed heavily. But before she could even try to find an explanation for why things were tense, he hastily continued.

"This is what you've both always wanted. You each hold one another in such high regard… All you spoke of was seeing each other, talking, being reunited at long last, having the opportunity to learn of each other in person.

"He won't tell me what caused such an immediate rift but I assured him—as I'll assure you—that I think it's completely natural for there to be some growing pains since you were raised apart and now are learning to be together in person. You may have formulated opinions in your head that are different in reality. I know that's true of him."

She allowed him to finish. Andru wasn't the lecturing sort and she was certain he'd been practicing this little speech. The least she could do was hear him to the end.

"Plus, you don't want the Senate to see any rifts between you both." Andru's voice dropped lower. "They'll find a way to capitalize on any perceived weakness, use it to cast doubt. I know my father would find every way possible to twist even the most innocent sibling squabble into something sinister. Being at odds will be good for neither of you."

"I know," Vi said, her voice just as soft. She looked over the blinding desert, lifting and adjusting the headscarf Jax had given her the night before to shield her face from the sun's assault. "Tell me, Andru, do they love Romulin?"

"The Senate? Or the people?"

"Both."

He thought a moment before speaking. "The senate *understands* Romulin. It's no secret between us or anyone that the Senate is uncertain about what they want the future of the crown to be." Vi resisted a retort that would do her no good. "But Romulin is a known entity—a safe bet, someone they can work with. Even if the Senate doesn't consolidate power further, they can fully trust the person on the throne."

"They don't see me as a safe bet." It wasn't a question, so Vi didn't phrase it as one.

"I don't think they would've sent me if they did," Andru agreed solemnly. "Apologies, princess."

"You've nothing to apologize for." Vi shifted in her saddle. "And the people?"

"Oh the people—court and commoners—love him immensely. They see in him the blood of your grandfather and great grandfather. Some say he has the wisdom of the last King Solaris, the strength of the first Emperor Solaris, and the kind demeanor of your late Uncle Baldair."

"All very strong, very Southern men," Vi murmured. A small smile graced her lips as her gaze focused on the flaxen haired man in question. It was good he had that much love. There would be much he'd need to bear in the coming weeks. Luckily Romulin's shoulders were wide and they could handle the weight, she hoped. "The people's approval would go far with the Senate."

"Yes, as I said—and as you know—he's a good ally. But more than that, he is your brother and you both love each other dearly. Neither of you is enjoying being at odds. One of you must bridge this chasm."

"I know." Vi gave a small nod. "I handled things poorly and needed the past few days to clear my head… to decide what to say to him next. I don't want to mess this up again. But I promise, I'll approach him tonight." She tried to give a reassuring smile, and was happy to see it was one Andru returned.

Rather than going right to her tent, Vi set to wandering after they broke rank for the day.

Dusk had overtaken the rock and sand of the desert. Behind her, in the far distance, she could still see the trees of the North, but they had shrunken, become shadowed, and now looked like little more than ominous black clouds on the edge of the horizon. Ahead of her, the sun still blazed, dying slowly in the western sky. Above, the stars were already beginning to kick off the covers of daytime and greet the world once more.

Vi grabbed the bracelet still tied around her wrist, worrying at the small bead of wood. How had she handled it when she and Ellene had scuffled? Surely they had. She *knew* they had. But all Vi could think of now were fond memories of the girl.

The soldiers mostly avoided her and Jayme as they moved through camp, and Vi ignored them in reply. Jayme was just as quiet, giving Vi her mental space when she could not allow physical space as well. She had originally set out to find her brother's tent, but a voice drifting over a gathering of soldiers quickly distracted her.

"When fighting a sorcerer, you need to keep an eye on their movements first—" Snippets of her mother's voice were carried on the wind like a precious token. Vi headed in the direction, toward a group of soldiers on a dune half-ringing two people opposite each other below—one was her mother; the other wore the black armor of the Tower of Sorcerers.

Vi recognized one of the men on the upper portion of the ring and crossed to her uncle.

"What's going on?" she asked.

Jax looked a little startled to see her. "Your mother is helping some new recruits with pointers for fighting sorcerers. They've been asking for some time if she would, and it seems your mother is up to the task this evening."

"Empresses do that?"

"Vhalla does. Well, these days she makes time whenever she's able, at least." Jax nodded, not taking his eyes off the woman in question as she continued instruction. "Connecting sorcerers and commons became her life's work after she was Awoken."

That was right—there was a time when Vi's mother hadn't been a sorcerer. Where she'd just been a common-born library apprentice working in the palace. Vi found herself forgetting in her mother's presence, since the woman walked as though she had been born to wear the crown on her brow.

"Being involved with the soldiers, keeping yourself accessible…" Jayme picked up the thought. "Anything that makes sorcerers not seem frightening is a good thing. I hear the way the soldiers talk about sorcerers even now."

Vi watched her mother move as she demonstrated her instructions to the soldiers. There was a decisive grace and a lack of hesitation that Vi had been working toward with Taavin for months now and she still didn't possess.

"Such small movements," she whispered.

"Indeed, but it wasn't always so. You wouldn't know it from watching her now, but she had the hardest time with not telegraphing her sorcery when she was your age." There was a fond and familiar note to Jax's voice.

"You've mentioned that. It's a skill I seem to have inherited."

"You have?" Jax looked to her in surprise. "When have you been practicing? I haven't seen you with the Black Legion once on this trek."

"I—"

Their conversation was thankfully cut short by Vhalla.

"Now, I think we should demonstrate two different affinities against each other." The Empress's voice echoed over the dunes. "Jax, would you care to step in the ring with me and show the soldiers how two different affinities can volley against each other?"

Suddenly all eyes were back on them.

Vi glanced between her mother and uncle, giving the former a small nod of both greeting and understanding. She didn't know how much Sehra had told her mother about her powers, but Vhalla knew they were different from the rest and Vi was grateful she wasn't—

"How about the crown princess?" a voice interjected before her uncle could respond.

The attention swung to the giant man who had made the shout. The soldiers around Fallor took a small step away, as if trying to avoid association with him. They were visibly nervous, eyes darting between Vhalla and Vi.

"I should not like to be seen as receiving favoritism," Vi said with stiff formality.

"Hardly favoritism! I think we would all like to see what our crown princess and future Empress is capable of." Fallor beamed up at her and Vi was forced to wonder if there wasn't a sinister glint to his too-white teeth.

Vi wanted to show him exactly what she was capable of with a strong *juth* lit right under his arse. But her rage quickly devolved into fear as the soldiers around Fallor began to murmur what sounded like agreement. Of course they would be curious to see the princess and Empress Regent spar.

"Are there any objections?" Vhalla addressed the crowd, and then the sorcerers in black situated on the lower dune. "Or perhaps any sorcerers who would like the honor instead?"

Vi's heart thumped a beat that had the word *please* attached to every pulse. Yet no one moved. She glanced over her shoulder at Jayme, silently pleading. The girl lifted her brow and scrunched it as if to ask, "What can I do?" Vi didn't have an answer; Jayme wasn't a sorcerer, she was just pulling at straws.

"I think you have to go up," Jax mumbled.

"No one?" Vhalla asked, her eyes settling back on Vi apologetically.

She didn't want to have to spar before all these people. But there were, as expected, no objections. She had been practicing her Lightspinning at length… to the detriment of her skills as a Firebearer. Vi swallowed hard. Taavin had said magic was magic—Lightspinning or Firebearing—they were both ways to focus a channel.

She could do this.

The group of soldiers parted for Vi to walk through as she descended to the flatter area where her mother stood ready. A pair of purple eyes caught hers, almost flashing in the near-darkness. Fallor stood a head above the rest, still grinning like a fool and looking easily like he could crush all the soldiers who stood a good half step away from him. Vi suppressed a shiver and focused forward.

I'm overreacting, Vi tried to tell herself. He was nothing more than a member of the infantry. A really large, really creepy, annoying member—but not someone who deserved her suspicion. Tonight was merely a coincidence.

Vi wiggled her fingers, feeling the sparks that lingered just beneath her skin charge around them. Should she try to hide her Lightspinning? Or try to draw simple attacks of fire with her magic as she'd first learned? She could conjure basic flames easily enough. Perhaps that was the best path forward...

"Just a simple round, then?" Vhalla suggested, loud enough that the soldiers could still hear what was being decided.

Vi gave a nod of affirmation. *Just a little bit of power*, just enough to convince them she was a Firebearer and nothing more. She didn't have to win the spar. It was likely better if she didn't beat the Empress Regent—Martis would say as much, wouldn't he?

"Are you ready?" Vhalla asked, sinking slightly lower. Vi gave a small nod, trying to look as though she was ready to do battle as well and hoping it was all a show. "Let's begin!"

Vhalla didn't hesitate. She sprang forward, unleashing the power in her legs as she launched from her stance. Vi stepped back, bracing herself, hands up, spark ready.

A wall of wind blew across her. Her heels sank into the sand as she was pushed back. Vi was reminded of Uncle Jax's fire walls and she pushed the spark into her palms, avoiding the instinct to craft a shield with *mysst*.

The wall of wind had been a diversion, and the Empress shifted her trajectory. Vi could see her moving with the air under her feet, speeding her movements and sending the sand scuttling away in divers. She spun, bringing a kick toward Vi.

Vi dropped low, pivoting around her bent leg. The other stretched out and led her turn, sweeping across the sand toward the leg Vhalla stood on for support. Fire crackled off her heel, picking up with a flare on her mother's wind, causing her to jump back.

"Clever move! Use your opponent's magic against them whenever you're able." Vhalla clapped her hands once and before Vi even had time to register the praise, she was launching forward for a right-handed thrust.

Vi stepped back, avoiding the jab. This was a spar, an exhibition, not a fight. Their punches were wide, their distance large. Her mother was playing up Vi's limited attacks. *It must look real to the soldiers*, hope whispered within her. She could convince them all she was a Firebearer.

Vi swung her hand toward her mother's side and fire cracked like she held a physical whip.

Vhalla dispersed her flames with a gust. Vi was ready, sending a bolt of flame with a flick over her mother's shoulder. She'd been expecting Vhalla to dodge in the opposite direction, but watched as her Mother stepped toward the fire. The flame caught her clothes, singing a hole by her collarbone—Vhalla stopping just in time to avoid further damage.

Mid-leap, Vi froze, her fire completely vanishing, her eyes landing on the barely exposed flesh. She teetered from one foot to the next, nearly losing balance and tripping over herself. Her stomach had fallen from her body, her mind was in full revolt, and her heart thrummed not from the exertion of battle but sheer panic.

For underneath her mother's clothes, concealed, barely visible through the singed hole, was a firm-looking, white portion of skin that seemed to almost glisten—as though it were a wet rock. Certainly not burnt flesh, as it should be.

Vi knew that marking. She'd seen it in her visions of the future. She'd seen it with her own two eyes at the clinic.

But nothing could've prepared her to see it on her mother's flesh.

"That's enough for one evening, I think," Vhalla said lightly. Vi would think her completely oblivious, were it not for the sudden shift in her demeanor. She was almost too casual, too composed. Vi wanted to run to her, hold her, weep, shake her, scream, and demand answers all at the same time. "As always, thank you all for your interest in learning more about sorcery."

Vi closed her eyes, trying to calm the pulses of magic that were ripping through her like a sudden shift in tide, sweeping up on the undercurrents of her emotions. She had seen it wrong. It was a trick of the fading light, the pale moonlight on the dunes.

This wasn't real.

Footfalls grew closer. "What happened?" Jax asked, looking between them. "Are you all right, Vi?" Jayme wasn't with him. That should've been Vi's first clue that he'd already known despite his confused look.

When she opened her eyes, she looked directly at her mother. Vaguely, the soldiers leaving registered to her—just enough to know that they were out of earshot. *If* she managed to keep her voice low enough.

"Tell me you're not afflicted," Vi whispered with a trembling breath. It was barely audible or screaming; there was no between for her right now.

Her mother's face was unreadable, her expression closed. It was Jax who gave away the guise as he looked from Vhalla to Vi, his eyes becoming soft and sad in a terrible way that Vi didn't want to ever see.

"No, no—" Vi shook her head, taking a step back, as if this was something she could run from.

All too fast, her mother crossed the gap between them and wrapped her hands around Vi's shoulders. Vhalla gave her a gentle shake, looking at her with eyes harder than a Groundbreaker's stone skin. All in one expression, she seemed to be able to communicate the simple message: *If I can keep myself together, so can you.*

But those words never left her lips. Instead, her mother instructed simply, "Come to my tent. We will discuss there."

13

THERE WAS NO sound in Vi's ears, just a dull ringing noise that she feared would be there for the rest of her life. Things were clicking together, locking into place. Questions compounded with more questions, crashing together around one terrible truth.

Vi pressed her eyes closed, wanting to shut out the whole world for just a minute. One minute so she could catch her breath and then—

"Vi?" her mother said with a gentle touch on her shoulder. Vi's head jerked up at the contact. "Come in, please."

Part of her desperately didn't want to, as if she could ignore the truth laid out before her. But Vi had no other option. It was better to hear it from her mother than leave her mind to speculation.

As soon as the tent flap closed between her and Vhalla, Jax remaining outside to presumably stand guard and send away any who would interrupt them, Vi started.

"Is it the White Death?"

"Yes." Her mother sat heavily in one of her chairs. Her tent was set up nearly identical to Vi's.

Vi swayed in place. She wanted to scream and shout, not at her mother, but at the disease slowly killing them all. Instead, Vi stumbled over, all but collapsing at her mother's feet.

"Were you going to tell me?" Vi looked up at her mother, her invincible mother, the woman who had risen from nothing to rule all, who had fought wars and triumphed—now made frail in the wake of a plague.

"I was."

"When?"

"After your coronation."

So if she hadn't seen it now, she would've never found out. "This… this is why Father left, isn't it?" Vi's shoulders were trembling, but no tears fell. She was too profoundly shaken and sad—past the point of tears. This was another emotion altogether, one she didn't even have a name for. "The Senate would've never let the Emperor leave, and Father wouldn't have risked it unless—"

"Unless my life was on the line." Vhalla was able to say what she could not. She sighed softly, sinking further into her chair and looking up at the ceiling. "But now it seems I will not see him again until we meet in the Father's realms of eternal night."

Vi rested her temple on her mother's knee. Her eyes were unfocused and the world blurry. Everything had a hazy numbness to it that muted reality and made the pain less agonizing.

She could tell her mother of her vision.

Vi could give her hope that Aldrik still lived. But she hadn't had a vision of him since the one in the ruins long ago. Perhaps Romulin was right and her insistence was misplaced. Perhaps Aldrik Solaris was dead. Vi pressed her eyes closed, as if blocking out the thought. But it persisted.

Her mother's hand fell on her hair, stroking it lightly. *She wouldn't tell her,* Vi decided. If her vision was wrong, or her father was dead, she wouldn't give her mother a cruel, false hope. "I'm sorry, my daughter, that I have never properly been there for you."

"You've done what you could." Vi reached up, gripping her mother's hand. She held it as she shifted, to her knees, and then her feet. Vi squeezed Vhalla's fingers tightly, as though it would be the last time. Her body acted in a way her mind refused to acknowledge; Vi refused to mourn. "Let the rest of us do what we can, now."

Her mother smiled faintly. "You've truly grown into your namesake."

"My namesake?" She'd never realized she'd been named after anyone in particular. Her name was slightly odd, so Vi always assumed her mother had invented it.

"Yes... I met a woman once. Well, multiple times. She was actually the one who gave me that watch." Vhalla nodded toward the watch around Vi's neck.

"This one?" Vi grasped it, looking down. This was the watch that connected her with Taavin—the one that bore his mark, the one he wanted her to take to Meru. "You recognized it?"

"Of course I did." Vhalla gave a small nod. "I would recognize that watch anywhere. I'd wondered what happened to it."

"Fritz said he'd kept it and sent it to me. Is it all right?"

"Yes, sweet girl. If any were to have it, I'd want it to be you."

Vi breathed a secret sigh of relief. She hadn't wanted to try to convince her mother to let her keep it. "Who gave it to you?"

"She said her name was Vi."

"Why was I named after her?" Vi asked softly. Things weren't adding up. Her brother was named after their great grandfather—the last king of the Solaris line before their grandfather proclaimed himself Emperor of the Main Continent. Vi was named after a woman her mother had met a handful of times?

Vhalla pressed her fingertips to her lips in thought. Her eyes seemed hazy and unfocused, though Vi couldn't tell if it was from exhaustion or from focusing on the past more than the present. When her mother finally spoke, it was more dream-like than the confident way she usually presented herself.

"She was... important."

Vi waited for more, and when the silence stretched on: "Important *how*?"

"Forgive me." Vhalla smiled. "I'm afraid that the more time that passes, the harder it is to remember exactly what happened when it came to her. Your old mother is going senile."

"You are neither old nor senile." *Nor dying.* No matter what, she wouldn't let her mother die. The family Vi had always envisioned would be together, even if she had to fight death itself to make it a reality.

"Well, in either case, she saved my life, multiple times. And every time, she seemed to be less real than the last."

"How well did you know her?" Vi asked cautiously.

"Not well."

"Would you say she was a… traveler?" The word stuck on Vi's tongue, weighing it down, filling her with anticipation.

"I don't know what she was."

Vi could tell her mother was tired and had revealed all she remembered already. For all Vi wanted to press for more information, she let it slide. If the woman who gave Vi her name was somehow linked to Sehra's traveler, Vi would only find out in time.

"Thank you for telling me, Mother—about both the watch and the woman I'm named after. But you should rest now. You look tired."

"I am." Vhalla raised her hand and Vi reached out, grabbing it one more time. "How was I blessed with such an understanding daughter? It will do me well to have the trials of the Empire passed off my shoulders. Forgive me for that."

"Stop asking for forgiveness; you've done nothing to forgive. Romulin or I would both be relieved to see you in a place where you can rest and focus only on your health." Vi leaned forward, planting a gentle kiss on her mother's forehead. "Now, get all the sleep you can before the march tomorrow."

"Thank you," Vhalla said softly, eyes dipping closed. "Forgive me also… that I repeat the mistakes of my mother." Her voice trailed off, already drawling with slumber so much that arguing further with her was pointless.

Vi took a few steps backwards, her attention settled on the rocky portion of her mother's chest, laid bare by a tiny singe. She took a deep breath, straightening with it, and strode from the tent—nearly bumping into Jax on the way out.

"Vi?"

"She's falling asleep." Vi looked up at her uncle. "See she gets to the actual bed so she's comfortable."

He was startled at her tone. So was Vi. She wasn't usually one to order him of all people. But things had changed. In such a short period of time, everything was becoming irrevocably different.

"Are you—"

"I'm fine. I will be fine," Vi answered, soft but firm. "Please, look after her."

"I always have." Jax turned his head toward the tent. "Your father asked two things of me. The first was to look after you. The second was to look after her."

"Don't let him or me down." Vi grabbed Jax's hand. "I— *We* need you."

"I will always be here for Solaris." Jax's eyes were shadowed and haunted. But soft, and as loving as she'd always seen them. "They call me the Crown's Dog. But these days, if I'm a dog, it's because the hearth I have found to guard is yours."

"Thank you," she whispered.

He merely nodded, pulling away, and stepped into the tent. Vi moved in the opposite direction. Her family was splintering at an alarming rate, and there was one bond she couldn't allow to sit fractured any longer.

Her brother's tent was only a short distance away—short enough that Vi managed to cross to it without an escort clinging to her shoulder.

Without hesitation, Vi gave a firm knock on the tent post. There was movement within, hushing voices, and then Romulin's face appeared illuminated by a small sliver of orange light.

"S-Sister?"

"We need to talk." Vi clasped her hands before her, knotting them over her stomach. "You're the only one I can turn to right now. I need your wisdom. I need the other half of my mind."

"I—Of course." Romulin looked inside and it was when he shifted that Vi locked eyes with Andru. The other man stood from where he'd been lounging, eyes on his feet as he crossed to leave.

"I'll leave you to it," he mumbled.

"Thank you, Andru." Vi watched him go. Luckily, he didn't seem too upset at being displaced. He'd been the one pushing her to make up with Romulin, after all.

"Well, come in then."

Vi followed behind her brother, stepping into a tent full of awkward tension. She ignored it. There wasn't time for their petty squabbles anymore.

"I wish," she started, "we had the luxury of time. I wish we could've grown up together, spent our years playing and learning alongside each other. But we didn't have that."

He gave a small nod, not yet knowing where she was going with her point but clearly agreeing with that basic sentiment.

"But I realize now, I wouldn't change it."

Romulin's eyes widened a fraction at that statement.

"We are in a unique position—you and I."

"What are you talking about?"

"I know about Mother."

The words clearly shook him to his core. He took a step backward, sitting heavily in one of his chairs. Romulin ran a hand over his face and shook his head.

"I didn't think she'd tell you so soon…"

"She didn't intend to. I found out by chance." Vi watched the opportunity to chastise her brother for keeping it from her come and go. A competitive, sisterly part of her hated that her twin knew something she didn't. The more logical princess knew it was a strength they had—they'd each studied vastly different knowledge, and together they formed a more complete whole.

Romulin wouldn't look at her. Finally, he spoke softly. "Do you see now?"

"See what?"

"This is why I was telling you that we need to focus on the here and now. We need to enjoy what we have—the love and joy we can find—because the road ahead is more challenging than anything we've faced so far."

"The road ahead *is* more challenging than anything we've faced. But we need to keep our eyes on it, focused on the route that leads where we want to go. We can't be so lost savoring the now that we don't seize tomorrow."

He finally looked back to her with his cool eyes. Vi leveled with his, not backing down, not flinching. She didn't come to fight, but she also wasn't about to budge on her opinion.

"I'm going to find Father," Vi vowed softly. "And I'm going to help him find a cure for Mother."

"Not this about Father being alive again." Romulin pushed off the chair's armrests and began to pace.

Vi stopped him, grabbing his wrist. "I need you, brother. You have always given me good counsel, helped me lay and implement plans, but now I need you to heed me—to trust me. As I'm going to need to trust you. It's my turn to give you counsel. Mother will need you when I'm gone, the whole Empire will. You're going to do what needs to be done. You've always known what that is; trust your gut and follow it."

"Vi... You can't really be entertaining this fantasy of running off and playing hero."

"I don't care about being the hero. I'm merely doing what must be done because no one else can or will." Vi released her grip, searching his face for the brother she'd always known in her letters, for the closeness she'd always felt. The moment she saw a glimpse of it, Vi reached out, clasping her arms around his neck and pulling him in for a tight embrace. "We will talk more. Take the next day and think if you must. But I will be leaving from the Crossroads, and before I do that, I want to know two things: That you know I love you. And that you will take care of Mother and keep this secret, sharing my truths only when you think the time is right. I trust your judgment above all else. So if you have any bright spots of advice to give me before I go, I welcome them."

Releasing him, Vi left him with those thoughts. He wouldn't tell anyone of her plans—she was certain of it. They may not see entirely eye-to-eye on this. But he was her brother, and he would look out for her above all else.

Before she knew it, she was back in the darkness of her tent, alone.

"*Narro hath hoolo,*" Vi whispered. Outside, Jayme's armor clanked as she settled into her post just on the other side of the tent flap. She had to be quiet, but she wasn't going to be dissuaded.

Taavin appeared, her emotions linked to each swirling glyph that etched him before her from thin air. Vi watched as he sharpened and came into focus. She took an almost hesitant step forward.

"What is it?" he asked softly the moment he saw her expression. The lilt of his voice vibrated deep within her.

"My mother has the White Death."

"Oh, Yargen's light, Vi, I am so sorry." Taavin crossed quickly, scooping up her hands in his.

Vi shook her head. "I'm not grieving for a mother who isn't dead. I'm not mourning someone who's not gone—someone who can be saved." She locked eyes with him. "Tell me she can be saved."

"I don't—"

"Tell me there is a cure on Meru. Or that once we lock Raspain away for good, the White Death will be gone with him. Once he's gone, and the spread stops, we can heal her," Vi whispered hastily.

"I... would hope." He sighed softly. "But I fear it won't be so simple... And I don't want to hurt you by promising things I cannot ensure will pass." His thumbs stroked over hers. In the darkness of her tent, there was only him, a man with pointed ears who shimmered slightly at his edges.

"You could never hurt me. You have given me so much strength."

"You still barely know me." Taavin looked at her sadly. "I've done terrible things. And even worse things happen to the people I've dared to love, Vi." His voice dropped to a thoughtful whisper, a hand loosening its grip to land on her cheek. She felt the pad of his thumb smooth over the curve of her face. But it was distant, the action unimportant to the words he spoke.

"People… you *love*?"

His lips parted slightly, shock manifesting on his face. So she hadn't heard wrong. She hadn't *felt* wrong. Vi gripped his hand more tightly; she wasn't going to let him go now, not for anything.

She pulled gently, leaning forward, her heart racing. She'd never done this before and certainly didn't think she was doing it right based on how Ellene had always described it—the young woman had always stressed that the man must be the first to move at all costs. That was well and good for someone who had time, for someone whose life was secure and stable. But Vi's was one misstep from falling apart.

It might not be love yet, Vi honestly didn't know. But she knew what she felt for this man was strong and different from anything she'd ever felt with anyone else. She knew she wanted him above all others.

"Don't do this." Taavin's breath warmed her nose and mouth. Even as he protested, he moved closer—closer than they'd ever been before. "There will be no going back."

"I certainly hope not," she whispered.

Vi's eyes dipped closed. The last thing she saw were his heavy lids and unfocused pupils. Darkness… and the moment his lips met hers, an explosion of color behind her eyelids.

She'd wanted this. For how long, Vi didn't quite know. But she wanted to feel him next to her, his hand shifting to rest on her waist, the other still on her face. She wanted to feel the embroidery of his coat under her fingers and not simultaneously feel the pressure to let go.

Nothing was guaranteed or certain. The world would rob them blind on a whim. Romulin had said to savor what they had before them and, like always, he was right.

He had Andru.

And Vi had Taavin.

14

S HE WAS STIFF, as was he.

They both stood rigidly against each other, struggling to move and simultaneously afraid that if they did it would bring an end to this moment. His lips hardly moved. They quivered under hers as Taavin drew a shaky breath across her mouth, his barely far enough away to find air.

Then, it was his turn to kiss her.

Vi wasn't sure how she'd known his intent, but she had. Every bit of her sensed his want to initiate before he'd even begun to move. He'd wanted to capture what he'd been yearning for just as she had. She allowed her mouth to be consumed by his and savored each new, thrilling sensation.

More confident, his lips parted slightly, begging hers open. A small sigh escaped her lips as they shifted, wet and warm, against his. Worries melted from her mind, trickling down her spine and leaving bumps in their wake, before pooling low in her stomach, transformed there into something wonderful.

His touch had turned pain into pleasure. His lips, worry into delight. Everything faded but him and the feeling of his warmth—no longer frustratingly a step too far away.

The world was not about to be saved by a kiss.

But if it could've been, that would've been the kiss to save it.

When Vi finally pulled away, she was breathless. They hadn't been kissing that long, she was certain of it. But she felt dizzy, and he looked as though he'd just run a marathon.

Blush suited him.

"Vi, I—" Taavin's grip tightened on both her shoulders, before he pushed himself away from her. "We can't. This, we can't."

"Why?" Vi asked, despite being halfway toward placing her mouth on his again. She wanted to do it over and over, to feel every way he moved and delight in it all. How had she gone so long in life without kissing? It was seven times as wonderful as Ellene had made it sound.

"Because we're half a world away." He brought a hand to his eyes and turned his back toward her, as though ashamed.

"And I'm going to come to you."

"We belong to different worlds," he said over his shoulder. "You're a princess, and I'm the head of a religious order."

"And we're the Champion and the Voice—which seems way more important than any of those other titles."

He turned to face her, trying to stare her down. Vi wouldn't cower. "Bad things happen to those I've been foolish enough to entangle myself with—and I've never even risked being entangled romantically. I've no idea what could happen."

"Well, at least we're both new to romance," she said with a small smile. He ignored her attempt at levity.

"Vi, this is serious."

"I'm being serious." She allowed the smile to slip from her face. "You say bad things happen... Well my mother is dying, my father may be dead, the world is ending. Just what else can get worse?"

"It can always get worse, I assure you," he cautioned. "I've seen it with my own eyes."

"I'm not afraid." Vi took a step toward him.

"You should be." Taavin's voice had dropped low, almost growl-like. "I'm trying to protect you."

"That seems a fool's errand." Vi grabbed his coat lapels, feeling the supple fabric. "Don't deny me this. This fire I feel between us is brighter than any magic I've ever known. You're the only thing holding me together right now."

"And you... you're the only thing that has ever made me fall apart."

All at once, his hand was in her hair again, his mouth crushed against hers. The kiss was clumsy, sloppy even. But it was also full of desire and yearning.

It was everything she needed.

A barrier had been broken down in her—a dam released. It had been holding back years of repressed desires and wants and everything else she refused to allow herself to feel. Now that Vi had torn it down, she was being swept downstream faster than she could recover.

Taavin pulled away once more. Vi pulled him back. She kissed him as if to devour him, teeth hitting awkwardly until they learned each other's rhythm.

Finally, they pulled apart once more, and this time Vi merely searched his face. Her hands drifted upward, following her eyes, caressing his cheeks, up to his ears— feeling the strange way they pointed. She finally buried her fingers in his hair, all the while he merely stared at her.

"What now?" he whispered, breathless.

"Nothing changes, overall," she confessed. "You're still in Meru and I'm going to get to you."

"Between us?"

"Tell me everything." She dropped her hands to his chest once more, feeling the broad swathe of lean muscle. "Tell me of yourself, of the man I've been kissing. Hearing you're the head of a religious order is a large part of who you are—and until now, I didn't know. I feel you know almost everything about me."

"You don't want to know about me."

"I do."

Taavin sighed softly. Catching her hand, he brought it to his lips, placing a thoughtful kiss on her wrist. The movement sent shivers up her arm and neck.

"What is it you want to hear?"

"Tell me about your room. Describe it in detail." Vi started there: something simple, harmless, easy to confess. "You've told me it was above Yargen's flame... that you can see Risen from your window."

"Yes... I can see Risen from my window." Taavin paused, looking toward her sitting area. He motioned for it and Vi led the way. Once they were settled, her side flush against his, he continued. "My room is shaped like an octagon.

"Through one set of doors, there is the entrance. Across from that is my bedroom, then a window, then my study, another window, my wash room, the entrance, and then a study area in the final two corners.

"The floor is wood, much the same as the room—octagonal and set against each other in a pattern..."

Vi's eyes closed as she tried to envision it. In her mind, she constructed it not unlike her own chambers in the North. But his sounded... smaller. She painted it in soft grays and whites, just as he said, gilded with gold. A single shelf—mostly religious texts and works of his own writing—occupied one wall. At one end was a collection of watchmaking tools, a hobby he said he'd picked up years ago. Embellishments on the door panels depicted lore from *The Word of the Goddess*—a religious text she also now knew existed.

"It sounds beautiful," she whispered when he finished.

"It is. A gorgeous prison."

"Why do you say you're imprisoned?" A protective streak, deeper than what she expected, ripped through her.

"I've told you."

"In bits and pieces..." Vi shifted, turning to face him. She hesitated briefly before taking up his hand. It was odd to think about the lines they'd crossed... how it might change them. Could she kiss him freely now if she wanted to? How would she know if he wanted to kiss her back?

"On Meru, there is the Order of the Faithful, and the Voice is at their head."

"So you're like a king?"

He sighed, running his free hand through her hair. Vi enjoyed the way it smoothed through the dark strands, tugging lightly on her scalp as he teased through a knot. "It's difficult to explain."

"Try me, I'm not stupid."

"Far from it," he agreed quickly. "Meru has a Queen; the Queen is anointed by the Voice and the Faithful. She is the one who rules—"

"But with your blessing." She was reminded of her first vision of her father—the woman in all the bolts of draped silk must be the Queen of Meru.

"Yes." Vi could see instantly how that would make Taavin powerful, even if he didn't wield the power of the crown himself. "The Faithful also have a strong arm—Swords of Light. Though most call them merely 'The Swords.'

"The man at their head... Lord Ulvarth, he is the one who keeps me here."

"Why?" Vi whispered, though she could guess.

"Because if I were ever to leave—to splinter from him and the Faithful—his power would be diminished. He gets away with what he does because the people think his actions are based on directives that come from the Goddess herself, funneled through me."

"And those directives don't actually come from you or the Goddess... do they?"

Vi said slowly, putting it together.

"They don't," he affirmed. "Well, not always. And if it is from me… I'm merely saying what Ulvarth wants me to in order to protect my own wellbeing."

"How does Lord Ulvarth get away with that?" Though again, Vi suspected she knew the reason.

"By keeping me here. If he is the only one who may speak with me, then who is to know?"

"But the people, surely they—"

"The people have only seen me a handful of times." Taavin gave her a tired smile. "I doubt they even remember my hair color, let alone what I would or wouldn't say. I may be the Voice of the Goddess, but Ulvarth is the voice of me. He is the only truth they know."

There were more layers to this; Vi could see them between his words even if she couldn't quite understand them. But there was little she could do about his situation until she was with him. For the time being, all they had to make the hours a little more bearable was each other.

She ran her fingertip down the outline of his scar. Taavin's eyes took on a worried expression. She barely had time to give him a reassuring smile before leaning in to kiss him once more.

He could have his secrets, for now.

The Crossroads were finally in sight.

The Western Waste had seemed like it would never end and then, suddenly, out of nowhere: civilization. The first sighting of it on the horizon was enough to set her heart racing. Now, every step closer filled her with apprehension and excitement.

This would be the end of her journey with her family, and the start of something a mere year ago she never would have expected.

"It will be similar to how it was when we came to get you," Romulin said from her side. "We shall be in front, just behind some flag bearers this time. Then some more flag bearers on horses. A couple guards around. Then, the rest of the infantry."

"Right," Vi murmured, watching as said flag bearers assembled posts to make tall staffs, to which they affixed pennons emblazoned with the sun of the Empire. She fussed with the headscarf that had been keeping the heat off her brow. A heavy, rope-like braid fell down the center of her back.

"You're not wearing your scarf anymore?" Andru asked from Romulin's side. The two were together more often than not. And, while Romulin had yet to say anything outright, Vi was beginning to assume that Andru had mentioned she was in the know.

"No, not for when we enter. I've been told I look like my grandmother, Princess Fiera. I think showing my hair and face could only garner favor."

"A brilliant idea, sister."

"Thank you." Vi gave her brother a smile. They had yet to really address what had happened two nights ago, but she took their easy rapport today as a sign they were headed toward some kind of peace—and that was the best she could hope for, before she set off for Meru. "I'll take it out of the braid when we get closer, otherwise the wind will make it a knotted mess."

"I admire that you learned the Southern braids from Mother," Romulin said softly.

"It was a nice gesture."

Mother.

They hadn't spoken much since Vi found out about her affliction. She stared at her mother's back, at the cape bearing the blazing sun and lined in Western crimson. Vhalla rode strong and tall. If Vi hadn't known better, she would've never suspected the illness ravaging her.

An hour later, they passed under the great northern gate of the Crossroads.

The Crossroads were unlike anything she'd ever seen. Certainly, the treetop cities of the North were magical and breathtaking in their own right, but the West was its own unique form of magic.

Canvas shades were pulled over the alleyways and streets to guard those below from the sun. The filtered light illuminated the white of the road ahead in reds and oranges. But the streets were mostly empty. Only a few lined their path forward, regarding them tiredly. Perhaps even warily.

Her eyes scanned over their heads, to the buildings behind them. Mostly squat and constructed of a smooth stone that looked almost like the sand itself, they had square windows and ashen timbers jutting out between floors.

Vi's attention settled on the doors. Painted in a rough hand over a few was a white circle. Others bore an X.

"The White Death," she muttered. She'd seen a similar mark in the North.

"Slightly different from the Northerners. Here, the circle marks places where the afflicted live... the X marks somewhere with a confirmed death. They haven't set up any kind of central clinic," Jayme said solemnly from Vi's side. "When I came through a few months ago, I don't recall seeing half as many marks."

"The plague has hit the West the hardest so far," Romulin agreed. His tone just as grim. "This is a better turnout than we had on our way up, if you can believe it. Though they look even less happy to see us..."

"Do you know how many?"

"How many the West has lost? Or how many have turned out to greet us?"

"The former," Vi clarified.

"Elecia will have more up-to-date numbers... last I heard, it was in the range of twenty thousand."

Vi gripped her reins so tightly the horse's head jerked sideways. She hastily loosened her fingers and gave her mount an apologetic pat.

"There must be a cure." Vi turned to Romulin, giving him a hard stare. His eyes darted between her and the people. She was putting him on the spot, confronting the harsh reality of their circumstances, but she didn't care.

"If only," Andru said softly. "I think hope of one passed with our Late Emperor."

The Imperial party marched into the center of the Crossroads—the center of the world.

It was a large square, lined with buildings easily three floors higher than the rest. Every building seemed to be more ostentatious than the last, as if in a competition for which could be the highest, or have the most windows, balconies, or adornments. If Vi had to pick a winner, it would be the one toward her right, straight behind a platform in the center of the square. The building had three large, circular, stained-glass windows stacked on each other. Vi could only imagine how much it must have cost for an architect to conceive.

At the center of the square where the two main roads of the Empire met—the Great

Southern Road and East-West Way—was a blazing sun in gold, cardinal directions pointing out toward each of the four departure points from the square.

The square was more filled with people than the road had been. Civilians stood to meet the approaching party, though it did not feel like a greeting. It felt more like a squaring off. They regarded the Imperial parade with shadowed eyes and slumped shoulders.

Surrounding them at the edge of the square was another small army, outfitted in Western crimson. They had been brought by the Lady of the West, who stood on a large platform in the center of the square, clad in black armor trimmed in red. Elecia had her hair undone, corkscrew curls standing in all directions like a crown that encircled her whole face. It was not unlike how Ellene had worn her hair, and Vi's heart ached at the comparison.

"It is my honor," Elecia's voice boomed over the square, "to welcome her highness, Vi Solaris, on her historical march home."

"Liberate us!" a woman screamed at Vi, lunging against the line of soldiers. "Liberate yourself and us from the tyranny of Solaris, reclaim your Ci'Dan name!"

Vi kept her eyes forward, focused solely on Elecia. She remembered the incident with the man during the solstice. As soon as chaos gained a foothold, there was no room left for reason.

"It is my honor to return to the home of my forefathers," Vi proclaimed, trying to speak over the growing whispers. "On my path home to Solarin."

"That is not your home!" a man shouted.

"Not your home!"

"*Not your home!*" The chant was picked up by the crowd.

Vi contained a bitter smile. They were right. She had no home, and she never would.

"The sooner we can end this, sister…" Romulin whispered, looking warily at those gathered. The crowd was beginning to shift, growing tenser by the moment.

Vi dismounted and guards pushed through the crowd ahead of her, creating a path to the platform. Jayme remained glued to her side, directing the other soldiers with waves of her left hand, her right on the hilt of her sword. The people forced themselves against the guards, trying to reach her. Jayme stepped in front whenever one stretched a hand too close.

Vi looked at their harrowed and strained expressions. These were not subjects looking to their sovereign in delight—but a people demanding answers from the party they deemed responsible for immense troubles.

"Lead the West to its former glory!"

"Will you help us?"

"Leave Solaris!"

She made it to the stairs, and had one foot on the bottom step when a shout stole her attention.

"They say Adela knows the cure! She killed Emperor Solaris for it. She'll sell it back to us, at a price. Is it true?"

Vi scanned the crowd as murmurs increased.

"Your highness," Jayme whispered hurriedly. "We shouldn't linger right now."

Vi quickly finished her way up the stairs.

"Her future Empress and I shall be discussing matters of the White Death, as we know—" Elecia attempted to speak over the growing unrest.

"Solaris is complacent!"

"No, the Easterner is!" Attention swept to Vhalla. "She was the one who made Prince Aldrik weak. She was the one who distracted him from his birthright when he could've seated himself in Mhashan during the rise of the Mad King."

"Remove the Easterner—" A voice seemed to echo off every building, booming over every other, silencing the masses. "And let Ci'Dan rule once more!"

A glint of light caught Vi's eye from a rooftop. Vi jerked her head in the direction, squinting against the sun. *An archer.*

"Mother! The roof—" Vi didn't get to finish, but luckily she'd said enough.

Her mother swept a hand upward even before her head turned. Wind gusted upward all around her, ripping a pennon from its flagpole. The fabric fluttered through the air, tangling with the arrow that had been blown off-course along with it.

As if the assassination attempt were a cue, the mayhem began.

15

"**M**OTHER!" VI STARTED for Vhalla.

"No, this way." Jayme grabbed her arm. Vi swung around, glaring at her friend. "I know you want to protect her, but you are useless dead. Trust the soldiers to do their jobs and get to the hotel. The sooner you're protected, the more we can focus on your mother and brother."

Vi looked back. The crowd had broken through the line of soldiers Vi had left behind her. A small group condensed around Romulin's horse. They brandished weapons at the encroaching masses. Vi watched as someone leaned down, picking up a rock to volley at him.

"Romu—" Before Vi could call out, a soldier lunged into the fray and Vi watched in horror as the square was plunged further down a spiral of violence.

"Listen to your guard, Vi. Leave it to the soldiers." Elecia started down the other side of the stair, her own guard quickly surrounding her.

Jayme gave a firm tug on her arm. Pulled off balance, Vi staggered along, half dragged down the other side of the platform.

"Vi Ci'Dan, come with me." A man lunged for her. "The Knights of Jadar are ready to be loyal once more to your rule."

Jayme drew her sword in a second, stepping in the man's way.

A wall of stone shot up from the ground between Vi, the assailant, and Jayme. Vi felt magic crackling around Elecia. It was not unlike Ellene's, though it was far more focused, more precise.

Vi looked behind her, free of Jayme and Elecia's attention for a brief second. Had her brother dismounted? Where was her mother in the mob? She knew she needed to be protected, but she couldn't abandon them either.

Yet abandonment had been her plan all along.

If she couldn't trust them to be protected in this moment, how could she leave them? Her thoughts mirrored the noise around her—shouts and cries with no logic to string them together.

She took a step, and two strong arms closed around her shoulders, practically hoisting her off the ground.

"Let me—" Vi began to shout, silenced and chilled by the voice in her ear.

"Go? No, we must get you to safety, princess."

Fallor.

"Unhand me." Vi pushed against his forearm. "This is no way to carry your princess."

"I'm merely doing what's safe for her highness. You seem to have been separated from your guard."

Vi looked frantically for Jayme and Elecia. She couldn't find the former in the chaos of the crowd. The latter was already up the stairs of what had long been the Imperial hotel in the Crossroads. Elecia turned, her eyes scanning, no doubt looking for Vi. But Fallor turned away. With his back to Elecia, there was no way Vi would be visible.

She kicked, struggling against his crushing grasp. His arms dug into her ribs, making her wheeze.

"What are you doing?" Vi twisted in his arms. "The hotel is that way."

Fallor looked ahead, a stupid smirk on his face as he manhandled her.

"Let me go or I will—" She pushed against his forearm, trying to wriggle free, but then stopped all movement.

"You'll what?" Her stillness must've been more intriguing to him than her struggles.

Vi's eyes were glued to the exposed skin of his wrist. Barely visible were three lines, tattooed in dark ink, jagged and gently curving. If those three points met… if the center line continued, then it would be…

A trident tattoo.

The mark of Adela.

Before she could finish her threat, or he could realize what she'd seen, Jayme sprinted into view. She had her sword at the ready, pointed over Vi's shoulder and right in Fallor's face. Vi had never seen a more fearsome expression on her friend's face.

"Drop her."

"Thank the Mother," he said stiffly, the expression sticking to his tongue in his odd accent. "I'm glad you saw us. Who knows what could've happened to the crown princess if you hadn't? I was merely trying to shield her from the rabble."

The lines on Jayme's face only deepened as Fallor let Vi down with sudden delicacy.

"You would do well never to manhandle—"

"Thank you, Fallor," Vi interrupted. Whatever threat Jayme was about to lob at Fallor would have been justifiable but ill-placed. The tattoo was still seared in her vision and she was eager to get away from the man, the sooner the better. "Let's go, Jayme."

Jayme gave a small nod and then hooked her arm with Vi's, before rushing through openings to get to the Imperial hotel. Luckily, the crowd was beginning to disperse, and the worst of the violence seemed to have ended.

"What—"

"I'll tell you later," Vi whispered hastily. There wasn't time to discuss now—they were already ascending the stairs. "Just know that I was right about him."

"Well this is a mess," Elecia muttered. The mob had been short-lived and not too bloody. Vi saw only one body lying face-down in a puddle of blood, and she hoped it was the archer who had tried to shoot down her mother. "You should get inside."

"Moth—"

"Her and Romulin are ahead of you, Jax and I are behind," Elecia answered before she could ask.

With that, Vi and Jayme stepped inside the lobby of the stately hotel, the whole staff standing at uncomfortable attention. As Elecia had said, her mother and brother were together in the far corner, by the stairs, talking with a silver haired man. Thankfully neither had visible wounds.

"... most regretful, forgive them, your highness," the man was saying. "They don't fully understand their actions. It is not the crown they hate, but this miserable plague."

"They will see mercy," Vhalla assured him. "It is a difficult time for all of us, Lord Etton. The crown understands that as much as any."

Vi stepped off to the side, pulling Jayme with her before she could unlink their arms. They faced the wall, rather than the group.

"Fallor is a pirate," Vi said hastily. There may not be another chance to tell her.

Jayme blinked at her. "*What?*"

"I saw a trident tattoo on his wrist when he tried to kidnap me." At least, she was pretty sure it was a trident tattoo. She hadn't seen all of it.

"You're right, it didn't look like he was merely trying to protect you..." Jayme murmured. The words had Vi's heart soaring that her friend finally believed her suspicions.

"He wasn't," Vi hissed. "Have you found out anything about him?"

"Not yet. I'm working on it..."

"Be diligent. I want you to find a reason to get him ousted from the army, for Romulin's safety. I don't know what he's up to, or why a pirate is so far from the sea, but I want none of it near my family."

"Romulin's safety? Your family's? What about yours?"

"I'll be—"

"Your highness," a maid interrupted. She was dressed from toe to chin, bound in tightly tailored fashions of the West that left so little to the imagination, it seemed slightly scandalous. "I am to show you to your room."

"Thank you." Vi started behind her.

Jayme took a hasty step to Vi's side. "You'll be what?"

"I'll tell you later," Vi said softly.

"You'd better. Remember, you promised to tell me everything. All I want is to do my job and protect you."

"I will tell you, the first chance I get," Vi whispered hastily and then started up the stairs behind the maid. She just didn't know if she'd ever have the chance... so it wasn't technically a lie.

The maid took Vi up the stairs to the second floor and down a small interior hallway lit by sconces. Each iron dish jutted out from the wall like a small stage for the tiny flames they carried to dance in magically.

"This will be your room." The maid stopped at the door at the end of the hall and opened it.

Light flooded the hall as Vi found herself looking once more at one of the large circular windows of the building's front, but this time from the inside.

It was like a fractured rainbow had been spilled on the floor, all the colors of the stained glass falling over the seating area right before the window. They stretched toward Vi's feet, and out to her right in the direction of a tall working table—similar to what she'd been given in her tent. To the left stood a modest bar. Also to the left were a pair of intricately carved wooden doors, detail so fine that Vi could almost feel the tingle of magic from the Groundbreaker's hands still on them.

"It is beautiful."

"I'll tell Lord Etton so." The maid dipped into another curtsy at the praise. "Your things will be brought up shortly. Is there anything else I can do for you right now?"

"No, I think I can manage from here." A few moments of uninterrupted silence actually sounded blissful. Yet the woman lingered, her eyes looking around the room, landing on Vi, and then fluttering off like two black hummingbirds, unable to stay in one location for too long. It reminded her of Andru. "Is there anything else I can do for you?"

"What?" The woman seemed actually taken aback. "Oh, no, forgive me, princess, I didn't mean—"

"It's good that I don't seem to be the only one losing herself in thought today. Especially given all that happened in the square," Vi interrupted gently. Her words landed right where she'd hoped they would, and the woman's shoulders relaxed slightly.

With a breath, the maid finally seemed to manage what had clearly been absorbing her attention the whole time. "It's good to have you here, my lady. Truly."

"It's truly good to be here." Vi wished her royal instinct hadn't kicked in. It seemed awkward to say, given all that had transpired.

"No, I misspeak." The woman shook her head, sighed at herself, and then tried one more time. It was her turn for the words to land. "Here, in this room. This was where your father stayed, whenever he passed through the Crossroads on visits to the West."

"Here?" Vi whispered.

"This room." The woman nodded. "His... news of him..." She shook her head, mouth pressing into a grief-stricken line. "It hit the West hard, my lady. So seeing you, here. It restores faith for all of us that we still have a place in this Empire."

"Of course you do, regardless of which Solaris sits on the throne."

The maid simply smiled. Vi saw lines she hadn't noticed before, a tuft of gray hair poking out from underneath her head scarf, a boniness to her hands that betrayed age as much as strength. *How old was she?* Not old enough to remember the West as an independent nation. But perhaps old enough to remember growing up in a recently annexed territory.

"Do call if you need anything, princess." The woman dismissed herself, closing the door behind her.

Vi turned back into the room; suddenly, everything seemed alive.

The motes of dust in the air were like fire. They sparkled in the sunlight, illuminating corners. She ran her fingertips lightly over the bar, then the back of the low sofa, then the table, as she made a wide loop of the room.

Her father had been here. She was already one step closer to him.

Vi stopped at the table. She fished out an iron key from her pocket, one she'd been diligently carrying halfway across the continent. Placing it down, Vi stared at it.

"Well, I'm here," Vi said to the object. "Now the real work begins."

16

"*NARRO HATH HOOLO.*" Vi uttered the incantation the moment the door closed behind her that evening. Usually, when she did, Taavin would first look at his new surroundings. But this time, he looked only at her.

So many things had been left unspoken between them—what were they, really? What could they be? Vi didn't have the answers, so she didn't concern herself too much with the questions. Right now, she wanted to savor the appearance of him and the way he seemed to freeze her in place and set every nerve on fire all at the same time.

"You've made it to the Crossroads, then?" His eyes finally left her, though only briefly.

"Yes."

"You're ready to leave?" His attention landed on the bag at her feet.

"I think so… I've packed everything I can think to bring. I took some food back from dinner, so I have some initial rations. I have some coin for the road. Clothes, of course. A journal with notes I took on the seas after my father went missing, and a map." Vi looked back to him. "Can you think of anything I'm missing?"

"No, but seeing as I've never exactly gone on a trip before, I may not be the best person to ask." Finally his eyes pulled from the bag to her. Taavin took a step forward. "Vi, I find you incredibly brave."

"I haven't done anything brave yet."

"I disagree." Another step closer. "And I think what you are about to do—leaving it all behind for the sake of our world—is the bravest thing you could do."

"Or the most selfish. I have a very vested stake in that world, after all." It felt oddly uncomfortable to let the compliment from him stick. Especially when part of her still felt like leaving her Empire was the most selfish possible maneuver. Ultimately, the outcome of her gamble would determine how history remembered her: brave or selfish. Loved or hated.

"Are you sure you want to do this? It's not too late for you to turn back."

"And leave my father out there? Leave a cure unfound?" Vi swallowed. Taavin had continued his approach and they now stood toe to toe. Her voice was quieter when she spoke again. "Never meet you in person? Touch you in person?"

Taavin lifted her hand gently, spreading his fingers against hers, palm to palm.

"This feels real enough to me."

Vi opened her mouth, but words failed her. How many layers were there to that sentiment? More than she could pick apart.

Before she could try, there was a knock on her door.

"It's my brother," Vi whispered. "I want some time with him... alone."

"I understand." With that, Taavin disappeared.

"Romulin," she said as she opened the door. He stood in simple nightclothes— loose fitting pants, a belted robe over a shirt—all in shades of Solaris blue and Imperial white. Vi was dressed all in black, ready for the road. "You came."

"I did." He looked her up and down, much as she did him. "You're really leaving."

"I am." It wasn't a question, so Vi didn't attempt to dodge an honest answer. "Come in."

"You're going to die, too," he mumbled as he entered. Vi glanced around the hall, seeing no one, and closed the door behind him.

"I'm going to find Father," she vowed. "And a cure for Mother."

"You're just running away from the throne." He frowned. It was harsh and callous... and, in its own way, completely right.

"Not intentionally so. Well, it's not my primary motivation."

"But you are, and you're leaving me saddled with it." He stormed over to the window, resting a hand on the wooden frame, staring out listlessly.

Vi studied him. She had been wrong—it added up in her mind all at once. Everyone wanted Romulin to sit the throne, but he'd never desired the honor. Perhaps all his careful advising was to ensure he would never be forced to assume the mantle.

Crossing over to him, Vi rested her hand on her brother's shoulder, looking out the window also.

"You were made to rule," she whispered. "You're far more suited for it than I, and you have the support of the people. I don't. I don't know if I ever truly wanted the throne, or if I merely wanted the family that came with it."

"If you want the family, stay with us—with me." His voice was suddenly small, the command almost weak. "Aren't I your family? Don't I deserve family too?"

"You are—you do. That's why I'm going to find—"

"Then why are you leaving me alone? Mother will die. You will die. And Father... Father is... If he's not dead, he'll die because you'll die on the way to get him, and I will be alone. I won't even have Andru. I'll be forced to marry a woman to produce an heir because I'll be the Emperor and that's what's required." The words weren't said in a fit of emotion or rage. They were uttered calmly and quietly as though they were facts he'd long since come to terms with. "Stay, Vi."

"You know I can't." Her chest ached as it tried to contort in a way that would allow her to accomplish two diametrically opposed goals. "Please understand."

"You know I can't," he whispered.

"You will in time," she said confidently. Vi squeezed his shoulder. "Rule well until I return with Father. Keep the throne warm for him and me. Then, I promise I'll take it back, and I'll wed, and produce all the heirs the Empire could ever want so none shall blink at the notion if you run away with Andru."

A smile cracked through his bleak expression.

"But please don't actually run away, because I'm going to need you both to help me with that brood."

"Assuming we have not adopted children of our own." Romulin rested his temple on her shoulder and Vi shifted her arm around him.

"Well, if you're doing that, then I'll just see to changing the laws that the heir must be by blood and then have no children of my own."

They both shared a small laugh at that. Romulin's arm snaked around her waist and they stood together quietly.

"I'm sorry for being tense around you, sister. I hadn't wanted our meeting to go like this."

"Me neither. But I understand... these are tense circumstances." Vi gave him a small shake. "When I return, we'll both have time to relax. Maybe even take a trip down to Oparium with Andru and stay at the summer manor. Jax has told me rumors of caves connecting to it that I'd love to mark on my maps."

"Always with your maps."

"I'll have so much more to show you of Meru, too."

Romulin pulled away, starting for the door. "You do know I don't like this, even still."

"I know." Her heart sank; she thought they'd reached an understanding.

"But I'm going to allow it on one condition." He stopped, his back to her. "You find Father and bring him back."

"I swear." Vi started over, grabbing her pack on the way, as he turned to face her. They embraced tightly. "I swear."

"Good. Now you should get going, while the night is young. I'll do my best to cover for you here, keep them busy come dawn for as long as possible."

"Thank you," Vi whispered as he pulled away. Her eyes were prickling, but Vi refused to allow herself to cry. She needed to keep her composure—be strong for her and him both. "Will you cover while I sneak out through the lobby? Make a distraction?"

He shook his head.

"What? I thought—"

"There's a better way for you to leave." He walked behind the small bar in the common area of her room. On the second shelf, he counted three bottles in from the left. Vi watched, fascinated, as his fingers closed around the glass neck of the unassuming bottle. It looked just the same as the others—mostly full and freshly polished. At least, until he went to lift it off the shelf.

The bottle did not move up, but forward, connected to a hidden latch on the shelf beneath. She heard the soft *click* of a lock disengaging. Vi stared in wonder, pulling open the whole shelf to reveal a secret passage.

"How did you..."

"When you came up here to presumably pack... I stayed after at dinner. The adults drank far too much and reminisced."

"As they do." Vi had seen as much when her mother and Jax, and Elecia and Jax, had been together in the North. She could only imagine how it was when the three of them were all in one spot.

"Yes, well apparently, Father did not enjoy feeling trapped in a space and requested this room specifically for that reason." Romulin's fair skin turned scarlet. "They wouldn't stop teasing about Mother sneaking in through this passage."

Vi's reaction was a cross between a grimace and a laugh. She did not want to think of her parents as rebellious, young, and full of desire. But it was also amusing to picture them that way, so free compared to the composed, careful adults they'd been forced to become.

"If you leave through here, no one will know you're gone until some time after breakfast. I'll tell them you weren't feeling well this eve, and to give you time to sleep. I'll try to delay as long as possible."

She looked at her brother. For all he said he didn't want her to go, he was doing everything in his power to help her. Perhaps some part of him did want to see her venture forward, claim a freedom neither of them had. Find their father for the good of their family and their Empire.

Or… perhaps… love in all its forms was simply complicated. And for all he did not want her to go, he loved her and wanted to support her. Would she not do the same for him if the roles were reversed?

"I love you, brother," Vi whispered, pulling him close one final time.

"I love you, sister. Don't forget your promises. Now, go… get a head start on the hounds they're going to send after you."

He all but pushed her into the narrow tunnel. Vi tripped on the sloping path, and caught her balance on the rough wall. She turned to get one last look at her brother before he closed the shelf behind her.

Lifting her hand, Vi uncurled her fingers and allowed the spark to lift off her skin, and ignite into a full flame. She lowered her hand away and the flame continued to hover right where she'd placed it, happily burning near her shoulder and giving light to the darkness. It was enough to scare away the shadows, but not enough to cast aside the thick curtains of cobwebs and what looked like years of dust that had settled on the stairs.

She stifled a cough, waving away the remnants of spiders—even they seemed to have abandoned the place. The passage was long and she had no idea what rooms it was nestled between. When she reached the end, a door blocked her path. Vi ran her hand over the smooth plate of metal—a Firebearer's lock.

Placing her hand on the strip of metal, Vi took a deep breath and cut off the funnel of magic to the flame over her shoulder. This would be easier to do as a Firebearer than risk blowing off the whole door with *juth*. She pushed her magic into her palm—*just enough*, she commanded mentally.

Her overabundance of care made it agonizingly slow, but the metal eventually heated to the point where a soft, reddish glow began to illuminate the passage once more. When it was molten hot, Vi pushed, her feet scraping against the stone as she sought to put all her weight against the heavy door.

It gave way, and she breathed a deep breath of fresh desert air.

Vi turned, settling the door closed as softly as possible, pressing it flush once more. *The door was one-way.* On the outside it was nothing more than smooth stone about to nestle into place with the wall.

"Good thing I wasn't going back in," she mumbled as she caught her bearings.

The narrow alleyway the door had put her in dead-ended against the other buildings on one end, the center of the Crossroads on the other. Vi pulled up the scarf around her neck, situating it to conceal her face as much as possible. She gave herself one last assessment before stepping out into the light of the street lamps.

Her clothes were of fine make, but she didn't think they screamed "princess". Her face was shadowed and covered, the scarf she used was sun-bleached and worn from the desert. And, more than any of that, she was alone. No one expected to see the

Princess Solaris alone, so hopefully they'd see no one at all when they looked at her.

Vi stepped into the main Crossroads and immediately headed right, away from the hotel.

She hugged the walls of darkened storefronts and avoided the welcoming glow of street lamps as though they were stage spotlights that could betray her. Her hands continually adjusted her headscarf, making sure that it was safely in place, and she felt her entire body tense whenever a passerby's feet entered her field of vision.

Her heart was in her throat the entire time, yet nothing happened. She began to feel easier as she rounded the corner to the East-West Way—the great street that connected Norin, capital of the West, with Hastan, capital of the East. Along this street was the great market of the Crossroads.

She pulled the key from her pocket, looking at the now familiar iron rose at one end. The woman had said the curiosity shop was somewhere along here, and the embellishment on the key was all she had to go on. She began walking the streets, crammed even in darkness with empty stalls, archways, and sunshades that offered protection from moonlight.

There were doors by doors by doors, all nestled in every way they could be conceived to fit—like crooked teeth in a too-small mouth. They were wedged between stalls and cornered at alleyways. Vi studied the lock on each one, the signs, the embellishments.

Her feet came to a stop.

Across the narrowed street was an unassuming iron gate. Thorny bars knotted together to ward away anyone from even so much as leaning on it. They came together at face-height to fold into a rose insignia that was rendered with alarmingly life-like detail.

As if in a trance, Vi crossed to it, pulling the key from her pocket. She knew it would fit before she even inserted it into the hole and yet, as she did, there was a heavy weight to her every motion. The lock disengaged with a quiet metallic clang.

Taking a breath, Vi pushed open the gate and stepped into the darkness that awaited her at the next Apex of Fate.

17

THE ROOM WAS not the sort of dark that fell over the land when the sun went to sleep. The darkness here was deeper, richer, and so impenetrable that not even light or noise seemed to exist within. It was so complete that Vi had to turn back to the gate leading to the Crossroads to assure herself that she hadn't gone blind.

The gate… had closed behind her without so much as a sound.

In fact, there were no sounds in the void she now found herself in. Her breathing rattled her chest, hitching in a panic that rose with the tone of her voice as she almost squeaked, "Hello?"

If there was ever a moment when Vi was certain she was going to die, it was then. But she didn't die. Nothing happened at all.

Vi took two more steps forward, bumping into a table in the darkness. She tilted forward, pressing both hands down for balance. Something crunched under her palms and Vi hastily lifted them, shaking away the dried flakes.

Did she even want to know what that was?

Summoning bravery and her flame, Vi looked. The whole table was scattered with flecks of deep crimson—but it wasn't dried blood.

"Rose petals?" Vi picked one up and it nearly disintegrated between her fingers, time weighing too heavily on the fragile petal.

Far in the back, there was a sliver of light—a red glow she hadn't seen before. It was ominous, terrifying, and she was certain it was where she needed to go.

Slowly, Vi stepped around the table. On the outer edge of the room were empty shelves—all save one, which held quills lined neatly in silver inkwells. They glinted in the light of her tiny dancing flame, as if winking back at her. Suppressing a shiver, Vi pressed on.

As she neared the sliver of angry light, a new scent tickled her nose. It was earthy, familiar, though Vi couldn't place it until she felt the crunch of dried grasses under her feet.

No, not grass.

"Wheat?" Vi crouched down, looking back. Nothing but darkness pressed in on her. She couldn't see the light of the Crossroads peeking through the iron of the gate.

Both the table of rose petals and the shelf of quills were invisible to her now. "What is this place?" Vi muttered as she straightened.

She'd thought it was a curiosity shop, but this was nothing like what she expected. The shelves were supposed to be packed with all kinds of tokens for clients to burn and hold when the Firebearer looked into the future. Vi would've thought the place abandoned, if not for the rose petals, quills, and wheat.

It was almost as if someone had expected her to come here, laying out the tokens like invitations. Was it possible the old woman had had a glimpse of the future before she left the West? Had she known Vi would come?

But if that were the case, Vi would have to believe there was some deeper meaning to the seemingly random things strewn about.

Her hand closed around the watch at her neck on instinct and Vi took a deep breath. She couldn't allow herself to get unnerved by this strange place. She was here for one thing—a vision. It didn't matter what the place was used for before, or after.

Crossing the path of wheat to the doorway, Vi pushed aside the heavy curtain that had been barely open a sliver. Inside the small back room was a recessed fire pit and a single fire burning like an invitation. The white-blue flame waiting for her, a silent instruction.

Taking a breath, Vi knelt before it, opened her eyes wide, and stared into the flame.

The fire nearly exploded, tendrils wrapping around her in an eager embrace. Yet unlike the fire Vi had created and manipulated before, this did not singe her clothes. It hovered just off of her flammable fabrics and caressed the exposed skin of her hands and face. It crashed on her like a wave; Vi couldn't have shut her eyes if she tried.

White. Her vision was nothing but white hot fire. A tingle rose in the back of her mind, her eyes widened further, and there in the distance of the whiteout was the silhouette of a man.

Vi found herself standing on a rocky beach, her father opposite her.

Father! She wanted to scream. But as was normal in her visions, Vi couldn't hear or feel. She could merely bear witness to a future that may or may not come to pass.

Aldrik Solaris stood with all the regal poise of an Emperor, perched on a large stone covered in blue frost. He stood as if in defiance to the grime that covered his cheeks and the shackles that weighed down his arms. His hair was greasy, stringing around a face coated in thick, dark stubble. Clothes that had once been white were soiled in filth.

Still he held his head high. Even when she shouldn't have been able to recognize him, Vi did. She knew her father from his bearing alone. Moreover, she knew him from his eyes—eyes as hard and dark as iron.

Next to him was a woman Vi didn't recognize. Her hair was white and extended down to her waist in loose, wispy locks that caught the faintest of breezes. While her face seemed youthful—no older than Vhalla's—she held a silver, bejeweled cane in her hand. The appendage caught Vi's eye.

The woman was missing her arm.

Frost floated off her hand and through the thin sleeve of her shirt. She had a hand made entirely of ice. Vi continued to stare, fascinated by the novel use of magic.

The woman lifted her cane, pointing out to sea. She said words Vi couldn't hear to her father, who remained expressionless. Vi turned, looking toward the source of the woman's attention.

Bright sunlight filled the horizon, blinding her. Vi squinted, unable to make out what the woman might be pointing at. Everything grew hazy, and Vi realized far too late that the light wasn't just from the sun, but the ending of her vision.

It wasn't enough.

She spun back around, looking for her father. He had nearly vanished, engulfed by the white light overtaking everything. Vi tried to run to him.

An expression of horror had overtaken her father's face as the woman grinned wickedly.

Father! She screamed with every decibel her mind could generate. *Father I will come for you!*

Perhaps it was all in her imagination, but his eyes seemed to drift in her direction, if only briefly. Vi held his gaze for one last second. One more moment to see her father living and breathing.

The fire receded all at once, releasing its hold on her and retreating to nothing more than red hot embers, a slumbering beast. Vi fell forward into the soot and ash, into the coals.

"Show me again!" she cried, flames burning between her fingers, trying to ignite the spent wood. "Show me more!"

But no more visions came. She couldn't plead with the Apexes of Fate, or make demands of them. They showed her what there was to see and nothing more.

Vi hunched over the remnants of the fire, breathing slowly. Her magic wavered and wobbled, the flame dancing with it. She stared bitterly into the orange and red glow, simmering like her resolve. Hoisting herself upright, Vi wiped her face, smearing soot but ensuring no rogue tears had slipped over her cheeks.

Standing, she looked down at the remnants of the fire, glowing like fading stars on charcoal.

Her father was alive. He was alive, and waiting for her arrival. Vi took a deep breath—she still had time to make it to him.

When she opened and stepped back through the door, the empty store was lit by the first hazy lights of dawn. The room was the size she'd originally expected it to be—small, with only two tables and some shelves along the walls. The gate was open once more, as if inviting her back into the world.

With a breath, Vi accepted the invitation, wheat crunching under her feet as she started for the exit. Adjusting her headscarf, Vi stepped into the early morning light with a deep breath and turned left—away from the hotel, and her family.

The East-West Way would lead her to Norin, the greatest port in the world, where she would find countless ships on which to secure passage across the sea to Meru. Further west still, across treacherous, pirate-infested seas, was her father—and the cure for an ailing Empire.

18

VI WALKED WITHOUT stopping.

She walked as the sun crested the desert sands, spreading its arms as it woke up in beams of light that broke on a cloudless sky. She walked as the men and women of the Crossroads awoke. She walked as merchants began to fill their stalls with wares and open the doors of their stores, spreading out their large sun canopies in preparation for the day.

Her mind was filled with two things only: her father and Meru. No matter what, she would get to him. She would learn of everything that had transpired since he left, how he'd survived, and what *exactly* he'd been doing.

Then she would get to Taavin, and embrace him. Together, the three of them would find a cure, of that Vi was certain. Then she'd return for her mother, and they'd all live happily ever after.

It was the perfect plan, too perfect to unfold without a hitch in real life, but Vi repeated the lie over and over again.

Ahead of her, Vi could see the edge of the Crossroads. The buildings had been shrinking, the stalls becoming less lush the further away from the center of the Crossroads she got, and now in the distance she could see a glimpse of the Waste and the road that snaked through it. She was so close to what felt like true freedom that she had to struggle to contain a scream of pure anguish as a hand suddenly grabbed her wrist, halting her.

Vi whirled, the spark igniting between her fingers. She pulled it back, freezing in place the second her eyes met those of the woman who had stopped her. A familiar set of irises looked back at hers, searching. They rested under knitted brows and a mess of brown hair.

"Jayme," Vi whispered. "What are you doing here?"

"Making sure you stay out of trouble… Or trouble stays away from you." Her voice was low, almost a growl, as her eyes darted around. She wore a heavy cape over her shoulders, but Vi could see she still had her sword and chainmail on underneath.

"What are you talking about?" Vi narrowed her eyes, looking from sword to woman.

At the sight, Jayme slowly uncurled her fingers from around Vi's wrist, easing her hand back down and taking a small step back. Vi returned the gesture in kind, lowering her hand and letting go of the fire with a sigh. She continued to look around them, though no merchants seemed to have noticed.

"Romulin told me you were leaving."

Every curse word Vi had ever heard flew across her brain at once. Her brother didn't out her to their mother, or the army at large. But he did tell Jayme—Vi's guard and friend. She could understand the logic, but she still resented him for it. Jayme was supposed to stay behind to protect him.

"You're not going to stop me," Vi declared, adjusting her head scarf once more, praying no one looked too closely at the odd exchange.

"I'm not trying to." Vi stilled. Jayme's eyes swept their surroundings again. "Not out in the open... this way."

They started toward a secluded alcove between two buildings. Not quite an alleyway, but not in the center of the street either. Jayme leaned against the opposite wall, arms folded. It was then that Vi noticed her friend had a pack on under her cloak. She'd come prepared.

"You're going to come with me," Vi said softly.

Jayme nodded solemnly. "It's my duty to protect and look out for you. I'm not letting you do this alone."

"You don't even know what I'm going to do."

"I have a hunch."

"Really?" It was Vi's turn to fold her arms over her chest.

"Yes, really."

"What do you think that is?"

"I think you're going to look for your father." Jayme fought a grin and lost as Vi's arms fell to her sides, defeated.

"Am I that transparent?"

"Only to those who know you." Jayme's hand fell on her shoulder, giving it a squeeze and a light shake. Vi didn't know why, but she found the weight reassuring as the woman leaned in slightly. "Fortunately for you, I know you, and I'm not going to stop you."

"Why? You should."

"I should," Jayme agreed. "But who will really be surprised that I've gone off with you? If anything, they'll expect it." Vi gave a soft huff amusement and agreement. "Plus, it may give your mother some peace of mind to know that her daughter has someone looking out for her."

Vi sighed softly. Her leaving would be enough stress on her mother. If there was something she could do to alleviate it, she should. As usual, Romulin's decision was flawless—even if it thwarted Vi's attempts to, just once, look after her younger brother.

"All right."

"Is that a, 'Yes, Jayme, I'm not going to fight you'?"

"Yes, Jayme, I'm not going to fight you. But I will stress that it'll be dangerous—"

"Since when have I been afraid of danger?"

"And I will be leaving the Empire."

"If I don't want to go, I'll turn back." Jayme straightened away, resting her hand on the pommel of her sword. "I'm more than capable of making my own decisions."

"Let's go then." There wasn't much more time to waste. Romulin may already be working to stall their mother, prolonging Vi's discovery.

"Lead on."

Vi stepped back out into the sunlight, starting once more down the road—this time, with Jayme at her side. From time to time, she would look over her shoulder, half expecting a small military party to be racing after her. But, much like the first time she'd snuck out in Soricium, Vi was surprised at how easy it was for her to slip away. Minus telling Jayme of her plans, Romulin had done well.

"Did you have another vision of him?" Jayme finally asked, long after there were no more buildings around them and only the endless sands of the desert.

"Yes." Vi didn't have to guess who *he* was. "Right before I left, I found another Apex and saw the future—this time, my father."

"He's alive then?"

"Perhaps, for now…" Vi shook her head. "It's hard to say, since my visions can change."

"But this seems like a good omen."

"I hope so." Vi adjusted the pack on her shoulders. "Did you find anything more about Fallor before you left?"

"I tried, but there wasn't much time. I was in the process of settling into the temporary barracks with the soldiers when Romulin sent for me. After that, I was more focused on packing… Don't give me that look." Vi raised a hand to her face, trying to feel what look she'd been giving Jayme without realizing it. "I made sure to mention everything you told me about Fallor to Romulin. He'll have someone else look into the brute and will be on guard."

"Good." Vi breathed a sigh of relief.

Jayme flashed her a bright smile. "I've always admired that about you."

"What?"

"How much you want to protect your family. I know that's why you didn't tell me you were leaving." The smile continued to play on Jayme's lips as she looked over her shoulder, eastward.

"Guilty."

"I would do anything to protect mine."

"I know." Vi reached over, giving her friend's hand a squeeze.

Jayme looked down, squeezing back as her eyes trailed up Vi's arm to her face. "I'm glad. That means you understand me."

"Of course I do."

The day progressed without incident. It was surprisingly peaceful. The lone cry of a bird of prey, soaring so high overhead that it was merely a silhouette against the bright blue sky, was the only thing to break the sound of the wind and whispering dunes.

"We should stop and set up camp," Jayme said finally.

Vi turned, looking back. The Crossroads was now a distant point on the horizon. She'd been watching it shrink for hours, but it still didn't seem far enough away.

"We can go a little further," she insisted.

"No." As if to accentuate her point, the woman dropped her pack right on the road. "We need to conserve our strength, and the sun is going down. We want a camp set up before the night's chill sets in."

"But—"

"Who's traversed the desert more, you or I?" Jayme asked pointedly.

"Fine, you... but let's make it far from the road. I don't want any search parties to see us."

"If they were sending a search party this way, they would've by now. I'd bet they're keeping the search local. The soldiers underestimate you; I don't think they'll suspect you're capable of wandering too far on your own." Jayme picked up her pack and started off the road anyway. "We'll set up camp off the road, but not too far. We want to avoid desert wolves or scorpions. We'll also avoid making a fire that would draw attention to us."

"I didn't see any animals other than a bird in the sky on the way here." Vi followed behind.

"That's because you've been marching in a huge party along the road. Creatures are less likely to frequent where there's established traffic."

"A desert wolf could make a good meal," Vi mused.

"You're the hunter between us. If you can nab one, go for it and we can cook it in the morning." Jayme shrugged. "I brought rations though, just in case."

"Me too." Vi set her pack down next to Jayme's about fifty paces into the desert sand. "At least enough to get me—well, us, now—to Inton."

"Inton?"

"It's a small town, well, more of an outpost really, a little more than halfway between the Crossroads and Norin. I figured we could resupply there."

"I've never heard of it before."

"A lot of maps leave it off, it's so small. I've only seen it on the enlarged Western-made versions Elecia sent me." Vi set down her pack, rummaging through and producing her journal. "This is just a summary... but we're about here and—"

"You *would* bring a map." Jayme chuckled, pulling multiple short poles and a large top from her bag. She'd brought several maps, in fact.

"You didn't even look."

"Because I trust you to get us wherever it is we need to go. I'm just here to make sure you get there safe and sound." Jayme began setting up one of the dome-shaped tension-rod tents the soldiers were using on the march.

"Can I help with that?" Vi shoved the journal of her map scribbles and notes back into her pack. "Or are you going to insist you set up my tent because I'm the princess?"

"Oh shut it with that and help me." Her friend laughed.

Jayme was a patient teacher, showing her how to fit the poles together and slip them into pockets that'd support the roof when arched. They filled pouches at the sides with sand and skewered the corners to weigh them down against the wind. Jayme explained how the Western design allowed the wind to smooth over the material, rather than picking it up in a gust.

Vi sat back on her heels, looking up at the sky. Without the city lights or military fires, it had never looked so bright.

"I don't recall the last time I saw you in such a good mood. Perhaps we should run away more often?"

Jayme laughed. Vi couldn't recall ever seeing her so free, so relaxed.

"I like being on the road. It's what I'm used to." She looked Westward. "Perhaps it's also knowing that we're so far in trouble with this stunt that, if we're caught...

well, there's no point in stressing about it because there's no escaping what is certain to be a swift and stern punishment."

"We won't be caught." Vi didn't know if she was reassuring Jayme or making a threat to the universe. "The further we get from the Crossroads, the less likely people will be looking for us."

"People in the West seem to recognize you well enough."

"That's true…" A thought crossed Vi's mind. "Let's not call me Vi any longer, just to be cautious."

"What?"

"Call me Yullia."

"Where did that name come from?"

"I think I read it in a book somewhere, once, maybe?" Vi shrugged. "Either way, it's as good a name as any."

"Yullia it is, then."

Vi stood, brushing sand off her legs. The sun had almost faded, but the large circular moon reflected off the dunes and gave more than enough light to see by. Despite walking all day, she didn't feel tired in the slightest. Perhaps Jayme was right, and there was something to life on the road.

"What is it now?" Jayme asked, looking up at her.

"I want to learn how to use a sword."

"Didn't Sehra's warriors train you when you were younger?"

"The basics… But I focused more on archery." Vi made a quick mental note to ask Taavin if there was a way to craft a bow with *mysst*. "You said you've grown up practicing with the sword—surely you can teach me something."

"I'm sure I can." Jayme stood, retrieving her sword and scabbard from just inside their tent. She unsheathed it, moonlight catching on the blade. "Here—"

Vi waved it away. Jayme took a step back, confusion on her face. Vi took a step, facing her. Her heart beat in her throat, but she wasn't entirely sure why.

"You're risking a lot for me, on faith. There are things I've told you about my magic, but there's a lot you still don't know." She sighed softly. "I'm tired of keeping this secret from my friend."

Jayme said nothing, merely watched and waited.

"*Mysst soto larrk.*" Vi stretched out her hand before her. It wasn't as seamless as Taavin's had been when they last sparred in the pit.

Taavin—thinking of him made her ache. It would be some time until she could summon him again, being around Jayme. Vi pushed down regret at the notion that she should've kissed him when she had the chance before she left.

Instead, she focused on willing the strands of light to spin from her glyph, outlining a sword similar to Jayme's that condensed into existence. It filled with color, solidifying as Vi wrapped her fingers around it. She felt the magic still entangled with her fingers. It was as though she wore little rings around each finger, connecting to the sword, and as long as she grasped the hilt, it would remain real.

To Jayme's credit, she didn't so much as flinch. She stood calmly as Vi demonstrated a power that she should not have, and that Jayme had never seen before.

"Well, that's a useful skill if I ever saw one," she said, finally. Jayme approached slowly, looking at the blade. "May I touch it?"

"Yes…" Vi watched as she ran the pad of her thumb perpendicular to the edge of the sword, inspecting its sharpness.

"It's real."

"Only until I let go," Vi clarified.

"What magic is this?" Jayme's eyes flicked up to hers. "I've never seen it before."

"Sehra taught it to me." It wasn't entirely untrue. "Those beyond Solaris possess magic like this, I've been led to believe."

"Well, then, this will make teaching swordplay easier." Jayme walked away, spinning her rapier in her hand in fluid movements.

Something wasn't quite settling right with Vi. "You're not... afraid?"

"Should I be?" Jayme arched her eyebrows. "This magic, fire magic, any other magic. You're still Vi Solaris, and will always be—nothing can change that." She settled her grip on her sword. "Now, we'll work on stance. One foot forward, the other back, like this."

Vi tried to follow Jayme's demonstration. But her mind was elsewhere. She should be happy to be accepted unconditionally, even with her Lightspinning. But the fact seemed so... impossible.

"Now, lunge!" Jayme cast one arm backward, the other forward. "This is a rapier blade, so you're not going to be flailing it about like a two-sided, heftier sword. You'll need to use finesse."

Vi tried to mimic her movements, pushing the worrying thoughts from her mind. She had the road to Norin to learn as much as she could from her friend. Even though tonight was quiet, Vi was certain danger lurked ahead, and she had to be ready with every dawn from here on to fight it.

19

TWO DAYS PASSED uneventfully.

They'd woken early and set out on the road, stopped at any well they passed to replenish their water, and walked until the sun set or their feet couldn't carry them any longer. At night, they'd hungrily eat through rations. Despite Jayme's prior warnings, the Waste seemed void of life and hunting was proving difficult.

They still worked to practice swordplay, but were more exhausted after each day of walking. On the eve of the third day, Vi's feet were so blistered that Jayme refused to teach her and, instead, they sat around the fire they'd finally dared to make for the sake of warmth before calling it an early night.

On the third day, the town they'd been waiting for finally came into view, and they arrived by nightfall.

Inton had its own road branching off the East-West Way that led into its heart. It was perhaps only ten—no, sixteen on counting—buildings large. One was a large manor-type house, its high wall the type Vi had come to associate with the aesthetic of Western nobility. No doubt it belonged to whatever lord maintained this small town's existence. There were two or three smaller houses, what looked like a sort of shared-living dwelling, then the other buildings needed to support those living in the town, such as a tailor and a smithy.

"I wonder if they have an inn," Vi mused.

"We need to save our coin for supplies."

"I brought enough to do both."

"Of course, the crown princess would leave with a small bank in her pockets."

"Yullia, remember?"

"Even in private?" Jayme arched her eyebrows.

"Especially in private, or how else will we be accustomed to it in public," Vi reasoned.

"Fair… So then you're just a wanderer, Yullia, on the move with a small fortune jingling your pack." Jayme shook her head. "That's believable."

"Maybe my parents are insanely rich." Vi was more mindful of where she was placing her feet. The stones of the road off the East-West way were worn, uneven, and rutted from centuries of cart wheels passing over them without much maintenance.

"Well, they are, technically."

"Yes, but Yullia's parents aren't the Emperor and Empress."

"You are truly a master of disguise," Jayme said dryly. Vi snorted with laughter. "Mother, you know you're in a small town when the inn, general store, and bar are all condensed into one."

Vi looked up at the building that had captured Jayme's attention. Sure enough, the bottom floor looked to be half-shop, half-bar—very likely the only source of entertainment in town. The upper floors had the letters I-N-N painted between the windows that lined it.

Inside, there was every manner of supply imaginable: food, home goods, crafting materials. There was a bladder that could have been for water or lamp oil. There were glass jugs of varying shapes and sizes that reflected her face—and that was a sight.

Her hair was a bird's nest. The plaits she'd attempted to weave into it had snarled into knots around the nape of her neck. Vi raised a hand, teasing it lightly, but everything just seemed to tighten at the prodding.

She couldn't stop a giggle.

"What?" Jayme asked, stepping over from the shelf of roasted nuts she'd been eying.

"I'm a mess."

"You stink, too. Let's see if we can get a bath with our room for tonight." Jayme continued up to the counter.

"You're not exactly sweet smelling yourself," Vi muttered.

The counter stretched between bar and store, but no one was positioned behind it. They both craned their necks, looking through an open back door. After seeing no one, Jayme lightly rang a small silver bell set out on the counter.

"Hello?"

There was some grumbling, movement, and a wiry-haired old man emerged. The whole of his head was white, and his beady eyes were magnified behind a pair of thick spectacles.

"Oh, you two are new," he said in a weathered voice.

"Yes, may we purchase a room for the night?" Jayme took the lead. "We'd also like to purchase some supplies."

"Right, right..." The owner opened a heavy ledger. "Just let me know what you need and I'll tally it all up."

"We'll take six of the jerky..." Jayme moved as she spoke, beginning to collect the items. "... six of these biscuits... This is for water, right? One of these, then..."

Vi left her to it, wandering the shelves toward the empty bar. The sparse bottles—dull with dust—were a contrast to the brightly polished and well-stocked bar that had been in her room at the hotel. It reminded her of her brother and his hand in her escape.

How was he handling it now? There was a dull ache in her chest as his words, begging her to stay, returned loud and clear in her mind. She was doing the right thing, she was certain of it. So... why did she feel guilty?

Movement distracted her. Vi turned, looking out one of the windows. The glass was far from perfect, distorting the bird that had perched on the windowsill. She walked over slowly, so as not to spook the animal.

It was a an eagle—ruddy in color—with pristine plumage, bright eyes, and the strangest circular marking on its brow. Vi leaned forward and the bird swiveled its head to look directly at her. Deep intelligence reflected in its eyes.

"V—Yullia?" Jayme called over.

"Yes?" Vi straightened and heard the flapping of wings outside the glass. She looked back and confirmed the bird had indeed taken flight at her sudden movement.

"Shall we go upstairs?"

"Sure." Vi adjusted her pack, glancing over her shoulder. "Did you see that bird? It was huge."

"I missed it," Jayme said through a mouthful of food. She handed Vi a candied lemon peel.

"Looked like an eagle."

"Not impossible, though hawks are more common out here in the desert," the old man interjected. "You'll see them from time to time."

"It was beautiful, whatever it was," Vi murmured, looking back to the window. But the bird was long gone.

Vi fell back onto the plush bed, looked at her pruned fingers, and proclaimed, "I am exhausted."

"Yes, but it's good to have had a chance to wash everything, and kind of the owner to allow us to use his laundry supplies."

"I thought I would dry up in the desert; after today I think I've had enough water until we get to Norin." First there had been laundry, then scrubbing themselves—it took nearly an hour to work a brush through her hair, and Vi hadn't missed the opportunity to soak tension from her aching muscles in a hot bath.

"You won't be saying that three hours into tomorrow." Jayme sat on the other side of the bed, swinging her legs.

"That may be true." Vi fought a yawn.

"Speaking of… We should get some sleep." The yawn was contagious, and it was Jayme's turn. "We won't have a real bed again until Norin."

Vi laid back and snuffed the candle on the table opposite the bed in the same motion. She expected sleep to come quickly, but found herself staring up at the ceiling as her eyes adjusted to the moonlight streaming through the open window. Her body was tired and her mind had never felt more awake.

It wandered down every possible mental pathway—her mother, brother, and father. She thought about Taavin and barely resisted the urge to try to sneak out of bed to summon him. Vi turned her head, looking at the back of Jayme's on the pillow opposite. *What would it feel like to have Taavin there?*

"Jayme," Vi whispered.

"What?" she grumbled sleepily.

"Are you awake?"

Something between a sigh and a yawn. "No, I'm good at sleep talking." A pause. "Yes, I'm awake, what do you need?"

"Have you ever lain with a man before?" Vi asked softly.

Another painfully long pause. Then Jayme twisted in bed, shifting under the covers to face Vi. She hoped the moonlight would hide her blush, now that Jayme was looking at her.

"This, coming from the princess who has 'no time for romance'?"

"I didn't—*don't*—have time for it. I was just… wondering." Vi's tongue wouldn't cooperate. Now that she'd started the line of thought, all she could think about was lying curled in bed with Taavin.

"Well, like I told you before, I haven't had time myself for relationships. I've been too busy." Jayme's eyes blinked slowly, sleep tugging at the lids.

"Some say a relationship isn't necessarily required for *certain aspects.*" Vi folded and unfolded her hands over her stomach.

"You think I'm a loose woman?" All exhaustion and sleep fell from her friend's voice, replaced by hurt and tension. Vi turned quickly.

"No, no. I just meant that I heard—"

"Commoners spread their legs whenever they please because they have no land or titles to uphold?" Jayme rolled her eyes at Vi's silence. "Of course you have. Let me be the one to break it to you, Vi: even some nobles will do that. Just as there are many who won't. It's all the same—low or high born. We all struggle through the same shite, have the same needs, and all do our best to live with what life hands us as best we can."

"Right…" Vi looked back to the ceiling. "Sorry if I offended you," she said softly.

"You didn't." Jayme rolled back over and Vi hoped she was telling the truth.

"I really am."

"You really didn't."

Another long silence stretched between them, which Vi's mind used to wander down the path of clandestine meetings. It struck a different memory, tangentially related to Jayme. Something Andru had said during a dinner that now felt like forever ago.

"Did you manage to see your friend in the Crossroads?"

"What now?" Jayme glanced over her shoulder, barely pulling her head off the pillow.

"Andru said you met with a friend in the Crossroads… a blonde woman."

Jayme stared at her and yawned. "I have no idea what he's talking about. Must have the wrong person. Now, go to sleep, Vi."

Vi sunk her head back onto the pillow and Jayme did the same. Her eyes drifted closed, then open again, and closed once more. No matter how hard she tried to quiet her mind, it refused. But her body was stubborn, demanding some form of rest, and Vi fell into a twilight-like sleep…

Time had passed.

She wasn't sure how much, but Vi could feel that it had. The moonlight in the room had shifted, dimmed somewhat. That meant the moon had dipped on the other side of the inn; dawn wasn't far. Vi shifted in bed, sinking further into the warm blankets. The ropes beneath her creaked.

The floorboards across the room mirrored the action.

Vi opened her eyes slowly. Her heart pounded, waking her with a rush of panic. *There was someone in the room with them.* Vi was certain she'd locked the door after coming in from the bath. Had they climbed through the window?

She shifted again, pushing Jayme with her foot. The woman groaned softly as a shadow took over Vi's side of the bed. Vi took a deep breath. She wasn't about to go quietly to some assassin in the night.

Throwing the covers off the bed, Vi brought her legs under her.

"What the—" Jayme was now awake, but Vi's attention was on the man wrenching off the blanket she'd thrown at him.

Vi held out her hand. "*Mysst soto—*" She froze, the chant stalled, magic dissipating with nowhere to go, as she locked eyes with Fallor.

20

ALLOR WAS LIKE a mountain in the small room. His clothes were sun-bleached and windswept. A thick, ruddy beard clung to his cheeks and accentuated the white of his teeth, exposed by a mad grin.

He looked like he was about to rip her to pieces with those giant hands of his.

Vi held out her hand, readying her magic again. But before she could even start the chant, Jayme lunged.

She plunged her hand into his gut. Vi didn't expect the man to even feel it, but Fallor let out a large exhale of air. If he was stunned, it was only briefly. He lifted his hands, balled them together, and brought them down over Jayme's head.

But Jayme was too fast; she spun behind him and grabbed her sword from the table. Vi heard the blade ring against the sheathe, startling her back into motion as Fallor's attention was split between them.

"*Mysst soto larrk.*" Vi held out her hand, closing her fingers around the sword that formed there. Her practice with Jayme had made the magic faster, more confident, and the blade feel even firmer in her hand.

"It really is true, then." Fallor laughed.

"Haven't I heard that before?" Vi growled back. "I think from the last assassin who tried to kill me."

"I'm not an assassin and I certainly don't want to kill you. You're worth far more alive. You've no idea the bounty they have on your head." He took a step forward.

"Take one more step and I put this blade through the back of your skull." Jayme said from behind him. From her vantage on the bed, Vi could see the woman had her blade on the back of the man's neck. Fallor only grinned wider at the threat.

"You think you have this under control?"

"I think you shouldn't underestimate us," Jayme answered for them both.

"We'll see!" Fallor doubled over, pushing himself back and into Jayme. Her sword went over his head before she was pinned against the table on the opposite wall.

Vi took her chance, lunging for him. Every combat tutor she'd ever worked with told her the same thing: when an opening presented itself, the living took it, and the dead never had the opportunity to learn better.

She was mid-air as Fallor straightened. His hand came out of nowhere, clasping around her wrist and pulling the blade over his shoulder. She hung, struggling against his grasp, but his muscles were like iron. He took a step away from Jayme; Vi heard wheezing at the same moment Fallor tightened his grip, a pulse of foreign magic rippling through Vi's body.

The sword vanished.

"Little Lightspinner, you think your magic is a threat to me?"

"Who are you working for?" Vi demanded, looking in his pale eyes. Whatever that magic was, it wasn't anything she knew. Which meant… Fallor wasn't from the Solaris Empire.

"The pirate queen herself." Fallor beamed from ear to ear as Vi's blood turned to ice.

"Adela," she whispered.

"Don't you touch her!" Jayme had recovered and charged full force into Fallor's back.

The man let out a roar and released her. Vi fell, stumbling slightly, hitting the bed and collapsing onto it. The point of Jayme's sword protruded from Fallor's side. She stared at it with a dark fascination as blood pooled, dripping down his shirt and staining it crimson.

"You upstart bitch." The words were as harsh as his guttural tone. But Fallor had a wild grin and a crazed look to his eye as he turned from Vi to Jayme when she withdrew her sword. "Fine…" He looked back to Vi.

Vi readied herself with another sword, but Fallor didn't go for her.

Instead, he lunged for the door, yanking at it. Wood splintered and cracked as he pulled it open without even turning the knob. He ran from the room, racing down the hall to the stair.

Vi was on her feet.

"You stay here," Jayme ordered, already halfway out the door.

"But—"

"I know you're safe here if I don't let him from my sight! Stay put!"

Vi would've fought more, but Jayme was already gone.

She didn't want to be left behind. She didn't want to leave Jayme to do the dirty work on her behalf. Vi pushed away from the bed, starting for the door. Then decided better of it.

She'd give her friend five minutes… five minutes and then she'd go help.

Vi strained her hearing, listening for any sounds of a struggle. She heard them bounding down the stairs and then out the main door. But then, silence.

Quickly, Vi repacked their things, shoving sundries into their respective packs. She stood, slinging both over her shoulder. One slow count to ten, and then she was after Jayme. Vi set to pacing, trying to push the visions of her friend dying a horrible death as far from her mind as possible with every step.

"That's it," she declared, reaching ten, and started for the door.

A single set of footsteps—light and nimble—bounded up the stairs. Jayme's hair was wild. Dark bruises puffed around her right eye, and she held herself a little crooked. But she was alive, and Vi didn't see any mortal wounds.

"Did he—"

"I killed him. I wasn't about to let him run to whatever pirate scum he had hiding."

Jayme crossed over, grabbing her pack from Vi before starting down the stairs once more, leaving Vi little other option but to follow hastily behind. "Old man's waking up. We need to get out of here before they find the body."

"But we didn't do anything wrong."

"Even if that's true, do you want to be held up long enough to try to prove it?" Jayme hissed.

"No…" Vi paused at the front desk, fishing through her pack. She put one heavy gold coin on the counter for the damage to the door as the man stumbled from his back room.

"What's the—" he muttered.

"Sorry for the door, thanks for letting us stay!" Vi shouted over her shoulder as she hastily followed Jayme into the night.

She searched around the inn for signs of the scuffle. The blood trail led around the corner of the building, footprints in the sand surrounding the drops. But it passed out of Vi's field of vision.

"Jayme, is the body—"

"Yes." Jayme glanced over her shoulder, three steps ahead and not slowing. "A town like this? They'll leave it to the animals. It's not worth their trouble to pursue us. We're outsiders, he was an outsider, they won't care for any of us and they're not going to mourn him. He'll be food for the wolves by tomorrow night."

"He was masquerading as a soldier. Do you think the army will send a search party after him?" Vi stumbled on the wheel ruts in the road she'd been so careful to avoid earlier.

"If the army hasn't sent a search party this far after *you*, they're certainly not going to send one after him." Jayme reached out a hand, helping Vi catch her balance. They stilled for just a second, catching their breath. Her friend seemed so calm, so stable, even now. "And you heard him, he was working for Adela… Or at least some kind of pirate claiming to be the infamous pirate queen. He may not have been on any kind of soldier roster at all. Maybe that's why so few people knew anything about him—he was pretending the whole time to get to you."

A shiver ran down Vi's spine that had nothing to do with the desert's icy chill at night. She could handle assassins lurking around corners—those were the devils she knew. But assassins lurking under the guise of people she should be able to trust? Vi didn't know if she could handle that notion.

"Then—" Vi swallowed, trying to find her words and make them sound stronger than she felt. "—Perhaps it's a good thing I got away from the army. Maybe I'm safer incognito."

"As long as you stay that way," Jayme agreed. "Now, come on, we'll get some distance between us and Inton and set up camp. Try to get a few hours of sleep before we continue on to Norin."

Vi didn't know if she would manage to sleep at all after the incident. But if anything would help, it would be further exhausting herself. She fell into step behind Jayme, focusing on the road while worrying the wooden bead on the bracelet Ellene had given her.

It didn't matter if the Adela Fallor worked for was real or not. He'd said there was a bounty on her head… and that meant more than just the elfin'ra were likely to be after her now.

As long as she was Vi Solaris, Yargen's Champion, nowhere was going to be safe.

Three days later, and without any other incident, the great city of Norin came into view.

Vi couldn't imagine a more perfect time to see the city than in the early hours. Towering walls of raw stone rose up and out, curved to sheer away dangerous sandstorms from the city proper. Even taller than those were the looming buildings that rose to meet the castle at its center.

The many glittering lights of lamps and houses sparkled on a shadowed background, the city cast in a dark outline by the first pastel rays of sunrise bleeding across the horizon from the east. It was as if someone had painted it with a starry brush—a beauty that took Vi's breath away.

Much like when she had left the Crossroads, the majority of the city slumbered. Houses were quiet and storefronts were occupied by only a few lone workers. Residential alleyways were still, windows just opening to let in the early breezes of dawn.

Also like the Crossroads, the architecture of the buildings mirrored that of the traditional West—squat, flat-roofed, structural beams poking out at the corners and edges here and there. But the construction here was, on the whole, even older. Which said something, given that the Crossroads had served as a central market of the Main Continent for centuries.

Norin was the ancient bastion of Mhashan—its original capital, the origin of the religion of the Mother. And it *showed*. The rich areas were steeped in old money, and the poor areas had a coat of grime that was just as ancient.

The streets were more full than she expected as they plodded along. There were other travelers and merchants, and men and women going to work for the day. None of them made any effort to stop or bother her and Jayme, though there were a few looks here and there—mostly at the soldier.

Where the Crossroads saw travelers of all types regularly, Norin was almost exclusively populated by those of the West. Jayme's fairer Eastern skin stood out here. Vi only slightly blended in, thanks to her father's bloodline. But overall, even she looked pale by comparison.

Vi's focus mostly stayed on the structure dominating the sky before her.

The castle had grown by the hour and now it was almost impossible to look anywhere without seeing some part of it. The edifice was imposing, rigid, and done in mostly black stone—a stark contrast to the sandstone she'd seen across the majority of the West. But she didn't know if the stone's coloration came from the stone itself, or centuries of exposure to the nearby sea.

"It's truly a marvel," Jayme murmured from her side.

"It is." Vi hadn't realized that they'd both come to a stop, admiring the structure. "How does it stack up to the Imperial Castle?"

"It's hard to say… They're both incredible. The castle in the South has more height."

"More than this?" Vi said, shocked.

"Well, it's built into a mountain... So it cheats. They're both impressive in different ways."

Vi gave a small nod.

"Were you planning on going to Norin's castle?" Jayme asked, shifting to face her. "After you managed to run away?"

"What? Oh no." Vi realized Jayme misunderstood her fascination. "I had thought it would be years until I laid eyes on it. But now... here I am."

"So, what *is* your plan?"

She knew Jayme likely wasn't intending to be accusatory, but her tone bordered on it. It's not like Vi could blame her. She'd dragged her through the desert on a mission that appeared to be half-baked to begin with.

"Well..." Vi started slowly, allowing the plan to solidify in her mind as she spoke. "I planned on going down to the docks, asking around, seeing if I could find work on a ship or stow away that could get me to at least the barrier islands, then..."

"Then... what? You just hope a ferry stops by to take you the rest of the way to the Crescent Continent?" Jayme put her hand on her hip, shifting her weight, and giving a small, frustratingly satisfied grin. It was the kind of grin she reserved for when she knew she was already right.

"Okay, you have a better plan?"

"I think I do." Jayme's body language shifted. For a brief moment she looked conflicted. But before Vi could ask why, she continued. "Do you know where the Le'Dan manor is?"

"The Le'Dan Estate is just outside of the Crossroads."

"Their main one is," Jayme agreed. "But they have another out here."

Vi was reminded of Andru's words once more. "Why do you know so much about the Le'Dans?"

"You'll find out." Jayme sighed. "Just lead the way to the estate, my cartographically-inclined friend."

Vi didn't even have to reach for the journal in her pack; the maps of Norin, with its off-center crescent shape wrapped around the greatest port in the world, filled her mind. There, diagonal from that point, was the castle. Making a triangle with the two was the main gate, where the East-West Way ended. Vertically toward the sea from the gate—though frustratingly without a direct access route—was the northwest ridge. It was the wealthy area of town with homes that dominated the same space as three or more smaller ones in the city on Vi's to-scale maps.

"It'll be this way." Vi opened her eyes and pointed. "But I really don't want to go to Lord Le'Dan."

"Why?" Jayme adjusted her pack and began walking, despite Vi's uncertainty. "He has ships, and he's an old friend of your family."

"He's a Le'Dan. He only does what benefits him."

"And you don't think helping the crown—helping you," Jayme hastily corrected before any passerby could hear. "Would be of benefit to him?"

"I don't want to reveal who I am." The road began to incline as they wove through the buildings of a city waking. "What if I do and he refuses to help? What if he keeps me under lock and key until Elecia returns, then hands me back over?" Vi's voice had dropped to a worried whisper.

"So don't tell him who you are until he agrees to help you."

"And we're back to why would he agree to help a no one? He's a *Le'Dan*."

The Le'Dans were splashed throughout history, thriving at every turn, even when they lost by traditional measures. The family had once vied against Vi's own lineage—the Ci'Dans—for control of the West. In the end, the Ci'Dans claimed the crown and the military, and the Le'Dans claimed the purse strings. Rivals became begrudging partners, then willing allies, and finally friends as the years progressed.

"Vi... trust me, just this once." Jayme sighed heavily.

"I always trust you." Vi glanced at her from the corners of her eyes. "Are you all right?"

"I'll be fine. I'm not looking forward to this either, honestly. And I don't want to argue about it any more."

With that, the conversation died.

They turned and began walking along a street aptly named "Golden Row." Every building was more ornate than the last. They had intricately carved doors and windows of delicate iron scrollwork and colored glass that undoubtedly cost more than some families made in a year. Most seemed to cater to fashion-based industries. There were cobblers, milliners, jewelers, and more tailors than she could count.

Based solely on appearances, her and Jayme were wildly out of place, and getting more than one questioning look from those who passed. Even though there had been no gates or guards, it felt as if they had trespassed on grounds where they weren't supposed to be. They were the "poor folk," the "lesser," and should thusly stay in their respective section of town. Every glare from the affluent citizenry seemed to try to convey the thought.

Vi was certainly unbothered by it, however. If anything, she found it amusing. To think that the men and women who turned up their noses at her were actually sniffing at the Crown Princess Solaris. It was almost enough to make her laugh aloud.

"We shouldn't be far now... up that way." Vi pointed to a narrow stair between two buildings.

"How do you remember your maps so well?" Jayme huffed softly up the steep stone steps. "Down to street names?"

"I can't explain it," Vi confessed. "Perhaps not being able to travel forced me to cement it, because I always thought of it. Walking here now... almost feels like I've done this before. I've gone over it in my mind so many times."

They were both breathing hard as they finally reached the top of the third set of stairs, grabbing their knees and thanking the Mother above for the fact that they had finally reached what seemed like the summit of the northwest ridge. For such a large piece of land, there were only a few homes. Every one was guarded with a tall wall and gatehouse to ward away all who didn't have express business.

"This certainly looks like the place." Jayme straightened and looked around.

"Yes." Vi stood taller as well, catching her wind. "Look, there."

She pointed toward a manor five down the row, distinctly larger than the rest. It towered two floors above the other tallest house on the row and seemed to have dominated the most prime piece of real estate. In fact, Vi wouldn't be surprised if the whole ridge had once been a singular estate, parsed out over the years for gifts, or strategy, or coin. It waved a large flag from its tallest rooftop bearing the Le'Dan crest.

"Well, we've come this far... Let's do this." Jayme marched forward, as though she was going off to war.

"Jayme, do you want me to lead the conversation?"

"No," Jayme replied, quickly.

"You seem—"

"Let me do this," Jayme snapped. Then she said, softer, "Please, Vi. This is not enjoyable for me, but I'm going to do it for you."

The expression on Jayme's face—one of agony—stopped Vi in her tracks. "Just what are you going to do?" she whispered, but Jayme had already continued on toward the front gate.

As expected, the gate house was occupied. The Western man who leaned against the side of his post looked at them dully, heaving a sigh when he realized they were headed for him. Pushing away, he straightened his leathers, puffed his chest, and rested a hand on the sword on his hip. Vi caught Jayme doing a similar motion from the corner of her eye.

"Turn around, we don't take beggars." He gave them a wave.

"We're not beggars," Jayme retorted. "Summon Lord Erion."

"Lord Erion?" The man sniffed. "His Lordship is far too busy for the likes of street urchins."

"We are no street urchins." Jayme had yet to back down. If anything, she stood even straighter. Vi stared at her friend, half in admiration, half in the smallest amount of fear at what had overtaken the woman. "Summon him, or you will regret not doing so."

"Is that a threat?" The guard's grip on his sword tightened.

"I think what my friend is trying to say—"

"Stay out of this." Jayme glared at her and promptly turned back to the guard. "Summon him or—"

At that moment, one of three sconces in the man's guardhouse lit magically. He glanced between them and the flame, hastening over to the gate as he said, "Go away, children. There's nothing more for you here."

The man huffed and puffed as he worked a large crank. The gate began to shudder before it slowly swayed open. Jayme didn't move an inch, standing right before the opening gate.

Vi waited nervously at her side. She didn't want to see her friend's guts spilled out on the ground because of a misunderstanding. She'd out herself as the crown princess before that. But what if no one believed her?

Her hand closed around the watch at her neck. Perhaps Lord Erion would know it? Vhalla had recognized it at a glance, but it had likely been a far more important token to her than the Western Lord.

"Are you going to make a run for it?" Vi whispered to Jayme, hiding her words underneath the loud squealing of the gate.

"That's a sure-fire way to get yourself killed. I've spotted two archers on the balconies making patrols. This place is even more fortified than it looks."

And it looked fortified to begin with. Vi scanned the main house in the distance, but saw nothing resembling an archer. Still, she was inclined to agree with Jayme. She knew from Sehra's warriors that good archers could easily remain hidden if they so choose.

"What're you still doing here?" The guard turned, wiping sweat from his brow, the gate crank forgotten. "Go on, get out of here."

"We're not leaving until you summon Lord Erion," Jayme insisted.

The man drew his sword. In one movement, Jayme pulled hers as well. The two squared off against each other.

"I don't think this is really necessary." Vi hastily stepped forward.

"What is going on here?" A man stood at the gates, attendant at his side. He had shoulder-length black hair, drawn back and away from his face. He had the tanned skin of a Westerner, but the bright blue eyes of a Southerner. It was a rare combination, but that—nor the stately clothes he was wearing—were what betrayed his identity to Vi. It was the skeletal metal hand that protruded from his right cuff, barely visible under the elongated sleeve.

"Lord Erion," Vi said hastily, stepping around Jayme. The soldier tried to step back between her and the guard as the guard made a motion as well. Vi paid them no heed. "I have come very far in search of you. I must speak with you. Please, grant me an audience."

Erion Le'Dan looked her up and down, squinting, slightly.

"My lord, my apologies, I was just telling the rabble to—"

Erion held up a hand, silencing the man. "And why do you think I should grant you an audience?"

"It's not her you'll want the audience with, my lord." Jayme stepped forward, three paces past Vi. She held her arm straight out, sword clutched in her fist. The point was not tracked on Erion, but angled harmlessly away, showing the pommel. "It's me."

Vi watched as Erion's eyes went wide and glossy. It was as if Jayme was holding out some kind of sacred treasure. But all Vi saw was the same pommel, carved with sheaves of wheat, that she'd always seen Jayme carry.

"Who are you?" Erion whispered, almost reverently.

"I am an Imperial guard." Jayme's voice had gone as hard and closed as her expression. "And my name is Jayme Taffl."

Taffl? Vi's attention swung to her friend. That wasn't her name. Jayme's last name was Graystone, not Taffl.

"What was your father's name, Jayme Taffl?" Erion crossed to her hurriedly. With both hands he took the pommel of the sword in his, rotating it slightly. Jayme allowed his inspection, but didn't loosen her vice-like grip.

"Daniel, sir. Daniel Taffl. He told me he served with you."

"Impossible..." Erion echoed Vi's single resounding thought.

"He's alive, sir. And he told me once if I were to meet you in my time serving the crown that I should tell you he's deeply sorry for that day. That he should've stepped forward and—"

"Enough." Erion held up his mechanical hand. "Ivos," the lord said to the attendant at his side. "Inform the Capricians that I shall not be in attendance for dinner this evening, as the daughter of an old friend has come to call."

Vi stared at the woman she'd called *friend*. The woman she thought she knew. The woman who was her confidant and ally, who had literally carried Vi's dreams and secrets across the land. The woman she now felt she was seeing for the first time.

Either Jayme was a clever, bold, and well-practiced liar—more so than Vi could've ever suspected, given how Erion had recognized the sword. Or her father really was Daniel Taffl—member of the Golden Guard, the most esteemed fighting squadron formed under Vi's late uncle, Prince Baldair. The same Daniel Taffl who had been an irreplaceable guard in service of Vi's mother.

The Daniel Taffl who was, by all counts, presumed dead.

21

"PLEASE, FORGIVE ME, my Lord, I had not realized." The guard at the gates continued to bow. "Esteemed guests of the Le'Dan, I beseech your forgiveness." Such a fast transition for someone who moments ago seemed so intent on removing them from the premises that he drew his blade.

"All is well," Vi murmured on their behalf as she entered. Her focus couldn't be further from the guard now. It was solely on Jayme as Erion led them into his manor.

The courtyard within the gates was a sort of T-shape.

There was a small amount of space between the wall where they'd entered, and the buildings to the right and left. In that space, flowers—Vi recognized them as Western roses—grew on trellises. The building to the left was a carriage house; three of the four gates were occupied by both carriages and horses, with the last vacant. *There must be an access road somewhere*, Vi reasoned, for she could not imagine how anything resembling a carriage could fit up the narrow walkways they'd traversed.

The building to their right was a workshop—an easy thing to determine given what she knew of the Le'Dan family trade, the feeling of Firebearer magic crackling the air, and the needlessly large windows that gave her a perfect view of the men and women laboring within. They toiled over worktables and benches, holding up sapphires as big as her eye and rubies larger than her thumb. It was clearly designed to communicate one thing: the wealth of the Le'Dan house.

But Vi wasn't concerned with that, just as she wasn't concerned with the five-story manor they entered at the other end of the meticulously paved walkway, or the ornately gilded entry hall they came to a stop in. Vi was concerned with one thing and one thing only: Jayme, and what now felt like a secret identity she'd kept from Vi for years.

Jayme avoided her probing stare completely, so adeptly that Vi was certain it was a conscious maneuver.

"Ivos," Erion commanded the elderly manservant at his side, "see to it that Jayme and…" He turned, looking directly at Vi. "Forgive me, my lady, I did not yet catch your name."

"For now, call me Yullia," Vi said with a wary glance to Ivos, hoping Erion would read into her hesitation. Even if Erion would end up helping her, the staff of nobles were known to have loose lips. Her own handmaids and tutors had been proof enough of that.

"Yullia, then." There was more than a note of curiosity in Erion's tone. "Ivos, see Jayme and Yullia to the summer rooms. You both look weary from what I assume has been a long journey. Please, take your time and freshen up. When you are ready, I will be waiting in the red study on the second floor. Any servant will be able to assist you there, should you find yourself wandering."

"Thank you, my lord," Jayme said stiffly. She should be stiff. Vi was glaring daggers at her back.

"Yes, thank you," Vi muttered, trying to manage decorum in the wake of her conflict over Jayme.

Erion gave him a nod and with a motion sent them on their way.

Ivos led them up the grand, arcing stairway to the right of the entry. They looped and continued upward again, and again, until they reached the fourth-floor landing. It was a small sitting area, framed by three doorways.

"The summer rooms are through here." Ivos went through the door directly across from them.

The set-up reminded Vi somewhat of her quarters in Soricium. There was a central sitting area with doors leading off from it. Two doors across from the entry were styled with glass and opened to a wide balcony that overlooked a rear courtyard and a fantastic view of the sea beyond. The other doors, left and right, led to lavish quarters equipped with low platform beds (as was Western custom) and *en suites*.

"Should you require anything, simply pull this cord," Ivos said after giving them the quick tour, motioning to a hanging tassel by the entry door. "Someone will be with you within moments. I shall return within the hour with a sampling of fresh clothes that should fit your measurements."

"Thank you, Ivos," Vi said without breaking her staring contest with Jayme.

The man gave a small bow, likely eager to excuse himself from the mounting tension that had become a tangible presence in the room. Vi held her breath, waiting for the door to click closed. Only then did she take a step forward toward the couch Jayme had positioned herself behind.

"Why didn't you tell me?"

"I can explain."

"Explain how you *lied* to me?" Her voice rose, fire igniting in her stomach. "I trusted you with my life, with my letters, and you couldn't even tell me your real name?"

"I told you my real name." Jayme frowned, her back rigid as a board, her hand on the hilt of her sword. *Let her draw it*, Vi thought bitterly. If Jayme thought the only spell she knew was to summon a sword, then she was severely underestimating Vi's danger as a sorcerer.

"You liar," Vi seethed.

"Don't call me a liar."

"When the shoe fits."

"Graystone is my real name—my mother's name."

"I'm to believe this whole time you have been the daughter of Daniel Taffl and chose to go by Graystone instead? Daniel Taffl—renowned, *dead* member of the Golden Guard?"

"My father isn't dead! You don't get to say he's dead, Vi *Solaris*." Jayme said her name like it was a curse. "Not when your family were the ones who left him to die."

"What are you talking about?" Vi narrowed her eyes. "You're raving mad."

"No, I'm the one with sense. And you're the ignorant princess, trapped in her tower and too focused on her own world—her own problems—to notice the rest of us dying."

"Excuse me?" Vi took a step back as though Jayme had slapped her. "I'm the one who's risking my life to try to find a cure for the White Death."

"And what do you think I'm doing right alongside you?" Jayme snapped back. She had her there, and Vi knew it. But before Vi could think of a good response, Jayme shook her head slowly. "You only see yourself and your needs. You don't really see anyone or anything else. Don't paint yourself as a martyr. You're doing this for you, Vi Solaris. Just like your father left the empire for himself—to save your mother."

"How did you…" Vi whispered. Jayme knew of her mother's illness.

"See, that's the problem with only focusing on yourself. You don't even realize what's going on around you—what's being said *about* you." Jayme stormed to her room. "And you're shocked I wouldn't want to share my father's identity with someone like you."

She punctuated the statement by slamming the door, leaving Vi's ears ringing. Vi stood in the main room, ready to call her back. She wasn't done screaming at her.

Instead, in a brief moment of sense, Vi stormed off to her own temporary quarters, slamming the door just as loudly. She'd only intended to lean against it for a brief moment and somehow she had sunk to the floor, knees at her chest.

"*Narro hath hoolo,*" Vi whispered listlessly. Luckily, the magic was so familiar to her now that she didn't even have to think about summoning the glyph. It was second nature.

A pair of booted feet appeared in her vision. Vi's eyes drifted upward—up the loose-fitting pants tucked into the worn boots at the knees, up to the robe he was rarely without, up to the eyes she hadn't seen in what felt like forever.

Somehow, her gaze had brought her whole body up with it. Vi was on her feet. She moved in a haze, pulled along by a base need and the knowledge that with Taavin came confidence, reassurance, stability in a world that suddenly seemed profoundly unstable.

Taavin's arms wrapped around her. Her face pressed into his chest, muffling her words.

"I missed you." She nearly choked on such a simple statement. More emotion than she could bare tried to compound in the spaces between each word.

She felt his cheek, warm on her temple. His lips brushed lightly against her ear as he spoke.

"And I missed you immeasurably." Taavin took a slow breath that quivered just slightly at the end. "But Vi, tell me what has upset you so?" He didn't comment on the room. He didn't ask where she was now. He didn't even ask for updates on her trials and progress toward Meru. All he focused on was what made her tremble in his arms. "I feel it… I feel you… What has made your heart so heavy?"

She didn't answer him immediately. She couldn't. If she opened her mouth now it would let out the tears.

"Vi, you're safe here," he murmured. "It will all be all right."

"You can't say that. You don't know that," Vi retorted, somewhat angrily. How could he proclaim it would all work out? She was far from home—far from everything she'd ever known. She was shaken to her core and she felt like she'd lost far more than she'd gained. Logically, Vi knew it was a moment of weakness. But logic was losing the battle against emotion at present.

"I do know that."

"How?"

"Because you are here, with me, in my arms… And so, everything will be all right."

It was illogical. There was no reason for her to believe it. No clear explanation for why it soothed her so. But soothe it did. Vi felt her shoulders relax. The tense knot in her throat gave way to a small hiccup. And a single tear of exhaustion and frustration rolled down her cheek.

"It's okay."

Vi pressed her eyes closed, feeling the intricate embroidery that covered his chest sink into her skin as she tried to remove all space between them. Nothing was okay. Her world was changing faster than she could keep up.

But his arms remained around her—firm and unmoving. Perhaps that was what he'd meant. *They* were okay. This one beautiful and unexpected thing she could rely on when everything else was gone—that was still okay.

She leaned into him further, if that were possible, and let out one quivering breath, then another. Magic was as hot against her wrist as his breath was on her cheek. And when she finally pulled away to look up at him, all Vi saw was his kind and unwavering gaze—filled with more adoration than she deserved in her present state.

Leaning up, craning her neck, Vi kissed him once for strength.

Then, languidly, she kissed him a second time, purely because she wanted to.

The third time, he kissed her. And the third time was the charm. For it was then that the world drifted away and she melted into him, sure that if she let go of the fear and anger trying to knot itself around her heart, everything would be all right.

22

FIRE CRACKLED AROUND her shoulders, the water in the tub hissing steam. Heating water was something she couldn't even dream of doing mere months ago. But now, her magic was more like an old friend than an estranged neighbor she only sort of knew from a distance. Vi drew her legs to her chest, working to get her thoughts in order.

She needed to speak to Jayme and apologize properly, with a clear head. That was first. Then, second, Lord Erion Le'Dan.

Vi practiced what she may say to Jayme over and over, but nothing sounded right. With a sigh, she finally emerged from the tub and started for the main room. She'd just have to figure it out as she went, and trust herself to keep her sense when the time came.

When Vi left the bathroom, she found clothes had been laid out on the bed in the other room—just as Ivos had promised.

It was certainly a sampling. Yet despite his assurances, nothing seemed to fit quite right. The tailored styles of the West were unforgiving to Vi's curves. If she found something that fit in the hips and waist, it was comically large around the calves and ankles. If it fit her lower legs, she could barely get the waistband over her bum.

In the end, Vi settled for something that was no doubt out of fashion—a small price to pay for actually complimenting the shape of her body. A silken skirt clung to her hips, falling to her knees before flaring slightly, as though the seamstress had intended for all the extra fabric. The top she chose was knit, and felt somewhat modest given how Westerners seemed to like their fashion.

Vi's hand hovered over the doorknob, hesitant. She collected herself with a deep breath. Vi opened the door.

"Jayme, I—"

Jayme was nowhere to be found. Vi thought about knocking on her door and apologizing as was the plan, but she instead headed for the exit. *She would apologize tonight.* She was reorganizing her priorities, not fleeing from them. Nothing would be gained if she forced her apology on Jayme right now.

The second floor of the manor was composed of all kinds of parlors and gaming rooms. A single, long hall stretched from end to end, lined in carved wooden sliding doors. Most were pulled open, creating a pleasant cross-breeze off the sea and through the manor. Due to the layout, she had little trouble locating the red study.

Aptly named, every wall was covered in rich red velvet, though most of it was hidden by the bookcases stained in a dark lacquer, same as the floor. A fire crackled in the hearth across from her, framed by two tall windows on either side. Erion Le'Dan turned, taking his eyes off the flames.

"You look lovely, Yullia." Erion raised his glass in what she presumed to be a small toast.

"My name isn't Yullia." Vi cut right to the chase, having seen no one else nearby—not even a servant at the door. Perhaps Erion had been hoping for a similar conversation.

"I know." Erion took a sip of what she presumed to be an amber colored liquor. "That much I inferred."

"You did?" Vi would play things carefully until she was certain they were on the same page.

"I have my suspicions," he affirmed. "I know when someone lies to me, especially when they telegraph it so well. I'm in regular contact with the Crossroads. And... I am a Westerner through and through. I have seen portraits of our last princess and first Empress Fiera." He gave her a long stare and Vi didn't let her own gaze waver.

"Then allow me to introduce myself again. My real name is Vi Yarl-Ci'Dan Solaris, Crown Princess to the throne of the Solaris Empire." He knew, and she may as well be the one to say it.

"A pleasure to meet you, Vi Solaris." Erion gave a small nod and took another small sip of his liquor. But he did not bow or prostrate. In fact, nothing about his demeanor changed and Vi liked him more for it. Erion motioned to one of the two sofas angled toward each other in front of the fireplace. "Would you care to sit?"

"Certainly." Vi took up a space on the sofa he indicated.

Erion, however, did not sit across from her. Instead he walked to a small bar in the corner of the room. "Would you care for something to drink? Kaha, perhaps?"

"Whatever you're having is fine." She didn't know what he was having, but didn't want to look ignorant or rude. She'd only heard about kaha—strong Western bean tea—from her uncle. And Vi would take her chances with almost anything other than that ominous-sounding concoction.

Erion gave her a look that made Vi wonder if she was about to regret this decision. He turned a small knob on the clawed hand that was holding his drink. A spring was released, and the fingers shot outward. Hand freed, he worked to open the bottle and poured a fresh glass, topping off his as well. Erion re-locked the fingers of his metal hand around his glass before delivering hers.

"Thank you," Vi said softly. Her eyes drifted to his prosthesis, but Vi tried to divert them. She didn't think her fascination would be interpreted as flattering given the horrific circumstances that surrounded him losing the limb to the Mad King Victor.

"You're welcome." Erion finally sat. "So, what is the cause for all this cloak and dagger? You have created quite a stir."

"I am on a secret mission," Vi began. "One of the utmost importance, on behalf of the entire Empire."

"And that is?"

"I'm going to find my father."

"Aldrik Solaris is—"

"He's alive." Vi cut him off at the pass. "I have future sight and I have seen him."

Erion paused for a long moment. Then he leaned forward, elbows on his thighs, an intent stare on his face. Now she had his attention. Vi gambled on his Western roots putting great stock into future sight, and it looked like her gamble was going to pay off.

"I have had many visions of my father, many." *Did two count as "many"?* "And I have every reason to believe he is alive on the Crescent Continent." So she was stretching things. Vi wouldn't make the same mistake she had with Romulin or Jayme and show hesitation.

"You're certain?"

"Yes." She didn't know how she could make herself any clearer. "He is alive. He is on the Crescent Continent. And he is waiting for me."

Erion leaned back in his seat and took another long sip of his liquor, looking at her from over top the glass. It reminded her that she had yet to touch her own drink, and Vi finally brought it to her mouth. As suspected, it was something strong that singed the hairs on the inside of her nose. The vapors tangled in her throat, causing her to cough.

"It's an acquired taste," he said with a small smile.

"I—" another round of coughing claimed her. "I like the taste. Just not the burning."

"You'll become acquainted with how to drink it," he assured her. "I presume you told your mother of these visions?"

"I…"

"You have not." Vi couldn't decide if Erion's expression was proud, amused, or merely curious. "Why?"

"I did not want to risk involving my mother," Vi began delicately. "The Senate is already skeptical of the crown."

"And you thought running away would help?"

"Actually, I think it will. We both know it's my brother they want to see sit the throne." A pause, waiting for him to challenge. Nothing. "They have no love for me—raised in a foreign land, Firebearer, only passable in the dance of politics." Vi wasn't attempting to downplay herself, merely speak truth. Erion seemed to appreciate the fact, as he didn't object. "My brother seated on the throne would be best for the Empire, I admit that fully. The West is loyal enough and, despite physical appearances, my brother has as much of my father's blood as I do. There's no reason it *must* be me on the throne.

"But…" Vi finally turned her attention back to him. "I am the only one who can find my father."

"Why do you think you can find him when all other search parties have failed?"

"Other search parties didn't have the benefit of future sight. I do." Vi closed her eyes, taking a breath. One of her hands wrapped around the watch that connected her to Taavin, drawing strength from the thought of him. "Because… while I'm certain those search parties did their best, they were looking for their Emperor. I am looking for my father. And I believe that motivation will be the key to my success."

Erion paused; the silence was heavy and uncomfortable. Despite herself, Vi continued to speak over it.

"Furthermore, I—" She fought to regain an iron grip on her emotions but they slipped free. "—I do not think I would be an effective ruler if I was forced to sit on the throne and watch my people die, doing nothing, when my father, their rightful ruler, is alive and may have the cure for the affliction ravaging our lands.

"The Empire will do well, thrive even, under the shrewd politics of my brother; the crown is secure. I will find our true sovereign and reunite my family. I will aide in finding a cure for the disease plaguing our citizens."

"And if you die?" He said it as if she hadn't thought about the possibility. As if she hadn't already considered the likelihood of that coming to pass.

"Then I die. Which is another reason I could not involve my mother. I could not have her knowing of that heartbreak while also enduring the heartbreak of knowing Father is out there as well, unable to return home. In that case, my true fate will remain a mystery to all but you and Jayme."

Erion leaned back in his chair. Finally, he took a long sip of his drink. It was as if she had passed whatever test he had been administering.

"And Jayme—what does she intend?"

"She's one of the few who knows of my visions. Whatever she intends is up to her."

"She should prove trustworthy, if she's anything like her father." Vi bit back a retort. "Where did you learn such craftiness? It reminds me of Jax." He almost seemed impressed. "It couldn't have been easy, sneaking away from your guards, enlisting one to help you—though I'm not surprised, given her parentage—and surviving the Waste."

"I have to find my father." It was all she could say because, in truth, she didn't know where the abilities had come from. She'd never even considered failure. Doing so felt like a betrayal of her family and the Empire. "Will you help me or not?"

Erion thrummed his fingers on the armrest of his chair. When they finally stopped, the conversation shifted in a way that sounded like permission.

"I will need a week to execute this. Organizing ships for these sorts of ventures is not easy since the Empire closed trade with the Crescent Continent. And I will need to devise the proper incentive for my business partners to ferry you beyond the barrier islands."

"Thank you." Vi took a cautious sip of her drink. "What do you seek in return for all this kindness?"

A thin smile formed itself on his dusky lips. "It's my honor to assist the future Empress. Surely, you don't think I'd ask for anything more than your gratitude for doing my duty to the crown?"

The word *gratitude* rang heavy. "Of course not, Lord Le'Dan."

It was not the first time her family had been indebted to his. The Ci'Dans may have won the Western wars for political supremacy with their military might, but they'd always been beholden to the wealth and influence of the Le'Dans. They were shrewd, cunning, and had a knack for politics that meant they were rarely on the losing side.

Vi was certain Erion was already two steps ahead in figuring out several ways that, no matter what happened to her, this act of kindness would benefit him.

"Then, to your venture." Erion raised a glass. "Should I not have a chance to toast your health and success—as I do not think we should risk speaking so openly on this again—let me do so now."

"To my venture." Vi raised her glass as well and then drained the rest of its burning contents.

23

THEY HAD GONE to dinner shortly after cementing their agreement.

Erion's wife—Rhalla—was a generous woman, both in manner and in hospitality. For a woman who hadn't been "expecting to entertain," she produced an enviable spread of Western fare. Vi had worked her way through the different courses. There were too many to finish all of them, but Vi still cleaned plate after plate. Now her stomach felt like she was carrying a stone in it.

She wasn't sure if she could have gone right to bed after a meal like that if she tried.

Now, she stood at the balcony of her room, which she'd admired from the first moment she'd entered. The scenery was a good distraction from the pain of her engorged stomach, and there was a calming safety to the darkness. Between the soft, distant crash of the waves, the wind in her hair, and the nearest barrier island a small shadow on the starry horizon, Vi would dare say she felt peaceful if she weren't waiting on pins for Jayme to return.

Erion hadn't lied when he'd said he wanted to talk with Jayme following dinner. He was keeping her half the night.

Vi sank to her elbows on the railing, holding out her hand and murmuring. The glyph was small and tight, flawlessly crafted. She could feel Taavin at her side without even looking.

"Do you think it wise to summon me out in the open like this?" He mirrored her posture, forearms on the wide railing.

"It's quiet and I haven't seen another soul for hours."

He didn't argue or put up a fight. The man's shoulder brushed against hers before settling flush against her. Even when he said nothing and did nothing, he still found a way to speak volumes to her rapidly fluttering heart.

"It's peaceful," he finally murmured. "You should enjoy it while it lasts."

Vi gave a small nod in agreement. The statement seemed harmless enough, but as the silence stretched, it drew her attention to his face. Taavin's eyes were narrowed slightly, looking out to sea with an intensity she wasn't expecting.

"What is it? What have you seen?" Vi finally took her gaze from the sea, and it landed on him. She rested her hip against the railing.

"It's hard to say." Taavin sighed, straightening his spine. His eyes scanned her face, and hers did the same to his. "My dreams and visions, they're increasing in frequency. The nurse says that my seizures and comatose states are lasting longer and—"

"Seizures? Comatose states?" Vi grabbed his hand as she grappled with the words. "What's wrong?"

Taavin gave her a small, bitter smile. "I told you that I have always been afflicted with visions of you—torturous visions." He rose a hand, tucking a strand of hair that had fallen from her braids behind her ear. The sea wind was eager to rip it from its spot once more.

"You said dreams," she whispered, worry filling her.

"Yes, sometimes they come in sleep." He paused, caressing her cheek. How could he hold so much longing, pain, adoration, and suffering in one expression? Why did she have to be the one to provoke such complexity? "Other times, they come as daydreams. My body seizes and shakes. I fall into a deep, involuntary sleep."

"When I summon you…"

"With *narro hath*?" Taavin shook his head. "When I feel the magic, I lay down willingly and allow it to overtake me. I could break the communication spell with *juth* if I so chose."

Vi breathed a small sigh of relief. It didn't make everything better—he was still suffering. But at least she wasn't knowingly causing it.

"Taavin…" Vi took a step forward, resting her hands delicately on his hips. Suddenly, her magical friend, tutor—*lover?*—felt far more frail than he ever had before. "I don't want to hurt you."

He leaned down, a small smile on his lips. Lightly, he kissed her forehead, wrapping his arms around her shoulders. Vi shifted her arms around his waist, and they held each other for several long breaths.

"At first, you were only pain… but now you have brought a light to my world that I will protect with as much ferocity as the Flame of Yargen itself." Taavin shifted, looking out to sea once more. Vi felt more than saw it as he re-situated his cheek and chin on her head. "And I fear what lies ahead that I cannot protect you from."

His grip tightened. Vi twisted, looking up at his shining emerald eyes. She could lose herself for hours in those stunning orbs.

"What have you seen?" Vi whispered.

"A storm, death in the water, frost, and you cast into dark waves."

"But you've said your dreams are merely of the past." Yet even as she spoke, Vi suppressed a shudder at those ominous words. "Could it be my grandmother instead?"

"I don't know." His fingers hooked under her chin. "What I do know is that I've had precious little to live for, Vi," he whispered. "I've been struggling to survive for years without knowing why, other than a frustrating sense of self-preservation. I never knew why I didn't just give in. But now, I think I do. I believe, somehow, I knew I would find you, and you would be the key to everything."

"What are you saying?" Vi whispered. His words clung to familiar corners—his thoughts echoing ones she hadn't dared linger on.

"You are not the only one who will be on a journey, Vi. I wish to see the world too. And I too will find a way out of my prison."

"Taavin, if you run away, what—" Vi never got to finish her question.

She was cut off by the sound of the door to the main room opening. Vi's head jerked in the direction of the noise to see Jayme step into the dark room. She looked back to where Taavin had just been standing, and found her hands clutching nothing but thin air.

Vi quickly dropped her arms hastily and turned to face Jayme. Moonlight streamed over her shoulders and through the propped-open double doors that led to the balcony. Yet she still had to squint to make out the woman hovering by the door in the darkness.

Her emotions rose, tension on tension, over worry for Taavin and what she needed to say next to Jayme.

Vi cleared her throat. "How did it go?"

"Good." Jayme abandoned her position with an ease that gave Vi hope. She strolled over, hands in her pockets. "I enjoyed hearing more about my father from someone who knew him well before the Mad King."

"Your father really is Daniel Taffl," Vi whispered softly.

"I told you I didn't lie." Jayme folded her arms over her chest.

Vi looked at her toes, then up to the woman, down again, and back once more. Somewhere in her bouncing gaze she found the resolve she was looking for. "Jayme, I'm sorry."

"For?"

"I'm sorry for doubting you, for the harsh things I said... And for not thinking through... well, knowing this makes a lot about you come into focus."

"Does it?" Jayme sighed. There was resignation in her walk, but instead of retreating to her room, she moved to the balcony. "Tell me, what of my father do you know already?"

"Mother mentioned him," Vi started. "She told me Daniel Taffl was a good soldier, a better swordsman, and one of the best men she'd ever known... But the Mad King had taken his toll on him. She said he was with her in her journey across the Empire, but they split ways in the East when she went West to collect the army. Then, when the Mad King marched on the East and put it to the torch, she lost all contact with him."

"She wasn't completely honest with you, then."

"We all have our secrets, don't we?" Vi muttered. "I know many don't like talking about the time of the Mad King."

Jayme gave a solemn nod. Her expression wasn't just pained, it was angry. "The scars from that man are still on this Empire. You see it in Erion and his hand. And you see it in my father."

"What really happened?" Vi took a step forward, resting her hands timidly on the railing, feeling as though she no longer deserved to share the space with Jayme.

"Your mother spoke true up to a point." Jayme gave a small, bitter laugh and shook her head. "She did find my father, free of the Mad King. But the man had already done his work. He took Erion's hand, but my father's mind.

"She returned him to his parents in Leoul and just left him there, trusting them to know what to do with him in that state."

"Leoul was put to the torch when the Mad King's armies marched from the South, reclaiming that territory. My father may not be of sound mind, but he had an intimate knowledge of the Mad King and his movements. That was what kept him and his family alive.

"Eventually, he returned to Leoul, met my mother, and had me."

"Why did he never reach out to anyone—Erion, my mother, Jax? Why call yourself Graystone?"

"My father did much better, I'm told, after having a wife and child… and having a farm to work again. But he always struggled talking about the old times.

"So my mother banned talk of it in the house—banned it altogether. Father didn't seem to mind; it kept him level not to think about the war or have people calling after Daniel Taffl. I didn't even learn who my father truly was until I was fourteen and exploring my own options to provide for my family."

"You said my mother didn't tell the whole truth… Your father finally reached out to her, didn't he?" Her heart was breaking for her friend. Jayme shouldered so much, and silently. When she gave a nod, Vi continued her speculation. "So my mother finds out he's alive and has a daughter looking for work. That's how you were appointed courier, and guard—an Eastern girl of humble background."

"Right again."

Vi shifted uncomfortably, looking out to sea. She ran a hand over her braids and let out a sigh. The information weighed heavy on her; she couldn't imagine how it was for Jayme.

"I'm so sorry," Vi whispered. "I truly had no idea."

"I didn't want you to." Jayme shrugged. "What good could come of it?"

"I'm your friend… I want to help you."

"Help me by letting it drop." Jayme pushed away from the railing. "I'd rather not have all this hanging over our heads. We have other things to focus on."

"Yes, we do…" Vi turned to face her friend. She tried to tell by body language alone how she was feeling. Jayme was a closed book, however. And all Vi was left to go on was her word and faith that she meant what she said. "Is all forgiven? Are we all right?"

"Yes, we're all right. Graystone or Taffl, I'm still Jayme." Jayme pulled her in for a small hug, then promptly started for her room. She looked exhausted, which was perhaps why Vi didn't try to stop her.

Or maybe the real reason Vi made no motion from the balcony was that she didn't entirely believe her transgressions had been forgiven.

24

Vi HAD EVERY intention of enjoying her time resting and relaxing in the days that followed. She was between two major stops on her long journey to Meru. She'd finally made it to Norin and secured a vessel. And, to top it all off, she was somewhere safe where she could enjoy the luxury of letting her guard down.

As it turned out, doing nothing was utterly agonizing.

The first day, Vi roamed the Le'Dan mansion. There were rooms on rooms—some large, others small, some crammed to the brim with furniture and artifacts like small museums, others mostly empty save for a single table or lonely chair perched on a platform like a throne. One of the handmaids, Samri, took note of her wandering and became Vi's impromptu guide.

She told Vi the history of the house, confirming Vi's earlier speculations that it dated back over a hundred years and the whole ridge had once been Le'Dan property. Vi listened with half an ear, distracted when her nose picked up a familiar scent. Parchment, ink, leather, wood—all the glorious trimmings of a library. Sure enough there was one, and Samri led her right to it.

Vi spent the next two days in the Le'Dan library pouring over ship schematics, tidal records, island maps, trade manifests, and any other book on sailing she could find. If she was going to set sail, she may as well learn all she could about what she was up against. It made for a valuable distraction… but a distraction nonetheless.

Things still didn't feel right between her and Jayme.

"Samri." The woman was rarely far now, currently stationed at the door of the delicately decorated breakfast room. "Where's Jayme this morning?" Normally, Vi wouldn't worry about Jayme not showing up for breakfast. But this was now the second day in a row she'd been gone. Coupled with Vi's simmering worry…

"I think she went out for a walk this morning, ma'am." Samri lowered her eyes when she answered. She couldn't be much more than thirteen, but her long black hair was pulled into a tight bun at the nape of her neck, and she stood as though she carried more years on her small shoulders than Vi.

It was a stark contrast to Ellene's reluctant transition to womanhood. Vi lightly touched the bracelet around her wrist. Perhaps she should write? No, she couldn't.

Even Ellene couldn't know of her plans, and Vi knew she was just grasping for an excuse not to look for Jayme.

"Do you know where she went?" Vi asked, lavishing a bread pocket with deep crimson jam.

"I believe she said she was heading down to the docks."

Vi took a bite of the bread and chewed through the bright flavors of strawberry and warm wheat as she debated. Perhaps she should leave Jayme to her own devices... But Jayme had said all was well between them. Vi wanted to see Norin and reassure herself Jayme had been sincere. Going out would achieve both of those goals.

"I think I'll join her," Vi mused aloud.

"Very good, ma'am. If you won't need me for anything else here, I'll see to setting out clothes for you."

"Thank you, Samri." Vi nodded her dismissal.

Breakfast finished, a quick freshening up, one fresh set of clothes, and Vi was on her way. The guard at the gate did nothing to stop her this time. In fact, he showed extreme deference, the likes of which Vi would expect a servant to show her as the crown princess, not as Yullia. *The perks of being a guest of Lord Le'Dan.*

Like when she had first entered Norin, the city was still waking up. Most of the opulent areas of town were quiet; the shops catering to people with more gold than sense were still. Not far from the port was a store bearing the name "Le'Dan" emblazoned in gold on the door. Vi paused, looking at the glimmering pieces the shopkeeper was setting out for the day. The Le'Dan family truly did good work. Vi wondered how many of the strange, sparkling stones had come illegally from Meru.

Further down were the more conventional storefronts, which eventually gave way to warehouses and fish auctions. Before she knew it, Vi found herself standing before the greatest port in the world.

The docks were well alive by this hour of the morning. Men and women with arms as thick as Vi's thighs carried barrels and hoisted heavy lines of rope, carrying them from place to place. At the far end of the docks there seemed to be some kind of bidding war, if the shouting crowd was any indication. Merchants bartered with other merchants, peering into crates and haggling over the contents inside. To Vi's fascination and mild horror, some of those contents were still able to knock against the walls.

The air was scented with brine, fish, and sweat. Birds of all shapes and sizes squawked, filling the air and lining ship rails and ropes alike. Underneath the hum ships murmured, quietly creaking and straining against their ropes, as if trying to return to the open sea. Most flew flags of Solaris on their tallest masts. But some had red sails of the West. Others had what she recognized as Western family crests dyed into the canvas.

Vi wandered, looking for what would be a Le'Dan ship... Perhaps the ship that would take her across the Barrier Islands.

"Hey, watch yourself!" a man barked at her.

"Sorry..." Vi mumbled an apology, distracted by the man's size. He was nearly as large as Fallor had been. There were people of every shape and size, surely. But some of the men seemed unnaturally large and hardened by the salt spray.

He continued on gruffly, paying her no mind. Vi turned, looking to a woman who was lounging against a pillar. A smoking pipe hung from her lips.

"Excuse me." Vi approached. "Do you know where Le'Dan ships are?"

"Le'Dan?" The woman took her pipe from her mouth, spitting on the ground at the name. "Don't go looking for work there, girl."

"I'm not a girl." The way the woman looked her up and down showed apparent disagreement.

"They're swindlers. They'll risk the lives of their crew for the sake of some coin, running the routes they run."

"I'm not looking for work. I'm looking for a friend, actually."

"Then your friend is the swindler." Vi sighed and started walking away. "They're back on the northern side. Go that way," the woman called after her, somewhat begrudgingly.

"Thank you," Vi shouted back.

Sure enough, back on the Northern side, Vi found two vessels flying Le'Dan flags. They were smaller than she would've expected, dwarfed by most boats anchored at port. Clearly the Le'Dans favored speed and nimbleness above all else. The smaller of the two ships had the words *Dawn Skipper* painted along its hull. It had two masts and four portholes on the side, and its figurehead was a simple, needle-like spear, keeping with the minimalistic look of the entire boat, save for the aft rudder. That was of comparable scale to the ships nearly three times the *Dawn Skipper*'s size.

Was this really the best she had to get her to Meru? Vi suddenly felt a kernel of doubt at her plan. This ship looked like it would tip in a modest swell.

"… good, I'm glad everything sounds like it's going smoothly."

That was Jayme's voice. Vi slowly rounded the hull of the *Dawn Skipper*. The dock stretched down its side, between the two Le'Dan vessels.

"Everything's according to plan," an unfamiliar voice responded. "I don't think there's any reason to think we'll be delayed."

"Excellent."

"Pleasure, as always."

Jayme was talking with a blonde woman who stood on the gangplank of the *Dawn Skipper*. Whatever conversation they'd been having had just ended. Jayme continued off the vessel, and the woman returned onto it.

Vi paused, debating if she should hide somewhere. She didn't want to upset Jayme by seeming nosy, or eavesdropping. But lying was likely worse. It wasn't Vi's fault she happened on something. She hadn't been intentionally lurking.

Before Vi could make up her mind, Jayme spotted her. "V—Yullia." She seemed surprised. "What're you doing here?"

"I wanted to see the port." Vi shrugged. "And the Le'Dan ships." She didn't know why she didn't just come out and say that she wanted to see Jayme as well, and make sure everything was all right.

"They're impressive, don't you think?"

"Smaller than I would've expected."

"They're fast," Jayme assured her. "So I'm told." Jayme continued walking away from the ship. Vi glanced behind, but the other woman had vanished. As if sensing Vi's confusion, Jayme offered an explanation without being asked. "Look, I trust Erion well enough… but I wanted to see it for myself. If we're getting on one of these things, I wanted to speak to the crew, make sure everything looked good. I'm not the most versed in vessels, but I at least wanted to know what we were in for."

"Oh… So that's what you've been up to." *Well, that made sense.* Vi felt suddenly silly for doubting her friend. "Good thinking."

"It's my job to look out for you." Jayme linked arms with her, and Vi's worries were finally laid to rest. "Now, let's sample some of the real Western fare. Not the fancy stuff Erion is serving us."

She had never eaten anything more delicious than *mannik*.

Vi had gorged herself on two of them and was now going back for a third from the street stall two alleyways off the docks in the poorer section of town. The woman behind the stall took her third coin and lifted the lid off the tall cooking basket to her right. Steam billowed up like a chimney, filling the air with the sweet aroma of sauced meats and steamed bread. She handed two more *mannik* to Vi with a smile. Of course she was nice to them, they were likely her best customers today.

"You're going to explode." Jayme half-spoke, half-laughed at her. She was perched on a wide stoop leading to the back door of a modest home. The door itself had multiple locks—all rusted and weeping with age. So they didn't seem to be at any risk of being in the way anytime soon.

"Not possible when I'm eating the most delicious thing on earth." Vi took up her space next to her, passing Jayme hers. She took another large bite, letting the gravy from the minced meat dribble down her chin.

"It is pretty good," Jayme admitted, nibbling the side of her own bun.

"More than pretty good," Vi insisted. "This is better than candied nut rolls during the solstice."

"Well, I'm glad we got to try some before we left."

"It won't be long now, will it?" Vi wiped her mouth with the heel of her hand, relishing the feeling of not being scolded for the unladylike act.

"A few more days and we should be off to the Crescent Continent," Jayme agreed.

"You won't find any ships going there," the elderly woman spoke up from across the alley. Both girls turned sharply, not realizing they'd been overheard. At their attention, she continued. "The Crescent Continent has blocked all travel on account of the White Death. Bold, since they gave it to us to begin with."

"Is there proof—that they gave it to us?" Vi might already know better, but she was curious to hear what misinformation was currently in fashion.

"What else could it be? Take it from an old woman…" She shook her head, as if disappointed. "I've been around these parts for many years and have heard many tales. That is a world wild with magic. It's why they only ever allowed our traders in and out of a single port on the Barrier Isles—they didn't want us to see what they had. Where else would a disease that first targeted a sorcerer's channels come from than a land like that?"

An evil god bent on destruction? Vi thought loudly. Outwardly, she merely shrugged. Jayme remained silent.

"Especially now that it's afflicting non-sorcerers, none of the sensible ships are sailing to the Barrier Isles." The elderly woman knelt down with a soft *"ooph,"* hoisting a tray of *mannik* from within her cart. She continued to speak as she restocked the steaming basket. "And those who go even that far are only the most foolish and greedy seafarers."

"Foolish and greedy?"

"Greedy, because they say that unscrupulous merchants on both sides will ignore the ban, meeting in the middle at abandoned atolls for the sake of goods. Nothing hikes the price of foreign wares like a trade ban." That was exactly what Vi imagined Erion was doing. "Foolish, because those waters have always belonged to Adela."

Adela. Vi's blood turned to ice. The mere mention of the name filled her with thoughts of Fallor and the last vision of her father. "What do you know of Adela?"

"You don't know the stories?" The woman huffed at her.

"Adela terrorized the seas surrounding the main continent for years," Jayme supplied. "But that was…" She thought for a long moment.

"More than a century and then some ago." A man who had been ferrying trash out the back door of one of the restaurants to a bin by the old woman's *mannik* stand joined in the conversation. "Adela is long dead, and don't go speaking her name around these parts. It brings storms and bad luck—though luckily not the pirate queen herself."

"Evil doesn't die, only bides its time," the elderly woman cautioned.

He gave a wave and started back for his store, pausing on his own landing adjacent to where Vi and Jayme sat. "The woman is batty and you're batty for believing her if you think Adela lives." Before Vi could speak in protest, defending the kind old woman who had given her the most delicious food known to man, he continued. "But she's right that those are pirate-infested waters, worse now they can pray on vessels traveling without the Empire's protection. I wouldn't be surprised if an impostor took up Adela's mantle. I don't know what test of courage you're looking to embark on. But turn away now before you stick out your neck too far and lose your head for it."

Vi took a bite of *mannik*, chewing it over as Jayme thanked the man for his warnings. The woman threw a rude gesture at the man's back.

"We should get back." Jayme stood.

"Sure." Vi rose to her feet as well, shoving the rest of her *mannik* into her mouth in one bite. But it seemed they could not escape without one more remark from the watchful woman.

"You are neither foolish or greedy." Her eyes settled right on Vi. "You are hopeful, and that is far more dangerous."

"Thank you for the warnings," Jayme said, practically tugging Vi along. When they were out of earshot she added, with a glance over her shoulder, "The man was right—she's batty."

"You think so?" Vi looked back as well.

"If Adela were alive she'd be… at least eighty? Ninety? Perhaps even over a hundred. So even if she is still among the living, claiming she sails the seas as a pirate is downright insane."

"So you don't believe the old woman… Or Fallor?"

"Nah. Though what the man said rings of truth. I'm sure someone claiming to be Adela is terrorizing the seas and thriving on the notoriety. Adela is the stuff of Southern bedtime stories meant to scare children into behaving."

"Is she really so infamous?"

Jayme gave a nod, continuing unprompted: "She was the most notorious thief in Solarin—perhaps that's why you haven't really heard of her, growing up in the North. Just when the King Romulin's guard was closing in on her for a whole number of crimes, they say she fled to the coast, to Oparium. From there, she turned her attention to the seas. As a Waterrunner, she was unstoppable on the waves."

"A sorcerer?" Jayme made an affirmative humming noise at Vi's interjection. "Just what the South needs—*needed*—another sorcerer to hate."

"This was before the War of the Crystal Caverns," Jayme reminded her. "I think most of the sorcerer hatred came from that."

"From all I've read, I'm inclined to agree," Vi muttered. "So you're not afraid, then?"

"Oh I'm terrified." Jayme shoved her hands in her pockets. "Of storms, and swells, and backstabbers, and pirates, and whatever awaits us on the Crescent Continent. But the one thing I'm not afraid of are ghosts."

25

TWO MORE DAYS passed before their time ran out.

"Miss Yullia!"

Vi was jerked awake with a rough shake of her shoulder. Samri stood at her bedside. "What is it?" Vi came instantly awake, pushing herself away from the nest of pillows.

"We have to go," Samri whispered hurriedly.

In the lower floor of the manor, Vi heard loud voices. There was a commotion, complete with doors slamming and the rumble of booted feet. It was a wonder she'd slept through it at all.

"What's happening?"

"There's no time, please, come with me." Samri held out a folded cloak. "There's clothes at the docks. Wear this until you get there."

Vi stood at the edge of her bed, hurriedly donning the cloak and rubbing sleep from her eyes. "Samri—"

She was cut short by a voice.

"Vi?" Jayme called. There was a knock on the door. "Do you hear the commotion? Should we leave?"

Vi opened the door quickly and motioned to Samri. "Already one step ahead of you."

"We must go," Samri whispered, standing at a wall. One of the panels had been opened, a servant's passage exposed. Vi wasn't even surprised by its presence.

"Should we grab our things?" Jayme asked. She already had her sword strapped to her hip. Vi had the journal of maps and notes on the sea in hand. They'd each gone for their most precious items.

"Samri said there are supplies at the docks," Vi said as she hurriedly entered the open passage.

"There's no time," Samri repeated, practically pleading. "Please, come."

Samri pulled the door closed behind them and latched it. There was already a candle flickering in a holder on the wall, and Samri slipped her finger through its ring before scuttling ahead. "This way, please."

Above them, Vi heard voices—men and women with the gruff militaristic tone of soldiers. She heard the words "princess" and "here," but not enough else to make out much more. Vi frowned; they'd been outed. She was right from the start not to trust the staff. If she'd come out with her name to Erion sooner, perhaps they wouldn't have even had the six days that passed.

"Miss Yullia?" Samri whispered, barely more than a breath.

"We're coming," Jayme answered for both of them, pulling Vi along and saving her from her thoughts.

"Yes, sorry," Vi breathed back.

The hall finally opened into a dank basement. The light of the candle glistened off the slick sheen of damp on the walls and the slimy grime of the beams supporting the floor over their heads—a floor that rumbled and coughed dust with every heavy footfall.

"Down here." Samri pointed to a hatch before heaving it open. "Down the ladder—there's only one path. It'll take you out to the cliff. Head right and around, then down to the docks. Speak to no one but a man named Marcus at a ship called the *Dawn Skipper*."

Right. Down. Marcus. Dawn Skipper. Vi repeated the important parts in her mind and then gave a nod. It was easy enough to remember, given Jayme's personal inquiries had already led them to the vessel once.

"He'll help you from there."

"Thank you." Vi reached out and rested her hand on Samri's white knuckles where they gripped the top of the hatch.

"It wasn't me," she whispered as Jayme started down the ladder. "I wasn't the one to betray you, princess."

"I know. I believe you." Vi nodded and looked down at the ladder in the ominous black hole before her. Crouching, she gripped the top of the ladder and swung her feet down onto the third rung.

"*Fiarum Evantes*." *Eternal flame*, Vi roughly translated the Western phrase. Samri peered over the hatch. Uncle Jax had taught it to her and Vi had been delighted as a child to experiment with the strange words.

"*Kotun un Nox*," Vi responded quietly as the hatch closed overhead. *Guide us through the night.*

She clung to the ladder a moment, her heart racing. It was as if the organ chose now to decide to rush nerves through Vi's veins. All at once, everything felt real. This was her last chance to back down from her plan. If she pushed forward now, she would find herself on the Crescent Continent with no plan for how to get back.

Vi closed her eyes, though it made no difference in the darkness.

"A little light, Vi?" Jayme whispered up. "So we don't slip and die on this death ladder."

"Right." When she opened them once more, fire ignited over her shoulder, Vi gripped the spine of her journal between her teeth and they descended.

The ladder ended at the end of a tunnel pathway that left them with only one way to go. She walked with a hand along the wall until the glow of the flame merged with the light of moonlight shining off craggy rock. Then, Vi extinguished her fire, giving time for her eyes to adjust, and headed out toward the silver moonlight that bled through a crack at the end of the tunnel.

Squeezing herself through, Vi emerged onto a rocky path along the cliff-edge, just as Samri had described.

"Careful," Vi said over her shoulder. Jayme was also pushing herself though. "It's—"

"Narrow and windy." Jayme finished, clinging to the wall as she emerged.

The wind howled, threatening to rip Vi's cloak off. Holding on to it was no better, as it only became a sail that could pull her down onto the rocky waves below. She may have been better without a cloak, as Jayme was.

One hand on the stones next to her, Vi turned right and began walking downward.

They walked for nearly an hour, inching along narrow sections of stone and the remnants of water-worn pathways from centuries of storms. The cliff ledge above them gradually lowered, until it wrapped around and dropped the two women off on a small platform behind a rusted gate. Vi gave it a pull; while it squealed in protest, it wasn't locked.

"Put your hood up," Jayme suggested. "All the way, I'll keep a look out."

Adjusting her hood over her head and linking arms with Jayme, she stepped into the streets of Norin for the second time in two days, this time under vastly different circumstances.

"Do you know where we are?" Jayme asked, her voice still hushed and tense.

"Make a left here," Vi suggested. "Anywhere down and away from the Le'Dan manor is best."

Eventually, the streets connected with one she recognized from her earlier wanderings around the rich shopping district. Jayme seemed to recognize it as well, and with their location known, they immediately struck out on a direct course for the docks.

Sailors already bustled about, heaving huge nets and crab traps onto ships. Most of the energy was around what appeared to be fishing vessels, so her focus remained on the other, quieter ships.

The *Dawn Skipper* was as quiet as it had been the last time Vi had wandered here, and she approached the vessel with tense anticipation.

A man sat on the thick post beside the boat's lowered gangplank. He had his arms folded over his chest, chin almost lowered on them as he dozed while sitting upright. He jerked awake, and a moment later his eyes were clear and appraising.

"We're looking for Marcus." Vi kept her voice quiet.

"You found him." The man's voice reminded Vi of the rumbling crash of waves, and with it she felt a shift of magic about him. All in her head, perhaps... but she would bet he was a Waterrunner. "Are you the girls Lord Le'Dan mentoined? The daughters of one of his servants who wants to take up seafaring? Holly and Arwyn, was it?"

Holly—yet another new name. It made sense to retire Yullia. That name was likely to be discovered as her alias. She didn't want it to trail across the sea as well. Best to let Yullia die on the Main Continent.

She glanced at Jayme, wondering how her friend felt about her own false name. She didn't seem to be bothered in the slightest. "Arwyn," she said with a nod.

"And I'm Holly."

"Right, then, on the boat with you both." Marcus led them up the creaking gangplank that squeaked with every crest of the water beneath. Vi followed close behind, not looking back once. "The Lord was gracious enough to send your things ahead."

"He's a generous man," Vi murmured, inspecting the ship's main deck. There was a sloping rise to the quarterdeck in the back, but otherwise not much else. It was a noticeable contrast to the sumptuousness she'd come to associate with the Le'Dan aesthetic.

"While he made clear your goals for this voyage—" Marcus stopped speaking long enough to give them a look that spoke volumes, "I'll expect you to pull your weight while aboard."

"I'm stronger than I look," Vi assured him.

"Me as well."

He snorted. "I have men for the heavy lifting. How are you each with cooking? Or cleaning?"

Vi would've preferred the heavy lifting—at least it'd come with some direction, she assumed. Vi had never cleaned her own rooms or cooked her own food in her life. Still, she didn't want to make a fuss and was certain she could manage. "I can't speak to cooking, but how hard can scrubbing be?"

"Not cooking for you, then. Mare will still have the responsibility of ration management."

"I can help Mare," Jayme offered quickly. "I'm a confident cook."

Marcus kept his attention on Vi. "What did you do in service of Lord Le'Dan?"

She hadn't given much thought to her cover story. Then again, she hadn't exactly had much time to do so. She was supposed to be a daughter of a servant in service to the Le'Dans. Vi's mind scanned over her memories from the Le'Dan estate.

"I worked in the smithy." Holding out her hand, fingers skyward, the tips of her middle and index ignited like candles.

At nearly the same moment the man's hand clasped around hers, as though he were catching a fly. Confirming her earlier suspicion, water dripped from his palm; Vi's fire snuffed out. Marcus scowled at her.

"Are you mad?" He tightened his grip and Vi fought a wince. "Fire on a boat is a recipe for disaster."

"I had control," Vi insisted.

"Bloody Firebearer," Marcus muttered, throwing her hand aside. Vi wiped it on the inside of her cloak. "Not again on my vessel, understood?"

"Understood." Vi barely contained a scowl. He was helping her, and he owed her nothing. She was merely Holly, the servant's daughter, after all. She had no right or room for righteous indignation.

"What else can you do?"

"I'm very good with maps," Vi offered after thinking a moment. "I've taken notes on the seas." Vi lifted the journal she'd been clutching for emphasis.

That seemed to give him pause but in a positive way this time. "Is that so? Perhaps there'll be genuine use for you yet... but that's up to Kora."

She hoped so. She didn't like the idea of being nothing more than cargo. But if that was what she must be, she'd be a quiet, harmless lump and give them no reason to question handing her off at their destination... wherever that may be.

Under the quarterdeck, down a few steps, were three larger cabins. On either side were additional stairs leading into the hull of the ship where Vi heard movement—no doubt the crew. She looked down past the swaying lanterns, barely making out hammocks tied up. Behind one of the doors, she heard ruffling feathers and the occasional squawk.

"You'll be in here." Marcus started for one of the cabin doors.

"We have our own cabin?" Vi asked skeptically.

"Of course not." He laughed at the ridiculous notion. "Women share. Not putting them in the hold with the rest of the lads. We only have two other lasses aboard. Lucky for you, one of them is our navigator. Perhaps you'll make friends."

He opened the door to a dark room. There were bunks bolted down on either side of the narrow cabin, the two bottom beds occupied.

"Your stuffs up there." Marcus pointed toward the top bunk on the right. "And yours is there," he said to Jayme, pointing to the other. "But you can fight between you for who gets which top bunk."

"You are so annoyingly loud, Marcus," one of the two occupants of the room hissed from underneath her woolen blanket.

"Your new hands are here. Make sure they don't get in the way, ladies."

With a palm in the center of their backs, Marcus pushed her and Jayme into the cabin and shut the door. Neither of the women stirred again. Vi and Jayme shared a look.

"Try to get some sleep," Jayme whispered, leaning close.

Vi gave a small nod and was left climbing the bunk Marcus had said held her things. Sure enough, there was an unassuming sack. Within was an assortment of functional clothes that actually looked as if they'd fit. She glanced over to Jayme to find the woman was looking on in approval, having made a similar assessment of her own bundle.

Erion's tailors had worked quickly to learn their measurements. Vi scanned the few clothes, shoved them back into the bag, and tried to push every negative thought and worry away with them.

Her hands smoothed over the familiar leather of her journal. This was all she had now. The further she went, the more she would give up. That was the way it had to be.

Vi looked down at her wrist. The fingers of her right hand rested on the leather wrap that remained firmly affixed, rolling the wooden bead over the skin of her forearm. The bracelet Ellene had given her, a watch around her neck, a journal of her notes, and the knowledge of her true name was all Vi had of her past life.

She was willing to give everything to find her father and a cure for her mother, and help her people. Yet she'd always assumed "everything" meant death. She never thought she could give up her life while still breathing.

The sun was beginning to wink through the slats in the porthole cover. Dawn was breaking, and she'd barely slept. Mimicking Jayme, she used her sack of clothing as a pillow and tucked her cloak under her feet. One ear continued to listen to the docks, waiting for the sounds of Elecia's Western Guard coming for her… but it was quiet, only the sound of water sloshing against the hull breaking the regular hum of sailors moving about.

Vi's eyes met Jayme's across the narrow room. They seemed to glisten in the low light. Vi's insides twisted; she hoped her friend was not fighting back tears of regret.

Are you sure? Jayme mouthed slowly.

Yes, are you? Vi silently said back.

Yes. There was no hesitation on Jayme's face.

Pride and admiration for her friend filled her. No matter what, Jayme was on Vi's side. The further they ventured, the more Vi realized the depth of her friend's loyalty.

With that not-insignificant comfort, Vi closed her eyes and worked to push all doubt from her mind. They had passed the point of no return.

All she could do for the moment was sleep.

26

"U P WITH YOU, ladies!" Banging on the door woke them all. "We're casting off!"

"We didn't have nearly enough time for this turn-around," a Western woman grumbled in a thick accent. Vi blinked down at her sleepily. Jayme was already stirring in the bunk above.

"Greed of lords," the woman in the bunk below Vi rasped. She was the first to stand, pulling a loose-fitting shirt over golden curls. She turned to face Vi, piercing her with her icy blue Southern eyes. "You, new girl, you're from the Le'Dan manor, right?"

"Yes." Vi pushed herself into a seated position—or rather hunched, as there wasn't much room for her to sit fully upright on the top bunk.

"You hear why we're being sent off again so fast?"

"No," Vi lied and shook her head.

"You?" The blonde turned her attention to Jayme. "You were the one coming around and asking if we were all ready to shove off at a moment's notice."

"I had a suspicion… But nothing more concrete." Jayme was beginning to dress, so Vi followed her lead.

"Of course neither of them knows anything." The Western woman stood, tying an apron around her waist. "You think Erion Le'Dan would tell that to the help?" Her dark eyes shifted to Vi, then Jayme. "I'm Mare, by the way."

"Oh, right, I'm Kora." The Southerner strapped a rectangular pouch to her thigh, belting it also around her waist. It had a sleek sheen to it, almost like oil.

"Holly," Vi said.

"Arwyn."

"Speaking of help," Vi slid off her bed, landing somewhat ungracefully. She regretted it near instantly; the floor was cramped with three people. "I heard one of you is the navigator?"

"That'd be me." Kora was craning her neck to look up to Vi, who was a good hand taller even though she was also likely a few years younger.

"I'd like to offer my services to you."

"You?"

"I'm good with maps and I've been studying the tides."

"Navigating is more than maps." Kora gave a bemused huff. "And it's cute you think that studying tides and being out on them are comparable experience."

"Well, I'd like to learn."

"I'm not here to babysit."

"Well, you have fun with that, Kora." Vi didn't like the snicker at the end of Mare's statement as she quickly departed the room.

"Wait." Jayme hopped off her bunk, hurrying after Mare. "I'm to help you…"

"I'm not asking to be babysat," Vi insisted, focusing on Kora and leaving Jayme to her own struggles with Mare. "I can help, I promise. I'm sure I can be of some use."

"Have you ever charted a course before?"

"Not entirely…" She had navigated through Norin—did that count? Vi didn't think Kora would think so.

"Have you ever identified channel walls based on surface currents?"

"No, but—"

"Adjusted based on wind or charted on stars alone?"

Of course she hadn't. Vi wanted to scream. Just taking a short nap before the ship came to life had been more time on the ocean than Vi had ever spent. "I've read many books and studied seafaring charts. I have the foundation. I'll learn quickly."

"This isn't—" Kora's next rebuttal was cut off by a booming shout from the top deck.

"Cast off!" Marcus's voice seemed to rattle the ship. If it hadn't, the purposeful footsteps of every man and woman aboard certainly did.

"Where are you going?" Vi asked, hastening after Kora.

"To the quarterdeck to get our heading." Vi started to follow eagerly behind but Kora rounded on her. "Don't leave your things about—tie them up like your friend did or they'll be scattered across the room with the rocking of the ship. Mare and I won't hesitate to step on them."

Vi dashed back into the room, scrambling up to her bed. Taking Kora's instruction to heart, she used the draw ties on the sacks she was given to string it to one of the supports of her bunk. Vi hastily tucked her blanket around the lumpy mattress, hoping it'd be taut enough to hold. By the time she jumped down again, Kora was gone, leaving Vi to emerge into the sunlight of the main deck alone.

People bustled about, curling ropes like giant serpents as they were thrown off from the pillars the vessel had been tied to on the docks. The last of some large crates were carried up the gangplank, carried by four straining men.

"Move, girl," one of them commanded, waving her out of the way. Vi obliged and they passed, taking the crate down into the cabin right across from the stairs on the first of the lower decks.

She searched for Kora, and found her on the quarterdeck talking to Marcus.

"… we'll be heading to Beauty's Bend." Marcus stopped short, following Kora's piercing gaze.

"What do you want?" Kora asked.

"I want to be of help."

"You want to be of help?" Vi nodded and Kora continued, "Then go down and help Mare."

"But I—"

"It is not too late to throw you off the boat," Marcus cautioned. "Listen to your betters, girl."

Vi backed away slowly, turned, and walked without any haste, hoping to catch more of their conversation. But she couldn't; their voices were too low.

Just before Vi could disappear below deck, the ship began to move. It crept forward so slowly away from the dock that Vi thought they were merely adrift. However, the distinct thrum of magic told her differently.

She looked back up at the quarterdeck, Marcus stood at the back end, radiating power. *He's using magic to push the boat*, Vi realized. Vi rushed over to the side of the vessel where the dock had been. Other Waterrunners were there, using their own powers to protect the pylons of the dock from Marcus's currents.

Vi stared in wonder at the sight. There was always a new, clever application for magic. Every sorcerer wore a bored look on their face, but performed tasks Vi assumed would require extreme focus. It was just a testament to their training and experience.

As soon as the vessel was maneuvered far enough away from the docks and other boats, a *pop* filled the air, and the sails snapped open to capture the wind.

They began to pick up real momentum then and the port of Norin, greatest port in the world, was swiftly being left behind her in a trail of white foam. Vi watched as her view was limited to nearby ships, and a few buildings, slowly expanding as more and more distance was gained. Just like that, she was off, out to sea… doing what had seemed impossible.

"What did you feel, Father?" Vi whispered softly to herself, a hand reaching up to hold the watch around her neck. Her father had sailed away from Norin; he had watched this same sight as he left behind the world he knew and loved in a last-ditch effort to save it. Was he afraid? Did he look back and think of her mother, their family? Or did he only press forward?

"Watch yourself." A sailor carrying a length of rope over his shoulder grumbled as he passed.

It snapped Vi back to reality and she turned for the opening below the quarterdeck. There would be no fanfare, no one waving after her from the docks. There would not be an Imperial farewell party as she was certain there had been for her father. Yet something about the quiet departure sat low in her stomach, making her uneasy. Without so much as a word of goodbye, she'd left her home—her continent, with no immediate plans to return.

Vi swallowed down the ill feelings and headed below to find Mare and Jayme. Her father hadn't aborted his mission; neither would she.

The women weren't in their cabin, so Vi explored the lowest deck of the *Dawn Skipper*. Descending the narrow flight of stairs, Vi's head almost scraped the ceiling—which was also the underside of the main deck. A few of the portholes were opened, allowing in just enough light to see by and more than enough for salt mist to dampen the room. At the very back of the boat were Mare, Jayme, and two other sailors, fighting to tie off crates.

"Can I help you?" Vi asked aloud, not wanting to startle anyone. They hadn't seemed to hear her approaching.

Mare wheeled in place, hands on her hips. "Kora's trying to saddle me with *both* the green gills now?"

Vi didn't know what "green gills" meant, exactly, but she could assume it wasn't a term of endearment. "Kora said I could help here."

"Go back and tell her you're her responsibility."

"She's going to say no."

"Don't let her get under your skin," Mare said with a shake of her head. "She's hard on new sailors. Especially ones who she thinks are encroaching on her job. She's fairly new herself, and we put her through a pretty bad gauntlet. She's likely just over-eager to put someone else through it."

"I don't want her job and I can put up with whatever tests she wants to throw my way," Vi insisted, barely stopping herself from saying that even if she did, it wouldn't matter because she'd be off the ship in a few days or weeks—however long it took. "I just want to be of use."

"All right, help us tie these in place. Your friend is good at knots—she can help if you need."

"She's my sister," Jayme corrected, and Vi realized she hadn't done the same for Mare earlier.

"I don't care if she's your lover's cousin once removed. All I care about is that these crates don't go sliding into our friends if we hit rough water in the night."

Doing as she was told, Vi began to slide rope through rings bolted to the floors and walls, wrapping them around the boxes. Her knot skills were quickly identified as sub-par, but the group didn't immediately send her away, especially thanks to Jayme's help—which was now a small victory. So she remained, clinging with every lurch of the ship to the same ropes she was securing, and trying to learn the knots Mare showed her.

"… we're headed out again so quickly?"

The conversation continued around Vi as she worked.

"Maybe she heard?"

"Holly? That's her name, right?"

Vi struggled with her current knot, trying to get it to hold as Mare's could.

"She doesn't know either." It was Jayme's voice that finally broke her from her thoughts. "And she's not deaf or mute."

"What, sorry?"

"They were saying your name, scatterbrain." Mare gave her a thump on the head with her fist. Vi was certain that it was intended to be playful, but Mare had arms like tree limbs and she was left rubbing the crown of her head. "They're asking about why we're leaving so soon. Your sister and I already said you don't know."

"Oh, yes, who knows why we're off so soon." Vi gave another tug on her ropes, looking at the other crates. They all seemed secure—and not a moment too soon, as the ship lurched again.

"*We?* You just got here." One of the Western men scoffed. "Don't go talking like you're one of the crew."

Vi pursed her lips to keep herself from objecting. She didn't need to be one of the crew. It didn't matter if they counted her among them or not. In fact, the less they liked her, the less they'd be inclined to even think about her when she disappeared. It was better this way.

"All I know is we're headed to a place called Beauty's Bend." She'd never seen such a place marked on a map before.

"Beauty's Bend?" One of the Western men said a hasty string of words in the old language of Mashan. "Out of all the spots… we're headed *there*?"

"You're sure?" Mare grabbed her shoulder.

"It's what I heard Kora and Marcus talking about on deck. But I don't know anything more."

"They're going to get us killed."

"Cargo must be important," Mare reasoned.

"Get us killed for cargo, even worse." The two men walked ahead, griping, Mare just behind them.

Vi and Jayme brought up the rear. She stared at Mare's back, debating asking why Beauty's Bend was so important. She'd find out soon enough, she supposed.

"Beauty's Bend is in a dangerous spot," Jayme whispered, slowing her feet. The rest of the crew ascended the stairs, leaving them to themselves.

"Why?"

"Imagine the Main Continent here." Jayme held up her right hand. "And the Crescent continent is here." Holding up her left hand and making a C shape with it, she angled it slightly to the left of her right.

"Yes, I know the layout without the hand symbols." Vi looked at her friend dumbly.

"Well, they help me so please indulge me." Jayme rolled her eyes. "The barrier islands arc around the Crescent Continent."

"Is Beauty's Bend here?" Vi asked, pointing at the center of the arc between the two continents.

"No… Beauty's Bend is up here." She pointed to the top of the arc. "It's the curve around the barrier islands."

"Up by Blue Lagoon? Or Teeter Island?"

"I guess, if that's what their names are." Jayme shrugged. "I've only heard it called Beauty's Bend. But sailors have their own codes and ways. Many times they don't want the names they call things to be on maps. Especially if they're dealing in more… illicit goods."

"Then how do *you* know it?" Vi was forced to ask.

"That's part of why I was out talking to people." Jayme gave her a friendly nudge, starting for the stairs. "You collect all the book knowledge, and I collect the information on the streets."

"Well, thank you for that, because my book knowledge is doing little for us right now." Vi caught up in a few wide steps. "Why do you think we're going all the way up to Beauty's Bend? That's beyond the end of the Main Continent, isn't it?"

Mare emerged from the cabin right as they were rounding the landing. "Because there are storms and worse between the barrier islands," Mare said, answering even if she hadn't been asked. "At the top of Beauty's Bend is the Blue Lagoon, perfect for trading."

"So it *is* Blue Lagoon." Vi glanced at Jayme with a smug smile.

"Whatever it is we're delivering must be important," Mare mused aloud as they started up the stairs.

"Why's that?" Jayme asked.

"Because Beauty's Bend is one of the few places we dare to drop anchor, rather than trading on planks or tossing between vessels or on rowboats. It's a hike to get to and we're sitting ducks if anyone should catch us. Whatever it is better be worth it."

Vi held her tongue, barely stopping herself from reassuring Mare that it was, indeed, worth it to find their Emperor.

"Aren't you worried about pirates?" Jayme asked.

"The pirates have to catch us first." Mare grinned. "And they haven't yet."

27

Vi HAD WANTED to make herself useful aboard the ship. Her body wanted to spill her guts over the deck railing.

Vi: zero. Body: one.

She spent the majority of the first two days trying to find her sea legs—they were determined to be elusive, and the consequences were an upset stomach unlike any Vi had ever endured. In turn, her suffering made her an object of ridicule to the majority of the crew, who seemed to think it was hilarious she was so affected by the rolling tides. Kora and Mare had kicked her out of their room, leaving Vi to curl up in a corner of the main deck to sleep.

Originally, Jayme had gone out to keep her company, but Vi sent her back below. She was a mess, and there was no reason for them both to suffer just because she couldn't seem to manage the swaying of the boat. At least from time to time, Vi got to watch Jayme being helpful to the rest of the crew in her stead.

She watched the world drift by. The sails billowed with the wind, adjusting as the ship made its heading northward.

The Main Continent was little more than a distant blur on the horizon, but Vi watched as it transformed from the rocky flat Waste to shrub trees, and then the towering jungle giants that were the northern forests. She'd gone south, and west, to go north again, to ultimately go west. If she were drawing her own course to Meru on a map, it would be the most inefficient zigzag.

But making it was all that mattered.

A biscuit appeared in Vi's field of vision.

"Hadn't seen you turn over in a while," Jayme said, chewing through her own ration. "Thought you may want to give this a go again."

Vi looked at the food warily. She had tried some of the doughy bread last night only to have it throw her stomach in full revolt. But the near-constant heaving throughout the day left her exhausted; combined with the hollow feeling in her stomach, Vi felt weaker than she ever had before.

"I suppose it can't hurt." She took the food, taking a mouse-like nibble of its edge.

"As long as you don't throw it up on me."

Vi gave a small snort of laughter. "I'll do my best."

Vi had expected Jayme to leave, but she sat on the deck instead, stretching out her legs. Her hair had been done in a tight coif, identical to how Vi had seen Mare wearing hers. Vi's own hair was a bit of a mess, slipping from its braids, but they were still tight enough to keep it out of her face—and safe from whatever *projections* her stomach offered.

She took another bite of biscuit, pleased to find it settling well in her stomach.

"Mare do the braid for you?" Jayme nodded, tearing a hunk of her food. "Glad they're being nice to one of us."

"They're nice enough to you," she said through her biscuit. "They're risking their lives for you, after all."

"Yeah, but not by conscious choice—they don't know they are." Vi shrugged.

"Does that make it less of a risk?" Jayme looked out over the deck and Vi's attention followed.

Two men leaned against the opposite railing, talking. The sun was hanging low in the sky, casting the whole ocean ablaze behind them. A few more milled about the quarterdeck with Mare, Marcus, and Kora. Vi counted ten people in total, including her and Jayme, which meant the other three men were below getting sleep before the night's watch.

"Don't let them dig too deep into you."

"Easy for you to say. You seem to be a natural at this whole seafaring thing." Vi rested her head against the railing, watching the sea speeding by. The *Dawn Skipper* was a nimble vessel, fast as far as Vi was concerned, though she had little to compare it to. She took another bite of her biscuit, mentally willing her stomach to remain calm. She was already feeling stronger.

"Kind of glad I am, actually," Jayme confessed.

"A lot easier than what I'm going through."

"They say you should be through the worst of it." Jayme gave her a pat on the back. "That it takes about two days."

"Mother, I hope so."

"I'm honestly surprised you made it this far." The statement was stripped back and bare—a brutal honesty only Jayme could conjure.

"Really?"

"You've lived a life of luxury and safety. I wasn't sure if you had it in you to cast that aside."

Vi gave a soft laugh. "Thanks for that." She took another large bite of her biscuit.

"You can't blame me."

"Maybe a little. I thought you knew me better than that."

"Maybe we both still have a lot to learn about each other." Jayme had a relaxed smile on her face as she looked out to sea. "A bit of salt and distance does us both good, I think."

"It could certainly be worse." Vi's eyes swept across the deck once more, lingering on Kora and Marcus. They were talking eagerly over the map Kora held. A cartography tool drifted over the map, passed from hand to hand as they discussed. Vi had such tools once, when she was still safe and ignorant. "Except for her."

"She's not so bad when you get to know her." Jayme saw what drew her attention. "I found out she's from Oparium." Southern port, closest to the capital; Vi visualized it on a map. "On a ship of mostly Western sailors, she has a lot to prove."

"Shouldn't someone from Oparium have as much salt in their blood as someone from Norin?"

"You know how the West can be when it comes to outsiders." Jayme shrugged.

"How every region of the Empire can be…" Vi frowned.

"She says we have another day, maybe two until we're there."

"Soon enough." Vi looked out across the ocean, leaning forward to press her forehead against the railing once more.

"You're not going to puke again are you?"

"No, give me another biscuit."

Jayme handed her another and Vi ate it, determined not to be bested by the sea.

It was the first crack of lightning that jarred Vi from sleep. She was upright in her bed in an instant, but still seemed to be the slowest of her group. The door was open, Mare and Kora a blur, Jayme behind them.

"Strike topmasts!" Marcus shouted as he ran out of his cabin behind them. "We're running the storm!"

Sailors were quick, pouring out from below. Determined not to be the last on deck, Vi rushed out after them. The wind howled and carried the fresh smell of rain, but the storm had yet to reach the vessel. It was a swell blotting out the stars in the distance.

A brilliant flash raced across the sky, splintering an uncountable number of times and lighting up the darkness for a brief moment before thunder rushed in. Vi stared up at the sky, dazed. She did not see the ocean, or the boat, but the end of the world drawing ever closer.

Had the lightning been red? Had she imagined it?

Another bright flare of lightning. Vi stared, both eyes open, unblinking. The thunder boomed, rolling with her stomach.

"Red lightning?" one of the sailors shouted to no one in particular—confirming this was not a natural phenomenon to them either.

"I don't care if it's red, blue, green, or pink. We're dead if we're caught in it," Marcus shouted.

It was red because Lord Raspian was gaining power—Vi was sure. What Taavin said was true. The dark god had been set free, and the world was slowly falling under his control as he gained strength.

"How can I help?" Vi pushed herself into motion. Gawking would do nothing.

"Out of the way, girl!"

Vi stepped back, heeding his warning. Other soldiers worked the ropes attached to the sail, wrestling with them in the wind.

Vi sprinted, narrowly dodging a rope snapping against the mast, to stand next to Jayme and Mare at the other end of the deck. Marcus had said to strike the sails. Doing so would drop the boom. Vi held out her arms.

"Vi—" Jayme didn't have time to finish her thought.

The heavy weight of the already rain-slick sail and wooden rigging slammed into them, nearly taking them both out. Vi knew bruises coated her arms, but somehow she managed with Jayme's help. But even her friend was struggling.

"Faster, crew!" Marcus shouted over the increase in wind. "If we don't reef the sails, we're not riding this!"

"I got you two." Mare's voice appeared over Vi's shoulder. Her thick arms strained as she helped Vi and Jayme cast the topsail aside. It was just in time to ready a second one.

"Pull slack from the reef line!" One man shouted.

"Holly, help me secure this!" Mare dashed across the deck, not even looking over her shoulder to see if Vi was following. "Hold the line."

Vi did as she was told, arms straining as the damp rope bit into her palms. She felt the muscles in her back strain as another gust of wind threatened to capsize the boat. The waves were picking up now, their white crests crashing nearly on deck, sloshing foam around her feet and the rest of the crew's.

"You're set, Holly."

"Where's my navigator?" Marcus shouted from the quarterdeck. Magic was heavy in the air around him and the raindrops caught on his power, slowing mid-air before falling limply straight to the ground.

"Here!" Kora called back, sprinting from the rigging she'd been helping other sailors with. Vi watched as she jumped to the quarterdeck.

Vi took a hesitant step forward. Kora had made it clear she couldn't be of any help. Shaking her head, Vi turned, looking for Jayme. Her friend was clinging to a rope other sailors were in the process of tying off. Vi hastened over to help where she knew she'd be of use.

"Give me a heading," Marcus shouted over the wind, loud enough for the whole deck to hear. "I can't see shite in this rain and dark."

The rope they'd been struggling with fastened, Vi looked in the opposite direction of the storm. She'd spent the day watching the Main Continent dwindle away. She would've seen clouds in the sky... Sure enough, it was still cloudless. That meant Meru was to their left, Solaris their right; if they were headed up to the Blue Grotto, they were moving northeast, and she'd lost sight of the Main Continent just before going to bed... given their speed...

Her mind whirred, then Vi shouted on instinct, "We're close to the Shattered Inlet."

Kora paused, looking down at her. She had a map that was quickly turning to pulp in the wind and rain. Her eyes narrowed slightly at Vi and Vi merely waited for her judgment. Either she'd believe her, or not.

"Hard to starboard!" Kora commanded to Marcus and the crew on deck. "Shattered Inlet at port!"

Magic filled the air. A sailor worked the helm and Marcus lent his skills as a Waterrunner to the waves below. The ship lurched forward.

"Holly, up here," Kora commanded. Vi was on the quarterdeck in an instant. The woman was still wary of her, but staying alive was winning out over any need to exert dominance. "Marcus says you're a Firebearer."

Vi nodded. She was... more or less.

"We need light. Get to the bow and cast your fire ahead of us. I need to see where the rocks are." Even though they were standing next to each other, Kora still had to shout to be heard over the howling wind.

"Understood!" Vi jumped back down to the main deck, slipped, recovered, and worked her way to the bow. Sailors cleared a path for her and Vi slammed against the railing as she slid to a stop at the very front of the vessel.

Vi cast out her hand and, for once, didn't even second guess her magic doing exactly as she commanded. In the distance, far enough away from the ship and high enough that they wouldn't speed into it, a ball of flame erupted in the night. It cast the black waters in an angry red glow, not unlike the ominous red lightning of the storm quickly closing in on them.

Glistening jagged rocks jutted up from the ocean—the Shattered Inlet, just as Vi suspected.

"I want sailors on the rails!" Marcus bellowed.

"Holly, you do that again. The rest of you look for rocks," Kora ordered.

Vi did as she was told. She was too soaked, exhausted, and frantic to even worry about losing control of her magic. She cast it out like she would for Lightspinning, but unlike Lightspinning, she relied solely on the instincts her father and Uncle Jax had instilled in her from the first moment she'd manifested.

"Rocks at starboard!"

The tiller squealed due to the rainwater coating it as the helmsman pulled on it, yanking the rudder below. Vi gripped the deck rail, her feet slipping. She squinted into the rain and cast out another ball of flame.

If they were in the maw of the Shattered Inlet now, then the Greater Atoll was right before them—Little Brother Bay next to it. Vi threw fire with every thought, clinging to the rail with her free hand, feet sliding beneath her as the ship jostled. If they made it through this, they'd have a straight shot to Blue Lagoon.

"Hard to starboard!" Kora commanded. "Correct back!"

The whole crew worked the vessel flawlessly. They navigated the perilous rocks of the Shattered Inlet, racing to the sea beyond. The *Dawn Skipper* rode the swift currents of wind pushed out by the storms and the powerful currents Marcus helped create with magic. By the time they broke free of the worst of it, the outer edge of the sky had turned a soft purple.

"Get the sails back up, lads and lassies, the sky seems to be calming," Marcus ordered. His voice didn't have the same bass as it usually did, the harshness of the gravel in his throat worn by a night of rain and magical exertion.

Vi reached up, breathless, grabbing the watch at her neck. *They'd done it*. Her magic, her maps, had played a role. She couldn't wait to tell Taavin. Vi slumped against the railing in relief.

A heavy hand fell on her back, clapping her once right in the center. Vi jumped at the contact, spinning to see Kora—she hadn't even heard the woman approach. "You were right. You do know your maps well for a landlubber."

"Thanks." It was high praise, especially coming from Kora.

"Now, excuse me while I see how off-course this made us so I can properly communicate how late we'll be to our business partners," she said dryly as she promptly turned and started below deck.

"You're welcome," Vi muttered under her breath and avoided pointing out that they hadn't really gotten off-course. Kora just wasn't going to allow herself to give Vi a genuine compliment.

"Don't give her that look. I think it was progress." Jayme approached, slinging her arm around Vi's shoulders. "Now, let's go below deck too, get dry, and get some sleep. You look dead on your feet."

"I feel it." Vi gave her friend a once-over. There was some expected bruising and rope burn, but no major injuries. "You don't look much better."

Jayme gave a low chuckle.

As they headed for their cabin, Kora emerged from the room opposite. She wore a thick leather glove, protecting her flesh from the talons of a mighty bird. Around the bird's foot was a small scroll.

Vi paused, watching as she passed.

"Vi, what is it?" Jayme asked, stopping as well.

Vi continued to stare at the bird. It was a massive thing, ruddy brown. As if sensing her attention, its head swiveled back and the bird let out a loud caw. She wasn't surprised Kora kept birds to communicate with other vessels—it made perfect sense, actually. She also shouldn't be surprised that the bird was a desert eagle. They were likely common in Norin.

But she would've sworn it had the same bright, steely eyes as the bird on the windowsill in Inton.

28

Vi was on deck shortly after dawn.

She was the second to arrive after the early call of "Land!" was shouted across the vessel. Vi raced up to the bow, straining over the railing, as if by leaning slightly closer she could urge them forward.

Jayme's hands appeared on the railing next to her and, for a while, they let the commotion on deck occur around them. Vi's heart was racing. Every step she took on this journey felt like a new point of no return.

"So, that's it," Jayme said, finally.

"That's it." Vi affirmed. As they continued to near, the isle grew. It looked much like Vi had imagined it: a sloping rise in the land, dotted with tall, wide-leafed trees and dense brush. The beach was white sand and curved around what Vi knew to be a sheltered grotto.

"I hope we haven't missed our counterparts…" Jayme murmured softly. "I want this all to go smoothly."

"You and me both."

"Ready the rowboat," Marcus ordered, stepping out into the sunlight on deck. "You three, get out the goods."

Mare was close behind him. "I'm going to try to get two new bladders of fresh water."

"You're not going ashore." Marcus turned to Vi. "They're in the boat with Kora."

"What? The green gills? Why them?" Mare pestered. "Isn't it my turn?"

"I don't think I opened the matter for discussion," Marcus said with a low growl. "You're getting one."

"We'll be in and out. I don't want us anchored longer than we must be here. You'll go ashore somewhere else if we need water."

"Fine," Mare huffed, walking over to them. Vi was expecting to have to defend herself, but was pleasantly surprised when Mare merely lounged on the railing. "You two see any red flowers, spiky pedals, almost fuzzy centers, grab them. They're called Fire Flowers and taste just like fresh cranberries."

Jayme and Vi shared a look.

"Sure," Vi merely agreed. It didn't matter she wouldn't be coming back. Mare was hardly the first person to whom she'd made a promise she had no intention of keeping.

The ship coasted into a sheltered lagoon.

The sails hung limply as they were stowed, loose rigging keeping them from catching the wind for the time being. A loud clanging noise brought Vi starboard. The anchor plunged into the icy clear waters with a splash and the whole ship rattled as the heavy chain clanked into the deep.

"You ready?" Jayme asked from her side, hand on the hilt of her sword.

"I think so." Vi started toward the rowboat. "I hope you don't have to use that."

"You and me both," Jayme mumbled again.

The rowboat was positioned just on the other side of an open gate in the railing. Vi recognized a large chest, already loaded in the boat's center. Two men were in the boat, working the ropes and levers. Kora sat in the bow.

"In with you both." Marcus nodded to the boat. Then, turning to Kora, he added. "You're sure about handling the negotiations? Gray Sail merchants can be shrewd."

"I'll be fine." Kora assured him. "I'll also have Earnt and Varus with me, too." She motioned to the two men in the rowboat, completely ignoring Jayme as she clamored in, sword and all.

"I heard Mare giving some ration requests as well," Marcus continued.

"I'm sure she wants the usual. All will be well," she reassured Marcus. "In and out."

"In and out," he repeated with a nod. "We'll start hoisting the anchor when we see you coming back."

After that, it was impossible to hold a conversation as the levers clanked and ropes creaked. Marcus walked away from the railing before they were even halfway down the side of the vessel.

"Sit there," Kora commanded, pointing to the crate. She pointed to Jayme next. "You, next to me. And stay out of the way."

Vi did as she was told, running her hands over the polished wood of the crate. With each shift of the rowboat she could hear a soft clanking, and the heavy fall into the water almost confirmed her assumption.

"That's full of gold and gems, isn't it?" Vi asked as the two men situated themselves side by side at the center of the boat to row. Kora sat at the bow, Jayme at her side. Vi couldn't help but wonder how much gold transporting a princess was worth. She couldn't imagine there was much precedent.

"It doesn't concern you what's in there."

"I know this isn't a normal trade." She struggled to keep her voice level—factual.

"You do, don't you…" Kora paused briefly, not more than half a breath, but time seemed to slow and hang on her next word. "Princess?"

Vi's nails dug into the crate slightly. "So Marcus told you?" She glanced at the other two men on the rowboat, trusting Kora to hear the unspoken question.

"Have to know what we're trading in order to negotiate." The island was growing behind Kora.

"How long have you known?"

"Long enough," she answered cryptically. "Who would've thought that a man like Marcus would give in to human trafficking? It looks like the times are driving everyone to extreme measures."

"It's not trafficking," Vi insisted quickly; she'd not have Marcus's reputation ruined on her behalf. "I asked to go on this journey."

"Well, I suppose that could be true. You're not trying to barter for your life at the first possible moment." Kora looked her up and down. "But why would you go so far from home, to a continent you've been led to believe harbors the source of the White Death?"

"I have to." Vi stopped herself there, heeding Romulin's words. She owed no one any more explanation than she desired to give.

Kora opened her mouth to speak again, but paused, cut short by an icy gust of wind accompanied by the grinding of sand as the hull of the boat met beach. She stood in the bow, looking back toward the *Dawn Skipper*. Vi was about to follow her gaze when the wind howled yet again, carrying on it the sound of shouting.

The unexpected gale drew her simple-spun clothes taut over her shoulders and set her hands instantly to shaking. In the span of time it took for them to row to the shore, the temperature had dropped precipitously. It should be impossible—they'd headed further north, not south. It should be warmer, not colder.

A speck of white landed on her knee.

Vi pressed her finger into it, watching as it melted into a damp spot on her leggings. *Melted.* Another damp spot joined the first, and then another. *It was snowing*, Vi realized in amazement. She'd spent her entire life without ever seeing the strange phenomena known as snow—ice falling from the sky in fairy-like motes of wonder.

Raising her eyes, momentarily entranced by the dance of flurries, Vi returned to the present just in time to see Kora tossing the body of one of the crew overboard. Jayme was in the process of slitting the second man's throat.

What?

What was happening? Vi was too dazed to even scream as Jayme let the body fall heavily over the side of the boat, blood swirling in the surf around them, staining the sand. She stared at her friend as she wiped her blade on the dead man's shirt.

"What?" Vi whispered, looking right at Jayme. Her eyes... were not the eyes Vi had come to know. They were eyes she'd never seen before. Brutal, cunning, careless.

"You shouldn't have gone so far from home." Kora shook her head as a mother would to a toddler who had stepped out of line. "Fool of a princess. It's in your blood, though. Not one Solaris has been particularly bright."

Vi opened her mouth to speak, then closed it again. There was a broken pathway between her mouth and her mind—a bridge that had collapsed, and she was now being swept away in the river rushing beneath it. She looked down at the bodies, another shiver running up her spine. Her eyes returned to Jayme, who had yet to say a word.

"Jayme—" Vi's dazed question was cut off by the sound of wood groaning.

She turned in the rowboat, nearly tipping over the side, in time to witness the end of the *Dawn Skipper*. A ramrod of bright blue ice had impaled the smaller vessel, cleaving it in two. Men and women—mere specks—jumped off the larger ship flying sky-blue sails. A frosty mist poured out from the main deck, as though the entire vessel was made of ice sweating in the northern heat.

"No..." Vi whispered. She watched as men and women jumped from the ramrod onto the sinking *Dawn Skipper*. No one would be left alive.

"I was just like you." Kora's voice was closer than she would've liked. But Vi didn't move away. She merely stared at the magic that seemed to writhe in the air covering the ice ship. "The first time I saw the *Stormfrost*."

"*Stormfrost*," Vi repeated blankly, watching the carnage unfold. The crew made quick work of their deed before returning to the boat.

"The vessel of the legendary pirate, Adela."

29

"JAYME." VI'S EYES darted between her and Kora. "Now would be a good time."

"A good time to what?" Jayme arched her eyebrows.

"Oh, she thinks you're going to kill me." Kora laughed, hopping out of the rowboat and almost skipping in the surf. "She and I go way back, almost as long as you two."

"What?" Vi looked to Jayme. Her friend—*friend?*—stood rigid, sword in hand, looking down at her. "What is she talking about? Aren't you... You killed Marcus's man to help us barter, right?"

There was a hairline fracture cracking Vi's understanding. Nothing made sense. The world was ice around her. It fell on her shaking shoulders, collecting in white drifts, melting through her clothes, soaking into her skin, and refreezing around her heart.

Jayme slowly raised her sword, pointing it at Vi.

"Get out of the boat," she commanded, her voice low and dangerous.

"What're you doing?" Vi didn't move.

"Out of the boat."

"Jayme—"

"Do it!" Her friend snapped. "I didn't work this hard to get you this far, only to kill you because you're just so bloody stupid."

"What are you talking about?" Vi whispered, standing slowly in an effort to perhaps coerce the woman into giving her answers through her compliance. "Get me this far?"

"Aren't you supposed to be friends?" Kora called from the beach. "Friends don't screw up friend's plots."

"Out." Jayme flicked her sword through the air, and Vi obliged, too stunned to do anything else.

The water made her suck in air as it splashed up to her thighs. It was like dunking in a vat of ice. Shivering and soaked from the waist down, Vi moved up the beach. Jayme sloshed behind her. When they were both on solid ground, Vi turned, surprised to find the sword point so close to her.

"Tell me what's going on," Vi demanded firmly.

"I don't take orders from you, or anyone else in your family, anymore." Jayme tilted her head, looking up at Vi in sheer rage. In that moment, Vi really wouldn't have been surprised if she shoved the sword clear through her torso.

"What's going on, Jayme. Tell me?" Vi dropped her voice to a whisper, glancing at Kora. She was waving her arms, signaling to the icy vessel at the entrance of the lagoon. "She won't hear now and—"

"Oh, I don't care if Kora hears. Kora knows everything. You're the one who's in the dark, Vi."

"What's... everything?" Vi whispered. Her voice was so tiny, just like Vi felt in that moment.

"See, Adela charged me with finding some new goodies..." Kora walked over. She could hear after all. "I docked up on Solaris and began listening around. Worked in the docks for a bit, got close to the Le'Dans—that was fortuitous. But it was when I was in the Crossroads that I really had my breakthrough with Jayme here." Kora rested her hands lightly on Jayme's shoulders.

"You... you're the woman Andru saw in the Crossroads." Vi looked from Kora to Jayme. "You said you had no idea what he was talking about."

"I lied," Jayme said it with an incredulous shake of her head. "You're so damn gullible, you believed me when it came to just about everything."

"I believed you because I thought you were my friend!" Vi didn't know if her voice broke in anger, or pain—likely both. The icy grip on her heart was spreading, building a cage. Every beat was slower, more strained. When it stopped, Vi didn't know what would happen.

"I was never your friend. I was the *help*. Your messenger. Your errand girl."

"I never saw you that way," Vi said gently, pleading. It was already far too late. She was pleading for a girl—a woman—who had never really existed in the first place.

"You're a Solaris. Everyone is your plaything, your toy," Jayme seethed.

"So Jayme began selling us information," Kora continued. "I hear Adela pays better than Solaris. I can't say I'm surprised; her coffers are likely deeper."

"My letters..." Vi looked slowly from Kora to Jayme. The world was blurring into gray under the squalling snow. Or maybe the world had been so gray and void of color all along. "You shared my letters?"

"It was easy enough. All I needed was to have a Solaris seal made, see to it that some official sealing wax fell into my hands. I had enough time in the palace and, like I told you once, us poor folk stick together."

"Those..." She felt violated, exposed, drawn out for the world to see. Her thoughts—raw emotions—poured into words only for her brother's, mother's, or father's eyes, cast out to the world. "Those were *mine*... How could you?"

"Like I said, easy enough." There was no emotion there. Not one ounce of regret.

"That was how we knew the Emperor Solaris was finally leaving the protection of his Empire, the course he'd be charting, and the vessel he'd be on."

"And now I'll bring Adela his heir, and she will make me one of her crew," Jayme said proudly. It was the pride that finally snapped something in Vi, the infuriating smugness that betrayed her frostbitten, blackened heart.

"How could you?" Her voice rose to a near scream. "You sold my father to them? That's my father, Jayme!"

"A father for a father!" she screamed back, spittle flying. Her voice echoed over the water. "Your family took mine from me."

"Daniel Taffl was a willing soldier!"

"My father gave more than a soldier gives. He loved your mother, and she turned her back on him. Had it not been for her, he would've left. But no, he stayed, and the Mad King got him.

"My father gave his life for your family and got nothing! He was destroyed Vi, cast aside, left to die. And did your family care? *No*, they didn't even go looking after him."

"Jax went looking!" Or so he'd said once. Vi thought he did. The details were blurring underneath the veil of sheer rage.

"Another dog of the crown!" Jayme's scowl deepened. "Your mother couldn't be bothered."

"She thought he was dead until you showed up looking for work!"

"Yes, and then they knew he was alive. They gave me a job. Such generosity. My father gave a life and they gave me *work*. And did they do anything else for him?" Jayme challenged. Vi stilled; she didn't have an answer. "No, they didn't. They left their mess to rot, as though they weren't responsible."

Vi took a small step back, then a shuffle forward. She was pulled in every direction. Pity for Jayme, for her father, for the life they'd endured. Defense of her own family. Did the punishment Jayme was exacting fit the crimes perpetrated against her? One evil, begotten of the next, in a never-ending cycle.

She clutched her head and let out a scream.

"I think she's gone mad." Kora chuckled.

"If you had told me, I would've done everything I could." Vi looked to her friend. "You and Ellene were the closest thing I had to family in the North; I loved you."

"And I hated you," Jayme responded without missing a beat. "You were a means to an end, preventing my lineage from forever being trapped under your family's heel. I will not be grateful for your pity and scraps. I will not live without justice at the feet of the very people who saw my father harmed and cast him aside when he was no longer useful.

"My revenge started with your father, it continues with you, and it will end when I dance on your mother's grave."

Vi's whole body trembled. A great and terrifying rage had reached a boiling point. Fissures erupted in her, power spilling out of them, feeding on a kind of hurt Vi had never known. Her heart had numbed, frozen over, and now shattered with an explosion.

With a cry of pure agony and heartbreak, Vi's magic exploded from her. It encircled them in a ring of flame.

"Make her stop this," Kora warned. "You said her magic wasn't very good."

"It's not," Jayme assured Kora.

The fools.

Vi lifted a finger, pointing it right at Kora. With a horrible detachment, she uttered, "*Juth calt.*"

To shatter.

She pushed her magic into Kora, through her. The woman took a sharp inhale of air, eyes going wide. Inside, Vi strung her magic through and around every rib. She wove her power into the sinews and fiber's of Kora's every inch.

So that when her glyph exploded, so too did Kora, coating the beach in carnage.

Jayme was off-balance with shock. Her sword point faltered before she held it up again. "So you do have fight in you," she growled.

"You should know that," Vi all but snarled in reply. She did not feel the fire that encroached closer as she took a step forward. But she felt the second life she'd ended already weighing heavy on her soul. "Didn't I *surprise you*, after all?"

"I won't hesitate to attack you."

"I think you already have." Vi stepped to the side in a quick motion. "*Mysst soto larrk*." The sword appeared in her hand as she lunged forward.

Jayme parried, taking a step back. Vi held her blade in place, leaning forward slightly.

"How could you?" she whispered to the woman who was once her friend. "How could you spend years with me, telling me you were my confidant, my ally? That you were out to protect me, all the while knowing what you were doing to hurt me?"

"Easily." Jayme slid her blade down to the hilt of Vi's. Vi jumped back. "And I would do it all again, given the chance."

"Did you ever care for me?" Vi let the sword down, throwing out her hands at her sides, as though attempting to take back her friend in her arms one last time. Tears streamed down her cheeks, evaporating in the heat before they could hit the ground. Let her friend return to her and let them wake from this nightmare together. "Did you ever see me as I saw you?"

"Never."

Vi let out a single cry of agony. It was the end of her. The last shred of her innocence burning on the fire that Jayme had lit.

"How could you?" Vi lunged. Jayme held up her sword. "*Mysst xieh!*" Vi all but shouted in her face, pushing away Jayme's sword with her shield.

They toppled onto the sand, Vi on top, Jayme's sword pinned. The fire swirled around them, closer than ever before. She looked down at the familiar brown eyes.

"I did all I could for you. Why was I not enough?"

"You never could have been. Your name alone was all it took for us to be enemies." Jayme spat at her face. Vi stared in dull disbelief. They couldn't be on further ends of the spectrum. "If you're going to kill me, then do it. It won't be the first Taffl your family murdered."

"Your father is alive! Don't you want to live and return to him?"

"Not if I return as another pawn of Solaris! I'd rather die free than live under your rule."

Vi shook her head violently.

"Kill me if you're going to," Jayme repeated her earlier demand. "I'm not going to grovel for my life."

"I don't want to kill you!" Vi pressed her eyes closed in agony. She was pulled in more directions than she could count. But all of them held her against the woman in the sand, caught in stasis between her life and the fire surrounding them.

"Then I'll kill you!" Jayme began to twist, breaking free of Vi's hold.

They rolled. Jayme came out on top. Her sword drew back—point toward Vi's chest.

The world held its breath for a moment alongside Vi Solaris.

She saw everything in perfect clarity. Her one-time friend, illuminated by the orange light of her wild, raw magic. The face of the traitor that Jayme had exposed herself to be was superimposed over the kind eyes Vi once knew. High above them, the sun hovered, as though the Mother was watching the squabbles of her children, waiting to see how it would all unfold.

Vi gave a soft sigh and drew back in her magic.

Jayme let out a cry—the last sound Vi ever heard leave her lips—as she plunged her sword downward toward Vi's breast.

"*Juth calt*," Vi whispered softly, almost gently. But what she said internally was, *shatter like me*.

It was an instant kill, clean, simple. Jayme shuddered, eyes rolling back, chest bulging slightly as Vi's magic exploded her heart from within. She slumped, slid sideways, and fell to the sand, dead.

Vi twisted her head, staring at the visage of what had once been Jayme Taffl Graystone, willing herself to feel something. *Anything*.

But there was a hole in both their chests now where their hearts had once been.

And no feelings came.

30

Her friend was gone.

Her friend had never been there to begin with.

Vi continued to lay in the sand, inches from Jayme. She stared listlessly, eyes unfocused.

Get up! a voice urged in her.

Why?

The voice didn't have a worthy retort, so Vi continued to lie there. Perhaps, if enough snow fell, the whole world would freeze over and put a great hold on everything. But the Mother was not so kind.

The world was ending, just not by ice.

The sound of sand beneath the hull of a rowboat brought Vi back to alertness. She finally pushed herself upward. Magic crackled off her, igniting the air with the rage that still simmered under her skin.

She didn't make it very far before two arms suddenly appeared, hoisting her up. They yanked her hands forward and before Vi even realized what was happening, a man clamped shackles made of what looked like shimmering glass—*crystal*, she realized dully—around her wrists. Her whole body was instantly heavier as the spark retreated from her.

Darkness. Nothing but darkness within her.

Vi slowly found her feet as the men began to pull her away from Jayme. She had to keep moving. There was nothing more for her here—her friend was gone.

Her friend had never been there to begin with.

Ten pirates had come to retrieve her, each more hardened and terrifying than the last. If Jayme's devious tasks had been some kind of trial to join Adela's crew, she couldn't imagine what horrors these men and women had wrought in the pirate queen's name. Vi hoped Adela had sent her best after the display she'd shown on the beach.

A fist balled itself in her hair. Pain barely registered to her anymore. Vi's entire threshold and understanding of what pain was had been shaken. She hadn't even set a new baseline. But the pirates were working to do that for her.

Whoever had a hold of her braids yanked. Vi's mouth opened on instinct to let out a yelp. But before she could, a ball was shoved between her teeth. The gag was cold. It burned her teeth and her tongue stuck painfully to it before the natural heat of her breath warmed it from the inside out.

"In the boat." One of the pirates pushed her forward.

Vi stumbled, eliciting snickers from around her. Balancing herself was awkward with the heavy shackles. But she straightened enough to look them each in the eye to convey a single thought; She had killed to get this far. They should keep treating her like the threat she was.

The rowboat glided across the lagoon. Two men for each oar made quick work of the lagoon. Vi kept her eyes forward, ignoring the debris-littered waters, the carnage, and the conversation happening around her.

"Who would've thought she had it in her?"

"She is Aldrik's daughter."

"He fought like hell, didn't he?" Vi glanced at the man who said the last part. His eyes locked with hers and a grin widened his face. "You hear your dear ol' dad's name? Wanna go running after him?" The man leaned forward, getting right up in her face.

The last person who got in her face and threatened her family was dead on the beach.

"Well you're too late. We got him locked up tight on our Isle of Frost... Pretty little bargaining chip, that. Can't wait to see what Adela cashes him in for."

"Shut up, Edgar," one of the other pirates snapped. "Adela won't like you talking to her."

"Upset Adela, and you'll answer to Fallor."

Fallor. Vi's eyes widened and she fought the urge to try to speak. Moving her jaw only seemed to further press the agonizingly cold ball gag against her teeth.

Of course Fallor was alive. Why would Jayme kill one of her own? They had likely been in cahoots the whole time. It must have been some kind of test, to prove Jayme's loyalty. Or perhaps it was all a set-up to deepen Vi's trust in her "loyal" guard.

The hull of the *Stormfrost* was nearly three times the size of the *Dawn Skipper*, making the smaller vessel look like little more than the remnants of a toy crashed on the battering ram. Vi saw the hulking form of Marcus, face down, amid the debris bobbing in the relatively still waters of the lagoon.

How many had died because of her? Surely, the crew knew the risks they were taking. But this was certainly more than they bargained for.

She struggled to keep her gaze forward. She couldn't allow herself to feel guilty. She had to worry about her own survival. That was all that mattered now.

Ropes descended on their little rowboat and the men quickly tied them off. Vi felt her stomach sink as the vessel lurched, hoisted from the water. It clanged against the side of the ship, sheets of ice falling into the water below. Like self-healing armor, the patches repaired nearly instantly with spindly fingers of frost reaching to cover the exposed wood.

The magic it took to create such a barrier—one that could regenerate on its own—must come from some immeasurable well. It prompted a dull, bitter thought for the darkened spark inside of her. But the ice itself jarred a different memory—her vision from the Crossroads, of the frosty beach. Given what the pirate had said... they truly did have her father, alive yet, somewhere.

The rowboat was maneuvered back into its place and not a second later Vi was all but pushed off with a gruff, "Out."

Vi complied, stepping onto the main deck of the icy ship, nearly slipping in the process. She barely managed to recover. Vi tried to force her spark around her feet to give them better purchase, but it was still dark in her. No matter how hard she tried to summon the magic, it refused to heed her call.

Vi didn't panic. Even if she'd had her spark, she was so outnumbered it was comical.

The crew was situated in a semi-circle around her. They didn't brandish their weapons, but had them very clearly at hand even though she was constrained physically and magically. Most of the crew were wrapped in heavy wool and thick furs—but some wore loose-fitting clothing more regularly associated with seafaring.

Those would be the Firebearers or Waterrunners, Vi assumed. Firebearers because they could keep their spark right under their skin for warmth. Or Waterrunners, because the ice would not affect them nearly as much. Or perhaps they had some other magic entirely—either way, it gave her a rough estimate of the number of sorcerers aboard.

Magic did not surprise her.

But seeing men and women outside of her visions who were not-quite-human still did.

While all were human-like, two had upturned noses and a pale blue flesh with shimmers of magic that ran over what appeared to be scales. There was a man like the one she'd seen in her vision with her father on Meru—he looked as if he possessed some reptilian heritage, as he bore opalescent organic plates on his skin, an elongated snout-like nose, and slitted eyes. Several were nearly-human, but with faintly glowing dots on their brows in place of eyebrows.

"Welcome to the *Stormfrost*, Vi Yarl Ci'Dan Solaris, crown princess to the Solaris Empire." A woman emerged from the center of the group, commanding Vi's full attention.

Her eyes held the ocean itself within, her hair held the winds of winter, and she walked with a cane held by an icy hand.

Adela. Vi recognized her from the vision at the Crossroads. But being in the woman's presence was staggering. An impossible amount of magic radiated from her. A large bird was perched on her shoulder—bright-eyed and ruddy-feathered. It was the same one Kora had sent the day before.

"You are not the easiest woman to catch. But if anyone was to do it, it would be me."

Vi glared at her, balling her hands into fists.

Adela ignored her silent anger, turning to the crew that had been with Vi on the rowboat. "Where's Kora and the lady of the hour—our dear Jayme?" Just the way Adela asked betrayed she already knew the answer.

"She killed them."

"My my, killing my crew." Adela walked over to Vi slowly. She stopped when she was a mere breath away. "What am I going to do with you?" she whispered, looking Vi up and down. For once, Vi couldn't read someone's assessment of her. Whatever thoughts Adela had, she was keeping them well away from her face. "Take her below."

Adela punctuated the statement by bringing her cane before her, tapping it lightly between their feet. Light shot out from its tip, spreading across the icy coating of the vessel and running up the masts. The sails unfurled at the silent command, and the ship began to move.

"We make headway for Salvidia immediately. The elfin'ra want her fresh."

Two men grabbed her at her elbows, hoisting her off the deck. Vi didn't even bother struggling. It wouldn't get her anywhere.

"*Oh—*" Adela stopped the men carrying her with a sound. "Do not take the gag from her mouth under any circumstances. I'm told she's a Lightspinner."

"To feed her?"

"Feed her?" Adela gently petted the bird on her shoulder. "It'll only take us six days to get to Salvidia. If she's anything like her father, I think she can sustain for that long without dying."

The men picked her up once more, dragging her below the main deck of the *Stormfrost*. The rest of the crew parted to make room, then continued about their duties, as if already bored with her. Vi was helpless to do anything other than be manhandled.

She needed to save her strength more than ever.

She had six days to plan an escape from the most infamous pirate in the world... or be handed over to those who would sacrifice her to their dark god and bring about the end of days.

31

V I SAT CURLED in the back of a prison cell made of ice.

It didn't entirely look like a prison cell—at least not the ones Vi had seen before in books and certainly not like the hanging cages of Shaldan. There were two flame bulbs frozen to the wall, fire managing to flicker within without ruining the integrity of the ice. There was scarce little else—a bed, and a place for Vi to relieve herself connected to the outer hull—though she had yet to make the attempt as that, too, was frozen over, and her shackles made it awkward.

The bed was the only thing not completely covered in ice. Vi was nestled in the furs that had been piled atop it, her back against the wall, facing the only point of exit and the one thing that made her feel as though she were in a cell. The opposite wall was made entirely of ice, like Adela's hand, bars spanning from floor to ceiling. Only a Waterrunner—and a powerful one at that—would be able to break through or alter the ice.

Or a skilled enough Firebearer.

Or a Lightspinner.

That is, a Firebearer or Lightspinner whose magic wasn't smothered to oblivion.

Fighting another shiver, Vi continued to stare listlessly forward. Drool collected around the gag in her mouth, dripping from her chin from time to time. Wiping it away was her only movement.

She had to focus on thinking of a way to escape. But all she could think of was her family. Was her father rotting away in a cell similar to this one on the Isle of Frost the crew had mentioned?

Escape, and kill them all, Vi thought darkly. The hole in her chest left by Jayme's betrayal was slowly consuming her bodily. If Vi could thank her now, she would; Jayme taught her an important lesson—just how far she would go for her family and her mission.

"Well, well… look at you now, *princess*," a familiar voice sneered. Fallor strolled into her field of vision, as if he was taking a walk through a park. "How far you've fallen."

Vi narrowed her eyes slowly, watching him.

"Oh, don't get up, princess, not on this lowly *soldier's* account."

She hadn't intended to. He wasn't worth the energy.

It was then Vi noticed the thick black brows he'd had painted on the last time she'd seen him were gone. In their place were four small dots above each eye that seemed to almost shimmer with a dark, crimson color.

"Wondering what these are?" He noticed her stare.

Vi gave a small nod. Let's see how much precious information she could get him to slip.

Fallor leaned into the bars, gripping them with his bare hands. Vi couldn't imagine how he would pry them off without losing a layer of flesh to the ice. He pushed his face forward, ruddy hair hanging around it in gnarly ropes. "They're the mark of the Morphi."

Vi tilted her head.

"You wouldn't know, as a dweller of the Dark Isle. You have no idea of half the splendid things in this world." He pushed away, still grinning like a madman. "And you never will. You'll rot here until we deliver you to the elfin'ra. And from what I hear, they'll make you wish you were back in Adela's generous accommodations."

Vi kept her face passive. The last thing she wanted to do was give this man any kind of emotion. Fear or rage—he'd delight in all of it, because it would give him the knowledge that he had power over her—that he could control, in part, what she felt. And Vi would be damned if she gave him the satisfaction.

"Seeing you, like this… so strong, so stubborn… you remind me of your father. He was like this too, you know, at first. You're making him proud."

The gag in her mouth ached. She wanted to spit every vile curse she knew at this man. But other than gnawing on the iron ball between her teeth, Vi worked to remain passive. At least until Fallor added, "But you'll break eventually, just as he did. And he was a delight to crush."

Vi launched off the bed and crossed the small cell in two wide steps. She glared at Fallor through the bars. Fists balled. Face lined with anger.

"Oh, you want to get to me?"

She nodded. She'd tear him apart with magic. She'd show him exactly who was going to be crushed.

"You want to speak?"

She nodded again, even though she knew he was just toying with her.

"Perhaps the elfin'ra will let you in five days. Enjoy your time here, princess."

Fallor left. Vi watched him stroll down the long hall she'd been dragged down, up until the point he vanished from her field of vision. Vi spun in place, leaning against the bars. The ice sent tingling daggers up her spine, clearing her head.

She couldn't allow herself to get so fired up; she would just play into their hands. But her emotions seemed fragile and scattered. Just when she thought—

Fire.

A thought crossed her mind, a wild idea… she turned, staring at the flame bulb. If she was lucky—and nothing about this situation led her to believe she was—one last insane idea may just be her ticket out of Adela's clutches.

Two days.

Two days passed.

At least, she thought it was about two days. Once a day, seemingly around the same time, Fallor came to "check" on her. He volleyed insults and jibes through the bars, meaningless verbal attacks that Vi let slide off her skin like vinegar off oil.

Each day she stared at him dully, balling her emotions deep within her. Focusing only on what must be done.

Each night, she ran through maps and rough estimates in her head. She had no idea exactly how fast the *Stormfrost* was moving through the tides, but she'd seen a similar ship in Erion's books. Using the reported speeds of that vessel and the fact that they had begun their journey on Blue Lagoon, Vi estimated they were somewhere near the easternmost tip of Meru.

It was just an estimate, however.

Until Fallor confirmed it on the third day.

"It's a shame you can't see it," he gloated in that terrible, skin-crawling tone of his. "To be close enough to Meru to lay eyes on the coast but unable to see it... You could've made history and completed your father's mission if you'd made it to the continent. But he failed, and so will you."

On and on Fallor went about her family's shortcomings. Vi fought a yawn. She had her information.

As soon as he left, Vi stood. Her plan was roughly constructed and risky at best—suicidal, more likely. But while Vi had no intention of dying, it would be better to die at sea than to hand herself over to the elfin'ra.

Vi stood, taking a deep breath. She turned to the flame bulb, starting over toward it. If Vi had been any shorter, she wouldn't have been able to reach it. But perhaps she had been blessed with height for just this moment.

Raising her arms over her head and twisting her wrists back, Vi said a silent prayer that no one would hear what she was about to do, then smashed her shackles into the ice covering the bulb.

Much like the rowboat as it slammed against the hull of the ship, the ice cracked and splintered, falling in pieces. Vi let momentum ricochet her arms back before redoubling her efforts and smashing forward yet again. More white fractures formed and broke into cracks. She repeated the process one more time—two—and on the third, it broke to the glass underneath.

Glass fractured, embedding into her palms. Before the flame could extinguish Vi jumped, turning. Her hair singed—the stink of it filled her nose.

She could burn off all her hair if that's what it took. She needed to burn through the heavy leather straps holding the ball gag in her mouth. If she could get off the gag, she could muster her Lightspinning. If she could do that, she could get rid of the shackles.

She hoped. This all hinged on the theory that the pirates had put both gag and shackles on her to stymie two different kinds of magic: the gag for her Lightspinning, and the shackles for her fire magic. If she couldn't speak, she couldn't say Yargen's words to summon her powers that way. If she couldn't access the raw power of her spark and channel it as fire, she was useless as a Firebearer as well.

Smoke filled the air and was quickly replaced by the wintry cool of the ship. Vi reached up, tugging at the gag on her cheeks. She struggled, inching her fingers back, working to try to reach the clasp. But she couldn't; she was still too immobile and the leather was holding strong.

Turning, she raced to the other flame bulb, repeating the process.

A loud *bang* broke her concentration briefly as she heard the door at the end of the hall slam open. Vi turned back to the fire behind a bulb of glass and thin sheet of ice. She smashed against it again. And again.

"What do you think you're doing?" The man behind the bars barked at her.

Vi ignored him, heaving one last mighty smash. The glass shattered once more. Her hands plunged straight through the wall behind, fingers crunching against the ice. Her wrists were in the last remnants of the flame before it extinguished.

But this time, the fire didn't die.

An explosion of light originated from Vi's wrist as the wooden bead from the Mother Tree heated and exploded in an array of fire and light. Vi felt it wash over her like the tides of the sea on which she was trapped adrift.

The man was thrown back in the blast.

He hit the wall opposite with a thud; the remaining icy bars shattered atop his hunched form. Vi felt magic—her magic. No, different. This was hers but not. Everything was sharper, more precise, as though this was the magic she was yet working toward.

Yargen's power originates from the Mother Tree. The rogue thought wandered through her mind, said in Ellene's voice.

Vi ripped the gag from her mouth. The shackles had been destroyed in the blast. Massaging her jaw and jumping over the limp body of the man, she made a dash for the stairs.

Her plan wasn't going quite according to expectations. But the result was the same—she was out. She had her magic. Now… she had to figure out how to get off the boat and to Meru.

The fire followed her, sprinting ahead like a ribbon unrolling upward through stairwells and ladders to the main deck. People attempted to approach her, twice, but they backed away from the flames in fear, shouting curses. Vi spat magic at them left and right, not caring who she levied *juth* against.

Vi emerged onto the main deck, surprised to find it dark. Fallor had been coming at night, not morning as she'd originally suspected. Not that it mattered now. She was too far along in her attempt to turn back now.

"Fire below!" a man bellowed, rushing out of the portal she'd just come through. Vi felt the crackle of magic at her back—a Waterrunner no doubt trying to subdue the flame.

"Fire above!" a woman shouted back, jumping from the quarterdeck to land heavily at Vi's side. As she stood, ice shards appeared in the air in a wide arc around her. With a flick of her wrist, they were sent hurling toward Vi.

"*Mysst xieh*," Vi said as she raised a hand. The glyph of light was ablaze and the ice hissed as it melted on contact. It was as though all of her magic right now had been steeped in flame.

A rumble from deep within the bowels of the ship stilled them all. Vi turned toward its source and like the frosty breath of an icy dragon waking, mist poured from the opening beneath the quarterdeck—where Vi had just come from. There was no sensation of flames beneath any longer, just the stillness of ice. The *tap tap tap* of a cane announced Adela's arrival. She emerged into the moonlight, the draped silks over her shoulders heavy with ice.

"Give this up and return to your cell," Adela cautioned. "You try my patience."

"Let me off this vessel, and I'll allow you and everyone on it to live." Vi didn't really think the threat would work, but damned if she wasn't going to try.

Adela laughed.

Tearing her eyes from the pirate queen, Vi turned toward the northwestern horizon. She could barely make out the silhouette of what she hoped was land and not clouds.

"I need you *alive*, girl; I don't need you well," Adela cautioned.

"*Juth starys!*" Vi didn't wait for the woman to make her first move. She sent a ball of fire in Adela's direction and began to run once more.

It would be safer to commandeer a rowboat, but it would almost ensure her recapture. Adela would find her among the dark waters and hoist her back into the boat. She would freeze the sea itself around Vi's escape and ensnare her. There was only one hope for a way out—to be lost in the waves.

"Remember you chose this," Adela said, almost bored. Lifting her cane with her icy hand, she dropped it onto the deck. A ripple of magic shot out, expanding until it reached in front of Vi before it propelled upward through the air, a solid wall of ice. Vi turned, only to find the ice spreading around and above her, forming a near-perfect cube.

It was so cold that even within her flames, Vi shivered. She looked through the nearly transparent wall at the sea beyond. *A little more*—it would not end like this.

Closing her eyes, Vi dug deep. She was exhausted, famished, worn to the bone; whatever magic had been unleashed from Ellene's bracelet was waning.

"Yargen please, just a little more."

Fire pushed against the ice, magic pitted against magic. Vi opened her eyes to see her progress, but there was nothing but light surrounding her. Yet she could feel it, the walls of ice that tried to contain her unstoppable fire, and pushed all the harder.

"*Juth calt*," Vi said, and put an end to her icy prison with a crack that seemed to echo through her very essence. It was followed by another, and another, and then—a rupture that shook the ship itself. Freed, her fire ran over the deck, leaving people screaming in agony, fleeing from its incinerating tendrils.

Vi turned, looking back to Adela. She found the woman encased in her own thinning shield of ice.

"You..." the woman whispered. "It was you, your magic that broke my treasure ward all those years ago." There was a joke somewhere in those words, judging from Adela's crazed laughter, but it was lost on Vi. "It was *you* who stole the Crown of the First King from me! You, a human girl!" She was screaming now. "*How?* Tell me how!"

Everything around them was burning as Vi's fire continued to increase in power. Men and women screamed, jumping into the water, pouring out from decks below. The ashen ice-soaked wood was quickly drying under the heat of her flames, the ancient tinder going up almost eagerly once freed from its cold prison.

"You would see your crew die and your ship burned to save yourself?" Vi wondered at the strange phenomenon she witnessed around her: Adela was drawing her power inward to protect herself. She was the only one untouched by Vi's fire.

"I've lived too long to die here and now," Adela said off-handedly, the ice continuing to surround her like a frozen coffin. "I have much to do, yet. And I know you won't kill me now, little princess. Because I have your father."

Time seemed to slow. The crackle of the flames had vanished alongside the screams of the pirates. There was only Adela and her savage grin with the sounds of Vi's breathing layered atop.

"I will find him with or without you. Nothing will stop me," Vi whispered. With a shout of agony, Vi placed all her focus on Adela. *"Juth starys hoolo!"* Ice sheered away in sheets at the initial fiery assault, evaporating before it could even drip onto the deck.

"Finally, a Solaris with real fight!" Adela pushed the ice forward.

Startled, Vi didn't have the chance to incinerate it completely, and was sent tumbling by the blow. She felt the tell-tale crackle of magic under her left shoulder and Vi rolled just in time to see a spear of ice protrude from the deck. Another crackle, another roll, this time onto her knees.

Adela lifted her cane, and a thick mist poured from the top. Like a weighted blanket, Vi could feel it sitting heavily atop her flames, trying to smother them. She stood, ignoring the force pushing her downward.

With a wave of her arm, and a shout of *"Juth mariy,"* Vi attempted to stunt Adela's magic. The woman dodged her glyph. Why did she ever try *mariy*? It never worked.

But Adela's movement redirected her oppressive mist, and that allowed Vi's flames to feed off fresh air once more, seeking more exposed timber to burn.

The pirate captain shifted her cane from hand to hand. Reaching out with her icy grip, her fingers elongated to dagger-like points.

"Mysst xieh." The shield blunted the icy lances. She was so busy with the first attack that Vi didn't notice new ones appearing at her flank.

Vi let out a scream—a noise she'd never heard herself make before—as pain poured from her like the crimson blood that spattered the deck. She looked at the blood, remembering the carnage she'd wrought on the beach.

This was how people died.

"And here I thought you were something special." Adela withdrew her hand, returning it to her side.

Pressing her hand into her side, trying to stave off the blood flow, Vi blinked at Adela in an attempt to regain her focus. *Better dead than in the hands of the elfin'ra*, a voice repeated in her mind. Life had been reduced to a terrible mantra.

"Halleth ruta sot. Halleth ruta toff." Vi attempted each healing spell. But it was a discipline she and Taavin had yet to study properly. She felt her skin knit and mend, already scarring in odd and uncomfortable ways with her clumsy attempts.

"Fire below is sorted," Fallor's shout broke through her concentration. But Adela remained focused.

She raised her cane once more, and Vi turned, running. She closed her eyes, seeking out the light that now seemed to be at the distant end of a tunnel—the light that had always burned so brightly for her was growing dim. *One more time*, Vi beseeched it.

Come to me, one more time!

She ran blindly into the railing. It knocked the wind from her and crushed Vi's arms against the wound she'd been attempting to heal. One last, brilliant explosion of light and flame was all her body had to give. She would take them all with her, burn them alive so they would not hurt another member of her family—or any family—ever again.

Vi tumbled forward into the air off the side of the boat. She went head first into the sea like a falling star, brilliant, before the dark waves crashed down over her.

32

"FALLOR, AFTER HER!" Adela's shriek was barely a whisper over the crashing waves in Vi's ears.

Vi pushed against the waters, trying to swim. Everything hurt, everything felt heavy. Her heart, her mind, her body, even her magic was at its limit. She'd given everything and now was dried up. There was nothing left for her to give.

She surfaced from the waves with a spout of air. There was the cry of a bird, loud and echoing overhead. Vi's hand hung limply at her side, her mind filling with the thought of the dark waves around her, bright sea foam, and an angry dawn reflecting in the water.

"D-D-Duroe," she managed through chattering teeth. The water was frigid, but warming the further she got from the boat. "Watt…" One more, one more and then anchor the glyph. "Ivin."

Vi didn't know if she was successful. But she felt the magic underneath her hand, tight in her grip, like a treasure she would never relinquish. Hopefully, it would shield her, and one of Taavin's last lessons on Lightspinning hadn't gone to waste.

Darkness.

The world was awash with darkness that smelled of salt and ash. She floated through it, adrift in a giant sea of impenetrable blackness. It was suffocating, heavy, drowning…

Vi pushed upward toward the early sunlight, gasping in air, just as another wave crashed down on her, bringing darkness anew.

She turned, belly up and barely breathing. The sea rolled and she rolled with it. Hazy images plunged into nothingness over and over, more times than she could count.

Judgment. This was her judgment for trying to change a desolate future. This was her punishment for thinking she and her family might triumph despite all odds.

The Mother watched her from above, threatening to burn her face where it protruded from the foamy sea. Vi pressed her eyes closed, unwilling to see the light once more. For the light had failed her. The light had not been enough in the one moment she'd needed it most. And now... now she waited for Adela to find her yet again. She awaited recapture and delivery to the elfin'ra.

Yet it was not Adela who took Vi into her hands... but the same Goddess she believed had forsaken her.

The roar of waves, the crash of her body against a rocky shore, the cool feeling of wet sand in her face—Vi forced her eyes open, blinking into the light. She couldn't move, and everything ached. There was a bloated, heavy sensation about her body that Vi had never felt before. Water flowed up into her nostrils with every new crash of the waves at her feet, causing her to sputter and cough.

Pushing herself upward, Vi made an attempt to stand—to merely crawl. But her hands, cut and torn from the glass she'd broken, slipped out from under her. She hadn't made it very far, but she had managed to get her nose and mouth above the tide, and that was good enough for now.

Darkness, once more.

A soft grinding noise eventually stirred her. There had been nothing but the sound of wind, the cry of gulls, and the rushing of water for hours—days? It felt as if she had been washed upon the beaches of the hourglass of time, destined to slip through its eye again and again as an invisible hand flipped the device—resetting it every hour.

The noise of grinding sand repeated, growing louder until it was close enough that Vi could recognize it as footsteps. Yet the moment she made the connection, the sound ceased. Prying her eyes open—breaking the thin crust of salt and grime that had nearly sealed them closed—Vi blinked into the late sunlight of the day.

A pair of booted feet stood before her. They were the shoes of a traveler—worn and dusty with scratches marring the surface of the leather so soft, it pooled around the ankles.

These were boots she knew.

Vi twisted her head, feeling shells grind against her right ear as she followed the legs clad in cotton upward to where the wide hem of a coat covered from knees to chest. It was embellished in gold with seaming that would have looked near-regal if it didn't also look positively ancient in its construction and care. Wiry bits of thread jutted from the fabric and patches helped keep the garment together.

The man tilted his head. A messy mop of what she knew to be dark purple—not black—hair caught the dim morning light like coal picking up fire. He stared down at her with emerald eyes offset against ruddy skin Vi would've associated with a Westerner if she were still in the Solaris Empire.

The Empire... Her mind curled sluggishly around the thought, clinging to it. Had she made it?

"T-T-Tav—Where am I?" she wheezed through cracked lips, speaking to what could only be an exhaustion-fueled vision. Vi looked down at her hands, confirming there was no magic there summoning him. That meant...

He crouched down, the better for Vi to see him clearly. There, the curved scar so familiar it might have graced her own cheek. She tried again to twist, but her side protested in sharp agony at the movement.

"Is it really you?" she whispered. It couldn't be. It couldn't be him, of all people.

"It is really me," he answered softly.

He reached out, scooping her upward, pulling her soaked form to him.

Vi allowed herself to curl against his chest, his arms locked around her. Taavin pressed a kiss into her forehead. Vi felt water on her cheeks, but she didn't know if it was from the surf or tears. Likely both.

"I have you," Taavin murmured, rocking back and forth slightly. "Breathe, for just a moment."

Vi ran her hand along his embroidered coat. She knew there was much left to do. A mountainous, impossible task lay before them. She didn't want to think of it now.

"Come, let's get you cleaned up." Pulling her arm over his shoulders and hoisting, Taavin pulled Vi up alongside him like a limp puppet. The man was stronger than he looked, a sturdy force unwavering even with the slippery sand and her unstable footing.

"Where are you taking me?" Vi coughed, saltwater and spittle coming up clotted with sand.

"There's a fisher's hut just on the other side of this ridge," he murmured softy. "We can stay there... long enough to see you mended."

Vi glanced at him from the corners of her eyes, studying his profile. She still couldn't believe he was here, that she'd come this far, that she'd managed to actually find him. Or, perhaps more incredible, that he'd managed to somehow find her.

The ridge of his nose was sharp, down-turning slightly at the tip. It was complimented by the sharp jutting of his chin that seemed equally pronounced when she took his almost hollow cheeks into account. Had he always been so gaunt? They were likely both worse for wear.

"You did well." Taavin stared straight ahead. "But things are only still beginning."

She had so many questions, so much she wanted to say and do now that he was here. So much had happened, how did she begin to tell him? But the only word that fell from her lips was, "Beginning?"

"We're running short on time, Vi. The end of the world is near, and we must be ready to meet it."

FAILED FUTURE

VORTEX CHRONICLES

BOOK THREE

*for every dream that failed
to make room for the one that came true*

E VERYTHING WAS A BLUR.

Each memory merged into the next, a hazy mess of color and sound and not-quite-consciousness.

She was on a ship of ice. Frost glittered through the dark memories, illuminating nothing but pain. An ocean of dark water enveloped her—nearly as cold as the vessel itself. She was lost in the vast sea, an invisible fragment among the waves, tossed between each swell, tumbled over reef and stone. There was the feeling of grit, rough against her...

Sand.

Breathing.

Just... breathing. Air sputtering between gasping lips. Heaving as her body expelled the water to make room for every life-giving breath it fought for.

Exhaustion.

More darkness.

Him.

Two hands hoisted her up and liberated her from the soggy grave she had consigned herself to. Arms covered in a delicately embroidered coat that her fingers would know anywhere wrapped around her, sure and warm.

A voice that resonated with her very soul.

Her hair was smoothed away from her face. She was still damp, and felt perhaps this would be her existence from now until forever. Air sucked the moisture from her, setting her body to shivering. Her brow couldn't dry; it was constantly slick with sweat.

Fever raged through her. At least, she thought so. Maybe he told her so.

Cold, hot, cold.

Mumbled words, sparks of light, more darkness.

Time persisted like this. For how long, Vi couldn't quite say. She was alive, but hanging by determined, ragged threads and a body too stubborn to give in.

She screamed herself hoarse as her wounds were ripped back open—something muttered about her clumsy healing needing to be "reset". She gasped as agony ebbed and flowed and her tissue was mended anew. Salves were smeared on her and potions poured down her throat; she had no choice but to drink or drown.

Every time her eyes opened, they stayed that way a little longer. Slow blinking seconds connected in her reforming consciousness.

Wind rattled against the drawn shutters on the sole window of the hovel where he'd stashed her. There was a hearth at her right side, always burning. Too hot, or not warm enough, never right in the middle. But the flames were a familiar and welcome companion. They were the only thing that made sense to her.

At her left was Taavin. He would curl up, leaning with his back against the door, light always surrounding him even when he looked as though he were sleeping.

How was he here? And where exactly was *here* anyway?

If she stretched far enough, she might be able to touch him. But Vi had neither the strength nor the energy to try.

Sometimes, she would wake to find him fumbling around in a trunk, open like a clam against the wall opposite the fire. She would hear the sound of corks popping before bright herbaceous smells cut through the briny air.

Other times, she opened her eyes and he was hovered over her, lips moving fast and soft. Most of the words she could identify if she thought hard enough—and thinking was very difficult. But a good many she couldn't. So Vi didn't expend too much effort on identifying which was which. She'd forget the next time her eyes opened anyway.

Vi blinked into the twilight.

This time was different than the others.

Her mind was sharper—clearer. She was present in the moment and keenly aware of her own excruciating existence. Her thoughts were still jumbled, but now felt like pieces she could put her fingers on and begin to snap back together.

Vi turned her head toward a soft clinking sound.

"Taavin?" Her lips stretched painfully, and the iron taste of blood swelled where the delicate skin cracked.

"Vi." He turned sharply, nearly spilling what was in the rough-hewn cup cradled in his hands. Their eyes met, and Taavin scrambled over to her in clumsy haste.

He was undeniably Taavin... Yet he looked so different than she remembered. Almost jarringly so. Enough that Vi had to blink, reminding herself that this was, indeed, the same man.

His hair was matted with dirt and grime. Dark circles she'd never seen before shadowed his eyes. The usual vibrancy of his coat was gone, replaced with gray twilight and accented by the dying embers of the fire casting long shadows over them. The only things that had any brilliance to him were his eyes—ever shining— and the small circle of light spinning around his left wrist. The glyph was drawn together so tightly that Vi couldn't identify what it was for.

"How do you feel?"

"Like death, but slightly more animated." Vi shifted onto her side, putting her weight on her left elbow and trying to push herself up. Every joint was stiff and aching. It felt like she hadn't moved in years.

"Don't get up too quickly. 'Animated death' may be an apt description given how I found you and what I've had to do to try to piece you back together properly." But Vi was determined, so Taavin helped her upright, situating her against the wall behind her. Vi knew the space had been narrow, but she hadn't realized that the top of her head was nearly touching one wall and her toes the one opposite while lying down. "Here, drink this—it'll help your body wake up. I've been keeping you in a sort of stasis to let your body focus on healing."

Vi accepted the cup from him, staring down at the muddy mixture within.

"I promise it looks worse than it tastes."

She took a timid sip. It was thick and grassy, but warm on the way down—almost like liquor, but without the strong burn. Vi took another sip, replacing the salt musk of the shack with the bright tang of the drink. This was the earthy note she'd smelled earlier and Vi found it almost pleasant.

"Do you remember everything? Remember me?" Taavin asked almost timidly. "Was your memory affected at all by the trauma?"

"Yes." Vi stared into the cup once more. "I mean, yes I remember everything—and you. No, my memory wasn't affected." The cup rested in her lap, over the rough-hewn blanket that covered her legs. Vi wiggled her toes. They didn't feel like her own... nothing felt like hers. It was as if her soul had been placed into a completely new body. "I think so, at least..."

Her voice faded to nothing. Memories stacked like building blocks around her, closing her in. Vi's fingernails dug into the grooves of the clay cup; the craftsman's mark still present in the indents of fingers fired into permanence. The dull ache in her chest assured Vi that this seemingly new body was, indeed, hers.

Every scar she now wore was like a map, showing how she'd finally made it to Meru.

"That's good," he breathed a small sigh of relief. "I've been worried I'd not done enough..."

"I'm fine." It was a lie. A lie to save her from having to fight her way out of the deep hole the truth put her into. Vi was many things... but after fleeing her home, abandoning her Empire, fighting for her life, facing off against a pirate queen, and putting a traitor to death... "fine" was none of them.

"How are you here?" Vi flipped the focus on him. Talking about herself was the last thing she wanted to do. "Aren't you trapped in Risen?"

"Clearly not." Taavin sank back off the balls of his feet, drawing his knees up to his chest. Vi watched him and debated passing the mug back. He seemed as if he could use the soothing properties of its contents as much as she could. "I managed to escape."

"How?" Vi looked around the shack. "How did you get here? And how did you know I would be here?"

Questions piled on questions. Nothing was adding up.

"Remember, I told you that you were not the only one who would be on a journey. I vowed to find a way out of my prison." His hand, timidly, rested on hers. "No, I always knew there was a possible escape. I just needed to have the courage to take it."

Vi stared at his hand, willing it to spark light into her chest as it had once before, but she still felt frustratingly little. Every emotion was dulled. Instead, she focused on that conversation they'd had forever ago on Erion's balcony. "You said you were having dreams too... of storms, and death in the water, of me in dark waves."

He gave a small nod.

"Taavin, you dream only of the past," Vi whispered.

"I thought I did." He looked away, lost in his own thoughts. "But the closer you got to me, the stranger my dreams became. Or perhaps it was merely the will of the Goddess that I would find you. Either way, the black sand beaches outside the Twilight Forest are unmistakable. When I had a brief but particularly violent vision of you on the sand, I knew I had to leave."

A violent vision? She knew he'd spoken of having shakes and going comatose during his visions... Was she nothing but violence to those around her? Was that what she was becoming?

"Then, on my way, I heard word of the pirate Adela sailing along the eastern coasts. I knew you were aboard a vessel. I had these unrelenting visions. It all seemed to compel me to go in a way I simply couldn't ignore; I feared for the worst."

He finally dragged his gaze back to her. Vi stared back, holding his deep and sunken eyes. They seemed all the more harrowed when framed by the gauntness of his face—a sharper edge to his cheeks than she'd ever seen. When was the last time he'd had a good night sleep? Or a full stomach?

"I'm glad you came, whatever the reason." Vi took another sip of the concoction he'd made for her. She didn't know if it was serendipity, the will of the Goddess, or some other magic at play, but she would count her blessings rather than question them.

"Me too. I don't know how long you were out on that beach, but I shudder to think what would have happened if I had been any later."

Vi looked down at his hand, still lingering atop hers. It half-hovered, trembling, as though he was afraid to touch her. Vi finally released the mug and twisted her fingers with his. He shifted closer at the unspoken request.

Both of them stared at the contact for several long seconds. She heard a hitch, and a quiver in his breath. But neither moved. Vi's gaze dragged upward to meet his.

Their shade of green was even more astounding in person. It was the only thing of brilliance in the dark world she now found herself in.

"You're really here," he whispered in wonder, despite the fact that he must have been taking care of her for days now.

"I am. Do I feel different to you in person?"

"Not really," he confessed with a soft laugh. "I can't tell if that makes me happy or sad." His other hand lifted, cupping her cheek. Vi could feel the thin layer of grime on her skin that smeared under the pad of his thumb.

"Why sad?" she dared ask.

"Because you came all this way and endured so much...maybe you summoning me through the watch was just as good."

"It wasn't." Vi placed the cup off to the side, shifting her hands so they covered his. One on her face, one in her lap. "I don't need magic to see you now. Your presence isn't governed by glyphs. Now you can be by my side whenever I need— every moment of the day."

"Only if you permit it."

"I'd permit nothing less." Vi closed her eyes, tipping her head forward to press her forehead against his. Taavin stayed there, giving her comfort without needing to be asked. "Besides..." Her voice trailed off, sandpaper covering her throat, her soul.

"*Besides?*"

Vi shook her head slowly. She needed him to help hold her together. Far from home, he was all she had right now—the only familiar thing in a strange land.

But somehow, needing him felt like weakness. It felt terrifying for a reason Vi couldn't describe.

"Besides," Vi started again, clearing her throat and leaning away, distancing herself from the moment and the sensation of frailty. "My coming wasn't purely social. We have work to do." Vi slowly raised a hand to her watch.

"We do," he said in solemn agreement.

"What do we need to do now?" she asked. There were two reasons she'd struggled and fought and killed to get to Meru, and this was one.

"I don't know yet… May I?" Taavin held a hand right before the watch. Vi ignored his closeness. How soft she knew his lips were.

"Go ahead." Vi rubbed the back of her neck, debating if she should just take it off.

The watch was the last connection she had to the world she'd been born into—to her family. It was perhaps the only thing that could prove she was, in fact, Vi Solaris. Even as her fingertips rolled over the screw-lock that held the chain fast, she couldn't bring herself to undo it.

A different sensation distracted her—the feeling of shorter hair than she was used to. Vi remembered the start of her escape from Adela—smashing a flame bulb and using the remnants of the fire to try to burn off the gag they'd forced on her. Some of the hair had singed away, and now it was shorter at the back of her head than the rest. She fussed with the ends that now extended barely past her shoulders.

The hair the West had so loved… she'd need to cut it. Like everything else, the thought passed through her mind with a dull ache and little other feeling.

Ignorant to her various internal battles, Taavin's fingers closed around the watch.

The moment the metal touched Taavin's skin, magic sparked, exploding out like tiny fireworks from the contact point. Glistening specks sparkled through the air and clung to the barely visible outline of glyphs unknown. Noise filled her mind—so loud and instantaneous that Vi couldn't tell if it was music or voices, singing or screams. Her breathing quickened. She may have even let out a small shout.

The colors and shapes overtook Taavin as well, encompassing them both for what felt like hours but surely must have only been seconds. His eyes flashed brightly right before the room returned to its dim light—though in the wake of such strange magic, it seemed darker than before.

Taavin's breathing was heavy. Vi's heart raced, and she was more alert than she'd felt since she'd woken. They both seemed to be waiting for something else to happen. Yet nothing did.

When Vi could no longer handle the silence, she dared to ask, "What was that?"

"I take it that hasn't happened before?" The intense stare he'd been impaling the watch with was now turned to her. A sensation similar to the first time he'd ever laid eyes on her crawled up her spine and Vi subconsciously leaned slightly away.

"No… What… what was that?"

"I don't—" A knock on the door interrupted him. Taavin looked back to her, his eyes frantic. "My wards broke." The words fell from his mouth, not an answer to her question but several times more horrifying.

"Your wards?" Vi breathed, trying to match how softly he was speaking. Her attention fell with his to his wrist—the glyph that had been there earlier was gone.

"Surrounding this place, keeping us hidden. Now they can sense me, and with that burst of magic—"

"Fallor," Vi finished.

"Fallor?" Taavin looked to her. "Adela's right-hand man?"

"He's after me," Vi answered hastily. "Wait… Who did you think it was?"

"The Swords."

"The what?" As soon as the question left her lips, Vi remembered a brief conversation they'd had in her tent when she'd first begun to demand information from him. "The Swords of Light? The Faithful's militia?"

"They're after me."

The door rattled again, preventing Vi from asking the thousand questions swirling in her mind about the Swords of Light.

"Get ready to run." Taavin grabbed her hand. *"Durroe sallvas tempre dupot. Durroe watt radia dupot."*

Light spiraled out from him. Vi recognized the chants to deceive ears and eyes. *Radia*, to hide. *Tempre*, to mask? *Dupot...* she'd never heard that word before. Had she? Her mind was in a haze, still sluggish from her injuries and whatever magic was still making her ears ring.

Glyphs surrounded Taavin, condensing onto his left wrist like bracelets. She knew what he was doing, and yet... Vi was struck with awe.

He commanded the magic with a deftness she'd never seen before—not from any sorcerer from any discipline. It put even the poetic nature by which her parents could command the elements to shame. It was more than sorcery, it was art—as breathtaking as a virtuoso musician or master dancer. The magic wasn't just an extension of Taavin.

It *was* Taavin.

The door to the shack was kicked in. Two men stood framed at the threshold, ice crackling around them, reaching inside of the shack. The remnants of the dying fire were snuffed and Vi's eyes worked to adjust to moonlight only.

One man was unknown to her, a nameless and bloodthirsty face. Her focus remained locked on the other: Fallor. The red of his hair and shimmering dots that lined his brow were unmistakable to her now. She'd know them by daylight, moonlight, and nightmare.

His eyes narrowed slightly, sweeping across the shack and past where Vi and Taavin were hidden.

"Search it," Fallor commanded. The nameless man stepped forward into the small space as Fallor remained in the doorway.

Vi bit back a shout of pain as she was tugged into motion. Taavin seized the opportunity, sprinting past Fallor in the doorway. Unfortunately, he misjudged the distance.

Taavin twisted to slip through, but Vi was caught-off balance. She tripped over her own feet; there was still a disconnect between her body's movements and her brain. Taavin pulled at her arm as Vi tried to convince her limbs to move properly.

Barely, just barely, her side brushed against Fallor's giant arm.

The man turned his head, moving on instinct—there could be no other description for how fast he lashed out. She'd touched him, and that meant the magic that had extended from Taavin to her, now extended to Fallor. *He could see them.*

Fallor's arm slammed against her middle, knocking the air from her lungs. It pressed further into Vi's abdomen as he pulled with bone-crushing might.

Vi looked to Taavin, watching his eyes widen slightly as she was ripped from his grasp. He was still moving in the other direction, hand around her wrist. But Fallor was too strong. She felt weightless as she was hoisted into the air. Taavin's fingers slipped from Vi's and she watched as he disappeared, the magic now concealing him from her without their contact.

"Found you," Fallor growled into her ear, a stomach-churning glee making the words all the more terrifying.

"*J*UTH—*" A LARGE HAND clamped around Vi's mouth before she could finish the chant.

"I think not." Fallor turned to his comrade. "There's another, get him."

"Adela only wanted her."

"She'll want this one," Fallor assured him with a confidence that shook Vi to her core.

They knew who Taavin was. That was the only explanation. Otherwise Fallor would've focused only on her.

Vi stared out into the rainy field surrounding the shack, looking for any sign of Taavin. Her stomach and jaw ached from Fallor's unrelenting hold. She hoped Taavin was still running as fast and far as he could get. She'd tangled with the pirates once and survived—she could do it again. She would never forgive herself if he was taken captive, too.

Yet for all she wanted Taavin to look after himself, Vi knew he wouldn't.

She was Yargen's Champion, and if the elfin'ra got their hands on her they would use her blood to summon their dark god Raspian. But even if that weren't the case… This was the man who had dared to escape his captivity, come to her, and nursed her back to health—he wasn't going to leave her behind. Which left Vi with one option before he would do something reckless and expose himself again.

Magic was magic, he'd said once. Every discipline was merely a way to manipulate and channel it. So Fallor could stop her as a Lightspinner by silencing her, but without Adela's terrible shackles, he'd never stop her as a Firebearer.

Closing her eyes, Vi sought out the spark within her. She imagined it springing forth, just as the light did. The only difference was that this power needed no words.

Heat shimmered against the rain, turning it instantly to mist. Fallor must've felt it, but he didn't react fast enough. Tiny sparks ignited in a blink, forming a wall of flame that hovered a few inches off Vi's skin and clothes. It pulsed out from her, forcing Fallor away.

She hit the ground. One hand slid out as Vi sought balance, slipping in the mud. It coated her side and she rolled with it. The taste of earth filled her mouth as she shouted, "*Juth starys hoolo.*"

A glyph formed around the men and the shack as she spoke. Vi squinted at Fallor, rubbing the mud from where it was running in her eyes with her other hand. There was a different shimmer of light surrounding the pirate, but she couldn't make out what it was before the fire she'd unleashed caught the glyph she wrought, erupting in a white-hot blaze.

Screams from the bloodthirsty man who had been investigating the shack filled the air, solo. There wasn't a chorus of cries as she'd expected—but then again, had she ever expected Fallor to go down quietly? Vi stared into the blaze, searching for his outline. The flames burned even brighter, and he was nowhere to be found.

Already ash, she hoped.

The cry of a bird of prey echoed off the cliffside as it rose higher on the updraft created by her flames.

"Vi!" Taavin's voice broke her concentration in tandem with his hand clamping once more around hers. "We have to go."

Vi remained still, staring at the burning hut with the pirate still inside. The screams were quieting. It was a terrible way to go, yet killing the man didn't yield even the slightest bit of remorse or guilt, and that fact made her feel terrible.

All around her was darkness—outside, in the stormy night, and in the hollow of her chest, a chasm opened by betrayal. Dawn would come with the morning—but would light ever breach the inky depths that threatened to drown her?

"Fallor is coming." Taavin yanked at her arm. "We have to go!"

"Fallor? I—"

An eagle's screech interrupted her. The bird she'd seen take to the skies was in full dive, wings tucked. An odd shimmer of light surrounded it. At first, Vi thought the distortion was merely the firelight catching on the rain, but it was more than that. Reality itself rippled, as if nothing more than a reflection in a shimmering pool.

With a magic Vi had never even imagined, the bird was gone and Fallor was there—as if one had disappeared beneath the shifting waves of reality and the other had surfaced. Momentum propelled him through the air as he plunged both of his feet into Taavin's chest, using the other man's body like a springboard. As he pushed away, the same ripple was already beginning to surround him, but Vi didn't watch this time as bird was substituted for man.

Her eyes were on Taavin. Agony singed through her, a silent cry caught in her mouth, left agape in shock.

Taavin wheezed, rolling in the mud, coughing and sputtering.

"Taavin!" Vi fell to her knees, sliding to his side.

"We have to go, on foot... They killed the horse." He barely forced out the words. "More... come."

Vi looked skyward. She searched the darkness and rain for any sign of the eagle, but there was none. With his strange magic, Fallor could be anywhere. In her mind, he was suddenly everywhere.

At any moment they would be attacked. If Fallor's magic could transform him into a bird, she shuddered to think what else it could do. She had to fight back, had to think of a glyph combination that could thwart whatever power he was using. But facing a magic so foreign to her, Vi was armed with little but panic.

"*Durroe sallvas tempre dupot. Durroe watt radia dupot.*" Taavin repeated his earlier words and Vi felt the glyphs slip around them both, cocooning them in his magic. "We have to make it to the trees."

"The trees," Vi repeated, forcing her mind to continue to function. She couldn't freeze up. Not now. Not after all she'd done to get here.

"Over there." He pointed with his free arm as Vi lifted his other and placed it around her shoulders. "We have to get to the Twilight Forest."

Twilight Forest. Her mental atlas flipped through its archives but came up empty. Not because she was panicked, but because she was now in a land she knew almost nothing about, running blindly into the night.

"Let's go." Vi pushed off from the ground.

Taavin was heavier than he looked and Vi hadn't felt so weak in a long time. She ignored the signs of fatigue, pushing her feet into a run over the tall grasses that covered the cliffside.

The flames from the burning shack had been smothered by the torrential rain, and a heavy mist clouded above the quickly cooling remains. Fallor wouldn't give up. And he wouldn't make it easy.

As the thought crossed her mind, a pulse of magic rippled out across the ground, tangling her ankles. Vi felt herself falling, clasping her hand as tightly as possible to Taavin's so as not to break the magicks that were hiding them. But it was Taavin who let go.

The power that had been concealing them shattered under the second pulse of magic that swept over the grassy cliff. Fragments of light swirled in the ripple before blinking unnaturally from existence. It was as if Taavin's power had never been there at all.

"*Loft Dorh Dupot*," Taavin snarled. Vi had never heard such a vicious tone from the man's mouth before and was taken aback by it.

Taavin held out one arm, fist clenched around the center of a spinning circle, as though he was holding an invisible tether. She followed his focused gaze to Fallor. Vi remembered when Taavin had used the same immobilization rune on her.

He'd said it was no easy feat, even if he made it look otherwise.

Which meant Vi had to act fast.

"*Mysst Soto Larrk*!" She sprang into motion, feeling light condense under her palm into the hilt of a sword. She didn't want to risk *juth* interfering with Taavin's magic. She'd take the fight to Fallor.

Vi was nearly to him when Fallor broke free of Taavin's magic with a roar. She shifted her grip on the sword, swinging it with all her might. Fallor dodged, the point of the blade missing his neck by a hair's breadth. She let out a scream of frustration.

"A sword?" Fallor caught her wrist. His fingers looped entirely around and then some, compressing her bones. "Did you learn how to use this from your *friend*?"

Jayme.

Vi's hand released the hilt under Fallor's crushing grip. The magic blade fell to the ground, unraveling into formless strands of light that faded quickly into the night.

"What was the poor wench's name who lived under your boot again?" he sneered.

The narrowing of her eyes was his only warning before magic exploded from her, unfettered. It was light and fire. Both and neither. It was every inch of agony she felt and had not even had a breath to properly address since waking.

Fallor jumped back from the flames. In the same movement, he unsheathed a dagger, nearly the length of a short sword, from his thigh. He reared back, driving it right toward her chest.

"*Mysst Soto Xieh*!" Vi proclaimed, staring up at Fallor, unflinching, as his weapon drove harmlessly into a spinning circle of slight. "Don't you dare mention that traitor's name in my presence."

Fallor stepped back, spun, and launched another attack.

"*Loft Dorh Hoolo*," Vi seethed. She poured every ounce of hate for the man—and Jayme's betrayal—into the words. Fallor was stopped instantly, frozen in time.

Even under the influence of her own word of power from the goddess, Fallor was barely tethered. Rain poured over her shoulders. Mud dripped into her eyes. But Vi ignored the burning sensation, staring at Fallor as she waited for Taavin's words.

Waiting for him to finish the job.

A crack of lightning arced overhead, dancing through the clouds, splitting toward the earth. Her attention wavered as red illuminated the entire bluff.

Red lighting.

Vi found herself flooded by a profound sense of foreboding. The watch at her neck felt hot and whispers tickled the edge of her hearing. She'd seen the phenomenon in the distance on the *Dawn Skipper*. Up close, the lightning was profoundly unnerving. In its wake, Vi felt surrounded by an enemy she couldn't see but could sense lurking, ready to attack.

Unfortunately, it distracted her from the enemy right before her.

"*Mysst Soto Xieh!*" Taavin spoke so hastily the words were barely distinguishable. A shield of light was before her once more, this time shattering under Fallor's blade.

Vi jumped and slid back, putting distance between her and the pirate. "*Mysst Soto Larrk.*"

In her right hand, a bow appeared; in her left, an arrow. Vi brought them together, hands moving with expertise born from years of training. She drew back the bowstring, feeling the aches in her shoulders that accompanied it. Vi ignored every protest her body made—every reminder that she wasn't operating at full health.

She loosed the arrow point blank; it moved only inches to sink into Fallor's shoulder. The arrow exploded into light as Vi reached back to where a quiver would be. Her fingers condensed around something solid—a new arrow where there had previously been none.

Nocking the second, Vi loosed it just as quickly. Fallor stumbled back, raising his hand up to his shoulder, covering the wounds she inflicted. Rain, tinted red by another burst of lightning, merged with the dark blood pouring from the wounds. Vi expected to find anger, rage, or frustration in Fallor's gaze when he trained it upon her.

She hadn't expected the laughter.

"You really think you're a killer?" Her hands were moving to prove him wrong as he spoke. Fallor narrowed his steely eyes. "Do it then," he challenged with a whisper. "Show me you're a killer and not some pampered princess. Kill me, and meet Adela's true rage."

Rainwater shook from her quivering hand. Her fingers cramped in their grip, tighter than death, around the bow. She stared down the arrow, looking at the point right over the soft spot in the center of the man's neck.

Kill him.

It would feel so good to kill him.

She wanted to. But she couldn't. She was trapped between something dark and twisted that kept trying to snarl her in its thorny embrace, and everything she once thought she knew about herself. All the while, he was right there, waiting.

Was he right? Was this why she hadn't shattered his heart as she had Jayme's or Kora's? She had been able to kill them in a moment of blind rage. But would she be able to kill so easily again?

No, she'd chosen this route because it would be more painful. *That was it*, a sinister voice uttered within her. It felt like a person Vi had never met had taken residence in the void of her chest.

"I want to kill you slowly," she whispered. "I will see to it that none of Adela's pirates enjoy a clean death."

Vi let the arrow loose, aimed right for his throat. She wanted to watch the blood drain from his neck in a river. But the arrow only had time to knick his flesh before an unfamiliar voice boomed over the pouring rain. "*Juth mariy.*"

The bow in her hands shattered into harmless light. Vi let out a cry of anguish and readied her magic for her next assault. Enough of letting him off easy. Enough hesitation. She'd end this now.

The familiar grip of Taavin's fingers closed around her. "*Durroe sallvas tempre dupot. Durroe watt radia dupot.*" They were concealed once more.

Fallor didn't look for them. Instead, he turned, squinting in the darkness at the top of the far ridge. There, mounted on white steeds, was a line of men and women illuminated by shining orbs of blue-tinted light cast above their heads.

"Oh, holy Swords," Fallor cursed. There was the tell-tale ripple of power that made her skin crawl and Vi watched as the man slipped between each pulse of magic, disappearing and reappearing as an eagle where a man once stood.

"We have to go." Taavin tugged on her hand. He was going to dislocate her shoulder before the night was up. "Quickly, before—"

"*Juth mariy.*" The man at the head of the group shouted again. Vi could make out little more than his golden armor and dark hair. There was an uncanny similarity between him and the man she'd come all this way to find.

"Father?" Vi said, small and weak.

"Vi, this way!" Taavin pulled on her as his concealment shattered. "We have to make it to the Twilight Forest."

He broke into an all-out sprint, leaving Vi little choice but to follow.

That man atop the steed wasn't her father, no matter how much the armor looked like that of Solaris. She was far from that world of white and gold. Far from her home.

And her father was still the captive of the pirate queen.

An eagle's cry sounded, punctuated by the man shouting, "Archers to the Morphi! Calvary, to them! Loose!"

Vi couldn't hear the bowstrings over the rain and rolling thunder that followed streaks of red lightning. Neither could she hear the hooves of the large horses in pursuit of them. But she could *feel* the beasts.

She pushed her feet harder into the earth as red lightning cracked once more, striking the forest ahead. Every leaping step she took had Vi's free hand pressing into her side, where the flesh felt like it was tearing open anew. She was too freshly healed to be fighting and fleeing.

Taavin slowed. He was wheezing, too, his hand grasping at his shirt above his chest. Vi slowed her pace, looking back to the horses.

"Taavin, we—"

"I know," he hissed. Glancing over his shoulder, he looked back at the horses quickly closing the gap between them. "*Durroe watt radia. Durroe watt ivin.*" He turned forward again, keeping close alongside her, the rings of light he'd summoned condensing around his finger. "Keep running, and don't look back."

Vi heeded his words, running with all she had. Taavin, for his part, managed to keep stride. But every five steps he seemed to stumble, then every three.

"Taavin—" She looked to his face with worry. His eyes were hazy and unfocused. Was he going to make it to the forest? What would happen if the Swords caught them?

"Keep, going," he panted. "We're almost there."

As they ran, nearly at the trees, Taavin's arm swung out, pointing. A tiny glyph still spiraled around his finger. Vi watched as a nearly identical copy of her and Taavin sprinted off at an angle.

An illusion.

The horses continued to charge, shifting course to chase after their fabricated copies. Taavin's illusions vanished into thin air as the mounted men and women overtook them. One of the knights let out a cry of frustration as Vi and Taavin plunged into the welcoming embrace of the tree line, and into the dark unknown that was the Twilight Forest.

THE MOMENT HER FEET hit the mossy, wet earth of the forest, Vi moved faster. She'd grown up in the jungles of Shaldan, spending her childhood leaping and swinging from branch to branch. The feeling of damp brush and leaves under her feet, the sounds of rain muffled by the leafy canopy—its familiarity was a balm to her panic. She felt more comfortable with trees above and around her than she had in months in the desert and open sea.

There had been a road that led into the forest, but her and Taavin continued to ignore it. Instead, he struck out between the trees. From the corners of her eyes, Vi watched him move. Since entering the forest, her footing had become surer, while his stumbles were happening with greater frequency.

Taavin didn't even so much as glance her way. His face was etched with a fierce determination that unnerved her. Not just because she'd never seen the expression on his features—but because she was afraid of what would happen when that expression vanished. It was the look of a man who was going to run himself until his body gave out. She took a half step closer to him so she'd be there if he fell.

Vi glanced back, looking to where the riders had been. The rainclouds had blotted out the moon, leaving them very little light to see by. She found herself hoping for the cracks of the ominous red lightning to catch a quick glimpse of the knights or Fallor, but there was no such luck and she didn't dare summon a fire.

With every winded breath, the ache in her side ran deeper. Vi pressed a hand into the still-healing wound, wondering how recently Taavin had ripped it open. The pain seemed to spread, shooting straight up into her head.

"Taavin—"

"I know." He slowed his pace, chest heaving with panting breaths. He was faring no better than she. "Looks like I was right…"

"About what?"

"None of them will dare to come into the Twilight Forest," he wheezed, slumping against a tree. Vi was ready, reaching out to support him. But the moment her hand brushed feather-light against his side, he winced and let out a long hiss.

"Your ribs." Vi pulled her hands away, looking at the place Fallor had made contact. "Let me see."

"Let's get out of the rain first. We may be able to find shelter closer to the cliffs— an overhang, perhaps."

They pressed onward, albeit at a slower pace. Vi was soon dragging her feet and Taavin was leaning against every other tree to catch his breath.

"We have to stop. We're not going to make it much longer." She scanned their surrounds for options.

Ahead, the trees gave way for a small stream. Vi looked up and downstream, searching for any sign of Fallor or the Swords. But there was none. In fact, they seemed to be the only life in the forest, the world still other than the whisper of water. Taavin took a step down onto the slick rocks.

"Be careful." Vi quickly leapt to his side. Her arm wrapped tightly around his waist, holding him to her and stabilizing him.

"You're sure-footed."

"I grew up in a jungle, remember?" Vi helped him across to the giant boulders she assumed he was heading toward.

Just as Taavin had suspected—or hoped—the terrain had become rockier the closer they got to the cliffs that met the sea. The banks of the stream became giant boulders that jutted out from the earth. Downstream, Vi could see more rocks than trees.

They made their way toward one particularly large outcropping, a dark gap betraying a space just wide enough for them to squeeze through.

"In here?" Vi asked.

"It's the best I've seen and we should get out of the rain."

"Let me go first and make sure there's enough room." Vi guided him toward one of the two giant boulders on either side of the opening, stepping away from his side only when she was certain he was stable enough to stand on his own.

Squeezing herself into the opening, Vi tip-toed into the dark before allowing a small flame to kindle above her palm. The passage grew so narrow, she was certain she'd have to give up and turn back. But the flame illuminated a more open space ahead, and somehow she managed to twist the curves of her hips in just the right way to pop through with only a small wince.

Sure enough, it was a small cave, formed by four massive rocks leaning against each other. It would barely be large enough for the two of them—but it was dry and certainly well hidden.

It'd do.

"Come on in," Vi called back. "I think there's enough room."

Taavin appeared as he side-stepped between the rocks. Vi reached out, offering a hand and helping him through the rest of the way. He emerged with a sigh of relief, immediately leaning against the rocky wall opposite, hand splayed on his chest where Fallor had used his body as a springboard.

"Sit, and let me see," Vi repeated her earlier demand.

"I'll be fine," he said, as if pain wasn't written on his face in large, block letters.

"Quit being stubborn."

He finally obliged her, sinking down the wall until he was seated. His legs extended until his toes hit the opposite wall, knees bent. Vi crouched at his side, twisting until she found a way to somehow sit comfortably and not be in his lap at the same time.

Her hands paused at the hem of his shirt, the fabric still slick with rain and clinging to every curve of his muscle. Vi raised her eyes slowly to his.

"May I?" she whispered.

"Go ahead." The words were stronger than hers, but far from what she'd call confident. He was as nervous as she was. This was uncharted territory for them both.

She wasn't undressing him. Well, she *was*. But not really. It was for medical reasons.

Her racing thoughts had her heart matching pace as she slowly lifted the shirt, exposing the tan skin beneath. His flesh was bumpy, thanks to the chill of the cave and the exposed damp. Vi continued to ignore the cut curves of his muscles and the line of hair trailing down to and underneath his trousers—an easy task the moment her eyes landed on his ribcage.

"Oh, Taavin…" she breathed.

He winced as her fingers lightly brushed the deep bruising that splotched his skin. "It's that bad?"

"It looks like you had a small mountain crush you." Vi lowered the shirt slowly. "I've used *halleth* before but—"

"Not very well."

Vi narrowed her eyes slightly. She'd been about to say the same thing. But that didn't mean she appreciated him beating her to the punch. As if reading her mind, he wheezed laughter.

"I could tell." Taavin hid a wince between his words. The fight and flight had stolen their focus from their injuries and ailing bodies; it seemed that the pain was settling in on him now, just like she hadn't noticed her aches until they'd slowed their pace in the woods. "The wounds that had been inflicted on you—you tried to heal them with *halleth*—it was clumsily done. The skin was all knotted and scarred in a way that was going to give you trouble long-term. I was forced to rip them back open and set them correctly."

That confirmed her suspicions about why she still ached so badly.

"I was learning on the run," Vi said defensively. "We haven't had a chance to go over *halleth* yet. And Firebearing doesn't cover any kind of healing other than cauterizing wounds."

"You're alive—that means you did more than enough," he said, trying to soothe. "With Fallor on your tail, I assume those wounds were from Adela?"

Vi gave a small nod, lips pursed.

"What happened to you on the way here?" he asked, daring to ask the question that must have been on his mind since he found her on the beach. "I spoke with you on that balcony not more than—"

"Two, three, maybe four weeks ago," Vi murmured. It felt like a lifetime to her as well. Being unconscious for a large chunk of that time certainly didn't help.

"Something has changed since then."

He was right. Something had changed. Jayme's betrayal had awoken a darkness in her that Vi worried she'd never be free of.

"Vi, what is it?" he asked softly, emerald eyes shining in the firelight. Did hers shine as brightly? Or had they dulled with the dust of the long road she'd traveled?

"It's nothing." *Besides being trapped in the dark prison of my thoughts.* "It took a lot to get here. That's all."

He opened his mouth to speak again and Vi knew what he was going to ask. He'd want details. He'd probe for information she wasn't ready to give. Those events were still lost in the depths of the black waters sloshing in the hole in her chest.

"It seems to have been the same for you," Vi countered. His turn to look away. "The Swords of Light, the strong arm of the Faithful, are after you?"

"Led by Lord Ulvarth, no less."

"Their leader?"

"Yes. Knight of the Sun. Lord of the Faithful. Beloved by Yargen. Sole attendant to the Voice." Taavin enumerated Ulvarth's titles, each more bitter than the last.

"That's a mouthful… Not that I'm one to talk." Taavin gave a small grin at her jest, one he quickly abandoned. "He was there, wasn't he?"

"He was," Taavin said. "At the front." The firelight danced on his skin, casting long shadows. For a man who was filled with the power of light, darkness seemed to love him.

"They want to bring you back to the Archives of Yargen, don't they?"

"As soon as they can. I don't think it's public knowledge that I've escaped yet. If word gets out, Ulvarth stands to lose his rank and title—or the people's faith, at the very least."

She was slowly piecing together the parts of Taavin's life from bits of information he'd dropped like breadcrumbs in a vast forest. A man who was the head of a holy order—who'd ordained the Queen of Meru by his hand. But a puppet for others, a captive to keep under control so that Ulvarth could have power over arguably the strongest organization on Meru.

Her heart ached for him as her blood boiled with rage at the Lord of the Faithful.

"Why does Adela want you? Because you're a Solaris?"

At the mere mention of Adela, Vi's midsection ached. "The elfin'ra have put a bounty out for me," Vi answered simply.

"And Adela will capitalize on anything, even the end of the world." Taavin cursed under his breath.

She'd even capitalize on the lonely heart of a gullible princess, Vi thought bitterly. But she kept her mouth shut.

"Vi, what is it?" Taavin's palm cupped her cheek, summoning Vi's attention back once more from the demons lurking in her heart. "Let me help you," he said gently.

"You've done enough." It was her turn to take care of him now. And Vi didn't want to give Jayme another thought or word. Doing so felt like letting the traitor win. "We should plan our next move. You have Lord Ulvarth after you, and I have Fallor—Adela by extension—after me. It's a lot to deal with."

"Our next move is to wait." Taavin shifted, wincing again as his hand fell from her face. Vi caught it, not wanting to let go his warmth just yet. She felt far too cold on the inside to lose his touch.

"We have to keep moving. We're not safe here."

"This is the one place we have a chance to be safe," he insisted.

"Why?" Vi remembered his mention that they wouldn't "dare" follow them into the forest.

"Because we're in the Twilight Forest, which is under the protection of the Twilight Kingdom."

"Twilight Kingdom?" Vi repeated.

"The Twilight Kingdom is inhabited by the morphi, those who command the power of the shift."

Twilight Kingdom. Morphi. The shift. Her head was spinning, trying to take in all the new information at once. "What's the power of the shift? Is that another discipline of magic on Meru—like Lightspinning?"

Taavin's eyes fluttered closed a moment as he took a shallow breath. He looked exhausted and Vi knew she should let him rest. But it was hard to do that when information that might keep them alive hung on his tongue.

"It is. But I admit... I don't know much. The shift is a forbidden topic for the Faithful."

"What makes it forbidden?"

"You saw the markings on Fallor's brow?" he asked. She nodded, remembering the glowing dots that he'd covered with grease paint when she'd first met him. "Those are the mark of the morphi. The Faithful teach that they—the morphi—are turning their backs on Yargen by anchoring themselves in the twilight—neither darkness or light. Because of this altered existence, they can *shift* reality—which is an affront to Yargen's goodness."

"That sounds like a more religious than logical reason."

"It likely is." Taavin let out a soft sigh, eyelids drooping. "As I said, I know little of this power. Only the morphi possess it, and they guard the secrets of the shift with their lives."

"Is it because of the shift that Fallor can become an eagle?" Vi asked. "He's shifting the reality of himself—his nature—into that of an eagle?"

"That is my understanding, yes. Physical change is just one of their skills. They can also distort or break Lightspinning magic."

"That's what he did in the field, to break your illusion?"

"Yes."

"So how does this Twilight Kingdom protect us, if Fallor is one of them?" Vi kept her focus on the pressing matter of their survival rather than any questions on magical theory.

"He's a morphi... but the Twilight Kingdom holds no love for him. He's a famous exile from their lands, forbidden from entering their territory."

"And the Faithful won't follow us into the forests because the shift magic is anathema to them?" Dislike of the morphi still seemed an arbitrary and ill-founded prejudice, but if it protected them, she wouldn't complain too much about it.

"More or less."

"Can we seek refuge in the Twilight Kingdom?"

"No, we'll rest here until I can recover." Taavin rested a hand lightly on his ribs. "Which may be some time since we've lost the contents of my trunk."

"Sorry..." Vi muttered. It had gone up in smoke with the rest of the shack.

"It's all right. I didn't have much left anyway after traveling for a good week."

"If we can't seek refuge, can we at least restock in the Kingdom?" She couldn't blame Taavin for wanting to keep a low profile, given who he was. But surely she could at least go and get what they needed?

"No. The Kingdom is protected by an impenetrable shift. Even if you could get through... you shouldn't."

"But I can—"

"The enemies of our enemies are not our friends in this case. Neither of us should venture to interact with anyone from the Twilight Kingdom." He spoke as though it were a declaration. Vi bristled at the tone but didn't object. He knew far more about Meru and its nuances than she.

"Why would they have a reason to be hostile to us?"

"For the same reason that I will not heal myself with *halleth*... The feeling of hatred is mutual between the Faithful and the morphi. If they sense Lightspinning in their lands, we will be hunted. We conceal ourselves here in body and in magic."

Which meant they weren't really safe at all. Vi turned toward the narrow entrance they'd squeezed through. The rain still pounded outside, perhaps intent on raising the water in the small stream and flooding them out like two rats. In the distance, thunder rolled.

"Raspian is getting stronger…" Taavin mumbled, his eyes finally closing for slumber. "The end of the world is drawing near."

Vi remained silent, allowing Taavin to slip off to sleep.

She didn't bother worrying him with the fact that this was the second time she'd seen red lightning.

THE FIRST THING VI felt was the reassuring warmth of someone next to her.

The soft dripping of the cave filled her ears. Wet *plops* thrummed a rhythm underneath the echoes of the quietly babbling stream that ran by the entrance. The world was far quieter than when she'd gone to sleep.

Vi slowly opened her eyes, her attention drawn immediately to the man at her side. The gray light washed out his features and darkened his hair nearly to black. It clung with grime and sweat around his face, the natural waves of it almost clumping into curls. Slowly, Vi raised a hand, lightly pushing his hair away from his eyes.

Her fingertip brushed the point of his ear, her hand lingering there almost of its own volition.

He truly was different from her. She'd always known it. Yet when she had summoned him with *narro hath*, he'd existed in the framework of her world. Now, she was an occupant of his, and even the princess who belonged nowhere had never felt so out of place.

She'd finally made it to him. Somehow, he felt farther away than ever. They were from different worlds, pulled together by fate. Two people who should have never met and seemed destined for nothing more than heartache.

Vi lifted her hand off his person, though he was still heavy on hers. He was far heavier than Ellene had been when she'd fallen asleep on Vi's shoulder during too-long stories around campfires.

Ellene.

Vi had begrudged her life in Shaldan. Those endless nights of storytelling, the expectations of royalty, her never-ending lessons, the seemingly insufferable captivity. How grateful she would be to have one more night to relax with Ellene and sip cider, safe and protected behind walls meant to keep the world out as much as Vi in. She had never fully appreciated how good she'd had it.

And now it was gone.

The young princess who had sat around those firesides was lost on a beach between the Dark Isle and Meru. She was no longer that innocent, spoiled girl. Vi took a slow inhale of breath. The anger that ebbed and flowed within her had no direction, and would serve nothing. She had work to do; she had to let it go… But she didn't know how.

"Vi…" Taavin murmured, face still pressed against her shoulder. He hadn't even opened his long lashes yet. She shifted slightly, trying to get a better look at his face.

The man was calling for her in his sleep. But her movement seemed to rouse him from the remnants of dreamland.

"Did I disturb you?" she asked softly.

"No." Taavin winced as he rubbed his sides. "I think I disturbed myself." She neglected to mention that she'd been the one to lightly trail her fingers along his face. "It's late."

"Is it?"

"Given how stiff I am, I think so."

"Good to know the stiffness isn't just me." Using the wall for support, Vi pushed herself upward. There wasn't much room to stretch, but she made a good effort of it. "I'm going to wash my face and have a drink."

"While you're out, will you get me a garnet skullcap?"

"You're not coming? Some fresh air would do you well."

"You may be right… But no." Taavin adjusted himself slightly. Vi didn't miss the wince. "I think I shall linger here for a bit more. I'm not quite sure if it's the best idea for me to be moving yet… The skullcap should help relieve the aches and soothe me back to sleep."

"You slept a fair bit." A frown crossed her lips. Could a person sleep too much? Vi suddenly wished she'd paid more attention to Ginger's brief clerical lessons whenever Vi landed herself in trouble. Another thing she'd taken for granted.

"The more I rest, the faster we can be on the road." He gave her what Vi could easily recognize as a brave smile in the face of great pain.

"Taavin, I'm worried—"

"Don't worry about me, Vi. I'm elfin; we're a hearty bunch and heal much faster than humans, even without any kind of clerical assistance." Heal much faster than *her*, he meant. Everything this morning served to remind her of their differences. "Garnet skullcap. Bright white flowers shaped like little bells. Deep crimson leaves—thin and slightly waxy."

Vi quickly repeated the description back to him. "Got it."

"Thank you, Vi."

She gave a nod. "I'll be back soon."

Vi sucked in her stomach and squeezed through the narrow passage and out onto the rocky bed of the stream. Raising a hand to her eyes, Vi shielded them from the bright white light of morning, giving them a chance to adjust.

Motion startled her near instantly. Vi ducked quickly, raising her hand, her spark crackling around her fingers. She jerked her head toward a nearby tree where the projectile had landed.

No, wait, not a projectile… Sitting in the tree was a bird as big as her forearm with a long neck and oil-slick plumage. It almost looked wet with how the light shimmered off its long feathers. Every subtle breeze sent rainbows across its back and breast. From hooked beak to bright blue talons, Vi had never seen anything like it.

The strange looking bird regarded her for a long moment before taking off with an undignified chirp. Vi watched it take flight, the mere sight of a bird sending small shivers down her spine. She wondered if she would ever be able to see a winged creature again without thinking of Fallor.

Vi set off, trying to leave thoughts of the pirate behind her.

In the daylight, the trees were an eerie gray color. Not quite the shade of bleached bone, but brighter than the ashes of a fire pit, and a hue Vi had never seen among the giant sentries of the North. These trees were tall—dizzyingly so. But they were thin from root to canopy. So thin that Vi wondered how they didn't topple over with the slightest of breezes that swayed their canopies.

The forest floor was covered with leaves and little else. There were no smaller shrubs, no fan-like fronds stretching out to block her path. She could see straight through all the trees like bars in a cage until the horizon blurred and it was hard to tell just where anything stopped and started.

That was the real reason she didn't stray far from the stream.

Every tree of the forest looked identical. Sameness and more sameness. It was a forest she felt she could get lost in forever if she wasn't careful.

"Red leaves," she murmured to herself.

She'd been walking for the better part of an hour in search of the skullcap. Vi was about ready to give up when she finally found it. Taavin hadn't specified what part of the plant he needed—and Vi knew all too well that not all parts of a plant were equal, at least not when it came to extracting medicinal properties. So she dug it out, roots to delicate buds.

"I think I have it," Vi announced as she squeezed back into their hiding place.

The skullcap slipped from her fingers, forgotten.

"Taavin!" She knelt at his side. The man's chin was slumped to his chest. His arms hung heavy, palms up. The last person she'd seen in such a state had been dying from the White Death. "Taavin wh—"

"I was merely resting." He lifted his head with a start, giving her a thin smile. "No need to fret."

Vi searched his face. *Lying.* He was lying through his teeth. There was plenty of reason for her to fret.

"You're not okay, are you?" she whispered.

"I will be." Taavin looked toward his feet, seeing the skullcap she'd dropped. "I see you found some."

"I did."

"Good. I'll just need the buds… two for now. Be careful to pinch them off so that you don't get any stem. Here, like this." His hands reached out, covering her fingers lightly. Vi split her attention between what he was showing her and his haggard expression. Even now, even after all that had transpired, a certain grace clung to him and wouldn't let go.

"Here, let me do the next." She focused on the task at hand and tried to replicate his motions.

"Perfect." Taavin took the bud from her fingers, chewing it thoughtfully before swallowing. With that, he leaned back, settling himself once more.

Vi shifted to face him. His feet were at her side, hers at his. Her eyes landed on his hands—folded over his lower stomach and slowly running over a golden bracelet Vi had never seen before. Had they been outstretched, she might have gathered them in her own.

This was the first quiet—and fully conscious—moment they'd had since meeting in person, she realized.

Suddenly, despite all that had transpired, she felt marginally awkward. Her hands couldn't seem to find a good place to rest. How had she been so comfortable around him before? How had she touched him like it was nothing? Vi ended up mirroring his pose.

"How long will it take for you to get better?" she asked.

"With enough rest and any luck, a few days at worst."

"A few days..." she repeated, her mind already turning over the implications of the thought. "I'll need to forage some sustenance for us." He'd said the Twilight Kingdom and Forest were the lands of the morphi, and the last thing Vi wanted to do was slay an animal that was secretly a person. Her thoughts wandered back to the dark bird—it was a good thing she hadn't killed it.

"Do you know what plants are safe to eat?"

"I was going to look for ones I recognized. I realize I'm far from home, but there's likely a few common varieties—Meru and the Dark Isle aren't *that* far apart. Certain mushrooms grow across the whole Dark Isle... I assume they'll be here too. Maybe some fruits or nuts that you can help identify?"

"Brilliant thoughts. Forgive me for forgetting how capable you are." A small, sad smile crossed his mouth. "I sometimes think of our captivity as the same. In reality, you were able to explore far more than me."

The aching and longing in his voice kept Vi from arguing. She hadn't ever really been able to *explore*. Not in the true, untethered sense of the word. But she had been awarded some freedoms. She'd had teachers who wanted her to know how to survive in the wilds if, or when, she needed to. She suspected none of them ever thought she'd have to put theory into practice—but here she found herself, somewhat prepared to face this newest challenge.

Even if she hadn't realized it at the time, she'd had luxuries Taavin had only dreamed of.

"When you're better..." Vi straightened away from the wall, resting a hand on his thigh. "I'll show you every edible plant I can find, and how to harvest them. I'll even show you the ones that I had to taste-test to find out if they're edible or poisonous."

"Don't you go taste-testing possibly poisonous things." His hand covered hers. "I don't want anything happening to you."

"Nothing will."

Taavin gave a dark chuckle. "You say that, when clearly so much has." Vi searched his expression as he effortlessly held her gaze. "You're not the same woman I first met."

"No one stays the same," Vi murmured.

"True... Then, you're not the same woman I stood next to on that balcony." Taavin's fingers worked to lace with hers. Vi's hand remained limp, giving him no encouragement. Yet she couldn't find it in her to pull away either. He was the only comfort she had in this strange world.

"Maybe you never really had a good measure on me to begin with," Vi contested as discomfort worked its way underneath her skin like maggots.

"Truly?" He arched his eyebrows. "You think I don't know you by now? You think I haven't spent my life learning your mannerisms? Memorizing your face?"

"You memorized a woman in a dream. I am not that woman. It was likely my grandmother, remember?"

"Maybe." He shifted slightly, sitting straighter. "Or maybe you're challenging me because you know I'm right."

Vi shifted, caught between wanting to pour out her soul to him, and bolt from the cave to avoid his scrutiny. She'd spent so much time trying to get to him that Vi hadn't really thought about what it would be like when they were together... all the time. When she couldn't dismiss him with a thought or wave of her hand. When his eyes continued to bore into her soul long after she wanted the relief of hiding from things she herself wasn't yet ready to address.

"Vi—"

"I should get to foraging, while there's still plenty of good light." Vi pulled away quickly. Fleeing from her problems would be her choice.

"Wait—" Taavin leaned forward, started to get up, then stopped mid-motion with a wince of pain. His back rested heavily once more on the wall behind him as he grabbed both of his sides. "Vi, I'm just trying—"

Vi ignored him, pretending she couldn't hear. Once more, she squeezed out into the sunlight, promptly starting upstream.

He was just trying to help. She knew he was. She paused to look back to the rocky entrance of their cave, briefly debating whether or not to return immediately and make amends.

Would it feel good, or terrible, to expose the angry darkness that swirled around in her now? What would he think when he learned of how she'd used *juth calt*?

Vi turned, continuing on, her back to the cave mouth.

At first, she wasn't very active in her foraging. It was more of a walk to try to clear her head. But the more time that passed, the less clear-headed she felt. If anything, things got murkier.

Mirroring her mindset, dusk fell.

"Twilight in the Twilight Forest," Vi muttered. Her feet slowed once more.

The world had certainly taken on an unnatural quality. The ashen trees looked even more devoid of color. Their leaves had become pale—not a fiery red as one might expect with the fading sun. And they cast long shadows on the forest floor, turning it dark gray. It was as though the whole world had been expunged of color and steeped in drab.

The trees in the distance seemed to waver briefly. Vi rubbed her eyes and squinted. Had she only imagined the ruler-straight trunks wobbling?

She stepped away from the rocky stream, scrambling up a large boulder, and started into the trees.

Her first thought was Fallor and his strange magic—*the shift*. Perhaps he had followed them into the forest despite being exiled? Vi balled her hand into a fist, curling the spark under her fingers.

Taavin had said they couldn't use Lightspinning without risking detection. Would her fire be all right? It would have to be, because she wasn't about to fight Fallor bare-handed.

The forest was uncomfortably silent. Nothing but gray sameness as far as the eye could see. She turned, glancing over her shoulder—

The stream was gone.

Her heart raced in earnest now. She couldn't hear the stream over the deafening stillness of the woods. She couldn't see it between the countless trees that seemed to close in on her. Vi spun in place. All she had to do was turn right around and go back the way she came.

It wasn't Fallor, anyway—it couldn't be. Perhaps it was some other morphi. Though Taavin had cautioned her to stay away.

As she spun in place, something caught her eye—another bit of wobbling, this time over the split trunk of a fell tree.

"What is that?" she whispered, slowly drawing near. The leaves crunched under her shuffling footsteps, but Vi could barely hear it. There was a murmuring buzz at the edges of her hearing, the closer she got to the oddity.

It was a tree trunk, split from the inside out. The smell of rot suddenly filled her nose, as though the tree had let out a dying breath. But the aroma was not deep and earthy as one would expect. It was rank and choking, like carrion. She would've long fled were it not for an unnerving fascination with the anomaly—as though she were looking at something she shouldn't.

Tiny sparks of red lightning jumped between each gaping crack in the bark, leaving black spots in their wake. Above it, the air seemed alive, shifting and writhing, distorting the trees beyond. There was a snap, a pop, and Vi could nearly make out lights where there had been none. It was as if the air were tearing open to expose the darkness that existed beyond the veil of her reality. A whole city of darkness, waiting.

Vi squinted and leaned closer in an effort to make out more details before the air shifted again and the city was gone.

She leaned too close.

A tiny bolt of lightning extended upward, striking her fingertip. Though it couldn't have been more than a pin-prick, it felt as though it darted under her skin, crackling across her muscles from finger to shoulder to brow, all the way down to her toes.

She must've let out a scream, but Vi couldn't be certain, because the murmuring in her ears magnified with the cracks of lightning that struggled to break through her flesh. Suddenly it was as if a thousand people were talking over each other at once, all trying to get to her. They said countless names, rapid fire, over a thousand muttered conversations Vi couldn't make out.

She gripped the sides of her face, trying to cover her ears and mute the excruciating, deafening noise. Slowly layering atop them all was a terrible rhythm, a singular repeated word, louder by the moment.

Die, die, die.

There was another bolt of lightning, this time jackknifing right for her heart—too quick for her to move away.

Light burst from the watch at her neck, cutting the impending darkness of the forest, keeping the lightning and auditory assault at bay. Vi stumbled backward, fell, scrambled back to her feet. She panted, breathless. But the only sounds in her ears now were that of her frantically beating heart, and every labored breath as she turned and broke into an all-out run.

"TAAVIN... TAAVIN!" VI PUSHED herself through the entrance of the cave, not caring for every rough bit of rock that dug into her curves. It barely registered as pain—barely registered at all. "Taavin," she repeated again as she gasped for air. As though his name was the only thing she could manage.

"Vi, what is it?" Through the pain, he forced himself more upright. Distress, but not for his own state, written across his features. "Are you all right? What's happened?"

Vi shook her head. The one voice, that terrible, earth-shattering voice demanding her death still lived in her ears. If she opened her mouth, it may come from her lips. That was how deep it now ran in her.

"It's clearly something." Taavin's voice had gone stern. "Don't shut me out."

She shook her head again, trying to focus on breathing. Trying to dig her nails into the rough wall behind her to keep her focus grounded in the here and now. She needed something stable. But the whole world felt like it could crumble at once.

"Vi—" A small yelp of pain broke through, yanking her back to the present. Taavin was rolled on his side on the ground, his elbow supporting him. Yet even now, he struggled to get back up.

"Don't." She stopped him with a word. "Don't get up again, you'll just hurt yourself." Vi sank down the wall slowly, crouching on the balls of her feet, knees to her chest and arms around her legs.

"Tell me." He reached out with the hand that wasn't supporting him, fumbling until he caught her fingers. "Did you run into a morphi?"

She shook her head no.

"The Swords of Light?"

"No."

"What, then?"

Vi stared at him. Her eyes felt dry, as though they'd been held open too wide for too long. She made an effort to blink them. Somehow, even that hurt. The same sensation she'd had when she'd woken returned: her body was not her own.

"I don't know what it was," she confessed. "There was red lightning around a fallen tree and—"

"Red lightning around a *tree*?" Taavin finally seated himself once more, no longer leaned over on his elbow.

"More like… inside the tree. Maybe it was struck during the storm last night? There was a tree that had fallen, and it looked odd. When I got closer, I could see red lightning jumping between its shattered trunk and it *reeked*. Taavin, it smelled of death."

His expression darkened. "What else happened?"

"How do you know something else happened?" Vi whispered.

"Because you aren't a woman reduced to shaking by a tree that smells of death and has red lightning… however darkly unnatural it may be."

Vi balled her hands into fists, willing her arms to stop trembling. He was right. She wasn't someone who quaked in fear. She swallowed hard, continuing when her voice was more level.

"The air above seemed… alive. Like it was writhing and ripping. Through it, I saw a city of darkness. Then, a bolt of lightning hit me and… *noise*. Terrible noise." Vi's hands slowly worked their way back up to her ears, as if she still needed to block out the wretched sounds. "Screaming, crying, talking, a thousand people—a whole world of people—all at once."

She couldn't put into words the sensation. She'd known the sound of every voice, as though she'd heard them with her own ears earlier in her life. Yet the words were muffled and unfamiliar.

"Is that all?" He pushed himself forward, sliding along the floor, reaching for her. This time, Vi extended a hand, allowing their fingers to knot together tightly.

This was real, she reminded herself. Taavin was real, and good, and safe, and that… what she had seen in the forest had been… had been…

"It was Raspian," Vi uttered so softly she couldn't be certain she'd spoken at all. "Above it all, I heard him, calling for my death." Taavin's fingers tightened around hers. "He's getting stronger, isn't he?" Taavin gave a small nod. "I saw the land of the elfin'ra, I heard their voices. He's rallying them."

"I'm not sure about that."

"But—"

"I agree… Raspian is getting stronger. He's sinking in his dark clutches wherever he can find purchase, as Yargen's powers weaken. We've seen it in the White Death, we've seen it in his magic streaking through the sky as red lightning. But I don't think the city you saw was of the elfin'ra. I think it was the Twilight Kingdom. I suspect his dark energy is distorting the shift around the city, weakening it. Perhaps, as you describe, tearing it."

"He's rotting the world from the inside out." Vi returned to one of her earlier conclusions.

"But this could be a good thing for us," Taavin mused.

"How so?"

"Because Adela and her like have eluded punishment for years by retreating to her Isle of Frost. The whole of the island is protected by a shift of its own."

"Adela knew the Faithful wouldn't rely on the morphi, not even to get to her." Vi pieced it together aloud, recalling what Taavin had said about the mutual hatred. That made the morphi an easy target for Adela to lure to her cause.

"But if Raspian is breaking down the shift, we may be able to find a way in to the isle. It was something we were going to have to confront, one way or another. This just provides us a simple solution."

Vi dismissed the fact that Taavin was ignoring the obvious, yet again; they could simply seek help from the morphi. Vi likewise filed the idea away, for now. Getting a morphi on their side appealed to her, loathe as she was to bring an unknown element into her plans. She didn't want to leave her father's rescue to the chance of a tear in the shift around the Isle of Frost—she wanted to know for certain she'd be able to get to Adela.

"How is Raspian doing all this without a physical form? Isn't that what the elfin'ra have been after, what they're hunting us to achieve?"

"Yes. For Raspian to reap the destruction he so desires and rebuild the world in his image, he will need to be flesh and blood … But as Yargen's magic continues to fade, Raspian can make bolder plays as he searches for a way to walk among us again."

"What can we do to stop him?"

"Rekindle the flame and restore it to the blazing beacon of life it's always been." Such had been his goal from the start. It had been the one thing he'd sought her out to do all those months ago.

"The watch protected me from one of the bolts of lightning," she said as she clutched the token. "Taavin, I think somehow, it has Yargen's magic."

He hummed in agreement, reaching upward. But rather than going immediately for the watch, his fingertips rested lightly on her cheek. They were almost scalding hot. Vi hadn't realized how clammy she'd become. He searched her face for a long moment before his hand fell, resting atop hers and the watch.

"You may be right. We don't know what it contains, yet, and I desperately want to uncover its secrets."

"How do we do that?"

"I'll need to use Lightspinning to investigate the magic within. Something I am in no position to do."

Taavin pushed himself away and settled back against the wall across from her once more. His eyes fluttered closed a moment and Vi watched the shallow rise and fall of his chest. She didn't know if he meant that he wasn't in a position to do so because of his current state… or because they were in a place he couldn't use Lightspinning.

Likely both.

"Well… you'll just have to get better quickly then." Vi pushed away from her wall, twisting and settling once more next to him. Their sides were flush and she soaked in his warmth.

"I'm trying," he murmured over a bite of skullcap.

"Try harder." Vi nudged him lightly, hoping she'd come off as playful. The emotion was rusty. It felt awkward to her, so she couldn't imagine how it was received.

A smile broke on his lips. "Yes, my Champion."

"Thank you, my Voice."

There was something dangerously endearing to the words. Perhaps their physical proximity added layers of meaning that weren't really there. Or perhaps it was the panic that still popped under her skin like electric shocks, driving her to seek out any feelings of safety and security she could.

"Taavin…" Vi whispered. His breathing had slowed, and she had yet to look back toward him, instead keeping her focus on the dancing shadows her small, flickering flame cast on the wall opposite them. She almost hoped he had fallen asleep.

"Yes, Vi?"

"You told me once, terrible things happen to those you love."

"I did." His voice had grown more lucid, and Vi felt guilty keeping him awake. What was she really trying to ask, anyway?

"Why did you say that?" He sighed softly. "You don't have to tell me."

"I've only ever loved one person, Vi—" She braced herself for the name of some lover she really didn't want to know about, instantly regretting her decision. "—my mother."

"What?" Her eyes were pulled to him in surprise. But Taavin wasn't looking at her. He stared off at the same wall she had been, seeing something entirely different in the shadows.

"Why is it so surprising I loved my mother?"

"I expected you to have a lover... I wasn't thinking of familial love."

He chuckled at that. "How would I find a lover? I was sequestered... The only person who really has unfettered access to me is Ulvarth."

"Right..." She didn't know what else to say. Vi had imagined servants coming in and out, attending him as they had her. Another thing she'd been wrong about. "What happened to your mother?" Vi couldn't imagine a mother condemning their child to such a life willingly. And given all he'd said on the matter, she fully expected the truth to be grim.

"Ulvarth killed her."

She wasn't surprised, not really. After everything Taavin had told her... Her lips pursed into a thin line.

"Ulvarth killed her, to get me." Taavin still wouldn't look at her. His expression was blank, matching the hollow tone of his voice. "There is always a Voice, Vi... When one dies, Yargen chooses another child to serve her for their lifetime. I always suffered from my visions—that was what ultimately drew Ulvarth to me."

"But your mother didn't want to give you up." Vi's mind wandered back to her own mother. Vhalla had made that terrible choice to give Vi up for such an excruciatingly long stretch. But if she hadn't... If the North had attacked during the rise of the Mad King, her mother and father may not have lived long enough to see Vi into the world.

"No, she said they were wrong. That I was merely a troubled boy, not afflicted by words of the goddess." Taavin raised a hand, running it down the side of his face over the crescent-shaped scar on his cheek. "The struggle wasn't much. What could a boy and a young woman do against Ulvarth and the Swords of Light?"

"You tried to defend her." The scar had an explanation, and a terrible, gut-wrenching one at that.

"I did. They wouldn't kill me... No... Ulvarth needed me alive. But he didn't need me unbroken."

"I'm sorry," she breathed. It wasn't nearly enough. Taavin didn't even address the paltry attempt at consolation.

"She loved me. So she defended me and died for it. If she had agreed to Ulvarth's demands, she would still be alive. Bad things happen to those I love and who love me. So I swore I'd never love again and put someone at risk."

Vi closed her eyes, ignoring the dull ache the words inspired. The halfway status of their relationship, the questions, the time spent wondering what they were... He'd never give them anything more than he already had, she realized. She heard it clearly between his words: *I can't let myself love you.*

Despite all she'd been though, that realization may have hurt the most.

"We should go to sleep," Vi murmured and extinguished the flame.

"We should," he agreed and, within moments, his heavy breathing told her that he had, finally, allowed the world to slip away.

But Vi was still very much grounded in the world. It was a world of men who cut down women to take their children. A world of red lightning.

A world where she had somehow allowed someone into her heart who may not want to be there.

TAAVIN HAD GOTTEN WORSE.

"You should drink something." Vi tapped his cheek gently. His head was limp, chin against his chest. "You haven't drank anything for two days."

His bloodshot eyes cracked open, blinking slowly in the dim light. Sweat beaded on his forehead. Two nights ago, when she'd returned from the red lightning incident in the wood, she'd thought she was cold from fear—that was why he'd seemed so warm to her. But the fever had been ravaging him then. Now, the infection from his broken bones and festering wounds continued to spread.

"Taavin, please, the fever is taking water from you; even if you don't feel you're thirsty, you need to drink."

"Vi..." His lips barely moved as he spoke.

"I'm here, it's me." She held out the wide, flat leaf she'd been cupping in her hand and using as a bowl to ferry water into the cave. "Please, drink."

"I..."

"Please." Vi brought the edge of the leaf to his lips. Taavin didn't have the energy to object further. Most of the water dribbled down his chin and onto his lap, but some got into his mouth. Surely, some had. "Good, that's it."

The knot in his throat bobbed and Taavin's eyes closed. Vi set the leaf to the side. He was fading. She didn't have to be a cleric to know when someone was dying.

"I'm going to find help," Vi whispered. A foolish and dangerous idea had been forming in her head for days now. One that she became less able to shake with each passing morning as he woke worse than the last. "Stay here, and hang on."

Vi emerged from the cave into the familiar haze of the Twilight Forest and struck out upstream as she had all those mornings ago. Part of her was already sick with the notion of what she was about to do. But there was no other choice. Inaction would result in Taavin's death. At least this way he'd have a chance.

How long had she walked that first day? Long enough for her mind to wander... but she hadn't really been paying attention to any actual distances. Vi's eyes scanned the trees to the edge of where the horizon became hazy, looking for a tell-tale wobble in reality itself.

Finding none, Vi stepped off the rocky riverbank and onto the leafy carpet of the forest. She hadn't found the last tear along the water—it had been in the woods itself.

Vi looked back the way she'd come. *No other option*, she repeated to herself. Going back meant Taavin's death. And that was a reality Vi was not about to face.

Tree by tree, Vi ran her fingers along the bark. Her spark tingled beneath her flesh, heating the air between her and the tree. She left singed fingerprints in her wake on every tree she passed. They were signposts for her to use to find her way back, and Vi sincerely hoped she would need to use them—that this foolish notion wouldn't kill her.

The sun was hanging low in the horizon and Vi had lost count of how many trees she'd marked when she finally saw a flash of red light. It was a tiny spark, barely perceptible in the wash of sunset amber. But it was the hope she'd been searching for.

Vi approached the abnormality in the fabric of reality with caution. Another tree had fallen, but this time, rather than landing on the ground, it was propped against its neighboring tree. Tiny bolts of red magic, like ominous fireflies, darted back and forth between the fallen tree and the ground. Scraps of bark were sheered off and hung at an odd angle, dangling in the air—perfectly still, even when breezes swept through the forest enough to rustle the leaves at her feet.

It had been the storm, Vi decided. The bolts of red lightning had struck trees in the forest, creating these abnormalities. She wondered if she went back to the bluffs, would she find red lightning crackling among dead grasses, like footprints of an angry god?

Murmuring returned to the back of her mind, the closer she came to the tree of red lightning. It was a dull, pulsing sensation, but one Vi knew would become sharper if she drew closer.

When she drew closer.

Vi watched the shimmering air in the triangle created by the upright tree, the lightning-struck tree leaning against it, and the ground below. She watched, and waited, keeping her distance. She waited long enough that her feet ached from her toes digging into the ground through the worn-thin soles of her shoes. It wasn't until twilight had fallen on the forest in earnest that Vi caught the first glimpse of the kingdom shimmering beyond—this time more clearly than the last.

Taavin's theory was that Raspian's magic had worn away the shift protecting the Twilight Kingdom—however *that* worked. It was time to put his theory to the test.

Vi gripped the watch around her neck so tightly that she feared she would break it. But that didn't prompt her to unfurl her fingers.

"Yargen, protect me." Vi didn't know if it was a prayer, a demand, or just a wish. She'd take all three, if that's what got her through.

Shifting her feet, Vi launched herself forward like an arrow loosed from the bowstring. Each step was wider than her usual gait, intended to build momentum as quickly as possible. Her body tipped forward, running head-first toward the pulsating air that grew more violent with red magic by the second. She threw her entire weight behind every step. There was no turning back.

There was only one way for her now—into the breach.

Every muscle in her body tensed on impact, ready for the agony she knew was coming. Lightning flared on all sides of her, blinding her, trying to snarl her in its brutal embrace. Vi kept pumping her legs, pushing herself forward, but she didn't know what she was pushing against.

Her eyes had closed instinctively, but now she forced them open. Lightning danced before her vision. It looked as though it was behind her eyes, shooting through her skull—in one ear and out the other. Between every bolt was nothing but pure darkness.

She clutched the watch tighter as the cacophony grew so loud, Vi could barely manage a thought beyond *forward*. She had to keep moving forward. She'd either free herself and be on the other side of this terrible bramble of magic in a world beyond, or she'd push straight through to the Twilight Kingdom as she'd hoped.

A thousand hands worked to keep her back as a thousand voices screamed at her all at once. Vi ignored the feeling of every electric grasp on her body. She ignored the noise as best she could.

Forward.

The word resounded in her chest and Vi realized she'd been saying it aloud the whole time. That was fine. It drowned out Raspian's call for her death. It kept her feet moving. It kept him from claiming her.

Underneath her hand, the watch seared white-hot. It throbbed with every pulse of magic washing over Vi's body. *Forward, and don't let go.* If she let go of the watch, she let go of Yargen. Without Yargen's magic protecting her, Vi knew she would've already been torn apart.

Her long march suddenly had an end. In the distance, beyond the flashes of lightning, there was darkness. Perhaps, it was death waiting for her. Either way, Vi continued relentlessly on and, with a shout, she freed herself of the clutches of Raspian's magic.

Vi took in a gasping breath, only to find the air suddenly thin. Suffocating darkness was around her, so thick that not even air could exist here. She opened her mouth, not getting enough air through her nose alone. But there was no more to be had in this still, blank space.

Still, she forced herself to take a step, and then another.

With every inch, cool light flared underneath her feet until it condensed into a shimmering, solid form. The glowing blue path of magic hardened into stone guided her through the darkness and toward the twilight. Every step brought magic rippling over her like wind, giving her a brief reprieve before the darkness closed in again. But just when her head was throbbing and her eyes felt as though they might explode from her skull, the world slowly rebuilt itself before her eyes.

It was not the world she'd known. The Twilight Forest had vanished before her eyes and was now replaced by a city appearing through shadowy trees that barely had form. With every step closer, there was a brief flash of air, then sound, then light.

Vi emerged from between two dark trees, which seemed now more solid than shadow, and collapsed to her knees. Surrounding her were shards of pale blue stone; they fell off her, like shards of glass, fading to a dull black stone as they hit the ground. She gulped in heaving breaths. Air had never tasted so fresh, or felt so good. Her eyes were blurry, face wet. Vi didn't know if it was from involuntary tears brought on by pain, sweat from the exertion, or immense relief to have made it through.

Likely all three.

Vi rubbed her eyes, sank to her heels, and blinked, taking in the new world before her. It was a city nestled in a valley. Tall ridges extended up on all sides, lined with the same dark trees that were now at Vi's back. It was as if the trees were made of smoke—less solid the farther back one went, turning into wisps of magic that trailed up to form a hazy barrier around the Twilight Kingdom.

A metropolis of wooded magic lit up before her. Large buildings with rope-bridges suspended between them towered overtop wide fauna that served as roofs for bustling markets and businesses below. The construction reminded her somewhat of the North, but with more glass and fitted stone. *There were no Groundbreakers here*, Vi reminded herself.

There were balconies of glass, shining in the moonlight. Some homes had siding that looked like dark metal laid in a pattern that reminded Vi of snake scales. Wood blended into metal set into stone. Nothing seemed right, yet it all connected.

Vi's eyes drifted upward to a moon that had never felt so close. She swallowed hard, her vision of the world's end seared in her memory. Like that vision, this moon, too, was rimmed in a bloody corona, stretching out into the stars scattered on a perpetually dusky sky.

Even here, Raspian had sunk in his claws. Vi wondered how long it would be until the moon in her world looked much the same. And that was when a terrible thought crossed her mind…

What if Taavin's injuries were not fully a result of Fallor's attack? What if the voice was falling prey to Raspian's effects on their world? And if he was—what did that mean for her own susceptibility to the spreading darkness?

Vi gripped her knees, hanging her head. Perhaps that was why, despite Taavin's allegedly superior healing abilities, he was so injured. Vi sniffed, rubbing her nose with the back of her hand. Memories of the White Death—of the clinic in Soricium—drifted through her mind.

No.

She wouldn't let this be his end.

Vi struggled to her feet, using the tree next to her for support. Somewhere in the city beneath her were clerics. She would find one and she would bring him or her back to Taavin by any means necessary.

With one shaky footstep after the next, Vi descended into the Twilight Kingdom.

V I MADE SHORT WORK of the walk down the grassy, sloping ridge that ringed the bustling metropolis. Leaning against the back wall of a building right at the edge of the city—Vi took a quick assessment of herself.

Her clothes were ratty and torn. They were sun bleached and salt damaged, hanging like rags on the line that was her too-thin frame. Vi pressed at her stomach and hips. There was less muscle there than she was used to and far less than she'd like.

Rubbing her temples, Vi tried to maintain her focus. It was a difficult task. Her head was still splitting and she could feel the invisible scars of Raspian's infernal lightning on the underside of her skin.

"Think, Vi," she commanded herself. Hearing her voice aloud helped her brain return to task. She glanced around the corner, looking at the group of people lounging on a shared patio area between two buildings.

They didn't seem to notice her, too busy carrying on laughing, drinking, and playing some kind of game Vi couldn't see and doubted she would recognize. She mostly ignored the conversation—which, fortunately, was carried out in what she knew as the common tongue—and focused on the people's faces. They each looked very much like what she would expect of a human... save for their eyebrows.

Dotted across their brows were faintly glowing spots like those Fallor sported. Every individual seemed to have a slightly different color and pattern. Vi leaned back, running her fingers along her own brow in thought.

There was no way she could create anything convincingly similar without using some kind of Lightspinning. Which meant she'd need to hide rather than masquerade. Perhaps there were humans among them, and Vi's worries were ill founded. But the Twilight Kingdom went to great lengths to protect itself from outsiders, and Vi had yet to see any non-morphi. She wasn't about to take a chance.

It took three side alleyways before Vi found one that wasn't swarming with people. Two men lingered at the opening by the road, their backs to her. Neither so much as looked over their shoulders as Vi slipped in, grabbing a dishcloth off a drying line and quickly tying it around her forehead.

She adjusted it several times, making sure it was secured tightly—tight enough to contribute to her already-throbbing headache. Vi ignored the pain, focusing on running her fingers over her brow and making sure everything from just above her eyes to halfway up her forehead was covered.

It likely looked ridiculous. But given the sorry state of the rest of her, a dishcloth bandanna was the least of her worries. Vi held her breath and kept her strides even as she approached the two men.

Calm—she had to be calm, even when it felt like everything pointed to her being immediately discovered as an interloper.

"Excuse me?" Vi asked. Both men turned, startled to see her. Vi folded her hands, keeping her eyes mostly down in an attempt to be demure and nonthreatening. Just because she was willing to fight tooth and nail for her and Taavin's survival didn't mean she wanted to. If it came down to that, her odds didn't look good.

"Yes?"

"Do you know where I can find the nearest cleric? I don't regularly come this way… and I'm a bit turned around."

"Cleric?" The man repeated, looking to his friend. The other shrugged.

"A healer, I mean?" Vi said tentatively, hoping her difference in word choice wouldn't be what ultimately led to her discovery.

"Oh, why didn't you say so?" The man shook his head, as though she was already burdensome, then looked to his friend. "Who's closest to here?"

"Sarphos has a shop. But he's rarely in it."

"Yeah, he wouldn't be."

"I think after that it's Rem?"

"Rem?"

"Five streets down and over, on seventeenth, the shop with the purple-colored awning."

"*Oh*, her."

"So…" Vi jumped into the conversation. "Purple colored awning on seventeenth," she repeated. "But Sarphos is closer?"

"If you want to try him." The man gave a shrug that showed how likely her success was. "He is in the opposite direction though… Only one street down." He pointed to another intersection diagonally across from where Vi stood. "He's in between here and fourteenth. But he's rarely there."

"Excellent, thank you." Vi gave a small nod and started in the direction the man had pointed. The two men resumed their conversation as if nothing had happened. As if her heart wasn't racing.

She adjusted her makeshift bandanna again and allowed her eyes to wander.

Men and women of all shapes and sizes, skin tones and hair colors walked around her, ignorant to the stranger in their midst. The only unifying factor among them was the glowing markings dotted above their eyes in place of eyebrows. But that wasn't the most fantastical element of the kingdom.

There was a menagerie surrounding her. Jaguars lounged on balconies, wolves trotted down alleyways, birds of all manner of plumage soared overhead, and towering beasts of scales and feathers that Vi had no name for raced each other down the main streets. Magic pulsed around her, strange and foreign. In a flash those same animals would be replaced by human-looking folk, quickly conducting their business before another pulse of magic brought them back into their animal forms.

Her head was still splitting. Her body still felt ravaged by the toll it took to get here. And Vi knew she should be alarmed with every step—she had more worries than fingers to count them.

But for a brief moment, her chest was tense with delight. Laughter hid behind her smirking lips as she beheld the splendor of the world in perpetual twilight. Every glowing stone and flower, person and dialect, was new.

Turning the corner, Vi scanned the various narrow storefronts. It reminded her somewhat of the market in the Crossroads, with everyone fighting over space. But there were no street sellers here—only quaint doors with signs dangling before them.

Vi looped the street twice before she finally noticed a narrow door crammed between two others. On it was a picture of a garnet skullcap and a mortar and pestle, *Sarphos's Supplies* engraved next to the image. Taking a breath, Vi pushed on the door, pleasantly surprised when it opened effortlessly.

A small bell overhead jingled happily at her entrance. Vi stepped into the crammed space. There were shelves of jars stacked three deep, floor to ceiling, on either side of her. Despite being shut tight, the jars emitted the earthy aromas Vi had associated with clerical salves her entire life. Herbs of all varieties dried from the ceiling, packed between linen bags containing unknown but sweet-smelling items.

At the very back of the store was an empty desk, and behind that a door.

And nothing and no one else.

Vi slowly walked, debating if she should just take something and run while the store was unattended. But she didn't know the first thing about what salve or potion Taavin would need. And worse, she realized she didn't exactly know how she'd get back short of running into that seemingly infinite blackness and hoping she ended up on the other side alive.

A risk that didn't seem wise to take more than once.

"Hello?" Vi called, resting her hands on the counter. Glowing stones hung like pendants on either side, giving the whole room a ghostly light. "Is anyone here?"

"Yes, coming!" a male voice called. Vi heard stomping overhead, then stairs creaking, before a man emerged from the dark doorway behind the counter. "Sorry about that. You caught me right before I was going to step out. How may I be of service?"

He had steel-colored eyes and the dots above them were the same sort of pale blue. His expression was soft, youthful. Kind and yet... painfully sad. Perhaps it was the dim light playing tricks on her, but there was something haunted about this ruddy-haired man.

"Are you Sarphos?"

"I am."

"Excellent, I... I need help." Vi folded her hands on the counter. Were she back in the Solaris Empire, she could always resort to commanding him if she had to. But here, she had no sway, no golden coin bearing the Solaris seal lingering in her back pocket to reassure her even in tough situations that there was always a way out. "Please."

"What seems to be the matter?" His expression grew serious, the dots above his eyes scrunching together.

"My... friend. He's in the Twilight Forest. He's wounded... I think he has broken bones that have become infected."

"Its difficult to diagnose someone from afar... can you bring him here?"

"I don't think I can move him. Can you come to him?"

"I'm afraid I can't—I'm needed at the castle."

Mother above, she would pick the cleric that had some tie to the royal family. Vi briefly debated heading to the other cleric the men mentioned, but she didn't want to waste time. "Please, I... I think he may die."

Sarphos's expression deepened into a frown. He lifted the counter where it was hinged on one side, and slipped through. There was barely enough room for them to stand side by side in the narrow shop.

"Tell me exactly what's wrong, what symptoms he's exhibiting, as much detail as you think would be necessary and then some." Even as he spoke, his eyes were scanning the shelves, hands reaching for jars.

"He had something heavy fall on his chest," Vi answered somewhat vaguely. She didn't think going into the fact that they had been battling with a morphi—even a morphi the kingdom had exiled—would help her cause. "There's a lot of bruising. I think at least one rib is broken. From there... lethargy, fever."

"Infection, likely." Sarphos grabbed three leaves from one jar, filled a small bottle with an inky substance from another, then two dried roots from a third. "Take these to him. He eats the leaves first, and then drinks the potion—but *slowly*. It'll likely make him sick if he goes too quickly. But he does need to get it all down. And then have him chew on the roots for the pain as needed until I can get to him. Come back to me tonight and I'll go out with you."

Vi accepted Sarphos's supplies, realizing two things at the exact same time. The first was that she had no way to pay for this. An Imperial "I owe you" was likely not going to cut it here. The second was that she had no idea how to get back to Taavin.

Sarphos was sidestepping away, already halfway the door.

"I don't know how." Vi hated how weak she sounded, and felt. She hated being forced to rely on the goodness in this stranger's heart because she had no other option. "I don't know how to get back to him."

"You lost a dying man in the woods?" he asked incredulously.

"No, I don't know how to get back to the woods."

"What?"

"I'm not supposed to be here." Vi pulled the cloth from her forehead.

Sarphos took a step back, and for a brief moment she was afraid he'd bolt for the door. He looked at her like she had begun speaking in tongues—like she was going to attack him at any moment.

"How are you here?" he whispered. "Only morphi are allowed in the Twilight Kingdom." Well, that confirmed one of her suspicions.

"Were it not an emergency, I wouldn't have trespassed on your lands," she assured him, trying to emphasize she meant no harm. If he raised an alarm, Vi doubted she could escape in time. "I just want to get medicine, that's all."

"No." He shook his head, still not taking his eyes off her. Like she was some kind of apparition. "*How* are you here?"

"There was a tear in the... shift, I believe. I fell through." That was technically correct. Still, Vi gripped her watch on instinct, remembering the full details of the ordeal.

"A tear in the shift? The shift doesn't tear."

"It can, and it is," Vi insisted solemnly. "I doubt you'll believe me if I tried to explain why, but—"

"What would a human know of the shift?"

"Frustratingly little." The statement was somewhat snappish. But Vi would practically kill for a decent explanation of the morphi's magic. "But I do know there are nefarious forces at play, and the world is rotting from the inside out."

"I can't say I believe you... But the fact that you're here at all is proof enough something is amiss." Sarphos looked her up and down. "Will you show me this tear you speak of?"

"Only if you help my friend. Come and heal him, and I'll show it to you."

Sarphos chuckled, and a small smile crossed his lips. In a world full of liars and backstabbers, the seemingly genuine kindness caught Vi off-guard. *Don't trust it,* a voice in her mind cautioned. Everyone was out to get something. Everyone had a goal. And she had no idea what this man's were or what he'd do to get them.

"I was going to help you anyway." Sarphos pulled a bag from a cubby near the floor by the door. He took the items from her, and Vi begrudgingly released them. It felt like she was letting go of Taavin's lifeline by relinquishing them back to him. "That's what a healer does, you know... heal people. It's my oath."

"I'll still show you the tear." Vi much preferred a clear this-for-that agreement. The idea of giving someone good faith grated against her new base instincts, re-aligned by Jayme's betrayal.

"And I appreciate that. The morphi need to know of it." Sarphos motioned to the rag. "You may want to wear that again until we're out." Vi nodded, donning the cloth once more. "Right, this way then."

With her stomach clenching with worry to the point of pain, Vi followed him back onto the streets.

T HEY ASCENDED THE MAIN street of the Twilight Kingdom. On one end was what Vi assumed to be the palace, given its grand gate, overall opulence, and positioning at the center of the city. On the other end, the road sloped upward over the ridge that surrounded the tree-line to a large archway that was the only break in the ominous black trees.

"Take my hand." Sarphos paused and extended his palm to her. "I'll need to guide you through the shift. Don't let go, or you could find yourself trapped in the in-between."

Vi still didn't fully understand the shift, but she did as instructed. She didn't need in-depth knowledge to know she wanted to get through as quickly as possible. Given her last experience, Vi didn't want to spend any extra time in the space that was neither here nor there.

"And keep quiet as we pass. It looks like Ruie is on duty today. At least it's not Arwin…"

She nodded, not even daring to speak now as they continued their approach.

A woman lounged at the side of the archway, arms folded, looking bored. She had bright golden hair that reminded Vi achingly of Romulin's, though hers was cut shorter. Billowing fabrics tucked into simple boiled leather armor covered her lanky, lithe form.

"Sarphos… didn't Arwin want to see you today?" she said dully, by way of greeting. "She's back at the palace."

"I realized I was low on a few supplies I'll likely need for her."

"Need a few things or…" Ruie pushed off from the stone column of the archway. "Are you ditching my sister to take someone special out for a late-night *stroll*?" She grinned wildly. "I don't think Arwin will take too kindly to playing second-fiddle."

"Wh-what? Stroll? You mean—no. Me?" Sarphos blubbered. Vi couldn't tell if he was embarrassed, or worried about what this Arwin may think. Either way, she committed the name to memory.

"Someone special perhaps?" Ruie took a few steps forward. "What's your name?"

Vi opened her mouth to answer, but Sarphos spoke too fast.

"She's no one. J-Just an apprentice of mine."

"I didn't think you took apprentices. You sure it isn't something more?"

"I don't mind if you say something." Vi gave a grin and a wink to Sarphos, trying to mirror Ellene's voice and facial expressions when teasing Darrus.

"I-I—"

Ruie roared with laughter. "Oh go on, then, don't let me keep you. She's clearly eager."

Vi gave a tug on his hand, taking a step forward. *Let him fall into step*, Vi pleaded mentally. She could almost feel the uncomfortable, nervous energy radiating off the healer who was now scarlet from the crown of his head down to his collar.

Luckily, he didn't actually die of embarrassment, and instead kept moving.

"And good for you Sarphos!" Ruie called after them. "It's good to see you happy after so long!"

Sarphos shot a glare over his shoulder before turning back to Vi. "I thought I said not to speak." He had the audacity to sound bothered.

"It got us through, didn't it?"

"Yeah, but now she's going to tell all her sisters," he muttered. "Oh, never mind." Sarphos sighed. "We're past it anyway. Now, to get through the shift—stay close."

Vi did as she was told, and they continued to walk into the darkness.

She squeezed his hand tightly, not caring if she hurt him. Better that, than allow him to feel her tremble. The last thing Vi wanted to do was go back into this void. But Taavin waited on the other side. At least this time she had a guide.

There was a pulse of magic so faint Vi wasn't sure if she imagined it. Vi took a deep breath and held it, remembering the thin air that came next.

"Not far, now," Sarphos said, low and steady as another pulse thrummed against her, then another, and another, as the world wobbled back into existence from the darkness, like ripples across a pond.

They stepped out between two trees and Vi took a deep breath.

"That was much better than when I did it," she said with relief.

"I'd imagine," Sarphos said. "The shift transforms things from what they are, to what they can be—though that shift is a special one made only by the royal family. We call the transition 'the between'—which is a place you don't want to be stuck in."

"I believe it…" Vi looked behind her, but there were just the same pale trees of the Twilight Forest standing sentry to a quiet night. All traces of the Twilight Kingdom were gone. *The shift transitioned what was to what could be.* She still had many questions about the magic, but they could wait. There were more pressing matters now. "Come on, this way."

Luckily, they'd come out in a location where Vi could hear the stream. She just had to hope they hadn't emerged too far from the cave… and that it was the same stream.

"So what brings a human to the Twilight Forest?" Saphos asked as they walked. "We don't get too many in our borders these days."

"I'm just passing through." Vi had no desire for small talk. This was business. She wasn't about to be his friend. "I would've been gone by now if it weren't for my friend's injuries."

"Where are you going after you pass through here?"

"I have to find my father."

Saphos fell silent. The quiet made the walk seem even longer, fraying the nerves at the ends of Vi's patience. All she had to go by to find Taavin was the stream, so she nearly wept tears of joy when her eyes landed on something familiar. She recognized a boulder—at least she thought she did. She picked up her pace.

"Wait, why are we running?" Sarphos called.

Vi's feet flew over the wet stones, slipping and splashing in the water. Her pant legs were damp up to her knees. But Vi paid it no mind. She was used to running in forests.

What she wasn't used to was this overwhelming, sickening, lightheaded feeling of worry and fear and excitement all wrapped into the shape of a single man.

She came to a stop at the unassuming cave, her chest heaving. "He's in there." She hoped. "Let me go first... there's not much room."

"All right." Sarphos leaned against the large boulders, catching his breath. "Call me when you're ready. I'll just be... you know... recovering from the most exercise I've had in months. Don't mind me."

It was easy to ignore his mutterings due to the racing of her thoughts. What if Taavin was gone? What if she'd somehow gone to the wrong place? *What if he was...*

She didn't finish that last thought.

Vi rested her hand on the rock, took a breath, and pushed through the narrow opening. She emerged into the near darkness, immediately aware of Taavin's form. But he made no sound or movement.

"Taavin?" Vi whispered, summoning a spark for light. "Taavin, please." She crouched down, shaking him lightly. But for the first time, he didn't respond. Her hand flew to his neck, seeking a pulse and breathing a sigh of relief when she found it.

"Sarphos!" Vi shouted, deafeningly loud in the small space. Taavin still didn't wake. "Sarphos, he's not moving!"

Sarphos pushed his way through the opening with a grunt, holding out one of the faintly glowing stones she'd seen illuminating the Twilight Kingdom like a lantern. Vi barely had time to shift herself onto the other side of Taavin to give the healer room. Her hands wrapped around Taavin's, clutching tightly, as if he'd slip away from her for good if she let him go. Her eyes drifted up to the morphi as he finished pulling his bag through.

"This is him?" Sarphos's expression darkened as he stared down at Taavin. His eyes narrowed in a way that Vi could describe as nothing other than pure loathing.

"Yes. You said you would help him," Vi reminded him, the statement coming off more as a curt demand. Then she added, softly, "Please help him." Taavin's pulse was so weak underneath her fingers. It felt as though he could leave the mortal realm any moment.

Sarphos's eyes dragged away from Taavin's prone form, turning to Vi. They stared at each other for several quick breaths—Vi's hastened in panic, Sarphos's in what looked like rage. She braced herself, ready to outright threaten the man's life if that's what it took.

She was ready to burn down the whole world to save Taavin.

"You told me it was your friend... You didn't tell me your friend was the worst, most despicable, wretched creature on this earth: the Voice."

"Wretched?" Vi would've been more angry if she wasn't so confused. "He's not—"

"Was this your plan all along, to lure me here?" Sarphos looked over his shoulder, through the crack in the rocks. "Where is your legion of Swords?"

"I don't want to kill you. I don't wish you ill at all." Vi made every attempt to speak calmly, but Sarphos's rising mix of panic and prejudice was making it difficult.

"Then why would you bring me before the Voice? You're one of them, aren't you? Faithful?"

"He's dying!" Her shrill voice echoed in the small cave. Taavin didn't stir. "Does this look like a man who is trying to kill you? He's fighting for his life."

"Good," Sarphos said darkly. "Let him die. Better for the rest of us."

Sarphos turned, about to squeeze through the opening. Vi stood, and with her rose a wall of flame, filling the narrow opening, licking the healer's face and clothes. Sarphos jumped back, patting a spot on his shirt that caught fire.

"What magic is this?" His eyes darted between the singed spot and her. But Vi ignored the question. Let her powers remain mysterious. There was danger in the unknown.

"You said you were a healer—that it was your *oath* to heal people."

"Oaths can be broken," Saphos seethed.

"I know that too well," she spat back. "Just as I also know that when negotiations break down, force may be necessary. Help him or you will not go back to the Twilight Kingdom alive. Help him or I will find the Lord of the Faithful myself and tell him that the Voice has died because of you."

The last thing Vi ever wanted to do was align herself with Ulvarth. But Sarphos didn't need to know that.

Sarphos continued to stare at her, narrowing his eyes slightly. "If you kill me, King Noct will demand retribution."

"I am not of your land, and I do not fear your king. I am from across the sea—across the Shattered Islands. I am from the Dark Isle, and this man is my only ally here. Do not underestimate what I would do for the people I love."

The glare Vi gave Sarphos hid her shock. She kept her feet on the ground, even if her head was reeling.

People I love… Love… She loved him. Her heart felt like it had just shattered into a thousand pieces only to have them all start beating in unison—a chorus that sang for Taavin alone.

Sarphos spat a curse at her in a language she didn't understand. Vi was unflinching and unremorseful. Sarphos, however, was slowly worn down.

"If I heal him… he will harm my people."

"He won't."

"If you're from the Dark Isle as you say, you have no idea what he's done, or what he'll do."

"I know him far better than you," Vi insisted. "I've known him for nearly a year now. He's not a violent man, regardless of what the Faithful do. They do it without him."

Sarphos grumbled and shook his head, running a hand through his ruddy hair. "You really must be from the Dark Isle if you think the Faithful move in any way the Voice doesn't command."

"Please, Sarphos, as a healer—help him… And I give you my word he won't harm your people."

"*She gives me her word.* What's her word good for?" Sarphos grumbled as he knelt down. Vi let him have his gripes; she'd clearly won. His eyes trailed over Taavin, taking quick stock, before flicking back up to her. "I didn't have you pegged as someone who could be so brutal."

Neither did she a few mere weeks ago. "You have no idea what I'm capable of."

"I suppose I don't," Sarphos muttered, placing his hands on Taavin's chest. Delicately, he lifted Taavin's shirt. Vi looked on warily, making sure he didn't get any smart ideas. But Sarphos was focused, his gaze serious. He had shifted from the morphi loyalist to just a cleric tending to a patient.

Vi held her breath, waiting for his assessment, and praying she'd done enough in time to save the man she'd fallen in love with.

V I'S GAZE LINGERED ON Taavin's face. He looked so frail and small—something she never thought she'd say of the man. But wounded and prone, he seemed all too fragile. Her thumb lightly caressed the back of his hand.

"It's not too serious." Sarphos pulled away and began to rummage through his satchel.

"This looks serious."

"It's *becoming* quite serious," he agreed. "But the wound itself is uncomplicated—some broken bones, internal bleeding, and an infection going unchecked brought about by improper hygiene. All of those things have a clear and simple fix. He should be back to his normal, tyrannical self in no time."

Vi pressed her fingertips to her lips, suppressing an involuntary noise of relief. Perhaps Raspian's distortions hadn't gotten on Taavin. She dared to hope.

"Prop him up for me."

Vi did as Sarphos instructed, shifting to slide an arm under Taavin's back. He was dead weight and nearly impossible to lift, but Vi managed it. Sarphos gingerly tilted his head back, parting Taavin's lips and pouring the inky liquid she'd seen earlier down his throat.

"Will he choke?"

"No, the potion will be absorbed before it even gets to where his lungs split off."

She turned her attention back to Taavin, continuing to hold him. Sarphos continued giving small doses of the medicine, counting quietly to himself. Just when the bottle was almost empty, Taavin's eyes jolted open and he erupted in a fit of coughing.

Vi shifted her arm further around him, patting his back as he wheezed and gasped. Sarphos inched away. She narrowed her eyes at the healer, silently reminding him of her threat if he dared to run. But Sarphos was distracted and soon, too, was Vi.

"Vi?" Taavin whispered.

"Taavin." His name was a breath of relief on her lips.

Vi leaned forward without a thought. Her forehead pressed against his and tightened her arm, their noses nearly touching. Her eyes dipped closed and for three blissful seconds she just listened to him breathe, feeling his frail form against her.

Feeling him wonderfully alive.

"You terrified me," she murmured, pulling away.

"That feeling is mutual. I thought you'd gone off on your own and left me." Taavin's hand tried to reach for her face, but only made it to her forearm.

"I wouldn't leave you."

Sarphos cleared his throat, reminding them both of his presence.

Taavin's eyes peeled away from hers. He turned slowly, looking Sarphos up and down. The morphi healer returned the glare inch for inch.

"You did wander far, I see…" Taavin muttered. She could feel the tension rising between Taavin and Sarphos.

"Sarphos is a healer of the Twilight Kingdom. He's the one who's helping you." *Helping*. Not helped. She hoped Sarphos's care would be ongoing until Taavin was back at full strength.

"I see…" Taavin ground out, his jaw tense. Though his face relaxed when he looked back to her. "How did you find a morphi healer?"

"She claims she went through a tear in the shift. Something I have not forgotten she promised to show me," Sarphos interjected.

"A tear? Vi, you didn't—"

"Yes, I did. And I haven't forgotten, I will still show it to you," Vi interrupted and gave Sarphos a look. He'd kept his side of the bargain, she'd keep hers. She turned back to Taavin, putting his protests to rest with a short, "You were weak and getting worse. I had no other choice."

"You have a choice now—don't go with him." Taavin grabbed her arm. "I don't want you leaving my sight… I don't want you going somewhere I can't get to." Taavin's palm finally found her cheek. Vi leaned into it slightly, her eyes dipping closed. He'd been the only one to touch her this way.

"As the crown princess of the Solaris Empire, I must keep my word." Vi gingerly trailed her fingers up his arm. "Just as you must keep the word I gave on your behalf, in exchange for Sarphos's help—that you will not harm any morphi while you're here."

"I will not harm a single morphi, so long as they don't harm you." Taavin's eyes swung to Sarphos.

"We do not harm unjustly." Sarphos seemed to emphasize the word *unjustly* an odd amount—as if to imply Taavin would. His rage toward Taavin was something Vi still didn't fully understand.

"I can protect myself," Vi reminded Taavin.

"I know you can…" Taavin sighed, his eyes shining in the dim light of Sarphos's glowing stone. "Please, be careful."

"I will be."

"We should go," Sarphos needlessly reminded. As if Vi wasn't aware her time was running short. "The king is expecting me."

"I'll come back as soon as I'm able," Vi vowed.

"If anything happens to you I—" His throat closed and he choked on the word. Taavin shook his head, continuing down a different path. "I finally have you in reach and I've barely had a chance to speak to you."

"And we keep getting pulled apart." Vi gave him a small smile. "I know… But the road to my father, to figuring out this—" she touched the watch around her neck "—isn't going to be a short one. We'll have plenty of time. For now, we both need to focus on starting that road at full strength."

"I agree with all that," he reiterated. "But it doesn't mean I want you to go."

Vi searched his eyes. Had their faces always been this close? Or had they been slowly moving together?

Near. Far. Near. Far.

Back and forth they swung, a pendulum that never lost its momentum. The closer she got to him one moment, the further he felt the next. Vi closed her eyes, taking a slow breath through her nose. She leaned forward, resting her forehead lightly against his one final time.

But Vi didn't kiss him, not with an audience. Not now, when he still looked of death and smelled of potion. She'd kiss him when they were next together—when they were both stronger. In her mind, that future joining of mouths and tongues was an unspoken promise—to whom, exactly, she wasn't sure.

"Be careful," she whispered, and quickly stood, giving a nod to Sarphos. The man now wore an entirely new, strange, expression. "I'm ready."

"Very well then. Until I return with stronger, more tailored potions, continue drinking that, and chew on those. And whenever you feel strong enough... do try to take a bath." Sarphos pointed to the various healing accoutrements he'd left before he pushed himself through the crack.

Vi looked down at Taavin once more, already regretting her decision not to kiss him.

"Taavin... I..." Her voice was barely more than a whisper.

"Yes?" Had his breathing hastened? Or was it her imagination?

"I hope you feel stronger soon. I'll be back as soon as I'm able." Vi side-stepped through the craggy opening, reminding herself of the one thing Taavin had made clear: terrible things happened to the people he loved. Thus, he didn't want to love anyone, or have anyone love him.

Under no circumstances could she let him know he'd well and truly stolen her heart.

"Ready?" Sarphos startled her from her thoughts as she emerged from the small cave.

"Yes, this way." Vi started on ahead, walking along the bank of the stream. Just once she considered ignoring her promise to Sarphos about showing him the tear. But Vi knew she had to keep her word. New plans were already forming in her head. "Thank you, Sarphos, for healing him."

"You didn't leave me with much of a choice."

"That makes me no less grateful."

"I suppose, in a way, I should be thanking you." Sarphos ran a hand through his ruddy hair.

"Why?"

"If I hadn't seen it with my own eyes... I would've never thought the monster capable of compassion, let alone affection."

They reached the singed tree that marked the point Vi had diverted from the stream. Sarphos at her side, Vi followed her earlier markers into the dark woods.

"Why do you call him a monster?" She didn't want to make small talk. But when it came to Taavin, she wanted to understand the source of Sarphos's vitriol.

"If you are from the Dark Isle, as you claim—"

"Which I am."

"—then there's no way you could understand. This is not your fight."

Vi sighed, pausing a moment to locate the next singe mark before moving on. "Maybe not… But Taavin is very important to me, and I'd like to understand the conflict as it relates to him."

"You may not be able to hear the truth, as you have already been taken in by Faithful lies. But if you can, trust me when I say that there's good reason why many in this world would kill me for not letting him die and rot in that cave. Even then, that would be a death far better than he deserves."

Vi wanted to tell him that Taavin had been honest with her about the mutual hatred between the Faithful and the morphi—that she knew it was rooted in fundamental ideological differences in each culture's magic. But the tear had come into view, and the conversation ended.

"What in the…" Sarphos murmured, slowly approaching the felled tree Vi had crossed through earlier.

"Don't get too close." She grabbed his forearm, holding him back. "It's not safe."

"It doesn't look safe." His nose scrunched. "And smells of death. You went through that?"

"Yes. If you watch closely, you can see the Twilight Kingdom, now and then, in the shifting air."

Sarphos stared intently at the air between the trees, but Vi's focus was on the leaning tree itself. It was almost entirely blackened, large splits exposing liquefied innards that glowed with red lightning. The tree looked as though it had been rotting for weeks since she had last been here—not mere hours. She bet that had they arrived a day later, it would've collapsed entirely.

"So it's true," he whispered. Sarphos must've seen the kingdom while Vi was distracted by the progression of the rot. "You can catch glimpses."

"Believe me now?"

"I still don't believe you could've made it through that and survived."

"It wasn't an…*ideal* experience." Vi's hand went to her watch. Without it and whatever power it held, she likely would've died.

"Well, then, I think our business has concluded." Sarphos adjusted the satchel on his shoulder.

"You won't tell anyone about Taavin?" Vi dared ask. It was too much trust to put in a single man, especially when Sarphos had every reason to betray them. She needed to move Taavin as quickly as possible. But Taavin couldn't be moved yet… Her mind began to whirl around possible solutions.

"So long as he doesn't harm my people."

"Give me your word."

"You have it," Sarphos said with all the sincerity in the world.

Vi wanted to believe him.

She wanted to take him at his word. She wanted to go back to the days when promises meant something. But they didn't any longer. A vow wasn't good enough, not when he had so much to gain by outing them. If she were in his shoes, Vi couldn't be certain she'd honor it.

That meant she had to ensure his silence another way; she had to keep him in her sights.

"Sarphos, wait," she called after him, just as he had taken a few steps.

"What now?"

"You're going to report this tear to your king, aren't you?"

"I am," he responded cautiously.

"Take me with you?" Vi did her best to phrase it as a question and not a desperate plea or command. The only way she could get him to agree was to endear herself to him, truly convince him it was in his best interest, or both.

"Why do you think I would take someone in league with the Voice to King Noct himself?"

"Because I have more knowledge than you on these tears—their cause and how we may be able to stop them." Vi held out her hands. "Because I am unarmed and no threat in the Twilight Kingdom."

"You had that strange fire magic before."

"Firebearing. It's called Firebearing." For a brief second, Sarphos looked almost intrigued by the notion. "It's a discipline of magic on the Dark Isle and is in no way like the Faithful's Lightspinning."

"It didn't feel like Lightspinning…" He stroked his chin. "You really are from there?"

"I really am."

"But there is nothing on the Dark Isle. It is a barren wasteland."

Vi chuckled. "I thought much the same of Meru." She braved a smile, hoping it came off as casual. Hoping he believed they were finding an easy rapport and she wasn't just looking for a way to keep him in her sights. "Take me to your king, let me tell him of my lands myself."

Sarphos twisted the strap of his bag. Vi wondered if his thoughts mirrored her own—twisting and turning over the various options before him. As she waited, Vi tried to keep her expression light, even though she was already working two mental steps ahead.

Taavin had mentioned a shift like the one around the Twilight Kingdom protecting the Isle of Frost… If she continued building this relationship, perhaps she could ultimately convince Sarphos—or King Noct—to help rescue her father.

"Oh, all right, come on then." Sarphos grabbed her hand. "But don't blame me if Arwin kills you on the spot."

Vi didn't have a chance to inquire further as pulsing magic enveloped them both. She barely had time to hold her breath before the darkness of the between pressed around her.

10

"TOOK YOU LONG ENOUGH," the woman at the archway at the entrance to the Twilight Kindgom droned. "Arwin has already come looking for you."

Vi knew she didn't imagine Sarphos suddenly going pale.

"What did you tell her?" he squeaked out.

"That you were out with your lady friend."

"Why did you say that?" Sarphos groaned, starting down the street.

"Why are you keeping it a secret?" Ruie called after them. "Is it because she dresses poorly?"

"I'd like to see how lovely *she* looks after sailing across continents," Vi mumbled, picking at the fabric of her shirt. They were the same clothes Erion had given her, back when she was pretending to be Yullia.

Should she use another name now? Vi looked up to the castle ahead of them, towering over all the people crowding the street. No… she'd already told Sarphos that she was the crown princess. And meeting another royal while being honest about who she was may just serve her well.

"When we get to the castle, let me do the talking at first." Sarphos interrupted her thoughts. "Arwin is going to be in rare form, I'm sure. She doesn't take kindly to delays and will be even more irritated when she finds out I've brought a human before the king."

"Who is this Arwin to you? An old flame?"

Sarphos tilted his head back, letting out a bark of laughter. It was rich and warm-sounding, comfortable. Good, she wanted him to be comfortable around her. The more she could endear herself to him, the better.

"No, *no*. Arwin is… Well, she was to be my sister by marriage, once. But that was a lifetime ago." Sarphos kept his eyes forward, focused on the castle, oblivious to Vi studying him.

"So there's history there." Vi didn't press the matter. He clearly didn't want to go into the details.

"To say the least. We'll likely have to get through her to see the King."

"How so?"

"She's one of his core guards and by far the toughest of them all. What she says, goes. But if I can get to King Noct before she gets to us, all the better."

Vi adjusted the bandanna around her forehead. Tough, headstrong, demanding—none of them were personality traits she exactly wanted to work with.

They entered the castle through another free-standing archway. The castle had no outer wall or gates. In fact, there was little to stop the populous from strolling in. In a city protected by a force like the shift, Vi could understand why they didn't feel the need for fortifications.

She wondered if Adela felt much the same. Vi could only dream of catching the pirate flat-footed.

"You finally came." Positioned at the door was another young woman. She had a shade of blonde hair similar to Ruie's, though slightly more ashen. Even so, the family resemblance was unmistakable. "Arwin is waiting for you."

"Tell her I need to speak with the king." Sarphos continued leading them into a large foyer, the girl falling into step alongside them.

"And who are you?" she asked.

"A traveler of sorts." Vi looked up at the ceiling, where a chandelier of glowing stones illuminated the open space with a harsh, bright light.

"Who is she?" the girl asked Sarphos, apparently dissatisfied with Vi's answer.

"She's a traveler."

"From where?"

"Enough questions, Emmie." Sarphos rolled his eyes as they stepped into a hallway in the back of the room. A curtain of small, white flowering vines was strung along the ceiling. These, too, gave off their own magical illumination. Enough to see by, but comfortably dimmer than the entry.

"Why do you only tell Arwin things?" Emmie puffed out her cheeks in frustration.

"I do not only tell Arwin things," Sarphos muttered.

That would be something to keep an eye on—how close Sarphos and Arwin really were. Vi didn't know much about the woman yet. But what she'd gleaned so far assured her that Arwin gaining knowledge of Taavin would be trouble.

"Go find Arwin and tell her I'm with the king." Sarphos shooed Emmie away. The girl gave a huff, but ran off anyway.

Vi paused, looking down the hall where Emmie had disappeared. She saw a different young girl running down in her place, a girl with corkscrew curls and that same streak of childishness. Vi would bet anything Emmie and Ellene were near the same age.

"This way—" Sarphos tapped her shoulder and turned to lead, but stopped abruptly. "I just realized, I don't even know your name."

Vi smiled slyly, proud that she managed to go this long without telling him. "It's Vi."

"Vi… right, this way, please."

They went through two more hallways and three antechambers before entering a rectangular room.

On the far side, an open wall faced a grassy glade where children ran and played; on Vi's right stood a throne crafted from an array of materials, including some Vi would never attempt to piece together; wood and stone were fitted against glass and metal. It was where she would expect to see their King seated.

But the throne was empty.

At Vi's left was a low table and sitting area surrounding it. A plump man sat with his back to the door, watching three children playing with a pair of wolves and a peacock in the field beyond. *This* sagely and content-looking man was not what she'd expected of the Twilight Kingdom's king.

But looks could be deceiving. Vi was a living example of that—with her tattered clothing and grime-coated fingernails, no one would believe her a crown princess. Which meant she'd have to work all the harder to convince these people she was. Vi folded her hands in front of her, rolled her shoulders back, and adjusted her posture.

"My king, forgive my intrusion." Sarphos rounded the sitting area, dropping to a kneel.

"You know you are always welcome in my home, Sarphos." The king spoke with a whispering, weathered voice. "Stand, please."

Sarphos did as he was bid as Vi came to awkwardly stand next to him. "Unfortunately, I have brought ill tidings."

King Noct had golden hair like Ruie and Emmie, that faded into a white beard. But rather than analyzing the familial resemblance between him and the girls, Vi's mind wandered back to her own family. She wondered if she was looking at a much older version of her brother in the man.

"Ill tidings," King Noct repeated. "I do hope this lovely young woman isn't the cause of such things."

"Your highness." It was Vi's turn to kneel. Sarphos may be welcome in this court, but she was an outsider. "I've—"

"Sarphos!" A shout interrupted her. "You got some pair of stones, keeping me waiting." A woman stormed in from a side entrance.

She had bright golden hair, braided back tightly and wound into a large bun at the top of her head. Tiny curls attempted to escape around her face. She was pale, but not unnaturally so like the elfin'ra. Her eyes were muted gray, and landed on Vi with cold, steely calculation. Vi had little doubt that the person currently sizing her up was the infamous Arwin.

"Is *this* the woman you've been hiding from us?"

"I'm not hiding anything!" Sarphos insisted.

"We were just about to find out who this lovely young lady is, and why Sarphos kept you waiting… before you interrupted," the king said slowly, as if fighting back a yawn the entire time.

"If there's a stranger in our midst, shouldn't you be on your throne, father?"

Father?

"I think not being on my throne is far less damaging to my appearance than you questioning me before said stranger," the king answered—though he didn't sound the least bit offended. Vi felt like she was more present to a family gathering than a royal court.

Arwin pursed her lips and gestured for Vi to continue. Vi took a deep breath.

"I've come from an Empire across the sea."

The king stilled. Then, he commanded slowly, "Tell me your name, child."

"I am Vi Solaris, crown princess of the Solaris Empire."

"Solaris?" Arwin looked to Sarphos, who seemed to shrink under the woman's stare. "There is no such Empire."

Vi fought a smile and failed. She remembered being in Arwin's shoes. The moment the veil was lifted from her eyes was fresh in Vi's memory. She had assumed the rest of the world knew about Solaris—that her people alone had been left in the dark. She had assumed wrong.

"There is, across what you call the Shattered Isles. On the Dark Isle."

"A forgotten and desolate rock?"

"Let her speak, Arwin." King Noct's voice had deepened, his tone becoming far more serious.

"I was born in Solarin, capital of the Solaris Empire, to Emperor Aldrik Solaris and Empress Vhalla Solaris. There, Meru's existence is not common knowledge. Shortly after my birth I was sent to our northernmost territory, Shaldan. I thought my wardship was a purely political arrangement, but it was more than that.

"There was a prophecy about my birth," Vi proceeded delicately. Given the morphi's relationship with the Faithful, Vi didn't know what their reaction would be to Yargen. *Tell the truth, just not the* whole *truth*. Half-lies were child's play compared to the web of fictions she'd had to craft along this journey. "It involves those known as the elfin'ra and Lord Raspian's return to this realm."

"Lord Raspian, elfin'ra? You speak like a Faithful," Arwin said, her voice dropping to a low growl.

"I am not a Faithful," Vi insisted.

"But you are a liar." Arwin stomped over to her. Without so much as a word of warning, she yanked the bandanna from Vi's brow. "Human," Arwin seethed, turning to Sarphos. "You brought a human among us? She could be Faithful."

Sarphos shrank backward. If Arwin pressed, he'd break. And if he broke, there was no guarantee of Taavin's safety.

"I said I'm not Faithful," Vi insisted. "The Faithful don't even exist in Solaris."

"Silence, Arwin." The King sighed tiredly. "Tell me more of the details of this prophecy?"

"My lord, I don't entirely know them all myself..." Vi looked down at her feet for a moment, hoping the body language of respect and deference was the same here as it was at home. "It has been passed to me in pieces, from my mother and from the woman who raised me. All I know for certain is that I have been chosen by Yargen to play a role in preventing the end of our world. I am Yargen's Champion. But what that means exactly... I'm unsure."

"And that is why you have ventured so far?"

"Yes, that... and to find my father."

"Prophecies, the Faithful's goddess, a human in the Twilight Kingdom..." Arwin paced between Sarphos and her father, staring down Vi at every turn. "She spews lies to you, father."

"Have you not seen it, Arwin?" Noct straightened in his seat. In that motion he went from a lounging old man to a king. "The bloody ring that circles our moon? It foretells the end of days."

"Or it's merely a phenomenon we don't yet understand. What's more likely? Ancient prophecies or a natural anomaly to be investigated?"

"Then there are the tears in the shift..." Sarphos said meekly, staring at his toes.

"Tears?" All eyes were on him. Vi watched as he fidgeted with the bag strap over his shoulder.

"Lord Raspian is rotting the world from the inside out," Vi said finally, when Sarphos didn't speak. "On the Dark Isle, people have fallen ill to a deadly plague from which there is no cure; we call it the White Death. There has been red lightning in the sky, now the corona around your moon, and I fear the tears in your shift are his work as well."

"Plague? Did you say plague?" Sarphos's head snapped up.

"Yes."

"What are its symptoms?" He was gravely eager. So much so that Vi had a horrible theory he already knew what she was about to say.

"Stony skin, milky eyes, bulging red veins, madness, and—"

"Sores that break and ooze white," he finished solemnly. Vi nodded in acknowledgement. "It's started to show here too."

"I'm so sorry," Vi said softly. "Our healers couldn't make headway with it. I don't think there's a cure beyond stopping Raspian."

"Don't doubt Sarphos," Arwin said defensively.

"I don't. He's already helped me once."

"The journey looks to have taken a toll on you." The king's voice was almost sad. Vi didn't need sympathy, but she'd gladly take it. "I shall open my home to you, Vi Solaris."

"You can't be serious," Arwin grumbled. Everyone ignored her.

"She is to be my distinguished guest," the king insisted. "See that she is made comfortable until she feels well enough to continue on her journey."

"I am to be saddled with—"

"Enough, Arwin," the king snapped, finally reaching his limit with his daughter's objections. "I have spoken."

"Yes, father." Arwin lowered her head.

"Bathe, rest, eat, and recover tonight, Vi… For in the morning, there is something of grave importance we must discuss."

"Grave importance?" Vi repeated.

"An object was bestowed on my forefathers long, long ago… well before history was recorded in your homeland. And I believe it belongs to you."

"I don't understand." What could he possibly have that belonged to her? Moreover, how would something like that even get to the Twilight Kingdom?

"I never understood either… until this moment. But we shall discuss in the morning, for it is late now and you could use some rest underneath the safety of a friendly roof." Noct gave a yawn, as if for emphasis, and when he finished, he waved them away.

Arwin placed her hand on Vi's shoulder, giving her a small shove toward the door she'd entered from.

"Manners, Arwin." Vi heard a soft snort over her shoulder. "When you have seen her settled… go with Sarphos to inspect these tears, and then return to me. There are things I must share with you regarding the Dark Isle."

Secrets on both sides of the ocean. Vi already knew what King Noct would say, and she didn't envy those revelations. It didn't take a prophecy to see that the hours looming before Arwin were destined to be filled with unpleasantness.

"Very well, father."

"I could help show the tears," Vi offered. Really, the last thing she wanted was for Arwin and Sarphos to be alone in the Twilight Forest. It would be too easy for him to out Taavin and she still had yet to get a firm grasp on their relationship. "Since I know of them."

"Can you find them confidently, Sarphos?" the king asked.

"I can."

"Then you should rest." Noct turned back to her with a small smile. "You look truly exhausted."

She was. But she wasn't too exhausted to try to protect Taavin. "I don't mind assisting."

"It's all right, Vi," Sarphos said. Vi looked to him and the man pointedly locked eyes with her. He gave a small nod that spoke volumes meant to be reassuring, yet it only put her stomach further in knots. "You can trust me to show her the tear."

And nothing else. Vi hoped that's what was left unspoken.

"Now that's settled… Arwin, please see her to the north tower?"

"If I must," Arwin grumbled, before escorting Vi deeper into the palace of the Twilight Kingdom—and farther from the healer who knew her secret.

“THERE WILL BE A guard positioned at the entrance to the tower you'll be staying in,” Arwin said without so much as glancing at her.

“Am I a prisoner?” Vi looked back to the throne room. Sarphos was still speaking with King Noct. What if they were discussing Taavin? How quickly would King Noct's hospitality turn to hostility? She should be ready to fight her way out of the castle at any moment.

“If it were up to me, you'd already be in irons,” Arwin muttered. Then, louder, “No, you're not a prisoner. But that doesn't mean I trust you.”

“I'm not here to make trouble.”

“That's what all troublemakers say.”

“I suppose they do.” Vi sighed. No one who was about to stab you in the back gave any warning. There wasn't any kind of armor that protected you from betrayal. The only defense was constant suspicion and vigilance. “I suppose I'll think of this guard as an attendant, rather than a sentry.”

“Whatever makes you happy, princess.” Arwin said *princess* as though it were a slur.

“Are you not also a princess?”

Arwin let out a massive snort followed by raucous laughter. “I am no princess.”

“That's what the daughter of a king is in my land.”

“In the Twilight Kingdom, the lineage is passed only through the male bloodline. Daughters become sworn guards of the crown.” It was a surprisingly straightforward and informative answer from the woman who had been entirely callous thus far. Even though Vi's questions on the logistics of royal succession abounded, she kept them to herself, not pushing the matter.

Up two floors, Arwin led Vi across a narrow arcade.

On one side was the courtyard she'd seen three stories below from King Noct's throne room. On the other side, the Twilight Kingdom was visible through the archways and stone pillars. Vi admired its ethereal nature as they walked to the tower at the far end of the walkway and up a final flight of winding stairs.

“You'll use this as your room.” Arwin stopped at a doorway, the second one up the stairs that spiraled around the tower, and pushed it open.

The soft light of the stars filtered in through a window that couldn't be bothered with glass. Instead, a curtain of white, glowing flowers modestly obscured the view. There was a comfortable looking bed, a side table with a washbasin, and a tall dresser that hopefully had a clean change of clothes. As the king promised, everything she would need to be comfortable for a good night's rest was there.

"One door down is the bathing room for this tower. I do recommend you use it." Arwin scrunched up her nose.

"Yes, I need it." Vi wasn't about to let herself be offended by the obvious.

"While you're in the bath, I'll see to finding you a change of clothes." Arwin walked back down to the first door. "Emmie will be positioned at the start of the bridge. Ask her if you need anything else."

"Thank you." Vi said, stopping before the bathing room as Arwin continued on.

"Don't thank me. I'm just following orders."

"Still, I'm grateful," Vi called after her. Arwin didn't look back.

The bathing room was small but heated to steaming perfection. The nearly scalding water of the tub soaked off grime and eased away her tensions. Her mind wandered to Taavin.

He was alone in that cave while she was enjoying the hospitality of the Twilight Kingdom's royal family. Hopefully, Arwin wasn't currently on her way to meet him. Sarphos was supposed to show her the tears, but could she trust him to do only that?

Despite the heat of the water, Vi's shoulders tightened.

As she wandered back up the stairs to her room, she wondered if there was a way she could sneak Taavin in. If Vi couldn't keep Sarphos in her sights at all times, perhaps she should try to keep Taavin closer. *No*, it'd be impossible, she quickly decided. Gaining the trust of the king and keeping Sarphos close was the best she could do.

When Vi returned to her room, she found the dresser full of lush fabrics in every color from pale grays to vibrant reds, embellished velvets and simple silks. There was everything she could imagine in every size.

She found a pair of voluminous trousers in a dark violet hue that tapered around the ankle. There was room enough for her hips and butt, and they were surprisingly comfortable. After that, Vi donned a thin sleeveless shirt, meant to be worn beneath the coat embroidered with matching silver vines along the hemline.

Vi lifted the jacket from the drawer. Its construction reminded her somewhat of Taavin's intricately embroidered coat—a tight-fitting, tailored torso that split into four panels at the hips. However, where his extended down to his calves, this looked like it wouldn't go past her waist. And where Taavin's coat had a small upright collar, this had a large cowl. Vi ran her fingers over the fabric. It was just as fine as his, from the deep yet colorful dyes to the cut and intricate stitching.

Vi clutched the garment to her chest, imagining what she held was indeed Taavin's. Imagining he was there. She pressed her eyes tightly shut and took a quivering breath.

"I hope I'm doing the right thing," she breathed into the fabric, as though it could somehow carry her words to him. "I want to protect you."

He'd said terrible things happened to the people he loved. But Vi supposed her track record was no better. The only other people she'd loved were plagued, captured by pirates, struggling to keep an empire together, and watching their people die with little hope of a cure.

Maybe they were both cursed.

Vi returned the coat to the drawer and closed it. Her hands pressed on the outside, as if she could trap all her insecurities within. As if she could smother them.

When her emotions had leveled, Vi walked over to the small washbasin. Grooming tools were set out around it, and Vi set to brushing through her hair. The process quickly reminded her of the discovery she'd made earlier: thanks to her escape from Adela, her hair was now at different lengths. Inspecting herself in the small hand mirror, Vi tilted her head left and right, looking at the longer hair on either side. She could braid it up and wait for it to grow out. Or…

A pair of shears caught her eye.

Vi carefully gathered her hair in her hands, suppressing a small shiver at the sound of the blades slicing through. Hair fell to the ground like the remnants of her past life. In just a few moments, it was over, and Vi's free hand played with the freshly sheared edge of her hair—now almost all one length, just past her shoulders.

She couldn't remember the last time it had been this short.

Staring at the pile of hair on the floor, she waited to feel something. Sadness, perhaps? Her hair was part of what had connected her to her grandmother, her father, and to her Western heritage.

And yet… Vi felt very little.

She had far more important things to worry about than hair.

A firm knock on her door jostled Vi from sleep. She'd barely had time to open her eyes before Arwin was barging in.

"Up. I have breakfast," Arwin declared gruffly, standing at the foot of her bed and holding a tray in both of her white-knuckled hands. The silverware on the tray clanked together as a result of her barely contained rage. "I will tolerate no complaints. I am not your servant girl to boss around."

"I wasn't going to complain." Vi yawned and pulled herself upright. Her room was identical to how it had been when she'd gone to sleep—there was no sunrise or sunset in the Twilight Kingdom, no day or night, just the perpetual half-light of its namesake. She looked at the breakfast Arwin held and resisted the easy jab that for not being her "servant girl," she sure looked the part.

"What are you smirking at?" Arwin muttered, setting the tray down heavily at the foot of her bed.

"I'm not smirking. I'm smiling because the food looks good." Vi reached for the sandwich, not inspecting it too closely before taking a large bite. She wasn't dead, and Arwin wasn't throwing chains on her… That must mean Sarphos hadn't told them about Taavin—or at least not told Arwin. Noct was still a wild card, but Vi suspected if he was a smart king, he wouldn't pass up the opportunity to at least capture a valuable enemy like Taavin.

No, Sarphos hadn't told them anything, Vi decided.

"Are you always so trusting?" Arwin's voice cut through the silence and Vi's thoughts like a sharpened axe. "Eating food put in front of you by strangers without so much as a sniff?"

"If you had planned to kill me, you could've done it when I was sleeping, or in the bath, or the first moment you saw me." Vi took another large bite for emphasis. Arwin looked away, staring out the window. When she wasn't glowering at Vi, there was a softness to the woman Vi was unaccustomed to. "Why are you so mistrusting of me? I told you I'm not Faithful and I mean no harm to your people."

The woman tensed. Vi could see the biceps in her folded arms tighten over her hands tucked by the insides of her elbows. She was wearing a sleeveless shirt today and the lines of her bulging muscles were on display. Perhaps another show of power, another subtle threat.

"You truly know nothing, do you?" Arwin said almost delicately. Her steely eyes drifted back to Vi. "You're really from the Dark Isle?"

"I am. And I know a great many things… But I admit there are serious gaps when it comes to knowledge of your land and people." Vi paused, allowing Arwin's continued scrutiny. "But I would like to learn."

"Why?"

Once more, her original question popped into her mind. What had happened that led to the morphi—Arwin—to have such a deep mistrust of all outsiders? Sarphos's words the night before still clung to her thoughts as well: *Why was Taavin a monster?*

Vi wasn't sure she wanted the answers, but she needed to know all the same.

"Why not?" Vi asked simply. "Aren't you curious about the Dark Isle?"

Arwin held her gaze for a long moment. Just when Vi thought she was about to give in, she uttered a simple, "No."

"But—"

"Finish your food. My father is waiting for you."

Vi did as she was told, and quickly donned fresh clothing in much the same fashion as the articles she'd found yesterday. She didn't really need to change—what she'd gone to bed in hadn't gotten dirty. It just felt good that she *could.*

Arwin led Vi down the tower, across the walkway, down another flight of stairs, across a hall, down yet another spiral staircase, and into what Vi would best describe as a council room. The walls were stone, vertical tapestries running from floor to ceiling depicting champions with dotted foreheads standing victorious in battle. Between the tapestries hung weapons, the low light of the glowing stones hung above the center table gleaming off their polished edges.

"I'll get my father." Arwin stepped forward and around the table toward the back of the room. Vi watched as the woman swung her arm in a circle, magic rippling across the wall like waves in a pond. The stones shifted, shimmered, and changed right before her eyes, redesigning themselves in the shape of an archway.

Vi had been watching the whole time, yet, if pressed, she wouldn't be able to tell someone how a solid wall transformed itself into a door. Luckily, Arwin didn't look back before slipping through the new passageway. She didn't see Vi's awe.

With nothing to do other than wait, Vi began to inspect the careful stitching and bright dyes of one of the tapestries. But she didn't get far before Arwin and Noct appeared in the archway.

"Your highness." Vi dropped to a knee.

"Rise, child." He spoke to her, but his focus was not on her. Rather, the king gave far more attention to the small wooden box he was carrying. Noct set it down on the table reverently.

"Are you certain, father?" Arwin asked. For once, she didn't sound indignant. She sounded… concerned. Worried. Ominous.

"I am." Noct turned his gaze to Vi. "My family has protected this with our royal shift for generations. But it is time for the weapon to be among the world of men once more."

He placed his hand down on the box and, in a single blink, it transformed into something entirely different.

Vi's eyes focused on the item wrapped tightly in a deep purple velvet. Time weighed heavy on the fabric, parts threadbare; the gold cord fastening was gray with dust. While Vi couldn't see through the wrapping, it left little to her imagination: a long pole, connected to something flat and curved at one end—a scythe, she'd surmise. Though that only made her more confused.

King Noct rested a hand on the non-bladed end of the weapon, then finally looked up at Vi. "Do you have any idea what this is?"

Her eyes stayed glued to it. The watch was heavy around her neck, hot enough to nearly burn her skin, but Vi hardly noticed. A piece of her had been torn from her body, thrown into a different place and time. The surreal feeling raked up her spine and sank into her skull, impossible to shake, as she stared wide-eyed.

"I don't," Vi said, her voice almost quivering. Though something insisted she did. She knew what it was… but not with her eyes. With something deeper rooted and less explicable.

"The prophecy you mentioned… you said you were chosen by Yargen as her Champion," King Noct began. "It reminded me of a piece of lore passed down in our family, generation to generation, dating back nearly a thousand years. My father told it to me, and his father to him—generations preparing one another should what I believe to be this moment ever come to pass."

Her heart was beating so hard Vi could've sworn she heard the watch chain rattling around her neck.

"This is not of the Twilight Kingdom. We were merely the holders of this relic— protectors or curators, if you will. It came from your Dark Isle." She should feel excited by that fact, shouldn't she? But all Vi felt was sickness rising. The surreal feeling of having one foot in the present and the other somewhere else lingered—her body torn in two. "I was told that long ago, it was used to cultivate the land of the Dark Isle so that it would be fertile for eons to come, giving life to the magickless people who sought refuge there. But its powers could easily be used to end that same life.

"A man, the grandson of Yargen's last Champion, smuggled this off the isle to ensure it never fell into the wrong hands."

"How did it get to the Twilight Kingdom?" Vi murmured. Her voice felt like it was echoing from a distant place.

"Queen Lumeria has sent spies to the Dark Isle over time. One of those spies was a morphi… back then, tensions weren't as high with the Faithful."

"Why were there spies?" She should be offended by the idea. But Vi had felt very little since the wrapped item had appeared. All she could feel was a deep need to *see it.*

"To ensure those on the isle weren't disturbing forces they shouldn't."

"A lot of good that did," Vi whispered. Raspian had been locked away in the Crystal Caverns, the destruction of which led to the rise of the Mad King Victor. That set in motion a series of events that ultimately led Vi to where she was now.

"So it would seem," Noct agreed solemnly. "But that long-ago descendant of the Champion saw this weapon preserved for the future Champion—perhaps for this very moment."

Noct reached forward and Vi watched as he undid the knots of rope keeping the velvet closed. One of the braided tethers nearly disintegrated beneath his fingers. Vi's heart raced until the fabric was at last thrown back—

All at once, her heart stopped.

There, shining dimly, was one of the four legendary crystal weapons. She knew it was true without needing further proof. She knew it in her marrow.

It glowed with a faint blue light, a microcosm of stars trapped beneath its glassy surface. Vi reached out a hand. She was drawn to it with an undeniable pull. She couldn't turn away if she tried.

Her fingers brushed the top of the blade.

The hazy light that surrounded the weapon slowly drifted over her hand and up her arm, before fading completely into her skin. It swirled within her, like a dust storm over the desert.

The desert.

Images flashed before her eyes, so clear Vi could swear she was standing at the event itself, watching them play out. There was an Eastern man with hazel eyes, working his way through a humble city that was ancient Norin. A shift in the magic, a spark of blue light, and he was now at the docks, speaking with another, passing over the velvet-wrapped parcel. Another shift, and Vi witnessed the man turning away from his precious heirloom.

A chill ran over her as Vi jettisoned back to the present. The sensation of being in two places at once had finally abated. Perhaps because she'd finally seen what she needed to—what the goddess had wanted her to see. Vi lifted her hand away from the weapon, the dim shimmer of magic clinging to her fingers for several seconds before fading.

She turned to King Noct, her voice barely a whisper. "It is a crystal weapon... But what do you want me to do with it?"

King Noct and Arwin were a half-step farther away than she remembered them being. They both stared at her with wary, awe-filled eyes. Vi took a slow breath, not daring to ask what they'd seen when her senses were overtaken by a time long past. She didn't want to know. With one touch to the crystal weapon, something within her had changed, and she wanted no additional proof of the fact.

"I want you to do what you were chosen to do—use it to save our world."

V I SAT ON A bench at one end of a large, rectangular training hall.
The floor was wooden, mats lined up on the back wall to her left, mostly forgotten. Archery targets hung on the far wall to the right; weapons of all shapes and sizes lined the wall across from where she stood.

But none of them consumed her attention quite like the weapon in her hands.

Every time Vi shifted her fingers across its surface, magic sparked and crackled within. Power seemed to flow from her to the weapon and back, growing more powerful with every turn. Her breath quickened.

"So, what are you going to do with it?" The question jostled her from her fascination with the magic within the scythe. Vi hadn't even heard the steady *thunk* of arrows sinking into the archery targets come to a stop.

"I... don't know yet."

"You don't know?" The woman huffed, as if disappointed, passing her bow from hand to hand. "Aren't you the Champion?"

"This whole Champion thing doesn't exactly come with a guide book," Vi muttered. There might be someone who could help her... but getting to Taavin wasn't an easy affair at the moment. Vi stood, holding out the weapon with one end on the ground. "Could you teach me how to use it, perhaps?"

Arwin tilted her head to the side, looking Vi and the weapon up and down. "It's a scythe—a *farmer's* scythe, not a war scythe. The blade's all wrong for proper combat. You really want it to be more vertical to get better access to the sharp edge."

"Well, it's all I have, so I'd better learn how to use it," Vi countered.

"Can't you reshape it somehow?"

"*Reshape it?* You think I can reshape something a goddess made?"

"Fair point," Arwin mumbled and crossed the room to a rack of weapons. She tossed her bow from one hand to the next; there was a pulse of magic mid-air, and when Arwin grabbed it again, she wielded a long pole off the wall with an axe on one side. "Even if I'm confident with pole arms... I still have no idea how I'm going to teach you how to use that effectively at all."

"I'd appreciate the effort," Vi said sincerely, meeting Arwin in the center of one of the painted rings on the floor.

"Do you even know the basics of combat?" Arwin asked, slowly twirling the halberd in her hands.

"I've had a bit of training," Vi answered somewhat coyly.

"The fate of the world rests on the shoulders of someone who's had 'a bit of training'?" Vi could feel the vibrations through the floor as Arwin slammed down the butt of her weapon. "We're all doomed."

She should be offended, but Vi couldn't stop laughing. Finally, she managed, "Maybe we are."

"You're really reassuring me now." Arwin's posture went slack, slightly relaxed.

"Let's be honest, you thought we were doomed from the moment you first learned I was Yargen's Champion."

"Can't say I believe all that. Maybe you're an opportunist with a good grasp of history. Maybe you noticed a convenient opportunity to claim you're something you're not, with few to argue against your claims."

"If I'm lying about being Yargen's Champion, I sure went to great lengths for that lie." Vi tried to mimic Arwin's stance, gripping the small handles that extended from the main shaft of her weapon. She barely had time to shift her feet into a wider, sturdier base before Arwin lunged without warning. Vi stepped back, adjusting the distance. She lifted the scythe on instinct, pushing Arwin's blade up and away from striking at her center.

The curve of the axe at the end of the halberd hooked on the main body of Vi's scythe. Arwin gave a firm yank, ripping the weapon from her fingertips. Vi was pulled forward and off balance.

Arwin shifted the halberd back in her hands, allowing the scythe to fall to the floor. She stepped forward, driving her fist into Vi's stomach. Vi doubled over, her muscles contracting around Arwin's hand.

The woman had a fist like a rock.

Wheezing, Vi grabbed her stomach and fell to her knees. When she lifted her head, it was to find the tip of Arwin's halberd at the tip of her nose. Arwin regarded her coolly down the pole arm.

"Was the punch really necessary?" Her stomach was still spasming. *Great Mother above it hurt,* and it reminded Vi that her midsection was still mostly fresh flesh. But she tried desperately to keep her face calm and hide as much of the pain as possible.

"Your enemies won't show you mercy. Especially not with a pathetic showing like that."

A chuckle escaped Vi's lips. "Don't I know it."

Arwin cocked an eyebrow at the bitter remark. She lowered the halberd, replacing it with her hand. Vi stared at the open palm, glancing back to Arwin. She wasn't about to take the bait and be an easy target once again.

"Come on, up with you."

Vi's fingers clasped around Arwin's and she hoisted her up so quickly that Vi's shoulder ached. Vi rolled it backward but said nothing. The woman started for the door.

"Wait." Vi stopped her with a call. Arwin turned, eyebrow arched. "Is that it? Are we done?"

"You actually want to go again?"

"As many times as you're willing." Vi picked up the scythe, adjusting her grip some. It had been too easy to rip from her hands before. Perhaps if she locked her thumbs around the main shaft, it'd provide better support.

"Why? You're fooling yourself if you think that thing will stand up against any trained combatant. At best, you'll have some range over a swordsman. But with the scythe curved as it is, you can't effectively use the slicing edge."

"So you've told me."

"You'll have to use it in more pulling motions, which will be hard to manage at distance."

"Then I'd better practice."

"Do you even have the stamina to swing it more than a few times?"

"Only one way to build my stamina." Vi wasn't backing down and she would make sure Arwin knew it.

"Why not just—"

"Because this may be our only hope," Vi interrupted. "Because all the crystals, and crystal weapons, on the Dark Isle have been destroyed. *This is the only one left.* If it came from the descendant of the last Champion, it may just be the only thing I can use against Raspian. I have no choice. So will you help me learn it or not?"

Arwin stared at her, long and hard, not moving a muscle.

"*Please.*" Vi had no choice, no pride. Just holding the scythe filled her with a sense of urgency. The idea of preventing the end of the world was no longer an intangible thing. Vi now held proof of what she'd have to do in her hands, and she couldn't be too arrogant to avoid admitting she was nowhere near ready.

"Very well then," Arwin said finally. "But I'm going to train you as I would any of my sisters. I'm not going easy on you just because you're a guest and princess."

"None of my enemies will go easy on me." The thin line of Vi's mouth turned into a bitter smirk. "Bring on the gut punches."

What followed was a series of beatings the likes of which Vi had never experienced before. She'd always thought Sehra's warriors had stopped going easy on her when she'd come of age. But like most things in her childhood, that too turned out to be a lie.

Arwin didn't miss an opportunity to trip her, smack her sides with the pole of her halberd, knock the scythe from her hands, or rap her knuckles for improper grip. Bruises covered her body and everything ached. She wasn't sure exactly how much time had passed. An hour? Maybe two?

But Vi knew it wasn't nearly long enough. She had just begun to feel comfortable with the weight of the scythe in her hands.

"That's enough," Arwin declared. "You're spent for today."

"For today?" Vi leaned heavily against the scythe for support, panting and wiping sweat from her brow. "Does that mean you'll teach me tomorrow?"

"We'll see. Don't push your luck."

"And here I had you pegged for not passing up the chance to knock me around some more."

"It may be one of the most fun things I've done in some time." Arwin cracked the beginnings of a smile. It wasn't much. But it was more emotion—*positive* emotion—than Vi had seen from her so far. The expression faded as quickly as it came, and Arwin looked between her and the door before starting toward a cabinet in the back of the room instead. "Come here."

Vi obliged her. Toward the back of the room, near the archery targets, was a tall cabinet. All manner of vial and supplies housed within. Vi knew a clerical stash when she saw one. Arwin selected a small jar.

"Drink this now, and then we're taking you to Sarphos for him to give you something stronger. You're still skin and bones and will be far too achy tomorrow to do anything if you don't take steps to ease the pain now."

"So we *are* sparring again tomorrow?" She was excited at the prospect, but the deep ache in her body tempered the fact. Vi leaned the scythe against the wall to take the jar from Arwin and sniff the thick, amber colored liquid inside.

"I said we'll see." Arwin wiped sweat from her face using the bottom of her shirt. "Though, I still suspect there's another, better way for you to use that thing... There must be. I can't imagine a goddess would outfit her warrior with something not designed for fighting."

Vi looked at the scythe as she took a long sip of the liquid. It was cloyingly sweet and as thick as honey—perhaps it was just honey with herbs and salves swirled within. But there was a distinct medicinal aftertaste that was so bitter on the back of her palette that Vi was glad for the sweetness.

"I wish I knew," Vi murmured. She was staring at a crystal weapon. A real, complete, legendary crystal weapon. She could feel its power, even now, thrumming quietly. It whispered secrets to her, inviting her to uncover them. Yet it spoke in a language she couldn't understand. Perhaps Arwin was right and there was some way to change the weapon. There was so much potential waiting to be unlocked, but Vi didn't even know where to start. "Unfortunately, the only people who may be able to help me are the Faithful."

Arwin leaned against the wall, an almost lazy, deadly smile playing at her lips. "Suggest going to the Faithful in my presence again and die."

"Why do you hate them so much?" She'd asked Sarphos. It was time to hear Arwin's answer... and hope it was something more significant than "because they're monsters."

Arwin searched her face as if Vi was hiding the answer to her own question somewhere on it. Finally, "You truly know nothing of the morphi and Meru, do you?"

"I imagine I only know slightly more than you know of the Dark Isle," Vi lied. She would bet she knew vastly more than Arwin knew of the Dark Isle, thanks to Taavin and Sarphos's information. But in the grand scheme of things, that was precious little.

"Fair." Arwin sighed, closing her eyes. When she spoke, it was the first time Vi didn't feel as though she was being spoken down to, or threatened. "The seeds of the hatred were sown about a thousand years ago, not long after the Great War between the entities they call the Goddess Yargen and the God Raspian."

"Entities?" Vi interrupted quickly. "So, you don't think they're actually divine?" Arwin surprised her with a shrug.

"Don't know. I've never seen them. They must be powerful if all the stories are true... But I could be a powerful goddess to a beetle." Her eyes drifted to the scythe. "That weapon, however ill designed it is, combined with the tears and the plague—it all makes a compelling argument for these supposed gods' might. But I don't know if I could confidently say something is divine when I saw it. So how can I trust someone else's claims?"

Vi hadn't considered it that way, and it was almost painful to do so. Some things about her world vision weren't ready to be challenged. Especially not when so much was already cast in doubt. "Well, that being what it is... you were saying? After this great war and the morphi?"

"Yes, well... Yargen and Raspian are said to have battled countless times—starting different eras of light and dark. After their last row, Yargen won dominion over the world—so the Faithful claim—and was seated in Risen for a time. In the aftermath, the elfin'ra were exiled from Meru and locked away on their island as punishment for their support of Raspian. Much like the morphi, their magic was seen as fundamentally twisted. The race of the draconis were eventually cast off as well... though that didn't happen for a couple centuries."

"Did the draconis help Raspian?" Vi had yet to hear of this particular people.

"Some did, some didn't. Find me a whole race of people who's entirely good or entirely evil and I'll eat my boot. But it didn't matter what they *did*. It mattered what people *said*. And people say a lot in the years following world-changing events.

"The core of Yargen's followers, the early Faithful, claim the draconis are descended from Raspian's great dragon, crafted by the god himself. They also say the morphi are tainted by Raspian as well, since our magic is said to derive from twilight—neither here, nor there—the moment when the sun gives up its hold to the darkness where Raspian thrives."

"But the twilight could also be the dawn," Vi contested.

"Thank you!" Arwin threw her hands in the air. "I'm pleased to see you have some sense. Certainly not a Faithful after all."

"So that's why you hate the Faithful? Because they have unfairly labeled your people as allies of Raspian?"

"If only that was the extent of it." A frown lined Arwin's face. "Around twenty, thirty years ago, the Faithful grew bolder and far more wicked. They were always bad, but they didn't have the power they have now. They increased their hold on Meru—on Queen Lumeria herself. They justified their actions by saying the word of Yargen had changed, and the people believed them. They were the first ones to say the end of the world was coming and, as a result, they were more active in cleansing those who would seek to aid Raspian."

"*Cleansing?*" Vi said the word slowly. It had a horrible taste.

"Their words, not mine. They've slaughtered innocent morphi and draconis under false trials in Risen. Really, it was all a display of power. The Lord of the Faithful knows no limits to his cruelty. The draconis don't leave their island just as the morphi can only exist safely here—that's why my father carved out this place for us using the royal family's knowledge of the shift."

"That's horrible," Vi whispered. The potion she held in her hands had been forgotten. No amount of balm could soothe the ache she felt for the people of Meru. "Why does no one stop it?"

"Like I said, their actions supposedly come from the goddess herself. Though I have my suspicions..."

"You don't think they're acting on Yargen's orders?"

"I can't imagine the goddess being quiet for hundreds of years and then suddenly demanding blood. Can you?" Vi shook her head and Arwin continued. "No, it's all the depravity of two power-hungry men."

"Who?" Vi whispered. She didn't want to hear the answer, because she already knew it.

"Who else? Lord Ulvarth wields the sword, but the one who gives him the orders and the power—the real evil—is the Voice of the Faithful."

*T*HE REAL EVIL IS *the Voice of the Faithful.* The words rattled in her ears, drowning out the buzz of magic from the scythe. The conversation took a blessedly lighter turn as they walked back to Vi's room, but the weight of earlier revelations was heavy on her mind and shoulders.

"Leave the blade here, we're going to Sarphos," Arwin commanded. Vi was too tired to argue.

Leaving the scythe without so much as a lock on her door didn't feel like enough. But it had been safe and hidden in the Twilight Kingdom for hundreds of years now, so Vi could only trust it would be safe for a few more days.

Though, knowing her luck, Vi wouldn't exactly be surprised if something happened now that the scythe had been revealed from its hiding place.

Up two floors, Arwin came to a stop before a large, open space. The domed ceiling overhead was framed by metal and otherwise open to the stars in the twilight sky above. Glowing stones hung like pendants over three tables that quite literally *grew* up from the floor—starting as stone, but transforming into branches that wove themselves in the proper shape. In the back of the room was a desk with a familiar red-haired man hunched over it. On either side of his work station were a series of tables, vials, mixing stations, and other workspaces.

Whatever Sarphos was doing must be intense, for his shoulders were pulled to his ears and his hand moved feverishly over the open page before him. Arwin cleared her throat and he nearly jumped from his seat.

"Sarphos."

He looked over his shoulder. "What is it now?"

"Don't look so happy to see me," Arwin leaned her hip against one of the tables.

"Why would I be happy? You're always breaking something," Sarphos muttered. "Or someone, I should say. What did you do to her?"

"She was worse for wear when she came in. Even mild training has her bruising." Arwin motioned between Vi and the table. "Up with you. Let Sarphos give you a once-over."

Vi obliged, pushing herself off the floor to sit on the edge of the table.

"Can I trust you with her?" Arwin asked, already starting for the open door. "I have to get to a meeting with the head of the city guards. *Someone* has been taking up all my time today."

"I'm not sorry," Vi called loftily after the woman.

Arwin just snorted before disappearing, not even giving Sarphos a chance to respond.

"You two seem to be getting along better," Sarphos observed thoughtfully.

"She still doesn't trust me." And that fact could be deadly to Taavin. No matter how much easy banter they exchanged, Vi needed to stay on guard.

"She likely never will."

"Good, the feeling can be mutual then."

Sarphos looked away from his potions, inspecting her in his peripheral vision. His expression made her wonder if she should've kept the thought to herself. But she had little energy to care about whatever verdict he reached about the callous remark.

These people are not your friends, Vi reminded herself. They had their own objectives and histories she didn't understand. They were a means to an end.

"Have the morphi not been kind to you?" Sarphos asked softly, as he placed a hand on her forearm. Vi thought the motion merely reassuring until she felt a pulse of magic reverberate through her body, probing uncomfortably between her muscles.

"Everyone has been kind."

"Yet you do not trust us?" Sarphos removed his hand from her and then pointed at her midsection where Adela had wounded her. "Lie back and let me see that."

Vi did as instructed. "I can't... because once anyone finds out who I am aligned with... the kindness will end."

"Mine hasn't," he murmured, lifting her shirt slightly. Vi looked down at the raised scar on her abdomen. It could've been much worse, given the original wound.

He worked in silence and Vi stared at the glowing stone pendant above her. There was an odd, hollow ache in her—one she didn't think any salve would be able to fix. One that would make tears prick her eyes if she wasn't careful.

"Thank you," Vi said finally.

"It's my oath to heal," Sarphos said simply and lowered her shirt.

"It's not your oath to keep him a secret." Vi didn't have to specify who *he* was. "Perhaps the opposite. So, thank you."

"I still don't know if it was the right decision." He looked her right in the eye. "Make sure you and he prove to me that it was. Prove to me that this prophecy you're involved in, your goals to help all the people of this world, are real. Prove to me... that I didn't just let the murderer of morphi survive for no reason."

Vi gave a small nod, accepting the vial Sarphos held out. She downed it, and the next, feeling steadily stronger. Over the third, she asked, "Take me to him?"

"I had already planned on it."

Vi opened her eyes to the eerie skeletal trees of the Twilight Forest and took a deep breath.

"Are you all right?" Sarphos asked from her side, releasing her hand.

"Yes. It's easier to pass through the shift if I keep my eyes closed and hold my breath. Much less jarring that way."

"Interesting," he murmured. "I've never passed through a shift with a non-morphi before now."

"Glad I could be your experiment." She tried to keep her voice easy. "I see you got us closer this time."

"Now that I know where it is, I can come here directly."

Vi wondered if she should interpret the statement as a thinly veiled threat—that he could lead anyone here in an instant.

"Saves us time." Vi stepped ahead, crossed the stream. Without another word, she side-stepped through the narrow opening of the cave.

"Vi?" Taavin called out. This time, his voice didn't come from the ground, but directly across from her. The glowing stone Sarphos had left the last time illuminated him faintly as he breathed a sigh of relief. "I thought I heard your voice."

"Sarphos is here too." Vi gave him a quick once-over. His eyes were attentive and bright, the luster had returned to his skin and his muscles seemed better defined. Even Taavin's hair looked clean. Whatever Sarphos had given him had truly worked wonders overnight.

Her relief was light and palpable, but only until Sarphos entered, and the atmosphere in the close space suddenly grew heavy.

"Sarphos." Taavin gave him a wary look.

"Voice," Sarphos responded just as curtly.

Silence, long and strained, stretched between them. Vi waited, holding her breath. Of course meeting Taavin when he was healthy—healthier—would be different for Sarphos than helping a dying man.

"Shall we just get on with it?" Vi broke the silence, and their staring battle. The less the two interacted, the better. Sarphos was already in too deep to back out now, and he knew it. Taavin still needed his help, and he knew it. At least, she hoped they'd both arrived at the same conclusions.

"Very well." Sarphos's tone took on a more detached and clerical nature as he set down the bundle of clothes he'd brought and stepped forward.

For his part, Taavin said nothing, holding out his arms and waiting. Sarphos poked, prodded, and pulsed his magic over Taavin. Vi folded and unfolded her hands before her. Her whole body was tense, every muscle trembling just beneath the surface, though she didn't entirely know why.

Was it because she was nervous either Taavin or Sarphos would snap, attacking the other? Was it worry that Sarphos would find something terribly wrong? Or was it because of what Arwin had said about Taavin and the Faithful earlier?

"Right, then… the healing so far looks good. There's still quite a bit of infection so I have a few draughts I'd like to make you." Sarphos stepped back toward the opening. "Give me a minute or five?"

"Take your time." Vi caught his eyes, trying to silently stress the words. Sarphos may have picked up on her meaning, giving her the slightest of nods before pushing back toward the entrance.

"You're certain we can trust him?" Taavin asked.

"Yes." Vi leaned against the wall behind her by the opening so she could listen for Sarphos's return. "If he was going to hurt either of us, he would've by now. If he was going to out us, he could've—I've tried to keep an eye on him, but I've hardly been with him every waking moment. No one in the Twilight Kingdom knows he's smuggling me out or helping you."

"It's just… the morphi…" Taavin rubbed the back of his neck, staring at where Sarphos departed. "They don't take kindly to Faithful."

"So I hear."

Taavin's arm dropped to his side. "I'd imagine… What exactly have you heard?"

"I've heard that the morphi have been sequestered—forced to hide behind the shift, to fight for their lives to have a mere place on this land." Vi took a step forward. "I've heard how the Faithful will slaughter them just to make a point. I've heard of the brutality of the Lord of the Faithful—that his bloodlust is impossible to sate. I've heard he murders innocents on nothing more than superstitions regarding their magicks." She was standing toe to toe with him, heart racing, struggling to keep her voice and her emotions in check. Yet when she spoke next, her voice had dropped to a whisper. "And I've heard that all of these atrocities come to pass at your command."

Taavin's eyes searched her face as Vi searched his. She held her breath, waiting for a reaction of any kind. But he gave her none.

"Tell me…" She reached up, grabbing Taavin's coat. "Tell me they're lying. Tell me the Faithful of Yargen aren't butchers hiding under the skirts of their goddess, using fear to justify their wicked actions."

Taavin said nothing. He continued to stare with those terribly beautiful green eyes. Vi shook him, anger rising in her once more. She was helpless against its rolling tide.

The darkness threatened to consume her whole. One more betrayal was all it would take, and she may never trust again.

"Tell me it wasn't you." Sparks crackled around her fingers, singeing his once-bright coat. "Tell me it wasn't you who ordered it!"

"I wish I could."

Vi released him. She wasn't sure if she pushed him or he stumbled back. But the net result was the same. Once more, they both stood against opposite walls in too-small space.

"Tell me… the truth." Vi forced out. "No lies, no half-truths." She shook her head and cast a hand through the air, as if she could dispel the shadows he'd spun around her—the mystery that had made him so horribly alluring. "Tell me what you've done. Tell me everything, like I asked of you in the West… and tell me why I shouldn't tell Sarphos to get the whole of the morphi army and kill you as he wanted to from the start."

"Other than the fact that if the morphi killed me, it truly would spell their demise?" Taavin said, painfully deadpan, worrying the bracelet around his wrist.

"Do not deflect!" Vi pointed her finger at him, wishing she could pin him down. His words were slippery things. "What is your role in all of this?"

Tell me you aren't betraying me too, her mind screamed.

Taavin took a deep breath, his eyes fluttering closed. "Everything I've said has been the truth. I was taken from my home as a child by Lord Ulvarth and the Faithful. They murdered my mother and burned everything she'd worked to create to the ground. I was troubled by visions—nightmares of you."

"This is not my fault," Vi growled before he could continue. If he was about to blame his actions on her, he had another thing coming.

"My actions are my own." The man had an uncanny and uncomfortable ability to read her mind. "But you need to understand where I was in life: I was alone, sequestered, *tormented*… And I was a pawn for Ulvarth to consolidate power. The Lord of Swords is nothing without the Voice. He needed someone as a figurehead—someone he could manipulate into saying everything he wanted. Someone who would live in fear of him and never utter a word about the truth of his twisted directives."

"So you told him what he wanted to hear," Vi concluded, all their past conversations falling into logical place.

"He locked me away with the flame at the top of the Archives of Yargen, denied me food and drink. Told me I would receive nothing until I espoused the words of the goddess. At first, I lied, making things up for him." Taavin's words became hurried, almost crazed. "But he would say, 'Taavin, you must have misheard. Listen again.'"

It was Taavin's turn to approach her. With every statement he drew nearer. Arms outstretched, as if begging her for something. But Vi wasn't sure what, or if she had anything to give.

"So I began repeating what he'd say to me—the things I knew, things he all but told me, he wanted. I became his parrot. If I knew he wanted a man condemned, or to march against a city, or to take over a celebration, I would say the words. He would have the Voice's proclamations… and I would eat."

"And with your words, you knowingly condemned innocent people to die." Vi stared up at him, their noses nearly touching.

"If that's what it took to survive."

"How many people saw you say these lies? Was it only Ulvarth? Or did the Swords hear as well? Did the citizens?"

"I did what I had to do to survive. But I took no joy in it. I didn't want to. I knew what I was doing and I loathed myself for it. But I was a captive; I was helpless." Taavin shook his head, running his hands through his hair. When he looked back to her, his eyes were haunted and far more sunken than they'd been just moments ago. This was the shadowed edge of his personality that he'd always kept hidden just below his hopeful, driven exterior. "What would you have done? Curled up and died?"

"I wouldn't have told a power-hungry lunatic to murder innocent people for no reason!" Her voice rose now and Vi shoved him away. Taavin stumbled, reaching out to the cave wall for support. She wouldn't have him looking down at her. "If I had to die to spare them, I would've."

"It's easy for you to say that here, now… but not when hunger is gnawing at you. Not when death is staring you down. You don't know what you'd do then."

"I do know what I'd do. Because I've seen death. I've seen it on my land, in my people, and in visions of the world's end that haunt me even still. I've seen it in the faces that tried to kill me as I risked my life every step to get here." Her voice had gone low. "And I risked it all, not for me, not for you, but for this world. For my family. So don't you *dare* tell me I wouldn't die for a cause greater than myself."

"I never wanted to hurt anyone." He was pleading now. "I didn't—"

"Just because you didn't wield the sword, doesn't mean your hands are clean of blood."

"Had I stopped him then, he would've let me die and found another babe to rip from their home! The Voice is reborn, Vi. Time and again. So even if I had died, it wouldn't have changed anything."

His eyes were ablaze and, for the first time, Vi's mind and mouth fell silent.

"If I hadn't done as Ulvarth asked, if I let myself die, I couldn't have stopped the Swords of Light when I was able. I wouldn't have been able to hear Yargen's words when they came in earnest. I wouldn't have been able to do the best I could from my powerless position for the people of Meru— *all* of them. I wouldn't have been able to help guide you here and begin to make sense of this." Taavin thrust his index finger at the watch and Vi felt it press painfully against her breastbone. "I wouldn't have had the ability to help stop the world's end. He would've let me die, done his will anyway for a few years, claiming he was acting on my last words as the Voice, and then placed another helpless child right back in the position I was in."

Vi looked from the watch to Taavin. Every emotion ravaged her thoughts. There was sorrow for him, frustration, hurt, confusion. He was in more pain than she could imagine—the agony she'd always somehow known was there finally laid bare—and seeing the hurt unleashed only sparked her own profound sense of suffering.

Above it all, anger thrummed within her. So much that her spark had taken residence in the hole Jayme had left in her chest. Pressing her eyes shut, Vi tried to find sense in the darkness. But there was none to be had, and she was forced to look once more at Taavin.

"I trusted you," she whispered.

"As I did you. I left Risen for you. I told you my story. Forgive me for sparing myself the trauma of sharing the more agonizing details of my captivity."

"How can I believe anything else you'll say? How can I trust you're not keeping something else from me?" Her heart was racing. They were at the point of breaking, she could see it. Yet she couldn't stop herself.

"How can I put my faith in you when you judge me for actions taken when I was in *captivity*?" he seethed back. "I never meant to break your trust, Vi. But know you are dangerously close to breaking mine."

"Maybe that's just what happens to the people we love." Her mind returned to one of the last thoughts she'd had when she'd seen him previously. "Maybe we're meant to hurt and be hurt. Maybe we're just meant to burn."

Vi took a small step away from him. Taavin caught her wrist. Sparks crackled, bright yellow, tangled with a hazy blue glow that Vi knew as the hallmark of his magic—of Yargen's power.

"Fine," he breathed. "If we're meant to burn, then we burn together."

They were both breathing heavily. His exhales were her inhales, until the air between them was thin and she felt dizzy. Vi stared up at his emerald eyes long enough to watch their crystalline depths go hazy. "Taa—"

His hand was in the back of her hair, grabbing, pulling. His free arm wrapped around her, holding her to him. Vi's eyes barely had time to close before his mouth crashed against hers.

Taavin's teeth scraped against her lips and Vi parted them with a soft groan, allowing him entry. The rock wall behind her dug into her back. She managed to squeeze her hands between them. Her fingers fought their way up his chest, to his face, tugging him closer.

Sunlight... Even in the darkness, he smelled of sunlight. He smelled of fields warmed in the afternoon, of the heat on fresh laundry pulled inside on a hot day, of joy and laughter over a cool drink in the balmy hours after dusk.

He shifted his legs and Vi's hips pressed forward slightly, their bodies completely flush. His fingers gripped her hard enough that they might leave bruises. Vi almost hoped they did. She needed proof this moment was real. She wanted something to look at later and remind herself it wasn't just a fleeting daydream.

Taavin finally pulled away a fraction, breathless, their noses rubbing and foreheads nearly touching.

"Perhaps you're right about us burning together, because only you can set me on fire." Vi leaned forward, catching his mouth for several more moments. Taavin kissed her slowly this time, almost sweetly, as if he was savoring every taste. As if they both somehow knew that these desperate, fleeting moments were the best they would have.

"Vi." Her name was husky on his swollen lips. "I've never had much… but this is all I have now. This whole world may need you and not know it, but no one needs you more than I do, I promise you that. I will make mistakes. But I need you to believe in me, trust me." His thumb caressed her cheek as his eyes locked with hers. Gut-wrenching pain filled her with that gaze. He was asking for something she didn't know if she could give any longer. "I need you to accept that this, however perfect it can feel, isn't. I want you to stay with me despite that fact. Stay with me because it is messy, and raw, and something we need but may also be terrified to want."

She pressed her eyes closed. Vi took a quivering breath. *Say yes. Just say yes.* She tried to will the word to her lips.

What would happen if she gave herself to him even more than she already had, and then he betrayed her? Would there be anything left unbroken in her after something like that?

"Taavin," her voice was raspy and thin, barely forced through a thick throat. "What if I can't?"

"Good sense would have me give up on you… But when it comes to you, Vi, I seem to be lacking in good sense."

Vi tightened her arms around his neck and shoulders. "I'm sorry," she whispered.

"As am I," he murmured.

"Sarphos will be back soon and I have so much to tell you. So much we should discuss… but all I want to do is hold you." Vi let out a small, bitter laugh. There was so much to say. She had yet to tell him of the scythe, of Jayme, of Adela. There would never be enough time for all the words unspoken between them.

"Then hold me, and let the world wait."

E VENTUALLY, KING NOCT'S HOSPITALITY would run out. Everything had its limits. And before that happened, Vi wanted to be as prepared as possible to start on the road again.

But with so much to do, she wasn't sure where to start.

Vi opened a heavy wooden door to a library, tucked away in a quiet corner of the palace. Cool air rushed to greet her, carrying the scent of stale leather and parchment. The atmosphere was that of opening a time capsule, the room still and coated in a thick layer of dust.

The only evidence that anyone had used this room recently was an open journal sitting out on the table, two empty inkwells and one still full laid out next to it.

The private library of the royal family was small, but tall, and every bookcase that lined its walls was packed. It was more than enough information to keep herself busy yesterday and today… perhaps tomorrow. But Taavin was getting stronger, and so was she. And that meant they needed to continue onward.

Her father was out there, and the longer she dallied, the longer he suffered.

Vi ran her fingertips absentmindedly along the spines of the books, working her way toward the back corner where she'd left off last night. Selecting a narrow, wide book, Vi lifted it off the shelf and brought it over to her table. She flipped through the maps within, landing on the page she'd been working from yesterday.

Settling into her spot at the table, Vi got to work.

"You really have a thing for maps, huh?" Arwin's voice startled her. Vi had filled five pages in the journal and half the inkwell was gone, so she must've been working for at least two hours. "You burned the midnight oil here last night, and were back at it before breakfast."

"I do love maps." Vi looked back down at her transcriptions. She'd been sketching from memory the map Sehra had shown her, the maps she'd grown up with on the Dark Isle. Now, she was making slow work of transcribing the coastlines of Meru— comparing them to what she knew, comparing them to the morphi's records of maps through the ages.

Two pages earlier in the journal, she'd been working on a route to Adela's Isle of Frost.

"Here, breakfast." Arwin held out a sandwich as she sat across the table from her. Vi took a generous bite, ignoring the smear of ink her fingertips left on the bread's hard crust.

"Thanks," Vi mumbled over the food, looking back at her work.

"Why do you like maps so much?"

Slowly, Vi looked up. The question was calm, genuine. There wasn't even a hint of a jab. So Vi answered an honest question honestly.

"I told you, I grew up captive."

"You said you were sent to the northernmost territory of your Empire, for politics and prophecy. Nothing about being captive."

"Well, it effectively made me a captive." Vi glanced up again from her journal, seeing pity in Arwin's eyes. She laughed softly, shaking her head. "It wasn't that bad. I lived a fairly good life…" Her thoughts went to Taavin's imprisonment. Yes, her time in the North could've been *much* worse. "But maps were my window to the world, how I made sense of all the space spreading out around me that I never thought I'd get to see."

"I see," Arwin murmured.

"What about you?" Vi dared to ask. "What are you interested in?"

"Mostly combat."

"Just combat? Nothing else?" Vi knew many soldiers who delighted in honing their skills. But underneath the armor, they were still people. They had passions and hobbies.

"Sometimes I sing." Then, as if suddenly regretting the burst of honesty, Arwin stood quickly. "But speaking of combat, I should get back to training." She nearly bolted for the door, catching herself on its frame and turning back to Vi. "So should you… I'm sure you'll be on your way toward the end of the world soon enough, and you're not going to kill any evil gods with your current scythe skills."

Before Vi could reply, Arwin left.

She spent a few more hours pouring through the maps, working as quickly as possible to get as much information down as she could from the records of the Twilight Kingdom. There was a wealth of information she'd never be able to comb through. As Vi returned the last book to the shelf with a sigh, she scanned the room one more time.

What if, somewhere in here, was information on the scythe? Its history? The history of all the mysterious crystal weapons?

She could spend months looking through every book, searching for information that may well not be there—that likely *wasn't* there. Arwin was right, she didn't have much time, and she had to make the most of what she had. So, clutching the journal to her chest, Vi left the library behind and made for the training room.

"I was wondering how long you'd keep me waiting." Arwin's brow was slick with sweat when Vi entered. A spear in her hand today.

"Thanks for waiting at all." Vi adjusted her grip on the scythe as she crossed over. Magic flowed through her, bright and immeasurably powerful.

"You need me." Arwin shrugged.

"I do." In multiple ways, Vi realized. A plan had been forming in the back of her mind while she had been working on routes to the Isle of Frost.

Taavin had said there was a shift protecting the Isle of Frost, like that surrounding the Twilight Kingdom. Originally, Vi had thought to try to get Sarphos to come with them. But perhaps Vi could convince Arwin to come along to continue her training with the scythe. It was another avenue to pursue and seemed more likely than convincing the soft Sarphos to venture out on a dangerous journey. Vi wasn't about to leave their access to Adela's stronghold to chance.

Vi considered the best next steps as they traded blow for blow in the sparring ring.

"Remember, distance." Arwin knocked the pole of her weapon with Vi's. "You have to manage the distance with that thing." Vi adjusted her feet, and Arwin held up her spear again. "Dodge and slash—catch my hip with the curved part of that weapon and pull."

They repeated the motions again, and again. They did them slowly and at a too-far distance to start, then sped up as Vi became more comfortable. Just when she thought she'd gathered the hang of it, Arwin changed the move.

"All right, put that to the side for now," Arwin finally commanded. Vi's arms were like jelly, limp at her sides the moment she let go of the scythe. "Let's practice a little bit of combat, now that we've run through drills."

All Vi could do was nod. She was winded, legs exhausted, arms failing. But she wasn't about to back down. Arwin walked over to the weapon rack, grabbing a wooden halberd. With a pulse of her magic, the polearm had turned into a wooden scythe, nearly identical to her weapon. She tossed it over and Vi was shocked she still had the reflexes and strength to catch it.

"Why haven't I been practicing with this the whole time?"

"We weren't moving that fast, or doing anything that dangerous, during the drills. I wanted you to grow accustomed to the actual weight of your weapon. But for sparring... I'm not going to even risk having you knick me with that thing. Who knows what it'd do to me."

Vi looked to the weapon, and agreed. It was likely for the best... She'd always heard crystals led to madness, and monstrous corruptions of mind and body. But the scythe had also been in the hands of the morphi for generations. Perhaps, somehow, they were immune... or perhaps they'd just never handled the weapon enough. Vi wouldn't take chances, in case it was the latter.

"I'll use different weapons each round. Your only objective is to land a killing blow on me."

"Understood," Vi said, and the sparring commenced.

With two weapons, Arwin formed an X to catch her scythe, pushing it off and digging the blunted wooden point of one into the soft part of her throat. When Arwin wielded a single sword, Vi had slightly more luck keeping the woman at distance—until Arwin caught the pole in her hands, yanking the wooden weapon forward and Vi with it. She stumbled and fell, blinking up at the sword in her face.

"I know you have more than that, up with you," Arwin commanded gruffly. They clasped forearms and Arwin pulled her upright. Vi swayed wearily and ignored every stinging pain in her body. "You were good on distance there; you just need to identify openings to attack better. Defense is only useful to create an opening for offense."

"I'll focus on openings, then," Vi said, and they continued on.

Arwin was nimble and skilled—a trained warrior through and through. No matter how many hours she put in, Vi wasn't about to make up for the difference in their years of experience.

And yet... when an opening presented itself, Vi took it.

Arwin's weight shifted—Vi recognized her preparation for a lunge. She dodged to the side. Swiping the blade low, Vi hooked Arwin's ankle and pulled. The woman was sent off-balance, dancing from foot to foot to try to stay upright.

Vi pushed the blade this time, hitting the fronts of her ankles. Arwin slammed the tip of her wooden sword into the ground, using it for support. She crouched low, about to strike again. But Vi was too fast.

She swung the scythe around, stopping it right at Arwin's neck.

For a brief second, they both panted, staring at each other.

"Well done." Arwin recovered her breath much faster than Vi. "Perhaps you have a fighter in you yet."

Vi eased the scythe away from Arwin, leaning against it for support. "I have a good tutor."

Arwin flashed her a genuine smile, taking the scythe and returning it with her wooden sword to the rack. Vi took the expression as a sign of hope—perhaps she really could convince the woman to go with her on her journey.

"Come along." Arwin started for the exit.

"Where are we going?" Vi grabbed the crystal scythe and followed Arwin out of the training room. They went through the normal doors, into the usual hallway, but then took an unexpected turn down a wing of the palace Vi had never been to before.

"You'll see soon enough." Arwin glanced over her shoulder, making sure Vi was still close behind. "You did well today. You deserve—and need—some recovery."

The potent scents of flowers and woody herbs filled the air on clouds of steam. Arwin led her into a bathing room. There, Vi discovered the source of the aroma—three large tubs, like barrels cut in half, filled to the brim with steaming water.

"Strip." Arwin pointed to a tall table on one half of the room, then to the tubs. "And soak. It does wonders for the body."

Vi hovered as Arwin headed for the tall table on the room's other side. She slowly peeled her sweat-drenched shirt off her skin, revealing a tight leather binding underneath before Vi could look away. Vi would have called it a corset, but it covered the breasts only—not down to the hips. Additionally, it had thick straps that wrapped over the shoulders and—most fascinating of all—it was fashioned to cover the entire breast, accentuating no cleavage, and was tied in the front.

"What?" Arwin caught her staring. "This?" She motioned to a fairly large, crescent-shaped birthmark underneath her collar bone.

"No, not that. Why do you bind your chest like that?" Vi blurted.

"Keeps them out of my way. They'd be way too painful to deal with if they were bouncing about during combat or practice." Arwin paused, mid-loosening of the ties. Her eyes caught Vi's. "What do you do?" she asked cautiously.

Mutual fascination filled the air to the point that Vi felt dizzy with it and couldn't help laughing. And the laughter felt so good that she didn't even bother trying to stop it.

"Look at us," Vi said finally when she was under control. "Fascinated by each other's lives, even when it comes to undergarments." Arwin gave her a small grin. "We have nothing like that where I'm from. Our underclothes are meant to tighten the waist or accentuate the bust."

"We have corsets too," Arwin said.

"I see."

"They're just not practical for my line of work." Arwin started for the laces of her chest leathers and Vi quickly averted her eyes, giving the woman some privacy. "I really don't care how small my waist is."

Vi set the scythe to the side and quickly undressed before crossing to the tub next to Arwin's. She stepped up onto the ledge that surrounded it, dipping her toes into the water—feeling around for the small step she knew must be there. Finding one, she brought the other leg over and sat. What Vi had thought was water turned out to be a bright teal substance that reminded her of the consistency of an egg yolk. Any potential to be unnerved by such a comparison dissolved as a rush tingled up her body to her head, making everything feel light. Every muscle in her body relaxed all at once.

"*Oh my...*" Vi sighed softly, sinking back into the tub, the back of her head resting against the edge.

"Nice, isn't it?" Arwin slung her arms over the side of her tub closest to Vi, chin resting on her forearms.

"I've never felt anything like it. It's as if my whole body has vanished."

"It's one of Sarphos's concoctions, actually. We worked on it together back before..." Arwin's voice trailed off. Vi looked over to see the woman staring off at nothing. Vi didn't question her; whatever memory had drawn her away was hers alone. The last thing she wanted to draw Arwin's attention to was her moment of vulnerability. "It's made from the shift," Arwin continued hastily, as though the pause hadn't happened at all. "Using water and other ingredients, he'll use the shift to merge them together and make something new—shift it into something else."

"He's a skilled healer, and an even better man," Vi murmured, thinking of all he'd done for Taavin and her, despite them being his supposed enemies. That would be another challenge if Vi somehow managed to find a way to convince Arwin to come along with her. How would she get her to ignore Taavin's identity? Perhaps it was better to go after Sarphos; he already knew who he was dealing with.

"He is. And nothing at all like his brother," Arwin continued.

"His brother?" Vi remembered when she'd first inquired about Arwin and Sarphos's relationship—he'd said something about Arwin being engaged to his brother. So the mention now had her more than a little intrigued.

Arwin pushed away from the side of her tub, mirroring Vi's position with her head lounged back. She stared upward, speaking more toward the ceiling than Vi.

"Sarphos's brother and I were engaged to be married. He was nothing like Sarphos—strong willed, a fighter, reckless, everything a young girl foolishly dreams—or lusts—about. There are times I wonder what would've happened if I knew what I know now, and had been smart enough to fall for the kind and stable Sarphos instead..." Arwin's voice was filled with longing. But Vi didn't know whether it was for Sarphos's brother, or a life that could've been with Sarphos himself.

"What happened to him?" Vi asked gently. "Not Sarphos, obviously, his brother?"

"He's gone now."

"I'm sorry." She straightened, moving the thick waters around with her hands, watching the flowers dance on the surface as she stirred up currents beneath. This could be her opportunity. Vi took a deep breath. She just had to find strength enough to be vulnerable... How was it, out of everything she'd done, that was starting to terrify her the most? "I'm afraid I may lose someone important to me as well."

"Who?"

"My father."

"You said you were here to find him. Why is the King of the Dark Isle on Meru?"

"Emperor—we don't have kings on the Dark Isle anymore," Vi corrected without thinking. Luckily, Arwin didn't seem offended. "My mother is sick with the White Death. So my father embarked on a journey to Meru to find a cure. He didn't know then what the cause was." *Didn't know his journey was hopeless*, Vi thought but couldn't bring herself to say. If only she'd known earlier. If only her father had known. Then he would've been safe and sound back with her mother.

"I take it this journey didn't go well?" Arwin asked solemnly.

"It didn't… He was captured and is being held hostage."

"By the Faithful?"

"No, he never made it to Meru. Adela captured him. Now she has him on her Isle of Frost and… I know he's alive… but every day that passes is another when his life could end. Even when I'm so close to reaching him." Vi turned to Arwin, surprised to see the woman stony-faced and serious. "Before I do anything else, I have to get to the Isle of Frost."

"You're going to the Isle of Frost?" Arwin whispered.

"Yes."

Without warning, Arwin stood. Vi looked away quickly, giving the woman privacy as she left the tub.

Had she said something wrong? Had she offended her somehow? Vi ran through the conversation in her head.

"Get out," Arwin commanded gruffly. Vi turned slowly, but the woman's back was to her as she tightened the bindings on her chest. "We're going to see my father."

"Arwin… I didn't mean to offend—"

"You didn't offend me." Arwin looked over her shoulder with a fire in her eyes. "But you have presented me with a unique opportunity."

U NIQUE OPPORTUNITY. V I DIDN'T know yet if she liked those words.

Arwin didn't say anything else as they left the baths, starting up through the palace wordlessly. Vi repeated the conversation in her head verbatim, wondering where she'd gone wrong. Perhaps it was bringing up Adela? Taavin had said that Fallor was a notable outcast of the morphi, and he was in Adela's service…

Vi suppressed a groan. She should've thought of that sooner.

Her mind swirled around the possibilities as they made their way along the spiral staircases of the palace, down to the throne room Vi had been first taken to days before. Just like then, King Noct sat on his large sofa, hands folded over his round belly, watching children play in the courtyard beyond.

"What is it, daughter?" the king asked, slowly drawing his eyes to Arwin. They drifted over Vi as well, pausing. "I see the weapon is becoming a part of you."

Vi shifted her grip on the scythe. It was less cumbersome than she'd originally thought it would be—perhaps because it was surprisingly light. Or because she could feel the power radiating through it underneath her fingers. Either way, carrying it was indeed becoming more instinctive.

"I don't enjoy letting it out of my sight," Vi said quietly. Then added quickly, "I know it's safe here, but—"

"But that is the right decision. You cannot be too cautious… and the weapon must get to know its new champion. Perhaps Arwin can fashion a sling for you to better carry it with." At the mention of his daughter, he turned to Arwin. "Why have you come with such a severe expression?"

"Father, there is something we have overlooked—a detail our guest has neglected to share."

"What is this?" The king looked back to her.

"Well… I had been telling Arwin about my quest to find my father," Vi started, glancing between the two.

"Yes, one of the reasons that you came to Meru."

"It's not that she's finding him—it's *where* her father is," Arwin said gruffly before motioning for Vi to continue.

"He's on the Isle of Frost, your highness," Vi said delicately. "Adela has him."

"The Isle of Frost…" the king repeated softly. His eyes drifted back to Arwin. "I know what you are thinking."

"Father, I must. This is my chance."

"I remain firm in my—"

"Your stance has always been that I cannot go alone," Arwin interrupted, "and that has been enough, because you forbade my sisters from going with me on my mission." Arwin took a step forward. "Well, now I will not be alone. I will have a companion on the journey—a companion who is not your daughter and will be going anyway."

"A companion who also doesn't know this land. Who is not a warrior like yourself and can't protect you."

Were she able to show the king her Lightspinning, he might think differently. But Vi kept her mouth shut.

"I can take care of myself—you know I can. She has the scythe and is improving. At the very least, she can guide the way—I've seen her with her maps, father." Arwin looked to Vi. "You know how to get there, don't you?"

"I do," Vi said with slightly more confidence than she felt.

"If you go, you will die at Adela's hand."

"Your highness," Vi interjected quickly before the conversation could take yet another repetitive turn. "I do not fully understand the depth of all you are discussing... But if Arwin wishes to join me, then I beseech you to let her." Vi glanced at Arwin. The woman had a desperate look to her eyes. Vi didn't know what she was bargaining for just yet—what had given Arwin this fire—but if it resulted in the help she needed, she would handle the rest as it came. "I must save my father."

"You must save this world."

"I know that," Vi nearly snapped back at him. The only thing keeping her voice level was her years of royal training. She had no idea how she was going to save the world—she was still just trying to save the ones she loved. "But I also know this: Arwin is the best teacher I'll be able to find for this weapon." Vi shifted her grip on the scythe. "How will I be ready to fight to save our world if I can't keep training?"

The king was silent.

"I also know that I won't be able to focus on defeating Raspian if I'm worried for my father's life. I want to save him *and* the world. All my life, I have been trying to reunite with my family... I don't want to live in a saved world where I cannot."

Noct pursed his lips slightly. She could tell she was trying his patience. But Vi took his continued silence as an indication that she still held the upper hand on the matter.

"I've been told there is a shift around the Isle of Frost—much like the one here. I'm hoping there are tears in that shift, too—tears I plan to exploit." Vi tried to counter his argument before he could make it. "But I'd rather not risk that chance. I'd rather know that once I sail for the Isle of Frost, I will be able to get to my father. If you don't allow Arwin to accompany me for her own reasons, let her come to train me and ensure I can get past the Isle's shift. Please, I—"

She stopped shy of begging, but only just.

The king closed his eyes and sighed. When he opened them, he looked out on the courtyard with a sorrowful expression. Vi knew she was asking him to risk his family for her to save hers. She knew it wasn't a fair trade. Just as she knew exploiting the world's end was an underhanded tactic.

But Arwin also had her own reasons for going. She could see it on the woman's face. Even if Arwin's presence would help Vi, she got the impression it would help

Arwin, too. She just wasn't sure exactly how.

"Did you not tell me we are to help the Champion?" Arwin asked, stepping forward. "Isn't that why you gave her the scythe and your hospitality?"

"I do not wish to give her my daughter as well."

Arwin knelt by her father. "You will not lose me, father. But I must put an end to the abominable shift that protects the bane of the seas—the shift that should've never been established and is a theft of our magic. I must put an end to the one who betrayed us."

King Noct looked only at his daughter, slowly lifting his hand. He cupped her cheek thoughtfully, lovingly. Vi's chest ached, thinking back to the few times she'd been with her own father and he'd looked at her with his heart in his eyes.

"If you take this burden on yourself, if you leave our lands... You know I must make it a royal decree. You will get no exceptions as my daughter."

"I understand."

"Then, my royal guard..." King Noct's whispering voice quivered slightly. "I command you to leave the protection of the Twilight Kingdom to atone for your past transgressions. I command you to venture beyond the embrace of the Twilight Forest. You are to go, and on your way, you will teach the Champion so that she may save our world. You are to destroy the shift which should've never been—and you are to ensure it shall never be formed again by killing the one who created it. Otherwise, you will not be welcomed back into this court."

Vi's heart pounded so hard in her chest that it rattled her lungs. Breathing suddenly felt harder than normal. Cast out? Succeed, or live in exile? What circumstances were these? When she'd envisioned Arwin coming, she hadn't envisioned anything like this.

Vi was playing a game, though she knew precious little of the rules.

"Do you understand?" King Noct asked solemnly.

"I understand, my king. And as your royal guard, I live by your words."

The next morning, Vi woke early. She dressed with more than enough time to get lost in her thoughts before there was a knock on the door.

"Come in."

Vi turned, surprised to see Sarphos rather than Arwin.

"I hear you're leaving," he said as he entered the room.

"So it seems." Vi leaned against the wall by the window, staring out at the bloody-ringed moon that never left the sky. "Can't say I'm surprised the King's hospitality has run short given that I'm responsible for his daughter's exile."

"King Noct holds no ill will toward you." Sarphos set a satchel down at the foot of her bed.

"I wouldn't blame him if he did," Vi said gently, giving him permission to be honest.

"Arwin made her choice."

I did a pretty good job of convincing him to go along with it, Vi thought to herself. She'd replayed the conversation again and again for half the night. Wondering if she'd done the right thing. But Arwin had been eager to go along first. So Vi tried to set the worry out of her mind.

"I prepared something for the road." Sarphos motioned to the satchel. "There's some crackers in there that can fill an empty stomach like a meal, a specially woven blanket that will keep you warm even on the coldest nights without being bulky, salves, of course, and—"

"Why have you been so nice to me?" Vi interrupted. "You hardly know me."

"Do I have to know someone to be kind to them?"

"Too much kindness… too much trust… It will get you hurt, or killed," Vi muttered bitterly.

"The opposite is also true—but it'll be a much lonelier death."

"What would you know about it?" she murmured.

"A lot more than you give me credit for." He sighed and stood. "I don't understand everything about you or your world. But I don't have to, to see that you're hurting." Vi opened her mouth about to protest, tell him to stop any kind of diagnosis he'd been performing on her. "Trust me when I say you're not the only one who's been hurt by people they loved."

Vi pressed her lips shut as Sarphos started for the door.

"Look after her, please."

"Arwin is far stronger than I, she can look after herself."

"But her emotions get the better of her and cause trouble." He stopped, and the long pause that followed was what brought Vi's attention back to the healer one last time. "I've already lost a brother, Vi," Sarphos whispered. "I don't want to lose a sister, too."

With that, the man was off and Vi finished readying for her journey alone.

She inspected the contents of the pack. In addition to all Sarphos had promised, there were a few extra changes of clothes, wrapped around vials. It didn't matter what he said, Sarphos was a fool for giving away his kindness as he did… She certainly didn't deserve it.

Vi put the journal she'd been working in atop everything else in the satchel, slung it over her shoulder, and strapped the scythe to her back over the opposite shoulder. The strap from the satchel and the scythe formed an X over her chest. But thanks to the undergarments Arwin had gifted her, neither dug in uncomfortably.

Also thanks to Arwin, Vi no longer had to carry the scythe by hand. The woman had taken heed of King Noct's suggestion and stopped in last night with a special strap identical to those she used to carry her pole arms.

"It looks good on you," Arwin appraised as Vi met her on the arcade walkway.

"Thanks." Vi gripped the strap.

"Though, unhooking the strap can make for a slow draw. You may not want to have the weapon wrapped as well, in case you need to get to it."

They started back toward the entrance.

"If I don't have it wrapped, it'll draw too much attention." Vi patted the fabric covering the blade. She suspected her magic would be the first thing she fought with the moment she was out of the Twilight Forest. Vi was still more confident with a sword in her hand than a scythe.

They walked through the entryway and out of the palace, starting along the same road Vi had now traversed many times. Other than the occasional person who gave a nod or wave to Arwin, there was no fanfare.

"Not much of a going-away party," Vi said under her breath, tightening the bandanna around her forehead.

"They're used to my coming and going," Arwin replied. Vi hadn't intended for the woman to hear. "I'm usually patrolling the edges of our kingdom, checking the barriers daily. They don't know that this time I'll be gone a little longer than normal."

"Don't you want to say goodbye to anyone?" Vi couldn't help but ask. Something about their departure reminded Vi of leaving Norin. A princess quietly departing her Empire… even if Arwin wasn't *technically* a princess.

"I said goodbye to my family earlier."

"Friends?"

"I don't have many of those."

"I'm shocked." The dry remark slipped through Vi's lips before she could stop it. Arwin looked over her shoulder in what could've been a glare, had it not been so obviously laced with pride.

"When did you get a smart mouth?"

"More like when did I get bold enough to share it with you."

"Don't get too bold," Arwin cautioned. Despite the warning, a grin was sneaking its way onto her lips. "Take my hand, I'll need the physical contact to get you through the shift. Don't let go."

Vi took her hand and refrained from pointing out that this would be the third time she'd passed through the shift. If Sarphos kept their secret up until the end, so would Vi. Even if one very big, Taavin-shaped secret was about to come to light.

Heart racing, Vi closed her eyes and sucked in a deep breath, allowing Arwin to guide her through. It seemed like a single step now—the transition between kingdom and forest becoming easier each time. Like waking from a dream, Vi blinked into the bright morning light.

She instantly raised a hand, shielding her eyes. She and Sarphos had only ever sneaked out at night. The light of the Twilight Kingdom was perpetually dim, the majority of illumination coming from unnatural sources.

"Your eyes will take a little longer to adjust… It's been a while since they've seen the sun. But don't worry, you'll be back to normal in no time."

Vi had an increasing amount to worry about, none of which had to do with her eyes. Squinting, Vi trying to discern her bearings. But there was nothing familiar. Trees, as far as the eye could see, and not the slightest bit of sound from the stream.

"Where are we?" Vi tried to ask calmly.

"Right near the western edge of the Twilight Forest." Arwin pointed. "We're about half a day away from Toris. It's a small fishing and trading town notorious for being a pirate stopover. We should be able to pick up a vessel there to get us to the Isle of Frost." Vi didn't miss the slight grimace at the mention of Adela's stronghold.

"Can we return to where Sarphos showed you the tear?" Vi's markings on the trees should still be there. With them, she could find her way back to Taavin.

"Why?"

"There's something I stashed in a cave near there. I want to retrieve it," Vi explained delicately.

"Oh, fine." Arwin rolled her eyes. "Come on then."

Scooping up Vi's hand once more and gripping it tightly, Arwin tugged her through the trees. Vi barely had time to close her eyes and hold her breath. Her lungs were on fire in a moment and her ears popped from the shifting pressure. But as quickly as it came, the uncomfortable sensation of the shift vanished and Vi opened her eyes once more to what had become a more familiar stretch of forest. She could hear the stream in the distance, and see the markings on the trees.

"Right, this way." Vi started forward, gripping the straps of her satchel. It was going to be a miracle if they didn't all end up dead. "Listen, Arwin… I want you to know how grateful I am for you coming."

"I have my own agenda."

"Yes, well… I still appreciate it." Vi continued. "And I hope that, on this journey, we can trust each other."

Arwin snorted. "I suppose I can trust you not to get yourself killed. Barely."

The cave came into view and Vi pointed at it. "That's where my things are. Wait here?"

"Get what you need and let's be on our way." Arwin folded her arms, resting against a tree, impatient.

Vi moved hastily, not wanting to sour the woman's mood even further. Uttering every prayer and good luck wish she knew, Vi crossed to the cave, set the scythe aside, and squeezed through the opening.

"Vi." Taavin's voice cut through her thoughts.

"Taavin." Vi looked over to him in the dim glow of Sarphos's stone. They stared at each other for what felt like an hour—long enough that Arwin should've come investigating. After their last parting, Vi was even more painfully aware of all that was left unsaid.

"Are you alone?" Taavin's eyes shifted over her shoulder.

"No. And it's not Sarphos who's with me."

"What happened?" Taavin's tone sobered and Vi wondered for a brief second if he'd thought she betrayed him.

"I can't explain fully right now, there's no time, and this introduction will be uncomfortable enough as it is. I'd rather not do it in a confined space." Vi sighed and rested her palm on his chest. "You have to trust me, all right? Please know, no matter what, I will never seek to bring you harm. Trust me like I trust you."

"What're you talking about?" His heart was beating faster underneath her fingers.

"You said it yourself—the morphi are not friendly to Fallor or Adela. Turns out, they have some unfinished business with the pirate queen and one of the royal guards wants to come and settle the score."

"*What?*" Taavin's voice dropped to a panicked whisper. He spoke so fast that Vi didn't have the chance to tell him Arwin stood far enough away that there was no way she could hear. "We can't bring a morphi along, especially a morphi royal. First, you saw how Sarphos reacted to me. Second, if they leave their kingdom, they risk exile. Third, they risk being hunted by any Faithful we run into."

"I know the risks. Moreover, *she* knows the risks." Vi dropped her hand, fighting the urge to glare at him and failing. "And so do you. You told me yourself of your hand in creating the decrees that would lead to the Faithful hunting her."

"And I told you not to judge me for the things I did in captivity."

Vi bit the inside of her lower lip and focused on the present. "We don't have a choice in this. Adela's Isle of Frost is shrouded by the morphi shift and I'm not about to leave getting to my father up to chance and hope that one of Raspian's tears allows us through. Getting to the Twilight Kingdom nearly killed me. That's not a viable strategy for us."

Taavin pressed his lips together into a thin line. Vi knew when she'd won. There was no better counter-argument. She'd run through every possibility already; having a morphi on their side was their best chance.

With that, she left the cave, trusting him to follow. But she didn't look back. Instead, she focused on quickly slinging the scythe over her shoulder once more and walking toward Arwin, trying to position herself right between the two.

Vi knew the moment Taavin emerged based on the change in Arwin's expression. It was a darkly fascinating thing to behold. She went from bored and grumpy, to horrified, to the picture of loathing in about an instant.

Spear in hand, Arwin let out a crazed cry and began sprinting toward Taavin.

CROUCHING SOME AND DIGGING in her heels, Vi braced herself as the woman approached, shifting to the side slightly and narrowly missing the point of her spear. She grabbed Arwin's shoulders with both hands, knowing full well she couldn't hold Arwin anywhere for any amount of time if she didn't want to be held.

"I need you to listen to me."

"Vi, you have no idea who that is." Arwin twisted from her grasp. Bringing an arm around, she pushed Vi behind her as if Vi was in danger.

"I know who that is." Vi gripped Arwin's forearm and bicep, clinging to the woman, futilely trying to stop her from moving.

"What have you done to her?" she growled at Taavin. Vi watched the man's eyes dart between her and Arwin, no doubt debating if or when he should step in. "What hold do you have over her?"

"He hasn't done anything to me, Arwin, listen!" Vi yanked at her arm. It was as unflinching as one of the giant vines in the forests of Soricium. "He's…" Her eyes drifted to Taavin for a long second. So much was left outstanding and unsaid between them. But now wasn't the time. And sorting through that mess would be a lot harder if he was dead. "He's my friend."

"Your friend?" Arwin wrenched her arm free and stepped back, facing Vi without letting Taavin fully out of her sight. "Your *friend* is the Voice?"

"I can explain." Vi held up her hands.

"You lied to me," Arwin seethed, raising her spear. "You lying traitor. Curse you, your father, and your family."

"I didn't lie." Vi worked to keep herself calm even as Arwin spit venom.

"You said you weren't Faithful!"

"I'm not."

"No? You're just aligned with the worst of them all." Arwin swung her spear in Taavin's direction, though her eyes remained glued on Vi. When she spoke, it was with a bitter detachment that hurt more than any word. "I knew you were seeking to infiltrate and betray us from the first moment I laid eyes on you and I was right."

Vi allowed her blood to run cold. She knew the pain on Arwin's face all too well. It was the look of someone you trusted showing their hand and coming up with cards you never dreamed they'd be holding.

"If I had wanted to harm the Twilight Kingdom, I could've," Vi said calmly. "If I had wanted to lead a legion of Faithful though the tears in the shift, I could've." Vi actually doubted that. It had been the watch that had protected her through the tear. But Arwin didn't need to know that. "If Taavin had wanted to move against your people, he would've."

"The Faithful are devious. They don't function based on logic or reason. They act on hate alone."

"You don't have to like us," Vi spoke through Arwin's justified rage. "None of us are pretending to be friends. Our only link is that we're all working toward the same thing."

"I will never be aligned with a Faithful, and especially not the Voice."

"You already are. I need him to teach me how to bring down Raspian, but I need you to get to my father. And you need both of us to settle your old score if you ever want to return home." They didn't have to like each other. They had to work together. That would be good enough for Vi and it should be good enough for Arwin. If they all knew where they stood from this moment forward, there would be no more betrayal, because there wouldn't be any real trust between them. They would trust in their shared goals, and nothing more.

"I don't need you," Arwin seethed. She swung her weapon and pointed the blade right at the soft spot of Vi's throat. "My father may have told me not to come back until I settled my outstanding score, but I think he'd make an exception for bringing him the body of the Voice and his accomplice."

"Harm her and you'll never see the Twilight Kingdom again," Taavin cautioned dangerously. "Harm her and I will ensure every sword and sorcerer at my disposal will rally against you."

"You will not leave here alive."

"Do not underestimate me." Taavin raised his hands. Vi could feel the power gathering under his palms, ready to be brought to life with a word. Power Sarphos had nursed back into him at Vi's command.

One wrong word, and the whole situation would explode into violence and death.

"Listen, both of you, just listen!" Vi pleaded, trying not to move too much. She would've suspected talking would be much harder with a spear through her throat. "We all want the same thing! This doesn't have to be personal."

"You made it personal," Arwin growled. "And I will never want the same thing as a Faithful."

"You do though," Taavin interjected before Vi could. "And I could give it to you."

"What're you talking about?" Arwin's eyes narrowed at him, but she had yet to attack, which Vi took as a victory.

"What do you want more than anything else?" Taavin asked. "You want to see Ulvarth dead, no? You want an end to the Faithful as conquerors? I can deliver that opportunity to you."

Vi watched Arwin shift her white-knuckled grip on the weapon. She was holding the spear so hard that it squeaked as her calloused hands rubbed against the polished wood. The woman seemed suspended in place by her own tension.

"How?" Arwin demanded finally.

"I will give you access to Ulvarth. I know where he lives and works. I know the people who attend him. And I know the back doors that connect them all."

"You lie. No such back doors exist into the Archives of Yargen. The place is a fortress."

Vi had never thought of a library as a fortress. Her image of the Archives, and just where Taavin had spent the majority of his life, were shifting faster than a morphi.

"The Archives of Yargen are old. They've been added to by countless Faithful over the years, each one more neurotic than the last. Each trying to find a new way to protect themselves, escape if needed, or slit the throats of their enemies as they lay sleeping."

"Exactly—slit the throats of their enemies as they sleep. The Faithful are underhanded, so why should I believe you?"

"Because I am proof that such passages exist. It's through them that I finally staged my escape."

"Why would you have to escape?" Arwin seemed genuinely confused. "Why not just command your way out?"

"Because he's been their prisoner for years, and hates the Faithful just as much as you do." Vi dared to speak.

"Silence, you," Arwin growled.

"I want nothing more than to see Ulvarth dead and the Faithful returned to a quiet order built around Yargen—not blood-lust or power." Taavin stole Arwin's attention again with the declaration.

She laughed, bitter and icy. "You're a dog that would bite your master?"

"Let's say my master didn't spare me the rod," Taavin countered with a dangerous edge to his voice. "You don't get to beat this dog and expect loyalty."

"Betrayers, the whole lot of you," Arwin whispered. But she was also clearly weighing her options. Vi did the same, hoping they came to an identical conclusion.

Arwin could try to kill her and Taavin here and now—maybe she'd be successful, but she'd likely die in the process.

Or she could help them settle not only the score with Adela for the sake of her family, but slay Ulvarth as well, for the sake of her people. If she could muster enough faith in Taavin's deal, she had far more to gain. In fact, Arwin would get everything she'd ever wanted. Except there was a loose end in Taavin's proposal—

"And what about you?" Arwin asked, gaze intent on Taavin. "I could slay Ulvarth and you could find another just as ruthless to carry out your decrees."

"They are not my decrees."

"You are lying to save your skin!"

"He's not!" Vi interjected.

"I said silence!" Arwin pressed the spear farther forward. Its razor-sharp edge biting into Vi's throat was far more persuasive than words.

"Hurt her and die."

Arwin's eyes swung back to Taavin and the expression on her face almost had Vi wondering if she'd heard something Vi had not. A devious, deadly smile crept across her lips. "What does she matter to you?"

"Everything." There was no hesitation. No holding back. "She is everything." Arwin's grip faltered slightly; the spear sagged as surprise settled in on her.

What are we?

Vi finally had her answer. She was suddenly too hot and too cold at the same time, keenly aware of the pain at her throat yet numb and tingling all over.

Everything.

She loved him. And he loved her… despite both of them knowing better. Despite neither being brave enough to say it in such plain terms. Those facts made no difference in the end. They had fallen in love despite themselves. They just had yet to be brave enough to say it aloud.

Taavin continued on as if the very world wasn't shifting beneath Vi's feet. Perhaps he was oblivious to it. More likely, his ground had shifted long ago. So had hers. She was only fully realizing it.

"Help us, help *her* get her father, do whatever you need to do to Adela, and then I will deliver you Ulvarth. And should his head not satisfy your need for justice—if I do not keep my word and do right by you and your people—then at that time, you may have me."

No! Everything in Vi screamed at once. She didn't care if it was justified, or righteous, for Arwin to seek Taavin's life. She didn't care if it was Taavin's right to make this deal. She didn't want to see him harmed. That was the sole thought in her mind.

Yet thanks to the blade at her throat keeping every breath shallow, nothing escaped her lips.

"How do I know you'll keep your word?"

"You'll have to trust me."

Arwin snorted. "Trusting a Faithful? That never worked out well for anyone. Just look at the spot I'm in now." Her eyes swung back to Vi. "*Her.*"

"*What?*" Taavin asked and Vi let out something of a whisper to the same effect.

"If I so much as think for a moment that you will go back on your word—if I even *suspect* it—I'll kill her on the spot."

"That's too high a bar. You will be suspicious of my breathing."

"Then you should make an effort to breathe less," Arwin snapped at him. "It'd do wonders for my mood, at least."

Vi searched the woman's face for any sign of warmth or familiarity, but there was none. This was the same woman who had accused her of being Faithful in the throne room. No, this was worse. This was a woman who had proof of the careful tapestry Vi had been weaving around her.

Vi didn't have the right to hope for anything from Arwin. *This was business*, her mind insisted. It always had been. Friendship was a luxury she could no longer afford.

"Do we have a deal?" Arwin asked neither of them in particular.

"I said—"

"You have a deal," Vi interrupted before Taavin could say something well-intended but foolish. "Help me get my father. Taavin will give you Ulvarth. And if at any point, you think we mean to harm you or the morphi, or that we will go back on our words… You have my life."

17

THE NEXT HOUR WAS uncomfortable, to say the least.

Vi looked to Taavin. Taavin glared at Arwin. Arwin watched her. None of them said anything. It was silence the entire walk through the forest. An uncomfortable, deafening silence of Vi's own making.

By the end of the day, Vi nearly wanted to scream just so she'd hear something in the too-still woods.

"We should make camp here." Arwin came to a stop just when the forest's edge was in sight. Through the trees, Vi could see a clear dividing line—not unlike where the jungles of Shaldan ended at the Waste. She wondered if this, too, was a scar left on the earth by the ravages of man's squabbles. "Get one more night of sleep somewhere that the only enemies we have to worry about are each other."

"We're not your enemy," Vi said tiredly.

"I'll be the judge of that."

"Suit yourself." Vi held up her hands as Arwin took a few steps backward.

"Where are you going?" Taavin asked cautiously.

"I'm going to find dinner for myself, and perch somewhere you two don't know of so you can't slit my throat while I sleep." Arwin pulled her mass of golden hair back with a line of cord. "But don't think I won't be watching you."

"How do we know you won't go back to the Twilight Kingdom and return with an army?"

"I guess you'll just have to… how did you put it? *Trust me*," she said with a mocking smile.

The air around Arwin pulsed. Magic rippled in several equidistant rings, distorting the forest around her as though it were the surface of water. Arwin took a small step, then jumped into the air, slipping between the rings. Vi saw the outline of a bird taking her shape, identical to the dark fowl she'd seen when she'd first emerged from the cave nearly two weeks ago.

Before Arwin's feet could touch the ground again, she was gone, and there was just the flap of dark wings as the animal soared away. Vi and Taavin watched her leave, until it was impossible to see her outline from the deepening darkness between the trees.

"We should consider leaving," he murmured. "She could go back and—"

"She won't go back." Vi sighed softly, removing her scythe and leaning it against a tree. "She's exiled if she doesn't finish her mission."

"If the king can make those rules, he can break them," Taavin cautioned.

"I know. But the king who breaks his own rules is a ruler soon to lose his crown."

"Spoken like a true princess."

"Perhaps because I am one." Vi removed her satchel next, setting it down heavily. "Besides, we've made her a good offer. She stands to gain a lot more than lose."

"What's been happening this past week?" Taavin asked cautiously, looking from the weapon she'd been carrying to the satchel Vi was rummaging through. "I've had precious little by way of information."

"I know, and I'm sorry." Vi sat, beginning to sort through the items in her satchel and looking for the blanket Sarphos mentioned. Of course, it was at the very bottom.

Vi took a deep breath and tried to fill in the gaps in Taavin's information with broad strokes. He remained silent as he positioned himself at her side to listen. The sun was low in the sky when she finally finished.

"So that's it, then?" Taavin nodded at the scythe. "This weapon the king claimed was from the Dark Isle and bestowed on you?"

"I believe him." Vi rested on her elbow and reached for the weapon, surprised once more at how light it was. Laying it across her lap, she slowly undid the upper strap and then unwrapped the cloth tucked around the blade.

Taavin let out a soft gasp. He slowly reached out a hand, then withdrew before he could touch it. There was a reverent expression on his face, as though he gazed on a holy object.

"I take it you believe his claims now, too?"

"Vi… This… It shouldn't exist," he breathed, eyes drifting up to her. "What do you know of its history?"

Vi ran her fingers over the shining crystal of the weapon. It was as if the whole thing—blade and shaft—had been crafted from a single, flawless stone. But there were no marks of the crafter, no sign of any tool on its surface. It was flawless in every way. She closed her eyes, feeling the magic pulsing from it, familiar and yet slightly unnerving at the same time.

The longer she was in contact with it, the more dangerous it felt.

"I've been thinking about that," Vi started thoughtfully. "Trying to piece it all together… I know Raspian's return aligns with the destruction of the Crystal Caverns—so I know the caverns were where he was sealed away. One of my final lessons from my tutors was how my mother had a role in starting the war that led to that destruction, beginning with a crystal axe she found in Soricium. And I know that, in the lore on the Dark Isle, there were four of these weapons—an axe, a scythe, a crown, and a sword."

"Yes, you have the main points…" His hand finally rested on the scythe. Magic swirled up from the crystals, wrapping around his forearm in hazy blue light—as if reaching out to him, before it sank into his skin. His eyes seemed to shine an even brighter green in the fading light.

"What am I missing?"

"Yargen's sacrifice." Taavin looked to her. "When Yargen defeated Raspian in the last great war, she broke off a piece of Meru, sending it into the sea and sealing away Raspian there for what was to be eternity. She then split herself—her power—to ensure he remained in place. A third was bestowed on the Champion as a staff of frozen fire. Another third encapsulated Raspian in the same frozen fire to prevent his return. And the final third remained here on Meru as living flame, to guide her world."

"Frozen fire..." Vi repeated. Before her lips could close, her jaw went slack. *Frozen fire.* "No, not fire," she uttered. What would frozen fire look like, if not magic captured in shining stone, faintly glowing with a power greater than any man had ever known? Stone that would turn to coal—obsidian—when the power diminished. "Crystal."

"Just so," Taavin said solemnly.

"But all the crystals are dark and dormant since the caverns were destroyed... why does this persist?" Vi stared at the weapon in her hands that still glowed with a life of its own over a thousand years since it was first created.

"As I said, the Crystal Caverns sealing away Raspian were one part of her power. The other part was given to the Champion in the form of a staff to guard the tomb and ensure none sought it."

"Then, this is not from the tomb... but from the staff?"

Taavin gave a noise of affirmation. "That's my belief. The Champion was to use the power of Yargen bestowed on him to guard the tomb and ensure none came to seek it out. For over two hundred years, the Champion kept his lonely watch. But as with most things in time, details become hazy... the severity of a threat is forgotten.

"Eventually, people came to the Dark Isle, and the Champion did not send them away."

"Why?" Vi couldn't imagine why the Champion would turn back on his duty. But she also couldn't imagine spending centuries alone. The notion that such could be her own fate, that it wasn't beyond the realm of possibility, crawled under her skin like invisible bugs.

"Why does any man turn from duty? Love, loneliness, family... I can only speculate," Taavin murmured softly. Vi wondered if he was speaking about himself and the duty he'd left by fleeing Risen for her. "But he wasn't foolish. The people he let on the Dark Isle were mostly human—all born without magic."

"Without magic? I thought everyone has magic outside of the Dark Isle?"

"The vast majority do... but once in a hundred, a child is born without. And this world is not kind to those without magic."

"So they left to seek out a new world, kinder to them," Vi finished, imagining ships of dozens setting out for a barren land—an empty continent without anyone to judge them.

She'd always been told that people in the Solaris Empire feared sorcerers for their magic because it was rare, strange, and dangerous. Perhaps the real reason they hated sorcerers so fiercely extended back past anyone's memory. Extended toward the first peoples of the early kingdoms. People who held a deep resentment for magic—any magic—because it forced them from their homelands.

"And the Champion let them settle, either out of loneliness, or because he believed that these peoples without our magicks could be of no threat to the tomb."

"But... Solaris did eventually develop magic." Vi thought of the elemental powers of her home. "You called the magic of my land fractured..." Then, it dawned on her. "The Champion used the power of Yargen within him to split the staff into an axe, a scythe, a crown, and a sword—the Crystal Weapons of lore."

"From the fractured magic of Yargen, new magic seeped into your world."

Taavin gave a solemn nod. "And that new magic, the lure of power, drew them to Raspian's tomb long after the Champion had relinquished his mortal form by giving up Yargen's power. It was her magic that was extending his life beyond the hold of time, and when he no longer possessed it, he left our world."

"We turned Yargen's magic against itself. We were the ones to destroy it," Vi said in horror.

Everything made sense. Such loathsome, horrible, wretched sense. The fear of magic ingrained in people from the start, bolstered by the Champion's warnings, and cemented by time. Conventional wisdom maintained that the crystals in the Caverns tainted people, perhaps as a result of a power mortal hands weren't intended to hold. Or perhaps Raspian's power was slowly escaping through them, and that was the source of the deadly crystal taint.

"But this means there's hope." Vi clutched the scythe tightly. "This is hope. In the ruins of old Shaldan, I saw a figure of a man and a woman fighting etched on the wall. I didn't understand it then… but it was Raspian and Yargen. The likeness must have been made by those who remembered their story. Yargen wielded a *staff* against him. If this comes from that staff, then maybe we can fight him with it. Maybe we have a chance."

"I can only hope." Taavin looked from the scythe to the watch around her neck, then to her face. "I know that Yargen's power seems to seek you out. And that the other living piece of Yargen is in Risen, with the archives. If there's any information that will help us crack this—" his fingers landed on the watch "—and figure out a way to fight Raspian… it's in Risen."

"We'll go there." Vi closed her hand around his. The man's skin was warm under her fingertips.

"As soon as we rescue your father." Taavin's fingers worked their way around hers, winding tightly together. A dull, sweet ache filled her chest. Even with the world on the line, he knew she would go to her family first. He knew her focus would be her father until Vi knew he was safe. And he was not doing anything to pry her from that task when he so rightfully could.

"Thank you," she whispered.

"For what?"

"Beginning to tell me everything."

"There's so much I've yet to say," he murmured, his other hand reaching up to lightly tuck a strand of hair behind her ear. "I'm just afraid to say it."

"Me too." Yet, in saying that much, she knew what was unspoken for both of them. She didn't need anything more for now.

"Just as I'm afraid I have already cursed you by it." Taavin brought her hand to his lips, kissing her knuckles. "I never wanted any of this to happen to you." Remorse flooded his words. Vi gave a small, bitter laugh.

"*Never?* Not even when I was just the woman who supposedly tortured you in your dreams?"

Taavin began to protest, but stopped when he saw the makings of a grin on her lips. "Hush, that didn't count."

His thumb brushed over her lower lip, his eyes dipping half-closed as he watched the motion with delicious intent. Vi's focus was shifting as well. The tiniest of touches flooded her with such bittersweet delight.

"If that doesn't count, then you couldn't have cursed me," Vi said gently. "Because the red lines of my fate were drawn by the goddess long before you met me."

He looked at her as if seeking permission. She tried to convey it to him as she held his hand tighter, as she leaned forward—awkwardly across the scythe still in her lap.

"Perhaps, we're both equally cursed," he murmured darkly, close enough to her face now that she could feel his breath on her mouth.

"Perhaps."

They were from two different worlds. When it all was over—assuming the world didn't end—she would still be the crown princess. He was still the Voice. They couldn't be anything else to one another.

What does she matter to you?

Everything.

Their lips brushed, feather-light. His mouth quivered slightly, and a groan escaped him. Taavin's fingers curled around her jaw and he pulled her closer.

The scythe was forgotten, sliding off her knees as Vi shifted her weight forward. He leaned back and she followed him. She couldn't breathe if she didn't know her lungs were in time with his. She couldn't move if his hands weren't on her. Taavin laid back on the leafy ground, Vi atop him. He was light and life and everything she'd ever wanted without knowing it.

She was clumsy and inexperienced. But what she lacked in confidence she made up for in enthusiasm. She allowed every shift, kiss, and caress to fill her, fuel her.

If they were destined for heartbreak, she would steal as many nights as she could along the way.

It took two days, but on the afternoon of the second, Toris at last came into view.

The town was set aside a small inlet. Cliffs stood tall toward the sea, but they gradually sloped down as they wrapped around the sloping hills to the valley where Toris proper sat. A winding dirt path connected the town with a larger stoned road that ran from the Twilight Forest out into the great plains beyond—plains mottled with dark brown patches that looked alarmingly like decay.

"Grim little place, isn't it?" Arwin muttered. She was still barely on speaking terms with them.

"I suppose," Vi agreed purely for the sake of not starting an argument. She didn't see anything that grim. It looked like any other town.

"It's been a sheer delight to patrol these past few days," Arwin continued. She'd spent most of her time ahead, rather than with them. The scouting served a purpose they hoped to capitalize on, but Vi also suspected it had given Arwin an excuse to get away from them. "But the pirates haven't moved since I first flew in; they're on the ship in the morning, wreak havoc in town, drinks at the brewery, back at night."

"You're sure they haven't seen or sensed you?" Taavin asked.

"I'm certain I would know if they had. One of them would've been after me in an instant if he'd known."

"Who?" Vi asked.

"Another morphi. He's been flying the edges of the Twilight Forest relentlessly."

"Fallor?"

Arwin rounded on Vi the moment she said his name. "You know him?"

"He's been after me." Vi watched Arwin closely. There were emotions Vi couldn't quite put her finger on in Arwin's reaction. Fallor was obviously an exiled morphi who had betrayed his people, but there was more than that in Arwin's expression. This felt personal. "Do you know him?"

"He's an exile of the Twilight Kingdom." Arwin backed away from Vi, looking to the cliffs.

"I know that. But what I mean is, was he anyone... significant in the Twilight Kingdom before he was exiled?" Vi clarified. "Anyone important?"

"Not to the masses."

"But to you." Taavin keyed into the unspoken implication.

"Back off, Voice," Arwin snarled. "Whoever he was to me is none of your business."

Vi's lips parted as her jaw relaxed. She put all of Arwin's past actions, statements, reactions together in a second.

"He's Sarphos's brother." The family likeness was undeniable, now that she saw it. "He's the one you were engaged to."

Who else would make a woman like Arwin leave her home and her post as guard to her father? Who else would have committed such a deep betrayal? Vi knew firsthand how hard it was to crack through Arwin's callous exterior. If she let someone in, and that person betrayed her, they would be forever dead to her.

Vi could relate.

Arwin's grip on her staff tightened. Her eyes were glued on Toris.

"What of it?" she muttered.

"We don't need personal feelings getting in the—"

"I will not have *you* lecture me, Voice." Arwin glared between him and Vi, a look that said she had seen them waking side by side more than once. "This is personal. All of it is."

So much for being just business, Vi thought grimly.

"Yes, Fallor was my betrothed. Yes, I was young and didn't see him for what he was. I made the mistake of trusting him. Those are the faults I've had to live with for years since."

"He was the one to set up the shift around the Isle of Frost, wasn't he?" Vi asked.

"Yes. He wanted to learn the royal shift—the way we pulled the Twilight Kingdom out of reality. He'd always been fascinated by the notion... but something changed. Mere curiosity became a relentless pursuit. I didn't know then, that Adela had already got to him. And fool that I was, I didn't want to lose him, so I gave in."

Vi stared at Arwin's detached and determined eyes. The woman had her jaw clamped so tightly, the muscles in her cheek twitched.

"When the time comes, I have to be the one to do it." She was talking about murdering a man she'd loved enough to marry at one point. "Neither of you will take this from me. I have to be the one to kill him."

"Are you sure?" Taavin asked, far too gently for a heart as ragged as Arwin's. "You and he were—"

"He's yours," Vi interrupted. Arwin looked directly at her now with all the same murderous intensity. "Adela took something—someone—from me, too. A woman who was a sister to me until I learned of her true nature. She was taken in by Adela, just as Fallor was. I had the satisfaction of revenge in her death. You will have your satisfaction today."

Arwin gave a small nod, the beginnings of what looked like a new foundation of shared understanding in her eyes. If Vi had read it correctly, it was coming from the last place she would expect. Without a word more, Arwin leapt from the crest of the hill on which they were standing. The shift rippled around her, and she was gone in a blink, a bird soaring off down to the town, ready to implement their plans.

"JAYME?" TAAVIN ASKED AS they started down the sloping field toward the main road into Toris.

"I don't want to talk about it." Vi looked over the crops and land as they passed between fenced pasture and open field alike. An uncomfortable quiet had overtaken the hill. The houses were still; not a single farmhand was out tilling soil.

"I haven't asked about her because I assumed she'd decided to stay behind, but you said—"

Vi spun, rounding on him. "I said I don't want to talk about it. She was a traitor, nothing more." Her voice dropped softer as she tried to quell the rage. Vi wrapped her hand around his. "I don't want her name coming from your mouth. I don't want to associate anything of you with betrayal." She'd already toed that dangerous line once on finding out the true nature of the Faithful.

"Are you all right though?" Taavin held her fast as Vi tried to pull away. "Jayme was—"

"Jayme was no one. She was a traitor. She betrayed my family. It's because of her Adela has my father. It's because of her Adela had me. I gave her a traitor's death and I don't want to speak about her ever again."

"Very well." Taavin released her and Vi quickly started on again.

It felt like she was running. But she didn't quite know from what. Just the mere thought of Jayme filled her with brutal darkness—not unlike the darkness that seemed to be settling on the land.

They quickly discovered the reason why no one was working the fields—the houses were abandoned. What crops there were had rotted where they stood. Tilled soil had turned to hard, cracked mud, small deserts breaking up what Vi assumed was once fertile farmland. An ox rotted where it fell, eye-sockets oozing white.

"Raspian's power grows," Taavin said, giving voice to their shared thought.

"How much longer do you think the world has?" Vi wondered aloud, gripping the strap attached to the scythe.

"Not long enough."

When they arrived in the town, there was no main gate to enter Toris. The buildings crept up from the earth. Most of the construction was waddle and daub, an ashy clay the same color as the raw earth of the central town square. By all appearances, it was not a wealthy place—but a few buildings boasted shingled roofs or intricately decorated glass in their windows. Where would money like that come from in a place like this? *Nowhere good*, Vi thought wryly.

"Good luck," Taavin whispered. "I'll keep you in sight. Stick to the plan."

"I will, and good luck to you too," she breathed back, before they promptly headed in opposite directions. Taavin wandered off to the side and Vi continued along the town square until it evolved into a market that extended right down to the docks.

Here, Vi could appreciate the majesty of Norin.

There were only two main docks and neither could tie up anything larger than a medium-sized vessel. The larger ones were anchored in the sheltered bay formed by the cliff sides, or further still, out at sea. Only dinghies were tied up at the docks.

It seemed incredibly... small. She didn't know what she'd been expecting, but after the greatest port in the world, followed by a magical city of twilight, Toris seemed lackluster. Though Vi supposed there were average or below-average towns everywhere, no matter how fantastical certain elements of the world were.

"Don't just stop in the road, girl." A man pushing a wheelbarrow laden with feed veered around her. "Daydreamin' kids."

Vi quickly stepped to the side and mumbled an apology. She positioned herself by the side of a building where she could see the whole market. She scanned the seabirds on the docks and the silhouettes against the late afternoon sky, looking for Arwin or Fallor, but Vi saw neither. Not that Vi could tell Arwin apart from a normal bird. The oil-slick plumage of the nightwisp was common in this region of Meru.

She settled into Step One of the plan: observe and be noticed.

After an hour of normalcy, Vi debated if she should move elsewhere in the town. She'd taken two laps around the market trying to make herself visible, and was just about to wander the docks when the sound of shouting filled the air.

Vi glanced over her shoulder and into the small store she'd been passing. Two men argued within, nearly coming to blows. The larger of the two scooped the smaller by the collar, pushing him out.

"Get out and stay out, you bloody cheat." The store clerk? Building owner? Gambling pit master?

"Just because you lose doesn't make someone a cheat." The man stumbled, but recovered before he ended up face-first in the mud. The larger man was already heading back inside with a shake of his head. "The nerve of some people," the shorter man muttered. His eyes drifted to Vi. A smile slowly spread across his lips. "All you want to do is play a game of cards and they cast you out, am I right?"

She hummed noncommittally, looking back to the market.

"Say, you wouldn't be interested in a game of cards, would you?" The man walked over, despite her showing no interest in him. That was a positive sign.

"I'm not really one for cards." She looked him up and down, trying to remember every detail Arwin had recited after her scouting. Could she be confident this was one of Fallor's men?

"Come now, that can't be true. I'll buy you a drink and we can play a game of cards—low stakes, I promise. We all enjoy a good game of cards now and then."

"Buy me a drink from there?" Vi pointed to the brewery.

"Only place in town." He gave a hearty laugh. As he tilted his head back, the collar of his shirt shifted, revealing the edge of a tattoo—three lines disappearing under fabric. A trident, she was sure.

Vi made a show of debating the proposition. But her mind was already made up. She had accomplished Step Two of the plan: find one of Adela's men.

"Perhaps you're right." She tried to make her agreement sound reluctant. "It's been a while since I let loose."

"Excellent, this way!" He linked his elbow with hers and pulled her off across the market.

Vi skipped a step to get in pace with him. She tried to take a quick glance around the market. There were shopkeepers talking with farmers about the harvest, rumors being swapped by two old men sitting at the docks... but no indication of Taavin or Arwin.

They'd better be playing their parts and in their positions.

Because Vi was about to initiate Step Three: offering herself up on a platter to Adela.

Vi would make herself an easy target and lure the pirates into a false sense of security. Then, when they were busy apprehending her, Taavin and Arwin would strike. With the pirates taken care of, they would steal their vessel.

Simple enough, and it was going off without a hitch so far.

Vi followed her escort into a dimly lit tavern. There were a few patrons scattered throughout, each scarier-looking than the last. Two burly men were seated at the far end of the bar. Another table was filled with a loud group well into their cups. Two others played darts at the back wall.

If Arwin and Taavin were to be believed about this town, most if not all were pirates—though not all Adela's men. Toris was a quaint fishing town on the surface, hub for the trade and sale of pirated goods underneath.

"What'll you have?" The man sat at one of the bar stools.

Vi did the same, feeling her legs slide into the divots made by countless patrons' thighs. "Whatever you're having is fine."

She needed to keep her wits about her and didn't plan on drinking much. Vi took one more scan of the bar while he ordered—Taavin and Arwin were nowhere to be seen.

"Two ciders, then." He motioned to the bartender. "The name's Charlie, by the way." Charlie raised his hand to his forehead, right between his brow, and lowered it. "And you are?"

"Marnie," Vi lied deftly, not knowing where the name had come from so easily.

"And where do you hail from, Marnie? You certainly have a strange accent."

"Monlan." Her days studying maps in the Twilight Kingdom had paid off. Monlan was a land-locked city, one she doubted pirates got to often. But for good measure, Vi added, "But my father was from Hokoh, so I grew up with a weird mix of accents." She knew very little about these cities other than the fact they were on opposite ends of the continent and surely produced different accents.

Vi was saved from having to elaborate further by the bartender placing down two heavy clay flagons.

"Two silver."

Charlie produced two silver coins from his pocket, laying them on the bar. On the front of the coin was a simple carving of three circles, a line intersecting them—a symbol Vi actually recognized. Her eyes widened slightly, trying to take it all in before the bartender collected it. She'd seen that symbol carved into the old trees of Soricium.

At least, she thought she had... Because the coin was gone with the bartender in a blink.

"To new friends." Charlie lifted his mug, holding it between them.

"To new friends." Vi lifted her mug as well, tapping it lightly against his. She brought it to her lips, taking a long sip. It drank somewhat like an ale, small bubbles tickling her tongue. But this was sweeter and had a bright, fruity quality—almost like an apple juice. Placing it back on the bar, Vi stared in wonder and said, with no acting required, "It's… really good."

Charlie gave a hearty chuckle. "Toris has a good brewmaster. He does creative things with palm fruits. Horse and Cask is one of my favorite bars to stop in when I'm sailing my route."

"What's your route?" Vi asked, hoping the query sounded casual.

"Oh, I go all over," he answered coyly. "I've been from Risen to Toris and beyond."

"So you're a trader, then?"

"Of a sort." *Pirate*. Definitely a pirate. "Do you have an interest in sailing?"

"I do, actually." Vi smiled sweetly.

"You must… Growing up in a land-locked city, I imagine a girl like you would find the high seas thrilling." He gave a nod to the scythe Vi had strapped to her back. "Though it looks like you may have been coming here to find work in a field. Too bad they're all going barren."

"I only told my father I was going to find work on a farm," Vi said lightly and took a long sip of her drink. "I wouldn't have traveled all the way from Monlan if I just wanted to farm."

"Then what do you want?" He leaned in slightly.

"Adventure," Vi said conspiratorially, leaning in as well. "You're right, I do find the idea of traversing the ocean thrilling. But not half as thrilling as the men on those vessels." She said it so effortlessly, so smoothly, that Vi even shocked herself. She was a far cry from the girl stumbling over her words at the Noru races.

His pupils dilated slightly—just as she'd seen Taavin's do right before she was about to kiss him. Vi glanced down at his mouth, licking her lips for good measure. And then leaned away with a playful grin.

"I like the sound of that." He gave her a smirk and was back to shuffling his deck. "So I know we discussed a game of cards, but let's make it interesting, shall we?"

"What do you have in mind?"

"We could gamble for coin?" The way he said it told Vi he had no expectations of that actually happening. So she played right into those expectations.

"I'm afraid I don't have much. It'd make for a boring game." Vi made a show of thinking hard. "Say, if you're a trader… your vessel must be nearby."

"Anchored off the other side of the cliffs," the fool announced proudly, further confirming all of Vi's suspicions.

"Then how about this: if I win, you take me with you to wherever it is you're going next?"

"And if I win?" The man asked with such obvious expectation. Vi hadn't thought of that and she quickly rummaged her mind—but came up with nothing. Luckily, he had an idea for her. "How about you still come with me… but you're not my guest. You're my deck wench."

"All right," Vi agreed quickly. It didn't matter what she bet. This was all going to end with him having a sword in his gut. "I'm feeling lucky."

"Let's hope you are, Marnie."

Charlie shuffled and dealt. Vi's eyes were focused on his motions, trying to catch the sleight-of-hand she knew was there. She was so intent on him that she didn't even notice the man who had entered from around the back door behind the bar.

A hand covered the cards and Vi followed the forearm up to a shoulder, to the man who had a smirk smeared across his ruddy beard. Fallor leaned against the bar as though he owned the place; even the bartender gave him a wide berth.

"You don't need to flip those," he said. Vi narrowed her eyes slightly, not wanting to show for a moment that her hands were trembling. "I can already tell you, your luck has run out." Then louder, to the other patrons, "The rest of you—out."

As though issued a command from a lord, the rest of the bar came to its feet. There was some grumbling from particularly red-faced patrons in the back corner, but no one objected. Even the bartender calmly set down the glass he'd been polishing and left through the back door Fallor had entered from.

Fallor wasn't supposed to be there. Vi's heart was racing. He had been in his bird form almost exclusively according to Arwin, patrolling the edges of the Twilight Forest. They were supposed to have a chance to take out his lackeys before he even knew they were there. Or, at worst, catch him mid-fight.

They'd planned, and Fallor had been one step ahead.

"Now, last I saw you, you were traveling with the Voice himself. Where is he hiding?" A pulse of magic rushed over her, disorienting and powerful. Vi vaguely recognized it from the field that night—it was the same magic that had disrupted Taavin's Lightspinning.

"I'll never tell you." If Taavin was still operating to plan, he was positioned somewhere in the square, hood up, as inconspicuous as possible, watching the entrance of the bar.

"No matter." Fallor turned his eyes to her. "He's not here now. Good. I wanted to speak with you alone."

"And what makes you think I want to listen to you?" Fire crackled around her balled fists, singeing the bar. "I'm much stronger than when you last met me. I could—"

"Spare me." Fallor waved a hand through the air, as though he could wave away her words like a bad smell. "If you so much as make one move against me, your father dies."

"What?" Vi whispered. The spark stilled, iced over with horror.

"Adela is the *pirate queen*—do you think she rules by being everywhere at once?" Vi stayed silent, allowing him to continue in whatever way he wanted. "No, she delegates, as any good ruler would. As I'm sure you would understand."

"Get to your point," Vi ground out through clenched teeth.

"I know you're not threatening me, are you?" Fallor looked to Charlie. Charlie leaned against the bar, fumbling with a large hoop earring in his ear. "Because, you see, Charlie here has an imprinted token of Adela's."

Vi's hand went to her watch at the mention of an imprinted token. She knew what that was. It was what had started it all—it was the same as her watch. Though Vi had never seen one made, she knew they could be used to communicate over any distance.

"He's not the only one." Fallor's grin grew wider, verging on the point of mad arrogance. "Each one of my crew has a token. If Charlie so much as thinks you'll use one bit of magic, he'll activate it. If he, or I, don't return in due time, the rest of my crew will activate theirs."

Each one of his words was like a hook to her flesh—digging in, pulling, peeling, exposing her. They had so quickly put together a plan... none of them had thought for one moment Fallor would have a better one to counter with.

"So, not one more word. Not one bit of fuss for my colleague here," Fallor commanded as Charlie slowly collected his cards. "You're going to come calmly onto my vessel, or your father dies. Do you understand?"

Vi bit the insides of her cheeks. She wanted to scream *juth* at him until her voice was hoarse. She wanted to burn the whole brewery down to ash, them inside. She wanted to sever head from spine with the blade of her scythe.

Maybe Fallor was lying. Maybe she could kill Charlie fast enough that he couldn't get to Adela. But could she kill Fallor before he flew away? Could she, Taavin and Arwin take him down in the middle of Toris—a town where the majority of the population would stand for Fallor? And even if they could, how long until the pirates aboard Fallor's ship would raise an alarm?

These were risks Vi couldn't take—not with her father's life on the line.

All she could do was nod.

"Good." Fallor pushed away from the bar, starting for the back door. "Now, remember Vi, your father's life depends on what you do next."

More than you know. Because while Fallor had out-planned them, he had also overplayed his hand. Vi knew what she was dealing with. And most importantly, Fallor had just confirmed *her father was alive*. He was too valuable a bargaining chip for Adela to let him die without gaining something for it.

All Vi had to do now was get out of this.

"COME ON, PET." CHARLIE grabbed her wrist and tugged. He was stronger than he looked, *much* stronger, and if Vi didn't go along she risked having her shoulder popped from its socket.

The moment they were out of the bar he turned, starting for the port. Vi's eyes scanned the crowd, searching for Taavin or Arwin, but she found neither. The sun was already setting, casting the world in a bloody glow.

"Let's get to the boat before dark. They say pirates are in this town… we wouldn't want anything happening to you, now would we?" Charlie gave a laugh at his own joke, carrying on for everyone to hear, knowing full well that even if someone knew what was happening, no one would dare stop one of Adela's men. "The path is narrow. Don't try anything funny or you may fall off."

Charlie pushed her ahead along the narrow way that wound along the cliff-side just above the docks. Vi glanced back over her shoulder. Where were Taavin and Arwin? By now, they were supposed to be following her in some form or fashion, ready to strike against Fallor when the moment presented itself. But if they did so in a way his crew on the ship could see… her father would be dead. Unless Adela was playing games about that, too.

Vi's hands balled into fists, her nails leaving crescent moons in her palms. She hated this game of cat and mouse. She scanned the skies until she found a large bird soaring on the updrafts off the cliffs. She couldn't make out its color, but Vi would bet it was ruddy. Fallor was flying high enough to stay in sight of the boat on the other side of the cliffs.

They had barely crested the top of the cliffs. Vi knew from Arwin's reports that there was a switchback on the other side of the ridge, leading down to a narrow beach. There, a boat was anchored not too far off—a rowboat used to transport men to and from the beach. Vi scanned the plateau; she couldn't see the vessel, which meant they couldn't see her—she hoped.

Vi intentionally tripped herself.

She caught the toe of one boot on the heel of the other. Her hand raked against the rough wall for support, but she prevented her fingers from catching. Vi allowed herself to fall hard, knee splitting underneath her clothes.

"Get up." The man took a wide step around her, hand on his earring. "Get up or—"

"I tripped." Vi looked up at him, pushing herself onto her elbows. "I tripped, that's all. I'm coming, I promise." She leaned back onto her heels, rubbing her palms on her pants, trying to stall for every second she could. "Shite... I scraped my knee." Vi made a show of inspecting the bloody spot on her clothes.

"I don't give a rat's arse about your knee. Get up or it's your dear old father who's getting his blood spilled."

Vi put her palms on the ground, tucking her head and trying to sneak a look over her shoulder. Fallor was flying lower—no doubt coming to inspect the disruption. Vi took a slow breath.

"I said—"

Magic crackled through the air. Vi could almost hear on the wind the blessedly beautiful words of *loft dorh* leaving Taavin's lips. There was a spark of light, and the eagle seized mid-air.

Vi turned back to Charlie. Fallor may have tried to throw a wrench in their plans, but those plans could still be salvaged. They just had to move very quickly and stay out of sight.

"Get up or—" The pirate never had a chance to finish his sentence.

"*Juth calt*," Vi snarled, going right for the heart.

Charlie seized, wide-eyed. He crumpled on the spot, just as Jayme had, blood dripping from his lips. She had vowed to Fallor that she would see Adela's brood suffer. But Vi found herself beyond caring. There wasn't time to exercise the dark art of vengeance.

The world was ending and all that truly mattered were results.

The screech of a bird drew her attention. A nightwisp—half the size of the eagle— shot through the sky like a black arrow. Vi watched as it twisted mid-air, wicked sharp talons leading the charge. Before the eagle could fall from the sky, the nightwisp had dug its claws into it, using momentum to pin the eagle against the cliff wall.

Vi turned away from Charlie's body, keeping herself crouched and praying the men on the boat hadn't seen their comrade fall. Down the path was Taavin, shifting his stance and readying more words.

"Taavin," Vi called as loud as she dared—hoping the wind and crash of waves masked whatever of her voice would carry. Taavin looked up to her. "They have imprinted tokens to talk to Adela. If the ship sees a struggle, they'll have my father murdered!"

His eyes widened, no doubt putting together all Vi had in an instant: they had to move fast and with certainty.

With a pulse of magic, Arwin replaced the bird, landing on the path and sliding back slightly. The dazed eagle shook its head, slowly regaining its footing. When its eyes focused, they were trained on the spear Arwin was pointing at its neck.

"*Loft dorh hoolo.*" Vi thrust her hand at Fallor right as he was about to take flight. Her glyph surrounded him, stalling him in place.

Even with *hoolo*, she could feel him wriggling and writhing against her magic. He struggled to break free of her tethers and Vi realized she didn't know how long she could hold him. Sweat beaded on her brow.

"You're not leaving." Arwin ruthlessly stabbed her spear through the bird's wing. "Free him of your magic."

Vi did as Arwin bid. This was her kill, her moment of revenge. They didn't have much time, but they had time enough for this.

Fallor rippled in and out of existence. When he reappeared, his clothes were torn, blood pouring from deep slashes in his chest that Arwin's talons had made. His arm was pinned to the path, blood pooling around Arwin's spear.

"Arwie, let's not—"

"Don't," she snarled. Vi would've snarled too if a man like Fallor had tried to give her a nickname like *Arwie*. "If you have any scrap of honor, any trace of the man I loved, you will stay in place and let me gut you from naval to nose."

"Because you love me, don't gut me," he pleaded hastily, holding up a hand. "I-I never wanted to hurt you."

Arwin slowly tilted her head to the side as Fallor spoke. Vi couldn't see her expression, but she could see Taavin's reaction to it. And that was enough for Vi to know it was every bit as venomous as her tone.

"You had a poor way of showing it."

"Let me fix it. I can fix this," Fallor continued hastily. "Who would you rather leave here with—me, or the Voice and a foreigner? Adela will pay anything for them. She'll be indebted to the Twilight Kingdom. She's a worthy ally to have on your side against the Faithful. With her ships, you could even stand up against the Swords' armada. Start with the seas, then attack Risen."

Arwin went very still.

"Arwin…" Taavin started cautiously. There must have been something on her face, if only for a moment, that made him uncertain. But his expression changed in the next instant, as the woman herself no doubt swung on a pendulum of emotions.

Vi watched as Arwin ripped the spear from Fallor's arm and, in one deft motion, gouged his throat with the blade. The man fell back, took one last gasping, gurgling breath, and died. Vi didn't feel one drop of pity or remorse. But right now, it didn't matter what she felt.

It mattered what Arwin did.

"Don't think this means I like either of you now," Arwin said softly. "It's not that I chose you."

"You had a job to do." Vi finished the thought.

Arwin slowly turned and gave a nod. That was enough for Vi to count on her for what needed to come next.

"The two left on the ship. If they suspect something is amiss, they'll contact Adela and she'll kill my father." Vi looked to Taavin. "You'll wear Charlie's clothes and we'll ride out on the rowboat. Arwin, you fly in from behind. We strike them both at once, but only when we're certain we can take them out cleanly. If one survives for even a second, it could be enough time to relay a message."

A jump off the cliff, followed by a pulse of magic, and a bird rising on the updraft was all the affirmation Vi was going to get from Arwin. But she didn't need more. Time was of the essence now.

Still, she found herself staring at Fallor for one last, long moment. He was dead. She imprinted his bloody corpse on her memory. He was dead, and he couldn't come for her again.

Vi turned away, crawled toward Charlie's body, and began to tug at his clothes. "Taavin, help me, he's heavy."

The man appeared across from her, wordlessly helping lift the dead weight to yank off Charlie's long tunic.

"How did you kill him?" Taavin asked warily.

"*Juth calt*—I shattered his heart."

"You what?" he whispered.

"I shattered his heart, maybe his lungs, too."

"I've never heard of *calt* used that way," Taavin said warily.

"Well, now you have." Vi held out the shirt. While she waited for Taavin to take it, she ripped off Charlie's earring with her other hand and pocketed it. "I've had a long road to get here, and I've had to improvise along the way. Now, wear this—the sun is getting low and I don't want to test their patience."

Taavin yanked off his shirt. It was the first time she'd seen him in such a state of undress. The scar on his face extended down past his collarbone. There were other scars, too. Smaller, fainter, curving and intersecting... almost as if someone had taken a knife and lazily drawn lines across his body time and again until their bloody art left a permanent mark.

No doubt from Ulvarth, she thought darkly

He finished tugging the tunic overhead, bringing her back to the present.

"Good thing pirates are embroiled in shady business." Vi lifted the hood of the tunic. "Of course they'd have sewn a hood to everything."

"Vi, you saw—"

"Later." Vi gave his hand a squeeze, knowing where his mind was. She didn't have to know the stories behind those markings to know that it was likely something very few had seen, and that he'd want to keep them hidden. "When we're on our new boat."

Taavin gave a small nod as he stood. Vi did as well, taking a step in front of him. She kept her head down, starting on the switchbacks with Taavin close behind.

"Remember, I'm your prisoner. Push on my back a little, make it a good show."

Taavin did, but the shove was so weak Vi had to intentionally put a stumble into her step. She fought the smallest of smiles. Even acting, he didn't want to harm or demean her.

Sure enough, there was a rowboat moored on the beach. Just off the shore was a single vessel—narrow and fast looking with one main sail and a secondary. Perfectly hidden from view of the town.

Two silhouettes were drawn against the setting sun, standing at the railing. Vi held up a hand, blinking into the sunlight as they trudged through the sand toward the small skiff. She didn't see Arwin anywhere.

"Do you see her?" Taavin asked, pushing on the rowboat. He strained against the sand—clearly not a trained deckhand. Vi hoped Fallor's other crew would assume Charlie drunk.

"No," Vi murmured. She wanted to help him, but she doubted Charlie would've asked for help, so she just stood there, waiting and watching the other two pirates aboard the boat.

"What if she left?"

"She wouldn't. She still has to disable the shift on the Isle of Frost." Vi hoped to the Mother above that remained true.

The skiff was in the water and Vi boarded first, Taavin behind her. He took up the oars, pulling them hard through the water and fighting against the waves crashing along the beach. Vi looked at the surf splashing up against the sides, remembering the last time she had been in a rowboat like this.

Then, she had been a prisoner. Now, she held the upper hand.

"When we get close enough that you can be sure to hit your mark... use *juth calt*,"

Vi said under her breath. Taavin looked up at her, panting. "I'll take the woman, you take the man."

"I don't think I can…" Taavin nearly stopped rowing, continuing in an instant. "I've never been trained to use it in that way. What if I explode their whole body?"

"Then there's less for someone to find when the corpse washes ashore." Vi stared at him. In that moment, it was painfully clear that he was sitting where she had been months ago. He had never killed—at least not with his own hands—and had never considered doing so. Vi swallowed hard, looking over her shoulder. "Just freeze one, I'll take care of the rest."

"Charlie," the woman cupped her hands to her lips and yelled. "Have you seen an ice moon?"

It was clearly some kind of code—a code neither of them knew the answer to. "Get a little closer," Vi whispered, glancing over her shoulder. Taavin kept rowing.

"Charlie," the man bellowed, "have you—" At that moment, he was cut short by a sudden jolt of magic. Vi heard him make a gurgling groan before he landed heavy on the deck with a dull thud.

"*Narro h*—" the woman began.

"*Loft dorh*," Taavin said, eyes focused on the woman.

Vi turned in the rowboat, careful not to knock it over or rock it so much that Taavin lost his focus. Arwin was on deck pulling her spear from the dying man. Before she could thrust it through the woman, Vi uttered, "*Juth calt.*"

With that, Taavin's magic was broken, and the woman fell limply to the deck. Arwin stood at the railing, looking down at them, regarding them both warily. Vi locked eyes with her, as if in warning.

As if to say, *Yes, beyond the Twilight Forest we are as deadly as you feared.*

"THROW DOWN THE LINES," Vi called up to Arwin as they positioned the rowboat under two arm-like pulleys at the stern. "I'll tie them off to the boat and you can hoist."

Arwin walked over to the low deck rail, looking down at them. She wore a stony expression that guarded her innermost thoughts. Instinct would have Vi just as guarded, but she kept her face calm, relaxed. She didn't want to risk escalating tensions in an already-tense situation.

Without a word, Arwin threw the ropes down and Vi caught them, quickly fastening them off to either end of the dinghy. "Stay here," she murmured to Taavin, pulling off her scythe and setting it in the boat.

Grabbing one of the ropes, Vi hoisted herself upward with a small jump that set the dinghy to rocking. Kicking out her feet, Vi landed them on the side of the larger vessel. One hand over the other, one foot then the next, Vi walked up the side of the ship with the help of the rope.

"What was that for?" Arwin asked.

"Now you don't have to pull alone." Vi rubbed her palms on her thighs, working out the aches in her fingers.

"That was unnecessary. I could've done it on my own."

"Or you could accept help and make it easier." Vi moved to one of the pulleys, making sure everything was looped through correctly. Unsurprisingly, the riggings seemed to be in top shape, ready to go at a moment's notice.

"All right, let's get our dead weight aboard."

They pulled together until the small boat was up at deck level, tied off the ropes to secure the dinghy in place, then Vi reached out a hand for Taavin. He wasn't too proud to take it, allowing her to help him over the railing and onto the deck. Vi reached in after him, retrieving her scythe and slinging it back over her shoulders. She was finding the longer she carried it, the less she liked being without it.

"You're fairly confident on a boat," he observed.

"This is the third I've been on." Vi shrugged. She had a strong suspicion that neither Arwin nor Taavin had been on a ship. Maybe Taavin. But if he had been, it wasn't in any kind of sailing capacity.

Vi knelt down, taking the earrings from both of the pirate's ears. They were identical to Charlie's, further confirming her suspicion that this was the token.

"Are those some kind of trophy?" Arwin asked.

"No, they're communication tokens to Adela," Vi pocketed them. "They could be useful... or perhaps not. Either way, I'd rather keep them than lose them to the sharks. Now, a little help please?"

Taavin and Arwin both helped Vi push the bodies to the railing, twisting them until they slipped through the wide gaps and off the sides of the boat. Vi fetched a bucket attached to a long rope, drawing up seawater and splashing it across the deck twice to remove some of the man's blood. There was still a long red streak on the main deck, but it was clean enough. Spending too long cleaning a pirate ship felt like an exercise in futility.

"All right." Vi wiped her hand across her brow, taking stock of the setting sun. It was little more than a sliver on the horizon now. Was it just her imagination, or was it setting earlier than normal? "We should set sail before anyone can find the bodies. I can imagine there's at least a few in Toris who will be sympathetic to Fallor and Adela's men."

"Or who will at least want Adela's gratitude and bounty for turning over the people who killed them." Taavin leaned against the railing, a few steps away from the red smears.

"Taavin and I will give the ship a quick once-over and see the status of things. Arwin, will you fly back and gather up our supplies?" When the woman didn't immediately respond, Vi turned to face her. She looked back at the coastline with a conflicted expression. "Ar—"

"I heard you." The woman leapt into the air, soaring upward and back toward the cliffs where she'd stashed their bags.

"What's her problem?" Taavin muttered.

"She got what she wanted, and doesn't know how to feel about it," Vi answered easily, beginning a quick inspection of their new vessel.

The ship was fairly simple, one mainmast and a foremast. The rigging she'd already used on the davits was some of the most complicated of all the ropes. There was a tiny cabin that was half in the hull and half beneath a shallow quarterdeck. A break in the smooth lines of the deck toward the bow betrayed a storage area Vi inspected immediately, confirming rations within.

"You think she regrets killing Fallor?" Taavin followed behind her.

"Regrets? No." Vi shook her head. Thinking of Arwin right now felt like looking into a mirror that reflected what was inside, rather than out. Vi could recognize emotions and feelings—all the ones she didn't want to see. "But I don't think it's so black and white. Fallor betrayed her, yes. But she also loved him, once. Those feelings were real to her before the discovery that they hadn't mattered to him."

"This isn't Jayme," Taavin whispered gently. Vi slowly lowered the storage hatch and turned, looking up at him from her crouched position. "Arwin has known who Fallor was for a long time."

"Some emotions are as sharp as knives that don't dull or rust with time." Vi stood, looking out over the water and seeing the dark bird gliding on the ocean breezes. "Even if you're right, after dreaming of his death for so long... how would it feel to actually get it? To have it be so easy?"

"I don't know."

"Me neither."

Jayme's death had been swift and sudden, and perhaps easier. Vi didn't have to live with the knowledge that the woman who had wronged her was still out there breathing. The chapter was closed, and while she still carried the wounds of it, she could try to move forward.

Arwin had been in stasis for years. Vi could only imagine how she must be feeling now.

The woman in question landed lightly on the deck, a pack over her back and Vi's bag strapped across her chest. She tossed them haphazardly into the cabin, reporting, "No problems with them."

"Arwin."

"What is it, princess?" Arwin sighed, leaning her staff against the entrance to the cabin. There was no door, merely a curtain stretched across the opening to keep out the night's chill and salt spray. She looked at Vi warily and, for a long moment, they merely held each other's gaze.

Vi didn't know what she'd intended to say. Had she wanted to tell Arwin that she understood in some way? Did she want to say it was okay to feel whatever it was she was feeling?

"Thank you for your help." In the end, Vi couldn't pry. Just as she didn't want anyone to pry about Jayme, she wouldn't inflict that on Arwin.

Rather than retorting back with something about having no other choice, or begrudging them both, Arwin gave a grunt in acknowledgement. That was the best Vi could hope for, and she let the matter drop.

"Taavin, how much do you know about rigging?" It was past time for them to be on their way.

"I grew up in the Archives of Yargen and spent most of my time making use of the fact. I may not have had a chance to apply knowledge very often, but I certainly collected it."

"Good, let's give you a chance to practice, then. You and Arwin will help get the sails ready while I plan a headway." Vi started for her satchel in the cabin, retrieving her journal and a compass. She didn't even make it back out before they were bickering.

"I wouldn't untie that."

"You said to untie this."

"No, untie *this* one." Taavin tapped on a rope knotted to a peg. "Not that one."

"Well you should be more clear."

"I'm being perfectly clear."

Vi ignored them, starting up to the quarterdeck. Consulting her maps and the compass, she quickly decided on the best headway. "Lower the sails. Taavin, as we sail out, please hide the ship."

"Why?" Arwin asked.

"I don't want anyone from Toris seeing us leave." She didn't want to give Adela any warning that they were coming. Though, despite her best efforts, Vi fully expected the woman to know. She was far too cunning not to. Vi was beginning to doubt that anything happened on the seas without Adela somehow knowing.

The wind hit the sails and Arwin finished tying them off as Taavin intoned, "*Durroe watt radia.*"

Light swirled out from him in glyphs that slowly wrapped up the whole vessel.

They spun slowly over the deck, cutting through the walls of the vessel harmlessly. Magic settled on every surface with a dull shine.

Vi adjusted the tiller, checking her compass as the ship began to turn.

Arwin made a noise of disgust. "Even your magic feels slimy."

"Slimy?" Taavin asked. Vi was genuinely curious as well. Could Arwin detect a tangible quality to Taavin's magic, or was this just another opportunity for her to make a jab at the Faithful?

"It slithers, feels like wet seaweed over bare skin."

"Your magic feels different for us, too," Vi spoke before Taavin could, stealing Arwin's attention.

"It does?"

"I wouldn't say slimy though... uneasy, perhaps."

"Yet another reason why the morphi are hated without cause."

"Doesn't that go both ways?" Vi looked down at the woman on the main deck. "I mean... if you describe Lightspinning as slimy... doesn't that also sow the seeds of dislike?"

"Don't talk like you know things, Dark Isle dweller," Arwin grumbled.

Vi chuckled softly and turned her eyes back to the horizon. There was the same empty feeling she'd known all too well lingering between the spaces of Arwin's words—the feeling of not belonging. She hadn't belonged anywhere in her Empire, now she didn't belong with those of Meru. Arwin was right: she didn't understand because she wasn't a part of this world.

But would she ever have the chance to be a part of anywhere?

"Ignore her," Taavin said, placing a hand on Vi's shoulder. She didn't realize he'd even walked over, a testament to how lost in thought she'd been. "Do you have a headway?"

Vi nodded.

"How long until we arrive?"

"Depending on the wind... Perhaps two days? Three at most?"

"I'll know when we near the shift that surrounds the isle," Arwin declared with a determined stare over the bow of the boat. "I'll feel it."

"That's helpful, then." Vi looked back to shore. The land had become a narrow strip of black in the darkening night. The vessel was, indeed, a fast one.

"If we have a couple days, let's sleep in turns and get decent rest so we're ready," Arwin suggested, starting up the quarterdeck. "I'll take the first." Coupled with her thoughtful expression, the offer sounded almost like an apology for her earlier remarks.

"All right." Vi released the wheel and passed the compass to Arwin. "Head due southeast. We won't start cutting south until we get to the Diamond Sands isles."

"Simple enough." Arwin said. "You two get some rest."

Taavin paused, his gaze lingering on Arwin. Vi couldn't tell if the woman was choosing to ignore his hesitation, or just hadn't noticed. Not wanting to risk either, she tugged lightly on Taavin's sleeve.

"Come on, she's right. We should catch some shut eye."

He followed her down into the cramped cabin, crouching through the curtained opening. Vi pushed aside the heavy tarp, hooking it on a peg.

"Leave it," Vi requested as Taavin went to swing the tarp back down into place.

"I'd rather it be open."

"Are you sure? The moon is full tonight—it may be quite bright."

"I'll sleep better if I don't feel like I'm trapped." Vi settled her scythe on the floor between the two hanging cots on either side of the narrow cabin.

"Trapped... like on Adela's vessel?"

She paused for a breath, then sat heavily. Vi rubbed her eyes. At every turn of her journey, no matter how much rest she managed to get at the end of the one previous, she somehow managed to feel even more exhausted.

"Yes," Vi said finally. "The idea of being tossed around in the hull of a ship again, confined, is one of the last things I think I could tolerate right now." In truth, there were a lot of things her patience was running thin on. This was just at the top of the list based on circumstance.

"Then we'll keep it open." Taavin took the bed across from her, laying down as she did.

Vi stared out the opening, the night sky barely visible over the rocking bow. Above her, Arwin stood, alone with her thoughts—and the knowledge of what she'd finally done to the person who'd harmed her.

Without warning, her chest was burning—brighter and hotter with every breath. She tried to slow her breathing, to stave off whatever was rising within her. But it was hopeless.

"Taavin," Vi croaked. "Are you still awake?"

"Of course," he whispered back. "What is it?"

"I..." Words escaped her. In the darkness, the burning of her chest flushed her cheeks and pricked at her eyes. All she wanted was comfort. Just the slightest bit of comfort. Why was that so hard to ask for? The longer the world forced her to be strong, the harder it was to accept weakness of any kind.

"Vi?"

"Can I sleep with you?" she forced out, finally.

Taavin shifted to face her, eyes shining in the darkness. Vi's shone as well, but for a different reason. He pressed his back against the wall and lifted an arm.

Slowly, heart racing, Vi moved from her bed to his.

The cots were far too small for two people. Vi felt like half of her was hanging awkwardly over the side of the bed, which meant Taavin undoubtedly had no room for his considerable height. Even if she'd wanted to be modest, there was no room to be.

Vi's eyes fluttered closed. No, she didn't care about modesty. He was warm. His arm snaked around her waist, hips twisting, legs intertwining... Taavin's whole body fit flush against her, as though it were made to be there. His comfort was enough to soothe the burning of her chest and racing of her mind.

"I find myself thinking, more and more, that I am cursed." Her fingers laced with his.

"You are not cursed, you are chosen." Taavin held her tighter.

"Are they really so different?" Being *chosen* had led her down a path she had never wanted to walk—a path laid well before her birth. "If I try, I can tie everything together. My mother's illness, my father's plight... It all leads back to the Crystal Caverns, Raspian's return. It's all connected. Were they being punished for me?"

"I can't claim to know the will of Yargen. None of us can."

Vi closed her eyes, shutting out the world. "What if it's all my fault? What if they suffered because they had to be the parents of the Champion?"

"Or what if everything was merely chance? Or what if their actions were what made you, out of everyone, the Champion?" His voice was low and soft, whispering across the shell of her ear. "I don't know what the truth is. I don't know if it lies here." His hand freed itself to rest on the watch around her neck. "I don't know if it's in the scythe. I don't know if there's a greater meaning to any of it."

"That's hopeful," Vi said sarcastically.

"I won't lie to you." The words sent chills down her spine. "I can't promise your mother will live, or your father will be saved. I can't assure that you will find your way back to your family and homeland, and selfishly... selfishly I..."

"You what?" she probed when he hadn't continued the thought after several breaths.

"Perhaps, selfishly, I don't want to see you go."

A sad smile crossed her lips.

Romulin had accused her of deserting her post. But everything Vi had done had been for her Empire and for the greater good of the world itself. If anything could inspire her to act selfishly, it would be Taavin. Perhaps, after all she'd been through, she wanted to be selfish, too.

"But..." Taavin continued, finally. Sorrow filled his voice, matching the sorrow that was beginning to fill her chest, extinguishing the burning fears that had risen there earlier. "I can guarantee one thing."

"What's that?"

"Should you want it... allow my arms to be your home. Here is home. Because, as I told you once, here is where you are safe."

The last holdouts of her stress and tension vanished. Vi sank further into his embrace, and his arm tightened around her waist, pulling her to him. There wasn't a part of her that wasn't flush against him, and Vi savored every bit of warmth he had, wrapping it around her like a blanket.

Despite feeling the most relaxed she'd been in some time, Vi disrupted the comfortable position they'd found to turn to face him. He didn't seem surprised; a small smile played on his mouth, and his eyelids were heavy but not with slumber. Her arms were tucked between them, fingertips on both of his cheeks. Vi looked from his lips to his eyes.

This was not the man she'd kissed in Solaris. She was not the woman who had seized a moment in a tent for fleeting joy. She saw him for who he was—tortured and hopeful. A man who had done wretched and wonderful things alike. And she was no different.

Imperfection fit them both well. Maybe life had carved enough parts out of each of them that they needed each other to feel whole.

She leaned forward, and Taavin moved to meet her. His breath was hot on her cheeks, lips soft under hers. He kissed her tenderly, almost timidly. Vi pressed forward and Taavin's arms tightened around her, drawing her close. A hand knotted in her hair. A sigh escaped from her lips between slow, languid, sensual motions that ignited something completely new.

Something worth holding onto as long as time allowed.

THE SCYTHE SAT STRETCHED across Vi's lap. Beside her, Taavin manned the helm as she ran her fingers along the smooth crystal. Magic swirled underneath her fingertips, trapped beneath its glassy surface. She'd spent the day running drills on deck with Arwin again and still felt no more confident using the weapon for battle.

"You'll master its use," Taavin said encouragingly from her side, as though he read her mind. "And I'll be scouring every book on the crystal weapons the moment we return to the Archives of Yargen for anything that could help you." Taavin pushed his sleeves back and massaged both his wrists, the golden bracelet shining in the light of Vi's flame, before grabbing the wheel again.

Suddenly, Arwin emerged from the cabin like a wild animal. She bolted on deck, hair a golden bird's nest, stance alert, head jerking about before her attention landed on them. "It's close."

"Is it?" Vi reached for her journal, opening it up to the maps she'd been referencing. They'd been sailing for about two days, so it wasn't impossible. Her maps were beginning to get as murky as the dark waters spreading beneath the hull of their boat the further they got from the Twilight Kingdom.

"I know the shift better than anything." Arwin turned slowly, looking to the left of the bow. "I can feel its magic in the air."

"How far do you think it is exactly?" Vi flipped her pages, looking at the sketched grid lines and trying to estimate where on their course they were.

"I'll know soon enough. I'm going to fly ahead and see if I can find it. I'll scout out a good point to enter through the shift." Arwin began to run for the bow. "For now, just stay on course. I'll find you!"

Before Vi or Taavin had a chance to reply, Arwin had leapt from the vessel, shifting into her form as a nightwisp and taking to the skies. Vi followed her with her eyes as long as she could. But she quickly lost sight of the woman in the darkness of the early morning. She didn't have a working clock at this moment, but the days seemed to be getting shorter, the nights longer.

Arwin returned a short time later, landing on two feet after a pulse of magic and starting right for the helm. "I'll take it from here to get us through the shift." Taavin stepped aside and allowed her to take the wheel. "There's a cliffside I think we can dock by without anyone seeing, near some caves that'll take us right into their stronghold."

"Will they know when we've crossed through the shift?" Taavin asked Arwin.

"I don't think so. They didn't seem aware when I crossed through in my nightwisp form." An intense look of focus was painted on her brow.

Vi stared forward at the open sea, her heart already racing. All of her maps—now safely tucked in her pack below deck—told her that somewhere in this vast ocean of nothingness was an island. But as far as she could see on the dark horizon, there was nothing but water below and a sea of stars above. The horizon remained unbroken.

There was a growing electricity in the air. The sensation of a terrible storm on the horizon pulled Vi's hairs on end from head to toe. She glanced over to Taavin, who wore as intense a look as Arwin's. Did he feel it too? Was she the only one who felt the edges of something transformative about to occur?

"Brace yourselves" was the only warning Arwin gave.

The ship rocked with a violent pulse of magic. Rigging groaned, the sail slumped in the still air. The world around them shifted: stars brightened, light kissed the edge of the horizon before darkening once more to the near-blackness of the hours before dawn. Vi kept her eyes open and held her breath.

Like a veil lifted, the Isle of Frost shimmered into existence before them.

It looked like a great storm on the horizon, a frigid mass of ice and snow fogging the air around a giant, craggy rock. Vi squinted, trying to see through the haze, but it was nearly impossible. The sea itself had begun to freeze all around the coast, the waves calmed by the unnatural atmosphere of the shift.

Somewhere, in all that, was her father.

Another pulse shook her. But Vi kept her feet under her, using only a hand on the deck rail next to her for support. She kept her eyes forward, waiting for the pop in her ears that signaled the shift passing.

"We're through. Take back the helm," Arwin said. She jumped down from the quarterdeck, heading to the bow much as she had before. "Full sails. There's not much in the way of wind here. Follow me." The woman leapt over the water and took to the skies as a bird.

"I have the helm." Vi rushed to Arwin's prior position.

"I'll man the sails."

They rounded the island, the only marker of their vessel the white foamy trail that faded into blackness behind them. A blustery gale picked up as they plunged into the perpetual frost swirling the coast. It crept under her clothes, clawing at every inch of exposed skin. Vi knew this cold. She'd felt it before on Adela's vessel.

She pushed the spark forward and felt its warmth bloom under her skin. Heat radiated off of her, melting snow to rain before it could settle on her. By the time they reached the ice that ran the perimeter of the coast line, her hair was slick against her face and neck.

"Shouldn't they have more patrols?" Vi asked in a low voice. She'd seen the first specks of light in the distance at the far end of the isle. "It seems too empty, too quiet."

"I imagine they feel fairly confident in their barriers… and the fact that no one in their right mind would walk into Adela's stronghold."

"Good to know we're all mad." Despite the weight of the situation, a grin struggled to form on her cheeks. "Here I thought I was alone in that."

"You're not alone. Not in any way." The thin line of his mouth almost made a smile.

Arwin continued to glide ahead, banking and turning on the swirling currents that surrounded the island. Vi worked to keep up, following her as closely as possible. But as the ice became thicker—its frozen tendrils reaching out into the surf—she began to fear for the vessel's integrity.

Luckily, Arwin seemed to think much the same. She did a wide loop before returning to their small ship.

"I think we should tie off here," Arwin announced. "The cliffs will keep their eyes off us, and there are no outposts I could find on this side of the isle. Those caves will be our way in." She pointed to a dark spot tucked into the side of a cliff.

Arwin and Taavin made quick work of striking the sails as Vi debated if she should take the scythe with her or not. Ultimately, she decided against it. She wasn't skilled enough yet to use it, and carrying it onto the island only risked it falling into Adela's hands.

After disembarking, Arwin guided them forward toward the yawning darkness of the cave. "I only scouted far enough to make sure this was an unguarded route. Once we cross onto the hillside beyond, we're all on our own."

Slowly, twilight filtered in, penetrating the blackness. It was carried on the icy wind and snow that piled at the mouth of the cave. The three emerged into a snow bank up to their knees, looking down over a small slope that ended with what could only be described as a pirate city.

Much like Beauty's Bend, the Isle of Frost was crescent-shaped, surrounding a lagoon packed to the brim with ships of all shapes and sizes. The coast of the lagoon was riddled with waterways. They snaked through ice-covered buildings, functioning as main thoroughfares for the pirate city below.

"How many pirates do you think there are?"

"Too many," Taavin said grimly.

"Enough to make our odds worse than grim."

Vi found herself agreeing with Arwin's assessment. This was certain suicide. They were walking into the hornet's nest. "Shall we, then?"

"Today seems as good a day to die as any other." Arwin gripped her spear tightly. "I'm going to dismantle the shift and then I'm back to the boat. Good luck finding your father."

"Wait, aren't you—"

"Going to help you?" Arwin interrupted. "I've helped you both more than enough to get here and I've my own business to settle. Hopefully, I'll see you both, plus a fourth, before things get bad enough that I have to set sail. It'd be a pain sailing that thing alone, so don't die."

Before Vi could get in another word, the shift pulsed around her and Arwin took to the skies.

Vi and Taavin trudged through the snow, sliding on packed ice and tripping on hidden roots and rocks. Vi glanced behind them, trying to cement the path of their return journey in her mind. The falling snow and blustering wind were already filling the tracks they'd made.

They stepped onto the narrow walkway that lined a canal. People were busy going about their business as they would in any city. She heard music drifting over the wind and snow from taverns; laughter rang out in harmony to a shouting match. Vi saw a man slam his hand down on a card table in a gaming parlor as they passed.

It felt chillingly normal.

She looked for someone who looked like they knew what they were doing. Vi scanned the men and women on the streets, and in the boats traveling the canals. She searched the signs and doorways for any indicators, no matter how subtle.

If Adela was smart—which Vi had no doubt she was—she wouldn't let everyone know where she was keeping a prized prisoner. Even if the whole isle knew Adela had the Emperor Solaris, she would keep his exact location a secret. Which meant Vi needed someone—

She stopped dead in her tracks, a flash of red in the twilight catching her eye.

"What?" Taavin asked.

"I saw an elfin'ra."

"*What?*" he echoed, but this time the word said a whole lot more.

"Come on." Vi started for the building she saw the man slip into.

"I don't think we should be going toward the people trying to maim or murder us in order to bring about the end of the world."

"This whole island is trying to maim or murder us," Vi whispered hastily back.

"Yes, but the whole island can't bring about an evil god with our blood," Taavin muttered.

They slipped into a narrow walkway between two buildings that ended in a cliff-side. At their backs were the cliffs they'd entered from—and if the bluffs before them were anything like those, then these too had countless passages winding within them, no doubt attached in some way to the building.

"What're you looking for?" Taavin breathed, his back pressed against the wall as Vi leaned forward slightly to peer into a window.

"Anything." It wasn't a good answer, but her mind was moving too quickly. She barely had time to form her thoughts, let alone explain them to him. The elfin'ra she'd seen was inside, standing at the side of a table surrounded by four others—one more elfin'ra, a morphi, and what appeared to be two humans.

Vi brought a finger to her lips, motioning to Taavin for silence. Leaning against the wall on the other side of the window, Vi pressed her ear to the frosted wood of the building. She covered her other ear with a hand, closing her eyes and focusing on the muffled words, only catching every few.

"... patrols are..."

"So far there's no sign..."

"They'll... up soon..."

"Adela will want... keep them alive..."

"... prisoner?"

"Guard change will happen... far he's being quiet and..."

"... keep a close eye."

Vi struggled to piece together the missing blanks. She listened until her pounding heart drowned out the soft words. Was she hearing correctly? Or was her mind playing tricks on her and feeding her what she wanted to hear?

They had little else to go on. Her suspicion that Adela would keep the elfin'ra close was supported by the conversation. Surely they were talking about her and Taavin showing no sign of coming to rescue her father.

There was a shuffling of chairs and Vi leaned forward slightly. Whatever little council she'd been overhearing disbanded. The two elfin'ra headed back, the others started for the door. Vi motioned for Taavin and they stepped back further into the shadows of the alley as half the group left the building, none the wiser that the very people they were on the lookout for were right under their noses.

Vi kept her ear against the wall, hearing the creaking of wood, the closing of doors, the dull metallic thud of locks being engaged and disengaged. She ran toward the back of the building, getting ahead of the elfin'ra moving through it. Leaning forward, Vi peered through the frost clouding the window of a dark room.

She squinted, making out shapes moving within it. A flash of red. Vi pulled back, pressing herself flat against the wall. Taavin mirrored her motions, trusting her without word or explanation.

"… thought I saw something." One of the voices from earlier drew near.

Vi wriggled her fingers, keeping her magic at the ready. The spark was eager, curling like lightning right at the edge of each of her movements.

Another voice said something Vi couldn't make out.

She glanced at the window, trying to make herself as flat and small as possible. The heat radiating off her beaded the frost into water at the bottom edge. *Please don't let them notice*, she silently prayed.

"It's nothing." Footsteps thudded away, carrying the voice with it.

Vi closed her eyes, breathing, counting to twenty. The room was completely still for the second half of her count. She dared to lean forward, peeking through the lower corner of the window.

The room was empty.

Vi stood, stepping around Taavin, pressing her ear back to the building. There were no more sounds of doors. No more footsteps.

"We're going in." Vi started for the main street with wide, hasty steps. She had no idea when, or if, the previous three people would return. Or if another group would soon arrive.

No one stopped them as they rounded the front. Vi's hand fell on the metal handle, pushing on it. But it didn't move.

A scream wriggled up in her throat, but it escaped as a few hushed words.

"*Juth calt.*" The metal around the lock splintered, cracking. Vi pushed her way in before anyone on the street could look in their direction. Rushing over to the table, Vi propped up a chair against the door underneath the handle. It wouldn't stop someone for very long, but it would at least keep the now-broken door closed at a glance, and make noise if anyone tried to follow behind them.

"Was that wise?" Taavin asked, as though she could somehow change her actions now. Vi shot him a dumb look that seemed to communicate the fact. "The morphi have a way to sense when Lightspinning has been used in their lands. What if Fallor has set up the same here?"

Vi hadn't considered that. "Even if he did, it's likely as Arwin said: he's the only one who would've been able to sense it. And even if there are morphi here who can sense it—they have Lightspinners on their crew, remember?"

Taavin nodded, looking over his shoulder warily.

"*Juth calt,*" she said again to the next door that barred their progress, glancing over her shoulder at Taavin and making sure he followed her into a narrow hallway. Vi continued to press straight back through the building and toward the cliff wall.

A short humming sensation pulsed through the air. The air pressure changed and Vi's ears popped. She rubbed them; Taavin did the same. They exchanged a look as a bell tolled, its frantic, high-pitched ringing echoed over the whole city.

"Any chance that isn't for us?" he asked grimly.

"Us or Arwin, and it doesn't matter which." Vi pushed forward, no longer holding back with her magic. "*Juth calt!*" It exploded from her, knocking down the final, heavily locked door at the end of the hall that led to the back room she'd seen from the alleyway.

"A dead end?" Taavin turned, looking back the way they came. So far, no one was in pursuit. But Vi suspected it wouldn't be long until someone was. If the pirates knew she would be coming for her father, then they knew right where she'd be headed.

"No, there's a passage here." She knocked along the back wall softly. Her hastening heartbeat led to trembling hands. But she tried to keep her rapping as quiet as possible. The pirates may know they were here given Arwin's presumed progress on the shift, but they hopefully didn't know where they were just yet. "Help me look."

Taavin lifted a hand. Vi felt the swell of magic like a rolling tide around her ankles. "*Uncose.*"

The unfamiliar word rattled her bones. Magic ignited around his fingers, exploding forward from the glyph—most of it bouncing off the walls in an array of sparks. However some sank in like water slipping through a grate.

"How…"

"*Uncose* means to expose truth," he explained, starting for the wall where the magic had vanished. "It's a word Yargen recently gave me."

"Convenient, when you were looking for a way out of the Archives of Yargen." Taavin pushed in a knot of wood and the whole panel slipped open—jagged at the edges to completely hide the passage behind. He motioned for her to take the lead and Vi did so without hesitation. "Can I use that word?"

"Unfortunately not… It's a word given to me by the Goddess herself. I doubt I could teach you if I tried."

"If we survive this, I may want you to try." Her voice dropped low as they started into the narrow passage. It was rough-hewn and natural in appearance—much like the caves they'd entered through—but this one was far better maintained and… she heard voices.

"… hear the bells?"

Vi recognized the voice from one of the two elfin'ra from earlier. She slowed as amber light danced off the outlines of stones, pressing her back against the wall. Taavin did the same on the wall opposite.

A second voice. "Do you know what it means?"

Vi pressed her eyes closed, taking shuddering breaths. She had to keep her head about her. She couldn't give in to hope—not yet. Not when there was so much risk still and so much at stake.

"It means your darling daughter is here." The first voice again. Vi inched forward. Her magic was building to an inferno inside her, ready to be unleashed on the whole room. It was a rage she didn't know she'd been carrying. A rage she knew could melt the whole island into the sea.

"She thinks she can save you." The second voice again.

Let there be only two.

She and Taavin inched forward to the mouth of what looked like a cavern. From Vi's field of vision she could see a row of cells. Two were occupied with the husks of other unfortunate souls Adela had deemed too valuable or too lowly to give the comfort of death—people she already knew she couldn't risk trying to save.

She was here for one thing only.

"She's like a lamb, coming to slaughter."

How many? Vi mouthed to Taavin silently. He held up two fingers, confirming her earlier suspicions. They could manage two.

A deep chuckle interrupted her thoughts. Its rasp echoed through the caverns and was attached to a voice richer than even Romulin's. Even weary and worn, Vi knew the sound. She'd know it anywhere in this wide world.

"I think it's you who will be slaughtered." Vi felt as much as heard her father's declaration.

"Do you think you can scare us?"

"No, and I think that will be your downfall. You should never underestimate a Solaris... least of all my daughter."

Magic swelled on pride. It flowed out of her as sparks of fire and light, dancing on waves of power and heat that scattered off her skin. Vi pushed from the wall, swinging her hand in the same motion. Power for the glyph was already collecting under her fingers before they turned. Vi took a breath.

"*Juth mariy!*" One of them hissed. The glyph shattered and Vi used it like a starting gun on a line.

They'd been paying attention to the wrong hand and the wrong glyph.

"*Mysst larrk,*" Vi breathed between wide steps. Her right hand was held behind her, grasping the sword that bloomed from the light under her palm. She swung it wide, putting all her force behind it, both hands clasped around the grip.

It sank with a satisfying crunch into the elfin'ra's side. Vi shredded bone and sinew, dark pride rising within her. It felt good to wield a sword again.

You should never underestimate a Solaris... least of all my daughter.

She'd prove her father's words right as he watched in shock and awe.

THE SCREAM THE ELFIN'RA let out was sweeter than any music she'd ever
heard.

"*Mysst xieh!*" Taavin's voice called out from behind her. A shield
appeared at Vi's side. Magic ricocheting off of it. "*Loft dorh.*" The elfin'ra at her left
was frozen still.

Vi had only taken her attention off the man before her for a moment, but it was
long enough for him to grip the blade of her sword with a hand, blood streaming
from between his fingers as he ripped it from his side and her fingers. She moved to
take a step back, but wasn't fast enough. His hand clasped her face.

His dark blood smeared across her skin, red lightning crackling between the blood
and his fingers as he pulled away.

"*Narro vah'deh.*" He rasped at her.

She knew what *narro* meant—acts of the mind. But *vah'deh* was a new and
foreign phrase. It rumbled across her uncomfortably in a dissonance that made Vi's
teeth clench to the point of pain. There was something distinctly *wrong* about it.
Something that made her toes curl and her head hurt instantly.

His eyes flashed a brilliant red, brighter than anything she'd ever seen. So bright,
her mind went blank. The world was awash in that crimson shade. Shadows carved
shapes from a bleeding reality before her, but Vi could no longer make sense of what
she saw.

This is wrong, something in her screamed—a voice she knew once. It was her
voice. But she couldn't figure out how it had become so distant. She couldn't fathom
anything. Her mind wouldn't move. Every time a thought formed it was gone, falling
through her fingers like the magic that poured from them.

Another scream and Vi awoke back to the room, not as she'd left it.

The elfin'ra who had been holding her was ablaze, thrashing to try to put out the
flames. The other elfin'ra had lunged for Taavin and the two tumbled on the floor.
Her head was splitting in two, pain seeping out from her ears. But Vi forced her
thoughts to work enough to conjure the symbol and sounds she needed.

"*Juth calt.*" This time, the other elfin'ra couldn't stop her. The one assaulting
Taavin crumpled as Jayme had on the beach, blood dripping from his mouth. Vi
turned in place, repeating the process before the remaining man could put out the
flames. "*Juth calt.*" As soon as the glyph was gone, Vi gripped her head, wincing in

pain. "Mother above," she hissed.

"Vi—" Taavin pushed himself from the ground, rushing to her. "Let me—*halleth maph*—better?"

"More or less," Vi mumbled. He had stinted the pain, but a dull throbbing in the back of her skull promised it'd be back with a vengeance soon enough. She needed to find out what that elfin'ra had done to her. But first…

She turned to face the jail cell, and the man within.

Her father was a shade of his former self. He looked more like the man on the beach than the man in her memories—but somehow, even worse. His clothes hung limp on his emaciated frame, torn and tattered. Dark circles lined his sunken eyes and cheeks. Icy shackles Vi recognized coated his wrists.

But his eyes were alight, shining in the darkness. They were eyes Vi knew well from looking into the mirror.

"Do you know who I am?" she whispered, even though Taavin had only just said her name. She was overcome by the inexplicable fear that he might somehow deny her. So much had happened. She was so far and away from the girl he'd last met years ago when he'd managed to escape the pressures of ruling to visit her in the North.

A smile spread across his cracked lips. "I would know who you are anywhere. Not even a haircut can hide you from me, my daughter."

"I've come for you." She took a slow step forward. Her voice echoed in the cavern. Or maybe it just echoed in her ears. Vi couldn't be certain. "I've sailed across the world for you. I've come to bring you home, father." Vi looked to the heavy padlock on his cell, not even bothering to search for a key. "*Juth calt.*" It fell with a heavy *clang* and Vi swung the door open.

"I should scold you for this—coming to such a dangerous place." Even as her father spoke, there was a prideful smile on his mouth. He stared up at her as though in a daze, as though Vi had become the Mother herself.

"Let's save the scolding for when we make it out alive." Vi knelt down, looking at Adela's icy shackles. "Taavin?"

"It's strange magic." He stepped forward, looking over her shoulder.

"It stints my power." Aldrik cursed under his breath—colorful language Vi had never heard from her father before.

"I know, I wore them once." Vi glanced up at her father, then to Taavin. "It took a bunch of fire to get them off me."

"Then I'd try fire," Taavin suggested. "If Adela really is from the Dark Isle, her initial training may be closer to that of a Waterrunner than anyone on Meru—like your training with fire. But you may want to hurry."

"Are you ready?" Vi looked to her father. Fire shouldn't hurt a Firebearer… but her magic seemed so different from his that there was a twinge of worry she may actually harm him.

"Yes."

Vi placed her hands on the shackles.

The ice was so cold it burned her skin. Even the initial flames Vi pushed forward were snuffed in a puff of steam. She narrowed her eyes, pushing through the barrier. More flames, more power.

"Taavin, *starys*," Vi ground out through clenched teeth. Her magic was hardly making a dent on its own.

Without hesitation, he uttered, "*Juth starys.*"

A glyph appeared around her hands and her father's. It swirled slowly in orbit above the shackles. Fire blazed inward from its outer rings in a breathtaking display of power. Vi was a wildfire compared to the measured elegance that was Taavin.

Fire around her. Fire within her. Fire within her father.

Call it forth, she silently pleaded. Sweat dotted her brow. Adela's power would be stunning if it weren't so stubborn.

All at once, the ice shattered, dissipating into steam before it could even hit the ground as water. Taavin's glyph vanished, but Vi's and Aldrik's hands were still engulfed in flame. Her father shifted his grip, taking her hands in his. Flames danced up their forearms, illuminating the grimy jail cell in bright yellows.

They slowly stood, the fire remaining on her father even after their hands dropped.

"Are you ready?" Vi asked him.

"To get out of here? More than ever."

She nodded at her father and turned, starting for the exit. Taavin fell into step beside her, his long strides almost putting him out in front. Aldrik took a step and stumbled. The sound of his body hitting the open bars of the jail cell rang in Vi's ears.

"Father!" She hurried back over to him. "What is it?"

"He's weak." Taavin assessed the obvious.

"I can't say they were the most mindful about how much, or what, they fed me," he said grimly. Aldrik's eyes, full of sorrowful dread, swung to her. "I'm sorry, daughter... after you came all this way..."

Don't consign yourself to die! She wanted to scream at him. Not after all she'd gone through. Not when the pieces of her family were finally all within reach. He was like a firefly: brilliant, blazing, and fading all too soon.

"You will not apologize to me," she said firmly. "You will move." Vi looked back to Taavin, a plan quickly forming in her head. "Taavin, I need you."

"Anything," he said hastily. Perhaps a little too hastily, judging from the sideways look her father gave her.

"Put my Father's arm around your shoulders. Support him. Get him to the boat."

"Vi—" She wasn't sure which one of them said her name first in that disapproving tone. But Vi wasn't about to let either finish.

"One hand, manage *halleth*—heal anything you can on him before moving, then sustain *maph* on the same hand to stint his pain so he can push through." Vi knew pain was only a small factor. Exhaustion and malnutrition were the bigger ones. But she could only do so much. "With your other hand, *durroe watt*. Only focus on those two. Conceal yourselves and get out of the city. Don't do *sallvas*."

"Why not *sallvas*?" Taavin asked slowly, horror already creeping into his voice. He knew what she was planning. He knew it from his sad eyes to the slight tremor in his words.

"I'll be making enough of a commotion that it won't be needed."

"You can't do this." He took a step toward her. Vi held out her hand, slowly walking past him with a straight arm barring him from coming too close, as though he was some wild animal.

"I can, and I will. Because you both need to get out of here alive and you and I both know you're no fighter."

"Vi, these pirates are deadly and well trained," her father cautioned.

"So am I." He'd seen what she'd done to the elfin'ra, hadn't he? "Wait a moment, begin healing, then move. I'll only need a minute to bring about destruction."

A sinister grin found its way onto her lips and Vi turned before either of them could notice. They didn't need to see her like this. She barely wanted to see herself like this, and some part of her curled up in the far back of Vi's consciousness, remaining oblivious to the horrors she was about to unleash.

She'd entered the isle unsure. She'd been taken over by sympathies for the people here. But Taavin was right: these people were murderers. It took seeing the brutality of the elfin'ra and the state of her father to remind her of that.

Vi's hands balled into fists at her sides.

She wouldn't forget it again.

Banging echoed to her through the cave, dull and distant. Vi pushed her feet harder against the ground, picking up speed. With a wave of her hand and an utterance, the opening to the cave was blown wide open with an explosion of splinters. The chair she'd propped against the front door rattled with another loud bang.

Vi imagined the men on the other side, slowly rearing back. Perhaps they had a battering ram. Perhaps they were just putting their shoulder into it.

She hoped for the latter as she shouted, "*Juth calt!*"

The whole front of the building exploded outward. Vi leapt through it, over the bodies that had been sent tumbling by the shockwave of her magic. Her feet hit the wooden walkway bordering the city's canals.

Vi pinwheeled her arms, preventing herself from tumbling in. She took a step and a small leap onto a nearby bridge and started running. She had no headway and no purpose other than to burn it all.

She was a blaze of fire through the dark night. Her flames licked through the permafrost of the buildings and ignited tinder as they had on the *Stormfrost*. But unlike the *Stormfrost*, Vi was at her best—she'd recovered, she'd been trained, and she'd learned how to channel the darkness within her.

A man lunged from an alleyway with a curved sword. Vi took a step back. Magic flew from her lips and hands—a shield to block, a blade of her own to plunge into the soft spot of his throat. She was moving forward again before the body even hit the ground.

Where was Adela? Adela must be here. She'd been expecting them—preparing for them. Where would she hide?

Sliding to a stop across snow and ice alike, Vi sent out a wave of fire, giving herself a moment's reprieve. She pulled one of the earrings she'd taken from Fallor's crew from her pocket and said, "*Narro hath.*"

The glyph appeared above the earring and the sensation of a communication channel being opened pulsed through her.

"Come and face me," Vi demanded and dropped the earring, letting go of the magic.

Her challenge issued, Vi continued through the city, zig-zagging as arrows were fired from rooftops and stoking more flames. She started heading away from the port, setting buildings and boats aflame left and right, then dashed across the bridges that spanned one of the canals and looped back. Pirates came at her from all directions, but none could manage her flames. They were all too disorganized, too startled, or too under-trained.

Without warning, a crack of ice snapped across the ground and a large spear jolted upward in an attempt to impale her.

Vi spun away at the last second, flame at the ready, turning to face the pirate queen.

Neither of them said anything. For a brief moment, they were the only two people in the world. But pirates filed in around Adela, emerging like rats from every alley and doorway.

"You finally show yourself," Vi called over. She smothered the flames around her fingers and readied her next attack. If the woman was smart—and Vi knew she was—half of the men surrounding her were Lightspinners ready to cancel her magic. All it would take was one good *juth calt*.

"Give it up, girl."

Vi would grant Adela this—even in the moment she should feel most panicked, most worried about defeat as her pirate city burned around her, she remained calm and composed. The command was said as though Vi was nothing more than a child who had wandered too far from home and needed to be scolded.

"I may have lost your father, but I will not lose you."

"Let me go, and I may let you live," Vi threatened.

"How long have we been doing this?"

What?

"We're alike... aren't we? It's how you got this far. It's how you destroyed my ice around the crown decades ago. You have their blood, too, don't you? Was it your mother or your father who was elfin? Who are your real parents?"

Vi took a small step backward, feigning shock; really, it was an excuse to look around and get her bearings. Let Adela yammer on about parentage in an effort to distract her—meanwhile, Vi sighted the cave she and Taavin had entered from. The snow leading to it was disturbed, but Vi couldn't be certain if it was their footsteps from earlier, or if those were fresh tracks from Taavin and her Father.

"Let's end this, finally. Just you and I, girl." Adela held out her icy hand. The fingers elongated, combining into a single column, and crashed into the ground. It was as if the pirate queen was merging with the isle itself. "The elfin'ra can kiss their Dark God's arse. This will be the night when one of us dies."

Vi was torn.

She knew she should run for it. She should make her way to the cave tunnels by all means necessary. This didn't matter.

Her vengeance didn't matter.

"*Mysst larrk,*" Vi uttered darkly, her eyes on Adela. The satisfying weight of a sword filled her hand. She sprinted into battle, bringing the sword across her body. Adela shifted slightly, magic pulsing with the movement.

"*Juth mariy.*" Vi made a flick of her wrist with her right hand, stopping the shift in power. She danced over cracking ice, her feet remembering every step Sehra's warriors had trained into her, every movement Jayme refined, each new step Arwin had drilled into her. Vi moved with the strength of each of them and with something none of them could give her—a power that had been bolstered by their teaching but was entirely her own.

Adela narrowed her eyes. There was another shift in the magic, but this time it seemed to split into several parts—none of which Vi could focus her sole attention on. The canal on the next street over came alive, a tidal wave of ice shards roaring over Vi.

She didn't have time for a word, so she swept her hand overhead, incinerating the deadly hail before it could reach her. Her left foot slipped out. Vi spun on her right, bringing the sword to Adela's shoulder.

The woman ripped her hand from its column of ice, fingers reforming at her magical command. The limb stopped her blade before it could strike true. Ice chipped off, but Adela was otherwise unharmed.

Vi leaned forward, closing what little gap remained between them. She had no reason to think this would work... and yet...

"*Narro vah'deh*," Vi echoed the words of the elfin'ra from earlier, whispering them as a lover would to Adela. She remembered every syllable with perfect, deadly clarity.

There was something about this twisted magic that she didn't need to understand the way she did Lightspinning glyphs. It was an abomination—an adaptation of Yargen's words gone wrong. It tapped into the most ruthless, brutal nature that hid in the corners of her humanity.

This magic thrived on hate—not logic or skill.

Adela's face glazed over. Her hands went limp. Vi saw the world both through her eyes and the eyes of the pirate queen simultaneously. Everything was doubled and vastly too large as Vi occupied the mind of her adversary.

It was a spell to control the mind of another, Vi realized quickly. This explained the world as she'd seen it earlier, when she had been under the same command. It also explained the screaming voice in the back of her mind that sounded identical to Adela, demanding freedom.

Vi pushed herself and the magic. *Die, die, die*, a voice in the back of her mind screamed. With Adela under her control, she could make the woman do anything. *Die, die, die!* The voice grew louder, and all too late Vi realized that it had not been the voice of Adela, but the same voice she'd heard at the first tear—Raspian.

There was a thunderous crack in her chest.

The whole world exploded with bright yellow, red, and blue light. Tendrils of red lightning shot out from Vi, exploding against the buildings around her and Adela. Vi was thrown backward, hit a wall hard, and slumped on the ground.

Everything the magic touched seemed to wriggle and thrash, like the tears in the Twilight Forest. Raspian's magic was breaking down the buildings, turning them to dust before her eyes. Turning the minds of the men it struck to madness.

Vi blinked, trying to bring her mind back into focus. Adela was hunched over on the ground, turning over the contents of her stomach. One of her men, still in possession of his right mind, levied a crossbow directly at Vi.

Move. She had to move. Vi pushed against the ground, struggling to regain her feet, to somehow dodge the incoming shot. Her whole body was a shuddering mess.

The man's finger squeezed the trigger and in the same moment one of the other pirates crashed into him. The bolt dug into the wood at the side of Vi's head, but she hardly flinched. She watched in horror as the now white-eyed pirate mounted the man who had once been his ally and began to tear him apart with hands and teeth, like a wild animal.

She'd be sick if she looked on any longer.

Move, she commanded herself again. Everything hurt. Red magic crackled over her skin, splitting it, only to have it heal with the blue and yellow tendrils of flame that coated her.

Somehow, Vi found her feet.

"G-Get her!" Adela struggled with words, pointing in her direction. But there wasn't anyone able to heed her command.

Vi looked over her shoulder and, for a brief second, debated going back to finish the job. This was her chance to kill the pirate queen...

Ultimately, she didn't take it.

Getting to her father would be sweeter than any revenge, and the longer she lingered here, the less likely it became that she'd make it back to him. She'd already made the mistake of lingering once.

Vi tried to move faster. Her head was splitting and body aching. Flames still licked over her body, dancing with red lightning. Every time she blinked, there was a red and violent edge to her sight.

A little longer. She was so close now. The darkness of the cave coated her and Vi paused, several steps inside. The mere idea of her magic was like torture, and yet...

"*Juth calt*." Vi pointed up at the entrance to the cave. The earth groaned and split, rumbling as the supports for its frozen mouth caved in. Vi didn't wait to watch the first rocks collapse with the power of her glyph. Instead, she turned and sprinted through the tunnels on the last bit of adrenaline she had.

Flames birthed with her every footstep, cutting through the darkness and smoldering against the wet, frozen rock. She heard crashes behind her. The island itself was trying to bury her now, chasing her through its frigid bowels. It wanted to punish her for the magic she'd unleashed on it.

Magic she still didn't fully understand and should've never touched.

Vi emerged on the other side just as the cave-in caught up behind her. There'd be no pirates getting through there and Arwin would figure out that she needed to fly around... If Arwin survived at all. Vi swallowed hard.

"Vi!" Taavin's voice cut through her thoughts.

Her attention jolted to the ship still tied to the thick ice surrounding the island.

"Vi!" Her father echoed, hands cupped around his mouth. "We're here!"

They'd made it.

She began sprinting once more. She slipped, falling hard, landing with a cry, but pushed herself upward, ignoring the red that smeared the blue ice from where her shirt ripped at her elbow.

Get to the boat. Get away. Get to the boat. Get away.

The mantra was on repeat in her mind. Vi leapt to the rope that dangled down the side of the vessel. With the last of her strength, she pulled herself upward. A strong hand closed around her belt, hauling her over the deck railing.

"*Juth calt*," Vi said with a glance at the rope tying down the vessel. It snapped in two. Between heaving breaths, she panted out a soft, "Go."

"Arwin?" Taavin asked, though he was already stepping away and heading for the ropes connected to the sales.

"She'll make it back," Vi murmured, blinking up at the sky above her. She'd never seen a sky so violent. Red lightning crackled overhead like the tentacles of a writhing beast, ready to escape. Dull light, the color of dried blood, seeped over the horizon, staining the sea, staining the sky.

Her father may be saved, but there was still much for her to do. Yet for now... Vi twisted, looking at the man who sat at her side.

Her father was saved.

"Father..." Vi lifted a hand. It felt heavier than lead.

"Daughter." Aldrik's fingers clasped hers. Neither had a strong grip. Adela had stolen both of their strength. "You did well."

Vi pressed her eyes closed, only just now feeling the wetness on her cheeks. Things were only beginning. He didn't understand what still awaited them.

"You did well," her father repeated softly.

Even though she knew all that lay before them, three words had never sounded so beautiful.

"Μ AY I?" Taavin asked, kneeling down on the other side of Vi. He held out his hands, his intent to heal her obvious. Vi gave a small nod.

But no magic flowed, and no words were said. Taavin looked on in horror.

"What is it?" Vi rasped.

"What happened?" Taavin whispered, reaching for her watch. As his hand drew near it, a spark of red lightning streaked from watch to finger and he pulled away quickly.

"What—" Vi struggled to prop herself up, looking down at her chest. The watch had cracked, half the cover had vanished—a molten line still smoldering in the metal. The glass that had protected the face was shattered and the face itself had been charred completely black. "I… I don't know." She looked up to Taavin, frantic. "What does it mean?"

"I have less of an idea than you. What happened out there?"

Vi was about to answer when the cry of a bird overhead stopped her.

Hovering on gusts and gales sweeping over the sea was a bird with a crooked wing. It coasted low before a bloodied Arwin tumbled onto the deck with a pulse of magic. Her eyes were dazed and unfocused, blinking slowly.

"They did *not* want me to break down the shift," she groaned, nursing her arm. Vi noticed her weapon was nowhere to be seen. "Yet, somehow, you look worse than me."

"Thanks." Vi fought to sit.

Taavin looked between her and Arwin. His eyes fell to the watch and that seemed to make up his mind. He quickly walked over to Arwin and hovered near the woman, looking down at her. "Want me to heal you?"

"Don't touch me, Voice," Arwin droned. The bite was gone from her words. Their hatred for each other had lost its venom, becoming more residual habit than impassioned feeling.

"Let him heal you," Vi called. "We need the hands to set sail."

There was a long stretch of silence and, finally, "Fine. Though if you tell anyone I let Lightspinning touch me, I will kill you."

"I thought you were going to kill me anyway," Taavin mumbled.

"I thought I was killing Ulvarth, and you were still to be decided."

Vi slumped, resting her forehead in her palm. The whole world spun, and it had nothing to do with the rocking of the boat. She had to get herself in order. They needed to get away from the Isle of Frost. Yet she stayed frozen, her hand clutching the now broken watch.

"Daughter." Her father's hand rested heavily on her shoulder, jolting Vi from her thoughts. "Is there anything I can do for you?"

She stared up in momentary awe. *He was really here.* It had been years since they'd last seen each other. Now, they were together for the foreseeable future—no meetings, no Imperial business, nothing to tear them apart. Nothing save the end of the world, that is.

"Actually, yes." Vi forced her mind to move again and not just gawk at him. "In the cabin there's a satchel. Bring it to me?"

Aldrik stood slowly, and walked even more slowly to the cabin's entrance. Vi watched him carefully. Even though she had been far more beaten up during the escape, he looked worse for wear. The gray streaks by his ears had never seemed wider.

Still, he moved with the grace of an Emperor. Every motion was fluid and purposeful. Even at his worst, he was still better than most at their best.

"Is this it?" he asked, returning with the bag.

"Yes." Vi placed it on the deck, rummaging through it for the vials Sarphos had given her. She quickly read through their various labels and found the two she was looking for, downing them in a large swig. "Thank you."

Vi wiped her mouth with the back of her hand. Sarphos's abilities never failed to impress her. It felt as though the potion never even reached her stomach, seeping into her blood and restoring strength to her muscles near instantly.

"Here—" Vi held up two more vials to her father. That only left them with one more—for disease, specifically, which didn't seem applicable at the moment—but if there was ever a time to use them, it was now. She also took out one of Sarphos's ration crackers. It looked like a biscuit but really did fill the stomach as though you'd eaten a meal. "Take these."

Her father didn't question, uncorking and drinking from the vials as Vi stood. Taavin and Arwin were on their feet as well.

"We should get moving." Time was strange for her at present. She couldn't tell how long she'd been on the deck, waiting for the world to settle back into place. Yet it felt like far too long. "I think Adela has enough on her hands but—"

"We don't want to be around when chaos turns to rage," Arwin finished.

"Taavin, you take the helm, Arwin and I will get the sails ready." Vi looked to her father, a small smile spreading on her lips at the mere sight of him. He was alive, and with her. It was every dream come true. She'd actually done it. "Father, you just sit tight and rest."

"I can help."

"We have this," Vi insisted. "The three of us sailed here, we know the ropes."

Her father relented, still slowly nibbling Sarphos's biscuit as he sat on the steps that led up to the quarterdeck. Taavin walked around him, and Vi didn't miss them sharing a small look that spoke volumes she couldn't hear. For now, she ignored it. They had a few days trapped on a ship together; there'd be enough time to deal with everything.

Arwin began readying the sails. They got the ship moving without so much as a word among them. Vi looked out over the Isle of Frost as they turned away; smoke plumed into the early dawn from the still-burning pirate town. Not one ship had limped out from the lagoon.

"I saw it," Arwin said softly, startling Vi from her thoughts.

"Saw what?"

"When I broke the shift around the Isle of Frost... I saw the spider-web red fractures in the veil between this world and the next."

Vi turned her gaze over the horizon, leaving the isle behind her. So what she'd seen in the sky hadn't been a hallucination of magic and pain. Taavin's words—some of the first he said to her when she arrived on Meru—echoed back to her: *We're running short on time. The end of the world is near, and we must be ready to meet it.*

"The world really is ending, isn't it?" Arwin whispered.

"It's heading in that direction."

"Can you truly stop it?"

"I'm going to try." Vi looked over at her companion, the woman's eyes locking with hers.

"We'll have to keep training you with that scythe, then." Arwin gave her a light pat on the shoulder, the touch brief but shockingly reaffirming. "So rest up today, princess. We're back at it tomorrow." All Vi could do was nod, startled by the woman's sudden change in attitude. "Speaking of... How many days are we going to be stuck on this thing this time?"

"That's an excellent question." Vi returned to her bag, grabbing the journal.

"I was about to ask for a headway—more than 'away from Adela'." Taavin joined the conversation.

"That headway sounds good enough to me for now," Arwin declared. "I'll take the helm. You should give her a look-over and make sure her wounds have healed..." Arwin glanced between Vi and Aldrik. "And I suspect you may want some time with your father."

"Thank you." Time with her father was a luxury Vi could barely comprehend. She almost didn't know what to do with it now.

"So where are we heading?" Arwin looked over Vi's shoulder at the map.

"Risen," Vi announced. She looked up at Arwin. "There, you can kill Ulvarth."

"You sound almost eager about that," Arwin mumbled with the tiniest grin on her mouth. Vi ignored it, looking to Taavin.

"And we can find out the truth about this." She held the watch, broken metal jutting against her hand uncomfortably. "And find a way to stop Raspian."

"Risen it is." Arwin took the journal from her, bending over to scoop the compass from the satchel. "North, then northwest after we pass the southern tip of Meru's crescent?"

"You have the right idea," Vi affirmed.

"Then I think I can manage for a while."

Taavin was already descending the stairs as Arwin went up. Vi looked over her shoulder again at the Isle of Frost. There were still no signs of ships in pursuit, and the land was growing smaller and smaller with each passing minute.

"Looking for the *Stormfrost*?" Taavin asked from her side.

"Yes. Though I don't think they'll give chase..." She thought back to the magic she'd unleashed—the pirates going crazed, red lightning mixing with blue and yellow fire. As her thoughts wandered, Taavin's hand drifted over her and he murmured spells. The haziness in her head began to clear and the last of the aches vanished. But before Vi could thank him, Taavin's fingers rested against the watch. This time, no magic lashed out at him.

"What happened?" he asked again.

"I used the words the elfin'ra had used on me to control Adela." She could still feel the echo of power rumbling within her like a dark storm.

"You used those words?" He looked up at her, his expression darkening. "Are you insane?"

"Maybe. It was that or die," Vi said firmly. She didn't want to be made to feel guilty for doing what it took to survive.

"Those words are Raspian's work... As Yargen's words evoke her magic, those evoke his." Taavin tapped the watch. "You invited his power into you willingly."

Vi clenched her jaw as she looked out over the ocean. She could continue insisting it had been to survive... but was it? Or had she wanted to find the most brutal way to end Adela's life? Where did her justice end and her darkness begin?

"No wonder it reacted poorly with the watch," he said grimly. "Yargen's magic was likely trying to protect you."

"Protect me from what?"

"Vi, *think*." Taavin gripped her upper arm to the point of pain. "Raspian seeks a living host to let him walk among this land once more, and fully usher in an Era of Darkness. To do that he needs one of us, or the ashes of the flame. If you *invited his magic into you*..." Vi felt her shoulders tense, and it had nothing to do with the pain of Taavin's grip. It felt like a crank was winding the muscles in her neck, making her head hurt all over again. "One way or another, as his power continues to grow, he'll find a way into this world. Let's not make it easy for him."

"I won't," Vi whispered. "I won't use those words ever again."

"Good." Taavin relented, quickly releasing her as if he hadn't realized he'd been holding onto her. His fingers trailed down her arm, wrapping around hers tightly for a long moment. "I don't know what I'd do if something happened to you."

Vi gave him a small smile. Their lives—their love, however unspoken it was—seemed so insignificant in the face of the needs of the whole world. No wonder neither of them could bring themselves to say it aloud.

"Now, I'm going to get some rest..." Taavin looked over her shoulder. Vi thought he was looking to the cabin, until she turned, realizing he'd locked eyes with her father. "You finally have your father. You should spend some time with him."

Vi squeezed his hand once before letting go.

Taavin crossed to the cabin and disappeared behind the curtain. Arwin was at the helm, focused and silent. Her father slowly stood and walked over to her. Vi's throat was thick with emotion, and tears prickled her eyes but didn't fall. Aldrik's eyes seemed just as glassy.

But the deeply ingrained stoicism of royalty won for them both.

They had shared words. They had been reunited. This moment felt different. This moment felt like the first time they were actually seeing each other, free from panic, fear, and worry.

Vi took a deep breath.

"It's been a while. I've much to tell you.

24

"I̶T STARTED WITH A watch…" Vi began as they sat at the bow of the boat. The seas were blessedly smooth, the salt spray from the hull cutting through the ocean misting her legs as she hung them over the side between the railings. "This watch—or what's left of it, to be specific."

"I recognize it."

"You do?"

Her father hummed softly. "Even charred and broken, I'd know it anywhere. After all, it was this watch that gave your mother her magic back."

"Magic… back?" Vi repeated.

"Have we never told you that story?"

"I suppose not." Vi had heard of rare cases where sorcerers lost their power through a process called *eradication*—diminishing magic to the point that it created a block in the channel. But she'd never heard of her mother going through it.

"When the Mad King rose up, he gravely injured your mother and, in the process, robbed her of her magic. There was a brief time when her command of the wind was gone." Aldrik's eyes drifted closed and he sighed, for a moment living in a time well before Vi's birth. "We didn't think she would ever regain her power. But it seemed she had made an unintentional vessel—that watch. It housed enough of her magic to reopen her channel."

"Fritz said that Mother was reunited with her power when the world was darkest, thanks to this. But I didn't know…" Vi turned the watch over and over in her hands. *Magic has an odd way of finding us when we need it most.* He couldn't have known when he'd sent the watch how right he'd been. "It gave mother a connection to her power; it gave me a connection with mine," she whispered, mostly to herself.

"Your magic, Vi…" Her father left the sentence hanging, clearly expecting her to fill in the blank.

"It's not like yours, after all." She looked back over the deck, toward the cabin. Her mind was an ocean of memory and Vi was sinking into its depths. "It's like his."

"His?" Her father turned, following her attention. "*Ah…* Taavin, you called him?"

"He's a Lightspinner. Like me." Her voice nearly quivered at the end. "I-I'm not a Firebearer."

Aldrik was quiet, looking back out over the sea for a breath. Eventually he turned to her, tilted his head, and asked, "So?"

"My magic isn't like yours, like grandmother's, like anyone in the Ci'Dan line or anyone on the Dark Isle for that matter."

"Just as Sehra predicted."

Her parents had known, thanks to the traveler, that she would have unique magic. At first, Vi had hated the traveler and what she'd done to her life. But now, sitting next to her father—a father she had rescued thanks to that magic—Vi found her rage had quelled. Had it not been for the traveler, Aldrik would be dead.

"Speaking of family, does your mother know where you are?"

"I'm not sure." Vi glanced at him, feeling as if she was about to be scolded. "I told Romulin. He may have mentioned something by now."

Aldrik shook his head, letting out a chuckle. Had her father always looked so old? Sounded so tired? It seemed he'd aged ten years in the five it had been since she'd last seen him.

"My foolish daughter... You could've been killed, you know." His face fell from the controlled mask of the Emperor into the raw emotion of a father.

"You could've been killed if I hadn't come to rescue you," Vi countered stubbornly.

"This streak of recklessness, you get it from your mother." Despite his words, her father had a proud smile, as if he were silently taking credit for the fact.

She blurted out rough laughter. "Mother would say differently I think."

"Exactly. She's reckless *and* stubborn." His eyes were glassy and tired. But still, no tears fell. This time it had nothing to do with the trappings of royalty, and everything to do with the fact that they were soaking in the relief of being finally, *finally* reunited.

"I know about her," Vi confessed. "I know why you left."

"You do?"

"Yes. And I want you to know that I'll save her, just like I saved you." Vi stared out at the sky. The bloody dawn had turned into a pastel blue with spots of white in the distance. Not a cloud of red lightning in sight.

But Vi could still feel Raspian out there. She could feel him in her blood now—in the weight of the broken watch around her neck. Taavin was right: Raspian's power was growing day by day, perhaps in part because of her. She had been the one to first sail through the storm of red lightning, to inspect the tears in the Twilight Forest, to throw herself into one of those tears, and then to use his words...

It was possible her actions were giving him footholds in the world. Vi's jaw tightened. It didn't matter; she'd be the one to undo him.

"Vi," her father said painfully soft, "Sometimes, you can't save everyone."

Vi jerked her head toward him.

Aldrik Solaris had always been an imposing figure. Dark hair, taller than most. He wasn't particularly broad, but he could command a room with little more than his presence and a look. Vi loved her father dearly, but he could be frightening to a young girl, especially when she'd done wrong. She had always seen him as an insurmountable force of nature.

But right now he looked like a tired old man.

"I will save our family," she vowed. "First our family, then the world." She'd saved him from the clutches of Adela; the rest suddenly seemed manageable.

"How did you even know to save me?" Her father shifted, bringing up a knee and resting his forearm on it. The skin of his shin was exposed through a long rip in his clothes. Everything he wore was in tatters—a shadow of former Imperial glory.

"I had a vision of the future, specifically of you on the Isle of Frost."

"So you can see the future?" Vi made a noise of affirmation. "You share that much with your grandmother—my mother—then."

"I thought so but... It's a different sort of sight." Vi tucked her head, running a hand through her hair with a sigh.

His father tapped her chin. "Do you not peer along the lines set out by the goddess?"

"I think so but—"

"Do you look into flames?"

"Well, yes, but that may just be because I—"

"Daughter, you are of her blood, as you are of mine, as you are of your mother's. You don't need proof in magic or tokens. You don't need the world to validate it. It's here." He tapped her breastbone under her collarbone and above her heart. "It's in the woman who's sailed across the world and risked her life to reunite that family."

Vi hung her head now. She would not allow the world to see the few stray tears fall. Her father's arms wrapped tightly around her for a long moment, his chin on the top of her head. As if he understood, as if he knew that for one long minute she needed to hide from the world and give in to the overwhelming emotions before she drowned in them.

She straightened, finally, rubbing her face when her tears would no longer betray her.

"But this talk of saving the world," her father finally continued. "You've risked enough, Vi. Come home."

"Father... I can't," she protested weakly. It was a tempting prospect, even before he elaborated.

"You can. You are the crown princess of the Solaris Empire. Your home is on the Main Continent."

Vi sniffed as a bitter smile crossed her lips. Her father still called it the Main Continent, and she had long since begun to refer to it as the Dark Isle. Vi could argue it was because that was how those on Meru knew it. But it was more than that.

She had called it the Dark Isle more because that was how she saw it. Her worldview had changed, and Vi didn't know what it would take for it to change back... if it ever would.

"You've done your share, return home," he repeated.

"What about mother?"

"You've been on the Crescent Continent longer than I. Do they have a cure?" Vi shook her head. "Then them summoning me to discuss a cure was a lie." Vi glanced at her father, filing that information away. Who had summoned him? Ulvarth, or the queen? Had Taavin known? Her heart protested against that last question. "Let's go home."

"But mother..."

"Your mother is strong. The strongest woman I have ever met." Nothing short of wonder, admiration, and love filled his voice. Vi watched as her father gazed out to sea, his brow softening. Only to nearly choke on his next words. "But I have been away from her long enough, and if ill is to befall her, I should be by her side, as she would seek to be by mine."

"But *I can save her*," Vi reiterated, stressing each word.

"How? Daughter, I believe you can move mountains. But I need your help filling in the blanks of how you believe so adamantly that you can accomplish something the most skilled clerics and sorcerers on the Main or Crescent Continents have not."

"Have you ever heard of the Champion of Yargen?"

"I can't say I have."

Vi chewed on her lower lip a moment, trying to figure out her next words. She knew of the rise of the Mad King and the fall of the Crystal Caverns. It would be an understandably trying topic for her father. How could she broach it all without sounding as though she blamed him? She didn't, of course. No one knew what the Crystal Caverns really were and it was not his fault they had been opened.

"Long ago, Yargen—we know her as the Mother, and Raspian—we know him as the Father, were at war."

"At war?"

"Yes, well, the Crones of the Sun got their stories a little twisted at some point in history. They're not lovers; they're sworn enemies. Anyway, when the war was over, Yargen won and sealed Raspian away. That seal was broken, and he's back now. He's behind the White Death."

"If you stop him, or seal him away again, the White Death goes away too?" Vi gave a nod. That was the same logic she had used—the same thought she'd hung all her hopes on these past months. "But how can you accomplish such a task?"

"Well…" Vi picked at the hem of her tattered, sun-bleached shirt. "Because I am Yargen's new Champion."

"You?"

"Yes, and because—hold on."

Vi scrambled to her feet. She had to prove to him she wasn't talking madness. Heart pounding against her chest, Vi sprinted over to the cabin, quietly leaned in so as not to disturb Taavin's slumber, and grabbed the scythe. She returned, sitting back down and setting it between them. Her father regarded the bundle warily and Vi took a deep breath.

"I think—know—I can defeat him because I am Yargen's Champion. Taavin is her Voice; he can hear her words and knows how to get to the flame of Yargen in Risen. That's the other piece of Yargen's power." Vi knew she was talking too fast, but couldn't slow down. She was working up to this moment and her words were in a race with her heart. "And because I have this."

Vi undid the straps wrapped around the scythe, pulling back the fabric covering it. Even in the bright, early morning light, it sparkled and shone with a magic that filled her with delight and hope.

At least it did until her father scrambled backward, looking on in horror.

"Throw it overboard," he demanded.

"Father—"

"That, Vi, is not the solution. *That* is the problem."

"I KNOW WHAT THIS IS," Vi insisted.

"You clearly do not." Aldrik reached forward, hesitated with his hand hovering above the pole of the scythe, then made up his mind. He grasped it, but not before Vi gripped it with both her hands on either side of his. She held on firmly as he tried to wrench it away and make good on his demand to throw it overboard. "If you knew what this was, you would not be holding it in the first place. Now let it go, Vi."

She knew that tone. It was the same tone that would have had her shaking as a child. But she wasn't a child any longer.

"No. You need to listen to me, Father."

"Vi—"

"Listen, please," Vi pleaded. But she knew that alone wouldn't be what got through to him. Vi knew she had to prove she wasn't the reckless child he thought she was. "I know this is a crystal weapon and I know their history. I know Mother found a crystal weapon that led to the rise of the Mad King and the destruction of the crystal caverns."

"Do you know it was that same crystal weapon that stole her powers?" Aldrik's voice lowered, becoming sterner by the moment.

"What?" Vi breathed.

"Do you know it was a crystal weapon that also began the War of the Crystal Caverns *before* the Mad King?"

She didn't. Her father was pointing out dangerous gaps in her knowledge left and right. "No," Vi said calmly, leveling her eyes with her father's. "I don't know those things, though I would like to. What I do know is that the Crystal Caverns are gone. All the other Crystal Weapons—fragments of Yargen's power—are gone with it. And this may be the last thing we have to stand against an evil god trying to destroy this world as we know it."

They engaged in a staring contest. Vi didn't back down. Her father sighed heavily, releasing the scythe and staggering away as though it had wounded him.

"Neither of us should be touching it…" he murmured, running a hand through his dark, limp hair. "You may have gotten recklessness and stubbornness from your mother, but damn if I didn't pass along that fire in your belly."

Vi felt somewhat proud. Continuing her efforts to calm the situation, she acquiesced to his request, slowly laying down the scythe.

"I think I'm able to touch it without issue since I have Yargen's magic—I've felt normal handling it for some time now. But you're likely right in that you should limit your contact." Vi didn't know if the scythe could taint him in the way the crystals of the Crystal Caverns were said to have tainted men who had come in contact with them. The scythe had been removed from the Dark Isle so early, perhaps it had escaped the slow weakening of the barriers holding back Raspian and the affects of his powers on the crystal.

It was a plausible theory. But to test it, Vi would have to risk the crystals twisting her father into a monster. So she wasn't about to find out if she was right or not.

Aldrik settled back into his earlier seat. Vi glanced at Arwin over her shoulder, but whatever thoughts the woman had about the outburst, she was keeping them to herself. Luckily, Taavin hadn't seen Aldrik nearly throwing their one crystal weapon overboard. She didn't want him to have a negative impression of her father.

"Vi, nothing good comes of a Solaris touching a crystal weapon."

"Father, I—"

"It was a crystal weapon that sparked a whole new thirst for conquest in my father."

"How?"

"Our family has a dark history tied to these. One we cannot seem to escape." Her father stared at the scythe as though it had hypnotized him. "Your great grandfather held one in his vaults—a crown stolen by Adela that was later recovered by my brother."

"Uncle Baldair fought Adela?" Vi had heard stories of Baldair's prowess with the sword. Still, she couldn't imagine anyone without magic standing against Adela.

"No. I found out much later he discovered it in an old pirate hideaway one summer at Oparium." Aldrik sighed heavily. Talk of his late brother always cast a cloud over him. Usually, Vi would change the subject. But this was the first time she couldn't afford to spare her father from these thoughts; she needed the truth. "But it was brought back, and my father eventually learned of that crown. He thought he could use it to someday conquer the Crescent Continent..."

"Grandfather was born with a taste for conquest," Vi tried to say as delicately as possible.

"It was a crystal weapon that led to my mother's death."

"*What?*" Vi had to open and close her mouth several times before she finally found words. "She died in childbirth."

"So the official story goes. But it was really because she was the last head of the Knights of Jadar."

"The extremist group?"

"They weren't always so." She'd been taught as much. But it was still odd to hear. "My mother as the head of the knights was said to have been in possession of their sacred relic—the Sword of Jadar, which was—"

"A crystal weapon," Vi finished with a whisper. "And then mother found the axe." Sword, axe, crown, scythe. They were all accounted for. And all of them had passed through her family's hands.

"Fiera was ultimately killed by men who sought to unleash the powers of the caverns. She died protecting that sword."

"Was the sword destroyed in the rise and fall of the Mad King as well?" Vi asked delicately. Her hushed tones had little to do with Arwin. Her father's eyes seemed more sunken and haunted with every word, despite his voice remaining level. These were old wounds, yet they still oozed.

"No, it was destroyed when I used it to kill a man. And with that act, I began the War of the Crystal Caverns."

"You..." Vi placed a hand on the deck, leaning, trying to catch her father's eyes. But he avoided her gaze at every turn. "Father, you—"

"It's the truth, Vi," he spoke firmly, leaving no room for doubt. "I was taken to the caverns. I was misled. But that is no excuse. It was my hand and my actions that led to the death and suffering of our people—that helped pave the way for your mother to be used as a tool and nearly die in search of that same power. Now you—" Aldrik reached upward, grabbing her shoulders, shaking her gently "—you wield one as well. And I will not see you suffer the same fate. These weapons attract lies as easily as foolish, power-hungry men."

Tears shone in his haunted eyes. Vi's lips parted, but no sound escaped. She was held in place by her father and by the weight of his truths.

"Father, this is different," she finally insisted, her voice weaker than she would've liked.

"Is it? Or is this just another turn of a vortex that every Solaris will drown in?"

Vi didn't have an answer. She wanted to. She desperately wanted to. But nothing came. And, as if sensing the crack in her determined exterior, her father continued.

"Leave this behind and come back to the Main Continent with me. Return to your family."

"I..."

"Vi, please. I have longed for our family to be together as much as you have. Leave the world to the hands of fate." Her father's arms tightened around her, pulling her to him. "Leave it all behind, and come home with me."

Vi closed her eyes, returning her father's embrace. No matter how old she became, part of her would always be the girl soothed by her parents' arms.

"Vi..."

She whispered, "I'll talk to Taavin about starting a course for Norin."

Her father tightened his grasp, holding her to the point of pain—though Vi couldn't tell if the ache came from his hold, or from within.

She was behind the helm, adjusting course slightly. The wood was weathered and worn, ashen from the beating sun. Vi felt the same heat on her cheeks, deepening the natural tan of her skin.

On her left was Meru and the end of the world she was expected to meet. On her right, across the Shattered Isles, was the Dark Isle and her waiting family. At her feet was the scythe that was part of a far more bloody history than she fully understood.

And she was trapped between them all.

Movement below deck wrenched her back to reality from her tangle of thoughts. A familiar mess of dark hair emerged from the cabin, the late afternoon sun picking up purple notes as the sky turned to red. The days were undeniably shorter now. Vi would bet they only had six or seven hours of daylight now—a change too dramatic to have anything to do with the summer months stretching toward winter.

"My father?" she asked as Taavin approached.

"Asleep. It seems to be restful," Taavin said softly.

"Arwin?" Vi had expected Taavin to emerge the moment Arwin entered the cabin after Vi had offered to take the second shift. But he hadn't, and Vi had been too grateful for the silence to investigate.

"Asleep on the floor." Vi gave him a look and Taavin let out a low chuckle. "I was just as shocked."

"I expected her to kick you from your cot."

"Me too." Taavin looked out over the bow of the boat, where Vi's eyes remained transfixed. "How long until Risen?"

"If we go straight there... perhaps two days?" Vi answered delicately.

"Why wouldn't we go straight there?" Taavin shifted mostly in front of her, making it impossible for her to avoid his piercing stare.

"I was thinking of making a quick stop in Norin."

"No."

"It would only add two—three days."

"Vi—"

"We can drop off my father." She decided not to bring up the fact that her father had begged her not to go onward with her plans to seek out her destiny involving the scythe.

"We risk being caught." Taavin frowned. "Moreover, what makes you think your father will let you go once he has you back on the Dark Isle?"

"I'm his daughter, not his prisoner."

"You're right, a prisoner would be better because he'd care much less about a prisoner."

Vi rolled her eyes and looked away, doing anything to avoid his gaze. "I don't want to bring him to Risen," she finally whispered.

"Why?"

"Because it was someone in Risen who contacted him—claiming they had a cure for the White Death." The surprise on Taavin's face reassured her that he hadn't known. It didn't rule out Ulvarth; in fact, Vi's bet would still be on the Lord of the Faithful. But she took solace in the knowledge that Taavin had no hand in this particular machination of Ulvarth's. "Why do they want him?"

"I don't know." Taavin shook his head. "I had no idea he was summoned."

"Then I'm inclined to believe it's not a good reason." Vi stressed. "I always told you that you'd have my undivided attention to figure out the watch—the scythe—as soon as my father is safe."

"But your father will always be at risk." Taavin grabbed the helm, standing right in front of her. "How long will you make the world wait in the name of your personal problems?"

"As long as it has to, because a world without my family is not a world I want to live in."

"None of us may have a world if you keep dallying."

"I am *not* dallying." Vi glared up at him and fought to keep her voice hushed.

"Every delay brings us closer to the end. Raspian's power is growing exponentially by the day. You've seen it. You must surely feel it, perhaps better than I. You can't deny it. And yet you stall."

They were in a deadlock, each holding a peg on the helm's wheel. Vi gripped and released the wood several times. It felt as though they were now at the moment when he would turn the wheel west, and she would spin it east.

There was a weighted, heavy sensation. Every nerve-ending firing. The spark was alive under her skin, flushing, radiating heat.

This moment had weight to it.

It was the same sensation she felt before they had entered the Isle of Frost. Perhaps their every decision now carried so much weight that nearly each choice affected the outcome of the world. Maybe this was how an Apex of Fate was formed.

The thought sparked an idea.

"Let's let the future decide." Vi was acting on a hunch.

"What?"

"I'll look into the future. I have the scythe. The watch has been broken, some of Yargen's power unleashed. Perhaps I will see a vision; perhaps I can command them now." Vi released the wheel, giving it to him. Taavin regarded her warily.

"And if you don't?"

"Then we'll keep arguing after." Vi sat, holding the scythe in one hand. "It can't hurt to try."

Before Taavin could say anything else, she summoned a flame in the palm of her other hand. The bright, yellow fire burned on and around her palm, snaking through her fingers. She held it at eye level, staring, waiting expectantly.

"Vi, I don't think…"

"It will work," she insisted. "I will make it work." Her grip on the scythe tightened. A shot of energy went straight through her—from the hand holding the scythe to the hand holding the flame. It tinged the flame with blue, barely visible at the edges.

"What the—" Taavin's voice was lost as Vi was pulled into a vision.

The world blurred and overexposed before slowly fading back into place. Things were hazier than normal. Nothing seemed sharp. Vi squinted, trying to make out the shapes being painted into a dark reality.

There was an arc of blue in the darkness, and a flash of red. The blade of the scythe came into focus first, floating mid-air, quivering with her strain as she tried to push it through a tangle of red lightning.

The blue-green magic that swirled within the blade illuminated her bruised and bloodied face. She had a split lip and swollen eye, and blood streamed down her temple to her cheek from trauma hidden by her matted hair.

Out of the darkness, a figure emerged opposite her future self. The lightning was his forearm, his face the haunted, skeletal visage of death itself. His hair writhed like snakes, silvery like moonlight. His mouth was a perpetually open maw of razor-sharp teeth.

The man's gaze shifted away from Vi's future self and toward *her*—as though he could look straight at her.

Raspian saw her.

Vi took an involuntary step back, though she didn't know how she would escape even if she wanted to.

In the vision, lightning cracked through the scythe. It shattered into a thousand pieces, magic propelling outward in a shock wave. Raspian grabbed for the throat of her future self and his nightmarish mouth ripped soft flesh from bone.

The Vi facing off against the dark god collapsed, grabbing her throat and gasping. She gasped as well, her consciousness blurring between reality and the Vi she witnessed die. Then, the air that filled her lungs was salty. Her throat was in one piece. And Taavin's face appeared over her.

"What did you see?" he asked solemnly, kneeling down by her, ignoring the helm.

"I... I don't know." Vi rolled onto her elbow, just in case she was going to be sick.

"Vi—"

"I don't know. I think it didn't work right because I forced it. Or because I let Raspian's power in me. Or because—"

"What did you see?" he demanded harshly, both his hands closing around her cheeks and jerking her face toward his. They were inches apart, his green-eyed gaze devouring her soul far more effectively than Raspian ever could.

"The scythe won't work," Vi whispers. "In the end... he wins."

Taavin's grip on her face relaxed. His eyes slowly widened as all tension left his face, his lips parting. He sat back heavily and breathed a soft, "No."

"I fight him, and he wins."

"No."

"I saw it."

"You saw wrong," Taavin snapped.

"And if I didn't?"

"Then we are headed to Risen, and we will find the information we need there to change this future. There's still time, there has to be time..."

Taavin stood, grabbed the helm and turned east, but set his gaze westward toward the fading sun. That was the problem with her vision: she didn't know what choice led to the outcome she saw. Was the scene she just witnessed the result if they chose to go to Risen, as Taavin wanted? Or if they headed to Norin, as she intended?

She rubbed her throat thoughtfully.

"For now, we stay on course. We'll decide if we are off to Risen or Norin later. I'll speak with my Father—" though Vi doubted she'd ever find the right words to explain that "—and make the best choice for us all."

Vi eventually relented to the need for sleep, leaving Taavin at the helm. He hadn't argued with her for hours, so she decided their plan was settled. Arwin was just stirring as Vi entered the cabin, but her father slept on.

As soon as she was horizontal, a deep and thankfully dreamless sleep overtook her as well.

When she woke, it was still dark.

Moonlight winked through the cracks in the curtain that closed off the cabin from the main deck. She blinked away the sleep from her eyes. Her head felt heavy and aching, but it was nothing compared to her body.

It felt as though a noru sat on her chest.

There was creaking and the sound of ropes straining... and *voices*. Her eyes widened and Vi shot upright, heart racing. More hushed voices than Vi could count lingered on her ears. She pushed off from the cot slowly, reaching over to her father. He was rousing as well with a soft groan.

"Father," she whispered. "Father, do you hear—"

Vi never finished her thought.

"The bastard betrayed us!" Arwin's scream cut through the night. "Vi—"

Vi bolted upright, grabbing for the scythe. But Arwin had been right—she couldn't get it unwrapped fast enough. The curtain to the tiny cabin was pulled open with such aggression that it ripped clean off its pegs. Vi stared in confusion, her mind struggling to process the face that looked at her. He had a beak-like nose and short cropped back hair pulled tightly against his head.

He wore golden armor, embellished with mother of pearl, and a heavy sword strapped to his hip. The man's bright blue eyes—almost steel-like in their iciness—peered down at her, shining in the moonlight. A terrible grin spread across his face.

"Aldrik Solaris, Emperor of the Solaris Empire," he said to her father, and then turned to her. "Vi Solaris, Crown Princess of the Solaris Empire… I hereby place you under arrest by the order of her Holiness, the Goddess Yargen."

It hit her all at once.

Vi was staring at the face of Ulvarth, Lord of the Swords of Light.

VI KNEW WHAT SHE SAW. But it didn't make any sense.

"You must be Lord Ulvarth," she said, as if saying the words aloud could remedy the disconnect between the realms of what should be possible and impossible. How in the Mother's name was Ulvarth staring her down?

"If you know who I am, this should go smoothly." His voice was a light and airy tenor. The man was clearly so full of his own hot air that she was shocked he didn't drift away. "I'm willing to grant you both the decency your stations deserve, assuming you grant me the decency of mine and do not resist capture."

"If you know who we are, you should not be arresting us." Her father tried to stand. But he was hunched in the small cabin. "Your queen sent for me. We are to discuss how the magicks of Meru could possibly be used to—"

"*I* was the one to send for you," Ulvarth interrupted. Vi only wished she could be surprised. "And I answer to no queen. I answer to the Goddess."

Vi balled her hands into fists. The scythe, still wrapped, was locked in her grip. If she swung it hard enough, she could cut straight through the cloth around it. But could a crystal blade cut through metal plate armor?

"What are our charges?" her father asked.

"You," Ulvarth spoke directly to Aldrik, "are charged with destroying the Goddess's confinement of Lord Raspian, and unleashing him—and the death and destruction he brings—back into the world."

"Raspian doesn't yet have a mortal form. He's not truly returned," Vi tried to counter. Even though she well knew that without a mortal form he'd still managed to kill countless people, thanks to the White Death.

Ulvarth turned to her and continued as though she'd said nothing. "And you are charged with kidnapping the Voice."

"*What?*" Every word Taavin had ever said about Ulvarth and his wicked nature was turning out to be true—not that Vi had doubted him. "I did no such thing."

"That will be for the High Counsel of Light to decide. Now, if you please." He stepped aside with a swing of his arm, as though he was ushering them into a party and not onto the dark deck of a stolen pirate ship.

Vi shared a look with her father, but neither of them seemed to have any better ideas about what to do. So they both emerged from the cabin and onto the deck. Several other knights in heavy plate armor stood in a semi-circle. Vi fantasized briefly about pushing them each over the railing and watching them sink far below the waves, no matter how hard they struggled against the weight of their plate.

"Where's Taavin?" Vi spun in place, looking Ulvarth in the eye. She was oddly satisfied by the fact that, even in his greaves, he was no taller than her.

With an emotionless expression and movement faster than she would expect of someone wearing such burdensome armor, Ulvarth slapped her across the face with the back of his hand. Vi was sent stumbling. She tasted blood in her mouth and knew from the instant throbbing it would leave a colorful bruise.

"That is *the Voice* to you, Dark Isle dweller."

"How dare you," her father snarled, fire crackling up his arm.

"Father, don't." Vi clasped her hand over his, extinguishing the flames and straightening. A smirk spread on Ulvarth's lips.

"Listen to the girl and keep your head about you… or we may just take it early."

"Where is the Voice?" Vi demanded, drawing up to her full height once more. He could not beat her into silence.

"We've already taken him aboard *Light's Victory* so you could not beguile him further." Ulvarth pointed over her shoulder and Vi dared to turn.

Not far from their own vessel was a large ship. Vi could hear voices drifting over the water and the creaking of its hull against the waves. Those must have been the noises she'd heard when she'd woken.

The whole situation finally began to come into focus.

"How?" Vi whispered. Certainly, they had been consumed with Adela and rescuing her father.

Vi hadn't so much as spared a thought for the fact that she wasn't the only one being hunted. For every step of theirs, Ulvarth had taken one just behind, following their tracks. She could imagine him casing the towns around the Twilight Forest—setting checkpoints on the main road. She could see him getting word from Toris that the pirates had been made fools of by a girl with a strange accent, accompanied by a morphi and an unknown Lightspinner.

It wasn't hard to piece together their intended route. Mother, the Swords of Light had likely known Adela had captured her father. He'd been coming to Meru under their order, after all. Adela may have even tried to sell him back to them.

Her hands clenched into fists at her side. She'd been so focused on herself and her own missions that she'd forgotten to account for the other pieces in play. And now everyone she loved was going to pay for it.

"Your hold over the Voice would not last forever." Ulvarth smiled, teeth shining in the darkness. "He was bound to call out to us."

A pulse of magic drew Vi's gaze upward. Arwin was perched on the stern railing. "There's no way they found us in a dark sea. He betrayed you, Vi! Don't trust him."

"What?" Something wasn't adding up.

"Archers!" Ulvarth shouted across the waves. Arrows peppered the back of the boat and water behind, but it was too late; Arwin had already taken flight again, disappearing into the dark night. "Keep your eyes on the morphi!"

Vi didn't know how they could—she had already lost track of the nightwisp. But a second pulse of magic above the large warship gave away Arwin's location aboard a mast's crossbeam.

"Taavin," Arwin shouted at the top of her lungs, so loudly that her voice was perfectly clear even over the crash of waves and creaking of boats. "I will not forget your promise to me. You will pay in full, and then some. I will have blood!"

The archers had readied another volley. But by the time they shot, she was off again. Vi watched as the nightwisp flew across the dark water, blending in with the sky and sea.

"Morphi scum," Ulvarth muttered. "My work is never done." Vi glared up at him and Ulvarth must have sensed it, because he locked eyes with her once more, an amused expression sliding across his face. "Do you have something to say, dark-dweller?"

Vi opened her mouth to speak, but before she could, Ulvarth continued.

"Consider your next words carefully. Come peacefully, use no magicks, and I shall not be forced to gag and shackle you." Ulvarth took a step forward, trying to loom over them. But he seemed so very small in Vi's eyes. To her, he was little more than a boy wearing too-big armor. "Come peacefully and you will receive an imprisonment befitting your station. Fight me, and you shall know the full spectrum of pain I inflict on all those who stand against Yargen."

He said it like he was doing them some great favor. Vi wanted to punch him square in his teeth. No magic required.

"We surrender peacefully," her father said for both of them.

As much as Vi wanted to object, she didn't. She'd reached much the same conclusion as her father—there was no point in fighting this now. They were out maneuvered and outnumbered and their best bet was to keep as much ground as they could beneath them as they tried to plan their next advance.

Plus, her jaw ached at the mere thought of another gag.

"Take them to *Light's Victory*," Ulvarth commanded his soldiers. "And torch this dinghy."

Vi looked back to the cabin. Her meager supplies. The journal with all her notes and maps. Once more she was ushered away from what little she'd managed to scrape together and claim as her own.

The knights directed them to the side of the vessel; Vi took a step forward. Ulvarth snatched the scythe from her grasp.

"Give that back," Vi demanded, knowing it was both foolish and futile. But seeing the man holding the weapon was enough to curdle her stomach. Ulvarth opened his mouth and it was her turn to interrupt. "You don't know what you're holding."

"You dare question me?"

"I will not fight you, but that is mine to carry."

Ulvarth leaned forward, passing into her personal space with a sneer. "Get in the rowboat before I change my mind."

Vi stood her ground, hands balling into fists.

"Daughter, come," her father said sternly. But she still didn't move.

"Listen to your father, girl."

With one last glare, and one last look at the scythe, Vi moved forward. She was oddly reminded of the *Dawnskipper* and her last moments aboard that vessel. Life on the high seas was exhausting, and seemed always to end badly.

She and her father slowly climbed down into one of the two rowboats. They sat side by side, right at the front, as the rest of the boat filled with Ulvarth and his knights. The remaining men and women piled into the other dinghy and were off rowing in an instant.

"A farmer's scythe, of all things to carry…" Ulvarth glanced at her from the corners of his eyes. "What a useless weapon."

Vi bit the inside of her lip, keeping silent. Perhaps if she let him believe that's all it was, he wouldn't investigate further and peel back the fabric.

"Unless your determination surrounding it is something more?" She remained silent. Ulvarth chuckled. "You'll talk eventually. They all do. Now, burn the boat," he commanded his soldiers.

Three soldiers set their stolen vessel ablaze with circles of light. Vi stared at it, watching as what had once been Fallor's ship burned into the sea. She wondered if she should feel something toward it, but she must've retreated once more into that dark place within her that Jayme had created. Arwin's words echoed in her mind: *He betrayed you.*

It seemed like no time had passed at all before she was back on deck, but this time aboard a far more massive craft than even the *Stormfrost*. *Light's Victory* was no doubt a flagship of the Sword's armada. Its sides were riddled with cannons and a long ramming spear dominated its tall front.

"Take them below," Ulvarth commanded to the knights still surrounding them, walking in the opposite direction.

Vi and her father obliged as they were led below the main deck. A long hallway with many doors stretched the length of the vessel before dropping off in another stairwell. Judging from the outside, the gun deck was beneath them now, which meant there had to be yet another subdeck for the crew to sleep.

"In here." One of the knights opened a reinforced door heavy with various locks. "You will have a guard posted day and night. If we so much as get a whiff of magic, Lord Ulvarth's patience and extreme generosity will run dry very quickly."

"More generosity than they deserve," one of the other knights muttered.

Vi and her father held their tongues as they walked into the small cabin. It wasn't what she'd been expecting in the slightest. It was sparse, but comfortable enough. Certainly a very different type of confinement than what Adela had given either of them. The linens on the two cots looked clean, the bedding plush and fresh. Water sloshed in a jug on the shelf, threatening to spill with every sway of the ship. She was already trying to figure out Ulvarth's goals in giving them this much comfort. What game was he playing?

The door closed behind them, and the sound of locks engaging brought her back from her thoughts.

"So much for a rescue," Vi murmured.

"Far better than my last imprisonment." Her father sighed heavily. He'd just been liberated and here he was, back again under lock and key. He sat on one of the cots.

"Mine too." She went over to the small porthole—barred—and looked out over the sea. The last pieces of Fallor's ship smoldered in the water.

"Yours?"

"Adela had me for a while, but I managed to escape."

"You escaped her?" Aldrik said, wonder softening his voice.

"I nearly died doing it." Vi looked back to the door. "I think if I tried to escape this imprisonment, I would die." She had no doubt she could make a good run of it. But there were too many trained soldiers here. They'd get her, sooner or later.

"We're not going to try to escape. It makes the most sense for us to get to Risen and sort this there. Perhaps their queen will be able to assist."

"I doubt it." Vi put her back to the wall, sliding to the floor. "Ulvarth said it himself—he doesn't answer to the queen."

"But—"

"The Swords of Light are part of a religious order on Meru—the Faithful—and they're trying to consolidate power. They're using fear of the end of the world to do it."

"Little good consolidating power does if you have no one to rule because the world ends." Her father made a good point, one that brought a tired smile to her lips.

"The only hope we have is Taavin. As the Voice of Yargen, he *technically* supersedes Ulvarth."

"Technically?" Aldrik must've heard the strain in her voice.

"Ulvarth will do what he wants, regardless of what Taavin says. And if Taavin doesn't say what he wants to hear, Ulvarth makes his life a misery," Vi said bitterly, not wanting to go into more depth than that.

"This Ulvarth sounds like a tyrant in the making," her father said solemnly. He'd know; he'd seen tyrants. Some claimed his own father had been one.

The words left a heavy silence in their wake. Vi took a deep breath, tilting her head back and staring at the ceiling. Her eyes drifted closed.

"I'm sorry. "I really was going to take you back to Norin if you'd wanted to go."

The floorboards creaked as her father stood, walking over to her. He slowly sat next to her on the floor and covered her hand with his. "Only me?" he asked.

Vi cracked her eyes open, tilting her head to look at him. She couldn't manage words. She couldn't hurt him with the truth, but she didn't want to lie to him either. She settled on a small nod.

"If there's even a chance I can save this world, I have to take it." The memory of Raspian was seared in her mind, the dark god tearing into her flesh. "No matter what happens."

Her father was deathly still. When he finally spoke, it was a repeat of words he'd said before. "This recklessness—you get from your mother."

"So you've said."

"Have I told you that you also inherited her profound compassion?"

Vi gave a small smile.

"There are so many things I would've done differently, were it not for her. Before your mother, I was a man who would have watched the world burn. She was the one to show me how my actions impacted others, and how to care." He let out a heavy sigh. "But that compassion has a cost, Vi. Trying to save just our Empire nearly took everything from her... Are you certain you understand what you would have to pay to save the whole world?"

"I do." The words felt like a lie. But she couldn't back down now and she couldn't hesitate. She'd made up her mind.

Her father pressed his eyes closed, not hiding a wince. He slowly shook his head. When he opened his eyes again, he couldn't seem to bring his gaze to rest on her.

"Why do you think it has to be you?"

"Because every step of my life feels like it was planned—everything led me here. You said it yourself: Solaris has a history with the weapons. You and mother have a history with the Crystal Caverns."

"Then you are paying for the crimes of your forebears."

"No, not just that." Vi squeezed his hand and leaned forward. "I was born with magic I wasn't supposed to have, in a land that knows nothing of it. I was given a watch that, somehow, connected me with the one man in this world who could help me understand myself—who had visions of my destiny before we ever met."

"Taavin." Aldrik turned to her. The way he said Taavin's name gave her pause. "The young woman... the bird woman..."

"Arwin, yes," her voice had fallen to a whisper.

"She said he betrayed you."

"I..." Every fear raced to be the first to overwhelm her. The memory of Jayme. Learning the truth about Taavin. Seeing nothing but betrayal in Fallor and Arwin's worlds. "He would never hurt me," Vi insisted. Taavin had said so; she had to trust him.

"Do you love him?"

"I... I do," she whispered. She hadn't even managed to tell Taavin yet. But it felt surprisingly good to say it aloud. "But it's also very complicated."

The makings of a tired smile spread on her father's lips. "Now you sound much like your mother, or how I imagine she sounded, when she talked about me."

"I didn't expect to. And I certainly wasn't looking for it to happen. The only love I've ever been certain of—ever looked for—has been yours, mother's, and Romulin's. I've never thought about anything else. I've never considered it because—"

"You never thought you had a choice." He stole her thoughts and gave them form. Vi must have given him a shocked look, but she couldn't be sure—her face had gone numb. Her father chuckled and continued anyway. "You forget, Vi, I was a crown prince before I was an Emperor. I, too, fell in love with someone I wasn't supposed to."

"How did you navigate it?"

"It was nearly impossible... and I messed up, greatly." Aldrik's gaze swung to the door. "As I fear he may have," he added very softly. Then, continuing louder, "But that love was the best thing I ever surrendered to. It gave me your mother, and it gave me you and your brother." His palm rested on the crown of her head, stroking her hair twice like he would when she was a child.

"I don't know if I can manage it all," Vi confessed. "I'm scared of being hurt and of hurting him."

"You may not have that choice. Love often decides for us. Do you trust him?"

"I do."

"Then you have to have faith in him, his decisions for himself, and in what you just said—that he will not hurt you."

Vi let out a heavy sigh, tipping her head back against the wall. Her chest ached and all she wanted to do was see Taavin. She wanted to curl in his arms again and merely exist quietly, hidden from the world, hidden from the pain of trying to sort through every complex and uninvited emotion she felt.

"How did you two meet?" her father asked lightly. Vi could tell the tone was forced, but the question was sincere.

"It's a long story."

"I think we have time."

Vi took a deep breath, and as she let it out, the whole story poured from her. It was a mess of emotion and facts, tangled together in a way she was certain barely made sense outside of her own head. The horrific visions of the world's end fell heavy from her lips, the scenes of the dying men and women in the clinic tumbling alongside them. She spoke of Jayme, recognizing her own shock on her father's face, her own anger at the betrayal in his eyes.

Vi finally spoke of Taavin. And, just like that, he transformed from her precious secret to a known person she held dear.

She detailed her trials on Meru, in the Twilight Kingdom, and finally on the Isle of Frost. Her father asked few questions, not because she was such a coherent storyteller but because he realized the telling was as much about catharsis as information-sharing. For the first time, she felt like all her burdens weren't completely on her shoulders.

Vi's voice was hoarse and ragged when she finished. Every detail had been explored and every truth confessed. Her father was the only person in the world other than her who knew everything.

When she finally laid down that night to sleep, Vi rested easier than she had in weeks.

Over the next three days, there was no word from Taavin or Ulvarth, which left Vi and her father to their own devices. The first day, Aldrik repaid the favor of her story with stories of his own. He elaborated further on the crystal weapons. He spun tales about his brother. And he told her stories about visiting the North when Vi was too little to remember.

On the second day they dared to ask for a deck of cards when food was delivered, both surprised when one was granted to them with dinner that night. So they played cards and discussed tactics, speculating what would happen when they finally got to Risen. The next day they discussed magical theories—not daring to practice—and played even more games.

Vi had never had so much time with her father all to herself and felt downright guilty for enjoying it. Their circumstances were terrible. But getting imprisoned with the Emperor seemed an effective way to secure his time and attention—attention Vi had never fully admitted she was starved for.

On the morning of the fourth day, they were woken by the same knight who had been bringing them food and leading them to the latrine. As usual, he strode in as though he were a god himself.

"Up with you both. We shall be anchoring off Risen shortly."

Risen. This was the city Taavin had grown up in, and the capital of Meru. Curiosity swelled in her with every step up the stairs and back to the main deck.

Sure enough, in the distance was a vast city. It was settled among rising hills that sloped to the docks and down to a wide river that cut the city in two. On one side a large castle dominated the tallest hill. On the other, a circular building smaller in overall size than the castle stretched taller into the sky.

Without needing to be told, Vi knew that the two were the residence of the Queen of Meru and the Archives of Yargen. She knew it in their opulence, and in the way their very construction seemed to square off against each other.

A city of stone stretched out before them. Buildings were packed against each other so tightly that Vi had no idea how roadways fit between them. Every one was three or four stories tall and had a tile roof with metal gutters—not unlike the buildings in that long-ago first vision of her father.

She glanced at him from the corners of her eyes. His attention was still on the cityscape, and he was none the wiser. Taavin had said that her visions of the future were malleable. Had she changed the one with Adela? Or had the pirate queen taken him onto the beach before they'd arrived? Would he still end up in that square before the queen to bear witness to the plagued man in the cage?

Had she changed the designs of fate at all? Or had she merely played into the path that led to the world's end? Vi grabbed the watch at her throat, nervous energy sparking across her skin, leaving goosebumps despite the warm air.

"It's magnificent." Ulvarth seemed to materialize from nowhere, leaving Vi to wonder what hole the snake had slithered from. "I imagine you're in awe of it, coming from a land so... uncivilized."

"It's clear you've never been to Solaris, if you think us uncivilized," her father retorted.

"I don't recall giving you permission to speak," Ulvarth said lightly, as if talking about the weather. "Do I need to have you fitted for a gag?"

Vi bit her cheeks, barely resisting the urge to rise to her father's defense.

"Which reminds me... when we arrive, we shall proceed to the Archives of Yargen."

At the mere mention of the Archives, she swung her gaze across the deck. *Where in the Mother's name was Taavin?* What had been confusion turned to frustration, and now to worry. All this while, Ulvarth had been threatening to gag and chain them... What if he actually had done so to Taavin?

Surely he knew that Taavin had escaped of his own accord. His blaming her was to save face for losing the Voice. She couldn't fathom the wrath Ulvarth harbored for Taavin.

While they docked, Vi looked for Taavin, continuing to worry over him.

Despite all Taavin had said, she realized she had vastly underestimated Ulvarth's cruelty. And she should've spent her time aboard worrying more over herself rather than playing card games.

THE SHIP ANCHORED JUST off the docks of Risen and they took tendering vessels to get ashore.

Vi sat with her father, silent once more. They were both keenly aware of the fact that any movement or noise could, and likely would, be used against them in some way. Ulvarth's efforts to lull them into a sense of security had come to an end. Vi turned into the salt spray splashing up against the side of the boat, allowing it to mist her face. She'd taken the time to rake her fingers through her hair and braid it. Her father had helped, knowing some of the more intricate plaits her mother usually wore. He had used a splash of water to slick his own hair back in the style he'd always worn.

They were a far cry from their regal personas, but it made Vi feel more put together and more like a princess. It made her feel less like some horrible sea goblin rising up from the muck to stumble through a gilded city.

The boat came alongside a dock that had a small army waiting. Ulvarth's Swords were a group larger than Vi had previously given them credit for. She counted at least fifty, and that was excluding all the men and women who had been aboard *Light's Victory*. She wondered how much of the whole militia of Meru was composed of the holy order—how many men and women were positioned in and out of Risen who reported to Ulvarth instead of the queen.

"My Lord." A man sank to his knees. He wore a bright purple sash around his shoulders pinned with a medal that Vi had never seen before. Ulvarth held out his bejeweled fingers and the man reverently scooped them in his hands, kissing his knuckles for an uncomfortably long time. "We have made all the necessary preparations."

Vi spared a glance for her father. Aldrik seemed calm and composed, but an uneasy panic was rising in her. But she knew everything Taavin had said about Ulvarth, who was not the calm, collected, respectful individual they'd been dealing with to date.

He was a monster.

"Good," Ulvarth almost purred. Without so much of a glance back toward them, he started down the dock, a wave of knights dropping to their knees as he passed—as if he were a god. "Get them in irons for the parade."

"Irons?" Vi blurted. Ulvarth paused. She didn't know if she was glad or not he'd heard. But she had his attention now. "My lord," she ground out the honorific, hating herself for every syllable. "We have complied with you without struggle. You said there would be no irons or gags."

Slowly, Ulvarth crossed back to her. The assembled soldiers seemed to hold their collective breath. What set her heart to racing was their curious anticipation—as though they were about to witness a show.

"You did, didn't you?" he said softly. "And I do thank you for making it very easy for me to get you here." Vi narrowed her eyes as a satisfied smile crept across his lips. Ulvarth leaned forward, whispering in her ear. Vi barely resisted the urge to shove him away. "Now continue to be a good pet and I'll let you keep your skin. I have hides of far more fearsome creatures than you hanging on my walls."

He straightened away, leaving the strong smell of peppermint clouding the air in his wake. Ulvarth turned and Vi took a half step forward, fantasizing about shoving a blade right between the vertebrae of his neck. But the only blades drawn were pointed at her.

Four knights had closed in on her in a moment. Their weapons rested right under her chin. Ulvarth looked back with an amused smile.

"Muzzle that dog. She may bite the hand that's feeding her."

"Do not—" her father stepped forward as knights with irons approached. Vi grabbed his forearm, stopping him.

"I've endured worse, Father," she said loudly. "I've endured worse and thrived while the people who forced me to endure it suffered."

If Ulvarth heard, he gave no indication.

Outnumbered and out-manned, the knights were met with no resistance when it came to shackling them. A gag was pressed between Vi's teeth. *At least this one isn't cold*, she thought darkly. Two gags were too many, Vi decided; she was developing a preference.

As the knights pushed them down the dock, another vessel came up to a pier one slip over from theirs. A litter was situated on it—so heavy with gold that Vi was shocked it didn't sink the boat. Twelve men strained to hoist it, carrying it off the boat and onto the docks so that the man within was never forced to have his feet touch the ground.

Taavin.

Drawn by an invisible tether, Vi stepped toward him. Arms restrained her. She struggled against them. Incoherent noises slipped around the gag in her mouth.

Taavin didn't so much as look her way.

He was dressed in golden plate, a long cape draped behind him. A legion of knights maneuvered to surround him. Pennons flew at the front and back of his detail. Taavin kept his eyes forward, face passive. Were it not for the breeze ruffling his hair, Vi would've thought he was sculpted from clay, not flesh and blood.

"Move!" A knight shoved her hard and Vi stumbled, barely keeping her feet beneath her. "If you stop, or try to run, or fight, we will cleave you straight in two."

Vi glanced over her shoulder at the man. He had golden hair and light brown eyes. He'd be plain, if not for the malice that permeated his very aura. She looked to her father, who stared back helplessly. He'd told her he'd endured much in his ascension to the throne, but Vi was left wondering if this could top it all.

Taavin was back in Ulvarth's hands. She and her father were captive. Her mother and brother were still back on the Dark Isle, left very much in the dark as to their predicament.

What had she accomplished? What had every step of struggle and effort until now been for?

Horns blared, echoing a short, lively tune off the tall buildings. The knights arranged themselves into a single line, falling into place. At the front of the procession was Ulvarth on a white steed—easily the largest warstrider Vi had ever seen. Behind him was a stretch of soldiers, then Taavin—the Voice that gave Ulvarth the power to lead, the foundation of his unjust rule. Then another long stretch of knights, a gap, and Vi and Aldrik.

Behind them was another gap before more knights, who kept their distance as though they were tainted.

"Lord Ulvarth has returned. Rejoice!" A voice boomed from the front, magnified by some kind of magical or mechanical device. Vi couldn't see which. "Lord Ulvarth has returned. Rejoice! The Goddess has smiled this day! Yargen's children celebrate, for his mighty campaign has been successful! Thanks to Ulvarth, the Voice has returned to Risen!"

The proclamations echoed off every wall as they entered the city proper. The knights must have been keeping the populous at bay. Because suddenly they were inundated with people. Citizens stood in line, pushing against each other to get a better look at the parade.

"Lord Ulvarth has returned. Rejoice!" the crier at the front of the line continued. Vi would've guessed Ulvarth, not Taavin, was Yargen's Voice, the way he was carrying on. "He has brought evil to justice. He has liberated the Voice from evil. He has recovered the Voice from the hands of those who would do him harm."

It was then Vi realized they were talking about *her*. She saw the people surrounding her for the first time, their skeptical and angry faces glowering from the shadows of their marbled buildings.

"Those who have brought the plague? Justice! Those who turned our fields barren? Justice! Those who unleashed the Dark God Raspian? Justice!"

Vi looked over to her father. His jaw was set so tightly that Vi wondered how his teeth didn't crack. His hands were balled in his shackles and fire crackled around them. But he kept his rage checked—for both of their sakes.

"She who took our Voice? Justice!" Cheers increased, the crowd chanting along, all crying for "justice."

Vi kept her eyes forward, no longer looking at the people and their lavish clothes or buildings. She could hear their jeers without needing to see their angry eyes. She would let their vitriol slide off of her, just as her father was. She would follow his example.

Something wet and rotten-smelling crashed into her temple. Vi stumbled, more from surprise than pain. She felt the slime from whatever it was—*food, rotten food? Let it be rotten food*—dribbling down the side of her face.

"Lord Ulvarth has returned. Rejoice!" the crier began anew, methodically repeating himself to the crowd.

It seemed all of Risen lined this wide road. All of Risen had come prepared with their best insults to levy and trash to throw. Vi and her father were pelted. The slimy, sticking, stinking things hurt less than the bottles and rocks—those Vi actively attempted to dodge. But the former coated her in yet another layer of grime.

Something particularly large smacked into her shoulder. This time she did stumble and falter. A knight grabbed her roughly, righting her.

"Keep going or lose your head," he snarled.

Vi found her feet once more, looking to her father. His dark eyes were filled with all the sorrow of the world. Sheer agony covered his face, agony that compounded the longer he looked at her. But when he spoke, his words were strong and even.

"Keep that head high," he dared to utter. "Even if you wear a crown of filth, you are still a princess of Solaris."

They can't take that away from you. The words were left unsaid, but Vi heard them with her heart more than her ears. She felt them—saw them, in every one of her father's movements.

Vi straightened, holding her head high, and continued their slow march to the Archives of Yargen.

At long last, they crested the top of the final set of stairs, reaching a large square. The heavy irons had cut into her wrists, blood dripping down her fingertips. But Vi continued to hold her head high. The small act of defiance was all she could manage now.

The Archives of Yargen towered over her in a single spire. At its base, triangular buildings stretched out like points on a sun, connected by glass-topped, floating archways and walkways. Every building was nearly five stories tall—taller than anything else surrounding it. But even they were only half the height of the main column.

Vi craned her neck awkwardly, jaw aching. Smoke billowed from a ring of windows near the top of the spire. *The Flame of Yargen.* Which meant Taavin's home—his prison—was just above that.

"Take him to the dungeons." Ulvarth's voice drifted back to her. The public had been pushed away from this square, leaving just Ulvarth and his small army.

Taavin was gone as well, but Vi hadn't seen where they'd taken him.

"And bring the girl to me."

The words took a second to register. It wasn't until her father was being forcibly ripped from her side that Vi understood. She turned for her father. Vi screamed against her gag—more incoherent sounds.

In truth, she didn't know if she had words at all. Her mind was pure rage, and the daze of such a new and overwhelming place, peppered with the sheer confusion of exactly how all this had happened.

Two strong arms closed around her, pulling her backward, hoisting her off the ground. Vi kicked her feet and thrashed. She was done being the polite princess. The masses were gone; there was no longer the need to represent the Dark Isle with regal pride, and Ulvarth's Swords already thought her a monster. She would prove them right to defend her father.

Aldrik looked back to her, worry in his eyes. He still said nothing. *How could he say nothing?* She was the one wearing the gag, but he was the silent one. It was a level of self-control Vi had yet to gain.

"You have fight in you, don't you?" Ulvarth stepped into her field of vision, blocking her view of her father. Vi twisted and struggled against the arms holding her, trying to catch sight of him again. But he'd been lost in the sea of golden armor, purple sashes, and cruel eyes.

She'd lost him again.

She'd lost her father.

Vi glared at Ulvarth. She'd show him how much fight she had in her. Fire crackled around her knuckles, popping underneath the iron biting into her flesh at her wrists. It didn't take much for the iron to heat to a red glow under her white-hot flames.

Ulvarth covered the flames with his hand. She didn't know if he had somehow smothered her fire—or if it was the sheer surprise of the motion that extinguished her spark. He leaned in, the thick scent of peppermint making her dizzy.

"Now, now, you've done so well. No need to fight."

Vi would spit in his face if she could.

"Especially not since I'm willing to make a deal with you."

Her body went still. Warning bells tolled violently in her mind. His mere proximity had her whole body aflame with caution.

"You'd like that, wouldn't you? A deal to save yours and your father's skins?" Ulvarth waited long enough that it became clear he was waiting on her. His mouth twitched into a brief grimace, but he kept his composure. "*Well?*"

Vi nodded begrudgingly, and the sinister smile returned.

"Good, I thought so." Ulvarth leaned away. "Take her to my throne," he commanded the knights holding her before starting off ahead.

Vi was all but dragged behind him, ushered into the shadow of the Archives of Yargen, through the lofty stone archway, framed by two open doors.

And into the Light of Yargen for the first time.

THE ARCHIVES OF YARGEN were barely comprehensible. They should be an impossibility. Surely a place like this couldn't exist.

Vi forgot her body for several blissful minutes as she was half-carried, half-dragged through the ground floor of the Archives. She was too distracted by the shelves on shelves on shelves of books. Surely, every piece of knowledge that ever existed was compiled and packed into the overflowing bookcases that lined the spire all the way to the top.

Rings of walkways—connected by stairways and ladders—spread out at varying intervals all the way to the top. At the summit, a brazier hung over the center of the room, larger and more opulent than any Vi had ever seen. Several archways extended from the bookcases to support it, with chains hanging from points on the ceiling to further secure its suspension above the center of the tall, hollow room.

She squinted at the flame. It was so bright that it lit the whole of the Archives like daylight, even though there were no other light sources positioned among the bookcases.

Underneath her feet was a tiled floor of mother-of-pearl mosaic grouted with gold. At the center, directly under the flame, was a large golden sun. At the sun's center was an intricate engraving of a glyph Vi recognized from the coin Charlie the pirate had used to pay at the tavern. It was the same glyph she'd seen carved in the trees in Soricium—three interconnected circles, stacked vertically with a line through their center.

"Keep moving." One of the knights shoved her and Vi stumbled forward.

They led her across the room, directly under the flame. From where Vi stood, it seemed massive—and she was at least ten stories beneath it. Vi couldn't fathom its size up close. Even from here, she could see sculpted women fanning outward and linking arms to hold the main basin with their frozen, reverent faces.

Above the flame was a stone ceiling—likely the floor of Taavin's room. His prison.

She had no further opportunity to study the Archives as the knights led her through a side door tucked between bookcases. They wound up a narrow stair sandwiched behind the bookshelves, illuminated by glowing stones—not unlike those in the Twilight Kingdom—and emerged in a hallway through one of the soaring arches she'd seen connecting the main archives to the pointed buildings fanning around it like sun rays. Through another carved and gilded door they went, into what Ulvarth had aptly described as a throne room.

He sat on a chair of gold, plush with purple velvet. A sun rose up from the back of his chair, its points giving the illusion of a crown on his raven hair. A sash was draped over his shoulder and he wielded the crystal scythe in his right hand. Just the sight of him holding the glittering weapon made her feel ill.

"Kneel." The brown-eyed knight who'd been manhandling her kicked the back of her knees. Vi fell hard, biting against her gag to keep back a shout of pain. "You're in the presence of High Lord Ulvarth, Lord of the Swords of Light, Destined Savior of Meru and Champion of Yargen."

Ulvarth's hateful eyes glimmered as he looked down on her. Vi had no doubt that while he didn't respect her land or people, he still delighted in seeing a princess brought to her knees before him. And a man that delighted in debasing others was a man who could never be trusted.

"If I remove your gag, do you promise not to try to use magic against me?"

Vi thought about it for a long moment and eventually nodded. He'd said something about offering her a deal, and she wanted to hear him out. Taavin was still at play in all of this. *He wouldn't betray her*, Vi's heart insisted for a countless time.

"Remove her gag, leave the shackles, and get out," Ulvarth commanded his knights.

"My Lord—"

"I did not ask for your opinion," Ulvarth said smoothly, almost lightly, as though he was making a passing suggestion and not levying a very obvious threat.

The knight removed her gag and left, closing the door behind them. Vi listened for their footsteps—they promptly stopped just beyond the door. Maybe she could kill Ulvarth, but she wouldn't make it out alive.

"Are you thinking of killing me?" he asked with a surprisingly smug grin.

"It's tempting." Vi rose to her feet.

"You won't make it out alive."

"So I gathered. It's still tempting." Vi gave him a mad grin. Perhaps she was mad for talking to him the way she was. But Vi had seen the death that was coming for her, and knew she wouldn't die here.

"Do you wonder why you're not dead yet?"

She doubted he'd believe her if she said she knew it was because she was currently fated to die fighting Raspian with the scythe he had his filthy hands all over. "I have the distinct feeling you're about to tell me."

Ulvarth lifted the scythe before slamming it down on the dais. The low thud was a cue and, on command, Taavin emerged from behind the throne. He wore the same finery she'd seen him in on the litter—gold and white. They were the Solaris Imperial colors as well, and for half of a second her treacherous mind wondered what he would look like as a Solaris Emperor, ruling at her side.

But now was certainly not the time or place to indulge such fantasies.

Especially not when her and her father's survival was up for debate.

"Our Voice has told me something most interesting," Ulvarth started. Vi didn't miss the hint of annoyance already in his voice. "He has told me that you are Yargen's new Champion, destined to defend the light against the coming darkness."

"And yet your men honor you with the title." Vi arched her dark eyebrows. Ulvarth's eyes narrowed slightly.

"You." Ulvarth's eye twitched. "The divine chose *you*. A small girl from the Dark

Isle. The daughter of the man and woman who wounded Yargen so—who went against her will and acted in favor of the dark god."

Vi pressed her lips together and kept her mouth shut. He hadn't asked her a question and she didn't feel like indulging his chatter. She glanced over to Taavin, but he had yet to make eye contact with her. Wherever he was mentally, it was a world away.

"What can you possibly do?" Ulvarth grumbled. Vi didn't have a good answer, but once more, he wasn't looking for one. Ulvarth adjusted his seat, narrowly avoiding a position that would make his sulking even more obvious. "It's no matter… you're here now."

"You said you had a deal for me." Vi had no interest in his pity party over not being chosen as Yargen's Champion. She suspected if he really knew the trimmings the job came with, he'd be happier without it. He was just another man who wanted power and none of the responsibility attached. Vi had dealt with men like him her whole life—she called them Senators.

"I do. You see, Vi Solaris, I am not a man without mercy. I would be willing to send you and your father back to your forgotten rock on one of the Sword's fastest vessels."

"What would you want in return for such a kindness?"

"The Voice has assured me that, with your help as Champion, we will be able to rekindle the Flame of Yargen and return it to its former glory."

Former glory? Rekindle? Taavin had said as much… But the flame she passed under looked incredibly glorious from where Vi stood.

"If the Faithful have any hope to make it through the dark age Lord Raspian will usher in, we shall need her barrier, at the least. Yet the flame is so weak, it can barely protect this temple—let alone all of Risen."

Vi gave a small nod. She heard his words but didn't fully understand them. Yet she had the distinct feeling Ulvarth was the sort of man who didn't appreciate questions.

"Should you rekindle the flame for me, and commit to eternal silence on the role your family played in weakening it in the first place, I shall let you and your father return to your isle and do… whatever it is you do on that desolate rock."

"And my role as Champion?" Vi glanced at Taavin. He was still avoiding looking at her. This had to be some kind of plan he'd put together… right?

"I think you mean *my* role as Champion." Ulvarth gripped the scythe tighter, as though that alone distinguished him as the Champion.

"I see…" Vi said. He saw the crystal weapon as a trophy. Even if he knew it could be used to stand against Raspian, Vi doubted he would. All he wanted was the flame rekindled and a barrier around Risen—the rest of the world be damned. Taavin had kept information from Ulvarth and that meant she had to trust him and play along. "In the meantime, while I rekindle the flame and keep my silence, you'll keep my father safe?"

"No harm shall come to him while he awaits trial for his crimes."

"My father committed no crimes against you or your lands. This is the first time he's ever stepped foot on them." Vi shifted her wrists, trying to adjust the pressure of the shackles. Her blood slowly dripped on the floor from where the iron had cut into her flesh on the long walk.

"Your father allowed Raspian to return to this world."

Vi expected him to seem more upset about such a truth, but he delivered the line with the same concern one might reserve for reporting the weather. That was proof enough that he was lying. Ulvarth knew it wasn't entirely because of her father that Raspian had returned. This was all just a game.

Think like him.

Something was wrong with the flame of Yargen, and Ulvarth couldn't fix it—not without her help. The man likely hated the notion of "lowering himself" to asking someone from the Dark Isle for help. If she succeeded, and he sent her away... he planned to take the credit.

"No harm comes to my father while he awaits your trial," Vi reiterated, confident she now understood the full terms of the deal. "You keep him safe, comfortable, and in quarters befitting his station."

"You think you can order me, now?"

"I'm not ordering, I'm bargaining. Didn't you say you had an offer? Well the offer has turned into a negotiation." Vi rolled her shoulders back, standing straighter and ignoring the weight of the shackles trying to pull her down. "You keep my father and me safe and comfortable. When I have finished rekindling the flame, you allow us to go home without any other hindrances. You make no move against the Dark Isle or my family ever again. And then I will say nothing of my role here. I will let no one know that it was really I who helped rekindle the flame."

Ulvarth's expression soured like a too-ripe fruit. Vi smirked. He hadn't expected her to figure his game and she hoped he hadn't figured out hers.

Rekindling the flame had always been part of her mission. But so was figuring out the secrets of the watch and the scythe. Her arrival in Risen hadn't gone according to plan, but she was where she needed to be—the Archives of Yargen.

Fate had yet to abandon her.

"Do we have a deal?" Vi tilted her head. "I do everything you need and you can take credit for all my work."

"You think I need you that desperately?" he sneered.

"I do, because you are only pretending to be Yargen's chosen Champion. You need me," Vi stated with all the royal arrogance she'd avoided her whole life. "Do we have an understanding?"

Ulvarth was silent for several long breaths. Vi wondered if his heaving chest was a method to attempt to calm himself down. If it was, it didn't seem to be working. But then again, he didn't scream at her when he opened his mouth again, despite the bright flush in his cheeks.

"I think we have an understanding," he said finally.

"One more thing."

"You are a greedy woman."

"Blame my royal upbringing." She was in rags, covered in filth. He was on a gilded throne. Yet in that moment, Vi felt like the more powerful person in the room. "I need free access to the Archives of Yargen, and to that scythe."

"You think I'm just going to let you wander with a weapon?"

"It's required to rekindle the flame." She had no idea what was required. But she wanted as long of a leash as possible. She wanted to get her hands on those books for more reasons than she had fingers and toes. And she wanted full access to the last crystal weapon.

"Very well. I will let you have access to the Archives. But take one step outside and you will not make it a second step."

"And the scythe?"

Ulvarth considered for a long moment, slowly turning to the statue called Taavin. "The Voice shall keep it, and perform any necessary research. He shall report to me on his findings and, as needed, you shall have supervised access to him and the crystal weapon."

Vi tried to keep disappointment off her face. The more she fought, the more he'd know he had something worth holding over her head. It'd give up the strength of her position. So instead, Vi kept her face passive, emotions hidden.

"Then yes, my lord. We do have an understanding."

"You have one month to rekindle the flame. One month before my patience and kindness expire."

Vi didn't know what she was doing, so she didn't know if that was long enough. Taavin had no reaction and gave no indication one way or another. He hardly looked like he was breathing.

"Now get out," Ulvarth snarled.

She gave a bow, just for effect, and turned for the door. The scythe thudded dully on the dais beneath her as Ulvarth struck it twice, signaling for the knights on the other side of the doors to escort her away.

"Remove her from my sight and find a place for her in the Lark's dormitories. Let them be forced to deal with her," Ulvarth commanded. "And for the love of Yargen, clean her before she stinks up the entire place."

THERE WERE THREE ASPECTS of the Faithful, Vi quickly learned.

The first were the laymen—Faithful who studied Lightspinning and followed the teachings of Yargen but did little else. They were civilians. Followers, but not active participants in the structure of the Faithful. The laymen were scattered across Meru.

Next were the Swords. Vi had had enough of them for a lifetime. And, judging by how they shoved her into the care of a beady-eyed, sagely man, the feeling was mutual.

The final aspect were the Larks of Light. These were men and women who had pledged themselves to Yargen. But where the Swords where the militaristic strong-arm of the Faithful, the Larks were the teachers, theorists, theologians, scholars, and preachers.

They were quiet, calm, and kind.

Three things Vi hadn't experienced in a long time.

"This way, young one." The elderly man's demeanor reminded her instantly of King Noct. "Let's take you to a bathing chamber."

"What's your name?" Vi asked. She rubbed her wrists, gently inspecting the clotted blood and torn flesh left behind from the irons.

"They call me Kindred Allan." He spoke without turning. Likely because every movement seemed stiff and painful for him. "And your name, young one?"

"Vi Solaris."

"Not the same Vi Solaris as the Crown Princess of the Solaris Empire?"

"You know of it?" Vi asked cautiously.

"It is the Lark's job to know of it," he said thoughtfully. "We record all Yargen's light touches, and even the places where it cannot, to keep record of all her designs and the ways mortalkind seeks to change them."

It was a pleasant surprise not to have someone immediately telling her how terrible her home was. Allan seemed emotionally detached, but genuinely interested. Vi counted it a victory.

Allan lead her down a spiral stair in a different building from the one Ulvarth had occupied. It was the northernmost point of the triangular buildings surrounding and connected to the Archives. Every flight of stairs opened to either a long hall or a warm room. There were crackling fires, and men and women working quietly at desks or talking, while sinking further into plush cushions wrapped in warm-hued fabrics.

"This way, your highness."

"Just Vi is fine."

"Is it not your custom to always use some kind of honorific or title in Solaris for royalty and nobility?"

"Usually, yes… But we're not in Solaris. And it's not common for those who are close to royalty." Besides, Vi had enough of being the crown princess for one day. She'd invoked her royal persona for Ulvarth and her walk through the city. Now, she felt too tired to deal with it.

"Are we close?" he asked.

"That depends on your actions, I suppose."

"Spoken like a true princess." He gave her a weathered smile as he opened a door, allowing steam to billow out. The room was tiled from floor to ceiling. A faucet continually poured hot water into a large copper tub, the overflow draining underneath the vessel. There was a small wooden stool with a soap bar and a few other scouring agents in jars.

Another shelf at her left had a variety of brushes, combs, razors, and other barbering tools. Over which was a mirror. *A mirror.* Vi hadn't seen herself in a mirror since the small one in the bathroom of the Twilight Kingdom.

She stalled before it, slowly bringing a hand to her cheek.

"I shall leave you to soak. Please enjoy at your leisure. While you are soaking, do pull the screen before the door. I shall send one of our female Larks to come with clothing for you and she will drape it over for your convenience and modesty."

"Thank you," Vi murmured, too distracted by her reflection to say more than that.

The woman she saw didn't reflect the woman Vi thought she knew. Her fingers trailed over cheekbones that were sharper than she recalled. As sharp as her father's— she could recognize now that she had seen him again so recently. The harsh sun of the seas had further darkened her skin, as Vi suspected from her arms, but her hair was still as black as midnight and as fine as spider's silk.

She slowly undid the braids she and her father had coiffed for their arrival to Risen. Vi turned her head this way and that, looking at how it fell just beyond her shoulders. There wasn't the slightest bit of wild body to it, not even with the kink of braids—nothing like her mother's and brother's.

She was, indeed, her father's daughter.

Stripping, Vi balled and burned her clothes. Once more, she incinerated everything of her last incarnation in life. What version of Vi would walk the Archives of Yargen when she emerged from the tub?

Pulling the screen mostly shut, Vi sank into the water, spilling it over all sides. It completely engulfed her and for a few moments she let the warmth soak off the filth that covered her. With the constantly running tap, the water was perpetually hot and the grime flowed over and away as she began to scrub.

Vi had just started rubbing her legs raw when the door opened.

"Princess?"

"Just Vi is fine," Vi called over the screen.

"Vi, then… My name is Serina. Allan told me to attend you. I have clothes here;

shall I drape them over the screen?"

"That sounds lovely." Vi rested her elbows on the edge of the tub, looking at the clothes that appeared by two dainty hands. A towel was draped last at their side.

"I'll wait just outside for you to finish to show you to your room… But do take your time. It sounds as though you've had quite a journey."

"Thank you," Vi said softly. For one moment, she thought about asking the girl to stay. Vi had questions about this place, about the Larks, and about the flame. But she ultimately decided to save them for Taavin.

She had no interest in making friends here. This was like the Twilight Kingdom—like Arwin. It was business. Vi retreated further into the tub, thinking of the morphi woman. She had definitely not grown any attachments to her, Vi insisted to herself. She only wondered how she was doing out of pure curiosity.

The door clicked closed and Vi finished, dried, and dressed. The robes were basic—not unlike those she'd seen the crones wear on the Dark Isle. They were a deep, sunset-red hue, cinched tight at the waist with a wide, golden sash. One benefit of clothes so basic—they were designed to swim on their wearer, and Vi didn't have to worry about how her hips were going to squeeze into anything.

Vi opened the door to find the woman waiting just as she'd said. She had silvery hair, though she didn't look much older than Vi, and bright hazel, nearly yellow eyes. There was something distinctly cat-like about her movements and Vi couldn't fight the notion that if the woman ever became a morphi, her shifted form would be some kind of lynx or leopard.

"The rooms are two floors up." She pointed upward as she walked to the stairs. "They're not much, but we've managed to rearrange ourselves so that you will have a room of your own."

"You didn't need to do that."

"We thought it appropriate," she said with a note of finality that suggested there were more layers to *why* they thought it appropriate than Vi understood.

They walked up the stairs, passing one landing that led into a workroom, and then up once more to a long hall nearly identical to the last. Her door was the first on the left. It was just as Serina had said—simple. A bed, a small desk, a washbasin, an empty bookcase.

"Should you need anything, you can ask any of the Larks." Serina paused, stalling before she headed back to the stairs. Her eyes dragged over Vi from top to bottom. She opened her mouth, promptly closed it, and turned.

"Ask." Vi let a slightly regal tone seep into the word, turning it into more of a command. "I know what it looks like when someone has a question."

With a guilty grin on her cherubic cheeks, Serina turned. "They say you kidnapped the Voice."

"So I've heard."

"Yet they tell me you are to be made comfortable while you are here…"

"And?" Vi kept her face passive.

"Those two things seem contradictory."

"They do, don't they?" Her attempts at stoicism failed, and a small grin made it onto her face.

"So are you our enemy, or our friend?"

"What do you believe?"

"I don't know. I don't have all the facts." Serina spoke as though that should be obvious. "That's why I ask... to collect them."

Vi smiled tiredly. Something about the girl reminded her very much of her mother. She couldn't put her finger on what, but it was there. Which was odd, given that she looked so young. The comparison already filled her with a dull ache.

"I'm not allowed to say much," Vi answered honestly. She would honor her deal with Ulvarth only as far as it benefited her. But Serina seemed sharp enough to figure out the undercurrents on her own—she was already seeking to piece together the facts. And while Vi wasn't looking for a friend, she could use an ally. "But I will say this: Taavin is the last person I would ever harm."

Serina seemed startled Vi had used his name so confidently. Eventually saying, "You seem honest enough about that."

"Good."

The woman continued to hover. Her eyes drifted down to Vi's hands. It was then that Vi noticed she was dripping blood onto the floor. The clots of her wounds, left behind by the shackles, must've been washed away in the bath.

"Would you like me to heal that for you?"

"I think not," Vi said, after a long moment's debate.

"It'd be no trouble."

"I know it wouldn't be as I, too, know *halleth*." She wasn't very good at it, but she knew it. Now the Larks also knew that she possessed Lightspinning. "I don't think I want to heal these with magic. I think I'd like the scars from Ulvarth's *hospitality*. It seems a fitting reminder of my time here."

Serina regarded her warily, as if seeing her for the first time. It was the same look Arwin had given Vi when they had stolen Fallor's boat, after Vi had killed a pirate with two words. Now, like then, Vi reached the same conclusion: *Let her be wary.*

Finally, Serina bowed her head, turned, and started for the stairs, not quite hiding her relief at the prospect of making her escape. Which only made Vi more surprised when her door opened again a short time later. Serina popped in just long enough to leave a small roll of bandages on the foot of her bed before leaving again without another word.

Vi debated her next move as she wrapped her wrists in the bandages. The mere mention of Taavin was all the direction she needed. She closed the door and headed back up the spiral stair the way she came, across the lofty bridge high above Risen, and back into the main tower of the archives.

She started up the first ladder she came to, arced around the wide landing that granted access to this stretch of shelves, then up a second stair. Up and up she climbed, higher and higher. It was nearly impossible to keep her attention on her destination among the ocean of books.

Close to the top of all the walkways, Vi was nearly level with the sculpted women holding up the brazier she'd seen from the first moment she'd entered. The light was blindingly bright and the fire that raged behind their arms was white-hot. How could anyone say this flame needed rekindling? If someone were to spark it further, they risked burning down the whole building.

Oddly, no heat reached her cheeks. She didn't feel the slightest bit of warmth from the blaze. Even as someone who first learned to interact with fire as a Firebearer, she still suspected she should feel *something*.

Vi squinted at it, holding her breath. She was waiting for something... but she didn't quite know what. A sign from the Goddess, perhaps? Taavin heard Yargen's voice in the flame; surely as her champion, Vi should hear something, too?

"Magnificent, isn't it?" Vi turned, startled. She grabbed the railing for stability, suddenly off-balance and aware of the dizzying height. Ulvarth had ascended the stairs opposite her, the imposing man slowly walking around the brazier. Vi regarded him warily, still gripping the railing. "I asked you a question."

"I thought it rhetorical, given it's obviously magnificent."

"I didn't bring you here to admire it." His voice went low and dangerous.

"Didn't you though? I am to find a way to reignite the flame, am I not?"

He smirked. "You don't already know how?"

"I couldn't go into it, really… It's something that can only be understood fully by the Champion and the Voice." Vi borrowed the morphi's explanation of their magic. He didn't seem to notice, but for her it felt like a double-edged blade to shove between his ribs. Vi had the satisfaction of one-upping him, and the knowledge that she'd borrowed an explanation from people he unjustly hated.

"I hope you're right, for your sake." Ulvarth gave her a sinister smile. "After all, your father starts his trials at the queen's earliest convenience."

"Let's hope it's a fair trial."

"Oh, I'm sure it will be." Ulvarth finally came to a stop only a few steps away. "You think me a monster." Vi kept her mouth shut and let that be answer enough. "But this is one thing I don't have to be monstrous about. Your father dug his own grave, by digging the world's."

She searched his unflinching gaze. Ulvarth may be a monster. He may be ruthless and calculating and obsessed with his own power. But there was confidence in those blue eyes. Not just arrogance, *confidence*. At least in this instance, he genuinely believed himself right and just.

"So maybe I am a monster. But you're the spawn of a monster. So you're really no different."

"Call me a monster and I'll show you my fangs." Vi sneered widely for emphasis. Ulvarth chuckled.

"A shame you were born a human to such poor parentage. We may have gotten along in another life, you and I."

Vi was certain she'd hate him in any and every lifetime. She hated him from his pointed ears to his mirror-polished boots.

Ulvarth sauntered away as though he owned the whole world. The megalomaniac likely thought he did. Vi tracked him with a piercing stare as he ascended the staircase to the next ring of walkways, then up one more ladder to the highest walkway. She began moving, as quickly and silently as possible, following behind him.

Up the first set of stairs, Vi wound back, looking for a sign of Ulvarth. He had disappeared. She quickly climbed the ladder, not even caring if Ulvarth saw her or accused her of following him. But when she finally ascended… he was nowhere to be seen.

Vi walked all the way around the wide rung of the archives, her fingers trailing along the books. There was nowhere for him to hide. And no door for him to walk through. The only exits were the stairway she'd ascended and the rectangular windows at the top of the bookshelves—allowing the flame's thick smoke an escape. But Vi didn't think Ulvarth had gone through one of those.

Tapping her knuckles against the railing, Vi looked at the pillars that supported the roof above the flame. From all Taavin had said, she suspected this ceiling was also his floor. The pillars between the openings were wide enough to be hollow and fit a man though.

Taavin had said there were many secret passages in the Archives and he'd used *uncose* to find those passages. Vi didn't have the same skill. But she would make up for it with her knowledge of blueprints, architecture, maps, and planning.

V I SCOURED THE BOOKS for an hour. She walked through the archives—up staircases and down ladders—until her legs and arms were tired. But she didn't stop until she located the tall shelves containing the information she sought.

"*The Building of Risen*," Vi mumbled, selecting the book from the shelf. She set it down on a stack she had already collected, then pulled two more. The Larks had said they recorded all knowledge, so surely, somewhere in this vast labyrinth, there was something on the construction of the archives.

She continued flipping, searching, ignoring the growling in her stomach and Larks moving in and out of the Archives. Vi scanned pages on pages of blueprints until she began to find ones that matched the structure she recognized around her. To a layman, the sketched cross-sections would be difficult to line up. But for Vi, the whole building was slowly rebuilt in her mind's eye.

Her focus stayed on the uppermost portions of the buildings, no matter how fascinating the rest of its construction was. The triangular buildings that stretched out from the central spire were a web of bridges and passageways. The foundation of the building was a feat of engineering—brilliant minds had outdone themselves here. There was more than enough substance for her to be engrossed for months.

Vi's attention drifted upward to the flame. She didn't have months; she had days, weeks at best. Tracing the lines in the book with her index finger, Vi could clearly see the layout of the uppermost portions of the archives—much simpler than the rest. Away from the outer buildings and their connecting bridges, it was only the hollow column of the inner archives, and whatever the architects had hidden in the walls.

Sure enough, just as Taavin had said, within the walls behind the bookcases were passages that swirled and crossed over each other.

"Where's an entrance?" Vi murmured. She suspected one of the bookshelves was false—it wouldn't be the first such trick door she'd seen. But she couldn't find any indication of a hidden doorway in the blueprints.

Not wanting to give up on the theory, Vi went up to the landing and paced one, two, three times, running her hands along the bookshelves.

They didn't yield their secrets.

She retreated back to her perch and her books. There was a way to Taavin from up there, but it may not be the only way. As Vi searched for alternate routes, she kept an eye out for Ulvarth—though there was no sign of him. He had been gone for a long time—long enough that suspicion frayed the edges of Vi's concentration. The only good thing about his absence was that she could search in peace.

Closing each of the books, Vi tried to place them exactly as she'd found them on the shelves, giving no indication what she'd been looking for. She returned the way she'd came.

Vi stopped at the entrance to the walkway that soared atop a giant archway to the Lark's halls. There was no one in sight—hadn't been for hours. Still, she waited for Ulvarth, waited for someone to show up. She waited long enough that the sun began to dip, changing the light that streamed through the glass ceiling of the walkway from gold to a deep amber.

"Very well then." Vi lifted a hand, Taavin's voice echoing in her mind. "*Uncose.*"

Nothing. No magic sparked. No glyph came to life underneath her fingertips. It was just as Taavin suspected, though Vi didn't regret trying. With the merest flash of disappointment, she proceeded with the manual route.

Rapping her fingers along the side of the bookcase that met with the stone of the outer wall of the Archives, Vi listened closely. Her first couple taps sounded dull, with little reverberations. The fifth rang hollow.

Vi looked up the wide panel of wood. At about chest height, there was a thin line in its surface—one she'd overlooked at first—and another a short distance away. Vi pushed in a few different places before the panel popped loose and swung open. She hoisted herself into the narrow tunnel, closing the door behind her with a fraying leather strap on the inside.

It had been some time since anyone had come this way, if the cobwebs and bug carcasses were any indication.

Vi trudged on, determined, until the tunnel opened up into a proper secret passage. Working to rebuild the Archives in her mind as she walked, Vi wound upward once more from the inside. She kept a low flame over her shoulder, just enough to see by, though she extinguished it the moment she heard voices.

"You will tell me its secrets, and hers," Ulvarth rasped, as though struggling to keep his voice quiet. Vi crouched low in the darkness, closing her eyes and trying to imagine how high up she was.

Second walkway from the top? Maybe?

"Don't think I will let you see her unsupervised," he snarled. Taavin, for his part, remained worryingly silent. "You will not make a fool of me again. You are mine."

A door slammed so hard that Vi could almost feel the stones of the archives rattling. There was the sound of metal sliding against metal, followed by heavy footsteps. She held her breath, creeping on hands and knees upward—just a little farther.

A glow stone cast eerie light on the inner wall. She stopped, flattening herself on the ground. Ulvarth stomped across the narrow hall, oblivious to her presence. Vi couldn't see what he was doing, but she could hear him fumbling with something, footsteps on the other side of her, and… silence.

Vi kept a hand over her mouth, trying not to breathe. Her fingers trembled. Not from fear, but from loathing she didn't know if she had ever felt so strongly before. She pushed herself off the ground and continued upward to a four-way intersection. Directly ahead, the passage sloped down into the darkness. At her left was a ladder and at her right, a short ramp up to a flat wooden surface.

That was when it hit her.

Each of the landings in the Archives was in the shape of a right triangle, jutting out into the hollow center. The walkway was flat and formed a right angle with the wall, but the hypotenuse sloped down and away. Initially, Vi had thought it merely an aesthetic choice. Now, she realized otherwise.

The passage to Taavin wasn't in the bookcases. It was in the floor. Casters invisible to the naked eye slid a trap door underneath the bookcases she'd been looping around, looking for one such secret passage when it had been right under her nose the whole time.

Cursing herself, Vi turned away from the ramp and toward the final option at the intersection—a ladder upward.

The passage narrowed slightly as she climbed, and Vi imagined herself in one of the columns above the bookcases—fire from the Flame of Yargen billowing out on either side. Farther on, a faint ambient light glowed.

Stepping off the ladder and onto a small landing, Vi found the source of the light—or at least, the heavy door around which wisps of light managed to escape past the heavy latch and lock tightly on the outside. Sandalwood incense curled through the door jamb.

Vi swallowed, working to get rid of the lump trying to form in her throat.

"Taavin," she whispered. Nothing. The panic from Ulvarth's departure returned in full force. "Taavin?" A little louder.

"Who…" his voice was muffled. But she heard footsteps nearing the door.

"Taavin?"

"Vi, is that you?"

"Yes."

"How did you—"

"Given everything that's happened, I think me figuring out how to get to you should be the least surprising thing," Vi teased lightly. "There's a lock on the door. How do I get in?"

"The lock is new. I think only Ulvarth keeps the key. He says he'll only let me out at specific times to collect whatever research I need." Her blood instantly boiled at the words. She had grown up in a beautiful prison as well… but never one with locks on the doors.

"If I break the lock, he'll know." It was still tempting to do it, just to mess with him. But Vi suspected Taavin would be blamed—and punished. She ran her fingers over the rung the heavy padlock was slipped through. Such a delicate-looking piece of iron for a door that was bolted so tightly. "But I have an idea."

"There's no way to fix the lock with Lightspinning," Taavin cautioned hastily, needlessly.

"I know. I'm not breaking the lock, and Ulvarth doesn't need to know."

Vi pushed the spark into her fingertips, rubbing the rung again and again. The iron heated slowly. She wanted it hot enough to be malleable, but not so hot it dripped off the door. She'd have to fix it before she left, after all.

Her left hand held the lock in place as her right worked. Vi dug her nail into the soft metal, pulling back and separating it. She widened it just enough that the padlock could slide out. Vi set it on the floor carefully, giving the metal time to cool before she undid the latch and opened the door to the face of a very shocked Taavin.

"That's the problem with metal locks." Vi gave a small smile. "They're not really the best at keeping Firebearers out."

He stuck his head through the open door. His eyes fell to the still locked padlock on the ground. Vi tapped the rung attached to the door that she modified.

"You heated the rung." He went to rest his hand on the now separated metal. Vi stopped him with a touch.

"It may still be hot."

"Fire truly doesn't burn you."

"No, and thank the Goddess for that holdover from my Firebearer training." Vi looked to her hand, opening and closing her palm for a moment before shifting her attention to him. His eyes were worried and sunken, face pale. He looked more harrowed being around Ulvarth for a few days then he had on the run or while dying in a cave. "May I come in?"

"What?" Taavin's attention was jolted from the door. "Oh, yes, of course."

He stepped to the side and Vi entered, though Taavin's eyes remained on the door and the dark ladder that stretched away from his quarters. Vi caught the longing look from the corners of her eyes. It was the look of a man presented with the notion of false freedom. They both knew if Taavin left, Ulvarth would find him—and the consequences would fall on both their heads. Besides, all the answers they needed were here, anyway.

He'd described his room once to her and Vi had worked to imagine it in her mind's eye. She'd been right about a few things, wrong about others.

The whole room was in the shape of an octagon—that much she'd managed to get right. The walls were, indeed, painted in soft grays and whites, but mostly white. The gray was a delicate embellishment in tiny patterns of birds, swords, and suns across the room. It was such a subtle contrast that in certain light, it disappeared completely.

A single shelf on the wall to the left of the door held a handful of texts. The bookend on one side was a bunch of inkwells. On the other, screws and scraps of metal rested, little cogs shining in the low light. He'd mentioned his hobby of watchmaking and Vi had entirely forgotten. They'd been forced to leave behind so much of their peacetime lives since starting this journey. Vi thought back to the hobbies she'd had, the things she'd enjoyed—things she may never be able to do again.

Other than the shelf, there was a single chair and ottoman, facing a lonely window on the wall opposite the door, one other window to the right.

"This is where you live," Vi murmured. It was obvious, but she had to say it aloud. It didn't seem real. It couldn't be.

"My whole life."

Everything was immaculately clean but worn with age. She tried to imagine a young Taavin, running laps around the chair to dispel the energy that graces all children—even children chosen by Yargen. She imagined a young man standing at the windows, looking out at the world beyond and wondering if he should scream for help. She imagined the man he was now, cultivated in his captivity, seeking solace in the tomes beneath him.

Turning back to face him, Vi found he was suddenly blurry. She blinked rapidly, trying to draw him into focus once more. She could imagine the man before her now sitting in his lonely chair, waiting for the "daydreams" that tortured him to pass.

"Don't look at me with those sad eyes," he said softly, crossing over to her. Taavin collected both of her hands in his, bringing them to his mouth and kissing her knuckles.

"I can see you," she whispered, her voice steady. "I can see you here... alone."

"I was never truly alone." His voice was low and warm on her skin. "I had you."

Vi laughed bitterly. "My face was torture."

"Until seeing you became my light."

Her fingers curled tighter around his and Vi guided him toward her. Moments like this, moments of quiet, were so rare that they were more precious than any token or object she'd ever held.

She reached upward, fingertips smoothing along his jaw. Tilting her head, Vi guided his mouth to hers. Taavin's eyes dipped closed slowly, as if he wanted to see her there until the last possible second.

A soft sigh escaped her at the blissful moment of warmth and rest. Their kisses had yet to solve anything for her, but they made the days so much easier to bear.

As gently and slowly as his lips had met hers, Taavin pulled away. Vi looked at him through heavy lids.

"Would you like me to heal these?" Taavin ran his fingertips over the bandages around her wrists.

"They're fine," Vi said, shaking her head. What she'd said to Serina about the wounds still stood.

Taavin didn't insist further. He must've seen the blood dripping from the shackles in Ulvarth's throne room. So perhaps he had some idea of why she was allowing those marks to remain on her flesh.

"I want to show you something." Keeping her hand in his, Taavin stepped away, guiding her toward the set of doors next to where Vi had entered from. He pulled them open to reveal a small, dark room.

There was nothing inside. No gilded statues. No signs or sigils.

On a single pedestal in the center of the room stood a plain marble candlestick holder with a flame flickering at the top. There was no wick for oil or candle wax. The flame burned impossibly, hovering just above the candlestick.

"This is it, isn't it? The real flame."

"Yes, this is the legendary Flame of Yargen," Taavin affirmed. "Or what's left of it."

Vi took a step forward, her eyes never leaving the small flame or the dull ash collected around its base. "What about the brazier in the Archives?"

"The flame used to burn that brightly, barely controlled. Now, it's nothing more than an illusion maintained by a few High Larks sworn to secrecy."

That explained the lack of heat, and Ulvarth's delight—she hadn't immediately identified the false flame.

"Why has it dimmed?"

"I suspect because of the destruction of the other parts of Yargen's power. The Crystal Caverns, the crystal weapons... they're all connected."

"We're all connected."

"What did you say?" Taavin took a small step forward into the room.

"We're all connected." She clutched her watch, thinking back to her father's words. Members of the Solaris family had been wrapped up with the crystals for generations, likely going further back than she understood. "Fate is a road that is made, laid by the generations before us."

"Vi—"

"And us," she turned to face him, clutching her watch. It felt hot under her palm in a way not even burning through iron had felt. "We're connected too, drawn together by her power. It lives in you, and in me, as it did in the crystal weapons and the caverns, and does still in the scythe."

Vi's hands went to the nape of her neck, slowly unfastening the watch. It was the first time it had left her neck in months, and she felt naked without it, bare before the Goddess. Taavin did nothing to stop her as Vi slowly turned toward the flame, compelled by an invisible force.

"I did what you asked. I've brought this to you." Beseeching the Goddess had just as much chance of working as her trying *uncose*. But she hadn't come all this way not to try. "Tell us, what do we do now?"

She slowly lifted the watch, and as soon as it drew level with the flame, the world was overcome with white.

Wind rushed around her, soundless. Even though it should whip her hair and tug at the robes she wore, Vi remained perfectly still. Untouched.

The world was completely dark, only the immediate radius visible to her. Underneath her feet was a barren landscape of pale gray ash, piled thick. Whatever fire had raged here had burned so hot that not even the stumps of trees or foundations of buildings had survived.

Cloying heat sank into her, trying to smother her, despite her detachment from the dead world before her.

She began to walk.

It was impossible to tell her direction, or what she was walking toward. But it was equally impossible for her to stomach the idea of standing still. If she stood still, *it* would get to her, something within Vi nagged. But she had no idea what *it* was.

Vi came to a stop.

A shard of obsidian jutted out from the ash—a dormant crystal. There was another not too far away, and another closer to the second. Vi followed the trail to a scattering of obsidian fragments. Her gaze landed on a hand, clutched around a large shard, even in death.

The woman was mostly covered by the thick ash, but one all-white eye still stared lifelessly at the world. Even with a sunken face, collapsed with rot, even mostly covered in ash, Vi recognized her own corpse.

Her pulse returned to her first as the vision faded. It beat like a war drum in her ears. No... it wasn't. It was a word.

Thrumsana. Thrumsana. Thrumsana, the soft voice repeated. It was strong, yet pleading—whispering, yet loud.

When Vi opened her eyes once more to the real world, light surrounded her, like flames condensed into glyphs she couldn't recognize. They spun against symbols wrought in a faint blue magic she recognized as Taavin's.

"Taavin," Vi groaned. The man lay across from her, his body twitching slightly. "Taavin." Vi pushed herself up, the magic fading. "Taavin," she shook him slowly. Her whole body felt leaden, her mind exhausted. Her magic spent. Yet she still found energy enough to worry over him. "Please, Taavin."

The minor convulsions stopped, and with them Vi's panic abated, though it didn't fully retreat until his eyes blinked open.

"Taavin, I think I... I..."

"I heard the Goddess," they both said at once.

"YOU... YOU HEARD YARGEN?" Taavin pushed himself up slowly. He seemed to be in as much pain as her.

"I think so. She said a word, one word, over and over, she said—"

He pressed a finger against her lips. "Don't say it out loud... not until it sits in your mind and unravels. Think of her words like an egg: you must incubate it before it hatches understanding."

"But—"

"What if it is a word to summon Raspian so that you may face him? Or level a city?"

Vi ran a hand through her hair, shaking her head. He was right, she didn't know what it was for and until she did, caution was the best path forward. "I came to Risen for answers... but I only have more questions."

"But we are getting answers." Taavin leaned forward, bending his knees and locking them against the inside of his elbows. "There are layers and layers of magic here—magic the likes of which I've only ever seen in one place before."

"Here?" Vi motioned around them.

"Here." He reached out, tapping the watch that had fallen to the floor between them. "I was right to make sure we came back to Risen. We need the watch and that scythe to reignite the flame. It's just as the traveler foretold."

Vi ignored the mention of the infamous traveler. "You were right to make sure we came back to Risen," she repeated. "Taavin... what did you do?"

He looked at her with those worried eyes. Vi slowly shook her head. She'd asked the question and now, suddenly, would do anything to not hear the answer.

He betrayed you, Arwin had said.

He betrayed you, and Vi hadn't believed it.

"No," she whispered. Vi placed a hand between them, leaning forward. "Taavin, what did you do?" He turned away. "Answer me," she pleaded softly. "Taavin, please tell me I'm jumping to conclusions."

Still, silence.

"Tell me you didn't contact the Swords." Adela had used communication tokens. Why wouldn't the Swords, or Ulvarth himself? Why would she assume Taavin hadn't been carrying one with him the whole time? Her eyes fell to his bare wrist; the bracelet she'd seen him wear through their whole journey was gone. "Tell me—"

"You wanted to go to Norin… and there was no time…" He had the decency to sound ashamed.

Vi pulled away. Her whole body had gone from acutely pained to completely numb. The word Yargen had told her vanished from her ears, replaced by ringing.

"You… You carried a token to contact Ulvarth on your wrist." Taavin wouldn't even look at her as she spoke. "Tell me, yes or no?"

He gave a small nod. Vi shifted onto her knees.

"You were contacting him the whole time, telling him where we were. You didn't escape. He let you leave. He let you leave to get me. This was all one big game crafted by both of you." Vi's voice rose, cracking like her heart.

"No. I only contacted Ulvarth at the end. I tried not to the entire time—not even when I was near death in that cave. I only contacted him then because I knew he would be tracking us and there was no way we would make it to Norin. He'd stop us first. And this way I could try to salvage—" Taavin grabbed her hand.

"Don't touch me," she seethed. He slowly released his grasp. "Don't you dare touch me."

"Vi—"

She stared at him and slowly shook her head. It didn't matter what he said or claimed. Whatever they were—whatever they'd shared—was breaking right before her eyes.

"Listen, please," he pleaded. "The days are becoming shorter, the nights longer. Raspian's power only grows. The end of the world is near and *we are not ready*. We couldn't afford a delay—if we even made it to Norin."

Vi stood, turning her back to him. Still he spoke. She heard his boots sliding against the wooden floor as he stood as well, relentless.

"I knew if we came back, we would figure out the way to end this—the way to save us all. Your father, your mother. Then you would be reunited with your family not in the final hours, but for a lifetime together.

"I wanted to give you everything you desired, but this was the only way."

Vi stared out at his small room—the lonely chair, the window to the world. The pity she'd felt was crumbling. It started a landslide that slipped underneath the dark waves she'd carried since her time aboard the *Stormfrost*.

"You don't know it was the only way."

"I knew delays wouldn't help."

"You couldn't know." She slowly turned, lacing and unlacing her fingers to try to keep the spark from springing forth and burning him alive. "Because you do not see the future. That is *my* destiny."

"And you have." He stared, unflinching in the face of her seething rage. "You have seen the future and it is one of failure. We must remove ourselves from this line of fate that leads only to our end."

"Well, you have brought me here." Her voice was quiet and quivering as Vi fought the urge to shout. "And the world is still headed toward its end."

"What?" he breathed.

"I saw it here, now. The scythe still breaks. I still die. Raspian still wins."

Taavin stared at her, dumbstruck. Vi watched him crumble under her unrelenting gaze. She looked down on him like the traitor he was, and he couldn't stand under the weight of her judgment. Vi took a small step forward and he stepped back so hastily that he gripped the wall to prevent himself from tripping over his own feet.

"The only thing you changed is that now I will have to watch my father die at Ulvarth's hand before I die fighting Raspian."

"We can still figure it out," he said weakly, less confident than she'd ever heard him. "We can still—"

"We? That's the other thing you changed, Taavin." Her voice cracked. Damn it all. It cracked. "There is no 'we,' not anymore."

"Vi…" His tone was pleading, begging. So much said in the single syllable. Yet her heart ignored it.

She was the fire of her forefathers. She was the bitter ice that had hardened her. She was the frozen flames of the Goddess herself embodied in crystal: hard, unmoving, unfeeling.

"Count your blessings," Vi whispered. "The last time someone betrayed me and my family, I killed her. But I guess I really did love you, Taavin. Because here you stand, and here you'll stay."

Vi started for the door. He didn't move to stop her. She briefly considered leaving the lock broken and letting Ulvarth's wrath befall Taavin—but if she sought revenge, now or ever, it would be by her own hand. Just as it had been with Jayme. Just as Arwin had shown her with Fallor.

So Vi returned the lock, sealing Taavin away once more, and vanished into the darkness of the secret passages of the Archives. She walked down the way she'd come, heart thundering in her chest, eyes blurry with anger.

She made it all the way back to the secret entrance, crouching to crawl through the passage. But Vi couldn't bring herself to move another step. She sat down heavily, leaning against the wall, knees at her chest in the narrow space.

In the darkness, the crown princess felt herself burning alive, from her heart outward. But she didn't cry. She didn't call for help.

She let the fires within burn.

Until there was nothing left but ash.

She was alone now.

Without Taavin, there was no one on Meru she could depend on beyond her father. But he was locked away somewhere Vi couldn't find and likely couldn't get to even if she could find it. So rather than wasting the effort, she focused on research. She focused on the one thing Taavin had been right about: the only path forward involved finding a way to prevent the world's end. And sulking wouldn't accomplish that.

Vi sat perched on a high rung of the Archives. From her vantage point, she observed the Larks coming and going. Much like their namesake, they flitted in and out, carefully selecting tomes to bring back into their chambers to study. She wondered how many recorded new histories, how many studied the old in order to provide counsel, and how many merely maintained the massive library.

After watching them for an hour, she stood and began nonchalantly following behind one man, then the next, lingering at the shelves long after they'd left. Vi watched as books were taken and returned. *What had them so busy?*

"*The Kingdom of Solaris,*" she murmured, reading the title of the most recently replaced book. Vi plucked it from the shelf and opened to the first page, where a large family tree spilled over onto the next four pages.

It was strange to see her father's name there among the rest and, in a fresh ink, her own. The book was on the lineage of the Solaris kings, and later, its emperors. The conqueror who had brought the continent to heel was none other than her grandfather, Tiberus.

Vi replaced the book and moved on to the next.

The War of Light. Lord Noct had mentioned the last great war in relation to Yargen and the Dark Isle. Vi flipped to the first chapter, scanning the text:

In the fifteenth century following the end of the last Dark Era, Lord Raspian escaped his previous imprisonment in the heavenly body, the prison of night's light.

The book was factual and dry, but the subject matter was so vibrant, so fantastical, that Vi read it more like a story book than a historical text.

A horn startled Vi from her reading. Her head jolted upward, looking on instinct to the open windows above the fake flame where the sound echoed from. It was a sweet melody that rang throughout Risen, bells accompanying the trill of the horns. She could've sworn she heard drums in the mix.

The sound drew nearer and Vi closed the book to listen. The music increased in fervor. It was bright and full of life—the sort of thing she'd associate with a celebration of some kind. All at once, it stopped.

The large doors to the Archives opened with a mighty groan and Vi sprinted around to get a better look, dashing down a set of stairs. She positioned herself opposite the doors peering at the group waiting to enter.

A company of knights were revealed to be on the other side of the door. But these were not Ulvarth's Swords of Light. They wore silver armor and had bright red plumage extending from their caps. Without any further invitation, they marched in slowly.

Behind the first line of knights was a row of men and women, dressed in heavy layers of embroidered finery. The only similarity among them were the silver pins they wore on their left breasts—each in a different shape. Behind this row of people came a single woman.

Vi couldn't actually see her face. In fact, the woman wore so many layers of fabric that she couldn't tell it was a woman at all from the shape of the body. But Vi knew it was a woman, because atop the long veil that covered her from head to toe was an ornate, silver crown.

Lumeria, the Queen of Meru, had come to the Archives.

She leaned over the railing slightly, watching as the queen passed underneath. They went through a door opposite the entry, toward one of the pointed buildings Vi had yet to explore. Two more groups of knights took up the final rows, and Vi waited until they'd passed under her to step back and sit against the bookshelves.

Ulvarth had said her father's trial would begin at the queen's convenience. If the queen was here, that meant his trial was beginning. Vi ran a hand through her hair; the sensation of it, free of braids, was odd, but she didn't have the energy to coif it.

She should keep reading, keep searching for ways out of the mess they were all in.

But she couldn't.

She was so lost in thought that she didn't hear the footsteps of someone approaching. Two unfamiliar booted feet appeared next to her and Vi followed them up to a silver-armored woman. She had bright blue eyes, ringed in purple. Eyes that stared at her for so long, Vi began to feel uncomfortable.

"Vi Solaris?" the knight asked, after that seemed like forever.

"Yes?"

"Your presence has been requested."

"By who?" Vi slowly tilted her head away from the bookcases, though she already suspected she knew.

"The queen." The knight took a step away. "If you'll please follow me."

Book in hand—because Vi wasn't about to risk a Lark taking it off the shelf again—Vi trailed behind the knight to ground floor. They walked through the same door the queen and her retinue had disappeared into, and across a tunneled walkway. The windows were laden with fragments of heavily tinted glass that distorted the world beyond.

From time to time, the knight glanced over her shoulder. Vi caught her odd looks. It wasn't suspicion, and Vi didn't get the sense the woman viewed her as a threat.

"Is something the matter?" she finally asked as the hallway split in two, absentmindedly scratching at the bandages around her wrists.

The knight paused, allowing Vi to catch up. They stood side by side before a staircase leading upward. "You look just like someone I once knew." Her voice was filled with a longing that made Vi inexplicably sad. "A good friend that I lost."

"I'm sorry," Vi murmured. The knight shook her head, refusing Vi's sympathies.

"Perhaps we will meet again someday, in a different place and time." It was an optimistic world view—one Vi couldn't share after seeing the end of the world. "I'm Deneya." She raised a hand to the center of her forehead, pushing aside the dark brown, almost black fringe there to touch her skin before lowering it.

Vi did her best to replicate the greeting. "A pleasure to meet you."

Deneya led her up the stairway and to a small landing. Another knight in identical armor was positioned by a door. He gave Deneya salute and opened the door.

"Please, come in." A voice summoned them.

The long room was dominated by large windows that ran the length of both walls. Vi was distracted by the inner wall that overlooked a courtyard. She knew she should be bowing before the woman at the far end of the room, sitting poised in her endless folds of fabric on the edge of a plush chair. But for a moment, all of her regal training was forgotten.

"I know this place," she whispered, horrified.

The last time she'd seen it, she'd been nothing more than a specter. She'd seen the carved gutters and tiled rooftops. She'd seen the covered stage where the queen would sit and before which her father would kneel. But that time, the square had been full. And now it was unnervingly empty.

She'd seen this moment long ago in a cave in the North.

"Do you?" The queen's voice sounded nothing like Vi would expect. For all the flowing silks and chiffons she wore, the woman's voice was low and sharp, every word enunciated in the thick accent Vi had come to associate with all of Meru.

"I saw it in a vision once," Vi explained. Secrecy wouldn't serve her now. Vi pulled herself from the window, crossing to the small sitting area where the queen waited. She dropped to one knee. "Forgive me for forgetting myself before you, your highness."

"I thought the Solaris family saw themselves as rulers of the world entire. Is it common for you to kneel before other nobility?"

"I've found 'the world' a bit generous to describe our borders." Vi lifted her gaze with a small smile. "And you are not even the first ruler I have knelt before since coming to Meru." The one downside to all the fabrics covering the queen was that Vi could not read the woman's facial expressions. She was left to judge her reactions from voice alone, and the length of pause she took to collect her thoughts.

"Please sit." Lumeria slowly raised a jeweled hand. Vi would move slowly if she was forced to wear that much silver on her fingers.

Vi stood, sitting on the stool across from the queen's chair. She very much felt like a child at her mother's knee.

"I have summoned you because I would like a word with you before your father's trial begins."

"How may I be of service?" Vi asked cautiously.

"Merely speak with me. I ask nothing more of you." Vi gave a tentative nod. She knew just speaking could be dangerous enough, especially when her father was about to stand trial before this woman. "Do you know what is happening with your father? Have they told you?"

"I believe the Faithful think he had some role in harming our world," Vi answered delicately. She didn't know how much Lumeria knew about the impending doom that awaited them all—or if keeping it a secret from the queen would be beneficial in some way. Proceeding with caution seemed the only choice.

"They believe he set free Raspian from the god's tomb on the Dark Isle." Lumeria paused for a brief moment. "This doesn't surprise you? I didn't think the War of Light was compulsory education on the Dark Isle."

"It's not. But I have had ample time to research and learn over the past year." Vi looked to the window. Everything seemed too bright, too harsh. "My father is not guilty—not to the letter of the accusations. The man who truly destroyed the Crystal Caverns and tried to harness their power was the Mad King Victor, and he is dead."

"Do you think Ulvarth will care?" She could almost imagine Lumeria's eyebrows rising underneath her veil.

"Hardly. He cares for little beyond himself. I think his sham of a holy crusade to undermine your power and work to put the real control of Meru in his own hands through brutal tactics is enough proof of that." It would be plain speaking between them, then. *How refreshing.*

"Tell me why he has yet to put you on trial."

"Because I am the Champion reborn," Vi answered honestly, deciding her best chance was to ingratiate herself to the queen. She had just lost one powerful ally on Meru; she could use another. "So I can help rekindle the flame."

"I have always known Ulvarth to be greedy, but not stupid," Lumeria murmured. Then, louder, "Can you rekindle it? Can you bring Yargen back to us and collect her scattered power from your lands?"

"Scattered power from my lands?" Vi repeated. She suspected she understood—she had heard about Yargen's fractured power—but sought clarity nonetheless.

"To seal Raspian away, Yargen split herself—one part into the staff she gave the last Champion, one part to the seal Raspian's tomb, and one part to the flame."

"As you know, the tomb is gone," Vi said.

"The staff, then. There are records it was split and—"

"Transformed into a crown, an axe, a sword, and a scythe," Vi finished. "Yes... But all that remains is the scythe."

Lumeria was silent for a long time. She folded her hands in her lap and Vi heard a soft sigh. Underneath the fabrics of her veil, the queen hunched slightly.

"Then it may already be too late."

"I have the scythe in my possession," Vi said quickly. "Well, Ulvarth has it. But it is here."

"I will pray for that to be enough," Lumeria said wistfully. "But a fragment of a fragment of the Goddess's power does not seem like it would be sufficient to stand against a god."

And Vi had the visions to prove it wasn't.

"Deneya, you may escort the princess back to the Archives now. Thank you for speaking with me, Vi Solaris."

Vi stood at the dismissal. Deneya guided her back through the door and down the stairs. They crossed the walkway in silence, the knight pausing at the entrance to the archives, hovering like the clearly unspoken words.

"Vi," she said delicately. "You have a path more difficult than any can comprehend. The only one who can truly understand it is the Voice."

She bit back protest that Taavin was clearly the last person in the world who understood her. If he did, he would've never put her and her father at risk.

"But should you ever need me, no matter the time or place, seek me out. My sword is yours."

"Thank you," Vi said, trying to hide her discomfort. She didn't trust the woman's eagerness. Perhaps Lumeria had put her up to the task.

Or perhaps she was another trying to get close to her for their own gain.

"Good luck, Champion."

Deneya gave a small bow, returning back the way she came.

Vi watched her leave before wandering back into the Archives. She returned the book she'd started reading on the last War of Light to its place on the shelf. Her mind was too full to try to process the knowledge within.

A fraction of a fraction of the goddess's power wouldn't be enough to stand up against Raspian.

It made sense and gave credence to her visions of Raspian shattering the scythe and striking her down. But all the other crystal weapons had been destroyed. Her father had told her that much.

Vi clutched the watch around her neck and for the first time wondered if, perhaps, the future of their world couldn't be saved.

If there was only one path forward—into the eternal darkness of death.

THE LIGHT STREAMING THROUGH the window of her room dimmed to night as Vi paced. It seemed like now the days were more darkness than anything else. The moon dominated the sky almost perpetually and daylight was only a couple hours.

Finally her feet came to a stop and Vi let out a groan of frustration. She knew what she needed to do. But it was the last thing she wanted to do.

Ulvarth would be at the trial, which meant he was tied up for at least a few hours. This was the perfect time for her and Taavin to work, though he was the last person she wanted to see.

She was up the stairs of the archives despite heavy feet, through the trap door she'd discovered during her last excursion, up the ladder, and worrying away the ring holding the lock on his door without so much as knocking. Vi allowed the padlock to clang as she set it aside, the only warning before she opened the door.

Taavin stood at the opposite window in all his heartbreaking beauty. He didn't so much as look at who entered.

Vi hovered in the doorway, trapped in the snare of wanting to scream at him and, at the same time, flee. Freeing herself from the hold of fear, she crossed the small room to the man. His eyes—distant, *different*—drifted to her. They felt like the eyes of a stranger.

Things had been damaged between them and they both knew it. Vi held his gaze for a long moment.

"Listen." She knew she had to be the one to get the first word in. "I am not here for you. We still have a duty."

There was the little matter of the end of the world, and Vi would let him assume that was all she referred to. In truth, her treacherous heart still bled from the wounds he'd inflicted that her past experiences had only made worse. She still felt for him. She wanted to be ambivalent, but her emotions had yet to catch up to her mind's stoicism.

A small part of her still loved him. And that terrified Vi more than anything.

"That's putting it mildly," Taavin said dully, leaning against the wall behind him.

"I met with Queen Lumeria." Vi stepped away, pacing. She noticed the scythe leaning against the doorway to the flame. Good, they wouldn't have to go hunting for it.

"Did you?" He looked back to the window, as if the sight of her was too painful.

"I think I know what we need to do." Her voice was little more than a whisper, though Vi didn't know why. "I think the watch holds Yargen's power. We need to use it and the flame to give more power to the scythe. When Yargen fractured her power, giving the staff to the Champion, he later fractured it further. It is only a part of her power, and it's too weak to stand against Raspian on its own."

Vi turned away from the scythe to find him staring at her. "It's not a terrible theory."

"I'm glad it makes the high mark of 'not terrible,'" Vi muttered dryly. "It's far better reasoning than the logic you used before betraying me," she mumbled under her breath.

"Vi, I—"

"Don't." She glared at him, equally angry now at herself for her own pettiness. "I won't bring it up again and you shouldn't either. We have to focus now… we can deal with all that later." Of course, there might not be a later, which suited her well enough. She worked to get them back on track, trying to keep her venom in check. "I think the word the Goddess gave me was for the watch."

"You *think*, or you know?" Taavin took a step forward.

"I know," she lied. She didn't have time enough to sit on this particular egg, waiting patiently for it to hatch. All she knew for sure was that merely thinking of using the word filled her with confidence. She was right; she had to be. Vi lifted the scythe and opened the door to the flame. "Come and hold this with me."

"Why me?"

"Because you're the Voice. You also have a part of her magic in you, don't you?" Taavin gave a small nod. "Surely that's important. We're trying to collect as much of the Goddess's power as possible."

Taavin crossed over, grabbing the scythe around her hands. Vi kept him at arm's length, but he still felt too close. She wasn't strong enough around him yet—her mental defenses hadn't been sufficiently fortified. Because her heart still wanted to love him—her mouth still ached to kiss him.

"Are you sure about this?" he asked softly, nervously.

"Yes," she insisted. But his worried look got the better of her. "Why?"

"I have this weird feeling… as though I'm in two places at once."

"What?" Vi remembered the same sensation the first time she'd seen the scythe in the Twilight Kingdom. "I've felt something like that around the scythe before."

"Right. Perhaps it's normal then." He looked up at her, the soft blue glow of the crystal illuminating his face. "Whenever you're ready."

Vi took a deep breath, then a second, a third. Her nerves rose alongside the pounding of her heart with each stabilizing breath. She let her mind go blank, staring into the swirling magic of the scythe, allowing herself to feel the heat of the flame of Yargen.

"*Thrumsana.*"

Glyphs appeared from the watch on her chest. Layers on layers of them—just as Taavin had said. They swirled around them, filling the room with symbols Vi didn't understand.

The voices she'd heard at the tears—whispers, cries, screams, songs, and shouts— filled her ears once more. The cacophony was softer than she remembered, sharper, but overwhelming to her senses as it seemed to flow through her.

Taavin let out a scream.

He fell, and Vi dropped the scythe alongside him in shock. He writhed on the ground, clutching his head. Vi stared on, helpless, as veins bulged at his neck and temples.

"Make it stop," he begged. "Make it stop!" he screamed loud enough that Vi was certain someone had to have heard.

"Taavin, Taavin!" His thrashes were too violent, not even allowing her to get near. "*Th-Thrumasana!*" Vi tried again, trying to imagine the glyphs going away.

They did not.

The magic began to shine brighter. The noise filled her ears. Taavin's mouth was locked in a soundless scream and Vi watched in horror as his whole body tensed and arched off the floor. The glyphs condensed on him like ropes, sinking into his flesh. He shuddered with each one that collapsed in on him.

Taavin gasped for air; tears streamed down his face, his eyes wide and unseeing as the assault continued. Vi covered her mouth, collapsing to her knees beside him. He may have betrayed her... but she had not wished this on him, had she? Had *thrumsana* somehow done this? Had the word somehow known the dark corners of her heart?

"Taavin..." Vi said his name weakly, helpless as more glyphs poured from her watch into him. She did everything she could to bring the magic within her once more, but the powers had a mind of their own and Vi was helpless.

He curled into the fetal position, crying out with each circle of light that crashed against him. His eyes were unfocused, his mouth hanging open, fingers contorted at odd angles with pain, his whole body quivering. All she had ever been to him was pain... and now she may well kill him.

Vi unhooked the watch from her neck and thrust it toward the flame. "Take it!" she cried. "Yargen, make it stop!"

The watch shattered. Light tinged with blue filled the room—but this was not a vision of the future overtaking her. It was Yargen's pure magic. And rather than seeking out the scythe as she had hoped it would, it all flowed into Taavin.

One final scream, and it was over.

He lay on the ground, limp and lifeless. Tendrils of magic swirled off of him, fading into the darkness. Soon there was nothing—no sound, no movement.

"T... Taavin?" Vi whispered, crawling on her hands and knees to him. Her eyes were still adjusting to the dim light of the flame. "Taavin." Vi rested a hand on his shoulder and he flinched.

At least he was alive.

"Taavin, I—"

"Get out," he rasped.

"But you—"

"Don't touch me," Taavin seethed. "Don't touch me ever again. Not in this lifetime or the next."

"I didn't mean for..." What hadn't she meant for? This to happen? Hadn't she loathed him for betraying her not hours before?

Nothing between her heart and mind made sense right now.

"I said out!" Taavin roared, sitting at once. The irises of his eyes were a green so bright and pale, it nearly matched the whites surrounding them.

Vi bounced to her feet and ran.

She sat alone in the darkness on the edge of her bed, clutching herself.

What had happened? What was that?

Questions swirled through her mind. Answers eluded her. Even after using the word, its meaning was no clearer to her. It felt as though a part was somehow missing. Perhaps that was why it had gone so awry. Perhaps a meaning was hidden in those seemingly endless glyphs.

Vi rested her elbows on her knees and sank her face into her hands. The watch was gone. One more token of Yargen had been destroyed and Vi doubted the flame seeming dimmer after was only in her imagination.

Slowly, she turned, looking out the window at the dark city. Maybe this would be the day the sun stopped rising altogether. The end of the world seemed more inevitable by the hour.

The door opened suddenly and Vi's eyes with it. She turned to face the man in the doorway slowly. Taavin stood, staring at her with a fire in his eyes she'd never seen before.

"We have to move," he said. "Now."

"Move? Where? Are you—"

"There's no time." Taavin's expression darkened. "The trial ended and your father will be put to death tomorrow."

It was her worst nightmare come to life. This was the reason she hadn't wanted to come here.

"If we hadn't—"

"Spare me." Taavin glowered at her. After the events earlier, it now seemed the rift between them spread both ways. "It doesn't matter I brought him here—none of this matters. I know now how to rekindle the flame and stand against Raspian."

"What do we have to do?" Vi asked softly. No matter the tension between them, it seemed they could still work toward this singular, common good. Perhaps when the world was saved, they could solve the rest—if things didn't become too broken between them along the way.

"Follow me."

Vi did, into the hallway and up the spiral stair that led to the walkway to the archives. As they crossed, Vi could hear noise and commotion growing. They were making preparations to kill her father. Vi didn't have to walk up to the railing and look down to confirm it. She felt the dark truth in the air itself.

"Through here." Taavin pushed on the same trap door Vi had used. "The Swords are patrolling the Archives. They expect you to try to escape."

Vi moved quickly and quietly, not arguing. She wriggled through the narrow tunnel and into the passage where she could stand. A small flame appeared over her shoulder, illuminating them both.

"What have you figured out?" Vi asked over her shoulder.

"I was right—the traveler was right. The watch was the key to everything."

"But—"

"Quiet," he interrupted with a whisper. "Don't talk here, it's not safe." They continued walking upward in silence, Vi's nerves setting her hands to quivering. The shakes only stopped when Taavin's firm grasp wrapped around her closed fist. "Wait here. Let me go ahead and make sure Ulvarth hasn't decided to pay me a visit."

Vi pressed herself against the wall to let him pass. They were practically stepping on each other's toes and his chest slid across hers. She wondered if his heart was beating just as hard as hers, or if she only imagined feeling it through the thin fabric of the Lark robes she wore.

He disappeared in the darkness and Vi remained leaning against the wall, rubbing the bridge of her nose. The one good thing about everything happening all at once was that she didn't have time to think or worry about any one thing. She needed to save her father, save the world, rekindle the flame... all while continuing to navigate the strained relationship between her and Taavin. She was so focused on surviving that she didn't have time to be afraid.

At least, until moments like this, when she was still and waiting.

Unfocusing her eyes, Vi looked to the flame dancing over her shoulder, the one that had been lighting her way. She scratched at her bandages; the wounds were constantly itchy now. Vi tried to keep her mind on the tangible so it didn't get too worked up over the possible horrors emerging from the shadows around her.

But it was Taavin who appeared next. Not a Sword. Not Ulvarth himself.

"Well? How does it look?"

"Safe, for now. Let's hurry."

Taavin started off into the darkness once more and Vi followed behind him. She paused, turning slowly. Their interaction was seared into her memory.

She'd seen it before, Vi realized with a sense of growing dread. It wasn't bright in her memory because it had just happened. It was seared in her memory because—

"Taavin!" she hissed, grabbing his arm. Her words burst forth as fast as her heartbeat. "I've seen this before. My first vision... Here..." Vi looked down at her clothes, the simple, drab robes—the cowl—the bandages over her wrists and hands. "We haven't changed anything." Her eyes darted back up to him.

"We haven't changed anything, *yet*." Taavin pulled his arm from her grasp and took a full step away, as if to see her clearly. His eyes burned brighter than the flame at Vi's side. They were wide enough to swallow her whole—the wide eyes of a fear Vi didn't know if she had the strength to acknowledge. "That's what we're going to do now, tonight... We're going to change this world."

Vi nodded her head like she understood and when he continued into the darkness, she followed. It was possible he was leading her to a trap, Vi realized. He could be setting her up for yet another betrayal.

She swallowed. She didn't want to trust him again. But if she couldn't trust him, she had to trust the fact that he had just as much of a reason to want to fix their future as she did. She had to trust in mutual goals, if not in the man himself.

Up the ladder, Vi found out how Taavin had escaped.

"You broke the door." She stared at the scattered splinters and the annihilated lock. "But Ulvarth—"

"After we rekindle the flame, Ulvarth won't matter." Taavin started in. He went to the shelf on his wall, lifting something from his watchmaking supplies. "Here, I made a new watch, you'll need to hold it."

Vi held out both her hands to accept the small token. When Taavin's fingers vanished, she stared at something nearly identical to the watch she'd carried across the world. The links were uncannily similar. The face was the same. The only difference was this one was shiny, new, so pristine that Vi could see her face reflected in it.

Whereas the one she'd been gifted, the one Vi had received from Fritz, showed its age in every scratch, dent, and smear of tarnish.

"What do we need to do?" Vi whispered. "Why do I need a new watch?"

Her mind was jumbled. She'd packed it so full of information and plans that it was now about to explode. This would be the final straw.

"Listen to me, there's little time to explain now, but I will soon. After you are settled, summon me as you once did. I can explain it all then."

"Tell me now?" she asked, wishing her voice was stronger.

Taavin lifted the watch from her numb fingers, fastening it around her neck as he spoke. "When the War of Light ended, Yargen fractured her power to keep Raspian at bay."

"One third to the tomb, one third to her Champion in a spear, and one third here in Risen as a living flame," Vi recited. "And we have a piece of that staff in the scythe."

"But the scythe alone... it isn't enough." He stepped away, starting for the open doors. The flame cast him in silhouette. "The scythe with the power of the flame, your watch, my power—it's not enough. We need all the crystal weapons to stand against him. We need the full power of Yargen."

"The full power of Yargen is gone," Vi needlessly reminded him. "The caverns, destroyed. The other crystal weapons—"

"Destroyed," he finished for her, glancing over his shoulder, the light of the flame illuminating his profile. "I know it all. Thanks to your word, I now know every step this world has taken for hundreds of years, time and again."

"So then how do we rekindle the flame?" Vi asked, taking a small step toward him. "If that power is gone, if the crystal weapons were destroyed, along with the other third of Yargen's power held in the Crystal Caverns... What do we do to reignite the crystals so we can bring her power back to the flame? What do we do to bring her power back so she can fight off Raspian?"

"It's not a what, Vi. It's a *when*."

WHEN.

When.

Her mind sputtered and came to a halt on the word. Vi stood, swaying slightly. There was magic in the world. Powers great and small. Powers to heal and destroy.

But there was no power that granted one the hold over time itself.

To have that… one would have to be a… a… a goddess.

"Vi." Taavin summoned her from her haze. Vi looked up, startled. She hadn't realized he'd crossed over to her. Now, he towered above her with every inch of his height. "You cannot lose yourself now. I need you here with me mentally. If we dally too long, we're met with a great deal of hardship. Ulvarth comes and… Well, what happens then doesn't matter because we're not dallying."

Taavin rounded behind her, pushing her to motion. He pushed her toward the flame and Vi's body only obliged because it was that or collapse in place. Luckily, her physical form moved on instinct, even when her mind refused.

"I'm going to say some words," Taavin was saying. Vi barely heard him.

None of this was real. None of this was happening. It couldn't be. He was speaking insanity. And yet her other option if she didn't go along with it was walking back down into a hornet's nest of Ulvarth's men who would execute her father by dawn—if dawn even came. If they hadn't already executed him.

What if Taavin had been lying about that to get her to move? What if they'd killed him in that courtyard and Taavin knew if he told her she would be a grieving mess? Could she trust him to tell her the truth?

Right now, the answer was a resounding no, and Vi felt as though she would be sick.

Taavin stopped pushing her and rounded in front of her. His hand cupped her cheek, but Vi could barely feel it. The motion was too familiar, too caring, for the strange man in front of her now. Madman or traitor—she didn't know who he was.

"This is the only way forward. This is the only way to save your family. Repeat what I say, Vi. And I will be there to guide you in the new world, I promise. This is my destiny as much as it is yours." He turned, his back to her, and knelt.

Destiny. She hated the word.

Vi was living a nightmare that ended with the world's destruction. For the third time in three short days, she was overcome by a sensation of déjà vu. She'd had a vision of this very moment and she knew where it led. She knew what was about to happen.

"N-no." Shaking her head, Vi stumbled a few steps back. "No, Taavin, I—"

Taavin stood slowly, looking to her. He advanced and Vi took another wide step—too wide. She stumbled, falling, landing hard because she didn't even bother to catch herself.

"No, not this... don't make me do this."

"Don't you hate me now?" His face was shadowed by the flame behind him, his mess of hair falling into his shining eyes. "Aren't I the one who betrayed you?"

"Taavin, if I do this, you will die." The words were a whisper, little more than a breath. "I have seen this—I told you. I will not burn you alive."

"It's because of me your father will die. I betrayed you, Vi."

"Stop," she pleaded. He was speaking truth right to the darkest part of her—the part she so desperately wanted to ignore.

"You wanted to take him to Norin if he wished, and I stopped that from happening."

"Taavin—"

"You must do this!" His expression was a cross between pained and impatient. "This is the only way. This is the only path forward."

"I'm not a murderer!"

"Then hate me more for making you one." Taavin knelt before her. Even as she shouted at him, his voice didn't waver and his gaze was set. He really was going to let her kill him. "Hate me because I will never let myself love you again. Hate me because you truly are the cause of all my torment. You are my nightmares. It was always you."

Hate me, because I now hate you, his eyes said. That same burning feeling she'd embraced the other night was sparking again within the charred husk of her ribs. She wanted to sob and let out all the tears it felt like she'd been holding in for a lifetime. But if they fell now, they would merely evaporate on her cheeks.

"You must do this," he reiterated, his voice gone soft. Taavin reached for her arm, pulling her upright.

"What happens if it doesn't work?" Vi croaked, standing on shaking knees. "What happens if you're wrong and I just kill you?"

"Death comes for us all." He echoed the same sentiment as the first time she'd told him he was going to die. He looked her right in the eyes, so close his features went blurry. Perhaps, somehow, if everything he was saying was true, some part of him had known even then. "And if I am wrong, death will come for me before you when Raspian walks this earth once more... and you will have the satisfaction of killing someone else who wronged you."

"You're not making any sense!" She wanted to slap him. "Do you hear yourself? This isn't logical and this magic, it doesn't exist, and—"

"The watch was power—my power mingled with Yargen's, and yours," he spoke over her hastily. His hands gripped her shoulders, hard. "Layers and layers of magic, Vi... countless times. Countless attempts to stop this failed future from coming to pass. You have to return the power that's in me to her, along with you, along with the scythe. Only that will give her enough power to send you back."

"You truly are mad."

"And you truly are the worst thing to have ever happened to me," he seethed, so close their noses almost touched. Part of her wanted to kiss him, kiss the pain away. The other part of her was more tempted by the minute to give in and kill him. He was begging for it, after all. "Now, help me do this."

Why was the line between love and hate so confusingly thin? She stared at his back, at the scythe positioned on the pedestal before the flame.

She wondered if she was about to trade some part of her soul—and if so, for what. It didn't feel like much of her soul was left. Whatever was still there after all she'd endured, she may as well give to the Goddess.

Taavin knelt and Vi hovered behind him, swaying unsteadily.

Without so much as looking back at her—without even reaffirming what it was they were about to do one final time—Taavin begin to chant.

The words blurred together into a litany that would be his dirge. She could stop this now. She could clamp her hands over his lips and silence those infernal words that were already flowing through her.

But if she did that... then what? Taavin would likely perish anyway, as fodder to bring about a dark god. She would likely die fighting that same god. The world would end. Her family would be forever lost.

Perhaps Taavin was the one to have it right all along—*death comes for us all*—and Vi was the one to have her worries tied around the wrong priorities.

Vi took a slow step forward. She knew her role. She'd do it just like she had in the vision she was given back in Soricium.

Her hands settled slowly on Taavin's shoulders. Light was already peeling off of him, merging with the halo of brightness surrounding the flame. Barely-formed glyphs seemed to wrap, collapse, and form anew in complex patterns Vi couldn't follow.

His magic, shimmering and bright, pulled hers forth as well. Together, it looked almost like a white-hot fire, but with a cool pale blue at the edges. Vi gave into the flow like a ship to a current. She shut off her mind and let him pull her along.

If she thought too much about what was about to happen next, she may not be able to do it. Her will might fail her.

She spoke.

Vi didn't know the words she was saying, she didn't know the meanings, but she echoed him anyway. She allowed the magic to be pulled from her. It felt almost like an invisible hand plunged into her chest, pulling forth all she was with a violence that seemed appropriate for an unnatural act.

They were two mortals, playing at godhood.

Taavin's head tipped back and he let out a scream as his magic exploded in a burst of flame, mingling with the fire of Yargen. In the distance, voices. Ulvarth or the Swords were coming to investigate. They must have discovered her absence.

But it was too late.

The Voice was immolating under her hands, with the help of her magic. The fire before them blazed brightly, brighter than anything Vi had ever seen before—so bright, she was certain to be blind when it faded.

The whole world was consumed...

And Vi was falling into the void it left behind.

THERE WAS NOTHING BUT light, so bright she squinted and her head ached. Vi tried closing her eyes, but she couldn't even do that to block it out. The light was in her mind, in her flesh. It seared through her from the inside out.

She felt every layer of skin boiling. Red lightning finally broke through, flesh disappearing into the void above her as she continued to fall. She felt her tongue crisp and her hair singe. She felt the burn down to the clean white of her bones.

There was nothing left of her. At least, Vi couldn't *feel* anything. All sensation had vanished from head to toe. She was a spirit, her body gone.

Tick.

Tock.

No… perhaps, there was something. The watch Taavin had given her still ticked. Vi was aware of magic swirling from the timepiece as time and space whipped around her like wind. From the magic that had been stored there with their final act together, life began again, and Vi let out a scream more animal than woman as everything rushed back all at once.

A new heart—her new heart—beat in time to the watch. Veins sprouted from it, unfurling outward like bloody ribbons. Bone and sinew became her foundation, sprouting muscle and then layering on flesh. Her nails grew back in place, her hair flowed past her shoulders.

And her freshly made, still-falling body began to finally, *finally*, slow.

Tick. Tock.

The end of the world is near, and we must be ready to meet it. Taavin's voice echoed and Vi turned, trying to find the source of the sound. Her new heart began to race.

Tick. Tock. Tick. Tock. Tick. Tock.

Vi covered her ears, trying to blot out the noise. The faster her heart beat, the faster the incessant ticking. It would drive her mad before she even—

"Young one," a voice that sounded like every man, woman, and child in the world speaking all at once startled Vi from her thoughts. There was silence, then the voice again. "My Champion."

"Y… Y…" Vi could barely form a word. Her mouth was new, foreign, strange.

She turned in place, aware she was no longer falling. But all around her was nothing more than bright light, swirling yellows mixed with blues and whites. The same colors and intensity as the flames that had engulfed her.

"I am here."

"Where?" It felt like eternity stretched in all directions, all possibilities contained within.

Vi looked behind her, and when she turned forward again she was startled to see the shadow of a woman. A long veil covered her face, bolts of silk hiding her form. A crown of pure light sat on her head.

"Queen Lumeria?" Vi said, finding her voice once more.

"No. It is I… I who have seen this world from its start. I who sowed the seeds of life. I who gave you ground to grow in. I who gave you light to grow by."

Yargen. Vi would've dropped to her knee, but she was too stunned. She also wasn't completely certain she could move her knees. Her body was as fresh and primordial as the light around her, yet it mirrored the woman she'd always been.

The magic of the Goddess was within and around her. But mortal flesh still covered that power. She was neither divine nor mortal. A familiar sensation for the princess who had never belonged in any one place—who had never been any one thing.

"Yes," Yargen spoke as though she heard Vi's thoughts, because of course she heard Vi's thoughts. Vi stared at the face—veil—of a goddess. "I am in everything. I am everything. My essence, my being, cannot be comprehended by you or any mortal mind. So this is merely a form your consciousnesses has created, to make me something you can understand—a meager shell for all I am…" She slowly raised her hands, fabric floating unnaturally weightless through the air. "Because *this* is all I am.

"Or, should I say, all I was." Her hands lowered just as slowly. "I have given you a boon once more, my Champion. Your mind does not deceive you—in you is the last of my power from this world, collected from what fragments were left. The flame has been extinguished. With it, the world you knew is gone."

"Gone?" Vi repeated in quiet horror.

"The world you were born into, the people you knew, the way you knew them, are no more."

Gone. Everything was gone. Everything Vi had ever loved, would ever love, vanished at the whim of a goddess. Her mind ached and Vi didn't know if it was from the struggle of trying to comprehend what was happening, or from what she'd already endured. She would cry in the face of such a truth, but Vi wasn't sure she even remembered how.

"Do not despair," Yargen soothed. "They are not gone forever. Just as you are not gone forever. You now possess a new shape… as shall they."

"What? But you said—"

"This is the only way to thwart Raspian. The only way we can prevent him from destroying my world of light. We must begin anew in the shell of the former world and preserve my power, this time, so that I may face him once more in our deadly, eternal dance."

"A new world," Vi whispered.

"Yes, but a familiar one. Everything as you knew it has been wiped away. But the lines of fate remain. The life that was cultivated can still thrive. Everything is as it was, but new once more."

"I... I don't understand." Vi shook her head. She wanted to. She desperately wanted to, because somewhere amid all the talk of the world ending was hope. Vi could hear it, and she lived for that hope, even if she didn't yet understand its foundations.

"You will, in time," Yargen assured her. "We begin anew. I return you to before the first moment where fate was changed. I place you back in a new world. You will be free of the bonds of time because my magic is in you. I have given you the power that lived in the watch your past self carried. I have bestowed the power of my Voice and the last vestiges of power from the flame on you as well.

"Together, we have scraped together my meager remnants to make this attempt at a world in which I am not weakened. When I rebuild this new world, you shall enter it as you are, knowing all you know. However, you shall be immune to time's flow, a traveler among mortals."

A new world. A traveler. If Vi understood correctly, the world was being remade with the crystal weapons still intact. But that meant...

"But what about *my* world? My father, my mother?"

"The only world that exists now, is the one we exist within. I am the fount of life and time. There is no other world."

Vi shook her head and fell to her knees. What was it for? *What was everything for?* She'd struggled and fought to spare the world from ending, only to see the world end anyway? Raspian wanted to destroy the world, so Vi fought against him... only to see it destroyed by a different god.

Yet, if Yargen spoke true, there was still a chance to save it.

The Goddess approached, stopping before her. Queen Lumeria's shifting silks floated through her vision as Vi stared up like a hopeless acolyte, beseeching forgiveness and mercy.

"Regain your birthright as Champion," Yargen intoned.

The spear that was bestowed. A voice that both was and wasn't her own replied from within her mind.

"Assume your mantle as Champion."

To defend the Crystal Caverns.

"See my power is never turned on itself again. See I am not weakened. See I am able to stand against the incomprehensible darkness that rages at the edge of your mortal world."

The air was sucked from Vi's lungs.

Light turned to darkness and she was falling again. Yargen vanished from before her and Vi was left alone. The wind sped around her. Her eyes dipped closed.

If she hit the ground at this speed, she'd die.

Perhaps that was the best end she could hope for.

But she couldn't die. For in her was the power of Yargen. Wasn't that what the goddess had said? And that power condemned her to remain adrift in the sands of time.

Vi gasped for air, opening her eyes wide. She lurched upward, the watch around her neck thumping dully against her chest. The world around her was bright— uncomfortably so—but not the same brightness she had just endured.

And certainly not the same brightness that peeled off her skin like some primordial, godly afterbirth.

Rubbing her hands over her arms and shivering in the heat, Vi looked around.

She'd thought of herself in the sands of time… but now she was just in regular sand. Hay was scattered at her side, damp-smelling and foul. Whatever animal lived here would need something fresh, if the animal was still alive at all. The stables she was in were completely empty.

People drifted past on the other side of the gate. None of them noticed her or looked her way. Perhaps they couldn't see her at all.

Vi stared down at her trembling hands. She opened and closed her fingers slowly. They still worked. She could keenly feel her nails digging into her palms when she balled them, just as she could feel the thin layer of sand shifting over hard-packed earth beneath as Vi pushed herself off the ground.

Swaying, she took one step forward, then another. She knew where she was before she emerged from the stable. The people were easy enough to identify, the architecture of the city even easier.

The city stables of Norin stretched on either side of her as Vi emerged along the main road. She remembered passing through these markets and streets with Jayme. At least, she thought she remembered…

Perhaps this whole time she'd been in one endless fever dream. Perhaps none of it had been real. Perhaps she'd been marching home with her family, took a detour to Norin she couldn't recall at this moment, and suffered heat fainting. She'd only dreamt her father gone, her mother ill. She'd only dreamt of Taavin and Meru and—

"What do you think will be in the proclamation?" a wife asked her husband as they passed. Her voice was low, and as weak as her body looked.

Vi turned and stared. Luckily, the woman didn't notice, because Vi didn't think she could wipe the shock off her face if she tried. The wife hadn't been speaking common. She was speaking the old language of Mhashan—and Vi could understand it with perfect fluency.

"Hopefully an end to this war," the man murmured in reply.

War. Vi's whole body continued to tremble. She ran her hands over her arms, trying to comfort herself. But her palms smoothed over fabrics she hadn't ever owned in a style she didn't recognize.

Dragging one foot forward, then the next, Vi began to march with the rest of them. Ahead was a castle. Her gaze drifted over familiar spires, working to make sense of them. She'd read enough to know the architecture of the castle of Norin anywhere. But seeing it now was impossible.

She had just been in Risen. Her head ached as her head tipped back and her eyes lifted. She squinted at the sun, wondering if Yargen was watching her right now—watching her attempt to complete the task she'd been given.

Watching her attempt to make sense of what on the Goddess's earth had just happened.

A crowd collected in an open area at the end of a long bridge that connected the castle and city over a dry moat. Guards were gathered in a semi-circle, blocking entry to the bridge. None of the populous seemed interested in fighting them. The people were harrowed and gaunt. Every man, woman, and child had the haunted eyes of a soldier who had seen far too much.

Without warning, a woman stepped up onto a tall box that had no doubt been carried out expressly for this purpose. She was just high enough to see over the people. Vi stared, slack-jawed, at an oddly familiar face. It was not identical to hers. But it was so close that it was like looking into a mirror.

Even from Vi's distance, she could see the woman had angular black eyes, jutting cheekbones, and a sharp chin. Her skin, a deep tan darker than Vi's own, paired with straight black hair. Hair identical to Vi's.

Vi opened her mouth to speak, but couldn't form words. Not that she knew what she would have said, anyway.

"People of the West," the woman began, "this siege has gone on for nearly ten long years. But I am Fiera, Princess of Mhashan, youngest daughter to King Rocham, and head of the Knights of Jadar, and I have received a vision from the Mother above. The end is near, and we must be ready for it."

SOVEREIGN SACRIFICE

VORTEX CHRONICLES
BOOK FOUR

to the hundred and eleven
who have my eternal gratitude

PROLOGUE

FIERA EASED HERSELF AWAY from the smoldering remnants of the fire she'd been using to peer along the Mother's red lines of fate to catch glimpses of the future. She sat back on her heels, hands on her thighs, and stared out the wide, open window that overlooked her dying city. She had been charged with the sole duty of protecting them… and she had failed.

"At least it will finally be over," she said thoughtfully. The words made her vision real.

For nearly ten long years, the Solaris Empire, led by Tiberus Solaris, had laid siege to Norin. Mhashan would not fall easily. Fiera had used the sword to see to that. And her father would never surrender; the blood of the greatest king to ever live, King Jadar, flowed through his veins and hers. They had a family name to honor, though their ideas about how exactly to do so couldn't have been more different.

She pushed herself away from the small fire pit, standing. Her scrying room was attached to one of her sitting rooms, accessible through a curtain. Fiera made her way across her chambers and into her closet. She'd need her finest to deliver this message. If they were to fall, they would fall with the same dignity they'd lived and fought with.

Dressed in deep crimson splashed with accents of bright silver, a decorative pauldron over one shoulder with chain mail draping off, Fiera stepped into the halls of the castle.

Things were quiet. But they usually were these days. Hunger was beginning to scrape the very bottom of every citizen's stomach. Most of the castle staff had been dismissed long ago with the command to conserve their energy. Fiera knew at least half of them were dead now.

Only an extremely loyal few remained at their posts.

Heading down a wide staircase, Fiera stepped into a side hallway accessible through a narrow door on the side of the stairs. When she was a girl, this hall had been filled with the sweet scents of perfume and fine soaps, imported from the Crossroads. Now, it was merely damp. Humidity beaded on the walls from the heated washing tubs. Sweet-smelling soaps had run out long ago; now, the best they could do to clean their clothes was boil them.

A middle-aged man tended the steaming tubs. Magic radiated off of him, sparking throughout the room as he kept each of the large, wooden basins bubbling hot. He went from tub to tub, stirring the contents.

"Hanc."

"Your highness." The man released the over-sized spoon he'd been holding and dipped low into a bow. When Fiera was young, an elderly woman would threaten to crack her knuckles with the too-large spoons if she was caught snatching soap shavings for her personal use. Fiera didn't know where the woman was now; she'd vanished like all of Hanc's other helpers. "What can I do for you?"

"I need you to collect all the bedsheets in the castle and begin stitching them together." Luckily, the tubs were filled with colored garments. That meant he should have plenty of white sheets at his disposal. "It doesn't matter if they're clean and the stitches do not need to be tidy—merely sturdy." He stared at her, clearly working to process the odd request. "I need you to do this with haste, as many as you can. Do you understand?"

"Yes, your highness," Hanc said slowly. Then, timidly, "Any particular way they should be stitched together?"

"Not really. So long as they are white—or close enough to white—and the banner you make is large, it should be enough."

"I shall do so when I finish this wash and—"

"You shall do so now," Fiera interrupted firmly. "There is precious little time. Remember, you need to do as many as your hands can bear in the coming hours and only stop when the time comes to use what you have produced." Hanc gave a small nod. Fiera wished she could tell him more, but it was better not to. They all needed to keep their faith in these final hours. Ignorance while doing so was the best she could give them. Fiera went to leave, but paused in the doorway. "One more thing."

"Yes?"

"Tell no one of this task save my brother. But wait to go to him until the time is right. Perform your duty as discretely as possible. Start with the sheets not on beds to avoid suspicion, then those in vacant rooms. Use my quarters if you need a place to work." Fiera doubted she would spend much time in them in the hours to come.

"How will I know the time is right?"

"Trust me when I say that you will." It would be obvious what he was making when the time came for it—if it wasn't obvious already. "Work with speed, Hanc."

"Yes, your highness."

Fiera left him and started back up the stairs. Her hands worried the familiar stone banisters as she wound up to the royal council rooms. A war council was convened at all times of the day, it seemed, though the discussions had dulled the longer the siege dragged on.

When she stepped into the stately room, the men and women who had been lounging in velvet tufted chairs stood instantly.

"Your highness." They bowed rigidly, hands at their sides.

"Captain." Zira, Fiera's head knight and right hand, saluted.

"Report on the city's status," Fiera commanded.

"Grain stores have been entirely depleted outside the castle," Denja reported, adjusting the scarf around her head. She had once been a councilor of commerce, and a good one at that. But the war had robbed her of much purpose other than rationing.

Perhaps, in the days to come, her skills with negotiation could be put to use again. "We're relying entirely on the sea now." Her eyes were now on Twintle.

"In the waters we dare to sail, fishing has been scarce… Though, the fishermen claim that with the season's shift, new fish should come to the area. There's still the reserve of dried fish at my warehouse at the docks," Twintle, councilor for maritime, picked up Denja's report.

"No breaches reported by the guard along the outer wall. No movements of the Imperial army since half their forces retreated two weeks ago," Zira added.

It was a standard report Fiera had been receiving for years now. The only variant was that each time she heard it, there was less and less to say. Most had thought she was far too young to be placed at the head of the Knights of Jadar five years ago when it happened at her seventeenth birthday. But war changed girls into women, and softness into steel.

"Any report of Imperial ships at sea?"

Twintle shook his head. "Not since our last effort to drive them away."

"The pirate Adela?"

"No sightings," Twintle said, with no small amount of relief.

Fiera nodded, relieved as well. They had enough to worry about. Adela could go terrorize the brutish and uneducated masses on the Crescent Continent.

"Open the grain stores of the castle to the soldiers. Denja, anything you can dredge up from the bottom of barrels in the castle or city is to be turned out. Ask the nobles again to search their larders—by surprise this time. Let's see if we can't find anything hidden away in their cabinets. All combatants have first claim. Let the people eat after our military, and then a curfew is in order. All non-combatants are to remain indoors."

"If I open my warehouse—" Lord Twintle began from the other end of the table.

"You will quickly run out. Yes, I realize." Fiera rapped her knuckles against the table twice; a ring in the shape of a silver phoenix rung out loudly. "This ends in the coming days. Feed our troops, give them strength."

"You had a vision." Ophain, her brother and eldest sibling, said softly from the head of the table opposite her. He still had not risen to greet her.

The man was a shade of his former self. Fiera remembered him towering over her with broad shoulders and a noteworthy amount of muscle ever since she was a girl. But he had been one of the first in their family to begin refusing food to help it last longer, and his perpetual fast had taken a toll.

"The Mother has blessed me with the sight," Fiera affirmed. "This ends. So if you agree with my will, brother, see it done."

All eyes shifted to Ophain. Officially, he was the head of the council as the crown prince. But Fiera was the head of the Knights of Jadar, the soldiers of the West, and that made her nearly his equal.

"I will see it done."

"Then I will be the one to tell Father," she said to him and turned to Zira. "After, I will address the people. Send criers for a royal announcement now and meet me in the armory."

"Yes, your highness." Zira bowed low, hovering there as Fiera left the room.

She rotated the heavy silver ring around her ring finger, worrying away at the smooth silver. *It would end.* She had told them the truth in that. Fiera paused, staring out a window lining the hallway. She imagined a city burning, ransacked by their enemies.

Was it wrong not to tell even her most trusted advisers *how* it would end?

Pushing the thoughts from her mind, Fiera continued on to her father's chambers. More and more often, she found him on his wide balcony. The sheer curtains that drifted in the open archways of his room obscured his form.

"Do I hear the soft footsteps of my youngest child?"

Nothing about her was still soft. "Yes, Father."

"Approach, girl."

Fiera did as she was bid. Even as the head of the Knights of Jadar, she was still a girl to her father, and no amount of cunning deeds or ruthless bloodshed would change that.

"What have you come to trouble me with?" Even as he spoke, silver crown heavy on his brow, King Rocham gazed out over the city. Fiera wondered if he, too, could imagine it burning.

"We are making preparations for the end." That brought his attention to her. Rocham's dark eyes set against leathered skin scrutinized Fiera, and she let no weakness show. "The Mother has gifted me with a vision."

"Finally," he murmured. "Well, tell me."

"This will all end soon."

"How does it end?"

"We will lose." This was the one man whom telling could make a difference—though Fiera doubted it would. She knew how deep her father's pride ran.

Rocham settled back once again to admire his kingdom, likely one of the last times he would see it in the bright afternoon sun. Soon they would be looking from this balcony at just another stretch of the Solaris Empire. The history and name of Mhashan would be wiped from the maps and reduced to "the West."

That was, assuming they still had their heads attached to their shoulders when Tiberus Solaris ruled.

"Then we shall die fighting." Her father stood and Fiera's heart sank. "As is our way."

"As the head of the Knights of Jadar, I must remind you our forces are tired and weak. If—"

"I was the one who gave you that title. It does not give you the ability to question me," he cautioned.

Fiera continued despite. "If we fight, the losses will be even greater than they otherwise have to be. Let us at least attempt peaceful negotiations."

"I tried to negotiate with the monster Solaris ten years ago. He is a power-hungry child who cannot be reasoned with."

"Father—"

"And if we are to lose," the King continued, not hearing her. "then I will die killing the bastard."

Were it not for her years of training, she would have shouted at him. Her hands would ball into fists and she would tremble with rage. But Fiera was a weapon. She'd been hammered, sharpened, and forged from birth.

Her brother would rule. Her older sisters were royal prizes—trophies to be married off as it fit the crown. Thus, her father had not needed her to be genteel. He'd needed her to be a soldier, a tool that could take the shape of whatever the kingdom required.

And that was what she had become.

"You will not kill him. With the size of the Imperial army, you will not even come close to him," Fiera said, level, as the king started into his quarters. "But perhaps we can—"

"I will take no more of your treasonous talk. The time for negotiations has long since ended. If Norin is to fall, then I shall burn it to the ground myself before I let Solaris sit on my throne." Fire sparked to life in the air over her father's shoulders.

Fiera merely stared at him, willing her face to remain passive. Not a single emotion would betray her by floating to the surface. She had weighted them all, burning them deep within the flames of her gut.

"And as the head of the Knights of Jadar, you will heed my orders. Go and ready the soldiers. Prepare them to take one last stand for King and country. Prepare them to die."

"Yes, sir." Fiera gave a bow and strode from the room, not one crack in her stony mask.

She strode down the hall and down a flight of stairs. The royal quarters were toward the top of the castle. Down and to one side were the council chambers, comprised of meeting rooms and offices. Down and to the other were the barracks, training grounds, and armory. Two strong pillars of the Ci'Dan family had lifted them centuries ago to royalty: diplomacy and combat.

Fiera strode between racks of swords in one of the oldest armories to the very back right corner, where an unassuming second door, bolted with a heavy lock, waited. At the door's side was a black-haired woman, eyes shining in the light of the mote of fire hovering over Fiera's shoulder.

"The criers have been sent. I gave them my horse to do it with," Zira reported, pushing away from the wall. "Ophain is carrying out the rest of your orders."

"To the letter?"

"To the letter."

"Good." Fiera tugged at a chain around her neck. The lock on the door had only one key—the one she was never without. Through the door was a narrow hallway, illuminated by an inferno at its end.

The wall of fire filled the stone passage, perpetually burning, just in case anyone dared try to break into this most sacred chamber. With a soft sigh, Fiera relaxed her flames. With it, the slow sap on her power vanished.

Maintaining the flame, day and night, was a leech on her. But a worthy one. For behind the wall of flame, a silver scabbard hung on a wall, embellished with rubies as large as a trout's eyes that picked up the faint blue glow emitted by the pommel.

"Zira, I fear this may be our last battle together," Fiera began as she reached for the sword. "The Mother told me little of our fates following the end of this war."

"If it is the Mother's will that I die this day, I do so with the honor of serving you," Zira said with ease. The woman was one of the greatest mercenaries ever to come out of the Nameless Company. She knew the face of death as early and as well as her own mother's. "May I make a request of you, princess?"

"Anything, you know it is yours."

"I know we spoke of my defending your family. However, if it is possible that this is our last battle together, I would like to stand by your side."

Fiera's hand ran lightly along the scabbard of the Sword of Jadar. The room was empty, save for the lone sword and a narrow table below. It made the weapon seem all the more powerful.

Yet the sword's strength was wavering. When the war started, her father told her where it had been hidden—slumbering, waiting to defend Mhashan—since the age of Jadar. Fiera had been the one to take the sword, learn what she could, and harness the latent powers of the crystal it was crafted from. Doing so had dulled the sword's energy and nearly killed her.

But the walls surrounding Mhashan had held for ten years.

"Then by my side you shall be. See to it that my brothers and sisters are protected by the best in your stead. Entrust the key to the old escape route to my brother, if need be."

"What about your father?" Zira missed nothing.

"The king can defend himself," Fiera said, deathly quiet. Her father had his chance to live for the people and refused. So she would let him die with his mistakes; his fate was on his shoulders alone. "Do not waste the loyalty of good men on him." Fiera pried her gaze away from the weapon to look Zira in the eye. The woman had been with her now for four years and, from the start, they seemed to have a bond that transcended words.

Fiera felt fate keenly. She knew its pull, just as she knew when someone's red lines were knotted to hers. She might not always understand the purpose right away, but the Mother revealed all in time.

"Understood," Zira said with a small bow.

Without a moment's more hesitation, Fiera lifted the Sword of Jadar and strapped it to her wide belt. It was cumbersome. But so were the trappings of leadership. She had born worse burdens and still walked.

Zira at her side, they left the castle together. A score of Knights joined them in the royal stables—right at the end of the long drawbridge that connected the castle to the city across a wide, dry moat. Fiera doubted her father would even raise the drawbridge. He'd convinced himself he was ready for this fight, ready to meet his end.

She, however, was not ready to meet hers. Someone needed to defend the people of Mhashan, even after they became citizens of the Solaris Empire. She held the sword that could do just that.

Fiera sought a life of service, not glory in death.

At the end of the drawbridge, their group of Knights met with another already there, filling in the gaps. They all wore red armbands bearing the seal of the Phoenix of the West, a sword clutched in its talons, emblazoned in silver. A crate had been carried out for her to stand on.

There were no cheers or fanfare as she stood atop the humble wooden box, looking out over those assembled. Fiera took a slow breath and clutched the leather-wrapped pommel of the sword. She tried to draw power from it—whatever power was left—so she could find the strength to do what must be done.

"People of the West, this siege has gone on for nearly ten long years," Fiera began, her voice echoing off the buildings that lined the square. "But I am Fiera, Princess of Mhashan, youngest daughter to King Rocham, and head of the Knights of Jadar, and I have received a vision from the Mother above. The end is near, and we must be ready for it."

"I CANNOT TELL YOU WHAT the final outcome will be—the goddess did not bless me with this knowledge."

Vi watched Fiera speak from among the crowd. She was still shaking, but no longer from the remnants of the goddess's power surging through her as she was thrown through time and space. Now, she shook because of the face she stared at.

Fiera was dead.

The woman standing before her, speaking before her, had long been a corpse in the world Vi knew. It should be all the proof she needed that the goddess had, truly, remade a new world. But Vi's mind couldn't comprehend it. Her head ached just trying to.

"But I can tell you that it will end soon," the princess continued to the blank-eyed, defeated masses. "We are feeding our soldiers and Knights with the last of the food stores, so they might better protect you. Whatever is left will go to women and children first, then all others.

"A curfew has been set on the city for civilians. Everyone is to be in their homes between the hours of one in the afternoon, until eleven in the morning."

She could hear and understand the language of old Mhashan—Vi realized—a language she'd only studied a handful of times with her tutors and had been very far from mastering mere hours ago. She was able to comprehend it without effort.

Hours ago? Or had it been days? Or years? How long had she been with the goddess? How long had it been since Taavin—

Her mind stalled, hand instinctively going to the watch around her neck. *Taavin.* Her last memories of the man were clouded with hurt and confusion, punctuated by a fire that burned so brightly it consumed him.

"That's only two hours we can be about," someone murmured from Vi's side.

"This isn't a curfew—it's more like house arrest," someone else said, oblivious to her panic. They were all oblivious to her. Not one person had the slightest idea that a traveler from a distant time was among them.

"If you do not have a timepiece, or can't otherwise accurately tell time by the sun, you are encouraged to err on the side of caution and remain indoors," Fiera continued, ignoring the growing murmurs rippling through the crowd. When she spoke, the people stilled, as though transfixed. Fiera had a magnetic quality Vi could feel influencing her, even through her relative panic. "This is for your protection. The only people that should be in the streets are soldiers."

Dawning recognition washed over Vi: Fiera was trying to prevent citizens from getting caught in the crossfire.

"You have one hour to collect what food and supplies you can before we all settle in for this long night." Fiera drew a sword and Vi nearly let out an involuntary shout of surprise. Her hands flew to her mouth, suppressing a strangled gasp as the princess lifted the shimmering weapon above her head. "Flame burn eternal!"

"And guide us through the night," the citizens around her chanted, going stiff with arms at their sides in a sort of Western salute.

Vi didn't say anything. She didn't mirror the salute. Her sole focus was on the crystal sword Fiera had lofted over her head.

A sword that should've been long destroyed, held by a woman who should've been long dead.

The princess left with her host of Knights. The rest of the castle guard walked through the crowd, encouraging people to disperse.

She turned on her heel and pulled up the hood of the tunic she was wearing. It kept the heat of the afternoon sun off her brow, and it kept her from making eye contact with anyone. Vi stayed with the masses until they mostly disappeared and she was alone once more in an all-too-quiet street.

A door caught her eye. It was unassuming, wooden, nearly identical to most others. But this one she remembered. Vi walked over slowly, running her hand along the wood. For some reason, this door stuck in her mind, vivid with the ghost of a white X that had been painted on it when she'd last been in Norin.

"No White Death," she whispered.

"Excuse me, can I help you?" Vi jumped, looking over her shoulder at a young woman who stood behind her. She couldn't be older than fifteen and carried a mostly empty basket—save for two tiny jars of what Vi recognized as spices and a hunk of dry fish meat. The young woman's eyes widened. "P-princess?"

"No, I'm—" Vi didn't get a chance to finish before the woman was on the ground, head bowed.

"Princess, you grace our humble doorstep. May I invite you in? What service can we give you?"

"I'm not the princess." Vi knelt down, pulling back her hood. Fiera's hair ran down her shoulder blades, where Vi's stopped just past her shoulders. The hair alone wasn't enough, as the woman studied Vi's face. It took longer than Vi would've expected for her to finally admit that she wasn't the princess. But then again, a commoner like her likely had only ever seen Fiera from a distance.

"But... you look just like her."

"I know, many have told me." Vi reached out, grabbed the woman's basket, and returned it to her. Every moment felt as though she was underwater, moving against the current.

I'm not the princess. She wasn't the princess this woman was thinking of. She wasn't Fiera. But she also wasn't a princess at all... not anymore.

The crown princess, Vi Solaris, was gone.

"What do you need, then?" The young woman took the basket, clutching it protectively, as though Vi had been trying to steal it rather than return it.

"I'm a bit lost." That was the best way to put it, though it was a drastic understatement.

"Lost? What area of town are you from?"

Vi's mind retrieved a map of Norin easily from the depths of her cartographic knowledge. She could pick anywhere and make it believable. But she wasn't from anywhere here, and picking somewhere at random wouldn't help her. She needed a quiet place to get her thoughts in order, not an easy way out of this encounter.

"I don't remember," Vi lied, rubbing her head for emphasis. She stood. "I woke up in a stable. And I don't remember anything before then." It was easy to inject the words with the slightest bit of panic and terror. She had more than enough of each to go around. "I don't know where to go and I don't know how to find out."

The young woman shifted, tucking a section of bangs behind her ear. "We don't have anything to give you."

"May I just sit on your doorstep, then?" Vi asked. "Your second floor juts out slightly and gives some shade from the afternoon sun."

"Fine." The young woman pushed past her. "Just don't think of trying to come in." She slammed the door shut behind her, and Vi was alone.

She crouched down and sat on the stoop. Her hands worried the watch at her neck as her brain tried to organize her thoughts.

An hour must've passed, for guards began to sweep through the city, telling the few stragglers on the streets that the curfew had come into effect and it was time to go inside. Just as Vi was about to use her Lightspinning to make herself invisible, a guard started her way and she cursed her luck. She couldn't blink out of existence now.

"You, it's time to go inside," the man commanded gruffly. Vi was focused on the red strip of fabric that circled his bicep. The symbol of the Knights of Jadar instantly unnerved her. But at this point in history, the group had yet to splinter and turn on her family. "Did you hear me? Go inside."

"I don't have anywhere to go."

"Get inside," the man repeated, pointing to the door.

"This isn't my home."

"Then go back to your home."

A bitter, raspy laugh escaped her lips. "If only. I don't have a home."

"Please, I don't want any trouble." The man sighed and glanced over at his fellow soldiers. They had already moved on. "If you truly don't have a home, there are shelters not far from the castle. I don't care where you end up. But I can't leave you out here. Anyone who's not a soldier or a Knight must be indoors, royal orders."

Soldier or a Knight. She could fight. The thought hovered in her mind for a long second. Vi opened her mouth before closing it again slowly. Would she fight against her grandfather?

On one side of this war was her grandmother, on the other her grandfather. Her heritage versus her Empire. Though it wasn't even *her* Empire anymore. Vi let out a groan and held her head.

"What's wrong with you?"

The door at Vi's right opened suddenly, the young woman from earlier in its frame. "She's with us—I mean, she's not. But we'll take her in."

"What?" Vi wasn't sure if she said the word in her surprise or just thought it loudly.

"Come on, inside with you." The woman grabbed her arm, helping Vi up.

"See to it that none of you are caught out past curfew," the Knight cautioned with a pointed look at Vi before starting along.

"We'll follow orders," the young woman called back. Without another word, Vi was ushered inside a tiny foyer connected to a narrow stair. There were no other doors and the top landing was dark enough that Vi couldn't make out much. The woman locked the door and leaned against it with a sigh.

"Thank you," Vi said softly.

"Don't thank me, thank Granny. She was the one who said I couldn't leave another woman out there to fend for herself." She looked Vi up and down and added with a mutter, "Though you seem perfectly capable."

"I still appreciate it." Vi didn't comment on her capacity to defend herself.

"Well, show that appreciation by not making us regret it." The young woman ran a hand through her short-cut hair. "The name is Lucina, by the way."

"Nice to meet you, Lucina."

"Do you remember your name? Or is that gone too?"

"It's gone too." Vi didn't know what compelled her to hide her name. No one knew of Vi Solaris in this world. Her name, however unconventional it was, would mean nothing.

Yet that was precisely the reason why she didn't want to share it. Her name was precious—the only thing that was truly hers that she still carried. Even the watch around her neck was different than the one she had received from Fritz. Her mother's watch had been destroyed, the replacement from Taavin now hanging in its place.

Call out to me. Some of his final words thrummed across her thoughts like fingers dancing on the strings of a harp. *When you are settled, call out to me.*

"Well, I'll need some sort of name. Can't just say, 'Hey, no-name girl,' whenever I need you."

"How about Yullia?"

"Yullia it is." Lucina ascended the stairs. "Granny is sleeping, so don't wake her." Her voice had fallen to a hush. "Granny sleeps in the living area on the first floor. I have a room on the second floor. You can take dad's old room."

Before Vi could inquire further, Lucina pressed a finger to her lips as they emerged onto a landing area that was utilized as a living space. There was a kitchen, a sitting area with distinctly low-profile, Western furniture, and a cot in the corner where an ancient woman snored. Lucina headed up a ladder in the corner to the floor above. Vi followed as silently as possible.

"You'll be in here." Lucina opened the door immediately to the right at the top of the ladder.

"Your father won't need it?"

"Dad's dead."

"I'm sorry," Vi said. But her tenderness seemed to confuse the young woman. "Did... I say something wrong?"

"Half of this city is dying or dead. It's weird to hear sympathies and I don't want them." Lucina shrugged and hastily changed the topic. "Remember, we don't have anything for you. All you're getting is a bed. If I even catch you looking at our food—" She drew a kitchen knife from her belt "—I won't hesitate to kill. No one would notice or care about another body."

Vi lifted a hand, placed her fingers against the flat of the blade, and pushed it away. "I'm not going to give you reason to fear me," she said firmly, locking eyes with Lucina. "I mean you no harm."

"Well…" Lucina hadn't been expecting Vi to take the threat in stride. She tucked the weapon back in her belt. "See that you don't."

The young woman started for the ladder and descended quickly. Vi made a point to close her door loudly enough that Lucina would hear it—but hopefully not too loudly that it disturbed the sleeping old woman whom she had to thank for this hospitality.

The room was small. A bed, a chest at its foot. A narrow window, barely large enough to let light in, faced the blank wall of another building.

Vi sat heavily on the bed, sinking her face into her hands, her elbows on her knees. An ache ran so deeply within her that she didn't know where it stemmed from, or what hurt most. Physically, her body felt fine. No, great. Not even the scars from Ulvarth's shackles marred her wrists. Yet her joints seemed to protest every movement, as if they carried an invisible weight.

Quiet had never been so loud.

"What is going on?" she whispered to no one. A hand dropped to the watch around her neck. Magic pulsed under her fingertips.

This watch—no, not *this* one… but a watch nearly identical to it had connected her with Taavin. It had begun this whole relentless series of events that had chewed her up and now spit her out in a place she had no business being.

"Curse you," she muttered, burying her face in her hands again. She didn't know who she was cursing. The goddess, Taavin, fate itself? All of them, *curse all of them*, for all she cared. "You told me to summon you? Summon a dead man?" Vi laughed, a sound that was crazy to her own ears. "Fine, Taavin. I'll honor your mad, last wish. *Narro hath hoolo*."

The words sparked in her mind, bright and true. Meaning poured from them into glowing lines of yellow light that spun from her like ropes of fire. They connected to form familiar glyphs.

From those glyphs came the outline of a man—a man she thought she'd killed with her own hands. A man whose brilliant green eyes could not be dulled by the sands of time no matter how many times they were turned over.

"T-Taavin?"

2

H E STARED AT HER for a long minute before looking around the room, much as he always had whenever she'd summoned him. As though this interaction was perfectly normal and planned.

As though she hadn't *killed him* hours before.

The facts compounded on the surreal nature of her current state, making it feel as though she watched him from outside of her body. Their roles were reversed. She was the specter, and he was the real person.

Because nothing about her world could possibly be real right now.

"I see you've found some quiet corner to hide in." He breathed a sigh of relief. "Where are you this time? I don't recognize this place."

"I don't recognize any of this." Vi was on her feet, working to keep her voice quiet. The building was sturdy and seemed well-built. But Lucina and her grandmother would definitely hear if panic got the better of her and she began to shout. Vi took a staggering step closer to him. "Taavin… where are you? What's going on? Are you all right?"

Her hands reached for him as she drew closer. Closer to the man she had killed. Closer to the man who had held and hurt her. Nearly close enough to touch, to reassure herself that this wasn't a psychotic break.

Taavin's fingers wrapped around hers. They weren't as solid as she remembered. Was this identical to how she'd first spoken to him in Shaldan? He'd seemed so real then, as though he'd been standing in the room with her. Now, the ghost of magic wriggled around his body. It created a barrier she couldn't seem to cross.

He uncurled one hand and pointed his index finger at the watch over her chest. "I'm here."

"The watch?" Vi looked down at the faintly shimmering glyphs that hovered over the token. "Yes, I remember it connects me to you, but where are *you*?"

Pain flashed through his familiar emerald eyes. Taavin opened his mouth, then closed it, as if unable to find the words. His finger had yet to move. "I'm *here*."

"In the watch?" Vi dared to ask. Taavin nodded. "But… how?"

"The watch was the key to it all." She remembered him saying as much in Risen.

"In it were my memories… all of them. In it, the Champion's future is ensured and preserved. In it, my consciousness now lives, so I may guide you."

"I don't understand." She wanted to. Vi repeated his words mentally, but she couldn't siphon out the deeper meaning clearly hidden beneath them.

"One moment." Taavin gave her hand a light squeeze and, without further warning, stepped away. He stretched out his arms before him and curled his open palms, as though holding an invisible book. His lips moved with low whispering tones; it must have been some kind of Lightspinning, but Vi couldn't make out a single word. She suspected that even if she could, she wouldn't have understood them.

This was a magic the goddess had given only to him.

The glyphs above her watch spun faster. Like a spigot, magic poured from the necklace into symbols that hovered between Taavin's arms. He watched them carefully as they piled, one atop the next, shifting and changing. The green of his eyes faded to the same pale blue as his magic, glowing brightly in the dark room.

Finally, Taavin lowered his arms, the light between them vanishing into the still air.

"All right, I think I've cobbled together the swiftest explanation that will make it easiest for you to understand," he began. "You met Yargen, correct?"

"Yes."

"What did she tell you?"

Vi sighed and closed her eyes, thinking back to her interaction with the goddess. She remembered pain, then life, then Queen Lumeria—who hadn't actually been Queen Lumeria, but Yargen masquerading as the sovereign.

"She told me… That she was restarting the world," Vi paraphrased. "Returning me to a time before her power had been turned against itself, and destroyed."

"Exactly. You know what time you're in, yes?"

"Norin fell in three hundred twenty-two." Vi raised a hand to her forehead and shook her head. "Just saying that aloud is madness."

"Yet you know it to be true. You can feel it in your marrow, just as you can feel Yargen's power. This will all be easier if you don't try to fight the truths before you."

"Don't tell me what I can and can't feel," Vi snapped. She was a rope fraying at all sides. "I'm sorry, I didn't mean to be curt," Vi said hastily. "It's a lot to process is all. I was just thrown back in time and now I'm talking with someone akin to a ghost. Not to say I'm not happy to see you, but…" She trailed off in the wake of Taavin's tired smile.

"I understand. You're not alone in feeling jarred by all this. From my perspective, I just died for the ninety-third time and it gets no easier."

"Ninety… third?" Vi repeated. He seemed determined to look anywhere but at her.

"This point in time is the furthest at which Yargen can remake the world with the limited power she had," he continued, determined to ignore her probing stare. "So it is where our work must begin. Your job is twofold. Foremost, your goal is to ensure the birth of a new Champion and another attempt, should you fail. While doing so, you must collect the crystal weapons in order to consolidate Yargen's power once more and prevent Raspian from ever being set free."

"So I am to change the past?"

"There is no past—not the past you knew, at least," he said gravely. "The only time that exists is the one in which Yargen exists. The world you and I knew, the world we were born into, is no more. She lives in this world now, in you."

"But this world exists along the same lines of fate… so it appears identical," Vi said, remembering more of what the goddess had told her. She sank heavily onto the bed behind her. "My mother, father, brother?"

"They do not exist, yet." He was silent for a long moment, then added softly and apologetically, "And the Aldrik, Vhalla, and Romulin who will exist, will not be the ones you knew."

She looked down at her hands. They were trembling again. Her whole body shook. Vi felt painfully cold, like no matter what she did, she'd never be able to warm up again. "I wanted to save them."

"Preventing the Crystal Caverns from being tampered with is how you will save them."

"No, the family I loved is gone—you just said so." Vi tilted her head up to the man as if pleading with him could change the terrible fate she found herself in. "The world was in danger, so I did everything I was told; I did everything to stop it from ending. I did it all to save my family."

"And this is how we will stop it so your family is never in danger again."

"The world—my family—merely ended at the hands of a different tyrant!" Vi was on her feet again, pacing. Her magic crackled, stronger than ever before, ready to collect in her palms and burn the whole broken world and all its pieces. "Raspian didn't end the world, so Yargen did? So we could try to fix a new version of it? How does that make any sense?"

"The timeline we were on was a failed future. It made sense to abandon it."

"The timeline." Her hands shook harder. "Don't call it a 'timeline' as though it's just dates and facts in a book. There were *people*, Taavin. Hundreds of thousands of people. A whole world of them. My family was in that world… and they're all gone now." Vi didn't remember approaching him, but her fists knotted in the simple tunic he wore—the same garment he'd had on when she'd found him in his room that fateful night. A night that might as well have been a thousand years ago. "Yargen killed them all."

"Yargen is life. Vi, don't think of it as them dying." His hands wrapped around hers again. His tone was soothing. "As it stands now, they never existed in the first place. But fate can see them born again in this world—a world you will save. You saw it yourself, the end of the world."

For a brief second, her eyes were as haunted as his, as visions of her falling before a dark god flashed across her mind.

"If we had remained in that world, Vi," he continued, "the cycle of light and dark would've ended. Raspian and Yargen would've battled again. But since she was weak and didn't have all her power, he would've killed her for good. There would've been no eventual return of the goddess, no great war, no subsequent age of light. Darkness and death would've ruled forever. It was the end."

"You're saying no matter what… the life of everyone in that world was forfeit? Every beautiful, hidden corner, every person, all would've been destroyed?" Her voice quivered alongside her hands. She had been born into a dying world and she was the only person to survive it.

Vi felt profoundly unworthy of each breath she took.

"Yes."

"I thought, as Champion, I could save it. Save… them."

"You were chosen for this world, where you stand now. It was the last Vi's failure that doomed the world you knew." A ghost drifted around his words, one that seemed to cloud his vision whenever his eyes settled on her.

Ninety-three times. His earlier words stuck in her mind.

"How many times have we had this conversation?" Vi whispered.

"What?"

"How many times have you explained all this to me?"

"I don't know what you're asking." The lie was so obvious Vi had to bite back bitter laughter.

"Yes you do. I know you too well, Taavin; I see behind any mask you try to wear." She swallowed, her throat drier than the Waste. "This isn't the first time I've asked, is it?" Taavin pursed his lips together and narrowed his eyes. "How many times, Taavin?" she reiterated. And then, just to twist the dagger, added, "How many times have you died by my hand? Has the world been rebuilt? How many times have we tried and failed to stop Raspian? How many *other Vis* failed?"

She didn't know why she was asking. She'd already figured out the answer.

"Ninety-three."

Somehow, hearing it from his lips was worse than she expected.

Vi's fingers slowly uncurled from the man's garb. She smoothed out the wrinkles thoughtfully, almost gently. The motion was a stark contrast to the torrent of anger brewing within her. Abruptly, she went to the narrow window. It was her only source of fresh air and she desperately needed to take a breath.

"Ninety-three times," she finally repeated quietly. The world had been destroyed, rebuilt, destroyed again, over and over, ninety-three times. It was incomprehensible to her.

Mortal minds weren't made for this.

Vi stared at the stone wall outside of the window, willing the wind to blow, to feel some movement in the air. But everything was stagnant, making a hot day only hotter.

"What makes you think we can do this now?" Vi asked without looking at him.

"Nothing." That drew her eyes back. Taavin elaborated without further prompting. "I don't know if we will be successful this time, or the next, or the time after. But I have faith eventually we will. I have to, otherwise we are trapped in this torturous vortex forever, always spinning, down and down."

They were cursed. She'd known it on Meru. He'd confirmed it now.

"How long have you known this was our fate?"

"Only when you used the word *thrumsana*. It unlocked the stored memories from my past selves in the watch, returning them to me. Then, I knew what must be done to finish the turn and start anew."

Vi narrowed her eyes slightly. She vividly remembered the power that had been unleashed when she used that word. Just as vividly, she remembered learning not long before that Taavin had betrayed Vi and her father to the Swords of Light. That wound had yet to be mended, and now Vi wondered if they'd ever have the chance. Did she have any right to still be angry with him for a father that no longer existed?

The thought made her throat close up.

He had betrayed her. She had killed him. Perhaps it was better to destroy the hurt of those transgressions with the world she'd known.

Mother above, her head ached.

"What do we do now?" Vi forced herself to ask.

"We need to be careful going forward." Taavin crossed to her side. "Very careful, for a number of years. Until you ensure Vhalla receives the watch, the birth of a new Vi—a new Champion—isn't guaranteed. Which means if you die… it ends for good."

"It *will* end for good." *Ninety-three times*. That was ninety-two too many. "We will end it, this time." Vi turned to him.

Taavin placed his hand at the small of her back, staring down with worried eyes. He wasn't as warm, she realized. Little things kept adding up that made his presence here torture. He wasn't really with her any longer. *Not really*.

"I told you once: I look back, you look forward. This is the curse you always felt, but never fully knew. You're forced to see the end of the world encroaching, and you feel an obligation to try, futilely thus far, to prevent it. Whereas I…" He swallowed hard. "I remember the past. I exist to watch and be a living record of your every action. To serve as your aide in finding what will succeed by ensuring you don't repeat what failed. I remember every time you've fallen and every hurt you've endured. And the only thing that enables me to carry on is the knowledge that someday, I will see you again."

Or some version of me, Vi wanted to say, but couldn't. The truth, even though they both knew it, was too cruel to speak aloud. If what he was saying was true, every Vi was a unique person that lived, fought, and ultimately perished underneath the wheel of time.

"So you must be careful, until Vhalla Solaris gives birth to a Vi Solaris in this age." Vi gave a small nod. She was too tired to fight. Taavin must've sensed as much. "You should get some rest. Norin will fall soon, and you'll want to be nimble to try to get close to Fiera and the sword when it does."

Vi grabbed his bicep before he could pull away. Her grip tightened, trying to press through the thin barrier of magic that kept him from her. "I want you to stay," she whispered. Pain flashed across his face.

"I wish I could. But you know how this works." He leaned forward, planting a gentle kiss on her forehead. "Now, rest."

With that, he vanished; the glyphs above her watch dimmed and faded, and the room seemed darker and lonelier than ever before.

An explosion woke her.

Vi was on her feet in an instant as shock waves rattled the city. She heard shouts, and the clash of steel on steel. Her heart raced as she stared at the door.

Vi took a step forward, and one back, then two forward. *Keep yourself safe*, Taavin had said. Another rumble shook the city, and she was off. Running, Vi threw open the door and was down the ladder in a breath, steps ahead of Lucina.

"Yullia!" Lucina called after her, following close behind. "Where are you—"

"Lucina. Lucina!" The young woman's grandmother was upright in her cot, calling out to her granddaughter. Vi paused at the top of the stairs, watching as her wrinkled hand reached out, grabbing at the air, milky eyes unseeing.

"Granny, I'm here." Lucina rushed over to her kin, sitting on the edge of the bed as another shock wave rattled the city. The two huddled together tightly, holding each other.

"Lucina." Vi summoned the girl's attention with her name. "I'm going out. You'll want to lock the door behind me."

"Out? Yullia, there's a *war* going on out there."

"I know, and I have every intention of fighting in it. Lock the door behind me." Vi didn't know if that was entirely true. She still wasn't sure if she could pick a side in this war—not when both sides were her family. Or at least… once upon a time, they had been family. Though the waters were murky, Vi couldn't help wanting to jump in with both feet. Sink or swim.

She sprinted down the stairs, unbolted the door, and stepped out into the dusty street.

When she heard the bolt engage behind her, she started off in the direction of an orange haze. The fires of battle were already burning the city; what was once the greatest kingdom in the history of the Dark Isle would fall before the sun rose.

3

VI RAN TOWARD THE carnage along the main street of Norin. Doubt nipped at her heels as she fell into step with men and women carrying various weapons—everything from forged steel to fishing spears. Her beacon was an orange haze glowing off smoke rising in the horizon. If Vi kept solely focused on that, maybe she wouldn't question too much what, in the Mother's name, she was doing.

She pushed against the masses who were fleeing as fast as they could in the opposite direction. Women carried wailing children tightly in their arms; those large enough to walk were half-dragged along the dusty ground.

At first, most of the people fleeing seemed unscathed, but the further she ran, the more Vi saw wounded and dying.

A man staggered through the street, soldiers and civilians alike parting to run around him. His clothes had been nearly burnt off; charred ribbons clung to blistered and reddened skin. He stared with a pleading expression and a gaping mouth that couldn't seem to find the right words to beg for help.

Suppressing her instinct to gag at the putrid scent of burnt flesh and hair, Vi stopped right before the man, not daring to touch him on his reddened and bubbled side.

"Come this way." His eyes swung to her when he realized someone was speaking to him. Someone had actually heard his soundless cries. "I can heal you," Vi said softly. Somehow, little more than a whisper felt loud when the man's crazed gaze was on her. It was louder than the sounds of fighting in the distance, or the crackle of flames that blazed at the far end of the main street. "Will you come with me?"

He made a choked noise, barely bobbing his head.

Vi took his left hand—the one that hadn't been burned in whatever blaze he had been caught in. She led him out of the street, making sure no one bumped or jostled him in the process.

"This won't hurt," she whispered. She wasn't good at *halleth*, but surely, anything was better than the pain he found himself in. Vi murmured under her breath, "*Halleth ruta toff.*"

She kept the glyph tiny and tightly wound right underneath her palm, holding it above the man's burnt forearm in such a way that he would see nothing more than a faint glow. Vi focused only on mending his forearm, ignoring the rising sounds of battle and the countless others in just as bad a state as this man. *Grow, mend, heal,* she willed to the flesh through her magic. When his forearm was no longer blistered and red, Vi moved on.

Section by section, she mended the worst of the burns. She tried to focus on what seemed the most life threatening, but Vi was no cleric. Her healing was clumsy, scarred and knotted, just as Taavin had said it was when she washed up on the beaches of Meru. But it was better than dead. It had to be better than dead, she insisted to herself.

Vi lowered her hand, having finished with the side of the man's face. His eyes were on her, much more focused than before. He swallowed once before rasping, "Thank you, your highness."

He thought she was Fiera, just as Lucina had. Vi pursed her lips into a thin smile.

"You're welcome." Vi didn't see the point in correcting him. No one was likely to believe him even if he remembered the details of their encounter come dawn. "Can you tell me what's happening? Do you remember?"

He gave a nod. The scar tissue of his neck seemed to pull, causing him to wince slightly. "The wall finally fell. The Imperialists blasted through. They're in the city."

Vi looked in the direction she'd been heading. The fires burned brighter now, almost like an angry dawn on the horizon. She had read about the fall of Norin, but it wasn't a breach in the wall that had brought the noble city to its knees after ten long years—it was by an attack on the sea.

The fighting at the wall was a distraction to give the ships carrying the bulk of the Imperial army time to enter the port.

But what should she do with that information? If she did something, could she see Norin fall faster and potentially spare more from this man's fate?

A hand closed around her watch and Vi briefly thought of summoning Taavin. But if she did, he'd know she'd run into the fray, putting herself in danger. Perhaps putting the future of the entire world in danger with her. *Ninety-three times.* She'd hurt him enough for one day.

"Thank you for the information." Vi stepped away, leaving the man to hover, clearly still dazed. She'd done all she could for him. "Head for the northwest corner of the city. Avoid the port and the outer wall at all costs."

Vi ran upstream through a river of people. Then, all at once, there was no one left for her to push against. She found herself among burning rubble, the crackle of magic blazing through the sky.

Men and women littered the ground around her. Some were burned to husks. Others still oozed crimson into the cracks of the road. Vi stared at the carnage, at those soldiers still fighting in the distance, flames glinting off their plate armor.

She had seen death, up close. But she had never seen war. Standing before it now, Vi felt frozen in place. She wondered if she should feel terrified, if she should weep.

There weren't any feelings though. It was as if any single emotion was insufficient, and so they all left her. Everything was numb. She was presented with the embodiment of *juth calt*: the world had been shattered.

Without warning, a tiny jolt of magic broke the stasis Vi was unwittingly trapped in. Her heart began to race. The bodies around her were more than just corpses; they suddenly became men and women, people with lives, daughters and sons. Vi fought against the swelling sickness that threatened to overcome her.

Another crack of magic—one Vi would recognize anywhere.

When she turned, a wall of flame blocked her vision. The fire roared with unnatural power, connecting one blazing building to the next. It was no doubt a dividing line. The break in the wall must be on the other side and someone very, very powerful was trying to contain the flow of soldiers within.

Yet even a heavy curtain of fire couldn't hide the pull of something greater—a god-like magic. Determined and drawn by an invisible tether, Vi marched forward toward the fire, allowing her own spark to swell within her.

You feel it in your marrow. Taavin's words echoed inside her.

"Yes," Vi whispered to no one. He had been speaking about the truth of her situation. But Vi felt something far greater in her bones. Within her was a power that recognized and sought out its own—the power of a goddess.

You will be free of the bonds of time because my magic is in you, Yargen had said.

Raising a hand, Vi used her magic to bore a hole through the flames that barred her path. It was surprisingly easy, given how impressive the fire was. Whatever Firebearer made it was weaker than Vi expected, for she gained control of the inferno as though it had been her own power all along.

A tunnel opened up before her and Vi charged through, quickly releasing her hold on the fire. On the other side, more carnage waited.

The chorus of battle she'd heard echo over the crackle of the blazes throughout the city was now reaching its crescendo. The large wall surrounding the city had been blown in, reducing nearby buildings to rubble. Debris scattered inward, men and women fighting around large chunks of stone. Those with crimson armbands and red plumes seemed to have the upper hand, pushing back the silver-plated soldiers in short capes of Solaris blue and white.

The same jolt of magic pulsed through her, stronger and closer this time. Vi's eyes were drawn to a far corner, where a woman was locked in the heat of battle with a group of three. She wielded a sword that glowed with a blue haze; power crackled off of it as she alternated between swinging it and casting balls of fire off her free hand.

Vi watched in awe as Fiera Ci'Dan made quick work of three soldiers. She wondered if Fiera had even the slightest idea of how much the weapon was influencing her power.

"Push them back!" Fiera screamed to the soldiers fighting their way up the mound of debris where the wall once stood. "Don't let them through! Show them the strength of Mhashan." Fiera began running and Vi picked up her feet as well.

Their paths intersected near the center of the battlefield. Without missing a step, Fiera shifted her weight, bringing the sword across her body in a swing at Vi. Vi reacted instantly, dodging backward. Fiera held the sword out, keeping her at length, and met Vi's eyes for the first time.

They stared at each other, panting, unmoving. Energy crackled underneath Vi's skin—something more than her own power or Yargen's. Vi knew it as the hair-raising sensation of fate playing its hand.

"Your face is… You…" Fiera struggled for words between heavy breaths.

"There's no time to explain. But I am not your enemy."

"*Who are you?*" Fiera said, as she looked Vi up and down, lowering the sword.

"I'm a traveler, and I've come a long way to tell you…" Vi trailed off. To tell her what? That she needed the sword? That she was the granddaughter of another Fiera from another world? Vi had been acting on instinct, pulled along by her gut, and now she wasn't sure if it had landed her in a good spot.

"To tell me what?" Fiera pressed, with an expression that told Vi she'd seen right through her uncertainty. Another explosion rocked the city. Magic sloshed off the blade in her hand and Fiera cursed and turned, frantically scanning the wall. "Guards in the First Legion, go through the opening, find where they're trying to breach the city a second time!" Men and women pushed farther up the rubble and Fiera started in their direction. Vi gripped her forearm, and Fiera's eyes darted between the clearly offending touch and Vi's face. "Unhand me."

"It's a distraction," Vi blurted. "Tiberus Solaris is coming from the sea."

"What? There's no—"

"They split their forces, weeks ago, I think." Vi struggled to remember her history. The fall of Mhashan had seemed like ancient history when she'd studied it with Martis. Now she was searching her brain for every last detail she could recall. "He's coming from the sea."

Fiera's attention volleyed between Vi and the soldiers. She let out a string of curses before settling her gaze on Vi once more.

"Tell me why I should believe you." The princess lifted her sword. Oddly, it didn't feel threatening. It felt like a challenge.

"Because I know what fate has designed." It was the only explanation Vi could think of, and she knew it wasn't a very good one. Yet somehow, it was enough.

Fiera sheathed her sword, turning to the carnage. "Schnurr!" she shouted. A man who looked far too young to be on the battlefield came rushing over. "See to the troops here. I do not want the Imperials to take one more step into our city."

"Yes, your highness." The man gave a salute.

"Honor guard, to me!" Fiera commanded. Three men and two women ran over as Schnurr ran back into the fray. "We're going to the docks."

They all saluted. Not one questioned her. Not one uttered a word of dissent. These men and women were ready to follow their leader to the ends of the earth or the ends of their lives—whichever came first.

Vi wondered briefly if she'd ever commanded such loyalty from anyone.

"You're sure?" Fiera turned to her once more. Vi nodded. "Onward, then!" Fiera swept out her arm and cut a tunnel into the flame, much as Vi had.

The princess and soldiers took two steps ahead as Vi stared in awe.

The magic had almost felt like hers... It had almost felt like hers in the same way Vi would know her father's magic from anywhere. She might be from another version of the world, but something still connected her with the woman who would become the grandmother to a new Vi.

The group plunged through the tunnel of flame. Without stopping, Fiera continued along the street. Their pace was a jog, which felt agonizingly slow to Vi. But she was in a simple tunic and trousers. The rest of them wore an array of plate and scale mail. She used the pace as an excuse to take sidelong looks at the princess.

The woman had a sharp nose and angular eyes set atop cheekbones even stronger than Vi's own. Her hair had fallen free of whatever tie it had been in and was now knotting down her back. She was real, breathing, *alive*. But if the events of this world were transpiring along the same time frame as they had in Vi's world... she wouldn't be alive for more than a year.

Or would she?

In Vi's world, Fiera had died in childbirth—no, her father had corrected that. She'd died protecting a crystal sword. Now Vi desperately wished he'd told her all the details. Though perhaps they didn't matter.

Perhaps nothing from her world mattered now.

Her stomach knotted as they continued down the main street, turning off at the intersection Vi had walked with Jayme months ago. The docks weren't far when cannon fire rattled the glass of the windows around them. All seven dropped, hands covering their heads as cannonballs ripped through the city.

"What was—" one of the soldiers began.

"The wall was a distraction," Vi said, standing. "The Emperor is flanking you, coming from the sea."

"You call the usurper *Emperor*?" The long-haired woman drew a dagger, placing it at Vi's throat. "And just how do you know all this?"

"I—" Vi wasn't prepared to explain, and luckily Fiera didn't make her.

"I trust her," Fiera interjected, rising to her feet as well. The woman holding the blade at Vi's neck didn't move. "I said I trust her. Put down your weapon."

"What if she's a spy? She speaks like an Imperialist. No red-blooded Westerner would call that destroyer of kingdoms 'Emperor.' She looks like she could get away with masquerading as you, even. What if they sent her to take us from the wall? What if the ship is the distraction meant to pull you away?"

"If she's a spy, we kill her at the docks and return." The other woman with hair cut so short it barely reached her ears rested her hand on her comrade's shoulder. "Listen to our leader. We only have a few minutes before those cannons are reloaded."

Ultimately, the woman with the dagger at Vi's throat did as Fiera commanded, and they were off once more. Vi rubbed her neck as she ran and remembered Taavin's words—if she died now, it was over.

But no, it was only over if she *failed*. If she succeeded in this world and stopped Yargen's power from being turned on itself, then it didn't matter if a new Vi was born. Because there would be no more destruction and rebirth.

Vi's mind was silenced as they rounded the corner and caught their first glimpse of the great port of Norin. Fires blazed in the ocean from ships that were sinking beneath its inky waters. Three large warships with massive battering rams had invaded the port, leaving debris in their wake. Each ship bore a white sail emblazoned with a golden sun.

The ships had already dropped anchor; two were using makeshift gangplanks to allow a near-endless stream of soldiers into the city. Half of the Imperial army had been crammed into those bloated hulls, and now they were encroaching on the castle of Norin, on the civilians that surrounded it, and on the troops battling at the wall from behind.

"Mother above," one of Fiera's men uttered in shock.

Cannon fire rang out, and they all dropped once more as shrapnel and cannon balls ripped through the paltry collection of Western soldiers and buildings alike on the docks. Vi continued to stare, watching them fall. For the second time since she'd entered this version of the world, she felt as though she was watching everything from outside of her body—a history book come to life in the darkest of ways.

"Traveler." Vi hadn't realized they'd ended up side by side until she glanced over and found the princess at her shoulder. "Is Tiberus Solaris on that vessel?" Vi nodded, hoping her grandfather made the same choice in this world as he had in her own. "Then we press onward." Fiera sprang to her feet. "Quickly now!"

Vi, Fiera's five Knights, and the woman herself came to a stop at the center of the docks, right before the main vessel that had been unleashing an artillery assault.

Fiera drew her sword and shouted, "Tiberus, face me!"

The world seemed to hold its breath. Even the soldiers that had been marching down the gangplanks of the other two ships paused as Fiera's voice reverberated off rock and sea. Vi prayed this world was unfolding like her own, that she hadn't started out by lying to Fiera.

"I know you're there. Come out and duel me like the honorable man you claim to be. I am the sword arm of the King of Mhashan. You will not conquer us until you have conquered me!"

"You have been heard, princess." A deep voice filled the air.

Standing at the bow of the ship before them was a man clad in golden armor, trimmed in silver polished so brightly it shone white in the pale moonlight. His hair was the same hue as his armor and his face was clean-shaven, almost roguish—Vi had only ever seen portraits of her grandfather and he looked nothing like the young man standing before them now. She searched his face, seeking out some familial resemblance. But the only thing her father had inherited from Tiberus was the pallor of his skin. Fiera's features had won out in every other way.

Fiera pointed her sword directly at Tiberus. Raw magic sparked from it, falling to the ground like dying fireworks. "And do you accept my challenge?"

"I will accept your surrender," the Emperor said haughtily, in a tone Vi recognized from her own father.

"You must earn it first."

"You've lost this war."

"He's as arrogant as they say," the long-haired honor guard muttered.

A sailor ran up to the Emperor, whispering something in his ear. As they exchanged words none of them could hear, Fiera remained poised, waiting. Her arm didn't so much as quiver despite holding out the long sword.

"You may have your duel, princess. With whatever time is left," Tiberus said ominously before disappearing from sight. Soon enough a rowboat worked its way from the side of the boat to the docks.

"Your highness—"

"I told you before, this ends tonight." Fiera glanced over her shoulder at them before turning to the castle.

Vi took a step forward. Something in Fiera's eyes compelled her. She had an understanding no one else did, save Vi herself.

"You know," Vi whispered softly. Saying nothing, Fiera gave a small nod.

"As do you?"

It was Vi's turn to nod. "Fighting the Emperor won't change anything."

"I realize." Fiera shifted her attention to the rowboat that pulled up alongside the docks. "But the longer I can distract him, the more lives I can spare in the city. If I can be the outlet for his rage, act as the embodiment of my family, then he might spare my siblings."

It was a noble goal. Vi would've admired it more if it wasn't leading toward her grandfather and grandmother dueling. Bringing Fiera here had been a terrible decision.

Taavin had said she was here to change fate.

What if she changed it in the wrong way?

Three soldiers quickly disembarked, followed by Tiberus, then two more soldiers. Were it not for Vi, they would've been evenly matched. In a way they still were. Vi wasn't about to fight for or against either side if it came to blows.

"Sheathe your sword and I'll spare your life." Tiberus wasn't very tall, Vi realized. Yet he spoke with authority that towered above them all.

In reply, Fiera hoisted her weapon, pointing it directly toward the Emperor.

Vi inched backward, her heart racing. Had Fiera and Tiberus traded blows in her time? She swiftly ran through her options for diffusing the situation. If one of them was killed now, would she—rather, the new Vi—even be born?

"Let it be death, then." Tiberus drew his weapon.

"Wai—" Vi never had a chance to finish.

Horns blasted through the city in a low, sad song. She didn't recognize the melody, but it had everyone else holding their breath. Fiera turned to the castle.

From the tallest tower, a makeshift banner was unfurled. It wasn't much, but it would surely be seen from anywhere in the city: the white flag of surrender was draped across the castle of Norin.

Like that, Mhashan fell.

"Zerian did it..." Tiberus murmured, turning back to them. "Kneel before your Emperor and you shall know my mercy."

Fiera's knuckles went white, but ultimately, she sheathed her sword. Vi watched as the princess fell to one knee.

"Your highness, do not kneel before—"

"We have lost," Fiera said back to them.

Tiberus turned to Vi next and she hastily dropped to her knee, bowing her head.

"Kneel," the Emperor demanded to the rest of the soldiers.

One man and the two women did as they were bid. But the other two remained on their feet.

"We will never kneel before Imperial swine."

"Kneel or die," Tiberus reiterated. "I am ready to give this city mercy, but do not test me."

"We are the Knights of Jadar—"

"And your commander orders you to kneel," Fiera snapped.

"Our commander would never bend her knee before a Southerner," one of the men seethed.

"The war is over," Vi said. "You see the banner." They all ignored her.

"Kill them," the Emperor ordered.

"No." Fiera was on her feet in a moment, blocking the Imperial knights. Swords were drawn from all angles, each pointing at someone different. "They are my responsibility." Fiera leveled her gaze at Tiberus. For his part, he had very little reaction.

Vi watched closely, seeing her father in both of them—seeing herself. She had given little thought to the blood that was spilled before her birth to build the Empire she would rule. She'd learned of it, but she hadn't comprehended the sacrifices or all the tough choices her family had made along the way to build what was known in her age as the greatest Empire the Dark Isle had ever seen.

"Go on, then," Tiberus said. It sounded like a challenge.

Fiera put her back to the Emperor and his soldiers in an incredible display of faith. "Kneel before our new Emperor."

"How dare you—"

"I said kneel!" Fiera shouted. "Mhashan has lost enough in the last ten years. We shall lose no more to foolish pride."

"I will die for my pride."

"Die, then." Fiera swung her sword in a wide arc. She didn't so much as flinch. In one movement, the princess struck down her once-loyal guards by slicing them both at the neck with deadly precision.

Vi watched as the corpses fell. With one swing of her sword, Fiera struck a bloody line in the ground that marked where Mhashan ended, and the rule of Solaris began.

VI STARED AT THE wide eyes of the men who had refused to kneel. Now, they were nothing more than two more bodies on the cobblestone streets of Norin.

"You, princess—"

"Fiera," the woman finished for the Emperor. There was an almost defiant air about her. "Princess Fiera."

"Fiera." The Emperor paused. Vi wondered if she was the only one who caught the brief expression of thoughtful surprise. "You were just a slip of a girl when last I saw you."

"It has been ten long years."

"Thank your father for that." Tiberus sheathed his sword, no more pleased than she was. "Speaking of, let us head to the castle. Perhaps now he will be more inclined to discuss the annexation of the West."

"My father is dead."

Vi tried to catch the eyes of the other three soldiers to see if they should stand as well, but an unspoken conversation was unfolding among them. Vi remained where she was.

"How do you—"

"Know?" Fiera wiped the blood from the crystal blade nonchalantly, incredibly calm given all that had transpired. "I know because I know my father, and he would've never surrendered this city to you. He would be a king of rubble before a servant to a foreign crown." She sheathed the weapon and Vi shifted her weight over her knee. She couldn't attempt to take the blade at this moment. Her best chance was to continue letting things play out and look for an opportunity. "I know because I have seen this future in the flames."

"Unfortunate you couldn't have seen a path to victory earlier," Tiberus said arrogantly.

Fiera didn't rise to the bait. "Your victory was the goddess's will."

Tiberus, for his part, didn't seem the slightest bit unnerved by the proclamation. He didn't so much as nod to address that he'd heard the incredible statement. But Vi could see in his eyes that he was filing away that particular tidbit for later.

She'd read that her grandfather had claimed it had been his divine right to unite the continent. Now Vi wondered if that idea had originated from him, or Fiera.

"Come, all of you. We start for the castle," the Emperor declared.

Soldiers fell into step around them and more were gained along the way as they trudged through the empty city roads. It seemed Imperial soldiers were patrolling around every corner of Norin, putting down the last fighters still loyal to the West. Tiberus's ploy to invade by sea had paid off.

Vi allowed herself to be shepherded along. Taavin had said to get close to the sword and Fiera. This likely wasn't what he'd had in mind, but the result was the same, which surely counted for something.

They walked in silence all the way to the large city square opposite the castle. Here, crowds of Western soldiers had been gathered. They were penned in by rings of Imperial troops that brandished weapons at them as though they were livestock.

"You three, with the rest of them," Tiberus commanded. Then, to Fiera, "You're with me."

"But—" Vi's objection was cut off by another.

"Princess, don't go with him," the long-haired woman in the group objected. "He will slaughter you with the rest of the blood of Jadar. Run now with the blade and—"

"Get in line with the rest of your lot," one of the Imperial soldiers growled, pointing his sword at them and motioning to the masses of surrendered Western soldiers.

"Princess!"

"Come on." Vi grabbed the woman's elbow as Fiera and Tiberus started along the castle's lowered drawbridge. "We have to trust that she knows what she's doing."

"And who are you to say that?" The woman jerked away. "You're not one of us," she said to the Imperial guards. "She's not one of us!"

"She looks like one of you. Now get in line."

"This is the will of the head of the Knights of Jadar," the short-haired woman to Vi's right said, giving the other woman a firm shove toward the opening in the line of Imperial soldiers. "Obey your commander."

"She's not our commander, not anymore," the man grumbled under his breath. "She murders the Knights she's sworn to lead. She kneels before foreign kings. She shames the Knights of—"

"Stay your blasphemous tongue." The short-haired woman just kept pushing.

The opening in the line of Imperial soldiers closed behind them and Vi found herself among a mass of Westerners, packed shoulder to shoulder with barely enough room to move around. This city square was large, but it was quickly filling to capacity. Half the people were coated in soot and blood. Vi took a deep breath, scanning the eyes of the Imperial soldiers brandishing swords in their direction.

Those swords were once intended to protect her. Her stomach knotted as her brain tried to readjust her instinct. Nothing was right. Not even her skin seemed to fit in the same way it once did.

"Are you all right?"

"What?" Vi brought her attention to the short-haired woman at her left. The other woman from Fiera's guard, who had threatened Vi at dagger point, was still whispering in hushed tones with the man.

"You're not one of us." She gave Vi a once-over. "You're certainly not a Knight of Jadar... and you don't look like a soldier."

"I'm neither," Vi affirmed.

"Fiera didn't know you. Though she clearly trusted you." The woman's eyes were drawn back to the princess, now nothing more than a distant speck at the end of the drawbridge. "If you're a civilian, you should try to get out now while you still have the chance. There's no comfort to be had in Norin, but civilians will fare better than soldiers in the days to come."

"Do you think they'll believe I'm not a soldier?"

"Fiera could speak for you."

"She has more important things to worry about." Staying close to the remaining Knights of Jadar might be her best chance of getting back to the princess—and the sword.

"You're a true Westerner, sacrificing your wellbeing for her. Trying to help lead us to victory."

Vi snorted. "I'm not a Westerner."

"But your features are Western—so Western, you could've convinced me you're a lost sister to the princess." Vi stopped a snort of laughter at that. "And you speak our tongue so well."

"I don't know my parentage," Vi lied, staring at Fiera and the Emperor until they disappeared from sight into the castle. "And the language I picked up in my travels. I don't really have a home."

Especially not anymore. She was alone. The only person she had in this world was the man who had stolen her heart and betrayed her—right before she murdered him.

Yargen had an interesting sense of humor.

"Well, if you don't have a home, do you have a name? I'm Zira."

"Yullia."

"While it was under unpleasant circumstances, it is an honor to meet you, Yullia. I believe the goddess sent you for our princess tonight, to fight for her and this land. Fiera is keen to the will of the Mother; that must've led her to trust you."

"You have no idea…" Vi murmured.

"Listen up!" An Imperial major stood at the foot of the drawbridge, right where Vi had witnessed Fiera give her last speech hours ago, and boomed over the masses. His pronunciation of Western words was poor and Vi suspected it made his decree even more grating to the ears of those assembled. "You are to be split at random and will be taken to manor houses that have been converted to shelters where you will be held until further notice. Do not resist and the Emperor will see fit to let you live."

"I wonder how long that kindness will last," the long-haired Knight mused.

"I'd rather be dead than take kindness from that man," the other Knight grumbled.

"Quiet, Luke. If you were determined to die, you should've stood at the docks," Zira said.

Luke continued muttering to the long-haired woman, though it was too quiet for Vi to hear.

Not that she was paying much attention anyway. Her thoughts were back in time. According to the history she knew, the Emperor spared the majority of Mhashan's forces…

But only after he'd made a display of killing off the generals, and quelled the resultant outrage.

The war had ended. But the fighting wouldn't stop for weeks.

Martial law was enacted in the city—at least, that's what they were told by whispering servants who were allowed in and out of the manor house once each day to feed the soldiers held inside.

"Here." Zira startled Vi from her thoughts by thrusting a hunk of bread about the size of Vi's palm in her face. "Eat it before someone kills you for it."

"Is this... fresh?" Vi grabbed for the food eagerly, taking a bite so large she was forced to chew with her mouth open. The bread was soft, crust hard, free of mold or weevils, and still had that distinct aroma of fresh-baked deliciousness—a scent she hadn't smelled in the two weeks since she was imprisoned with the rest of the soldiers. "How did you—"

"The girls say that provisions have arrived from the East. It seems the Emperor has starved us enough and now wishes to win us over by filling our bellies."

Luke started a familiar litany of muttering. "If he thinks the West will bend before him for a few loaves of bread—"

"He's absolutely right," Vi interrupted, swallowing hard to get the rest of the too-large bite down. She needed water, but there was none to spare in the manor. Everything was rationed tightly; they were given just enough to be kept alive. So Vi bit the tip of her tongue until saliva coated her mouth—a trick Zira taught her. "The people have been defeated, shown the Emperor's power, made to feel desperate, and now, when he shows them kindness, they will be all too eager to accept it. It's hard to think straight when hunger is gnawing at you."

She had been learning as much the hard way these past two weeks. In the process, Vi was finding a new, dark appreciation for Taavin's time spent under Ulvarth. How readily she'd judged him for his actions back in the Twilight Forest. Part of her still did. Even during the longest nights of hunger pangs, Vi still didn't think she'd condemn a group of people to slaughter.

But she was only two weeks in. And he'd spent years in such a state. She twisted the watch at her neck, longing to summon the man once more but not having a scrap of privacy to do it with.

"*The Emperor.* You still speak like one of them."

"Well I'm in here with you, Luke." Vi took another bite of bread. "So either I'm not one of them, or I'm really stupid for not getting myself out before now."

"None of us are getting out of here alive," Kahrin sighed, her long black hair hiding her face. She was a far cry from the woman who threatened Vi when they first met. "They've taken all the generals, and half of the Knights of Jadar... We're next."

"We're not dead yet, so eat." Zira sat on the other side of the wide windowsill where Vi was perched. The other two remained in their spots on the floor. It was a corner of the room they shared with ten other random soldiers—men and women whose names Vi hadn't bothered to learn. "The princess will need us."

"The princess is dead."

"Shut your mouth," Zira growled.

"Do you really think the Emperor will be satisfied with just King Rocham's head? No, he'll want more royal blood to spill in a glorious display of power. And who better than the youngest child, the woman who led our army against him?"

"Fiera isn't dead," Zira insisted in the face of Kahrin's determination.

"If she was alive, she would've come for you of all people by now. You were always her pet."

"She's not dead." Vi tore off another chunk of bread, chewing it over and staring out the window.

"What do you know, *traveler*?" Kahrin spat. Her tone made plain that she had yet to relinquish her theory that Vi was a spy.

"More than you ever will."

"How dare you—"

"Enough," Zira snapped. "You three are exhausting me."

They all ate their remaining scraps of bread in relative silence. Luke mumbled something about the food sitting heavy in his stomach and making him sleepy, "likely drugged by Imperialist swine." Kahrin must've decided she was bored of being ignored, because when Vi looked over her shoulder next, she was gone.

"Do you know she's alive?" Zira asked softly, her voice hushed.

Vi gave a small nod that felt like a lie. What did she know? Precious little. The ability to gaze along the Mother's lines of fate was one thing, but she hadn't had a vision since entering the remade world. It was like she was trying to navigate a new city using ancient maps. She'd been biding her time, waiting, seeing how things played out. Tiberus and Fiera nearly exchanging blows on the docks had ignited a fear Vi hadn't expected. What if she messed something up? What if, in trying to improve the future they were now heading toward, she somehow made it worse?

She needed to speak with Taavin again.

"You have the sight too, don't you? Like she does?"

"I do."

"I heard what you said to her, at the docks..." Zira looked back to the window. "She told me of her vision before the battle. She knew we would lose. She knew her father would die."

"And yet she fought for Mhashan anyway." The meager piece of bread was gone all too swiftly, and Vi's stomach was grumbling even louder than before. But ignoring angry stomachs had become something they were all quite good at.

"Yes, she fought for Mhashan... but not to win. She wanted to save the people— to prevent as many as possible from dying. I don't understand the dance of royals, but I must believe that these deaths we hear of, however gruesome they might be, are still part of her plan. Fiera was always good at minimizing losses."

"The hard part of having royal blood is deciding how you spread the suffering. Who will bear the burden—many, or a few? Who? And how do you choose? Do you spread it as thin as possible, or is it better to absolve some and force others to pick up the weight entirely?"

"Are you certain you're not a bastard of King Rocham?" Zira chuckled at Vi's expression. "You speak like a royal."

"I've spent my share of time around them, I guess you could say."

"In your travels?"

"In my travels."

Booted feet came to a stop at the entrance of the room. There were no more doors in the manor; they had all been ripped off when the Imperial soldiers evicted the house's noble residents and declared it the new containment shelter for the former army of Mhashan.

"She's there. Zira Westwind is there." Kahrin pointed at them and spoke to the Imperial soldiers on either side of her. "The one with the shorter hair."

"Westwind..." Vi repeated softly. The name was familiar to her in a way she hadn't been expecting. "Your name is Westwind?"

Zira didn't have a chance to answer as soldiers approached. "Come," a broad-shouldered man barked in Mhashanese. Zira stood without protest.

"Where are you taking her?" Vi asked, jumping from the windowsill. The man ignored her and she repeated herself, forcing her tongue to make the sounds of the common language she'd spoken all her life, "Where are you taking her?"

The two soldiers stopped, gaping at her in surprise. They weren't the only ones; the soldiers of Mhashan wore expressions of curiosity at her deft outburst.

"That is none of your concern," one of the men finally said, before they dragged Zira out of sight.

There was no word of Zira, and none from Kahrin or Luke either. After Vi's outburst in common, they began to shy away from her—prior suspicions of her being some kind of Southern spy reignited. Without Zira, Vi didn't have the energy or inclination to refute them.

Three days passed, and Vi became bolder about wandering the manor. She was growing tired of being cooped up, tired of waiting. Perhaps it would be better if she could remember more of the immediate details following the fall of Mhashan, but her studies—or her memories of them—were lacking. She needed the counsel of the man who was tasked with looking back for her. But every room she entered was filled with people.

"How is it outside?" she asked one of the girls passing out hunks of bread. It had tasted so good three days ago, but had since grown stale. "Any progress?"

"Some." Vi stepped off to the side, leaning against the wall next to her. "There's rumors they might be lifting the martial law soon."

"Rumors don't hold water. Did they kill Zira?"

"I don't know who Zira is, but the killings in the square have ended."

That much was good, at least. The Emperor must be feeling more confident in his control of Mhashan. The next step would be—

"Criers today announced that tomorrow, there will be a ball held for Mhashan's court."

"A ball?" Vi repeated. After weeks of ruling with blood and an iron fist, there was to be a party?

"I think it's odd, having a party so close to so much bloodshed. But who understands royals? The ball is to follow some kind of announcement in the square opposite the castle."

An engagement announcement. The Emperor would secure his hold in the West with a marriage. Vi finished off her bread with one more large bite, thanked the girl, and left. If there was a ball, the castle would be open; he'd want as many nobles as possible to attend.

Vi waited for nightfall. She'd staked her claim in the corner of one of the rooms—crowded enough that no one would notice one person missing, empty enough that she could have the dark corner of what was once a closet to herself.

"*Durroe watt ivin,*" Vi whispered, standing and sliding into the skin of one of the Imperial soldiers she'd been watching for weeks. The brief flash of light didn't seem to wake any of those sleeping.

Carefully tiptoeing from the room, Vi stepped into the hall and walked with confidence. Magic was hot under her hand and the illusion blurred the edge of her vision. But it was far easier than the first time she had attempted a similar deceit—escaping out of the fortress of Soricium as Jayme.

"Lolan, don't you usually take the mornings?" one of the guards asked as she approached the exit.

"Usually. I'm covering half a rotation," Vi said softly, with the same Southern accent Ginger would use. Vi had picked this particular guard for her masquerade because she'd never raised her voice above a whisper. "Excuse me."

Keeping her head down, Vi stepped out into the street. The guards at the door said nothing more. They believed the illusion completely.

Vi took a breath of fresh air. Freedom filled her lungs.

She started down the street toward where she knew the Le'Dan's shop would be.

5

S HE KEPT THE ILLUSION of Lolan's skin most of the way through the city. Vi passed three other Imperial soldiers who each gave her a bob of their heads before continuing on their patrols. It wasn't until she reached the opulent area of town where the Le'Dan shop stood proud that Vi stepped back into a side alley, crouched, and finally let go of the magic running thin against her palm.

Letting her eyes adjust to the darkness, Vi remained low, waiting. The city had been quiet for weeks, which meant the patrols were becoming more scarce. Even without them, the citizens stayed hidden away. Tiberus had conditioned them all now, whether they realized it or not.

After the next patrol passed, she eased out of her stance and looked to the building across the road. The first floor was a shop; a window above. Perhaps a loft for some kind of security or shopkeep to sleep in? Vi had no doubt that the Le'Dans would keep their goods heavily guarded, especially now, when the people around those valuable goods were hungry and desperate.

She hastily crossed the street and came to a stop at the door.

"*Durroe sallvas tempre,*" Vi whispered, willing the magic to spin outward and encompass both her and the door. "*Juth calt.*" The inside mechanics of the lock built in to the door shattered with a *pop*, and Vi eased herself quietly inside. Her magic hid the jingling of the bell overhead.

Vi willed the glyph for concealing her sound to hover across the entire store. She stepped behind the counters and pulled back the fabric covering the cases. Jewels shone like colored stars in the faintly glowing light of her magic.

"No… not one of these." Vi replaced the cover, turning away from the cases. She didn't need showpieces designed to accentuate the Le'Dan family's skill. No, she needed something smaller, something no one would notice was missing, *hopefully*, until tomorrow night at the earliest.

Vi rummaged through the drawers behind the counters. There were all manner of jeweler's tools in the first four. She stepped lightly to the back of the room and kept her magic strong. With a glance, Vi checked the street. No sign of soldiers yet.

"Something, something…" Vi murmured to herself, trusting her magic to keep her thoughts from anyone who might be slumbering upstairs. In the back of the room, tucked between two towers of drawers, was a thin case. Vi opened it and her eyes settled on rows of pieces tagged with names, dates, and amounts. Some were marked as paid, some weren't.

She settled on a statement ring with a Western ruby the size of a quail's egg propped up by two silver phoenixes on either side. Underneath the ruby, the jeweler had emblazoned the Le'Dan family crest.

"Marla Le'Dan," Vi read the name off the tag before pocketing the piece. She didn't know who Marla was, and Vi knew most of the names of the important Le'Dans throughout history. Which meant this woman was perfect—Marla was someone people might recognize by name, but likely wouldn't know personally. And if the Le'Dans hadn't found a way to get her ring to her yet, Vi suspected Marla was outside of the city.

The rest of the night unfolded with the same ease as breaking into the Le'Dan shop.

Vi made her way through Norin, slipping into the skins of various Imperial soldiers when necessary. She visited a dressmaker, furrier, and cobbler, relieving each of the pieces she'd need to enable the next phase of her plan.

Each of the stores was flush with goods covered in a thin layer of dust. Clearly, no one had been shopping for months, especially not in the more expensive areas of town. It made it easy for Vi to collect all her necessary supplies before dawn, giving her enough time to slip into an abandoned house just as morning broke.

She knew she should sleep, but her first moment of privacy had Vi extending her hand, reaching for one man.

"*Narro hath hoolo.*" Three simple words, and he stood before her.

"Vi," he said with immense relief. Taavin's arms wrapped around her, pulling her to him. Vi buried her face in his shoulder, pressing as close as she could, willing his embrace to feel as sturdy as she'd once known it to be. "It's been three weeks. Don't worry me like this."

"I'm all right." She shifted enough to look him in the eye. "See?"

"You're skin and bones… and in dire need of a bath."

She couldn't disagree. But rather than linger on that topic, Vi asked instead, "How do you know how long it's been?"

"From within the watch, I might not know what you're doing, but I have a sense of how much time is passing. My consciousness is stored there, so when I'm not in this world, it feels almost like twilight sleep—not really awake, but not fully asleep either." Taavin released one arm, running his finger across her forehead as if to brush away stray hairs. The ghostly touch was feather-light, and the strands that had escaped her braids barely moved. "What's happened?"

"I found Fiera," Vi began delicately. "Though, in doing so, I ended up getting myself captured."

"*Captured?*"

"I'm fine," Vi insisted once more.

"What did you do?"

"It doesn't matter. What matters is—"

"It does matter," he interrupted firmly. "I exist to chronicle time and keep record of your actions. I can't do that if you don't tell me them *exactly*. Our best hope for figuring out what will save this world is ruling out what won't."

With a palm on his chest, Vi pushed him away lightly. She folded her arms to guard herself—to try to hold in the truth. He was already worried enough. Vi walked over to the boarded window of the parlor where they stood. She could feel his gaze as keenly as the beams of sunlight that streamed through the cracks in the boards.

"I went out to find Fiera the night Mhashan fell."

"You went out?"

"Yes, into the fray." Vi could tell from his tone he was putting the events together.

"You went out into the field of battle knowing that if you died, this world is doomed?" Taavin stomped over, though the floor didn't so much as creak—his footsteps held no real weight. "What were you thinking?"

"I had to see it," she said without looking at him. Her eyes saw that night, replaying its events. "I had to see it with my own eyes. It made all of this real." She finally locked eyes with him. "Besides, didn't you say the first thing I must do is get the sword?"

"Yes, but—"

"Well, I have a plan to do that now."

"Is it just as reckless as your last plan?" Taavin frowned.

"I'm not sure if I should tell you. You might just scold me for it."

"Yes, I'm going to scold you for risking your life when the fate of our world hangs in the balance." Taavin gripped her hand, the touch a pale shadow of the intensity in his eyes. "*Think* about it, Vi. One mistake and the best that can happen is this world is headed for another future of death. The worst? An age of darkness from which there is no escape—death of all things, the atrophy of our world, a perpetual midnight without stars."

She squeezed his hand back just as tightly, looking up at his emerald eyes. "And if I do nothing, we are equally stuck in this loop, which is its own form of torture. I must act if I am to end this."

"But do so cautiously," he insisted. "Just telling someone the truth about yourself could tip the scales and change fate in a way none of us expect."

Sighing softly, Vi turned away, feeling her brow relax. He wasn't wrong. There was still so much about her predicament that she didn't understand. But she knew that doing nothing wasn't the solution either.

"Let me tell you what it is I plan to do next," she said finally. "You have the memories of all my failures; perhaps you can help poke holes in my orchestrations to give me the best chance for success."

She heard him breathe a sigh of relief.

"That, I can do."

The last time Vi had laid eyes on the square at the drawbridge of the castle of Norin, it had been filled with the winners and losers of a ten-year war. Soldiers had held their heads in triumph and defeat. Now, it was filled with common folk and nobles alike. But the only soldiers were those in Imperial plate, bearing signets of the Solaris Empire.

Her layers of skirts swayed with her hips and flowed around her heeled shoes. Over her shoulders was a shrug; the ruddy feathers that adorned it reminded her of Fallor. In a dark way, it felt as though she was wearing the skins of an evil she'd vanquished.

Vi had managed a wash and found a mirror that enabled her to put a strategic plait in her hair. She'd woven the braids in a fashion her mother would wear for Imperial events. Most everyone else wore their hair down and loose, some swept theirs up with a simple braid wrapped through it. But none had quite the same intricate knots as Vi, and her style drew more than one look.

"Hear ye, hear ye." A man stepped up onto a stage positioned at the foot of the drawbridge. Knights fanned out before him, swords drawn with their points driven into the earth. "It is my honor to bestow on you your first Imperial announcement."

"*Honor*," a man snorted from somewhere behind Vi.

"In six months' time, your Emperor, ordained by the Mother herself to unite this continent, will be wed to the one much loved by the sun and much loved by your land." The ruffles at the crier's neck bounced up and down as he spoke. Each heaving breath carried his voice further than the last. "The Emperor Tiberus Solaris announces his betrothal to Lady Fiera Ci'Dan!"

Horns blasted and soldiers threw confetti into the sky over a confused crowd. Whispers collected to form a sound loud enough to be heard over the bellowing instruments. Frightened, concerned, and angry eyes sought each other out in turn. The commoners were less likely to keep their opinions to themselves.

"She would marry him?"

"The unbendable Fiera?"

"She was the leader of the Knights. Now she's nothing but an Imperial whore," the male voice from earlier muttered darkly.

At that, Vi glanced over her shoulders. But she couldn't see who behind her might have spoken. Was it the angry-looking commoner? One of the nobles behind him? Someone further back?

Vi looked forward once more, trying to push the remark out of her mind. She'd heard mention that Fiera's engagement to the Emperor Solaris had not been taken well. And why would it have been? Having seen the fall of Mhashan with her own eyes, she understood why the people were upset. Vi turned her gaze to the ground, wondering how much blood from the Emperor's killings had flowed right where she stood.

Still, the horns continued their celebratory trill, as though the people were as excited as the shimmering bits of paper happily floating through the air.

"Now, now!" Everything quieted as the crier raised his hands once more. "Members of the court, we invite you to join the Emperor in his first soiree in this land, to celebrate this most glorious union. Those who are not of noble birth, fear not, for you shall also enjoy minstrels and food."

"We do not want minstrels. We want our king—King Ophain!" a man shouted. "We do not want Tiberus's blood-soaked charity. We want our free—"

The declaration was cut short with a crunch and gurgle that echoed louder in her ears than the horns had. Vi couldn't see who had been shouting, but she knew he would never shout again.

Silence fell heavy atop simmering resentment.

"Now, please, enter the castle, Western court. Enjoy and be merry, all!" the crier finished, as though the outburst had never existed.

The mass split into two groups—nobles marching forward along the bridge, slowly filing into two lines, and commoners who were held back by the guards surrounding the crier's stage. Vi rolled her shoulders and adjusted the long, feathered coat that covered them.

With every step, she retreated further into her mask; by the time she arrived at the Imperial soldiers holding scrolls of names, she was no longer the woman who had been wasting away in a prison or a cat burglar stealing garments. She was Vi Solaris, crown princess to an Empire lost.

"Name," the soldier demanded.

"Marla Le'Dan." Vi worked to add a thick Western accent over the name.

"Marla… Le'Dan." The soldier checked his scrolls and then leaned over, murmuring something to the woman behind him. He turned back to Vi. "I don't seem to have your name."

"Excuse me? I am of the Le'Dan family. How can you not have my name? Do you know who my family even is, *Southerner*?"

"I don't have your name on the lis—"

"Then find another list," Vi insisted. "Or perhaps this should be proof enough." She held out her right hand, the ruby catching not only the soldier's eye but the eyes of the other Western nobles around her.

The soldier looked back to the woman he'd deferred to before. She stepped forward and inspected Vi's ring. "Let her though."

"Thank you." Vi gave a huff she hoped conveyed that the transgression against her noble person would not be forgotten.

She fell into step with the stream of people passing through the glistening royal stables that flanked the wide entry, toward the grand doors of the castle. Vi glanced over her shoulder; the Imperial soldiers were already focused on the next people. No one around her seemed to be paying her any attention.

Vi made her way to the edge of the crowd and stepped back into the shadow of one of the stables before slipping behind a low wall unseen.

Hurriedly, she shrugged off her coat and pulled pins from her braids, allowing them to fall into a much simpler style. She ripped at the flowing skirt she wore over a clinging dress, casting it aside with the coat and incinerating it with a burst of magic. She yanked the ring from her finger, tucking it into a hidden pocket of her dress as she slipped back into the crowd without anyone so much as giving her a glance.

Smoothing over her dress once more, sufficiently satisfied with her altered appearance, Vi stepped into the great hall of the Western castle.

Her feet came to a stop as Vi let out a soft gasp. It was more magnificent than she could've imagined. The architect's sketches and blueprints Elecia had sent hadn't done the castle justice. Columns supported wooden rafters that soared high enough for gigantic iron chandeliers to hang unimpeded. At the far end of the room was the throne area—a place Vi could barely see over the heads of those gathered.

Stained glass along the upper walls picked up the glow of a thousand tiny flames, burning magically in the chandeliers and otherwise empty glass bulbs throughout the room. Vi took a step, placing her hand lightly on a column. This was her family's home. She ached at the thought and part of her—the part that shared blood with the Ci'Dan family—wanted to weep for all they'd lost despite all she herself had gained.

"There you are," a male voice said from behind her. "I knew you said you were thinking of getting a feel for the attitude of the crowds, princess, but I didn't think this was what you had in mind."

Vi startled, realizing he was speaking to her. Even from behind, he'd mistaken her for Fiera.

The man was a Westerner, through and through. He had short-cropped black hair and muscular shoulders that framed a barrel chest. His clothing was twice as fine as the average person's. But what made his identity as plain as the nose on his face was the thick chain around his neck—cast in gold and weighted by a diamond that could make even a Solaris blush.

Vi was face to face with Richard Ci'Dan.

"You'll never believe what's happened. I came down early myself because I was told my cousin Marla was here. Foolish Imperials, they know nothing, or they'd know Marla is—"

"I think you have the wrong person," Vi said softly.

Richard stopped himself mid-sentence and stared at her. He blinked several times, tilting his head, before taking a step forward to get a better look. He searched her face with a gaze as tender as it was knowing before that same expression became distant and inquisitive.

"You're *her*, aren't you?" he said finally.

"And just who do you think I am?"

"The traveler the princess foretold."

6

"SHE FORETOLD... ME?" VI leveraged all her royal training to keep her surprise in check.

"She did. She said a traveler would come who wore her face."

Vi wore a knowing smile. Fiera's actions were gaining clarity. "Yes, I have come from very far to meet her."

"Sorry to say you don't have any hope of a private meeting. A public audience, perhaps tonight. But no one has been able to get to her, not even one of her oldest and dearest friends." He sighed heavily and looked toward the empty thrones at the far end of the room. "She's been kept sequestered under lock and key with that wretched man."

Vi took a small step toward Richard, looking toward the thrones as well. She said nothing, and the silence greased his tongue.

"I shudder to think of what he's done to her—what he's threatened her with—to bring about this union."

"Perhaps he loves her?" Vi suggested.

"Loves her?" Richard balked. "The man loves one thing: war. He's long been married to death itself. He doesn't love, he conquers."

"Have you met him?" Vi had always been told that, above all else, Tiberus had been over the sun for Fiera Ci'Dan. That while he had stolen her land, she had stolen his heart.

"No. Just how much socializing have you been able to do recently?" Richard's eyebrows arched. "Forgive my tone, and that I've yet to learn your name, Lady..."

"Yullia."

"Lady Yullia." Richard took her hand and brought it to his lips. "An honor to meet you."

"And you as well."

"You have an uncommon name. Might I ask where—"

Two doors at the far end of the hall opened and interrupted Richard before he could finish. A hush fell over those gathered. They turned collectively to the group of three standing in the doorway.

"Ophain, Lord of the West!" a crier announced as the man in front stepped forward along a white runner. "Sisters to the Lord of the West, Lady Tina and Lady Lilo." Two women stepped out, walking side by side.

"Lord of the West," Richard murmured at Vi's side. "He should be *king*."

Vi remained silent, watching the procession. Ophain was heartbreakingly similar in features to her father, save the hooked nose and slightly longer hair that he wore tied at the nape of his neck. Tina, the older sister, was spindly and elegant. Lilo was stouter and, despite all that had transpired, wore a serene smile on her face.

Perhaps she was smiling because she'd somehow avoided engagement to the man who had conquered their homeland. Both women making their way down the long runner to the dais were older than Fiera, and both were currently un-betrothed. They would've been the more expected choices.

"My friends, my noble kin," Ophain began as he reached the top of the dais. There were only two chairs behind him, Vi noticed, and he sat in neither. "I realize this celebration has come under… unconventional circumstances."

"That's a way to put it," Richard mumbled. He wasn't the only one.

"However, it is just that—a *celebration*," Ophain emphasized. "My darling sister, the youngest and I think we can all agree the strongest among us—" Lilo gave a nod from Ophain's left "—has been chosen as our future Empress. She is a woman whose hands were only for the sword and now, they will help hold up the Empire."

Any other proclamation, under almost any other circumstances, would have been met with cheers. But those gathered were silent. Slowly, a few people clapped—mostly the Southerners in attendance—and then a few more. A depressing showing for a crowd that dressed for a party but felt as though they were attending a funeral.

"Thus, it is my honor to present the Emperor Tiberus Solaris and future Empress Fiera Ci'Dan!" Ophain motioned to the back of the room, where the doors were still open wide.

Two figures emerged from the darkness and into the light of the hall. The Emperor wore the sun crown—a golden circlet with fiery sunbeams stretching up from its base. His crisp, white, double-breasted jacket and tailored trousers were a clear attempt to distance himself from the more flowing styles of the South.

Fiera walked in stark contrast beside him. Her crown was a simple silver band across her brow. She wore a tightly tailored, crimson dress with a split all the way up to her hip. Underneath were black leggings and boots that appeared to have the dust of training fields still on them. Silver pauldrons adorned her shoulders and a sword Vi would recognize anywhere was strapped to her hip.

The only thing connecting them were their hands. Tiberus escorted her with his elbow out, palm parallel to the floor. Fiera's hand rested atop.

They didn't look like they were walking into a party in their honor. They looked as though they were walking to war. Yet the effect seemed to work on the crowd, for as they passed men and women alike dropped to one knee and bowed their heads.

Vi was no exception, though she was one of the last to kneel, waiting long enough that Fiera's attention came to her and her alone. Vi held the woman's eyes until her knee met the floor. Fiera turned forward quickly, keeping her reaction to Vi's presence concealed.

"My newest and well-loved subjects," the Emperor started when they reached the dais. Fiera's siblings had stepped back to stand behind the thrones. "It is my honor to stand before you today. Not just as your ruler, but as your future kin."

Vi glanced over to Richard. His jaw was clenched tight, veins bulging in his neck.

The man looked like he wanted to scream more and more with each passing second.

"It is my most sincere hope that you all will join us in celebration, now and over the next six months, as we prepare to join in union in the Cathedral of the Mother."

The room remained silent. The Emperor stared out at the crowd for another long moment before he stepped back and assumed his seat in the gilded throne tufted in blue velvet. Fiera, however, remained.

She swung her gaze across the room, a hand resting on the hilt of her crystal sword.

"Lords and Ladies of Mhashan," she began in Mhashanese. The Emperor didn't have much of a reaction, which told Vi that Tiberus was confident in what she was going to say. "I was your princess. More than that—I was your sworn protector. My father appointed me the head of the Knights of Jadar so that I may keep you all safe.

"I still hold that duty dear to my heart. I know you might not always understand how, but I fight for you. I will continue to fight for you until my dying breath. However, fate guides us to unexpected places. I no longer defend you on the field, but from a throne—a throne where I know I will find happiness. I am happy. Join me in that, my kin. Eternal flame."

Fiera finished with the common Western colloquialism—*fiarum evantes*. The term was both greeting and farewell, meant to inspire good will.

"Guide us through the night." *Kotun un nox,* Vi said aloud, when no one else would.

Others picked up the sentiment, echoing her. The words rippled through the crowd. One by one, they uttered the expression as a form of solidarity with their once princess and now future empress.

Fiera sat on her throne. As soon as she was settled, minstrels playing harps and lutes picked up a merry tune set to the fast beat of a drum. It was jarring to the very clearly uncomfortable atmosphere. But someone had planned for this, and servants passed wine around on trays. The nobles eagerly grabbed for the goblets, searching for anything to quench the awkward feeling that hung in the air.

Richard took one more long look at Fiera and Tiberus before turning, starting eagerly toward a servant passing drinks. Vi took a hasty step, falling into place at his side.

"I need a drink," he muttered. "Something stronger than the stuff they're serving here... but this is a start." He lifted a goblet off a tray but Vi refused it when he offered. She fussed with the skirt of her gown instead.

"Have faith, Richard Le'Dan. The South isn't all bad," Vi encouraged lightly with a pat on his chest. Lucky for her, he too wore a military-style jacket with pockets over both pectorals—one of which now held the ring Vi had lifted from the Le'Dan store. Taavin had cautioned her not to keep it beyond tonight. This was a much better solution than casting it in some dark corner. "You might even learn to like it someday."

Before he could retort, she walked away, her mission with him finished. One by one, men and women were lining up to pay respects to the Emperor. Vi stepped into the line and waited her turn.

"Emperor Tiberus Solaris," she said in Southern Common when it was her turn. "Lady Fiera Ci'Dan." Vi switched deftly to Mhashanese to address the princess. "It is my honor to come before you both and wish you well." Vi dropped to a knee.

"And what family do you hail from?" Tiberus asked. All of the other nobles had made it a point to very clearly state who they were when they swore their allegiance.

Someone in the shadows was no doubt keeping a tally of which families weren't here.

"I have no family, your grace." Some murmurs. Vi could see movement from the corners of her eyes and wondered if the guards were already coming for her now that she'd identified herself as the person who did not belong among all the members of the Western court. "But I do come bearing an engagement gift."

"A gift?" Fiera asked, eyes locked with Vi's and filled with awareness. The question stopped short the guards who had just about surrounded Vi. The room was silent once more.

"Fiera Ci'Dan, you will bear a son." Vi pitched her voice as ominously and with as much gravity as possible. "He will have your flames, and sit on the throne of his father."

A small smile worked its way onto Fiera's lips as a guard approached, whispering in the Emperor's ear. Tiberus looked at Vi with renewed focus.

Vi opened her mouth to speak again, but was interrupted.

"Kind words, indeed," the Emperor said lightly. "A shame you felt the need to lie to say them. You are under arrest for masquerading as a member of the house Le'Dan. Guards, please take her to the dungeons. We shall sort out what to do with her later."

Vi stood, offering her elbows to the guards who were already reaching for them. She didn't struggle or try to get away. Instead, she walked like a princess, all the way out of the party and into the depths of Norin's castle.

They locked her in a cell without fanfare and promptly left. Vi waited for their footsteps to disappear down the hall. Fiera knew she was here.

If she waited, the princess would eventually find a way to get to her. But Richard's claim that Fiera was being kept under tight watch lingered—highlighting the advice Taavin had given her.

The party will be depressing for Fiera. She'll retreat to her rose garden.

"*Durroe sallvas tempre. Juth calt.*" Vi did away with the lock on the cell in the same manner as she had broken into the storefronts.

She went down the long hall that lined this wing of cells, magic gathered under her fingers. The one other prisoner was lying on his cot, back to her, and didn't stir as she passed—her footsteps completely silenced by her magic. One end of the hall stretched deeper into the dungeons; the other, where she'd entered from, was hazy with light. Vi glanced around the corner to find the guard on duty slumped in his chair, much as he had been when she'd entered.

Vi closed her eyes, debating what chant to use. There was one bit of Lightspinning she had yet to try. Should she risk a new piece of chanting, or try to make herself invisible while moving through a room? Invisibility in motion was nearly impossible; the choice practically made itself.

"*Loft not,*" Vi breathed, her own eyes feeling heavy and fluttering closed for a long moment. *Not* was a subset of *loft*—to sleep—and in the same family as *dorh*—to immobilize. The word was warm on her tongue and the glyph that haloed over the guard's head settled on his shoulders like sunset.

He let out a large snore and Vi crept though the room, still keeping the sounds of her footsteps silent. As soon as she was down the hall and out of earshot from the now slumbering guard, Vi let go of both glyphs and immediately whispered a few more words to step into the skin of one of the guards who had escorted her to the prison. With the man's face, she strolled easily through the halls and stairwells.

Vi ran her hand along the banisters as she ascended through the quiet passageways. The castle felt unnaturally empty. Servants weren't buzzing around and guards had seemingly limited patrols. It felt like a great beast, now slumbering, waiting until it would rise once more to be the bastion of the West.

Elecia had sent no shortage of maps of Norin and architects' drawings of the castle to Vi while she was in Soricium. She had deemed it "important for Vi to learn her heritage." Vi's chest tightened at the thought that she'd never have the opportunity to properly thank her cousin for how she'd prepared her.

Vi went up and up. She stepped through doorways and underneath carefully embellished archways. High above the royal family's quarters was the library. It was hexagonal in shape and extended five stories up with nothing but bookcases lining each wall. Had the original builders of the castle of Norin known of the Archives of Yargen? Were they aware of the distant influence that still held sway over their aesthetics?

Making her way up and around the library with a side stair, Vi paused at a doorway wedged between two bookcases. It was unassuming and unlocked.

The thick scent of roses assaulted her senses as Vi stepped out into the rooftop conservatory. Western breezes filtered through open windows in the high glass panels that capped the garden. The quiet sound of trickling water added a layer of serenity that had Vi's tense shoulders relaxing. She began to walk the gardens, looking at the various flora and fauna—mostly Western roses, Fiera's favorite.

"You're here."

Vi turned, meeting Fiera's gaze as the woman stood in the doorway. Fiera blinked with surprise, but it passed quickly and was replaced with a knowing smile.

"I am."

"I was wondering when you'd come."

"FORGIVE ME FOR BREAKING free of your prison." Vi's attention shifted, turning to the sword still strapped to Fiera's hip. Her whole body ached at the sight of it and Vi barely held herself back from giving in to a moment of weakness and just ripping it from Fiera's body.

"Part of me suspects I should be pleased that you have."

"I mean you no harm."

"So you've told me, and so you've illustrated." Fiera took a step forward and lifted her hand. "Shall we stroll?"

For a quarter of one lap of the lush garden, they didn't say anything. Vi kept glancing at the woman at her side while Fiera kept her gaze forward and relaxed. Still, her hand remained on the sword hilt.

"I sense fate in you," Fiera said finally, "in a way I have never sensed in any other."

"I'm afraid I don't understand what you mean."

Fiera paused only long enough to glance at her from the corners of her eyes. "You're a poor liar."

"Don't mistake half-truths for a lie." Vi chuckled. "I don't understand what you mean when you say you 'sense fate.'"

"Yargen has chosen me to see along her lines," Fiera started, leaving Vi to wonder if her deflection had been so easily dispatched. "Sometimes, I feel compelled to look along those lines—more so than other times. Sometimes, I don't need to peer along the lines at all to know that someone or something has great importance in those designs."

"Or perhaps you are sensing places and moments where fate has been changed," Vi suggested, narrowly avoiding the term *Apex of Fate*.

"A good way to put it." Fiera gave a small nod. "You... you are the embodiment of that feeling. When I see you I feel I know you—like somehow I've always known you."

Fiera came to a stop and Vi with her. They faced each other, nearly identical in height and build. If anything, Fiera was slightly more curvaceous than Vi. But otherwise, they could be mistaken for identical twins at a glance.

"Perhaps it is because I look at you and see my face."

"An oddity, indeed." That was something she had no idea how she could explain away—not even with half-truths.

"Yet, this feeling runs much deeper," Fiera continued. "When I have tried to scry into the flames for you, I see nothing. The sight has been absent since we met, all other sensations dulled, save for you."

"But you told Richard Le'Dan you foresaw our meeting?"

Fiera laughed softly and shook her head at the mention of Richard. She wore a tender smile on her lips, one tinged with sadness.

"Richard wouldn't understand if I tried to explain it to him. He is not like you and me. He doesn't understand these feelings," Fiera said tenderly. "I told him that because I knew you would seek me out, as you sought me out the first time. My hope was that the more people I told of you, the greater the likelihood of you being led to me."

"How?"

"I had a feeling." Fiera shrugged and crossed to a bench. She patted it, inviting Vi to sit next to her. Vi obliged. "May I know your name now, traveler?"

"Yullia."

"Yullia, a beautiful and unique name." A knowing smile spread across her lips. "And tell me, Yullia, what is it you seek?"

The sword you carry. Vi knew it wouldn't be that easy. The crystal sword, known to the West as the Sword of Jadar, was a sacred relic. If she was going to steal it, she needed a bit more of a plan than grab and flee.

Move slowly, Vi reminded herself in Taavin's words. She had time, *decades* of time. She didn't have to take the sword in one night.

"I wish to be at your side—guiding and protecting as I am able," Vi said finally, after weighing her various options. "I can serve you in many ways, and perhaps we will find one that is the best for your needs. I am confident with a sword, and with magic. I am wise to the ways of the world. And I can see along the Mother's lines as well."

Fiera hummed softly. "I should tell you no. I wouldn't want to get a reputation for accepting people easily into my employ. Especially those who break our laws."

"Will you tell me no?" Vi asked, genuinely unsure of the answer.

"I will tell you that I am a woman of faith—and I believe in the Mother's will that guides us all. You feel of fate, and speak like one who has the sight." Fiera stood. "So kneel, traveler Yullia."

Vi pushed off the bench and did as she was instructed.

"Do you swear fealty and loyalty to me, and to the Solaris crown?"

She didn't even have to fake the broad grin at the question. "Yes."

"Then consider yourself a member of my guard, formerly the Knights of Jadar…" A smirk pulled up the corners of Fiera's lips. It was somewhat coquettish and the first playful thing Vi had seen about the otherwise perfectly composed royal. "I'm still working on a new name."

"No names needed." Vi rose to her feet. "I am here for you, your highness. Not for a title."

"And I have been truly blessed in that." Fiera stood and began walking once more, but her shoulders had more sway to them, her steps far less rigid. Just like that, a barrier between them had been lowered, if not entirely removed. "You are not the first the Mother has sent to me in this way."

"Who was—" Before Vi could finish, three people appeared in the doorway.

"There she is." Tiberus let out a sigh of relief, crossing over to Fiera and scooping up her hands. He didn't even so much as glance Vi's way. Vi wouldn't be surprised if he didn't even realize there were other people around him. It was a far cry from the Emperor Vi saw in the great hall. "You worried me—all of us—wandering off without Zira at the very least. It's too dangerous still for you to do that. The association with me will have people out to harm you."

"No one in Mhashan would harm me. And I had to come and meet with my new guard." Fiera motioned to Vi and the Emperor slowly turned his head to look at her.

"You're the criminal."

"I'd prefer 'party crasher'." Vi shrugged.

The Emperor's expression grew more concerned at her nonchalance, but lightened instantly when Fiera let out a burst of laughter. He finally chuckled as well.

"You are an odd one, aren't you?" Tiberus shook his head with a slight smile, all the while his eyes still on Fiera. "I suppose if my beloved trusts you, so shall I."

Most of the stories Vi had heard of her grandfather were about him at the end of his decades of conquest. They were tales of an older man, hardened by war. The man before Vi now was barely in his thirties and he looked not a day past twenty-five.

"Yullia?" a familiar voice interrupted the conversation.

Vi grinned. "Hello, Zira."

"I thought it was you!" Zira hastily walked and clasped Vi's shoulder. "Forget how she made it out of the jail cell… how did you make it out of containment? You do have an interesting set of skills, don't you?"

"You could say that."

"A set of skills we will use for our Empire," Fiera insisted to Tiberus. "I have made her my guard and would seek not to have her punished for impersonating a noble tonight, or sneaking out of the soldiers' confinement. She was merely following the will of the Mother, and my will, to stand at my side."

"Then it shall be done." Tiberus gave a nod to Vi and, like that, she was absolved of all crimes.

"Thank you, my love," Fiera said lightly, almost sweetly. It was yet another stark contrast to the stiff, formal woman Vi had seen in the main hall.

"You are to be my Empress, the sword protecting my back, and will rule at my side. I wish for you to know always that your voice is heard." Tiberus cupped Fiera's cheek and Vi gave a glance to Zira, who was barely refraining from rolling her eyes.

"Zira, will you see that Yullia is settled in a room?" Fiera asked, turning away from Tiberus's affections. "There are more than enough open. You can place her wherever you think is appropriate."

"Yes, your highness."

"Zerian, please escort us back into the party. They'll wonder if we're gone for too long," Tiberus said.

"And leaving nobles to wonder only leads them to gossip." Fiera sighed. "You're right, we should be along." Tiberus offered Fiera his elbow and she took it, starting away. But not before Fiera paused once more to say, "I look forward to working with you, Yullia."

Vi stared at the familiar dark eyes. Fiera's spell-like quality of speech made Vi feel as if she were the only person in the world. Perhaps it was this quality that made others eager to bend over backward for the princess.

"And you as well, princess." Vi gave a small bow of her head. Zira and Zerian exchanged a nod and the man escorted the two royals back into the library. Vi glanced over at Zira, whose whole body now seemed racked with tension. "Is everything all right?"

"My eyes tell me I'm seeing the men who are responsible for King Rocham's death and the fall of Mhashan, while my mind reminds me they are no longer my enemies." Zira shrugged, shoved her hands in her pockets, and began strolling forward. "It takes some getting used to."

"I can imagine," Vi said thoughtfully and fell into step at Zira's side. "Does she love him?" As though Fiera's love would make the circumstances easier to bear for Zira.

"I can't tell," Zira answered candidly. Vi was grateful they'd already had the opportunity to build a rapport; talking came easily, and there was no need to dance around topics when they'd spent days imprisoned together. Then again, Zira didn't seem like the type to dance in any context that didn't involve holding a blade. "I know she loves her people. She loves this land. And if loving him saves those things, she will love him to the sun and back."

Her grandfather and grandmother's love had been the stuff of legend, and Vi had believed it. Though now, she wondered... A begrudging political arrangement wouldn't have done nearly as much to keep the West loyal and begin the slow process of endearing the South to their future Empress and Emperor. It made sense the story would be spun in brighter light. Vi's chest tightened and her breathing grew short, but not from the stairs she and Zira climbed.

Despite having been taught all her life that marriage was a political transaction for someone born to her status, Vi had looked to Fiera and Tiberus as a model for how a political union could straddle both love and politics. The thought suddenly seemed so naive now.

"Here, these quarters belonged to one of Fiera's other generals who's... Well, let's not linger on the details."

Vi walked into the room. It reminded her of a smaller version of the hotel in the Crossroads: a carefully carved sliding screen separated the bed from a sitting area, and two doors at her left likely led to a closet and bathing room.

The memory briefly misted her eyes. That hotel had been the last place she'd seen her brother. Those few weeks they'd spent together on the road were all she'd ever have now, and they weren't nearly enough.

"Make yourself as comfortable as possible," Zira continued, oblivious. "Do you have personal effects anywhere in the city I should collect?"

"No, I travel light."

"As a former mercenary of the Nameless Company, I respect that." Zira smiled. "I'm sure I can find more than enough spare clothes for you before morning. We'll need you dressed properly as one of her guards because tomorrow, you'll face something far scarier than an Imperial army."

"What?"

Zira turned from the doorway, a wry grin on her face. "The Royal Council."

ZIRA WAS GOOD TO her word and brought Vi two trunks of various clothing to choose from. As usual, the slim-cut styles of the West were nearly impossible to fit into if they weren't perfectly tailored to the wearer. But Vi found something that didn't look comically large or small.

She braided her hair in large parts, knotting the ropes together up and away from her face at the back of her head. There were already enough similarities between her and Fiera; Vi didn't want to encourage them further. Keeping her hair up rather than wearing it loose as Fiera did would be a good point of differentiation.

The council met just outside the royal quarters, which made it right down the hall and around the corner from Vi's room.

When she entered the chamber, she was greeted by only four familiar faces—Fiera, Zira, Ophain, and Zerian. Tiberus was surprisingly absent and everyone else was a wary stranger. Vi would tread lightly while she determined if she needed to earn their favor.

"We should discuss the matter of the soldiers first," Lord Twintle, councilor for maritime matters, pressed as soon as Fiera opened the meeting to concerns at large. "They are the men and women of the West, men and women who put their lives on the line for their kingdom."

"Their kingdom is no more," Zerian interjected. "In the eyes of the Empire they are war crimi—"

"They are equal citizens with a chance of serving the Empire," Fiera said, cutting him off quickly with a look before he could say something that would likely raise tempers. "Lord Twintle, I know your son is in one of the containment shelters."

"Containment shelter? You mean prison."

Fiera ignored the remark and continued, "We're doing all we can at the moment for our soldiers. But returning the city at large to a point of comfort and normalcy is our first priority. That way the soldiers see there is nothing more to defend and will integrate back with society more smoothly as citizens of Solaris."

"They will always want to stand for Mhashan," he mumbled. Fiera ignored him.

"Lord Twintle's eldest son is Luke," Zira whispered in Vi's ear. "He's been vying to get him out of the prison for weeks."

"Speaking of that normalcy, Lord Twintle, how is trade? And fishing?" Fiera asked.

"Fishing is better now that we aren't dodging Imperial vessels."

"And Oparium?"

"We're still talking with the dock master there regarding getting into port."

Vi stared at the notes, letters, ledgers, and maps spread on the table before her. She had heard of council meetings like this from her parents—even fantasized about one day being a part of them. Now that she was here, and with the knowledge she held, it was proving difficult to remain silent.

"Until trade improves," Vi began, and all eyes immediately swung to her. More than one councilmember looked surprised by her boldness. "Might I suggest we import additional rations from the East? I believe they are going to have a rather impressive year for grain; they might be able to spare more than they're letting on, in an effort to conserve in case of a poor harvest next year. But I'm confident the Mother will bless their fields again."

"And just who are you again?" Lord Twintle asked dully.

"My name is Yullia."

"I didn't ask for your name," he drawled. "Let me put it more simply for you: why should we care about your thoughts? Especially since they are the thoughts of a criminal."

Vi merely shrugged. "Care or don't. I merely offer my wisdom."

"And your wisdom is welcome," Fiera insisted with a glance to Twintle. "Yullia is gifted with the goddess's sight. Perhaps even more so than I." There were several skeptical glances at that statement. "I am certain when she gives us her thoughts, they are worth listening to. I'll speak with the Emperor regarding reaching out to the Lady of the East for additional supplies."

"Perhaps in that same missive he can introduce me to her," Ophain suggested from Fiera's right. "As I might need to deal with her directly in the coming years."

"I'll bring it up." Fiera nodded to her brother.

Vi studied Ophain as he leaned forward, making a few notes in his personal ledger. He seemed to be taking the situation with surprising grace. Then again, he was heir to the last king of the West and had somehow escaped being murdered following the end of the war. That would be enough to make anyone grateful.

"If we are thinking of asking the East for further assistance, we should check the current storerooms to ensure our counts are accurate," Denja, a councilor for commerce mused. She had a thick accent—one Vi couldn't quite place. It didn't sound entirely Western to her ears. "I have been sending messengers regularly, but I worry the Imperial soldiers have been dipping in without approval."

"Imperial soldiers would never," Zerian insisted.

"Then perhaps they haven't been taking careful notes." Denja smiled thinly.

"We shall go together," Fiera suggested.

"Do you think that's wise?" her brother asked.

"I've been shut up in this castle for too long." Fiera sighed and collected her papers. "The engagement has been announced and the people should know I'm not being held hostage until my wedding day. Besides, I'll have my knights with me."

Her gaze lifted to Zira and Vi. They both gave a nod to the princess.

"Knights," Twintle murmured. "But they're not anymore, are they?"

"I've yet to decide what the fate of the Knights of Jadar will be," Fiera said. She quickly returned the conversation to its previous topic, looking to Denja. "Do you have time now?"

"Of course, your highness." When the councilor bowed her head, the beads attached to the ornate headscarf she wore clanked softly.

"Excellent. I leave the other matters in Ophain's capable hands." Fiera started around the table. Denja, Vi, and Zira following behind.

"Where are you from, Yullia?" Denja asked as they walked. "You speak Southern Common and Mhashanese quite well."

"I've been gifted with languages," Vi said honestly. When Denja continued to stare expectantly at her, Vi knew she hadn't dodged the initial question. "I've traveled all over. I've never quite had a home and couldn't tell you where I was born or who my parents were." Vi kept Taavin's words in mind as she danced around the question; telling people who she was could have unintended consequences.

"How heartbreaking, an orphan alone in the world." Denja didn't sound for a moment like she was genuinely sympathetic. "And now you stand in direct service to one of the most powerful people on this continent. That's extraordinarily lucky."

This continent. The words stuck out to Vi like an absent compass rose on a map.

"And where are you from?" Vi asked, trying to keep her voice light. "You have the bright blue eyes of a Southerner." So blue they almost had hints of purple.

"I am from the south of Mhashan," she answered easily. "Right along the border. Some Southern blood made it into my family tree."

"I see." Vi didn't trust those unnaturally colored eyes, full of suspicious knowing. But for now, Vi put the sense behind her. She had other things to focus on—like getting a moment with Fiera to discuss the sword.

They stepped out into the royal stables and continued out toward the drawbridge that connected the castle to the city. However, before they could depart, an Imperial soldier blocked their way.

"Your highness, do you require a guard detail into the city today?"

"I already have my guards," Fiera motioned to Vi and Zira.

Even though Fiera's unspoken dismissal was clear, the soldier didn't move. "The Emperor has insisted that you are to be protected at all times."

"And I have told you that I will be. And I am quite able to protect myself, thank you." Fiera patted the steel sword on her hip and looked the man up and down. "I'd venture I was training long before you ever even saw a sword."

He pursed his lips together but managed to squeeze out, "This is an order from the Emperor."

"And I am the future Empress," Fiera retorted. "I wish to go out into my city without a pack of soldiers around me. The war is over, sir, and the people should know it."

"The city is unsafe."

"What do you know of the city?" Zira asked, a lazy grin on her face. "I think her highness and all her advisors have a clear sense of just how dangerous it is or isn't."

"Now, stand aside," Fiera ordered firmly. "If the Emperor has a problem, he'll take it up with me."

"Yes, your highness." The soldier finally relented and stepped aside. Vi could feel him and the others in his squadron watching as the four women passed.

"Do you think it's actually dangerous?" Denja asked.

"They're Southern. Judging by their sunburnt cheeks, they'll likely try and claim the sun itself is dangerous," Zira remarked dryly.

Fiera let out a low chuckle. "Perhaps, for soldiers, the city poses some threat. But I want the people to see me among them without Southerners surrounding me. To know that the Mhashan they once knew has not vanished, regardless of its name— and that I am still with them, regardless of mine."

After a beat of what felt like companionable silence, Vi cleared her throat. "Speaking of Mhashan," she began delicately. "The Knights of Jadar…"

"Don't start sounding like Twintle," Zira muttered with a roll of her eyes. "The man is relentless."

"Of course he is. He's one of the last living commanders of the Knights." Fiera sighed heavily. "It was an honor he doesn't want to see stripped."

Vi's stomach flipped on the thought and settled the wrong way. She couldn't recall Lord Twintle in any of her readings or discussions, but that didn't make him unimportant. From this point on, in Vi's world, the Knights had devolved into a shadowy, separatist organization that stood against her family.

"I don't wish to speak about the Knights a moment longer. That is my burden and decision. No need to cloud our otherwise good day with it." The note of finality in Fiera's voice brooked no protest. "Denja, can you please outline our goal for this excursion?"

"Certainly, your highness. There are new stores for grains and other supplies brought in by the Empire around where the old wall used to be…"

Vi tried to pay attention to the conversation with half an ear, but her eyes were on the houses around them. The dictates of martial law were being lifted bit by bit; citizens were getting a few more hours each day to be about. But this hour was not one of them, and the city felt like a ghost town.

She glanced over her shoulder, unable to shake the perpetual feeling of someone watching them. The silence in a city so large was eerie—an unwelcome fifth companion.

Slowing, Vi caught Zira's eye and the woman adjusted her pace until the two of them were side by side. Denja and Fiera took the lead, talking about current stocks and trade. Vi kept her voice hushed.

"Zira, do you feel like someone is watching us?"

"I feel like a thousand someones are watching us." Zira looked to the upper floors of the buildings around them. Vi saw a curtain abruptly close in one of the windows. "But that is the point of this, as our princess has decreed."

"Yes but…" Vi couldn't put her finger on the uneasy feeling that crackled up her spine like the phantom sensation of the red magic of an evil god. It was akin to the nervous energy she'd felt before sailing into Adela's stronghold. "I can't shake the feeling that *something* is about to happen."

"Should we head back to the castle?" The question was genuine, and Vi appreciated it down to her toes. Zira had no reason to give her so much faith, especially not when her worries were ambiguous.

"No, I don't want to turn us around for a mere feeling." Vi shook her head and tried to shake the sensations with it, but they clung to her like leeches. "I'm sure it's nothing."

The four made it without incident to the storehouses. Vi felt far better the moment she saw the Imperial guards standing out front of the large barn-shaped buildings. Vi and Zira walked a quick perimeter as Denja and Fiera consulted with the quartermaster. The whole affair took less than an hour and was blessedly over without incident. They were on their way back when bells tolled over the city, reigniting Vi's paranoia.

"The citizens are allowed out for an hour after the bells," Zira explained.

Sure enough, doors began to open and people wandered, blinking into the streets. They seemed dazed, their senses dulled by long hours cooped up inside. One by one, they turned their faces skyward; the sun was the first thing their eyes met, as if to burn away the haze in their eyes. As if to greet it like an old friend. For the first block, none of the people even noticed the princess in their midst.

"Y-Your highness." A woman was the first to turn their way. "You are free." She dropped to her knees.

"As I have always been. As are we all."

"The conqueror… what has he done to you, m'lady?" another young woman dared to ask.

"Only steal my heart." Fiera gave a smile so tender and warm it could melt ice.

One look, and Vi nearly forgot all her prior questions about the genuineness of Fiera's love for Tiberus—only to have them rushing back even stronger. Did she have a genuine smile? Or was it the look of someone desperate to save their home—someone who knew the safety of her people depended on them believing a beautiful lie?

It wasn't her business, Vi tried to remember. She was here for the crystal weapons. She had enough on her plate when it came to love.

"He has stolen your heart, and your fire." A male voice cut through Vi's thoughts. The little crowd collecting around Fiera suddenly seemed far larger as Vi searched for the speaker. "The Fiera who led the Knights of Jadar, who was truly blessed by the Mother above, would've never given into the false sun."

Vi's eyes settled on the man, who had short black hair and a closely trimmed mustache. Zira took a step closer to Fiera, situating herself between the princess and her detractor.

"You might not be able to understand," Fiera said, keeping her composure rock-solid and voice as soft as feathers, "but I truly do love him. He brightens my fire. And I will ensure he protect us all."

Motion from Vi's left caught her eye.

Like a bull rushing forward, a cloaked man pushed through the crowd. Vi's eyes barely had time to land on a flash of silver. Zira wasn't moving and wouldn't notice in time, Denja had yet to react, Fiera was looking the other way—

"*Mysst soto larrk*," Vi hissed under her breath, moving as she spoke. She drew her hand across her chest, moving as though she was drawing the blade from a hidden sheathe in her sleeve. Vi hoped it was enough to hide the flash of the glyph that created the weapon she now held.

Steel met steel as Vi pushed Fiera aside, stopping the assassin's blade. But the hooded man paid her no heed. Instead, his dark gaze swung to Fiera.

"You should've died with your father," he uttered darkly. "Traitor."

T HE WORDS WERE THE man's last.

The hand-guard of Vi's dagger was flush to his blade. She slid it upward, the short pommel of hers butting against his. Vi used the force to beat the blade away; she had momentum, and the man was caught off-guard by the sudden assault.

Twisting, Vi threw her body into a lunge and sank her blade into his ear. As Vi withdrew, he crumpled.

She spun in place. Zira had already engaged the man who had first drawn their attention and had him on the ground in an instant. People were screaming, fleeing; chaos radiated around them, but Vi's eyes scanned the windows and rooftops. The memory of the Knight's attempt on her mother's life at the Crossroads was suddenly fresh and—

Motion caught her eye.

Vi lifted a hand and sent a tendril of flame in a burst toward a rooftop. She used the motion to release her dagger back into her sleeve, the flash of fire and fabric hiding the unraveling remnants of light. Whoever had been on the roof darted away and didn't return to the building's edge. Vi linked arms with Fiera, briefly startled by how warm the woman was to her touch.

"Your highness, we must move you—"

"I will not be moved." Fiera pulled her arm back, an offended expression at being manhandled briefly taking over her features. She spun in place, looking to the man Zira held at sword-point on the ground. The princess crossed over like a beast stalking prey. "Who sent you?"

"No one sent us." The man narrowed his eyes at Fiera. "We didn't need to be sent by anyone, because we no longer need a leader. We shall lead ourselves as we stand by our mission—to defend Mhashan from Southern invaders."

"The war is over."

"The war is only beginning." A smile spread across his mouth. "Kill me, like you did the other Knights of Jadar. Those who made the mistake of being loyal to you until the end."

"You are not my knight," Fiera whispered.

Vi continued to scan the buildings. Denja, for her part, remained incredibly calm—far calmer than Vi would have expected from a commerce minister. Vi's attention landed on her and they locked eyes for a long moment.

Denja had been the one to suggest going to the storerooms, hadn't she? It wouldn't have been hard to find dissenters and organize an attack with a few hours' notice.

"No, I am not *your* knight. I am Mhashan's Knight, one of the true Knights of Jadar," the man insisted. "We have broken free of you. We do not need your orders."

"You speak treason like it delights you."

"Truth is what delights me."

"I will not give you another chance to—"

"No, you won't," the man interrupted. "Just like you did not give your once-loyal Knights another chance on the docks that night."

Vi frowned. Of course word would spread of what had happened at the docks. Most likely, Luke or Kahrin had started the rumors—Zira wouldn't. Luke was Twintle's son and Twintle could connect back to Denja. Lines of betrayal unfolded like a deadly map before her, one where a single misstep would lead one to death.

"What will it be, princess?" the man continued. The commoners watched from a wide distance. "Will you—"

Fiera clamped her hand over the man's mouth. Fire poured from between her fingers and down his throat. Vi did not grimace or turn away; this was how Jax had described her father's method for killing people.

Vi wondered if Aldrik was even aware of the similarity with his late mother. That the action was a dark, unlikely, perhaps even unintentional connection between them.

The man collapsed to the ground, his skin red and bubbling as Fiera straightened away. She smoothed out her clothes and tossed her hair over her shoulder, starting for the castle without a backward glance.

"No one touch them," Fiera declared as they passed the ring of wide-eyed onlookers. "Do not burn them this evening for a Rite of Sunset. I want them to be strung up and branded as traitors. Let there be no doubt that my Empire has no room for those who stand against me. The only true knights are those at my side."

Every man and woman seemed to hold their breath while Fiera's eyes were on them. They were utterly captive to their fear. And while Vi could see a certain amount of shock in their stares, she was keenly aware that none of them seemed surprised.

Fiera was a double-edged sword. One side of her could slice through a man's most iron-clad defenses with startling sweetness. The other side of her could cut a man down beginning with his ankles and working up from there.

The most fearsome thing was that Fiera clearly knew what she was, and had learned to wield her skills with deadly precision.

"Knights of Jadar," Fiera muttered, pacing her personal quarters and worrying the heavy silver ring on her finger. Immediately after returning to the castle, Fiera had made her will known regarding the bodies of the traitors, sent Denja away, and summoned Vi and Zira to her rooms. "They called themselves 'true Knights of Jadar.'"

"They wouldn't be able to pass even the initial tests to become a Knight," Zira muttered. She lounged in a large wingback chair by one of the windows of Fiera's room, one leg draped lazily over the armrest. "They are cutthroats turned opportunists."

"They make a mockery of my family." Fiera clenched her hands into fists so tightly they trembled. Tiny tendrils of flame snaked through the air around them. "Being a Knight of Jadar was the greatest honor in all the West."

Vi watched Fiera's rage from where she leaned against the wall by the doorway, arms folded and holding her elbows. She tried to keep herself detached from the princess's plight by reminding herself that this Fiera was not her family. Vi was merely here as a traveler, doing what she needed to do before leaving without a trace.

Yet the raw hurt that swirled almost visibly in the air around Fiera brought up emotions from the void that was always threatening to swallow Vi whole. Fiera's eyes were glassy, as though she was nearly at the point of frustrated tears. Still the fire within them burned.

"What do you think?" Fiera asked Vi.

"Pardon?"

"I asked your thoughts, Yullia." Fiera motioned toward her with an open hand, flames still writhing around her fingers. "Do you agree with Zira that these are opportunists and I do myself more of a disservice by giving them a platform with my anger?"

Vi only had to make a show of thinking about the answer. "I don't think this was an isolated attack, unfortunately."

"You don't." Fiera's hand dropped to her side.

"I think there are those who cling to old Mhashan like a security blanket. Those who would've rather fought with every last breath for every last brick, regardless of the cost."

"Those like my father." Fiera pinched the bridge of her nose with a sigh and shook her head, walking over to one of the three large windows that dominated one wall of her sitting room. They towered over her, making even Fiera seem small. "He wanted to defend Norin until it was ashes. He would've seen every last man and woman of the kingdom die if that's what it took to prevent Mhashan bending to Solaris."

"Foolish men and their foolish honor." Zira tipped her head against the side of the wingback, looking to Fiera. The princess was still avoiding eye contact with both of them.

"Foolish people who cannot see the world changing around them," Fiera said thoughtfully. "We are a people surrounded by desert. Yet somehow, there are those who cannot see how power shifts like sand in the wind. It blows one way, then another. You can never expect it to be in the same place for long.

"Mhashan was not made strong because of our cities of immovable stone. The Ci'Dan family did not rise to prominence because we were rigid. It was because we could adapt."

Vi continued to stare at the princess's back. Fiera would give up everything to save what she loved. Not to preserve the world as she knew it, and had always known it—but to see it thrive, to continue on even if that meant letting it change.

A thought settled at the forefront of Vi's mind: when she had gone to Meru to be the Goddess's Champion, what had she been fighting for? Had she wanted to see her family thrive in whatever form that took? Or had she only wanted to see her family as she had envisioned them?

"The fact remains that not all possess your wisdom," Vi said, silently including herself in the sentiment. "And those men and women will band together."

"He said the war was only just beginning." Fiera turned away from the window at last. "You said you believe the attacks will continue. How do you think they'll strike next?"

"All wars need a general. In the case of the Knights of Jadar, that general is designated by a singular object—"

"A sword," Fiera finished for her. "They will never lay their hands on my grandfather's sword."

"It sees the light of day rarely enough," Zira murmured.

"They will go after it though, regardless of where it is. If they even sense the edge of its power, these false Knights will hunt it." Vi braced herself for what she needed to ask next. "If I'm to be effective as your guard, I need to know where it is."

For the first time, Fiera didn't immediately acquiesce. Vi supposed she should be grateful; Fiera's caution surrounding the sword was their first line of defense.

"It took me three years to lay eyes on it." Zira stood. "Why do you think she should show you? You've only just entered her service."

"Because my only goal is to protect it," Vi said as earnestly as possible. She pushed away from the wall and allowed her arms to fall to her sides, abandoning her previously defensive position. "Because I have a sense about it, just as I had a sense earlier this day about the attack."

"What sense?" Fiera looked between her and Zira.

"She did tell me as we were walking to the storehouse that she felt uneasy. But then again, we all did."

Fiera debated this a moment before slowly approaching Vi. She searched Vi's face and narrowed her eyes slightly, as if she could extract any falsehoods from Vi's eyes alone. Vi worked to make sure she didn't hesitate, which seemed nearly impossible under the woman's relentless inspections.

"I need more from you," she said finally. "Your words, the feeling of fate steeped in the air around you… it has gotten you this far. But I need more from you if I am to bestow this most prized secret on you."

It was fair, more than fair. Vi had earned Fiera's trust thanks to the woman's senses. But she'd found the extent of that good will and now the real work would have to begin. Taavin had cautioned her as much.

"I see more than the future," Vi confessed softly, her voice nearly quivering. She was walking a very fine, very dangerous line. "I was chosen by the Mother herself to defend this world and the sword will play a role in that. Keeping it from falling into the wrong hands is all I desire."

"Chosen by the Mother?" Zira repeated, though Vi couldn't tell if her tone was one of belief or incredulity.

"It's true," Vi continued, speaking directly to Fiera. "And if you take me to the sword, I can give you proof of my claim that will satisfy you." Fiera was immobile as a statue, listening, waiting. It was that expectant tension that had Vi adding, "Should it not, then kill me there and I will take the secret of the sword's location to my grave."

The princess took a step backward, then nodded. She glanced to Zira and said, "I'm going to accept Yullia's offer. Keep your blade ready."

Zira gripped the pommel of her sword and Vi's heart began to race.

Fiera was ever the double-edged sword and Vi walked the ridge down the middle. Would she end on the side that would protect her? Or was the sharper edge about to be turned against her?

Her future with Fiera balanced on what happened next and, unfortunately for Vi, she had no idea what she was about to do to earn the trust she needed.

10

L UCKILY, VI HAD A bit of a walk to think about her plans. Even better, the walk
was done entirely in silence. Fiera led them down through the castle with Vi in
the middle and Zira behind her.

As Vi walked, she scribbled down a mental list of things she could do to prove
to Fiera she was meant to have the sword. She could try to look into the future and
if that didn't work, perhaps summon a glyph? That would seem mysterious enough.

They entered through empty passages clearly meant for soldiers—those men and
women still locked away at the order of the Emperor. Fiera led them past a desk that
must once have belonged to the quartermaster, and through one of three doors that
led to a mostly empty armory. Every part of Norin had been impacted by the ten-year
siege. The city was like a carcass that the Empire was slowly, bite by bite, licking
clean.

Fiera went to a door in the back, lifted a key with a chain around her neck and,
with one more glance back at Vi, opened the door.

Beyond the threshold, a narrow hallway glowed orange thanks to a curtain of
swirling flame burning at its end. The fire was nearly white-hot and would no doubt
be difficult for even the most powerful of Firebearers to pass through.

Fiera waved dismissively and the flames vanished. Vi was left blinking into the
sudden darkness in the moments before the princess summoned a mote of flame for
them to see by.

"How difficult is it to maintain that flame all the time?" Vi asked.

"I've grown accustomed to it," Fiera answered. "At first, it seemed like a great
deal of power constantly draining from me, making me weak. But our magic is like
our muscles—the more we stretch and flex our powers, the stronger they become. I
hardly notice it now."

Vi believed her. Fiera's powers were as breathtaking as all the stories she'd been
told growing up made them seem.

They continued forward, past the stones that still glowed faintly from the residual
heat of the flames and into a tiny room. It was unadorned, save for the sword hung on
the wall before Vi, and a narrow table beneath it. Fiera reached for the blade without

hesitation, unsheathing it.

"The Sword of Jadar," she said with quiet reverence. "Bestowed by King Jadar onto his youngest son—the one who did not inherit his flames—so he could use its powers to defend Mhashan and the throne." She held out the blade, pointing it directly at Vi. "You have seen it. And now I will have the proof you promised."

She should feel threatened. But Vi's heart raced purely because of how close the crystal was. She could feel the waves of power rippling from it. Every swirl of the magic within it delighted her, enthralled her.

Vi's plan to prove her good intentions had been formed out of a series of guesses. But in that moment, she no longer needed a clear way forward. She didn't need to overthink.

She acted on instinct.

Lifting her hands, Vi's fingertips lightly landed on the edges of the blade on either side. It was sharp enough that it could bite into her flesh but it didn't. It wouldn't. This was the will of the goddess; Vi and the sword were of the same make, now, and it would not harm her.

Power lifted off the blade. The faint glow that perpetually surrounded the sword curled like tendrils of smoke, reaching for Vi with a nearly sentient quality. Like the scythe, the power crashed on her, and the sensation of being two places at once overtook her.

They stood in the center of the Dark Isle.

Two women and two men were semi-circled around one older man who had the same pointed ears as Taavin. He still appeared youthful, yet his eyes were ancient and ringed with dark circles. Clutched in his left hand was a tall staff of glittering crystal as bright blue as a clear morning sky.

Vi knew the man was the former Champion. Looking at him was like looking in a mirror that twisted her outside reflection while exposing what was within. He spoke to what she assumed were his children, but his eyes remained on her—as if he could see the one who would come after him, even then. As if somehow, across all time and space, he was aware of the future Champion in his midst.

Lifting the staff, magic burst from his hands, merging with the glow of the crystal as he broke off the first quarter of the staff.

The fragment glowed so brightly that Vi was left blinking, struggling to make out what was happening; the four kneeling before the Champion covered their eyes. But the light and magic faded, revealing a scythe he bestowed on his youngest daughter.

The Champion repeated the process, giving an axe to the next daughter, and a sword to his youngest son. On his eldest's brow, the Champion settled a crown of crystal.

As soon as the man's hands left the crown, his body aged. Vi watched as the magic left him like fireflies returning to the sun high above. He swayed from side to side as muscles vanished and his clothes became limp sacks. His skin and hair grayed and his lips curled in.

But his eyes—those eyes that had witnessed the passage of time from beyond its reach, thanks to the hand of Yargen—stayed the same. They were not surprised. They were not in pain.

Vi only saw acceptance and relief in the man's final moments.

All at once, her awareness returned to her physical body.

As it had with the scythe in the Twilight Kingdom, a soft glow coated her skin, extending from the sword. The magic disappeared like smoke as the vision left her.

Fiera and Zira looked at her with startled and slightly worried expressions.

Vi lowered her hands from the blade, taking a step away. She moved slowly so they wouldn't spook and attack her, and because her head was still spinning, settling back into this time and place.

That vision had been far more vivid than the last. With the scythe, she'd experienced shifting images, feelings, sensations that connected into a story Vi could piece together. This had been a complete scene from start to finish.

"They glow blue, not red..." Zira whispered. "Like the sword."

Vi lifted her hand to her temple and wished there was a mirror in the room so she could confirm Zira's murmurings were about her eyes.

"What are you?" Fiera asked as she lowered the sword.

"I am chosen by the Mother to defend this world," Vi repeated softly, hoping this act of exposing a part of her true nature didn't adversely affect the future she was working toward. For reasons she couldn't quite explain, Vi trusted Fiera and Zira more deeply than she likely should. "You will not understand who—what—I am. But you must keep what you have seen a secret. The fate of your world depends on it."

Zira took another step back. But Fiera was less shaken. She delicately rested the tip of the sword on the stone floor and sank to one knee. She bowed her head.

"Chosen of the Mother, you have my allegiance."

"Fiera—"

"*Zira*," Fiera interrupted sharply. "You saw her. You witnessed her magic. Her blue eyes. Her communing with the sword itself. You must have felt it too—the sensation of fate."

Zira looked between Fiera and Vi. She swayed slightly, but dropped to her knee after only a moment's hesitation. "My fate is linked with yours, Fiera. It was declared by the Mother. If you are loyal to her, so am I."

Vi took a slow breath. Yargen's power still surged through her. The blade beckoned her with whispering invitations only her ears could hear.

"I require the blade."

"Require it?" Fiera lifted her head first, then the rest of her. Zira followed the princess back to her feet as well. "This blade has been in my family for—"

"Hundreds of years," Vi finished. "Yet you do not know where it came from... not really. Nor what it can be used for." She motioned to the sword. "In that blade is a great and terrible power. The longer you wield it, the more you risk it twisting your body and mind, as well as the bodies and minds of those around you. It calls out to the false Knights of Jadar who rely on lore they don't understand in an attempt to return themselves to prominence."

"I cannot give it to you."

"You must," Vi insisted.

"The princess said she cannot, so she cannot." Zira stood, her hand back on the sword at her hip.

"The sword will be used in my wedding to the Emperor as a ceremonial piece," Fiera began. For the first time, Vi saw doubt on the ever-self-assured woman's face. "But... after... I had intended to seal it away. Even had you not said so, Yullia, I'm aware that this weapon holds a great power that mortal men aren't meant to hold. Perhaps, I might entrust it to you at that time." The princess shook her head, as though she was dismissing the notion as soon as it came to her. "No... I must think on it."

Vi wanted to insist on Fiera's compliance, but she'd already made progress. The longer the princess simmered on what had transpired here, the closer she'd be to realizing the truth of Vi's words.

For now, an openness to giving up the sword would have to be good enough for Vi. Pressing the matter, looking desperate, wouldn't suit her.

Fiera returned the sword to its scabbard, the scabbard to the wall. No sooner was it back on its pegs than footsteps sounded in the hall. All three women turned, startled.

Two figures approached from the darkness of the hall: Tiberus and Denja.

"There you are, my bride." Tiberus, once more, went immediately for Fiera. For him, nothing else seemed to exist in a room when she was there. "I have been worried to the sun and back for you."

"I'm fine." Fiera squeezed his forearms lightly and took a step away. Even though she wore a smile on her lips, Vi could see the discomfort behind her eyes. She didn't appreciate the suddenly crowded room any more than Vi did.

"Denja told me what happened on the streets, and that you refused your guard detail."

"I had a guard detail." Fiera motioned to Vi and Zira. "Why don't we all head to a sitting room to discuss these matters? It'll be far more comfortable."

"What is this place anyway? You've not taken me here before…" The statement trailed off as the Emperor looked around. His attention was quickly consumed by the sword. "This was what you held that night… This must be the Sword of Jadar."

These weapons attract power-hungry men. Vi keenly heard the words of her father once more. If Tiberus's expression was any indication, the Knights of Jadar were no longer the only ones who were out for the sword.

"Yes," Fiera said begrudgingly as she stepped in front of her betrothed. She rested her hands lightly on his upper arms in an attempt to guide him away. "We shall use it at our wedding to bless our union and then it will be sealed away forever."

"Here? Will it be here?" Tiberus asked, a little too eagerly.

"No, I will find a new spot for it." Fiera swept her gaze across the room, landing on Denja. Vi didn't miss the subtle confusion that furrowed Fiera's brow. "Too many people appear to know of this location." Then, like magic, her whole expression softened. Fiera gave Tiberus the sweetest, most endearing smile one could imagine. "Now, my love, come with me to procure some refreshments? I'm both parched and starved from all the excitement this morning."

"Yes, the excitement…" Tiberus looked back to Fiera and his focus returned. "You must tell me what happened."

"Of course." Fiera linked their arms, leading Tiberus out of the room. Denja fell into step behind, Vi and Zira pulling up the rear. Fiera locked the door and Vi could feel the *pop* of magic as she lifted the curtain of flame in the hallway once more.

"Zira," Vi said lightly, loud enough for Denja to hear but not so loud that it distracted Fiera and Tiberus. "Do you have time now to show me that sword technique you were telling me about earlier?"

"Yes, I think now would be a wonderful time," Zira said easily, without even missing a beat.

"Excellent."

They paused at a landing, Zira taking the lead. "If you three will excuse Yullia and me, there's something I promised to show her in the training ring."

"Good of you to do so." Fiera picked up on the ruse. "I appreciate you taking such an active interest in Yullia's training."

"I have other matters to attend to as well," Denja said stiffly, adjusting the scarf around her head. "If you'll all excuse me."

"Thank you again for informing me of the incident today," Tiberus said to the blue-eyed woman. "I appreciate that someone made it a point to notify me of actions taken against my betrothed."

"Certainly, your grace." Denja bowed. "I am here to serve." After taking two steps backward, Denja turned, disappearing down the hall.

Vi bowed as well, Zira mirroring the motion before leading them in the opposite direction as Denja. They rounded down two staircases, to a storeroom attached to an empty training pit. Zira closed the door behind her and settled on one of the room's many unmarked crates before asking, "You wanted me alone and now you have me. What is it?"

"Denja. How did she know of that room?"

"I don't know, but I don't think Fiera told her."

"I don't think so either." Vi paced, running her hands along the dusty boxes of training equipment. "Which means she figured it out, interrogated someone else who knows, or followed us."

"Before today, only Fiera and I knew of it."

"Not even her siblings? Ophain?"

"If they know, I'm unaware. But I doubt they would've spilled the secret just because some random councilor asked."

Vi stopped pacing. With stilled feet, her mind felt like it could move faster. "How long has Denja been in the employ of the royal family?"

"Right around the time the war began, I believe. I've only served our princess for three years, so I can't say for certain." Zira pushed herself off the crate. "Long enough that if there was something to worry about when it comes to Denja, they would've already found out."

"Not always," Vi said softly. "Some betrayals take decades to mature." *Like Jayme.* "In the coming months, we must protect the sword at all costs."

"So you've said. What happens if it falls into the wrong hands, as you say?"

"Would you believe me if I said the end of the world?" Vi gave a bitter grin. Zira let out a laugh that told Vi just how seriously she took the warning.

"You really are an odd one." Shaking her head as the laughter faded, Zira started for the door. But her hand stalled on the handle. She looked back to Vi and—for one brief second—Vi could see the woman taking the words seriously. "We'll keep it safe."

"I hope so."

Zira gave her a nod and left. Vi crossed over to the window that overlooked the empty training field. They would keep it safe this time. She wouldn't allow the world to repeat itself once more. There wouldn't be another Vi pulled from her home to be Yargen's Champion. There wouldn't be another Taavin to suffer at the hands of fate.

The cycle *would* end. Now that the sword was within her grasp, the real work could begin.

11

I N THE DEAD OF night, the halls were empty, and the castle was quiet.

Vi made her way with ease, glyphs wrapped around her wrists. One masked her sounds. But should someone see her, the other gave her the face of a random Imperial guard.

Once in the armory, Vi closed the door behind her, grabbed one of the swords off the racks, and propped it lightly against the handle. There would be no surprise guests this time. She wanted to know the moment someone came in.

Though, hopefully, her paranoia would prove unfounded.

The lock on the door to the sword's chamber was easy to melt away with her magic. She repeated the same process she had in the Archives to get to Taavin after Ulvarth had locked his door. Vi melted and bent and separated the ring holding the lock in place, rather than destroying the lock itself, and set it aside. That way, she could return it to its previous position.

As a Firebearer, Fiera no doubt knew of this flaw in the protection of the blade. That was why she kept the curtain of flame burning at all times within the hall. But the princess had also said she barely noticed the magic leeching away from her anymore. Vi surmised that if Fiera were asleep, she wouldn't notice any slight fluctuations in that magic at all.

Lifting her hand, Vi moved forward deliberately. Her fingertips dipped into the flames first. It was warm—Fiera's power undeniable. But it didn't burn her.

She didn't want to assume full control of the flames, merely adjust them. Pushing her magic out from her extended hand, a hole barely larger than her wrist appeared in the wall of fire. She extended her magic further, stretching the opening little by little until it was wide enough for her to step through, flames raging right at the edge of her power.

On the other side of the fire, Vi released her hold, allowing the flames to ease back into place.

"*Narro hath hoolo,*" Vi uttered, her eyes locked with the sword on the wall. She didn't so much as look at Taavin when he appeared.

"This is record time for you getting here." He took a step forward, looking up at the sword. "What did you do?"

"What you told me to: I befriended Fiera and found the sword. Then I came to it." Vi crossed in front of him, lifting the weapon off its pegs.

"You need to be more specific. It's my duty to record all you do, and because I keep that memory, you do better every time… until, eventually, we succeed."

"We'll succeed this time," Vi insisted, focusing on the scabbard.

"While I admire your confidence, we won't know for sure until your sight shows us a future where Raspian is safely sealed away."

"Have a bit of faith." She finally allowed her attention to stray to him. His eyes were twice as brilliant and three times as hard as an emerald. "Believe in me."

"I do."

"You don't." Vi set down the blade on the table, taking a step away from it. Every time she was near the weapon it consumed her attention—but she wanted to give Taavin her undivided focus. "You don't think we'll succeed this time, otherwise you wouldn't be so cautious."

"I'm cautious because the world needs me to be."

"Because you think I'll fail."

"It's not what I think that matters. It's what's happened ninety-two times…" he murmured, glancing askance. Vi refused to allow it, stepping into his field of vision.

"When you look at me, you see me combined with ninety-two other versions of myself. You see actions I have not taken, but still could. Moments when I succeeded and, more often than not, failed. You see me in a way that I can't even imagine myself." She looked at him from head to toe. "But when I look at you… I only see one Taavin. The Taavin who taught me my magic and guided me across Meru, who betrayed me and my father. The Taavin I still loved even when I thought one more betrayal would break my heart. The Taavin I watched burn—" Her voice broke and she allowed herself to fall silent.

She didn't want him to sweep her into his arms and kiss her fiercely with lips that weren't really there. She wanted to feel like he understood—like he heard her. When he remained silent, she continued.

"All I have is you, Taavin," she whispered. "But you're stuck with those other ninety-two versions of me, and part of you is already expecting to meet the ninety-fourth. You'll never be with just me again."

"You're wrong," he said hastily. Emotions broke through all at once. His eyebrows pinched, his lower lip quivered slightly as he spoke. His hands trembled, as if wanting to reach for her, but they remained in place. She wondered if he, too, was held by the same invisible tethers that kept her rooted to the floor. "You are the only one I am with… the only one I have ever been with.

"You consume every thought I have. There's not a corner of my mind you don't fill. Or—" He was before her now, toes nearly touching. So close she could feel the phantom warmth that radiated off him like magic and sunlight. Vi raised a trembling hand, resting it on his chest, feeling the simple fabrics where there had once been intricate embroidery.

"Or?" she repeated, looking up at him through her eyelashes.

"Or my heart," he said finally. "You vex me. I have hurt you and you've hurt me in ways I cannot describe. And even now, I love you. I love you in a way I don't know if I deserve."

"You do," she whispered. She needed him here, now. She needed this love as much as she wanted it.

"I'm not sure." Taavin chuckled softly. The tip of his middle finger brushed against her temple. Soon his fingertips were in her hair, smoothing it away from her face, knotting in the strands at the nape of her neck.

"It's not your decision to make." Her head tilted upward, obliging his unspoken guidance. Her eyes dipped closed. "You'll be hurt again," she breathed across his lips.

"So will you."

It wasn't quite a kiss, but a trembling of lips brushed together. Vi pressed forward eagerly, and Taavin obliged. His arms tightened and she was swept against him.

Vi pressed her eyelids tighter together. This kiss… *it wasn't the same*. She willed her mind to ignore the slight shimmer of magic, the heat of the glyph at the watch that brought him into her world, the thin barrier that couldn't be lifted between them. She wanted to scream, and the only way she could keep the feeling contained was to smother it with his mouth.

When they pulled apart, his cheeks were lightly flushed. His fingers caressed her face.

"What should we do now that I have the sword?" Vi pulled away, flashing him a smile when she saw the confusion in his eyes at the swift change in topic.

"You still need to tell me how you got to it so swiftly." Taavin rested his palm on the small of her back.

"Right… Well, I went to the ball just as we had discussed…"

Vi recounted the events of the morning, the attack on Fiera, and her efforts to convince Fiera to take her to the sword.

"What did you say to her, specifically?" Taavin didn't miss when she'd glossed over that part. "Usually Fiera is far more cautious with the sword."

"I told her I was chosen by the Mother herself to defend this world and that I need to prevent the sword from falling into the wrong hands."

"Vi, you can't let them know who you are and why you're here. If the Dark Isle gains knowledge of the Champion, it could change the course of events."

"Just how easy is it to change the course of events?" Vi asked. "If I've failed ninety-two times, it must not be that easy."

He crossed his arms, a sour expression dousing his features. "You're right. It's not entirely easy." Taavin sighed, bringing his hand to his forehead. "Think of time as a river, flowing along. There are three types of things you will find in that river.

"The first are leaves floating along—these are people, pulled along by the course of fate, thrown this way and that by the flow of the world around them.

"The second are stones—things that are immovable. They will happen regardless of what you do. The river runs around them, its current and pace distorted by these events." He held up two fingers.

"So… some things can't be changed?" Vi said quietly. Taavin nodded. "What if Raspian being set free is one of those things?"

"It's not," he said quickly. "Raspian being set free is a result of other actions, not an action itself."

Vi thought about that a moment and finally hummed in agreement. Raspian was set free because of the crystal weapons being destroyed. Prevent those actions, and he wouldn't be freed.

"And the third thing in the river?" she asked.

"You—the dams and floodgates you create to guide the currents. The few locations where the river is quiet enough, or shallow enough, or narrow enough, to change how it flows."

Vi leaned against the table, Taavin at her side, the sword behind her. She hung her head, eyes on the floor, staring at nothing. She had to function like a surgeon of fate—cutting and stitching carefully, or the whole world would bleed out and die.

"The Apexes of Fate," she said slowly. "I can *make* them?"

"Yes. You, the previous Champion, and the crystal weapons."

"That's why there were so many in the North," Vi realized. "Because the axe was there for a long time and helped shape the North itself?"

"Exactly."

"So here in Norin, there must be many, too?"

"Indeed. And now that you have access to the sword, we will seek them out in time. At the Apexes, you will peer into the future, and there we'll learn if your actions have led to a change in fate overall."

"So where is the first one?"

"Don't be so eager. You've done enough for now. Lie low for a bit, build trust."

"There isn't time," Vi said hastily. "Fiera will be wedded soon, and then Aldrik will be born. That's when the Knights take the sword, and my father told me that Fiera dies trying to protect it. We have months, Taavin, to prevent that from happening."

"Remember what I said about stones in the river," he said cautiously. Vi didn't miss the ominous undercurrent to his words.

"Are you saying Fiera is—" Vi didn't have a chance to finish.

The flames at their right brightened as a woman pushed her way through. The fire licked around her skin but didn't touch it, thanks to a protective barrier. When she was through, that barrier shattered with a snap of light.

"*Mysst soto sut*," Denja said instantly. Light spilled from her palms, weaving and solidifying into the shape of a war axe she hoisted with ease. Her muscles bulged against the thin fabric covering her arms. Her bright blue eyes leveled with Vi, Taavin having vanished. "We should talk, you and I."

12

MAGIC COLLECTED UNDER HER palm, ready to be unleashed. Vi bet they were about to do a lot more than talk.

"We clearly have a lot to discuss." Vi's eyes darted to the weapon. Denja was a Lightspinner. No wonder Vi didn't hear the crash of the sword she'd propped against the door. Denja had likely used *durroe sallvas tempre* to hide her movements. "Why don't you release that, and we can do so calmly?"

"Why don't you summon one of your own like you did in the streets?"

Damn. She'd seen. Vi pressed her mouth into a thin smile. "I really don't want to hurt you."

"I've yet to decide what I want to do with you," Denja said casually. "I know you're not one of the queen's women. And I'll assume you know that travel to the Dark Isle isn't permitted, so I'll give you one chance: why are you here?"

What Vi wouldn't give to have a simple answer to that question. Instead, she said, "How do you know I'm not one of the queen's agents?"

"If you have to ask, you're not." Denja had some kind of communication with Meru, Vi would bet. "You're wasting a lot of what could be your last breaths not answering my question."

Vi locked eyes with the woman, swiftly debating her options. She could fight her way out—kill Denja. It wouldn't be hard to get in a *juth calt*. Even Taavin had been surprised when she'd used the words in that way. Then again, there was always *juth mariy*—destroy magic; Denja would use that on her the moment she started chanting.

Firebearing, then?

No, killing one of the Queen Lumeria's agents would create more problems than it would solve.

"Really? Nothing to say for yourself?" Denja narrowed her eyes, blue and almost purple-ringed. She slid her feet forward and sank into her stance. "Then—"

"Your name isn't Denja," Vi whispered. Her whole body relaxed, overcome with a sense of knowing. But this wasn't magic. What she felt was the overwhelming relief of recognition. How had she not noticed sooner?

"What?" She seemed genuinely startled, her grip relaxing slightly. Perhaps, Denja recognized her too, with some phantom echo of past lives they'd shared.

"Deneya?" Vi asked softly, trying to superimpose the face of the slightly older knight who had taken her to see Queen Lumeria over top of the woman before her. "It's Deneya, isn't it?"

"So you know my name. That's possible for any good spy to find out." Deneya tightened her grip again. "Especially one who could be working with the elfin'ra."

Vi balked. "The elfin'ra are still sealed away on their island, aren't they?" They should be, if Vi's memories and understanding served her. The elfin'ra were sealed away along with Raspian, a barrier on their island tied to the Crystal Caverns.

"They're constantly looking for ways to escape. Or finding agents to serve them who are not limited to the island." This woman was vastly different than the level-headed, quiet knight Vi had met briefly. Yet her eyes were the same as the woman who had found Vi in the Archives.

"Deneya, a world away, you promised me that I would have your sword if I sought you out… Well, here I am, seeking you out."

"What're you talking about?" Deneya chuckled. "You're not going to distract me, agent of evil."

Vi sighed heavily. There was no way Deneya was going to believe her, not without doing something drastic. Vi would just have to hope Taavin forgave her.

"I'm going to use *narro* now, to summon someone who can help explain things. Will you allow me this?"

Deneya seemed to weigh her options. She lifted her axe, resting it over Vi's left shoulder. The blade was a hair's width away from the flesh of her neck.

"If I hear even the start of a chant that begins with anything other than *narro*, your head comes clear off."

"Fine," Vi agreed easily. "*Narro hath hoolo.*"

Taavin appeared off to the side as he usually did—rebuilt from glyphs of light until he looked nearly solid. Only the faint outline of magic around his form betrayed that he wasn't actually there. He looked from Vi to Deneya, then back to Vi.

"Well, this is early," he murmured. Then, with his attention squarely on Vi, "Did you miss where I told you to keep yourself a secret and act cautiously?"

"Believe it or not, I'm actually trying to keep myself alive right now." Vi ground out the words. Couldn't he see she had a war axe at her throat?

"What sorcery is this?" Deneya whispered, staring at Taavin.

"Can you tell her who I am? You know her from before, right?"

"Yes, I do." Taavin turned to face Deneya. "Deneya Tallois, daughter of Arullia and Rox. Currently the first knight in Lumeria's Order of Shadows. She who has been on the Dark Isle defending the Caverns for the past hundred years… It is a pleasure to meet you, again."

"H-how?" Deneya stuttered. The axe at Vi's neck quivered and nearly bit into her flesh. Deneya was too startled to notice. "Begone elfin'ra specter!" She swung the weapon toward Taavin. It cut straight through him as though he was made of nothing but mist. It didn't seem to harm him, but the sight was a phantom blow to Vi's gut.

"I am not wicked. I am the eternal Voice of Yargen," Taavin continued calmly. "I have served her for hundreds of years. In my last lifetimes, in this, and in the next."

"You are not the Voice of Yargen. She is—"

"Fathima, and she has been the voice for the past two hundred years," Taavin finished. "And she will perish in the next twenty to thirty years… depending on certain factors, which will give room for Ulvarth to make his power play against Lumeria."

Deneya frowned, lowering her weapon—though she still held it so tightly, her hand trembled. Vi took it as a good sign that she had yet to brandish it against them again.

"Earlier, you said *hoolo*." Deneya looked to Vi. "One of Raspian's words? Is this man his work?"

"No," Vi said quickly. "You would feel it if it was." She remembered the sensation of the elfin'ra using the word on Adela's Isle of Frost. It was unmistakable.

"And the dark god is sealed away, unable to give new words," Taavin continued for Vi.

"Then... what are you?"

Vi took a deep breath and Taavin remained silent, yielding her the floor. Deneya finally relaxed, releasing the axe. It unraveled into strands of light and disappeared.

"I realize that what I am about to say is hard to believe," Vi began, working up her courage. "I am the Champion of Yargen, and I have been placed here by the goddess herself to defend this world from Raspian's return." Vi worked on bite-sized pieces of information.

"The Voice would've sent word if Yargen was giving us a Champion once more," Deneya said cautiously.

"As far as this world is concerned, we don't exist." Taavin smiled bitterly.

"Think of us more as travelers, passing through," Vi added.

"If you're truly the Champion, prove it to me. Tell or show me something that only the Champion can do."

"Have you ever met a Champion before?" Vi asked.

"Well, no..."

"Then how will you know it's something only the Champion can do?" she challenged.

"I..." Deneya let out a low chuckle. "You're almost drawing me in to this insanity, both of you."

"Deneya," Taavin said firmly, silencing the woman. "With the help of the proctor, you cheated your way through the written portion of your examinations to enter into Lumeria's Order. You did so not because you couldn't remember the information—but because the words dance on the page before your eyes, and you knew you wouldn't be able to finish in the allotted time."

"How do you—" Deneya took a step back, horror overtaking her features.

"Your tutor, the proctor, died in a skirmish in the south of Meru, leaving you alone with the truth of what you both did. Despite his assurances, you have always worried that you are not good enough for your post."

"I..." Deneya looked between the two of them. Vi could see the hasty rise and fall of her chest as her breathing quickened, panic settling in. "I never told anyone that," she whispered.

"You told her." Taavin gave a nod at Vi. "In a past life. You trusted her because she is the Champion and because she is a woman worth trusting."

Vi felt a frisson of heat rising to her cheeks at his praise.

Deneya took a step backward, her back meeting the wall. Slowly, she began to laugh, shaking her head. "This is madness. This is impossible."

"But here we stand," Vi said.

"Glad one of us knows where we stand because I'm not sure which way is up anymore." She cast a wary eye over Vi and Taavin. "I need time to deal with all this."

"Fine." Mother above, even Vi was still processing what was happening to her. And she had the benefit—if one could call it that—of living through the goddess rebuilding her body to send her back in time.

"But while you do so, swear you will not act against the Champion. And swear you will not report back to Lumeria or anyone else on Meru of her presence here, or of my existence," Taavin cautioned.

"Why?"

"I'm walking the razor's edge of fate and the only way we're all getting out of this alive is if I have as much control as possible," Vi said confidently, perhaps more confidently than she felt. "I don't need more variables I can't control complicating an already-complicated situation. You're the only one in this world who knows who I am. I don't want to regret that trust."

"Not even Fiera?" Deneya had a look of genuine surprise.

"No." Though Vi suspected Fiera had some inkling of what Vi was, even if she didn't have the words to describe it. "Do I have your word?"

"On one condition."

"I don't remember this turning into a negotiation." Vi folded her arms over her chest.

"It's not every day I get to negotiate with the agent of a goddess." Deneya smirked and swung her eyes to Taavin. "You seem to know so much. Perhaps you know what I'm about to barter for?"

"It varies." Taavin's answer only seemed to unnerve Deneya more. She stared at him for another long second, but abandoned whatever thought she had as she looked back to Vi.

"You give me no reason to suspect you're up to anything. No funny business. Be on your best behavior." Deneya's attention turned to the sword. "And that... I don't know what it is you intend to do with it. But if you're seeking it out, you must have some plan for it. Whatever that is, you don't get to act until you tell me. I'm on this Yargen-forsaken rock to watch over those weapons and the tomb. So if you do something with the sword—or any other weapon—you're right in the line of my duty."

Vi looked back to the sword, then Taavin. He had told her they needed to act slowly and be cautious. Making this promise to Deneya seemed in line with that objective. Vi also couldn't make her play on the sword until after Fiera's wedding.

"Fine, I accept your deal," Vi said casually, trying not to convey any hesitation or doubt. The Champion wouldn't waver. She had to be steadfast in her decisions.

"Good, because I'm tired and desperately want to go to bed and find out this was all a bad dream." Deneya yawned for emphasis. "When I see you tomorrow, it should go without saying, none of this happened." Vi locked eyes with the woman and gave a small nod. Deneya returned it, stepped backward, and uttered, *"Wein."*

A glyph shot out from her midsection. Splitting into two, one rose vertically to the crown of her head and the other dropped to her feet. The two circles of light faded as they swirled around Deneya, as though they were wrapping her up in a magic casement. Power glittered across her skin as she stepped back through Fiera's flames unharmed.

"Wein," Vi repeated thoughtfully. Just like Taavin's word, *uncose*, it did nothing for her.

"She received that word from Yargen before she came to the Dark Isle. It acts like a personal shield from attack. It's most like what you know as Groundbreakers' stone skin," Taavin said factually, as though it were obvious.

"If you know so much, why didn't you warn me she was coming?" Vi rounded on him.

"I didn't think it'd happen so soon." He lifted up his hands defensively. "Perhaps it's your recklessness that's speeding things up. Recklessness… like summoning me to appear before her."

Vi cursed under her breath, working to calm the spark crackling up her spine. "I didn't know what else to do. And when I figured out she was from Meru, I just thought…" Vi shook her head, feeling the spark abate. "I don't know what I thought."

"I'm sorry for snapping, too." Taavin heard the apology in her tone. His hands clasped over her shoulders. "This is exactly what I'm trying to protect you from— what I was telling you earlier. There is *variance*. Very few things are perfectly identical in any of these recreated worlds. Even though there are stones in the river, the little leaves bob and sway along the water's currents—each acting according to its own will."

"Even so, you could've told me it was going to happen eventually. You could've prepared me so I wasn't caught off-guard."

"Foremost, I didn't think it'd happen for weeks yet. And truly, I didn't see how it would have helped you any. I couldn't give you specifics even if I wanted to. Maybe you would've had this confrontation in a council room after everyone had dispersed. Or on a training field. Or in a hall one night on your way here." He spoke with such certainty that Vi had no doubt all of those things had, at some point, happened. "All I would've accomplished by telling you would have been putting you on edge nearly all the time."

"I want to know," Vi insisted. "You want to know what I do in this timeline? I need to know what I've *done*."

"I don't want you to act rashly." He smiled tenderly. But Vi only felt more frustrated. "Take things slowly. We'll figure out the best way to take the sword when the time is right."

When would the time be right: before or after Fiera's death?

Vi kept the question to herself. She didn't want to worry him more. And there was only so much she could accomplish in one night. It had been a long few days, and she was very tired.

"Very well," Vi agreed finally. "I trust you."

"And I trust you." He leaned forward, placing a gentle kiss on her forehead. It was little more than the ghost of warmth. "Now, go rest. I can feel your exhaustion."

Vi nodded and released the glyphs.

"Do you trust me?" she whispered to the empty air. If he trusted her, he would arm her with information. But all Vi was getting were crumbs and a heavy dose of skepticism from him; should he give her anything more, she'd take it and run head-first into the end of the world.

13

"YOU MUST SET THEM free." Fiera slammed an open palm against the council table. "It has been long enough."

"*Weeks*, it has been weeks," Tiberus growled. His patience was visibly running thin, the man's hair a mess from constantly raking his fingers through it. "It's not nearly enough time to let loose those who called not only for my death, but the death of my men—and perhaps now the death of you, since you are to be my wife."

"They are my soldiers and would never harm me," Fiera insisted.

"Like those men on the streets would never harm you?" He arched his eyebrows.

"Those were riff-raff, not my men." Fiera leaned forward. "All you are doing, Tiberus, is risking gratitude turning into resentment."

Vi volleyed her attention between the two most powerful people on the continent. Technically, Tiberus's say was the only one that mattered. But he deferred to Fiera in a far greater way than an Emperor should. She still didn't know what Fiera felt for the man. But Tiberus's feelings were clear enough in his actions.

Zira leaned over, whispering, "Do you think they'd notice if we just walked out?"

"Be my guest and risk it if you'd like," Vi mumbled.

The whole council had been confined for at least a half hour as the debate raged on. Everyone looked uncomfortable.

Vi caught Deneya's eyes across the table, but the woman glanced at her for only a second. The fact that it had been a week and she had yet to say anything to Vi, or act out of the ordinary, was a testament to her training from Queen Lumeria.

"You're being utterly unreasonable." Fiera threw up her hands. "You were the one who set out to conquer. You can't expect the rest of the continent to roll over like Cyven."

"I do not expect the West to handle their change in rulership with the same grace as the East." It was a low jab from Tiberus, one that made Lord Twintle's head turn and eyes narrow.

Vi closed her eyes and took in a slow breath. She had to work to prevent it from coming out as a heavy sigh. Fiera was all fire and passion, no doubt playing up those traits because of how easily they got under Tiberus's skin. Usually, this enabled her to push him in the direction she wanted him to go.

"May I propose a compromise?" Vi asked, allowing the remnants of her years as a royal to seep back into her tone. She couldn't tolerate this a moment longer.

The Emperor appeared startled she'd spoken up, but Fiera gave her a trusting smile and said, "I'd love to hear it."

"Thank you." Vi stood. "Your graces, I think I—we all—understand your respective wishes. My proposal is this: release the confined soldiers in several rounds in the coming weeks. The first round would be soldiers willing to put their skills to use and serve in their new Empire's army. Also in that round would be the sons and daughters of any nobility."

She gave a look to Twintle, remembering Luke, who was still trapped in the encampment.

"The next round would be those who do not wish to fight, but have a valuable trade skill. Put them to work and keep their hands and minds busy with rebuilding their city, so they do not think to turn against you.

"The final round would be those remaining." Vi thought a moment, running the suggestion over a final time in her head. "If any have nefarious intentions, they will likely show their colors as they lose patience."

Vi finished and glanced between Fiera and the Emperor. The former had gone stony faced and Vi couldn't discern if the suggestion was pleasing or upsetting. The Emperor on the other hand was far more transparent with his emotions, giving Vi hope when he finally said, "Your new knight speaks wisely."

"Thank you, your grace." Vi bowed her head and sat.

"What do you say, my love?"

"It's a fair suggestion," Fiera finally relented. "A week between each round?"

"A month," Tiberus fired back.

"Two weeks." Fiera's mouth quirked into a tiny grin. Fondness alighted in her eyes, brought out by the banter.

"Very well." Tiberus chuckled. "Two weeks, and let none claim that Tiberus Solaris does not bend before his bride." He stepped away from the table and everyone stood on cue. "Now, may I steal that bride for a drink before dinner?"

The royals departed, and everyone in the room seemed to immediately sit straighter, a weight lifted.

"About time." Twintle gathered his papers, shoving them unceremoniously into his folio. "Our loyal Westerners have rotted in their prisons long enough."

"They have been kept comfortable," Zira said firmly.

Vi remembered her time in the "containment shelter" and how quickly the once-glorious manor house devolved into squalor when crammed with soldiers who didn't have proper access to something as simple as a bath. She wasn't sure if *comfortable* was the right word.

"Comfortable? You think confinement is comfortable?" Twintle grumbled. "I cannot wait to hear just how comfortable my son has been these past weeks when he is back in his home where he belongs."

"Luke comes from good stock. He'll be—"

"Good day to you all," Twintle cut Zira off curtly, striding out of the room without a backward glance.

The other councilors gathered their things quietly, the tension in the air slowing their movements to a glacial pace.

"What a mess," Zira mumbled.

"Empire building is rarely tidy." Vi stood. "At least we found an acceptable solution."

"One can only hope they both think it's acceptable come morning."

"What about Kahrin? Will she be out with Luke?"

"No, she'll likely get out with the tradesmen. She's the daughter of a miner to the north of Norin and became a Knight seeking glory. I think she's had enough of fighting for one lifetime." Vi could only hope that was true. The fewer angry Knights of Jadar she had to contend with, the better. Zira sighed. "I really do hope this is the last of it. Fiera needs to focus on planning her wedding... it's coming up soon."

"Yullia," Deneya interrupted them. "May I borrow you for a word in my office?"

"Certainly."

"This way." Deneya started out the room. Vi shrugged at Zira as if she had no idea what this could be about, then followed the minister down the hall and into a closet-like office. She closed the door behind them, locked it, grabbed Vi's hand, and uttered, "*Durroe sallvas tempre.*"

A glyph formed between their locked palms.

"You certainly have my attention." Vi looked between their hands and Deneya's face.

"I didn't want to risk anyone else overhearing." Deneya's grip was firm and unflinching. "I've been thinking about what you said and I must ask, what is your goal here?"

"I already told you, I—"

"Yes, agent of Yargen or some such." Deneya shook her head. "What are your goals as that agent—Champion, rather—acting on behalf of Yargen? What are you hoping to achieve?"

"To protect—"

Deneya pressed her free palm to her forehead and sighed. When she spoke again, it was with the same tone Vi would use to explain a difficult concept to a child. "I understand all that. You're here on behalf of Yargen, protecting the sword. Our goals really aren't that different."

"I doubt they would be," Vi said cautiously.

"If you're truly are here on behalf of the Goddess, it's my duty to assist you. Tell me how I can do that."

"Information," Vi said after a moment. "You've been ingrained in this world longer than I have. I need information on people, specifically the Knights of Jadar and those associated with them before the fall of Mhashan. They've already begun moving against the sword."

Deneya thought about this, humming softly. Then, as if her mental tally came up with the same answer Vi already knew, she gave a nod. "They haven't been too pleased with Fiera's engagement."

"If their attack on the street is any indication."

"That's only the start of the whispers I've heard."

"Oh?"

"Information gathering is part of my duty to the queen. I go out at night and sit in taverns. Most don't recognize me, so I hear murmurs of the citizenry. Some seem content—they're happy the war is over. But others are more in line with the thinking of the old king. They'd rather burn than bend the knee. They see Fiera doing so as the ultimate betrayal."

"Foolish…" Vi mumbled. They couldn't see, or were willfully ignoring, that Fiera's engagement was likely what saved them all. And was possibly the ultimate sacrifice on her part—to be married to a man who had conquered her land for the sake of her people.

"I'm sure the rumors will get worse when the soldiers are set free. A lot of the Knights are still in there. I'll work on procuring the full roster of names for you."

"Thank you," Vi managed, somewhat surprised by the sudden kindness. "Let me know when you have it." Vi moved to leave, but Deneya held her hand firmly, almost yanking her back.

"Be careful," Deneya said solemnly. "Getting close to the royal family without having eyes on me took me years. You've ascended swiftly and publicly… They're already whispering about you."

"I'm not worried," Vi lied. In fact, she was suddenly very worried. This whole time her eyes had been on Fiera, at the expense of noticing who had their eyes on her. "I have this under control."

Vi hefted the Sword of Jadar overhead and brought it down in a vertical slice. She slid her feet to the side, dancing around an unseen opponent, drawing the blade in a side slash. She stepped back, shifted her grip, and thrust forward into a lunge. Her movements were slow and deliberate, more meditation than combat.

Soon enough, Deneya would arrive to go over the list of Knights she'd procured. And before then, Vi needed to speak with Taavin.

She went to put the blade on the table, pausing. The vision of the Champion splitting the staff remained ever-present in her mind. *How had he known how to do that?* Vi tried to push the question from her mind, uttering, "*Narro hath hoolo.*"

"You're back here again." Taavin looked around.

"Yes. I've been doing just as you asked for the past two months and laying low." She stared at the sheathed weapon on the wall. Despite herself, the memories of the last Champion still lingered. "Taavin… do you think there's a way to manipulate the crystal?"

"Why do you ask?"

"My last vision… the last Champion split the staff. Do you think I could split the sword?"

"We're trying to preserve Yargen's power, not split it," he needlessly reminded.

"What if—"

They were interrupted by Deneya emerging through the flames at the entrance to the small room. The woman's bright blue and purple-rimmed eyes darted between them.

"Sorry to keep you waiting."

"It's all right. Tell me what you've found?"

"You're not going to like it." Deneya frowned. "The Knights of Jadar are picking right back up where they left off. Nearly all of them."

"How so?"

"They've been gathering at Twintle's house at odd hours."

"When?"

"In secret, at night… I've reason to believe they're meeting right now."

"Then what are we waiting for?" Vi started for the flames. "We should go and see what they're—"

Taavin stopped her by grabbing her hand with his ghostly grip. Vi swung around to face him. Her heart began to beat faster, already knowing what he was about to say.

"No."

"But—"

"*No,*" Taavin said more firmly. "Our goal is not the Knights of Jadar."

"The Knights of Jadar are trying to take the sword. They're likely plotting it right now. Knowing what they're scheming will only help us."

"She has a point," Deneya muttered, and Vi liked her that much more for it.

"You know why you can't." Taavin leveled her a look that told Vi everything.

She couldn't, because her rebirth wasn't yet assured. She hadn't given the watch to Vhalla Yarl yet. So there was no guarantee of a new Vi Solaris, a new Champion, if she failed.

If she failed.

"What if this is what I need to do for us to succeed, and I'm not, because we're being so cautious?" Her words were softer than she expected, nearly pleading.

"What we need to do to succeed is keep the sword safe."

"And if we know what the Knights are doing, then—"

"I don't want to see you risking your life. I can't live with that knowledge," he added, softer. Vi hated his tenderness and how it quelled her frustrated anger.

"Hello." Deneya waved, drawing both of their attention. "Yes, hi, I'm still here." She smiled broadly. "How about this? If you can't go for… whatever reasons the Voice has, I'll go in your stead? I'll just keep watching them as I have."

"A fine suggestion," Taavin said. He had yet to release Vi's hand.

Both eyes were on her. Vi bit the insides of her cheeks, but finally said, "Fine, go now… and let me know what happens."

"They'll be none the wiser, I promise! *Wein*!" Deneya dashed through the flames, gone as quickly as she'd come.

Vi stared at the fire, her hand still in Taavin's. When he finally released it, it fell limply at her side.

"What is my purpose here?" she whispered.

"To protect the Crystal Caverns."

"Is it?" Vi spun, rounding on him. Fire was alive in her, burning down her arms, cracking into life around her knuckles. "Or am I just a vessel shepherding us into another repeat of the world's end?"

"Of course not."

"Then you must let me act. The Knights of Jadar are gaining strength while I help Fiera pick out flowers for the Cathedral of the Sun and minstrels for the reception. They are going to act against my family for generations. They will *kill her* if I don't stop them."

"Your only focus should be the sword," Taavin reminded her gravely. "What happens to everyone else—Fiera, Zira, Tiberus—is not your concern."

"They are my family!"

"Your family is gone and will never come back!"

The words echoed through her ears; Vi staggered back. She swayed, but righted herself. A buzzing sound vibrated her brain and the world blurred for a moment, tilting in a sickening way. He'd only spoken the truth, a truth she'd known. Why did it hurt so much?

"Vi, I'm sorry," Taavin said hastily.

"No," Vi whispered. "You're right." She forced a smile, but felt her cheeks curve into what was certainly more of a snarl. "My family is gone, and I'm clearly a fool for caring about these people."

"That's not—"

"Leave me." Vi waved her hand and released the glyph. Blissful silence filled the air as Vi was left alone with the sword. She stared at it, wondering how a single object could cause so much pain.

Vi approached the weapon slowly. Her eyes were on the sword, but her mind was on the Knights of Jadar. While she was here, waiting, they were plotting. Everyone else was acting as Vi drifted along.

This feeling was worse than being in bed for a month with autumn fever. Worse than waiting her whole life for her family to retrieve her.

"Nothing good comes of a Solaris with a crystal weapon," Vi murmured, putting her hand on the scabbard. "You were right, Father."

She hung her head and felt her eyes burn. Vi took a shaky breath, and then another. She remained like that until her muscles were stiff and her feet ached. She stayed in that tucked-away armory room for so long, the sun was streaming through the windows as she made her way back to her quarters.

There she remained until she was certain she wouldn't betray Taavin's trust and run off after Deneya.

14

VI STARED OUT THE window at Norin. For months, it had been slowly blossoming before her eyes like a bloom that had been trapped in the permafrost of war now poking through the snow. People were beginning to take to the streets again; the Western militia in its entirety had finally been freed of their confinement.

She was used to looking down at cities. She'd spent the vast majority of her life doing just that as she was kept in the fortress of Soricium. Now, it was Taavin's caution keeping her here. She was relegated to council meetings, training grounds, and working with the crystal sword in secret, trying to figure out the depths of its power… As Deneya did the real work of keeping track of the Knights of Jadar and their ever-growing strength.

"… ask her again. I don't think she's listening," Zira said from where she and Fiera stood.

"Yullia?" Fiera repeated herself.

Vi jerked. "Yes? Sorry."

"Don't apologize, all this bores me to tears, too." Zira collapsed into a chair, her long legs kicking out and falling limply over the armrest.

"It's not that bad," Fiera mumbled. "Yullia, I was wondering what you thought of the dress color. Of course, silver or red would be traditional Western colors, but white or gold would be more fitting from an Imperial standpoint."

Vi walked over to the table, looking at the swatches of fabrics the royal tailors had sent for Fiera to review. The whole, cluttered mess represented what Vi had always expected of a royal wedding—a political headache where one misstep could be the difference between a smooth ascension and a long-term nightmare.

"If I'm honest, I think the white and gold is stunning." Fiera lifted a scrap of fabric covered in layers of golden petals. In the light, it sparked almost like flames. She layered it atop pure white silk, humming. "Yet I worry it will ruffle a few feathers in the Western Court if I don't show anything of home."

"The Western Court is a relic now and they need to get over themselves," Zira muttered, tipping her head back. If Vi had to bet, she would guess the woman found the toils of war easier to bear than wedding preparations.

"Even if Tiberus has formally disbanded the Crimson Court, they are still influential families in this land. And he also invited most of the members to be a part of the Southern Court whenever they choose to attend."

"And how often do you think they'll head south?" Zira asked dryly.

"That's not up to me." Fiera's usually composed tone slipped to the edge of annoyance, prompting Zira to stare out the window as Vi had been. "Anyway, Yullia, what do you think?"

Vi took the fabrics from Fiera's hands, feeling the sumptuous textiles between the pads of her fingers. Her clothes had once solely been made from cloth like this. Now, Vi felt as though she shouldn't be touching them. She returned them to the table after only a few seconds.

"I'm inclined to agree with you—all white and gold could spell disaster. The nobility of the West finally seem to be settling with this idea, and you've ensured Mhashan you will still rule as their princess while being a Solaris."

"She should wear what she wants," Zira insisted. "It's her wedding."

"It's not though," Vi said before Fiera could get a word in. "She is a symbol first and everything here—" Vi swept her arm over the table "—conveys a message about what that symbol stands for."

Zira blinked blankly at Vi. Her mouth opened, closed, and she looked away again. Vi turned back to Fiera only to be met with a strange expression.

"I hope I didn't overstep." Vi bowed her head.

"No, you stole the words from my mouth," Fiera said brightly, patting her shoulder. "You really are a natural at the ways of diplomacy." Vi snorted at that. "Now, my astute friend, tell me what color my dress will be."

"How about a compromise? Wear gold on white for your dress. But then your jewelry could be silver and red."

"Yes, a silver crown inlaid with Western rubies." Fiera's expression lit up at the idea.

A silver crown. The thought drifted through Vi's mind on a memory. Her mother had held her once as she'd fallen asleep, indulging all of Vi's then girlish curiosities on the details of her wedding to her father. She had worn a silver crown…

"I think a silver crown would be beautiful," Vi said in a tone softened with nostalgia.

"It's settled, then!" Fiera clapped her hands together. "I love it."

"Excellent." Zira pushed herself away from her chair. "Is that all we had for today?"

"For now." Fiera placed a hand on her stomach. "I'm starving."

"After all the breakfast you ate?" Zira gave her a startled look. "I wouldn't eat for a month if I cleaned my plate like that."

"Planning takes a lot of energy!" Fiera gave a laugh and started for the door alongside Zira.

Or she was already eating for two. Fiera had given birth to Aldrik in all-too-short a time after the wedding in Vi's history. Just long enough that no one questioned her father's legitimacy, especially since the Emperor had always acknowledged him as his son.

If she was pregnant, that meant they were headed along the same path as Vi's world. Not that she could've expected it to have changed; she hadn't done much to shift any fated events.

"Yullia, are you coming?" Fiera asked, pausing to glance over her shoulder.

"Yes, of course," she said. What she really wanted to do was stay in that spot and beg Fiera to listen to her as Vi warned her against all that was to come. For it wouldn't matter what dress she wore, or who she upset, if she was just going to end up dead before the year was up.

"Zira, while I'm at lunch, will you do me a favor and fetch the sword? Tiberus and I will be rehearsing the ceremony with the Crones this afternoon."

"Why not just use a regular sword instead?" Vi asked. She didn't like taking the sword out of its hiding place.

"I suggested as much," Fiera sighed. "But Tiberus was insistent... He's not been quiet about finally seeing the legendary Sword of Jadar. I hope if I indulge him some, it'll lose its wonder."

It never would, but Vi didn't have the heart to tell Fiera that. "Are you rehearsing at the Cathedral of the Sun?"

"No, we'll do it here."

"At least it's not leaving the castle, then."

"My thoughts exactly." Fiera gave them both a smile and passed the key to the armory over to Zira. "Now, if you'll excuse me, I don't want to keep Tiberus waiting." Fiera turned, starting up the hall.

"Princess—" Zira began, quickly stopping herself.

"Yes?" Fiera looked startled at the outburst.

"It's nothing." Zira put her hands in her pockets and smiled. "Have a good lunch."

Vi followed Zira down toward the armory. If the sword was being taken out of its hiding place, then she was going to stay glued to its side. But her thoughts wandered from the sword.

"What was that?" Vi finally asked, when it was clear Zira wasn't about to say anything.

"What was what?"

"The thing you were going to ask Fiera."

"It's nothing."

They arrived at the armory and Vi held her breath as Zira undid the lock, waiting to see if she noticed anything amiss. But if there was a sign of Vi's nighttime experimentations and practice with the sword, Zira overlooked it. In fact, even as she took the sword off the wall, her gaze was a thousand miles away.

"Zira—"

"My family is here," Zira finally let out with a heavy sigh. "My mother and daughter."

"Raylynn?"

Zira froze for a full half-minute before turning slowly. "I don't recall ever telling you my daughter's name."

"Perhaps you... forgot?"

"I think I'd remember."

"Perhaps the Mother gave me a vision of the girl."

"Did she..." Zira murmured, looking at Vi as if seeing her for the first time. "Perhaps you can help me."

"With what?"

"Come, and let me tell you on the way."

They strolled through the castle, winding down the now-familiar pathways. She ran her fingertips along the walls, feeling the grooves of the stone underneath her nails. There had been another Vi before her who had walked these halls. Had she made the same motions? Were her fingerprints running along the tracks of the fingerprints of ninety-two other Vis throughout time?

"A few years ago, Fiera told me that when she met Raylynn she would look into the girl's future," Zira started.

"Like a curiosity shop?"

"Yes, exactly. I made the mistake of telling Raylynn and now she won't stop asking about it. I think that's part of how she convinced my mother to drag her here." Zira looked to Vi with pleading eyes. "I know I shouldn't ask this. But I don't want to trouble Fiera, not now, not with all that's going on. And I know that five is a little young to scry into a child's future, but—"

"I'll do it," Vi interrupted, touching the woman's elbow. "I'll pretend to be Fiera and try to peer into the future."

"Are you sure?"

"It's the least I can do after all you've done to help me." She smiled, hoping the expression hid her uncertainty. Unlike the future-seers at curiosity shops, Vi had much less control over what she did and did not see. But she also had Lightspinning at her disposal, and could make a convincing show of it.

"Thank you." Zira squeezed her hand once as she led them through two side rooms and into a mirrored reception area with a few low chairs.

There, an older woman sat on her feet and held up her palms, as a young child punched and kicked them.

"Faster, Raylynn," the elderly woman demanded sternly. "You're spending too much time on both feet. Bounce!"

The girl tried to do as her grandmother bid, focus knotting her brow. Her golden hair, a striking contrast against the deep tan of her Western skin, swished as she moved.

"I don't think she's meant to be a brawler. I think she'll hear the song of the sword like her mother," Zira said.

"Mommy!" the girl squealed, sprinting over to Zira. Zira crouched down, taking her daughter into her arms. "Can I come live with you in the castle now? I want to defend the princess, too."

"You will defend whatever and whoever you wish." Zira tapped Raylynn's nose. "When you are old enough to hear the calling."

"But I can fight." Raylynn wriggled from her mother's grasp, bouncing from foot to foot. She threw jabs into the air identical to the ones she'd been practicing with her grandmother.

"You can fight better than half the men I train, my little dagger." Zira laughed, ruffling her hair. The woman's tone was entirely different around her daughter. She still had the sharp edge about her that Vi would always associate with Zira, but it was tempered with a tenderness unique to a mother's love.

"Thank you for gracing us this day, your highness." Zira's mother dipped into a low bow, her forehead touching the floor. "You honor us."

"Princess, I will be your new guard!" Raylynn proclaimed, thrusting a hand into the air. "I am here to report."

Vi let out a laugh and crouched down as well. "You will be a mighty guard indeed, someday. Though you should listen to your mother and give yourself time to see what cause calls you."

Raylynn lowered her arm, thinking about this. "If you say so, your highness."

"Now you've met my daughter, Raylynn." Zira scooped up the girl, pulling her into her lap. "And this is my mother, Sophie."

"It's an honor to meet you both." Vi gracefully eased herself onto one of the legless and armless chairs across from the family. Raylynn's golden hair was a stark contrast to the rest of them. Her father's identity was a mystery Vi would not be asking about, given that the girl was conceived after the South invaded. "Zira has told me so much about you."

"She told me you would look into my future!"

"Raylynn, please," Sophie half scolded, half sighed.

"Yes, I will. Would you like me to do that now?" Vi glanced over at Zira. The woman bobbed her head yes.

"Yes please." Raylynn bounced from her mother's lap. "Gran and I brought things to burn. She said this wouldn't be like a normal curiosity shop, so we'd better be prepared."

"Your grandmother is very wise. Be sure you continue to listen to her."

"You hear that? Even the princess says you should listen to Grandma Sophie," Zira said.

"Yeah, yeah." Raylynn rolled her eyes at her mother. "I know that." She hastily returned to Vi with a collection of items retrieved from the satchel at the older woman's side. "Here, I brought these."

Vi scanned what a five-year-old girl had determined was precious enough to burn for a sacred purpose. She held a clump of cotton, two dried leaves, and a bottle containing a shot of amber colored liquid.

"Are they good enough?"

"They're wonderful," Vi assured. "I'm going to hold out my hands and make a fire; you drop them in one by one, all right?" Raylynn nodded, an adorable intensity overtaking her. "Here we go."

Vi rested her elbows on her knees, sitting cross legged. She leaned forward, made a bowl out of her hands, and allowed her spark to fill the empty space. Fire ignited, eagerly filling her cupped palms. It burned brightly, shining off Raylynn's delighted expression.

One by one, the girl dropped each item into the flames, almost reverently. After uncorking the bottle and pouring the liquid over the fire, her hands clutched the dagger that was attached to the small belt on her hips. Three items to burn, one to hold. Vi took a breath, readying an illusion with *narro*, but as her eyes caught the flame, the genuine sensation of future sight overtook her.

The world blotted out, blurring into white, and Vi found herself standing a mere stone's throw from the castle her body was in.

Fiera and Tiberus stood together at the center of a crowd, hands joined with a red ribbon wrapped loosely around them. Zira stepped toward them, drawing the crystal weapon she wore on her hip. A Crone of the sun spoke, though Vi couldn't hear the words. Even if she could, her focus remained on the glimmering Sword of Jadar.

Zira lowered the sword with purpose, resting the flat of the blade over top their joined hands. Flames sparked, harmlessly singeing the ribbon to ash. Tiberus beamed and Fiera returned the smile. Zira lifted the sword once more and as she held it aloft—

A blade gouged through the soft flesh of her neck. Blood ran down the ceremonial armor Zira wore in a river that raced to pool at her feet. The phantom sounds of gurgling, of Zira's knees hitting the ground hard as the blade was withdrawn, filled Vi's deaf ears.

She watched with disturbing detachment as a man she didn't recognize grabbed for the weapon. Chaos collapsed in on the couple. The last thing Vi saw was Tiberus pulling Fiera close to him, panic in his eyes.

Vi blinked, suddenly seeing the flame in her open palms again. Straightening, she let go of the spark and looked out the windows along one wall to avert the worry in her eyes.

"What did you see?" Raylynn asked eagerly.

"Give the princess a moment, her eyes haven't even stopped glowing." Zira hushed her daughter sternly.

"I saw…" Vi started softly, but lost all train of thought. That certainly hadn't been how Vi expected this to go. Her future sight wasn't a trained skill like it was for the purveyors of curiosities. Her future sight only happened at places where fate changed. Would the Cathedral of the Sun become an Apex at Fiera's wedding?

Her eyes drifted from Zira to Raylynn.

She'd heard stories of Raylynn Westwind, the only female member of Prince Baldair's illustrious Golden Guard. She'd joined shortly before the young prince's untimely death. The stories Vi had heard were striking—the sort that stuck with a girl first learning to hold a sword.

"Your life, Raylynn," Vi finally began with confidence, "will follow your mother's in service. But where your mother follows a crown of silver, the one you serve will be a crown of gold, like the hair of your head."

And the hair of Prince Baldair's head. Perhaps Raylynn could prevent Baldair from meeting his young death if she felt she were destined to be his guard. If she grew up to become even half the swordswoman her mother was, it could be enough to change his fate. Memories of her father talking with such longing about his brother, a broken relationship he could never repair, flooded and propelled her.

"You will live by the sword, and through it you will fulfill many duties. These duties will be heavy, but you will carry yourself gracefully till your final hours. And through it all, you will find your home." Finishing with something ambiguous seemed far wiser than getting too specific. As much as Vi wanted to meddle with the outcomes of history to spare her family, Taavin's cautions stuck.

"You honor us with your sight of the Mother's plans." Sophie dipped once more into a low bow. Zira stared in slack-jawed awe.

"Do you hear that, mommy?" Raylynn stole her mother's attention. "I will carry a heavy sword, just like you!"

"That you will, my little dagger. But the sword I'm carrying today isn't heavy. In fact, it's very special. I only have it now for the princess's wedding. Would you like to see it?" Raylynn nodded and Vi was forced to watch as the crystal sword was unsheathed once more, casually exposed to even more eyes. "This sword is—"

"The Sword of Jadar," Sophie gasped.

"Is it so special?" Raylynn asked, running her little fingers along the flat of the blade. The girl was calm and at ease, even in the presence of a legendary weapon.

"Very special. Can't you hear its song?" Zira tilted her head. "Remember, we must—"

"Listen to the blades, and dance and sing with them." Raylynn finished. She tore her eyes away from the sword. "Did you give my mother this sword?"

"It belongs to my family," Vi answered doggedly.

"Can you give me a sword when I am in service to the golden crown?"

"Perhaps."

"I want a sword like mama's."

"A sword like this cannot be made. It came from the Mother herself, very long ago." Zira sheathed the weapon.

"But her visions come from the Mother, and she's so powerful!" Raylynn looked between them all, as if one of them could explain why this fact wasn't obvious. "If you can't make another sword, can you give my dagger power just like it?"

"Stop bothering the princess and mind your manners, Ray," Sophie said sternly, cutting off the conversation. She stopped the girl from unsheathing the dagger.

"Now, the princess and I have to go get ready for her wedding. It'll be very soon." Zira gave Raylynn one final squeeze and stood. "I'll meet you both tonight for dinner. Thank you again," Zira murmured as her mother and daughter exited. "Do you think I'm a bad mother for this deceit?"

"No." It was Vi's turn to give Zira's hand a squeeze. "I think you just did a very, very good thing."

If Vi's suspicions were right, she had just witnessed her first real opportunity to change fate.

15

V I GAZED UP AT the domed ceiling. A statue of the Mother held out a giant basin of fire that lit the entire cathedral—the second-most impressive structure in all of Norin. It was yet another piece of architecture that reminded her of the Archives in Risen.

Beneath the great statue were smaller ones of the Mother in various poses and expressions. Those statues melted into the relief sculptures of the Father that rounded the room. He looked up at the visages of the Mother above in yearning.

Vi inspected the tender face of the deity who would be Raspian. The sculptor knew nothing of the god's actual likeness, just like the Dark Isle knew nothing of his real relationship with the Mother. All Vi saw in his longing eyes was a drive to once more subdue the goddess that ruled above him.

"So much history they don't even know they're a part of." A familiar voice startled Vi from her thoughts. Deneya had seemingly materialized at her side. "Every time I come here it reminds me of home—in a strange, not-quite-right sort of way."

"It's a bit like a distorted mirror, isn't it?" Vi murmured.

"That's one way to put it." Deneya glanced at her from the corners of her eyes. "Now, why did you summon me?"

"I need your help today."

"Oh?"

Some Crones emerged from a nearby door, beginning to light sconces throughout the room. Vi walked in the opposite direction, keeping her voice so low it was barely audible over the echo of their footsteps in the cavernous space. "I need you to protect Zira."

"Zira has always struck me as a woman capable of protecting herself."

"The Knights are going to make a play for the sword. I had a vision."

Deneya stopped walking. "When?"

"About two weeks ago."

"You didn't think to mention this when we spoke with Taavin last?" Deneya arched her eyebrows. The three of them had been meeting weekly.

"Slipped my mind."

Deneya rolled her eyes. "Whatever you have to tell yourself. That's between you and him."

"Exactly," Vi said firmly. Her stomach was still in knots because she had yet to tell Taavin of her vision, her slight maneuvering—*encouragement*—of Raylynn, or her bold plan. But this was her moment to spare Zira from an untimely death *and* prevent the sword from falling into the hands of the Knights of Jadar. Asking for forgiveness would be easy when she succeeded. She hoped. "At the point in the ceremony when Zira lifts the sword overhead, she'll be struck from behind. I need you to move through the crowd and counter the attack."

"So just focus on Zira. Not Fiera or the sword?"

"I'll worry about the sword and Fiera. Just save Zira."

"Simple enough." A smirk curled Deneya's lips. "I always wanted to run circles around the Dark Isle dwellers with Lightspinning. But it's against my code while I'm here."

"But you'll help me do this?"

"Of course. You're the Champion—exceptions can be made for you." And Deneya looked all too eager to make those exceptions. "Things were boring before you came."

"Hopefully, if I do my job right… they'll be boring again." Vi's attention was drawn to the main doors of the cathedral—the only entrance and exit onto the streets. As if sensing their discussion, Zira appeared. "Now, if you'll excuse me."

Deneya fell into step, whispering hastily, "I have something else I need to tell you, when it's all over."

"What?"

"No time now." She lifted her eyes, looking to Zira. "Good day, captain."

"Good day, councilor. Is everything all right?"

"Yes." Deneya smiled. "Just checking in with Yullia here about the final count of the guards so I can ensure they are paid correctly. Now, if you'll excuse me, I need to change before the ceremony." Deneya bowed and departed.

"Are you ready for today?" Zira asked.

"I think so. You?"

"No," Zira answered bluntly. "I've fought countless men in dozens of battles. But this has my hands trembling."

"You'll be fine." Vi patted the woman on her shoulder.

"Do you mind if I go over the ceremony once more with you? I don't want to forget." A nervous Zira was more endearing than Vi could've imagined.

"Not at all."

"Thank you." Zira promptly turned to a back door.

Vi's eyes were drawn to the sword on her hip as Zira moved. Vi's head bobbed along as Zira went through the ceremony a final time. But her attention was on the sword.

She would protect it, and the woman, at all costs.

She wouldn't accept any other fate.

Two hours later, Fiera arrived by covered carriage. Soldiers stretched sheer panels between poles that obscured her as she entered the cathedral. The gathered crowds cheered and threw flowers, praising their soon-to-be Empress, as if their happiness for the union had been there all along.

Vi watched from an upper floor, scanning the guards that lined Fiera's walk. How many of them were Knights of Jadar loyalists? How many were ready to stab the woman in the back if the opportunity presented itself?

When Fiera entered the cathedral, Vi spiraled down the narrow iron staircase that took her from the top of the spire she'd perched in down into a side wing, and out into the cathedral proper. The main chamber was beginning to fill with nobles and dignitaries and Vi stepped lightly, unnoticed by most.

She scanned the crowd carefully, trying to discern who might be surreptitiously positioning themselves, waiting for the time to strike. Vi made a note of every man and woman who chose to stand behind where Zira would be in less than an hour. By the time she waded through the sea of people, Vi had committed their faces to memory.

Vi slipped into a back hall that connected to a waiting room where Fiera sat in a chair by the window—looking far more composed than Vi had expected.

"Are there a lot of people yet?" Fiera asked, perking up when Vi entered.

"It's filling quickly." Zira was nowhere to be seen. Having the sword out of sight put Vi on edge. She glanced at the two handmaids who hovered in the corner of the room. "Out with you both."

They glanced at each other, but left when Fiera commanded a gentle, "Please excuse us a moment." The princess turned back to Vi, dark eyebrows arched in question.

Vi stared down at the woman, wondering countless things at once. Was the cut of her dress—tight below the bust, but flowing loose around her abdomen—happenstance, or an intentional concealment? Had she looked into the future at all during these past weeks? Did she have any sense of what was about to transpire?

Not knowing the answers to those and several hundred other questions, Vi slowly drew her sword. Acting on instinct, she rested the point of the weapon in a crack of the floor and knelt before Fiera.

"Princess, soon to be Empress..." Vi looked up over top of her white-knuckled hands. "I shall not abandon my post before your throne, on this day or any to come. I am loyal to you, and any actions I take are an extension of that loyalty."

"What have you seen?" Fiera asked. "Tell me. I am burdened by the sight as well, and accustomed to living with its revelations. You do not need to shoulder this truth alone."

"There will be an attack during your ceremony."

"Who else have you told?"

"No one," Vi lied easily, and Fiera believed it without question.

"Not even Zira?"

"I need her to act without knowing."

"I see." Vi actually believed she did. "What do you need from me, then?"

"Faith. Trust."

"You have had those from the first moment I laid eyes on you," Fiera said softly. It was a gift Vi still didn't feel she'd earned, but was grateful to have.

"When the moment comes, trust me to protect you."

Fiera nodded just as their conversation was interrupted by the door opening. Lord Ophain stood in its frame. He was dressed in deep crimson finery from head to toe, a heavy silver pendant around his neck that Vi recognized as the mark of the Lord of the West.

"Dear sister, it's time," he said gently, walking over. Vi stood and stepped out of the man's way, allowing him to take both of Fiera's hands. Ophain was accustomed to servants and guards in his presence; he didn't so much as look at her twice. "Are you ready to do this?"

"I am," Fiera said with a small smile. "There is only happiness and love ahead. The war is done, and this shall put it to rest."

The fight for Fiera's life was only just beginning. But Vi said nothing as they left, arm in arm. She slipped out through the side door and joined the masses gathered to watch the first Empress Solaris be crowned.

It had become difficult to walk in the great room of the cathedral. People had filled it to the point of pressing against the guards on the outer ring. Vi looked for the faces of the men and women she'd seen earlier. She sought out people she might know. Some she was certain she recognized, others she was certain she didn't. But her recognition or lack thereof was not a reliable measure for traitors. Vi could thank Jayme for that lesson.

Soft gasps and murmurs distracted her when she was halfway through her first sweep. Vi jerked her head upward, toward what was stealing everyone's attention. Fiera had entered and, at the same time, the Emperor made his grand entrance from the upper doorway in the dome. As Fiera walked, her gold-trimmed train stretched behind her in equal measure as the Emperor's golden cape.

They made their way to each other in the center of the room. There, in an outer circle, was a row of soldiers. After that, a row of Crones, Fiera's sisters, and Zira.

"My lords and ladies of the West, our esteemed guests from the South and East, I welcome you all to this most joyous occasion," Ophain's voice boomed as they reached the middle of the chamber. "It is my honor as Lord of the West to present my sister to our Emperor so they might be joined in marriage." Ophain presented the hand of his sister to Tiberus.

"Eons ago," the head Crone began to speak, wasting no time. "The Father lived in a land of eternal night. It was in that darkness that he met the Mother. She was a brilliant star…"

Vi tuned out the ceremonial storytelling. Her eyes continued to scan the crowd, even more attentive as she positioned herself directly behind Fiera. Deneya would defend Zira, and from this vantage Vi would get a look at the attacker if she was lucky. But her vision hadn't shown her the aftermath of the attack, and Vi would be ready for whatever came.

"The Mother watches over us, bringing life and joy. The Father watches over our timelessness, seeing us safely into the lands beyond." The head Crone produced a long red ribbon from inside her robes. It was the same one Vi had run back to the castle for earlier. She pushed forward into the crowd, ignoring the glares and rude gestures of those around her. "From our births to our deaths, we are bound to the plans they have laid. We walk the red lines they have given us."

Not if I have something to say about it, Vi silently added. She was the one who could change those red lines—if she was bold and brave enough.

"By this, it is not for us to question those who are called to each other, just as it is no more our place to question those called to greatness. To do so would be an affront to the divine."

Vi heard the scoff of a man to her left. She looked in his direction. He murmured something to another gentleman beside him. Vi stepped through the crowd, squeezing through an opening to get closer to the man. The ripple effect of shifting people caught his attention.

Their eyes met and he gave her a thin smile before looking forward again. The other man he'd been whispering to shuffled through the standing masses. Vi caught only a glimpse of the back of his head. *Luke?*

"Princess Fiera Ci'Dan, daughter of the last King of Mhashan, may the Mother bless you with the greatness of her warmth." The Crone carefully laid the ribbon, looping it over the couple's joined hands. Vi looked between them and the man who had vanished into the crowd. She couldn't go chasing after him. She had to stay close to Fiera; the time was near. "Emperor Tiberus Solaris, first Emperor of this great land, chosen by the sun, may the Father bless you with his resolution."

The Crone carried on with her blessings, wrapping their hands with each one. At the same time, Vi worked her way through the mass of people, pushing bodies aside when they refused to move. She was right behind Fiera as she and Tiberus recited their vows to each other.

For a brief moment, the world was calm. Happy, even. Fiera smiled brightly as she promised to be the Emperor's, to honor him, to serve him, to hold him to a standard befitting an Emperor of all, for all. The Emperor nearly teared up as he promised the same—that he was hers, that he would love and cherish her, that she would forever be the brightest ray of the Solaris sun.

The future was hopeful in that breathtaking minute. And Vi witnessed the first glimpse that told her, beyond all doubt, this unlikely couple had come together to be greater than the sum of their parts.

Then the Crone spoke again: "The Mother bestowed on Mhashan a weapon to guard us all." Zira unsheathed the sword. "May your love be as strong as this blade, as unyielding as its edge. And, should she above bless this union, may her fire touch the fate that binds you both."

The Crone stepped back as Zira raised the sword above her head. Movement caught Vi's eye. Zira dramatically lowered the weapon over top their joined hands. Vi sank into her legs, ready to spring. Women around her wept tears at the ceremony's beauty. Vi readied herself to kill.

Fire ignited between the ribbon and the blade, burning it away as ash. Vi held her breath as Zira lifted the sword. *This was it*. This was the moment she died.

Instead, like the fire that burned in the sculpted brazier above the center of the room—flames erupted at Fiera's back, igniting chaos in the crowd.

16

Z IRA SCREAMED, STUMBLING FORWARD.

Vi launched herself forward as well, pushing a Crone and Princess Tina out of the way to barge into the inner circle of the wedding ceremony. Zira's back was singed, her clothes hanging by threads. But for the time being, she was very much alive.

People began to move, the crowd rumbling as if the earth itself trembled beneath them.

"Everyone stay back!" Vi shouted at the top of her lungs. She reached for the head Crone, pushing the elderly woman away. Vi spun, grabbing Zira and pulling her toward her, Fiera, and Tiberus in the same moment.

"How dare—" the Emperor grumbled. Before he could finish, Vi conjured a thin wall of flame with a thought. It burned white-hot and towered above them, nearly touching the bottom of the stone basin the statue was holding aloft in the dome above.

"It's an assassination attempt." Vi glared at Tiberus. "Keep your wife safe and don't move."

Sweat dotted his brow, but the Emperor kept silent, the reality of the situation sinking in. He clutched Fiera to him, so tightly that Vi couldn't make eye contact.

"Zira, stay here and protect the sword."

"I can fight," the woman insisted, pain turning her voice into a snarl.

"You're hurt and—"

"Mother above I will turn this sword on you if you don't let me at the bastard who did this!"

"Fine." Vi was grinning like a fool. As if this was something she wanted. Something she enjoyed. "Fiera, you guard the sword."

"It has always been my duty." Fiera pushed the Emperor away enough to take the sword from Zira's hands. She looked the least frightened of them all. The only thing that filled her dark eyes was the light of Vi's flames, and absolute trust that Vi had only ever seen one other time—in the eyes of the men and women who had followed Fiera into battle that night.

"Ready?" Zira asked over the crackle of flames.

"Take this." Vi quickly drew her sword, handing it to the woman.

"What about you?"

"I'll find—"

A sword sliced through the wall of fire, nicking the Emperor's side. He yowled in pain and turned with a growl. Blood stained his hip red, but it wasn't a fatal wound.

"We've wasted enough time." Vi grabbed Zira's hand and pushed an opening into the fire, just wide enough for them to slip through, before closing it once more. They ran head-first into a man on the way out.

Head over heels, the three of them tumbled. Vi rolled, stomping feet around her crushing her back and ribs as the panicked masses fled. Grunting, she pushed herself off the floor, flames following her every movement, sending those who would run into her away in burning pain.

"*Mysst soto larrk.*" A sword appeared in Vi's palm, her flames masking the strands of light and glyphs that condensed into the weapon. In the back of her mind she continued to focus on the wall of fire protecting Fiera and the Emperor; at all costs, she'd maintain it.

That brought her attention back to the barrier. Three men were slashing at it blindly, getting as close to the flames as they dared. They must think the wall of fire was Fiera's and that the princess was the one to kill to see it undone.

A dark delight filled her at the notion. This was becoming too easy.

More fire erupted at her side, identical to the flames at Zira's back and stealing her attention. Zira pushed the charred man off of her, scrambling to her feet.

"Thank you, a second time."

She'd thought Vi was behind the fire. "You're welcome," Vi said as she rapidly scanned the shifting crowd for where Deneya was firing off *juth starys*. But the woman had hidden herself well, and Vi brought her attention back to the men slashing for the Emperor and Fiera. "Let's take care of them."

"My pleasure."

They moved in tandem. Vi had been running drills with Zira long enough that she was familiar with how the woman moved. But moreover, she was confident with a sword now. Killing came easily. Vi sliced the first man down without a thought before moving onto the second.

Zira parried another. They fought off the immediate threat with backs to each other in an odd dance of death.

Vi bared her teeth, panting and snarling as she looked across the blood-smeared floor of the cathedral for more threats. Most people were out now, the other conspirators included. They must've turned tail when they realized their plan wouldn't bear fruit.

"We need to follow them!"

"No." Vi stopped Zira with a straight arm. "You get the Empress and Emperor to safety. Bar up the room she was in earlier. Let no one in but me. I'll go after them."

"Yull—"

"This is an order!"

Zira blinked, startled at Vi's audacity. Vi kept her brow furrowed, lips pursed, and the tension in her muscles the same as when she had been in battle. Zira's mouth fell open, shock softening her jaw. She closed it with a nod.

Vi released her control of the flames. "Go!"

The Emperor and Empress looked around, dazed. Tiberus blinked several times, no doubt seeing blue from the fire. Fiera was faster to recover, swinging her gaze from Vi to Zira.

"This way." Zira stepped forward.

If Vi left now, she might have a chance to follow any remaining attackers. It'd be the best opportunity to weed out those who were actively hunting the sword. Vi looked over to the group of royals, nearly at the door.

She wouldn't leave until they were safely away. Vi tightened her grip around her sword. Zira was still alive. She wasn't about to see her killed now.

As soon as the door to Fiera's preparation room closed behind them, however, Vi was off. She raced behind the last of the guests flooding out onto the streets.

"*Durroe watt radia*," Vi whispered as she crossed the threshold of the cathedral. When she emerged, it was in a new skin.

Vi swung her head left and right. She decided on the direction where the majority had gone. Moving quickly to catch up with those still fleeing, she listened carefully.

"The new Empress is dead."

"She's not dead!"

"They really did it."

"The Knights actually did it. He pulled it off."

"He didn't pull off anything. That was an utter failure."

Vi spun in place, trying to locate the speakers. She slowed her pace to a walk.

"What do you think they'll do next?"

"They can't accomplish anything without the sword."

Two men were walking into a bar not far from her. Vi stepped lightly behind them, trusting her Lightspinning to prevent them from identifying her.

"I think I know a way they could get it."

"*Shh*, you idiot, not on the streets." The taller of the two men glanced over his shoulder, but his eyes swept over Vi as they hastily entered the bar.

She was quick behind them.

"… him at the warehouse. I think the next meeting is—" Vi caught the last of what the tall man was saying as she entered.

"Excuse me, miss, we're closed for the day," the barkeep interrupted abruptly. The two men startled and looked directly at Vi—but what they saw was the face of a random woman who attended the wedding. A woman who, blessedly, neither of them recognized.

"I'm sorry." Vi put on a thick Western accent. "I got separated from my companions, I didn't know if they'd come in here."

"They're certainly not in here. Closed to mourn the tragedy at our princess's wedding. Out with you," the barkeep barked.

Mourn? Or conduct private business? Vi looked between the groups of men, but merely gave a sweet, innocuous smile. "I'm sorry for interrupting."

With that, Vi left.

The streets were mostly empty as she trudged back to the cathedral. When she ascended the stairs once more, it was as a woman the world knew only as Yullia.

"Using your spinning to conceal yourself like that is clever." Deneya leaned on a column by the doors, arms folded. "You have other tricks for the words?"

"Maybe. And maybe I'll show you if you continue to be useful to me." Vi couldn't tell if the curve of her mouth was a roguish smile or a more threatening display of teeth. She was in a deadly mood.

"I'm useful enough to keep Zira alive like you asked." Pushing off the column, Deneya walked over to her. "I also saw who delivered the first blow," she said in a hushed tone, looking out over the city while Vi stared absently into the cathedral.

"Meet me later in the usual place, then."

"Usual place?" Deneya groaned. "It's dark and dull and hard to get to. Let's go out tonight."

"It's secluded and no one will overhear us." Vi shot her a glare. Deneya just grinned as though her goal all along had been to rile Vi up.

"My office instead? I have their fire whiskey, good stuff—"

"Fine." Vi was beyond arguing. She still had work to do. What they were doing could be a game to Deneya, a fun opportunity to meddle with the affairs of the Dark Isle. But every action had the highest stakes for Vi. "I don't know when I'll be there, so you'd better wait."

"All the more reason to meet in my office." Deneya strolled down the steps. "I'll have my books and bottle to keep me company while I wait."

"Keep your head about you," Vi called down.

"Won't be a problem." She raised a hand, touching the scarf on the side of her head, just where the tops of her ears would be. *Elfin.* The woman was elfin, Vi realized. That was why she was never without a scarf.

Vi shook her head and went inside, heading right for Fiera's door. She knocked softly.

"It's me." She heard the locks disengage and the door cracked open, Zira brandishing the sword. She relaxed the moment her eyes met Vi's and opened wide the door.

"You find the bastards?"

"Unfortunately not. They blended into the crowd." Vi stepped inside, still locking the door behind her. "Is everyone all right?"

"Tiberus is—"

"It is just a nick, do not fret," he interrupted Fiera. "I've had worse out in battle. You, however, will need to see a cleric."

"You worry for nothing," Fiera mumbled, glancing askance.

"We'll arrange for a guarded carriage to take you both back to the castle. There, you can both be looked at by clerics," Vi said. "And following, we'll need to discuss protection of the sword going forward."

"I have every intention of sealing it away." Fiera shifted in her seat.

"Sealing it away?" Tiberus muttered. "Why seal away a weapon like that, when you could turn it against your enemies?"

That was the last thing Vi wanted. She stepped forward, kneeling before the Emperor and Empress. For a brief second, her breath caught in her throat at the sight of them—a regal couple, young and strong. She was witnessing a moment that even the most skilled painters never could have captured. A moment she should never have witnessed.

"My Emperor and Empress," Vi started reverently. "I am your loyal subject. I defer to you in all things. But if you will, I implore you to accept council from this lowly one." She was laying on the decorum thick, but Vi knew enough about Tiberus now to know he was one to appreciate it. "The Knights of Jadar will grow in strength with or without the sword in their possession. They see it as their right."

"Which it certainly is not," the Emperor snapped. "Treasonous scum."

"It is not," Vi agreed. "But reality and the perceptions of men rarely overlap."

"What would you have us do?" Fiera asked.

"Hide it as you intended," Vi said delicately. "But it needs to be a place no one will know—a place they cannot even hunt you to find."

"How do you suggest I do that?"

"Give it to me," Vi said boldly, her gaze unwavering. If she didn't exude confidence, how could she ever expect them to invest it in her? "Give me the sword, and then not even you will know of its location. You cannot be captured or killed to find it."

"You think we should trust *you* with the sword? You overstep much for a guard," Tiberus said down his nose at her.

"She knows her place and acts within it." Fiera reached out to touch her husband's hand lightly. "It is something I have considered before. Furthermore, she's right... this is not something either of us should do. We do not live for ourselves any longer. We live for our Empire—and for our unborn son."

Fiera rested her hand on her stomach. Vi had never been so fixated on something that couldn't be seen. One motion could say so much, but Vi didn't know what language the message was in. Did this mean she was pregnant now? Or was Fiera merely referencing the prophecy Vi had given her months before? She narrowly resisted asking outright.

"You..." The Emperor seemed torn. Torn between his growing family and the peace a contented royal family would foster, and his thirst for conquest. His gaze volleyed among the sword, Vi, and Fiera. But ultimately his wife and unborn child won out. "You are right."

"Then I will entrust the sword to you, Yullia." Fiera's mouth turned upward into an easy smile. She almost looked relieved. "Tell no one what you do with it."

"I will take its secrets with me to my grave."

17

*S*HE HAD THE SWORD.

Vi had to replay the day's events in her mind as she stared at the faintly glowing weapon in her bedroom that night to make sure she wasn't dreaming. There had been the preparations, the wedding, the attack. She had summoned a carriage to take Zira and the royals back to the castle before slipping out a back door herself, the sword wrapped tightly so that not even a glimmer of its divine blue light could be seen. Her shoulders had been tense as she wove through the city, the grin she wore so wide that it hurt.

Her heart was still racing as she summoned Taavin.

The man looked from Vi to the sword on her bed. Like a moth to a flame, he slowly crossed to it, entranced. Taavin ran his fingertips along the blade. Yargen's magic sought him out as it did Vi. It seemed to seep into him and, for a brief, breathtaking second, the thin lines of magic that hummed around the edges of him faded.

He was there, in the flesh. She crossed over to him and rested a hand on his shoulder. He turned, startled. His eyes widened. He must have felt it too.

"Taavin, you're…" He was solid underneath her fingertips. Vi snaked her arms around his waist, acting on instinct and awe. She could feel his heartbeat racing. Or perhaps the frantic beating was actually her own.

"Vi—" Taavin moved to embrace her and lifted his hand from the weapon. The shimmering magic returned to his form. The warmth and smell of him vanished.

"The sword," she whispered. "It makes you… real." If she could string it around his neck, she would.

"Yargen's magic is a power unlike any other. It's the embodiment of life itself," he said thoughtfully, more to the sword than her. But Taavin brought his gaze back to Vi, his thumb caressing her cheek. "But I am always real, for you."

Vi put on the bravest smile she could, unable and not trusting herself to say anything else.

"Now, tell me, how did you manage to procure it so quickly?"

Her arms tightened around him. "Don't be cross with me," Vi started, already searching his eyes for the edges of anger.

"*How* did you procure it?"

"I had a vision," Vi began hesitantly.

"When?"

"About two weeks ago."

Taavin released her and took a step back. "Two weeks, and you didn't tell me? Where did you have it? What was your vision of?"

Vi finally told him of Zira's request, looking into Raylynn's future, and what it had ultimately led her to. She watched his expression darken more with every word. Her heart was now racing for an entirely different reason—the adrenaline of warring emotions.

When she finished, Taavin turned, putting his back to her.

"Taavin, I was only doing what I thought was best. What I thought would lead this world—"

"No, you were doing what *you* wanted to do," he interrupted harshly. "You weren't acting on behalf of this world. You put yourself in danger to strike against the Knights of Jadar. You didn't even consult me."

"You would've told me not to do it."

"Of course I would've!" He spun, looking at her with rage-filled eyes. "You're not thinking this through."

"I am," Vi insisted. "I played it safe. I did what you asked. And all it led to was the Knights of Jadar gaining enough time to strengthen and organize an attack. If I had been acting offensively sooner, then maybe I could've prevented the attack on the wedding from ever happening." He was silent, glowering at her. "If I hadn't acted, Zira would be *dead*."

"That's it, isn't it?" Taavin whispered.

"What?" Vi was taken aback by his sudden quiet.

"This wasn't about the sword, or the world. It wasn't about dealing a blow to an organization that threatens your family. This was about her."

"It was about the sword," Vi insisted.

"No, you wanted to save Zira." He took a step forward, raising a finger and pointing at her. "You wanted to save her, because you *always* want to save her."

"And is that so terrible?" Vi met him step for step. "What's so awful about not wanting to see a little girl grow up without her mother?"

"Because you can't save Zira." Taavin shook his head sadly. "And you can't save Fiera, either."

It was an arrow that fired straight and true, landing right through her heart. Vi staggered back. She grabbed her chest, clawing at the physical ache there.

"You don't know that," she whispered.

"Their deaths are stones in the river."

Vi shook her head, as though she could shake off his words. She couldn't—they'd burned her. His words singed her chest, making her feel hot all over, like her bones had become cinder. "No," she said softly.

"Vi, listen to—"

"You listen." She brought her eyes back to him. "I saved my father when the world presumed him dead. I saved him from Adela. I had a vision of Zira dying today, and she yet lives. I am the one who is to change fate and save this whole, damned world. Do not tell me I can't save two women."

"It doesn't work that way." The pity in his eyes was the worst part.

"Have I ever saved her before?" Vi volleyed back to him. He narrowed his eyes. "Has Zira ever survived the wedding before?"

"No," Taavin reluctantly admitted.

"Then you don't know." Hope was a wave crashing down on her, extinguishing the blaze that had nearly consumed her. "You don't know, because this is new."

"I have ninety-two other histories that guide my wisdom."

"But you don't *know*."

"I know there are some things that, no matter how hard you try, don't change."

"Then I will try harder," Vi insisted.

"I grant you that you've kept Zira alive longer than ever before. But Yargen will come for her life, as she will Fiera's. Perhaps the assassin that came in the night ten attempts ago will return once more, looking for the sword—"

"Then I will have guards posted at her door."

"Two attempts ago she was involved in a skirmish with the Knights while patrolling the city and was cut down."

"Then I will do the patrols," Vi continued to counter. "Rather than tell me what I can't do, help me accomplish what I can. Help me find all these avenues to spare her by telling me how she's died before."

"Or she dies at the hands of a thief who gets the jump on her while she's sleeping along the road during one of her trips, long after you've left her side." Vi narrowed her eyes slightly and balled her hands into fists. Before she could say anything again, Taavin continued. "And if you save Fiera from one death, she's murdered in equally horrible ways. Or falls victim to an accident no one could prevent."

She stared up at him, searching for a lie in his words. But Taavin's eyes were stony clones of their usual warm selves, cold and unfeeling. The backs of her eyes prickled, though Vi couldn't quite explain why. She hadn't felt like crying in months. Why now?

It wasn't that she knew Fiera *that* well. Certainly, she'd come to love the Empress in an unexpected but not entirely surprising way. And the woman did have her undeniable aura that made people willing to follow her to the ends of the earth.

But this feeling was more than that.

This was her stomach flipping upside down until her throat knotted. It was her eyes burning and her breaths becoming shallow. This feeling was worse than staring down Adela, or Ulvarth... perhaps even worse than burning Taavin alive.

"Why?" Vi whispered. "Why would Yargen do this?"

"There is the greater cycle of fate, the one we are trapped within and trying to free ourselves from. But there are also smaller turns, turns within families. Cruel fathers who raise cruel men who become cruel fathers themselves. There are some things we cannot escape."

"No." She shook her head. "I am here to change it—to break those cycles. And I refuse to believe that a goddess who supposedly wishes to look after all her people would trap them in destructive cycles they can't free themselves from. If anything, that is the work of Raspian, and I will give it no credence."

"I know your pain," Taavin said firmly and with a slightly pleading edge. "I understand your hurt. Watching the ones you care for suffer, over and over again. Being helpless to stop or change it, no matter how hard you try. Seeing someone you love more than anyone or anything else in this accursed world trapped in a loop for nearly a thousand years.

"Feeling every blow, pain, and betrayal as though it's your own. Each one worse than the last. Yearning not to feel... but you—I can't avoid feeling, because the moment I lay eyes on you, I feel everything."

His hands were on her face. Vi blinked up at him, startled. She hardly remembered him crossing to her. His words were more entrancing than any of Yargen's. The way he said them was like a prayer, or a Lightspinner's chant.

Taavin's thumbs smoothed over the curve of her cheeks and he held her there. In his eyes she saw all the wonder and pain the universe had ever held. It was enough to make her knees weak and heart ache.

"If you know this pain... then help me end it," Vi whispered. "Help me break not just one cycle, but all of them. Then we'll all be free."

He smiled sadly and his eyes drifted from her lips to her forehead, where he placed a tender kiss. Vi pressed her eyes closed, a deep ache reverberating through her. She needed him. Her hands grabbed the back of his arms above his elbows.

"I'm trying to help you," he murmured. "But you have to let me. You have to listen, and be careful. The best chance we have to end this is caution. But if we don't end it, we have to see you reborn. Be careful until then."

Taavin pulled away and when Vi opened her eyes again, he was gone. She spent a moment focusing on every long breath of air, but each one felt thinner than the last. When he left, he took all the oxygen with him.

Vi grabbed the sword as though she could somehow strike down the barriers that stood in their way. But all she did was sheathe and hide it. The currents of emotion she was wading through were her own. There was still work to be done—work that wouldn't end just because she wanted and needed more time to sort through her own experiences.

The castle was alive now, even at night. Servants tended to duties they didn't have a chance to get to during the day. Vi donned the skin of one random helper she'd seen most afternoons in Fiera's chambers as she made her way to Deneya's office.

Two raps on the door and it opened promptly. Deneya looked her up and down.

"I heard you needed help sorting your bookcases," Vi said, keeping the masquerade even though no one was around.

"My bookcases are fine. Though I wouldn't mind help with laundry. Folding is a pain." Deneya gave a smirk, one Vi returned. "Come on in." Vi entered and released her illusion. "It's just *durroe*, right?"

"Yes, though it helps if you pick a real person. It's harder to fabricate someone who doesn't exist with enough detail to keep the illusion stable."

"You speak from experience?" Deneya walked over to her desk, where there were two glasses set out alongside a half-empty decanter. Deneya had started without her.

"I do." Vi adjusted the sword at her belt to sit in one of the chairs facing Deneya's desk. "Though, I admit, it's been a while since I first began using *durroe* this way. Maybe I would have more luck with a fabricated person now."

"It seems to be working well, no point in pushing to change it." Deneya glugged a heavy pour from the decanter into each glass.

"That's precisely the reason to change it." Vi wore a grin as she accepted her glass. "Given the reactions I've received from the people of Meru, it's been far too long since someone re-imagined how the goddess's words can be used."

"Some would say re-imagining the words of the goddess is blasphemy."

"Beware of the ones who do—they're the real enemies of Meru. And, as the Champion of Yargen, I say it's fine."

Deneya chuckled and held out her glass. "I like you, Yullia. Cheers to saving a royal family today."

"Cheers." Vi tipped the edge of her glass against Deneya's and took a long sip of the dark amber liquid in her glass. It tasted of spiced caramel, surprisingly sweet. "And it's Vi. My name is Vi."

"Vi," Deneya repeated thoughtfully. "Why Yullia, then?"

"It didn't feel right to use my name when I came here, for a whole host of reasons." She watched the liquid swirl in the glass as she slowly rotated it.

"Then thank you for telling me."

"I know your true name. It's only fair," Vi answered offhandedly. As though she hadn't just allowed Deneya past a barrier.

Deneya took another sip of her drink and Vi did the same. She vaguely remembered the drink Erion Le'Dan had given her all those months ago. Was this the same? Or different? Better or worse?

She fought to dredge up the memories—the only proof that that time had existed at all. Vi set her glass down on the armrest of the chair.

"You said you saw who was the first to attack?"

"Yes."

"What did he look like?"

"Western, tall, bushy mustache... you couldn't see it in what he was wearing, but he has a scar on his forearm, too."

"You know him then?" Vi asked hopefully.

"*Know* is a strong word. I've seen him before." Deneya set her glass down and crossed her arms.

"Where?" Vi settled back into her chair, quickly adding, "No, let me guess. Heading in and out of Twintle's estate?"

"Half right. One of Twintle's warehouses down at the docks."

"Idiots," Vi half sighed, half mumbled. "They're no longer meeting at the estate?"

"I'm not certain. They've become much better at hiding their tracks," Deneya said with a note of frustration.

"Either way, Twintle is their ringleader."

"It seems so, and that brings me to the other thing I had to tell you." Deneya's eyes sparked with knowing. "Twintle contacted Zira, offering to resume some of his old Knightly duties and assist overseeing security at the last minute. Said it would be his honor."

Vi was sure she hadn't heard of it because Twintle no doubt hated her after she suggested the soldiers be released in stages, resulting in them being imprisoned longer. He would've done everything possible to keep her out of the decision-making process. "Slimy snake," she mumbled.

"He's definitely the one leading. He has the means and the coin," Deneya said with a note of agreement. "But I think Luke is helping organize. He's a convenient mobilizer so Twintle can continue to fulfill his duties and keep suspicion off his family."

"I see." Vi swirled the drink in her glass, thinking back to her conversation with Taavin.

"So, who do we go after? Luke, Twintle, or neither? I doubt Taavin would approve," Deneya said, not knowing how spot-on she was.

"No, he wouldn't." She took a long sip of her drink, savoring the burn while she thought about what Taavin had said. He'd claimed that, regardless of what she did, there were people she couldn't save. But that wasn't about to stop her from trying. She was in uncharted territory now, after all. At the very least, she'd make the lives of those who would harm the family of a future-Vi as miserable as possible. "We're not going to go after Twintle or Luke."

"Who, then?"

"All of them. Every Knight that would ever swing a sword against Zira or Fiera." She had saved Zira once. Now, Vi had to keep her alive, and prove to Taavin that boldness was the key to ending this vicious cycle once and for all.

18

"WHERE HAS TWINTLE GONE, exactly?" Vi asked as she and Deneya walked through the midday streets of Norin toward the port.

"He has a manor between here and the Crossroads, not too far from the latter. Last I heard he was taking a short leave of absence to return home and spend some time with family before summer is up."

Houses in the city, houses in the Waste. The old noble families of Mhashan had more homes than Vi currently had pairs of trousers and seemed to change them with equal frequency.

"Family, or networking with the old lords and ladies who still harbor ill will toward the new Empress along the way."

"My money would be on that."

"Mine as well." Though Vi also entertained the idea of him turning tail, embarrassed by his failure at Fiera's wedding.

"Then this is a boring gamble." Deneya chuckled lightly. Sometimes, like now, Vi deeply appreciated her casual disregard for the weight of the situation surrounding her. Perhaps it was because Deneya didn't see herself as a part of the Dark Isle, and its trials were mere amusements to her. Or perhaps she'd genuinely been so bored for so long here that even the slightest activity was a genuine delight.

Either way, it forced Vi to relax some. Her demeanor had Vi working to remove herself in a similar way—look at all that was happening from the outside. It didn't directly affect or relate to her, not really. She only had one goal and that was to do whatever it took to prevent the Crystal Caverns and weapons from being destroyed while saving as many people as she could in the process.

Of course, this distance was fabricated and skin deep. At her core, Vi couldn't deny the simmering hatred she felt for the Knights of Jadar for what they had done and would do to her family—a hatred that only grew by the day.

"Either way, he won't be here to deny the search, and no one else in his employ should be able to refuse me."

"You're confident in that?" Vi asked, glancing over at Deneya. The world blurred at the edges of her vision with bright shifting light. She was using *durroe* for an illusion once more. This time Vi had experimented with basing the masquerade off the face of a real person and the body and clothes of a different real person—a hybrid of real to make something fake. According to Deneya, her work was as flawless as it was the first two times she'd seen it.

"Look at me. Do I look like a woman who has ever not been confident in her life?"

"No." Vi refrained from bringing up Taavin's mention of her cheating on an exam during their first interaction. She'd looked very uncertain then.

"Good. You play your part, I'll play mine. We start with the two warehouses on the left side and work our way to Twintle's."

Vi didn't quite like the plan. The idea that they would go to other warehouses under the guise of a surprise inspection before arriving at Twintle's—theoretically giving Twintle's men time to learn they were coming and hide any evidence of the Knights—still rankled her. But Deneya was confident in the best approach and Vi would give the woman the benefit of the doubt. She'd yet to disappoint her.

The first warehouse was on the far end of the docks; Vi could smell it long before they arrived. It belonged to a prominent fish trader and Vi resisted the urge to cover her nose as she perused the rows of fish nearly the size of her, laid out for bidding. She was more than ready to depart when Deneya issued them the all-clear.

The next warehouse belonged to a logger, barging lumber from the North. Vi stared up at the massive chunks of wood, knowing they were mere fractions of the sentries she'd grown up in. She wondered how long until this man's business was shut down due to the Emperor's encroachment on Shaldan.

Finally, after spending the better part of the morning in the first two warehouses, they were on to Twintle's. His was around the middle of the bustling docks, toward the richer side of town. Vi paused, staring out at the ships. Her eyes swung to the far corner, the oldest stretch.

On all of her maps, those docks had always been there. They were the humble start of the greatest port on the Dark Isle. They had been there… when the scythe left.

The vision Vi had on Meru was in the forefront of her mind: an Eastern man with hazel eyes, standing at those docks, bestowing a scythe-shaped velvet-wrapped parcel on a ship captain. That was the spot where the scythe had left this land and—

"Are you all right?" Deneya startled her from her thoughts.

"Wh—oh, yes." Vi glanced back to the far end of the port.

"What is it?"

"Nothing, it's nothing." She shook her head. "Just remembering something. Let's carry on."

There were two men posted as guards on either side of the narrow entrance to Twintle's warehouse.

"Good afternoon gentlemen," Deneya said lightly. The two men gave gruff nods, regarding them warily. Deneya leaned over, glancing at the ledger Vi held open. "I see this is… oh right, Lord Twintle's storehouse. Of course."

"What business would you have here, ma'am?" the shorter of the two men asked.

"You might not know me, but I am Denja, the councilor for commerce." Deneya held out a hand and Vi slipped a piece of paper into it, just as they had for the first two warehouses. On it was Fiera's handwriting and both the royal seal of Mhashan, and a much more recent Imperial seal. "Everything should be in order verifying my credentials."

"Yes, councilor, how may we assist you?"

"I am performing inspections on warehouses today at the docks. Standard procedure to make sure all goods have been properly accounted for and the recent Imperial taxes levied against them."

The two guards shared a glance. Vi couldn't tell if they were genuinely surprised or not to see them and it made her shift her weight uncomfortably from foot to foot.

"We're afraid the Lord isn't present at the moment."

"Oh, that's right." Deneya brought her index finger to her jawline. Feigning ignorance was not the woman's strong suit. "He is traveling right now, isn't he? But here or not, this is something none of the traders are exempt from. If you could just allow us inside, my assistant will catalog goods and I'll cross-reference that against taxes paid yesterday."

"Lord Twintle explicitly instructed that we were to allow no one in until his return," one of the guards said hesitantly.

"As I said, no one is exempt." Deneya put her hands on her hips. "Please don't make me hike all the way back to the castle to get the Imperial guards and do this by force—none of us wants that."

The guards had a quick mental conversation that ultimately ended in a shrug from the taller man and an indifferent expression from the shorter.

"All right," he said. "But be quick about it. And we'll need to escort you the whole time."

"Very well."

With that, they were inside.

The warehouse was a simple build—little more than a brick box. Windows lined the upper portion of the walls just under the roof, no doubt to let out the rising heat from the Western sun. But they were currently shuttered, which meant the building felt like an oven.

It was surprisingly empty. Larger crates lined the walls along the outside. Rows of smaller ones that came up to Vi's waist stretched away from the door for about half of the space. In the other half, they were stacked in mountains. The logic of the two sorting methods was lost on her.

"While my assistant verifies the goods, could you please show me the most recent ledgers?"

"Of course." The shorter man went off to a far corner with Deneya, rummaging through a chest. That left the taller man with Vi.

She walked down the first row of crates, straining to open a heavy lid. Inside the box, settled on a nest of wood shavings, were some of the largest sapphires Vi had ever seen. Most were rough-cut, but they would still produce several stones of enviable quality in the hands of a skilled jeweler.

"Jewels," she murmured. "I thought Twintle was keeping fish and food?"

"That was only for the siege. His fleet was the smallest and fastest—they could slip past any Imperial vessels. Now he's sold off most of those wares." The man paused, narrowing his eyes at her. "I would think you would know that as the assistant to the councilor."

Vi laughed brightly and moved onto the next crate. "I'm sure you know how it is… they never tell the help *anything*. Just expect us to read their minds."

"Isn't that the truth." He shook his head sadly.

"So he deals in gems now." Crate after crate was filled with sparkling items that would fetch incredible prices. Where did Twintle get the money to invest in such a pricey business? And just how much was here?

"Rumor on the docks is the Le'Dans are quite sour because of it."

"Oh?" Vi paused, sliding up to the man. She made it a point to glance over at Deneya and the other guard. "Say, what's your name?"

"Adeem."

"Adeem," Vi repeated. "I do love good gossip, especially when it involves nobles."

"Who doesn't?" He chuckled. "All I know is that Richard Le'Dan has come by twice and both times were... quite contentious."

"I see."

"Twintle said that's part of why he's hired us to guard the place. He's worried the Le'Dans will come during one of his secret meetings."

"Secret meetings?" Vi could feel the muscles around her ears tense, as though they were trying to widen themselves so she could better hear what he would say next. This was what she had come here for.

"They happen at night. I think it's Twintle's suppliers and movers. Men and women—mostly men, though—come carrying crates in and out."

"What do they look like?" Vi asked, trying not to sound too eager.

"Twintle is very secretive about his trading practices... They all wear red hoods, like a Crone."

Vi laughed. "How odd," she said lightly, though inside she was barely bottling her excitement. Twintle had moved the meetings of the Knights of Jadar from his home to his warehouse and he was amassing wealth for the Knights there. He was likely distributing it as well. Everything lined up with the bits of information Deneya had collected. "Do you know when the next meeting is?"

"I imagine when the Lord is back. He usually holds them once per week, right at the end." The guard shrugged. "Though, again, it's not as if they tell me anything."

"Right..." Vi's eyes landed on a stretch of chests locked with heavy padlocks. She began rummaging through her bag. "Adeem, can you be a dear and please go fetch me a quill? I seem to have misplaced mine."

"Of course." He eagerly scampered off.

Vi leaned over, crouching behind one of the chests to hide her motions. "*Juth calt.*"

The lock was off and Vi set it aside. She opened the chest hastily, not even wasting time with a glance in Adeem's direction. Rubies winked up at her in the low light of the warehouse's flame bulbs.

Rubies... Vi closed the chest, straightening away and looking at all the other identically locked chests. Chests of Western rubies.

"Here you go." Adeem had returned, and he wasn't alone.

"Everything checks out on my end," Deneya said in a tone that implied she wouldn't be able to stall for much longer. Which was fine—Vi already had the information she needed.

"Mine as well. Thank you both for your flexibility in this." Vi made some marks in a ledger and smiled brightly at both the guards, imagining her illusioned cheeks dimpling.

"Yes, thank you." Deneya started for the door. "I'll be sure to let Twintle know that he has cleared inspection and remains in good standing with the crown." They emerged back into the sunlight. "You two have a lovely day."

Vi gave a wave, hastening beside Deneya before there were any further exchanges.

"Find anything?" Deneya asked when they were out of earshot and halfway to the next warehouse. They had three to go to ensure the surprise inspections couldn't be questioned.

"Two things, actually."

"Oh? Do tell," she asked eagerly.

"The first is that he has chests of Western rubies."

"How many?"

"I counted at least eight."

Deneya hummed. "That should be past the legal limit. King Rocham imposed mining sanctions on the stones about two decades ago. Though, knowing Twintle, he'd argue that it was a law made by an old king and is currently unclear under Imperial law."

"So not illegal, and not inherently nefarious?"

"Not nefarious, though suspicious… Good Western rubies fetch prices that can make your head spin. The reason Rocham banned them was because of an attack by Adela on a mine not far from the coast at the southern border. Combined with the difficulties surrounding their mining."

"I see," Vi murmured, eager to change the topic off Adela as quickly as possible. "The guard—Adeem—also told me that Twintle has been hosting gatherings of his 'suppliers.'"

"Now that sounds interesting." Deneya stopped walking to give Vi her full attention.

"It was. Men and women apparently coming and going in red hoods. Hiding their faces. Keeping others out at all costs." Vi glanced back at the warehouse. "I think we might have discovered the Knights of Jadar's new meeting spot and, even better, I think I know when the next meeting is."

And that meant the next time all the Knights were gathered, she would be ready to strike.

19

TWINTLE WAS GONE FOR about two months. His absence forced Vi to be patient, and to sit with her decision to take an active position against the Knights. The time also gave her ample evenings to continue working with the Sword of Jadar.

After Raylynn questioned if Vi could make the girl her own crystal weapon, Vi was no longer practicing with it as she would any other sword. Now, she focused on the magic, imagining it brightening and changing underneath her fingertips as it had with the ancient Champion.

The sword was suspended between Vi's knees as she slowly pushed and pulled at the magic that surrounded it. The magic was becoming a tangible thing, like a taffy that oozed between her fingers if she tried to hold onto it for too long, but solid enough for her to get good draws against it. She could sit for hours, moving it between her hands. Each time she turned it over she felt something new and different, as if a distant corner of her soul was ignited by it.

"As fascinating as it is to watch," Taavin said from where he sat across from her, "I'm still not sure what you're trying to accomplish."

"That makes two of us," Vi murmured, holding her focus. She'd made a cage of her fingers, the air within shimmering. "But you said I've not tried to manipulate Yargen's magic or the crystals the ninety-two other times. So why—" Vi glanced at him and her concentration was broken. The magic snapped back into the sword with a palpable *crack*. Vi sighed. "Why not be rebels and explore this as a possible tool to help us end this cycle?"

"The way we end this cycle is by making sure nothing happens to that sword and, sooner over later, getting it as far as possible from this city." He stared at her for a long minute, shook his head, and proceeded to become fascinated with a corner of the room. Vi hated how even when she was frustrated with him, the angular lines of his heartbreakingly beautiful profile softened her. She returned her attention to the weapon.

"I think I can do it, because I think I've made crystals before," Vi confessed.

"*What?*"

"It was when we were on Meru. When I crossed the shift to enter the Twilight Kingdom."

"You told me nothing of crystals then."

"I had a lot on my mind." Twist, pull, hold. Vi wrangled the magic like her memories. "I was more focused on keeping you alive and saving my father than anything else. There were those tears in the shift, formed by the red lightning. When I passed through on my own for the first time, the magic in the watch protected me."

"You mentioned that. How do crystals come into play?"

"Well, when the magic emerged from the watch, there was shimmering blue. It condensed and hardened around my feet. It protected me. When I made it through to the Twilight Kingdom, tiny shards of obsidian surrounded me. The shards looked identical to dormant crystal."

"I see…"

"It makes sense, don't you think? The crystals were formed from Yargen's power. They contain her power. It's as if the magic condensed…" Vi put pressure on the ball of magic she held in her hands. "… enough that…" Sparks flew between her fingers, increasing in brightness and density. "… it was given physical—" All at once the magic broke free and snapped back into place "—form," Vi finished and finally turned her eyes to him.

Taavin gazed at her with a peculiar intensity she hadn't seen from him yet. Only he could make her feel on edge and completely relaxed at the same time. "Perhaps you're right."

"Mother above, did it hurt to admit that?" Vi tilted her head back and let out a burst of laughter. Lifting the sword off her lap, she set it to the side and gave Taavin her full focus.

He ignored the remark. "Perhaps that's the variable I haven't been considering."

"The incident in the Twilight Forest?"

"Yes. All this time I focused on what you did and what happened to you when you were sent back. I never stopped to consider how the events that happened *before* you fully assumed your mantle as Champion shaped and formed what came after."

It seemed rather obvious to her, but Vi resisted saying so. She'd already made one playful jab and they were having what seemed like productive discourse.

"I think there was a unique sequence of events at play," he continued. "Lightning strikes, you getting to the Twilight Kingdom, noticing the obsidian, and piecing together how those shards relate to the watch's magic… all random variances between worlds."

Taavin stood with purpose. Holding out his hands, his lips began to move quickly. It never took him too long to draw on the wisdom of his past selves. When he finished, his attention was on her.

"Well?"

"I already knew there was no record of your obsession with manipulating crystal, but that confirms it."

"Does this mean we can say with certainty we're on a new timeline?" Vi jumped up from her chair. "Zira is alive, nothing has befallen her—"

"And some events will still transpire regardless," he said firmly.

"Maybe not, you don't know."

"I—"

"You don't *know*," she emphasized, then waited for his challenge. It never came.

"We could be on a new timeline. Possibly a successful one. There's only one way to find out."

"You want to go to an Apex of Fate."

"Yes, and I think I know where one is." She'd been waiting for a convenient opening to convince him this was the right course. Tonight was that night.

"Where?"

"The port... where the Eastern descendant of the Champion gave up the scythe to send it to Meru." His frown told her she was right in assuming it was an Apex. "The port is safe. I can conceal myself. It's low risk." Taavin ran a hand through his hair. He clearly didn't want to agree with her. Vi persisted in the wake of his silence. "The wedding might have changed everything, and we don't know."

"You're right. You need to look into the future. And I know I must let you do this. Yet..." Taavin crossed over to her, scooping up her hands in his. His thumbs ran against her knuckles.

"Are you really the same person who had me sailing to Meru?" Vi said softly. "You fret over me leaving the castle now."

"I'm not the same person." He gazed at her through his lashes. "That man didn't understand the cost of losing you—not for the world, and not for him."

"But I am the same woman who made that journey," she said tenderly, tightening her fingers around his. "I am the same woman who boarded a vessel and left her home behind, who fought pirates and *won*, who accidentally made crystals. I might look like those ninety-two other women, but I'm not. I'm me, Taavin. Regardless of who I look or sound like, I am unique. This chance, this very moment, is ours alone. Don't condemn me for others' failures."

He nodded. "I know." She wasn't sure she could believe him. "Which is why I'll merely ask you to be safe on this excursion."

"I will." His warming up to her boldness only made her feel all the guiltier for keeping her other actions regarding the Knights from him. But hopefully, by the time he learned of them, she would be telling him their future was secure.

The port of Norin was bustling at all hours of the day. A vessel was always coming in or leaving. Fish needed to be hauled for the morning's market. Sailors looked to blow off steam before they returned to the sea.

Yet there was a unique quiet to the port at night. People went about their business with the hushed tones darkness brought. Most saw by the lights of lanterns at pubs, the glow of their pipes, or stars in the sky.

Vi was reminded of a different time she'd journeyed to the port of Norin in darkness. Jayme had been with her then. Those days had been her final moments on the Dark Isle of her world.

She paused, sweeping her eyes across the port, remaining alert, before tucking her head back down and starting off toward the oldest section of the docks. The salt covered stones beneath her feet had seen more history than libraries. And, if she was lucky, they would show her history yet to be made.

At the far end was the old dock, rotted and sagging. A mix of nostalgia and respect still kept its pylons in use, but only dinghies were tied up here now.

Vi stared out at the sea, envisioning what the scythe had shown her. She saw the slow curve of the land to her left, the cliff rising up to support the rich section of

Norin.

"It was here," Vi affirmed to herself. She glanced around. A man slumbered against a doorstep. The houses were dark. No eyes seemed to be on her. Still, her heart raced.

She crossed over to the sea wall and sat on its edge, her feet dangling just above the dark water. With one last glance around, Vi cupped her palms in her lap and summoned a mote of flame.

It didn't take long before the world was overcome with white.

Color came into focus first. Then, blobs formed hazy shapes that quickly gained clarity and form. A mass of people moved together. They swayed and swirled in time to music Vi couldn't hear.

Their faces were painted with expressions of joy. Hands clapped soundlessly. Golden strips of paper rained from the sky. Vi held out her hand, trying to catch a piece of confetti. But it fluttered straight through her.

Pennons bearing the seal of Solaris reached out for the breeze, their golden stitching picking up the sunlight. It was a celebration unlike any Vi had ever seen, in a place she had only ever imagined.

Surrounding her was a semi-circle of triangular bleachers that rose up like points on a sun. Men and women were packed within them, drinking, talking, cheering. She didn't need to hear their joy; she could feel it. It was a palpable, pulsating thing.

The song stopped, and with it the dancing. The crowd turned their focus to the high stage lined by wide columns. This was the Sun Stage. She recognized it from the drawings Romulin had sent her.

Then, as if by thought, he appeared.

Every emotion welled in her all at once at the sight of her family. Her father led, mother at his right hand. His hair was salted as she remembered it. Her mother's was perfectly coiffed. It was a trick of the mind, but Vi could almost smell the faint scent of eucalyptus that was always in their perfumes. Romulin was at their side, just as she remembered him.

Which meant…

Vi searched for her future self.

She wasn't there.

Her heart started to race. When was this? What was this celebration for? Was she in the North *or*… Had she changed the future so dramatically that Vi Solaris was no longer a part of it?

Vi's thoughts came to a screeching halt as Romulin collapsed.

The young man seized on the ground. Vi tried to take a step forward, but she was rooted to the spot. People were running around her, guards were being called. Her mother held her brother, hoisting him upward. Her father barked orders. Romulin's head rolled back, his mouth hanging open like the gaping mouth of Raspian himself.

Red lines ran down his cheeks—tracks of bloody tears. They had the same glow as the red lightning cracking through the sky. Romulin's sky blue eyes had gone milky, and a pale white foam oozed from his mouth.

Vi screamed. She screamed and screamed but no sound came. She flung every curse she knew at the world, at the heavens, at the injustice of it all. She screamed until there was nothing left to say, and the vision came collapsing back in on her.

She panted, back on the sea wall, her fire extinguished, her body doubled over on itself. Her throat was raw, so raw she could vividly imagine Raspian ripping into it. She slowly raised her head, staring out across the sea.

If the White Death still came for this land, she had changed nothing.

"No," Vi rasped, forcing her spine to find strength enough to straighten. If her brother was the one who was diseased—not her mother—*something* had changed.

Vi pushed herself away from the wall, pulled her hood tight and started off, her bones shaking with every step.

She had begun to shift fate. But she hadn't altered it enough. Saving Zira, working to thwart the Knights' attention at the wedding, and getting the Sword of Jadar sooner than she ever had before… none of it was enough to stop Raspian from being set free.

Clenching her jaw, Vi glared at Twintle's warehouse as she passed. Changing fate would take something bolder, and more daring, than anything she'd tried until now.

"Y OU AREN'T EXPERIMENTING AS much with the sword lately," Taavin observed.

"I know." Vi yawned so wide her jaw popped. "I'm too tired these days." Vi was nearly going cross-eyed from exhaustion.

"What has you burning the candle at both ends?" he asked thoughtfully.

"By day I fulfill my duties to the crown, enough to keep a low-profile here… I train with Zira, lunch with Fiera… and most evenings I have nightcaps with Deneya." That wasn't all she'd been doing at night.

"You don't have to do this, you know." Vi knew what he was about to say before he said it. It was a discussion that was creeping up more by the day. "You have the sword, Fiera has trusted you to hide it—you can leave."

"If I leave too quickly, people will notice and might suspect I have the sword."

"It's been months since the wedding."

"And all it takes is one suspicious act." Vi gave him a tired smile. "Weren't you the one telling me to be cautious?" She stepped behind a folding screen set before her closet, changing into a nightgown as she spoke.

Taavin averted his eyes. "I am, but at a certain point, inaction is just as risky."

"Make up your mind." Vi emerged from behind the screen with another yawn.

"At some point, you'll have to take the sword and go."

"I know. But I'll do it when the time is right. And that time isn't tonight."

"Yes, I'll let you sleep." Taavin walked over, cupping her cheek thoughtfully. His eyes scanned her face. "Do try to get some rest tonight. You look exhausted."

"I will." The lie cut her gums on the way out. The smile that followed it hurt more.

"Sleep well." Taavin leaned forward and planted a gentle kiss on her forehead, vanishing before he could lean away.

Vi stared at where he'd just been, steeping in the guilt. It wasn't the right time to take the sword away. And it wasn't the right time to get some sleep.

She went back behind the screen, changing into dark clothes and grabbing a blood red hood that matched Adeem's description of the robes worn by the men and women who attended Twintle's meetings. This way, she could blend in without need of an illusion. Vi wanted both hands free in case she needed to use her Lightspinning when she entered into the lion's den.

Twintle had returned from his travels a week ago and Vi had been perching herself on a rooftop several down from his warehouse each night since. She suspected he'd call a meeting sooner rather than later and she wanted to be ready the second he did.

Her feet knew the way to the docks by heart. She'd practiced the route to and from the warehouse each night. She knew that when the time came, she would want to be able to run through the back alleys and keep off the main roads without second-guessing herself.

Tonight, she sank into the shadows of an alleyway as two men caught her eye—Twintle and Luke. They spoke to each other in hushed and hurried tones on their way to the dock, though Vi couldn't make out any individual words. Vi waited until they were down the road before hurrying through a back alley to lean against the corner of a building to watch them proceed. The men were none the wiser to the woman following in their wake.

She took the back way around Twintle's warehouse. There was only one entrance and exit, so Vi waited, crouched low, listening to the murmuring voices within and the footsteps approaching without.

Every man and woman uttered a soft phrase, "Rulliad," before being permitted entry.

Rulliad meant loyalty in the language of old Mhashan. Really... one would think they would be more creative than that when it came to their passwords. Still, it made things easy.

Vi yanked the hood she'd fashioned over her head.

With nothing to protect her but confidence and trust in her magical skills, Vi strode to the entrance. Neither of the guards were the ones Vi met when she had come with Deneya, which made her wonder how often Twintle's paranoia had him changing his hired swords. She hoped she and Deneya's inspection hadn't cost the others their jobs... but didn't linger on the thought.

She had more important concerns.

"Good evening," one of the guards said in Southern Common.

"Rulliad," Vi replied without preamble. He gave a nod and she walked in.

Everyone gathered around the mostly open area with the stacks of crates. There wasn't much mingling and most people kept to themselves. Not one person had lowered their hood, which made it easy for Vi to remain hidden.

"We'll begin in another two minutes—we're waiting on just one more," Twintle said, stepping forward. He and Luke were the only two people who had lowered their hoods. Likely because everyone knew exactly who was behind the organization of this meeting. But there was safety in anonymity among the rest of the members—they couldn't out each other if captured.

As soon as one more man entered, Twintle began as promised.

"I know it has been some time since we all last met. But today I come to you with exciting tidings." Twintle turned to address the crowd in full. "I left our beloved city of Norin and returned to the Waste. There, I communed with the people we fight for. Those who still stand with the Mhashan we have always known.

"Here in this city, they call us extremists. Those beyond these walls see that if we are extreme, we are only extreme in our love for this land. Those beyond these walls stand by us, cheer us on, to stand by our rich heritage. Those beyond call us heroes."

"Don't be taken in by Solaris!" a man from across the room called out.

"Yes, yes my brothers and sisters, we are the ones impervious to the allure of Solaris lies. Solaris claims they stand for the West, but they are making the West poor with their demands of tithing to pay for the remnants of their war. They are the ones making the West weak by sending our girls and boys south to fight for their cities of stone and ice."

"We shall stand against them!" another called.

The whole room was being worked into a frenzy by Twintle's words. People shifted in place. Murmurs of support grew to outright cheers.

"We shall be the ones to stand against Solaris tyranny!" Luke stepped forward. "We shall be the ones who honor our oath to defend the poor. To upkeep tradition. And to honor the sacrifices of all those who came before us."

"But we cannot do this with our glorious fervor alone." Twintle's voice dropped to a hush and everyone hung on his next words. Vi had never seen an orator quite like him. It was more than the skill of a virtuoso musician. Every man and woman Twintle had gathered was their own instrument, and he could play the orchestra. "To restore Mhashan to its former glory, we need a power that affirms our divine right."

More whispers, all resounding to an eerily soft chant, as if everyone gathered was under some kind of spell. A single word passed from person to person in hushed tones: *sword*.

"Yes, we need the Sword of Jadar. The sword once bestowed by King Jadar on his magickless son. The sword that was destined to defend Mhashan. We are its rightful owners now that the blood-traitor princess has turned her back on our ways. And with the sword's power, we can restore the throne to someone befitting of its honor. We will not be like the coward whore to the sun. We will unlock the power it was made to unleash on this world and with that power we will liberate ourselves from the tyranny of Solaris."

Applause, cheers. Vi watched as some men got so overwhelmed with excitement they nearly threw off their hoods. It was a type of spell that had just as much power as Yargen's words. Though Vi found herself immune. She watched it all unfold, trying to detach herself from the situation.

Yet in the back of her mind... a bonfire of rage burned for all the hatred and hurt these words would sow.

"You've made progress on the sword, then?" a man asked, more skeptical than Vi expected.

"I have," Twintle said proudly. "With this last trip to our brothers and sisters in the Waste, we have established a network that stretches far beyond this city. We have amassed wealth. And, in this, I have procured access to the one person who can steal from Solaris—the one person who has evaded Tiberus ever since she cut down his father and stole his family's treasure."

"You're mad," a man near Vi murmured. No one but her seemed to hear.

Twintle was mad. Because if he was talking about the one person Vi was thinking of, it would mean he had made a deal with—

"Adela," Twintle finished her thought. The fires that had been burning in the back of her mind crackled against her clenched and shaking fists.

"The bane of the seas?"

"The pirate queen?" another gasped.

"Yes, the *pirate queen*," Twintle proclaimed, glaring around the room as if challenging anyone to move or speak against him. No one did. "Sometimes, the enemy of our enemy is our friend. Adela will gladly help us strike against Solaris. She has even reduced her rate for the delight of this job."

"You would trust the sword to a pirate?"

"She'll just take it," Vi mumbled. Luckily no one heard. None of them had ever dealt with a force like Adela Lagmir before and it showed. Adela would gladly take the job, pocket every Western ruby she was likely demanding of them, and take the crystal sword for herself if she even had an inkling of the power it held. The mental image of the Knights scrambling to get it back—of them being betrayed like her family had been—delighted her like a black flame, dark and burning.

"She will lend us the help of her crew. Through them, she will provide knowledge and manpower with the wild magicks of the Crescent Continent. We shall steal the sword back when it is being transported to the South with the Imperial party. From there, it is not far to the Crystal Caverns." Twintle held up a worn journal. Vi squinted but she couldn't make out the writing. "I have procured the writings on Jadar's search for Windwalkers, about his belief that the sword could unlock enough power to see Mhashan rule for millennia to come. This is only a fraction of what was collected from the Burning Times, but it will be enough that we can access the true fount of power in the depths of the Crystal—"

Twintle paused, lowering his hand slowly. All eyes were dragged to the doorway where Twintle was now focused. There a man stood, leaning against a crate, panting heavily.

"Forgive me, brothers and sisters, for my delay," he huffed. "I was—"

Twintle held up a hand, stopping him. His eyes swung across the room, lips moving in a silent count.

"Bar the doors," Twintle commanded, deathly quiet. "There is a stranger hiding among us."

Everyone looked around and Vi did the same, not wanting to be easily identifiable as the odd one out. She could use *durroe* to hide herself. No, they'd already accounted for her. They'd launch a search if the count was off now. But they wouldn't find her if her illusion was solid enough.

"We are the sword—" Twintle started loudly.

"That stands against the darkness!" Everyone answered boldly, proudly, and in unison.

"Her," a man next to Vi shouted, approaching. "She didn't say anything."

"You there, lower your hood," Twintle demanded.

"Tell us your name," the man asked.

"My name?" Vi said softly, looking up at him through her eyelashes and past the edge of her hood. She should run. She *should* get out of there as quickly as possible—Vi had her information on what the Knights' next move was and they still didn't know who she was. This could still be salvaged without taking too many actions that risked fate.

But something rooted her to the spot. The spark that had been crackling within her was ready to ignite into flames. And as she gazed up into the eyes of this spiteful man—a man who would kill everyone she'd ever loved if given the chance—something within her snapped with an audible crack.

"Your name." The man reached for her hood, catching hair with fabric. But she didn't cry out in pain. She didn't even give any indication he was hurting her. She calmly met the eyes of the Knight she was about to kill.

"My name is *juth calt*," Vi whispered darkly.

He shuddered, stumbled, and fell back—dead before he hit the floor. Several other Knights jumped away and drew their swords. These were men trained in war. They weren't about to be swayed so easily.

The first lunged for her and she just stared at him, smiling.

"*Mysst xieh,*" Vi hissed. The words blurred together, but a shield of brilliant light sparked in the air before his blade could hit her. Vi ignited flames around the shield with a thought. He stumbled backward.

"What sorcery is this?" The man looked at his sword as though it had betrayed him and blinked at where the fire had been.

"The sorcery of the Mother." Vi waved a hand and cast an arc of fire around her. It burned white hot—hotter than it had burned for Taavin. Men and women bounced backward, throwing hoods from their heads, exposing faces of pure ugliness beneath.

The fire caught, leaping from crate to crate. Soon, the warehouse would be up in flames. Its contents wouldn't burn—the jewels would survive. The masonry of the building would endure. But she wanted to see them scatter like rats.

She wanted to see them burn until they were husks. She didn't care about fate or crystals. She wanted vengeance.

She wanted—

"Firebearers, get those flames under control and get her!" Twintle's voice cut through her thoughts.

Vi blinked and it was like coming out of a trance. Bloodlust had made her foolish. "*Durroe watt radia.*" Vi did what she should've done the whole time and made herself invisible.

The Firebearers among those gathered finally got control of the flames, but not until after they had consumed a fair bit. Others had already run out of the warehouse.

"Where is she?" Twintle demanded. Nothing more than a small spark illuminated the area. "Where did she go?"

"Father, there was an arc of flame all around." Luke moved the dark soot with his boot that formed a crescent shape around Vi. "We would've seen her—"

"She said she was the Mother," someone else whispered.

"Impossible." Twintle approached, blessedly stopping at the line she'd created in the stone floor. "The Mother does not have mortal flesh, and if she did... she would stand beside our noble cause."

None of the other men and women questioned his claim, though Luke seemed skeptical.

"A Waterrunner must have helped her escape. Search the area," Twintle commanded, then looked back in her direction, ignorant that their eyes were locked. "Turn over the whole docks. I don't want anyone to rest until the strange sorcerer and her accomplice are brought to me."

21

I T WASN'T UNTIL AFTER they left that Vi's heart decided to knock against her ribs. Nausea rose up and she brought her free hand to her mouth, holding in quivering breaths.

She would've killed them all and delighted in it, even if that meant this world ultimately failed. Some part of her, a part she desperately wanted to ignore, knew that if she indulged in these urges there was no recourse. The worst that happened was the world ended, again. It'd be the ninety-third time. How bad could it really be?

Vi shook her head and closed her eyes, urging the thoughts away.

Yet they lingered.

They clung to her like Raspian's magic, the tiny sparks of red lightning that had danced underneath her skin after she'd used the tear his magic had made in the world to get to the Twilight Kingdom—after she used his words. But she had also witnessed Yargen purge those tendrils of his magic from her when she was being remade.

These urges were her own. She couldn't blame a dark god or desperation born of a dying world. Controlling herself and staying the course was on her own shoulders.

Taking a deep breath, Vi forced herself to calm and began moving. She relaxed her spell and pulled up her hood once more. She could hear people moving outside, low voices drifting in through the doorway. Vi crept forward, scanning the docks; most of the Knights had fanned outward and were now far away.

When she slipped out, the nearest Knight had his back to her, and Vi disappeared into the side alleyway.

She ripped the hood from her head, throwing it on the ground and running from it as though it was about to give chase. As though that was the source of the darkness she'd felt. She weaved through the city, eventually sprinting onto the main road. The castle grew in her field of vision and Vi didn't even bother slowing her pace as she dashed by the guards stationed at the end of the drawbridge.

"You there—"

"It's Yullia." Vi spun, bouncing from foot to foot, stalling long enough for them to see her face before turning and resuming her run. They didn't give chase.

Her side burned as she took the castle stairs two at a time—up the main staircase, then through a door into a narrow spiral stair. She bounded down a hall, not far from where the council chambers were. Vi didn't even bother stalling to check if Deneya was there. Instead, she went right for her room.

The door snapped against the wall, reverberating with a low thud as she threw it open. Vi had to resist the urge to slam it in her haste. Instead, she slowly closed it, locking it behind her.

She raced to her bedside and hoisted the heavy down mattress, flopping it over onto itself. Underneath the mattress were woven grass panels, supported on slats of wood. Vi dug her nails into a panel, prying it upward. She set it aside and then carefully removed one of the wood slats.

With trembling hands, Vi retrieved the Sword of Jadar from its hiding place.

She clutched it to herself, shaking, holding onto it like a child she thought she'd lost. As though the Knights had found it while she was gone. As though she was the one being played the entire time.

Vi cursed under her breath and ran a hand through her hair, trying to get a hold of herself. She had killed before, she'd kill again. Yet something still rattled her about the feeling of how… *easy* it could be. She loathed the delight she could find in it, the feeling that there would be little repercussion.

Risking the end of the world should be repercussion enough. She'd sworn to end this and wouldn't let her emotions get in the way.

Staring at her hiding place and reflecting more calmly on the events of the night, Vi knew it was time to act. Taavin had been right—she had to get the sword away from Norin, especially with Adela closing in. A plan formed in her head and Vi stood, starting for the door once more.

Down the hall and to the left was another room, nearly identical to hers. Vi gave a few soft knocks. Zira was a light sleeper. Anyone who made a living fighting for their life and others had to be.

"Yu—" Zira's eyes dropped to the sword the moment she opened the door. A frown crossed her mouth briefly before it formed into a hard line. "What is it?"

"I have a task for you," Vi whispered softly. "But it won't be an easy one."

"What is it?"

"I need you to die."

"Excuse me?" Zira narrowed her eyes slightly. Vi had the distinct feeling that if she hadn't built up such a solid rapport with the woman, she would already be cut down.

"Not literally. May I come in and explain?"

"You'd better." Zira stepped to the side and Vi entered. Her fingers had gone numb from how tightly she was clutching the weapon.

"The sword needs to be hidden—above all else."

"I don't disagree."

"I want you to take the Sword of Jadar, tonight, and flee the city." Vi leveled her eyes with Zira's, knowing full well what she was about to ask. "I need you to take it, and I need you to die in the eyes of the people."

"So no one comes after me?" Zira reasoned.

"Exactly. We will say you were doing rounds and were cut down by a man in the alleyways." The alleged attacker would, of course, be revealed as a Knight of Jadar. "I will procure a body and there will be a Rite of Sunset held for you tomorrow afternoon."

"Fiera will know then."

Vi had been debating this ever since the plan began to solidify in her mind. "Yes. We can trust her with the knowledge that you are alive. But she won't know you have the sword. She can't know."

"What will she think then?"

"I will tell her we devised a plan to counter the Knights, and they needed to suspect your death. Which isn't untrue." Vi wiggled her fingers on the blade and tried to relax the bowstring-tight tension in her shoulders. It did little good.

"And what will I actually be doing while I'm 'dead'?" Zira asked.

"Take the sword and go to the Nameless Company, visit your daughter, and stay hidden for a time. Let no one there know you have it."

"But they can know I'm alive?" Zira arched her eyebrows.

"Am I wrong to say I trust the Nameless Company to keep the secret?"

"Not in the slightest." She grinned with pride. "The Nameless Company would all die fighting before they gave up my secrets… and we don't discuss the business matters of others."

"Go and hide there." Vi took a deep breath. "After a month… maybe two—enough time that things have calmed here—begin to head East with the sword." The crystal weapon needed to get as far out of reach as possible from the Knights of Jadar. And the East had managed to keep a crystal weapon safe before. She hoped they could do it again. "I'll meet you in Cyven. Linger near the old senate hall there."

Zira looked away and Vi could almost see the wheels turning in her mind as she ran over everything once more.

"If I leave now, wait two months, and then head East, there is a chance I won't make it back for the birth of Fiera's child."

"I know." Fiera was already well into her second term. The primary cleric overseeing her care was fairly tight-lipped about exactly when she suspected the baby had been conceived, which meant Vi's suspicions about her pregnancy during the wedding were likely well founded.

Aldrik's legitimacy was shaping up to be a thinly veiled lie. He had surely been conceived out of wedlock. But the Emperor was adamant that nothing untoward had happened before their wedding night. And if the Emperor declared his wife could have a child in less than the normal term, such would be the official truth as far as the rest of the Empire was concerned.

"I promised her—"

"I'm sure," Vi interrupted, somewhat harshly, "this will not be easy for any of us. But Fiera understands the sacrifices of her position. She always has. And part of why I am doing this now is for the safety of her and the babe. I want the sword gone well before she's vulnerable."

I don't want her to die, Vi stopped herself just short of saying. She wouldn't risk this world's failure for revenge on those who had wronged her family. But she would risk it to save lives.

No matter what Taavin insisted, Vi wanted Fiera to live. Her father needed a mother, the Empire needed its Empress. Her job was to prevent the Crystal Caverns from ever being tampered with, and who was to say—perhaps preventing Fiera's death was the key to all that.

If Fiera lived, the Emperor might remain a more measured man. He might never seek out Vhalla to open the Crystal Caverns. He might even ease some of his brutality in the North.

When Vi looked at everything through that optimistic lens, the future had never seemed brighter.

"We have to do this," Vi said softly, pleading. "We must, at all costs, keep the sword safe. This is greater than you, or me, or even Fiera. More hangs in the balance than I can explain."

Zira approached her silently. Vi felt the weight of her stare and was struggling to keep her knees locked under the pressure it put on her shoulders in addition to all the pressure that was actually there. Zira reached out, resting her hand lightly on Vi's white knuckles. With a reassuring magic only mothers seemed to possess, Vi stopped trembling.

"I will take the sword tonight and go."

"Mother bless you," Vi breathed in relief.

"While I gather my things, go and wrap it in leathers for me. I want it bundled so tightly that you can hardly tell it's a sword at all." Their roles had switched, and now Zira was giving the orders. "Then meet me down in the dungeons."

"The dungeons?"

"You remember the way, I trust?"

"It was the first area of the castle I had the pleasure of touring," Vi said with mock delight. How far she had come from that night. "Let's move quickly, there's no time to waste."

Vi waited in the hallway that led down to the dungeons. It was a singular pathway—easy to block and defend against any kind of breakout. A guard lingered farther on, keeping watch. Though, judging from his heavy snoring, the only thing he was watching were the insides of his eyelids.

"Sounds like Topperen is on duty tonight," Zira murmured as she approached. "I was hoping that would be the case." She passed an iron key to Vi.

"What's this?"

"A key to the cell we need to get to."

"You're not locking me away again, are you?"

Zira snorted. "The time for that has passed. Come along."

They padded down the hall, tiptoeing into the faint glow of the room beyond. Sure enough, an elderly man was sleeping with his head tipped back, mouth open, drool cascading into the stubble of his cheek. He didn't so much as stir as they inched across the room.

Once back into the relative darkness of the first row of cells, they moved faster again. Two men slept with their backs to the bars of the first two cells. Vi recognized the cell she had been thrown into as they passed it.

Zira led them down to the far end of the hall, to a black door nestled into a shadowed alcove. On the other side was a spiral stair, and down that was another hallway of cells that led to another black door.

Down they went—three, four levels of jail cells. Each level became more maze-like, with branches of halls leading off of it. Each level was more rough-hewn, carved into the bedrock that ran underneath the Waste.

Vi stared at the countless empty cells, wondering why there were so many. They seemed to stretch endlessly on into the darkness. All too soon, she answered her own question: the Burning Times. One of the darkest parts of Western history, during the reign of King Jadar, when he rounded up the Windwalkers of the East and used their magic for nefarious purposes.

She looked at the sword she was carrying. How many had died for this sword? Stopping the vicious cycle spiraling around the Crystal Caverns seemed as hopeless as counting every cell in this seemingly never-ending dungeon.

They came to a stop at an unassuming cell. With her thumb, Zira smoothed away the grime and cobwebs that coated the lock.

"Unlock it," she ordered, and Vi did as she was told.

Zira entered the cell and went back to the cot in the corner. The furniture nearly disintegrated when she pushed it to the side and they were both left coughing through clouds of dust. But, as the haze settled, Vi could see a staircase winding down.

"A passage out," Vi said, stating the obvious.

"Not used in over a year now. We might need to get a new cot to hide the entrance."

"When was it last used?"

"During the siege, for scouts."

"Is this the only hidden way out of the castle?"

"Yes."

That explained why they never sent more than scouts. It was a secret too precious to be entrusted to many. And the passage appeared to be too narrow to fit more than a single person at a time—certainly not a way to get the mass amounts of soldiers it would take to launch a surprise attack out of Norin.

"Why didn't King Rocham flee through here?" Vi asked.

"Because he was going to die on and for his land. The idea of flight or surrender never crossed the man's mind. I only learned of it when Fiera entrusted me with that key—to save her siblings if that's what it took."

"Where does it lead?" Vi peered down into the darkness. It was so intense that not even the light of the torch Zira was holding could penetrate more than the first three steps.

"Southwest. It'll let me out of a cliff side."

"Just south of the ridge where all the nobles live?"

Zira paused, staring at Vi for a long moment. "Yes... How did you know?"

"I'm good with maps, and the terrain of the city made it an easy guess." She wondered if this path was anywhere close to the one out of the Le'Dan estate.

Vi handed out the sword to Zira. With it, she felt like she was giving up a part of herself. She had never felt more vulnerable than when she watched Zira's hands closing around the weapon. Doubt fluttered through her mind; the memory of Jayme's betrayal rode on gossamer wings. Instinct told Vi not to trust Zira. But here Vi was, trusting despite every betrayal she had endured.

She was here in this world to bring about the end of cycles. And she'd start with the cycle of people she cared for betraying her.

"I'm putting all my faith in you with this." Vi raised her eyes to Zira's. "Don't let me down," she added softly.

"I wouldn't. Letting you down would be letting Fiera down. If nothing else, trust that I will always do everything in my power to see the wishes of our Empress done. And she wishes the sword to be safe."

It was nearly painful to uncurl her fingers from around the leathers. But Vi did it. "Fiarum evantes," she whispered.

"Kotun un nox," Zira replied, and then disappeared into the darkness.

Vi watched her go, grabbing the watch at her collarbone. The hairs on the back of her neck were on end. Her ears were filled with whispers and the sounds of distant drumming.

This was a moment fate shifted. Vi could feel it.

But had she changed the course of time for the better?

22

THERE WAS THE SMALL matter of procuring a corpse before dawn.

Vi made her way quickly back through the labyrinth of passageways. She trusted her instincts to lead her back and tried not to question too much. Questioning would make her pause, second-guess, and turn around or change course. Doing so would only waste time and get her lost.

Still, she breathed a sigh of relief when she emerged onto the top level of cells.

"*Durroe sallvas tempre*," Vi whispered to mask her footsteps. She treaded lightly past the elderly guard and through the castle.

Out of the castle and across the drawbridge, Vi glanced at the horizon. The sky was still completely dark. She had a few hours before dawn, and before any suspicions could be raised.

Vi made her way through the city to the Cathedral of the Mother. Detached from the main building and off to the side was the city's morgue, where all bodies were held ahead of Rites of Sunset. Bracing herself for the smell, Vi walked into the halls of death.

She was pleasantly surprised that it did not reek of decay. Instead, there was a chalky, herbaceous smell in the air. A Crone was stationed at a wide desk set in the center of the mostly empty, rectangular room. Behind her were rows of tables on which bodies were laid out. Over half of the tables were empty, but several had human-shaped figures underneath dark red cloths.

"Fiarum evantes," the Crone murmured sleepily, bringing her milky eyes up to Vi.

"Kotun un nox," Vi replied dutifully. "Crone, I fear my friend might have fallen today... Do you have any bodies here that have yet to be identified?"

The Crone lifted a gnarled finger, running it down the page of the open ledger before her. Vi was impressed her eyes could still see well enough to read at all, especially in the low light of the room. She tapped a few notes.

"Four are unidentified. Was it a man or a woman?"

"A woman."

"Three, then." The Crone pushed herself upward and Vi could hear the bones in her joints popping.

"Crone, please—" Vi rushed around the table, resting a hand lightly on the elderly woman's back and holding out the other for support should she need it. "Could you tell me which they are? No need to trouble yourself."

"If you don't mind, sweet child?" The Crone gave her a smile. "That would be most kind."

"I don't mind at all. Which tables are they?"

"These." The woman tapped the outlines of three tables in her ledger that corresponded with the back three on the right-hand side. The word "unknown" was scribbled by each of them.

"I'll return promptly," Vi said as the woman settled back into her chair.

The night was going well, almost too well. But given how it had started with the Knights of Jadar, Vi could use a few lucky breaks. In the back corner there were the three bodies. Vi peeled back the coverings of the first two—the third was far too short to be Zira.

Of the two remaining bodies, Vi decided on the woman on the right. Their builds were similar, and whatever misfortune had befallen her was gruesome enough to leave cuts over the majority of her face.

"I'm sorry," she whispered softly to the woman. "But this sacrifice is for all of us."

Vi went back to a clerical table and grabbed a knife. As she cut the woman's long hair to vaguely resemble Zira's, Vi wondered who this person had been. Was she someone important? Or was she someone the world had long since overlooked?

Her heart ached. At the very least, this woman would have dozens mourning for her—even if those mourners were misinformed.

"Yargen bless you," Vi murmured as she covered the body in the sheet once more and burned away the chunks of hair in a flash of fire.

She went back to the Crone and informed her that the body was that of Zira Westwind—that the Empress herself would come to mourn for the loss of her friend and chief guard at sunset. The Crone took Vi at her word and scribbled in the ledger dutifully, even adding that the cause of death was an attack by the Knights of Jadar during guard duty. With that settled, Vi returned to the castle.

Fiera wouldn't be up for a few more hours yet, and Vi didn't feel the need to wake her. Nothing would change if Fiera found out her machinations a few hours later. And Vi could use the time to plan her next moves.

Safely back in her room, Vi settled her bed into place before sitting on it heavily. She rubbed her eyes with both her palms. It felt like forever since she'd last had a good night's rest. But it would wait a bit longer.

"*Narro hath hoolo.*"

Taavin appeared before her, and Vi dragged her eyes up from the toe of his boots to the top of his head, eventually landing her attention on his eyes. He stared down at her; whatever he saw softened his expression.

"You were supposed to be sleeping."

"I know." Vi shook her head and closed her eyes. She couldn't handle the guilt of all she'd been hiding from him. Summoning him had been a bad idea.

"What happened?" he asked softly.

"A lot," Vi whispered.

"You don't have to tell me if you don't want to."

Vi looked up at him and let out a bitter laugh. "I thought I had to tell you everything."

"You should... But I hope you do it because you want to—because you want to save the world. And because you want to confide in me. I can do little else for you right now beyond lending an ear."

"You do more than you know and I don't deserve it." Vi took his hand in hers and hung her head. She'd trudged through a long dark night; she felt like the sun would never rise again.

"You do."

"I don't, because I've lied to you. I've deceived you."

"I know."

Of course he did. Two words had never been more heartbreaking. "Because I always lie to you at this point?"

"No, Vi, because I know you." Taavin knelt before her. "Because I can see it in your eyes."

"Taavin, I didn't—I *don't* want to hurt you." She squeezed his hand. "Somehow I had to balance that with doing what I felt was right."

"I'm fine, Vi. I've endured worse." His grim nature about the fact put a stone in her throat. "I'm more worried about you."

"For the future of this world?"

"For your own sanity," he said gently, covering her hand with his. "I love you just as you are and I want you to be open with me about everything."

"My recklessness included?"

"Your damnable recklessness that might just save our world included." The corner of his mouth quirked up in a smile that was far too endearing for their discussion.

Vi swallowed the lump in her throat and took a slow breath. She wanted to take him into her arms. She wanted him to kiss her until she knew or wanted nothing else.

But she couldn't. Not until he knew everything she had done and still wanted to kiss her after.

"You were right, I wanted to save Fiera. I still do. I want to save her, Zira, everyone else I can, *and* this world. When I saw the vision of my brother... I knew I had to be bolder. If I was to make this the last time for all of us, I had to do something I'd never done before. And I knew you would say no. So I didn't ask..." Vi proceeded to tell him of the past few days. She told him of the long, dull nights watching Twintle's warehouse. She told him of the Knights seeing her, of her fleeing, and giving Zira the sword.

When she finished, Taavin merely continued to stare at her, holding onto her hands tighter than she had clutched the Sword of Jadar before giving it to Zira. But Vi couldn't tell if it was in anger, worry, compassion, or some likely mix of all three.

"Tell me I haven't done the wrong thing," she whispered, her voice hoarse.

"You have never needed my assurance before." He didn't say the words in such a way that would lead her to believe he meant to cause pain. Yet the lack of immediate support cut her deeply all the same.

"But I want it now." Vi took a quivering breath. Perhaps it was the lack of sleep, perhaps it was all the events that had transpired adding up to a tally that was too high. Or perhaps it was his eyes that were making her come undone. "You're correct—I'll continue to do what I feel is right. I will take council, but ultimately make my own decisions. I will not feel regret or guilt for making the best decision I could at any given moment, given all the information available to me but—"

Her throat was thick and gummy, and she choked on her next words. "But…" Vi continued, or she might not have continued at all. "I want someone to say that what I'm doing is all right. Because in this moment I am so tired and unsure. In this moment, Taavin, I do not feel strong and I am laying myself bare before you asking—begging—for you to lend me some strength before morning comes and I have to face the world alone once more."

His thumbs smoothed over the backs of her hands in a motion Vi couldn't be certain was entirely conscious. Taavin listened intently and was silent when she finished. Vi braced herself for his reaction and readied herself to send him away before he could turn his back on her.

"Vi Solaris," he murmured softly. Nothing had ever sounded more delightful than her name gliding across his tongue. A name that she hadn't heard in so long, it made her ache. "You have done nothing wrong. The burden on you is one that no one can understand, not even I. And you handle it with all the grace of your forefathers. You do your parents proud."

She hung her head as her face twisted in pain. Somehow, he'd known exactly what she'd needed to hear. Every last holdout of her strength vanished and she leaned forward.

Her face buried into his shoulder; his arms wrapped around her. Vi dug her fingers into him, grabbing at the tunic he wore, trying to cross through the barrier that coated his skin like oil that she couldn't wash away.

"I wish you were here," she whispered.

"I am here."

"I wish you were real," Vi corrected, pulling away.

Taavin hooked her chin, his thumb pulling lightly on her lower lip. Through lowered lashes he murmured, "Let me show you how real I am."

He pulled at her and she leaned forward. With a soft exhale, his lips brushed hers. She trembled at the barely-there touch. Slowly, he returned his mouth to hers in a toe-curling, tender kiss.

Vi's hand balled into a fist. She wanted to yank him closer. She wanted him to kiss her until her head spun and she was breathless. Yet she couldn't move. She was putty under his shifting hands.

One hand caressed her cheek. His fingertips ran along the edge of her ear—as though he was as fascinated with their differences as she was. His other hand ran up her side, boldly tracing the outline of her breast, but not lingering. It joined the other and he held both sides of her face, kissing her more firmly now.

She leaned back. It was an invitation, one he accepted. Taavin crawled onto the bed and on top of her.

"Say my name again," Vi whispered as their lips parted briefly.

"Vi Solaris," he obliged, husky and deep.

"Tell me you love me," she demanded.

"I love you. I have only ever loved you. I will only ever love you."

Vi pulled him down onto her. She caressed his back and savored what warmth and weight she could feel. Taavin kissed the soft flesh of her neck, a feather-light trail that ran up behind her ear and back down to her collarbone.

"I can't feel you like I once did," she confessed dejectedly. "Now the sword is gone, and I fear I never will again."

He pulled away, propping himself to hover over her. Vi trailed her fingers down his face and chest. She didn't know how much was forced imagination spiced by longing, and how much was truly tactile sensation.

"It's not the same," he admitted, and the admission hurt more than she expected.

"But your words sound as they always have." Vi shifted away, inviting him instead to lie next to her. The space between them made her ache instantly, but even when he curled around her, that distance didn't truly vanish.

She needed him in a way she'd never needed anyone.

In a way she didn't think she'd ever be able to have again. Why hadn't they made the most of their brief moments together in Risen?

"Tell me," she murmured, her eyes sinking closed as she rested her head on his chest. "Have we ever made love?"

"What?" His whole body went tense.

"Before, perhaps?" She didn't have to say, *before I killed you.* "In one of the other worlds?" There could've been another Vi who was bolder than her on Meru. Or a Vi who found his current form to be enough to touch, and kiss, and explore in ways she couldn't bring herself to no matter how much her body burned with want for him. The feeling of him not really being with her was too great a barrier to cross. "Did we embrace as true lovers?"

Vi tilted her head up when he didn't immediately respond. Taavin looked at her with those same lusty eyes. He was seeing something that told her the answer before his lips did.

"Yes."

"Tell me of it?" she breathed. "Tell me how I felt. Tell me how we moved. How you touched me. I want to hear it all." If she couldn't experience it, she would live vicariously through another version of herself.

"Are you certain?" He shifted uncomfortably.

"If you're willing."

"Of course I am. Those are the sweetest memories I have," he murmured, pressing a firm kiss against her mouth to punctuate the sentiment. "The first time was on Meru, in Risen..."

Taavin spoke unhurriedly, and Vi hung on his every sensual word. Each turn of phrase delighted her. Phantom memories ignited within her as though her body remembered what her mind could not. She felt herself burning from the inside out with a fire she'd never known before.

A fire that felt like it could light the whole world.

23

V I DIDN'T GET ANY sleep that night. Come morning, her clothes were rumpled and her skin was flushed from the fire he'd set in her. For the first time, she felt as though she'd lived a hundred lives with him through his endless stories.

And it wasn't enough.

It wouldn't be enough until she could taste him like those other Vis had.

Vi stared at the window. She hadn't shuttered it the night before, but the paper screens were slid closed. The morning's first light was drawing a slow line across the floor and when it hit the bed, Vi knew her exhausting night would officially transition into an exhausting day.

"You never slept," Taavin mumbled from behind her, kissing her neck tenderly. His fingers traced lazy circles around her stomach, pushing up her shirt farther with every pass. It was a game he seemed to be playing—how far he could undress her before he put her clothes back into place.

It was a line they hadn't dared cross all night. If they hadn't crossed it last night… they never would. Not as long as he remained a specter.

"I didn't."

"You should've."

"If I slept, you would've disappeared."

He sighed softly. Vi twisted in his arms and Taavin placed a gentle kiss on her forehead, mumbling, "You have to rest."

"I will tonight, I promise." Her body wouldn't give her a choice. "I wanted to see one morning with you."

"We don't get such luxuries." He smiled sadly.

"I will find a way for us to have them."

"All right, my princess." Taavin let out a chuckle that was part laughter, part scoff, and all disbelief.

"You don't think I can?"

He hummed, a relaxed smirk draped on his face. She wanted to kiss it off. How dare he look so frustratingly handsome first thing in the morning.

"I will pull you into this world if for no other reason than to force you to have morning breath and bags under your eyes and bed head with me," Vi threatened.

"I would give anything in the world for that. Anything to be a normal man, and for you to be a normal woman. But that is not our destiny."

"I'm writing destiny now." She wanted the statement to sound strong and full of conviction. But her voice was tiny and wavering. The more she thought about her task, the more impossible it seemed. Especially now with the sword out of reach. What had she been thinking, sending it away? "And I will find a way to bring you back into this world."

His shining green eyes consumed her focus. Vi was only vaguely aware of his hand lightly running up and down her spine. Taavin took a deep breath and Vi readied herself to combat his obviously forthcoming objection. But instead he kissed her one last, long time.

"You should go," he said.

"I should."

"Do you need me to vanish to make it easier for you?"

Vi laughed lightly and pulled herself from his arms. Their parting hurt, like what she imagined a plant to feel when it was ripped from its roots. "I will summon you again."

"Please do."

At long last, she relaxed the spinning glyph around her wrist and watched him vanish into the air. The parting was familiar, but it hurt more now than she remembered. In a few short weeks on Meru she'd somehow managed to grow accustomed to his physical presence. She'd taken it for granted.

Now, she would do anything to have him back.

Fiera took breakfasts most often in her chambers now, so Vi headed there. The halls smelled of eggs and freshly cooked rice, but the only servants in sight were those who attended to bathing and dressing.

"Good morning," Vi greeted the handmaid outside Fiera's room. She and the two guards surrounding her all nodded. "I have a matter of grave importance to speak with our Empress about."

"Please wait just a moment." The handmaid held up her hands. "Cleric Joan is in with her now—she should be finished shortly."

No sooner had the girl stopped speaking than the heavy wooden door opened and a black-eyed woman emerged. She was as gnarled as a Crone and her skin had long been leathered by the sun. Her hair had turned to white, but she looked at the world sharply. There was still strength in her steps.

"Tell the kitchens I would like her to have plain rice this morning, one sliced prickly pear, and some more of the barley tea from the East," Joan instructed the handmaid.

"I think Jake said they have run out of the tea."

"Then tell him to pull some out of his arse. Or use these supreme culinary skills he keeps bragging about to make something similar. These are not my demands—they come directly from our Empress."

"Yes ma'am!" The handmaid sprinted down the hall. Joan's attention landed on Vi.

"Fiarum Evantes, I'm—"

"No time for or interest in formalities, I know who you are. This whole city knows who *you* are," Joan said dully. "You have a severe look on your face. Whatever it is you have to say, say it well and don't upset her much. This pregnancy is becoming hard on her and if she keeps her stress and work up, she's headed for a difficult labor."

"Understood." The cleric spoke like an officer, so Vi responded like a soldier.

Without another word, Joan left and Vi allowed herself into the royal chambers.

An entry hall opened up to a large sitting area connected to a wide balcony that stretched the length of the quarters. The Emperor and Empress sat out on the balcony, a table between them. Tiberus had draped his coat over the back of his chair. Fiera wore her hair long and unbound, her simple dress cut generously to accommodate her protruding stomach.

"Is breakfast already—" Fiera turned, her expression dimming when she realized food hadn't arrived, then brightening again when she realized who had arrived instead. "Yullia, what a delightful surprise!"

"It is impossible for newlyweds to have a morning alone," Tiberus grumbled, just barely loud enough for Vi to hear.

"Forgive my interruption, your highnesses. Were this not a matter of supreme importance, I wouldn't have come so early."

"Matters of supreme importance seem to follow you," Tiberus said with a glance at her. He had a stack of papers Vi vaguely recognized. They were nearly identical in format to the trade and grain reports her father used to study.

"Your highness, they follow *you*—I am merely graced by proximity."

"Your flattery is improving." He didn't even look up this time.

"Well, I do seek your indulgence."

"In what?" Fiera asked.

"I would like a word alone with you," Vi responded directly to her.

Fiera looked between Vi and Tiberus. "Anything you say to me, you can say to my husband."

"Very well." Vi couldn't blame her. It was a stretch to separate them at this point. She knew Fiera's primary goal was to keep peace in her growing family for the sake of all of Mhashan. Even with the Emperor's heir growing within her, she still acted cautiously. "It's regarding Zira," Vi started delicately, remembering what Joan had just told her. "I'll say foremost, she's well."

"All right," Fiera said slowly, understandably confused. She turned to Tiberus but the man shrugged slightly to indicate he had no idea either. "Why wouldn't she be?"

"Because this sunset we will go to the Cathedral of the Mother to mourn her death."

"I don't follow."

"The Knights of Jadar are getting bolder, your majesties. Just last night there was an attack down at the docks resulting in Lord Twintle's warehouse being burned." Vi resisted a satisfied smirk.

"Traitorous snakes, I told you to cut them off at the head." His words lacked any real bite. Clearly, this was an argument they'd had too many times for scathing words surrounding the Knights to still cut deeply.

"I told you there were good men among them—men who now fight for Solaris." Fiera gave a sideways look at Tiberus and then turned her attention back to Vi. "So I assume Zira is off taking some kind of action against them?"

"Yes, I've acquired intelligence about their network in the Waste. We hope to cut off their support and force them to the surface. But for our plans to work, they must believe Zira is dead—she must be an unknown factor in play."

"I see." Fiera stroked the bulge of her stomach in thought.

Tiberus glanced up at her and Vi was caught in his ocean blue eyes for a long second. In them, she saw the eyes of her brother.

"You really are a dangerously clever one."

"And I use my cleverness to support Solaris." Vi could read between the lines. She knew what he was really saying.

"Let's hope so, and that Zira is not the latest convert of the Knights. Otherwise we'll have to kill her, too."

"Zira would never betray me," Fiera insisted to Tiberius. Then, she said to Vi, "I will do what must be done this sunset to mourn her. But regarding a body to burn—"

"Fear not, I've already taken care of the logistics," Vi interrupted.

"I'd better not ask for specifics, then, and merely thank you for your continued service to the crown."

Vi gave a low bow. "The honor is mine," she said and dismissed herself.

On the way out, when he no doubt thought she was out of ear-shot, Vi heard Tiberus say, "You should keep an eye on that one. Someone who is always at the center of trouble is likely the cause."

More than you know, Vi wanted to say. The world was a puppet, and it was her job to pull the strings.

She headed right for Deneya's office, checking her watch along the way. It was still two hours before the council was scheduled to meet. That should be enough time.

"Deneya," Vi said as she entered. Thankfully, the woman was behind her desk. Vi had learned that Deneya gave herself extra time in the mornings to prepare for meetings on account of how the numbers and letters "danced" across the page.

"Whenever you show up with that face, it's rarely good."

"I've never claimed to be a good omen."

"Then you're living up to expectations." Deneya returned her quill to its inkwell and leaned back in her chair. "What do you need me for this time?"

"I need you to adjust the docket for today's meeting."

"That's usually Ophain's responsibility. Take it up with him."

"He likes you better," Vi countered.

"I can't argue that." Deneya stood. "What am I having him adjust?"

"The head of the city guard will need to discuss the Knights of Jadar."

"Why?" Deneya asked cautiously.

"To talk about last night's arson of course. Poor Lord Twintle."

"What did you do?" Deneya almost sounded delighted. "And how dare you for not taking me with you to do it. I would've loved to *juth starys* the man seven ways to the next world."

"Hopefully there is no next world," Vi mumbled.

"What?"

"Change the docket. I have to file a report with the head of the city guard." Vi started for the door. "A murder and arson in one night… The Knights were busy."

"Wait, murder? Tell me—"

"No time." Vi shot the woman a smile over her shoulder and was off down the hall.

Despite getting little to no sleep, she felt great. Control was an intoxicating thing. And Vi was finding she couldn't get enough.

"Forgive me for my tardiness." Twintle arrived for the meeting at the last possible minute. The man had still donned his impeccably tailored and pressed clothing, but there were hairs out of place and stubble was on his chin that wasn't usually there.

He looked like a man who had not slept an hour the night before and Vi delighted in it.

"The man of the hour," Euclan, head of the city guard, said from the end of the table.

"We're all sorry to hear of last night's misfortune," Ophain said with sincerity.

Vi resisted the urge to tell the royal that Twintle was the last one he should feel bad about. Twintle was the one attempting to orchestrate the fall of Ci'Dan and Solaris. Vi kept her mouth shut and a small smile in place.

"Yes, my misfortune…" Twintle said cautiously, looking from person to person. His eyes lingered for a little longer on Vi.

"The Knights of Jadar are getting too bold." Ophain shook his head. "That's why Euclan is here today to discuss what we can do about them."

"The Knights of Jadar?" Twintle repeated, confused.

"Yes, the arson at your warehouse is believed to have been sparked by them," Euclan said.

"That's… not possible." Twintle shuffled back a step.

"I understand how hard it is to see an order that you yourself were a part of fall so far. It guts me to see it." Ophain balled his hand into a fist. "Fiera has pleaded with our Emperor for leniency. But I think the time for such things has long since come to an end."

"Especially given the murder."

"Murder?" Twintle was on repeat and Vi relished his confusion.

"The Knights of Jadar murdered Zira Westwind last night when she was on patrol," Vi said sadly. "She was ambushed and cut down. They acted like a band of thugs to bring down one woman." Twintle narrowed his eyes at her and Vi could see the veins in his neck bulge. She sighed heavily, intentionally mistaking his expression to rub salt in the wound. "I know, it's heartbreaking. There will be a Rite of Sunset for her this evening."

"Then…" Twintle finally ground out, "allow me to suggest we focus on mourning the loss of one of our own, rather than worrying about my warehouse. I'll be able to get it back in order straight away. It was only property, after all. A loss of life is far more severe and our focus should remain there."

"Good of you." Ophain gave Twintle a nod as the lord took his seat.

"That still leaves the matter of defending our fair city from the Knights of Jadar. The murder of one of our Empress's right-hand women should be treated as nothing less than an attack on the crown itself. I would propose…"

Vi tuned out Euclan and instead focused on the quill she was twirling in her fingers. However, the sensation of a pair of eyes on her quickly stilled her hands. Vi slowly lifted her gaze to meet Twintle's. His stare was unwavering. The man was barely controlling his rage.

Without so much as blinking, Vi looked back to Euclan and pretended not to notice Twintle's intense stare for the rest of the meeting. He somehow knew this all circled back to her.

Part of her hated the fact. It meant he'd be watching her every movement. But a part of her was satisfied by his discovery.

Let him hate her.

Let every Knight of Jadar hunt her down. She would find a way to bring about their end, and save this world.

24

IT HAD BEEN NEARLY three weeks since Zira left with the sword and there hadn't been any word or further issue from the Knights. Vi's days had become almost routine, each starting with her practice with Yargen's magic.

Magic was magic. Taavin had told her so once, long ago, when Vi was first attempting to make sense of her powers. All sorcery was a means to harness the gift of Yargen, everything made possible by words, or feelings, or sparks of power.

Yet, in her, Vi could feel something different and distinct. Something that hadn't been there before. She could feel her own powers of fire and light. They crackled under her skin and sprang forth with a command. But there was also something more.

Something Vi had long since decided was the power of Yargen itself.

Holding out her hand in the early morning light, Vi focused on pooling that magic within her palm. Yargen had entrusted her with the remnants of her power from an old world. So why shouldn't she be able to use it like any other magic?

A hazy blue glow collected around her fingers. Vi narrowed her eyes and took a slow breath. She worked to distance herself from each inhale and exhale. The slightest jostle would disrupt the intense focus it had taken to get this far.

Tiny flashes and motes of light appeared in the thickening haze of magic. It felt as though she held a small microcosm in her fingers. Every muscle was rigid, her joints aching from holding herself in a precise form.

More power. Vi attempted to dredge it up from every nook and cranny. Her hand began to tremble; sweat beaded on her brow. She was going to lose it.

All at once, the power snapped back into place with a *pop* she could feel in the center of her chest. Like the rush of Deneya's spiced liquor, Vi shivered as it flooded her veins and made her head spin. Pulling out Yargen's power at all was nearly impossible. But if she had more…

If she had the sword.

Vi pushed the thought from her mind. Everything was going according to plan. The last thing Vi would do was muck it up by seeking out the sword.

She'd be reunited with it soon enough, anyway. But first, she had to ensure Fiera survived through her childbirth.

Shrugging on a cropped vest over her tailored, sleeveless shirt and tight-fitting pants, Vi departed her room for the day. She ran through the day's obligations in her mind: she would oversee the soldiers' training, get the reports from Euclan on the city guard, then ensure rounds and rotations for the soldiers were in order.

Zira had done a lot more to keep the castle and city guard running than Vi had given her credit for. Since Vi was the one to send her away, it was now her responsibility to oversee those obligations. Luckily, she'd been trained for the majority of her life to delegate, plan, and lead.

"Euclan, tell me what I need to know," Vi demanded as she entered the cramped guard office next to the training field.

A silver pot of steaming kaha was set beside two clay mugs, adjacent to two bowls heaped with steaming rice topped with egg and shallot. She'd begun to form a routine, and fortunately the castle staff had picked it up quickly. It made it easy for Vi to remain efficient in these busy mornings.

"Twenty guards have requested leave."

"Twenty?" Vi asked as she poured kaha for them both. When she was younger, she would've taken it with some kind of cream or sweetener. But much like she'd found a taste for liquor, Vi had discovered she liked the bitter liquid first thing in the morning. It sharpened her senses even after the longest nights. "That seems a little high, doesn't it?"

"Bad timing, but most of the men have never interacted with each other. Thank you." Euclan took his kaha, drinking it slowly. "I thought perhaps it could be something nefarious... but four of them are imminently awaiting children—"

"So many babies," Vi murmured.

"The post-war phenomenon," he chuckled.

Vi ran her nail along the edge of her mug. *Children.* She'd always expected she'd have some of her own for the purpose of heirs at the very least. But now... Vi pushed the thoughts from her mind.

"In any case," Euclan continued. "I thought perhaps it could be the Knights of Jadar infiltrating our men. But that doesn't seem to be the case."

"I appreciate your vigilance." The Knights of Jadar had been quiet. Vi suspected they were off licking their wounds and planning their next attack. "Let's continue to play it safe—take twenty of the best from the castle tonight for the city patrols."

"You don't need them here?"

"I'll figure it out," she said confidently. "Now, what's next on the docket?"

Vi shoveled food into her mouth as Euclan ran through the day's obligations. Her bowl was clean when he finished.

"As usual, thank you for your time."

"It's my job, now." Vi wiped her mouth with the back of her hand.

"You're a natural. We're lucky to have someone like you to replace—" Euclan was interrupted by the training-side door opening.

Vi's eyes met a familiar pair of dark orbs. She'd know that terrible, spiked haircut anywhere.

"Forgive my intrusion." Luke gave a low bow.

"We were just finishing," Vi said before Euclan could get a word in. "Thank you for your hard work, sir. We'll meet again in two days' time as normal."

"Fiarum Evantes."

"Kotun un nox."

Luke stepped to the side, allowing Euclan to pass. The two exchanged a nod, but little other indication of formality. Vi appreciated the fact. She didn't want to see Luke too friendly with anyone who came in and out of the castle.

"You say it well," Luke said.

"Say what well?"

"That colloquialism of Mhashan."

Vi picked up her mug and took a sip. The kaha had gone cold. But she wanted to keep her mouth busy for a moment to think through what to say next. "I am Western."

"No red-blooded Mhashanese would ever call themselves Western," Luke replied with a dangerous edge to his voice.

"What do you want?"

"Where would I find Lord Ophain at this time of day?"

"Lord Ophain?" Vi repeated. "Why?"

"Is it common for guards to question nobles on their business?"

"Only in the interest of castle security," she replied.

"Do you think I'm a threat?" He smiled thinly.

She'd lose either way. If she said no, she passed up the opportunity to question him further. If she said yes, he'd know she had some idea about the role he might be looking to play.

"The son of the illustrious Lord Twintle and a former Knight of Jadar? Of course I don't think you're a threat." Vi set her mug down lightly, resisting the urge to throw it at his smug face. "This way, please."

She led him into the castle and wound upward through the staircases and long hallways to the royal chambers. There was an audience room at the start done entirely in crimson trimmings and bright red lacquered wood. Vi sat Luke down there, stationing a guard at the door to keep an eye on him before she went and got Ophain herself.

"My Lord, forgive me for troubling you so early." Vi dipped into a low bow as Ophain answered his door. "Lord Twintle's son has come calling for you."

"Ah, yes, that is this morning." Ophain looked back into his room where food still sat out amid a mess of papers.

"I've placed him in the sitting room. Do take your time, my lord. He'll be comfortable while he waits."

"Thank you, Yullia." Ophain smiled at her. It was a wide, toothy expression. Whenever he smiled, all similarities with her father vanished.

"You're welcome."

Vi dismissed herself, but rather than heading back to Luke, she trusted the guard to do his job and instead headed for Deneya's office. She didn't like the fact that Luke was here, and if anyone would have a clue as to why, it'd be Deneya.

She knocked on Deneya's door and waited. Then knocked again when there was no reply. Vi checked her watch. It was late for the woman not to have arrived yet. Luke's presence was making her paranoid and Vi's mind ran through every possibility of misfortune that could've befallen Deneya before she showed up.

"You had me worried." The words burst from Vi as she nearly ran the length of the hall to the woman who'd just emerged from the spiral stairwell. Deneya blinked at her, startled.

"Worried? Why?" Deneya glanced around before adding under her breath, "And aren't you usually the worrisome one?"

"Exactly, don't take my title." Vi fell into step beside the woman. "Now, unlock your office, I have something I need to ask you."

"Say please." Deneya stopped at the door, grinning at her.

"Please," Vi said sweetly, batting her eyelashes.

"All right, in with you."

Vi stepped inside, spinning in place to hold out an eager hand. "Do you have today's matters?"

"I grabbed it from Ophain before coming here." Deneya slid a slip of paper from the stack she held and handed it to Vi.

"So you saw Ophain, then. Did you see Luke, too?"

"Luke? Why would I?" Deneya asked, but then immediately followed up with, "*Oh…*"

"Oh? Oh, what?"

Deneya sighed, cursing under her breath in a tongue Vi didn't recognize. She went behind her desk, setting down the satchel. "That explains it, then," she mumbled, rummaging through the bag.

"Explains what? You seem to be having a very good conversation with yourself. Care to share?"

"Yes, sorry." Deneya handed Vi another letter. On the outside was a broken wax seal. The wax was black, imprinted with two swords fesswise—the Twintle family crest.

Vi scanned the papers, reading aloud. She didn't know if Deneya had the chance to read them yet, and the woman seemed to appreciate it when Vi offered another set of eyes.

"Lord Twintle has cast off his fleet for Oparium… seeks to establish a trade route with the South…" Her attention drifted to the docket for the day's council meeting. "Councilor Luke, maritime." Vi returned the papers to Deneya. "So Twintle is gone, and Luke is here in his stead."

Deneya nodded. "Everything happened quickly last night. Though I can't say why."

"What did you find out?" Vi asked. Deneya had continued to case the city at night for information, searching in areas Vi didn't have time for.

"Twintle had business on the seas, so he left." Business by itself wasn't particularly alarming. But when it came to the Knights of Jadar, Vi was suspicious of every movement. "It makes sense Luke is operating in his stead."

Vi sighed. "I suppose it does. But I still don't like it."

"He's likely just trying to move some of those rubies you found."

"I'm worried it's more than that." Vi tapped her knuckles on Deneya's desk in thought.

"How so?"

"In his last meeting with the Knights, he said he was trying to work with Adela to get the sword."

"What? You didn't think to mention the pirate queen's involvement before now?" Deneya rounded the desk. "That seems rather important."

"Things were quiet, the sword is gone and should be on its way to the East by now." Vi shook her head. "I continued to hope that the mention of working with Adela was merely the ravings of a madman seeking to make himself look stronger and more influential than he actually is."

"You're right about Twintle being a madman." Deneya folded her arms. "Mad enough to actually go through with it."

"And if he's gone out to sea, there's a possibility you're right." Vi cursed under her breath. "Keep a close ear on the ground for any indication of Adela's actions."

Deneya nodded. "Though I suspect she won't step foot on this continent herself... She has middle men for that."

"Good." Because if Vi saw her again, she just might kill her this time.

"There's one other thing," Deneya cautioned.

"Tell me it's good news. I could use some."

Deneya shook her head solemnly. "Your name is being whispered among the Knights."

"My name?" Vi wished she could be more surprised. But she'd toed the line too boldly with Twintle following the warehouse incident.

"Not much else. But they're cautious and suspicious about you. Be careful, and trust no new friends."

Vi gave a bitter laugh. "You don't have to worry about that. I'm skeptical of everyone."

"Even me?" Deneya arched her eyebrows.

"Even you," Vi replied, though the words didn't ring entirely true. Deneya had worked her way underneath Vi's barriers. Just as Fiera and Zira had.

"You're usually better at lying than that." Deneya gave her a sly grin. Vi snorted in reply.

"Don't push your luck." She started for the door. "I'll see you at the council meeting."

"Drinks tomorrow?" Deneya asked, as though they were casual friends and not allies discussing espionage.

"Usual time and place," Vi replied and stepped out of the woman's office, bracing herself for the council meeting.

"You have to relax at some point," Taavin scolded. "Being on edge all the time is killing you."

"Being on edge keeps me alive," Vi muttered. She was laid back on her bed, her head in his lap as he rubbed small circles into her temples. Even with the quiver of magic between the pads of his fingers and her skin, his touch could still relax her.

"It's been, what, six weeks since Zira left?"

"Just over five."

"Five, then. No real movements from the Knights of Jadar, Fiera is well, Zira is alive."

"I don't know for sure if Zira is alive." She wished she'd found a way to communicate with the woman. No contact was for the best—it kept both of them and the sword safe.

"I have a feeling you'd know if she wasn't."

"How?" Vi opened her eyes, looking up at the man hovering over her.

He still had the crescent-shaped scar on his cheek—a mark of his old life. All of Vi's scars had vanished when she had been reborn in this new age. Her body was unblemished in its remade form. Some part of her envied the man for retaining his marks. Her scars had been like war medals, showing all she had survived.

"I just do." Taavin shrugged.

"Helpful." Vi allowed her gaze to go unfocused as her eyelids dipped closed once more.

"When are you going to reunite with her and the sword, again?"

"Once I'm confident Fiera is safe. Likely after my father is born." The statement had an odd ring to it, since Vi knew the Aldrik who would be born wasn't really her father—her real father was lost with an old world. Her mind knew the truth, but her emotions were still catching up. "Fiera seems ready to pop any day now. Shortly after she gives birth, there will be a blessing on the child. I've already asked Fiera to start letting it slip around servants that the Sword of Jadar has gone missing and lament over how it won't be present for the blessing."

"You intend to drive the Knights from the city, and away from Fiera, by letting them know the sword is elsewhere."

"That's my hope."

"And you think the servants can get word back to the Knights?"

Vi bobbed her head yes. If Deneya was to be believed, word was getting out of the castle somehow. The most obvious break in the chain would be a servant, someone easily overlooked by most nobles.

"Everything just has to stay according to—" Vi was interrupted by a knock on her door.

"Who's that?" Taavin whispered.

"I don't know," Vi mumbled. "Stay out of sight. I'll release the glyphs if someone's about to come in."

He nodded, stepping into a corner of her bedroom as Vi side-stepped through the sliding screens into her sitting area. She opened the door to find an unfamiliar servant waiting there, a letter rested on a silver tray.

"Apologies for bothering you. A courier arrived with this and said it was of supreme importance."

"What type of courier?" Vi asked, picking up the letter. It was folded into thirds, a wax blob holding it closed. There was no insignia to indicate who it might be from.

"A city courier. I have no other information, m'lady." The young man bowed. "Good evening."

"Good evening," Vi replied before locking the door behind him.

"A letter?" Taavin asked as he emerged.

"Yes, and a strange one at that. It's sealed, but there's no crest." Vi flipped it over. "Yullia" was scribbled on the front with the words "imperial guard" underneath. She pressed on the folds, popping the letter open like an eye. Like this, she could make out the words inside. "Not sealed well." Vi frowned, thinking of Jayme reading her letters.

"'I require you for a matter of grave importance. Meet me at the Hog and Bone Inn, room fourteen. *Fiarum evantes*,'" she read aloud.

"That's it?" Taavin moved to her side, reading over her shoulder, confirming the answer to his question. "Speaking of suspicious things…"

Vi set the letter down on her chair, intentionally leaving it where it could be found by someone looking for her if something went awry. She grabbed a cloak from her closet and strapped a sword onto her hip.

"Wait, you can't be thinking of going." Taavin grabbed her wrist.

"Of course I am."

"What if it's a trap by the Knights?"

"Then I'll kill them all and show them I'm not one to be trifled with. Then they'll know their best course of action is to clear out of this city," Vi said with all the vitriol she felt for the group.

"Think about this logically…"

"I am."

"No, you're acting on emotion and indulging your vendetta. You're reaching for too much, Vi. First saving everyone, now eradicating the Knights of Jadar. *Some things are meant to happen*, and preventing them will be met with failure at best, or at worst…"

"At worst?" Vi prodded when he trailed off.

"At worst you could create a world where you're not born again. Where there is no Vi Solaris."

"If everyone I love lives long and healthy lives in that world, then so be it."

"You don't mean that."

"I do." Ever since her vision at the docks, Vi had come to terms with the idea of not existing herself if it meant the world was safe. If Vhalla, Aldrik, and Romulin lived on, even if they weren't really her family, it would be enough for her.

"And if you fail in this timeline and there is no new Vi—no Champion—they'll all be condemned to death by Raspian's blight."

Vi bit the insides of her cheeks and scowled at the door. "I know all this. I'll be careful, I promise."

"Vi—"

She dismissed him with a wave of her hand. Taavin vanished, though his words lingered. They clung to her like he had, holding her in place.

Was he right? Was she overreaching?

Vi shook her head and started forward, out her door, down the hall, and out of the castle. She had everything under control. She was the one with all the power, pulling the strings.

She had nothing to fear.

25

VI KEPT HER HOOD up and her head down all the way to the Hog and Bone Inn. The inn wasn't far from the main entrance of the city, a fairly straight shot from the castle. But Vi took a longer route. She wandered down side streets and sprinted through alleyways.

She glanced over her shoulders and remained as alert as possible. But the night was quiet, and she arrived at the quaint inn without issue.

The building was four stories tall, long but not particularly wide. Its storefront was well lit with two iron lanterns and she could hear the sounds of mugs clanking and music from the bar within. Not wanting to raise suspicion by lingering, Vi entered and headed directly for a back hallway.

It looked like rooms one through ten were on the first floor, so Vi proceeded to the second. Sure enough, the first room she crossed had the number eleven painted on the door. Halfway down the hall was fourteen.

Vi stood outside the door, contemplating the latch for a moment. She could mask her face with *durroe*, see who it was first and then come back as Yullia. She could force entry and catch them flat-footed and off-guard.

Balling her hand into a fist, Vi went for the simple and most direct approach—she knocked, and held her breath as the door cracked open.

Her eyes met a familiar dark pair. They were framed by a short-cut fringe and hair that didn't extend past the ears. Even though the woman's clothes were different, Vi recognized her with ease. That meant anyone else could too.

"What in the Mother's name are you doing here?" Vi half-whispered, half-snarled. Then looked around quickly to make sure the hall was still empty. Thankfully, it was.

Zira opened the door slightly wider, and Vi took the invitation, allowing herself in. The swordswoman didn't speak until the door was closed once more and locked. "I had to come and warn you."

"Warn me?" Vi did a quick sweep of the room. A bed against the wall to the right, a chamber pot in the corner to the left, a dresser… the lack of things made the sword's presence all the more noticeable. "You brought the sword back? You even made a stand for it?" Vi balked at the little wooden stand, emblazoned with a silver phoenix.

"It felt right to give it a place of honor, even when I was on the road."

"I told you not to let anyone know you even had it." Vi spun, advancing on the woman. The conspicuous stand was the least of her worries. "Are you mad?"

"I had to bring it with me. I wasn't about to entrust it to anyone else," Zira said, defensive, holding her ground as Vi intruded on her personal space.

"Of course not, because you were supposed to take it East. By now you should've been past the Crossroads, by now it should've been long free of their reach." Vi wanted to scream. She'd never been so angry. She never expected someone to make her feel more vicious than Jayme had.

But here they were.

"I am only here one night," Zira said calmly, levelly, as though speaking to Raylynn during a tantrum. "Only one night to warn you."

"You leave *now*."

"Then let me say what I came to say. I'm here anyway."

"Very well. Speak."

"I did as you said—I went to the Nameless Company and waited. Eventually, word of my 'death' arrived back to me. I left the Nameless Company and traveled on the road through the deep Waste, places where the Knights of Jadar are strong. There, I learned that they're planning an attack on the castle with forces they've gathered from Adela. They say they have powers beyond what we can imagine. Powers of the Pirate Queen and—"

Vi held up a hand for silence. She took several deep breaths, more like panting, to prevent herself from shouting. Her plans... all her careful plans... were coming undone because of one woman's foolish honor and ill-thought decision.

"I know about the plan to work with Adela," Vi said, dangerously composed.

"You do?" Zira seemed honestly surprised. "They were speaking as though it was just coming together, as though—"

"Why do you think I sent you away?" Vi gripped the woman by the collar. Zira's hands flew up, grabbing Vi's wrists so hard the bones popped. But Vi continued to cling through the pain. "What do you think prompted the sudden urgency?"

"Unhand me," Zira commanded, deadly soft.

Vi obliged, but only reluctantly. She spun away before she really did try to throttle the woman. Vi ran a hand over her hair, smoothing away the pieces that had escaped the taut braid she'd woven through and around a knotted bun.

"All right, listen." Vi looked back to Zira. "We can still fix this. You take the sword and go now, tonight. It isn't safe in this city." Especially not with Twintle on the move. "Go back to the Nameless Company once more, wait just a week or two to make sure no one is following you, then continue on."

"And you'll still meet me in Cyven?"

"Yes. I'll find the sword wherever you are, have no doubt about that." Even now, it called to her. Perhaps it was all the work Vi had been doing to further explore and manipulate Yargen's magic. But she felt it even more keenly than before—even with it wrapped tightly in layers of leather, even without touching it. "I'll leave now. Wait just a little, to let anyone following me do so, then you slip out after."

"All right." Zira nodded curtly. "Yullia, I was only trying to—"

"I know." Vi met her eyes. "I know you were trying to protect our Empress. But you must have faith and believe me when I say that protecting Fiera is my current, sole goal. All of this is for her, and her child."

"Very well. I'll trust you, and meet you in the East."

"Good."

Without another word, Vi stormed out of the room. She barely resisted slamming the door behind her to punctuate the conversation. She knew she'd acted rashly. She understood Zira's motivations. She'd apologize later. Right now, she was seeing red, and sparks were crackling against her hands. Her fingers were clenched so tightly they hurt. But Vi was afraid that if she unraveled them, her spark would get loose and burn the whole place down.

Vi emerged into the cool desert air and gulped it down like a tonic that would soothe the flames raging within her. She walked several paces into the street and stopped. Tilting her head back, Vi looked at the stars above and tried to relax the tension throughout her body.

A familiar voice interrupted her thoughts. "Are you all right?"

She didn't believe for a second that he or his smug grin actually cared about her. Luke strolled out from the inn. *Had he been in the bar when she'd entered?* Vi struggled to remember.

"What do you want?" Vi asked.

"Is that any way to address a lord?" He arched his eyebrows. "I think not. It's odd to see you in this area of town, at this time of night."

"I didn't notice you paid such close attention to my comings and goings," Vi said flatly.

"I think people notice what you do a lot more than you give them credit for."

"I'm flattered." Vi started back toward the castle. She needed to get Luke away from the inn before Zira left.

"I'm glad I could flatter you. I do hope you have a good night, Yullia. I'll see you at tomorrow's council meeting. I can't wait for Euclan's report. The Knights of Jadar are becoming so infamous, next we'll hear about them killing ghosts."

Vi stopped dead in her tracks. She was so focused on her general annoyance with Luke, so overwhelmed with her hatred, that Vi didn't realize what he had been doing—stalling. She hadn't asked the right questions out the gate. Like, why was he there at this time of night? Or, had he followed her?

Her stomach went sour. Without another second's hesitation, Vi sprinted back into the Hog and Bone.

The bar downstairs was as cheerful as it had been when she'd left. Though three patrons who had been hunched around the corner of the bar were now gone. The hairs on the back of her neck lifted upright.

No, no, no, her mind repeated over and over.

Movement at the very back caught her eye; in the alleyway behind the inn, the flutter of a cloak rippled in the dark before the door snapped shut.

Vi dashed out the back door and into the dingy alley. Darkness clung like grime in all the corners. Two men and one woman were arguing about thirty paces away.

"... payment and then you'll have it."

"Give it to me now," the man on the right snarled.

Vi didn't have to wonder what "it" was, given that the woman was holding the sword.

"Drop it and I'll let you live," Vi lied. She was going to kill them all.

The three turned. Vi's heart dropped though her stomach at the sight of the woman.

Across her forehead in place of eyebrows were three faintly glowing dots.

A morphi. There was a morphi in Norin.

"*Juth c—*"

"*Juth mariy.*" The man on the right stopped her magic, shattering it before it could form. He said to the woman, "Go, they know the deal."

The woman holding the sword leapt into the air and the dark wings of a large crow stretched out between the pulses of magic. The Knight of Jadar stared, slack jawed, as she flew away. He blubbered, trying to make sense of what he had just witnessed—until the other man uttered a quick, "*Mysst soto larrk,*" and cut his throat then and there.

"They said a 'strange sorcerer' was here," the pirate said with a smile. "I assume you're one of Lumeria's?"

Vi didn't even dignify him with a response. "*Juth calt.*"

The man crumpled, dead on the spot. Yet another from Meru who hadn't considered all the creative ways Yargen's words could be used. She looked upward, scanning the dark sky. But the morphi was already gone with the sword. And that meant—assuming "they could pay" as the pirate had said—it would be in the Knights' hands before dawn.

Cursing aloud, Vi rushed back inside. She ran past the doors and up to the second floor. The door to Zira's room was slightly ajar. Vi pushed it open to confirm her worst fears.

Zira lay dead on the ground in a pool of her own blood.

Vi was transfixed by the body, bile rising in back of her throat. It wasn't for the gruesome way in which she'd died. But for what it meant.

Yargen will come for her life.

You can't save everyone.

Some things are meant to happen.

Every terrible phrase Taavin had uttered in caution seemed to echo up through Zira's gaping mouth. The woman's wide eyes judged every inch of Vi for not heeding them.

The floorboards slammed into her knees as Vi collapsed. Her shoulders hunched and she dug her nails into the wood, feeling it splinter beneath her nailbeds. She exhaled ragged breaths, somewhere between tears and screams.

26

S HE HAD TO MOVE.

She had to pry herself off this hard floor and keep moving. The Knights were likely to investigate, especially when the sword was delivered short of one of their own and one of Adela's men. But Vi was still barely managing to breathe. Her thoughts were jumbled.

"*Narro hath hoolo.*" The moment Taavin's shoes blinked into existence, Vi blurted, "I messed up. I should've listened to you, to my father. I messed up."

His knee met the ground before her, his knuckles hooked her chin, and Taavin slowly raised her face to his. "Tell me how this happened."

It was a soft command, but a command nonetheless—as if he somehow knew that she needed his tenderness, but she also needed orders. They might be the only thing that kept her moving through the shakes that were still trying to take control of her limbs.

"Zira, she came back, the Knights, Adela's men—" Vi stopped herself short, her eyes following Taavin's to the dead body in the room. She restarted, "The letter was from Zira. I came here and met her. She'd learned of the Knights' plot involving Adela and came back to warn me—for Fiera's sake. She brought the sword with her.

"I told her to leave... but I was too late. I don't know if the Knights followed me, or if they'd intercepted the letter and read it. For all I know, one of Adela's men was the courier who delivered it—she seems to be good at using letters to her benefit.

"But by the time I realized, it was too late."

"They killed Zira and took the sword," he finished what she couldn't say.

"Yes... There was a morphi who flew away—a crow. I'm sure they'll bring it back to wherever the Knights are waiting and Adela will have her rubies and they'll have the sword. Assuming she doesn't just take it for herself."

Taavin shook his head. He turned away from Zira, stood, paced to one end of the small room and back. He shook his head again, and again before grabbing it and letting out a groan as if he were in pain. "I thought... I really thought this was it. I let myself believe."

"I can get it back," Vi said, stronger than she'd felt in the past hour. Something about seeing him hurting, in pain, and doubting her brought her strength and conviction rushing back. He needed her to be strong and keep herself together. She was the one who could act and change fate. Vi stood. "I *will* get it back. I know their plan and I know where they're going. I heard them talking about taking the sword to the Crystal Caverns at their meeting. Do you think Adela will help them further?"

Taavin, unresponsive, stared at Zira's cooling body. Vi knelt down and gently pressed the woman's eyelids closed. His gaze didn't waver, and Vi wrapped one arm around his waist, guiding his eyes to her.

"I cannot imagine what you've seen. I know this is likely one more body on the pile," Vi whispered. "But I need your help now. I need you to stay with me and help me fix this." He finally nodded, clarity returning to his eyes. They were both on the cusp of falling apart, barely held together by each other. "In any of my past times, did Adela help the Knights of Jadar after they got the sword?"

Taavin pulled away and held out his hands. He mumbled words of Yargen and power flowed from her watch. Vi waited as he finished culling through all of his memories.

"They maintain a relationship with her, but they've usually only had one transaction at a time, then a longer stretch of time before the next."

"She's no doubt too expensive for them." Vi thought about how hard Twintle had to work to salvage enough rubies to buy just a few of Adela's crew. She looked at the blood-soaked floor again and hated that working with Adela had been a good investment for them. "It's just the Knights and me. I'll ride off and intercept them before they get to the Caverns."

"If you can find them."

"Good point." The Waste was large and it seemed unlikely she'd know the exact path they'd be traveling. "Then I'll go on ahead, and meet them at the Caverns. I'll stop them from turning Yargen's magic against itself."

She started for the door, but was stopped by two arms wrapping around her waist. Taavin squeezed her tightly from behind. Always at her back, always defending and supporting.

"You know just when my bones are rattling," she whispered. "And right when I need you to make sure none pop out of place."

"I know you," Taavin whispered back. "Good luck protecting our world."

The well wishes weren't enough. But nothing he could've said would've been enough. Perhaps he knew it too, because Taavin vanished without another word.

Vi swallowed hard, strode down the hall, and left out the back door of the inn, alone.

The castle was in chaos the moment she arrived. Servants sprinted from room to room. Some carried flowers, others were clerical assistants hauling towels and blankets; most carried food, to the nobles gathering in the main hall, or to the royals waiting in an antechamber not far from the Imperial quarters.

Vi didn't have to ask anyone what was happening. It was obvious enough to her, even without future knowledge.

She trudged up the main, grand stairway of the castle. She ignored the inquiring looks of nobleman and servant alike, as if she'd somehow become someone who knew things the rest of them didn't.

She'd thought that, hadn't she? A bitter smile crossed her mouth. She'd thought she had the upper hand on all of them. Humility was a necessary elixir for her now.

"It's only clerics beyond this point." A young man stopped Vi in the hallway. He wore the usual pale blue of the Southern clerics. The same robes Ginger had worn. "There's a place you can wait right down the hall."

She'd seen the place. She'd ignored it. But Vi didn't point that out. Instead, she smiled and said, "Thank you."

Turning on her heel, Vi walked down the now familiar hallway, realizing this would likely be her last time. She ached all over, but it was hard to put her finger on the exact reason why. Was it because she'd warmed up to this place and its people? Or was it because it was another familial home she was walking away from?

Side-stepping into an alcove, Vi uttered a quick, "*Durroe watt ivin,*" and stepped into the skin of the young cleric she'd met outside of Fiera's door weeks ago.

This time, when Vi passed by the man in the hallway, he merely gave a friendly nod and let her pass.

It was quiet in the Imperial chambers. Ginger had explained the birthing process well to Vi and she'd made it out to be a painful affair and understandably noisy as a result. But there was an almost serene stillness to the air. At least until Fiera's snappish comments broke the silence.

"Out. Out with all of you, I've had enough of your prodding! I will summon you when the pains come with any kind of regularity. Now leave me be to what peace I can manage."

Vi hastily stepped off to the side, positioning herself in a doorway at the end of a bookshelf. From this position, she was mostly concealed from the flow of clerics that streamed out of the room. Vi waited several moments to ensure there were no stragglers before she continued on to the bedroom.

The Imperial bedroom was as lush as Vi would've expected it to be. A bed large enough to fit four grown men was framed by a headboard that stretched halfway up the tall wall. A circular canopy was hung from the ceiling, the gold metal railing mirroring a crown, and supporting bolts of fine white silk fanned out behind the headboard. Pillows were piled high and would've dwarfed any other woman.

But Fiera remained imposing. Even amid all the excess, she somehow commanded the sole focus of anyone who entered the space.

Now, her angry eyes were turned to Vi.

"I told you all to get out. I understand what is happening to my body and will summon you when it is time or I am in actual pain. I have been stabbed through in war; I can handle a few contractions. Now, leave—"

Vi released her magic, allowing the illusion to dissipate like fog on the wind. Fiera, to her credit, didn't shout or cry out. Her eyes narrowed slightly and her head tilted, as though she was trying to figure out what she had just seen.

"Come closer." Fiera lifted a hand off her stomach and motioned to the bed. "Sit." Vi did as she was bid and eased herself onto the edge of the bed. "Who are you, really?"

Vi gave the woman who would be the grandmother of a new Vi a sad smile. "That's a difficult question, because sometimes I'm not sure anymore."

She looked to Fiera's stomach protruding like a massive hill underneath the thin sheet. In there was the man who would be her father. *No,* the man who would be the father to a new Vi. A new family she'd never known.

She still loved that man. And she always would. Just as she already loved the Romulin and Vhalla of her vision, and the Fiera that lay before her. Even though they were different people, they wore the faces of her family. They fit into the person-shaped voids left behind by the past world exactly.

"I've come from a time very far away… but one that looks very much like this one," Vi said softly, bringing her eyes back to Fiera. Taavin had cautioned her against sharing who and what she was—and she never had in any time before. If there were ever a time, this was it. She was already deep in a mess of her own making; how much could being honest with Fiera hurt? "I'm not the same person I was, then. And tomorrow I won't be the same person I am today."

"Time is relentless."

"In ways you can't imagine."

"That magic…" Fiera trailed off and winced. Her hands smoothed over her stomach and the pain seemed to have vanished as quickly as it came. She didn't seem worried, so Vi wasn't either. "Are you from the Crescent Continent?"

"What?" Vi whispered. This was shaping up to be a night of surprises.

"Tiberus told me about it not long after the wedding. Naturally, I didn't believe him until I began rummaging through my father's old records—the ones he'd always kept hidden. There's little written, but there's more than we think there. Tiberus thinks there are powers worth fighting for. Tell me, if he does fight for them, would he be successful?"

"Tiberus's fate is decided," Vi said as gently as possible. "He's long since chosen his path."

She couldn't bring herself to say that Tiberus would eventually fall to another as thirsty for power and conquest as himself. He'd fall before he ever had the chance to attempt attacking Meru. Though, knowing what she did of Meru, that fact was likely for the best.

"I know." Fiera's eyes were sad enough that they said everything her lips did not. She knew the man she'd married. "And my son?"

"What?"

"You can see the future, can you not? Or was it all a lie?"

"I can."

"Then tell me: what is my son's fate?"

Vi took Fiera's hand, wrapping her fingers around the Empress's. "Your son will live a hard life. But he will grow to be a good man. He will be the kind of man who loves his family and his people fiercely. He will defend them at all costs. He will be the kind of man who will board a ship and sail into pirate-infested waters for the woman he loves."

Her voice cracked toward the end. Sorrow flooded her and the only lifeline Vi had was Fiera's hand. She clutched it tightly.

"Good." Fiera's eyes closed as an expression of relief overtook her. She seemed to sit easier on her pillows.

"You didn't ask about your fate."

Fiera looked at her once more, a small smile playing on her lips. "I don't have to."

"Have you seen it?"

"Yes—in your eyes, right now." Fiera squeezed her hand. Vi felt herself unraveling.

"I wanted to save you," she whispered. "I've tried so hard. I've tried everything to save you."

"The Mother has a plan for us all. I'm glad I could protect my people when Tiberus came. That I could honor my family and see the Ci'Dan bloodline live on… it is enough." Fiera gently stroked her stomach.

Vi hung her head, shaking it from side to side. "Her plan for you ends in death. It always does. I've tried more times than you or I can fathom to save you. To give your son the mother he deserves."

"Perhaps there are things my son cannot learn if I am there." Fiera wriggled her hand free, cupping Vi's cheek. "I am not afraid of my future."

Her expression was open and honest. Vi studied those brave eyes, memorizing them, imprinting them on herself. Everyone told her she had Fiera's face. Perhaps, through all this, she could gain her bravery, too.

"I have to go now. I can't stay and try to protect you further from the vicious fate that wants you dead," Vi said, though she didn't move. Fiera was stable, warm, and confident even in the face of overwhelming odds. Part of Vi was trying to steal it through osmosis.

"Where will you go?"

"I tried to protect the sword. I spoke true when I told you that it was my sole duty to defend it and this world… Because of me, Zira gave her life to that end. But the Knights of Jadar have the sword now. And if they go to the Caverns, they will seek to—"

"Use the sword to unlock the power there," Fiera finished. Another wince and another massage of her stomach.

"How did you know?"

"The sword was locked away for a long time… But when the war with Solaris began, my father told me where it was hidden. It was my duty to use the sword to keep our people safe. So I read as much as I could on the old records from the Burning Times." Fiera grimaced at the last two words. It had nothing to do with her body and everything to do with the dark aura cast by mentioning the long-ago period during which the West captured and murdered Windwalkers in the East. "The records held information on the sword—not much, but enough."

"What kind of information?"

Windwalkers were the one affinity on the Dark Isle that was said to be immune to crystal taint. Knowing what she knew now, Vi would postulate it was because of what aspects of Yargen's magic they inherited from the scythe. Or perhaps it was because the scythe had long been removed from the continent. Either way, she made a connection that she never had before: The Burning Times were Jadar's first attempt at unlocking the power of the Crystal Caverns.

"Mostly how the sword could be used to free the deeper power in the Caverns. But the writings had enough on the power within the sword itself that I was able to fortify the barrier that helped protect Norin for so long."

"You… you formed a barrier," Vi whispered. That night of the surrender, she had seen Fiera and the sword—how the wall around Norin had held against all odds. It was more than just the magic of Groundbreakers. Fiera had imbued the wall with the power of Yargen. It explained why the sword had felt weaker than the scythe. "I-I should've spoken to you much sooner," Vi blurted. Guilt swelled like summer heat. If she'd only spoken with Fiera rather than keeping everything a secret, she would've had an ally in figuring out the power of the crystals rather than struggling on her own. "What can you tell me about this barrier? How do I form it?"

"I don't think I could teach you—" another hiss of pain and a deep breath "—at this exact moment."

For the first time in her life, Vi cursed her father.

"Tell me what you can," she implored. "There isn't much time. The Knights have only just taken the sword and if I go after them now—"

"I would if I could." Fiera squeezed her hand. "But it took me years of study to learn and gain even the smallest mastery of that magic. However…"

"However?" Vi asked cautiously. Fiera had a glint in her eye that Vi wasn't entirely certain she liked. It was the sort of spark Vi usually associated with a bad idea. She knew it well, because she'd seen it in the mirror many times.

"I could do it."

"What?"

"After my son is born, I could go with you."

"You— you'll— I haven't given birth before but I know enough to know you shouldn't be riding hard across half the Empire immediately after," Vi said bluntly.

"Weren't you the one to tell me my life is forfeit?"

"I didn't mean—"

"If it is the Mother's will that I die, regardless of what actions you or I take, then allow me this. Allow my death to mean something as my life has meant something."

"I cannot allow this," Vi insisted. "It's suicide. What you're suggesting is suicide."

"If you have magic that allows you to wield flames and take the faces of others, do you not also possess healing abilities beyond those of our clerics here on the Main Continent?"

"I do…" Vi said hesitantly. Well, she didn't. Her use of *halleth* still hadn't progressed very far. But Vi suspected she knew someone who had a much better handle on it.

"Then heal me, relieve my pain, and let me go with you. Perhaps then it won't be suicide like you say. Give me the chance to surprise you and fate itself. Perhaps your error has been trying to save me, when I need to save myself." Fiera settled back on the pillows, wincing once more. "This is my choice. Honor it."

It was a demand Vi finally obliged. She would do her best to see Fiera's will done, and keep her alive as long as possible. Her plans might have been ruined, but she had stayed this long to be by her grandmother's side—no, her friend's side. She would stay longer.

"Very well."

"Good. You know, you're nearly as stubborn as I am." The grin Fiera wore made Vi wonder if she suspected more than she let on. "Now, fetch me a quill and parchment while I still have a clear head and can focus enough to hold a quill. I wish to leave a letter for my sisters."

27

VI HOVERED IN THE alcove she'd hidden in before, wearing the face of the young cleric, this time with Fiera's letter in hand. She watched as Fiera called for the clerics and they bounded through the door, no doubt having been waiting outside the entire time.

Demands flew from Fiera's mouth and the healers began to flit in and out, bustling to meet her orders. Her contractions were coming closer together. She was demanding a draught to speed them further, to "get the child out" of her at all costs.

In the chaos, Vi slipped out unnoticed.

She walked through the halls, waiting until she was alone to release her illusion. Down a narrow wooden stair with handrails so worn by time that they were oiled to a shine, and through a side hallway, Vi let herself into Fiera's old room.

The smell of cinders overwhelmed her. Every heavy velvet chair and curtain was coated in the scent of incense—an aroma too potent to have faded since Fiera moved into what were now the Imperial quarters.

Vi headed for the bedroom, remembering what Fiera had said.

My sisters and I used to leave notes for each other...

They had a system, she'd explained. Fiera seemed to think that once it was known that she was missing, her sisters would execute a covert search. If either of them entered the bedroom, they'd head straight for the ornately carved headboard.

Kneeling on the mattress, Vi pushed on one of the carved suns and it slid to the side, revealing a tiny, hollow space. She placed the folded-up note inside, careful not to break Fiera's seal, then slid it back closed. Vi didn't know what the woman had written. But she trusted Fiera wouldn't betray Vi's true nature. Trusted her enough not to give into curiosity and temptation.

After, Vi headed down to the council. They were all gathered in the chambers and, from the sounds of it, Deneya had brought in her spiced liquor for everyone to enjoy. The fact complimented her plans nicely. If everyone was slightly sauced, they'd notice oddities on a delay.

"You there." Vi stopped a servant as he was about to carry a carafe into the room. "Tell Councilor Denja to step out, please?"

The boy gave a nod. After a few seconds, Deneya emerged as requested. The moment her eyes met Vi's she strolled over, her pace quickening when she was out of sight of the rest of those gathered.

"I'm not going to like this, am I?"

"You didn't like anything about me from the first moment—admit it."

"Sounds about right." Deneya put her hands into the pockets of her trousers, a motion that reminded Vi painfully of Zira. "What do you need, Champion?"

"How committed are you to this post?"

It was likely the Knights would pin the bodies in the alley and inn on Vi or Deneya as repayment for Vi's earlier movements against them. When Fiera vanished, there would be suspicion around that, too—especially since Vi and Deneya would vanish alongside her.

At best, Vi hoped Fiera's letter would absolve them both. Perhaps the royal family would strive to save face by keeping Fiera's disappearance a secret, claiming she died on the birthing bed as they had in Vi's time.

But by now, Vi knew better than to hope for the best.

She had to plan for the worst.

"Lumeria instructed that I was to keep an eye on the events of the Dark Isle, specifically surrounding the Crystal Caverns," Deneya said somewhat cautiously. "Though how I do that, specifically, is up to me."

"Excellent. The Crystal Caverns are just where we're going."

"Excuse me?" Deneya balked.

"I don't have time to explain in detail."

"When do you ever?" She sighed heavily.

"But we're going tonight. How good are you with *halleth ruta*?"

"Quite excellent, if I do say so myself." Deneya puffed her chest slightly.

"Superb. You'll be the one to heal Fiera, then."

"*Excuse me?*"

"I can stop her from feeling pain with *halleth maph*, but my flesh mending needs work. You'll need to go up there as soon as the room quiets following the birth, masquerade as one of her servants or clerics, heal her, then sneak her out. Meanwhile, I'll be readying us to go. I'll take the Empress's warstrider and—"

Deneya grabbed her shoulder, shoving her against the wall. Vi blinked, seeing stars for a moment. The world came back into focus with Deneya's face right before hers, their noses almost touching. The woman was much stronger than Vi had given her credit for.

"Stop, and explain this to me properly if you want my help."

"The Knights of Jadar got help from Adela's pirates. I underestimated them." Accepting fault was a bitter pill, but the more she did it the easier it became, and the faster Vi moved on from it. "There was a morphi and a Lightspinner. The morphi got off with the blade before I could stop her. The Lightspinner is dead."

"Bloody pirate queen," Deneya snarled, though not at Vi.

"If we don't go after them tonight, we might not get to the Caverns before they do. We can get a head start because the Knights need to detour to get the sword from Adela. If they get to the Caverns before we do, Raspian is free. It's over."

Deneya looked at her with her brilliant, purple-ringed eyes. Vi could almost feel her prodding, poking into her brain for the slightest hint of a lie. She must've found none, because Deneya released her.

Vi eased away from the wall, rolling her shoulders. "Help me?"

"What did you say I told you once? The other me in that other world of yours… Seek me out, and my sword is yours."

"Well, is it?"

"Yes." Deneya nodded. "Lumeria put me here to watch over the Caverns. I've been here for decades and you, in a few months, have accomplished more than I could toward that end. I'm aligned with you, Vi, before all others."

"Good. Then pack lightly, but make sure you have all you need. We won't be coming back. After, get to Fiera. She knows of Lightspinning and about Meru. You won't surprise her."

"She does?"

Vi ignored the woman's shock. "She does. When you get her stable, meet me at the entrance to the dungeons."

"Very well." Deneya was clearly still skeptical about the whole plan—which Vi hardly blamed her for—but she didn't question further.

They parted ways and Vi returned to her room, rummaging through it for a pack and two bags. She loaded the pack with basic clothes and supplies. On the way through the castle, she ran to the guards' storerooms for a few salves and potions, then the kitchens for rations, filling the other two bags with as much as they could carry.

Vi headed for the dungeons next. She cursed her luck that the same elderly man as before wasn't stationed at the entrance. It was a young guard whose name Vi couldn't remember. She stashed the bags behind a sculpture two hallways up and then sprinted back down, gulping air to catch her breath so she wasn't winded.

"Report," Vi commanded as she strode into the room.

"Captain!" The man jumped, stuttering over his words. "Nothing new to report. All is quiet."

"How many do we have jailed?"

"Currently, just three here."

"Their crimes?"

"Unruliness… a servant charged with castle theft… one of them is suspected of being a Knight of Jadar." He read off a list.

"No issues from them?" The guard shook his head. Vi forced a gentle smile. "Then I think you should go upstairs and enjoy the festivities."

"Pardon?"

"It's not every night an heir is born. Go, celebrate with the rest for three hours." She hoped it'd be enough time to get Fiera through. If not, Vi would figure out something else when the time came. "I'll take care of things here." Vi punctuated the sentiment with a conspiratorial wink.

"Are you sure?" The man was already headed for the door.

"Absolutely. Go on, have fun, time's ticking." Vi glanced at her watch for emphasis, and when she looked up, he was gone. She counted down a minute before following behind him, backtracking to her supplies, and then returning to the dungeons.

Down into the darkness, Vi wound through the mazes of cells. Even though she'd only been down this way once, Vi walked with confidence. Her mind had instinctively made a map of the area.

With the key Zira had entrusted her with, Vi opened the cell door and pushed the cot aside. She summoned a mote of flame, and her courage with it, before stepping down into the inky blackness of the underground tunnel.

The rapid beating of her heart slowed as Vi ventured further down the path. The tunnel was rough-hewn—cut out from the rock in some places and mortared with stone in others. Every now and then she had to duck underneath a rotting support beam, or side-step so her and the bags could fit through. But the pitch black of the tunnel's entrance was far more intimidating than the tunnel itself.

There was only one path and it felt like forever. Eventually, much as it had with Erion's escape route, Vi saw the first traces of pale moonlight on the rock. She extinguished her flame and stepped out onto a wide ledge that overlooked a small ravine with the ocean on the other side.

To her right, the cliff stretched upward, peaking at the rich area of town. To her left, the path continued down and away from Norin—out of sight, thanks to the large wall that still bordered the sea on this side. The walkway would be wide enough for a horse, Vi decided as she made her way quickly along it.

She went down far enough that she could see how the path wound through the rocky outcroppings of the cliff, hidden by archways and overhangs, twisting around large boulders, before the path finally blended into the open Waste at the far southern edge of the city.

Armed with this information, Vi sandwiched her bags between two large rocks and sprinted back the way she came.

By the time she arrived at the stables, her side ached and her lungs were burning. Even having worked to keep up her stamina by training with the soldiers, Vi could tell the past few months had been relatively easy on her. She felt soft in places she hadn't in what seemed like years.

"How to get the horses…" Vi murmured, hovering in the shadows near a side door to the castle.

People streamed in and out of the main hall. There were guards everywhere. She could go into the city and steal a random horse. That would certainly be easier.

But Vi didn't want any horse. She needed a warstrider—no, *two* warstriders. The beasts were bred for long, hard rides through the Waste's sands. They had the size and stamina to support two people and supplies with ease. They were her best chance of getting ahead of the Knights.

Vi had a black and white warstrider mare named Midsummer she'd inherited from Zira. The woman wasn't able take the horse with her, given the circumstances of how she'd left the castle. The creature had been a gift from Fiera and was almost as impressive as the Empress's all-black stallion, Prism.

"All right," Vi said with conviction. If she couldn't convince herself this half-baked lie would work, then how could she expect anyone else to believe it? "Let's do this."

During the next lull in the flow of people, Vi strode out into the stables focusing on one boy who was busy keeping up the tack room.

"You there." He turned to her, looking exhausted. "I need my mount saddled, as well as the Empress's, and taken out. Plain leathers, please. Nothing ceremonial."

For a brief second it seemed like he was going to inquire further. But either he was too tired, or Vi's rank was too high for him to question. The boy nodded and began going about the request.

Vi glanced down the stables. The stable master was hunched over his ledgers, intermittently barking orders at the others. Word must have spread like wildfire of Fiera's labor and some of the nobles who had longer rides were coming into town.

"All set," the boy said, before dragging his feet toward the stable master for his next task.

Sure enough, both horses were ready. Either he'd done quick work or she'd been distracted for longer than she thought. Vi mounted Midsummer, grabbed Prism's reins, and calmly started toward the drawbridge.

A couple nobles and stable hands glanced at her. But Vi kept her pace unhurried, natural. She kept her shoulders back and eyes focused ahead with intensity. She employed everything she'd ever been taught to make herself appear like she was meant to be there, doing what she was meant to be doing.

"Woah there, hold up, just where are you going?" The stable master ran out, stopping her just when she was about to cross onto the drawbridge. Vi didn't have to feign her annoyance.

"I'm taking the Empress's horse to where he'll be boarded for the next few months."

"Excuse me? Boarded?" The man put his hands on his hips and sighed with a shake of his head. "Why does no one tell me anything?" he mumbled.

"Things have been a little hectic," Vi said apologetically. "I only found out last-minute that the Empress has arranged for him to be boarded with a master of horse outside the city. Since she won't be able to ride for a few months, given her condition, she wants to see Prism exercised and trained around young ones. That way he'll be in prime condition when she's ready to ride again with the young prince."

Was training horses to be around babies and children a thing? Vi knew it was for noru.

"Right, right, to Ronaldo I'd bet?" Vi nodded, not having the slightest clue who Ronaldo was. "Makes sense, given he bred the bastard." Despite insulting the mount, the man patted Prism's neck fondly. When he spoke next, it was to the horse, "You be good now. None of that biting, you big oaf."

The man wandered away, and Vi left the castle and city without issue. Once in the Waste, she rode along the outer edge of Norin and back to the rocky area where the path met the sands. Vi tied off the horses and loaded their saddlebags with her supplies. For the second time, she wandered back through the tunnel, up into the dungeons, and back to the jailer's room.

Now, she had nothing to do but wait.

She paced the floor. She poured out a glass of some suspect liquor to take a sip and then abandoned it. She sat for a few minutes, only to find herself unable to be still. She jumped back to her feet.

Every minute that passed felt like a red-hot poker stabbing her palms or feet, making her fingers twitch and her steps hasten.

She couldn't speed up the process of Fiera's labor. She'd risk getting in the way, or not being here when they arrived, if she left. She had to trust Deneya and Fiera... and Yargen, that this would all work out.

Footsteps echoed down the hall and Vi sprinted to the door, sliding to a stop. The young guard she'd dismissed earlier looked at her, startled.

"S-Sorry to keep you waiting." He clearly mistook her eagerness.

"It's no trouble," Vi said sweetly. Likely too sweet. Her voice was bordering on once-I-stop-being-kind-you-might-end-up-dead. "Merely eager to hear of the status of our Empress."

"That's what I came down to tell you." He beamed from ear to ear. "A Ci'Dan is now the crown prince of the Empire."

Vi tried to stop a bubble of emotion from shooting up her throat, but she couldn't, and it burst forth as an oddly suppressed sound of joy. The man who would become the father to a new Vi had been born. Relief flooded her. It engulfed her in a feeling of rightness that she had finally, finally seen something come to pass according to plan.

"That is truly good news." Vi beamed. Now, Fiera would be sending the clerics away so she could get much needed rest. Deneya would be swiftly healing her. "I can only imagine the party going on up there."

"It's one for the books, that's for sure!" He laughed, quickly sobering when he added, "How about you go and enjoy it?"

"I think you'll have a far better time than I. Take the rest of the night off. There's no issues here."

"Truly?"

"Truly."

The young guard didn't waste another second before sprinting back the way he'd come. Vi continued to hover at the entrance, waiting. She waited there until her foot began to tap, until she had to begin pacing again.

Her watch read just shy of six when Vi heard a single set of footsteps again. She'd have to send him away once more. What excuse would she use this time? Vi was racking her brain when she emerged from the jailer's room.

Unnaturally blue eyes met Vi's own. Nestled in Deneya's arms with sweat-slicked hair and deep circles under her half-open eyes was Fiera. The woman who could always command a room with her mere existence had never looked so small.

They stared at each other long enough that Fiera lifted her head off Deneya's shoulder. Softly, she said, "We should go now. They'll be searching for me soon, and we have important work to do."

28

WITH THE SUN RISING at their left, they rode hard through the blood-red sands of the Waste.

Fiera was situated in front of Deneya on Prism. The saddle the horse had been initially strapped with was now attached to Vi's mount. Apparently, it was easier to ride double on a horse without a saddle—things Vi had never learned growing up in the North with noru and stable masters always attending her.

The Empress was mostly limp, her head tilted back against Deneya's shoulder. Luckily, the elfin woman was significantly bigger, so she seemed to be having no trouble holding Fiera astride as she drifted in and out of consciousness. Around both of Deneya's forearms near the elbow were brightly shining glyphs that mirrored the one around Vi's wrist.

Halleth maph. Stint pain. Vi focused on Fiera's body overall. Deneya focused one spell on her body as a whole as well. And then one specifically on her nether-regions. Layered as such, Fiera should feel nothing. If she did, she was doing an excellent job hiding it. Not even the bounding of the horse seemed to bother her.

Vi twisted in her saddle, looking behind them. Norin was already a dot far on the horizon. She lifted her free hand and uttered, "*Kot Sorre.*"

Kot was a new word Vi was learning on the go, thanks to Deneya's instruction. She remembered it mentioned in Sehra's book long ago, but there wasn't much on it other than it was a word that covered movement. *Sorre* was to push and *sidee* was pull.

The words burst from her with a surprising amount of force, enough that it had nearly startled her out of her saddle the first time she'd used them. A glyph shone in the distance where Vi directed it, pushing across the dunes. The sand slid over their tracks, covering them.

They continued throughout most of the day. In her time, the Crystal Caverns had long been struck from the maps. But it hadn't been hard for her as a child to suss out where they had been based on various stories, accounts, and poorly modified cartographer's notes. Due south-southeast of Norin was a long stretch of Waste, small, nameless villages dotting the vast sands until they reached the pine forests of the South. Then there would be the town of Mossant. Further south from there were the Caverns.

It was a general idea, but if Vi's instincts proved correct they would be on a more direct path than the Knights of Jadar. They would get to the Caverns first. They had to.

"We need to stop," Deneya said, calling over wind and sand. "The sun is getting high, and we need to give ourselves and the horses a break."

Vi knew that the only person among them who truly needed to rest was Fiera. Deneya's phrasing was merely kindness.

"You're right," Vi reluctantly agreed. She wanted to push onward until the horses' legs gave out and collapsed at the opening of the Caverns. But the journey was going to take at least two days, likely three, even at their aggressive pace. They had to rest eventually. But so would the Knights. No one could make the trek in one burst.

There was nowhere to seek shelter from the sun, so they arbitrarily came to a stop. Vi dismounted first and helped Fiera down; Deneya followed. Fiera had about as much life in her as a limp rag. While Deneya set up a desert tent she'd brilliantly thought to bring, Vi gave Fiera some water from one of the two bladders she'd packed.

"So much blood," Vi murmured.

"You'd be surprised how much blood a woman's body can hold," Fiera said between sips. "Though this is natural for after birth—so the clerics would have me believe."

"How do you feel?" That was the most important thing in Vi's mind.

"I don't feel much of anything," Fiera said lightly, resting her fingertips on the back of Vi's hand and drawing their attention to the glyph around her wrist. "Likely because of these. Are they difficult to make and maintain?"

"Not really, not when you get used to them. I imagine it's much like the wall of flame you kept to protect the sword." The mere mention of the sword soured and silenced her. If only she'd done something more. She should've taken it herself and left Fiera to fate. Her staying had done no one good.

As Vi silently admonished herself, the tent went up and the three huddled in the shade.

"You should rest," Deneya said to Fiera.

"We all should." Fiera laid back, trying to make room. Neither Vi nor Deneya moved to take it. Within moments, she was out.

"Relax your *halleth*," Deneya instructed Vi. "You should recover some of your magic as well."

"So should you."

"Once I know she's deeply asleep, I will."

Vi did as she was told and they both watched Fiera. The woman didn't even stir. Deneya relaxed one of her glyphs as well. Fiera groaned slightly in her sleep, but otherwise, no change.

"I can keep this one." Deneya held up her arm. "Let her get some good rest. I healed most of her tissue… so what's taxing her should only be the physical and mental exhaustion."

Vi looked at Fiera for a long moment and then turned back to Deneya. She didn't want to see the once strong woman so frail. "Thanks for healing her. I'm apparently shite with mending skin."

Deneya chuckled. "It's more of an art, that's for sure."

Vi drew her knees up to her chest, pulling them close and resting her chin on them. She stared out at the desert. In the middle of the day, the Waste was blindingly bright.

"I shouldn't have let her come," Vi murmured, thinking back to her conversation with Fiera on the birthing bed.

"Why did you? I didn't question before, but now I'd like to know."

"She's studied the crystals, more than I have, with books I didn't even think to search for." *If there was a next time…* She dared think the words. She would be sure to tell Taavin to tell the next Champion to seek out tomes from the Burning Times. Perhaps her instincts to manipulate the crystals were right. She just needed to go in a different direction. "She can make a barrier that I'm hoping will be enough to keep the Knights of Jadar and anyone else out of the Caverns. If no one gets into Raspian's tomb, no one meddles with it and he's never set free."

"She doesn't look like she's in a position to do much of anything." Deneya sighed. "I hope she'll make it."

"Me too." Vi still couldn't look back at the woman and mother she still felt like she'd condemned to death. Raylynn would grow up without a mother because of her. Now… if Vi wasn't careful, this world's Aldrik would as well. Her hand had struck the chords of fate and there was dissonance all around.

"I'll take first watch and give the horses some water." Deneya stood. "You should get some sleep."

Vi didn't object. She laid back, wiggling as close as she could to Fiera in the small tent without disturbing the woman. They were face to face, and Vi reached out. With just the side of her pinky, she touched Fiera's open palm. The woman slept on.

I'm sorry, Vi mouthed the words, not daring to say them aloud. She was sorry for so much that Fiera had and would endure. Sorry for what, regardless of what Taavin said was fated, she felt like she was taking from the world—taking from Aldrik.

But if this worked… Perhaps it would all be worth it.

Perhaps Fiera could yet be right.

Before the dawn of the second day, they crossed into the South. Shrub trees grew up from the Waste. Stubborn grasses became pine-carpeted forests as the canopy stretched higher and higher above them.

Vi still felt a rush tingling through her as the first blustery wind caught her cape, sending it flapping behind her.

"Lyndum," she whispered.

"Pardon?" Deneya asked quietly so as not to disturb the sleeping woman leaned against her. The horses were moving slower now, due to exhaustion and the new terrain. Snowbanks were in the distance, their vast, blinding whiteness as fascinating as it was unnerving to Vi.

They were out of the harshness of the desert, but stepping into a frosty world Vi had never known.

"This was supposed to be my home in another world," Vi confessed. "But I've never come here before."

"Just who were you in this other world?"

Vi looked to Fiera. The woman's head was tipped back and her jaw hung open. She slept more than she was awake. But every time she woke she seemed stronger than the last.

"Her granddaughter," Vi admitted. "Well, the granddaughter of a woman very much like her. I know that's likely impossible to believe but—"

"I don't really think so," Deneya interrupted. "You have the same face."

Vi chuckled softly. "Everyone told me so. Now I got to see it for myself and… I don't know, we seem different enough. She's stronger than I am."

"Self-doubt doesn't suit you."

"Maybe it's not so much doubt as it is finally being honest with myself about my own limitations?"

Deneya clicked her tongue. "Humility, reasonableness, they're good traits. Can't argue, won't argue. But… I've seen a shift in you these past few days. You were so self-assured. Now you seem like you're doubting each step you take."

"Failure has a high price, and I'm paying it." She had some hesitations now, what was the harm in it? "Taavin was right this whole time and I didn't listen. I might not be able to make up for it now… nonetheless, I'm trying to be more careful."

"Take care in deciding where to step, so when you do, you're certain of your path," Deneya advised. "You keep looking back. Those decisions have been made and the ink in the history books is already dry. Keep your eyes forward."

Vi nodded, twisting the reins in her fingers. Deneya was right: forward was the only path for them now. Forward into the snowdrifts that stretched across the forest floors from the last vestiges of winter. Forward to the place where every line of fate collided.

"Now, how much longer until we're at this town you mentioned?"

"Mossant? If we push, we might get there before the day is done."

"Good, I'd like a bed."

There wasn't much conversation for the rest of the day. Each of them was dead tired. The inside of Vi's thighs ached and her fingers had gone numb. They'd prepared for the Waste, but Vi hadn't packed appropriately for snow and cold.

In Mossant they restocked and slept at an inn for a night. The horses had time to rest and be fed properly. They were warm and safe. It was the best possible thing for them right before their final push to the Caverns.

The main road in and out of Mossant lead to the Great Imperial Way. That was the road they had come in from. But the road they left on was far less maintained.

It was more of a hunting path. Branches reached out for them, trying to snag on their packs and clothes. The overgrowth was annoying and, to Vi, oddly comforting. Had a group of Knights come trudging through, they would've left their mark on the frail branches. The absence of any such tracks meant they were still ahead of the Knights—for now.

That night, they laid eyes on the entrance to the Crystal Caverns. They came to a stop at the edge of a ridge. Switchbacks led down to a valley where Vi could see they curved up and around once more to a narrow cliff.

"So, that's it, then," Deneya spoke first. Her breath appeared as a cloud in the fading light of day.

"That's been the cause of my family's shame…" Fiera murmured. The birth hadn't been too hard on her—or Lightspinning was far superior to Waterrunners and clerics of the Dark Isle—and the Empress was far more alert after staying at the inn than she had been in days.

Set into the mountain face was a large, pointed archway carved directly into the stone. It was a gaping hole that Vi suspected was positively massive up close. Carvings of wyrms and men surrounded the archway.

Raspian.

A shiver ripped through her. She could almost feel his presence curdling in her stomach like cream mixed with vinegar. She felt the edge of his magic in the air like red electricity right before it collected into a bolt of lightning.

"How could anyone see this as something to tamper with?" Vi mused aloud.

"Men are ambitious fools," Fiera said dryly.

"Judging from the snow, we're still ahead of them," Deneya observed. She sounded as uncomfortable as Vi. "Let's get this over with."

29

THE MOON HAD JUST risen when they arrived at the entrance on foot. Their horses were tied off down the mountain, behind some large rocks and out of sight. Vi used *kot* to hide their footprints once more.

Deneya went in first, followed by Fiera. Vi approached the entrance but stopped, hovering where the snowdrift met the stone pathway within. An invisible force pushed outward like the dying sigh of a dragon. She stared up at the icicles that lined the top of the archway, imagining they were teeth. Imagining they might come crashing down on her at any moment.

"Yullia?" Deneya called back. "Is everything all right?"

Nothing was right about this place. "I'm fine."

Vi crossed the threshold. The moment her boot met the crystal-dusted floor of the Caverns, turquoise magic pulsed outward like a ripple in water. She felt magic ebb and flow from her as ripples reverberated all over the stones, bouncing off each other, reaching every corner. They illuminated the magical veins in the walls, columns of crystal becoming sources of light.

"What did you do?" Deneya asked.

"I don't know." Vi shook her head and took another step forward. This time, there were no other pulses of magic.

"Well, now we have some light, at least." Fiera gave a slow turn. "It's large enough to fit a palace in here…"

Now that she could see properly, Vi assessed the Caverns. A pathway had been cut through the center—perhaps it had been made that way from the beginning—leading to another smaller archway. The ceiling was so high above them that it was merely a hazy blue, motes of Yargen's magic falling toward them like snowflakes.

"A palace of death," Deneya muttered.

"What?"

"Don't you feel it?" Deneya asked Fiera. Vi could. "This place… it's *wrong*."

"Wrong or right… let's set up this barrier." Vi turned to Fiera. The faster they could get out of here, the better. Perhaps, if they moved quickly enough, they could get out of sight before the Knights arrived and there would be time yet to return Fiera to the West. Vi's heart skipped a beat, nearly tripping her on hope.

"Let's go farther in." Fiera pointed to the inner archway. "I need a smaller opening to attach the barrier to. I can't just make it in the air and the main entrance is too large."

"All right," Vi agreed, solely to buy herself time to think. She needed to protect the Caverns—to prevent people from entering entirely. If Fiera needed something to attach the barrier to, then perhaps she could use *juth calt* to collapse the archway? If she did that, then—

"What's that?" Deneya asked, taking a few hasty steps forward.

They'd crossed into another antechamber, smaller, but the crystals were larger here. They felt older. Their power ran even deeper below the earth, to a realm beyond Vi's perceptions.

Deneya squeezed through the center of two massive stone doors, barely pulled open.

"What's in there?" Vi called.

"I don't know," Deneya's voice echoed back.

Vi and Fiera shared a look before they proceeded up a few stone stairs and into the final chamber of the Crystal Caverns.

Here, crystals spiraled outward from a center point. They were embedded into the stone and glowed faintly, a dull thrum of power brightening and dulling with every step Vi took around the perimeter. The stones at the edge of the area were three times the size of her, brought to wickedly sharp tips.

She walked to the center of the room, crouching down and running her fingertips over the ground where all the magic seemed to pool together. Deep below the stone, encased in a place that was only partly anchored in this world, was an evil she knew by name. Vi slowly stood, backing away from that deep and rumbling pulse that made her tremble.

"The doors will do," she declared. "This is the source of it all. This is where the true power lies." She looked to Deneya. "This is where Raspian is trapped and where no man must reach."

"Raspian?" Fiera repeated, understandably confused.

"A dark god," Vi answered, starting for the doors once more. She didn't want to linger longer than necessary. It felt as if any moment the ground would crack and Raspian would reach through the mantle of the earth to consume her and all of Yargen's power whole. "The one thing we must ensure is never set free."

Fiera narrowed her eyes slightly at her. Out of everything, this was what made her skeptical. Vi finally found the limits of what Fiera's mind was willing to accept.

"Let's close the doors to this room and seal them." Vi wondered if the doors had been sealed once before. Perhaps King Jadar had been the one to find a way to open them with his captive Windwalkers. "Denja, help me?"

"What about the other crystals? Those out here?"

"I think... the Crystal Caverns were originally just this room and, over time, the magic spread to take over the whole cave," Vi mused. "The crystals are older and older the further we go back. But the crux of it all is here. This is what we have to protect."

Back in the second antechamber, Vi and Deneya faced the doors.

"*Kot*, at the same time, then?" Deneya asked.

Vi nodded.

Together, they uttered, "*Kot sidee.*" It felt as though someone pulled a rope through her chest as the magic came toward her. Vi took a step backward, watching her glyph crash against the other side of the door in tandem with Deneya's. The heavy stone groaned loudly, and closed with a heavy *thud*.

"Will this work for your barrier?" Vi asked Fiera.

The woman was in a daze, staring blankly at the room they'd just been in. She took a step forward and, for one second, Vi thought she was about to ask them to open it once more. Vi saw the same hunger in her eyes that she'd seen in Tiberus: hunger for power.

"Can you make a barrier over the doors?" Vi asked again, gently resting her hand on Fiera's shoulder.

"Wh—*oh*, yes, I think I can." Fiera blinked several times, as though the world was coming back into focus.

"Show me how to do it."

"I usually have the sword for it…" Fiera started uncertainly. After they'd sprinted across half of the continent, now was not the time to hesitate.

"There are a lot of crystals here. Perhaps you can show me the motions using the magic of those instead." Vi encouraged her to continue.

"With the sword, I imagined the power imbuing the stone the Groundbreakers had built. It knotted with their magic and reinforced it. As though the sword was the pin holding every magical chain together."

Vi could imagine it. But imagining something and putting it to practice were two very different things. And there were obvious gaps in Fiera's summary.

"How did you do it?" Vi pressed.

"It's hard to explain. Magic… *appeared* in my mind. Something I can't make sense of—like a Crone speaking in tongues. But the sword was what helped me make sense of it all."

Crossing over, Vi took the woman's hand in hers, giving it a squeeze.

"The sword isn't here now. But I am, and I will help you," Vi vowed. "I know this magic, too. In a different way from you. But together, we can do this."

Fiera opened her mouth in hesitation, then gave a small nod, abandoning any protest.

Together, they strode up to the door, standing at its right side. Fiera timidly rested her hand on one of the large crystals. Vi mirrored the motion, closing her eyes, and allowing herself to feel the magic within.

"Come to me," Fiera whispered, her voice thin and almost afraid. "Mother, come to me."

Vi tried to feel the magic seeping up from her marrow as she'd practiced, meeting the crystal under her palm. She drew on the crystal, allowing it to fill her, allowing it to be a catalyst. Yargen was within her. If Fiera had faith in the goddess, then so would Vi. She would entrust her mind and her actions into Yargen's hands.

The stone drew her closer and Vi breathed, "*Thrumsana,*" her lips nearly touching the smooth crystal as though she had been subconsciously about to kiss it.

Magic flooded her. It swelled up from the crystal and ripped through her. Vi was helpless to the currents and allowed herself to be pulled along them. There was sound, but not of the same sort the first time she'd used the word. This was not the chaos that had assaulted Taavin.

A thrumming disturbed her thoughts. Vi opened her eyes once more to find Fiera drawing lines of flame along the door. But rather than burning orange, they burned blue.

"Fiera…" Vi whispered in awe.

The woman held out her left pinkie, swirling it through the air, as though she were a spinner drawing magic onto the spool. With the index finger of her right hand, she drew across the door. Lines and circles, interconnecting. The flames burned low and bright, lingering long after she finished them.

Vi quickly stepped around to Fiera's other side. She grabbed one crystal with her left hand and took Fiera's magic spinning hand with her right. Fiera looked at her a moment, her trance-like state startled.

"Keep going," Vi encouraged. "Let me be a catalyst for you."

Fiera nodded and then turned back to the door as though she was facing off against a great opponent. She took a deep breath, and threw herself back into her countless lines of flame. Vi drew out the crystal's powers just as she had practiced all those nights with the sword. But when Vi had extracted the crystal's magic before, she hadn't known what to do with it. Fiera did. So she funneled the magic through her and into Fiera.

The woman's flames began to harden, condensing into crystal. Fiera worked faster—every motion more decisive, every line wrought with fierce determination.

She slumped, nearly falling back. Vi caught her only because she'd already been holding the woman's hand.

"I'm fine," Fiera said before Vi could ask. "I must finish this… I must."

Fiera continued with her determined fervor. Blue fire illuminated the room as much as crystals did. But every wild motion of Fiera's hand seemed to throw her off-balance. Her cheeks were gaunt, her eyes dull.

"Fiera, stop this," Vi whispered.

"What you said… it told me, I have to finish this. I heard it. I heard what must be done."

Thrumsana… Taavin had told her never to use a word of power unless she fully understood what it did. This was the second time she'd used it on instinct. Just like the first, someone was suffering for her carelessness, trapped by the magic *thrumsana* unleashed.

"Fiera—"

"It's nearly finished."

"Vi," Deneya gasped. Her shock was so apparent that she didn't even think to use the name Yullia in front of Fiera. "It's a glyph. It's a word of Yargen."

Fiera pressed her palm into the center of the flames. Everything erupted at once. Fiera was thrown back, Vi with her. They tumbled and Deneya rushed forward, catching them both on an arm and easing their fall.

Vi looked from Fiera, slumped in Deneya's arm, body limp and eyes closed, to the symbol on the door.

Just like with Sehra's book, sounds filled her ears. The fire crystalized, cementing itself as fragile crystals on the door. In it, Vi saw a glyph of Yargen. A word that Vi had never heard or seen before.

"*Rohko*," Vi breathed.

The chorus in her mind snapped into harmony. Everything came together at once as the thin crystal lines Fiera had made spiderwebbed out, growing as though time was progressing at twice its normal speed.

In less than a minute, the doors were covered by faintly glowing stone. And the innermost chamber of the Crystal Caverns—Raspian's tomb—was sealed.

30

"Fiera, Fiera," Vi said, shaking the woman. Deneya had laid her down carefully on the walkway, murmuring *halleth* over her again and again.

"There's something strange about her." Deneya's head jerked up, her eyes worried. "I can't describe it. Her magic—Yargen's magic… There's something *in* her now, something that wasn't there before."

"Crystal taint," Vi whispered in knowing horror. "Because their powers are fractured, the affinities on this continent can be tainted by Yargen's magic. She'd avoided it with the sword now and I dared to think…" Vi cursed under her breath. She'd been the one to pump Fiera's body with power from the crystals. "I don't have time to explain it properly—we just have to get her out of here. She'll be fine if we can get her away from the crystals."

"Then let's go." Deneya shifted and slid her arms underneath Fiera, lifting the woman with ease.

"Are all elfin so unnaturally strong?" Vi asked. She'd seen Deneya carry Fiera like that to leave the castle. The woman didn't even grunt with the exertion. And Fiera was no small woman.

"I make it a point to train regularly." Deneya gave her a smug grin, then turned her head further, looking back at the door that was now sealed. "What happened? And that word you used, it made her create the glyph in flame…"

"It's one Yargen gave me," Vi affirmed.

"What does it do?"

"Excellent question…" Vi reflected once more on the past two times she'd used it as they walked through the archway and back into the main chamber of the Crystal Caverns. "I think it awakens some kind of knowledge or awareness in someone?"

"Like *samasha* to a Lightspinner just beginning?"

"Perhaps something like that." It felt like a lifetime ago that Vi had *samasha* used on her and she had to work to remember what Taavin had said the word meant. "But for more than just the words of Yargen. I think to some greater truth or purpose."

"I'm surprised Taavin hasn't told you not to use words until you're certain of what they mean. In this time, that's a standard warning from the Voice."

"Oh, he did… But perhaps Yargen gave me that one because of my recklessness." Vi wondered what Taavin would think when she told him of how the word had been used again. After all she'd done, Vi doubted he'd be surprised.

Movement at the entrance of the cave caught Vi's eye. In the time it took for her to look, the archer had already loosed his arrow. She opened her mouth, but no sound came. The projectile moved faster than thought, faster than she could react.

For those brief moments, they'd felt victorious. The world had been hopeful. And Vi had almost dared to feel safe.

The arrow lodged itself through Fiera's neck and into Deneya's shoulder. Deneya dropped to her knees with a shout. Vi stared at the crimson tide pouring from them both.

So much blood. How did Fiera still have blood left to bleed? The macabre thought was the only one Vi could wrap her head around.

"Vi!" Deneya snarled, snapping off the fletching of the arrow and sliding Fiera off of it. The woman was limp on the ground, as dead as Zira had been.

Halleth. Her mind placed the word on her tongue. But Vi was silent. There was no word to bring back the dead.

Vi slowly lifted her gaze. The world was fuzzy. The haze of the crystals had never been so bright or thick. She felt drunk, and everything seemed to have a nauseating tilt. Her motions and thoughts had a sluggish delay.

She saw the men running toward them. The archer nocking another arrow.

"*Juth calt,*" the words slipped through someone else's lips. They couldn't be hers. Everything had gone numb. The archer seized and fell. Vi wrought her wrath next on the man running through the opening of the cave. Again, she repeated, "*juth calt.*"

Kill them all.

Clearly that was the simplest solution. She should've done it from the start. Holding back was a fool's decision.

She was the agent of the goddess, a traveler between worlds. What good was humanity to her now?

The Knights of Jadar had been an enemy of her family. In every world, they rallied against Solaris. In every world, they resulted in the death of Vi's grandmother and left her father motherless. It had been her vision to break that cycle.

A vision that was now tunneled.

"*Juth calt.*" Another body fell, and fire exploded in front of her face.

Vi was tackled off to the side, a heavy body on top of her. "*Wein,*" she heard Deneya say in her ear. Magic engulfed them and another burst of flame charred the woman's barrier but left her unharmed.

"Get off of me," Vi demanded. "Get off of me!" she roared. "I'll kill them. I'll kill them all!"

Vi pushed on the stump of the arrow, still in Deneya's shoulder. The woman howled and reared back. Vi launched to her feet.

"Keep her at bay!" Twintle shouted and more flames erupted around Vi.

"Do you think you can hurt me with your fractured magic?" Vi asked as she stepped through the fire, emerging on the other side. "I am part goddess. What do you think your flames will do?"

A Waterrunner was the response to her question as ice formed around her feet. Vi tugged against it, allowing her spark to roar, echoing the chaos in her mind. The ice turned to vapor as Vi glared at Twintle.

"I should've done this months ago," she snarled. "*Juth calt.*"

His body limply meeting the floor was the sweetest sound she'd heard in ages.

"Watch out! *Wein!*" Deneya shouted, stepping in front of Vi, her body acting as a shield. An arrow bounced harmlessly off of the protective barrier her word of power formed over Deneya's skin. "There's too many of them, we have to get out of here."

"We can take them." Vi motioned to the bodies on the ground. With two words, she'd killed four men. "They're nothing compared to us."

"I will not twist Yargen's words in that way." Deneya grabbed her wrist. "How you are using *juth* is the work of elfin'ra."

"It's the work of the Champion," Vi countered.

"What sorcery is this?" a voice echoed from within the antechamber, distracting them both. He very clearly wasn't talking about their magic. "It won't open." Vi rushed toward the center aisle once more, looking back at the Knights who fought against the barrier of crystal that covered the doors.

They slammed the sword of Jadar against it again and again. But the barrier held. Vi reached out for one of the pointed crystals protruding from the floor at her side. She forced her power into the stone, exerting her will and feeling it rush from crystal to crystal, maintaining the barrier at the door. The sword wasn't even chipping it. The fools had no idea how to wield the power of Yargen.

"What have you done?" the nameless Knight shouted at her.

Vi merely smiled. She smiled like a madman, baring her teeth, even as an arrow punctured her arm that was grabbing the crystal.

"Flee," Deneya yelled at them, her voice echoing off the high rooftop of the Caverns. "Run, as quickly as you can. Hide back under the rock you crawled from and never show your face again. Fiera's blood lives on and will guard these Caverns until the end of time."

The men began to run back toward them and Vi watched them sprint past. They regarded her with wary eyes, as though she was the blood of which Deneya spoke. The three were almost at the entrance to the Caverns when she rapid-fired, "*Juth calt. Juth calt. Juth calt.*"

One by one, they fell. The crystal sword clattered to the ground at the entrance, skittering away from the last man's lifeless hands. The rest of the Knights had already fled down the mountainside and Vi doubted they would dare return for the sword. Especially not if she killed them first.

Vi took a step forward, ready to give chase.

"Enough." Two strong arms wrapped around her like the thick ropes of a ship. Vi writhed against them and Deneya hoisted her upward. The pain in Vi's arm seared in a way that almost felt delightful. "Enough!"

"I should've killed them ages ago when I had the chance." Vi kicked her feet, trying to break free of Deneya's hold. The woman was a rock behind her.

"But you didn't because it's not you," Deneya shouted in her ear over Vi's grunts and snarls. "You didn't because you aren't a cold-blooded murderer."

"Clearly I am!" The darkness had finally overwhelmed her. Vi felt completely charred. Just when hope had begun to take root again, she burnt it away. Giving in was easier. "I am worse than them; I can be worse than all of them."

"But you're not. And you should never try to be."

"This is what the world needs me to be."

"The world needs compassion from its Champion, not killing. You can kill a thousand men, Vi, but their blood won't quench that fire burning within you."

Vi went still and pressed her eyes closed. Her head dipped and her chin nearly touched her chest as she hung limply. Deneya set her back down gingerly. When it was clear Vi wouldn't fight any longer, she unraveled her arms.

"I don't know what pain fuels your flames, but I can see you're burning alive."

Her head jerked upward and Vi stared, slack-jawed at the woman. She felt seen. For the first time in a long time, someone other than Taavin could see her. Really see her. It was terrifying and vulnerable, but in an oddly welcome way. Vi gave in to the sensation, leaning forward and pressing her forehead against Deneya's uninjured shoulder.

"I wanted to save her," Vi choked out. "I wanted to save her, and Zira, and I wanted to stop the Knights."

"I know." Deneya stroked her hair like a child. Like they weren't awash in blood and surrounded by bodies. "But you protected the Caverns."

"No…" Vi pulled away and looked to Fiera. "*She* did. Even though I was the Champion, she was the one who sealed the Caverns." Vi staggered over and knelt down next to Fiera's body. She tucked a stray strand of hair away from the woman's face, thinking back to Zira. She hadn't even given the woman a proper Rite of Sunset. "Help me?"

Deneya nodded and walked over. She first healed her shoulder and Vi's arm, murmuring, "*halleth ruta sot,*" twice. Then she scooped up Fiera and brought the body out onto the cliff. The snow was churned up, rocks jutting out where footsteps had crunched through to the ground below.

"Set her there." Vi pointed to a mostly clear area. "We'll send her off at sunset."

"What about the rest of them?" Deneya and Vi both turned back, looking at the carnage still littering the Caverns. "You can't leave them be."

"I could. They're traitors and murderers." Vi thought back to how Fiera had handled the traitors in the streets. What had been mere months ago now felt like years.

"All men deserve a proper sendoff. Even the worst among them," Deneya insisted. Out of everything Vi had expected the woman to be for her, a moral compass wasn't one of them.

Vi barely stopped herself from disagreeing. She wanted to. But the sentiment struck a chord with her—it sounded like something her mother would've said.

Vhalla Yarl, the woman Vi knew, was gone now. But every act she took was still a testament to her memory. That world was gone, save for what lived on in her. Was she becoming a woman her mother would be proud of?

"Pile them up off to the side. I'll burn them all at once." *It was better than they deserved,* a nagging voice told her in the back of her mind. But treating them like men, rather than meat, quieted the darkness that had consumed her and reminded Vi of her humanity. If only slightly.

Deneya carried the bodies from the deepest part of the Caverns. Vi couldn't quite lift the men at the opening, but she could push them along with the careful use of *kot sorre.* By the afternoon, the bodies were all lined up in the snow, waiting to be burned.

Vi finally went over to where the sword had fallen. She stared at it for a long moment, as though all the blood that had fallen had been wrought by this singular blade. Finally, she hoisted it for the first time in what felt like an eternity.

The weapon shone brightly with power. The whole of the Crystal Caverns seemed to glow brighter for a moment as the hilt met her fingers.

This was the magic she had been expecting all along. The sword no longer felt thin and weak, but recharged with the essence of Yargen. The more pieces of Yargen's power Vi drew together, the stronger they all became.

"Well, you have it and the Caverns are sealed... what now?" Deneya asked, sitting with her back propped against the archway.

"That's an excellent question." Vi twisted the sword in the light before setting it down carefully on a bed of crystals. *"Narro hath hoolo."*

The magic spun out from her watch as it always had. But instead of being the usual orange-yellow glyph, this time it was a pale blue. Vi watched as Taavin was cut out from the empty air, color seeping into his outline before the magic vanished entirely. She watched as he blinked, focus coming to his eyes before he turned to her.

"Vi—" Taavin stopped himself mid-turn, frozen.

"Taavin?" Vi asked cautiously, taking a small step forward. The wind tousled his hair and Taavin shivered, as though he could feel the cold. As though he were—her hand closed around his. "Are you?"

"It's the magic of the Caverns," he murmured, pulling his eyes from the crystals surrounding them and looking to her. "It heightens everything."

It makes you real, Vi wanted to say. She could feel the puffs of cool air that curled by her cheek. Vi searched his eyes, wanting to touch him all over. Wanting to savor this moment. But knowing it was not the time or place.

"You made it," he continued, as if he wasn't feeling the same ache she was. "And the sword?"

"Here." Vi took a hasty step away and grabbed the sword. "And Raspian's tomb has been sealed once more."

"Sealed?"

"We can show you," Vi offered.

As they walked back through the Caverns, Vi and Deneya gave him the quick run-down of everything that had transpired. Vi filled Taavin in on the conversation she'd had with Fiera. Deneya told him of her healing Fiera, and the woman's determination to come and defend the Caverns—to right the wrongs of her forefathers.

The short walk to the sealed door wasn't nearly enough time to cover everything. But they got through the broad strokes before Taavin's focus was drawn elsewhere. He let out a gasp the moment he laid eyes on the door.

"What... what is this?" His confusion had never delighted her more.

"Rohko," Vi said aloud. The word was as strong as a cornerstone, able to support the immense weight of a building without cracking. "Is this barrier... this word from the goddess, is it new?"

She hoped against hope, and Vi nearly let out an involuntary noise of relief when Taavin gave a small nod. He was still trying to consume the doorway with his eyes. It wasn't enough; he slowly approached the doors, resting his fingertips lightly on the crystal barrier that seemed to have already grown thicker.

"You have the sword. The Knights didn't get in. There's a barrier," he murmured, as if trying to keep it straight in his own head.

"I'm no expert at all this. But we did well, I think." Deneya folded her arms over her chest.

"Only one thing will tell—" Taavin turned, looking down at Vi. "Have you peered forward yet?"

"Not yet." She didn't know if she was ready to. She didn't know if her heart could take what she might see. If she saw a future of light, what did that mean for the rest of her time as a traveler in this world without a home of her own? If she saw a future of darkness... Did that mean the sacrifices made to get here had been for nothing?

"You have to," Taavin said, as if he, too, was riding the tumultuous currents of her thoughts.

Neither of them wanted to hope. Ignorance would be kinder.

But the goddess hadn't been kind to either of them when she'd given them this duty.

Vi held out the sword between two open palms and took a deep breath. She drew power from the Caverns—in through her feet, leeching it from the air like moisture to a plant. A blue flame erupted over the flat of the blade before her and Vi stared directly at it, her heart racing.

She wasn't ready. But that didn't matter. The world washed in white.

And all Vi could do was brace herself for the future.

31

THE LIGHT FADED INTO darkness.

Vi blinked several times, looking around. Slowly, shapes came into focus. A thin, bright line of crimson circled the horizon perfectly. It continued in all directions. But Vi couldn't tell if it was from an early dawn, about to break, or the last light of sunset vanishing from the world.

The color bled upward, casting the clouded depths of the sky in a bloody ombre. At the top, the clouds parted, the heavens had opened, and stars stretched to infinity. It was as though she stood on the top of the world. Everything stretched outward from this place where the earth and sky met.

A crack of red lightning struck from sky to ground. There, on the steaming rock, was the hulking, godly form of death and darkness incarnate. Raspian's skin was red and shining, like a blood-filled ruby. From his skeletal visage to his writhing hair, Vi knew the face of death. He turned his eyes to her, snarling and baring his razor-sharp teeth.

Oddly, she wasn't afraid.

She stood in a well of calm and strength. There was a prevailing sense of rightness with the world. Rightness at facing off against this wretched creature.

Once and for all.

Vi took a step forward without thinking. More like, the body she was in stepped forward. Most of her visions had Vi as an outside observer, but this time she was rooted in another form. A form that sprang wildflowers from barren earth with a single step.

A hand appeared in her field of vision—her hand, or the hand of the person she was in. Every color of the rainbow splashed across the woman's body, brilliantly bright, deep and rich. The colors were so vibrant, Vi thought they'd sear into her eyes forever and make everything else seem dull.

Clutched in the woman's hand was a blue staff.

The staff of the Champion.

Raspian tilted his head up to the sky and let out a cry that seemed to shake the earth itself. The woman braced herself, guarding against a shock-wave of magic that radiated out from the man. Vi tipped her head back and gaze skyward to see the moon had appeared in the center of the clouds. It was cracked, like an egg, a dark red yolk pouring at Raspian's feet and collecting in the shape of a great dragon.

Still, the person Vi occupied didn't panic. Though Vi certainly felt like she should.

As the dragon took its shape, cut from primordial essence, Raspian lifted his hand, pointing at the staff the woman still held outright.

"*Let it be done*," he said without moving his jaw. The words seemed to resonate as thoughts, grating sharply in Vi's mind. She wanted to wince, but she was subject to the vision before her.

She couldn't turn away, even if she'd wanted to, as Raspian lunged for her. Lunged for the woman whom Vi knew at her core was Yargen herself.

Vi returned to the world with a sudden jolt, right as Raspian launched his first attack. The sword clattered to the ground as it slipped from her limp hands. Her arms swung at her sides and Vi staggered, forward and back. She gripped her head with one hand, her stomach with the other. The unnatural calm of Yargen had left her, and now Vi was filled with a panic that tasted like sickness.

"Vi." Two hands on her shoulders. Stable, sturdy, warm, all the things she'd been missing for months. "What did you see?" Taavin asked softly.

She shook her head, leaning forward and pressing her face into his shoulder. Taking a deep breath, Vi inhaled the scent of him. Somehow, he still smelled faintly of the incense that burned in Risen a world away, and sunlight on a warm summer's day. She missed those scents a painful amount.

"Vi, you need to—"

"Give her a moment, she's been through enough," Deneya snapped.

A soft huff of amusement slipped through Vi's lips and Taavin's arms closed around her. She let out a sigh. *Let this embrace never end*, Vi wished.

She did not pray. Because she knew what gods would be out there to hear her prayers. Vi didn't want to leave her delicate wishes in either of their warring hands.

"Raspian is set free," she finally whispered.

Taavin released her, almost pushing her back as though her words had burned him. He held her at arm's length. As though with her, he could hold away her vision and prevent it from coming to pass.

"What?"

"Raspian is set free," she repeated, louder. "He gains a physical form, I saw it."

"I don't understand." Deneya took a step forward, physically inserting herself into their conversation. "We sealed the Caverns. You have the sword. How do they manipulate the tomb?"

"There are other crystal weapons. The crystals will never be safe," Taavin muttered. His arms dropped to his sides and he slumped, swayed, righted himself, and then swayed again.

"No, they'll never be safe on this land," Vi agreed easily. Perhaps there was some of Yargen's unnatural calm still in her. Or perhaps feeling Taavin there had given her a peace she'd long since given up on.

No matter what, they were opened. They couldn't stop the Crystal Caverns from being destroyed, not even after ninety-three times. Not even after what had seemed like their best showing yet, despite all Vi's shortcomings.

Vi slowly ascended the steps to the crystal-coated doors. She ran her hands along the stone. Feeling the deeply rooted magic within.

Destruction always reaped destruction.

"Maybe that's it."

"What is?" Deneya asked. Even Taavin stopped his murmuring.

Vi turned to face Taavin, bracing herself for what she already knew his reaction would be. "Maybe that's been our error all along."

"What has?" Taavin lowered his hand to look at her with his piercing green eyes.

"All these times, we've been trying to stop the Caverns from being opened, stop Raspian from being set free."

"That is your job—to change the fate of the world and prevent that."

"But what if there's another way?" Vi asked. The words felt like blasphemy ignited by a spark of red lightning in the darkness. "I'm supposed to change fate, but keep enough the same that I'm reborn. I have to alter the outcome of events, but accept that some things will always happen. Don't you think it sounds rather impossible?"

"If it were easy—"

"—we would've already done it, I know," Vi finished hastily. "Think about it," she implored him. "What was the problem in our world? What were we trying to stop?"

"The Crystal Caverns were destroyed and Raspian was set free." Taavin played along.

"Now, think about it in a different way. Why was Raspian being set free a problem?" She'd talk him through it so he'd understand. So she could vet this mad idea that had overtaken her.

"Because he's evil and darkness incarnate."

"Because Yargen *couldn't stop him*, because her power was fractured by the crystal weapons being destroyed across time," Vi corrected. "If Raspian was set free, but Yargen had all of her power, she could face him once more. It would be like every other war of light and dark through the ages."

"Stop." Taavin held up both his hands. "You're thinking about *letting* Raspian be set free?"

"Yes. And I know how it sounds," Vi added hastily. "But no matter what we've done, throughout the history of the Dark Isle, men have sought out the Crystal Caverns. They will continue to. Even if we're successful, Yargen's magic and Raspian's tomb will never be safe as long as they're within the reach of power-hungry people—here on the Dark Isle or anywhere else.

"What if, rather than stopping the Caverns from being opened, we focus instead on merely preserving Yargen's power? We store it in the Caverns. We allow the crystal weapons to be brought here as time dictates so a new Champion can be reborn, just in case I'm wrong."

Taavin nodded approvingly at that sentiment.

"We preserve the events that must happen to see a new Champion born. We allow the crystal weapons to come here, and allow the people of this world to *think* they've been destroyed. On the surface, it will all look the same—or same enough. But we'll hold the ace. We'll transfer the power from the crystal weapons into the Caverns, rather than allow them to be destroyed."

"Can you do that?" Deneya asked skeptically.

"With enough time to practice." Vi lifted her hand off the crystals, feeling the way the magic clung to her. She'd seen Fiera work to manipulate the crystals. She'd already begun exploring the notion herself before that.

"So we allow time to progress, ensure that all the stones in the river and Apexes of Fate are attended to, to see a new Champion reborn," Taavin started, somewhat hesitantly. "But when the weapons are brought here, throughout time, you'll transfer their power to the Caverns?"

"Yes." Vi knew what she was about to say next would be the hardest for them to swallow. "Then, when all of her power is here, we will be the ones to open the Caverns, properly."

"Wait…" Deneya tilted her head to the side, processing. "Tell me I can't be following this right. You want to be the one who sets Raspian free?"

"If I do it, I'll make sure all of Yargen's power is collected beforehand so she can do battle." *And she will win*, that quiet calmness from her vision assured Vi. "Once she is victorious, she will seal him away somewhere new—somewhere far from this place and far from the knowledge of men who would try to tap into power they don't understand for nefarious purposes. It'll not only ensure success in this time, but the safety of the world for eons to come."

Taavin turned away from her, as if he couldn't even bear looking at her when she presented him with this theory. He ran his hands through his dark, plum colored hair, short waves curling around his fingers.

"He can only be set free by destroying the seal on the Crystal Caverns, which means turning the part of Yargen's magic that's contained within the crystal weapons against the portion of her magic that's here in the Caverns. Which results in the Caverns weakening and ultimate destruction."

"But does it have to?" Vi asked, an honest question. She let it hover in the air, waiting to see his response. When there was none, she repeated, "Does it have to? Or… do you not know?"

"I can't claim to know all the details of her power. I have the benefit of experience, but that still only comes from trial and error."

"And have we tried this?"

"No."

"What happens if we fail?" Vi dared to ask, though she already suspected the answer.

"Everything repeats again." He turned back to look at her with his dread-filled eyes.

"Then I think it's worth trying," Vi said definitively. "Maybe, with a few years' time here, I could learn how to use the crystals for purposes beyond just transferring their power. With all of Yargen's power collected here, I have to believe we can break the seal without destroying her magic." *Rohko* was in her mind—to seal. If the word could make a seal, perhaps it could also be used to break one. "And if I'm wrong in that assumption… then the new Vi, the new Champion, will face whatever happens then."

"Your plan works, assuming Yargen is able to return to the world and—"

"She does," Vi interrupted Taavin. "She was in my vision, facing off against Raspian. What if that vision wasn't of failure, but of success? What if that's what she wanted us to work to all along?"

Vi descended the stairs hastily, crossed over to him, and stopped short as she was pinned in place by his wary eyes.

"Is she always this insane?" Deneya asked Taavin. Even in his state, he managed a nod. Vi ignored it.

"If we're working to see a Vi born in this age, we know when the crystal weapons will come. Their fate is linked with Solaris. They'll all return here, in the end, in the hands of my family… And I'll be ready to meet them when they do.

"Thanks to your memories, I'll know where they'll come from. I know how they'll get here. I can shepherd time along. Rather than trying to completely alter fate, I'll just nudge it in the right direction."

Vi had no idea if her plan would work. But she was ready to defend it and continue defending it. She no longer just wanted to keep Raspian sealed away. She wanted to see Yargen usher in a new age of light. She wanted the one thing she'd always wanted: To keep her family safe.

And Solaris would never be safe as long as the crystal weapons and Caverns existed on the continent.

Deneya folded and unfolded her arms, as though she was uncomfortable in her own body. Taavin paced several times. The silence grew heavy.

"You know what you're suggesting, right?" he finally said. "You know what it means for the people you love?"

"I do," Vi whispered softly.

"This idea of guiding time, guiding events that happened before…"

"Means people will be hurt as they have always been," she finished for him, for once reading his mind. "People will die," she corrected herself, not wanting to mince words. "They'll die like Fiera did. They'll suffer under the blight of the crystals on this land."

Vi swallowed hard, looking at the crystals that surrounded her. This was the physical essence of Yargen's power—the power of life, light, and creation. But it had only ever spelled death for those she loved. It was a stain on her family's history. One that Vi would take up the torch from Fiera to burn away.

"But those deaths will mean something, this time. We're on the right path. This time, it ends."

CRYSTAL CAGED

VORTEX CHRONICLES

BOOK FIVE

for the Man
my muse, my light

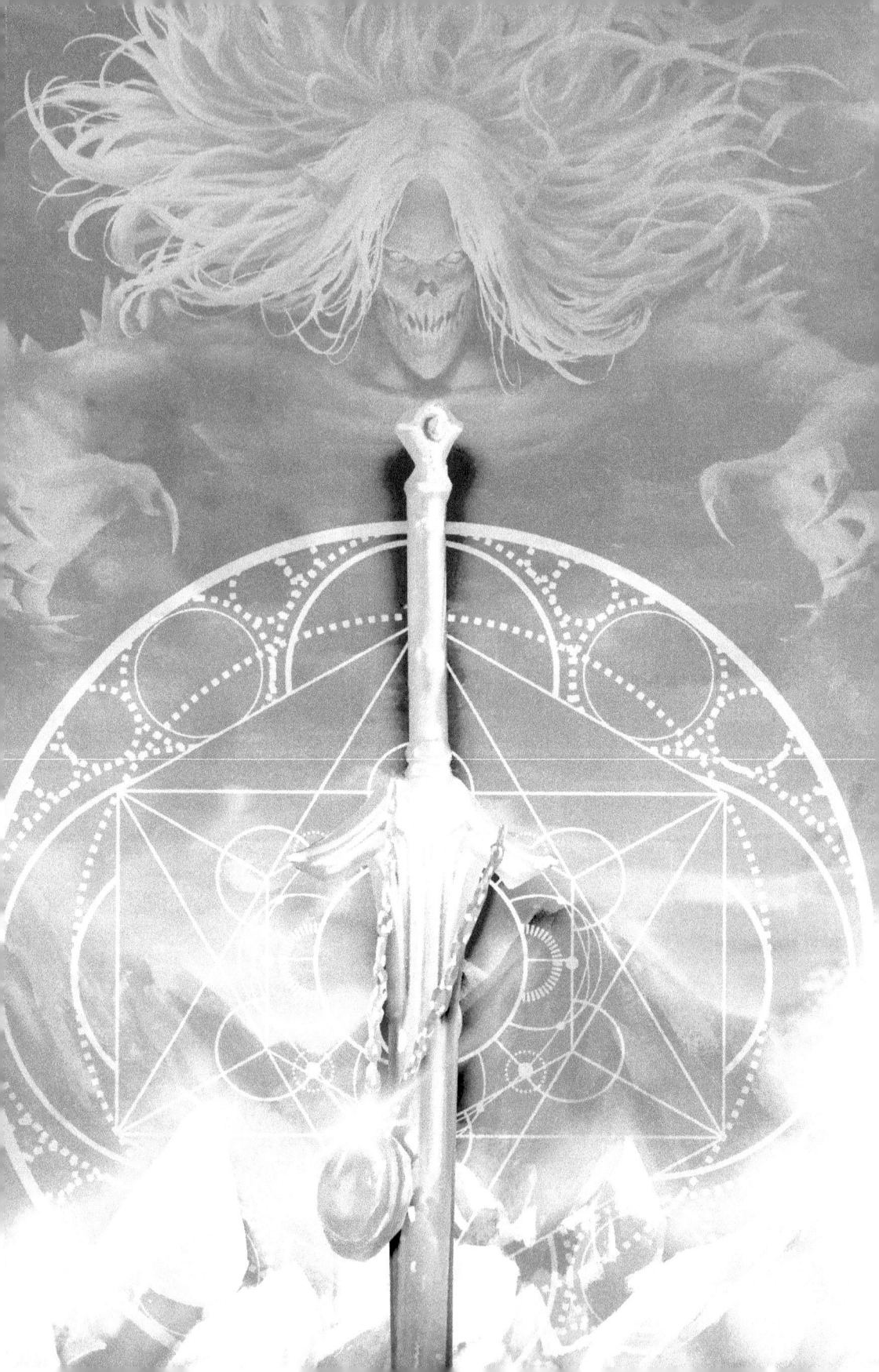

1

THE BLACK-BARKED PINE IN THE early morning almost reminded Vi of the Twilight Forest. Morning's first light glittered through specks of snow overflowing from too-heavy boughs down to shimmering snowdrifts. Vi paused to admire the beams of light, the snowdrifts, the crisp air, and the homey aroma of the fire that plumed smoke out of the chimney of the cabin behind her.

Each morning, she woke and was greeted by the quiet serenity of nature. For fourteen years, she had indulged in the bounty of this remote corner of the Solaris Empire. But it was all about to come to an end.

"I think that's it." Vi deposited the last of Deneya's work into the back of the cart attached to Prism—the massive warstrider previously owned by Princess Fiera.

"Did you get the quiver?" Deneya asked from where she was checking the saddle.

"I did, and the knife set." Vi scanned the items in the cart. It was a scant amount, but all of impressive make. At least, she was impressed. Vi had never suspected her elfin companion capable of such craftsmanship, but time and necessity had been the best teachers. While Vi worked on her magic, Deneya had kept her hands busy with leather and steel work.

Deneya rounded back, yanking on the woolen hat that Vi had knit for her two winters ago to hide her pointed ears, and assessed the load. "I think I'll fetch some decent coin for that set."

"I hope so. I'm tired of roots, pickled vegetables, and trying to cook frozen meat." Mosant was the nearest town, and they held their market once a month. Whenever Deneya went to market, she always came back with items that, a lifetime ago, Vi would've considered trivial. But now they were luxuries beyond compare.

"At least frozen meat doesn't go bad," Deneya said. In the summers, they had to either slowly smoke and dry their meat, or store it deep in the perpetually frozen caves of the mountains. "In a few months, when you're lamenting over meat gone foul because of the heat, I'll bet you'll be begging for next winter to arrive."

"Probably." Then again, Vi didn't expect to see next winter in this cabin.

Fourteen years they had lived in the woods at the far foot of the mountain that housed the Crystal Caverns. Fourteen years, and Vi still looked the same as she had when she'd first woken in this world. Save for the length of her hair. It was now down to her waist, usually woven into a simple, thick braid.

On the inside, however, Vi felt a world away from the young woman she'd been.

She'd learned to survive on her own, and how to go with and without. She'd learned how cold a night without shelter could be, what hunger really meant, what necessity could teach a person. She learned all the things a princess would've never been taught—all the things a princess would never have needed to know.

"I'll see what I can find for us," Deneya said, jolting Vi from her thoughts. "I have a trinket for the tavern owner. Maybe she'll spoil us with some roast hare again."

"We can only hope."

"You going up today?" Deneya's attention turned to the narrow path near their cabin that cut through the mountains.

"Of course." Vi touched the watch that never left her neck. It was tarnished and scratched, no longer the mirror surface Taavin had given her.

"Go on, then, while it's light and you can see the ice on the paths," Deneya encouraged.

"You should go, too. I don't want you traveling at night when the wolves are out." Deneya chuckled and Vi cracked a grin. They both knew the remark was more jest than worry.

"I am the wolf." Deneya's smile split into a wicked smirk. "More fresh meat."

"And more pelts." Vi stepped away as Deneya mounted Prism. "Safe travels."

"You as well. And good luck in there today!"

Before Vi could reply, Deneya clicked her tongue and Prism started his trudge through the snowy forest. The creaking of the cart covered any response she could've given. Not that Vi had any words worth saying.

Good luck in there. She needed more than luck. She needed results.

Their cabin was simple but well made. Deneya's brawn and knack for construction was a compliment to Vi's knowledge of architecture. It'd taken about a year to complete. But since then, they'd added onto it every summer. First it was the stables for their two large warstriders—Prism and Midsummer—and now their yearlings as well. The next year, before the summer rains, they'd replaced the initial thatching with wooden shingles of bark they'd sheared from trees. Another summer they'd laid wooden flooring inside. A different winter they cobbled the loveliest stones they could find over the hearth to make a mantle.

Inside there were two beds, a table, and two chairs. Vi walked over to the corner by her bed and lifted the sword that had been left behind in the Caverns years ago by the Knights of Jadar. She still wondered, from time to time, what the Knights said about that night. Did they recall it clearly? Or was the truth written and re-written through oral embellishments throughout time?

From their cabin, it took her about an hour and a half to walk up to the Crystal Caverns. She could do it in less time. But there wasn't a rush to anything these days. Time had continued its steady march as Vi worked in the shadows, determined to make the impossible happen.

Vi emerged from between cliffs and stepped into the light of the snowfield that coated the base of the mountain where the path up to the Crystal Caverns began. Tracks in the pristine white blanket weren't uncommon. There were a number of animals that continued to wander the mountainsides, even in the heart of winter. But these tracks were different, and fresh.

Someone was here.

Staying close to the rocky mountainside where there was less snow to show her footprints, Vi made her way to the tracks that led up toward the Crystal Caverns. She crouched beside the largest boulder she could find, wedging herself in a cranny.

"*Durroe watt radia,*" she whispered. A glyph appeared around her wrist and magic shimmered at the edges of her vision. A cloak of invisibility settled on her shoulders and she prepared herself to wait.

After about an hour, she heard the whinny of a horse and the clop of hooves over the mountain path. Her muscles had long since seized and gone numb from the waiting. But Vi remained rigid, watching. Her time in the wild had taught her nothing if not patience.

The horse came into view. The broad-shouldered rider atop wore a hooded cloak of deep blue that covered almost all of his face. Vi leaned forward, as though that would help her sight penetrate the shadow the cowl cast.

He continued forward, oblivious to her, down the path he'd arrived from and eastward—the direction one would take to the Capital. Vi waited until he was long out of sight before releasing her magic and making haste up the pathway to the Crystal Caverns.

The moment she entered, Vi pushed magic out through her feet, the crystals illuminating in response to the arrival of the Champion. She searched, but nothing seemed out of place. "*Narro hath hoolo.*"

The words passed her lips easily. Glyphs shone above her bundled chest, hovering over where the watch was underneath. A man with deep plum hair, bright green eyes, and a crescent scar on his cheek stood before her.

He appeared from a slowly rotating glyph that unraveled to carve his outline from the thin air. But when the light faded, he remained. In this place, with the power of Yargen in the very air, he was more real than ever.

"Good morning," Taavin greeted her warmly, though the expression fell flat when his eyes settled on her. "What is it?"

"There was a man here." Vi continued to look around, running her fingertips over the crystals, feeling the magic stored within them and searching for some sign of trauma.

"What kind of man?" Taavin asked, tone grave.

"I couldn't see his face. He wore a simple woolen cloak of navy blue."

"From the Capital?"

"He headed back in that direction. But I can't say for sure." Vi's hand fell at her side. "I don't know what he did here. I can't feel anything different in the crystals."

"Then whatever he did, it wasn't anything significant."

"It worries me, though, seeing someone come to the Caverns."

The world had been quiet for the past fourteen years when it came to the Crystal Caverns. There had been a traveler only one other time—a Western man who arrived shortly after Fiera's death—likely in search of the sword or evidence of what had transpired. Since then, it had been quiet. The sort of quiet that Vi had allowed to lull her into a false sense of security.

"Based on previous timelines, people tend to become interested in this place again around now," Taavin said quietly, scanning the shimmering blue crystals.

"I know." She had made Taavin tell her of the different iterations of the world time and again, over and over, until she knew many by heart. Vi looked down at the sword clutched in her hands. "That means there isn't much time."

"You're close, and you know it." Taavin rested his hand heavily on her shoulder. Every time she summoned him here, Vi savored the slightest of touches for how real they felt. "Perhaps today's the day."

"Perhaps," Vi murmured.

Years ago, Raylynn, Zira's daughter, had asked Vi to make her a crystal weapon. Her answer then had been no. But if the girl were to ask today... Vi's answer would be different.

"I should get to work." She stepped away from him and Taavin assumed his position not far from her, leaning against a crystal. His tall form cut against the light with an agonizing handsomeness that still, even after all this time, stirred desire within her.

Her need for him didn't cool no matter how much she wanted it to. Seeing him like this would always be bittersweet. The truth of his nature was a barrier they'd never been able to surpass.

Focusing, Vi unsheathed the Sword of Jadar, set the scabbard aside, and held the hilt with both hands. She slowly lowered it and, when the very tip met the ground, a jolt of magic burst through the Caverns. The sword was made of crystals—the raw power of Yargen given physical form in the world—so its magic slotted in with the Caverns naturally.

Uncurling her fingers one by one, Vi pulled her hands away, holding them out. Magic arced like a cold, slow-burning fire between her palms and the weapon. She could feel it wrapped tightly around the backs of her fingers, trying to collapse in on itself and return to the sword. Vi twisted her wrists and lifted her hands upward. Her muscles strained, trembling, as though she were lifting a colossal weight.

But she made her mind calm and focused. She controlled this power—not the other way around. Turning her wrists inward once more, Vi felt the last dredges of power drain from the sword. The magic wrapped around her hands, but it almost felt as though it seeped into her. Making a cage with her fingers, she brought the magic together in a ball before her. It fought against her grasp, seeking freedom.

She continued to compress the magic, forcing it inward. The pale blue of raw magic became a blindingly bright light. Sweat dripped down her neck as she focused on condensing the magic.

Pop.

Blinking into the relative dimness, Vi stared at the crystal that hovered in an aura of seafoam blue between her hands. She had drawn the magic from the sword and condensed it down into a *new* crystal. She let out the breath she'd been holding. Vi hadn't dared breathe for the first part of the process.

Twisting her right hand so the crystal hovered just above her palm, Vi lifted her left.

Just as Fiera had done all those years ago, Vi tapped a nearby crystal jutting from the ground and beseeched the magic within. It came forth as she rotated her wrist with painstaking precision. *Come along now*, was her silent command. Magic spun out from the Caverns, condensing into glyphs with no meaning. Perhaps they were words, but neither Vi nor Taavin could read them. So if they had meaning, Yargen kept it hidden.

She poured the power into the crystal she held. The stone's glow intensified, but it didn't change shape or color. Yargen's magic defied time and space. An immense amount of power could be held in a vessel as large as the Crystal Caverns, or as small as the palm of her hand.

The lights in the Caverns began to dim and Vi slowed the rotation of her hand through the air, slowing the draw of power. Two tethers stretched out from the crystal floating above her palm—one to the Caverns and one to the sword.

"Keep going," Taavin commanded.

"What?" Here was where she usually stopped, allowing the magic to spill back into the dimming sword and Caverns.

"Just from the sword," he clarified. "Not the Caverns. Collect all the power from the sword and transfer it to the stone."

"But what if—"

"We do it all again, then."

Do it all again. He didn't mean today's practice. He meant the whole cycle of time they were trapped in.

"No," Vi whispered, mostly to herself. "We won't." This was to be their last time. She had vowed as much to herself, to the world, even if the world would never know it.

One way or another, this vortex would end.

Vi twisted her hand and severed the trembling thread of magic that connected the crystal in her palm to the sword, lifting it away. She watched as the last of the sword's power was extracted.

The weapon transformed into obsidian as the power drained. Once the last dredges were removed, it fell to the floor and shattered into pieces. The magic once held within the sword now hovered above her palm.

"Now, return the power to the Caverns," Taavin commanded.

Vi spun the crystal she'd made through the air, feeling the power unravel from it.

The magic didn't need much guidance from her to return to the crystals surrounding it. Yargen's magic naturally sought out its own. A phantom thread pulled through her. Magic that lingered on her palms was drawn away with the rest. All at once, the crystal hovering above her palm stopped spinning and fell. It had gone dark, just like the sword.

Vi stared at the obsidian around her feet, panting softly. She jerked her head upward. "The sword is gone."

"Make a new one."

"I've never made a sword."

"You just made crystal. You'll merely make it in a different shape this time." Taavin pushed away from the stone he'd been leaning against, his preternatural casualness belying the tension thrumming through Vi like the reverberations of a lightning bolt.

Vi turned back to the nearest crystal jutting from the floor. It was nearly twice the size of her. She rested both hands on the sides of the stone. She'd chosen this path; she could do this. Yargen's magic was around her, within her.

"Easy now, just as before," she whispered.

Magic shimmered underneath her fingertips in response.

Once more, Vi pulled power from the stone. It was easier this time. If working with the sword was like drawing from a pond of magic, this was an ocean. She had much more to work with and the magic sought her out eagerly.

Stepping back, Vi repeated the process and drew out the magic by spreading her hands. Yargen's raw essence shone brighter and brighter, the more she pulled. How much power had the sword held? She couldn't remember. But she doubted anyone but her and Taavin would be able to tell if the new Sword of Jadar was weaker than the last.

Bringing her hands together, Vi watched as the magic condensed once more into a crystal. This time, she kept flooding the stone with power. Glyphs she didn't recognize but inherently understood appeared within her mind: *grow, change, shape*. They were magic given form and tied to her will, forcing the stone to grow as she commanded. Crystals jutted out from that initial seed, becoming hilt and blade. In a blindingly bright minute, a new sword hovered in the air before her.

Taking the hilt in her hand, Vi pulled the blade from the magic forge in which she'd created it. The leftover power soaked back into the Caverns. Some lingered on the sword, flooding into her. As it sank into her bones, she felt a rush straight to the head.

Her thoughts spun dizzily until her attention settled on the weapon in her palm.

"It worked," Vi whispered in awe. A theory, inspired by a five-year-old, supported only by the existence of some black stone that had surrounded Vi after Yargen's magic had protected her once… she'd finally proved it right.

Two arms circled her waist. Vi dropped the sword, startled. A yelp became laughter that echoed off the soaring ceiling of the Caverns as Taavin leaned back and lifted her feet off the ground to spin her in place.

"Put me down!" Vi managed through bursts of laughter. Her sides hurt, though she didn't know if it was from his crushing grip or from laughing more than she had in what felt like years.

"You did it!" Taavin's voice bounced off every crystal as he spun her once more before setting her down. He grabbed her face with both hands and brought his lips to hers. Vi savored the feeling of his breath, hot on her cheeks, and the warmth of his palms, even if it was all over too quickly. "You did it."

"You helped a bit, along the way," she said breathlessly when they broke apart.

"Just a bit though." She couldn't tell if he was being sincere or if he realized he'd been a monumental part of her success. Perhaps he was playing along with her jest. He continued, "It's time for you to return yourself to the world and begin enacting this plan in earnest."

"I know." She'd known for years it was coming. But somehow part of her was still terrified. The truth was, she might never feel ready despite all her convictions. Perhaps that's how it was when the fate of the world hung in the balance. "Walk back with me?" Vi asked, sheathing the new sword and starting for the entrance to the Caverns. "Deneya will need to hear our next steps, too—and she's probably been back from Mosant for at least an hour."

"You could always summon me when you return?" Taavin asked, though his footsteps matched hers. "It's not as though you can't summon me there."

"I know." She had used *narro hath* at the cabin two years ago. That night, she and Deneya had returned from Mosant, where they'd found a bottle of the same spiced liquor they drank together in Norin. Taavin had laughed and reminisced with them. He'd regaled them with tales of Vi's former selves and worlds that were both similar and different.

But he couldn't partake in the festivities, not really. He couldn't drink with them. He couldn't take her to bed as Vi had discovered she'd wanted.

Vi had never allowed herself to summon him there again. The torture of seeing him, wanting him, but not having him, was something she couldn't regularly bear.

"Is it so much to ask to stroll with you?" she asked, pushing away the ache the thoughts left in her.

"I suppose not," he said with a soft chuckle.

They emerged into the sunlight and magic instantly shimmered around Taavin's shoulders. That magic was a reminder of what he really was. In the Caverns, he seemed like any other man. But he was consciousness tethered to a watch and held together by a goddess's words.

Even still, when he offered her his elbow, she took it and ignored the sensation of a thin barrier between them. She ignored that his feet didn't leave footprints in the snow. Vi pulled him close, and savored what already felt like one of the last peaceful moments they were going to have for a long time.

Someday soon... I'll make you real, Vi wanted to say, but the words remained a vow on her heart rather than lips.

She looked down at her hand, feeling the tingle of magic still underneath her fingers. Yargen had remade her body between worlds. The goddess's power was within her—it sought her out. It was the same power that allowed Vi to manipulate the crystals. She was determined to continue exploring the seemingly endless possibilities of the magic. What kind of last-chance-to-save-the-world Champion would she be if she didn't at least try to push the boundaries?

It took about an hour to walk back to the cabin. The late afternoon sun hung low in the sky. They didn't say much, though they didn't need to—just being together was enough.

Deneya was outside, just finishing covering their cart with a tarp to keep the snow off.

"About tim—*oh*, you're here too." Her eyes settled on Taavin. "Is that a good sign or a bad one?"

"I'll let you decide," he quipped in return.

"I had a breakthrough."

"Did you do it? Did you transfer the power in full?" Deneya set down her axe. Vi nodded. "By Yargen's flame, you actually did it!" The handle of the axe had barely fallen into the snow and Deneya was clapping Vi over the shoulders. "Well, this calls for a celebration. It's a good thing I got the roast hare."

"Thanks to Yargen for that." Vi's stomach growled as if on command.

"Come, tell me everything over food." Deneya headed right for the cabin door, holding it open for Taavin. What Vi considered a feast was already set out on the table.

"You set the table," she observed.

"And you say I never do anything nice for you."

"You let the food get cold is what you did." Vi grinned at Deneya as they sat across from each other. Taavin took his place at the foot of Vi's bed.

"Oh, I'm so sorry, *princess*. Let me save you from your portion." Deneya reached over to take her plate.

"I wouldn't do that if I were you. I'm armed." Vi brandished the knife that was set out by her fork.

"Not the mighty Champion and her terrifying, blunt-as-a-butter-knife dagger." Deneya gasped. Vi gave a mock snarl, playfully jabbing the air in Deneya's direction until the woman let go of her plate. "Mercy, I'm unarmed."

"Perhaps I should level the playing field, then." Vi set down the knife, forgetting the food a moment, and untied the crystal sword from her hip. Deneya stopped laughing.

Vi drew the sword and held it out before her, parallel to the ground, at eye level. She focused on it, feeling the magic that collected together and gave the crystals shape. Vi tightened her grip, imagining her hold on the magic becoming greater in turn.

Change shape, she willed the crystals. Magic moved through the blade, invisible to anyone but her, and collected in the far tip of the sword. The blade thinned, transforming into a pole. The magic at the end jutted outward.

By the time the light faded, Vi was holding an axe of crystal.

"You've been making more progress than you've let on," Deneya said with quiet awe.

"You can hold it." Vi stretched her arm across the table.

"You're sure?"

"Yes."

Deneya took the weapon and twirled it once. She stood, swung it two times, and let out a low whistle. "I could cleave so many heads from shoulders with this."

Vi laughed.

"She's accomplished incredible things," Taavin said warmly. Vi glanced at him, the pride in his voice nearly making her blush.

"So, you can manipulate crystals however you please in addition to transferring power between them and the Caverns." Deneya turned back, passing her the axe. "It's what we were hoping for, isn't it?"

"Yes." Vi took the axe in both hands. She was silent a moment, intense focus overtaking her as she shifted the magic within the crystals once more. Like ice melting in sunlight, some of the crystals vanished, others jutted out, smoothed over, and the sword took shape once more.

"When the crystal weapons are taken to the Caverns, Vi will be there to transfer the power and—"

"The magic weapons won't actually be destroyed and the Caverns will remain intact," Deneya interrupted Taavin. "Then we'll combine the collective magic of the crystal weapons, the Caverns themselves, and what's trapped in the flame of Yargen in Risen to give a physical form to the Goddess herself. Then she'll duel Raspian in another battle of light and dark, yes, yes, I know."

"For a battle that the fate of the world hinges on, you make it sound boring," Taavin remarked.

"The fate of the world has been boring these past fourteen years," Deneya quipped without looking at him. She shoveled food into her mouth and Vi took the opportunity to do the same. "What I'm asking is... now that she can do this, what are our next steps?"

"We'll approach the weapons in order, based on Taavin's knowledge of past histories and stones in the river of fate," Vi mused aloud. "First is the sword. We know where the scythe is, so that won't be a problem."

"Glad getting to Meru is listed as 'not a problem'," Deneya muttered. Vi ignored her obvious disbelief and continued.

"The axe is safely hidden away in the North—or it should be."

"It's never been found before the War in the North." Taavin gave Vi a nod.

"That leaves the crown, then," Deneya said from behind her hand as she chewed. "Where do we think that one is?"

"Almost impossible to say. The crown is always so variable in its location." Taavin scowled. The crown was never a pleasant topic of conversation. It had the most variables and made them all nervous.

"For the time being, we work with the stones in the river. We try to vary the timeline as little as possible," Vi said calmly. "We'll go to the Capital and see Aldrik gets the sword so he can fulfill that stone in the river of fate: him bringing the sword to the Caverns."

"You're giving him the sword?" Deneya blinked in shock.

"Of course not," she said with a laugh. "I'm going to need you to make me a new one."

"*Me* make a new—" Deneya stopped herself, comprehension dawning on her face "—*oh*, I get it."

"And, honoring the stones in the river, will help ensure the birth of a new Champion," Taavin said with an approving nod.

The words grated her, but Vi didn't let it show. How were they supposed to look toward success if they were constantly planning for failure? For the time being, it wasn't a question she was ready to pose to him. They were on the same page, and the night was going beautifully.

She swallowed the uncomfortable thoughts with a hunk of rabbit and washed it down with a long drink.

"Then it's clear where we're headed next." She punctuated the statement by setting down her wooden cup heavily.

"Back to Norin?" Deneya said with a smirk, knowing full well what Vi was about to say.

"If you'd like." Vi played into the woman's jest. "But I'll be heading to the capital of the Solaris Empire."

"About time."

"About time?" Vi snorted. "Imagine how I feel... it's taken about thirty-two years and one rebuilding of the world for me to get to the home of my forefathers."

Solarin, the capital of the Solaris Empire, was nestled atop a twin-peaked mountain. At the very top of the city, stretching toward the taller of the two summits, was the Imperial Palace. It spilled downward into stone buildings with tiled roofs.

Even from the switch-back road leading up to the city, Vi could see the castle's golden-tipped spires and gigantic pennons forever fluttering in the mountain breezes.

"It's smaller than I imagined," Deneya said from the horse next to her, Midsummer. Vi rode Prism. Both women held lead ropes for the yearlings trailing close behind.

"Smaller, really?" From where Vi sat, it was massive. And they were still a good half hour down the mountain.

Deneya shrugged. "Nothing on the Dark Isle compares to Risen."

"You can't compare Solaris to Meru." Vi chuckled. They spoke of a world not too far from their own, yet the travelers around them continued on none the wiser. Anyone who overheard their conversation likely wouldn't believe or make sense of the remarks anyway.

They arrived at the main gate of the capital in good time. Their warstriders towered over most men and beasts; even their young offspring were the size of a regular horse. Rather than trying to fit in, Vi worked to stand out with her Western horses and dark hair.

"Excuse me, sir." They rode for one of the Imperial guards stationed by the gate.

"May I help you?"

"I'm looking to speak with the master of horse at the Imperial palace. We bring a gift for the young prince's fifteenth birthday and coming-of-age ceremony." Vi motioned to the yearlings and added the slightest hint of a Western accent to her words.

"That ceremony isn't for months yet."

"Horses take time to settle and train," she countered calmly.

"Head down the main road. It's hard to miss the castle entrance. You'll ask for Augus when you get to the stables," the guard answered dully.

"Thank you." Vi gave him a nod and they continued plodding along the main road of Solarin.

A sensation much like the first time she'd stepped foot on Meru overtook her. Icicles shone in the morning light hanging off undisturbed windowsills and gutters. Men leaned over balconies, taking drags off pipes that filled the air with sweet smoke. Music she didn't know lofted over the sounds of people talking.

This was the place where she should've lived… in another world.

The palace was built in layers up the mountainside. At its lowest point were long rows of stables that reminded Vi somewhat sadly of the castle in Norin. They were stopped by two guards at the gates.

"Business?" one of the men demanded.

"We're here to speak with Augus." Vi motioned to the all-black colt with a stripe of white on his forehead. "We have a gift for the prince."

"A moment." The guard ran into the stables and returned with a barrel-chested man who had a thick coating of golden hair over his forearms.

"I hear you've got something for the prince." The man pushed up his sleeves a little farther. "Well, bring him in, let me see the creature."

Argus led them into the stables, heading for an empty stall toward the back. Both women dismounted when they came to a stop. Vi untied the lead rope of the black yearling from her saddle, passing it to Argus. The stable master did a quick round of the horse and let out a low whistle. His eyes swept across the four mounts.

"Where'd you come across these lovely creatures?"

"My father was a horse trainer for the royal family." Vi thickened her Western accent slightly.

"Your father? Does he have a name?"

Vi wrung her hands, looking askance. "I shouldn't say."

"I can't rightly give the crown prince a gift that I can't verify."

"Clearly they're warstriders of good stock," Deneya huffed.

"Yes, I can see that, but the Emperor will insist."

"Then the Emperor is—"

"It's all right, Danya," Vi said hastily, interrupting the woman with the fake name they had agreed on. She looked over at the stable master, attempting to be the living embodiment of insecurity. "Between you and me?"

"Yes?" The man's eyebrows arched.

"My father was Ronaldo." There were a few events that Vi would never need Taavin's help recalling, and the night she escaped Norin with Fiera was one of them. The stablemaster in Norin had assumed she was taking Prism to Ronaldo for boarding, following the birth of the prince.

"Ronaldo... you can't be talking about *the* Ronaldo? Legendary breeder for warstriders?" Vi gave a meek nod. "I thought he only had two sons."

"I'm not..." Vi intentionally fumbled her words.

"Vivian was conceived on the wrong side of the sheets. Or barn, as it were," Deneya finished for her.

"Ronaldo, the dog." Augus shook his head. "Right, well, this all explains the apparent quality of the animals. You willing to part with the other yearling as well? Perhaps the whole family? I know the black one with the stripe is a gift for the prince. But I could pay you for the others."

Vi and Deneya exchanged a glance. They hadn't really discussed this. They'd managed to stretch the gold Vi had taken from Norin for years due to their own resourcefulness, with help from Deneya's profits selling her wares. But it couldn't hurt to have a little extra coin.

It also didn't hurt to have a swift getaway on good horses they didn't have to steal.

"I hadn't planned on it," Vi started slowly, hoping her hesitation read as a bastard daughter's love for tokens gifted from her father. "The other yearling we might be willing to part with." Vi looked at the creature. "But the parents..."

"The yearling is a start." Argus stroked his chin. "How long are you staying in the city? At least a year?"

"Hopefully longer than that. We wanted to find work," Deneya answered. "Perhaps establish a life here."

"You seem like an able-bodied young woman. I could put you to work here, in the stables. Even board these fine beasts at no extra cost to you."

"Really? That'd be great!" Deneya flashed him a bright smile.

"Excellent. And perhaps, if you're still here come summer... you'd let me breed these two again and sell me that foal too?" Argus showed the root of his kindness. "Warstriders of this caliber are hard to come by, and I would be remiss to let you go so easily."

He gave a genuine chuckle. The whole time the stable master had been stroking the mounts. Vi doubted he even realized that he'd gone through all of their bridals, checking them.

"Perhaps," Vi relented. Deneya had a job in the palace without too much effort. The longer the man thought they'd be useful to him, the better. "Thanks for offering my friend a job."

"No trouble. I could put you to work as well? Daughter of Ronaldo would be a welcome addition to my staff."

"Thank you, but I'm hoping to find a job that doesn't involve horses. I've mucked enough stables for one lifetime."

Argus chuckled at that. "Well, if you change your mind, come back. And you, Danya, I'll see you with the sun tomorrow."

"Of course." Deneya forced a smile so false that Vi had to struggle not to laugh at it.

"If you'll excuse us, we're meeting an acquaintance in the Imperial Library."

"Is that right? Marc!" Argus called for the guard from earlier, who begrudgingly stepped over. "Take these two up to the library through the castle." He looked back to them. "Much faster than going through the city."

Vi and Deneya said their thanks and followed behind Marc into the palace of Solaris.

Gooseflesh covered her arms the moment they crossed the threshold and Vi let out a sigh of equal parts delight and awe. They went into a side hall that wound around the throne room and receiving area. Her breath hitched as they turned a corner, the room opening into a sitting area. Vi delicately lifted a hand, feeling the fitted stones of the wall.

She touched the masonry of the palace like she was greeting a long-lost friend.

Every twist and turn of the candle-lit halls thrilled her. Every stairwell that rounded back on itself, overlooking Solarin on each landing, sent shivers up her spine.

She knew this castle better than anywhere in the world, even though this was the first time she'd stepped foot in it. She knew the pathways that would head to the royal wing, guarded with a stunning gold gate. She knew the secret servants' halls her mother spoke of and that she'd delighted in finding on her maps.

She knew the moment they laid eyes on the library doors.

The heavy door glided over the plush carpet silently at the guard's slightest push. The smell of leather and parchment filled her nose. Vi's eyes settled on the gold-gilded cherry wood bookcases that lined up in rows down the center hallway of the library. She stared at the center circulation desk, and the ancient looking man behind it who didn't even so much as look up from what he was working on.

With a soft click, the doors behind them shut, and Vi was snapped back into reality.

"It's just as she said," Vi whispered. She was drawn to the books as if by a trance. Her hand closed around one of the metal sliding ladders that allowed people to reach the tops of the dizzyingly tall shelves.

"What is? Who?" Deneya asked.

"My mother." Vi ran her fingers along the spines. She looked ahead to the outer wall she knew was lined with windows. Her mother had spoken fondly of a particular window where she would always sit to read. Would Vi be able to tell which, even though Vhalla had yet to step foot in the castle in this world? Would she feel it in her marrow as keenly as she could feel Yargen's magic? "She always said she wanted to introduce me to her friends here."

"I doubt your mother's friends will show up for a few years yet." Deneya laced her fingers, placing them behind her head as Vi let out a soft laugh.

"Her friends weren't people… they were books."

"Books? Your mother sounds like a dull person."

Vi grinned at Deneya. "My mother's life was anything but. You'll see soon enough."

They reached the end of the bookshelf and Vi looked down the long line of windows. Each one had a seat carved out beneath its glass. Cerulean pillows turned them into comfortable reading nooks.

Vi couldn't tell which one had been, and would become, her mother's.

"So, now that we've met your mother's 'friends' and I somehow ended up with a job that will involve literal shit… it's your turn."

"Yes." Vi tore her eyes from the windows. "You wait here while I—"

"I'm not waiting with a bunch of books." Deneya's tone reminded Vi of the woman's disdain for reading. "I'm going to explore the city and begin to get a lay of the land."

"Where will I find you?"

"In the closest pub to this frosty library, I'd bet."

"Are you exploring the city or getting drunk?" Vi asked dryly.

"It's been a while since we had the comforts of a city." Deneya grinned.

"Keep your head about you and the gold in our pockets, please."

"I always have my head about me. And I have a *job*, remember? I'll be spending my coin how I please." Deneya stepped away with a wave and vanished among the rows of books.

Vi watched her for a moment before going in the opposite direction. She'd made it into the castle. Now it was time to break in to the Tower of Sorcerers.

THERE WERE A FEW principles Uncle Jax had taught her since Vi was a little girl. Right at the top of the list was that the South hated sorcerers above all else.

Vi hadn't understood why when she was younger. She'd merely accepted it, as children do. But experience had taught her that the hatred went all the way back to the original, magic-less settlers of the Dark Isle, fleeing persecution on Meru. While that history had long been lost on the general public, it established Vi's expectation for her time here.

Starting with finding the Tower of Sorcerers.

The Tower was hidden in plain sight to prevent the servants and citizens of Solarin from being on edge all the time. There was a main entry accessible to the public, though even that was difficult to find. Vi knew where it was, of course. But she was closer to a back door. Sneaking in would have a far greater impact.

She stopped along one of the many hallways of the palace. She'd taken the long way to get here, savoring every step. No one stopped her. It was miraculous how far she could go when she walked with confidence.

Vi stood in front of a seemingly plain stone wall. On one of the stones was a symbol of two halves of a circle, broken apart and off-set from each other. It was a simplified version of the Broken Moon, the symbol of the Tower of Sorcerers.

Glancing around the hallway to make sure no errant servant would see her, Vi tapped the stone and watched her finger disappear within it. It was an illusion, carefully crafted and maintained by one of the Waterrunners in the Tower. She side-stepped through the wall with confidence, into a nearly pitch-black tunnel.

At the far end was a single flame bulb by an unassuming, unlocked door. The door led to a winding pathway that spiraled up higher and higher. Circular common areas were on her right, taking up the center of the tower. Doors to individuals' rooms were on her left. Flame bulbs lit the interior passage every several steps.

She passed by a group of people on her way up. They stopped talking, then quickly exchanged whispers and glances at the sight of her. But just like the servants she'd passed on the way here, no one made an attempt to speak with or stop her.

At the top of the tower was the office of the Minister of Sorcery. In her time, this room had been occupied by Fritznangle Chareem. This was where he would've greeted her and welcomed her as a new member of the Tower when she finally came home.

For a brief moment, Vi rested her fingertips on the door and closed her eyes, imagining that moment as she had so many years ago. Try as she might, she couldn't find the fantasy. Even opening her eyes and staring at the door, Vi had a hard time summoning what had been one of her more favorite daydreams.

The child who had dreamed them was long gone.

Vi gave a knock on the door and an unfamiliar voice responded, "Enter."

Letting herself in, Vi stepped into the generously sized office. The Minister of Sorcery sat at a desk, running a hand through his sand-colored hair. Books were crammed into shelves. A workstation bubbled with something sweet-smelling Vi couldn't place. She did a visual sweep of the room before her eyes met the bright blue ones of the Minister. His attention was focused solely on her.

"I don't know you." Egmun didn't mince words.

"Unfortunate for you, but easily remedied." Vi sat herself in one of the plush leather chairs that faced the desk. She tapped her fingers on the armrest, acting as though she was already somewhat impatient. "I'm here for a job."

"A job?"

"Yes."

His eyes narrowed. "You're not of the Tower."

"Not yet. Though I'm looking forward to being a part of it." Vi smiled sweetly at the face of the man whom she planned to play like a fiddle.

"Usually one would schedule a meeting with me, and I would meet them in the reception hall at the base of the Tower."

Vi couldn't tell if he was cross or impressed for the unorthodox way she'd gone about this. Egmun likely didn't know himself. "Yes, I thought this would be faster. Cut right to the chase."

"*How* did you get up the Tower without an escort? Someone must be stationed at the public entrance at all times to prevent wanderers like you." He tapped his fingers against each other; magic rose around him like a tide.

"I didn't use the public entrance."

"How did you get to a private one, then?"

"I have my ways." Vi tilted her head. "Wouldn't you like those ways to be under your employ?" He was curious. She'd tempted him with a nibble of knowledge. From here, she'd slowly feed him more in just the right amounts until he was eating from her hands.

"Do you enjoy avoiding questions?"

"Insofar as it suits me." Vi smirked.

"What's your name? Will you at least give me a direct answer for that?"

"Vivian."

"Vivian," he repeated. "And is there a family name to go along with that?"

She shook her head. "Just Vivian."

"I assume you have some kind of magic, otherwise you wouldn't be here looking for a job in the Tower of Sorcerers. Judging from your looks—you're a Firebearer?"

Vi lifted her hand and summoned flames around her palm. They snaked and wriggled between her fingers, illuminating the room in a red-orange glow. She extinguished them by balling her hand into a fist.

"Yes, well... I have enough Firebearers. Sorry to disappoint you." He pursed his lips together and looked back down at his desk. "If you excuse yourself without issue I will spare you the trouble of calling the guard for trespassing on the Tower uninvited." Vi didn't buy his dismissal for a moment. She'd bet anything that if she stood and walked off, he'd follow to see what secret passage was the Tower's weak spot.

"I never said I was here to offer you my skills as a Firebearer."

"You're still here?" Egmun glanced up at her.

"We both have something the other needs, and I think we should work together," Vi continued calmly, folding her hands over her lap. Egmun was now staring at her, saying everything with his eyes. Vi let the moment drag out. She was making a bold move, but the magnitude of her plans could hinge on little else. "I consider myself a researcher of crystals as well."

"I don't know what you're talking about."

"Of course you don't." Vi smiled and stood, walking over to one of the windows with purposeful strides as she spoke. She acted as though the office was her own. "Then I'll just talk *at* you for a moment, and let's see if anything sounds interesting to you...

"I grew up in the West reading about the power of crystals and hearing all the colorful stories that surround them. Stories of a power unlike any other. There was one thing, more than anything else, that entranced me—the Sword of Jadar."

"The sword is long gone." His whole attention was on her now.

"So they say... So I want people to believe." Vi glanced over her shoulder as the man jumped to his feet.

"You have it?" He was so hungry for the answer that he was nearly drooling over the question. Vi had been away from people for so long that she'd forgotten just how foolish power-hungry men could be.

"I do."

"Are you a Knight of Jadar?"

"If I was a Knight of Jadar, would I be offering the sword to a Southerner?" Vi arched her eyebrows. "The Knights seek the sword to bring back the might of Mhashan. They're old men yearning for a renaissance of their glory days because they can't handle that the world has changed." Vi allowed venom to seep into the words. "Mhashan is gone. And I don't want to use the crystals' power to bring back the past."

"Then what do you want?"

To save the world. "Must I want anything more than the pursuit of knowledge?"

The hard line of his brow softened at the question. She'd disarmed him. Just as Taavin had advised her, Egmun was a man who thirsted for knowledge above all else. Curiosity was an irresistible carrot for him that Vi now dangled at the end of a stick.

"Prove you have the sword," he finally demanded.

She clicked her tongue. "It doesn't work that way. Like I said, we each have something the other needs. It doesn't serve me to give you my bargaining chip without first getting something in return."

"The Sword of Jadar is quite the bargaining chip. What could I possibly offer you of equal value?"

"The crown prince."

"What do you need him for?"

"If you are as well-researched on the crystals as your reputation has led me to believe, then I assume you know about the barrier in the Caverns?"

"You mean the door?" he clarified. It didn't entirely confirm her suspicion that he was the dark-hooded man she'd seen at the Caverns, but it did support the theory.

"Yes, it leads to the heart of the Caverns, where the true power is. The sword can unlock that power, with the right ritual." The best lies were grounded in the slightest bit of truth. "But the barrier was formed by the late Empress Fiera."

"It's true then, the rumors of her death?" Vi nodded, wondering just what rumors had been flying about while she lived in the shadow of the Caverns. "Then, that means…"

"We need the crown prince to get to the true power. His magic is similar enough to his mother's. He'll be able to undo the barrier if we train him well enough with the crystals," Vi finished for him. She didn't actually know if Aldrik could undo the barrier alone or not. Fiera seemed to have an instinct for Lightspinning, despite all odds. Perhaps her son would as well. If not, Vi would be there to make sure there were no hiccups.

"*We?*" Egmun repeated, sounding somewhat offended.

"The sword is nothing if the door can't be opened. And opening the door is useless without the sword because you will not be able to access the heart of the Caverns without it." Vi crossed back over to him, perching herself on the edge of his desk. Placing her palm flat against its surface, ignoring the papers, Vi leaned toward the blue-eyed man. "Like I said, we need each other."

"How do I know I can trust you?"

"You don't. It'll have to be an act of faith on your end." Vi shrugged. "But if I were you… if I were a man of your talents and intellect, I wouldn't let an opportunity like this go. You don't have much to lose. Either I speak true, and the Sword of Jadar along with all the power in the Crystal Caverns could be *yours*," she whispered the words, letting them hang in the air. "Or I'm lying, and you can kill me for trespassing in the Tower of Sorcerers, or some other invented crime, whenever it suits you. I'm sure the Emperor will take your side over a random Westerner if it came to that."

Egmun considered this for a long minute.

"I do think I have an opening here at the Tower, for someone of your talents." Vi hummed as an invitation for him to keep talking. "Perhaps I could invite you to stay here as a personal assistant of mine? That way you're not troubled with the day-to-day, and your mind can be free to work on other projects."

"That would be wonderful." Vi leaned away and slid off the edge of the desk.

"Excellent. Now, regarding the sword—" he said eagerly.

"I'll show it to you when the time is right. Our deal is still fresh, minister, let it harden before we begin worrying about the next steps." Vi smiled. She needed to buy herself some time in the palace to search for the crown. The longer she could delay bringing Aldrik and the sword to the Caverns, the better. "In the meantime, I would like to get settled into my new quarters."

"Your… quarters?"

"Why, yes, I believe it's common for teachers and students of the Tower of Sorcerers to be given their own rooms?" Vi arched her eyebrows. Egmun pursed his lips, but didn't object. As long as she had the sword and knowledge to dangle before him, he would do her bidding.

"I fear the Tower is rather full at the moment."

"What a shame," Vi said, making it clear she really didn't have time for excuses with her tone alone.

"Though, I do have a room I think I could make do, if you're not too picky." He rummaged through his desk, producing an iron key. "This way, if you please."

The man led her out of his office and they wound even higher up the Tower.

"Beneath my office are the quarters I use," Egmun said. They stopped before an unmarked door, which Egmun unlocked before passing Vi the key. "This is an unused storeroom, which I will gladly appoint for your use."

Vi stepped into the chambers and waved her hand. Flames sparked to life in the braziers around the room. There wasn't much in it. Mostly empty shelves and cabinets lined the back wall. A few crates were piled up about the room and a doorway led to an attached bathroom.

"I think it was originally intended to be the minister's quarters. But I've never known a minister to use them since the lower chambers are much larger." Egmun shrugged. "Will this do?"

"Nicely."

"Excellent, I'll have Tower members start setting it up for you immediately. While they do, perhaps we can discuss our business further?"

"There is nothing more to discuss until you show me you can provide the prince."

"Tomorrow morning then," he said definitively. "Meet me in my office just before dawn, and you will meet Prince Aldrik."

"Most excellent." Vi smiled, as though the statement didn't curdle her stomach. She'd taken this young man's mother. Now, she'd lead him down a path that would result in extreme hardship.

"See you bright and early, Miss Vivian." Egmun spun on his heel and started down the Tower.

"I wouldn't miss it for the world."

4

Deneya was true to her word. Vi found her in the second pub she checked with only the faintest flush to her cheeks. Her wits were still about her, and Vi filled her in on what had transpired with Egmun over a flagon of her own.

Night had fallen when she made her way back to the Tower. Vi strode with confidence up the main, spiraling walkway. The names engraved on silver nameplates and set on the doors to her left caught her eye.

She stopped, staring at one.

Friznangle Chareem.

Vi ran her fingers over the carefully engraved letters. Her other hand touched the watch around her neck lightly, remembering Fritz's original gift ages ago. How old was he now? Ten? Twelve? Vi didn't know. But this man was the one who had always given the watch to every new Vi. This was the current shade of the man who had given her Taavin a world ago.

She was still very much at the beginning of her journey. Yet Vi felt like she was catching a glimpse of the end.

Footsteps echoed up from below and Vi hastily stepped away from the door, starting up the tower once more. She kept her head down and her pace swift all the way back to her room, lighting the braziers once more on entry.

This time, the light didn't fall on a storeroom in disarray. Egmun hadn't lied about getting the Tower students to set up the room quickly. Where once there were crates, now a narrow bed stood beside a desk with a single chair. The shelves had also been emptied and dusted.

She locked the door behind her and uttered, *"Narro hath hoolo."*

Taavin appeared, inspecting the room as he usually did whenever she summoned him in a new place.

"You're in the Tower?"

Vi brought him up to speed. By the time she finished, she had completed several laps around the furniture and was now perched on the top of one of the low bookcases in front of the window.

"Then everything is going according to plan," Taavin said after a long stretch of silence.

Vi gave a nod. "This will give me enough time to look for the crown."

"And Egmun will be the one to take Aldrik to the Caverns to fulfill fate's needs, ensuring we continue toward the birth of the next Champion."

"Yes. I'll need to ask Deneya to continue working on the sword we'll illusion to fool Egmun. That way he doesn't get his hands on the actual crystal weapon." She went to pace, but Taavin grabbed her forearm. He pulled her a step closer to him, resting both hands on her shoulders.

"If everything is going well, why do you seem so restless?"

"It's hard to explain." Vi glanced askance. "I know what I'm doing. I know what the path I've chosen means: that people will suffer because of my actions. That instead of trying to stop that suffering, I will play into it, hoping it leads to success. And if we are successful, everything will have meaning."

"Or the world will be rebuilt and their suffering is lost."

"Yes, or that." Vi retrieved the unassuming, shimmering crystal that held all the power of the Sword of Jadar from the depths of an inner pocket on the long, threadbare coat she wore. She turned it over in her fingertips, watching the magic shift and swirl with each pass. The magic clung to her, begging her to absorb its power and use it to shape the world to her will. With a thought, she could make it grow into the sword if she so desired. "I was thinking about the weapons."

"All right?"

"When Yargen sealed Raspian away, she split herself into three—one part to the Caverns, one part to the staff of the Champion that would later become the crystal weapons, and one part to the flame of Risen."

"Yes?"

She could hear the confusion in his voice. This was something they'd been over countless times. Vi shook her head, trying to remain focused. A thought was taking shape.

"The flame in Risen... I keep thinking about it. When the world was rebuilt—when my body was rebuilt by Yargen's hand—it was because of the power stored in the flame. We unleashed it."

"Yes." This time, the word took on a heavier meaning. Taavin already knew what she had pieced together—she could hear it in his voice. Vi met his eyes, not allowing him to hide from her.

"You know what I'm about to say, don't you?"

"If my suspicions are correct."

"And you're so rarely wrong." It suddenly felt as though someone had punched her in the gut. She tensed every muscle and braced herself. "Tell me what happened to the other Vi's, after a new Champion was born? If I'm the ninety-third Vi, what happened to the ninety-second, after she failed at her mission?"

"She gave her power back to the flame."

"I'm a part of Yargen, now," Vi said softly. "My body isn't really my own." She'd known it wasn't from the first time she'd set foot in this world. She'd known it down in her marrow as keenly as she knew Yargen's magic was there. "If we succeed, my body will return to her as well."

"You don't know that." He took a step closer.

"How else could it happen?"

"How does she manage to both rewind time and begin a new world? Even we don't fully understand the ways of the divine." Taavin rested his hand on the crystal, wrapping his fingers around hers. The motion was meant to take her hand. But the moment his fingers met the stone, he became that much more real. His touch was firmer, warmer. The faint glow that had emanated from him vanished entirely.

Vi twisted, careful to keep him as close as possible. Releasing the crystal into his palm, Vi ran her hands up his tunic and twirled her fingers in the hair at the nape of his neck. As long as the crystal touched him, he was as good as real.

She brushed her lips against his. Taavin ducked his head, leaning forward for another, longer kiss. She wanted to linger there forever, in ignorant bliss for him.

"Don't worry yourself so much about these things," he spoke against her mouth. "There is much that must come to pass before it's even a concern. Each event more unlikely than the last."

"Are you trying to make me ignore my responsibility as Champion?"

"At least for tonight," he said with a sultry note. Vi felt him grin against her mouth and it prompted her to mirror the action. Sometimes, there was simply too much to worry over.

Troubling herself with what would happen when all of Yargen's power was collected was pointless until she actually collected that power. First, she needed to worry about getting the crystal weapons and figuring out where the crown was hidden. But even before all that… she'd worry about the man before her.

She pushed him gently, allowing the back of his knees to meet the bed frame. Taavin sat heavily. The bed groaned under his weight—the ropes supporting the mattress tightened—and the sound jostled her from the trance his touch could put her under.

Vi blinked at him. His hands were on her hips as she straddled him, one still clutching the stone. Taavin looked up at her from underneath heavy lids lined with long lashes. His lips were already begging for hers again.

But all she could do was stare, running her fingertips down his cheek.

"What is it?" Taavin whispered.

"When you touch this, you're real. As real as you were in the Crystal Caverns," Vi mused gingerly. "I think if I linked your consciousness to the crystal, I wouldn't need to maintain *narro hath* and you would be here with me."

"Vi…" His free hand tapped at the watch around her neck. "I am always here for you. Isn't that enough?"

It should be. Some didn't get half as lucky. But she was needy. And there was some streak of selfish princess in her when it came to this man where Vi would never learn to leave well enough alone.

She wanted him. All of him.

"You are always enough." Vi kissed the tip of his nose lightly. "I just want all of you."

"You have all I am."

"I still want to try linking your form with the crystal," she persisted.

"You might have successfully managed the sword. But this is different. And the last thing you want to do is ruin the magic of the watch. Meddle with that incorrectly, and you really will lose me, along with your and your future selves' chances to save this world by benefiting from my collected memories."

"I know I can," she insisted. "Let me try."

"No, we must be cautious." A note of finality in his tone made Vi relent.

She sighed and pressed her forehead against his. "I want you like this." She wanted to feel warmth from him. To breathe in his scent. To feel his smooth skin and silky hair under her fingers.

"Do you think I don't want it?" He caught her lips again, planting a firm kiss as he pulled her closer to him and further away from the idea.

"I want to roll over and find you in the night. I want to come back and see you here, waiting to greet me," Vi whispered between short, sweet kisses.

Taavin leaned back, pulling her with him. He twisted, and Vi found herself beneath him. Their weight made the mattress sink further into the ropes as he continued to clutch the stone in his palm.

With *narro hath* he was real to her.

With the power of Yargen, he could be real to the world.

"I want to go about my day and run into you," he murmured, kissing her cheeks. "I want to catch your eyes from across a square, or a hall, or a library, and share a smile that only we would know. A smile to assure you that by night you will find your way into my arms once more." His lips moved down her neck and Vi let out a soft sigh.

I need you to give me a place to hide from the world when I need, Vi wanted to say. She had no reprieve, not really… not since she had fallen in love with him only to end his mortal form. The arms that had become her home were taken from her, just like everything else.

"It's a beautiful dream," Vi whispered.

"Indulge in that beautiful dream, tonight." Taavin brought his lips back to hers. Vi kissed him so firmly that when he pulled away, he was breathless. "Indulge in us, because that's all we have."

His words were like honey warmed in sunlight, bright, sweet, and oh so tempting. She found herself stuck in them as much as she was stuck in place, helpless beneath his wandering hands. It had been fourteen years since she had a room to herself, and the ground of the Crystal Caverns was far too cold and hard.

"I can't," Vi whispered.

"You can't?" He slowly pulled away and sat up on the bed.

"I need to start looking for some leads on the crown," Vi murmured, standing. She also had some research she wanted to do.

"Now?"

"No time like the present." Vi hooked his chin with her finger and pulled his lips to her for one more firm kiss. When they pulled apart, she gave him a beaming smile. "Perhaps I'll let you be the one to keep me up all night soon." Vi held out her hand expectantly.

"Don't tempt me." Taavin passed the stone back to her.

She leaned away and released her focus on *narro hath*. Taavin vanished.

With the stone in her pocket, Vi wandered down to the Tower library—a smaller and more private collection, separate from the Imperial Library. It was late, but she doubted she'd be able to sleep tonight. Her mind was far too full.

The library was dark and icy cold. Vi pushed her spark to burn beneath her skin, warming her as her breath fogged the air. There was a hearth on the far side of the circular room, but Vi didn't light it. She didn't want to draw attention from any other late-night wanderers.

A mote of fire appeared at her side, just enough to see by. The gold embossing on the spines that lined the shelves winked at her as Vi explored the library. She flipped the stone over and over in her pocket, her thoughts centering around it.

If she could manipulate the crystals to make weapons, she could manipulate them into the shape of a body. Crystals were Yargen's magic given physical form. Her presence in this world was proof of that. The body Yargen gave Vi between time, when the world was remade, was a result of Yargen's magic making a physical form.

Furthermore, if Taavin's consciousness could be anchored in a watch, it could be placed in a hypothetical body. It was all theory, yes. But she had facts to back up that theory.

Still, she knew no matter what she said, Taavin wasn't going to let her experiment... at least not until she could offer him some assurances that she would succeed.

Vi came to a stop by a back section of worn, tucked-away books. Most of the titles had flaked off their spines. Still, one volume caught her eye. She knew she should be looking for clues to the crown, but Vi couldn't stop herself. She hooked her finger on the book, sliding it from its place.

"*The Windwalkers of the East*," she murmured and flipped open the first page. It was a record, put together by none other than the current Imperial Librarian, Mohned Topperen. *Topperen*. The name was familiar to her—beyond the stories her mother told—but Vi couldn't place how or why.

The manuscript was an account of the Burning Times through interviews with one of the last surviving Windwalkers. Vi scanned the pages, which covered everything from magical theory to terrible experiments involving human sacrifice meant to unlock the true power of the crystals. Fiera had learned how to manipulate crystals by reading accounts from the Burning Times. Perhaps, if Vi did her own research, she could find something that would give her the additional evidence she needed to convince Taavin to let her experiment.

A pair of footsteps approached and Vi snuffed her flame on instinct. She hastily shut the book and returned it to the shelf. But she hadn't been fast enough.

"Who's there?" a male voice called into the darkness.

"*Durroe watt radia*," Vi whispered under her breath, stepping back against the wall.

"I'll give you one more chance. Show yourself."

Fire burst into life in the hearth. It cast long, shifting shadows on each of the bookcases. Vi could see its light shining through the tops of the books between the shelves from where she stood.

She saw the orange glow falling on a young man who needed no introduction. Her heart began to race.

Vi had wondered what she'd feel when she first laid eyes on Aldrik Solaris. The man who, in another world, had been her father. The man whose mother she'd taken from him.

There were too many emotions within her now to count, blending together into something impossible to name.

His dark hair went past his shoulders, unbound in a style Vi had never seen her father wear before. He was awkwardly tall, mostly legs and gangly arms—a body half grown and still trying to fill itself out. Vi recognized that phase. She'd been there herself.

This is not your father, Vi reminded herself. Yet her eyes, her heart, tried to tell her otherwise. The magic glyph around her wrist trembled with her hands.

He walked down the rows of shelves, searching. "I could've sworn..." Aldrik mumbled. Vi remained stone still, and the young prince eventually shook his head and rubbed his eyes. It was late, and he no doubt wrote off her faint light as a trick of his mind.

The prince set out purposefully for another section of the library. She watched him over the tops of the books. Every muscle was tense; she wouldn't have been able to move if she'd tried.

What is it you're looking for? Vi silently asked as Aldrik scanned the shelves with intent.

He slid a book from the shelf, his dark eyes almost meeting Vi's as she stared at him, entranced.

"Groundbreakers and their fortifications in Shaldan," he muttered to himself, scanning the first few pages. "Sky fortresses... impenetrable magic walls..." He stopped, eyes on a page. Aldrik snapped the book shut and started back down the row and out the library.

The fire in the hearth extinguished, leaving darkness in his wake.

Vi stepped out from her hiding place, listening carefully to the fading steps before relaxing her glyph.

"Groundbreakers, *hmm*?" Vi murmured. The prince was reading about the North when no one was looking. He was trying to hide his interest and Vi knew the reason why.

The Emperor was beginning to make moves against Shaldan.

And that meant she had less time than she thought to find out what happened to the crown of the first Solaris king, and get out of the capital.

5

"AH, PUNCTUAL I SEE," Egmun said as they met in the hallway outside his office door.

"I wouldn't want to be late after all you've promised me."

"What I promised, and will deliver." He ran a hand over the doorknob and the ice that blocked the lock withdrew into his fingertips. "Please, come in."

As they entered the office, the Minister went right for the cabinets in the back of the room. From the uppermost, he retrieved an unassuming box. Egmun set it on his desk reverently and Vi approached with apprehension. Engraved on it was Western writing, worn with time, and Vi knew what was inside before he opened the lid. The minister lifted a shimmering crystal from within.

"They're magnificent, no?"

"Where did you get those?" There were four more stones nestled against the plush velvet lining of the box.

"Western heirlooms." Egmun turned the crystal over in his fingers, the faint, blue light catching on the outline of his face and turning his pale hair to the same icy blue as his eyes. "They were a bit tricky to get my hands on, I admit. But I managed. The Knights of Jadar still claim I stole them." He chuckled. "I'm sure they'll claim I stole the sword, too, once it inevitably becomes known that it has returned to the world under my possession."

"I hope information about the sword doesn't get back to the Knights."

"Truth is like cupping water in your hands." Egmun glanced at her. "Impossible to keep to yourself for long."

"Well, either way, you don't seem like the sort of man who cares much for what others think." Vi leaned against his desk and plucked one of the smaller stones from the box. It shimmered brightly underneath her fingers, the magic calling out to her. Vi almost had to make a conscious effort not to absorb the frail power within. Vi suspected these crystals had been severed from the Caverns long ago, during the Burning Times and the reign of Jadar. She wondered if the Windwalkers she'd read about last night in the library were the last ones to have held these stones.

It didn't seem like enough power was collected in them that Vi needed to worry about their presence affecting her plans at all. She was trying to preserve Yargen's power, certainly. But Vi's plans hinged on the raw essence of the goddess, not tiny offshoots of magic from that essence.

"I've never seen a crystal have that reaction before." Egmun startled her from her thoughts.

"It's just a different way to draw out the magic. You use the flow from your own channel to pull it along." Vi pulled the lie out of thin air.

"I've never tried that before... or read anything about that." His eyes had an undeniably cautious glint.

"I picked it up in my readings in the West. This method is more similar to how the Windwalkers work with the stones."

"Not many tomes on the crystal magics still exist in the West. The Emperor took most of the writings with him when he returned south following the late Empress's death."

"What did you say about truth? Like holding water in your hands?" Vi smiled thinly and returned the crystal to the box, hoping to end the conversation. Egmun placed his crystal back in the dip in the velvet.

"You said you weren't with the Knights of Jadar."

"I'm not," Vi insisted.

"Yet you have a fascination with the stones one would expect a Knight of Jadar to have. You have knowledge one would expect only a Knight to possess."

"Don't assume just because I am Western and appreciate the power of the crystals that I must also be a Knight of Jadar." Vi straightened away from the desk. "I don't assume that just because you are Southern and obsessed with items of great power that you are working on behalf of the Emperor to gain weapons for him to use against Shaldan." She let the words *unless you are* remain unsaid.

Egmun laughed from his belly. "Fair, fair." He shook his head, as though the notion had caused him great amusement. "Though I'm not working with the Emperor and have proof of that."

"Oh?"

"You'll see soon—" He was interrupted by a knock on the door. "There they are now." Egmun smiled in a most devious way. He passed her a folio on his way to the door. "Here, take this ledger and record what happens." Vi accepted it wordlessly, allowing the tides of fate to pull her along. "Good morning, my prince. Victor."

Victor. Vi recognized the name from her studies as a girl. She also recognized it from Taavin's tales of past iterations of their world. This man was always behind the ultimate destruction of the Crystal Caverns, usually involving the crown of the first Solaris King somehow.

He was the one whose name her mother cringed to speak, and her father scowled to hear. He had been the source of suffering in their lives. Vi could only wonder what he'd end up being to her now.

His eyes met hers as Victor entered the room with a relaxed gait. She kept her face passive save for the small smile that had worked its way onto her lips. In this world, she would be the one to find the crystal crown, not him.

"Good morning, Egmun."

Another voice stole Vi's attention. Her gaze shifted and Vi saw Aldrik clearly for the first time. His dark eyes settled on her and Aldrik froze in place.

"Who's she?"

"She's a recent graduate of the Academy of Arcane Arts in Norin," Egmun lied deftly.

"Does the Academy still accept students?" Aldrik asked, clearly unsure of the answer.

"Graduate? You don't look like you could be any older than I am." Victor rubbed the makings of a goatee on his chin, which was currently little more than a ghost of stubble.

"We all progress differently." Egmun said, going behind his desk. The two young men assumed their seats in the chairs opposite. Vi remained poised, her folio at the ready to take notes as instructed.

"Yes, not everyone is as slow as you, Victor," Aldrik said with a grin. He clearly intended the words to be mischievous, but even Vi could tell they struck a sensitive spot instead.

"And what is your name?" Victor asked her, pointedly ignoring the prince. He clearly had a well-established relationship with Aldrik, seeing as the prince let his doggedness slide.

"Vivian." Vi bowed her head. "It is an honor to be observing two of the Tower's most illustrious students."

"So you told her about us?" Aldrik lounged, looking between Vi and the box. "About everything?"

"She has a good handle of the situation herself." Egmun gave a nod. "Vivian is well studied on the matter of crystals." Just the word "crystals" felt like crossing a threshold from which there was no turning back. "She's my new research assistant."

"I thought you knew everything?" Aldrik quipped. He was the epitome of a young prince, from the way he draped himself across the chair to the way he said the first thing that flew into his mind without any concern or filter. Vi felt herself inwardly cringe in embarrassment on Aldrik's behalf… and her own. She was old and wise enough now to know that she had been much the same once. "Isn't that why we're bothering to learn from you?"

"We all have something more we can learn," Victor said firmly. "Now, don't embarrass yourself in front of our guest."

Aldrik glanced back at her, awareness of how he had sounded appearing across his face. Vi held his eyes for a long moment—long enough that he was the one to break the stare.

Egmun slid the box across the desk and clicked it open. "Shall we begin?"

Vi watched with a mixture of curiosity and horror as the two young men picked up the stones. They each held them in their open palms and closed their eyes, an intense look of focus overtaking them. She twisted the quill between her fingers, eventually forcing herself to jot down a note. Writing after living in the woods for so long felt uncomfortable and awkward.

Perhaps it was just the situation that was uncomfortable.

"Good, join your power with the stone's. Try to connect your channel with it."

Egmun was stealing her words, though it did the young men little good. Vi kept her eyes on the crystals. They didn't change in the slightest.

"Let's start slow," Egmun continued.

Victor and Aldrik conjured ice and flame respectively, sometimes pitting their elements against each other, sometimes seeing how long they could sustain frost and blaze, and how intensely the magic could collect. Vi made some arbitrary scribbles, but mostly just gnawed on the end of the quill in thought. They weren't accomplishing much other than exposing themselves needlessly to the crystals for about half an hour in the name of seeing how crystals impacted their magic.

"That's enough for today. We don't want to risk your minds and bodies becoming corrupted from crystal taint." The minister finally stood, motioning to the box. "Please, return them."

"It feels strange... letting it go after you've had it." Aldrik curled and uncurled his fingers as if he were still imagining holding the stone.

"Strange how?" Vi asked.

"I forgot you were there." Aldrik blinked at her several times, as if he'd just returned to the plane of existence. Then, realizing he hadn't answered her question, continued, "You can feel it fueling your magic, making it stronger, sharper. When I hold it, I almost feel like I could make or do anything."

Victor was intensely focused on the box.

"And you, Victor?" Vi asked. "What do you feel?"

It took several seconds for him to shake his blank expression, for his eyes to regain clarity. The man pushed himself away from the chair, standing with a start. "I feel like I want more." With that, he abruptly left the office.

"Victor we haven't even—" Aldrik tried to call after him, but was met with a closing door. "What's gotten into him?"

"He's likely just jealous of your prowess," Egmun said.

"Well, he and I are on the same page. I want to practice more, too."

"I'm glad to hear that." Egmun returned the box to its hiding place. Vi's focus remained on the door. "But that's all we are going to work on today."

I want more. The words stuck with her. As soon as he'd said them, Victor had stormed off with purpose. A dangerous question crept into Vi's mind: *Had Victor already located the crown?*

Vi set down her notes and made her way out as Aldrik and Egmun spoke. Egmun gave her a questioning look. "Please excuse me, I just remembered an appointment I must attend," Vi said hastily and left the office.

She couldn't waste any time beginning her search, especially now that she knew Victor might already be ahead of her.

The Tower hallway was empty. She strode down the spiraling pathway, keeping her eyes peeled for Victor, but there was no sign of him. She'd waited too long to follow.

Cursing softly, Vi headed toward an unmarked door on the outer ring of the tower. Behind this door was a narrow path—a secret passage that connected the Tower of Sorcerers with the palace proper. Vi emerged into a servant's hall and, after orienting herself, started for the Imperial Library. She hadn't seen much that would be useful in the Tower Library, and the Imperial Library's collection was easily ten times the size.

On entering, she stepped hastily between shelves, easily avoiding the attention of any library staff without the need of flashes of Lightspinning. The last thing she wanted was someone asking too many questions about what she was doing.

"Histories... Histories..." Vi murmured to herself as she passed between the towering bookcases. Eventually, she made her way to a section dedicated to the histories of the Solaris Empire, organized by dates and rulers. The history of the Solaris Kingdom was tucked away in a corner of the tallest shelf, requiring her to climb one of the rolling ladders to reach.

Vi plucked the first book and skimmed the pages.

"Too long ago." She returned it and grabbed the next one. "The crown of Solaris was bestowed on the eldest son of the original Solaris. It was a boon given to him by the Mother, ordaining him to rule this land," Vi read aloud.

The words *boon given to him by the Mother* were underlined in mostly faded blue ink.

Vi flipped ahead a few pages. More words were underlined in the same pale ink.

... a powerful Waterrunner, the crown bestowed the Mother's blessing on him.
... then he crafted the first Solaris castle entirely of ice...
His son did not have magic. However, with the crown, he could inspire loyalty in those around him with powers unlike any other...

The book was littered with faint blue lines scribbled throughout. Some were dotted, some were double lined. A few passages were even circled. Vi furrowed her brow and ran her finger over a note at the end of the book. Scribbled in the corner on the back of the last page, it read:

One - Blue.

"One, blue," Vi read aloud. "What does that mean?" A frown crossed her lips. She didn't know what kind of notation system or code this person was using. But she did know one thing with confidence—someone else was tracking the history of the crown.

Vi just hoped it wasn't Victor.

Vi's head jerked up as she was startled by a knock on the door—three fast raps, followed by two slower ones. Rubbing her bleary eyes, Vi glanced out the windows. The midnight oil was burning in the mostly dark city below and that meant she'd been at it for at least five hours straight.

Putting down the book she'd been combing through, Vi opened the door without hesitation. Only one person knocked that way.

She was met with the face of a Tower apprentice—a pale-skinned young woman with straw-colored hair.

"I wasn't expecting anyone," Vi said with a tired smile.

"Well, when you become a hermit for a few weeks, you run the risk of people seeking you out." The young woman's eyes darted down the Tower hall. "Now, let me in before someone sees I don't belong here."

"I doubt that would happen. For how secretive they are, the Tower doesn't seem like it has the best security." Vi stepped to the side to let Deneya enter, and she watched the illusion vanish from her shoulders.

"Can never be too careful." Deneya hoisted a folio in the air. "I found it."

"You did." Vi carefully grabbed the time-worn folio from Deneya's hands. She opened it on the table, pulling out the papers one by one.

"Don't get your hopes up. There's not much there about the theft of the royal treasure." Deneya leaned on the back of one of the chairs. "All the names have been redacted."

She wasn't wrong, of course. Four lone sheets of paper were all that remained recorded of the greatest heist in the history of the Solaris Empire.

"Why would they blot them out?"

"I have a theory. Here, look at this one." Deneya held up a sheet of paper. She pointed to one of the names that had been poorly inked away. The pen scribbles were hasty, and only covered half of the letters.

A—la

"Whose name does that look like to you?" Deneya asked with a grin.

"Adela." The ink in the books had been too faded to be recent. The person who made those notations to find the crown's location wasn't Victor. "She was the one searching for the crown and who ultimately stole it."

"That's my theory. Also why they blotted out all other references of her name."

"Men and their superstitions," Vi muttered. She remembered how just the whispered name "Adela" had been considered bad luck in Norin.

"My bet would be pride for this one. Losing your family's heirlooms and treasure is one thing… letting your father be murdered by that same thief and then having her slip through your grasp? Too much for a young, budding Emperor to handle."

"Do you know what happened to the rest of the records?"

"If there were more, they're long gone. It's a miracle I could find these."

"Thank you for your hard work." Vi paused her reading to look Deneya in the eye when she gave her thanks. Having another set of eyes on everything she was piecing together—another set of hands to double the work—was invaluable.

"I am in Lumeria's Order of Shadows." Deneya smiled gleefully. "Collecting information like this is my job. The Queen will be all too happy if it's also information on the bane of the seas."

"Adela," Vi whispered. She lifted another sheet of paper. "The thief fled to the coast. The treasure was never recovered." Setting down the paper, Vi quickly went to the shelves underneath the windows in the back of the room. Vi had grown tired of constantly going back and forth to the library, so she'd been ferrying books back and forth for weeks now in secret.

"You're amassing a little library," Deneya observed.

"I've had a lot of time to read lately," Vi murmured. She'd discovered reading to be different than she remembered—especially when it came to histories. She read both the black ink of the words *and* the white space between them. There were phantom memories within her; sections of her subconscious remembered past worlds and connected them in ways that should be impossible.

Likely, the memories weren't her own at all. They were Yargen's. But that was a truth Vi left in uncharted territory, for now. Taavin was right: they had enough to worry about.

"Here it is." Vi located the book she was looking for and crossed back to Deneya, handing it over.

"*The Imperial Summer Palace in Oparium.*" Deneya opened to the middle and was greeted by blueprints that were now familiar to Vi. "Architectural drawings?"

"Yes, I had to get into the Imperial archives for this one... Unlike my other stolen books, I'll need to return this soon. But for now, look at the foreword." Vi's mind was moving so fast her mouth could barely keep up. "The date, specifically."

"Construction began in 308." Deneya glanced up at her. Vi held out the paper she'd been reading. "The theft was in 307." Comprehension lit up Deneya's face.

"The theft of the Imperial jewels that dated back into antiquity was in 307. King Romulin Solaris was murdered the same year, leaving Tiberus Solaris to become King. Then, the man who was to declare himself Emperor the very next year decided to make his first act as a ruler building a summer home?"

"Young men are fickle creatures."

"You know Tiberus," Vi said seriously. "He wouldn't let Adela's transgressions go."

"Then what do you think it is?"

"The manor is a front for something, I'd bet."

"A front for what?"

"I don't know, but look." Vi took the book back from Deneya's hands and rested it on the table, flipping through. "These plans are incomplete... There are sections missing. Doors lead to nowhere and hallways crop up from nothing."

"How can you tell?" Deneya shifted, looking over her shoulder.

"I just can. See, here, there's—"

"I'm going to stop you there; I'm not going to understand anyway." Deneya laughed. "I trust you."

"I don't know how you can understand how to make leather and smithed goods, but claim you can't grasp architecture."

"We all have our strengths." Deneya held out her hands and shrugged with a small smile, but her expression turned serious once more. "So where does this leave us with the crown?"

"Adela successfully stole it, of that I'm confident." Just saying it aloud made Vi's toes curl with how *right* it felt. "She must have fled to Oparium. It's the largest port near Solarin."

"Makes sense for the most infamous pirate the world has ever seen. Tiberus followed her in pursuit and... built a house with incomplete architectural drawings?"

"I don't understand that bit either," Vi admitted. "But that's a mystery for another time. The first order of business is to make sure Adela actually got the treasure out of the palace. We have to rule that out with as much certainty as possible before we go chasing another lead." Vi doubted that Taavin would go with her on a gut feeling when it came to this. She needed more proof of her theories before they took action.

"If she didn't get it out of the palace, wouldn't someone have already found it?"

Vi glanced back at her collection of books—a wealth of history on the Solaris family. Theirs was a bloodline that ran all the way back to the eldest son of the Champion.

"No," Vi said. "This place is old, very old, and it's been built on time and again. Who knows what may be hiding in its depths?"

THE MOMENT DENEYA LEFT, Vi summoned Taavin. He barely had time to orient himself before she asked, "Do you know where Adela's room in the Tower of Sorcerers was?"

"Excuse me?" Two emerald eyes blinked at her in startled confusion.

"Adela's room, when she was a student of the Tower... do you know where it was?"

Focus crossed his face and Taavin shook his head. "A moment." He held out his arms and murmured the chant that connected him to all the knowledge of their past iterations. As the light faded from him, he shook his head again. "This isn't something you've asked me before. Why do you need to know about Adela?"

"I think she's the one who took the crown—well before the point at which the world is being rebuilt time and again. The crown's location has always been variable. Her stealing it may have been a stone in the river, but everything else about how she did it—"

"Changes," Taavin finished thoughtfully. "Adela would be an agent of chaos in the world."

"Exactly. I need to figure out if the crown left the palace or not." Vi filled him in on all her discoveries—the books, Deneya's records, her gut instinct. "If it's here, we have it. If I'm right, and it's not... then it's either in Oparium, or with Adela herself."

"Let's hope it's not the latter." Taavin sighed and raked a hand through his hair. "I'm sorry, I don't know where her room was."

"Do you know *anything* about her? Beyond the obvious? Any memories of her, no matter how insignificant, might be helpful."

"You seem desperate."

"I am." Vi folded her arms. "Victor might be ahead of me in the hunt for the crown. I'm not sure." She shook her head at the whole situation—at the mere thought of Victor getting his hands on the crown. In her world, when he had, he'd used the crystals' power to challenge the Solaris family in a bloody coup. He'd become known as the Mad King for his twisted ways, and any effort Vi could make to thwart or postpone his nefarious tendencies would be effort well spent.

"I see." A pained look crossed his features. "I'm sorry, Vi. I don't have much knowledge on Adela beyond what you likely already know."

"It's all right." Vi crossed to him and took both his hands in hers. She gripped them tightly. "The knowledge you've given me has already done so much. I can take care of this." Leaning forward, Vi placed a chaste kiss on his lips, quickly pulling away. Now was not the time for romance. Deneya's revelations had lit a fire in her. "I'll let you know what I find."

"Where are you—" She'd dismissed him before he could finish.

"Sorry," Vi murmured to the empty air and left her room. The night was young, and the iron of her mind was hot—ready to strike.

She wound about halfway down the Tower to a central room. Long tables stood empty, projects scattered about them, waiting for their Waterrunners to return in the morning. Around the outside of the room were narrow doors that led to private workshops.

Vi peered into the darkness, imagining Adela here. The woman was sixteen, or maybe just seventeen. She had the same icy blue eyes. Her hair was blonde, not white. She was younger, but as confident and arrogant as the Adela Vi knew. She sauntered around the Tower and this room like she owned the place.

This was the shade of the woman who had marked up Imperial Library books, if Vi's theory was right. She plotted the greatest theft in Solaris history right under the eyes of the royal guard and family. Adela had been so confident that no one would suspect her, she even left a paper trail.

"You wanted someone to find you, didn't you?" Vi whispered into the imaginary face of the young Adela. She could almost envision the teenager smirking back. Adela would want someone to piece together her brilliance.

What good was a history-making theft without leaving enough behind for the bards to spin tales of her infamy?

Vi's midsection tensed with a phantom pain and she suppressed a shiver, remembering where Adela had gouged her with an icicle. She hated the thought of playing into Adela's plans. But letting the crown slip through her fingers was not an option.

To the right of the door was a narrow bookshelf. Each of the books on it seemed to contain records of the projects and supplies used by Waterrunners within the Tower. Vi went right for the year 307.

Sure enough, a familiar pale blue ink was neatly scribbled next to various dates throughout the year. The Tower records had been exempted from the systematic expunging of Adela's identity. Likely, in part, because her name wasn't actually written anywhere.

Vi focused only on what she assumed to be Adela's entries.

A.L. — Storeroom duty.
A.L. — Borrowed seven tokens from the storeroom.
A.L. — Training grounds, Waterrunner combat.
A.L. — Storeroom duty.
A.L. — Waterrunner combat.

A.L. — Absent.
A.L. — Storeroom duty.

The combat made sense to Vi. Adela was frighteningly good in a fight. She'd bet the absence was a trip to Oparium to plan her getaway. Perhaps that was when Adela had even purchased a ship.

"What was your obsession with the storeroom?" Vi murmured, replacing the book back on the shelf.

One by one, Vi opened each of the doors on the outer ring of the workshop. Black disks hung by each one, and every room was identical to the last. A single flame bulb hung over a center pedestal that had water in a shallow indent on top. Vi could only speculate as to the function of the rooms, but she was certain none of them was a storeroom.

Working to quell her frustration, Vi went to leave and it hit her. She froze, staring directly across the hall at an outer door marked *Waterrunner Supplies* rather than the name of an apprentice of the Tower.

"You arrogant pirate," Vi said with a small grin.

Luckily, the storeroom was unlocked. Inside were a few shelves on either side covered in all manner of baubles, books, quills, inkwells, and parchment. Vi closed the door behind her and brought a hand to the watch around her neck.

"*Narro hath hoolo.*"

Taavin appeared before her. "We're in... a closet?"

"A storeroom, more precisely. I think this was integral to Adela's plan."

"How so?"

Vi didn't appreciate his skeptical tone. But she didn't begrudge him it, either. "Perhaps she hid the crown here. Or maybe it leads to another secret passage. The palace is full of them."

"I'm surprised you don't know every last passage there is." Taavin folded his arms over his chest.

"I've been working on it." Vi gave him a mischievous grin. "I don't suppose you can use *uncose* to expose any hidden exits?"

"Not in this form, unfortunately." Taavin looked down at his palms and Vi barely resisted the urge to tell him that she would make him real. One way or another, someday soon, he would have a body and his magic once more.

"It's all right, help me look." Vi began scouring the shelf to the right of the door.

"I don't think we have to look very far."

"What?" Vi turned to find him pointing at a narrow strip of wood that ran the length of the wall, floor to ceiling, in the back corner. Cobwebs clung to it and Vi nearly coughed up a lung as she disturbed the dust to expose the wood to the light of her flame. The firelight clung to the carved shape of a trident, gouged deep. "Adela's symbol," she whispered. "How did you even see this?"

"Elfin eyes," he said with a grin.

Vi narrowed her gaze in his direction. "You just started in the right side of the room is all." She took a step back, pulling a heavy barrel away from the corner. She followed the strip of wood up, over, and back down, where a clean line ran behind one of the shelves. "I think it's a door."

"How do you figure?"

Rather than answering, Vi lifted her hand, pressing it to the wood. It went up in eager flames, turning to a pile of ash. Sure enough, hidden behind the wedge was a miniature handle mostly obscured by the shaded alcove.

"Like that."

"Why would Adela mark the entrance to her hideout?" Taavin asked as Vi gripped the handle, pushing her shoulder into the door.

"Two theories. One, she planned to come back here, or send someone else back here. Two, she wanted to be found by whoever was clever enough to follow her." Vi grunted and pushed harder. The stone door groaned on hinges that didn't want to open. "With any luck, we'll find the crown right—"

Vi paused as the door finally opened in full and she stared at the room beyond.

Dust had settled on every surface, from the mostly empty bookshelf to the cot. Vi's attention was drawn to the threadbare tapestry hanging by threads. A rudimentary trident was stitched on it.

"Was this her room?" Taavin asked, entering.

"No... she would've been given a Tower bedroom as an apprentice. This must've been her hideaway."

"She lived a double life even then. A bed as an apprentice... a bed as a pirate," Taavin murmured as Vi crossed to the bookcase. Notebooks were still lined up on it.

She grabbed one off the top shelf, but it had nothing but notes on Waterrunner combat. Vi returned it as her eyes settled on another row of Adela's records. Each journal on the lower shelf had a different colored spine, and a number.

"One, blue." Vi took the first notebook. Within were scribbles in what was now an all-too-familiar ink. "Each of these notebooks corresponds to a book she'd read in the library." Vi flipped the pages. "There's a whole system here—circles, dots— these are the cyphers to all her markings."

Separately, Adela's notes didn't make any sense. They were jargon about ships, seafaring maps, and histories. But with the library books in tandem, Vi was getting a complete picture of how Adela had tracked the crown through the ages and planned her getaway.

"What does it say about the crown?"

"I don't know yet, other than she wanted it." Vi scanned the pages. "She knew it could give her great power. That seems to be enough for most mortals."

"Most... *mortals*?" Taavin repeated quietly. Vi tensed and looked up from the notebook. His emerald eyes searched hers with intense purpose.

"I'm not quite mortal, not anymore," Vi whispered. "We both know that."

"I've never heard you say it in such a way before though."

Don't look at me like that, she wanted to say. It was the same look he'd given her in those ruins a lifetime ago. A look that saw something in her she herself wasn't ready to see.

"Well, it's a good thing I'm not mortal." Vi closed the book and returned it to the shelf. "Otherwise I couldn't do what needs to be done."

She took another book off the shelf to avoid staring at him. This one wasn't a notebook, but a proper manuscript instead. It was all about the port of Oparium, the closest port to Lyndum, and how it had been built. There were underlined passages regarding the difficulties the builders had in constructing the town and port due to the craggy, cave-pocked rocks and cliffs surrounding it.

Scraps of papers caught her eye. Balancing the book in one hand, Vi unfolded the leaves. Rough sketches made up the lines on rudimentary maps of what appeared to be tunnels.

"What's that?" Taavin asked.

"Her heist." Vi held up one of the maps. "Adela found a room to store her information here in the palace. I'm sure she had another secret passage she used to escape, because if she was caught it would've been recorded in the guards' records. But since her name was blotted out, I can only believe that she—and the crown—at least made it to Oparium. I'd bet she used these tunnels when she was there to evade the encroaching Imperial guards." Vi put the map down, moving to hold up another when a slip of paper fluttered to the floor.

"What's that?" Taavin asked, crouching down. Vi mirrored the motion and picked up the note.

She recognized the script. *No*, she recognized a handwriting *very* similar—this writing looked just like her father's and was too close to be chance. Vi read the inscription aloud:

"My darling A.L.,
I know you've been fascinated lately on the histories of Oparium. I encountered these maps in the archives and thought of you. Consider it a gift.
Forever yours, T.S."

"A.L. must be Adela Lagmir," Taavin said, looking up to her.

"I would assume." Vi returned the maps and the note to the book. The other ledgers could stay—they contained nothing more than notes and plans Vi already knew about. This book was coming back with her.

"Who do you think T.S. is? He seems fond of her."

"Isn't it obvious?" Vi started for the door. "Who else could take a book from the archives? Who else would Adela want to become close to?" A look of clarity overtook Taavin. "T.S. must be Tiberus Solaris."

"Your grandfather and Adela were... intimate?"

Vi cringed at the word. "I don't know about *my* grandfather. Though, it would explain why Adela hates and has always hated my family so profoundly, if he wronged her somehow..." All those years ago, when Vi had infiltrated a meeting of the Knights of Jadar, Twintle had said that Adela had reduced her rate to work against Solaris. The memory of the remark suddenly took on new meaning.

"Then she would want to get back at Solaris whenever possible."

They emerged back into the storeroom and Vi returned the barrel to where it had been. Hopefully, no one would notice the lack of wood or deep groove in the back corner. But, if they did, these were the sorts of things Adela's legends were made of. Vi could almost picture some Waterrunner gleefully telling his friends about the discovery.

"We need to get to Oparium and explore these caves." Vi tapped the book in her hands.

"Not until Aldrik goes to the Caverns with the sword." Taavin grabbed her shoulder and shook her gently. "We can't deviate from the stones in the river. A new Champion must be reborn."

"Taavin, we have the weapons in our grasp. Now is the time to act." Vi gripped his forearm, staring him in the eyes. "We can seize this opportunity and save our world."

"And if we fail, we have doomed it." His hold on her tightened. "You know what's at stake."

"Better than anyone."

"But not better than me." In his haunted eyes she could see every one of the ninety-three worlds he'd witnessed. "Aldrik must go to the Caverns. Give him your fake sword, if you must. But we will see the stones in the river honored. Yargen cannot just choose a new Champion from the masses and start the world over again. It must be the daughter of Vhalla and Aldrik Solaris, just as it was the first time. It's the only way to preserve this loop."

Vi swallowed once, twice; it took three times and a nod for the lump in her throat to finally go away. She knew what he said was true. In some deep and terrible way, she knew it to her core.

"All right," Vi whispered. "We do what we must here. And then to Oparium."

A FLURRY OF KNOCKS woke Vi with a start.

Adela's notebook fell from her chest and landed heavily in her lap. The maps were scattered around the bed. More knocking followed.

"Impatient…" she mumbled, cursing under her breath. Dawn was just breaking through the curtains of her room and after being up half the night, she'd planned to sleep in. "Just a moment!" Vi said, louder.

Swinging her legs off the side of the bed, she flung over the duvet to hide the books and parchment in its fold. Standing, Vi crossed to the door and grabbed the black jacket that hung on a peg next to it. She slung it over her shoulders, smoothed out her hair and clothing, and opened the door just as another set of knocks were about to begin.

Vi blinked grumpily at the blond man staring back at her.

"Victor, to what do I owe the pleasure?" Vi glanced around the hall. He appeared to be alone. "I don't believe we have lessons this morning." *And never this early*, she thought bitterly.

"Egmun has demanded to see you." Victor looked her up and down. Vi had no doubt done a poor job of hiding that she was still in her clothes from the day before—clothes she'd just been sleeping in. "Do you need a moment to put yourself together?"

Vi arched a single eyebrow and, rather than saying anything, strode out of her room like a princess. She locked the door behind her and returned the key to her pocket. Without waiting for him to lead, Vi descended toward Egmun's office.

"Are you his errand boy now?" Vi asked dryly.

"I'm his *most valued* assistant."

"I bet you are."

Victor paused in front of the door to the office of the Minister of Sorcery. A smirk spread across his lips. "I know I'm not up half the night, snooping through Tower storerooms and stealing Mother-knows-what."

Vi kept a sneer at bay, barely. She was too tired to deal with this petulant child. Vi took a step forward but Victor straightened. Even though she was higher on the slope of the hall, they were still eye to eye.

"Don't question what I do," Vi cautioned, "for it is far beyond the realm of what your mortal mind can comprehend."

"Mortal mind? Just who do you think you are?"

"I am the one who has seen the end, and will see the beginning of your destiny," she said ominously. It took everything in her not to have him flat on the ground, threatening him within an inch of his life. Only Taavin's abundance of caution, and Vi's fragile self-control, held her back. "Now get out of my sight."

"With pleasure." Victor didn't back down, right until the end. He took three steps backward and turned.

Vi watched him leave, firing curses at his back. Somehow, he knew she'd been in the storeroom. That made it only a matter of time until Victor found Adela's room. He was smart enough to piece it together, and all the pieces were secreted there.

The only thing that kept her from chasing after him was the knowledge that she had taken the key book on Oparium that contained Adela's maps. Additionally, the journals were useless without the library books also in Vi's possession. Trusting she was one step ahead, Vi knocked on the door to the minister's office.

"Enter," he said sharply. Vi did as he bid and found Egmun pacing the room. He stopped, spinning to face her, the moment the door closed. "I need to see it."

"You'd do well to not make demands of me in such a tone. I'm not one of your lapdogs." Vi was too tired to play along. He seemed genuinely taken aback.

"And you'd do well to not risk this shaky alliance we've formed. You need the prince, after all."

She didn't. Taavin did. But Vi was dutifully following his instructions still. Here she was, keeping the world on the rails, while Victor could be off hunting for the crown. Her lead on him slipped with every moment she wasted on Egmun.

"Bickering will get us nowhere." Vi pinched the bridge of her nose and sighed. "What have I done to earn such mistrust?"

"Nothing, and that's much the problem. I have given you everything these past weeks. I've given you food, shelter, access to the prince, even the ability to rummage through my Tower without an escort." Victor had run right to Egmun after tracking her last night. "And you've given me no indication other than your word that you have the sword at all."

Vi narrowed her eyes, though her displeasure was mostly directed inward. She'd been too focused on her movements and hadn't been accounting for the desires of others. The first night she'd seen Aldrik in the library, researching the North, came back to her.

"The Emperor is taking an interest in the Crystal Caverns, isn't he?" she said softly, so as not to speak over the pieces clicking together in her mind. Egmun's startled eyes said all she needed to know. The Emperor was interested in the Crystal Caverns because he wanted to go to war with the North and was looking for a secret weapon to bring with him. "You want to get there before he does."

Egmun was silent for a long moment. Then, "Yes."

"I'll show you the sword."

"You will?"

"Yes, but you must stay here and do not track me to its hiding place. I will know if you do."

"You really have it?" His voice was hurried and thin, as if he was afraid the truth was something that could break if he spoke too loudly.

"I always have."

Vi shut the door to the office firmly behind her and began down the halls. The spark had lit an inferno in her stomach, the likes of which she hadn't felt in some time. She wouldn't be surprised if steam was coming out of her ears.

She wanted to give chase down the hall and find Victor. She wanted to demand he tell her what he had seen of her movements, what books he had read, how close behind her he was. But that pursuit would have been futile.

Victor was a mortal, chained to fate, destined to heed the whims of two heartless gods. She couldn't concern herself with him any more than she concerned herself with the rats that ran through the sewers underneath her feet.

The walk to the stables did little to calm her. When Vi arrived, she could feel the sparks crackling around her knuckles. She scanned the mostly empty stalls, looking for a woman she recognized.

"You look like you're ready to murder someone," Deneya said, emerging and wiping her hands on a rag that she returned to a belt loop. "Don't think I've seen you like this since Norin. Welcome back."

"I need the sword you've been working on."

"It's not ready."

"It's going to have to be."

Deneya sighed and shrugged. "All right, follow me."

Vi followed her up a side stair that wound inside the outer wall of the palace surrounding the stables. Inside the wall was a series of doors that led to rooms for each of the stable hands, fitted with a bed, table, dresser, and a single window that overlooked the horses beyond.

"Here." Deneya lifted a short sword from behind her dresser, holding it out to Vi.

"It isn't long enough."

"He doesn't know that."

Vi pulled the sword from the scabbard. It was almost unnaturally light. The metal was nearly white from the alloys used.

"I was going to make a longer one. This was merely a first attempt. But it seems we ran out of time."

"You're right, he doesn't know the difference." Vi held out the sword before her, staring at the weapon intently. "*Durroe watt ivin.*" Yellow glyphs, tinted with white, surrounded the sword. They sank into the weapon and painted it with new colors. Bright splashes of blue swirled against deeper shades, nearly purple. Sparks of magic drifted off the weapon. Vi gave it a swing, watching the illusion cling to the blade.

"It's more convincing than any other illusion I've seen here. I'm sure he'll buy it." Deneya laced her fingers and placed them behind her head. "But what's the rush?"

"He's suspicious of me." Vi sheathed the sword. Even though it could no longer be seen, her magic fed the illusion. "I need to give him something."

"Then I'll pray to Yargen it works."

Vi nodded. "Be ready to move, too. You might want to start gathering your things."

"So early? I thought we needed to see them to the Crystal Caverns?"

"We'll see. The crown isn't here; I think it's in Oparium."

"Then you know where all the weapons are."

"The crown's location is still just a hunch."

"And if your suspicion is right, you want to move to get the weapons all at once?" Vi nodded again. "I bet Taavin loves that."

"Yes, well..." Vi looked at the sword, promptly ignoring the remark. "I should be getting back to Victor."

Deneya stopped her from leaving by grabbing her wrist and locking eyes with Vi.

"Remember, Vi, he's only seen how you fail. Never how you succeed. You're the Champion, not him. You're the one who's going to show us all how this ends." Deneya continued to hold her gaze. Vi opened her mouth, but couldn't quite find words. So she shut it slowly, settling for a third dip of her chin. "I'm following *you* into this future, not him."

"Thank you." That was all Vi could think to say. It wasn't nearly enough, but it was everything she meant.

"You're welcome." Deneya released her and the woman's lighthearted manner returned. "Now, off with you. Go quell the rage of a sorcerer who thinks he's powerful."

"With pleasure."

Sword in hand, Vi made her way back through the palace to the Tower of Sorcerers. The good thing about having spent years studying the architecture and maps of the Imperial Palace meant that if she didn't want to be seen, she didn't have to be. There was always a passage, and a passage deeper still, winding within walls and behind doors to get someone from where they were to where they needed to go.

Muffled voices indicated Egmun wasn't alone, but Vi knocked anyway. "Enter." And, for the second time in one day, she did.

Egmun was seated behind his desk, Victor across from him. The young man gave her a satisfied smirk. Vi ignored him completely.

"I have what you requested."

"Show me." Egmun's eyes never left the sword. But Vi's darted to Victor. "He knows of the crystal weapons."

"Very well." In a sweeping motion, Vi unsheathed the sword. It was whisper silent; the steel hardly reverberated underneath the illusion that remained solidly in place.

"There it is," Egmun breathed, drawn to his feet. "It's really there." He walked around his desk, as if he were approaching a sacred relic. Vi continued to hold out the sword as he approached, holding her breath, waiting. Egmun's fingers trembled as he reached upward. They came in contact with the illusion. Vi's magic held. "It doesn't feel the same as the other crystals."

"This much power wouldn't. It's far more refined, not wild like the stones you use. This has been honed."

"Yes, I read all about how Jadar honed the crystal with the blood and sacrifice of Windwalkers," Egmun said lightly, as if stating a passing fact about the lineage of Solaris and not the most heinous period of the Dark Isle's history. "Finally, after all this time, it's—"

"Minister." Victor stood, breaking the moment.

"What?" Egmun turned to glare at his young apprentice. But Victor wasn't deterred.

The young man reached out his hand. With one finger, he touched the hilt at the guard, running up along the blade. Victor's eyes narrowed. When he pulled his finger back, a line of red was cut into it.

"It doesn't feel like our crystals, Minister, because it's not." Victor leveled his gaze at Vi. She met it and kept her face passive.

"What are you talking about?" Egmun balked.

"Look closer," Victor practically snapped at the man. It seemed to jostle Egmun out of the power lust that had clouded his eyes. Now, he inspected the sword far more intently. "You're a Waterrunner too. You know illusions."

"What do you see?" Egmun asked.

"It's a subtle… shift. Only visible when you touch it. A good illusion, indeed. But not a perfect one. There is no such thing as a perfect illusion."

Vi watched as her hopes were crushed under the heel of Victor's boot. Egmun wrenched the weapon from her hand. He waved it around, watching it carefully. Then, Egmun began to laugh.

"Well done, Victor. You passed our test. You may go."

"Minis—"

"I said go!" Egmun barked. Victor dismissed himself, but not before giving Vi a rather satisfied side-eye. She had to hold herself back from reaching out and snapping his neck then and there. The world would be better for it. Of that, she was nearly certain. Once the door was closed, Egmun brandished the sword at her. "What is this?"

"The Sword of—"

"Lies!" he roared, slashing it through the air. "Lies, lies, lies." Egmun slammed the weapon into the side of his deck and Vi watched it leave a deep gouge. Sure enough, her illusion writhed as the weapon wriggled. He pointed it back at her, advancing. "You, you're a Firebearer. I saw it. You can summon flames."

Vi held up both hands in an effort to be non-threatening. But tiny fires illuminated each of her fingertips. Both to prove his point, and to show that she could fight back if she wanted.

"How are you doing this?" He stopped. "Unless… unless you have an associate. Someone working with you. Was that why you were in the Waterrunner storeroom?"

"No one is working with me," Vi insisted calmly. "The illusion is mine."

"Impossible."

Vi lowered her hands and with them, the illusion fell alongside her hopes.

"That's impossible," he repeated, looking between her and the now unveiled sword.

"It's not when you know how to use the power of the crystals. I *do* have the Sword of Jadar. But I will not show you until we are leaving for the Caverns with Prince Aldrik." Vi locked eyes with the man. "Consider this demonstration my proof of the sword."

"You—"

Vi wrenched open the door behind her and stopped him mid-sentence. "You will summon me when we are to leave for the Crystal Caverns and not a moment sooner."

Before he could answer, she slammed the door and retreated to her room, where the empty scabbard in her hand and the silence that surrounded her were solemn reminders of her failure.

8

VI PACED HER BEDROOM, looking out over the city of frost that glistened like fire in the light of the sun disappearing over the Western mountaintops. Solarin shone brighter than ever before, for every day brought them closer to the prince's coming-of-age ceremony. The relentless march of time continued against her, seeming faster and faster with each passing hour.

"We need to leave," Vi said to Taavin, worrying the crystal stone that contained the power of the Sword of Jadar between her fingers. "We should take the Sword and go, get the crown before Victor can, and put an end to this."

"We need to stay. Aldrik must go to the Crystal Caverns with the sword, otherwise we risk disrupting the flow of time so dramatically that a new Champion won't be born," Taavin said calmly, clearly trying to soothe her anxious energy. Vi bit her tongue. "You have already proved you can transfer the energy from the sword to the Caverns. All will be well. You'll preserve Yargen's essence."

Vi curled and uncurled her fingers over the crystal in her palm, feeling the magic move and stretch. Manipulating Yargen's power was becoming more and more instinctive by the day. The time she'd spent scouring the Tower and Imperial libraries for information on crystals, however little there was, seemed to help. It took a lot of reading between the lines, but there was knowledge there that enhanced her nightly practice.

"What if—" A knock on the door interrupted the thought, saving Vi from herself. It was three fast raps, followed by two slower ones. Vi opened the door to an illusioned Deneya.

"He's on the move," Deneya said as she entered, casting her magic aside with a flick of her wrist.

Several curse words lit across Vi's mind. But she kept her voice level. "What's happened?"

"Egmun went out this evening. He rarely goes by horse anywhere, so I followed." Deneya was still in her stable clothes, hay clinging to the rough wool covering her forearms. "He met with some Westerners down the mountain, at one of the last inns for travelers."

"Did you recognize these Westerners?"

Deneya shook her head. "But you know humans, they age so fast. I couldn't tell you for certain if they weren't boys the last time we were in the West."

"What did they discuss?"

"It was hard to hear from my hiding place. I had to remain inconspicuous so I stayed outside, underneath a window by the booth where they sat. But I know I heard mention of the Sword of Jadar." Vi let out the string of curse words this time and ran her hand through her hair. Deneya continued, "It seems you haven't given him enough. Egmun doesn't believe you have the sword."

"So he found the Knights of Jadar to make sure *they* don't have it." Vi's attempt at an illusion was costing them more than she could've imagined.

"And, in the process, let them know that *he* does," Deneya said grimly. "They attacked him on the spot, accusing him of somehow stealing it."

"And Egmun?"

"He's all right. Slipped out in the fray. Two Knights tried to follow him but their horses were spooked by a bear emerging from the woods."

"A bear?"

"Like this one." Deneya waved her hand and uttered, "*Durroe watt ivin.*" A large grizzly bear materialized in the corner of the room, roaring soundlessly. She released the illusion as quickly as she made it. "It was more convincing when I had *curo* with it, for the roar."

"Thank you for helping Egmun out of there." Vi turned to Taavin with worried eyes. "What do you think?"

"I think your time is running short." He stood from where he'd perched on the low bookshelves by the window. "You can't risk getting caught off-guard and having the sword stolen by Knights intercepting you. Aldrik taking the sword to the Caverns is a stone in the river, as I've told you. The sword will find its way to him… one way or another. But if you want to transfer the power, we ought to be the ones to see both prince and weapon to the Caverns."

"I know." Vi chewed over her thoughts, which were unpleasant as a piece of raw fat. She looked down again at the stone in her hands. "I'll have to get him there tonight."

"How?" Deneya asked.

"I don't know yet, but I'll think of something." In one fluid motion of light and magic, there was the hilt of a sword in her hand where there had previously been none. It was shorter than the original Sword of Jadar, just the right size to fit in the scabbard Deneya had made.

"You've gotten better with the crystals," Deneya said, tilting her head to the side. Her eyes drifted to Taavin. "She been practicing when we're not looking?"

"She must've been," Taavin thoughtfully replied.

"No time to go over it now." Vi returned them to the matter at hand. "Deneya, ferry some items between here and the horses. We'll take Prism and Midsummer—get them tacked and ready."

"You want me to follow behind on the way to the Caverns?"

"No, get out ahead. Go to the cabin and stash our things there. I don't know what will happen, so I want you to be nimble and ready."

"All right, anything in particular you want me to ferry?"

Vi pointed the sword at two packs in the corner. "All my things are collected."

"You were ready to go?"

"I knew we'd have to move soon... I was just hoping it wouldn't be like this." She'd hoped to head right to Oparium and bypass the Caverns entirely. But there was no way to win Taavin over to that plan. "I need to go to Egmun."

Taavin grabbed her arm, stopping her. Vi swung to face the ethereal man. "Be careful," he said, far more tender than the moment deserved. "Remember, everything you're doing is a risk. And if you die now—" he touched the watch around her neck lightly "—if you don't get this to Vhalla when the time is right. There is no Champion reborn."

"*I know*, and I'll be careful." Vi was growing weary of Taavin's well-intentioned reminders. She'd been spoiled by fourteen years when he didn't feel the need to press the issue nearly every day.

"Your eyes say something different." His touch was feather-light, but Vi was as immobile as if he'd snared her.

"I'll be careful," she repeated, softer, gentler. Vi leaned forward and kissed him lightly on the lips, releasing her hold on *narro hath* before opening her eyes.

"It's a cruel existence," Deneya said faintly, looking at where Taavin had stood just moments before.

"It is for all of us, don't you think?" Vi shrugged and left before Deneya could answer.

She would take the sword and present it to Egmun now. It was only two weeks before the coming-of-age ceremony and Aldrik would be busy for at least one of those weeks. If she pressured Egmun hard enough, in the right ways, he'd spill about the incident with the Knights and from there—

"By the Mother." A gasp interrupted her frantic planning. Vi looked up. Egmun was there, staring up at her with a mixture of awe and, to her surprise, horror. "You look like Fiera reborn."

"So I've been told." Vi lifted the sword, pointing its tip at him. The subtle threat was intentional. "You wanted the sword. I want the prince. Tonight, let's put an end—"

"I had a meeting with the Knights of Jadar," he interrupted her a second time.

Vi lowered the weapon. She didn't even have to feign annoyance and irritation, just surprise. "You *what*?"

"I had my doubts," he began. "Perfectly rational... When we first met, you spoke of Fiera's death with confidence. My research shows that the only people there when she died were the Knights. Then, after the fake sword, after I thought you had help from a Waterrunner—conspirators... Well, what would you have thought in my position?"

He took a breath to continue, but it was Vi's turn to interrupt him. She stepped forward, lifted the sword once more, and put it under his chin.

"I would've known when I looked upon an entity greater than myself. I would've known not to question," Vi said, dangerously quiet. Even though he was held at sword point, Egmun didn't look the slightest bit scared. His eyes were wide with anticipation, thrill, and a shameful lust for the immense magic contained within the crystal. "Can you feel it? The power this sword holds? Does it make you shiver and shake and yearn for more?"

He swallowed, the lump in his neck nearly scraping against the sword point.

"There's more of this magic to be had, much more." Vi slowly lowered the weapon and his eyes followed. "We've wasted too much time. We go to the Caverns tonight."

"Tonight, there's no—"

"Let's step into your office." Vi glanced over her shoulder. Deneya would be coming down any moment with supplies to load before departing. She looked down the hall as well to avoid appearing suspicious. Egmun obliged her suggestion and Vi continued the moment the door was closed. "Soon Aldrik will be too focused on preparations for his coming-of-age ceremony. We should go now and break down the barrier. We can sort the rest later if needed. I can secure the prince. You go secure the horses necessary for our flight."

"*You* will secure the prince?" Egmun arched his eyebrows. "Don't you think I should?"

"I know where he is at this time of night." She'd run into him in the library more than once when she skulked around the Tower in the dead of night. Like Vi, he had a tendency to take books and not return them with any speed, so she hadn't put together a clear picture of everything the prince was researching so faithfully. "I know how to make him bend to our will."

"If you're confident, then." Egmun nodded, a satisfied smile spreading across his lips. "I'll meet you down at the stables."

"Very good." Vi sheathed the sword and emerged into the Tower hall once more. Just ahead, a Tower apprentice carried two bags slung over her shoulders.

Deneya. Good, she got out without suspicion.

Vi descended the spiraling walkway of the Tower. For a short stretch, Egmun's footsteps followed her. But he soon veered off, departing through one of the doors that connected Tower and palace. Vi continued on, straight for the library.

A man was seated by the lit hearth. Blessedly alone.

Aldrik's head bobbed as he fought off sleep. He didn't notice her approaching. His chin had met his chest when her feet came to a stop right before him.

Vi watched the boy for just a moment. He was fourteen, barely a man. A slip of a thing still in transition to the Emperor that would someday lead a united Solaris Empire. So much of the world's future rested on his shoulders. All Vi could do was guide him in the right direction. When it came down to it, the actions had to belong to him, and Vhalla, and all the other mortals confined to time.

"Wake up," Vi said gently, kneeling down and shaking his shoulder lightly. "Your highness, wake up."

"What?" He blinked sleep from his eyes. His tone became sharper as his eyes focused on her. "Vivian... Is this a dream?"

"No, it is not. Though you might wish it were come the dawn." *More like a nightmare.* "I need you to listen to me, there's precious little time." She couldn't keep Egmun waiting—he'd start to wonder. "Tonight, we must go to the Crystal Caverns."

"The Crystal Caverns, why?"

"There is a barrier there, one only you and your magic can undo. It must be done, for the fate of this world... for the future of Solaris." His eyes widened slightly as she spoke and Vi knew she'd struck the right chord. "Your father will bring the North to its knees with the power of the Caverns. But only you can unlock it."

"Why now?"

"Because there are those who would move against you and your family." Vi lifted the sword. "*You* must be the one to act. Should this sword fall into the wrong hands, it will spell disaster for us all." Or at least another blasted revolution of the world. And Vi had vowed no more of those. This world would be it, the last time the vortex spun. "Before we go... there's something I wish to give you."

Vi pulled out the key to her Tower room from her pocket. "Minister Egmun allowed me use of the uppermost room in this Tower, but I fear I will not need it after tonight."

"Why?"

"Because that is how the wheel of fate turns," Vi said ominously. She wanted to seem mystical, too improbable to be real. "I have a feeling the room will prove useful to you."

Vi thrust the key in his hand, closing his fingers around it. Aldrik's hand wrapped around hers tightly, the key between them. He stared up at her with eyes so similar to Fiera's, similar to *hers*.

This man is not your father.

"Tell me what's really happening."

"I can't."

He ripped his hand away and stood, looking down at her. "You were insolent, right from the start. You're lucky you have such utility to Egmun and my family or I would've seen you thrown in the dungeon."

Vi lifted a hand to her chest and gave a small bow to hide her amusement. Her smirk would only make him more upset. "Thank you for not doing so."

"You said we must go." Aldrik shoved the key she'd given him into his pocket. "Carry on, then."

"Very well." She was on her feet as well, out the library, up, and across to one of the other doors that led to the palace. Aldrik faltered in the hall.

"The minister?"

"He will meet us at the stables." Vi held open the door for the prince. "Come along, now."

They walked in silence through the narrow hallway that connected the Tower to the palace. When they emerged, Aldrik immediately went for another side hall and Vi trusted him to lead them in the fastest way possible down to the stables. They passed a long stretch of windows that overlooked an inner courtyard. A lush garden flourished within—a greenhouse in the shape of a birdcage that Vi knew had been made to house Fiera's roses.

It was supposed to have been a gift from the Emperor—but it was a gift never seen by his bride.

The two emerged onto the dusty grounds of the stables. Two horses were out, tacked and waiting. Vi glanced around, seeing no sign of Deneya or their warstriders. She took a deep breath, ready to let out a sigh of relief. Everything was going according to plan.

A sharp pain seared through her abdomen. Vi's next breath emerged as a gurgle. The metallic taste of blood filled her throat.

She gawked, blood pouring from her mouth and down her chest. It mingled with the blood flowing around the point of a sword made of ice sticking out of her abdomen.

There was a sword of ice *sticking out of her abdomen*. Her first thoughts went to Adela. The bloody pirate queen had somehow found her after all these years. She'd known of Vi's hunt for the crown.

Yet another thing she'd missed.

Vi blinked several times, trying to force her eyes to focus around the pain. Aldrik's mouth was fixed in a soundless scream as he gaped at her. The presence of the boy was the only thing that didn't make Yargen's words of power come immediately.

The sword withdrew, and without its support, Vi fell limply to the ground.

9

"M-Minister, explain yourself," Aldrik demanded, his voice shaking.
Egmun appeared in Vi's field of vision. The sword of ice he'd been
holding evaporated into mist. "She was a traitor to the crown. I was
exploiting her for as long as she was useful." Egmun led a blindfolded man with a
rope, a gag suppressing his pleas for help. "Just like this one."

"What's going on?" Aldrik looked up at the minister with none of the ferocity
his question held. "She told me we were heading to the Crystal Caverns, that people
were acting against my family."

"That is true." Vi watched as Egmun rested his hand on the young man's
shoulder. She gritted her teeth to keep from saying anything. "They are called the
Knights of Jadar; they've hated your family since well before you were born, and
she was one of them."

Aldrik looked to her and Vi pressed her eyes closed. Let him think she was a
Knight of Jadar. Let her be branded as that—another nameless, faceless, unimportant
traitor of the crown.

Let him think whatever he wanted but let them leave, because she'd bleed to
death soon.

Her eyes opened as two hands slipped under her arms. Vi groaned as Egmun
hoisted her, dragging her through the mud into an open stable.

"You thought you could have the power?" Egmun whispered into her ear. "You
will *never* know the power of the Caverns. But I thank you for all you've done to
help me get to it."

"And this man?" Aldrik asked, unaware of Egmun's sinister remarks. He held
the bound man by the rope until Egmun returned.

"He is merely a run-of-the-mill criminal." Having discarded Vi's body like a piece of refuse, Egmun forced the bound man onto the saddle. "We will need him in the Caverns."

"For what?" Aldrik asked, following Egmun. He spared one glance back at her, though Vi could hardly make out his expression. Her head was swirling.

"I will tell you on the way." Egmun crossed over to where she'd dropped the sword. He hoisted it reverently—like it was the final piece of his plan falling into place as he slid it through a rope attached to his belt. "We must ride before dawn."

Vi closed her eyes, pressing her hands into the wound to try to stave the bleeding. Her whole body screamed in agony. She waited until she heard the rumble of horses departing the stables before she took a quivering breath.

"*Ha-hall-halleth…*" Her lips fumbled over the words. Yargen above, give her strength. "*Halleth,*" Vi started again, more determined than ever. She had to mend her torn flesh. She didn't care how gnarly the scar. If she didn't get on a horse now, everything would be forfeit. Red lightning cracked behind her eyes as she squeezed them shut, reminding her of what she fought for. Vi worked to dredge up strength as blood flowed freely from her. "*Halleth—*"

"*Halleth ruta sot.*" Light flared around Vi's body, illuminating the grime-coated walls of the horse stall. "*Halleth ruta sot,*" Deneya repeated.

Vi twisted, confirming that the voice wasn't a hallucination brought on by pain. The woman moved her hands over Vi's body. Glyphs soaked into Vi's torn flesh. She could feel her skin knitting underneath Deneya's skilled hands. "*Halleth ruta toff,*" Deneya finished, pulling her hand away.

"What are you doing here?" Vi asked, rubbing the freshly mended skin of her stomach.

"By the light, woman, you just had a sword through you and you've not so much as a single tear on your cheek. Are you even human?"

"No." Vi sat upright. "It's hardly the worst I've endured. The prize for worst pain goes to my body being rebuilt between worlds," Vi said grimly as she pushed herself to her feet. There were aches and pains, but it was nothing *halleth maph* couldn't fix. "I thought I told you to leave."

"Well, aren't you glad I didn't?" Deneya walked out of the stable. "I was collecting my things from my room when I saw you."

"What about the horses? I didn't see them in their usual stalls."

"They're here." Deneya led her quickly down the long stretch of stables and out the main entrance to the castle. Sure enough, both horses were there, their reins looped lightly around a post at a tavern. "I hadn't put Midsummer back in since I followed Egmun. So all I did was take Prism out."

"Why aren't there guards posted?" Vi looked around, still making haste for the mounts.

"I'm sure there will be soon. Egmun sent them away. I didn't catch what he said, but they were sent running."

"Likely some lie about the Knights of Jadar attacking," Vi mumbled as she swung herself up onto the saddle. "That way he could argue my corpse was one of them."

"Things *really* didn't go well with the illusioned sword."

"I told you as much." Vi grimaced as she mounted. Deneya followed her lead. "Mistakes or no, this is all for nothing if they make it to the Caverns without us and destroy the sword. Let's go."

With a kick and call, Prism bounded down the main road of the city with Midsummer right behind. The glyph *halleth* was still around Vi's wrist, stinting any lingering pain. Her skin had been mended, but no glyph could return all the blood she'd lost. Her vision was blurry, and Vi felt faint.

"Look, there." Deneya pointed as they departed through the main gate of the city. "I think that's them."

Sure enough, on the switchback down the mountain, two other horses with three riders between them rode out through the night.

"Let's slow down. We don't want to give them room to be suspicious," Vi declared.

"Egmun thinks he killed you."

"Egmun will jump at his own shadow right now."

"Do you think he'll hurt Aldrik?" Deneya asked gravely.

"Not until Aldrik lowers the barrier." Vi cursed under her breath. "After that... Well, let's hope he doesn't try." She watched as the horses below turned, winding further down the mountain. "They'll take the direct path there, I'm sure of it. You and I will go the long way. Straight for the cabin and around the mountain from the other direction."

"Riding through the woods could take double the time."

"Perhaps for riders who don't know them as well as we do." Vi grinned wildly. Challenging fate itself required all the arrogance she could muster. "And for riders who don't have purebred warstriders."

"These beasts are getting pretty old." Deneya patted the neck of Midsummer.

"Hardly. Warstriders don't hit their prime until at least thirty years." Vi watched as the other two horses crossed into the tree line below before giving a light kick, spurring Prism into motion with her heels. It was a good thing warstriders could live till seventy. She'd been counting on it from the first moment she'd taken these horses.

The mounts didn't disappoint her. They expelled plumes of white from their noses into the brisk, late winter air. The wind pricked her face and made Vi feel more alert and awake despite the blood loss. Her heart raced and her watering eyes gained clarity somewhere between their turn into the forests and winding around the mountain near their cabin.

The horses began to slow as they emerged from the back path to the Caverns. Vi could see the outcropping of rock she'd hidden in months before, to watch Egmun ride off. She hurriedly dismounted and Deneya followed.

"Tie the horses out of sight," Vi whispered, knowing how voices could carry over rock and snow.

"I don't think they're far ahead." Deneya did as Vi instructed, pulling the horses into an alcove as Vi continued on. She could hear the rumble of hooves over the mountain pass, slowing as it became narrow and treacherous.

"They're not. We just have to stay out of sight." Vi leaned around the rocks, looking up the path. The swish of a horse's tail was barely visible.

"*Durroe watt radia*," Deneya whispered, and Vi followed suit.

The chant was to conceal, a far easier task for something that wasn't moving. Whenever Vi glanced behind her, through the blurred and hazy edges of her vision, she could make out Deneya's form sliding over the rocks like running water distorting a riverbed. It wasn't perfect, but she suspected that the two men, in their haste, wouldn't look back long enough to notice.

Victor's keen eye for illusion wasn't here, thank Yargen.

They rounded the pathway and saw Egmun and Aldrik up ahead. Egmun was saying something to the young prince as he jerked the man he'd brought off the horse. Vi grimaced. She'd read about Jadar's attempts to use blood to open the Caverns. Apparently, that was something Egmun put stock in.

The three went into the Caverns with Vi and Deneya following closely behind.

Yargen's magic cast a blue aura on the fog that hung in the air. Egmun lifted a stone, dropping it to the floor. Vi used the distraction to slip into the Caverns. As was usually the case, the crystals illuminated at her presence. The magic greeted her with a familiar embrace, as if begging her to take the power that was here—to rejoin with it, once and for all.

Egmun smiled smugly at the light as he straightened.

I bet he thinks he did that, Vi thought bitterly.

"This way, your highness." Egmun led Aldrik through the main entry and into the antechamber with the confidence of a man who had walked among these crystals many times. Every few steps, he gave his prisoner a shove. The man attached to the rope carried on blindly, shivering in the dim light.

The poor sod had no idea where he was, or what awaited him.

Vi took a step forward to follow and Deneya grabbed her wrist. Their magics merged, and the woman was visible once more.

"What do you want me to do?" Deneya whispered to Vi, her voice no louder than the plops of water in the depths of the Caverns.

"Whatever you think needs to be done." Vi leveled her eyes with the elfin. "I trust you."

Deneya gave her a long, hard look and then a small nod. Vi stepped away, feeling her magic slip back into place around her. In the Caverns, Lightspinning was more of an art than a science. It was less about what words spoken and precise glyphs conjured, and more about intent.

Harnessing the true nature of Yargen's power was more like how she'd been initially taught magic: instinct. The more she worked with it, the more she understood it in a way that defied words, even the words of the goddess.

"Behind here," Egmun said, motioning to the crystal-covered doors at the top of a few steps, "is the heart of the Caverns. It is where the true power lies."

"Where we must go to help my father to victory," Aldrik murmured, repeating Vi's words from earlier.

Vi crept ever closer. The fingers on her right hand twitched, ready for magic, as her left hand remained balled in a fist, keeping her invisible.

"Just so." Egmun nodded. "You are the one who needs to undo this barrier. Only your great power can fell it."

"How do I do it?" Aldrik asked, looking up at the minister. He didn't seem to question for a second that he was the one destined for this greatness.

"Touch the crystals, and allow your magic to do the rest," Egmun answered cryptically. The man didn't know how to lower the barrier; Vi had never told him. And it didn't seem Fiera's instincts for the crystals had passed on to Aldrik. Lucky for them both, she was there. It wasn't how she imagined the sword meeting its end, but she had no other options.

Aldrik stepped forward, his hand held out rigidly as he ascended the stairs. Just once, he looked back over his shoulder and Vi froze, not wanting him to see the shift in her illusion. But the prince's eyes went to the minister. Egmun gave a nod, and

Aldrik reached out to touch the thin layer of crystal covering the doors

"*Rohko*," Vi whispered, feeling the magic flare. *Rohko* was the word Fiera had uncovered in the crystals when she'd made the barrier. Vi could still sense the glyph holding the stones together.

Now, with that same word and her will, she'd see it dismantled.

The crystal glowed brightly in tandem with Vi's intensifying focus. Spiderweb cracks spread out from underneath Aldrik's hand and in a burst of light and sound, the stones came crashing down. Aldrik stumbled back, dazed. The minister stepped forward, catching the boy by the arm.

"*Kot sorre*," Deneya murmured from her side. *To push.*

"*Durroe watt ivin*," Vi whispered hastily. A flash of light hovered around Deneya's glyph, concealing it. The men were still blinking from the release of the barrier; Vi suspected they hadn't caught a glimpse of the true powers at work as the doors swung open.

"Wh-what's going on?" the blindfolded man had bitten through his gag. "Where am I?"

"Quiet, you," Egmun snarled, jerking the rope around his wrists so hard that the man tripped and fell in a heap.

"Was that necessary?" Aldrik said, still dazed, looking between the prisoner and Egmun.

"He is a criminal, the lowest of the low." Egmun wrenched Aldrik forward by the arm as the prisoner scrambled to find his feet once more. "Come, both of you. Destiny awaits."

You're not wrong about that, Vi thought grimly.

She'd practiced the transference of power from the weapon to the Caverns for fourteen years. After her breakthrough, her confidence and skill had increased at a shocking rate.

Yet a shiver still rattled her teeth.

It all came down to this. The sword Egmun held wasn't a decoy. She had one shot at seeing the sword's power returned to the Caverns. If Egmun's magic won over hers, if his clumsy attempts at manipulating Yargen's power bested her transference, the sword would be broken and irreparable damage done to the Caverns.

She would fail. And if she failed now, she failed the entire world.

Egmun led Aldrik and the prisoner into the depths of the Caverns. Vi could almost see Raspian's invisible hands reaching outward, seeking the world he was shut off from, yearning for release. Every vertebra in her spine vibrated in a resonance that screamed "no" the closer she drew to the final room in the Caverns, the place Raspian had been sealed away. Every sensation was deeper, heightened, worse than the first time she'd come to this place.

With a kick to the back of the man's legs, Egmun brought the prisoner to his knees in the center of the stone floor. Vi crept to the door, perching herself by a crystal at its side to remain hidden.

"Prince Aldrik." Egmun took a step toward the boy, who wore a mixture of fear and wonder. "Someday, you will be Emperor. Do you know what that means?"

"I-I do."

"So you know that justice will fall to you." Egmun took another step forward. "It was your mother's last request to your father to spare you these duties as long as possible."

Vi didn't recall Fiera ever making any such request. If anything, the duty-bound woman Vi had known would've wanted her son to grow up entrenched in politics, learning from them, and becoming cunning enough to stay alive.

"My mother?" Aldrik asked with such hope, Vi's heart ached.

The mother she'd taken from him. Had Fiera lived, perhaps Aldrik would've never sought out his father's attention to the point of resorting to crystals. But, had he not, he would've never come here, and the world would've been a failure.

Everything connected in ways that not even Vi could always see. Which was as thrilling as it was dangerous.

"But you will soon be a man, won't you?"

"I will."

"It is rather unfair, no? For your father to be treating you like a child?" *Ah*, so that was Egmun's game. Vi's nails dug into the crystal at her side. Egmun was using the young man's desire to prove himself against him. "Are you prepared to be the crown prince this realm needs?"

"I am." Even though it was positively frigid in the Caverns, sweat dotted Aldrik's brow.

"Then, my prince, for justice, for the strength of Solaris, for the future of your Empire, slay this man." Egmun dropped to a knee and freed the sword from where he'd tied it to his belt. He offered the crystal weapon to the prince.

"But…"

"This man has stolen from your family; it is a treasonous crime. He is not innocent."

"Should my father not—"

"I thought you were a man and a prince." Egmun's annoyance with Aldrik's hesitation was showing. Vi loathed herself for sympathizing with the wicked man. *Get it over with*, she wanted to scream. She wanted to know if her whole future was forfeit or not. "I did not take you as someone who shied from justice or power, Prince Aldrik." Egmun paused dramatically. "Why are you here?"

"For my father, to conquer the North."

"With this, all will bend to you." Egmun smiled encouragingly.

Aldrik took the sword and Vi's heart nearly lurched from her chest. Every hair on her body stood on end. *So… close.*

"M-my prince, m-mercy please. T-take my hand for m-my theft. Spare m-me," the man begged through sobs.

"Minister…" Aldrik hesitated. He'd never killed a man before, Vi realized then. A mere week before his coming-of-age ceremony, he would make his first kill.

"The guilty will say anything to you, my prince, to save their skin. This, too, is a lesson." Egmun stood and seemed to be holding his breath.

Aldrik unsheathed the sword and passed the scabbard to Egmun's eager palms.

"M-mercy," the man begged.

"*Kill him, Aldrik,*" Egmun nearly shouted.

Aldrik set his jaw and hoisted the sword over his head. He paused with the blade stuck at the apex of his swing. Vi held her breath alongside the whole world.

He swung the weapon down.

Vi lifted her hand at the same time. Her other palm was flush against the crystal at her side. Magic sparked around the sword, almost like flames.

The strike was clumsy. The man groaned and gurgled, his pleas for help vanished.

Aldrik raised the sword again, bringing it back down. Carnage splattered across the center of the room.

But Vi's focus remained on the blade.

She allowed the magic of the Caverns to combine with hers, to guide her as she mentally reached out to the weapon. Vi could feel another magic in the air. Egmun was trying to act on the crystals as well.

Pathetic, Vi thought snidely. This power was hers—hers to claim and hers to control.

The sword shone brighter, as though the power within was trying to burn through. Aldrik slashed twice more before the man lay limp on the ground. The sword clattered to the stone below.

That contact of sword to Caverns was all she needed.

Crystals flared around the perimeter of the room. Aldrik shielded his eyes. Egmun thrust out his arms, as if waiting for the power to sink into him.

One crystal connected to the next, and Vi wove her magic between them all. The stones inlaid on the floor illuminated and, for the first time, Vi understood what they were.

The light that shone between them connected to form a glyph. Setting her eyes on it filled her mind with a roar of sound. It was as if every person in the world screamed a single word in agony, a word so loud she could barely make it out.

Suladin—a glyph of sealing.

A word Vi didn't yet dare speak aloud.

Keeping her focus on the sword, Vi held out her right hand, reaching for it. The glyph around her left kept her invisible. The weapon was too far for her to touch, but through the bond of the Caverns, she could feel it.

Her fingers tightened around the magic of the sword, yanking it like a tether and sending the magic back into the Caverns. Power flowed into the stones around her. She felt it rush through her body, leaving her breathless and dizzy.

The glow of the crystals faded.

And the Sword of Jadar turned to obsidian, fractured, and dissolved into dust.

10

"WHAT?" EGMUN LOWERED HIS arms and spun as the light of the Caverns faded. "What did we do wrong?" he shouted to the ceiling above. The echo of his voice was the only reply.

"M-minister... I... I don't feel so well." Aldrik swayed. His eyes were still on the mangled body before him.

"She... it's her fault," Egmun seethed, ignorant to the boy. Vi almost felt proud that he was laying blame at her feet. "She knew what must be done and kept it from me and now—"

Aldrik interrupted Egmun's ravings by turning up the contents of his stomach. Egmun jumped back to avoid the vomit splattering on his shoes.

"We should go, you foolish boy."

"Foolish?" Aldrik looked up at the minister, as though in a daze.

"Your power was not enough," Egmun sneered. "And now your desire for power has opened the heart of the Caverns once more to any who would dare use it against your Empire."

"I only did as you asked!" Aldrik pleaded.

Vi's breath caught in her throat. This young man, this *child*, who stood stained with blood and bile, would one day become the rough-tongued, harsh man her father had always been rumored to be. It wasn't Fiera's death that had set her father on a torturous path of transformation. It was this moment.

Either way, it was her fault.

She tried to steel herself, but everything ached. The only thing she could tell herself was that this was all worth it. She would make it worth it. It didn't matter if he was aware of the vortex or not, this would be the last time Aldrik would suffer the loss of his innocence in such a brutal way.

Rumbling filled the Caverns, as though a mighty beast within was starting to wake. Vi looked around, as startled as the two men. The sound was followed by a burst of light that rose from the floor and flowed out the Caverns, rushing to the opening like a torrential river of magic.

"We must go," Egmun said grimly. "Before the crystal taint claims us." He grabbed Aldrik's arm and wrenched him from the room.

As the two sprinted out, Vi knelt down, dipping her fingers in the river of light. It felt like nothing. There was no power here, only air.

Vi lifted her eyes and released the glyph for *durroe watt radia*. She stepped out of the inner chamber and through the doors just in time to see Deneya emerging from where she'd wedged herself between two crystals. The two men were long gone.

"Think I need to keep this going?" Deneya held up her arm, a strip of golden magic rotating by her elbow.

"Maybe for a bit longer." Vi dragged her feet down the steps on the other side of the door, but she didn't quite make it to the bottom before she sat heavily. She still felt dizzy. Though Vi couldn't tell if the dizziness came from her earlier wound or the current of power still rushing through her. "Just until we're certain they're far enough away."

"*Durroe watt ivin*," Deneya murmured, flicking her other hand toward the entry. Vi saw a haze of light fill the air.

From Egmun and Aldrik's perspective, the beast that was the Caverns had been woken with a roar, unfurled its tongue, and was letting out a sigh of pure magic.

"Clever." Vi appraised Deneya's handiwork.

"Thank you." As Deneya spoke the words, she tilted her head in a motion that said both, "don't worry about it" and, simultaneously, "I know I'm pretty great." Vi couldn't help but chuckle and shake her head. Deneya came over, glyphs still hovering around her forearms. She sat next to Vi. "I doubt we'll be seeing them back here anytime soon."

"They'll be back soon enough."

"Why?"

Vi sighed heavily, running a hand through her hair. Most of her braids had slipped out. "Because the river of fate moves forward, and the War of the Crystals Caverns is next."

"People fight over the Crystal Caverns?"

"Fight *against* the Caverns."

"How does one fight a cavern?"

"I wondered that myself, when I first learned of it." Vi thought back to her lessons with her tutors. The War of the Crystal Caverns had seemed like impossible lore. "In my world, the magic of the Crystal Caverns seeped out into the land and tainted the people and animals; they called it 'crystal taint.' The crystal taint disfigured man and beast, changing their minds and bodies into monsters.

"I think the taint comes from Raspian's power mingling with Yargen's in the crystals, once the glyph holding him back is weakened."

"Monsters, wonderful," Deneya murmured and looked back through the doors. "But we don't have to worry about any of this. You got the power out of the sword and into the Caverns, right?" Deneya leaned back and finally relaxed the glyphs. The illusion of magic faded and the air was still once more.

"I did…" Vi rested her elbows on her knees and folded her hands. She could almost hear Taavin.

Apparently, Deneya could, too. "Taavin is going to say there needs to be a war, isn't he?"

"I think so." In Vi's world, Vhalla's father had fought in the War of the Crystal Caverns. His valor in battle earned him a spot in the palace guard—a post which he ultimately gave up for his daughter to become a library apprentice. Which was an appointment that ultimately led to her meet a certain crown prince.

"You have a plan for that?"

"I've an idea... but no reason to think it'll work."

"Lovely." Deneya pushed away from the stone, pacing once, then stretching, as if unable to release all the nervous energy tensing her muscles. "Well, this whole scheme of yours hinges on you doing things that have never been done and have no reason to work."

"You have so much faith in me," Vi said dryly.

"I do." Deneya put her hands on her hips. "You know I have faith in the fact that you seem to be able to accomplish anything with sheer force of will." She shook her head and gave a look around the Caverns; Deneya's gaze turned skyward before falling back to Vi. "Honestly, I've always been rather shocked by this whole 'ninety-third try' business. You've struck me as the sort of person who can move mountains with nothing but an almost suicidal, ignorant determination."

"Thank you for saying so, I think." Vi grinned, an expression Deneya returned in kind. Speaking of sheer force of will, Vi pulled herself to her feet. There was still work to be done. "I intend for this to be the last time, for all of us."

"As long as it's the last time because you succeed."

"Agreed." Vi rested her hand on a nearby crystal, feeling how the magic within the Caverns had changed once more. It was just like her first experimentation in transferring the sword. Now, she had to take out that power and then some in an act that would make good on another promise—one she'd silently made to herself, and to a man of light, for nearly fifteen years. "Now, may I task you with heading back to our cabin and starting a fire?"

"You may." Deneya adjusted her heavy winter coat before heading out of the Caverns. "But I take it you won't be joining me just yet?"

"You know I still have some work to do here."

"Leave work to the morning; it's been an exhausting night," Deneya encouraged.

"No. I want this done before dawn. I suspect that once Egmun and the prince arrive back at the Capital, it won't be long until the Emperor finds out about what happened here. I want my business with the Caverns to be concluded before then."

"Concluded?" Deneya echoed skeptically.

Vi chuckled. "Concluded for at least a few decades."

"A few more decades of living in our cabin. Excuse my uncontrollable excitement."

"Maybe not in the cabin," Vi called to Deneya's retreating form. The woman paused, glancing back. "I think I'd rather go to the beach."

"The beach?" Deneya balked. Vi laughed at the expression, which proved the levity needed to break up the long night.

"I'll explain fully later."

"You'd better. I could use some warmth and sun again and couldn't bear it if you were merely teasing me." Deneya paused, almost at the entrance of the Caverns. "Be careful in here. Don't make me regret leaving you by yourself."

"I won't," Vi called back. With that minimal reassurance, Deneya left. "Right, then." Vi looked back into the heart of the Caverns, taking a slow breath.

She thought of summoning Taavin, but opted instead to remain silent and alone. Taavin would stop her, and Deneya's words had made her bold.

Vi went back up the stairs, through the doorway, and into the heart of the Crystal Caverns.

The magic was alive here. It welcomed her, surging through her veins. Vi held out her arms, inviting it to flow into her. This was Yargen's essence—the power that fueled the seal on Raspian, and the power that would challenge him once more.

Vi stared down at the stones embedded in the floor—the ones that formed the glyph that maintained the dark god's cage. She walked across them, her steps harmlessly connecting one to the next, until she reached the center of the room. Kneeling down, Vi rested her palms on one of the stones and closed her eyes.

She envisioned the Sword of Jadar. She dredged up memories of the scythe she'd held in another world. She recalled every last detail she could—how the objects felt under her hands, how much power they held.

"We'll start with that much," Vi said aloud, speaking to the crystals as though they were a sentient partner. For all Vi knew, they were. They held Yargen's essence after all; she couldn't rule out that they also held some of the goddess's consciousness. "Yargen, help me do this," she whispered. "I need him at my side."

Vi lifted her hands from the stone, drawing the magic in shimmering threads up with them. She twisted her left hand, palm to ceiling, and continued feeding magic from her right. Once enough power had collected in her upturned palm, Vi condensed it into a new crystal.

This would be the seed from which Taavin's new body would grow. She continued to string more magic from the Caverns into the stone, stopping when she'd reached the amount the Sword of Jadar had held.

Glancing to the heavens, Vi uttered one final silent plea to Yargen—*Let this work*—before continuing.

The crystals in the room flared and dimmed. Magic was drained from the stones along the outer ring of the room. It filled the crystals on the floor. They shone once more, the glyph they made barely visible in the beams of light reaching upward.

Siphoning this power, Vi felt something quiver between each draw off the Caverns.

Raspian could feel the weakening of power that confined him, she was sure. He could feel *her*. Just as keenly as she could feel him pressing, scraping, reaching, seeking a way out of his prison.

The phantom torment of red lightning cracking through her seared under her skin. She could feel the shadows of scars across her bones from where it had ravaged her body. Vi set her lips into a thin line and fought to keep her focus on her task.

"You'll be free enough to have your little finger escape," she said grimly to the dark god, not knowing if he could hear. "No more. No less."

The outermost stones on the floor began to dim against the brightness of the glowing stone in Vi's hand. It was a blue brighter than the sky, purer than the ancient ice of glaciers. It was bright enough to illuminate almost the whole of the Caverns and yet, looking into it didn't hurt. It felt... comfortable. Like staring into the eyes of an old friend.

With a flick of her wrist, Vi flattened her right hand and severed the connection with the Caverns. She could feel the remaining magic settling back into place, spread thinner, like water over a dry riverbed.

Sweat ran in rivulets down her neck and temples. Even in the chill of winter, holding the crystal, holding her focus, was extremely strenuous.

Vi placed the shining stone down gently before her. She ran her hands over it, murmuring, "*Kot sorre. Kot sidee.*"

Push and pull.

The magic was a tangible thing beneath her fingers. Vi manipulated it like a sculptor. She saw the crystal extend upward and downward. The stones smoothed and curved, taking on new shapes. Vertebrae appeared. Ribs stretched up from them. There were femurs that led to kneecaps, and ultimately toes. Collarbones sat beneath a strong jaw.

A skeleton of crystal was before her. The basis of her vessel. But it was nothing more than crystals in a new shape.

She wanted to lean back, sit on her heels, and catch her breath. But Vi couldn't allow herself to. Everything was fresh and new, waiting for the next layer of magic to be spun around it.

"*Halleth ruta sot. Halleth ruta toff.*" Halleth worked to create new flesh on an existing body. Why could it also not create new flesh for a new body?

A voice whispered in the back of her mind. The words were so faint that Vi couldn't decipher if it was instinct, or Yargen herself encouraging Vi in the right direction. "*Mysst ruta sot.*"

Mysst, to craft.

Ruta sot, inner flesh.

The words shouldn't have worked together. But here, in the Caverns, drawing on the raw power of Yargen, combined with Vi's unshakable determination, they did. It was as if she had the goddess's blessing to bend the words of the gods to her will.

For the first time, Vi truly made the words her own.

She was reminded of the moment she was rebuilt between worlds. The light intensified to the point that Vi could see nothing else. And from that light, substance took shape. The sensation of her veins unfurling like ribbons from a fresh heart was keen in her mind. Vi felt skin stretching across the form before her like a blanket, warm and safe.

When the light faded, she was left with the body of a man.

Reaching forward, she cupped the cheek of this lifeless body. It was still a vessel. There was no thought, no essence within. But Vi could see her plan taking shape. She could almost feel him there, and wondered if the warmth underneath her palm was the lingering magic in the air... or a fresh body seeking out life.

Vi gripped the watch with her left hand, white knuckled. With her right, she still caressed the man's face. Her eyes focused there.

Draw him out.

Lifting her hand off the watch as though it were a crystal, the magic of Yargen within followed her motions. She could see it in countless overlapping glyphs that hovered in the air. If she had to guess, there were ninety-three in total. Each one held the memories and essence of a different Taavin, including this one. They all combined together to compose the man she loved so dearly.

"*Narro hath loreth.*" Vi said the words to imprint a communication mark on the token—to first anchor Taavin's consciousness into this new vessel. On instinct, she repeated "*Hoolo, hoolo,*" over and over. *Stabilize, elongate, hold.* It was the first word Yargen had given her—the word that had truly brought Taavin to her.

Now, she would imprint that word, that glyph, over top of this body. Hold him there. Keep him within it. Let his consciousness be supported by the bedrock of her will and Yargen's magic.

"Come to me," Vi murmured as the magic sank into the flat plane of his chest. "Taavin, come to me. *Hoolo*."

The body was still, unresponsive.

"*Kot sorre. Kot sidee*." She would push and pull the air through his lungs and the blood through his heart. She saw his chest rise and fall with her words. But the moment she stopped, the body was lifeless once more.

"Taavin," Vi choked out. Exhaustion was knocking at her edges, cracking her resolve. "You can do this, Taavin," she pleaded, as though it wasn't all riding on her shoulders. "Yargen, please." Vi dropped her head to the man's bare chest, holding him as though he was already Taavin.

Vi took in a quivering breath. She could feel the magic seeping out of him. She could almost see the flesh turning gray and with it, her hopes dimming.

"*Narro hath hoolo*," Vi whispered. But what she really meant was, *wake up. Please, my love, wake up*.

There was a snap, like a tether breaking. Magic sizzled from the watch around her neck and she was thrown back. Her head hit one of the crystals embedded in the stone floor.

Everything went white and Vi blinked away stars with a groan. The sound echoed through the Caverns as she clutched her head, feeling for blood that thankfully wasn't there.

Twisting onto her side, her vision still hazy, Vi propped herself up onto her elbow.

There was another groan.

But this time the sound hadn't come from her.

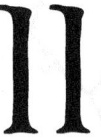

11

VI RUBBED HER EYES. Red lightning popped behind her eyelids and she snapped them open, looking around. The Caverns looked unchanged. But it felt as if the ground had been upturned, and the air had filled with invisible poison.

Her assessment of the environmental change passed when her gaze fell on a very naked man propping himself, his movements stiff.

"T-Taavin?" she asked weakly. For a terrible moment, she was overcome by fear that somehow everything had gone wrong, and she'd given a body to Raspian himself.

But the man brought his gaze to her, and she beheld the eyes that had never shone more brilliantly, set on an unscarred face. She knew it was him before he even spoke.

"Vi."

Her arm gave out, as though the sound of his voice reverberating through her took the last of her failing strength. Vi slipped back to the ground, but she didn't cry out. She laughed.

"Vi, are you all right?" Taavin rushed over, putting a hand on her shoulder.

"I'm fine—just tired." She made it a point to keep her eyes on his and not let them wander anywhere else. Especially further south than his collarbone. "Are *you* all right?"

"I've never felt better. I feel like—" He stopped short and looked down, taking in his full form for the first time. "I'm naked. And *cold*."

"Sorry." Vi laid back, staring up at the ceiling so he knew she wasn't taking advantage of the situation. "Making a physical vessel for you to occupy was a lot. I didn't figure out how to fashion clothing at the same time."

He gently rested a hand on her cheek. Taavin guided her eyes to his. Just the sight of him brought a noise of joy that was part hiccup and part laughter. An icy tear rolled down her temple.

Wordlessly, Taavin shifted, reached forward, and scooped her up. He sat and held her in his arms. *His arms.* They were sturdy, and stable, and warm. All things that made him distinctly real.

For the first time in over a decade, Vi was home.

She buried her face into the crook of his shoulder and breathed. He still smelled of warm summer days. Vi wasn't surprised. Yargen's magic lived in him now. He was made of the light itself.

"What did you do?" His voice was both stern and soothing.

"I made you a body."

"How?"

"I was inspired by how Yargen made a new body for me between worlds. I tried to mimic the process."

"Vi, that's impossible."

"Clearly not." She pulled away and looked to the doorway. Her unease only continued to heighten the longer they were in this center chamber of the Caverns. "I drew power from the Caverns, made your bones out of crystals, and wrapped muscle and flesh around them. You always said Yargen's magic was life," Vi explained hastily.

"I didn't mean like this," he murmured, kissing her temple lightly.

"Deneya wasn't wrong when she suspected I've been practicing. I have been, nightly, since getting to the capital. Transferring the power from the sword to the Caverns wasn't difficult. Neither was transferring the power from the Caverns to your body, or your consciousness from the watch to that body." She glossed over her moments of panic. He didn't need to know about that.

"We don't know what this means. You've never done this before. You could've risked my memories if you failed."

"What's done is done. And you're here now." Vi pulled away to look him in the eye. "I thought this through, Taavin. You want to ensure the world follows the path of the stones in the river. If the Caverns remain strong, there won't be a War of the Crystal Caverns. So—"

"So you stored the magic of the Sword of Jadar and some from the Caverns in me... to weaken the barrier on Raspian without actually harming or losing any of Yargen's power." He admired her with shining eyes. "You're brilliant. Reckless, but brilliant."

"Thank you." The War of the Crystal Caverns was a convenient excuse. Vi hadn't done this for the world. She'd done it for herself. She didn't know what pulling Taavin out of the watch would ultimately mean. But since this would be the last version of the world, Vi didn't worry too much about it. Not that she would say as much to him. "Maybe you'll start to trust my reckless ideas more."

"I likely should." She didn't miss the shiver that ripped through him as he spoke.

"We should go."

"We should," he agreed.

Yet they had a hard time moving. Standing would mean separating, at least for a little, and neither of them seemed to really want to do that at the moment. Vi could hold him until the day the world ended, now that she had him once more.

"Let's at least get out of this chamber." Vi rephrased her earlier statement, forcing them both into action. "We've lingered for too long."

"Yes, lets..." The way Taavin looked around and then scowled at the ground beneath them told Vi everything she needed to know: he felt the terrible aura that now hovered in the air of this place, too.

Vi pushed herself onto her feet and swayed a bit. She was only steady by sheer force of will.

Taavin rushed to her side, wrapping his arm around her waist. "I got you."

"I'm the one who's supposed to be helping you."

"You've helped me enough," he said as they hobbled down the stairs and into the antechamber.

"Here's good, set me down." Taavin did as instructed and Vi sat with a heavy sigh. She leaned back against a crystal, willing just a little bit more of Yargen's magic to seep into her and give her strength. With a thought, fire ignited around them in a semicircle, casting a warm glow over them.

"That's better."

"My horse is down at the foot of the mountain." Vi glanced toward the opening. "I have some clothes there. Nothing will fit you right. But it'll be *something* so we can get to the cabin. I just need another minute to regain my strength and then I'll make my way down."

"I don't want you trekking over that icy path in this state. I'll go."

Vi laughed at that. "You'll go? You'll freeze your bits off."

"I will not." He looked at her with a scowl.

"You will." She grinned in reply. "And I'd rather like those bits to stay attached." She'd meant it as a jest. But the words were softened by sincerity. Her cheeks were warm, and not because of the fire.

"Would you?" he murmured, his face close to hers.

"I would," Vi whispered. "I've dreamed of this moment for years."

"Really, *this* moment?" He arched a single dark eyebrow. "This moment where I'm naked in a cavern, a stone's throw from Raspian's tomb, holed up to escape the elements and figuring out how not to freeze to death?"

"Goodness, I forgot how annoying you can be in person."

"No, you didn't. You could just send me away when you wanted."

"And now I can't."

"And now you can't," he echoed tenderly. Taavin reached up, tucking a strand of hair behind her ear. His fingers lingered. They ran down her cheek, along her jawline, to her ear and back around the nape of her neck. His fingertips pressed into her and Vi tilted her head forward and up on command.

Their lips met.

Soft, was the first thought that ran through her mind. He was so soft. The thin barrier of magic between them was gone.

He was here. And he was hers.

Vi shifted, pressing forward until their sides were flush. He wrapped his arms around her while her fingertips spread across the unbroken, unblemished plane of his chest.

"My scars are gone," Taavin whispered huskily.

"They are. Mine disappeared too when my body was remade in this world." Part of her already missed every nook and cranny of his old body. "All the more reason for me to explore and discover this new form you're in."

His hand grabbed hers as it grazed over the raised muscles of his abdomen.

Taavin swallowed hard and locked his eyes with hers. "Yes."

"Yes, *but*?"

"Not here." He glanced over her flames and toward the open door. "Not so close to *him*."

Vi let out a groan of discontent. Taavin wasn't wrong. But she wanted him to be. She wanted to object to his postponement of this inevitable and most delicious moment between them.

She pried herself away.

"Where are you going?"

"To get my horse." Vi stepped through the flames.

"Are you sure you can—"

"You stay there and stay warm so you don't get frostbite and ruin that body I just made. I'll be fine. If anything was going to motivate me… this was it." She gave him a wink, and marched out of the Caverns with purpose.

Vi practically flew down the mountainside. Her heart was pounding and her magic was thin. She could feel every ache in her tired body. It had been a long night, and the first makings of a gray winter dawn were on the sky by the time she mounted Prism.

She raced back up the mountain and rode Prism into the entry of the Caverns, his hooves echoing off every surface. Vi ignored the sensation of Raspian, now as clear as Yargen's essence, permeating the entirety of the Caverns. She dismounted and rummaged through the clothing she'd packed. Luckily, unlike the last time she'd ridden out from a capital city, she was far more prepared for winter.

"Come on over." Vi relaxed her magic and the flames vanished. Taavin appeared in the archway of the antechamber, clutching himself and bracing against the winter winds that blew in through the cave mouth. Vi held out a pair of oversized trousers—one of the few things she'd lounged in, the brief moments she had time for lounging—and then a woolen knit shirt that should have enough give to fit his taller, broader body.

"This is comical," Taavin chuckled. It was a deep and rumbling sound, resonating within her more than anything else he'd ever said or done.

"I could never look at you and see anything but perfection."

"You're just trying to sweet talk me," he said as she threw one of her older cloaks over his shoulders. All she needed to do was keep him warm enough to get back to the cabin. Tomorrow she could ride to Mosant and find better-fitting clothes for him.

"I am. Is it working?"

"Yes." He caught her lips before she could pull away, his hands wrapping around hers.

"Good." She stepped away, a slight sway and twirl to her step. "Now, let's go home."

She mounted first, he swung up behind her. Judging from how tightly he clutched her, Taavin didn't have much experience riding horses. She'd take it easy on him if she wasn't so worried about him catching a chill on the way back to the cabin. And if her lower stomach hadn't become something molten hot at the sight of him.

They left the weakened Caverns behind and rode into the hours just before dawn. Clouds were gathering in the southern skies with what looked like the last blizzard of the season on the horizon. There were worse fates than being snowed in for a while, Vi supposed.

Smoke drifted into the gray sky from the chimney of the modest cabin. The windows splashed golden streaks across the snow. Midsummer was in the stable and it looked like Deneya had even found dry hay from their stores.

"Yargen bless, it's *cold*." Taavin's teeth chattered. "Or is it just my senses being heightened in this new body after not feeling the world for so long?"

"Both, likely." Vi and Taavin dismounted and she led Prism into the simple stable attached to the cabin. Trudging in the same line of snow as Deneya, she opened the door without preamble.

"How did it—" Deneya sat up from her bed, freezing the second her eyes landed on Taavin. She narrowed them slightly and tilted her head. "He…"

"I made him a body."

"You… made him… a body."

"I haven't seen you this flummoxed since we first met." Vi laughed lightly. She hadn't laughed so much in months—years. Things were finally going her way. After years of practice and waiting and praying, things had gone right.

"People don't make bodies."

"Women do it all the time."

"Firstly, babies don't count for what we're talking about here. Secondly, they don't count because you made an adult man's body out of thin air. Thirdly, do not dodge the topic." Deneya stood, walking over to Taavin. She poked his shoulder lightly. "You seem a lot more real than you used to."

"It's an adjustment for me, too." Taavin had a relaxed smile on his face, as though he'd just eaten a full meal. "I apologize that my presence might make things tighter for a while. You only have two beds here and—"

"You can share mine," Vi interrupted without hesitation. Both of them seemed surprised, though Vi didn't know why. It seemed like a perfectly reasonable solution to her. Perhaps neither expected her to be so brazen about it.

Despite what her body looked like, Vi wasn't a blushing young woman anymore.

"Right, well…" A knowing smirk played on Deneya's lips. She looked Taavin up and down. "Those clothes clearly don't fit you."

"They're mine," Vi said. "I was planning on going to Mosant tomorrow to buy some new ones."

"How about I go now?" Deneya promptly grabbed a satchel off the peg by the door and shoved a few coins into it.

"You don't have to. I can—"

"I really don't mind going." Deneya shook her head and gave Vi a pointed look. "It's only an hour into town. I can ride leisurely, maybe grab a hot meal. I should be back by noon."

Oh. A smile slipped across Vi's cheeks. She understood now. And respected Deneya all the more for it. The woman was a true friend.

"Right, then, you should get off your feet. You look dead tired." Deneya started for the door, pausing before she opened it. "Have a good, ah, *rest*." She left with a wink and not a word more.

They were alone. Taavin and Vi stared at each other as the sounds of Deneya's horse rumbled away. It didn't sound like a leisurely pace. But Vi had every reason to believe the woman would slow as soon as she was out of ear- and eye-shot of the cabin.

"Does she always leave just before dawn to head into town?" Taavin asked.

"Can't say she's ever done it before."

"So I should take this to mean she cares deeply about me and my new wardrobe?" He wore a smug, knowing grin. The look suited him. It'd look even better if it was the only thing he was wearing.

"I can't speak for Deneya… But I can speak for myself." Vi crossed the distance between them and rested her hands on his hips. "I think I care deeply for you."

"Care deeply?" He arched his eyebrows. "Vi Solaris, I think you *love* me."

"A bold claim, sir."

"I'm pretty confident it's true."

She kissed the smirk off his lips, then trailed her fingers up his body. They caught on the hem of the sweater she'd given him and pulled upward. She'd seen him fully naked. No matter how much modesty she'd tried to offer him, it was impossible not to have noticed the naked man standing before her.

Vi saw no point in hesitating now.

She wanted him. She'd wanted him for years. She'd yearned to run her fingers up his stomach and chest and twirl them in his hair, to the point of dreaming about it for days on end.

Taavin broke away from her mouth and trailed sweet kisses down her jaw and neck. His palms mirrored the movements of her own. They ran up her chest, fingers quivering with hesitation.

"Touch me, for the love of every god, Taavin, touch me," Vi groaned.

He obliged. His hands found their way up her shirt. The man's touch was searing hot—hotter than the glorious heat melting her from the inside out.

Her clothes were on the floor and the mattress sagged beneath her. It reminded her of their first night in the Tower. Kissing him then, holding him as he held the crystal. Now, the crystal was in him, and he was with her. No limits. No holding back.

Vi gasped as he explored with his mouth and hands. Her breathing hitched as he found a particular spot and Taavin caught a moan with his mouth. It fed his already eager movements, quickening them.

When he pulled away he was as breathless as she was. "I love you," he murmured.

"I love you," Vi whispered in reply. The firelight was generous to his sharp curves, casting stunning shadows over his body as it hovered above her. She tightened her grasp on him as he shifted. The distance between them diminished to nothing. "I will never let you go again."

"Please don't." He pressed himself against her, holding her tightly.

"I will save this world. And when it's over, it will just be us." It was a dangerous promise. Even if she could manage to save the world this time, she didn't know where it would leave them in the end. Yargen's magic was within him—in her—power that Vi knew they'd eventually need to return to see the goddess ready to take on Raspian.

Taavin sighed softly.

Pressing her eyes closed, Vi pushed the thoughts from her mind and bit his shoulder gently. She'd focus only on tonight and this release she'd been yearning and waiting for.

Delicious frustration built within her. She wanted him to move. She wanted him to be still. She wanted to sleep in his arms and do nothing. She wanted to do *everything* with him and to him.

"Let's not talk about the world." He pulled away, kissing up her cheek to rub the tip of his nose against hers. "Let's just focus on our world tonight. Right here, right now."

She nodded eagerly. And, as if he'd been waiting for that permission, Taavin moved, kissing her as he did.

Vi allowed her mind to go blank. For a few hours, she would burn hotter than the fire in the hearth, the spark within her, or the magic that remade the world.

THE WAR OF THE CRYSTAL Caverns started with trumpets and the echoes of military horses clomping through the mountain pathways and valleys. It was just over a week since Aldrik and Egmun had left the Caverns, and the start of the war signified that it was time for Vi and Deneya—and Taavin—to leave their cabin behind once more.

As they passed alongside the military party, heading in the opposite direction, Vi reflected on her lessons from years ago.

The Solaris army would march to the Caverns and become transformed into monsters. They would blame it on the crystals, never knowing the real culprit was Raspian. The untainted portion of Solaris's army would battle against the twisted version of itself for just over a year. Then, none would return to the Caverns for years to come.

In Vi's time, the next man to head to the Caverns and seek their power was Victor. He would use the Cavern's strength—Raspian's strength—to stage a bloody coup. He was the man she was working to stay one step ahead of. That meant she had to leave the War of the Crystal Caverns behind her, in the hands of fate.

Vi's focus was on the crown of the first King Solaris. They followed Adela's path and headed south to Oparium in search of the crown.

The port town was nestled in a valley in the mountains east of Solarin. The coast of Lyndum was mostly cliffs, making this cramped valley the only place to construct a larger port. It was nothing compared to Norin, and barely a slip for dinghies compared to Risen. But it was the best port the early Kingdom of Lyndum had, and it was where Vi suspected Adela had escaped to after fleeing with the crown treasure of Solaris.

When she'd first laid eyes on the city, months ago now, Vi had been optimistic. The crown was either hidden here, or with Adela herself. She'd either find it, or narrow down its location with confidence once more.

Now, all Vi felt was frustration.

"Months, we've been here for *months*, and not a single lead on QA or the treasure," Vi muttered. Southerners were even more superstitious about Adela than Westerners. Deneya had made the mistake of mentioning her name once, and their information gathering was near-instantly stinted. Now, the pirate queen was always "QA"—even when they were in the very back of what had become their favorite place to escape their shared hovel, The Cock and Crow brewery.

"It's not like someone's just going to come up to us and say, 'You know, you look like people in search of an infamous pirate treasure. Why not follow me and I'll show you where it is?'" Deneya quipped.

"It'd be nice if they did… or gave us *some* kind of lead." Vi sank her chin into her palm, looking out over the brewery. It was as lively as it ever was, and haunted by the same faces. "Nothing changes here."

"People are enjoying themselves after the end of a war." Taavin stretched, leaning back in the booth beside her. "They don't want excitement right now. They want stability and comfort."

"A shorter lifespan really does give some perspective." Vi envied them, in a way, for their ability to carry on dancing, laughing, and joking, ignorant to the world's imminent demise.

"I'd argue the opposite." Deneya took a long sip of her brew. "They can only focus on one existential threat at a time. Once that's settled, the world is all right."

"They can only do that because there are people like us to worry about all the others," Taavin murmured.

Vi brought her attention back to the ale slowly growing warm in its flagon. She took a sip and refocused herself.

"What's our goal tomorrow?" Vi produced the worn book, still filled with the maps Tiberus had gifted Adela years ago. Vi had added onto those maps over the past months. "I'd propose we head north through the tunnels."

"Seems as good as any idea." Taavin pointed at one of the winding tunnels. "You mean this one?"

"I was thinking so."

"Might as well keep crossing them off one by one." Deneya took a long drink. "Eventually, we'll go through them all." The woman met Vi's eyes. "What if the crown isn't—"

The door to the tavern opened and a rowdy bunch came singing in, interrupting Deneya. A noisy crowd wasn't particularly uncommon. What made Vi turn her head was the language they were singing in.

The throaty tones of Mhashanese filled the tavern as they finished the last refrain and devolved into laughter. They continued to carry on, heading straight for the bar. The leader among them, a man with dark, spiked hair, ordered from the young woman behind the counter.

"A round of your finest for my crew."

"Comin' right up." Maleese wasn't bothered. Even though she couldn't be much older than seventeen, the young woman was accustomed to bawdy sailors running amok in her bar. She'd clearly grown up among salt-crusted, curse-spitting men and women. "Not often we see Westerners in here," she said on behalf of every patron in the bar who was carefully regarding the newcomers.

"We're not Westerners," the man said. Vi knew that voice. How did she know that voice? She fought to place it, shifting in her seat.

"I hear it too," Deneya whispered over the top of her ale.

"Hear what?" Taavin leaned closer to say.

"The voice is familiar, but I can't place it... I want to see the man's face."

"What are you, then?" Maleese set four flagons heavily on the bar and went back to filling four more from the tapped keg. "Look Western to me."

"We're Mhashanese," the man said proudly. A notable distinction to make.

"*Oy*, Violet," Maleese called over to Vi. It was the name she was going by now. "You *Mhashanese* too? Have I had it wrong this whole time?"

The man at the bar turned his head. Vi locked eyes with him.

He was older now, resembling more and more of his father by the day. The father Vi had killed with two words.

Hello, Luke, Vi thought darkly.

"You can call me whatever you like, as long as you keep the ale coming," Vi said with a wink. A few of the other patrons gave her an approving nod or cheer in agreement.

Luke took his drink off the bar and walked over. He had a relaxed smile—more of an arrogant grin.

"*Fiarum evantes*," he said to the table.

"*Kotun in nox*," Vi replied deftly.

He paused, staring at her for a long minute. "Do I know you?"

"I don't know how you would." Vi shrugged.

"You look like a woman I once knew. But by now she would be..." He trailed off, and then shook his head, as if dismissing the notion. Luke had become a middle-aged man, and Vi still looked eighteen. Even if he recognized her perfectly, he clearly doubted his eyes. The man continued speaking in Mhashanese; knowing him, it was likely some kind of test. "Not common to see Westerners in the land of gold hair and snow fields."

"Could say the same to you," Vi replied in the old Western tongue. Even though she knew her pronunciation and grammar were flawless, thanks to Yargen's magic, it still felt odd to pronounce the words once more. "What brings you here, brother?"

"We're starting a sailing route between here and Norin. Regular runs on fast ships." He swept his eyes across the table; Deneya and Taavin both gave nods. They had begun inking Taavin's hair to make it black. With the deep tan of his skin, he looked the part as much as Deneya. "I don't think we'll have much room for passengers. But for the right price, I could liberate you from this icy prison."

Vi chuckled. "Perhaps we should take him up on it?"

"I miss the desert sun." Deneya sighed longingly.

"I'm afraid we don't have much in the way of money." Vi turned back to Luke. The son of the maritime minister in the West. A loyalist of the Knights of Jadar still, no doubt. In the face of an old enemy, Vi saw an interesting opportunity. She lowered her voice and leaned forward, speaking conspiratorially. "Not a lot of opportunities for us here."

"I've no doubt." He muttered something she couldn't make out, but it ended with "Southerners" in a nasty tone.

"Perhaps... we could work for passage?"

"I have all the crew I need."

"One of us can do the work of two men without tiring," Deneya boasted.

Taavin remained silent. His expression was passive at a glance. But she could see the questions in his eyes. *What are you doing?* he silently asked.

He'd just have to trust in her. It was a skill Vi was still teaching him.

"Is that so?" Luke hummed at Deneya. "I believe it of you. But these two…"

"We're stronger than we look," Vi insisted. "Give us a chance. You won't regret adding additional red-blooded Westerners to your crew." *Red-blooded Westerners*— she'd heard the Knights of Jadar using the term and hoped it struck a chord.

"I'll be the judge of that. But consider me intrigued. Plus, I'm always happy to help out my kin." Luke held out his flagon and Vi knocked hers against it before they both drank. "Come to the docks tomorrow. We'll put you through the wringer. If you can keep up, I'm sure I can find a position for you three."

"Thank you, sir…" Vi paused.

"Lord," he corrected. "Lord Twintle."

"Lord Twintle." Vi gasped, then bowed her head low. "Forgive our impropriety." Taavin and Deneya followed her motions. No matter how much time passed, Vi was certain a Twintle would always appreciate people prostrating before him.

"You know of me?"

"Oh yes," she said eagerly. "Who of Mhashan's blood doesn't know of the illustrious Twintle family? You stood up for the old ways when very few would. Or so I've heard…"

"Luke! Are you going to spend the whole night over there?" A burly man lumbered over, throwing his arm amount Luke's shoulders. "Your crew would like a drink with their benefactor."

"Yes, Cole, I'll be over." Luke looked back to them, pointedly at Vi. "And I look forward to seeing you three bright and early at the *Lady Black*."

The two men went over to the pack of Westerners, talking as they left. Vi saw Cole glance back on more than one occasion. She busied herself with her flagon as she stole glances from the corners of her eyes. She didn't remember a man named Cole the last time she'd been in the West.

But that had been nearly twenty years ago, which was plenty of time for Luke to find new allies. Especially now that he was the new Lord Twintle.

"Want to tell us what that was about?" Deneya asked in hushed tones. The Westerners were no longer paying them any mind.

"And why we're trying to get on a ship with *Twintle* of all people." Even though Taavin couldn't have recognized the man by face, he recognized him by name.

"To find an enemy, we have to go were enemies lurk," Vi whispered back. "Twintle is up to something. If he's coming to Lyndum willingly, I'd stake my life that whatever he's up to is big, and intended to work against Solaris. He and the rest of the Knights have had decades to lick their wounds from the blows they were dealt at the fall of Mhashan, and my cutting their ranks in the Caverns. They're emboldened again, and their coffers are fat."

"You think they might be planning something with QA."

"I can't be certain, but they've done it before. Why not go to her again?"

"And your rationale is there's only one way for us to be certain—to get on his ship," Deneya continued.

"Yes. Either Adela didn't manage to get the treasure off the Dark Isle and it's here somewhere, or she took it, and it's on the *Stormfrost*. If it's the latter, the Knights might be our best way to get to her."

"Clever, I'll give you that." Deneya grinned and stood, sliding out from the bench of their booth.

Vi and Taavin followed. They slipped out the main door and into the cool night with only a glance from Twintle. It was the last weeks of summer, and the chill of autumn was already beginning to settle on the world.

Taavin linked his arm with Vi's, allowing Deneya to walk ahead. He lowered his voice. "Are you sure about this?"

"Do you have a better idea?"

"I don't like the notion of working with the Knights."

"Trust me, I'm not a fan of it either."

They arrived at the single-room hovel they'd been staying in near the market. Most nights, Vi longed for something better. But it was a roof over their heads and they didn't have much in the way of gold or silver—some pilfered treasure Vi had stolen from the palace before they left, Deneya's meager wages from working in the stables, and whatever coin Deneya's craftsmanship brought in.

In the back corners of the room were three pallets. Two were pushed together, the third on the opposite side. They went about their business, readying for bed with habitual precision before crawling under their respective blankets.

"Think the beds on the ship will be better than this?" Deneya asked the darkness.

"There will be bunks or hammocks, if it's anything like the other vessels I've been on," Vi answered, twisting both her body and her words as she dodged the heart of the question.

Taavin slotted into place behind her, one arm stretched out underneath her pillow. The other wrapped around her waist and tugged lightly, bringing her close.

"A hammock sounds nice. Fewer bugs probably." Deneya yawned. "I bet it sways with the rocking of the ship. Lull us to sleep like babes."

Vi laughed. "The first time I was on a ship, I was nothing like a babe. More like a drunkard, vomiting everywhere."

"It can't be that bad. The ride over from Risen was easy enough."

"Risen," Taavin murmured sleepily in her ear. Warmth flooded her at the sound of his voice so close, at the feeling of his body flush behind her. Vi savored every precious sensation. She'd been taking them for granted since he'd gained his body. "If we get all the weapons—" he yawned "—we'll need to go to Risen and get the flame, to get Yargen's essence within it."

"I know." Vi had been accounting for it from the start. She kept track of where Yargen's essence was stored: the flame, the Caverns, the three remaining crystal weapons, Taavin, and herself. Every night, Vi reminded herself of the count. Because the question of what would happen to her and Taavin when the time to summon Yargen came always circled back into the front of her mind. "One step at a time. First we have to find the crown."

"And get all the other weapons."

Thoughts of Risen brought her mind in another direction. "Deneya."

"*Argh*, I was just about to fall asleep. What?" she said with a flair of drama.

"You were not about to fall asleep." Vi grinned. "What does Lumeria think has happened to you?" It had been over ten years since Vi had last heard of Deneya checking in with the queen.

"I told her when we last spoke that business here would keep me from giving updates to her regularly. I'm sure it'll take about fifty years of silence before she starts to wonder."

"Makes sense," Vi muttered, her lids becoming heavy.

It didn't even occur to her that she had just found the idea of someone checking in once every fifty years reasonable. Fifty years would've been half of her lifespan once. Now, it was little more than a moment.

With every day that passed, she drew closer to the end of the world and further from the world she'd known... and the woman she'd been.

Vi woke up before her friend and lover.

Taavin's breathing was slow and easy. The sunlight from underneath the crack of the door was already bright enough to see by. Vi twisted in Taavin's arms. He sighed softly in his sleep and tightened his embrace slightly.

She ran her fingertips from the point of his ear down his cheek. His eyes fluttered open at the touch.

"Sorry to wake you," Vi whispered, soft enough that Deneya wouldn't hear.

"Waking next to you is nothing to be sorry about." He blinked the morning's haze from his eyes. "How did you sleep?"

"Wonderfully."

He must've seen something on her face. "Is everything all right?"

"I hope so," Vi started cautiously.

"What is it?"

"I'm going alone this morning."

His brow furrowed. "All three of us are going—" She silenced him with a finger across his lips.

"Listen... I don't know what 'wringer' Luke will put us through to see if we can keep up with his crew. But even if somehow you two can hide your ears for the test... you'll never be able to conceal them long-term on the vessel. All it will take is one gust of sea breeze to take off your caps or bandannas, and then everyone will see them."

"We can illusion them."

"Those same sea breezes will make your hair wild. You won't be able to predict its movements with an illusion."

"We'll illusion the whole head of hair, then," he countered.

"And you don't think that would ever look suspicious?"

"Dark Isle dwellers don't understand what our ears mean. We could say it's a birth deformity."

"One you both share?" Vi arched her eyebrows.

"We'll say we're siblings."

"Even though you look nothing alike?" Vi barely refrained from rolling her eyes.

"We both have black hair."

"*I* have black hair, Taavin. You have bottles of ink."

"There are bottles of ink in Norin as well. We can keep up the deception," he insisted.

"I need you both here." Tired of arguing, she got to the heart of the matter. "You need to keep exploring the tunnels and caves to look for the treasure. This way, we can divide our efforts: I'll go and ensure Adela doesn't have the crown while you two remain here to look."

"You have no guarantee they're working with Adela."

"And you have no guarantee they aren't." Just when she was on the verge of exasperation, he cracked a grin and pulled her closer. There wasn't a bit of space between them and she was left breathless as Taavin leaned in and placed a gentle kiss on her lips.

"I understand, and I know." He sighed. "I'm not going to fight you further."

"Really?" Vi asked skeptically.

"If I tried, I think I would lose."

"You would, because I'm right about this."

"And I know it." Taavin kissed her lightly once more. No matter how much time passed, the act still sent sparks up her arms that were their own, unique type of magic. He pulled away and murmured, "I still don't want to let you go."

"If it's any consolation, I don't want to leave your side. But whenever I'm docked here, I'll be with you."

"And the weeks or months when you're sailing to and from Norin?"

"I'll yearn for you—for where I am home." Were she able, she'd hide from the world and spend forever in his arms. Taavin's embrace was one of the few places she still felt fully herself. She was Vi, here, nothing more or less. "Hopefully, I can gain some kind of lead on Adela early and I'll return to you quickly."

"Or maybe we'll find something and call you home."

Vi nodded and heard Deneya begin to stir. Before the woman was up and about, Vi leaned in for one more kiss—for one last, longing second when they were entwined. Then she pulled away.

There was work to do.

Deneya was understandably frustrated by the notion of not getting to go on the ship and prove her prowess. But she ultimately agreed with Vi that it would be for the best.

Then, with just a pack to her name once more, Vi emerged into the early morning.

She made her way through the narrow streets and alleyways of the compact city down to the docks. Vi instantly knew which ship was the *Lady Black*. It bore Twintle's family crest on an oversized sail.

"And what'll you be wanting?" A gruff sailor sitting at the end of the gangplank stopped her as she approached.

"I'm here to see Lord Twintle," Vi said in Mhashanese, hoping to earn some favors with the man.

"You really think the Lord sleeps on a ship when he has the comforts of port?" *So much for winning him over.*

"Then I'd like to speak with the man named Cole."

"That's cap, captain, or Captain Dower to you," the sailor corrected.

"May I please see Captain Dower?"

The sailor stared her down for several long seconds, spit something he'd been chewing into the strip of water between the boat and the dock, and finally pushed away from the pylon he'd been leaning on. "All right, green gills, come along. You'd best hope it's something good to be troubling the captain this early."

Vi followed him onto the main deck of a narrow ship. She was instantly reminded of the *Dawn Skipper*. The *Lady Black* was a little larger, designed to carry more cargo, but both vessels had clearly been designed with speed in mind.

"You wait here," the sailor ordered, disappearing into the captain's quarters at the stern for a minute before reemerging with the man Vi recognized from the night before as Cole—Captain Cole Dower, she now gathered. "This is the one looking for you, sir."

"Thank you." Cole dismissed the man and looked Vi up and down. "You had two others with you last night."

"They decided the high seas are a bit too intimidating for them."

"So the scrawniest came instead." Cole shook his head and turned away. "Go home, girl."

"No." Vi stood firm. But the man didn't so much as glance over his shoulder. When he continued toward his cabin, Vi had no choice but to scamper after him. "I said I would not leave."

"Well, there's no room for you here." Cole opened the door and disappeared into his cabin, leaving Vi standing on deck, a bit dazed.

This was a test. Her trial period had begun and they were going to see how determined she really was.

Vi did a quick scan of the deck and then started toward a man who was pulling out a bucket and mop. The ship was fairly quiet in port. But that didn't mean there weren't chores that needed doing.

"Give me those."

"Who are you?" the man asked, but he was already handing her the mop.

"Your new crew mate," Vi declared, hoping she'd be right by the end of the day. "When I'm done with this, what can I do next?"

The man gave her a long list. After she finished swabbing the deck, Vi coiled rope and sanded a portion of the wall underneath one of the windows in the crew's quarters. She worked without question or comment other than, "What's next?" or "What else can I do?" until the sun hung low in the sky. The narrow opening to the cargo hold kept catching her eye, but Vi ignored it, for now.

If there was one thing she'd learned, it was how to be patient.

"I thought I told you to go home."

"I'm almost done with this for the day," Vi replied, not even looking back to confirm what she already knew from the voice alone: Captain Dower had come to check in on her.

"I have no pay or berth for you. Go home."

"I don't have a home, sir," Vi said. The feeling of Taavin's arms, closing tightly around her, filled her mind. He was the only home she had.

"Is that supposed to illicit sympathy from me?"

"No," Vi answered, dipping her brush into the heavy paint and caking it onto the wall she'd spent the better part of the afternoon sanding down. "I'm merely stating facts."

"Then my facts remain as well: I have no room for you. Now, off my boat," he growled.

Vi calmly finished the section she was working on, returned the brush to the bucket, went to where she'd originally collected the paint from, closed the bucket, and dropped the brush in a soaking basin. When she emerged on deck with Cole, she noticed more than a few eyes on her. A group of sailors who were drinking on the quarterdeck went silent. Vi strode down the gangplank and settled herself on the pylon opposite the guard.

"Get going, girl," Dower called down.

Vi wondered briefly how old Dower was. Thirty? Forty, perhaps? They might be nearly the same age, and here he was, calling her "girl."

"You told me to get off your boat, sir. I am off of it. You said nothing about the docks and don't control them."

"Suit yourself," he grumbled and disappeared.

That night, Vi slept on the docks in a twilight haze. She was ever aware of the heavy footfalls along the creaking wood, always listening for a threat. When dawn came, she unfolded her cold, damp body and ascended the gangplank to begin her work once more.

Once more, Captain Dower told her he had no room and no pay for her.

Once more, Vi slept on the docks.

It took a week.

Twintle suddenly appeared on the boat without warning, looking quite smug. He didn't so much as spare her a glance as he went right for Dower. Vi hoped that Taavin and Deneya had been keeping an eye on the man while he was in town.

The call to cast off was made soon after.

Dower said nothing about having no space for her as they readied to set sail.

13

THE PASSAGE FROM OPARIUM to Norin took about four weeks, round trip, depending on weather. They usually stayed in Oparium for two weeks when docked, and in Norin for a month or two.

In total, the trip to and from Oparium usually took about two and a half months.

Vi had done that trip four and a half times when things finally got interesting. They were docked in Norin when a woman with a scar over her left eye boarded late in the night. Vi had seen the woman on the docks when she was off the boat with the other sailors in search of a drink or card game. But she'd never had much of a reason to pay attention to her. That was… until now.

"I'm here to speak with Cole."

"Not often a Southerner comes knocking in Norin." Vi folded her arms over her chest. She'd worked her way up through the ranks swiftly and deliberately, to be one of Cole's agents. He trusted her to not let just anyone onboard the ship.

"Twintle sent me." The woman tucked her hand into her coat and produced a folded letter sealed with the same symbol emblazoned on the sail.

"Well, then, don't keep the captain waiting with your lordly business." Vi pushed away from the dock pylon and led the woman up the gangplank.

A Southerner… what would have Twintle working with a Southerner? Whatever it was, Vi was certain it wasn't good. But perhaps, hopefully, this marked the start of a lead that would bring her to Adela.

Whatever the woman and Cole spoke about was short. She was strolling back down the gangplank with the same smug smile in only ten minutes. Vi worried the chain around her neck and wished, not for the first time in Norin, that she could still summon Taavin.

A few hours later, when the decks had long since quieted, a red-cloaked figure emerged from the night's haze. Vi shifted off her perch, instantly alert.

"*Fiarum evantes,*" Luke said, just as he had all those months ago.

"*Kotun in nox*," Vi replied, eying the red cape around his shoulders. Did the Knights of Jadar still meet in that warehouse? She'd cased it a few times without success, but perhaps she should do so again.

He started up the gangplank, but stopped only a few steps up and faced her once more. "You were that girl we liberated from the South. What was your name?"

"Violet," Vi said.

"That's right. You were the one who knew of my family." Luke paused, hands folded behind his back. He looked more and more like his father as his hair began to salt. "How did you put it? That my kin, 'protected the old ways'?"

"It's what I was always taught growing up here in Norin. And it's made working for you an honor, sir."

"Is that so?" He stepped forward, looking her up and down in the dim light of the docks. "How old are you, Violet?"

"Twenty, sir." She looked like she could be twenty, right? The longer Vi was alive, the harder it was to feel any age.

"You were a toddler when this city fell, then."

"But I grew up with the stories. They were vivid enough that, even as a girl, I felt like I had been in those battles."

"You remind me of a woman I knew, then," he said, his voice going soft with memory. Vi smiled innocently. He'd said as much in Oparium.

"Who?" *Let's see if you can remember this time.*

"I can't recall." Twintle shook his head. Couldn't? Or didn't want to? Vi didn't ask. "But more importantly, I have a proposition for you."

"Oh?" This was the most Twintle had spoken to her in the past year. They'd otherwise had only brief, polite interactions.

"I'm going to expand the business ventures of this vessel. We'll need an *adaptable* crew. One that is loyal above all else. Dower only has good things to say about you and your work ethic. I've never seen you fraternizing with the wrong crowd."

"I'm flattered you've taken such an interest in me."

"It's one of my duties to see that the young men and women of the West are both protected and raised with our ideals. You do share our ideals, don't you?" Vi nodded. "Good. Then perhaps I could put in a word with Dower and you will remain one of the crew."

"I'd be honored." Vi didn't like the idea that she was at risk of getting kicked off the ship. It would make returning to Oparium difficult, at the very least. She watched Twintle start up the gangplank once more. Vi stepped forward before she could think better of it, stopping him with a soft, "Sir?"

"Yes?" He turned, his expression one of surprise.

"In the stories of the old West my parents told me… red-hooded knights were always the saviors." Vi motioned to the cape he now wore. "This made me remember those words."

"I see." He had a knowing smile.

"If such knights existed, it would be my life's goal to serve them." Vi stopped herself there. If she said too much, she'd risk suspicion.

"That is most good to know." Luke bowed his head and Vi mirrored the motion. He disappeared up the gangplank and onto the ship.

The next morning, the whole crew was brought on deck. Dower walked the line of them, looking each up and down.

"For many of you, this is your last day of service to Lord Twintle and the *Lady Black*." Murmurs rippled through the assembled crew. "Many of you have been top-notch sailors the likes of which any captain would be lucky to have. I've communicated this to the Lord and he will be offering you a generous severance and a glowing recommendation for any future captains you wish to sail under."

"If we're such good sailors, why is he letting us go?" one of them asked.

"Because Lord Twintle is having the *Lady Black* take on a new directive that requires a specialized crew," Dower answered lightly. *Nothing to worry about here; don't read too closely into this*, Vi mentally filled in the blanks for him. "Now, please step forward if I call your name…"

"Louis." That was Cole's first mate. Expected.

"Joyce." The woman was a Western Waterrunner, but that was all Vi knew about her.

"Violet." Vi stepped forward, relieved to be included. If she stood with Louis, she stood with the group that was staying.

"You three will remain. The rest of you can go."

"A-All of us, cap?" the man from earlier stuttered in shock.

"Yes, you're dismissed." At Cole's final command, the crew of the *Lady Black* trudged belowdecks to gather their things. Vi stood a little straighter as he addressed them once more. She was still the newest of the lot and the one with the weakest relationship with Cole. "Louis, wait for me in my cabin; we need to go over what we'll be looking for in our new hires. Joyce, see to the crew below and escort them off if need be."

"Make sure there's no trouble, you mean." She had a wicked glint in her eye.

"Behave," Cole cautioned her before turning to Vi. "You, join me on the quarterdeck."

Vi did as she was told. Anticipation built with each step toward the back of the vessel. Cole went straight to the railing, glancing over his shoulder to make sure no one was around. When he spoke, he didn't look at her.

"You're here on the direct order of Twintle. If it were up to me, you'd be leaving with the rest of them."

"Thank you for that," Vi said, somewhat dryly. She folded her arms and leaned against the railing, looking in the opposite direction. "Or should I say to pass on my thanks to Lord Twintle?"

"Don't get me wrong, you're a fine sailor, Violet. But this is going to require loyalty—something you haven't really been tested on."

"What is?" She wanted him to say it outright, whatever *it* was. Vi was more than ready to know if all of this following Twintle was actually going to lead to information on Adela and the crown, or not.

"Know I won't hesitate to gut you and tip you over the railing should you betray us."

"Noted. Now tell me what we're doing."

"We need to make some special deliveries into the South. Henrietta—you met her last night—is going to help us with that." The Southerner with the scar over her eye.

"What kind of deliveries?"

"You don't need to know that."

"Are we still docking in Oparium?"

"Yes."

"Will Henrietta be part of our crew?"

"In a matter of speaking. We'll pick up some new crew members that are specially trained for this work." Vi opened her mouth for another inquiry but Cole interrupted her. "That's all you need to know for now. Do as you're told. Keep your head down and your mouth shut." Vi physically shut her mouth on the recommendation. "Good. We set sail with our new crew tomorrow."

Vi watched Cole descend to the main deck amid the steady flow of departing sailors. Twintle was clearly up to something. The question was… what? And, more importantly, was Henrietta working for Adela?

Every time Vi laid eyes on Oparium, her heart fluttered to the point of breathlessness. She'd made five runs now with the *Lady Black*, working with Henrietta and her crew.

Henrietta turned out to be the captain of a small smuggling operation that was now under Twintle's employ. A day before the *Lady Black* reached Oparium, they'd drop anchor in the sheltered cliffs of the southern mountains and meet up with Henrietta and her crew. Vi and the rest would connect the two vessels by a few precarious planks and carefully offload heavy crates of Western rubies onto Henrietta's boat.

Henrietta would then sneak the crates of rubies into the South through some secret dock to avoid taxes and questions raised about where they were going. Judging from the rumors Taavin and Deneya had heard, Henrietta was using Waterrunners to illusion her ship to look like the *Stormfrost*. No one in town wanted to investigate a ghostly-looking vessel that might belong to the infamous Adela.

But where the rubies came from, what the money from their sales was going toward, who was buying them, and whether Henrietta was actually in league with Adela were all things Vi had yet to find out. Despite having so many unanswered questions, every time she returned to Oparium, she did so with optimism… and excitement.

Taavin, Taavin, Taavin, every pulse whispered. Vi paused at the deck rail, watching the city come into focus through the early morning fog. She knew he'd be waiting at the docks for her. Sometimes Deneya was there, sometimes not.

But as the ship neared port, Vi knew immediately that something was wrong. A host of city soldiers were lined up, waiting where the *Lady Black* usually tied off her ropes. Vi, along with the rest of the crew, regarded each other skeptically. No one said anything until Cole was on deck, staring down at the portmaster and the head of the city guard.

"What's the meaning of this?" Cole asked.

"Your ship is temporarily embargoed," the head of the guard announced.

"Under what cause?"

"We have reason to believe you're not accurately representing your goods," the portmaster said meekly.

Cole scoffed. "Your men inspect our goods every time."

"This time the city guard will do it," the head guard said, taking control of the situation once more. "No one on or off the ship until my men have time to go through every box and bag in your hull."

"Be my guest. I'll lower the gangplank now."

"Unfortunately, I can't spare you the men now." The head guard smirked.

He couldn't spare the men? But he had a whole score of them lined up for their arrival. *Typical power play.*

"When do you think you can spare them?" Cole ground out.

"We'll see." Yes, the city guard was toying with them, no doubt ensuring that they would be punished regardless of whether or not they were found guilty.

She swept her eyes over the docks, looking for Taavin, as the head guard appointed someone to watch their ship day and night. Taavin and Deneya likely knew what was going on, and the real meaning behind this holdup. She just had to get to them.

Vi waited until nightfall. There wasn't much to do on the ship, and it was hard to slip away from the crew unnoticed. She made the excuse of a trip to the latrine. When she was there, she uttered *"durroe watt radia,"* then slipped out the next time a sailor opened the latrine door.

She'd been practicing her Lightspinning. Vi couldn't shake the feeling since making a body for Taavin that she had been given permission to challenge the conventions of how the magic worked. Nothing seemed impossible anymore—not even moving while invisible, without any kind of distortion. It still wasn't perfect. But with more power, perhaps it could be.

Perhaps with the scythe…

Padding lightly on the main deck, Vi headed for a spot she'd identified earlier, where the crates stacked on the docks were high enough for her to jump. She listened to the creaking of the ship, memorizing the patterns the waves made. During one loud groan of the vessel, when no one was looking, Vi jumped off. She left a rope right at the deck's edge that she could push down with *kot sorre* later to get back aboard.

"Durroe watt ivin," she whispered quickly, replacing one glyph for another. Vi slipped into the second skin of a Southerner, and made her way through the city to the one-room abode Deneya and Taavin still occupied.

Vi didn't even bother knocking.

"What the—"

"It's me." Vi closed the door, relaxing her illusion.

"See, told you she'd make it." Deneya gave Taavin a look of triumph. "And you were worried."

"We were just discussing how we'd break you out," Taavin said, standing. He crossed over to her and, without hesitation, enveloped her in his arms. "I was worried I wouldn't get to see you this time."

"If the world itself being rebuilt couldn't keep me from you, nothing will." Vi held him tightly and sneaked in a kiss before they broke apart. "But what's going on in the city? They've finally decided to investigate all the pirate talk?"

"The rumors of Adela have gotten worse," Deneya said. "Henrietta is getting bold or sloppy, but sightings of her vessel have increased and it's roused all kinds of suspicion."

"Too bad it's not actually Adela," Vi muttered.

"First time I've ever heard someone say that." Deneya snorted with amusement. "Any confirmation if Henrietta is actually working for Adela?"

Vi shook her head. "Though I'm beginning to wonder if her ability to masquerade her ship as the *Stormfrost* without Adela coming to put an end to it is proof enough."

"Adela could be on the other side of the world. She might not even know."

"There have been some other developments since you were last here," Taavin said. "Notably, the prince has come to town and things seem to be escalating swiftly with his presence."

"Again? He came last summer and nothing changed." Vi didn't need to ask which prince. According to all rumors, Aldrik had grown to be a harsh man, shaped by the cards Vi had dealt him with her own hands. Only Baldair left the capital with any regularity.

"There's been a murder on the royal estate during one of his infamous parties," Deneya picked up the explanation. "He's now looking into the Adela rumors as a result."

"What made him link the murder to Adela? Or Henrietta?"

"According to talk on the town, the murdered woman had the mark of Adela carved into her dead body," Deneya said grimly.

"Henrietta's getting greedy," Vi muttered. All good things had to come to an end, especially when those good things involved smugglers teaming up with traitors. Despite what was claimed, there was never honor among thieves. "Do you think Henrietta has a lead on Adela's treasure?"

"I don't see how she couldn't. She's been docking in the Caverns and using their tunnels for over a year."

Vi folded her arms, a scowl on her lips. She'd hated the feeling of stagnancy for years. It was becoming harder and harder not to just rush in and smoke out the smuggling rats with her own flames.

"I take it you still haven't made much progress investigating the tunnels with them there?"

"We've had to be cautious," Taavin said grimly. "We don't want to disrupt fate too much."

Vi barely resisted screaming.

"But we did find something," Deneya said hastily, as if sensing her agitation.

"What?" Vi asked eagerly.

"It'll likely be easier if we showed you."

They each donned an illusion, stepping into the skin of a Southerner so as not to stand out. The three traveled down the winding staircases that descended to a rocky beach not far from the port. From there, they went north, until the beach was nothing more than a narrow line of rocks where the waves ended. Soon, there wasn't a path anymore, and large boulders blocked their progression. The stone was slick with sea spray and it made the going slow.

Eventually, they came to a narrow pebble beach, and Deneya took the lead. The cliffs had completely hidden the town from view. Vi followed along to a point where the sea flowed in to a giant cavern.

"We've seen a ship go in and out of here—judging from your description, and those of the other sailors in town, likely Henrietta's."

"You couldn't investigate the caves anymore, so you investigated the cliffs," Vi said aloud as it dawned on her. "That's brilliant."

"This isn't even the most interesting bit." Taavin stopped at the water's edge. "We'll get wet from here on."

They swam across the deep channel—definitely deep enough for Henrietta's smuggling vessel—to the rocky beach on the other side. From there, they continued walking, climbing, and scrambling across boulders and cliff faces that had long ago fallen into the sea. There were a few other channels they had to swim across, and just when Vi was about to suggest they just *tell* her rather than show her whatever it was they were bringing her to, the roar of water could be heard.

"What's that?"

"What we want to show you." Deneya walked ahead this time.

"About a month ago, we came across this." Taavin pointed.

They stopped at another opening in the cliffs. Water roared out of the mouth of a cave in giant splashes, foaming with white, and racing to the sea. All of the other openings had water flowing *in* from the ocean. But this one was like a giant spigot someone had long forgotten to turn off.

"Some kind of spring, or waterfall created by mountain run-off?"

"We thought that too since the water is icy and fresh," Deneya said.

"But look closer." Taavin pointed to something wedged between the rocks just under the water's surface. It was a speck of gold, shining in the moonlight.

Vi crossed over and knelt down. Reaching into the chilly water, she retrieved a coin from where it had been stuck for what appeared to be a long time, judging by its worn surface. Vi flipped it over in her fingers, summoning a mote of flame to see by. On the side of the coin that had not been blasted by water for years, an imprint was still legible.

"Solaris," she murmured. But this was not a coin used by the Solaris *Empire*. "The Kingdom of Solaris." Vi stood. Now that she knew what to look for, dozens more flashes of gold illuminated the night. "Then this means…" She turned her gaze back toward the sheer rocks. Vi could think of only one way ancient treasure would be collecting here—Adela's stolen gold was somewhere close. The treasure, and the crystal crown, had never left the Dark Isle. "We should go into the caves tonight."

"I wanted to when we found it a month ago. He wanted to wait for you." Deneya gave Taavin a look. Vi's attention went to the man as well.

"You didn't need to do that."

"You are the Champion. It is your right to find and protect the crystal weapons." The sentiment was sweet, even if it made Vi tremble with agitation.

"Then we go now."

"Henrietta's crew will be docked in the caves. It's not safe to go through them now. We could risk altering something in the flow of fate that would result in a new Champion not being born."

"*I* am the flow of fate!" The words burst from her with a ferocity Vi didn't know she possessed. Taavin and Deneya both gaped at her. Vi pushed slick strands of hair from her face, fighting to compose herself. "We are trying to stop the world from ending. This is it; this is our chance. We get the crown now—we know where it is. Even if we change things, we will have all we need to stop the world from ending. All of the other crystal weapons are waiting for us. A new Champion doesn't need to be reborn."

"And if you fail?" Taavin stepped forward.

"I won't."

"If you do?" he repeated. "Are you ready to condemn every man and woman on this earth to death? Are you prepared to know that *you* alone were responsible for the end of light and life? Are you ready to usher in an age of darkness from where there is no return?"

"Taavin, that's enough," Deneya said gently. But Taavin didn't back down. He continued to lock eyes with her in an outright challenge.

"I won't fail," she repeated, though her voice was weaker than it had been a moment before.

"Guarantee me you won't," Taavin demanded. Vi was silent. It was a promise she couldn't make. "Guarantee it!" His voice echoed off the cliffs, briefly overpowering the waves.

Another shout of frustration struggled to rise from her throat. All Vi let escape was a meek, "I can't."

"Then we do as I say." Taavin put his back to her and stalked away.

Vi glared at his back, her eyes burning with frustrated tears. *What was the point?* She wanted to ask. What was the point of any of it if they weren't willing to take risks?

Clearly, she didn't have an answer. She fell into step behind him, and didn't speak another word about the crown.

14

VI SHOULD BE EXHAUSTED. After being up half the night and sneaking back onto the *Lady Black*, she'd only managed a few hours of shuteye. But she was up and tending to her duties, more alert than ever.

Her spat with Taavin was still mostly unresolved. At least, it felt unresolved. They hadn't spoken for the rest of the night.

Vi finished swabbing the deck and looked out to the cliffs. The crown was there. It had to be. She took a deep breath. One more week, and the *Lady Black* would leave without her. She would go get the crown, and then… *What?*

Her path forward seemed murky and uncertain. Taavin was the only person in the world who could shake her like this.

"Drop the rope ladder!" the guard on the deck called up, distracting her from her thoughts.

Another of her shipmates looked at her and Vi gave him a nod, a non-verbal, *I got this.* Hopefully this would be the head of the city guard here to make his check. He would find out that everything matched up, since the *Lady Black*'s illegal cargo had been offloaded days ago.

She crossed over to the railing, adjusting her braids to look over at who was coming to call. All the air in the world vanished.

Three men stared up at her: the young prince Baldair, Erion Le'Dan, and a familiar set of dark eyes that Vi would have known anywhere. She knew them as well as her father's because another version of this man, in a lost world, had been like her father. Tears stung her eyes as emotions bubbled up that Vi couldn't contain.

Jax.

"Don't just gawk, girl. This is an Imperial prince who's waiting on you," the guard scolded, jostling Vi from her shock. She knelt down and tossed the rope ladder over the side of the ship.

Vi rushed over to Cole's cabin. "Prince Baldair is here," she said hastily.

"What the—oh, by the Mother's love," he grumbled. "All right you lot, all hands on deck," Cole commanded. The crew lined up in their usual places for greeting Twintle.

Vi fidgeted as the three men tipped over the railing, landing on the deck with small bounces. She forced herself to stay still, pushing her emotions away.

"They sent a prince to inspect my goods?" Cole tilted his head to the side.

"It should be an honor to have the attention of an Imperial prince," Erion retorted. Even though Vi had only met his father briefly in Norin, she could see so much of Richard Le'Dan in him. But his blue eyes were that of a Southerner. She'd told Richard he'd learn to love the South. It looked like she'd been right.

"Oh, I'm *honored*. I just don't want to waste your time." Cole chuckled and spread out his arms. "I'm Captain Dower, and it's a pleasure to meet you, Prince Baldair. Let's settle this matter behind us. My cabin is this way. I'll let you review my logs and written inventory, complete with signatures all the way from Norin."

"My prince," Erion started as Cole was leading them to the cabin. "May I propose we go with the good captain while Jax goes directly to the hold? We can check at the same time."

"Good suggestion," Cole said, knowing he had nothing to hide.

"I leave it to you." Baldair passed the papers he was holding to Jax.

"Jax?" Cole stroked his scruff thoughtfully. "Unique name, that. I heard of a man named Jax a few years back. Did something monstrous, somehow didn't lose his head, and became a dog of the crown instead."

Vi bit the inside of her cheek. She saw the flash of hurt in Jax's eyes at the horrible brand he couldn't escape, not even in the South. Yet he grinned, pushing the pain away and pulling a mask in place.

This was certainly the start of the man she'd known as her uncle. But he was rougher, less polished and confident.

"You caught me! Though you're a little late, as the crown got me first."

"This matter has long been decided and need not to be discussed further," Baldair said with a firm tone.

"I don't know if I want such a man—"

"If Jax isn't endeared to you, you only have yourself to blame," the prince said sharply. Vi barely resisted cheering. "I trust Jax to do the right thing more than any other guard in this city."

Jax took the last of the papers from the prince and asked, "Where's this cargo hold?"

"Louis, you show him," Cole said, starting for his cabin.

Vi struggled to resist the urge to do it herself. But she had no reason to insist she be the one to show him. Violet didn't know this man.

So she was left standing uncomfortably as Louis led Jax below decks to the dark cargo-hold.

She milled about the deck as she waited, using the time to think. If the prince cleared the ship, she could get off. The ship would offload and be out of port. Then—

A conversation disrupted her thoughts.

"Fallen lord, how dare he step foot on this ship."

"Henrietta wants us to teach the royal and his lackeys a lesson for poking their noble noses into our business. They've been rooting around where they don't belong since they got to Oparium and hosted that little soirée of theirs."

Someone *shh*-ed. "Don't say her name so loudly."

"They're going to find out if they keep investigating."

Vi strolled over to the railing to get closer to the whisperers without looking suspicious.

"Stay calm and don't act rashly."

"Twintle doesn't pay us enough for this."

The conversation was between some of Henrietta's crew and Dower's. Usually, a few of Henrietta's crew stayed with the ship after they traded off the rubies. They were there to make sure that everything went according to plan—that was all the explanation Vi ever got.

Movement distracted her. She saw Joyce walking down into the hold. Vi pushed away from the railing as magic rippled the air. The last thing Vi saw was dagger of ice in the woman's hand.

At the same time, Dower's door opened.

The next few seconds unfolded as the world slowed to a fraction of its speed. Magic ignited below deck while Joyce retreated above. Vi lifted her hands and blocked the woman's path with fire. Joyce had gone rogue.

Vi's fire melted away with a hiss of steam as water pushed against it. A trident made of ice appeared in Joyce's hand and she lunged. Vi clamped her mouth shut so Lightspinning didn't escape.

She could go for the rest of her life without ever seeing an ice trident again. Joyce dropped her other hand, spreading ice across the deck, slowing the rest of them as she launched herself over the railing.

"Stop her!" Jax shouted as he emerged from below, alight with fire. He threw himself over the railing in hot pursuit of Joyce.

Vi followed on instinct.

They pushed through the crowds on the docks, already dissolving into panic. Vi watched Joyce cut down any who stood in her way. Behind her, Vi could hear Erion and Baldair shouting, but she worked to keep up with Jax. Instinct told her to do so above all else.

They rounded market streets, not far from the hovel. Joyce headed down a side alley and Vi was just close enough to see Jax disappear through an illusion in a cliff-side. Sprinting over, Vi ran her hands along the surface of the wall; sure enough, they sank through a misty illusion concealing a narrow passage.

She plunged through.

"Stop and I might make this painless for you," Jax's voice echoed ahead. Vi pushed her feet harder as magic erupted.

The narrow passage opened up into a cavern that had an interior cliff with a sheer drop down to the sea. It was no doubt one of the openings she'd seen the night before, with Taavin and Deneya. White hot flames assaulted Joyce as she levied a volley of ice spears with a wave her hand. Jax lifted his arms on instinct. Vi did the same, bringing a thin veil of flames to cover them both.

"What're you doing here?" He blinked at her.

"Helping you!" Vi shouted back. "I'll keep her pinned, you kill her!"

With a scream, Jax lunged forward for Joyce, fire alight. He missed his target. Vi watched him twist and Joyce caught his leg, ice coating his foot.

He certainly wasn't the skilled combatant he'd been in Vi's time—at least, not yet.

"You never should've chased me." Joyce looked to her with a snarl. Then turned to Jax. "You shouldn't have gone asking about Adela Lagmir."

Joyce pushed Jax away and his arms pinwheeled. Vi caught him, helping right him, but let go just as quickly to lunge for Joyce with flames alight.

The Waterrunner parried her blow for blow. Vi had spent decades learning and perfecting her Lightspinning. Her Firebearing had improved naturally with her combat instincts, but she wasn't nearly as good with it.

If only she could use her chants.

"I'm not letting you go," Vi growled, throwing a ball of fire.

"Petulant child."

Jax was all flaming hands and feet as he rejoined the battle. He was more of a liability than a help in such close proximity. Vi found herself dodging his attacks as frequently as she was avoiding Joyce's.

The awkward dance distracted her and Jax reached out, searing a spear of ice that was meant for her. Vi's breath hitched. He'd overextended and left himself exposed. Joyce impaled him to the hilt on an icy weapon and Vi bit back a cry of agony on Jax's behalf.

This could still be salvaged. If she let his consciousness fade due to blood loss then she could use her Lightspinning to finish off Joyce and heal him. Assuming Jax didn't die in the gamble.

"What a noble soldier," Joyce sneered as Jax coughed blood. "You shouldn't have gone looking for the pirate queen if you didn't want to find her." Joyce pushed him away and Jax staggered backward.

Vi stepped forward. Joyce levied a spear of ice against her. Vi melted it and uttered, "*Juth calt.*"

Two simple words, and Joyce was dead with a flash of light. *Now, for Jax.* Vi was just in time to see him stumble back into the open air beyond the cliff. Gravity mercilessly pulled the dying man down into the dark waters below.

"Jax!" Vi screamed, lunging into that void as well. She would not let him die.

Saltwater went straight up her nose and Vi surfaced, sputtering and looking around frantically for Jax. The tide was heading out—her first lucky break. They wouldn't be pushed deeper into the Caverns.

A lifeless body rolled over in the currents, dipping below the surface.

"Yargen above, don't you dare die on me," Vi snarled. Looking behind her, she said a quick "*Kot sorre.*" The glyph pushed on the water, giving them forward momentum.

As she tumbled in the waves she made, Vi reached for Jax. Dark waters, swirling with blood, surrounded her. Sand crunched beneath her feet as she found footing. Her elbows scraped against pebbles and rocks.

Her arms closed around the man and she pulled him to her. Vi tipped her head back, surfacing for air, clutching onto him for dear life. She gasped as they beached on one of the rocky shores she'd walked with Taavin and Deneya only a night before.

The wound was bad. Jax was coated in blood. But his heartbeat was weak and fluttering under her fingers. Water gurgled up from his throat as his lungs struggled to inflate.

Vi closed her eyes, dipping her chin down as she laid her hands over his chest. She could feel the man's shaky breaths, his struggling body, his quivering magic, his fleeting life. She could see it all as clearly as she'd seen Taavin's body, inside and out, when she'd made it.

"*Halleth ruta sot*," she whispered. Glyphs illuminated her hands. She opened her eyes, both seeing and feeling his skin mending.

"*Halleth ruta toff*," Vi continued. She moved deliberately, as if guided by an unseen teacher. Light and skin merged, weaving together and becoming one. Vi gave herself to instinct and her body moved as though it were no longer her own.

It was afternoon when she finally finished the job. Vi looked up at the young man. She reminded herself for the dozenth time in a few hours that this was not her Jax.

But... she would look after him to honor the memory of the Jax she'd known. He had spent the latter half of his life looking after her. Even if this Jax had nothing to do with the man who had made that sacrifice, Vi would look after him. She would repay that favor as best she could.

Vi twisted and sat with a sigh. She wiped the salt water that mixed with sweat from her eyes—certainly, these were not tears from emotions she didn't have names for—and looked out to sea. Jax slumbered at her side, breathing steadily; Vi would wait for him to wake naturally. She'd monitor him. And when he was ready, they would take on Henrietta's crew together.

A sigh at her side had Vi stopping the tune she'd been humming. She didn't know where she'd heard the song, or where it came from. Phantom memories that didn't quite feel like her own paraded through her head as she'd sat watching the waves, thoughts and visions that scattered like rats as Jax stirred.

"The Mother did not want you yet," Vi said faintly. Perhaps that was what had allowed her to pull him back from the edge of death—Yargen's blessing. At the edges of her vision she could see him turning to look at her.

"You're the sailor," he said slowly. Vi nodded in reply. "You saved me?" She merely nodded again. Not going into too much detail was for the best. "Where are we?"

"I don't know exactly." Though Vi had a very good suspicion. "We got dumped out here after you fell off the ledge and I went in after you."

Jax finally sat and Vi paid careful attention to his movements. Luckily, nothing seemed out of sorts. She watched as he inspected the holes in his clothing, pressing on newly mended flesh.

"How long was I out for?"

"A few hours."

"How did you heal me?"

Vi fought a smirk at that question. "Magic," she answered coyly. He stared at her, disbelieving, and Vi laughed. He'd never understand Lightspinning, and she wouldn't tell him. "Fine, fine, I had a salve on me. So you're doubly lucky I was here," she lied.

"*Why* did you save me?"

Her insides knotted at that question. He was so shocked someone would, and clearly confused as to her motives.

"Should I not have?" Vi leaned against the cliff at her back. Jax just shrugged and silence passed between them. They should get moving; things in town were no doubt escalating quickly. But she stayed where she was, saying gently, "I know who you are."

More panic across his eyes.

"I know you are Jax Wendyll, the man they call the 'Fallen Lord' in Norin," she said. She'd been in and out of the port for years now, she'd heard the stories. But she'd mostly ignored them. She knew the type of person Jax was in any world. "I know that, three years ago, you were tried for the murder of the Zower family, including the young Lady Zower to whom you were engaged.

"I know you were conscripted to the crown for your seemingly heinous crime."

"My crime was heinous," he retorted.

"It *seems* it."

"What would you know?" he snapped. "Who are you anyway?"

For one brief moment, Vi was back with Fiera on her birthing bed. She thought of telling him he had been like a father to her in another place and time. "Just a traveler," Vi said simply. He snorted.

"You're not 'just' a traveler."

"Perhaps not 'just.'" Vi grinned. He was astute. More than he realized. "But I have traveled from far away to investigate this Adela Lagmir impostor and her treasure." It was technically true. Just not in the way he'd interpret it.

"So you've heard of it, too?"

Vi nodded—that was one way to put it. "They've been running a criminal ring for over a year in the coves further south of here. Ships dock and unload cargo... some legal that they're avoiding tariffs on, others not so much. The coves are all connected, as you know. It's a maze, but that's how the real Adela gave the Emperor the slip about thirty-five years ago."

"Along with her treasure," Jax bitterly lamented.

"I wouldn't be so sure about that. Just because you haven't found the treasure doesn't mean it isn't here."

"What do you know?" His skepticism and self-doubt were becoming less jarring and more tiring by the moment.

"Help me take out this pirate queen impostor, and I'll tell you what I know about the treasure. I want to be the one to find it." She could imagine Taavin's face when he heard what she was doing. But *she* wasn't the one going rogue and finding the treasure. She was just following along with the prince and his merry band to make sure they didn't find it first. She was allowing fate to play out and give her the opportunity to get the crown.

If she lied to herself enough, perhaps even she'd believe it.

"Fortunate for me, that's an easy deal to make." A rush of relief overcame her and Vi beamed from ear to ear. "I would've done it anyway," he added, as though trying to somehow make it seem like the whole thing was, at least in part, his idea.

"I suspected we were aligned when I saw you chasing after her." Vi stood, dusting the sand and stones off her clothes. She had what she wanted, Jax was healed—no point in lingering. "Your little investigation into the treasure and soirée with the prince helped fluster the ring into making a mistake that has led me right to them."

"And now you're planning on going after her?"

"Will you help me?" Vi didn't understand the question—she thought the matter settled.

Jax sighed and pulled himself up to his feet as well. Vi regarded him with a careful eye, making sure her healing was as good as she thought. He didn't even stagger. "You're lucky we happen to be aligned."

"I think you were the lucky one." Vi smiled thinly. He would've died had she not been here. Taavin had never mentioned anything about Jax dying, and finding a time to ask when they were more at peace with each other was now high on Vi's list. Not that it mattered now. But she needed to make sure he wasn't keeping potential futures from her to spare her heartache.

He certainly hadn't with Fiera.

"Thank you," he said sincerely.

Vi waved away the notion and started along the beach. "I scouted an entrance up here. It's a bit of a climb, but if we fall heading for it, we fall into the water."

"What's your name?"

The question struck her harder than she'd expected. *You know me*, her heart wanted to scream. But her mind knew better. She searched his expression. There was no familiarity there.

She was no one to him.

Even after all this time, this new world could still cut deeply, and it would hurt more with every year that passed as the people here grew more and more to look like those she once loved.

"It's not important," Vi finally said.

"I must have something to call you."

"I've gone by many names. You pick." *Vi, pick Vi out of everything in the world*, her heart asked as she began to walk again.

"Fine, I shall call you," he paused and Vi's heart pounded, "Nox."

Vi chuckled. How dare she, after all this time, have hoped for anything else.

"Very well, if that's the name you choose."

"One more thing."

"What?" Vi stopped just as she'd been about to start climbing.

"You never told me why you saved me. If you were here to kill the Adela impostor and put an end to this criminal ring, why throw away the chance you had on saving me? Even if I could help, you had your quarry."

"Who said I threw away my chance? The woman we chased was not the leader."

"That's still not answering my question." And curse him for seeing so.

"Because all men are worthy of saving." Vi saw him open his mouth, no doubt with an objection. She cut him off at the pass. "Even—no, *especially* you, Jax."

His lips parted in shock and Vi turned away, beginning to climb. If she looked at him a moment longer, she would tell him there had been a young princess, long ago, who still thought of him like a father.

15

"**S**O, HOW ARE WE going to find them?" he asked as they headed deeper into the darkness of the caves.

"Patience." Vi shrugged as if she didn't know where they were going. Vi knew exactly where they needed to go to find Henrietta and her crew. If she led Jax there, perhaps she could encourage him to continue searching for the treasure. And if she *happened* to be there when he found it, she wouldn't have gone against her word to Taavin.

"And what if we get lost in here?"

"Then I suppose it's a good thing we're both people who've lived colorful lives. We'll have a lot to talk about while we wait to die." Vi gave a smirk over her shoulder. They weren't dying here.

"This, coming from the woman who wouldn't even tell me her name," he muttered.

"Well, maybe if we're on the brink of death, I'll tell you everything. Though, it'd take more lifetimes than we have."

"You love playing the mysterious card, don't you?"

"I am what I am." Vi shrugged. She didn't always know what that was anymore. "Quiet now. The ship docks in an inner cove to the south of town. I'm trying to listen for the workmen."

They continued into the darkness, winding through the dripping caves by the light of her flame. The sounds of people talking grew and Vi stopped, turning in place to stop him as well.

"I don't know where this is going to put us out." She feigned ignorance. He'd be suspicious if she knew too much. "We should stay low, make for good hiding the second we see it," she whispered in his ear. Jax nodded as she pulled away and followed her into a crouched position.

Vi waved away her mote of flame as its light merged with the ambient light of the cave beyond. She stopped for a moment, allowing her eyes to adjust, only to find Jax staring back at her.

"Do you want a 'we might be about to die' kiss?"

Vi fought the urge to burst out laughing with the competing urge to vomit at the suggestion. "This is not the place where you die," she whispered, cutting through his levity. "But this is the place where you will kill again." Vi grabbed his hand tightly. "You have to fight. You must fight for yourself, fight to live." *Not just now, but through all the years to come.*

Jax opened his mouth to speak and Vi silenced him with a finger. In him, she still saw the Jax who had raised her. But now she was the adult and he was the child in some ways.

"Just be quiet, and take the advice of a friend, Jax." Vi moved again before he could say anything else.

The cavern narrowed to a chute and they crawled forward side by side. It opened into a large room, though their vision was obscured by boxes and crates. Vi recognized them as the same boxes she'd helped unload from the *Lady Black* days ago.

"… their bodies recovered." Vi recognized Henrietta's voice. "None of you are to rest until their bloated corpses are here on a spike to warn the next captain who even thinks of challenging us." So Dower would take the fall for Vi running after Joyce.

"Henrietta, they've surely been lost to the sea." That was the voice of the woman who'd been on the *Lady Black,* murmuring dissent before Joyce attacked.

"Silence! It was your incompetence that got us into this mess. I'll hear none of it."

"Henrietta is their leader," Vi whispered to Jax. "You'll know her by the scar over her right eye. Go for her first." She'd never seen Henrietta in action, but suspected the woman was lethal. Anyone bold enough to use Adela's name had to be.

Vi took a deep breath, steadying her hands. They trembled in excitement, anticipation. It had been years since she'd felt like she'd accomplished anything, and now everything was happening all at once.

She emerged from the narrow opening into a bowl-shaped cavern. Vi rushed over to a larger crate and scoped out the six talking. Jax joined her shortly after. At least he was keeping up. Though, judging from his expression, only barely.

Vi took his hand once more. Fire licked from her fingers to his, as though she could give him her strength. His breathing slowed and he nodded. Vi faced forward, ready to—

"Drop the boxes," a booming voice shouted. Vi heard a groan from Jax. "You are under arrest by the will of the crown for smuggling, theft, murder… and many other horrible things."

She'd always heard her father was "silver-tongued." Clearly, that was a trait he'd inherited from Fiera. Because his brother was sorely lacking in eloquence.

Henrietta laughed. "Kill him."

Vi didn't waste a second longer, launching herself at the six smugglers. She'd told Jax to go for Henrietta. If he could handle that, she'd take on the other five.

Fire erupted around her hands as Vi swung, shooting a tendril of flame at one of the men still focused on Baldair and Erion. He screamed as the fire consumed him, though the sound was cut short as the fire was doused. Vi dodged backward, narrowly missing a spear of ice thrown.

She side-stepped, dodging another spear, and swept her foot across the ground. A wall of flame sheared off. The burnt man fumbled with his sword, determined to fight until his last breath. The woman shielded herself with a wall of ice that promptly became steam. Vi went for her—she was the more troublesome one.

With a flash of flame into the veil of steam, Vi stunned her, closing the gap. She grabbed for the sword the man was fumbling with, drawing it from the scabbard. Vi sliced his throat and swung for the Waterrunner. The woman had recovered, but her attention was elsewhere as she now engaged Erion Le'Dan.

The Waterrunner sunk a blade of ice into Erion's side. Vi crossed the distance with a lunge and threw out her magic. "*Juth starys*," Vi hissed under her breath—she wasn't taking chances on the smuggler countering her attack. The woman erupted into white-hot flames.

"Up with you!" Vi shouted at Erion. He blinked, startled. The lot of them were young men, fresh to bloodshed. She'd have to keep pushing them, especially knowing what trials their futures held.

Jax needed her help next and Vi launched herself back into the fray. She moved around him, preempting his motions; she knew his openings and could cover his vulnerabilities now that she'd fought with him once before.

Among the four of them, they dispatched Henrietta and her crew easily. Vi surveyed the room, making sure no others were about to spring toward them, as Jax went to his comrades.

"Erion, you got one on your hip."

"It's not that bad," Erion said bravely and pressed his hands into the wound.

"Nox, do you have any more potion?" Jax asked her. Vi shook her head. Lightspinning wasn't an option now.

"I'll burn it to stanch the bleeding." Jax leaned forward, flames licking around his fingers.

"Nox? From the *Lady Black*? The sailor who chased the smuggler?"

"She saved me."

"And the rest of you," Vi added as she adjusted her braids. This didn't seem like a group that valued girlish modesty, so Vi wouldn't play that card. She slipped into second skins easier than pairs of leggings. "I was told you were a noble fool, but that truly exceeded my every expectation."

Baldair, the golden prince, the playboy prince, the head of the Golden Guard— his reputation preceded him even after his young death in Vi's world. Though, seeing him now, at sixteen, it was hard to imagine him as any of those things. All he looked like to Vi was a spitting image of Tiberus.

"Jax, I didn't realize you were now in the business of babysitting lost, sassy children." Baldair laughed, his words lacking bite.

"I think I'm the babysitter," Vi mumbled as she began searching the crates.

"What're you looking for?" he asked.

"It's not here, either." Vi sighed. She should be happy that Henrietta hadn't found the treasure. But that meant the hard work was still ahead of them.

"You still haven't told me what we're looking for."

"Adela Lagmir stole the crown of Lyndum and fled with the other wealth of the last king." Vi straightened, placing her hands on her hips. "When the Emperor—your father, Baldair—chased her down the coast, she fled, giving all the impression that she'd taken the treasure with her. But I *know* it's still here."

"How are you so sure she left it?" Jax asked. "You said, if I helped you, you'd give me information on the treasure."

"I overheard them talking when we were docked in the port here to unload stolen goods," Vi lied. "They said someone was searching the caves and found 'it.' I assumed 'it' must mean the treasure. What else?"

"I think you're right." Baldair reached down, grabbing a wad of folded papers from his boot. "And we just so happen to have the map."

"You do?" Vi couldn't believe it. "Someone made a map to the treasure?" Someone who was very stupid to write such a thing down.

"Renalee had apparently been searching for the treasure for some time."

"Well, show me," Vi demanded, not bothering to ask who Renalee was.

"The city guard is coming; we can ask them for help." The young prince hesitated.

"I'm not interested in waiting." Vi tried to wave the idea away casually. Involving the city guard was a terrible idea—that was a whole lot of variables Vi didn't want to deal with. "Besides, it would mean more people can get their hands on it. Don't you want to be the only one to touch it, to hold it? Think of what the history books will say about 'he who finally rested his hands upon the lost treasure of Adela.'" What did young men want more than glory? Vi was betting on very little.

"It's *my* family's treasure. If anyone gets to hold it, it'll be me."

"I think I deserve this," Vi said with a roll of her eyes. "Especially after I helped you."

"Lay out the papers, Baldair." Erion was the one with sense in the group. Vi could tell that much. "I'm sure there's more than enough treasure to go around."

"Now you want a cut too?"

"I agree with the lady; I think we've all earned it," Erion said to the prince coyly. "What better way to end the summer than actually finding some long-lost pirate treasure? We've already hunted a ghost, stopped a murderer, and caught smugglers red-handed. We earned it."

"I agree. At this point, it's basically our divine right," Jax chimed in.

Vi snorted. *Divine right*—they had no idea.

Baldair relented with a chuckle, laying out the papers. He connected different curving lines stretching across multiple sheets to form a map, and Vi's mind was already committing each to memory. Some of the tunnels she knew from exploring herself, or seeing the maps of Deneya and Taavin's explorations. But other tunnels were paths they'd yet to go down. Dead ends and switchbacks were already recorded. The hard work was complete.

"All right," she declared once the map was solidly in place. She didn't need a moment more with it. "Let's go." The other three looked at her with surprise but fell into step.

They made their way through the tunnels, Vi dragging a dagger she'd lifted from one of the dead pirates along the wall to mark the way in case she returned with Taavin and Deneya.

There was some brief debate when they met a fork in the road. Ultimately they went right—something about a woman wearing an earring contributing to the decision.

At the end of the path was a dead end. Though wind howled through it. The four set to feeling out the walls, eventually finding an illusioned tunnel.

On the other side was another cavernous space, large enough to fit two of the *Lady Black* side by side. The platform they stood on was just wide enough to stand comfortably without fear of falling. Beneath them, at the bottom of a sheer drop, was a swirling whirlpool. White caps battered the rocks, and the churning waters made it impossible to tell its depth. Though Vi knew, somewhere beneath it all, was a short tunnel that cut through the cliff and let the water rush out to sea.

Stretching from the middle of the room was a column. Nestled at the top was a block of ice that had a mountain of treasure frozen within. That treasure was further protected by the column's distance from all the walls, the sheer drop, and the deadly water below.

Vi looked from water to ice to treasure as the men spoke.

"So then who made the ice?" Baldair was saying. "It's still frozen solid, so it must have been recent."

Vi doubted that. "Adela," she chimed in.

"I thought Adela was dead," Erion said cautiously.

"Just because she hasn't been seen in a few decades doesn't mean she's dead." Vi shrugged. It was the best tip she could give them on Adela, and she hoped to Yargen they listened. "And she seems to be as greedy as ever."

Adela never got the treasure out, so she froze it in place to prevent anyone else from getting to it as if to say "see but don't touch." It seemed like a very Adela thing to do.

"It doesn't matter who's making the ice—made the ice—if we can't even get to it," Baldair said. "We have no Waterrunners in our party to cross the gap."

"Should we go back to town and look for one?" Erion thought aloud.

"I don't think we need to," Vi said, her mind working swiftly to avoid bringing more people into the situation. "Adela was a smart woman—or it seems." Vi was loathe to pay Adela a compliment, but intellect didn't play favorites between good and evil. "She wanted to keep the treasure from anyone else, but it wouldn't be impossible to believe that at some point, she might need to send someone who was not a Waterrunner to fetch it. Maybe she would've made it more difficult for them… but there has to be a path."

"Or Adela was a murderous madwoman who wanted to keep her prize only to herself and send anyone who attempted to claim it to a watery grave," Erion said grimly. Vi hated that a part of her agreed that it was possible.

"No… I don't think so…" Vi looked up to the ceiling that was mostly cast in shadow. The only chutes of light were coming from three-fourths of the way up on the walls around one side of the room—the side that faced the beach where she'd found the coin, she hoped. "We merely have to see past another illusion."

A dark line of shadow caught her eye and Vi lifted her hand, sending a burst of fire up to the ceiling.

"Look there." She pointed to the line she saw, the firelight illuminating it. "I would bet that's wide enough to shimmy around."

"How did you even see that?" Baldair murmured.

Vi focused solely on moving forward. She was so close now, and all she wanted to do was get to that treasure.

"There are cut hand- and foot-holds here." Vi gripped a narrow outcropping of stone. "Had to be some reason why someone wasted the time. I would bet that behind that pillar is a bridge of some sort, connecting it to the far wall. We just can't see it from here, and Adela knew this would be the only entrance."

Jax boldly followed behind her as she began to climb.

"Jax, wait, what're you doing?" Baldair stole Vi's words from behind her lips.

"Someone is going to go over, right? We're not really going to get this far and just wait for a Waterrunner, are we? We all know I make the most sense. It's not like my life really matters, not like yours or Erion's."

"Your life most certainly matters," Erion blurted, warming Vi's heart. "If you are reckless here, I will pull you from the Father's halls myself."

"You're our brother," Baldair said, joining Erion's cause. "And I don't want to see you die here."

"Is that an order, my prince?" Jax asked in an almost timid tone that nearly betrayed all the brokenness she'd seen in his eyes.

"It is," Baldair affirmed. "Stay alive, Jax."

Vi continued her climb so she wouldn't be caught staring at the unorthodox little family—the start of the illustrious Golden Guard. Jax's feet scraped the stone behind her as they shimmied across the narrow ledge that rounded the room. Vi glanced at him from time to time, wondering if she could, somehow, convince him to turn back. But it would be suspicious if she pushed too hard. So Vi said nothing and prayed his balance was good enough to stay on the path.

Finally, on the other side of the cavern, they descended onto a narrow ledge that had a wooden bridge connecting it with the column in the center of the room.

"Do you think it's safe?" Jax asked.

"We came this far. Are you really going to turn back now?" Vi hoped he'd say yes, but knew from his determined expression, he wouldn't. "I'll go first."

"Wait—"

"What?" She stopped, one foot on the bridge.

"Be careful." He eased away.

Vi gave him a faint smile. "Worrying about little ol' me?"

"Have you looked at this bridge?" He grinned and pressed himself against the wall, putting as much distance as he could between them.

"It's all I'm going to look at," she muttered, shuffling her weight onto the planks of wood.

The bridge held as Vi walked, arms outstretched for balance. She crossed without the boards even creaking. Vi went immediately to the ice, taking a deep breath and whispering "*Juth starys*" before Jax could cross.

The fire burned underneath her right palm, outstretched to the ice. Vi lifted her left hand, summoning tendrils of flame to hide the glyph that spun there. The ice was certainly Adela's magic and it would need more than the splintered elemental affinities of the Dark Isle to bring it down.

Motion caught her eye. Jax was at her side, hands lifted as well, fire burning from them. She kept her gaze forward, focused, digging into Yargen's power and pushing it outward. She begged for the magic that lived in her to seek out its own and find the crown hidden underneath this frosty tomb.

Her hands were nearly on the crown after years of searching. The thought made her almost dizzy.

A monumental crack in the ice was accompanied by a rumbling roar that echoed against the cavern walls. Vi pushed harder. Steam filled the Caverns as the magic that gave the ice shape gave way beneath their joint efforts.

She saw Jax slump, panting. Vi launched herself forward into the haze.

The gold was so cold it nearly burned her fingers. Vi pushed through it, scattering coins across the scant platform, discarding them into the waters below. She knew the water was moving fast enough to carry the coins—at least some of them—out. There was enough gold here to buy a ship, and she needed the wealth far more than any of these young men did.

"What're you doing?" Erion shouted.

"S-Stop!" Baldair bellowed. "That belongs to the crown."

Vi ignored them, taking bags of gold, ripping them open, and tossing them over. It rained coins and jewels into the raging waters. She'd secure as much gold as she could for her, Taavin, and Deneya. In the process, she'd find the crown.

"Nox, stop!" Jax reached for her and Vi swung. He dodged backward and Vi grabbed for another bag.

Where was the crown? Yargen above! The damn thing must be here. Her mind raced as panic began to fill her. What if the past years of searching were for nothing? If the crown wasn't here, then where was it? Did Adela have it, after all?

Had she already failed? Had Victor beaten her here and this was his ruse, not Adela's? The thought nearly made her scream. It would be too much to bear.

"Jax, stop her!"

Jax kicked at Baldair's command and Vi dodged. She tumbled, rolled, and righted herself.

"Don't touch it!" she yelled. She needed him to wait a moment, just one moment to—

"What're you doing? Tell us, we can help you!" Jax pleaded.

As if you could.

Vi's eyes landed on the last, plump bag that'd been hidden at the bottom of all the other treasure. She lunged for it and Jax stepped on her hand. Vi pulled away with a hiss and grabbed a bunch of coins, throwing them at his face. When he was distracted, she grabbed the final satchel.

If she could get it all in the water, she could search through it later. The crown must be in this bag. It would be in her possession and this whole infernal vortex would be put to an end once and for all. If she got the crown here and now, she could get the scythe, and the axe, and then—

A hand grabbed the bag as she began to hurl it forward.

"No!" The word burst from her like fire, hot, singeing, painful.

The canvas ripped and its contents exploded. Vi twisted, off-balance. She stepped hastily, trying to recover. Her eyes landed on the gold-plated crown that now sat lonely on the mostly empty column of stone. Yargen's magic called out to her longingly.

Vi's arm rose. It was there, so close—she'd almost had it.

Her vision shifted. Jax was reaching for her—he was still going to try to save her. Even after she'd knowingly begun to try to push him away. The tiniest smile crossed her lips as Vi tipped backward.

Jax's compassion was the only thing she could find joy in, given her failure. Cursing herself and her arrogant greed as she fell, Vi took a deep breath right before she plunged into the icy water below, and allowed the currents to carry her out to the sea.

16

V<small>I ROLLED ON THE</small> stone and sand for the second time in the span of a day. Gold coins clanked and scraped against the rocks around her. Treasure glittered across the beach in the early morning light.

Dragging herself far enough out of the icy water that she could breathe without sputtering, Vi brought the spark under her skin. The water evaporated in shimmering waves of heat. She gulped in air by heaving lungful, staring up at the bloody sky. Spending years on boats and ships had turned her into a strong swimmer—strong enough to navigate the currents through the short passage out to the beach beyond.

She waited until her breathing slowed and her chest stopped burning, murmuring curses on the exhales. Failure felt like a noru on her chest, keeping her pinned. The crown had slipped through her fingers and who knew what the young men would do with it now.

Eventually, Vi pried herself up, left the gold behind for now, and began the long walk back to the hovel.

She didn't even knock on arrival, allowing herself in. The room was empty and Vi helped herself to the bed, inhaling the familiar scent of the blankets as she collapsed and fell into a dreamless, exhausted, sleep.

"Vi," Taavin said, shaking her shoulder. "Vi," he repeated. She cracked open her eyes. "Oh thank Yargen."

"You worried us," Deneya said from over his shoulder.

"Sorry, things happened quickly." Vi sat and Taavin helped her up. His fingers laced around hers as Vi rubbed her eyes with her other hand.

"You're being reckless again," he murmured.

"I had no choice." Vi shook her head, her hand falling. "The prince and his group were going after the crown. I was trying to get to it before they did. I knew once it was found, taking it would be nearly impossible."

"We know they found the treasure." Deneya sat on her bed across from them.

"The whole town is abuzz with it."

"That was fast."

"Word moves fast when it comes to ghostly prizes." Deneya grinned. "What happened?"

"Jax, Erion, and Baldair showed up at the *Lady Black*..." Vi started, telling them the events of the past day that had ultimately led to her failure. "... but I didn't manage to get the crown."

"So they have it, then," Taavin said faintly.

"I can only assume."

"Years..." Deneya trailed off, staring at nothing. But she didn't have to finish her sentence; they all felt the shared sentiment. They'd spent years hunting for the crown. Now, all that time meant nothing.

"They had a map. Someone else was searching the caves," Vi said.

"We had no idea." Taavin shook his head. "But perhaps all will be well. In all other worlds, the crown has come to light after the War in the North began, at the earliest. We can find out what they did with it later."

"In all other times, we hadn't been meddling as much with the crystal weapons." Vi folded her arms.

"What if we steal it back?" Deneya said, suddenly eager once more. "You studied the Imperial estate here. You know the manor. You just said there were secret tunnels connecting to it—hence why the blueprints you showed me ages ago were so strange. We could sneak in."

"We could," Vi said uncertainly. Deneya was right, Vi knew the manor. And now that she'd seen the prince's map, she knew how the caves connected to it. "But I think they'll have tighter security now that they have the lost treasure—or at least a small portion of it."

"Nothing we can't handle."

"I appreciate your confidence," Vi chuckled softly.

"We can't take it." Taavin put the notion to rest. "You're right, we've been meddling. If the crown goes completely missing at this point, it's impossible to say what would happen. We can't risk the birth of a new Champion."

"I grow weary of your obsession with Vhalla Yarl's womb," Deneya shot the curt remark at Taavin.

"He's right though," Vi said. "If it went missing now, they'd hunt for it."

"They didn't care to hunt for it for decades," Deneya countered.

"But now they know it exists. They'll know someone stole it. Getting the crown only worked so long as its location was a mystery."

"We can handle them if they come after us; it wouldn't be the first time we've fallen off the pages of history." Deneya was making it difficult for Vi to think rationally. All she wanted to do was go after the crown *right now*. But rushing in with Jax hadn't yielded results.

Patience, she reminded herself. Time and again, patience was the best way forward.

"What if I made another crown and you illusioned it again?" Deneya suggested.

"No," Vi said immediately and firmly. "That didn't work last time." She rubbed her midsection, remembering the price she'd paid for it. "If Victor sees it—"

"And we have every reason to believe he will," Taavin interjected, "if past worlds are any indication of how Victor might act now."

"Victor will see right through any illusion."

"How did he see through it the first time?" Deneya asked.

"A shift in the light," Vi said, recalling that fateful encounter.

"Well, you're more powerful now. I think—"

"Wait," Vi whispered. "*Shift...*" Vi stood and began to pace. Her mind was racing. Her gut was laying a new path before her. "This could work."

"What could work?" Taavin asked hesitantly.

"We have to go to the Twilight Kingdom to get the scythe. We also need to keep the crystal weapons in their places to ensure the birth of a new Champion." She looked to Taavin as she spoke.

"Yes, that's our top priority."

Not saving the world? Vi wanted to ask. She knew where his priorities lay and she'd indulge him right up until the moment she couldn't any longer—a moment Vi could now see on the distant horizon.

"We go to the Twilight Kingdom and collect the scythe. There, we have them use the powers of the shift to make a crown that looks like the crystals. Something real, tangible, not an illusion for Victor to see through."

Then, while they were there, Vi would use Fallor to get to Adela. They needed passage to Risen to get the flame and, ultimately, someone crazy enough to take them to the island of the elfin'ra.

"That... might work," Taavin relented.

"There's just the one small problem of the Twilight Kingdom being a sea away."

"I already planned for that." Vi looked to Deneya with a grin. "We now have enough old Solaris gold to buy a ship. All we need to do is collect it."

"Then we should do that," Deneya said with a nod.

"You look tired. Why don't you rest? Taavin and I can go and collect it." Vi grabbed two packs and handed Taavin two more.

"All right, I can tell when I'm not wanted. Go and have your alone time." Deneya was already nestling herself into bed.

"We'll be back soon," Vi said with a grin.

She and Taavin slipped out the door and into the dark town. There seemed to be fewer people about, likely because they were all clamoring somewhere else over Adela's treasure finally being found.

Vi opened her mouth, surprised when Taavin spoke first.

"I'm sorry."

"What?"

"I said, I'm sorry." Their eyes met. "The other night, I was harsh."

Vi gripped the strap of one of her packs tighter. "You're only trying to do the right thing."

"Yes, but doesn't excuse me when I act an ass."

"I snapped at you first," Vi said tenderly. "I'm sorry, too." Their shoulders brushed as they walked down a staircase that would lead to the beach by the cliffs.

"We're both trying to do what's right, and that's never an easy thing to do." He took her hand and Vi didn't hesitate to lace her fingers with his. The squeeze of his hand pushed forgiveness into her, a sentiment she tried to push back.

"There's something I want to ask you about," she said, pausing as their feet met the sand.

"Yes?"

"Jax, his life…" *and death*, she couldn't bring herself to say aloud. "Is it a stone in the river?" When he didn't immediately answer, she pressed, "Have there been worlds in which he died here and now?"

She almost told him not to say anything. She had her answer by the look on his face alone.

"I can't decide what his fate is," Taavin said, finally. "Some worlds he lives, and some worlds he dies. His life seems to be a variable, not a stone."

Memories flooded her, rushing like the seawater around their ankles as she started walking again, rounding the cliffside. Vi watched the little rocks being carried out by the tides, the larger ones stuck in place. "Why didn't you tell me?"

"I couldn't."

"That's not an excuse." The words could've been sharp and angry, but they weren't. She wasn't about to risk their restored peace. "You could've told me at any time. But you didn't want to because you didn't want to hurt me."

"Am I that transparent?" Taavin blinked into the morning's early light and Vi appreciated his profile. There might never be an hour of her life where the sight of all his sharp angles didn't fill her with a mixture of sorrow, joy, and longing.

"I know every corner of you, inside and out."

"I suppose if anyone would, it's you."

"Tell me about everyone else. Who does the goddess demand? Who can live? I won't fight Yargen's fate," she added hastily. "But if I can save someone, I will."

Taavin searched her face and sighed. "Regardless of the path we walk, Tiberus, Twintle Junior, Schnurr—"

"Schnurr?" Vi interjected.

"You met him, briefly." The words brought back a fleeting memory of a young boy in a war zone.

"He was with Fiera the night Mhashan fell—the young man with the moustache, who she directed to keep fighting at the break in the wall."

"And he becomes a leading member of the Knights of Jadar. He'll be one to watch as the years go on."

Vi groaned. "I should've killed all the Knights when I had the chance."

"They're a necessary counterweight. Without their presence, people wouldn't be driven to actions we need them to take."

"In any case…" Vi didn't want to speak about the Knights a moment longer. They made her blood boil. "Tiberus, Luke, Schnurr. Who else dies regardless?"

"Of the people you may be familiar with, Craig and Baldair."

She kept her face passive. Vi had never met her Uncle Baldair in her own world. He'd died years before her birth, before the war in the North had even ended. It was a wound on her father's soul deeper than she could comprehend. Though Vi had tried to, conjuring thoughts of Romulin passing until her heart couldn't bear it a moment longer and then multiplying that feeling by several hundred.

Baldair. His death was one she found herself longing to postpone.

"Very well." They were nearing the outlet of roaring water now littered with pieces of ancient Solaris gold. "The rest of them I still want to save, if I'm able."

She looked to Taavin and he held her attention. *Don't deny me this*, she wanted to beg. Saving the world was a large, unimaginable task. Saving the people her heart still loved was a more reasonable goal.

"You know our purpose, right?"

"I do." She knew his. She knew hers. And Vi knew a moment would come when only one of their desires persisted.

"Then yes, I'll help you save them if you're able... and if it doesn't alter fate too dramatically," Taavin said. It almost sounded like agreement.

It had been six months since they arrived in the West.

The desert heat felt like the embrace of an old friend. The people, the smells, the food, all carried a surprising nostalgia for her. But she hadn't come here looking for an opportunity to reminisce. She'd come because the Crossroads was the one place they could turn pilfered, ancient, Solaris coins into usable Imperial gold on the black market.

They took every opportunity to exchange their coins. Even still, they sat on two plump bags of un-traded pirate gold and knew where more was, should they ever need it.

It was enough money to buy a wedge of property nestled within the busy market of the Crossroads—one with an iron gate for a door that Vi fashioned Fiera's roses onto, exactly like the property Vi had stolen the key to from the spice seller in Shaldan a world ago.

They had enough money to enjoy themselves from time to time. Much like tonight, when they had decided to visit the sparring pits at Taavin's suggestion. Vi found out why he'd made the out-of-character proposal the moment they arrived.

"He's grown up a lot," Taavin observed from her side, taking a sip from his flagon as his eyes remained on Baldair.

"Has he?" Vi wondered. She still saw very much the young man that had been in Oparium the year prior. Seeing him here with Jax and Erion had been a surprise. "He still looks like a foolish child."

"You speak like an old woman." Taavin grinned at her.

"I can't be old if I'm ageless." She grinned back at him then returned her attention to the men on the far side of the sparring ring. They carried on, jesting, betting on the fighters, drinking their brew, and remaining willfully ignorant to the battle that had begun to rage in the North—a battle Vi couldn't yet bring herself to see. "We should leave here, soon."

"I thought you wanted to change a bit more coin first."

"I don't want to saturate the market with old Solaris gold, especially not now that the prince is here. If he sees some, he may get suspicious. We have enough to get passage to Meru, and we already bought the shop." Vi rubbed the familiar key in her trouser pocket. She'd carried its otherworldly twin a long time ago.

"You should stay on this continent a little longer."

"Why?" Vi glanced at Taavin, suspecting what he'd say next would have something to do with why he was so insistent on coming out tonight.

"They're going to need you. Specifically, the prince and... her." Taavin motioned to the ring where two fighters entered.

The room went quiet for Vi. She could see the men and women still cheering on the fighters. The announcer called out the names of those about to spar. Swords rang out against scabbards as they were drawn.

But it was all a distant hum as her eyes fell on the adult Raylynn Westwind.

"I can't," Vi whispered, more to herself than anyone else.

"In the last world… she and the prince died in the coming weeks." Taavin's words were a dagger to her gut.

"I got her mother killed. I can't have anything to do with her." The words were like ash coating her mouth. *I got her mother killed and I left her body in a puddle of its own blood like the foolish child I was.*

"She doesn't know that and she could use your help."

Vi swallowed her fear and guilt. He was right. Raylynn didn't know what she had done—that her mother was just another in a long list of casualties in the fight for a new world.

"I thought you didn't want me to meddle too much?"

"I told you Raylynn's life was variable, didn't I? And you told me you wanted to save the people you could," Taavin said gently. After their tense moments in Oparium, the gesture was not lost on her, and Vi's heart warmed at his words. Taavin kept his eyes forward. Raylynn had begun to move. She was just like her mother—the sword was an extension of her body. "I have heard of these people through you, across so many lives. Seeing them now…"

"They're real," Vi finished for him. The crowd erupted at Raylynn's victory.

"Let's save them."

"When and where?"

"She'll take on Luke." Vi jerked her head to Taavin and he grinned at her. "She blames him for her mother's death and wants vengeance. She'll take the prince with her to get it. In your world, he died on the way to Twintle's manor. It's possible that Raylynn will also die rushing in to take on Twintle."

Vi brought up a map of the West in her mind, placing a pin where Twintle's manor was. "We have to head to Norin anyway. Helping keep them alive can be on the way."

"My thoughts exactly." Taavin laced his fingers with hers and brought her hand to his lips.

Vi gave him a determined nod.

They left at the same time as Baldair and his golden companions. The three men went after Raylynn, but Vi and Taavin headed toward their home. They filled Deneya in on their plans—she had just returned from trading a few more of their coins. The three packed their things and started off into the desert, toward the town of Yon.

It took Baldair and Raylynn nearly two weeks to arrive. Enough time that Vi and her company had bought temporary residence in a cramped apartment out back of a local metal worker's home. Enough time that Vi could begin to listen to the people in town, and figure out who was a Knight of Jadar, who was in their pockets, and who supported the Knights. By the time Raylynn arrived, Vi was wondering how the clever girl who had gifted her with the idea of making her own crystal weapons had grown into a foolhardy woman. She was walking into the lion's den willingly, challenging local combatants, winning handily, then strutting back to the inn where she and the prince were staying like she owned the town.

Vi was positioned by the window of their temporary abode. From there, she could see the inn. There was no glass, so she leaned against the wall to keep out of sight. Heavy footsteps approached—a familiar gait.

"Midsummer is almost finished being saddled. Prism is ready," Deneya said, walking over to sit with her. "Any changes?"

"No, all is quiet." Vi kept her eyes on the inn. Taavin had told them this was the town where Baldair died during Vi's original time. *But not tonight.*

They continued to stare out the window and, for a moment, Vi's eyes drifted to the dark-haired woman. Deneya was poised, quiet, and ready. There wasn't a trace of doubt or the edge of restlessness about her.

"How are you not bored of this yet?" Vi asked.

Deneya shrugged. "What else would I be doing? Living comfortably in Risen? Getting fat off the Queen's pension and taking my secrets of the Dark Isle with me to a faraway grave?"

"Maybe you'd be her personal guard?"

"That's what I was in your time, right? I wasn't an agent of the Order of Shadows?" Vi nodded. "I just don't see it." Deneya shrugged. "Me? A queen's personal guard? No."

"In a way, you're the crown princess of Solaris's royal guard." She grinned at Deneya and the woman rolled her eyes.

"I thought you weren't the crown princess?"

"You're right." Admitting as much had long since become easy. "I'm not. I'm just Yargen's Champion, much less prestigious," Vi said sarcastically and looked back to the inn and the quiet, dark night. "If you weren't doing this—if you could do anything—what would you want to do?"

"I could do *anything*?" she asked and Vi nodded. Deneya hummed thoughtfully. Her gaze was distant as she looked out the window. "Maybe head north to Dolarian, the land of the Draconi. I've heard that some of them can breathe fire and some can even fly. Though there is no greater lore than—"

Deneya was silenced as they both looked at the dark shadows crossing the ground below.

"It's time." Vi stood, hastily leaving their hut. Taavin straightened away from Midsummer and they shared a look that said it all. She swung up on Prism. "I'll meet you both after."

Prism sprang into action with the slightest touch. He was a good steed, just beginning to get on the other half of his prime. He'd have good years ahead of him yet—Vi was counting on it. She rode into the dark night as the inn glowed red from within, like the waking eyes of some primordial evil.

Glass shattered and two dark figures leapt from a high window. Vi gave the place a wide berth, swinging around the town's perimeter and flying over the dunes. She slowed Prism as she neared a side alley by the inn and jumped from the saddle.

With a thought, the fire that was now consuming the building was under her command. She could feel the inkling of magic fighting against her at the edge of her consciousness, but the Firebearer the Knights had employed was weak.

Stepping through a wall of fire and into the lower floor of the inn, Vi heard creaking from above, voices shouting. If they were shouting, they were alive. Acting on instinct, Vi sprinted upstairs and skidded to a halt. The fire parted, arcing around her, giving her a view of the man and woman.

"Baldair, Raylynn, come with me."

"Who—" Baldair began dumbly.

Raylynn grabbed his hand and yanked him forward. Vi trusted her to keep the man in tow as she descended the stairs, pushing away the fire. She led them out the way she came. Prism was there waiting, not bothered in the slightest by the rising flames.

"Take the horse." After years of riding him, she trusted the mount to keep them safe. "Take it and go. Do not seek out what has been lost," Vi cautioned. It was the best she could do. She couldn't outright say, *the crystal sword is long gone*. "Protect, instead, the weapon that has yet to be found. Do not seek the tomb. Do not let anyone seek the tomb."

"Do I know you?" Baldair took a step toward her. "Wait, aren't you... Nox?"

"This isn't the time," Vi scolded. Though she didn't step back or give up her ground. "My control will waver soon," she said with urgency, though she could've held the flames in position for a decade if she'd wanted to. "Go, go now!"

Baldair cursed and mounted Prism, but Raylynn continued to stare.

"Princess Fiera—"

"Go," Vi urged.

"Damn it, Raylynn, we have an opportunity and we need to take it. Let's get out of here!" Baldair shouted. But Raylynn was rooted to the spot, her eyes on Vi. "Raylynn."

The woman stepped to the prince, who helped her into the saddle. Vi watched the motion, already familiar and tender. She couldn't help but remember the slip of a girl who came to have her future told by a princess, and who yearned to serve the crown.

Raylynn had Vi's help then, just as she had Vi's help now, and didn't realize it in either instance. Vi smiled faintly and, while they were distracted, stepped into the burning building once more, allowing the fire to close behind her.

"Look, look there!" she heard a man shout outside, followed by a snap of the reins and the gallop of a horse.

"Zira, your daughter is safe for a little longer." Vi took in the burning inn around her. The moment of tenderness immolated on the flames.

17

"ARE YOU CERTAIN ABOUT just leaving it here?" Deneya asked as the waves off the coast of Meru crashed against her midsection.

"It's a mostly sheltered cove, we've anchored it at low tide, and no one comes this way." Vi listed off all the reasons she'd been repeating to herself for the past day while they decided what to do with the sailboat they'd bought in Norin. If Vi's plan worked out, they wouldn't need the small vessel again, anyway. "I don't want to go all the way to Toris and risk someone seeing it docked there for too long."

"But we risk coming back and not seeing it at all."

"Then we buy another boat."

"Oh, right, we'll just buy another boat, because money can solve all our problems. Perfect princess logic, that," Deneya muttered as she sloshed up the black sand beach to where Vi and Taavin were waiting. They carried two packs apiece and not much else. Deneya had the heaviest satchel of them all—the one completely filled with clanking gold coins.

While the gold of old Solaris had no meaning on Meru, gold was gold. If they needed to, they could smelt the coins into bars.

"I shudder to think of what your opinions of me would've been if we'd met earlier." Vi held out a hand, helping Deneya free her feet from the cloying sand of the tides.

"Everything happens in its own time, just as it's supposed to," Taavin said thoughtfully. It sounded like an echo of his bygone days as the Voice.

They started up the beach toward the lowest point of the sheer cliffs. There was no man-made path, which was why Vi had picked this particular location to anchor. No one seemed to come this way. But she could see a path up the rocks if they were careful.

It was noon by the time they reached the top. Deneya massaged her aching hands and rolled her shoulders while Vi and Taavin stood unbothered. Vi wanted to tell herself it was because the woman carried the heaviest satchel of all of them. But she knew it was more than that.

Vi wasn't tired now, just like she'd never grown weary on their crossing from the Dark Isle to Meru. It was the same reason she could pilot their vessel through the night and have enough energy come the dawn to adjust the rigging on their single sail.

With every step she took in this world, she was further from her own, and further from the mortal casing she used to know. Whether she wanted to or not, she was truly embracing her new body and purpose.

"The Twilight Forest isn't far." Vi pointed when Deneya had caught her breath. "Let's try to get there before nightfall."

"Heading for the Twilight Forest, intentionally." Deneya shook her head. "Never thought I'd see the day."

"Ulvarth hasn't yet begun his campaign against the morphi, right?" Vi looked to Taavin, who nodded once.

"Ulvarth doesn't begin making his moves for a few years yet, usually."

She turned back to Deneya. "But you still hate them?"

"*Hate* is too strong a word. Personally, I feel little toward the morphi, good or bad. But I know it's a tense subject for the Faithful, and Lumeria has made it clear that we don't want to give a reason for those tensions to boil over."

"Smart woman," Vi said under her breath.

They discussed the delicate politics of the Morphi and Draconi as they walked. Vi remembered what Deneya had said in Yon regarding the Draconi and noted the excited fascination in the woman's voice—rivaled only by the warm tones she used to speak about Queen Lumeria.

Perhaps, when all this was over, Vi could meet the Queen once more, but not as a tired girl. She'd meet the queen as… Vi's imagination abandoned her when she tried to picture herself beyond the fall of Raspian.

Perhaps she and Deneya and Taavin could continue adventuring, buying skiffs and sailing to the world's edges. They could go to the isle of Dolarian and see if there were truly fire-breathing, winged beasts or if it was all just lore. Vi tried to imagine herself sailing to the far reaches of the maps in her mind, which was somehow easier than picturing herself sitting comfortably on the Dark Isle.

No matter what, when it came to who she would become, her mind's eye was blurry.

Borrowed time, a voice seemed to whisper from somewhere within her.

Yes, I'm on borrowed time, Vi thought in reply, touching the watch around her neck. Her body was a gift from the goddess, one she'd eventually have to return for the world to be saved. The thought should panic her. Vi felt as calm as the tall, still trees of the forest. But the thorny thoughts snagged her like the underbrush as they pushed deeper into the Twilight Forest.

"How do the morphi feel about Lightspinning at this point in time?" Vi asked. Taavin looked to Deneya.

"What?" Deneya glanced between them. "I haven't been on Meru in a few decades. How am I supposed to know?"

"One way to find out. *Durroe watt ivin.*" A ball of light appeared above Vi's open palm. It reminded her of the orbs she and Sehra would make when she was first learning her magic. Lifting her eyes from the illusion, Vi looked around the forest, waiting.

Deneya and Taavin both took a step closer. The three of them stood back-to-back, watching for any signs of movement. Collectively, they held their breaths until Vi dismissed the shining glyphs above her hand.

"I suppose they don't have as hard of a stance toward Lightspinning as they did in the world we left," Vi observed.

"Further proof that Ulvarth hasn't begun closing in on them," Taavin said bitterly.

"Let's keep going." Vi started off in no direction in particular. "We'll meet a Morphi sooner or later."

By late afternoon, their wandering intersected with the main road through the Twilight Forest and the three continued along it. There were no posted signs anywhere along the way, so they merely kept walking, hoping to be found. After about two more hours of wandering, they came to a bridge across a stream.

Vi paused, her hands on the worn stone, looking out over the water that flowed down and away toward the cliffs they'd climbed earlier.

"What is it?" Deneya asked.

"I wonder if it's the same stream we stayed near the last time we were here," Vi said thoughtfully, looking to Taavin.

"Perhaps, though I've had enough of that cave for several lifetimes." He grimaced. The man's mood only seemed to sour the longer they were on Meru. Vi couldn't blame him. This forest, this land, was a place of memories for them both— good and bad mixed together.

"Let's make camp soon," Vi suggested. "Get off the main road again and find somewhere that looks dry enough." She tilted her eyes skyward, peering through the break in the trees. "It looks like it'll be clear night, so we don't have to worry about rain."

They hiked for one more hour and then did as Vi suggested, breaking off the main road and finding a space between several trees where they could set up camp. Vi ignited a fire using *juth starys*, yet again, her Lightspinning didn't seem to summon the morphi. As night fell they split some of their hard baked bread.

"I'd love to get my hands on some more of the crackers Sarphos gave us," Vi said through her food.

"The ones he magicked to fill an empty stomach?" Taavin clarified and Vi nodded. "That'd be nice."

"Who's Sarphos?" Deneya asked. "And what's this about magic crackers?"

"Sarphos is a morphi we met the last time we were here." Vi chewed thoughtfully. "He was the younger brother of one of the people we're looking for now... though I have no idea if he'll be around yet." *It should feel stranger to think about someone not being born*, Vi thought to herself. But it had become quite normal. "He could use the magic of the shift to make a cracker that filled you up as if you'd eaten a meal. That power is one of the reasons why I think they could use the shift to make a fake crystal crown."

"I don't want any shift crackers." Deneya scrunched her nose. "But I would give my sword arm right about now though for some rovash."

"Rovash?" Vi asked as Taavin made a satisfied noise.

"I'd almost forgotten," he said wistfully. "I only got to eat it on high holy days." Taavin looked to her. "Rovash is a celebratory roast—giant spotted pheasant stuffed with dates, figs, and bread left over from the temples' holy celebrations."

"Cookeries would bake it slow over root vegetables." Deneya sighed wistfully. "If I'd known it'd be so long until I had it again, I would've bought a whole bird just for myself."

"You would've exploded," Taavin said with a small smile.

"Death by rovash would be an honor." Deneya grinned in return.

"Maybe we can all get some together... when this is all over," Vi said almost timidly, the thoughts from earlier still exercising their strong hold. Her companions fell quiet.

"What happens, when this is over?" Deneya asked delicately. None of them had ever discussed the topic aloud. It felt taboo. Like if they even uttered anything about the world being saved, it wouldn't come to pass. "You put Yargen back together with all her pieces like some divine puzzle and she beats Raspian into submission, heralding a new Age of Light. There's much rejoicing and a saved world ... *Then* what happens?"

Vi looked to Taavin. He gave a tiny shrug. "Your guess is as good as ours. We've never made it that far before... never made it this far, even." He finished the last bite of his meal and looked at his hand, flexing his fingers. She wondered if he, too, was imagining the crystal skeleton within him that held his consciousness and gave him life.

"We should go to bed," Vi suggested abruptly. "Got a long day ahead tomorrow."

"Of what? More wandering?" Deneya said smartly, stretching out on the leaves they'd piled up as pallets.

"If that's what it takes."

"Would you like to sleep?" Taavin asked, touching her arm lightly and summoning her attention to him alone. "I can take first watch."

"No, you go ahead, I don't mind. You sleep less than the rest of us anyway." Vi smiled. He looked surprised, as if he hadn't realized she'd noticed. His expression softened a corner of her heart.

How could I not notice? she wanted to ask. She noticed, just as she noticed he ate less than the rest of them but could go the longest without tiring. She'd cataloged every little thing about him—from the way he ran his hands through his hair when he was deep in thought, to how he tapped his foot when he drank alcohol. She'd visually traced his figure like lines of a map so that she'd never forget how to get him back again if the world took him from her.

"All right, wake me if you feel tired."

"I will." Vi squeezed his hand and leaned in to plant a soft goodnight kiss on his mouth.

He settled down on his palette and held her gaze for a good while. They stared at each other through the firelight, as though communicating telepathically. Though Vi was left wondering what, exactly, he was thinking.

And when his eyes closed, she was left with nothing to do but peer into the dark void of the forest around them.

The night passed uneventfully. Vi sat with her back against a tree, scanning the woods. She didn't know how much time had passed, but eventually her eyelids began to feel heavy. They dipped closed, staying shut for a little longer each time.

A rustling sound came from behind her and Vi's eyes shot open.

She stood, whirling in place to find herself face to face with a spear pointed at her throat. Behind the blade were the steely gray eyes of a young girl with two golden buns behind each of her ears.

"State your business, Lightspinners," she demanded. Skeptical, forceful, though not outright brutal. This was not the same harshness that Arwin had greeted her with in Vi's world.

Deneya and Taavin were on their feet, but Vi held out a hand, both silencing them and stopping their movements. She leveled her eyes with the girl and gave her a smile.

"Hello, Arwin." Arwin's eyes went wide at Vi's use of her name. Then they narrowed as she thrust the spear forward threateningly. The girl opened her mouth to no doubt question, but Vi spoke over her. "Please take us to your father. We have business with King Noct."

Vi was fairly certain that she and Noct were the only comfortable people in the throne room.

Arwin had been eying them sideways since they first met and she reluctantly agreed to take them to the Twilight Kingdom. Taavin was understandably uncomfortable in this place. Even if he knew this was a different Twilight Kingdom than the one they had last interacted with, it was hard to forget old conditioning. Deneya looked fascinated, but was very clearly aware that she was an outsider in this world of glittering twilight.

But Vi stood easily. She'd been here before, in this very room, standing in front of this very man. Though he'd admittedly looked somewhat older then. The beard had been thinner in her world. That must be what it was.

This time there were no children playing in the courtyard to consume his attention. He'd stood when they entered and regarded them as a monarch would. Then, he settled himself on the throne.

"It is not common for Lightspinners to come demanding me." He shifted. "Are you from the Queen?"

"No, we're not," Vi said, not so much as glancing at Deneya. The king didn't need to know there was a member of the Order of Shadows in his throne room. Deneya's business wasn't to spy on the Twilight Kingdom, anyway. "We've come from the Dark Isle."

"The Dark Isle?" Noct tilted his head to the side. "Two elfin and a human, all Lightspinners, from the *Dark Isle?*"

Vi had anticipated this skepticism. She'd encountered it before. But this time she knew exactly how to handle it.

"I am Yargen's Champion," Vi said confidently. "I have come from very far to collect that which is my birthright. I know that, deep within your palace, you hold a crystal scythe. It was bestowed on your family to keep safe until the Champion came seeking it."

"H-how?" Arwin stuttered, taking a step back.

"How, indeed." Noct smiled, his eyes shining. "How could you have come across that information?"

"I told you, I am the Champion." Vi put on the air of mystery she used when giving advice or fortune to those on the Dark Isle. Her voice was a deep whisper, her words shrouded in an air of knowing beyond that which mortal minds could comprehend. At least, that was how she hoped it sounded. "I have seen across time and space. I know Yargen's will and have heard her voice. I have witnessed the red lightning that heralds the end of days. Before this world is torn asunder, you must give me what I seek."

"All very impressive." Noct was unfazed. It'd take more than some lofty words to impress those on Meru, who were accustomed to more fantastical magics existing around them. "But your long-eared friends here could've known the truth from ages ago and told you."

"Elfin live long lives, but not that long," Taavin countered for her. "Give her the scythe and you will see that she speaks true."

Noct still looked unconvinced.

Vi chewed on the inside of her cheek, keeping her expression passive. In her time, the tears in the shift had been enough to convince Noct that she wielded a mighty power. If he didn't give her the scythe, what proof could she offer him of her abilities?

Luckily, the scythe wasn't her only mission here. There were other reasons Vi had sought out the Twilight Kingdom. One of them might just serve her now.

"Your highness, may we speak in private?"

"I will not leave your side with these strangers, Father," Arwin said firmly.

Noct was clearly intrigued by the request. "Approach me, and whisper what you have to say in my ear."

Vi ascended the dais and crossed to the throne. She leaned forward, cupping her lips around the king's ear. Arwin inched closer, her hands on her spear, ready to attack. Vi didn't point out how foolish the girl's protectiveness was. If Vi had wanted to kill Noct, he'd already be dead. Instead, she whispered.

"Your daughter Arwin favors a boy named Fallor—or will soon, if she does not already. But he will betray the trust of your family. He will gain and take the knowledge of your sacred shift to Adela. They might have already gotten to the boy. Keep us here and I will use my knowledge as Champion to protect your daughter and your throne."

Vi straightened away, Noct watching her carefully. She took two steps backward, bowed once more, and stepped off the dais to wait for his verdict.

The king stroked his beard, eyes settling on his daughter for a long moment.

"We shall go to the scythe now, and see if your words are true about your powers. If you are who you say, I will trust your other claims, and you and your companions will have rooms in the guest wing to stay in for as long as I see fit to host you," he said finally.

Vi bowed once more, a smile creeping onto her face as she did. Her fingertips nearly crackled with the phantom memory of the scythe in her hands.

18

NOCT LED THEM DOWN a series of halls and a familiar winding stair into a council room that Vi knew all too well.

The walls were stone, with vertical tapestries running from floor-to-ceiling depicting morphi champions standing victorious in battles. Weapons hung between the tapestries, the low light of the glowing stones above the center table gleaming off their polished edges. Taavin inspected one of the hanging pieces.

"Is this the battle of Marthas?" he asked, breaking the silence with genuine curiosity.

Noct paused, clearly startled, but a sincere smile spread across his lips. "Why, yes it is."

"Marthas… when the elfin'ra finally surrendered?" Deneya had joined Taavin at the wall.

"Just so."

"I didn't realize there were morphi there."

"Many don't." Noct chuckled, but the sound wasn't warm or amused. It was sad. "Much of the morphi's contributions to and alignment with the Kingdom of Meru has been expunged from common memory."

The battle of Marthas, Vi silently repeated to herself. For a moment, her vision was hazed as what felt like memories played before her eyes. Memories Vi wasn't supposed to have but found bubbling to the surface all the same.

The elfin'ra gathered on the large island in the watery center of Meru's great lagoon. She could see the men and women surrounding them as if she'd stood there as well, the queen banishing them off to a distant isle and beseeching Yargen for the strength to seal them away. Vi felt her words as much as heard them—no, she didn't feel it, someone else within her did.

Help came in the form of the last Champion.

"That's Arnoch, isn't it?" Vi said faintly. The attention was now on her. "The warrior depicted," she clarified.

"It is." Noct's smile widened. "Impressive that you know your morphi history. Now, excuse me a moment." He stepped around the table and disappeared through the door in the back of the room. Arwin lingered, eyes on Vi and hands glued to her spear.

"How did you know that?" Deneya asked.

"Yes, *how*?" Taavin repeated, much less amused than Deneya.

"I read it in the Archives when I was there, long ago," Vi lied. She knew she hadn't read it. But she couldn't describe the imagery she'd seen. She didn't even know where it'd come from. Just laying eyes on the carefully stitched picture sparked something in her that wasn't entirely her own. Luckily, she didn't have to elaborate further. Noct returned with the scythe, tightly wrapped in familiar purple velvet.

Arwin looked between them, but unlike the last time, the girl wasn't bold enough to question her father.

The king placed the weapon on the table and undid the knots on the ropes holding the velvet closed. Even knowing what she was about to see, Vi's heart raced in anticipation. She was ready for the familiar shining crystal, glowing with the power of the gods. It wasn't until that moment that Vi realized she still carried the loss of the crown with her. She needed to feel a fresh surge of Yargen's essence in her veins.

Without hesitation, she reached out a hand to the blade.

The hazy light that surrounded the weapon drifted over her hand and up her arm, before fading completely into her skin. The magic consumed her vision as though a tide of power was rising from within. Vi drew on it further, allowing herself to drown in this now familiar sensation.

The world came back into focus washed in darkness. She recognized the feeling of standing in another place and time. The future sight hadn't entirely been expected, but she welcomed it; Vi wasted no time in looking at her surroundings. She was on a cliff-side, a quaint town in the distance.

She squinted, looking at the town, specifically. *Mosant?* Her eyes fell on what was certainly the bell tower for the goddess's chapel there.

Vi turned her head to her right, where people stood. As usual, she couldn't hear what was being said. A group on horseback were mounted before a windmill. Vi watched as an old woman stepped out to greet them and was rewarded with a sword through her eye.

Vi's attention shifted to the vaguely familiar, mustachioed man holding the sword.

The world continued to oscillate in and out of focus. The next person to gain clarity was a young woman, hunched over in her saddle. The men were untying ropes around her and they hoisted her down. Her head was hung, but Vi didn't need to see her face. She knew that brown mass of unruly hair anywhere.

The Knights of Jadar had Vhalla Yarl in their clutches.

Vi tried to step forward. Moving through the vision was like trying to swim through a thick jelly. Yet she wanted to keep up with the men as they carried Vhalla into the open windmill. Shackles with embedded crystals were around her wrists and she put up no fight as she was thrown onto sacks of grain.

The door closed behind them, and ended what limited view Vi had been given.

No one said anything. But when Vi's consciousness returned to the Twilight Kingdom, just the breathing of her companions seemed loud.

"What did she do?" Arwin squeaked. Vi lowered her gaze to the pool of velvet on the table. A pile of obsidian shards and black dust was cradled in its luxe embrace. "She just touched it, and… now it's gone." Arwin inched closer to her father. The heel of her spear tapped on the floor with her shaking hand.

Vi lifted her eyes, looking to Noct, then to Taavin and Deneya. They all stared at her with wide eyes and soundless, slightly agape mouths. She curled and uncurled the fingers that had touched the scythe. The feelings there were muted, as if the appendage was no longer her own. However, pins and needles raced down from her elbow, and sensation returned as her head cleared.

"The power is within me now," Vi declared.

"How did she do that?" Arwin tugged on Noct's sleeve, looking up at him.

"Our mortal minds aren't meant to know how she did it, because she is the goddess's Champion," Noct said softly. "And we will now do everything we can to help her, because she is here to save us all from an impending age of darkness."

"Your help is required." Her voice didn't entirely feel her own. Vi's mind rocked back and forth with the tide of power that swirled in her. "I need you to make something for me, using the shift." Her eyes fell on Arwin.

"Me?" she squeaked.

"Yes."

"I…" The girl shifted her grip on her staff and took a more relaxed stance. "I will do whatever I can to assist you."

"Good. We shall begin after my companion makes a crown for us to work with. Now, if you'll excuse us, we are weary from our journey." Vi wasn't tired in the slightest, but she didn't want to be in the room a moment longer. She needed to sit down for a minute and try to get her racing mind under control.

"Yes, of course. Arwin, show them to their rooms in the guest tower."

Arwin nodded and led them with confidence. But Vi didn't miss her wary eyes looking back toward her now and then.

How cute and how fleeting she is.

"How did you do that?" Taavin grabbed her hand, jarring Vi from the thought. He slowed his steps, allowing them to fall behind so Deneya and Arwin didn't hear his whispers.

"I didn't do anything. It just… happened."

"That's exactly my point. You've always shifted the crystal's power willingly. It's never just happened, and you've never *absorbed it*."

"I've never worked with them to such an extent before. I understand their power and their will." *Their will…* The will of Yargen. Yes, that's what it was. Yargen was alive in each and every weapon, as she was in the Caverns, and the flame, and in Vi herself. All Vi had to do was listen. "It sought me out. It… lives in me."

"That shouldn't be possible."

"Why?" Vi asked him sincerely. "I am of Yargen's make, as are you." She held his hand tightly. "Can't you feel it?"

When they touched, magic darted back and forth between them. A connection deeper than the love that had traversed the ages spanned their physical forms. They were one and the same—each given physical shapes by the will of Yargen.

"I don't absorb power from the crystals." He pulled his hand away.

"But you could."

"I won't." Taavin looked forward.

"Why are you so unsettled?"

"Because I'm afraid."

"Of what?" Vi hadn't felt better in weeks. For the first time, she felt absolutely confident she could take on Raspian if she collected enough of Yargen's essence.

"Of not knowing what you're becoming." Taavin stopped walking, turning to her. Vi stopped as well and melted under the warmth of his viridian gaze.

"Taavin, I'm me." Vi took both of his hands in a firm but gentle grasp. "I've always been, and always will be."

He searched her face and opened his mouth after a moment's hesitation.

"Are you both coming?" Arwin called. She and Deneya had stopped ahead.

"Yes, of course!" Vi squeezed Taavin's hands. "Let's go."

The man remained rooted, staring at her for one more long breath. Finally, he nodded. Vi kept his hand clasped tightly in hers.

Part of her held on to the man who made her feel human, the man who was home.

The other part was governed by the essence of the goddess that was always just beneath her skin. Vi had to fight against uncomfortable urges all the way to their rooms. If she hadn't, she may have given into temptation and unraveled Taavin's magic to satiate the ravenous hunger waking in her—a hunger that needed to be fed with Yargen's essence alone.

"You want me to do… what?" Arwin asked, looking at the crown Vi had handed her.

"I need you to make it look like the scythe did."

"The shift can't make a crown into a scythe." Arwin's brow furrowed. They sat across a table from each other in a lounge that Vi had declared her own. After the incident of her absorbing the scythe's magic, no one seemed to question her much.

"No, not a scythe." Vi paused, thinking a moment. "Hold a moment."

She held out her hands and felt magic rush to her fingertips. Yargen's power pooled in her palms. Her stomach felt gutted by the mere notion of giving up the scythe's power. It had only been a part of her for a month while Deneya had worked to fashion a crown for them to work with, but it had felt like a lifetime.

Just like she had in the Caverns, Vi drew the power into a single location and condensed it down. However, unlike the Caverns, the well of power Vi leeched from was herself. As Yargen's magic collected in the air around her fingers, sparks of Vi's magic tethered it together. With a soft *pop*, a crystal appeared.

Reaching upward, Vi grabbed the stone and it writhed underneath her fingertips. Spikes of crystal grew from the "seed" of magic, then arced around and rose to points. Even though she had only seen the actual crystal crown from a glance, Vi knew its every detail, and she created an exact replica in crystal.

"I need you to make that crown—" Vi pointed to the one Deneya had made "— look like this one."

Arwin gawked at the crystal crown in Vi's fingers. The whites of her wide eyes nearly devoured the gray irises in the center. "How?" she said with a quivering lip. "How do you make something from nothing?"

"As Yargen wills," Vi said airily, smiling at the child. She set the crystal crown gently on the table. "Now, let's begin."

The girl studied the crown in her hands with a furrowed brow. Her magic shuddered, rose, and thrummed across the surface of the metal crown Deneya had crafted. Vi watched with new eyes. She saw the metal unravel and piece itself back together with every pulse of magic.

The shift was seeing the *between* of what something was, and what it could be. That had been how Arwin had explained it in her time. Or perhaps that was knowledge Vi was summoning from an otherworldly part of herself, just like the name of the morphi warrior who had helped fell the elfin'ra.

Arwin put the crown down on the table next to the one Vi had made. The metal had changed, becoming gnarled in places and smooth in others as it jutted like crystals. But it was still undeniably steel.

"It's not right," she said dejectedly.

"Try again," Vi encouraged.

"You should get one of my sisters to do it." Arwin slouched in her chair.

"I don't want one of your sisters to do it."

"Why?"

"Because I know you can." And because Vi wanted to endear herself to the girl. She wanted Arwin to trust her with her secrets, just as Arwin once had long ago. She wanted to be there the moment Arwin was ready to open up about any budding romance with Fallor, however long it took. "You will be stronger for it, and you want to be strong, don't you?"

"I do." Arwin ran her finger over the steel points of the crown. "But I don't even know how to use the royal shift yet."

"You will learn soon, I'm certain."

"Ruie says she's going to teach me soon!" Arwin covered her mouth suddenly. "I wasn't supposed to say that... you're not supposed to learn until you're fourteen."

"How old are you now?"

"Eleven... But I've been told I'm advanced in my magic."

"By who?"

Arwin paused, a blush overcoming her cheeks that instantly made her scowl. "No one."

"No one?"

"A stupid boy."

Ah, so Fallor was already present. No wonder Noct was ready to trust Vi.

"Well, he must be smart and not stupid, because I think you're advanced in your magic, too."

"You do?" Arwin slowly lifted her gaze to meet Vi's.

"I do. Which is why I want you to try again."

Arwin did as Vi bid. Time and again. That day, the next day, and in the coming weeks.

The girl worked tirelessly for three months as Vi watched silently.

She felt every pulse of magic, absorbing it into her as she had the power of the scythe. Cyphers of sorcery had been given to her in a tongue she couldn't read but somehow understood. Vi saw the glyphs behind her eyelids as she slept. She felt the knowledge they imparted to her in every action.

Day after day, that knowledge assured her of one thing: *You can do this.*

At first Vi thought the resounding confidence related to Arwin, and being patient enough to see the crown made. But day by day that theory waned. Her fingers began to itch as she watched Arwin work. Her magic reached out between Arwin's pulses.

Vi learned the secrets of the shift not through direct teaching, but by watching one day after the next, until, finally…

"Do it again, but slower."

"What?" Arwin's head jerked up from the crown she held. It was the fourth one Deneya had made. The girl had succeeded in changing the crown from steel to a faint blue glass.

"Slower, this time," Vi said again.

"All right." Arwin was clearly uncertain, but she wrapped her fingers around the crown anyway. At the first pulse of magic, Vi reached across the table and wrapped her hands around Arwin's. "Wha—"

"Keep going," she said without taking her eyes off the crown.

Another pulse of magic.

The first pulse was always connecting with the item. The second was learning it, inside and out. Vi understood what Arwin was doing in the same way she'd come to understand the crystals.

When she manipulated Yargen's magic, she first collected the power, learning it. Then, she envisioned what she wanted to be made. The shift was taking the raw essence of something, unraveling it, and then tightening it back in a new shape.

The thought brought them to the third pulse—unraveling.

Vi watched with keen eyes as the crown unraveled between fast pulses of magic. They were too quick for normal eyes to see. But Vi's eyes weren't normal. They were goddess-given, forged by Yargen between worlds.

Fourth pulse—remaking.

She tightened her fingers over Arwin's and pushed her magic through the girl. Vi's brows knotted with focus. The blue glass hardened further and reshaped slightly. When they pulled their hands away, there was a nearly identical replica of the crown Vi had made in shape. All it lacked was the glow and swirl of magic crystals held.

"You just…" Arwin pushed her chair away from the table, but didn't seem to trust herself to stand. "You're a *human*. You can't use the shift."

"I am the Champion, and magic is magic," Vi said with unfounded confidence. "If it doesn't obliterate, it is of Yargen. And it's merely a matter of learning how to use a new set of powers."

Arwin bit her lip, clearly debating the accuracy of this. Vi couldn't blame her. She knew what Taavin had said about the morphi and how their power was viewed as deriving from Raspian.

Mortals and their misinformation. Vi's heart ached at the sentiment.

"Will you teach me?" Vi said.

"Teach you what?"

"Everything you know about the shift."

Arwin stared at her and gripped her seat with white knuckles. Vi feared if the girl let her chair go, she might topple over.

Despite her rigidity, Arwin managed a nod.

19

TIME PASSED EFFORTLESSLY.

Vi took her young tutor's lessons on the shift to heart. She studied Arwin's hand motions and listened intently to her words. But what the girl didn't say was the best teacher. Vi felt every pulse, every pull and tug on the threads of magic and life that made up each and every object within the world.

Taavin had said Yargen's magic was life. But it was so much more. Yargen's magic was existence itself. It was the world, cut from the chaos that Raspian sought to reap. Every mortal magic was a different way to understand and interact with the raw essence of life itself.

Her understanding helped Vi learn the shift—something she was certain she couldn't have done a world away, or even in this world, a few years ago. But that understanding didn't replace time, patience, and practice.

At first, she helped Arwin adjust the shift. Then, the girl began teaching Vi how to do it on her own. How to draw out the power and change an object from what it was to what it could be.

The weeks pulsed into months without Vi so much as realizing.

"How much longer do you think it will take?" Taavin asked her from where he sat on the couch in the center of the room. A common space was located between their room and Deneya's in the guest wing they occupied.

"Not much longer." Vi leaned against the arm of one of the chairs opposite. She'd only just returned from working with Arwin and could still feel the magic under her hands. "I'm nearly there."

"Good, we'll need to return to the Dark Isle."

"Not before Deneya has uncovered a link to Adela."

"We don't need Adela to get back." Vi heard the frown in his voice before she even turned to look at him. "We have a vessel."

"It's been a year. Do you really think it's still in the cove where we left it?" Vi asked with an arch of her eyebrows. Then, before he could speak, "Even if it is, do you think it'll be seaworthy?"

"I don't like the idea of working with Adela."

"I know you don't." Vi sighed, turning away. She grew more and more weary of this conversation. "But we'll need the strength and speed of her ship to get the flame... and to get to the isle of the elfin'ra."

"That's if—"

"It's happening at sunset," Deneya interrupted, barging in. "Sorry to interrupt, I know you both usually have your date this evening but—"

"But it's important." Vi straightened away from the chair. "Tell me what you've learned."

"Fallor will be meeting with an actual member of Adela's crew at sunset on the southwest ridge just outside of the forest."

Vi and Taavin shared a look. They'd been tracking Fallor's movements in secret. Messages had moved in and out of the city through merchants Fallor was working with as a page in the city guard. The *Stormfrost* had been spotted not far from Toris— confirmed through scouting done by Noct's eldest daughter.

"I'll go ahead and let you both know how it goes." Vi held up her right hand. She wore a silver ring on her middle finger that matched an identical one on Deneya's hand. The woman had given the token to Vi as a gift, imprinted with her communication mark should they ever be separated.

"You'll go alone?" Taavin was on his feet as well.

"There's no way I'll be able to get on the *Stormfrost* if all three of us go together. Adela needs to feel confident that she can overpower me."

"What if something goes wrong and she actually does overpower you?"

"She won't." Vi gave him an assured smile.

"You've seen Vi in the training grounds," Deneya said in her defense. "She can handle herself better than any of us... And has three times the strength," she mumbled the last part.

"This is Adela we're talking about." Taavin's face was as stormy as the sea he'd pulled her from all those years ago. Vi stepped over to him and grabbed his shoulder gently. "I do trust you, you know that, right? But I—"

"Worry," Vi finished for him with a small smile. "I worry for you too, more than you can know."

"Not to break up the moment, but if you're going to go, you should go now."

"I know." Vi gave a solemn nod to Deneya. "You two should pack up while I'm gone. We'll be leaving this place once I get Adela to agree to help us."

"Leaving?" Taavin repeated with surprise. "I thought you said you were *nearly there* with the crown. We can't leave until we have a replica."

"No, I just said I was nearly there. Nothing about the crown." She gave him a somewhat sheepish grin. "We have the replica. It's in the workshop."

"*What?*"

Deneya followed her into the hall. "If you've had the replica this whole time—"

"I haven't had it the whole time," Vi interjected. "Just for the past ten weeks or so."

"Fine. If you've had the replica for the past ten weeks," Deneya rephrased her words with frustration, "what have you been working on?"

"I'll show you later," Vi called over her shoulder with a grin. "Follow behind me and I'll see you both on the *Stormfrost*."

Down and out the estate, Vi moved quickly in the twilight. She knew Fallor's rounds, likely better than he knew them himself. She'd long since mapped out the young man's movements just like she had mapped out the whole city that was the Twilight Kingdom. Even when he thought he was wandering at random to lose any people who might be tracking him, he wandered in consistent circles.

When she found him, he was finishing up a conversation with a merchant. Vi couldn't hear what they said, but the merchant gave him a token and disappeared into the shadows of an alleyway.

Vi ignored the merchant, focusing only on Fallor as he walked up the quiet residential street. He headed right, and Vi followed in parallel through an alley. She twisted between rubbish bins and around opening doors to step back out onto the main street.

Fallor had pulled his hood. He was trying to lose himself among the crowd. But Vi followed twenty paces behind easily. He looked around nervously from time to time, and Vi would side step—always just beyond the edge of his periphery. He'd recognize her if he got a good look. Fallor had seen her and Arwin working together enough times.

So she lingered at the edge of the city, leaning in a doorway, watching as he walked up the rise to the gateway of the kingdom. The moment Fallor passed through the swirling, fog-like magic, Vi sprinted up behind him.

"Champion, would you—" Ruie attempted to say as she passed. The young woman was on guard duty for the night.

"No time." Vi gave her a short wave and plunged herself into the haze that surrounded the Twilight Kingdom.

She pushed magic out around her in a quick pulse. It cocooned and stabilized her in the between space. Another pulse of magic, and Vi felt her powers running like a bridge between the city where she had been, and the forest where she was headed. With a third pulse, Vi pushed herself along the pathway.

Reemerging in the real world outside of the Twilight Kingdom left her off-balance. Pinwheeling her arms, Vi grabbed onto a tree. It wasn't exactly a smooth landing, but it worked.

It worked.

A grin spread across her face as she sprinted through the trees. When the muscles of her legs began to grow tired, she felt a barely-perceptible shift. Yargen's magic was in her bones. It was her flesh. The essence of the goddess was woven within her just as the power of the scythe was.

The trees were a blur and Vi was hardly breathless. She focused solely on heading to the southwest ridge as Deneya described. Vi skidded to a stop before she lurched through the treeline just east of Toris. Pressing herself against one of the tall trees, she crouched low, the leaves of the forest floor settling around her.

Vi squinted into the setting sun, focusing on the woman and young man speaking at the crest of one of the rolling hills that cascaded down to the humble fishing town. The woman sat on a rock, talking as much with her hands as her mouth, though Vi couldn't make out the words. The sun glistened off the jewelry she wore, sparking in the light. Two large hoops pulled down her pointed ears. They were no doubt communication tokens, if the Adela of this world was anything like the Adela of Vi's. The woman removed an earring and passed it to Fallor.

Vi scanned the surrounding hills.

The lone woman was high up—visible for a wide distance. Others were watching her, they had to be. But wherever her fellow pirates were hiding, Vi couldn't see them.

Fallor talked with her for about an hour. At the end of their conversation, he tried to pass the token back to the pirate, but she refused with a sickeningly sweet smile. Anger flashed across Vi's chest, bouncing between her ribs, making her breath hot. But she promptly squelched the feeling. This wasn't her fight. She wasn't here to help him.

She was here to get to Adela.

Yet... Vi saw someone else in Fallor. A young Jayme, impressionable and filled with hurt that Adela would fan into rage.

Fallor took to the skies with a pulse of magic. The woman watched the eagle, ignorant that someone else was watching her. Vi slid up the tree in tandem.

The pirate wasn't a morphi, which meant she had to walk back to Adela. That meant there was a skiff somewhere nearby. Vi stepped from the trees and at the same time said, "*Loft dorh.*"

Immobilize.

The glyph that sparked at the tip of her pointed finger was no longer the bright white-yellow it had been. Now it was tinted with blue on the edges, glowing nearly the same color as crystals. Vi felt a surge of magic at her left. She could almost hear the inhale of a man emerging from his hiding place.

"*Juth mariy.*" An audible *crack* filled the air as she destroyed the Lightspinner's magic. There was one other pirate, at least. Vi began running toward the woman she had under her command.

She remembered holding Fallor with *loft dorh*. It had been a nearly impossible act. She'd keenly felt his every struggle against her magic tethers. But her grip now was so tight, the only thing Vi could feel was the woman's panicked heartbeat under her grip.

A pulse of magic shot across the field.

The first pirate was a Lightspinner. The other was a morphi. Adela was nothing if not prepared.

Vi stopped her forward momentum, bracing herself as the morphi's magic disruption washed over her. She focused on her glyphs. They wavered; the woman moved for a second as Vi's control flickered. The pirate collapsed with a cry, but was then held in stasis again as Vi's glyph sustained the shift.

Now, it was Vi's heart that was racing. Her left hand burned with power from the glyph. Her bones singed against her muscles. She could feel Yargen within her, seeking release, seeking to be whole again, as Vi drew on the goddess's essence.

"Get away from her!" a man shouted.

Vi didn't give him a chance to say anything else, levying another "*Juth mariy*" in reply. There was another pulse of magic, and Vi's glyphs nearly flickered out of existence. But they held enough for her to make it to the kneeling woman.

Ruthlessly, Vi grabbed the woman's hooped ear and jerked her face forward. *Loft dorh* faded. The woman was held in total shock of Vi standing over her. To the pirate's eyes, Vi was a human who wielded Lightspinning that couldn't be broken by the shift.

"*Narro hath,*" Vi uttered, almost with a sinister note.

She felt the magic spring to life, her suspicions confirmed. All their waiting and watching had paid off. Vi had finally tracked down the elusive pirate Adela.

No, *more than that*, she had initiated a direct communication with her.

"Adela," Vi said sweetly, feeling the magic pull taut. "I have your crew. And while I know you don't care all that much for their lives, I will tell you that I have something much, much better. Something that will make you rich beyond compare. Something that will ensure your name is uttered in fear and wonder by every child for thousands of years to come.

"Let me on *Stormfrost* to parlay with you, and you'll know what it is."

Silence. Vi didn't even hear the wind moving over the grasses or the other pirates readying their next attacks as she waited.

"And who are you?" Adela's chilling voice was recognizable anywhere. Vi hated that it was as known to her as her own mother's.

"Yargen's Champion." Vi smirked. "The one who broke your magic in Oparium." Another pause. The other pirates stilled, some form of communication happening on the side. "Well? Don't test my patience, pirate queen."

"You intrigue me, Champion. Come aboard, if you dare."

Vi released the woman's face and her glyph vanished. The pirate collapsed at her feet, gasping for air and scrambling away. Vi looked down at her, magic surging from a font that would never run dry. It filled her to the point of being overwhelming.

"Take me to Adela, and you may live."

20

A SURREAL SENSE OF familiarity crept up on Vi as she stepped foot on the *Stormfrost* for a second time that felt like the hundredth. Much like the first time in her own world, the crew had gathered on the main deck. Adela was among them, identical to how Vi had first seen her, down to her icy cane.

Vi stood, motionless. The crew around her rigidly maintained their positions. They were the string of an invisible bow that Adela held in her frigid grip. One word, and they would lunge to strike clean through her heart.

Adela, for her part, wore a slightly amused smile. She stared at Vi and Vi at her. They waited each other out in the stillness, waited to see who gave first.

Vi knew it wouldn't be her. Time was one of the many things she had on her side. Time had made her *very* patient.

"You claim to be the one who broke my magic in Oparium." Adela's tone and look told Vi that she sincerely doubted that fact. "I thought the claim insanity. Perhaps just as much as your claim of being Yargen's Champion returned. Or maybe the real insanity is you willingly coming to the *Stormfrost* like a sheep to slaughter."

Adela smirked and the flash of blades being drawn caught Vi's eye. The crew looked at her like a prime cut of meat.

"I did not come here for slaughter," Vi said calmly. "I came to strike a deal with you."

"Yes, so you claim. Get to the striking, girl."

Vi was discovering one of the greatest annoyances of her current state was perpetually looking like she was eighteen. "Not among your crew."

"Any deal you strike with me can be done here and now," Adela insisted. Vi slowly shook her head. "Then I will let them kill you."

"It'd be a shame for me to raze everything you've built and kill every man and woman on this ship simply because you are stubborn."

"You think you can kill us?" a pirate broke rank and shouted.

"Do you doubt me?" Vi looked to the man and watched as he took a step backward. She turned her eyes back to Adela. "I will not speak among the rabble. This is your last chance. Parlay in private and have everything you desire. Or meet your end. I care not. The vortex continues with or without you."

Adela narrowed her eyes slightly. "Very well, come to my cabin."

The crew parted for their captain. Vi could feel their eyes gouging at her throat, making up for what their weapons could not do. But they made no motion against her. As long as Adela tolerated her, so would they.

Adela led her back to an entrance underneath the quarterdeck. It opened into a large cabin with windows lining the stern of the vessel. Ice stretched between beams of wood in place of glass, the world beyond blurred through the frost. A large desk was opposite a bed. Shelves lined the wall to her left, the books and scrolls held in by narrow rails. Two seats were positioned in front of the windows.

"Please, sit." Adela motioned to one of the leather chairs. "If it's not too cold for you." She smiled thinly.

"I'm not one you need to worry about." Dredging her spark to the surface, the air around Vi crackled, shimmering with heat. As she sat down, the thin layer of frost covering the leather evaporated into steam. She could feel Adela's magic pushing in against hers, trying to cover the chair once more. But Vi held the ice at bay with minimal effort, winning their first tug-of-war as Adela sat across form her.

"You're human, a Lightspinner, and you also know the elemental magics of the Dark Isle." Adela tapped her cane, punctuating each item. "You're like me."

"In some ways," Vi admitted. "I will not stop until I get what I want. I am not afraid to be ruthless. And I did grow up once, long ago, on the Dark Isle, just as you did."

"Is there elfin in your parentage as well?" Vi shook her head. "Pity, you'll be dead soon enough, then."

"I am timeless."

"Yes, this Champion business." Adela lifted her icy hand off her cane, waving it through the air as though the notion was nothing more than a fleeting thought. "Tell me what it is you want. And why I should let you leave my ship alive."

"What do you know of the crystal weapons of Yargen?" Vi asked, ignoring the opportunity to reiterate that there were only two options: Adela working with her, or everyone dying.

"Crystal weapons? Very little."

"I suspected as much, or you would've never left the crown of Solaris unprotected."

"It wasn't entirely unprotected," Adela said gruffly. "My magic was powerful."

"For one such as yourself, yes."

"Tell me about these crystal weapons," she demanded, tapping her cane on the ground.

"I'll tell you that these weapons are worth little to you and everything to me. If I do not get them, it will spell the end of the world." Vi looked out the windows. Adela—at least the Adela of her time—didn't care about the world ending. It was an intangible concept to a woman who only valued things she could put her hands on. "I need your help in getting them to where they need to go. Specifically, I need the

Stormfrost."

"I am the pirate queen, not a ferryman at your beck and call."

"You are a mercenary by another name who will take jobs from the highest bidder regardless of who or what they are." Vi gave her a hard look. Surprisingly, Adela didn't look offended. She smiled wider, or perhaps it was a sneer. "I am the highest bidder."

"All right, put your gold where your mouth is, then. What is sailing on the *Stormfrost* worth to you?"

"I can give you access to the treasury of Solaris."

Adela threw her head back and laughed. "I *had* access to the treasury of Solaris when I wasn't even twenty-five. I took all I wanted and that treasure ended up being worth so little to me, I couldn't be bothered to go back for it. Do better." Vi had expected this reaction. But she couldn't be blamed for starting low in her negotiations.

"The Archives of Yargen." That got Adela sitting straighter. She wasn't laughing now. "I know pathways in and through them. I will give you access to those pathways."

"And get the Swords of Light away from the Archives?"

"You'd have to promise me more than the use of the *Stormfrost* to get me to do that." Vi wasn't even sure if she *could* do that. But she wanted Adela to think she could.

"What will the use of the *Stormfrost* entail?"

"I need you to deliver me to a few places, pick me up in a few others. Perhaps some comrades of mine as well. Nothing too difficult for the great pirate queen."

"That's a rather open-ended request. I have my own empire to run here on the seas. I need to know how much of my time you'll take to determine if what you're promising is worth it."

"I won't call on you more than five times in the span of the next ten years." In ten years, the Caverns would meet their end, one way or another; a new Vi would be born; and she would long know if her efforts to save the world had ultimately resulted in failure.

"Humans," Adela said, as though her own parentage wasn't part human. "Always thinking so narrow."

"I'm attempting to strike you a fair deal."

Adela hummed, looking out the windows at the sea drifting by. She caressed the top of her cane made of ice, smoothing away jagged shards as they grew around her fingers. Being part elfin explained her immense power, and her longevity.

"Access to the Archives of Yargen for five trips in the next ten years, whichever comes first," Adela summarized before bringing her bright blue eyes back to Vi. "You have your deal, Champion."

"One more thing."

"You are not accustomed to how negotiations work, are you?" Adela narrowed her eyes. "One puts everything on the table foremost."

"The boy, Fallor…" Her voice trailed off. The thought had vanished from between her fingers and Vi struggled to bring it back. Why had she brought up Fallor again?

Ah.

The memory of Arwin, soaking in the bath, staring at the ceiling, trapped in a bubble of pain and longing and what-ifs. The shade of Jayme on the boy. Fallor was nothing in relation to stopping the vortex, but she had made a promise to save the people she could, hadn't she?

"You are to cut ties with him."

"We have been working—"

"This isn't negotiable," Vi said firmly.

Adela pursed her lips. "Very well, we have other morphi we've been working on recruiting." Adela shrugged. "Or are they off-limits too?"

"Recruit away." Vi leaned back in the chair, folding her hands over her stomach and staring out at the ocean. Perhaps the Isle of Frost getting a shift was the stone in the river, and some other morphi would betray King Noct and his family. Perhaps she'd somehow made it worse. But for now Vi hoped that Arwin would have a few extra years of happiness. If she was lucky, regardless of what else came to pass in the world around her, she would have a hand to hold when the day was done.

She'd handle Jayme when her and Adela's deal was up. By then, she would have even more power. The pirate queen would agree to anything just to avoid angering her.

"Where will we be delivering you first?" Adela asked, still somewhat begrudgingly.

"First, we'll wait for my friends to join us. Then, to Norin."

"And you will tell me of the way into the Archives?"

"I will tell you how to get into the Archives once our deal has concluded and you have taken me to my fifth and final place."

"What assurance do I have until then?"

"I'm sure you'll think of some way to make my life miserable if I don't follow through." Adela smiled knowingly at that. Vi held out her hand, a plain, silver ring on her left middle finger. "*Narro hath.*" The connection sprang to life with the glyph hovering around the ring. "It's settled, come to the *Stormfrost*," she said, short and simple, before closing the connection.

"Who are your friends?"

"Curious, aren't you, for a woman who's all business?"

"Keep your secrets." Adela turned, looking out to sea. Vi couldn't tell if she was bothered or not.

"One of them is an elfin from Risen. The other is another elfin but from much farther away... where I'm from." *More or less.* Vi decided to answer Adela's question anyway. She was never going to be friendly with the pirate queen. But the more cordial they could become, the better. "May I ask you something?"

"You may ask." But Vi didn't miss that Adela made no guarantees about giving an answer.

"Why Solaris?"

"Pardon?" Adela swept her icy gaze back to Vi. It would've made her shiver, once.

"Why do you hate Solaris? You stole the crown jewels. You worked with the Knights of Jadar. You'll go out of your way to bring harm to Solaris, even offering discounts to people acting against the family."

"Was it you who killed my man in Norin years ago?"

"Yes." Vi would've expected Adela to be upset at that, but she only seemed amused.

"I was wondering when Janice informed me there was a Lightspinner..." Janice must've been the morphi that night. "I had bet it was one of Lumeria's men."

"You still haven't answered my question."

"Oh, yes, why do I hate Solaris?" Adela's wispy, white hair hovered like an aura at the slightest turn of her head when she looked to Vi. "Why do you think?"

"I think it's because Tiberus scorned you," Vi said boldly. "Because you loved him and he—"

Raspy laughter and wheezes cut her short.

"Because I *loved* Tiberus? That sod?" Adela shook her head several times. "No. Though he might have thought I did. His affections suited me, I'll be the first to admit. Tiberus was a means to an end for me to see if I could get the treasure."

"Then it's not about Solaris?"

"Why would it be?"

"Because…" Vi faltered. Her voice trailed off. Everything she'd known Adela to be. Everything the pirate queen had done.

"You thought this was all about a man?" Adela continued to get a chuckle out of Vi's shock. "No, girl. This is about me, and my power. Tiberus was a stepping stone, a test run, to see if I could become what I knew I was destined for.

"I want every so-called ruler on this earth to know that their dominion ends at the sea. I do not hate Solaris any more than I hate Lumeria, or any other ruler across the various kingdoms, empires, and republics of the earth." Vi chuckled softly. "You find my ambitions amusing?" Adela looked at her from the sides of her eyes.

"Not at all. What I find amusing is that you and I will do anything to get what we want. And you are the last person I ever expected to find kinship with." All the hatred Vi had felt for Adela was melting away like the ice on the chair around her. She didn't *like* the woman. But she was starting to *understand* her. Part of that transformed her disdain into ambivalence.

Adela fought to carve out her place in the world. What made her any different from anyone else?

21

AAVIN AND DENEYA ARRIVED on the *Stormfrost* later that day, brought on the vessel by a skiff, and Adela showed them to their temporary quarters. Vi was reminded of the *Dawn Skipper*—two bunks, a table between them, and not much else.

"I don't want to say I doubted you but…"

"You doubted me." Vi grinned at Deneya. "I'm not offended. Adela's reaction was a coin flip."

"It was, and I'm relieved this worked out." Taavin crossed to the window, looking out at the sea that was now drifting past them as they moved toward the Dark Isle once more. "What did you have to promise her to get her to agree?"

"Nothing of consequence." Vi folded her arms and leaned against the closed door.

"Why do I get the feeling you're lying?" Deneya said uncertainly.

"Consequence is a matter of perspective."

"She's avoiding answering for a reason." Taavin faced Vi. "What were the terms of the deal?"

"We have ten years, or five trips on the *Stormfrost*, whichever comes first."

"Is ten years enough time?" Deneya asked.

"It all ends soon."

"That sounds ominous." Deneya sat heavily on a bunk.

"You still haven't told us what Adela expects in return," Taavin pressed.

"As for what I offered her… I offered a way into the Archives of Yargen."

"You *what*?" Taavin and Deneya said in unison.

"I had to give her something. But that was all I offered her."

"That's all, she says, as though handing the Archives to Adela isn't anything major," Deneya muttered.

"You didn't though." Taavin took a step toward her. "Did you?"

A smile curled Vi's lips. "All I promised her was a way in to the Archives. I didn't guarantee it'd be safe, and I didn't promise her a way out."

"You mean to ensnare her." Deneya was now grinning as well.

"I mean to prevent the world from ending. What the people of Risen do is up to them." Vi shrugged.

"I'll make sure the people of Risen are ready to protect the flame," Deneya proclaimed.

"The flame will be gone long before then." *And you'll be the one to take it*, Vi added mentally.

"If we take the flame from Risen, there's no more rebirths—no more turns of the vortex," Taavin said solemnly.

"As I said, it all ends eventually. It must."

He stared at her for a long moment. Vi could almost feel him reading her thoughts through her eyes. She tried to shield herself from it with an encasement of Yargen's magic around her.

"You have plans," he said finally.

"Of course I do."

"Care to share them?"

"When the time is right."

"You act like you don't trust us." Deneya rolled her eyes.

"I trust you both with my life."

"Then why didn't you tell us what you planned on offering Adela?" Deneya asked.

"Because it was inconsequential."

"What about your work with the shift?" Taavin's voice took on a hard edge. Even Deneya stilled as the atmosphere in the room became nearly suffocating. They'd found out. They must've heard from Ruie when word spread that she escaped through the shift surrounding the Twilight Kingdom without the help of a morphi.

"Is it true?" Deneya whispered. "Did you really go through the shift without the help of a morphi?"

Vi nodded.

"How?" Deneya shifted uncomfortably. "You shouldn't be able to... none of us can. Only morphi can master the shift."

"I'm not quite sure how," Vi finally admitted, staring down at her hands. "I got a feeling when working with Arwin. A feeling that led to an understanding."

"You can understand the shift."

"I can," Vi answered. But she didn't know if that was entirely the truth. Did *she* understand the shift? Or did the goddess within her, working through her mortal form? "Perhaps it's a boon. Now I will be able to make all the crystal weapon replicas so that the major events surrounding the crystal weapons remain unchanged."

She looked to Taavin as if she was the one giving a peace offering. If she could make crystal weapons, they could continue along his mission of ensuring the birth of a new Champion. Surely, he should be thrilled.

"Speaking of..." Deneya reached for her pack and produced the fake crystal crown she and Arwin had made. "We have it."

"We'll return south and find what Baldair did with the actual crown. Hopefully, it'll be an easy swap," Vi proclaimed. "We'll go by way of Norin so we can stop in the Crossroads and collect some gold from our hideaway." She looked to Taavin. He still regarded her with a thoughtful and somewhat wary gaze. "If my plans meet your approval as well?"

"The stones of fate in the river are unchanged. We're still heading toward the birth of a new Champion and protecting the future of this world in the process." His words were approving, but his body language said otherwise.

Vi reached out, taking his fingers and trying to smooth away the tension between them with her thumb on the back of his hand. A smile broke across her lips, one he reluctantly returned. Her fingers tightened. She had to hold onto him, for as long as possible, because holding him felt like holding the last remnants of the woman she'd once been.

Adela took them just south of Norin. They were taken ashore by rowboat and left without fanfare. In the distance, the *Stormfrost* was barely visible. By the time they reached Norin that evening, there were already whispers of the legendary pirate Adela being spotted.

They left the rumors behind and began the long trek to the Crossroads.

When they arrived a few days later, it was late, and the stars had been their only companions on the road for the final hour. Even the center of the Solaris Empire was relatively quiet.

"Glad to see it didn't burn down." Deneya looked up at the vacant storefront Vi had purchased years ago as she slid her key into the iron rose lock.

"It won't burn down," Taavin said confidently. "This place is going to play a pivotal role in the future of our world."

A deep rumbling distracted them. Vi and Taavin shared a look. Both turned to Deneya.

"Was that your stomach?" Vi asked with a laugh.

"It was a long walk today." Deneya rubbed her stomach. "Here, take my pack, I'm going to go find some food." Vi accepted the woman's pack and Taavin gave a nod. "I'll be back with sustenance soon."

Deneya headed off in the opposite direction as Vi and Taavin stepped into the darkness of the store. The shelves were perpetually vacant. Darkness clung to every corner. Vi crossed to the back of the room; there, hidden behind a curtain, was another doorway. This led to a narrow stairway and up into a cramped second-floor apartment.

Vi dropped her pack heavily and rolled her shoulders. Taavin's hands covered the sore spots, rubbing slowly. Vi sighed as he took a half step closer to her.

"You should take a hot bath."

"I should, and you should join me." She smirked into the darkness. "It's been a while since we've been alone."

"Now that sounds a delight," he whispered into her ear, lips brushing against tender skin. Warmth flooded her, from the top of her head to the bottom of her abdomen. "I'll draw the bath."

He stepped away and Vi caught his hand, then his gaze. Taavin locked his fingers with hers, pulling her hand to his face and kissing her knuckles thoughtfully. He straightened, a mischievous smile quirking his lips.

"Don't keep me waiting," Vi said softly, her voice gone deep with yearning.

"Never." Taavin stepped back, keeping his eyes locked with hers until the last moment he disappeared into the bathroom. He could have her yearning with just a look or a simple touch in an otherwise chaste location.

Being back on the Dark Isle, with him, made things feel simpler once more. At least for a little while, they could find moments to pretend he was a normal man, and she a normal woman. Their love could be uncomplicated.

As he rummaged in the bathroom, she set about sorting their things. The chest of gold coins from old Lyndum was right where they'd left it. They'd have to convert it once more into usable currency, restock supplies, and then head south. Vi closed the top of the chest and walked over to the lone window wedged between the buildings on either side of their narrow shop, as though their place was a weed that couldn't be contained.

She opened the window, allowing the room to air out with the cool desert breeze. Vi rested her hands on the sill, leaning out, savoring the sounds of revelry that hung on the crisp night. Laughter echoed up to her, drawing Vi's attention down to the street.

Two men clung to each other, swaying like willowy branches. They were both clearly intoxicated; their dark hair was thrown every which way. She watched with a little smile as their steps mirrored that of a rolling tide, up and down and not quite stable.

Oh, to be that young and—

Vi clutched the windowsill.

"It can't be. It's too early," she whispered. Her eyes didn't lie. "Those idiots." Vi spun, racing through the room, not even bothering to change. Taavin had just emerged from the bathroom, naked to the waist, and the sight of him stopped her in her tracks. Vi let out a groan, resting a palm on his chest. "I need to make sure two drunks make their way home safely."

"What?" Taavin called after her as she started down the stairs.

"It's Aldrik and Jax. The Imperial army is here, *now*," Vi called back before dashing through the store and emerging out on the street beyond. She was only several paces behind the two men and closed the gap quickly. She could've stabbed them both between the ribs before they noticed her at their backs.

Vi rubbed her eyes, pressing to the point of pain and stars popping behind her lids. Then she pinched her cheeks till they were splotchy—though it might have been impossible to tell on her tan skin in the middle of the night. She began running, head down; her shoulder clipped the taller man and she stumbled, sprawling on the ground before them like a proper damsel.

Aldrik was nearly taken down with her. Jax held him up with the arm that was already around his waist. The booze slowed their reactions and they both reached to help her up on a delay.

"Aaaare—" a burp "—are you allrisht?" Aldrik tried to ask.

Clearly, this was not one of his prouder moments.

"I'm fine," she said curtly, batting their hands away and collecting herself off the ground. Vi stopped herself, blinking the tears she'd pressed into her eyes so they'd roll down her cheeks as she looked up at them. "My prince!" Vi bowed, bringing her forehead to the ground.

"Shhhh." He brought a finger to his lips. "I'm incognitooo. Haaving a night of fshun."

"Sorry, miss." Jax extended his hand and Vi ignored it, helping herself to her feet. He looked like he was barely managing to keep Aldrik upright. Jax tilted his head so far he nearly fell over. "Do I know you?"

"I doubt it." Vi played with the short ends of her hair. She'd cropped it back to her ears before arriving on the Dark Isle. Long, short, long, short, her hair was the one thing that she could easily make sure was never the same between each meeting.

"I'm sure I do," he insisted.

"Forgive me for being blunt, but I think that's the alcohol speaking." Jax grinned wider at the remark and Vi smiled as well. "I'm a lowly one who wouldn't have the honor of meeting a prince or an illustrious member of the Golden Guard."

Aldrik burst out laughing. "She, she called you a *member*."

Vi had no idea why that was supposed to be funny. But Jax laughed along, snorting as he tried to regain control of himself.

"Well, now you have. Please do keep our appearance a secret? It's my fault the prince is out so late, and I don't want him or I to get in trouble."

If you wanted it to be a secret, you shouldn't be walking down the middle of the main street drunk, Vi nearly snapped. What she said instead was, "My lords, the Crossroads at night is not the safest of places. Perhaps I could have the honor of escorting you? I know these streets well, and I planned to enlist in the army come morning. I'm quite capable of being your temporary guard."

They had *not* planned on enlisting in the army come the morning. Their plan had been to head south, switch the crown, and *then* head North. But Vi didn't miss an opportunity when fate handed her one.

If she did this favor for them tonight, it was likely that they would keep her close at the front.

"Let her," Aldrik declared. "Secoond pretteh lady of the nighhht."

Second? Just what did that *mean?*

"Come on, then, walk with us back to the center of the Crossroads," Jax said lightly. The brief moment of recognition had passed and they began to walk. "Why do you want to join the army?"

"To serve the Empire." Vi sniffled, rubbing her eyes until a few more tears squeezed out.

"What'sh wrong?"

"I got in a fight with my parents about it," Vi said, looking at her feet. The sorrow in her voice at the mention of parents was genuine; it was compounded when she looked over at Aldrik. He had the bump in his nose now that she remembered her father having. His cheeks were gaunter than the last time she'd seen him. Deep bags clung underneath distant, harrowed eyes. "They don't want me to enlist. But I'm a woman grown. And well…"

"Yooou ran away from hoome."

Vi nodded at Aldrik's slurred words.

"You should go back," Jax said firmly.

"Jax, don't lose-us sholdiers."

"You only get one family. Hold them close."

She'd been worried about the two men getting a dagger between the ribs by a cut-purse in the night. But it was Jax who caught her off guard, striking her breathless. Vi took a second to compose herself. Her family was, and would always be, a soft spot. She formed an answer befitting the seventeen-year-old girl she'd once been, and not the timeless traveler she now was.

"I do hold them close," she insisted. "But they have to understand I'm doing this for them. I'm fighting for them. So they can have a better life. They have to understand that this is *my* choice, not theirs."

"Yooou're doing ah goodthing." Aldrik patted her on the shoulder and his hand stayed. He blinked into the brighter lights of the center of the Crossroads as they entered their aura. "Not like me. Not like someone who's done terrible things."

"That's enough for tonight. We're not far from your bed." Jax led them over to the Imperial lodging. Three, large, circular windows kept an eye on the square below. "Wait here just a moment, I'll be back," Jax said to her, giving her no time to reply before disappearing inside with Aldrik.

Vi sat on the stoop, elbows on her knees, staring at the other revelries happening at a bar across the square. Her mind was on Aldrik, on those haunted eyes— the ghosts of her actions haunting his nightmares. She clutched her hands so tightly together that her nails left crescent moons in her skin.

The door behind her opened again, startling her. Jax hopped down two steps, wobbled, and sat with a sigh.

"He'll be fine," he said.

"'Fine' is an interesting word choice for the hangover he'll be nursing." Vi glanced up at the second-floor window that she knew to be her father's room. "Does the prince drink to excess often?"

Jax's long silence was answer enough. When the "No" finally came, Vi knew it was a lie.

"Well, that's good, I suppose," she lied right back, pretending she didn't hear all his unspoken hesitations.

"And, for that reason, I appreciate your discretion about tonight's events."

"I don't really have any friends. So I've got no one to tell. Not that I would tell anyone. I'm looking to be in service to the crown and I know what's best for the crown isn't rumors of what the prince does during his downtime."

"He gets precious little of it."

"I'm sure," Vi murmured. "But he still has it better than he thinks." What Vi wouldn't give to be a "tortured" princess again.

"I wouldn't count on that."

"How so?"

Jax shrugged and Vi let that topic of conversation die. She didn't want to seem too eager for information on the prince.

"You said you wanted to enlist, right?"

"That's right."

"Come find me in the morning." Jax stood. "You can be under me, or Raylynn, depending on if you have magic or not."

Vi didn't have to force or fake her smile. She could enlist in the army and be near Aldrik. Moreover, she could fight along Jax and Raylynn. The idea of continuing to protect them both was appealing.

"Are you certain?"

"Yes, just remind me I was when the sun is up. Nights like this have a tendency to be forgotten." Jax laughed.

"I will."

"See you in the morning then—" Jax paused, holding out his hand.

"Gwen," Vi said, filling in the blank. "My name is Gwen."

"'Soldier Gwen' has a nice ring to it, don't you think?" Jax clasped her hand and they shook on both their second introduction and a deal.

"It does," she agreed. "Almost like it was fated to be."

V I, TAAVIN, AND DENEYA enlisted under Raylynn. Since Vi was the only person among them who could conjure her magic in the elemental ways of the Dark Isle, it was too much of a risk for them to try and join the sorcerer-warriors of the Black Legion.

Instead, they were foot soldiers—part of the nameless, faceless masses that exercised the will of the Emperor in his thirst for conquest.

Part of her thrived in the anonymity. It guarded her heart from seeing the Northern peoples she'd once considered friends and kin put to the sword. Being no one allowed her to move without raising attention or suspicion.

The other part of her clung to her identity. That was what motivated her to look after Jax and Raylynn, intervening on their behalf in more than one battle. Her small acts had no bearings on the outcome of the world's fate, but protecting them both honored memories of people she'd cared for.

"Thank you for today," Vi said to Deneya as she sat heavily around their campfire. The smell of burning bodies and ash was still thick on her from earlier in the day. "You really helped with Raylynn."

The very woman leaned against a tree some distance away, hair slicked to her neck with sweat, talking with Baldair. With every turn in the conversation, Baldair took a half-step closer. He never missed an opportunity to be by her side.

Their unspoken love was obvious to everyone but them.

"We'll have to leave her side, soon." Taavin didn't mince words. "Aldrik will sustain his injury soon."

"Yes, the one that brings him to Vhalla. Because nothing says 'fall for me' like being wounded and helpless," Deneya said dryly.

"You've been saying he'll sustain his injury 'soon' for months." Vi glanced at Taavin.

"Things aren't happening exactly when we expected."

"The world is changing. We're getting closer to the end of the vortex." Vi poked at their campfire with a stick, watching the flames dance.

"It's just variation," Taavin insisted. Vi shared a look with Deneya. The man wasn't going to admit they were on their final course until they were extinguishing the flame of Yargen. Vi had accepted that much.

Vi stood. "I'll be back. Off to the latrine."

"You know where to find us."

She always did. The campsites were mostly the same—only the terrain changed. The three of them set up their tents together, maintained their own campfire, and kept to themselves. The moment someone made a passing attempt to befriend them, Vi or Taavin would say or do something extremely off-putting.

They were the odd ones—odd, but effective. Too weird for anyone to want to spend much time with, too valuable to discharge.

"Do you think he's really going to do it?"

"Of course he won't. He's mourning, not suicidal. Well... I don't *think* he would."

Two men murmured by a campfire. Their backs were to her and neither seemed to realize Vi was there. She shifted her weight onto her back foot and floated her front foot forward before shifting her weight. The need for silence seemed suddenly paramount.

"You don't have me convinced... Listen, I'm worried. We should go after him. The attack today was hard on him."

"He was delivering a message. He'll be back within an hour and you'll feel foolish for this."

"What if I don't?" The man turned his head and Vi slid behind a tent, creeping around the back to remain out of sight and within earshot. He lowered his voice to a whisper. "What if I have every right to worry? It was his son in that village. There were no survivors and you heard the way he was talking. He had a whole plan on how he was going to get close to and attack Prince Al—"

"Stop that nonsense," the other man hissed. "You're going to get him killed for treason with that talk and there's no point to it."

"You don't know that. You didn't see his poisoned dagger. He was *serious*."

Vi pressed her eyes closed and took a breath. She started off in the opposite direction, away from the men, rounding back through camp in a different way than she came. She crouched down at Taavin's side, clasping his shoulder.

"That was fast."

"We have to go."

Taavin did one quick scan of her face. "What happened?"

"I overheard two men talking about someone going to attack Aldrik," Vi whispered.

"He's supposed to be wounded in battle. That's how it's always happened."

"I know what's *supposed* to happen, but that's not what's *actually* happening," Vi interrupted curtly. "Something changed."

"Too many somethings," Taavin murmured, glancing at the fire, as if he was the one who could find truth in flames.

"We need to move, *now*." Vi stood.

They both followed her into the woods. Aldrik's camp wasn't far—probably an hour by foot for a normal soldier. She wanted to cross the dense forest in thirty minutes. If anyone could do it, it was her.

Not looking to see if her companions could keep up, Vi began to run. The trees blurred around her and, seemingly in a blink, they emerged into the camp. Rising above the other tents was a large, square canvas structure.

She was so close.

Magic flared. The inside of the tent glowed orange.

They were too late.

Fate had sneaked past them. As Vi's eyes had been on Raylynn and Jax, thinking she had a bit more time to look after each of them before Aldrik required her attention, fate had made a mad dash for the prince.

Vi pushed past soldiers. Two guards positioned at the outside of the tent didn't even have a chance to stop her.

"What're you—" they tried to ask, but she ignored them, barging into Aldrik's tent.

A charred husk of a man was on the floor. The prince had his hand pressed against his side. He was on his knees, hair a mess, covering his face as he lifted his dark eyes to her. His jaw was clenched shut and he swayed.

"My prince, I'm here to help you." Vi rushed over. Aldrik slumped against her. His eyes were hazy. The man was an inferno to the touch. "*Halleth maph*," Vi murmured. The prince was too far gone to hesitate using her Lightspinning.

"Don't heal him entirely," Taavin cautioned.

"But—"

"It's not what we expected, but this wound will be what takes him south."

"He can head south when he's not on the verge of death." Seeing Aldrik like this made Vi panic more than she would've wanted.

"Trust—" Taavin was interrupted by the two soldiers bursting in the tent behind them.

"The prince has been poisoned," Vi said hastily. She could feel the foreign substance attacking his body. "He dispatched the assailant, but he's wounded. He needs to return to Lyndum for healing."

The soldiers looked at the carnage, at the blood soaking her shirt.

"*Now!*" Vi barked, standing. Taavin took Aldrik's other side. "Fetch his horse and every other warstrider or hearty breed."

"Who are you to give orders?"

"I don't have time for your strutting and self-importance," Vi sneered, looking down at the man as she passed. "Your prince is dying. I am the woman trying to save him. That's all that matters."

The other soldier snapped into action, running from the tent and shouting, "Horses! Get Baston and five more mounts!"

As they emerged, six horses were trotting over, already saddled and ready to ride. War made people prepared to move at all times.

The soldiers helped Vi and Taavin hoist Aldrik into his saddle. They tied him to the saddle and packed healing herbs into his wound, bandaging it. Deneya was one of the women quickly stocking their mounts.

"I'll sneak off and head west," she whispered hastily. "I'll grab the crown from our place and meet you south."

"Thank you." Vi squeezed her hand.

"I'm ready to be out of here." Deneya followed Vi over to one of the other mounts. "You need to go. The prince doesn't look good," she said, louder.

"The Minister of Sorcery will be able to extract the poison from his blood," Vi declared to those assembled as she mounted one of the horses without permission.

"Who in the Mother's name do you think you are?" Some major Vi didn't recognize balked at her and Taavin as they saddled up. "Those are my—"

"There's no time!" Vi shouted and snapped her reins. As she passed the large, familiar black horse Aldrik was riding, she gave it a light smack on its rear.

The mount's dark eyes met hers and Vi could've sworn she saw recognition there. He might be called by another name now, but Vi would know Prism anywhere. The beast followed closely behind her.

Four soldiers, Taavin included, took up the rear as they began to race across the continent.

The North was a blur. The Waste even more so. The party stopped at the Crossroads, briefly, demanding fresh horses for the non-warstriders among them, food, and clean bandages for the prince. Two soldiers threw around the idea of staying and sending for Western healers, but Vi overruled that decision. Just when the debate grew heated, Aldrik gained enough clarity to side with her. She wasn't sure if it was Yargen helping her in that moment, but Vi said a quiet thank you to the goddess anyway as they set out once more.

Hooves thundering on the Great Imperial Way filled her ears. The noise was monotonous and deafening, and the only sound any of them could hear. When they left Shaldan, they had all been too panicked for small talk. Now, they were all too exhausted.

Sweat rolled down her neck, plastering her clothing to her skin underneath her armor. The heat of the desert made the appearance of the Southern treeline in the distance a welcome sight. She was even grateful for the storm clouds on the horizon. The idea of rain was a balm to her sun-beaten cheeks.

She was such a fool.

Rain pounded down around them nearly non-stop after they entered the forests. Tiny rivers ran around the horses' hooves and down the road. She went from constantly wiping sweat out of her eyes to blinking away rainwater.

A yell distracted her from her riding trance. Vi looked over her shoulder in a panic. A horse was down, its rider shouting curse words as his leg was pinned under it.

"You're not far." One of the other soldiers riding a standard mount pulled on his reins, rounding back to the other man. "You three go on ahead. Get the prince there. It's a miracle he's held on for this long," the woman shouted over the rain.

"You heard her, let's go!" Vi kicked her horse's heaving sides to force it up the steep incline toward the Capital.

Horns trumpeted off every wall. The sound echoed around them all the way to the palace. Vi followed the calls to a side wall where two large doors were opening.

Palace servants rushed to meet them. They went immediately for Aldrik, who nearly fell into their waiting arms the second he was untied. Vi dismounted and her knees bit into the stone of the Imperial Palace as she slipped and lost her footing.

"Soldiers, report!" A man rushed out to meet them. Vi blinked up at him and then, with the help of her horse, stood.

"The crown prince has been poisoned. Fetch the Minister of Sorcery. Have every cleric help him." It was more of a command than a report.

"We couldn't identify the poison, but the Imperial library will have the answer," Taavin interjected from her side. He looked as wobbly as she was. But his head was clear enough not to forget the most important part. "Have the library staff summoned to look up information on Northern poisons—poisons in general. Anything will help, just get every library apprentice on the task."

"With haste." Luckily, the guard on duty didn't seem to mind their barked orders, or at the very least he understood where they came from. "Marcus, help them inside. I'll go to the clerics."

"Sir!" Another soldier saluted and then guided them into the palace. The four of them entered through a side receiving room, shivering and soaked to the bone. Vi looked over her shoulder, staring at the door Aldrik was taken through. "I'll take your full report later. For now, let me find you food and some warm clothes."

"That'd be much appreciated," their companion said through chattering teeth.

"I'm going off to the toilet," Vi declared.

"Me too," Taavin said eagerly. Perhaps a little too eagerly. It had been a long ride, so Vi hoped his enthusiasm wasn't conspicuous.

As they left, their companion told Marcus about the soldiers they left behind on the road. Vi closed the door firmly behind her and started through a tunnel that connected to another large hallway. Voices could be heard behind several doors and Vi paused, looking to Taavin.

"What now?"

"We've done all we need to."

Vi leaned against the wall, scrutinizing him. "We went to war. We raced across the continent, keeping him alive—not healing him, to get back here and do... nothing."

"The magical Bond your parents form is a stone in the river."

"A Bond..." Vi murmured. Bonds were legendary things—two sorcerers whose lives were wholly intertwined in such a profound way that they could never do harm to one another. A Bond could even keep one sorcerer alive while the other was mortally wounded. "I suppose something that powerful *would* be a stone in the river."

"Even knowing it was a stone—or, *believing* it is—I was worried there. Things are changing and I admit to wondering if Aldrik could actually die."

"I don't like that thought." Vi pushed her soaking hair away from her face, slicking it back. "I'd always assumed Aldrik and Vhalla's lives were stones in the river."

"As have I," Taavin said hastily. "But uncharted territory has my nerves aflame."

Vi nodded, looking in the direction where commotion echoed in the hall. "Should we go oversee things?"

"I don't think we should risk it. He's here and the library staff has been summoned. It's best not to muddle fate further with our presence."

"Then our focus becomes finding and replacing the crown." Vi pushed off the wall and began to wander aimlessly away from the voices and commotion as she focused on their new task. Taavin followed her into narrow and narrower corridors. Her mind was leading her in a specific direction, some map or blueprint in the far recesses telling her where to go. Vi trusted her subconscious self.

"That will be work for the morning," Taavin said eventually.

"What do we do tonight?"

"Whatever we want." Taavin took a step closer to her, wrapping an arm around her waist. "You're a hard woman to get alone these days."

Laughter sprang forth, tired and airy. "All this was a long ploy to get me alone, Taavin?"

"I'll say it was worth it." Two strong arms closed around her. In one deft motion, Taavin hoisted her upward. Vi immediately sank into the cradle of his arms, resting her head against his shoulder limply.

"You seem happy," she murmured.

"No. Just relieved." He pressed his lips against her forehead. "Where are we headed?"

"I don't know," she murmured. "Somewhere quiet." Sure enough, they'd ended up in the bowels of the palace, deep enough that no sorcerers even maintained the candles or torches on the walls.

"I think you've achieved that." Taavin paused at an open doorway. A dust-covered bed stood stubbornly against time. "Does this look good to you?"

She hummed as she assessed their option. Vi murmured "*Kot sorre*" and pushed the dust from the bed with a glyph that also bunched the threadbare blanket. "Better."

"Good." Taavin carried her to the bed and laid her down. Vi caught his shirt as he pulled away. She used what strength she still had left in her to yank him forward. Taavin stumbled, catching himself with a hand on the pillow by her head. Dust filled her nose, nearly making her cough, but Vi suppressed it as his lips met hers.

She would not allow anything to break this kiss.

His fingertips smoothed over her cheek and, despite the exhaustion he must be feeling too, he kissed her hungrily. His tongue probed hers gently, eliciting a soft sigh from her. When he finally pulled away, he stayed close enough for their noses to touch.

"Thank you," Vi whispered. She wanted to get the words out before sleep claimed her. "Thank you for being here no matter what."

"There's nowhere else, no *time* else, I would ever want to be."

23

TAAVIN'S ARMS WERE TUCKED around her, enveloping her in a cocoon of warmth. Vi shifted in an attempt to nestle farther back into him. His body curled around her back and his breath tickled her ear lightly.

The halls were quiet. It was as if there wasn't another soul in the entire palace—as if this space they had found was out of time itself. She trailed her fingers along his forearm to his hand. Even in sleep, he laced his fingers with hers.

"Good morning," Taavin whispered in her ear, his voice husky and low. She closed her eyes to savor the sound.

"Good morning."

"How did you sleep?"

"Like the dead."

"I'm glad you came back to life for me, then." He chuckled and it reverberated through her own ribcage.

She twisted to face him. "I'd never not come back for you."

He leaned forward, nuzzling her nose with his, before planting a sweet kiss on her lips. It was too brief, and an embarrassing whimper escaped her as he pulled away. He let out another chuckle and leaned forward again to claim her mouth. His arms tightened, and they remained locked in this embrace as the minutes—it could've been hours, even—slipped away.

Taavin kissed her fiercely. He twisted, bringing his weight atop her. Vi sank further into the mattress.

Her world was him—his exploring hands, his hungry kisses, and his ragged breaths. He didn't have to say anything else. She knew. She could taste it on his mouth. She could feel it in the way his fingers caressed her.

The day slipped away from them. Dusk settled on their sweat-glistened skin as it winked through the narrow window that ran along the wall above the bed. A beam of gold elongated along their feet as they lay, entwined and breathless.

"It had been too long since we had a moment alone," Taavin murmured, kissing her forehead.

"Yes, well, we've been busy. War will do that," Vi said with a smile.

"I never thought I'd say this, but I miss the Twilight Kingdom."

Vi laughed. "It was peaceful there."

"When you weren't studying the shift in secret." His tone had a disapproving edge, but it was just playful enough to let her know the affront had long since been forgiven.

"Admit it, you're glad I did."

"It makes things convenient," he grumbled, and kissed her anyway.

"Speaking of the shift… Deneya will be here soon. We have to start looking for the crown."

"That's tomorrow's problem." He shifted atop her again. "Tonight, you're mine."

Tomorrow's problems promptly became today's.

Taavin went to hunt through the records in the Tower of Sorcerers for any mention of the crown being discovered. Vi navigated the depths of the castle and back up into the servants' quarters. There, she lifted three sets of uniforms from a supply closet while no one was looking, and took them back to the hideaway she and Taavin were using.

He was still gone, so Vi changed alone and returned through the hidden passageways and servants' halls to get to the royal quarters. Neither of the guards positioned on either side of the golden gate stopped her as she made her way quietly past them. Pitcher in hand and pale blue tabard over her shoulders, she looked like any of the other servants coming and going to attend the needs of royals.

A short hall after the gates opened up into a large atrium. Vi's feet slowed as she crossed the tiled floor. She came to a full stop, staring in awe. The fact that she was supposed to be a servant who had traversed these rooms countless times was lost for a long moment and she shamelessly gawked, taking in the sight.

A stained-glass dome with the sun at its apex washed the mosaic of the palace set into the floor in a myriad of colors. The dome contained the Dark Isle, Barrier Islands, and Meru off to the side.

Her eyes followed a golden staircase back down to the main floor. Two hallways stretched out on either side. Vi imagined Romulin running up and down these halls to let out energy. No… that was what *she* would've done, had she grown up here. Romulin no doubt spent a good portion of his time in his room, or a sitting area, quietly studying like the golden child he was.

Now having met Baldair, she could see what everyone had said about her brother inheriting some of his features and charm. But there was still a good deal of Aldrik and Vhalla in him as well. Romulin had been a healthy mix of the family—the best of them, in Vi's eyes.

Her eyes stung, watering suddenly.

Turning away from the atrium, Vi headed left down a long corridor lined with doors. She was drowning in emotions she wasn't expecting, and her body was trying to let them out through her eyes. Vi picked one of the doors at random and gave it a knock.

When no one answered, she cracked it open, murmuring a soft, "Excuse me?" The room was empty, likely reserved for esteemed guests or extended family. Most of the furniture was covered in drop-cloths, dust weighting them down.

She stepped back out of the room and moved on to the next. One by one, Vi crossed the doors in the hall, finding them all empty. Most were bedrooms, but there were handful of sitting rooms, offices, and a dining room interspersed throughout. Vi crossed back through the atrium, ignoring the staircase for the time being—as it surely led to the royal chambers—and headed down the other wing.

There were fewer doors here and they were spread wider apart. As Vi roamed down the hall, a cleric emerged from one near the end. His eyes met hers.

"Oh good, perfect, thank you." He quickly made his way to her, taking the pitcher from her hands.

"Yes, of course." Vi passed it to him. "The prince—is he all right?" she asked hastily.

"He is, thank the Mother." Vi didn't have to feign her sigh of relief. The Bond must've been formed. "It's been a miraculous recovery, a true blessing. Now, excuse me." The man immediately returned to the room from which he'd come.

That must be Aldrik's room. Vi turned to the door at her right. If the one to her left was Aldrik's, then…

Sure enough, she had found Prince Baldair's quarters. Vi stepped inside and locked the door behind her. The younger prince was still out at the front and wasn't due back for some time.

The main room was clearly set up for entertaining. A dining table was situated by the window, covered in a drab cloth. Between it and the door was a gaming area, complete with a billiards table and bar. The outlines of sofas and loveseats made up a sitting area.

Walking through the door at her right, Vi found the prince's bedroom. The four-poster bed was bare and the air was stale. The bedroom connected through a dressing room to a bathroom that had two doors, the second leading her back into the main room.

"Was this where you lived, Romulin?" Vi murmured, running her fingers lightly along the tabletop as she walked by the window. Had he been given this room as the younger son? Or had he taken what was currently Aldrik's room, since he'd been the royal child who was actually present?

Vi drew her attention inward, trying to imagine herself returning home to this room. She would've been happy enough, she supposed. At least, she thought the girl she had been would've found joy in this place.

This was not her world, and the emotions attaching her to the people and places in it became more and more like the tarp-covered furniture by the day—covered, unused, dusty.

"To work," Vi said, refocusing herself.

She started in the prince's bedroom, searching the most obvious places first. Vi crawled under the bed, feeling underneath the platform for any hidden compartments. She lifted the mattress, double-checking that there wasn't enough room for something like the crown to be hidden underneath.

Next, she checked behind the headboard and explored the mantel around the fireplace. She ran her fingers over the embellishments and carvings, pressing and pulling. Her fingers hooked on a small lever, hidden by a raised section of trim. She pulled, and there was a soft *click* to her right.

One of the built-in bookcases sighed as Vi pulled it away from the wall, revealing a narrow passageway that ran behind the bookcases to the chimney. It was certainly a hiding place for the prince—judging by the racy literature and sentimental tokens dutifully stored within.

But the crown wasn't there.

Vi placed everything back exactly as she found it and closed the hidden passage. She continued her sweep of the bedroom before moving on to the dressing room. All the while, Vi tapped the floor with the toe of her shoe, listening for fake boards.

Most of the prince's clothes had been packed away when he left for war, which made scouring the shelves easy. Vi found two other secret compartments built in false bottoms of the shelves. One had a lock of golden hair, a silver dagger, and a pile of notes. Vi promptly closed the compartment out of privacy, suspecting the hair to be Raylynn's.

The other compartment held a key, the outline of which was visible in the dust when she removed it. Vi flipped it over in search of markings that could offer a clue as to what it might unlock. The skeleton key was fairly large, but otherwise plain. The only embellishment was the Solaris seal stamped at the end.

Unhelpful.

Still, Vi pocketed the key and resumed her search. The key clearly hadn't been moved in some time, judging from the outline it left behind in the dust. It must unlock something important for him to hide it. She just hoped that "it" was more than a chest filled with scandalous tomes of daring women.

As she'd expected, the prince's royal apartment was filled with secret nooks in almost every room. Vi scoured the place from top to bottom, not stopping until she could be confident she'd explored every one. She found ten in total, including one servants' entry and passage that was void of any possible hiding spots.

The crown wasn't in any of these locations. Nor was anything that the key could unlock.

She was just placing the last of the fabric over the furniture when the ring around her finger grew warm. A glyph sizzled in her mind, begging for release. "*Narro hath,*" Vi murmured.

"Miss me?" Deneya's voice echoed to her from across the connection.

"Terribly."

"Then your agony will soon be over."

"How far are you?"

"I'm just about to start up the switchbacks now."

"Meet me in the Imperial Library." Vi paused, remembering what day and age she was in, now. Vhalla was present in the castle. Her chest tightened in a way that begged avoidance at all costs. "On second thought, the servant's entrance, the one not far from the water gardens."

"See you soon."

Vi released the glyph and did one last sweep of Baldair's room. Wherever the prince had hidden the crown, it wasn't here. Vi pursed her lips and left, heading down through the castle to meet Deneya.

The servant's entrance was busy at all times of day. Boards lined the main entry with schedules and memos. Someone was always coming or going, and no one paid Vi a second glance in her palace robes.

She perched herself on a bench just outside, watching the night fall as she waited. Soon enough, the silhouette of a woman cut against the watercolor sky as

Deneya crested the hill.

"You're a sight for sore eyes." Vi stood.

"I'm marvelous, I know." Deneya smiled down at her. "It's good to see you, too."

"Let's find a place to board the horse. I doubt we'll get to use the palace stables again."

"Unfortunately." Deneya dismounted.

"I think I know a place."

"Lead the way." Deneya walked alongside Vi as she headed for an inn with a long row of stables that were usually unoccupied. "Any issues up here?"

"No, your end?"

"None."

Vi glanced at the pack the woman had over her shoulder, then to the saddlebags. "You have it?"

"Of course." Deneya patted her backpack and Vi could imagine the shimmering crown inside. "You find the real deal yet?"

"No, but we only just got here a few days before you."

"I know, that's why I thought you would've certainly found it by now." Deneya grinned.

"We need your help, clearly."

"Yes, you'd be lost without me," she proclaimed loftily.

"I did miss you." Vi nudged her shoulder against her friend's.

She snorted. "I doubt it. You've had a few days with Taavin all to yourself and judging from the glow around you, the alone time did you well."

Vi laughed and didn't even bother with a denial. "Yes, but now that you're back, it's nothing but work again. We must find the crown soon."

"What's the rush?"

"I'm not sure... a feeling?" Vi looked over her shoulder, feeling as if someone was following her. No one was there. The memory of the Tower—of Victor watching her movements without her realizing—was an unexpected companion in the castle. "I know Victor is usually the one to find it. And knowing what I know of him, once he finds it, he won't let it go."

"So we have to beat him to it," Deneya surmised. The statement brought Vi's thoughts to Baldair's empty room.

"Yes. But my fear is that we're already too late."

V I, TAAVIN, AND DENEYA BROKE the palace into segments in order to search for the crown.

Vi continued to search the royal quarters. Baldair might not have hidden it in his chambers, but he'd have access to every room in the Imperial wing of the palace. There were plenty more secret locations that were all potential hiding spots, and lots of locks for her to try the key on.

Deneya began looking through ledgers used by the palace guard. Vi supposed it was possible for Baldair to have entrusted the relic to his loyal soldiers. Though Deneya returned empty-handed day after day, which slowly squashed that theory.

Taavin remained assigned to the Tower of Sorcerers. He reported on overheard rumors, mostly from students; there were more tales of Vhalla's doings than anything relating to the crown. Whispers flew about how she had fallen from a tower rooftop and flown, how the crown prince was her personal tutor, and how Minister Victor wanted nothing more than to see her enrolled as the Tower's newest student.

Time whittled away Vi's patience. The crown began to haunt her dreams. Night after night, she could imagine herself touching it, feeling the magic of Yargen seep into her. Day after day, she searched for that sensation, imagining feeling it on the briefest shift in the air.

Just when she was about to turn the whole castle upside down, fate and stones and rivers be damned, the military returned to the capital.

Vi, Taavin, and Deneya watched from the upper ramparts as palace staff and citizenry alike funneled into the Sunlit Stage, waiting for the military party to march up the mountain and make its grand arrival.

"They look so small and insignificant," Vi murmured.

"From this high up, everything looks small." Deneya leaned against the stone, looking down.

Vi wondered what the world looked like to the gods. Did they stand on walls higher than this? Walls that kept mortals from their divine domains? She could imagine Yargen staring down, and every mortal in the world being little more than grains of sand to be swept around by her hand.

"Here they come." Taavin pointed to the military party as it arrived. Cheers erupted for the Emperor and Baldair as they entered, a deafening roar that rolled across the whole mountainside.

"They certainly love him, don't they?"

"They do." Vi stared down at the speck that was Baldair. Somewhere in his mess of golden hair was the knowledge of what he'd done with the crystal crown.

"I feel bad for Aldrik... to be so hated when your brother is so loved," Deneya mused.

"His hardships prepare him for what's to come."

"That's grim."

Vi shrugged in reply.

"Now that the prince is back, does the plan change?" Taavin asked.

"We'll see." Vi stepped away from the stone railing and headed back inside the palace. "I'm going to see if I can steal a moment with Baldair."

"Why does she get all the fun?" Deneya asked Taavin.

"Because this is her destiny."

Vi came to a sudden stop. How she truly hated that word.

"What is it?" Deneya asked.

"I'm going to go this way. I'll meet you both back at our rooms later."

"Good luck." Taavin leaned forward, planting a warm kiss on her cheek before he followed Deneya in the opposite direction, down to their hideaway in the bowels of the palace.

Vi moved quickly through the servants' passages. She was one of many hustling to get from one place to the next. The return of half the royal family, even when expected, had turned the castle on its head.

Servants flowed in and out of the Imperial wing and Vi fell into step with them. By now, the guards had seen her come and go so many times that they hardly paid her any attention. Most of the people went up to the royal chambers at the top of the golden staircase. It was the one place Vi had yet to look because it was rarely unattended.

A war raged within her as she debated if she had time to head up there now. In the chaos, she might be able to poke around unnoticed. Ultimately, Vi went to the right for Baldair's rooms. She doubted he would've hid the crown up in his parents' chambers, unless he'd given it to his father. But if Tiberus Solaris had a crystal weapon, the whole world would know it.

However, on returning from a long trip, Baldair might immediately want to check the location of his prize. If she was lucky, he'd lead her right to it.

The servants were bustling in and out of the young prince's room, carrying trays of food and drink. Vi stepped off to the side, heading for the bedroom.

"Just where are you going?" a man asked.

"I'm checking the linens," Vi said.

"I was just in there, the bed is made."

"Did you check the towels?" The man nodded. "Extra sheets?"

"Why would the prince want extra sheets in his room?"

"Do you really need to ask that? This is Baldair we're talking about."

"Oh, Mother above." He muttered something else under his breath.

"Come on, I need your hands." A woman tugged on the servant's arm, successfully pulling him away from Vi.

As he left, Vi could hear him murmuring, "I haven't seen her around before…"

She disappeared into the bedroom, which was thankfully empty. Vi headed right back for the fireplace and pulled on the secret lever she'd found before. The bookcase opened with a soft *click* as the mechanism disengaged. Vi hurried over and stepped inside, closing it behind her. She listened through the wood as the commotion continued in the common area. Servants bustled about in the bedroom.

Then, silence.

Vi counted to fifty, then opened the hidden door slowly. On light feet, she stepped out and closed the shelf behind her. She'd learned every creaky board in this room from her investigations, and Vi made her way soundlessly into the dressing room, then into the bathroom. There wasn't another soul to witness her collecting towels into her arms.

She poised herself in front of the bathroom door that connected to the main room. The bundle of linens was shoved under one arm. Her other hand was on the doorknob.

Closing her eyes, Vi took a deep breath. Who would she be? Who did she need to be in this moment?

"Yargen, guide me," she whispered. It wasn't quite a prayer. More like… asking a friend for a favor.

The door to the main room opened, heralding male laughter, and Vi sprang into action. She pushed open the bathroom door at the same time as Baldair and two other young men entered through the main door. Her eyes met his.

"My prince!" Vi said, startled. She juggled the towels, allowing them to scatter to the floor. Baldair's laughter stopped and he regarded her with a confused and somewhat amused expression. Vi dropped to the floor, hastily gathering and folding the towels. "I'm so sorry. I was supposed to be gone, I know. But I realized the towels had not been properly refreshed for your arrival and I was terribly worried by the thought of you putting a musty towel to your face."

The words raced from her with an anxiousness Vi hadn't felt in some time. She couldn't place the source of the feeling. Her mind was a dark lake, smooth and glassy. Perhaps Yargen had heard her request and this was exactly what the prince needed to see and hear: a panicked young woman, unassuming, innocent, and ready to flatter him.

Two armor-clad feet appeared in her vision, followed by knees. Vi brought her gaze up to the prince who had knelt across from her, making a clumsy attempt at folding a towel.

"Forgive me, your highness," she murmured. "Not only have I ruined your return… but you are now doing a servant's work."

"There's nothing to forgive." He handed her the towel with a roguish smile. "Every time I return home, I hope a lovely woman is here to greet me. Really, I should be thanking you."

"You're truly incorrigible," a man Vi recognized as Craig muttered as he shut the door.

"I think what the prince is trying to say… is that you have nothing to worry about." The other man was at Vi's left, and passed her a much more carefully folded towel.

She paused, taken aback by the familiar face.

I know these eyes.

Daniel. Vi had seen him in the North, but only ever at a distance. This was the first time she'd been close enough to him to see Jayme in his features.

Her stomach twisted.

"Thank you," Vi murmured, collecting herself and the towel from Daniel's hands. She was here on a mission. Vi cleared her throat. "My prince, I understand if you need to report me to my superiors for not having everything prepared for your arrival."

"You don't really think I'm going to do that, do you?" He chuckled and stood.

Vi finished the last of her folds, standing as well. "I don't want to assume the will of a royal."

"I'm not my brother." Baldair shrugged. "Though, perhaps you could do me a favor?"

"Anything!"

"Help me out of this armor?" He knocked his breastplate.

"Really, Baldair? You're not here more than an hour and you're already trying to get some woman to undress you?" Craig said over a mouthful of food. He'd wasted no time in heading right for the spread laid out on the table.

"The task requires an extra set of hands," Baldair insisted.

"Mother forbid we're the ones to help you." Daniel chuckled, strolling over to the table as well.

"If you think I can help, then it'd be my honor." Vi smiled up at the prince.

"Then, follow me—"

"Wait," Craig interjected. She and Baldair turned. "Do… do I know you?"

"I don't know. Perhaps our paths have crossed in the palace," Vi said. "I've been here for a few years now," she lied deftly.

"Have you ever been a soldier?"

"I know the eyes of a soldier when I see one," Baldair proclaimed. He rested his thumb on her chin, knuckle underneath, and turned her face toward his. The prince made a show of studying her eyes. Vi supposed this would be the part when the young woman he flirted with would swoon. But she still floated in that glassy, dark lake of her mind. "These eyes are soft, tender. They haven't seen the trials of combat."

Vi smiled sweetly and batted her eyelashes, keeping her laughter at bay.

"I could've sworn I saw you in the North," Craig insisted, unrelenting. "I know your face from a battle."

She knew of the battle he referred to. It was in their first year—a night filled with fighting and fire, a night when Vi had helped Craig save Raylynn.

"My apologies, my lord." Vi kept her eyes down, the smile falling into an expression that resembled distress. "I really don't think—"

"Oh you've gone and upset her again. Don't mind him, Miss…"

"Ivy," Vi said hastily.

"Ivy, a lovely name."

"And possibly poisonous," Craig mumbled. Baldair shot him a glare.

"Follow me, Miss Ivy." Baldair led her into the bedroom.

"Yes, my prince."

"'Baldair' is fine." He stood in front of an armor stand, arms out.

"You'll have to tell me what to do, Baldair." Vi said the name as though it were a new pair of shoes—uncomfortable and not yet broken in. Her attempt seemed to delight him.

"Start with the sides, there are clasps there—yes, you found them."

Of course she did. Vi fought the urge to roll her eyes. It wasn't as if she'd seen every type of armor known to the continent. Vi diligently worked on getting the prince out of his armor, refraining from being too hasty or skilled but not allowing his instruction to carry on for too long. She didn't want to hamper their conversation.

"How is the front?" Vi asked as she continued to undo the buckles and clasps. "Will the war be over soon?"

"You didn't hear my father's declaration at the Sunlit Stage?"

"I was busy."

"Oh, right, well, we expect the North to fall soon."

"You don't sound happy about that." She helped hold the armor as he slid out of the main breastplate. Vi waited as the prince situated it on the armor stand.

"I'm happy the fighting will be over." Genuine conflict shone in his eyes. She realized this was the first time she'd ever had the chance to really talk with the man.

"You don't like war."

"What?" He roared with laughter as Vi helped him out of his chainmail. "I'm the creator of the Golden Guard, the most illustrious fighting force in all of Solaris. War isn't something I shy away from."

"I didn't say you did," she said thoughtfully. "I said you don't *like* it."

Baldair focused on the chainmail that pooled in his hands for a long moment. "Who *likes* it, really? Other than madmen." His voice was soft and somewhat distant, his expression oddly vulnerable.

"I agree with you." Vi knelt down to unfasten his greaves. "You're right. Who would say they liked war? War is awful and the longer it goes on, the uglier it becomes."

"You're not wrong."

"You know, I grew up in Oparium." Vi shifted the topic.

"You did?"

"Yes. When I was growing up, we didn't have many stories of war, but we had plenty about pirates."

"I bet you did." He chuckled. Vi stood as he stepped out of his greaves.

"That summer… when you and Lord Jax and Lord Erion came to Oparium, that was what made me want to come to the castle." Baldair faced her. "My prince—"

"Baldair."

"Baldair," she repeated, glancing away as if still modest about using his name without title. "May I ask you something?"

"Anything, fair maiden."

"I heard a rumor you found the treasure. Is it true?"

Fear flooded his blue eyes. "I—"

"I'm sorry. Even if you had… I know, you can't say." Vi physically took a step back as she distanced herself from the topic. Baldair relaxed visibly. "I only thought of it now because of a story my grandmother told me when I was a girl."

"A story?"

"A tale of a vortex, of circles, of things repeating time after time—life and death, suffering and sacrifice, all hung in this vortex," her voice went soft and ominous. Baldair hung on every word. "She said there was one relic that could stop this vicious cycle of pain. It was the crown of the first Solaris king, bestowed on the true ruler of this land. That true king could command any loyalty, even loyalty from fate. He could bend destiny to his command."

His eyes widened slightly.

"Though, knowing granny… they were nothing more than stories from her softening mind." Vi shrugged and gave him a conspiratorial smile. "I merely thought, if such a power does exist… that you, a man of honor, would be the one I would want to wield it." She paused, allowing him to be enamored with her words for one more long moment. "If you did find it, then perhaps it's your destiny to use that power and save us all from war itself."

Baldair continued to stare at her before quickly plastering on a fake smile. "It's a wonderful story indeed. But I'm afraid you're right about it being nothing more than a story."

"No doubt. Now, is there anything else I can do for you?"

"No, thank you. My stomach insists on food in short order." He laughed lightly as they reentered the main room.

"We were getting worried." Craig's tone was the exact opposite of the sentiment.

"I gladly return him to you." Vi gave a bow.

"Gladly?" Baldair balked.

"Gladly." She winked and Craig and Daniel roared with laughter. "Excuse me, my lords."

Vi stepped out of the room and practically bounced down the hall. She'd put the crown in his mind, and Baldair would feel the need to go and check on it, if nothing else. But perhaps he'd also want to test if her words were true.

The prince was going to lead her to the crown. Now, all she had to do was—

She stopped in her tracks.

Victor crossed the main atrium, oblivious to her presence, and headed up to the Imperial quarters. Vi didn't know what business he had with the Emperor. But whatever it was, she could be certain of one thing: it wasn't good.

25

S HE WAS BEING IRRATIONAL.

There was no reason to think Victor's mere presence was a foul omen. Perhaps, when the Emperor returned, he summoned all the ministers one by one to give him updates on happenings in the palace. That seemed just as logical as the next thing.

Logical.

But not accurate.

In the years she'd traversed this world, across time and back, Vi had learned to trust her gut. More often than not, it was right. Sometimes, she had the wrong response—but the gut had the right sense.

Vi gripped the golden banister, staring up the staircase that led to the highest point of the palace. Without a second thought, she continued onward. Her brain tried to wander. The stubborn organ wanted to daydream about her parents living here and her being a girl, in this palace, rushing to meet them—all the trimmings of the happy childhood she never had.

Vi pushed away the thoughts and kept herself in the moment as she entered the Emperor's chambers behind another servant.

"Victor," Tiberus said from a nearby room. Vi followed the flow of servants and staff into an open antechamber, where the Emperor stood among weaponry and military fanfare. "You know I am very busy right now with the festival starting soon."

Victor's visit wasn't expected, then.

Vi kept her head angled away as she rounded the room to Tiberus. She held her breath as she accepted a piece of ornate plate from one of the servants undressing the Emperor, much as she had done for Baldair minutes ago. Tiberus didn't even so much as glance her way.

"I know, my lord." Victor's voice was deeper than she remembered it. He was still a boy in her mind. But the person before her now had the gaze of a man who'd set his sights on a prize. "But you told me to come to you with the results of my research on your future campaigns."

"Give that here," a woman hissed at her.

"Sorry," Vi mumbled.

Two blue eyes met hers. The woman tilted her head. "I don't know you."

"I'm new," Vi said hastily, turning away and going back for another piece of plate. She kept her focus on the conversation.

"You have found something useful?" Tiberus continued.

"Very useful. But tell me first, where is your eldest son now?" Victor said with a gleeful note. Vi was shocked he wasn't bouncing on his heels.

The Emperor turned to face the minister and arched a single brow. "Leave us," he commanded.

Servants filed out of the room with their heads down. Vi had no choice but to follow or be discovered. She trailed toward the end though, letting others go before her so she could listen as the Emperor continued to speak.

"Were it not for your manner, I would presume he would be making the necessary preparations for our court dinner for the start of the festival of the sun."

Vi rounded the corner as Victor said, "What do you know of the common girl named Vhalla Yarl?"

She barely resisted the urge to charge back. Pushing away the memories and daydreams of her own creation was one thing. Vi could keep herself focused. But hearing her mother's name on this man's tongue lit the spark in her like nothing had in years.

She's not your mother.

Vi knew that. She did. But the fire in her gut did not.

"Vhalla Yarl?" Tiberus repeated. "The name is not familiar. I usually make little effort to remember the names of the lowborn."

Vi continued to hover just outside the doorway. She folded her hands and kept her eyes forward. She was as still as a statue, even while the spark was an inferno within her.

"He has not sent one report to you about her? I'm sure it just slipped Aldrik's mind." Victor paused and Vi could almost imagine his wicked grin widening. "I am sure her name will be well known by you soon enough."

"Why?" Tiberus asked cautiously.

"Your son is with her now."

Why was Victor doing this? Vi kept her thoughts level. Was this to spite Aldrik out of a vendetta he'd long held against the prince for being the magical favorite? Or could it be more?

Victor knew by now that Vhalla was a Windwalker. Taavin's reports on the whisperings of the Tower had told Vi that much. All the sorcerers of the palace were abuzz with the presumed presence of a Windwalker.

If Victor was mentioning Vhalla to the Emperor, it could mean that he was trying to convince Tiberus to go hunting crystal weapons now that they had a Windwalker in their pocket. Victor was trying to make Tiberus the next Jadar, and convince him to use Windwalkers to get the crystals.

Vi had to switch the crown as soon as possible.

"Aldrik?" Surprise was apparent in Tiberus's voice. "Aldrik is not one to fraternize with—"

"Just what do you think you're doing?" The blue-eyed woman was back, grabbing her elbow and yanking Vi away from where she hovered in the doorway.

"I was waiting to see if the Emperor needed anything," Vi said, wrenching her arm away.

The woman's fingers snapped back around Vi's arm and she yanked again. They were back in the main room. Several curses nearly flew off Vi's tongue. Cursing the woman was better than splitting her in half. "You were eavesdropping."

"I was not."

"Foul girl!" The woman was a blur as she slapped Vi. She blinked, dazed. Vi had taken worse strikes, but this one was utterly unexpected and caught her off-guard. "I know what it looks like when one of your ilk is eavesdropping. It's why I don't have the likes of you up here."

"The likes of me?" Vi rubbed her cheek. Clearly, this woman was the mother hen of the Imperial domain. She'd been lucky not to run into her sooner.

Her eyes raked over Vi. "Dirty shoes. Windswept hair. Basic robes. Tell me and tell me honestly, were you appointed up here today or is this some clever little attempt to see the Emperor and his family up close and personal?"

"I was appointed," Vi said. *As if anyone would be honest in this situation.*

"If you're lying, I will have the guards cut out your tongue and hang it with the laundry."

"The guards won't do that," Vi blurted before she could stop herself. The woman only seethed further.

"Tell me who appointed you and you won't have to find out what the guards will and won't do."

"I was appointed by—"

"She was appointed by me," Victor said from the entrance to the Emperor's personal armory. "She's attending me today, to assist me in getting ready for the Imperial events this evening."

"Minister." The woman stepped away from Vi and bowed her head. "I am compelled to regretfully inform you that I caught her listening in—"

"Surely you were mistaken," Victor interrupted in a tone as icy as his magic. "She is one of my most loyal servants in this palace." He approached her. "Isn't that right?"

"Yes, my lord," Vi ground out, bowing her head.

"Good, come along then." Victor started for the door and Vi was helpless to do anything other than follow. She kept a few steps behind him on the stairs. Magic sizzled on her fingers, on her tongue. Even though there was a good distance between them, she felt ensnared; she was looking for the most immediate escape. Victor startled her when he spoke. "They hate us."

She kept silent, which forced him to glance over his shoulder.

"They hate us, *sorcerers*, because they don't understand. And what they don't understand, they fear. And what they fear, they seek to snuff out of this world." She pursed her lips, letting him soliloquize to his heart's content. "But I'm not like them. I do not fear what I don't understand." He reached the bottom of the stairs and stopped, turning to face her. Vi looked down at him, remaining a few steps away. "I do not understand what you are. But I do not fear you."

"You should," Vi whispered ominously.

A smirk cracked his lips. "No... you're like me, just a few steps ahead on this journey, aren't you?"

"More than a few." Vi's chest tightened to the point of quivering. He saw her. Somehow, out of everyone, Victor had been the one to see right through her. He could see she wasn't like the rest. Until now, Taavin had been the only one to peer into the corners of her that no one else could see. Vi hated that Victor, of all people, would be the second to do so.

Let him see your sharp edges, a voice whispered to her. *Let him see you have achieved what he can only dream of—an evolution from the shell of humanity that holds him back.*

Vi's hand tightened around the banister.

"As far as I'm concerned, you work with me, or you are against me." He took a few steps back, giving her additional space. Vi didn't move. "The choice is yours."

At that moment, Baldair emerged from the side hall, nearly stumbling right into Victor. "*Oof*—Excuse me, Minister!"

"The excuse lies with me." Victor took a step to the side and Vi saw the mask of a kindly sage slip over his features with the deftness of an actor's well-practiced costume change. "I shouldn't get in the way of determined princes."

"I wasn't looking where I was going." Baldair shook his head and his gaze met Vi's. She held it. He backed away as though he were staring down a monster.

"Is everything all right, my prince?" Victor glanced between her and Baldair.

"Yes, of course!" Baldair chuckled. "Now, if you'll both excuse me... I have a bottle of wine I've been saving for something special and I think the festival celebrations will be just that occasion." He retreated quickly and Vi descended the last of the stairs with forced slowness, not wanting to look like she was ready to race after him, even if she was.

"Even the prince fears you on instinct," Victor said to her in whispered awe, so that none of the servants passing them would hear. "I'm right. You are the woman from all those years ago."

Vi glanced at him from the corners of her eyes. So many had written off her similarity to a young woman they'd once met to faulty memory. Just a bit of insistence, and her agelessness had thrown them off her trail. But not Victor.

"I know you are." He took a step forward. "I feel your magic. It is the same."

"You cannot comprehend what I am. My being was not made for a mind like yours." The words resonated from deep within and Vi followed their will on instinct.

"It's the crystals, isn't it? They gave you this power. They have made you ageless." He stepped forward, encroaching on her personal space and staring down at her. "What else do they enable you to do?"

"More than you could possibly know," Vi sneered up at him. She turned to leave.

"Help me find them. Work with me. I am not Egmun. I will be a willing student."

Vi froze, then slowly turned to face him once more. "I would see this world burn again before I worked with you," she whispered.

The man before her was nothing more than an extremely gifted sorcerer. He had a sordid history. He had experienced triumphs and pitfalls, most of which Vi didn't understand.

He was as flawed as any other human and just as capable of great and wonderful deeds.

Except in Vi's world, this man had murdered the people she called family. In

Vi's world, he'd nearly cost her parents everything... just as he had in various ways across every other world, according to Taavin's recollections.

This man wasn't a stone in the river. He was a glacier, cold and unfeeling. That was how she would treat him.

"Then it is to be war between us," he whispered ominously and, for one brief second, Vi wondered if this moment had been an opportunity to guide him into more than the hateful man she had always heard him to be. Was it her insistence that he was wicked that pushed his wickedness over the edge?

"It has always been war." Vi put her back to him and strode out of the Imperial quarters. Her feet were hasty beneath her, but her head was held high. This wasn't a retreat. She was keeping two steps ahead of him.

Two became four.

Four became six.

She slipped into the back passages and began to run. Vi sprinted through the darkness, into the depths of the palace, keeping in a scream.

Though what she longed to scream about, she didn't quite know.

Vi slowed her feet and took a breath. She side-stepped behind a tapestry and emerged in a hall that led to the wine cellars. The soft clank of a lock disengaging in the distance caught her attention.

So, Baldair really was heading to the cellars.

"*Durroe watt radia*," Vi breathed and felt invisibility slip over her as she moved forward. "*Durroe sallvas tempre*." A glyph wrapped around her other wrist, masking the echo of her footsteps.

Light danced on the barreled ceiling ahead as Vi emerged into a large, underground wine cave. The walls on all sides, three floors down, were lined with casks. Most seemed new and well-tended. But farther down, the shelves became cluttered with cobwebs and caked in dust.

At the bottom floor, the barrels were locked in vaults. The wine was kept prisoner down here, most likely for its own safety. Some vintages had been exclusive to the Solaris family for generations. One bottle could be worth a fortune.

Baldair stood by a vault in the far corner. He held a torch in his hand and peered through the bars into the inky blackness.

"It's safe," he murmured. "No one has come for it."

Vi walked over, standing behind him, just far enough away that he wouldn't feel her breath on his shoulder. She followed the prince's gaze to the bottom left corner. The cask there looked like any of the others. Vi wouldn't have thought anything was different about it if not for the prince's sole focus on one, single barrel.

"And no one will use it," Baldair said firmly, walking away. The light of his torch retreated with him, enveloping her in darkness. Vi watched as that mote of flame danced all the way up along the walkways and out the entry high above.

"You're the wisest of them all," she whispered.

Baldair likely didn't even understand what the crown truly was. But he did understand that some powers were not meant for mortal hands. She pulled the iron key from her pocket and slotted it into the lock on the vault door.

It fit perfectly.

Vi extended her *sallvas* glyph to envelop the whole vault as she unlocked the door. Iron on iron squealed loudly as she swung open the bars. But Baldair was none the wiser, if he was even still close enough to hear at all.

She knocked on the barrels. Sure enough, the one in the lower corner sounded hollow. With a grunt and brute force, she pulled out the barrel. It was lighter than a wine cask should be and there was no sloshing liquid within. The top was nailed on clumsily, as if it had been removed once by an unskilled hand.

"*Juth calt.*" Glyphs flared around the nails, splintering the wood. Pale blue light washed over her face as Vi peered down into the barrel. Her pulse quickened; her breath hitched. She reached forward without hesitation, like reaching for a lover, a child, a part of herself that had been missing for eons.

Her fingers closed around the crown. The light brightened in intensity until the world went white.

She stood in a room beyond time. It was blindingly bright, yet she could see perfectly. Heat washed over her, but she was quickly cooled by unseen breezes.

A window was cut from the brightness. Vi looked through it, out onto the greatest map she'd ever seen. Hills and valleys rolled into plains and mountains. All kinds of people occupied these lands, making them their own. Cultivating them with the magic she'd bestowed on them.

She had bestowed magic?

Someone moved her head for her. The world around her changed as Vi's eyes looked in a different direction.

No, she wasn't looking through her own eyes. Because Vi saw herself enveloped in a bed of light opposite the body she occupied, staring back at her. Vi saw her body was hollow and fading. She had not been made for this world, and now she had no place in it.

This was the end.

Or, perhaps not.

"Time for time," a voice said, speaking with the force of every man, woman, and child on the earth below them.

"Time for time." The words echoed, but Vi didn't know who spoke them. Was it her? Or was it the body she was in?

She was suddenly falling. The vision slipped away as Vi reemerged into her physical form, where it lay on the cold floor of the Solaris wine cellar. She blinked several times, staring into the dim light her body was emitting.

Just like with the scythe, Yargen's essence had sought her out and she was helpless to try and refuse it. The magic seeped into her flesh, rejoining its other severed pieces and leaving only shards of obsidian behind. One by one, she would collect the last remnants of the goddess's power within her.

She would add up the pieces of Yargen until what the world had known as Vi was nothing more than that hollow, fading ghost.

Time for time.

"I know what I must do," she whispered to the living goddess within her. Vi would give her time on this earth for Yargen. The goddess demanded a body—in particular, the one Vi was merely borrowing.

She knew her true purpose now. Yargen had shown it to her. To fulfill it, she first had to peel herself off the floor. The next step was crushing the obsidian shards to dust under her boot. Then, she carefully put the barrel back where it was. Vi didn't suspect Baldair would return so soon after ensuring the crown was safe, but just in case he did, she didn't want him to be suspicious.

After that, it was merely a matter of planting the fake crown for Victor. "It's all going according to plan," Vi murmured. She knew Yargen could hear her. The goddess was watching and waiting in that ethereal prison for the moment she could be whole and present in the mortal realm once more. As Vi's presence faded in the world, Yargen's brightened. "We'll switch places, and you'll save this world."

Vi ascended the stairs and out of the wine cellar. As she walked, she fiddled with the watch around her neck. It had suddenly become heavy, constricting.

It felt more like a noose than a necklace.

26

"WE'RE LEAVING," VI ANNOUNCED as she entered the shared room she, Deneya, and Taavin had been using as their base of operations while in the palace.

"You found it." Taavin didn't mince words.

"I did." Vi looked at her palm. "The power is already in me."

"Where was it?" Deneya asked.

"Baldair hid it in a vault in the cellars." Vi held up the iron key. "That's what this was for."

"A miracle he kept it hidden and safe." Taavin sounded genuinely impressed. Vi was forced to agree.

"We're going to take the shifted crown and place it in a treasure vault or storeroom somewhere." Vi went to the back of the room, retrieving the fake crown from the sack where they kept it.

"Not return it to Baldair's hiding place?" Deneya asked.

"No, if we put it back in Baldair's hiding place, we risk Victor raising the prince's suspicions when he finally moves to take the fake crown. If Baldair has reason to think it's gone, he might raise the alarm and prompt everyone to look for the crown."

"Which would likely involve going to his father," Taavin murmured.

"Exactly." If the Emperor thought he had a crystal Weapon before the War in the North was over, it could change things dramatically. "Furthermore, the last thing we want is Victor to feel rushed to inspect the crown, or take it to the caverns when we're not ready, and risk him finding out its fake." No matter how good the shift looked and felt, Vi still feared Victor would somehow see right through it.

"So how do you propose we orchestrate Victor finding the fake crown without

Baldair realizing his hiding spot was compromised?" Taavin stood from the chair he'd been sitting in. It was positioned opposite the sofa where Deneya sat, a now-forgotten carcivi board on the table between them.

"Before we leave, I'll sneak into Baldair's room and return the key to its previous hiding spot. Baldair has already checked on the crown once and believes it secure. If we don't give him a reason to, he shouldn't check again," Vi postulated. "Deneya, you take the crown and hide it in a vault somewhere. Falsify some records with the guard that will leave just enough of a trail for Victor to follow over the coming months. Let's not let him find it too quickly."

"You got it." Deneya stood and crossed to Vi, taking the crown from her.

"And I assume I'll give Victor his first breadcrumb?" Taavin asked.

"That was my thought as well."

"I approve of this plan," Taavin murmured. "It keeps things tidy. No need for Baldair to go making waves. And Victor stays on track with the crown."

"We're glad you approve. You know how important it is to both of us." Deneya shot him a playful look and Taavin rolled his eyes.

"I'll go take care of this." Deneya held up the bag with the crown. "And let you know what trail I can set up."

"Then tonight, I'll sneak into the Tower," Taavin said.

"And I'll sneak into Baldair's room at the same time." Vi remembered the servants' passage she discovered. With her glyphs, she could slip into his closet unheard and unseen. "We can start for the North tomorrow and get the axe."

"There's a stop we'll make first in the Crossroads."

"For what?" Vi asked, not able to spare her voice from exasperation at the idea of another delay.

"I'm going to let you two talk that over. Be back!" Deneya fled hastily.

"Vhalla will head there with the army, and that's where you must read her fortune. In doing so, she'll charge the watch with her essence and link it to us and Yargen. That's the key to ensuring the—"

"Birth of a new Champion," she finished for him. Vi stepped forward, looming over the chair in which he sat. "There won't be another Champion."

"Vi, let's not do this." He sighed.

"There won't be," she said softly. "I've seen it, Taavin. The crown showed me."

She could almost hear the echo of his heart racing. His eyes widened a fraction, their pupils dilating. The air around him thrummed with anxious energy. Her fingers twitched, begging to reach forward and take the power of the Caverns from within him.

Return it to me.

He stood suddenly and stepped away from her and the movement jarred Vi from the almost trance-like state she was in. Her hand was outstretched, as if she had been about to grab him. But Vi hadn't given her body permission to move. She snatched her hand back, holding it to her chest as if it were wounded.

"What have you seen?" he whispered.

"The end of it all." *It ends with me*, she wanted to say. She would be the last one standing, before she gave the goddess her remaining hours. "We are on the right path." Vi studied his face as conflict raged across it. "I expected you to be happy about this news."

"Hope is a fragile thing." Didn't she know it. "For all I want to believe we're on the right path… the stones in the river remain. Our duty remains."

"Seeing the birth of a new Champion is not your duty," Vi said sharply. "Saving this world is."

"Part of saving it is ensuring it doesn't end," he retorted. "We finish things here and head West to the Crossroads. From there, we'll rejoin the Imperial army and swap the axe."

Taavin started for the door, but Vi remained in place. She wished she could make him understand, wished things were still simple, as simple as they had ever been, between them. But something held her back… only for a moment.

Vi broke free of whatever tethers were holding her, raced after him, and wrapped her arms around his waist. She clutched him tightly, her cheek on his back. Taavin's warmth seeped into her and thawed the icy indifference that had been trying to encase her.

He felt like him, and she like her.

Yargen's magic was quiet.

"There's a point when we won't be able to run from it anymore," she whispered.

"I know."

"Do you?"

"I do."

All they had ever had was borrowed time. Eventually the choice would have to be made to risk everything, and that choice was nearly upon them. The moment she held the axe, there would be no going back. The flame of Yargen would be extinguished. Its magic would be used to restore Yargen in Vi, and its ashes used to summon Raspian.

"Then we'll follow along until the axe," Vi said, sparing him the agony of spelling it out bluntly.

His hand covered hers. "Thank you."

She nodded and closed her eyes. For a little longer, they could enjoy these fleeting moments of peace; they could enjoy each other.

Because if what Vi saw truly came to pass… neither of them was long for this world.

It took the army a few months to finally arrive in the Crossroads. The military arrived carried on the back of desperation, a sandstorm on their heels.

Tales of Vhalla Yarl were whispered on every tongue in the days following. People spoke of her bravery, of the power of the Windwalker, of her running into the storm head-first and saving them all. Vi was certain there were embellishments here and there; much like the rumors Taavin heard in the Tower of Sorcerers, every story was more fantastic than the last.

But there was also truth there.

Vhalla Yarl had performed a feat that had endeared and indebted thousands to her.

Then, one morning, out of nowhere, Vi woke up from a tortured dream feeling filled with purpose. She slipped out of bed, well before Taavin or Deneya rose, and silently dressed. Her two companions didn't so much as stir as she donned the traditional robes of a Western future seer.

She traversed down the stairs and silently began to get the shop in order, placing things just so on instinct. Her hands moved like a puppet's, obliging silent commands she'd been ignoring since absorbing the crown. An hour had passed when she realized she wasn't alone. Vi didn't know how long it had been, but Taavin stood at the foot of the stairs that led up to their apartment.

"What is it?" The man was shirtless, his broad chest and sculpted abdomen on display. Vi knew it well. Her fingers had run over those carved muscles countless times since the day she'd made them. Seeing him sparked yearning. It sparked emotions in her that wouldn't serve her well today. So she looked away.

"It's today."

"What is?"

"Vhalla Yarl will come to me today."

"How do you know?" He approached.

"I just do." Vi shook her head, staring at the door that led to the main market of the Crossroads. It seemed so long ago that they'd purchased this place and she'd sculpted roses in honor of Fiera.

The sentimentality made her weary.

"Then today it is," he said without a trace of doubt, slipping his fingers into hers. Vi faced him.

"I need to do this alone," she whispered.

"You've never operated the shop alone."

"I know."

"What will you do about the illusions for your eyes? How will she believe you're peering into the future without them to make your eyes glow red?"

"I'm not sure." Vi shook her head, trying to shake off the creeping, crawling hands working their way up her spine. They'd grab hold of her mind and who knew when they would give it back. Her fingers tightened around his, holding onto Taavin like a tether. "Please, trust me," she whispered.

"I do." He cupped her cheek thoughtfully, bringing her eyes to his. "Immeasurably and completely."

"Thank you." She leaned forward, kissing his lips gently. "You and Deneya wait upstairs. I'll come up when I'm finished."

He nodded, his nose rubbing against hers. But he didn't step away. "Is everything all right?"

"What?"

"You haven't been the same since we left Solarin… Is everything all right?"

"I've been fine." She rubbed his arm reassuringly. At least, she hoped that's the impression she gave.

"Don't lie to me." He pulled away, staring down at her. "I see you."

"You always have." Vi looked back to the door. The market was setting up for the day. "I'll be better once we have the final crystal weapon in hand."

"Do you really think that?" he murmured under his breath.

"What?" Vi wasn't sure she heard correctly.

"Nothing, it's nothing." Taavin smiled. "Good luck today." He finally retreated.

Vi returned her attention to her preparations. She opened the shop for the day by unlocking the iron gate and pushing it aside.

"One more thing," Vi murmured. She unhooked the chain from around her neck and slowly placed it into a box on one of the shelves. How Vhalla was supposed to see it, of all things, Vi didn't know.

But this was how it was meant to be. Of that, she was certain.

There was nothing more to do but wait.

"Let's look in here," a man's voice said in the afternoon near her doorway. The sound shot electricity up her spine and she stood straighter, pausing her pacing to look.

The curtain to the shop lifted and Vhalla appeared, followed by Daniel. Vi watched as the brown-haired woman entered the room, running her fingers over the cases at its center.

"*Irashi*, welcome." The western tongue put her into character, and Vi sauntered over to Vhalla and Daniel. She leaned against the cases containing all manner of objects gathered for future telling. "Welcome to the finest curiosity shop in all the land. And what can I help you with today?"

"I think we're just looking." Vhalla stepped back, as though Vi was about to bite her.

"No one is 'just looking.' All desire." Vi folded her arms. "Tell me, what is yours?"

"Sorry to disappoint. Let's go, I'm hungry." Vhalla grabbed Daniel's arm, steering him to the door.

"There is not one curiosity you have, Vhalla Yarl?" She stopped short at Vi's use of her name. Daniel stepped forward, holding out an arm, as if to guard her. Vi smiled thinly at the unnecessary protection. "I know your winds will not tell you what the flames will tell me."

"How do you know my name?" Vhalla whispered.

"I can know many things, and tell more, if you wish it. The fire burns away all lies." She spoke on instinct, giving herself to the sensation that had roused her from sleep and had guided her all day.

"You're a sorcerer."

"I am a Firebearer." Vi nodded.

"What's your name?" Vhalla found some bravery, pushing away Daniel's arm and stepping forward.

"I've had many names. I could give you one, or I could let you choose a name for yourself. Then it will be something we alone can share."

"Tell me the name you would like me to call you. Invented or otherwise."

"Vi," she said simply, after little debate. If anyone in this world was to know her true name, it would be Vhalla Yarl. "Would you like me to read your curiosities?"

"Read our curiosities?" Daniel chimed in.

"I am a Firebearer. I am one with the flames, and with my eyes I can see into the future. You come to me with curiosities, *questions*, in your heart, and I will give you the answers."

"I'll do it," Vhalla said suddenly. It brought a smile to Vi's lips though the smile didn't feel quite like hers. This wasn't her joy. This was the contentedness of the goddess within her.

"You must pick four things: three to burn, one to hold." She motioned around the room.

"Are you sure this is a good idea?" Daniel whispered into Vhalla's ear.

"It'll be fine. Why not live a little? I am here, and somehow she knew my name," Vhalla replied as she scanned the items available to her.

The first thing Vhalla chose was a silver plume from a jar of quills.

The next item Vhalla chose was a bunch of wheat, followed by a handful of rose petals.

But the most important thing was the last thing—something to hold.

Vhalla lifted a chain from a box and Vi let out her breath slowly as not to be an audible sigh of relief. The woman had selected the silver watch Vi had worn through time, and the one that would ensure the birth of a new Champion.

Time for time.

"This… this is what I will hold." Vhalla crossed back to her.

"An interesting spread. Come." Vi took the goods to burn and led Vhalla to the back room where a fire burned in a pit on the floor. "Are you certain you wish an observer?" Vi looked pointedly at Daniel who had followed them. "I will read the futures as I see them."

"I suppose… if you don't mind?" Vhalla said to Daniel.

"I'll wait right out here." Daniel got the hint, and slipped back out the heavy curtain and into the main shop.

With that settled, Vi knelt before the flames. She raked her hands through the coals and Vi began by making a few soot marks on Vhalla's cheeks and brow. She hesitated for just a moment, staring into the brown eyes of her mother.

No, this wasn't her mother. *Focus. Don't get lost in old memories.* She didn't want to feel anything toward this woman.

In that moment, Vi didn't want to feel anything at all. She gave herself fully over to the guiding hand of Yargen.

"Vhalla Yarl, blessed bird of the East. The one who can soar without wings. The first chick to fly the cage. The first to return to our land." She leaned back and began to throw the items into the flames. With each one, she poured her magic into the fire to make it roar.

The flames danced from white to orange, to a crimson so deep it was nearly black. The color changing was new, and Vi had no idea what it meant. She leaned forward on instinct, dipping her face into the flames.

"The present burns away, leaving the future to rise from its ashes." Vi reached down, grabbed a fistful of ash, and threw it into the air. "You will march to victory, and it will be won upon your silver wings." *Go to war, Vhalla, and win.* "But the winds of change you will set free will also shatter the tender hope on which you fly." *Victor will rise to power, and nearly everything you thought you loved will be threatened.* "You will lose your dark sentry." *Only to see him rise again as an Emperor.*

Vhalla clutched the watch with white knuckles as she spoke. Vi could almost see the girl trembling.

"Two paths will lie before you: night and day," Vi continued. "Go west by night. Fade into the comforting obscurity of a shroud of darkness. You will find a familiar happiness there, if you can ignore yearnings for the sun."

Go west? Why go west? She wanted to ask. But her mouth was not her own. Panic rose. Vi wanted to claw at her throat, but her hands weren't her own.

"The other road will burn away your falsehoods by the light of dawn. You will own your wants for all to see. But take caution, for the fire that will expose you will give birth to an even greater power that will consume the land itself.

"And now, for payment."

"Ah, right." Vhalla put down her sack, her hands still trembling as she fished for gold.

"I do not want coin."

"What do you want then?"

"That watch." Vi's hand pointed to the one Vhalla had been holding. The one that had been carried from another world, marked by Yargen, and was now imbued with Vhalla's energy.

"This one? All right, of course."

Vhalla passed it over, and as she did, Vi felt a shock of magic shoot up her arm. It was the same feeling as when she touched a crystal. Her watch had always been an item of fate, but its purpose had shifted. The token now waited for the moment it would be returned.

"Our current business has concluded." Vi stood. Vhalla slipped into her shoes, all but running toward Daniel. Vi watched as they left, adding ominously, "Heed my words, Vhalla Yarl," before the young woman disappeared onto the street beyond.

She collapsed with a gasp, clinging to the door frame to keep upright. Her body had been held by puppet strings as she'd acted out the motions at the commands of another.

"This was what you always wanted, isn't it? A puppet in mortal form?" Vi rasped, feeling sensation return to her limbs. Her skin tingled in response, as if to say a delighted *yes*. She pushed herself off the ground, standing as tall as she could, but knowing just how small she was. She'd seen it, from Yargen's view: the world was little more than a speck. "You'll have it. But not for a little longer. Give me a little longer." Vi's attention drifted to the stairs.

Inside her mind, began a persistent background percussion.

Tick... tock...

The countdown ran not to the end of the world. But to the end of her.

27

ORICIUM WAS A DESOLATE wasteland compared to Vi's memories of the thriving capital of the North.

They arrived with the military as soldiers once more. The Imperial forces had been split after an assassination attempt on Vhalla's life failed. Baldair, Aldrik, and the Emperor all took a different path to Soricium, in yet another variation from the worlds Taavin knew. Unfortunately, Vhalla traveled with the Emperor. And since Vi, Deneya, and Taavin were under Baldair, they had a long march without eyes on Vhalla or Aldrik.

Vhalla was the first to arrive in the Northern capital. Alone. Something had gone wrong involving the prince along the way. Vi heard stories of Vhalla's heroism, and much like in the Crossroads following the sandstorm, each one was more impossible than the last.

There was no one they could ask for the exact details. So Vi, Taavin, and Deneya spent their days agonizing, holding their breath, and waiting. Surely, Vhalla and Aldrik couldn't die. At least, she wanted to believe that. But if the goal was to change things, then she had to become comfortable with *anything* changing. These people didn't mean anything to her, not really.

Yet, as the days passed, Vi realized she didn't want to imagine a world without Vhalla or Aldrik. They were not her parents, but much like Jax, they wore the faces of the people she loved. She wanted to save this world for them, even if they were nothing to her.

Or rather, she was nothing to them.

When she finally did see Aldrik and Vhalla, together again, in the flesh, Vi felt ten stone lighter.

"I knew they'd be fine," Deneya said as she followed Vi up to the top of the ridge that surrounded the basin that contained Soricium. They went to the axe together, Taavin catching some of the few hours of sleep he needed back in their tent.

"You did not." Vi glanced over her shoulder. No matter how many times Vi came up here, the sight still jarred her. The Empire had burned and cut down every tree of the forest, save for the most sacred, which remained safe behind the walls of the fortress.

"I did," she insisted. "Yargen is looking out for the girl."

Vi snorted. Yargen was too busy clawing at Vi's ribcage and skull, seeking control over her body, to focus on Vhalla Yarl. "Either way, I'm glad."

"Is the tomb far?" Deneya asked, changing the conversation.

"No, it's just beyond the top of the ridge." Vi led Deneya into the forest, following a familiar path. This was a new world, but her feet still knew the way.

"Seems like such an obvious place for the axe to be."

"Only because we know what to look for. The North is filled with ruins like this. The Empire doesn't know what's important and what isn't."

Deneya folded her hands and placed them behind her head, strolling. Ahead, the towering stones of familiar ruins loomed. Vi's feet slowed.

"It was night the last time I came here, too." The ruins looked almost identical to how they did in her memory. "It was the first time I saw the end of the world."

"Let's hope this time is more cheerful." Deneya clasped her shoulder. "We're only here for a look, right?"

"For now." Though Vi was already bracing herself for the first time her fingers closed around the axe. Each of the crystal weapons showed her a vision more vivid and important than the last. "The entrance is this way."

She led Deneya to the far back side of the ruins. Unlike when she had last been here, when obsidian had lined the opening, there were now live crystals with jagged points barring entry. In her time, her mother had taken the axe, and the crystals had died. It was the very act Vi and Deneya were working to circumvent.

Resting her hand on one of the crystals, Vi reached out into the network of magic and affirmed that the crystals stemmed from a single source. The axe was within, still safe and sound. The stones crackled and shrank to her will. Exercising control of them was becoming all too easy.

"After you." Vi motioned down the path.

"Oh, why thank you, fair lady." Deneya gave a bow with a flourish that made Vi bark with laughter.

"But of course, oh noble knight." Vi held out her hand as if she was escorting Deneya to a ball. With a snicker, Deneya took it and they dusted off the nobility neither of them needed any longer, parading forward.

Deneya's laughter faded as they reached the circular center of the ruins. Crystals lined the walls, pulsing faintly with magic. Moonlight streamed through an oculus in the roof, casting an eerie ring around the axe embedded in a crystal-covered pedestal.

"This is it, then."

"It is." Vi gazed at the axe, as though it were about to grow a mouth and begin speaking to her. If it could, the secrets it could tell. Judging by the power that hung in the air, the axe hadn't been moved since it was originally placed here by the daughter of the Champion. It was one of the few places on the Dark Isle where the crystals hadn't ever been touched. "This is a place of great purpose," she whispered.

"It makes me feel uncomfortable."

"Does it?" Vi tore her eyes away to look at Deneya.

"Yes... as though everything here is on a delay. Or that we've stepped into another world."

"Perhaps we have…" Vi trailed off. Her attention was on the axe once more. Her presence was already empowering the weapon, imbuing the air between her and it with divine energy. She thought of the otherworldly place Yargen waited.

"Then all the more reason for me to get this over with as quickly as possible." Deneya stepped forward. Vi matched the movement and the woman held out a hand. "Don't worry, I won't touch it. Just taking some measurements."

Vi eased away, folding her arms to keep them from lashing out. She'd lunge for Deneya to keep her from the axe.

Turning, Vi put her back to the weapon as Deneya began to measure the handle and blade. Some part of her couldn't bear to see another person so close to the crystal weapon.

Nervous energy rose within her and Vi began to pace. This wouldn't take too long. Deneya didn't need much. She needed to make an axe that was *relatively* close in shape and size, not perfectly identical. Vi would use the shift to handle the rest. They would leave soon.

What was taking so long?

She lapped the tunnel once more and froze as she reached its mouth. Soft voices echoed to her.

"Has anyone ever gone in?" That was undeniably Vhalla Yarl's voice. She was here. Yargen above, why was she here?

"In? No," a masculine voice responded, one Vi recognized but couldn't quite place. It wasn't Aldrik. Which then begged the question: *Why was Vhalla here in the middle of the night with a man who wasn't Aldrik?*

Too many questions, not enough time for answers. "*Durroe watt ivin.*" An illusion fell like a curtain over the opening. Just in case they somehow saw through it, Vi blocked the entry, crystals growing with a wave of her hand.

"What the—"

Vi clamped her hand over Deneya's mouth. "They're here," Vi whispered.

"Who?" Deneya said just as softly when Vi released her face.

"Vhalla Yarl and someone else."

"Taavin said she wasn't coming until the end of the war."

"Taavin was wrong." Vi cursed under her breath. "I've illusioned the only opening… they should leave." Her eyes drifted to the crystal axe. She should've just taken it and been done with this place.

They waited in breathless silence. *Let them leave*, Vi willed. She didn't know what it would mean if Vhalla somehow got the axe now.

She'd listened to stories of nearly a hundred worlds from Taavin's memories, and in none of them did Vhalla Yarl get the axe before the war was over.

"Wait, what are you doing?" Vhalla's male companion asked.

"We have to go in through the top," Vhalla responded.

Deneya cursed under her breath and turned to Vi. *Now what?* she mouthed as Vhalla and the man continued discussing the impossibilities of the climb.

"*Durroe watt ivin,*" Vi said and felt an illusion slip over her shoulders.

"Lovely makeover. You'll be so mysterious you'll scare her away." Deneya spilled her sarcastic words hastily.

"That's the hope," Vi replied back in all seriousness. "We don't want her taking the axe until we've had a chance to replace it with the fake." She had no interest in repeating her mistake in letting others take the crown.

"So you're going to scare her away." Comprehension lit up Deneya's face brighter than the soft light of the crystals.

"Try to. Help me?"

"Always."

Soft panting stole their attention. "*Durroe watt radia,*" she and Deneya both whispered in unison, a moment before Vhalla leaned over the opening above and let out a soft gasp as she beheld the contents of the cavern within.

Don't do it, Vi pleaded silently as she watched the woman inch toward the edge.

Her plea went ignored, as Vhalla stepped off into the empty air. Magic flared up around the young woman with the unique signature Vi recognized from her own mother. She fell gracefully to a large crystal, until her foot slipped and she whacked her head.

Vi bit back a groan. Out of everything Vhalla Yarl faced, Vi would rebel against fate and all the gods that wrote it, if Vhalla died from a clumsy slip and fall and *that* was what ended the world, somehow.

But Vhalla, thankfully, didn't die from a tumble onto a rogue crystal. She stood, walking through the room in awe, touching the tips of crystals along the way. Vi watched as they responded to her magic, tilting her head slightly. The pulses of power were similar to Vi's own early experimentations with crystals.

Vhalla's eyes were on the blade, as she approached with shuffled steps. She inspected it, closed her eyes, and took a deep breath. As if sensing Vi's watchful gaze, she looked over her shoulder, and then back to the weapon. Vi could see Vhalla's uncertainty and chose to capitalize on it. Dropping her illusion, Vi heard the softest of whispers from Deneya at her side.

As Vhalla's finger met the crystal of the blade, the whole room lit up.

Deneya's illusion of light faded into feathers cascading to the floor. The woman always had a flair for theatrics. Vi had known that since Egmun and Aldrik in the Crystal Caverns, and prayed it helped them once more.

"Leave it," she said, loud enough for Vhalla to hear.

Vhalla looked in her direction, eyes wide, like those of a prey animal.

"Leave the blade; do not take Achel from its tomb." Vi used the old name for the weapon, given by the Northerners. It was the name she'd known from stories told around campfires growing up. Vi rested her hand on the crystals behind her, allowing them to create an opening back out to the forest beyond. She'd long since let go of her illusion over the entrance. "Heed my warning and leave. Do not touch the magic of the Gods, Vhalla Yarl."

"Who are you?"

"I've had many names," Vi gave her standard response as an illusion slipped over her, washing her in light.

Deneya grabbed her wrist, and they both were enveloped by Deneya's other glyph, which rendered them invisible once more. Vi shared a worried look with her friend. They both returned their attention to Vhalla Yarl, waiting to see what fate held.

The whole affair must've overwhelmed the young woman, for she was on her knees, gasping for air. Or perhaps the magic of the crystals was too much for her, after all. Vi felt energized by them, but even she could recognize that the air was thick with their power in this ancient place. Vhalla stood and went for the axe. For one brief, glorious second, she hesitated and turned to the opening Vi had created.

But Vhalla didn't move as Vi had hoped. Instead, she gripped the handle of the axe and freed it with a tug.

Vi covered her mouth to conceal a groan. The noise was part frustration and part the uneasy sensation of all the magic that had seeped out of the axe over the centuries returning eagerly to its origin. The crystals around them went dark as the blade briefly shone brighter. Without magic to support them, the stones began to crack and shatter.

Vhalla Yarl sprinted past them, axe in hand, into the dark night as dormant crystals fell.

Deneya held her arms over Vi's head, shielding her from the rain of glass-like stone. She watched as Vhalla sprinted by them, axe in hand. Vi nearly lashed out to tackle the woman for the weapon.

When the stones were done falling, Vi went to the opening and looked around. There was no sign of Vhalla or her companion.

"Now what?" Deneya said gravely, emerging to stand at Vi's side.

"I'm not sure exactly," Vi said thoughtfully. "But this means we can't rely on anything from here on to be as we expect. We're done playing by Taavin's rules."

28

"THINK ABOUT THIS," TAAVIN pleaded as Vi stormed out of their tent. Deneya gladly stayed behind to pack their things. She clearly wanted nothing to do with the heated debate between Vi and Taavin over their next steps. "It makes a lot more sense to try to get into the fortress after the war is over, when they're negotiating the terms of surrender."

"*If* Tiberus negotiates those," Vi retorted.

"He negotiated for the West and that was after a ten-year siege. There was much more bad blood then to prevent such talks."

"He had brides to pick from, and he was a different man then."

"Fine, you're not wrong," Taavin mumbled.

"No, I'm not." Vi spun, fighting to keep her voice down so she didn't draw attention to them. "Who's to say he won't torch the fortress and all its sacred trees like he torched the rest of the North?"

"Are you doing this because you think it's the right thing, or is it personal?"

"This has nothing to do with me!"

"It has everything to do with you. Ever since you first stepped foot on this world, you've been trying to circumvent what must be done. You've been pushing against me."

"Maybe because you need to be pushed."

"I'm not doing this. This is against every plan—"

"Forget the plans, Taavin. Vhalla was there tonight. *She has the axe*." Even though it wasn't the first time she'd told him, Taavin still looked shell-shocked by the words. "We don't know what will happen next. We have to act. And, yes, the only thing that's important to *me* is getting that axe and seeing Raspian defeated by

Yargen, whatever that takes." She had to force the final words out. "But I know this matters to you. And out of love and respect for you—"

"For me? Not the world?" he blurted the interruption.

"Yes, for *you*, you frustrating man." Vi grabbed his hand, squeezing tightly. "I'm trying to honor your wishes because I love you. This is your one chance for me to continue setting up the life of a new Champion. Either we go to Sehra tonight and leave this place after, or we leave now and forget the next Champion entirely."

"You infuriating woman," he growled, taking a step closer to her. Taavin wrapped his arm around her waist, yanking her to him. "You have always made me act against my better sense. No matter the time, place, or world."

"I'm not sorry," she murmured with half a grin before his mouth crushed hers.

He kissed her like they were hidden away and not standing in the open among the moonlit tents of the Solaris army. He kissed her like it was their last chance to hold one another. She guessed every kiss from here on would be just the same.

"I know you're not," he muttered hot and low over her lips. "Thank you."

"You're welcome," she whispered in reply, eyes darting from his mouth to his eyes. Vi didn't dare tell him that there were one or two things he might tempt her with to prevent them from leaving tonight. She could already taste desperation on him for every moment they had left.

"Now, what's your plan to get in?" Taavin took a step away, though their hands were still interlocked.

"I'll need you to illusion us both—make us invisible in the darkness, or nearly so."

He pulled her down behind a nearby tent. Taavin looked around, then said, "*Durroe watt radia*." They stood, moving once more past the tents, this time with a glyph of invisibility swirling around them. "What next?"

"I'm going to hope that Yargen already gave me something I can use." Vi looked up at the large stone wall that encased the fortress. "She gave me a word for making and removing barriers, and this wall was made by Groundbreakers, which are a fracture of her magic."

"All right, I see your logic. But if this doesn't work?"

"Then we force our way in with *juth calt*." Vi shrugged. "It'll be louder and more chaotic. But we're invisible, so we'll slip in through the fray."

"Tactful."

"We're in 'making this up as we go' territory, remember?"

"Unfortunately." He sighed, though a grin pulled at his lips. If Vi didn't know better, she'd daresay he was enjoying this. Going off script was the slightest bit thrilling—if they ignored the fate of the world that hung in the balance.

They walked through the darkness toward a back section of the Imperial army where soldier's tents were fewer and siege weapons were in greater numbers. It meant there were less people here to take notice of them.

In the darkness, she and Taavin approached the wall. Vi ran her palm along the smooth stone. Normal workmen and tools couldn't create something this perfect. It was a wall fashioned entirely with magic.

Closing her eyes, Vi sent small pulses of her own power through the wall. She tried to understand it, much like she would a crystal. She stood there for several long minutes, breathing and feeling.

"*Rohko*," she whispered, imagining the barrier that was the earthen wall peeling back like a curtain. There was a soft groan and the sound of stone grating on stone. Vi opened her eyes, shocked to find an opening, much like she imagined. "Let's go, quickly!"

Archers patrolled the walls, so Vi had no doubt one of them would soon notice the break in defense. They rushed across a narrow flat area, void of anything, to a secondary inner wall. Vi repeated the process, "*Rohko*," and the wall opened for them, easier than the last.

She said a mental thanks to Yargen and pulled Taavin through. They emerged on the other side of one of the great trees of Soricium. Vi looked up. She never thought she'd be so glad to see the familiar branches. After spending years trying to concoct ways to escape from under these boughs, seeing them above her made her eyes prickle with tears.

"We should keep going," Taavin reminded her softly.

"You're right." Vi shook the nostalgia from her eyes and pressed on into the fortress.

She knew the pathways and stairs like old friends. Not much had changed between this world and her own. Perhaps Soricium was one eternal constant, built hundreds of years before rebuilding a world in rewound time even became a thought to Yargen. This one place stood, and would always stand. Or so she hoped.

Still, the Emperor torching it all still seemed a too-viable possibility.

They crossed a bridge and Vi paused. She stared down over the rope rail to the masses huddled below. Everyone who was able had retreated into the fortress before they erected the walls and the Empire closed in. Half the city was cramped together, living in squalor. But they lived.

Vi gripped the rail.

"If we truly succeed in seeing this world continue on… No more war for this continent," Vi whispered into the cool night air, speaking more to Yargen than Taavin. "Too much has been lost on this earth already."

Taavin didn't reply. He merely stood as witness to her quiet, idealistic vow, waiting until she was ready to proceed forward once more.

Up and up they spun on staircases, crossed bridges, and ascended into the heights of the canopy. Vi remembered the quarters Sehra had occupied before her mother died and she became Chieftain. They were the same quarters Ellene occupied after. She paused on the landing, raising a finger.

"That's where my rooms were," she whispered into Taavin's ear so she didn't alert the guard that patrolled the bridge between where they were and Vi's old chambers.

"I've never seen it before." His breath was hot on her ear as he whispered in reply. "I can imagine you here."

"Can you?"

"After all the stories you've told me, yes."

There was no time for further conversation, however pleasant the reprieve. Without hesitation, Vi allowed herself into Sehra's room.

She moved through the archways of woven branches into a side hall that connected to a balcony. That balcony flowed into a room that only had three walls. Curtains of flowers gave privacy to the room's occupant and reminded Vi distinctly of the Twilight Kingdom.

There, sitting upright on the bed, green eyes shining in the dim light, was Sehra. Vi released Taavin's hand and stepped out from the glyph. From Sehra's point of view, she appeared from thin air, and the girl's expression showed the fact.

"I'm not here to hurt you," Vi said in the old tongue of the North. The accents were familiar to her, no power of Yargen needed.

"Who are you?" she asked, sliding to the edge of her bed.

"A friend." Vi pushed vines of bell-shaped flowers aside, stepping into the girl's space. Sehra would be about thirteen at this point, she guessed. But even youthful, Sehra had the same intensity she'd keep all her life. Vi dropped to a knee to seem less threatening. "I will not hurt you."

"You're of Mhashan?"

"I'm of Yargen."

Sehra stood, crossing purposefully over to Vi. Her every movement carried regal poise beyond her years.

"You know of Yargen?"

Vi held out her hand and whispered, "*Durroe.*" Just like all those years ago, a miniature glowing orb appeared in her palm. But this time, even without the clarification words, the orb was sharp. It was a perfect ball of light, hovering.

Sehra lifted her hand; the moment she was about to touch the shimmering illusion, Vi released her magic and grabbed the girl's fingers lightly. She covered Sehra's hand with her other hand. The girl regarded her warily, but did not pull away.

"I've traveled from where your fate leads. From very far, indeed…" Vi searched the familiar face. It was Sehra, all right, merely twenty or so years younger than Vi remembered. "I've come because there is something you must do."

"For Yargen?" she asked. Vi nodded. "What must I do?"

She wished everyone else would be as easy as Sehra, who knew enough of the old magics, even at this point, that a small display was all the proof she needed. All that, combined with the knowledge that Sehra in Vi's time had been instructed by a traveler, led Vi to determine the most direct path was the best one in this instance.

Manipulation and suggestion hadn't really gone well for her tonight, anyway.

"Soricium will fall," Vi said apologetically. The words hurt to tell the girl. But her war-weary eyes were unfaltering in their attention. "When it does, you must see that your mother demands to negotiate the terms of surrender." Sehra nodded, continuing to listen intently. Vi braced herself for what had to come next. "When Mhashan fell, the Emperor engaged Princess Fiera—"

"You wish me to betroth myself to the Empire's dark prince?" Shock and disgust leaked into Sehra's voice.

"Fate is often most cruel when we hope it to be fair." Vi took a deep breath. She was toeing the line of saying too much, and she knew it. At least Sehra had come up with the idea of an engagement on her own. "You will return home a free woman. You will have two daughters… One of your own blood, and one of your enemy's. Yet both will have the power of Yargen."

"A Solaris will have the power of Yargen?" she whispered.

"You must nurture this power. When the time is right, take the eldest child. For her life, for yours, and for the lives of your people."

"You have made clear the will of Yargen."

"Good." Vi stood, releasing the girl's hand. She wanted to embrace Sehra tightly and tell her that everything would be all right. Vi might have, if a commotion wasn't rising outside on the walkways and bridges. The smacking of sprinting feet could be heard. Someone banged on Sehra's door.

"Sehra?" Za called through the door. Vi smiled knowingly. That relationship didn't exist beyond protector and protected. Sehra was yet a child, after all. The door opened. "There's been a tunnel discovered in the walls."

"Good luck," Vi whispered to the girl. She reached her hand back and felt Taavin's warm palm close around hers. The glyph surrounded them both once more, and Vi disappeared from existence as Za rounded the entrance of the room.

"Are you all right?"

"I am, Za," Sehra said firmly, still looking at where Vi stood. "I need you to take me to my mother."

"It's not safe."

"It is. There is no one unwelcome in the fortress." The girl turned to her guard, looking twice her age as she commanded, "Now, we go to the chieftain. There are things I need to discuss with her."

Za gave a bow and led the girl from the room.

"Why go to her, and not her mother?" Taavin asked when they were alone.

"I wanted the relationship with her in case our paths ever cross again. She'll be the one in the South. And the Sehra of my world said a traveler instructed her about what to do. I didn't have a sense that I needed to obscure things."

"A sense…" Taavin rounded to look her in the eye. "You said you had a sense in the Crossroads as well."

"I did."

"That sense might be the will of Yargen, flowing through you."

"Who knows." Vi looked out over the branches at the Imperial camp beyond so he didn't see the truth on her face. "Let's go."

"Just where are we going?" he asked, though he was already following her.

"The axe will be too guarded here. We'll meet them back at the Crossroads and take it from her then—before it makes its way south and into Victor's hands."

Vi's fingers twitched. *Soon.* So very soon the last of the crystal weapons would be in her possession.

29

"I AM SO TIRED OF trekking across this continent!" Deneya moaned from her bedroll.

"Keep it down." Despite herself, Vi chuckled. She very much shared Deneya's sentiment. "There might still be Northerners in these woods."

"After two nights ago? I doubt it."

Two nights ago... Those had been the final hours of Shaldan. They'd heard the fighting in the distance, echoing eerily through the towering trees. Vi could almost feel the earth weeping for the deaths of its children as she'd lain staring up at the canopy with wide eyes.

"I wonder what happened." Vi glanced in the direction of Soricium. "*How* it happened, rather."

"One war looks much like the next," Taavin said solemnly.

"You're right. At least we didn't have to be there for this one." Vi stared at the fire she kept burning magically between them. Part of her willed Yargen to give her some kind of sign in the flames that they were on the right path. The other part of her was afraid of what she might see. "We should get going for the day. We want to make it out ahead of the army."

"It'll take them weeks to move a mass of that size," Deneya said with a yawn. "We can get a few more hours of shut-eye."

"We've slept late enough."

"Lies."

"Don't you want a bed?" Taavin tried to reason with her.

Deneya just rolled onto her side, gathering more leaves under her head. "Look at this pillow, so lavish. Don't be jealous."

"Deneya—"

"Deneya is sleeping." She snored loudly for emphasis and Vi couldn't resist laughing. It felt good to laugh. So good that guilt made an attempt to follow it as if to ask how dare she be even remotely happy right now. But Vi shut out the negative emotion.

There was always someone hurting in the world. Someone was suffering every moment of every day. Sometimes, that person was her.

Vi wouldn't feel guilty for brief moments of joy.

"Shame that we'll have to leave Deneya behind." Vi extinguished the hovering fire with a thought and began rolling her own bedroll. "She was such a good companion."

"Indeed. Certainly did a few things along the way," Taavin said, packing up as well.

"What were they, again?" Vi asked Taavin with a grin.

"You know, I can't recall."

"They must've not been very important, then."

"Perhaps it's not a shame we'll have to leave her behind after all."

"All right, I'm up." Deneya sat. "And before either of you gets smug, it's only because you're both that terrible at teasing. I couldn't stand to listen a moment longer."

Taavin laughed and the sound was a recharge to Vi's system. Between the tense moments of guiding fate and holding the world together with straining threads, there were still traces of normalcy—moments of pretend. These, more than anything, were the moments that kept her human.

She vowed to cling to them until her last breath.

Traveling so light, it took them only a moment to pack up their basic camp. Vi led the way through the forest. She knew these trees from years spent underneath them. The thought they might have been in different locations than her world never even crossed her mind.

Even if the trees were different, she knew how to read secret signposts made by Northern scouts, hidden from Imperial eyes.

The sun hung high overhead when Deneya stretched out a hand. "Stop."

"What is it?" Vi asked.

"I hear it too." Taavin nodded at Deneya.

"Hear what?" Their long ears were picking up something Vi couldn't.

"A horse, in the distance," he said.

"Northern?" Deneya asked.

"No, they'd be riding noru," Vi said.

"This is definitely a horse."

"Are there many?"

"Just the one, I think." Deneya looked to Taavin. He hummed in agreement with her assessment. Deneya faced Vi. "What do you want to do?"

"Let's wait and see who it is."

They crouched behind the massive trunk of a tree, hidden by shrubs and branches. Soon enough, Vi heard the clops of hooves through the forest. The rider wasn't going particularly fast.

A messenger? Vi wondered.

Her eyes widened when the horse came into view, a rider slumped over in the saddle, barely keeping herself upright. Twigs and leaves stuck out of brown hair Vi would recognize anywhere.

"What is she doing here?" Deneya hissed.

"Don't ask me." Taavin panicked at the sight of yet another thing going off-plan. It fell to Vi to act.

"*Durroe watt ivin*," she hissed, stepping from underneath the branches and into an illusion. Her eyes were blue, skin paler, hair lighter. She looked as generic as any other Southern soldier as she called out, "Vhalla Yarl?"

Vhalla straightened instantly in her saddle, looking over her shoulder. She gripped the reins of the horse tightly. Her wide eyes darted between Vi and the path ahead, clearly ready to bolt.

"Did they send you after me?" Vhalla asked warily.

"Send me after you? Who's 'they'?"

"Who are you?"

Vi put her hands in her pockets and sighed. She glanced sideways, slowly bringing her eyes back to Vhalla. For good measure, she chewed on her lower lip, dragging out the obvious uncertainty.

"Mother, I can't lie to the Windwalker... Who am I? I'm nothing more than a coward." Vi chuckled tiredly, slipping further into the character she was inventing on the spot. "I should ask if they sent *you* after *me*."

"Why would I...?"

"I'm a deserter," Vi said plainly. "Got too scared of the idea of that last great battle and fled. We all did."

A shadow crossed over Vhalla's face. "We?"

Vi motioned to Taavin and Deneya. They emerged from their hiding places with their ears hidden underneath illusioned chunks of hair.

"We just want to go home and see our families again."

For a brief second, a look of disgust flashed in Vhalla's eyes, but it faded before it could gain momentum. The woman looked back at Soricium and sighed heavily.

"I suppose I can't blame you. I'm barely shy of being a deserter myself."

"The Windwalker, you'd never—"

"Don't tell me what I'd never do," she nearly shouted. Vhalla's lower lip quivered and it was then Vi noticed her bloodshot eyes.

Sehra lived.

That was the only explanation for Vhalla's presence. Aldrik had been betrothed to the chieftain's daughter, as planned, and Vhalla couldn't handle it.

"You have no idea what I've done," Vhalla continued.

Vi raised her hands as if to show she was unarmed in both weapon and word. This was not the mother she knew. This was a war-weary and fragile young woman, pushed past the point of breaking.

"Sorry."

"No, I'm sorry." Vhalla shook her head. "I should go."

"Where are you going?" Vi asked.

"I... I'm not sure." She sniffled and wiped her nose with the back of her hand. "I was thinking of the Crossroads. Seems like a good place to disappear."

Go west by night. Vi's own words echoed back to her. Had Vhalla left in the night, striking out for the West when all seemed lost, when she needed comfort?

Vi had let Yargen lead her in the Crossroads when she was speaking with Vhalla. Had Yargen foreseen this meeting? There was no other way for Vi to interpret the situation. Yargen had hand-delivered the woman before her.

And Vi wasn't about to let her go.

"Then, the way I see it, we're headed in the same direction and none of us wants to be found. Why not travel together?" Vhalla was clearly uncertain, so Vi added, "It'll be safer for all of us to travel in a larger group."

"I don't want anyone to know where I am."

"Who are we going to tell?" Vi motioned around her. "The army isn't here, and a bunch of deserters certainly aren't going back to report in."

Vhalla fumbled with the reins and then dismounted with a sigh. "All right. I need to walk the horse for a bit anyway so he can catch his breath. We can go together for at least a little."

"What made you depart so quickly?" Vi asked casually, taking a few wide steps to walk alongside Vhalla. Deneya and Taavin hung back. The young woman shot her a venomous glare. "Sorry!" Vi held up her hands. "I didn't mean—"

"I know." Vhalla sighed, her hands going up to the watch around her neck.

The pocket watch-turned-necklace was almost identical in size and shape to Vi's. But where the cover of Vi's watch was mirror smooth, Vhalla's watch had a sun split in half by a wing. It was a symbol Vi didn't recognize. But if she was forced to guess, she'd surmise Aldrik had made it for Vhalla—assuming the Aldrik of this world kept similar hobbies to her father.

Vi might not recognize the jewelry, but she did recognize the motion. *Like mother, like daughter*, she thought with a somewhat bitter note.

"I know you didn't mean to upset me," Vhalla continued. "I left because…" she trailed off, and just when Vi had given up on the woman speaking again, she continued, "because I found out something that made a part of me feel as though it were dying."

"Dying?"

"It's hard to explain." Vhalla smiled weakly. "My heart exists beyond myself. My life is not wholly my own. And the parts of me that were in another's hands were crushed in an iron grip."

The cryptic words told Vi two things. The first was that she had been correct in her assumption about Sehra's engagement. The second was a little less clear, but Vi was certain Vhalla was referencing the magical Bond forged between her and Aldrik all those months ago.

She wasn't surprised to see the young woman dancing around the topic. Bonds were rare and precious things. Knowledge of them could be used against the sorcerers who formed them.

"I think I understand," Vi said delicately.

"You do?"

"Maybe?" Vi gave Vhalla an encouraging smile. If Vi hadn't been there the night Aldrik returned south, if she didn't have fate's full picture, then she likely wouldn't have grasped all the layers to what Vhalla was trying to say. "At the very least… I have some idea of what it feels like to have a vulnerable part of yourself existing outside your skin."

Vi didn't know if it was her or Yargen who felt the sentiment more keenly. Despite herself, her eyes drifted to Taavin.

Vhalla's intention to walk with them "a little" melted into the rest of the day. Vi didn't dare point out that Vhalla was now setting up camp with them.

"Are you sure you want to stay with our motley crew?" Deneya asked.

"Don't scare her away," Vi scolded with a laugh, and a quick glance at her friend to say she wasn't entirely joking.

"It's funny," Vhalla murmured, focused on her bedroll. "I thought I wanted to be alone. But it turns out, it's nice to have some company."

"We're honored to hear it. Traveling with the illustrious Windwalker—"

"Can you…" Vhalla trailed off, straightening away and looking out into the dark forest. "Can you not do that?"

"Do what?" Vi was honestly confused.

"That 'illustrious Windwalker' bit. I'm not illustrious. I'm not… I'm not anything, right now."

Vi opened and closed her mouth, struggling to find words. The self-deprecating statements had been ongoing throughout the day, peppered through their conversations. One side of her wanted to smack and shake the woman, shout at her that this wasn't Vhalla Yarl at all. The Vhalla Vi had known was proud, and strong, and self-assured, but gentle to boot. She was everything a daughter aspired to be.

This Vhalla was meek and soft-spoken, oozing out between the cracks of a thin-shelled, tough exterior. This Vhalla believed every horrible thing she said about herself and more. They were the words of a young woman trying to find her place in the world and doubting at every turn.

For all her words frustrated Vi, they also softened a part of her heart to the point of aching.

"You're wrong." Taavin was the one to speak. Vhalla was clearly surprised that the man whom had been silent for most of their journey today spoke. "I won't even apologize for saying it plainly. You're wrong, Vhalla Yarl."

"What do you—"

"Know? What do I know?" He arched his eyebrows at her and chuckled with a small shake of his head. "When it comes to matters of importance, I know a fair bit." Taavin picked up a stick, poking at Vi's fire before throwing it in. "I come from a—uh—faraway town." That was certainly one way to describe Risen. "In this town, there's much lore surrounding fate, destiny, and the red lines of the Mother that link us all.

"Our stories teach that everyone on this earth has a purpose and a role to play. Their choices guide them to key moments in this grand, shared story. Even—no—especially you."

Vhalla continued to stare at him, eyes shining in the firelight. She sat, settling herself in her bedroll. "I can't, or won't, argue with your stories. I'll see you all in the morning." Clutching her pack to her chest, she rolled over and pretended to go to sleep.

Deneya slapped Taavin's shoulder. "You jerk, you upset her," she scolded with a whisper.

"I was just trying to help!"

Vi ignored their conversation, staring at Vhalla. Whatever she felt for the woman, Vhalla was on her own journey, just as Vi was on hers. She couldn't lose sight of what she must do.

Right now, her eyes settled on the strap of the bag Vhalla was holding. She was never without that pack, always keeping it close and clutching it whenever one of them drew near. Her heart began to race, and with every beat, Vi heard a resounding *yes*.

The axe was in that bag. Vhalla had taken it with her. All Vi had to do now was wait for the opportunity to take it from the lone, unguarded Windwalker.

They traveled together, all the way to the Crossroads.

There wasn't much time for plotting or planning on the road out of fear that Vhalla would overhear. But Vi assumed her companions were aware of the situation. She hadn't been patient when she'd made her move to take the crown. She would be patient now and move slowly and methodically.

"It's good to be in civilization again," Deneya said with a stretch. "I want to bathe for days."

"Me too," Vi said, glancing at Vhalla. She'd grown quiet as they'd neared the city. "I suppose this is where we all part ways. No questions asked, just like you wanted."

"And your secret is safe with us," Taavin chimed in. "No one will hear you're in the Crossroads from any of us."

"If I even stay here," Vhalla said quickly, a little too forced. She was definitely planning on staying here, at least for a little. "Thank you all for the company. The journey somehow seemed faster with you all." Vhalla reached up and took her second pack from where it was strapped to the saddle. "You can have the horse."

"Are you sure?" Vi asked.

She nodded. "I stole it after the last battle." Deneya roared with laughter that cracked a grin on Vhalla's face. "So I recommend changing the leathers from military issue, at least."

"We will." Vi took the reins. "Thank you for this gift."

"Take care, all of you." Vhalla waved and headed down a side alley.

"Follow her," Vi said with a glance at Taavin.

"Meet back at our shop?"

She nodded. The man stepped away and ducked behind a rubbish pile. She could see a ripple in the air when he emerged from his hiding place, now invisible. Vi only caught the faint distortion because she knew what to look for.

"Deneya, you still have the measurements for the axe?"

"I do."

"I need you to make or procure one as soon as possible for me to shift."

"On it."

Deneya departed as well and Vi went back to their shop alone. She tied the horse in the back alley, setting out water. Then, she brought their supplies to the apartment upstairs. It was evening when her friends returned.

"She's sleeping in an alley with one eye open," Taavin reported.

"We can make that sleep heavier with *loft not*." Vi held out a hand for the axe Deneya was holding. The woman passed it over.

Holding out the weapon, Vi encased it in a pulse of magic. It had been a long time since she had used the shift, and the magic felt rusty. On her third try, she finally got the weapon perfected into something she was convinced could fool Vhalla.

"It's unnerving watching a non-morphi do that," Deneya murmured.

"Don't worry, it's the last weapon—you won't have to see me use the shift again."

"I wouldn't say I was worried…"

"Taavin, lead us to her." Vi remained focused. Her fingers itched with yearning for the crystal weapon. She was close to it, terribly close. The axe was the final piece that would make everything fall into place.

Cloaked with *durroe*, they proceeded through the Crossroads as unseen specters. Her heart raced with every twist of the back alleys and maze-like streets. Behind every turn could be Vhalla and the axe. Any moment could be the last when she felt this insatiable yearning, this intolerable incompleteness.

Taavin came to a full stop.

"She's not here."

"Where is she?"

"I don't know." He dropped hands with Vi and Deneya. The illusion vanished from around them and Taavin frantically searched the empty alleyway. "She was here. I saw her fall asleep."

If Vi had been in Vhalla's shoes, she'd have kept moving. She'd sleep in spurts and always look over her shoulder. She wouldn't linger in the same place for longer than she had to, and she would change her appearance at the first opportunity.

Even after all this time, it still seemed she was her mother's daughter. Yet Vi had failed spectacularly at using that to her advantage.

With a grunt of rage, Vi spun, punching the wall of the building next to her. A singe mark was left behind from the crackle of flame around her fist, but her skin wasn't split. There wasn't even a bruise.

Taavin and Deneya regarded her with expressions she didn't recognize and didn't bother trying to decipher.

"We'll find her. Whatever it takes, we'll find her," Vi swore. The axe was in this city, and she'd be damned if she was going to let it slip through her fingers.

30

VHALLA HAD BEEN RIGHT to head to the Crossroads. It was arguably the largest city in Solaris, sprawling in all directions. It was also one of the densest and boasted a diverse population.

If there was anywhere the Windwalker could slip away, it was here.

The days bled into each other. Day after day they split up and searched, looking high and low. The hunt for Vhalla was like running on a track. Vi was exhausting herself and getting nowhere.

She wasn't sure how she could know every inch of the Crossroads and not be able to find one woman. But Vhalla Yarl clearly didn't want to be found. So she remained hidden.

"What's the plan for tomorrow?" Taavin asked, looking at the various maps Vi had purchased that were currently spread out across one of the tables in their shop. Vi had continued operating the curiosity shop in the hope that, for some reason, Vhalla would come back.

She hadn't.

"We're chasing a hare in a forest," Deneya murmured, staring at the red, blue, and green ink that marked different areas they had each explored. "This is pointless."

"We have to find the axe." Vi cracked her knuckles, folding and unfolding her hands to try to alleviate some of the restless energy that perpetually lived within her.

"I know that." Deneya folded her arms, leaning away from the table. "But I'm saying how we're approaching this is pointless."

"What do you mean?" Taavin asked.

"If you hunt a hare in the woods, you don't chase it all about. It'll outrun you, hide in holes you can't reach into, run to places you didn't know were there because it knows the woods better than you."

"Vhalla doesn't know the Crossroads better than I do." No one on the continent had a firmer grasp of all the maps of the world, Vi was certain.

"Clearly, she does."

"Fine, then how do you catch a hare in the woods?"

"Two ways." Deneya held up her fingers. "One, you use a fox—a beast that knows the woods as well as the hare."

"Fresh out of foxes."

"Vi, she's trying to be helpful," Taavin said with a sigh, running a hand through his hair. Deneya ignored them both.

"Two, you set a snare." Vi pursed her lips but remained silent, motioning for the woman to continue. "I think we have a snare coming our way in the form of the Imperial army. If Vhalla Yarl is here, she'll be drawn out by them—by the presence of Aldrik."

"Or go further underground. You heard her on the journey here, she was well and truly done with the prince."

"But she's not. She never is," Taavin said. "I think Deneya is right. This could be what draws Vhalla from her hiding place."

"I propose," Deneya continued. She pointed to the center of the map, at the heart of the Crossroads. "We have two of us right in the thick of it all between now and when the Imperial army arrives."

"You want to watch over the hotel where the Imperials usually stay," Vi realized.

"Yes. If she's going to try to see Aldrik, he'll be there. And she might try to sneak in beforehand."

Vi tapped her fingers on the table and then turned to Taavin. "You have any other ideas?"

"I wish I did… but all of this is new. I don't have a single past world to leverage." Discomfort flooded the words. He clearly hated that he didn't know what was coming next and Vi couldn't blame him. He was the one who'd always known what was happening.

Now, he was starting to have to play things by ear.

"All right, we'll take turns on who stays in the center square. The other one of us will patrol the city."

"What if she comes back here?" Deneya asked.

"One of us should keep an eye on the shop," Taavin said. "Both of Vhalla's visits to the shop are stones in the river. The second time is when the birth of a new Champion is cemented and the watch is given… While it doesn't usually happen until after the Caverns are destroyed, things are changing and we can't be too careful."

"I agree." Vi chose the path of least resistance. Even though Vhalla was still operating on the future Vi had told her when she was last here, there was a possibility she'd come back sooner.

Anything was possible.

Vhalla not coming back to the shop at all wasn't something they could entirely rule out. More and more of the world was changing, and that meant Vi had to come to terms with the idea of a world without a Vi Solaris.

"It's crowded today," Taavin murmured from Vi's side. He wore the face of a

Westerner. Vi was illusioned as well; they weren't taking any chances with Vhalla recognizing them.

"It is… Excuse me, sir." She tapped the shoulder of a kindly looking gentleman at her side. "Do you know if there's some kind of event happening today?"

"You haven't heard? Lord Ophain is coming ahead of the Imperial Army," the man said. "He's holding audiences for the public. I recommend you get in line if you'd like a word with him. I think it'll be hours before you'll get in, even if you line up now."

"Thank you for the advice." He nodded at her and left. She then spoke only to Taavin. "You should get in line."

"What?"

"Get inside that hotel and take a look around. Make sure she hasn't been hiding among the staff this whole time."

"I think the staff would recognize her, given her acclaim…"

"One would hope, but we well know how people only see what they want to." Vi squeezed his hand. "Come back tonight and report on whatever you've found."

"All right." He moved to leave, but Vi held fast.

She pulled him close, giving him a gentle kiss. "Thank you for all your help."

"It's my duty." Taavin smiled and gave a wink. "And my honor to follow you to the ends of the earth."

"Let's hope it's not the end," Vi called after him. She watched him leave with a small smile, one that slowly fell as she turned away. When he was at her side, the world was good and everything would be all right.

When he left, the world was cold. The only thing that gave her warmth was the flame of her purpose, the driving force of why she was even on this earth at all—to summon Yargen once more.

"Soon," she murmured to the goddess.

Soon. The word resonated within her, as though in reply.

Vi began to make rounds as the square filled. More and more people lined up, ready to seek an audience with Lord Ophain. Vi scanned each of them, looking for a pair of brown eyes she'd recognize anywhere.

When the Lord of the West arrived, the crowd erupted in cheers and fanfare. Vi kept her eyes off the man atop his warstrider and his military detail. She looked among the people, her eyes landing on a lone woman sitting atop a pedestal bearing a lamppost.

The woman wasn't cheering with the rest of them. She observed the world around her with brown eyes that had serious intent. Vhalla was smart enough to wear a scarf to hide her hair, but it didn't throw off Vi.

She made a wide loop, moving unseen through the crowd. Vi made it a point not to stare for too long, lest Vhalla sense her presence. Finally, she perched herself on a stoop high up enough that she had an unobstructed view of Vhalla's back.

The sun drifted lazily though the sky and Vhalla moved herself into a shaded nook. Vi remained as still as a statue. The woman didn't even so much as glance her way.

When the afternoon heat had scared away most of the people, a man emerged from the hotel, tapping his cane. He spoke in a booming voice that echoed across the square.

"Lord Ophain has taken to rest out the midday heat. Audiences will resume in the evening. Do not hold the line, we will form a new system upon your return."

Vi scanned for Taavin in the dispersing remnants of the crowd, but she couldn't distinguish him from any other Westerner. His illusion was too perfect and she hadn't bothered to study it carefully.

Vhalla moved, and thoughts of Taavin vanished. She went for the hotel and entered after a brief discussion with the man holding the cane. Vi shifted her weight from foot to foot to alleviate some of her energy. She hoped Taavin was in that hotel.

All she could do from where she stood was be patient, and wait.

The doors of the hotel opened shortly after Vhalla had gone in and Vi straightened from the wall she'd been leaning on. But it wasn't Vhalla who departed. It was a man with a thick mustache wearing a band of red crimson around his bicep. There was a symbol on the band drawn in black. From Vi's distance, she couldn't make out the details of the symbol, but she knew what it was.

A phoenix holding a sword in its talons—the symbol of the Knights of Jadar.

She scowled at the man from afar as he moved through the square. He consumed her attention with a familiarity she couldn't place. How did she know him? *Did* she know him? Or was this eerie sense of recognition merely the ghost of a memory from a past life?

Vi tore her eyes away, bringing them back to the hotel. The Knights of Jadar weren't her quarry right now. Vhalla was, and she couldn't miss the moment the young woman departed.

After another hour, a woman emerged from the hotel wearing the same headscarf as Vhalla. She kept her head down, and Vi couldn't see her face, but she followed anyway. Either this was Vhalla... or Vhalla had switched the scarf with a decoy and, in that case, Vi hoped Taavin had been inside to keep eyes on the real Vhalla Yarl.

Keeping her illusion wrapped tightly around her fingers, Vi followed a few dozen paces behind the woman. Tucked into a side street was a narrow bookstore. Vhalla went inside and Vi took her time strolling by. She saw Vhalla—for now she was sure it was her—retreat upstairs through the window.

Vi stepped into an alley where she could still see the building. At the very top, near the roof, was another tiny window. Vi held her breath, waiting.

A soft blue light subtly illuminated the ceiling of the top-floor room.

"Found you," Vi whispered.

She began to run.

Vi sprinted through the Crossroads and made record time back to their shop. If she hadn't known better, she would've guessed she'd flown rather than ran. Taking the stairs two at a time, Vi raced upward to their apartment, grabbing the satchel their fake axe was stored in.

She didn't bother to wait for Taavin or Deneya—she sprinted back to Vhalla's apartment. Her heart beat in her throat, making it hard to breathe. Otherwise, despite all the running, she was hardly winded.

The shop was dark. The woman she'd seen behind the desk was gone.

Vi rounded the building, looking for a back door. There was none.

"*Durroe sallvas tempre,*" Vi whispered, approaching the door. She glanced in through the windows, looking for signs of life. When confirmed all was quiet, Vi tried the handle.

Locked.

Vi let out a cry of frustration. She wanted to bang the door down. She wanted to storm in and grab the axe by force if that's what it took.

But she took a breath and stepped away, releasing her magic.

Vhalla had made a temporary home here. She felt safe. Vi knew where she was, knew she had the axe. All she had to wait for now was an opportunity to take it. The last thing she wanted to do was risk raising Vhalla's suspicions, sending her on the move again.

Still, Vi stood frozen, staring up at the window. She imagined the feeling of the axe in her hands. Her eyes fluttered closed as the phantom swell of power overtook her.

"Soon," Vi whispered again.

Soon, that same voice replied in agreement. Louder, this time, than the first.

31

THEY WATCHED VHALLA IN shifts over the next few days. One of them always had eyes on the modest bookstore. Sometimes, Vhalla worked behind the shop counter. Sometimes she wandered. But the other woman—the one Vi had presumed to be the actual shop owner—never left the building.

Someone was always there. And Vi didn't dare risk entering while they were.

When she wasn't watching the store, she tried to sleep. But that was an ever-elusive thing. Whenever she tried to still her mind, her thoughts went instantly to the axe. As if she could search for it even in dreams.

"You're still awake," Taavin said with surprise as he appeared at the top of the stairs.

"I am."

"I thought you were trying to nap."

"I was."

"Going well?" He made a soft *hmm* noise.

"Clearly." Vi tore her eyes away from the ceiling to look at him. Just the sight of the man nearly moved her to tears. "Hold me, please?" she whispered softly.

Taavin didn't hesitate. He set down the food he'd gone to procure, not even bothering to put it away on their shelves, and laid down next to her. He scooped her into his arms. Vi twisted so her cheek was on his chest. Her eyes fluttered closed and she gave a soft sigh.

This was the reason she could keep breathing. Her sanity was held together by his arms.

"I'm so frustrated and exhausted," she admitted with a sigh. "I'm exhausted of hunting—of this gnawing, needy feeling I can't shake." He was silent and let her speak, his arms tightening slightly. "All I want to do is move. And yet all I want to do is stop. Stop it all. Stop this relentless march of time toward an end that I both want and don't want.

"I can't explain it. But I'm being torn apart from the inside out." Vi pressed her eyes shut and pushed her face further into his chest, as if she could fall into him and away from the world.

"I know," he whispered, kissing the top of her head. "I know."

"You can't."

"I do."

"How?"

"I see you, Vi." His arms tightened around her as though he was trying to meld them like clay into one being. "Sometimes, what I see frightens me, or I don't understand it, or both. But I still see you. No matter how much time passes or what duties are piled on you. I see you."

"At least someone does." She smiled weakly.

"I always will."

"It's always been you."

"Vi," he spoke tenderly, his voice deep with emotion. Vi listened to it resonating through his chest. "When this is over—"

"Don't," she whispered.

"When this is over," he continued. "I hope I'm with you, in some form."

"I…" Her voice cracked, and Vi couldn't find words. Luckily, Deneya saved her.

The ring around her middle finger grew hot and Vi bolted upright. Taavin's arms fell from her and the mantle of duty replaced them. The moment of weakness had passed; Vi almost felt foolish for having it at all.

"*Narro hath.* Deneya, what is it?"

"They left, both of them. Bring the false axe." Deneya's voice echoed in her mind. "I'm going to follow to see where they go."

Vi stood. "We have to leave."

"What is it?" Taavin asked as she released the glyph.

"The shop is unattended."

Taavin was on his feet as well. Vi grabbed the satchel with the shifted axe and they were off. Taavin, luckily, could keep up with her as she sprinted through the Crossroads.

"*Durroe sallvas tempre,*" Vi said as she skidded to a halt. A glyph surrounded her hand.

"*Durroe watt radia.*" Taavin grabbed her fingers, making them both invisible.

"*Juth calt.*" Vi wasted no time exploding the inner mechanisms of the door lock. The storekeeper would never figure out how exactly all the pins broke at once.

Inside, Vi dashed up the stairs. In the upstairs apartment, her eyes landed on a ladder that led up to an attic moments before her hands landed on it and she scrambled upward.

The axe wasn't there.

She knew it before she began searching. But Vi searched anyway. She tore through the contents of the room and turned over the bed. Taavin helped, but they were done quickly.

"It's not here." He gave sound to her thoughts.

Vi cursed. "*Narro hath.*" A swirl of magic appeared around the ring she wore. "Deneya, it's not here. She must have it."

"I know."

"What?"

"I was just about to contact you. There's trouble on this end. We're in an alley behind a restaurant due west of the shop. She has the axe and is threatening some unfriendly looking men with it."

"Don't move, we're on our way." Vi released the glyph and jumped down the ladder. Taavin followed without question, even though he hadn't heard the other half of the conversation. What was Vhalla thinking, showing the axe like that?

Foolish woman.

Foolish mortal!

Vi headed west and found the restaurant. Just as she was rounding the side, she saw a man bolt out from a nearby alley. A sense of familiarity overtook her. Who was he? She'd seen him before.

A shout cut through her thoughts. "The Windwalker—the Empire's monster— has returned to wage war upon the West!"

Men and women emerged from restaurants, parlors and homes. They paused in the street, listening to what the shouting man had to say. "Look down there and find your brethren lying in pools of their own blood. Faces ripped open as only she can do."

Vi moved toward where the man was pointing, but Taavin pulled her back.

"Don't. She's going to be on the run. Chasing won't help now."

"We can get the axe," she seethed at him.

"It's true!" a new voice called. "Th-there's three! They're dead!"

Whispers and glances multiplied around them.

"Go find her! Give her to the Knights. We're the only ones who have ever been able to tame her kind. Clearly Solaris cannot be trusted."

"The Knights of Jadar." The mere words were poison to everything good in her life. "I should've known this all comes back to them."

"They're framing her for murder," Taavin grumbled.

"Not framing," Deneya said. She'd joined them. "Vhalla really did murder those people. But they didn't look like they gave her much choice."

Vi stared at the alleyway quickly flooding with people. Taavin was right. A manhunt was on and Vhalla would slip between all of their fingers once more.

As much as she wanted to rage and punch the wall at her side, she fought to keep a level head and refused to let her spark get the better of her. The Knights wanted Vhalla. The Knights knew she had a crystal weapon. They would no doubt try to unlock the Caverns to rebuild old Mhashan. That was all they ever wanted.

"By Yargen's light," Vi whispered. "That's it."

"What is?" Deneya took a step back as Vi spun to face her and Taavin. Vi's arms wrapped around their shoulders, pulling them close; she kept her voice low.

"I know where they're going. I know what's going to happen."

"How?" Taavin asked skeptically.

"I had a vision, when I touched the scythe."

"And you didn't tell us?" he balked.

"It didn't seem relevant at the time. Listen—*listen*—it was Vhalla. She was tied to a horse and was in Mosant. There were men with her, Knights of Jadar."

"How do you know it was the Knights?" Deneya asked.

"Let's talk as we walk." Vi's mind was moving too fast for her feet to be still.

She began heading back to their shop. "I know it was the Knights, because I saw one of them here, when Ophain arrived. He had a mustache and an armband with the Knights' sigil. I didn't make the connection until just now."

"If you're talking about the fellow with the magnificently ridiculous mustache, he left the restaurant with Vhalla tonight," Deneya said eagerly.

"I know, I saw him too. He's going to capture Vhalla. I don't know how, but he will, and he's going to bring her to the windmill on the mountainside of Mosant, no doubt on the way to the Crystal Caverns."

"A mustached man… Knight of Jadar… Schnurr!" Taavin's murmurings evolved into a single excited name.

"Yes!" Vi could see it now. Schnurr had been under Fiera's command years ago during the fall of Norin. The man she'd seen in the square had been a much older Schnurr.

"His death is inevitable, in all worlds," Taavin said. It was an echo of a conversation they'd had on the beach in Oparium, something she should've paid much closer attention to. "I wasn't even thinking of tracking his movements because he usually meets his end during one of the battles in the North."

"So he's never captured Vhalla before?" Deneya asked.

"No," Taavin said gravely. "Perhaps I was wrong about Schnurr, and his life is variable."

Vi had no desire to see Schnurr's life left to the hands of fate. Not when she wanted to wring the neck of every Knight of Jadar personally. But her focus was the axe, not the Knights or the man who seemed to be their current general in the gap Twintle left.

"We'll go to Mosant." They arrived at the shop and Vi hustled inside. "Taavin and I will."

"What am I doing?" Deneya asked as Vi rummaged through her bags.

She pulled out a small box and opened it. A hoop earring was inside—her communication token with Adela. "I'm going to call the *Stormfrost* to Norin. You're going to Risen."

"Vi, you can't mean—" Taavin started.

"This is it," she interrupted firmly. "This is the moment, Taavin. This is what we've been working toward, what every Vi and Taavin has worked toward for the past ninety-three turns of the vortex. We're not following Yargen's red lines of fate anymore. We're drawing them ourselves."

"And what if we get it wrong?" he challenged, though his protest wasn't as strong as Vi had once remembered.

"Then this ends. One way or another, this ends." Vi looked to Deneya. The woman had been a steadfast and loyal companion. "What do you think?"

"I get a say?" Deneya arched her eyebrows.

"You've been with us through all of this… I think it's only fair."

"I never much liked the idea of being the ninety-third version of myself. I like the idea of the world being trapped in a futile loop even less." Deneya grabbed her traveling pack from the corner of the room with determined movements. "I'd rather see the world end than be chained to the wheel of fate."

Vi looked to Taavin.

His eyes were fraught with frantic hopelessness. Vi crossed to him, wrapping her arms around his waist. She held him in an effort to bring comfort to him, as he had brought it to her.

"It's all right," she whispered, placing her forehead on his and looking him in the eye. Deneya packed, giving them some privacy with her back to them. "We can do this."

"If she goes to Risen, if she extinguishes the flame… that's it."

"I know."

"There's no more lingering essence of Yargen to restart the world. The last of her autonomous consciousness will be lost."

"I know." Vi sighed softly. "Everything ends eventually."

He pressed his eyes closed and held his breath. Vi braced herself with him. They would take these final steps together, holding and helping each other along the way.

"All right." Taavin opened his eyes and stepped away. "Deneya, when you go to Risen, you'll need to get to the Voice…"

Their conversation faded away as Vi sprinted downstairs and began to saddle the horse Vhalla had given them. Deneya would extinguish the flame and bring its ashes to her. Vi would extract the magic from within them just as she would extract the magic from the axe, and the remaining power in the Crystal Caverns.

After that, the only piece of Yargen's essence that was left was—

Her hands hovered midmotion, forgetting what she had just been doing. She let out a small whimper as if she'd been punched in the gut.

Taavin.

The only other remaining piece would be Taavin. Vi pressed her eyes closed and breathed for a moment, working to calm her swelling emotions.

Everything ends eventually.

Luckily, she wouldn't be far behind him. She would rejoin with the goddess, too, in a way. Vi remembered her fading corporeal form from her other vision. After Taavin was gone, all that would remain was Yargen, and the dark god she was destined to battle.

32

V I RODE IN FRONT, Taavin tucked in close behind her, as they made their way through the Crossroads. He clung to her as she navigated the narrow roads to the Great Imperial Way that would take them south. Vi didn't know when the Knights would capture Vhalla, but she suspected they hadn't in the two hours it had taken to see Deneya off.

Even still, Vi rode hard. Hard enough that Taavin had to remind her to ease up. They would surely arrive in Mosant before the Knights so long as they didn't kill the only horse they had.

They traveled by moonlight at night, and covered their heads during the day to keep safe from the oppressive sun. When the icy winds of the great Southern pines overtook the landscape, Vi knew they were close. The moment they entered the pine forest, Vi guided them down a hunter's trail.

By dawn, they arrived, their breath turning into clouds that caught the morning's first light.

"Look, there." Vi raised a hand, pointing to a windmill high on an upper ridge of Mosant. "If they're coming from the deep Waste rather than the main road, they should be able to navigate up the other side of that ridge without townsfolk ever seeing them."

"Is it the same one from your vision?"

"I think so, but there's one way to find out. Come, we'll go through the forest and keep out of sight."

Her plan made their pathway up the ridge much slower. At a certain point, Vi made the decision to tie off the horse in a circle of trees. There were ample shrubs holding on to their brilliantly colored leaves to conceal the mount. Continuing on foot, they scaled the mountainside, higher and higher until they could see the path that led to the windmill.

Vi stared at it, examining the door, the cracks in the worn stone; she took stock of every last detail and compared it to her memory of the vision. When she was satisfied, she finally said, "It's the same," and breathed a sigh of relief.

"So Vhalla will come here, then."

"She'll be *taken* here."

"Assuming we're not too late."

"I don't think we are." Vi scanned the ground for signs of a struggle. "They killed a woman in my vision in front of the steps. Even if they removed the body, there would be blood."

"And there hasn't been rain to wash any bloodstains away." Taavin ran a hand through his hair. He wore an uncertain expression. "So we're either *very* late, or slightly early."

"I'm confident in the latter. We had a head start on them."

Vi sat down in the brush, situating herself against a tree where she could see the front door through the leaves. Taavin crouched down next to her. After the first hour, he shifted to lean against the tree as well. By the time night fell, he was sitting with his side flush against hers.

"They might not be coming tonight," he murmured. The first spoken words in hours startled her.

"You're likely right."

"Want me to make camp down the hill, with the horse?"

"You can, if you want. I'd like to stay here and keep an eye out. It was night in my vision, so who knows when they might arrive."

"All right." Taavin stood, brushing himself off.

Vi listened to him go. She tipped her head back against the tree. The night was still and the evening birds were singing. Even when the world was nearing its possible end, the birds still sang as if nothing was wrong. Footsteps approached, and Vi turned to see Taavin there, holding their blankets.

"I thought you were going to make camp?"

"I am making camp." Taavin sat right next to her and threw the blanket over both their legs. He leaned forward, tucking it in on the sides. "You didn't really think I was going to leave you here alone in the cold, did you?"

"Maybe I did." Vi gave him a tired grin. After riding through the night, she was exhausted.

"I should be offended by that."

She laughed airily and rested her temple on his shoulder. Taavin gave her a light kiss on the crown of her head. He stretched an arm behind her with the corner of the second blanket in hand. Soon enough, she was bundled against him.

"Do you want to rest?" Vi murmured, already feeling sleep overtake her.

"No, I'll take first watch."

"All right." She yawned. "Wake me if you see the Knights."

"I will," he promised.

Vi slept surprisingly well that night. The next morning, she and Taavin watched the windmill's sole occupant—an elderly woman—make her way into town. She did not so much as glance in their direction as she passed the thick brush concealing them.

The woman being alive meant for certain they'd made it before the Knights, which helped Vi sleep even sounder the second night. It was still possible that things had changed so much between her vision and now that they wouldn't bring Vhalla here. Vi mentally gave them two more days before they would split up; he would wait here and she would head off to the Crystal Caverns.

Even if the world had changed since her vision and Knights didn't come to the windmill, she knew they would end up there. They always did. In every world, the crystal weapons sought to be returned to the Caverns.

Vi was dozing when the thunder of hooves startled her. She straightened and listened carefully.

"I hear it too," Taavin whispered as he hastily folded their blankets.

Sure enough, a group rode up. Vi recognized Schnurr at its head. Vhalla was tied to a horse in the center, looking even worse than she had in Vi's vision with heavy shackles, inlaid with crystals, around her wrists. Vi balled her hands into a fist and gritted her teeth. She wasn't sure which made her angrier: the fact that the Knights of Jadar were a perpetual thorn in her side, or what they had done to Vhalla.

She and Taavin remained crouched low, holding their breath, and watched what unfolded through breaks in the brush.

The elderly woman they'd seen before came out to greet the travelers on her doorstep. She couldn't get out a word before Schnurr skewered her through the eye with his sword. Vi didn't even wince as he cast the woman aside. Her corpse landed in an identical position to the vision Vi had seen.

"It's the same," she whispered as quietly as possible into Taavin's ear.

"Good."

She didn't know if she'd call this "good" but it was at least playing out just as Yargen had showed her. The Knights of Jadar untied Vhalla from the saddle and carried her in. Vi watched for a second time as the woman was thrown unceremoniously onto bags of grain. The group followed her inside and the door closed behind them.

"What now?" Taavin whispered.

"I... don't know," Vi admitted. "This is everything I saw."

Taavin pursed his lips, clearly thinking over their options. "Well, we know they're going to take her to the Crystal Caverns."

"Yes, and we can't let them do that."

"Do you want to free her, then?" he asked. "We're not playing by the rules anymore, right? We don't care if we change fate. This is it."

Vi struggled to find words. "Who are you, and what have you done with my Taavin?"

"I will always be your Taavin." He gripped her hand.

"Let's wait and observe," Vi declared. "We'll move when an opening presents itself."

"You've always been good at seeing opportunities."

She gave him a weary smile and brought her attention back to the windmill.

Night fell. The movement in the windmill settled and Vi assumed everyone had lain down to rest. She wondered how much closer she'd let them get to the Crystal Caverns. She'd killed Knights there before; she could gladly do it again. Perhaps she'd ambush them when they left. The creative and delicious possibilities for destroying them were endless.

"What was that?" Taavin whispered in the still night.

"I didn't hear anything."

"Listen," he hissed and cupped his hand around his ear, leaning toward the windmill.

Vi did the same motion and closed her eyes, focusing. Sure enough, there were dull thuds coming from within the windmill.

"Wind scum!" someone shouted.

"*Durroe watt radia,*" Vi said as she bolted from the brush, dashing over to one of the windows. She was barely tall enough to see inside, even if she jumped. But she bounced like a fool to get glimpses of the fight raging within.

Vhalla, still cuffed, was managing to hold her own against the Knights. She was fumbling with a key, trying desperately to remove the cuffs.

Vi jumped again.

The tides of the skirmish had changed. The Knights were advancing. One held the crystal weapon. Vi's heart raced even faster.

"Kill the wind bitch!" a man shouted. The other raised the axe.

She could let Vhalla die. If they weren't working toward the birth of a new Champion any longer, Vhalla wasn't technically needed. She could let them fight it out, kill whoever was left, and take the axe. No one would know what happened to it. If she let Vhalla and the Knights die here and now, everyone who knew about the axe's whereabouts would be dead. In one fell swoop, every loose end would be tied. It'd be clean. No one would come hunting for Vi and she'd finally, *finally* have the axe.

Vi pushed the thoughts away in horror.

No, that wasn't clean in the slightest. That wasn't right, or just. There was still no magic from Vhalla. The woman wasn't fighting back with the ferocity Vi knew she possessed.

Vi had to intervene.

She threw out her hand and cast a ball of flame toward the door. The wood caught instantly and the flames darted within, as if her magic was seeking out the axe itself.

"Vi, that's enough!" Taavin hissed from their hiding place. Her eyes were on the dancing flames eagerly consuming her magic and growing in size. She imagined those sacks of wheat they'd thrown Vhalla onto; it would burn just like the wheat Vi had thrown into the fire in the curiosity shop. "Stop, or you'll kill Vhalla too!"

She withdrew, both in person and in magic. Vi retreated into the bushes, lowering the flames just as Vhalla emerged, sprinting down the front steps of the windmill.

The young woman looked around frantically. "Aldrik?" she called.

Your prince didn't come for you. But from a world away, Vi had. She didn't know if she'd saved Vhalla, or risked killing her with her improvisation. Yargen only knew the truth.

Vhalla wasted no time mounting a horse. She still had the axe, stashed away now in a saddlebag. Vi continued to stare, eyes glinting in the firelight, wondering if saving her and burning the Knights had been the right decision... or if it had somehow cost them their world for a final time.

As if sensing her piercing gaze, Vhalla glanced over her shoulder in their direction as Taavin gripped her ankle and whispered, "*Durroe watt radia.*" Vi hadn't even realized her glyph had fallen when she'd started the fire.

If Vhalla saw anything, it was only for a moment, before Vi vanished from existence and remained the unseen hand of the Solaris Empire.

33

VHALLA RODE INTO MOSANT. Vi emerged from the brush, watching her descend the ridge. Men and women, up at this late hour, greeted her.

"What now?" Taavin asked. She hadn't even heard him come up to her side.

"She'll be too well-attended for us to take the axe here."

"Why not just grab it?"

"Because if we grabbed it by force, Vhalla would fight us. Knowing her, she'd do so to the death. I don't know if she fully understands what she has or not... but given how carefully she's kept it secret, I think she has some idea." Vi had employed similar logic when she'd decided not to take the crown.

"If we're committing to this being the end of the vortex, then we don't need her anymore." His thoughts had run parallel to hers, and Vi hated it.

I need her, a voice all Vi's own shouted from within. "I don't want to kill her," Vi admitted.

"You could've fooled me with that fire."

"I know. It was impulsive."

"Your impulses have always been as wild as your flames."

One side was her, the other was Yargen. Success or failure seemed to depend on if she was the one in control or not. *Had Yargen been the one in control of that fire?*

"I don't *want* to act impulsively," Vi murmured, dismissing the notion with a shake of her head. She had to move forward. "The least impulsive thing to do would be remove ourselves for a while and stop chasing after the axe. We know where it will ultimately end up and we can wait for it to arrive."

"The Caverns."

"Exactly. No matter how much has changed… I know Victor. The only time he'll relent in his search for the power of the crystals is when he's dead," Vi said bitterly, her eyes still on Vhalla below. "Let's allow fate to bring the axe to us."

People were beginning to stream out of their homes. Vi noticed more and more turning in their direction. The windmill still burned.

"It's time to go." She retreated away from the ridge and Taavin followed her. They hiked down to their horse and rode through the familiar forest, back to the cabin that still stood at the foot of the Crystal Caverns.

The grip of winter was undeniable. It wouldn't be long until the first snowfall of the season blanketed the entire mountainside. Vi sat at the entrance to the Crystal Caverns with Taavin, waiting as they had every day for weeks.

"What if they're not coming?" she was finally forced to wonder aloud.

"They always—" He stopped himself short, realizing that referencing what had "always" happened was now unhelpful. "Maybe things have changed too much and Victor won't go after the axe. We could go to them and see what's been happening? There may be an opportunity to take it at the palace." Vi chewed over this idea. "We'll take the main path toward Solarin. There's no way we'll miss them on the way."

"If we leave now, we'll make it just after nightfall." Vi stood and extended her hand to Taavin. "One last time to Solarin?"

He took her hand and Vi helped him up.

Sure enough, they made it to the palace in the early evening. Their gold was starting to run dry, but at least they had enough to board the horse. Vi and Taavin slipped into the palace—an act that was now second nature—and headed for the Tower of Sorcerers.

The Tower was quiet. Vi and Taavin moved unseen. She'd been planning to head to Victor's office first—at least, until she saw a haggard man stumbling into the Tower library.

"Where are you going?" Taavin hissed as she tugged him in that direction.

"It's Aldrik."

"So?"

"Wherever Aldrik is, Vhalla usually isn't far behind. She was the last one to have the axe, so it makes sense to check with her first."

Taavin relented, and followed her into the library.

The crown prince swayed, rubbing his eyes and shaking his head. He looked drunk, but Vi couldn't tell for sure. He began rummaging through the shelves, picking up a book and dropping it heavily on a table before reaching for the next.

Just what had transpired here while they were waiting for the axe? Was the prince's state some indication of foul play?

As if guided by fate, Vhalla appeared in the doorway. The young woman watched the man for a while, before announcing her presence with a soft, "My prince."

"What—when did you get here?"

"Aldrik, what's wrong?"

"Baldair. He's sick, Vhalla."

Vi watched the exchange. A rush of heat went to her head and her stomach churned, as though she was the one who was sick. She'd overlooked the first rule

Taavin had taught her in these past weeks of waiting: Yargen always demanded her due. Even in changed worlds. The ink on the pages of some people's destiny was long dried.

"It's serious, isn't it?"

"It started as a cold, aches, chills. It's autumn fever."

The two continued speaking, but Vi tuned out the majority of the conversation. She should feel grateful, she presumed. In her world, Baldair died the first time he headed to war. He'd been barely eighteen. She'd prevented that; now, he was twenty-two. She'd bought him three years. It hardly seemed like much of anything at all, but to the people who loved him…

She could see the pain on Aldrik's and Vhalla's faces as they spoke of a man they so clearly loved. *Family*. She remembered what it felt like to lose that.

The two left the library and it was only then that Vi realized her ears had been full of ringing that was just now beginning to fade.

"Are they going to see him?" she whispered.

"Yes," Taavin replied from her side.

"He's going to die."

"I think so."

Vi released her glyph.

"Where are you going?" Taavin was on his feet as well, appearing out of thin air.

"I don't know yet." Vi looked to him, holding out her hand. "Come with me?"

He took her waiting palm and that was all the affirmation she needed. This man was going to follow her to the ends of the earth, but asking him to follow her into the room of a dying man felt like too much.

Vi wandered the palace. Her feet felt the weight of every Vi before her. The ghost of every Solaris was over her shoulders, looking down at her, wondering how—with all the powers she possessed—she could not stop such misfortune from befalling them.

Vi ignored them. She had done her best. Every version of herself had done her best. That much was all Vi could believe.

She walked to the entrance of the royal quarters. Vi could almost smell the sick in the air from where she stood, hidden behind a corner so the guards didn't see.

"What do you want to do?" Taavin asked in a whisper.

"I want…" She shook her head, sending the notion that had been creeping across her mind scattering like rats. "I want to get away from here. There's nothing… there's nothing for me if I stay."

They retreated into the depths of the castle and slept in their old hideaway. But nightmares of Baldair and Raylynn filled her mind. They haunted her all throughout the next day, and those thoughts brought Vi back to the entrance of the royal quarters. Taavin had agreed to wait for her in the Tower library at her request.

She needed to do this alone.

Vi disguised herself as a cleric to pass by the guards. Then, she waited outside the prince's door. She stood in the hallway till her feet ached, unable to bring herself to enter, doubting every movement until now.

Just when she was about to turn away, Aldrik bolted from Baldair's room. Vi quickly stepped down the hall and uttered *durroe* so he wouldn't see her suspiciously lingering. When Aldrik returned, it was with a cleric. Vhalla Yarl was escorted out next; she was covered in blood that wasn't her own. Aldrik brought her through a door across the hall and Vi seized the opportunity.

She relaxed the glyph around her fingers. With the clothing of a cleric, she boldly stepped inside Prince Baldair's chambers. Clerical supplies filled the once-happy room like tiny tombstones.

"Just one of you?" a man said. Vi recognized him by his attire as a head cleric.

"I think more are coming," Vi said, hoping she wasn't wrong. She had no idea what she was doing, but it was too late to back out now.

"Good, we need the hands. Now, bring me those rags."

Vi grabbed a pile of rags that had been set on a low table by the door. She carried them though a side door and into the prince's bedroom. Here, the stench of illness was so thick that Vi was surprised she couldn't see it in the air.

The golden prince was coated in blood, doubled over and coughing.

"Don't just stand there, girl. Put them down and hold this," the man said sharply, motioning to the bucket in his hands.

Vi placed the rags at the foot of the bed and did as she was told. The head cleric left the room immediately and Vi could hear him clanking around the clerical supplies as Baldair heaved monumental coughs, blood and spittle coming up with each one. When he seemed to find a reprieve, Vi reached for a rag to gently wipe his face.

His cerulean eyes were half-hidden behind heavy lids. But he seemed to gain a moment of focus when he looked at her.

"Hello," she whispered.

"He—" He was coughing again, and Vi held up the bucket once more to catch everything that came out.

The door to the main room opened and closed. Discussions flew through the air and among the hasty words, Vi gathered the head cleric's name was Julus.

"I'd like a salve and potion there, suppressants, mostly—something with mint and valerian," Julus commanded.

"Understood, sir."

"You two get rid of these bloody rags."

"What can I do?" Aldrik asked.

"Just stay back, my prince. You'll only risk contamination."

"He's my brother—"

"Let us handle this."

Vi lingered in the room, somehow retaining her job as the blood collector and mouth wiper through the night. She watched as they poured potions down his throat that the prince instantly coughed up. Vi was there to catch everything in the bucket—exchanging it for a fresh one when it was full of fluid and soiled rags. The clerics were relentless, determined to find something that would stick on Baldair's sweat-slick skin or stay in his stomach.

Aldrik paced in the main room. Now and then he would come in carrying something Julus ordered, only to be sent away again. Vi watched him drift in and out and an idea crossed her mind.

There was something the crown prince could do.

"I'll exchange this one myself," Vi murmured, standing with her bucket. Another cleric instantly filled in the gap she left behind. Vi wandered out to the main room. There were definitely fewer clerics as the night dragged on, and it made the lone man dressed in black stand out all the more.

Vi set the bucket down in a corner. She wiped her sweaty palms on her thighs and approached.

"My prince," Vi said quietly.

He nearly jumped at the sound of someone addressing him. "What?" Aldrik said curtly, staring down the bridge of his crooked nose.

"I'd like to request something of you."

"*You* would like to request something of *me*?" He arched his eyebrows.

"Yes."

He sighed dramatically and looked back out the window. Vi would've interpreted it as dismissal if not for his sharp, "Well, what is it?"

"Do you know where to find Raylynn?"

"I don't concern myself with my brother's concubines."

"She's the best swordswoman in the world, far from a concubine," Vi said and allowed her tone to communicate she didn't appreciate his word choice.

"Yes I know where she is." Aldrik sneered at her. But Vi remained passive in the face of his gruff exterior. That confused him all the more.

"Please bring her."

"Who do you think you are, commanding me?"

"You want to help, don't you?" Vi snapped back. She gave him an intense stare that she usually reserved for people she was threatening. Aldrik straightened away, as if she'd slapped him. More likely, he had seen his own expression used against him. "Get her."

Vi walked away, satisfied when she heard his retreating footsteps.

She continued to help the clerics. As Baldair finally seemed to settle, they left the room one by one to get some sleep. Soon, she was one of three, and there was still no sign of Aldrik.

"One of you should stay. I want him monitored around the clock," Julus commanded. "I'll be of no use unless I get some rest, and the Emperor will want a full report in the morning."

"I can watch him until dawn," Vi volunteered before anyone else could.

"Fine, you do it." Julus yawned. "You, go to the Tower and get Waterrunners from Victor, or a Groundbreaker. We're going to need all the hands we can get. This won't be pretty tomorrow."

"Yes, of course."

There were more orders, but Vi didn't hear them as they left the room, leaving her by herself. She wasn't alone for long. Within the first hour, Aldrik appeared with a worried-looking Raylynn.

"Thank you, my prince," Vi said as she rushed over to them.

"How is he?" Raylynn asked.

"Dozing," Vi replied. Baldair was in a hazy, half-drugged sleep. Not the ideal condition for the conversation she wanted to have. But she had to work with what fate gave her. "He'll have clerics with him around the clock from now on."

"That's a relief." Genuine kindness crossed Aldrik's features. It was the first time she saw a glimpse of her father in the otherwise harsh man.

"Now, Raylynn, there's something I wish to discuss with you. My prince, you should get some rest."

"First you think to order me, now you'd dismiss me?"

"Are you not tired?" Vi arched her eyebrows in a mirror of what he'd done to her earlier. It gave him the same pause as her earlier look. Vi could've sworn she saw recognition somewhere in his assessment of her. Even if his conscious mind wouldn't admit it, Vi wanted to believe that somehow, he knew who she was. "Keep up your strength. Consider it cleric's orders."

His eyes darted between Vi and Raylynn before he turned away, muttering gruffly, and closed the door behind him.

"And who are you?" Raylynn folded her arms over her chest.

"A cleric."

"No, you're not," she said, starting for Baldair's room. "No cleric orders Aldrik around like that. Besides, I know your face."

Raylynn delivered the statement so calmly, without even turning, that Vi stopped dead in her tracks. She stared at the woman's back, waiting for her to turn around with a smug grin. But she never did. That truth was delivered plainly and Raylynn moved immediately to Baldair's bedside.

Vi followed slowly behind and looked at the scene she had orchestrated. Baldair lay in bed, drifting in and out of consciousness. His eyes fluttered open as Raylynn reached for his hands.

"I'm here," she whispered. "It's me."

It had always been her at his side. Vi had seen it from a distance. She'd heard whispers from the soldiers. The man known as the "Playboy Prince" had found his singular golden woman long ago.

"Ray…"

"Don't speak, you idiot," she scolded lightly, running her fingertips over his forehead. Baldair's eyes drifted, but before they could close, they landed on Vi. Focus overtook him once more. "Yes, she's here, too."

"Who… are you?"

Vi was in two places at once. But this wasn't the sensation of the unique visions crystal weapons gave her. This was brought on by memory. She was in a different room, standing before a different bed, occupied by someone who would've been a family member in a different world, who was destined for death.

She was honest then, and she would be honest now. She'd come here not for fate, after all. But for herself. For the love of family that transcended time and space.

"I'm the one who did this to you."

"*What?*" Raylynn seethed, turning sharply.

"I'm the one who pulled the strings of fate to bring you here, to this moment, Baldair. The flame of your life was supposed to be extinguished years ago." Vi dragged her feet over tiredly, pulling up a chair that had been cast aside so the clerics could have room to work. "I'm the one who tried to keep you alive." She looked from Baldair to Raylynn. "And I got you to help me do it without you realizing it." She thought back to reading Raylynn's future as Fiera. Raylynn had dutifully defended a golden crown, just as Vi had hoped.

"I don't—" Baldair wheezed and Vi braced herself for another coughing fit. But the cleric's medicine held and he finished, "understand."

"I know." Vi smiled tiredly. "It's hard to explain. I don't entirely understand some days myself… even still."

"You were the one who saved us that night in the West," Raylynn said. Vi nodded. "It wasn't the princess."

"Fiera is dead. I was there when she died."

"Impossible. You'd have to be at least thirty—forty, even. You don't look a day past eighteen."

"I've been eighteen a long time." Vi sighed heavily. Her body would be the one thing she would be ready to give back to the goddess when the time came. She'd mourn the loss of her mind and its thoughts—its memories—but her corporeal form was tired of feeling very old and very young all at once. "I've come from a world away, on a mission to save this one."

Baldair looked at her in a fevered haze. Vi would be shocked if he remembered any of this come morning. But Raylynn's expression was completely believing. The woman had her mother's eyes and intuition.

"You brought us here for a reason, to tell us the flame of Baldair's life will be extinguished?"

"Yes."

"Why?"

"I don't fully know myself." Vi shook her head. "Perhaps because I felt I owed this to you after meddling in your lives for so long."

"Nox?" Baldair whispered.

"That is one of my names, yes." Vi smiled tenderly at him. "I wanted you to know that I'm sorry. If I could save you, Baldair... Raylynn, if I could've saved your mother, or Fiera, I would have. It wasn't for lack of trying. But the goddess will have her due and—"

"Enough," Raylynn said faintly. She gave Vi a tired smile. "I'm not afraid of death, Nox. And I'm not afraid of giving myself to the Mother."

Vi focused on Raylynn. "Baldair will not survive this. In some ways, that might be a blessing. If the future remains unchanged—" which was a bigger "if" than any of them could know "—there is a storm coming that will claim the lives of many in this city. Even if I saved Baldair now, I'm certain he would be taken then. Fate would catch up with him in more brutal ways each time his life was stolen from it. But if *you* were to leave—"

"No."

"But you could—"

"I will stay by his side to the end." Raylynn met Baldair's gaze. The prince's ocean-blue eyes were filled with tears. "*On my terms*," she added.

But what Vi heard was, *I love you.*

"If you stay here much longer, you might not survive." Vi didn't know how she could make the woman understand that while Baldair's life would come to an end regardless, hers wasn't conscripted by fate.

"Death comes for us all."

The expression knocked the wind from Vi. She remembered Taavin's words and how ready he was to give himself over to fate. Before her were two people who had accepted much the same.

"It was fun while it lasted," Baldair said to the woman gently caressing him.

"It was," Raylynn agreed.

Vi stood wordlessly, excusing herself from the room. She gave the lovers space until dawn, waiting in the main room of the royal apartment. A new cleric arrived shortly after and Raylynn left with Vi.

They departed the Imperial wing of the palace together, stopping at an intersection in the servants' halls. Raylynn paused, and Vi stood silently beside her.

"Thank you," Raylynn said finally.

"You have nothing to thank me for." *Not yet, at least.*

A tired smile crossed her lips. "Then why do I have the distinct feeling I have quite a lot to thank you for?" Vi's lips parted. Raylynn held out her hand. "So, thank you."

"You're welcome," she managed to squeak out. Vi's fingers closed around hers and they clasped palms tightly.

With that, the golden-haired swordswoman departed in the opposite direction, as though this was the moment their fates diverged. Vi watched her go. Vi *let* her go.

Silent tears streamed down her face and fell to the floor in heavy drops. Vi fled to a quiet room where she could mourn alone. She wept for all the hardship and hurt, for everyone she'd lost all over again, and for the family she'd never known.

34

V I STAGGERED BACK TO the Tower library. She impressed herself that she managed to change into black robes lifted from a storeroom along the way. Sure enough, Taavin was there, waiting on a window seat, reading, and looking as if he didn't have a care in the world.

"You were gone quite a while." He closed his book slowly. Dawn was breaking over his shoulder.

"Prince Baldair is dead."

Taavin observed her, saying nothing. He didn't even move. Vi wondered if he was judging her for what she confessed to the prince and Raylynn. She wouldn't be surprised if somehow he knew what had transpired.

"Is he?"

"Yes." Vi closed the distance and determinedly wedged herself between Taavin and the window. His arm wrapped around her. His embrace was the one thing that could keep her together. "Well, I don't think he's dead yet, but he will be very soon."

Taavin was quiet for a long moment. Vi met his eyes in the reflection of the window. "Will we be searching for the axe today?"

"I don't think so. The death of the youngest prince will be the catalyst. All of this is going to come to an end very soon."

"You think so?"

Vi nodded. "If Vhalla has the axe, I think she might seek out the Caverns on her own to try to find some cure for him, or a way to cheat death."

"Ah, cheating death—you get it from your mother."

"Not funny," Vi said deadpan.

"Forgive me." He kissed her neck lightly and Vi wriggled closer to him.

"Let's just… wait here for a while and see what happens? I'm tired, and just want to exist quietly for a while."

"Certainly."

At some point, she fell asleep in his arms. Around her, the day began like any other. Guards showed up for work, servants cleaned the halls, and the Tower initiates went in and out of their library, looking oddly at the anonymous couple in the corner.

Once more, time drifted around them and they remained untouched. Vi didn't feel the turning of the hours. She didn't feel hunger gnawing at her or exhaustion pricking her eyes. Taavin's arms were stasis. They were the strength she needed to stand when the moment came.

And it came in the form of two familiar voices.

"… if there's one thing Elecia would hate more, it would be being someone else's puppet."

Aldrik and Vhalla sprinted by the library opening. The man was half dragging her, leaving Vhalla to take two steps for every one of his long strides. Without needing to be asked, Taavin stood and extended his hand to Vi.

"What will your father…" Vhalla's voice faded away as they continued racing up the tower.

"Shall we?" Taavin asked, almost thoughtfully.

"Fate won't let us linger much longer. *Durroe watt radia.*"

Taavin echoed her and they sprinted behind the prince and the Windwalker. Vi and Taavin passed the Minister's office in time to see the lone uppermost door in the Tower closing.

"I gave him that key," Vi whispered.

"What?"

"Years ago… that was the room I was in when I first came to the Tower. Aldrik was just a boy. The night I left, I gave him the key."

Taavin was silent for a long moment. Then, he whispered with fragile optimism, "Perhaps this is all how it was meant to be. Perhaps this really is the time we will succeed."

"Let's hope."

Aldrik stepped out into the hall once more and began to stride down and away. Vi heard the click of the lock engage behind him. He was trying to protect Vhalla from his father? Had she overheard their conversation correctly?

"Let's get a head start. They'll go to the Caverns tonight. I know they will."

They left the palace and rode out of the city. Vi set their course, heading down the Great Imperial Way, not taking the expected shortcut to the Caverns.

"It had to snow," Vi grumbled. She doubted *kot sorre* would work in snow as well as it had in the sands of the Waste. She imagined strange-looking snow banks at the ends of ditches where her glyphs pushed through the powder.

"I suspected that's why you were swinging wide."

"We should have time. We'll go to the cabin first and leave the horse there. We'll continue on foot. It'll be less noticeable than the horse's tracks." She prayed there was enough time for all of it.

But Yargen looked over them. She and Taavin made it to the cabin in record time. They started the hike to the entrance of the Caverns, Vi walking ahead with Taavin stepping in the footprints she left behind. Then they repeated "*kot sorre*" over and over. Their glyphs grazed the top of the powder, pushing and piling it to cover their tracks.

Just as they reached the cliff in front of the entrance to the Caverns, two horses could be seen in the distance.

"You think that's them?" Taavin whispered.

"Who else would it be?" Vi looked to Taavin. "Listen, if this goes wrong—"

"It won't."

"If it does… I'm sorry, for risking it all."

"Don't apologize." Taavin reached up, tucking a stray strand of hair behind her ear. "All you've done, you did for our world. Yargen could not ask for a better Champion."

Vi swallowed all the emotions he inspired by just looking at her. She still had so much she wanted to say to him, and time was running out. But there was no opportunity now and she had to focus on what was to come next. "We're going to need all the chants we can get in there."

"I have an idea."

"What?"

"Follow me." Taavin led her into the Caverns, the stones glimmering under their feet. The world seemed to hold its breath. Almost all of Yargen's power was now condensed in this one place, split across her, Taavin, and the Caverns themselves. "It's a word Yargen told me long ago… but I could never make it work right in Risen. Perhaps it was meant for here and now."

"What are you talking about?"

Taavin gripped a nearby crystal and uttered, "*Chronot*." The entire cavern flared, a rune sinking into every crystal that lined the walls. It made them all glow with fractured portions of the glyph, power illuminating every corner. Time itself seemed to hold its breath in the presence of the magic.

"Slow," she whispered.

"What?" He seemed incredulous at the translation.

"*Chronot*, to slow…"

"Yes, it makes glyphs cling longer. You should be able to cast two to four at a time but… how did you know that?"

"I heard it, in the word."

"That's not possible," he whispered.

"But I did."

"Only Yargen—" The sound of hooves silenced him. "*Durroe watt radia. Durroe sallvas tempre.*" Taavin chanted first and Vi followed. She tapped a crystal lightly, willing the Caverns to darken to their dormant state.

"There! There's his horse," Victor shouted, though his voice was different— deeper in some ways and pitched in others.

"We have to hurry!"

"Carefully!"

The mounts kicked up a confetti of ice and snow as they skidded to a stop on the ridge beyond. Vhalla was astride one. But Vi blinked at the man on the other. Aldrik?

No… Magic coated the man so thickly that Vi wondered how Vhalla couldn't feel it. Victor was using an illusion of Aldrik to get Vhalla to the Caverns. Which was clever, she'd grant him that. Perhaps he doubted Vhalla would give him the axe otherwise.

It also explained why he was doing his best impersonation of Aldrik's voice.

"We need to go. We're close now," Victor said with Aldrik's voice as he dismounted.

"Right…" Vhalla regarded the massive entrance to the Caverns warily. Vi suspected the woman's expression was identical to her own when she'd first laid eyes on the place. Even if Vhalla couldn't sense Victor's illusion, she could pick up on the gravity of this ominous space.

Something caught Victor's eye. He turned toward the valley. "We need to go!"

Vhalla worked to keep up with Victor, plunging herself into the darkness of the Caverns. Vi took a steadying breath as she laid eyes on the axe. She didn't know the details of what was about to happen. But she knew that, one way or another, the power would finally be hers.

Victor placed a crystal in the Caverns, much as Egmun had, and the space illuminated once more. Blue and white light washed over them and magic cascaded down from the ceiling like stardust.

"There's no time," Victor muttered.

As the two continued forward through the first archway, Vi released Taavin's hand and he quickly used *durroe* to conceal them both in sound and sight again. She could no longer tell where he was, and in the Caverns, it was nearly impossible to make out his magical signature from any other crystal. Vi pressed forward, listening in on the conversation that was continuing before her.

"…we missed Victor along the way," Vhalla said as Vi approached the archway that led into the antechamber. She was just in time to see Victor grab her. "Aldrik, your hands are cold. Let me go." Victor laughed at her rising panic. The sound pricked uncomfortable goosebumps into Vi's flesh. "Let me go!"

"No, I don't think so, my little Windwalker." Victor had dropped his poor attempt at Aldrik's voice. "Do you know how long I've bided my time? Waiting, *waiting*! Everything has been going according to plan, and you will not take this from me now."

My plan, Victor. I've been the one who was waiting, Vi thought darkly as she watched him shed his illusion. Victor had tricks up his sleeve she wasn't expecting, however. He produced a crystal from his pocket, slammed it into the base of Vhalla's neck, and coated it with ice to keep it there. Vi scowled, her spark tickling her fingertips. Victor had clearly taken it upon himself to do some additional crystal research.

She combated the urge to protect Vhalla.

Vi's focus was on the doors that Victor brought Vhalla toward by force. A new barrier was there, albeit a clumsy one. Vi had wondered what exactly happened to "end" the War of the Crystal Caverns. She always suspected that people merely stopped going there, thus, no more monsters. But judging from the traces of Aldrik's magic in the new barrier over the doors, the man had inherited some of his mother's intuition when it came to the crystals.

Victor lodged an insult at Vhalla and threw her against the doors.

"*Rhoko*." Vi held out a hand to help the barrier fall.

She watched as blinding magic wrapped around Vhalla, tightening across her. Vi could feel an aspect of the woman's power knotting with the crystals. Victor was using the young woman as a catalyst, trying to unlock the door himself.

If Vi released her glyph now and destroyed the barrier, Vhalla's magic would be wrapped in with it. There was no time to separate the two; they were intertwined. Vi panicked. Severing the magic could result in Vhalla losing her power.

Your mother found the strength to overcome overwhelming odds and be reunited with her power, thanks to this.

Fritz's words appeared in Vi's mind, as if ushered there by Yargen herself. He'd written them on the letter attached to the watch he'd gifted her. Vhalla had lost her magic in her time, too.

Have faith, Vi commanded herself. Everything was on a course for success. If she didn't believe that, she couldn't complete this task.

Closing her hand into a fist, Vi yanked her arm back. The thick barrier of crystals on the door shattered.

"*Kot sorre,*" Taavin whispered from somewhere nearby. The doors swung open, giving Victor access to the heart of the Caverns.

The man rambled madness to Vhalla as he carried her within, throwing her down like a rag doll. Ice coated the Windwalker, keeping her in place. Vi blinked, swaying, but kept her footing. Destroying the barrier had left her momentarily stunned.

"What is he doing?" Taavin whispered at her side.

Vi watched as he laid crystals around Vhalla's prone form. *What* was *he doing?* Vi worked to get her mind moving again after the burst of energy.

"Don't lump me in with the incompetent fools who are so hungry for power that they are blinded by it," Victor boasted to Vhalla. "I am of a far greater stock." He believed that because of Vi. "Egmun thought he could take this power, but he didn't have *you.*"

It clicked for Vi, then, and she wanted to scream. She'd been so focused on driving the momentum to get the weapons to the Caverns that she hadn't thought about how old actions would echo in the future. Around and around the world spun, mistakes made and made again.

"He was Egmun's student. He knew the same things as the former Minister... he's going to use her as a sacrifice." She kept her voice a whisper.

Taavin's hand clasped over her shoulder and he was visible to her once more. The touch barely registered through the numbness that tingled over her flesh like dark magic. "*What?*"

"I will kill you," Vhalla swore through chattering teeth.

"Will you? I would certainly love to see that."

"I will. *I promise.*"

"That would be impressive, as this place will soon become your tomb." The Minister affirmed Vi's suspicions.

"Are you going to let her die?" Taavin asked. His eyes were filled with genuine uncertainty.

"I don't want to." But Vi couldn't promise she wouldn't.

Vi stepped forward, out of Taavin's grasp. He disappeared from sight. Trusting her invisibility to remain in place thanks to *chronot,* Vi strode forward into the living core of the Crystal Caverns. She ignored the raving lunatic and prone woman as she walked around the edge of the room. The only reason she could ignore them was because she could feel the dark god underneath her feet, waking.

She'd given Raspian a taste of freedom for the War of the Crystal Caverns, and now he knew his time had come.

"I fear, my dear, that you must die without ever seeing my new world order,"

Victor was saying. "But know that your death will build a society that favors sorcerers for eons to come."

Vi positioned her stance wide, connecting her magic with the crystals around her as Victor wielded the axe. She was ready to make the transference. It would shatter the axe before it could wound Vhalla. That was how this would end, Vi decided.

But right as Victor was about to deal his final blow, a tall shadow appeared in the distant entryway, barely visible through the archways and doors.

"Aldrik!" Vhalla screamed.

"Vhalla!"

Mother above! Vi nearly shouted.

"It seems you shall be the first Solaris to die by my hand!" Victor said with glee.

Oh, Yargen, this was becoming a mess. Fire and ice battled as Aldrik and Victor levied their magic against each other. Chaos took over the Caverns and Victor finally put a temporary pause to it when he blocked the prince's progress with a wall of ice in the doorway.

"*Rhoko*," Vi whispered, hating herself for using the word. But she had to regain some control and contain the situation. Her magic flowed through the crystals on either side of the door, strengthening Victor's barrier of ice. Aldrik slammed into it, *hard*, and winced. He banged his fists against the frozen wall, bloodying them. No fire or rage was going to break through her barrier.

Vi's chest ached as she watched the frantic prince staring at Vhalla. Her hand pulsed with the magic that was keeping them apart. This suffering and the deaths that would follow would mean something when she ultimately succeeded. That was the only thing she could cling to.

Za and Sehra were in the Caverns now, too. Vi was grateful they came and escaped the Capital, until one of the warrior's arrows managed to pierce her barrier with a flash of light. Sehra was using her limited Lightspinning to try and get through.

The chaos had distracted her from Vhalla and Victor. Somehow, Vhalla had freed herself and the two were now struggling over the axe. It had only seemed a second, but it had been long enough. Victor snatched the axe and had it over his head.

A scream rose in Vi's throat and was stopped short as Victor swung the axe down, carving through Vhalla from shoulder to sternum. Vi saw glyphs appear where the crystals met her flesh. She recognized the shapes as *halleth*. Taavin was working to ensure Vhalla survived this so Vi could focus on what she was meant to do.

The axe shone brighter, as though the magic within was trying to explode outward. Vi reached toward it with her mind and closed her magic grip around Yargen's power, pulling it from the blade. The bright light of future sight tried to overtake her. *Not now, not yet*, Vi begged.

She kept herself grounded in the present by grabbing for the power that surrounded her. If she kept absorbing Yargen's magic, she could keep the visions at bay. The crystals in the room flared brightly. The axe turned to obsidian, falling from Victor's grasp.

Kneeling down, Vi pressed her palms into the floor and closed her eyes, remembering the word she'd seen glowing in this place years ago. "*Suladin*."

Magic lifted off the stones and flooded her senses. Victor was still shouting. Attacks were being levied against him. Vi's world was a hazy blend of light and magic. She saw the intricacies of the barrier that had been crafted to seal Raspian and, for the first time, began to understand them.

She pulled at the edges of the glyph, trying to uproot it from where it was anchored. "*Juth calt. Juth mariy*," Vi whispered over and over, focusing on the cornerstones that kept Yargen's power in place.

The world tilted, and a streak of red lightning shot across her skull. Raspian could sense that the cage holding him was weakening. He fought to be released once more.

The power surging through her made Vi dizzy. It swelled her veins to the point of pain. Everything within her hurt, and then was healed instantly by Yargen's magic. Her mind was overwhelmed.

Tilting her gaze up, she tried to focus on the real world as the edges of her vision became hazy.

Victor reached down and picked up a crystal. He used it to channel power, not even realizing what he was reaching toward. The eyes of the dark god flashed in Victor's briefly.

No!

Aldrik was there now. The barrier she'd made must've been destroyed when she'd focused on gaining the power of the Caverns.

Vi couldn't tell if everything was happening incredibly slow, or very fast. Time had gone sideways. She was losing the battle to keep her mind in the present.

Aldrik scooped up Vhalla, fleeing with her as the Caverns began to break beneath them. Victor followed close behind.

The crystals around her exploded as the last of Yargen's essence was absorbed into her and Raspian was freed. The burst shattered the doors to the barrier room. The ground cracked beneath Vi, while rocks jutted up around her. Victor didn't even turn to look over his shoulder. He was so focused on tracking down his prey that he was ignorant to the true work being done.

Raspian's essence roared forth. It sought out the man who had gained just a taste. Just as Vi was a channel for Yargen, Victor had become the first channel for Raspian. He would taint the world with the dark god's magic, not even realizing the power he had.

Vi's vision grew tunneled. The power was about to overwhelm her. She couldn't fight it any longer.

The last thing she heard was a man's scream, before the world went white.

35

THE BLINDING WHITE OF the vision faded with the crackle of power. She moved, casting another beam into the darkness that engulfed her. She was shooting blind, her target evading every attack.

Spinning, she searched the desolate wasteland for any sign of Raspian. Vi moved across the ashen stone and rubble of a great civilization that had been reduced to dust. Her feet hardly hit the ground; her body no longer felt like her own.

Lightning cracked behind her. She spun on instinct, readying an attack. A plume of smoke rose from a dark spot on the ground where lightning had struck the earth, but there was nothing else.

A growl at her ear was the only warning she got before rows of razor-sharp teeth sank into her shoulder. Two clawed hands wrapped around her. They dug into her abdomen, flaying her alive. Lightning sparked through her, rising within her until she was limp and lifeless.

Then, darkness.

The vision slipped away like a veil.

Vi cracked her eyes open. They were crusted with sleep, or perhaps it was blood and sweat, given how much everything hurt. She raised a palm to her temple, feeling a tender spot where her head must've met a bit of jagged stone when she collapsed. Vi let out a groan and sat.

A fire crackled happily in the hearth next to her. Snow fell outside the window, piling high. She looked to the bed across from her—it was perfectly made. Deneya always tidied up her bed before leaving for the day.

Massaging her temples, Vi closed her eyes. That had been the most horrible dream. Red lightning sparked behind her lids and they shot open once more.

It wasn't a dream. She could already feel Raspian's essence on the earth like oil on water.

The door opened and her attention went to the man in its frame. Given his tired and worried eyes, she wasn't the only one who could sense Raspian's renewed presence.

"How do you feel?" Taavin asked, crossing over to her bed and sitting on its edge at her side.

"Fine." The aches were already dissipating and she didn't need him worrying about her. She needed information. "What happened after I passed out?"

"They made it out alive. I kept Vhalla stable for as long as I could—not healing her so much that it would raise questions."

"But enough to keep her alive," Vi finished for him. She looked to the window once more. "That was unnecessary."

"What?" He took her hand. "Didn't you—"

"It doesn't matter. Raspian is free. Though some of his magic went into Victor."

"I could sense it," Taavin said with a cautious note. As though he was suddenly wary of her. "He headed toward the Capital."

"Expected. Blood will run in the streets of Solarin." The words were passive; though she physically spoke them, she didn't feel them. She was a mouthpiece of sorts, it seemed. Perhaps she was in shock. The dream—no, vision—she'd had was fresh in her memory. That was the only thing her mind could focus on. "It's time to go to Salvidia." Taavin stood, pacing. "You're uneasy," she observed.

He looked at her with that same wary gaze. Vi couldn't recall if she'd ever seen it from him before. He finally stopped, his back to her.

"I know that we've committed to this being it, the final time," he said delicately.

"Yes, in me is now the essence of Yargen that was in the Crystal Caverns and three crystal weapons. All that remains is to collect the remaining essence from the ashes, and the final crystal weapon in you."

His back straightened. Taavin was taut and stiff as he slowly turned to face her. Hurt shone in his eyes.

Had she said something wrong?

He'd already known this truth.

"I know," Taavin said softly. "But Victor has a trace of Raspian's power... would it not be better to see him ended? In case Raspian's essence was inadvertently split, as Yargen's was?"

Vi thought about this a moment and then shook her head. "No, if he had the actual essence of Raspian, he'd be dead. His body is not made for such things. He has a fracture of the dark god's magic... much like a crystal shaving. It's a bit of magic, but not the essence itself."

"Better to be safe?"

"I'm confident." Vi swung her feet over the side of the bed.

"I know," Taavin said hastily, crossing over to her. "I know we've already given up on ensuring the birth of a new Champion. But lingering here for a few more weeks—that's all—and giving the watch to Vhalla couldn't hurt, could it?"

"Why do you seek to delay the inevitable?" Vi was reminded that even though she'd blessed him with an immortal body, he still very much had a mortal mind.

"A little bit of assurance that somehow, maybe, if this doesn't work... there's hope."

"I am the hope of this world."

Taavin knelt before her. "Then, if not for the world, what about to ensure there is a new Vi born? Not for the world but for... somehow, for us. A new Taavin will be born, and then—"

"I don't care about the birth of a new Vi." He recoiled as though she'd slapped him. But Vi had spoken plainly, calmly, and without emotion.

"Vi, stop this," he whispered. Taavin shook his head and brought his shining green eyes back to hers. "If not for you, or me, or us, then for Vhalla. She lost her magic in the Caverns. If you don't return the watch to her, she'll have no chance of getting it back once more. Victor will surely kill her."

"Vhalla's death matters not to me."

"How can you say that?" He blinked up at her. "A day ago you were seeking to save her *and* the world."

"Those were sentimentalities of a narrow mind."

"What are you saying?" Taavin stood and, instead of pulling away, leaned forward and wrapped his arms tightly around her. Vi stiffened under his touch. Something in her was fighting to escape. A war for her heart and mind threatened to tear her apart. "This isn't you," he whispered in her ear. "Sentimentality, love—these aren't narrow-minded. These are the greatest gifts we have in this world. The only things that make this world worth saving."

Vi felt a snap inside her, and she could move again. Her hands were her own. Warmth flooded her and Vi reached for the man it poured from. She wanted to drown in it, in him.

Tightening her arms around him, pulling him onto the bed with her, Vi whispered, "All right."

"Yes?"

"We'll give the watch to Vhalla. But not for anyone to be born and not even for her magic." She managed to say the words before that cool and detached feeling overtook her once more.

"For what, then?" he whispered.

Vi pulled away, just enough to look him in the eye. "For you, Taavin. For a few more stolen moments with you."

Victor's influence spread. With even a sliver of Raspian's power at his disposal, the man wrought turmoil across the continent. It seemed to follow behind them as Vi and Taavin made their way to the Crossroads one final time.

But they made it without issue, and Vi had never been more relieved to see their quiet shop and second-floor abode still standing, waiting for them.

"I was half worried it wouldn't be here," she said as she dismounted in the back alley and tied their horse to a post.

"The West always holds out against Victor. At least for a while."

"Just like they held out against the Empire. It's a stubborn land."

"Ah, so stubbornness is in your blood."

"What little blood I have left."

"Don't speak like that, please," he said as he followed her inside.

"I'm sorry." Vi drifted up the stairs, setting her pack and saddlebags down heavily.

Two arms closed tightly around her. They stood in the center of the room, Taavin at her back, clutching her tightly. He buried his face into her shoulder, kissing her neck lightly.

"Don't be sorry," he whispered. "Just be with me."

"Because you'll be gone soon," she breathed. His grip tightened further but he didn't say anything. The silence was unbearable. "I know I've chosen this. But I'm not ready, Taavin. I'm not ready to lose you."

"You never will be."

She twisted, keeping his arms around her. Vi grabbed his face with both her hands, smoothing her fingertips up the cheekbones and browline that she knew so well she could carve it from memory. "If I let you go now, I'll be alone," she barely managed to say around the lump in her throat. She closed her eyes, keeping the distinct prickle of tears safely behind her lids. "I can't do this alone."

Taavin leaned forward, kissing her gently. It was another postponement of the inevitable, but Vi gave into it. The less she had to think about what the next days would hold, the better. For all she knew, this was the last time she could lose herself in the weight of Taavin's body over hers.

He took a step, forcing her to take one backwards. They shuffled to the bed. Taavin's hands slid up her sides, pulling the loose tunic she wore with them. Vi raised her arms over her head, allowing him to undress her.

Her back on the bed, Vi beckoned him atop her. She trailed her fingers down the expanse of his skin and then back up to his face. The man was magic—magic in his bones, magic in the way he moved. This was what she wanted to give herself to, forever. Every shift of their bodies was fire and life, the last brilliant burst before their own flames would be extinguished.

If they were meant to burn, then they burned together.

"In another world," he breathed heavily, pressing his forehead against hers. "I would've married you."

Vi laughed, then responded, equally breathy, "The crown princess of Solaris and the Voice of Yargen… Do you think it would've worked?"

"Of course." He nipped at her earlobe and then kissed down her neck to her collarbone. "It would've united two continents. Our union would've shocked and changed the world."

Fantasizing about such a thing was pain and delight in equal measure. Vi closed her eyes and imagined it as his fingers laced with hers. She imagined she made love to a husband. She imagined their union was one the world could know about—that their lives were their own.

The daydreams continued as he lay next to her, Vi's head on his chest. She traced the lines of his muscles, drawing different ways to connect them as though they were glyphs yet to be discovered. Taavin kissed her forehead from time to time. His own fingers moved lazily on her bare back.

Dawn had come and she was ready to spend the day with him. She was ready to have eternity with him, but all they had was a few short hours before nightfall. As the day continued its relentless march, Vi finally pulled herself from the bed. She sat with her back to Taavin, the watch heavy around her throat.

"It's time. I feel it." Just as she'd felt it the last time Vhalla had come to the curiosity shop.

Taavin stood, moving before her. He hadn't bothered dressing; Vi savored every inch of his glorious frame.

"I'll be the one to return my consciousness." He held out his hand. "All you need to do is give me the watch."

Vi lifted her hands to her neck, slowly unfastening the clasp. The token was heavy with the weight of destiny. She held it over his waiting palm, her hand trembling.

In the end, he didn't make her do anything. Taavin closed his fingers around the watch, taking it gently from her. Vi looked up at him, silently begging him not to do this.

There was no other choice. This was the end for them. She'd known it was coming all along, and yet she still spent every minute breaking inside.

"If you succeed and the world isn't rebuilt again. If you somehow make it on the other side alive... See this watch still finds its way to the next Taavin." His emerald eyes met hers. "Give him his memories." Taavin cupped her cheek, his fingers in her hair at the nape of her neck. "Let all of me return to you, Vi."

"I will," she lied—the most beautiful lie of her life. She'd seen Yargen's vision. Time for time. The goddess would have her body and return to this world. Taavin's collective memories, everything that made him Taavin, would be locked in a watch, and Vi would be lost forever as a castaway from a bygone world. "I love you, Taavin."

"And I love you, Vi Solaris. I always have, and I always will. My life was never complete until the moment you returned to it. You gave me meaning. You gave me my past and my future." He bent over and claimed her mouth hungrily. She grabbed his shoulders, digging her fingertips into his soft skin. When he pulled away, Vi let out a soft whimper, one he ignored. "It's time."

She stood, watching as he stepped back. Taavin held the watch, his lips murmuring fast and low. The only words she could make out were "*Narro hath loreth,*" to imprint a communication mark.

There were a thousand words she wanted to say. A thousand more times she wanted to tell him she loved him. She was the ninety-third Vi to let him go, but this time hurt more than any of the others. She didn't need to look into the past to know that.

She had held him, loved him, in an impossible time and place. The light of Taavin's glyphs began to consume him. They covered his entire form. His eyes opened and, one last time, they met hers.

Then, his gaze became unfocused. His pupils dilated. He fell to the ground, the watch clattering across the floor.

Vi dragged herself over to him. The world spun as she knelt over the body he had occupied. She touched his arm, trailed her fingers to his shoulder, gently rocking him.

"Taavin," she whispered, staring at his wide, soulless eyes. "Taavin." Vi choked on his name and doubled over.

She sobbed.

Tears flowed freely, her shoulders shaking. She gasped for air. The only pain she'd ever known that came close to this was the knowledge that her world was gone. That everyone she'd loved had been undone with a goddess's broad stroke.

But this.

This.

He was gone, and she would never see him again. This was the end of their love story. This was the last moment she had with him and she hadn't found the words to tell him how much he meant to her. She had decades with him and had never found those perfect words to encapsulate it all. She needed at least another hundred years and then some.

"Taavin, please." A high-pitched wail escaped her. She didn't care if half the Crossroads heard it. Let the world hear her agony. "Please don't go," Vi begged futilely. "Don't take your warmth, your love—it was all I had left." The begging was catharsis. She pleaded with the cruel gods whose game she was trapped in. And yet, without those same gods, she would've never met him worlds ago.

Vi buried her face into his shoulder, weeping until the tears no longer came. She expelled the last of her humanity, the last of her feeling, through her eyes. This was their curse, after all.

They had never been made for happy endings.

Finally, when the sun hung low in the sky, Vi peeled herself away from him. With one hand on his shoulder, she whispered, "*Juth mariy*. Come undone."

His skin began to glow. Pure light peeled off his body like ashes cast from an invisible fire. The magic she had made that held him together unraveled all too easily. Beneath it all was the crystal she had taken from the Caverns. It was the essence of Yargen that had lived in the Sword of Jadar, the Caverns, and the scythe.

She allowed that power to flow into her, as if she could steal some of the last of his essence. After getting a taste of it, Vi couldn't help absorbing it hungrily. It dulled some senses and heightened others. Yargen's power was a balm to her pain and she invited it into her.

All she was missing was the Flame of Yargen.

She was nearly complete.

Blinking, Vi saw the world with new eyes. Everything seemed to have a vibration to it, a faint outline of magic that she had never seen before. In everything was both light and darkness, woven together and held in perfect balance. She looked down at her hands and saw the power of Yargen shining over top them. Tiny glyphs of words she was certain she would've never understood before had meaning.

The language of the gods was becoming known to her. With two of the three parts of Yargen within her, there was no Lightspinning she couldn't do.

Taavin's body had been reduced to obsidian dust. There wasn't even a lock of his hair for her to keep as a memento. Vi reached for the pocket watch. It was all she had left of him, and now she had to give it away.

She dressed slowly in the same robes she wore the last time she met Vhalla in this place. It no longer felt like a costume she donned to play at fate.

Downstairs, Vi destroyed the few remaining objects on the shop's shelves with *juth*. It was an empty catharsis, and did little to make her feel better. Finally, she pulled back the curtain and lit a single candle.

Memories danced like shadow puppets in the flame of ninety-two other moments when a Vi had stood ready to perform this task. Each was a vision she shouldn't have. Each carried an instruction for what must be done, but Vi didn't want to expend the effort to understand what was being asked of her.

She didn't want to think—Mother above, she barely wanted to breathe. Everything was too confusing and wholly too much. Taavin was gone, there was little reason left for Vi to remain in the world as she was. Her time was up. She was ready to submit to Yargen.

"I don't want to do this," Vi whispered into the darkness. Her hand was still clutched around the watch. It had been Taavin's final wish to see it given to Vhalla to ensure the birth of a new Champion. She wanted to honor that, but… "I don't have the strength to give him away."

Then don't, a voice whispered from within. *Let me. I know what must be done, and you have given me enough strength to do it.*

Yargen's words were as clear as her presence. Vi could imagine the goddess standing behind her, hands on Vi's shoulders, ready to swap places. Vi closed her eyes and let out a soft sigh.

"Thank you," she murmured. "I leave it to you."

Her physical eyes opened once more. But all Vi continued to see was darkness. Tonight was the beginning of the end as Vi relinquished her body to Yargen's will.

When she came to, hours later, the watch was gone. Vi could only assume that it had been given to Vhalla, but her mind was blank on the details. Try as she might, Vi couldn't quite graps why the watch had been so important in the first place.

Every time she reached for the explanation she knew existed, the words evaporated like morning dew.

36

CONSCIOUSNESS HAD FADED IN and out over the past few weeks. She would go to sleep somewhere, and wake up somewhere else. Her movements were sometimes jerky and sometimes fluid. Vi could feel the goddess settling in, as gracefully as trying to squeeze into a too-tight pair of trousers. Except, the trousers were her skin.

But mortal bodies and mortal minds were surprisingly flexible things... or at least, they could be when prodded enough. The transition wasn't easy, but Vi's awareness slowly returned with consistency, and she started to remember more hours than she forgot. For as much as Yargen wanted to be fully in control, they were still missing a piece of the goddess's essence. Thus, for now, the goddess had to continue to work with Vi, making her will known with whispers or outright commands.

Vi stood at the top of the palace, watching the battle for the future of the Dark Isle unfold. How she'd made it back to Solarin and sneaked past Victor's barriers in the city was unknown to her. Aldrik and Vhalla had ridden into the city with an army from the West, North, and East. Vi didn't move from her spot the entire first day of the battle. The second day of fighting dawned and Vi saw the tides of war already shifting in their favor.

It wouldn't be long now.

She twisted the watch that bore the sun and wing around her neck, staring out the window. This was not her watch. The watch Vi had carried had been smooth and unblemished. That watch had carried something important to her...

... something...

What it was eluded her now.

She'd last seen the watch she now wore on Vhalla's neck, when they were leaving the North after the end of the war. How it had jumped from Vhalla's person to hers was a mystery lost in the darkness of that last, long night in the Crossroads. It was a mystery Vi didn't try to remember. Yargen assured her it was better not to think about it. And, frankly, it seemed so insignificant in the face of all the horrible things she'd seen and let transpire over the years.

Day by day, her emotions became more muted. Perhaps it was survival, since she was now sharing a palace with the mortal lunatic, Victor, who was becoming more and more twisted by the powers his body was not meant to house. Raspian was chewing up Victor alive, savoring each bite of the mortal man.

Or perhaps she was unfazed by the horrors, and the human part of her had left entirely with Taavin. All that remained was the Champion, a vessel waiting to become the goddess.

Taavin. The name had her eyes fluttering closed as she allowed the memory of his hands to touch her all over. It was because of him that she was still here.

She'd told him she would see Victor ended before heading to Salvidia. She would look after Vhalla Yarl. Had it been a vow to him or herself? Had it been a vow at all?

Vi couldn't remember anymore. It didn't really matter. She was here, now, and Victor would be dead soon. A few days more in the grand plan didn't make much of a difference.

Reaching into her pocket, Vi retrieved an earring and uttered, *"Narro hath."*

The connection stretched out into the ether. Vi watched the circling rune as she waited in silence. There was a long pause before Adela's voice was heard reverberating toward her, as if the woman stood on the other side of a long cave.

"I was beginning to think you'd died."

"I am beyond death."

A noise somewhere between a chuckle of amusement and a sigh reverberated through to her. "Always the odd one... I assume this is the moment where you call on me?"

"Yes. You will go to Risen and collect Deneya—my companion that you dropped there about a year ago. She'll be waiting to meet your men to the south of the city. Then you will come to Oparium, where I will meet your men in the Cock and Crow. Finally, we will head to Salvidia so that I might put an end to this vortex."

"Fine, fine." Adela dismissed matters of the world's fate with a yawn. "This will use up your remaining trips. You won't have a way to get back from Salvidia."

"That's acceptable."

"Is it? I hear the elfin'ra are thrilled for fresh meat since their barrier fell. Can't imagine what they'd do to the Champion of—"

"That's for me to worry about, not you," Vi interrupted.

"Very well." Adela made a clear effort to sound both tired and bored of the situation. "I will head to Risen and then meet you in Oparium."

Vi dropped the communication glyph and the connection fizzled. She returned the hoop to her pocket and brought her attention back to the fighting far below. Howling wind slammed against the castle's main entry, battering the heavy doors. Vhalla was there, assaulting it with her gusts.

"Rhoko," Vi murmured and watched the crystals Victor had caked the doors with shatter. "You'll need your strength, Vhalla Yarl. Save it for the real battle."

As the army poured into the castle, Vi descended to meet it.

On her path through the various hallways, she unlocked every door that was barred. With waves of her hands, she sent Victor's imitation crystals scattering, though more were likely to grow. Raspian's power radiated from Victor's body, condensing in the halls he frequented.

They looked like Yargen's magic to the naked eye, since they were also godly power given form. But Vi could feel how wrong these stones were. They would soon all be destroyed when the man himself perished, then Raspian would need a new mortal vessel—one that would allow him to face her.

Vi continued to walk calmly as the sounds of war filled the air. She descended to the cleric's old rooms, mostly abandoned now, and donned some clerical garb. Vi put a cloth over her face and knotted her hair simply at the top of her head. Then, she set out to find the clerical portion of the army, adopting her new identity.

Running full tilt to the stables, Vi searched for signs of healers. She saw a few arriving at the end of the vanguard, led by a woman with dark spiral curls—Elecia.

"My lady!" Vi ran over to her. "There's a wing of the castle that I think would be perfect for triage," Vi blurted before Elecia could say anything. She kept her voice frantic, as though she was panicked and not deathly calm. "I can show you—it's a hall not far from here."

"Show me," Elecia demanded. "You five, take the men you think we can save and follow us."

Vi escorted them through the castle to a central dining area that had originally been for servants and staff. It connected up through a stair to the old clerical wing. She looked to Elecia. "Will this do?"

"Well enough. I know where we are. Go and make yourself useful by directing other clerics and wounded here." Elecia spoke to the five who had carried wounded soldiers with them. "Lay them out here, the worst on those tables. We'll overflow to the garden down the hall if we need to."

Vi went to leave, but something stopped her. It wasn't a whisper of the goddess, but words from the young woman she'd once been. *If* she was successful, and the world didn't end… This was the last moment she had to adjust anything in the Solaris Empire.

These final hours were her last chance to right any wrongs.

"Elecia." A sliver of the girl she'd once been returned with the memories of the sting of a betrayal most cruel.

"What?" she said sharply, turning.

"Wounds of the mind can be more damaging and harder to heal than those of the flesh," Vi said. "The man with the sword of wheat lives. Tell the remaining members of his golden brethren to seek him out. They will do what must be done."

Daniel is alive, Vi wanted to say. *Look after him.* But she couldn't. It was hard to speak straight now. Her mouth—her entire body—wasn't really her own anymore, and every action was a negotiation.

"All right…" Elecia said uncertainly and confusion alight in her eyes.

"Excuse me," Vi gave a bow and spun on her heel, leaving before the woman could question her.

She didn't head back down to collect other wounded men and women still lying on the streets of the city, as Elecia had instructed. Instead, she strolled out to a garden and positioned herself hidden among the shrubbery, where she could watch a birdcage greenhouse.

This is a place of fate.

Aldrik appeared, frantic, Vhalla dying in his arms. There was no sign of Victor. He was defeated then.

She'd been right: the magic he'd siphoned from Raspian was little more than a taste. If it had been anything of substance, Vhalla and Aldrik wouldn't have been able to end him. She could already feel the dark god's magic leaving this place like a heavy fog lifting. It dissipated into the ether between the worlds of men and gods, to search for its next host.

Aldrik ran out and then returned with Elecia. But the curly haired woman soon darted from the greenhouse, shouting, "I'm going to try to find Sehra!"

The instinct was right. Out of everyone, Sehra was the only one with enough magic to heal Vhalla. But the girl was not versed enough—not powerful enough—to cure the wounds Vhalla had.

Durroe watt ivin. The words echoed from within. She didn't need to speak them aloud anymore. She was as much the words as the words were her. The glyphs bent to her will, rising to the surface, and giving her Sehra's face.

She stepped forward and drifted down the path before entering the greenhouse.

The first thing she noticed was the smell of roses, potent and bright, warm and oddly familiar.

Where did we smell these before?

Ah, yes.

These were Fiera's roses. Just one inhale took her all the way back to the early days on this world. But that had been a different Vi then, a less *evolved* one. A Vi who had wants and fears—all things she was now able to set aside.

"Sehra," Aldrik pleaded with tears in his eyes. "Save her please, your magic, can it—"

"I understand." Vi's eyes rested on Vhalla. Their last meeting in that long, dark night had been so contentious and painful. Those were emotions she hardly felt now, looking at the girl. Crackles of red lightning illuminated the air around Vhalla, visible only to Vi's new eyes. Her magic had been cast out of balance. *Raspian was a wicked entity, indeed.* Kneeling next to her, Vi spoke gently, "You did well. The crystals' magic is diminishing. They were never meant to be used as they were, manipulated for man's greed. They weren't left with that intent."

"What?" Aldrik asked.

"You saw them. They turn brittle and shatter under their own weight. They will be gone by dawn." *And I will take the magic of the divine off this land for good.* If Vi had one wish left, it was to see that nothing of Raspian, or Yargen, ever returned to the Dark Isle.

"Princess, we need to act quickly," Aldrik urged. "She's dying."

"I know." Vi's attention remained solely on Vhalla. "Vhalla Yarl, after all that you have been through, do you still want to be upon this earth?"

"How can you ask that? Of course I do."

"*Of course,*" Vi repeated. Fate still had plans for Vhalla, after all. Plans that Vi's yet mortal consciousness couldn't fully grasp. "Very well. I will grant you the power of Yargen one more time. I will change this fate set before you."

Her body moved and both of Vi's hands were on Vhalla's cheeks. She felt a small smile cross her lips. Was this what happiness and contentment felt like? She couldn't remember.

Halleth.

The word flowed through her. There weren't any modifiers, any need for clarification—simply, heal. With a tender touch, Vi guided every frayed and out-of-place thread of magic within her body back into its rightful spot. She mended wounds. She sought to return Vhalla to the state she was in before this darkness had settled on the land.

Satisfied, Vi pulled her hands away and stood. She swayed slightly, looking at Vhalla and Aldrik for what she knew was the last time. These people she'd watched over for years. Now, she would leave them to live out their days as they were meant to do.

"Are you all right?" Aldrik asked her.

"I am, but time is short. I'm no longer meant for this world." She had a dark god to settle the score with.

"Sehra, we can seek out another cleric."

"No need." Vi paused at the door. "You did well, but things are only beginning. The vortex still spins." And the only one who could end it was her.

"Sehra!" Vhalla jumped to her feet.

"If that is the name you choose." Vi gave her one last smile and slipped out the door, walking away from the lives of Vhalla and Aldrik one final time.

SEA MIST SPRAYED HER face as Vi sat serenely in the rowboat that carried her far out around the corners of the cliffs of Oparium. Her hands were folded neatly in her lap, feet tucked under her. She swayed with the rolling of the ocean, never off-balance, always expecting the next wave that would jostle the little vessel.

The pirates who were escorting her, however, had less luck. They were tossed back and forth in the gray seas. A storm brewed on the horizon; Vi searched it for red lightning.

The *Stormfrost* stood anchored in a wide-mouthed cove. The mist that peeled off of it in sheets acted as a natural camouflage, mostly obscuring the vessel in fog. But there wasn't much travel in these waters yet. Victor had died a mere day ago, and significant rebuilding had to happen before anyone was trading in the seas around the Dark Isle.

The pirates gave her wary glances from time to time, more when they hooked up the rigging. The natural magics surrounding their bodies, the ones Vi was learning made up every living thing, vibrated with apprehension. She made them anxious, which amused her.

At least, she thought it was amusing to her.

One of the men reluctantly offered her his hand to help her on deck and Vi accepted it. He went rigid at her touch and then massaged his palm when her fingertips left it. A smile quirked her lips. Yes, these mortal anxieties were, indeed, amusing, much like she imagined a mother would be amused by their child fretting over a rip in the dress of a beloved doll.

"I was beginning to wonder when you would come," Adela griped, tapping over to her with her cane in hand.

"Everything in its own time. No sooner. No later."

"Yes, well..." For the first time, even Adela seemed off-put by her. "Your friend is below. I trust you remember the cabin."

"Thank you," Vi said and gave a nod.

She descended belowdecks as Adela shouted, "Raise the anchor! Let's get out of this backwater place!"

A woman emerged from a cabin door. Her bright blue eyes met Vi's and they were flooded with relief. Deneya threw her arms around Vi's shoulders. Vi slowly lifted her arms and gently patted the woman's back as she believed a friend would.

"It has been forever."

"Not that long."

"Okay, you're right, it's been about a year." Deneya laughed, pulling away. Her face suddenly became somber. She scanned the otherwise empty hall. "Where's Taavin?"

"His consciousness returned to the watch. Why? I do not know. It was his will I believe. The watch is within Vhalla's possession and the essence of Yargen that his body was constructed from is within me now."

"Okay… that was a lot." Deneya clasped her shoulder, giving her a light shake. "I'm not ashamed to admit that I only followed half of that. And that's okay but, Vi, what really happened?"

"I have told you what has happened."

"No, I mean, with you."

"I have told you what has happened," Vi repeated, slightly more curt. She couldn't blame the mortal for not fully understanding, but it would be tiring to say the same explanation over and over.

"No, you're…" Deneya trailed off again. Confusion furrowed her brow. "You're different now."

"I know."

"It's all the crystal magic, isn't it?"

"Yes."

Deneya stared at her expectantly. Vi suspected she was waiting for her to explain further. But Vi didn't make even a remote effort to do so. It was clearly too much for Deneya to understand.

"How are you holding up?" Deneya asked delicately.

"I'm fine. Do you have it?" Vi shifted the topic of conversation.

"What? Oh. Yes."

"Show me."

Deneya led Vi back into the cabin. It was the same as last time—two bunks on either side of a small window. Beneath the window was a table and on the table was a golden box.

Vi opened it and, with her new eyes, saw the glyphs of a thousand divine words swirling around every speck of ash.

"When they find out the flame is gone, they'll likely kill the Voice for it," Deneya said gravely.

"She served her duty to this world." Vi hoped the words would cheer Deneya, though they didn't look like they did. "She was meant to die." Still, no change in her expression. Vi sighed. "You see, because she died, I will be able to become—"

"I understand what you're saying," Deneya interrupted. "What I don't understand is how you can say it that way."

"What way?" She'd merely been stating fact.

"As if someone's death means nothing." Deneya approached her. "When I last saw you… you negotiated with a pirate for a single boy's life who was nothing more to you than a friend's lover—a friend from another world, even. You enlisted in the army just to save the daughter of a woman you'd once called 'friend.' You fought fate to save a man whom you, in fact, had no relationship with, because he shared the same face as the man who'd raised you." Her purple-ringed eyes searched Vi's. "What happened to that woman?"

"She's gone," Vi said, lightly touching Deneya's forearm. "But it's all right, because I am here now. I will protect this world."

"I don't know who *you* are. And I don't even know if I want you here." Deneya shook her head and stepped away. "What Champion sees the lives of those they're sworn to protect as forfeit? What world is worth protecting if everyone in it is just a piece on some game board for higher powers?" Deneya waited for a response, but Vi kept her mouth closed. She could see the woman didn't really want to hear anything she had to say. With a sigh, Deneya opened the door. "If you need me, I'll be on deck."

Deneya was in pain. The idea of people dying still hurt her. Vi looked to the ashes for solace. Deneya couldn't see the lines of magic that connected everything and everyone to keep the world in balance, like Vi could. She didn't know how life continued on within those unseen connections.

She was oblivious to the meaning in everything.

That was all right. A slight smile crossed her lips. Mortals could be like that, couldn't they? And their shortsightedness made them endearing.

She sat on the lower bunk that did not look like it had been slept in. She took the open box, placed it in her lap, and remained transfixed on its contents.

"But you understand, don't you?" Vi whispered.

I do.

"You will help me see that all these deaths have meaning? That there is no pointless suffering… even if they cannot see how their pain has a hand in fate?"

I will.

"Thank you." Vi beamed from ear to ear. "Is now the time?"

Not yet. Enjoy your final hours on this earth.

"When it happens, will it hurt?"

No, it will not hurt. When it happens, you will not feel anything.

"Good," Vi murmured. She closed her eyes, thinking of the most logical path to Salvidia. It would take them at least five days to get there. That was a lot of time to sit with a goddess. "I would like to ask you something."

You would like to ask me a great many things.

"True." She chuckled faintly. Laughter felt weird now. Even breathing felt strange, as though it was an unnecessary task her body insisted on doing. Yet, when she tried to stop, her lungs burned until her mouth gave in. "Tell me of the world beyond Salvidia? Tell me what lies beyond the seas, beyond the large continent to the southwest of Meru?"

You wish to know of the whole world.

"Yes." Vi closed her eyes, remembering the vision Yargen had given her of the room high above the world. The place where everything was seen and known.

You will know it, child.

"When?"

When we reach the final stop on your journey, I will give you the opportunity to know everything.

Vi stood on the deck of the vessel as they approached the isle of the elfin'ra. It was a barren place, with stone structures cutting up the horizon like pretend mountains. Somewhere, in the center of it all, were those ritualistic ruins that had stood for centuries. The same ruins Vi had seen in one of her early visions.

In that vision, there had been a body wrapped in a bag. A blood-offering had summoned Raspian in the failed future she'd been born into. Taavin had explained to her then that there were three ways to summon Raspian—the blood of the Voice, the blood of the Champion, or the ashes of the flame.

In this world, Vi came willingly. They would not need her blood because the ashes of the Flame of Yargen would be freely given to summon the dark god.

"I'm not asking my crew to get any closer," Adela grumbled at her side. "I hope you're a strong swimmer."

"Give me a rowboat, that's all I require."

"Fine, then our deal is done."

"There are terms that persist." Vi faced the pirate queen. "The boy Fallor."

"Yes, I understand, I'll never touch him." Adela looked forward. "Now stop staring at me with those creepy eyes."

Adela feared her now, too. The fear that vibrated at her edges was different than the others. Adela still denied being afraid to herself. The pirate had stopped allowing fear to enter her mind long, long ago. So the fear was suppressed and muted. But it *was* fear, nonetheless.

Adela demanded a rowboat be readied. Vi followed close behind.

"Here's your rowboat." The pirate queen motioned to the vessel. "Now I've done all you asked. Tell me of these passageways into the Archives."

Vi looked at Deneya. In her hands was the box holding the ashes of the Flame of Yargen. Just from the way she held herself, she stuck out in the group of pirates. She could never fit in here, and Adela would take her far from Risen if Vi didn't do something.

Perhaps Deneya had been wrong, and there was just enough humanity within her to save an old friend. Vi silently thanked Yargen for making her wait to absorb the last part of the goddess's essence.

"Deneya will show you the passages. Take her back to Risen."

"I'm coming with you," Deneya said, stepping forward.

"No. This is not a place for mortals," Vi said softly. "Go back with them to Risen, and show them what you know of the Archives." Vi suspected Deneya had learned much when she'd gone to procure the Flame.

Deneya searched her face and Vi tried to silently encourage her agreement. This was the only way she would get back to Risen. Vi was out of negotiated trips.

What Deneya did once there was up to her. She could try to flee. Or she could tell them about a passage into the Archives, only to have an ambush waiting.

"All right." It seemed Deneya was smart enough to figure those things out. She stepped forward, awkwardly hovering before Vi. "Be careful saving the world, I guess."

Vi nodded her head. "All will be light."

With the box in hand, Vi sat on the railing of the *Stormfrost* and swung her legs into the rowboat with ease.

"Lower me," Vi commanded, and the pirates followed her orders. As soon as the rowboat met the water, Vi glanced at each of the ropes holding it. With *juth calt*, she destroyed each one. Then, she envisioned the glyph for *kot sorre* in the water behind her. She pushed it forward and the skiff moved over the waves toward the isle of the elfin'ra.

A group of men and women had collected on the beach. They'd likely been drawn over by the sight of the *Stormfrost* in the distance. In Vi's world, this meeting might have been the moment Adela crawled into bed with the elfin'ra. Perhaps even in this world, the pirate queen would've allied herself had it not been for Vi sending Adela away.

The skiff beached itself and Vi released her mental hold on the glyph. The elfin'ra surrounded her in a semicircle. They whispered under their breaths, but none made any motion to attack. They all watched as Vi stood and stepped onto the sand and surf of an island that had been surrounded by an impenetrable barrier for thousands of years.

Finally, a man stepped forward. Vi recognized him from her vision and assumed him to be some sort of high priest of Raspian.

"Who are you?" he asked.

"I am here to meet with your lord," she said to him. "I have brought you the ashes of the Flame of Yargen so that you may summon him. And so that we might once and for all bring an end to the vortex."

38

THE HIGH PRIEST LED her down a beach path that quickly became gravely as it meandered between boulders and then buildings. The isle on the whole was smaller than Vi had expected. Yet she wasn't surprised by its size. No, *she* was surprised; but the goddess who was taking over her mind and body was not.

"Why would Yargen come to us?" the high priest asked casually. He was merely curious, not disbelieving.

"Because this world is held in balance by him and—" Vi almost said *me* "—Yargen. Due to the actions of man, it has been thrown dangerously out of order. I have been working to correct it for thousands of years."

"*You?*" The man looked her up and down with his red eyes. "You are her Champion?"

"I am." There were murmurs at the admission behind her.

"Tell me why I shouldn't slay you here and now and use your blood to summon my lord?" The man grinned wickedly at her. "That way he might usher in a new age of darkness without the burden of Yargen's strongest warrior."

"Because you cannot kill me," Vi said lightly. Part of her was amused at the idea of them trying, though Vi couldn't tell if that was her own feeling or the goddess's. "And because I bring you the ashes willingly."

"I say we kill her now," a woman shouted behind her.

A man clearly agreed because he lunged for her. Vi turned her head and thought, *juth calt*. He seized and fell to the ground. Another woman screamed and rushed over to him, shaking him as a trickle of blood came out of his pasty lips.

"Foolish," the priest sighed, as if the man's death was little more than a frustrating inconvenience. Vi sympathized with the sentiment. "Please, no more of that," he said to the group behind them. All of the others nodded in unison. "Our lord will need your blood fresh for his glorious return. To waste your life is to go against his will."

They crossed into a desolate city square. More people were beginning to follow them as they marched through the cobblestone streets. The elfin'ra on the whole were an emaciated people with hungry eyes.

"Why do you worship Raspian?"

"I'm surprised you would ask." The man glanced at her.

"I admit to being curious."

"Very well… On Meru, there were once temples for both Raspian and Yargen. But after her last victory that ushered in this age of light, Yargen cast Raspian's temple out to sea on a lone island." Vi wondered where that isle might be. Perhaps it was Salvidia. "Unlike all the other times they had done battle, this past time she sealed him off in an unnatural way and ruled that none should worship him."

"There were those who worshiped him before?" Vi tried to imagine a time when worshipers of Yargen and Raspian lived side-by-side. Thanks to the goddess, she had hazy visions of such a thing occurring on ancient Meru.

"Oh yes. What is light without the darkness? Or darkness without the light? I do not revere Yargen." He scrunched his nose in a scowl, accentuating the point. "But I understand her role. I merely choose to relish the darkness. I choose the chaos his beast makes in our world. We all choose this because we believe that in nothingness exists true equality."

Equality through the destruction of all things… Vi certainly didn't agree with the notion. But as the Champion of Yargen, she wasn't supposed to. Perhaps, as he said, all she was meant to do was understand it.

They ascended an endless flight of stairs to a ridge. On the other side, a pathway sloped toward the sea. It ended on a plateau where a lone altar stood. Vi glanced behind her at the red-eyed men and women who had followed them to this point.

All these people were willing sacrifices for Raspian.

She wanted to tell them that their lives still meant something. But in their eyes, their greatest purpose was the one they stood ready to fulfill. She could see it in each one of them, how they walked with relaxed faces, as though in a trance. The closer they got to the altar, the more the elfin'ra moved as one unit, breathing together, marching together.

The moon was high as Vi crossed the threshold of the stones that surrounded the altar. At the center was the relief carving of a dragon, curling around on itself to form a perfect circle. A line had been drawn through the middle and cleaved the whole image in two, off-setting the halves. The image was meant to represent Raspian's dragon breaking free of its lunar prison, ready to reap chaos on the world.

All those assembled moved around the symbol. They formed a second row, then a third. When everyone was in position, five complete circles of elfin'ra stood shoulder to shoulder around the altar.

The head priest positioned himself at the center of the circles, before the altar.

"Bring me the ashes," he commanded.

Vi opened the box. This was the moment she let go of herself. Yargen had made her body with the intention of its eventual return to the goddess. Fulfilling that intention wouldn't hurt. Yargen had told her that much.

Bringing the box to her face, Vi tilted her head down and inhaled deeply. The ashes filled her nose, mouth, and eyes. The magic they contained blinded her and burned her from within, singeing every corner of her body. But there was no pain.

She felt only warmth, like sinking deeply into a familiar bed, the blankets layered so high, she never wanted to escape.

Her inner organs seared away. Underneath the once-tender flesh was crystal, and more crystal. Just as she had been in Taavin, the crystal was alive in her. It had always been.

Yargen? she thought. Vi's existence was more inward than outward now.

I am here with you. I am *you.*

Vi coughed and a waterfall of ash cascaded from her mouth and back into the box. Slowly, the world came back into focus. She could see and hear, but her body was fully in Yargen's control. She thought she'd been ready to fully relinquish control, but being a mere observer in her own skin rattled a corner of Vi's consciousness that she thought had been long smothered.

"Summon him for me." Vi felt her mouth form the words, but she did not feel herself say them. Her arms stretched outward, carrying the box forward. Her arms were awash in light, every color swirled atop them, settling into her skin before shifting again. Judging from the reactions on the elfin'ras' faces, this was not her vision alone. This was her new body—the body of a goddess returned.

Together, Vi thought frantically.

A subtle hum was her reply.

I want to take this final step together. I can help you.

How? Yargen demanded. Vi could feel the rest of the unspoken question. How could a mortal help a divine being?

You have fought him as yourself, time and again. He knows you, Vi insisted. *He does not know me. Let me help you end this.*

Eternity drifted through her mind as the goddess debated her proposition. *Very well, mortal. So it shall be.*

The sensation of her body returned to her with tingling waves of magic. In her mind, she stood side-by-side with Yargen. It was not the same control as before; Yargen was not forfeiting out of necessity because her essence was not complete. Yargen was *allowing* Vi this final act.

"Scatter the ashes on his mark, and we shall begin," the priest boomed.

The elfin'ra parted so Vi could enter the symbol. She did as instructed, scattering the ashes all around her. She stepped back out of the symbol, discarded the box, and watched as the elfin'ra closed back the circles again, all looking to their high priest.

The head priest raised his arm and drew a dagger from his belt. He sliced himself from forearm to palm. He held his wound over a stone chute that directed his blood into the carving of the split dragon below. The crimson river flowed unnaturally fast down the carved channels, filling in the outlines. As soon as the symbol was drawn in blood, it began to glow a bright red.

He began chanting, words fast and low that Vi barely recognized. She understood them though Yargen's ears as the language of the gods, but trying to comprehend them with even a fraction of a mortal mind was impossible, so she didn't try. She was beginning to learn the limitations of her shared space—what she could and couldn't control, how much Yargen would let her understand and do.

The men and women of the circles raised their arms, joining their voices with their leader's. The chanting grew louder and louder; some were wailing the words by the end. They threw their heads back in what looked like ecstasy, eyes rolling back.

Dark, ominous clouds rolled in overhead. The wind picked up around them, swirling to this spot, as though there were a void before her, sucking in the air.

Vi widened her stance, bracing herself. Even in a place of darkness, her magic connected with the earth. She felt Yargen's powers grounding her, connecting with the land beneath her feet.

The head priest descended from the dais with a purposeful stride. His face was red from shouting, and his eyes glowed a brilliant vermilion. He stared at her issuing a silent challenge; Vi readied herself, allowing ripples of magic to pulsate from her form.

When the man reached the center of the circled zealots, everything reached a crescendo in a bolt of blood-red lightning.

It struck the man, sparking off and sending the other men and women around him flying back. Their bodies, dead, littered the ground. Magic arced through the air like the rebirth of a cosmos, all condensing on a glowing figure rising from where the leader of this dark ritual had once stood.

A roar cut through the ringing in Vi's ears as the man tilted his head back and let out a primordial cry. He should be dead; the lightning had struck him square in the chest. Instead he wore the red light as a second skin, seeming to grow in size before Vi's eyes.

She'd seen all this before. Perhaps that was why she was so calm. She'd seen it in her vision of her failed future, and Yargen had seen it countless times. This was how it always began: a battle to determine which god would rule the next cycle of the world.

The man's jaw elongated with his screams. She watched as it jutted painfully outward. Vi heard the crunching of bones and witnessed new growth to make room for rows of razor-sharp teeth. His skin became hard and leathery as it stretched across plated armor underneath. His face became even more sunken and skull-like. His hair floated around him, swirling with the magic tempest he was birthed within. His eyes rolled back completely, exposing whites that seemed to glow faintly.

Lightning continued to strike around them. The electricity burnt away each of the bodies, as if rabidly consuming what scraps were left of the mortal essence that had brought both divine beings back into the world. Raspian continued to grow, remaking the mortal form that was given to him into something he found suitable.

Then, all at once, the wind died, the lightning ceased, and the world was still.

She didn't have to look around to know that time and space had shifted. Reality distorted around the weight of the gods. The landscape had become even more barren, every building crumbling to dust. The horizon had all but vanished. Over Raspian's right shoulder, the moon hung, cracked and bleeding, about to give birth to a wyvern that was ready to consume the world whole.

This suspended reality, outside of time, was a temporary battleground for them. It was the place the opposing gods could exist simultaneously: not quite the mortal realm and not quite the land of the divine. They could decide the victor here—who would return to the real world and rule, and who would be trapped in this liminal space until the next great battle.

Vi didn't dare take her eyes off the dark god. She watched him warily. At any moment, he would attack, and their final battle would begin. The memory of her final vision, following the destruction of the Crystal Caverns, cut through all of Yargen's influences and stood out in her memory.

The vision, that's why you need me! Vi tried to communicate hastily with the goddess.

Vision? What vision? Vi didn't have a chance to respond as Raspian raised a hand, pointing a clawed finger at her. Lightning punctuated his every movement. He opened his mouth and sound filled her mind.

"You *finally* meet me once more, Yargen."

39

"IT'S TIME," YARGEN SAID through Vi's mouth, using the language of the divine. Vi felt her lips make the sounds and understood the meaning of the words, but she couldn't have repeated them if she tried. "Go willingly into your darkness. Meet me once more in a thousand years."

"After you trapped me in that pit? No, perhaps you should feel what it's like to be contained and smothered with no natural way out."

He lifted his hand and Vi felt the magic collecting there. Yargen acted before she could.

She moved, tilting to the side, her hand swinging back. A spear of light trailed the line of her fingertips through the air. Her hand closed around it. She flung it forward.

The spear crashed against Raspian without so much as stunning him. He lifted his hand and a crack of lightning shot into the sky above. It arced through the clouds and came down as a hailstorm of bolts.

Vi dodged each one quickly. She retreated, gaining distance. Each attack carved static electricity through the air, giving her a split second to react before a bolt of red lightning scarred the earth where she had been standing.

Raspian lowered his hand and lumbered forward. He swung his other hand upward to cleave the land beneath her feet. Her body was sent tumbling back, head over heels. She dug her hands into the earth, seeking purchase. Just when she found her footing, a large rock fell atop her back and Vi cried out in pain.

She might be sharing her mind, but Vi felt every blow as though it was solely her own to bear.

"What a weak mortal form you chose this time," Raspian said with his booming voice. "You have committed yourself to one girl, Yargen, when I have had generations of devotees ready to bleed for me. I took the essence of hundreds. What can one mortal do for you?"

We have to get on the offensive, Vi urged the goddess within her. *He's larger and slower. We can out-maneuver him.*

She lifted her head and brought her hands under her shoulders, pushing upward with a grunt and finding her feet. With a strength no mortal should possess, she dislodged the boulder. Her focus returned to the dark god just in time to see Raspian swinging a clawed hand down toward her.

Vi's instincts kicked in. *"Mysst xieh!"* The words escaped her, even if they no longer needed to be said. She reached across her abdomen. *Mysst soto larrk*, Yargen's voice echoed in her mind as her magic wove a sword into existence. Fingers around the hilt, Vi drew it as if from a sheathe and slashed it across Raspian's lower stomach.

Light flashed off the sword like steel on flint. There wasn't so much as a scratch left behind on his gut. Raspian swung up with his other arm, reaching for her face. Vi bent backwards.

Wildly off balance, she flailed. Yargen's instincts kicked in. Her right foot swung out, her left bent as she tipped backwards, and she allowed herself to fall. A word Vi didn't understand echoed across her mind. She plunged into the earth as though it were a pool of water. The once-hard stone vanished into puffs of light.

Suddenly, she was falling through the sky.

Vi twisted mid-air and looked at the ground beneath her, desperately trying to keep up with the goddess. Raspian spun in place, looking for her. His thunderous steps shook the ground.

A spear of light was back in her hands. Wielding it in both, Vi was ready to use all the momentum of her fall to sink into his shoulder, but a bolt of lightning shot her down from the sky.

Smoking and spinning off-course, she shoved the spear into the ground before her body met the hard earth. She spun around the weapon before it vanished. When Vi landed on the ground, she broke into a run. Raspian had turned to meet her.

Vi stole back control of her body from Yargen. She bounced backward at the last moment, flipping through the air. She'd never done such acrobatics in her life, but being divine had its perks. Yargen seemed to know Vi's intentions at the same time, if not before, they crossed Vi's mind.

When she landed she reared back. *Misst soto gotha.* A bow appeared in her hands and Vi released three arrows at once. As they flew toward Raspian, she threw out a hand, allowing her spark to run rampant. It was a hybrid of her Firebearer magic and *juth starys*.

Fire erupted around Raspian's feet and he let out a roar as one of her arrows sank into a soft spot between the bony plates that protected his body.

So he can be wounded, Vi thought.

Not easily, Yargen replied.

Raspian recovered faster than Vi expected. He raised his arm in a straight line and the earth mirrored his motion. Clay grew like a Groundbreaker's wall. The hand Vi had thrown out in the attack was enveloped in slime. Vi tugged and tugged, but the red earth hardened before she could free herself.

The dark god approached. She could feel static building in the air. Vi readied an attack when her free arm moved without her permission.

Mysst soto laark. The glyphs for the words appeared around her hand as it closed on a sword. In one motion, without any hesitation, her body moved and sliced off its own arm.

Vi screamed, though mostly in her own mind. No blood poured from the wound.

It hardly hurt more than any other blow she'd taken, but the shock of cutting off her own arm made her dizzy.

Yargen was in control. She sprinted away from Raspian, pouring power into the severed stub of her arm. Crystals emerged, taking the shape of a new elbow, forearm, and hand. By the time her fingers closed in a fist, the appendage looked as normal as the last.

A wave of red magic erupted behind her. Vi looked over her shoulder, watching it crash over every rock and ledge. There was no way she could outrun it.

Spinning in place, she crossed her arms before her, kneeling. *Mysst xieh rohko hoolo.* The words combined in a way Vi had never expected, but with Yargen's full power surging in her veins, a cocoon of light surrounded her just before the rush of Raspian's power overtook her.

Sharp snaps, like whips against the outside of her barrier, filled her ears. Vi kept her eyes closed, breathing and focusing on nothing more than putting power into her shield. She felt it beginning to crack, worn thin under the assault. Lightning reached in, searching for her like flailing tentacles before fizzling out.

As soon as it faded she bounced upward, pushing the barrier out from her in a blinding flash of light. Raspian roared in frustration, holding his eyes. Vi moved for him. *Mysst sut.* This time, an axe was in her hands.

Wielding it two-handed, she leapt and swung it against the side of his face. Raspian recovered, turned, and opened his mouth. He caught her weapon between his teeth, clamping down and shattering it.

Vi tumbled with her remaining momentum, thrown over to his side. Raspian lunged for her. The weight of worlds threatened to smother her as the god was atop her. He grabbed her shoulder with his claws, pressing her into the ground.

We need to move! Fall in the sky! Vi thought loudly, willing her body to sink into the earth and appear elsewhere.

Too soon.

"*Loft dorh!*" Vi shouted as Raspian swung a claw for her face. He froze, tipping forward, off-balance. Vi scrambled out from underneath him, his claws ripping her shoulder.

On her feet again, Vi spun as Raspian regained control of himself. *Chronot!* Vi thought. It had been Taavin's word. But Taavin had gained the word from the goddess who was now within her, and the magic blessedly worked.

Vi's glyph remained steady on Raspian, fading slowly. *Thank you, Taavin.* She spared a brief thought for the man she loved and the moment she did, her heart beat faster. She felt her breath. She tasted the metallic tang of panic in her mouth. She felt human and *alive*.

Summoning an axe to her hands again, Vi swung it overhead at the nape of Raspian's neck. It stuck, sinking deep into his skin. Magic, not blood, oozed around it, releasing into the air as a dark and rusty haze.

Raspian's features softened. He became clay-like and was absorbed into the earth before Vi's eyes. She spun, searching frantically for him.

Thrusting her arm into the air, a bolt of power shot upward, reflecting off the swiftly cracking moon. In this distorted reality of the gods, it seemed like everything was connected in odd ways. The sky was closer. The ground was malleable. The stars were gone unless they decided to put them there.

Her magic illuminated the barren earth. Light rained down as droplets that seared the ground like acid. A roar echoed across the sky as Raspian emerged from below with an eruption of lightning and lava.

Kot sorre. Vi pushed the lava back with a glyph in each hand, holding it at bay. She locked eyes with the god who was trudging over to her as the molten earth cooled. The sky was still filled with fading light and she could see every gnarled element of his nightmarish form.

Durroe watt ivin. Nine illusions fanned out from her, surrounding Raspian. Vi ran to the right. The other illusions danced around her, darting in and out, trading places. She was the living version of a street urchin's card game—find the queen. Raspian was twisting, trying to keep track of her.

Vi lifted a hand, firing a bolt of pure light at him. Every other illusion repeated the same motion. Raspian swung at one, his claws sinking through it. The mirrored version of her dissipated on the wind as her magic struck him in the back. She danced again, struck again.

"Enough games!" Raspian snarled. He tilted his head back and roared at the sky. Vi didn't have time to react before lightning rained down all around her, one bolt striking her square in the chest. She felt it arc between her ribs. Her body seized as she fell to the ground, wheezing.

Blinking into the void above her, Vi gasped for air.

Keep moving.

She didn't know if it was her voice or Yargen's that commanded it, but Vi struggled to her feet. Her whole body continued to seize and tremble as the lightning created a cage over top of her, pinning her to the ground.

A clawed hand closed around her neck. The red magic sank back into Raspian's arm as he hoisted her into the air. He held her aloft as she gripped at his forearm, gasping for breath.

"An age of darkness will rule this land once more." His terrible voice echoed in her mind as his lifeless eyes locked with hers. Every nightmare too horrible to be remembered come dawn lived in those eyes. "A thousand years of destruction. A thousand years when the land is razed and the earth is reset."

Vi pressed her eyes closed, blocking him out. Aldrik, Vhalla, Taavin, Romulin, Jax, a new Vi—everyone she'd loved in the world she'd been born into still lived in this world. Even if they were not the same people she once knew, even if they never knew her as she was now, they were living, breathing people who deserved a future.

"They deserve a future," she wheezed, opening her eyes. Eyes trained on his shoulder, she snarled a defiant, "*Juth calt!*"

The taut skin stretched over the unnatural armored plates of his body exploded with shards of bone. Raspian roared and his arm went limp at his side. He dropped her and Vi scrambled away, gasping for air.

Halleth, halleth, halleth. Heal me, Yargen, she begged. The light within her flashed brightly atop her skin like a protective coating. She felt the interior damage from Raspian's lightning mend. She felt the tissues in her throat reconnect.

But as she ran, the ground went soft beneath her. She was suddenly up to her waist in murky water. The light above her was going dark. Blood spilled from the fractured moon, flooding the land. Vi tilted her gaze upward and saw an eye open in one of the larger cracks.

She felt like she had been holding her own against the dark god. But the longer the fight dragged on, the more control he was gaining over this temporary bubble they fought in. Soon, she would be drowning in his essence. His beast of chaos would be free of its cage and carry him back to the real world. She would be trapped here forever.

The water was rising. Vi worried that she would soon drown underneath its currents.

Raspian walked atop the water, crossing to her with ease. Vi continued to wade through. She glanced over her shoulder, panicked.

How do I kill him?

You cannot kill him. If our power is whole, neither of us can die.

Then what do I do? Vi frantically asked the goddess within her. *He's gaining the upper hand!*

We must seal him away.

We, not *you*. They were in this together. She had worked for decades toward this moment, to recollect the goddess. And even though she had lost everyone along the way, Yargen still stood by her.

Vi looked down at the water before her. *Mysst xieh.* A glyph appeared and Vi jumped onto it. *Mysst xieh.* Another glyph. She jumped from spinning magic to spinning magic atop the water, racing away from Raspian. She crossed the deepening channel created by the breaking moon toward the bank on the other side.

Her feet on solid ground again, Vi looked back to Raspian, but he was gone. She found high ground and held out both her hands. *Uncose*—Taavin's word for "expose truth." Light flashed across the land, the river of blood evaporated, and Raspian was visible once more.

Vi raced down, bounding across the stones. *Kot sidee!* She pushed a glyph onto him, forcing him to brace himself. *Mysst soto tonc.* A spear appeared in her hand, and she threw it at his head. He grabbed it but in doing so didn't notice how she closed the gap in one giant leap, a sword in hand. Vi plunged it into his gut with a mighty scream.

Darkness exploded from the wound. She released the weapon, watching the magic unravel and the sword disappear as it sank into him. Raspian's glowing, dead eyes fixated on her as darkness sprayed like noxious gas from his body. It filled the air around her, threatening to suffocate her.

Soon, the world was blotted out entirely and the faint glow of magic that coated her body was the only light she could see by. Even the sky had vanished.

Vi spun, looking for any sign of him. She raised a hand, firing a beam of light into the darkness, and then another. She was shooting blind.

Uncose, she tried again. The light flashed out along the earth, but it did nothing for the darkness in the air. Vi moved over the desolate wasteland, climbing over rubble and buildings and what must be the remnants of the lives Raspian's loyal followers had made. Her feet stopped in the center of the glyph of the dragon, split in two. Vi spun in place, still searching.

Lightning cracked behind her, sparking a surreal sense of familiarity. She was in two places at once. She had seen this before.

The vision.

She turned, looking to the lightning on instinct. A plume of smoke rose from the dark spot on the ground, but there was nothing.

She heard the inhale. He was behind her. This was the moment of her vision, a truth that she had seen but that eluded Yargen. This was why she was meant to be in this battle. Vi only had time for one choice, one decision, one word, before his claws and teeth overcame her.

Wein.

Glyphs shot out from her midsection. One rose to the crown of her head and the other sank to her feet. A thick coating stretched over her skin, turning it to stone. A protective barrier, identical to the one Deneya had used that fateful night in the Caverns, now covered her.

Raspian was dedicated to his attack. His teeth and claws struck her barrier, bouncing off harmlessly. Vi spun, no longer turning away from the face of darkness itself. His gigantic arms were outstretched, ready to crush her.

Grasping both sides of his face, her brow furrowed, Vi snarled aloud, "*Suladin dupot chronot hoolo.*"

Suladin—seal him and lock him away once more for a millennium.

Dupot—enhance this power and make it stronger than ever before.

Chronot—slow its natural weakening over time.

Hoolo—stabilize and elongate.

Half of the words were hers and half were Taavin's. They had come from the goddess, but she and Taavin had made them their own. She heard him within her, across time and space, his voice echoing inside her.

The glyphs that surrounded them condensed into crystal. It started at Raspian's feet and began to creep up his body. He roared, swinging for her. Vi released his face, leaving crystal handprints embedded in his flesh, and stepped out of reach.

Her mouth began to move. The language of the gods spilled from her tongue almost like a song. The words were light and airy; they boomed power and whispered twisting glyphs into existence. Despite Raspian's struggles, the crystals continued to grow up his body, caging him.

With a final roar, Raspian promised he would one day return—as he always did.

Then, silence.

Stillness.

The crystals grew toward the moon. They would patch the cracks and smooth over the edges of chaos that nearly escaped into the world she loved.

Yargen's chant hastened, faster and faster. Vi felt power siphoning from her body like someone was pulling an invisible rope from her navel. Light flickered around her, growing ever stronger, fading, then brightening once more as the goddess's essence was drawn out to power the crystals.

This was how the Crystal Caverns had been formed, Vi realized. History was repeating itself. Yargen would split herself again. A new cavern would be made to entomb Raspian, hidden on a new land. And when that tomb was inevitably breached, Yargen would be too weak to fight him.

"Yargen," Vi whispered aloud. Her voice was her own—quivering, tired, scared, and human. "Do not split yourself again. The world needs you whole. Stop this vortex."

Silence within her was the goddess's response. Vi hoped she wasn't too late. She swallowed hard.

"Take me. Take my life. Seal him with all of my magic. Buy time for this world with the time left in me."

Are you certain?

Vi closed her eyes, a tired smile crossing her lips. One final time, the memories of all those she loved flooded her. She thought of the faces of every person she adored—those lost in her world who had lived on in her memories. After this, they would be gone for good.

And she would be gone, too.

"Do it," Vi said with conviction. "This is my destiny. This is what you brought me all this way for. The world still needs you."

Another few seconds of stillness before light exploded out from her. Vi watched as the raw essence of Yargen peeled away from her body. She couldn't stare directly at the goddess; Yargen was too blinding and too incomprehensible in this form. Vi squeezed her eyes shut.

Flames seared her from the inside out as her spark was set free one final time. Every layer of skin boiled off of her bones. Her tongue crisped and her hair singed. She unraveled in the reverse of how Yargen had made her. Cycle after cycle of becoming condensed into this singular moment of release, lifetimes in the making.

And Vi gave herself over to the brilliant void of nothingness.

Tick…

… Tock

Tick…
… Tock

Tick… Tock.

Tick. Tock.
Tick-tock.

Something ticked softly in the distance. A sound she shouldn't be able to hear—because she shouldn't have ears, at least not working ones.

She was dead. She'd died.

Hadn't she?

Who was she, anyway?

"Vi Solaris."

Ah, *yes*, that was her name. Or rather, it had been one of her names. She'd had so many of them. *Vi Solaris*—it was a good name. She'd thought that before, hadn't she? Yes, certainly. That name had meant something to her… something important.

"Vi Solaris, it is time to wake up."

It wasn't so much *waking* in the way Vi had once understood it. More like going from a state of stasis to a state of awareness. The light around her was blinding. She could see every color blending together into a brilliance far greater than what mortal eyes were meant to see.

She was a spirit—an idea of life. She was a slice of consciousness in the primordial void, drifting for who knew how long.

I know this place.

"Yes," a familiar voice said. Every man, woman, and child in the world was speaking all at once through the voice.

I shouldn't be here.

"No, this is not a place for you."

Her back settled on something solid. She had been drifting like a leaf through space and had finally settled somewhere soft. Vi blinked, which was odd, because she didn't really have eyelids in this state. Or maybe she did have eyelids? She blinked again. Yes, there were definitely eyelids of some kind.

Around her, a room came into focus. Marble columns supported a ceiling so high she couldn't see it. A bed of plush feathers and clouds surrounded her. A woman with long, black hair stood by a wide window that overlooked the whole world. Vi found herself inhabiting the vision she'd seen after absorbing the crown, but this time from a different vantage.

A familiar face of angular cheeks and sharp eyes regarded her. A silver necklace hung around the woman's neck. The chain was weighted down by a vaguely familiar silver pocket watch that had a sun and wing on its surface.

Ah, that was where the ticking was coming from.

"You look like Fiera this time." Vi smiled, though the expression felt weak and tired.

"Do I?"

Vi remembered the last time that she had been in a similar space with the goddess, a place where eternity stretched on forever. How painful it had been before, to lay eyes on Yargen's raw form. She was grateful now that Yargen took the shape of something—someone—easier to comprehend.

Before.

What had happened before?

"The battle with Raspian," Yargen reminded her gently.

Yes, that was it. The pieces clarified and slotted back into place, one after the other.

"I died," Vi whispered. She sat up. A body was attached to her essence now, though Vi had the distinct feeling that what she perceived as a body was merely another aspect of Yargen's magic. It was another way her mind tried to comprehend an impossible place and situation.

"In a way."

"Death seems fairly black and white."

"I have carved earth from nothingness. I have breathed life into creations of crystal. For me, very little is black and white." Yargen crossed over and sat on the edge of the bed. "Yes, you gave the raw essence of life itself—such a powerful thing—and the body that housed it back to me, so that Raspian could be sealed. But consciousness does little to seal away dark gods."

"You took my body and life essence, but not my mind."

"Just so."

"Was what I gave… enough?"

"Yes." Yargen smiled with Fiera's lips. It was as tender and warm as the real princess's.

"Then the world…"

"The world you helped shape will be safe from Raspian for another thousand or two thousand years, perhaps more if we're lucky. Things were not rebuilt, this time." The smile became slightly coy and her eyes a little sad. "Eventually, he will break free of that containment. Or mortals will somehow find a way to set him free, whether they know what they're doing or not. Though I have made sure he is well hidden, this time."

"I see." Vi smoothed her hand over the foggy blanket atop her, watching glittering starlight dance underneath her fingers.

"Do not despair." Yargen rested her hand on hers gently. Magic and life shot through her. Vi inhaled sharply. Feelings were starting to return. Vi felt like laughing and weeping, singing and screaming, all at once. "That is simply the order of things. When he returns, I will be ready."

"You are not fractured, then?"

"Do I look fractured to you?"

"I've been told my eyes can lie to me around the divine, so I've stopped trusting them in moments like these."

Yargen chuckled at that. The sound was pure delight and as sweet as bells. "You have been an amusing one to watch, all these revolutions of the vortex."

"It's really all over then…" Vi looked out the window. She saw nothing but a bright blue sky, clear and filled with light. She brought her attention back to Yargen. "So why am I still here?"

"That is something I have debated for many mortal years now."

"Years?"

"For me, it has only been a moment." Yargen stood once more, looking down at her with Fiera's fiery eyes. "I have been thinking while I harbored your consciousness, keeping it safe from the passage of time. What is a just reward for a Champion who has served me so faithfully across the ages? Then, it occurred to me…

"Do you wish to return to that world?"

"What?" Vi whispered. Something jolted in her chest. It felt like a heartbeat, the first of what could be many.

"You enabled me to return the watch to Vhalla Yarl, and a Vi Solaris was born into the world you have saved. This new Vi's body is as you know it, though the world is slightly different than you remember. Your actions did cause ripples of change these past eighteen years. However, if it would please you, I could return your mind to that form."

Vi considered this, trying to wrap her head around it. "What would happen to the new Vi's consciousness? Would she know what's happened?"

"No, she wouldn't. You and she are mirrors; it would be a seamless merger of your awareness. Though there might be some memories and feelings from your separate childhoods that would get confused from time to time—memories you won't be sure which one of you made."

"Would it feel like two people at once?" Vi had that sensation before with Yargen. She wasn't keen to have it again.

"No. You would have one mind. One, final Vi Solaris."

"Would I feel like me?"

"Mortal feelings are elusive to me."

Vi looked around the room, considering this offer. She would be returned to the body of the ninety-fourth Vi Solaris, born into the world she'd saved. It would be a chance to live in a time that was not ending. And, if Yargen was to be believed, it wouldn't result in pain or confusion for the girl who was currently walking in that skin.

"What's the alternative?" Vi dared to ask.

"I would fully join you with my essence. You would live forever as an aspect of me. You would know every corner of this world and whatever comes next in a way a mortal never could, just as I promised."

"Are my parents and brother alive in this new world?" Yargen had mentioned ripples of change caused by her actions. Just because there had been a Vhalla and Aldrik when she'd left the Dark Isle didn't mean they still lived now.

"They are."

Relief made her dizzy and a sound somewhere between laughter and a sob escaped her. There were changes, but the people she held dearest were still there. She could still have a life with them—the life she'd been robbed of. "Tell me one more thing: is there a new Taavin?"

"Yes."

"Then I wish to return," Vi said gingerly, a smile working its way onto her lips. "I would rather live one life with them than an eternity without." Vi paused, then added hastily, "No offense, your magnificence."

Yargen laughed in delight once more. She crossed over to the bed and leaned forward. "I didn't expect you to choose differently."

Vi stared at the watch around the goddess's neck, realizing where it had come from. It was the timepiece Yargen had traded with Vhalla during that long, dark night. That meant the watch with Taavin's essence was still out there.

"Time for time," Vi whispered.

Yargen lifted her hand, touching the watch with a smile. "When Aldrik gave this to Vhalla, he bestowed on her his minutes, his hours, his days. I think he would be very pleased to know he was really giving them to you."

A thousand questions danced on her tongue but she remained in stunned silence as Yargen leaned forward. The visage of Fiera melted away to pure light. The goddess placed a single, tender kiss on Vi's forehead.

The air was sucked from Vi's lungs as she fell backward and descended from the realm of the divine one final time.

The room vanished into a misty light. Wind sped around her. Her eyes dipped closed and—

Vi woke with a gasp. She jolted forward, covers thrown from her shoulders and pooling around her waist. The smell of fresh wood, sap, and the damp tang of morning filled her nose. It was a familiar, nostalgic scent—one she hadn't smelled in a long time.

She looked around in the darkness. The walls were smoothed and polished. Overhead was a gnarled ceiling of decorative roots and branches that spilled down, weaving into the four corners of her bed. Across from the foot of the bed was a dresser, adorned with carefully painted portraits in gilded frames.

Turning, Vi peered at the candle on her bedside table. Her breath hitched as she lifted a hand.

The candle lit on command.

Vi threw off the familiar covers, standing. She grabbed at the sleeping gown she wore, feeling the cotton. She rushed over to the corner of the room. There, a pile of supplies was neatly stacked in the corner between the dresser and the window. A quiver she knew so very well hung on its peg, bow attached. She ran her fingertips over the fletchings of the arrows and the Solaris sigil emblazoned in the quiver's leather.

This was her room. Everything was just as she remembered it: the clothes she'd laid out for her birthday hunt, the candle she'd struggled to light. That meant she had woken at the dawn of her seventeenth birthday once more.

That also meant—

Vi sprinted from the bedroom. Her heart was racing faster than her feet. Every emotion was competing for dominance within her. Yargen's hold over her body and mind had been so slow that Vi hadn't realized for how long her emotions had been muted. It seemed like it'd been forever since she'd truly felt anything.

A strangled noise of hope and fear escaped her mouth as she rushed into the main living space of the quarters. The couches were in a slightly different spot than she remembered. Or… were they?

Yargen said time had continued along while her consciousness had been in stasis. There were changes and variations from the world she'd come from. Vi shook her head, turning to the door that led to her personal study. Only one thing mattered right now.

She yanked on it so hard that it slammed into the wall as Vi rushed into the room. Every map was where she remembered. The table where she'd drawn them was as much of a mess as she'd last left it.

Five presents were stacked atop the drafting table, neatly piled and out of place in the room.

"Don't let this have changed," she pleaded. *Let Fritz's gift be a stone in the river.*

Vi pushed aside four of the gifts and reached for a small parcel wrapped in black silk. It was feather-light and a had a black envelope slid under a black ribbon. Vi's fingers trembled as she ripped open the seal on the letter—the Broken Moon of the Tower of Sorcerers. The symbol of the Tower was something she needed to change the instant she got back to the palace. She couldn't look at it now without seeing Raspian's followers.

But Sorcerers and the sorting of symbols could wait. Vi hurriedly skimmed the letter that began with, "*Dear Vi*" and ended with, "*Your friend who cannot wait to meet and teach you, Fritznangle Chareem, Minister of Sorcery.*" She didn't need to read every word. She knew what it said.

Unwrapping the silken scarf, Vi found a silver pocket watch. She smoothed her fingers over its tarnished face. Her hands clutched it so tightly that her fingernails dug into her palms and her knuckles were white.

Vi dropped to her knees, tears flowing down her cheeks. Every emotion rushed through her at once. It made her tongue thick and her words awkward.

"*Narro haath,*" she dared to whisper.

Light sparked around her clenched hands. It formed the shape of a familiar glyph, one she understood better than ever. Magic raced across the ether, connecting her with the man whose communication mark had been imprinted long ago on this most precious token.

Silence.

And then, a familiar voice.

"What... Who—"

Vi covered her mouth, tears still falling in rivers down her cheeks. A new dawn broke through her window. With all the strength she could muster, Vi managed to say, "Hello, Taavin."

EPILOGUE

V I STOOD ON THE bow of the greatest vessel ever constructed for the Imperial Armada. She had spent her last month in the North drawing out ideas for the plans, based off the *Stormfrost* and what she had seen in Meru's fleet.

Of course, an actual shipwright in Solarin had to go through all of her drawings and turn them into usable blueprints. That process had taken nearly four months of convincing him that, yes, there were ways to build ships in the manner she'd drawn. He merely needed to expand his way of thinking and broaden what he considered "possible." Leveraging her family's relationship with Erion Le'Dan had ultimately helped expedite the process.

The construction had taken just over a year in a dry dock to the north of Norin.

It had been two agonizingly slow years until she'd christened the ship and they'd set sail. All of the patience she'd learned seemed to have been a casualty of her battle with Raspian. But in the end, the time it took to build was a good thing. There were other matters that had to fall into place.

Diplomacy took time, especially between two continents that had been closed off to each other for centuries.

"Is that it?" Ellene bounced from foot to foot. Vi had expected more of a fight from Sehra when she'd proposed that Ellene come along on this first diplomatic trip. But the moment Vi pointed out that this was the perfect opportunity for Ellene to spend some time studying Lightspinning in the land that invented it, Sehra instantly agreed.

"Yes. Careful, or you'll fall over the railing."

"I will not. I'm not that clumsy."

"You certainly are," Jayme said dryly. She leaned against the railing to Vi's left. Her back was to the land that had just come in sight.

"I am not!"

Jayme shot Vi a knowing grin that seemed to say *It's just too easy to rile her, isn't it?*

In the seventeen years Vi's consciousness had floated in Yargen's primordial stasis, the world had continued. But things were different in this world—different, and in so many ways, better.

There was no Adela terrorizing the seas of the Shattered Isles. After thieving from the Archives, the pirate queen decided to make herself scarce. Which also meant that Jayme was never recruited to act against Vi.

Because of what Vi had mentioned to Elecia, Daniel's existence was discovered much sooner. Elecia had told Jax, who went East immediately after the end of the war, and multiple times after. He found Daniel and, while he respected the man's wishes to remain mostly anonymous, he sent word to Aldrik and Vhalla. The royals had kept Daniel's life private and the man well taken care of.

So while Vi could still sense Jayme had mixed feelings about certain things, especially when it came to the crown's conquest and Mad King Victor, she didn't see the precursors of betrayal in the woman's eyes.

"I'm really glad you're both here with me," Vi said tenderly.

"Oh goodness, here she goes again." Ellene rolled her eyes. "You're not going to get all sappy on us for the next hour, are you? You've been terrible ever since you turned seventeen."

"No, I haven't!" She laughed, knowing well her friend was correct. Emotions were lovely and Vi had enjoyed feeling them again over the past two years. Perhaps a little too much, at times. "I'm just glad we could make this voyage together."

"I'm excited to see what the Crescent Continent holds." Jayme finally looked over her shoulder at the strip of land growing in size in the distance.

Footsteps approached from behind them. "I think that goes for all of us."

Jax and Elecia joined them at the bow. Elecia was dressed in finery that befit the Lady of the West. But Vi was still growing accustomed to seeing Jax in formal ceremonial garb.

She had memories of their wedding. Or rather, the Vi who had grown up in this world had those memories. The ceremony had taken place in the Cathedral of the Mother in Norin, and what Vi could picture was a breathtaking affair.

Elecia had grown impatient with Jax about five years ago. He was always stalling their relationship for "no reason." First it was heading to the East. Next it was setting up a new Golden Guard in the South. Then it was accepting a position to watch over Vi in the North when the first appointee—a man Vi had been too young to remember—retired.

In a way, Vi had now lived the best of both worlds. Her first childhood was full of memories in which she'd grown up with Jax as her surrogate father. But she also had memories of him finally chasing after his happily ever after. Now, she got to see him standing hand-in-hand with the woman he'd loved in every world.

Fortunately, while she could parse the memories apart, nothing was confusing or painful. It didn't feel as though she was competing with someone else for headspace. Yargen had been blessedly correct in that respect. And, as far as she could tell, the people she loved were none the wiser that her consciousness had undergone a transformation.

Vi turned her attention back to Risen.

The world spun, seasons changed, and people changed, but the one constant remained: love—the love of friends and family, the love that bound people together through the ages.

That was the love she now sought.

"You should go below and get ready, Vi," Elecia said thoughtfully. "We'll be dropping anchor before you know it."

"You're right. Excuse me."

Her cabin was one of the largest on the vessel. It was positioned in the back, with grand windows overlooking the sea. In many ways, it reminded her of Adela's cabin. Vi smiled to herself every time she entered, wondering what the pirate queen would think if she knew she'd inspired the flagship of Admiral Crown Princess Vi Solaris's budding armada.

The clothing she'd requested was neatly laid out: a fitted pair of leggings with a white split tunic that bore the Solaris crest. A wide belt attached a ceremonial sword to her hip. Everything was carefully embroidered in gold thread, reminiscent of a coat she knew so well she could draw it from memory.

On top of the tunic was a simple envelope. Vi lifted it, flipping it over. She'd said goodbye to her family when she left—that had been the hardest part, especially after getting to live nearly three years with them in Solarin while all the logistics for her voyage were being worked out.

The Senate was still adamant that it was too risky to have both heirs running all over the world and putting themselves in harm's way. But Vi got the impression Romulin would be all right staying in Solarin and working with Andru, the son of the head of Senate, and Minister Fritz.

Before she left, Vi had tasked them with brainstorming and ironing out some details for her next big idea. It was still in its infancy, but in a few years' time, if all went according to plan, Solaris and the Kingdoms of Meru would be reunited. And that called for a celebration to shake the ages.

Vi would oversee the diplomatic elements of treaties and alliances. Romulin, Andru, and Fritz would run with her wild ideas of lavish parties, friendly sorcerer competitions, and other ways to share knowledge and culture. She couldn't wait to see what would ultimately come to pass.

Her parents didn't come on the voyage because they refused to be separated. Not because they couldn't be; they simply didn't want to be. Vi didn't argue with that reasoning. She knew better than most what they'd gone through to be together now.

On the back of the envelope was a golden seal bearing the sun. She slid her finger underneath to break it, then slid out the letter and sat on the bed to read it.

Our dearest daughter,

We asked Elecia to give you this on your arrival to the Crescent Continent for one final reminder of home before you step off onto a new land for the first time.

Vi cracked a smile at the first line. It would be her first time... in this body.

We will of course remind you that these negotiations could open trade that would change our Empire and the lives of our people for the better. But we know you already understand this. After all, you were the one who somehow managed to open discussions with a closed off land that we, and our forefathers, had long since written off.

You will conduct yourself with grace and poise, of that we're certain. You've grown into a young woman wise beyond her years. We are so proud, and have every faith in you.

But the most important thing we wished to remind you of is that this is an opportunity for a grand adventure. This is the start of your journey. This is the moment you begin to write your story.

Go and explore. Seek adventure. Seek the world we have always seen you dreaming of.

When you are ready to return, your throne will be here waiting. We, and your brother, will be here waiting with all our love. But don't worry for us. We'll be fine.

For the first time, she could believe it. Solaris had a bright future ahead of it.

Our love goes with you. We cannot wait to hear all the stories you will have to tell when you return… Whenever that might be.

Your parents

Vi brought the letter to her lips and kissed it gently. "I love you too, mother, father," she whispered against the parchment. She could almost detect the faint scent of her mother's perfume, mixing with the smoke that always seemed to coat her father's clothes.

She read the letter twice more before setting it aside and beginning to dress. It felt like permission. It felt as though, somehow, her parents understood. One story had ended, but thanks to Yargen, she had a new one just beginning. Vi couldn't stop beaming from ear to ear, and she bounded back on deck in time to see the details of Risen coming into focus.

They anchored as close as possible to the port—close enough that Vi could see the ceremonial delegation that lined the docks, ready to receive them. Her heart raced as she took her position in the front of the rowboat that would take her ashore.

Elecia and Jax were behind her. Ellene and Jayme were behind them in a separate vessel. Vi worried the silver ring in the shape of a phoenix that she wore on the middle finger of her right hand. It was not Fiera's exact ring, but her father had commissioned it from old schematics found in the Le'Dan archives as a gift for her eighteenth birthday.

The rowboats pulled up to a low dock and Lumeria's guard was ready to receive them. Men offered her assistance, bowing their heads as they helped her out of the small boat. Somehow, Vi managed to disembark without stumbling, and she said a quiet thanks to the sun above.

Lumeria stood down the dock, hidden behind her veil and flowing fabrics. A line of honor guards stood on either side, creating a walkway for Vi. She approached stiffly and bowed low.

"Your highness, Queen Lumeria, it is an honor to meet you."

"It is," she replied in her whispering tones. "Or should I say, meet again? Which would you prefer?"

Vi straightened in shock. She had told Deneya years ago that she could share the truth with Lumeria in her reports, but… she hadn't been expecting Lumeria to actually *believe* the stories. Jax and Elecia arrived at that moment. She was prevented from questioning as they bowed.

"Your highness, I present Lady Elecia of the West and her husband, Lord Jax."

"Welcome to Meru, Lady Elecia and Lord Jax."

Vi turned to the next two. "This is Lady Ellene of the North—she is blessed with Lightspinning—and her honor guard, Jayme." Vi had changed Jayme's post before they set sail.

Even though things were better in this world, Vi still thought it was healthier for her and Jayme if the woman reported to Ellene. Besides, Vi didn't know where her travels would take her, and Jayme needed to remain on the same continent as her father as much as possible.

"Welcome." Lumeria raised her voice slightly, and said, "See that the dignitaries and their guards are shown to the palace."

Soldiers stepped forward, each one appointed to a different person. Vi watched as they paired up with her friends and family. There was not a single trace of foul play, which was a welcome change from the last time she'd stepped foot in Risen.

"I am to be your escort."

She met a familiar pair of blue eyes. "Deneya," Vi said with a sigh of relief, and threw her arms around the woman.

"This is a nice change from the last time I saw you on the *Stormfrost*. It's good to see you again," Deneya whispered as she held Vi in a crushing embrace. She pulled away abruptly and looked Vi up and down with narrowed eyes. "It really is *you* this time, isn't it?"

"Yes, it is. I'm goddess-free."

"Good. I mean, not good. Yargen don't smite me, I just like my friend. Now, Vi, follow me." Deneya stopped her rambling and started after the rest of the procession.

"I'm glad nothing horrible befell you for… you know." Vi stopped herself before she could say "stealing the Flame of Yargen."

"I'm just glad I made it back in time." Deneya and Vi had lost their communication token when Vi's body had been destroyed. Without it, they'd only been able to exchange a few letters, in which they didn't dare write too much. So there were still large gaps Vi was ready to have filled in between now and when they'd parted ways on the *Stormfrost* twenty years ago.

"In time for what?"

"To make sure my Queen knew of Lord Ulvarth's treachery." Deneya shook her head sadly in the face of Vi's shock. "Stealing the Flame of Yargen and framing the last Voice."

"Then the Voice survived?" she asked hopefully.

"Unfortunately, the woman had already been put to death."

Vi winced. She felt every bit of guilt and sorrow she should've felt on the *Stormfrost*.

"Tell me, at least, that Ulvarth faced the same fate."

"That's the greatest crime of them all. He's been stalling trials and leveraging favors from friends in high places to spare his neck from the executioner's block." Deneya scowled. "Lumeria is fed up and, for now, has locked him up and thrown away the key. Hopefully being away from public eye will cool his influence, and she can revisit the matter in the future."

"Good to know that justice for the wicked being elusive isn't exclusive to Solaris." Vi had spent the past few years entrenching herself in Solarin's politics. Some of the records she'd read—like a sham trial involving her own mother—made her skin crawl.

"Indeed." Deneya paused. "Are you all right with a detour?"

"If we have time?" Vi glanced back to Lumeria.

"She made sure we have time for this." Deneya stepped off into a side alley and Vi followed. It was right before the public crowds began to thicken, ready to watch and welcome the first dignitaries from the Dark Isle in centuries.

Deneya led her down the narrow alley to the back of building that lined the port. They climbed several flights of rusted stairs toward the top floor. Deneya stepped up to the door, opened it with a flourish, ushered Vi inside, and closed it behind her.

Inside was a simple room—a meeting space for traders, perhaps, judging by the tables and chairs. A row of windows overlooked the port and Vi could see her own vessel in the distance. The sun glistened off the sea, casting everything in a warm glow. Including the man who stood, framed by light.

Vi moved forward in a trance. She held her breath until he turned to face her, then exhaled his name like a prayer. "*Taavin.*"

"Vi Solaris." He still regarded her warily. It was the physical embodiment of the verbal distance he'd kept in all of their communications through the watch she now wore.

She approached slowly, as though he were an animal that might spook. "It's good to see you."

"Yes, well. I only agreed to this meeting because you said you had something for me." He was as stiff as Vi remembered him being the first few times they'd met. The memories brought a nostalgic smile to her lips, and that only seemed to frustrate him more.

Just as there had been a Vi born into this world, so there was a Taavin. But like all the other ninety-three Taavins, he lacked his memories.

Reaching up to her neck, Vi undid the chain there. She held out the silver pocket watch to him. Taavin accepted it with both hands, running his fingers over it.

"This… is what has my mark."

"Yes." Vi motioned to one of the sofas. "Let's sit?" He followed her, still fascinated by the watch.

"You said when we were in person, you would tell me how you got this."

"It will be easier to show you." She paused, hesitating. The crescent-shaped scar was missing on his face, and his hair was shorter than she remembered, but everything else about the man was the same. Should she force him to endure the memories of his past selves? Was it cruel to bestow that on him once more?

Give him his memories. Let me return to you, Vi.

"Show me… how?"

"I'd like to give you a choice," she said softly. "It will be a lot to take all at once. It might hurt. And once I give you this knowledge, I can never take it back."

He chuckled deeply. "I'm not afraid of whatever magic you have."

"Then you wish to know?"

"I did not help you come all this way to stop now."

Vi closed her eyes and took a deep breath. She opened them with purpose, looked him right in the eye, and said, "*Thrumsana.*"

Glyphs appeared from the watch in his hands—layers and layers of them. They swirled around him, filling the room with symbols that Vi could still understand even though Yargen was long gone from her body and mind. In every shining symbol, she saw an entire turn of the vortex written in the language of the gods. She saw joy and sorrow, victory and defeat—she saw herself and Taavin in every one.

Taavin dropped the watch and clutched his head. He trembled, groaning. Vi reached for him.

"It'll be all right." She wrapped her arms tightly around his shoulders. "It'll be over soon."

His shakes became violent but Vi only held him tighter. The magic began to shine brighter. Taavin's ragged gasps grew longer and longer. The watch had fallen to the floor and it now glowed white-hot from the endless release of magic. Vi clutched the man in her arms, watching as the watch cracked, released an exhale of fire like a dying breath, and then disintegrated to dark ash.

The magic faded and the room returned to normal. Taavin pushed her away roughly, staggering to the windows. He placed both hands on the panes and continued to inhale and exhale loudly.

Vi stood, waiting for his verdict. Would he truly remember her? Would he still be the Taavin she knew?

Would he hate her for the pain she'd forced him to endure one final time?

She dared to approach him. He still didn't turn. "Taavin?" she whispered, hoping and pleading at the same time.

He spun in place, looking at her with shining emerald eyes. Vi saw recognition. *He knew her.*

A surprised, strangled noise escaped her as something like a laugh of relief. Taavin moved for her and Vi stood in joyful shock. *This should be impossible.*

And yet, those were his arms wrapped around her. His hand on her face, in her hair. His lips pressed to hers—him kissing her as though they were still saying goodbye. Vi's fingers knotted in his clothes, tugging him closer still. She deepened the kiss, as if to remind him that this was *hello.*

The world wasn't ending any longer, though it still contained its share of problems. Light and darkness, chaos and order—everything was precariously balanced. Vi knew better than most that every action was what kept them—all of them—from slipping into despair.

A kiss couldn't change any of that. A kiss wouldn't ensure the happiness of Meru and the Solaris Empire, and all the people within for years to come. A kiss wouldn't be the end of the brutal dance of light and darkness.

But if one kiss could, this kiss would be it.

Get a BONUS SCENE!

Want more Vi and Taavin?

Want a sneak peek of where the Air Awakens world will head
in the next novel set in this universe?

Head to my website and subscribe to my newsletter to get a
BONUS SCENE that takes place 2 years after the Epilogue:

http://elisekova.com/vortex-bonus-scene

WHAT'S NEXT IN THE AIR AWAKENS WORLD?

A TRIAL OF SORCERERS

ICE IS IN HER BLOOD.

Eira Landan was the most unwanted Waterrunner in the Tower of Sorcerers until the day she decided to compete for a spot in the Tournament of Five Kingdoms. She knew going against the best sorcerers in the Empire wouldn't be easy. Eira expected a fight. She didn't expect that not everyone would make it out alive.

A new young adult, epic fantasy series filled with magic, action, rivalry, and love.

Don't miss out. Lean more:
http://elisekova.com/a-trial-of-sorcerers/

There's even more to the Air Awakens world! Flip to page 996 to see other series you can read right now.

APPENDIᕰ

About the world of Vortex Chronicles

Want even more about the world of Air Awakens than what's in this book?

Visit Elise's website at:
http://elisekova.com/books/
to see all of her titles.

PRONOUNCIATION GUIDE

There is no "wrong way" to pronounce any words in this book. However, if you would like to know how Elise Kova pronounces some of the trickier words and names...

Arwin: Are-win
Curo: Cure-oh
Deneya: D-eh-knee-ya
Durroe: Duh-row
Ellene: Uh-lil-een
Halleth: Hall-eh-th
Ivin: eh-V-in
Jax: Jacks
Larrk: Lark
Maph: Maff
Meru: Muh-rew
Noct: N-ah-kt
Radia: Rah-de-ah
Ruta: Roota
Sot: Sought
Taavin: T-ah-v-in
Tempre: Te-m-pray
Toff: Tough
Vi: V-eye
Xieh: Zay

COMMON TERMS

Definitions to common terms found in the Air Awakens world. Presented alphabetically.

• **Affinity** - term used to describe the type of magic a sorcerer has
• **Affinities of the Self** - secondary powers attuned with each elemental affinity
• **Aires** - term for the world, used outside of the Solaris Empire
• **Awoken** - when a sorcerer's magic is opened in full, giving them access to their channel
• **Broken Moon** - the symbol of the Tower of Sorcerers, stylized as a dragon curled in on itself and split in two, each side off-set
• **Channel** - the source of a sorcerer's magic that can be "opened" to give them better/easier access to their magic
• **Commons** - a person without magic
• **Firebearer** - a sorcerer with fire magic
• **Groundbreaker** - a sorcerer with earth magic
• **Manifest** - when a sorcerer's magic first shows itself, usually in a small way
• **Sorcerer** - a person with magic
• **Tower of Sorcerers, aka, "The Tower"** - a school of magic in Solarin, capital of the Solaris Empire, attached to the Imperial Castle
• **Waterrunner** - a sorcerer with water magic
• **White Death** - a plague that causes the diseased's skin to turn hard, pale, white eyes, madness, and ultimately death
• **Windwalker** - a sorcerer with wind magic

ELEMENTAL AFFINITIES

In the Solaris Empire, there are four elemental affinities among sorcerers. Every sorcerer can only perform magic within their affinity.

While magic is not in the blood, many families share the same affinity and the magic between family members of the same affinity is usually similar. However, two sorcerers can give birth to a commons and the reverse is also true.

Affinity: Firebearer
Element: Fire
Most Common Region: The West/Mhashan
Affinity of the Self: Future Sight

Affinity: Groundbreaker
Element: Earth
Most Common Region: The North/Shaldan
Affinity of the Self: Healing

Affinity: Waterrunner
Element: Water
Most Common Region: The South/Lyndum
Affinity of the Self: Listening to the Whispers of the Past

Affinity: Windwalker
Element: Wind
Most Common Region: The East/Cyven
Affinity of the Self: Out of Body Projection

LIGHTSPINNING

Lightspinning is a form of magic found beyond the Solaris Empire/Dark Isle. This magic can be utilized in any number of ways based on intent and the words its caster uses. The words are said to have been given from the Goddess Yargen.

The chants Lightspinners use have a structure of: [High level Discipline] [Secondary to the Discipline] [Clarification] [Any Personal Words of Power from the Goddess]

Words of Power

High Level Discipline: Halleth (Heal)
Secondary Word(s): Ruta (Mending of Flesh), Maph (Stint Pain)
Clarification Word(s): Sot (Inner), Toff (Outer)

High Level Discipline: Juth (Destruction)
Secondary Word(s): Calt (Shatter), Starys (Incinerate), Mariy (Destroy Magic)
Clarification Word(s): —

High Level Discipline: Durroe (Deceive)
Secondary Word(s): Sallvas (Sound), Watt (Eyes)
Clarification Word(s): Curo (Create a New Sound), Tempre (Mask a Sound), Radia (Hide/Conceal - Eyes), Ivin (Create an Illusion)

High Level Discipline: Mysst (Craft)
Secondary Word(s): Xieh (Shield), Soto (Weapons)
Clarification Word(s): Larrk (Sword), Gotha (Bow), Tonc (Spear), Sut (Axe)

High Level Discipline: Kot (Movement)
Secondary Word(s): Sorre (Push), Sidee (Pull)
Clarification Word(s): —

LIGHTSPINNING (*Continued*)

High Level Discipline: Narro (Acts of the Mind)
Secondary Word(s): Hath (Activate Communication Mark),
Samasha (Awaken the Words)
Clarification Word(s): Loreth (Imprint a Communication Mark)

Personal Words of Power

Deneya
Wein (Stone Skin)

Taavin
Chronot (Slow), Dupot (Enhance), Maath (Mute Magic), Uncose
(Expose Truth)

Vi
Hoolo (Stabilize/Elongate), Thrumsana (Awaken Truth), Rohko (Barrier)

Words of the Elfin'ra

Vah'deh (Mind Control)

MAP OF THE SOLARIS EMPIRE

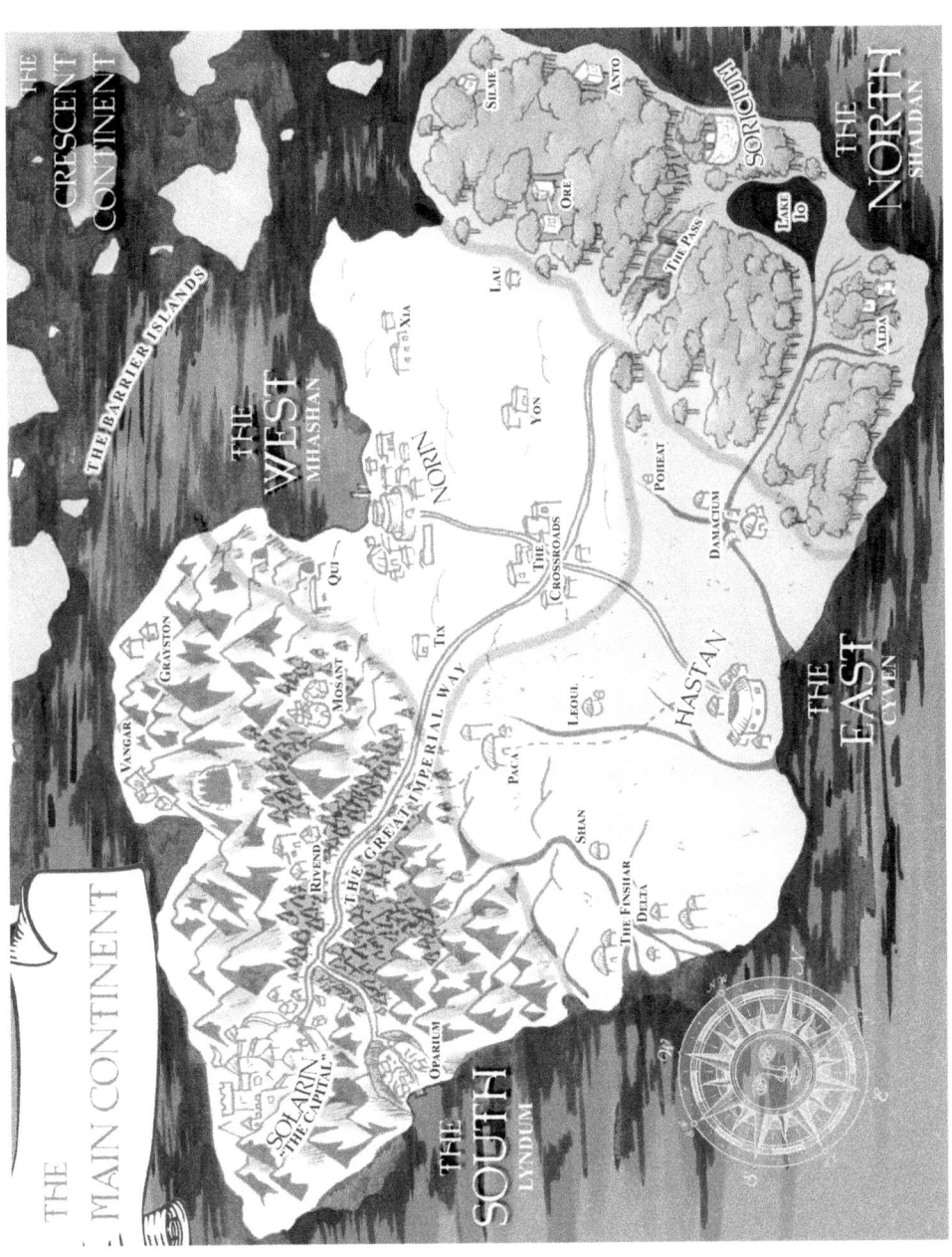

SEHRA'S MAP OF THE WORLD

DETAILED MAP OF MERU

THE STORY OF DIA

Dia was born when a falling star was caught in the boughs of the tallest tree in Soricum. As she fell, the branches swayed and shook, bestowing life and a mortal form on her. Her skin was made of the bark of the tree, and her hair shone with the godly stardust still captured within it.

She healed the sick and taught the first clerics in Soricium how to use the earth to make salves, potions, and poisons with the knowledge the gods blessed her with. She showed how to craft the first sky cities, cutting through the branches with a magic axe bestowed on her by the Goddess Yargen and rebuilding them effortlessly. She carved Lake Io, the reservoir for all of the North's fresh water.

However, as time went on, Dia began to feel distanced from the changing people.

Their magic was far less potent than hers, and some were born without it at all. Dia vowed to find a way to ensure the magic of her people remained. Before she wandered into the jungles of Shaldan in search of the wisdom of the gods, she left behind two things to her people.

The first was her daughter, the first Chieftain, born from a seed of what was now known as the Mother Tree.

The second was her axe. When Dia departed, her daughter sealed the axe away, vowing that none were of pure enough body and mind to use it other than Dia herself.

Some say that Dia truly found the wisdom of the gods in the jungles and she continues to wander them to this day. That her power was so great she found the antidote to life's greatest poison: death.

The last time someone claimed to see the woman, Dia looked no older than any prior time. The stars still shone in her hair, her skin remained firm and weathered like the bark of the tree she came from.

ABOUT THE AUTHOR

ELISE KOVA is a USA Today bestselling author. She enjoys telling stories of fantasy worlds filled with magic and deep emotions. She lives in Florida and, when not writing, can be found playing video games, drawing, chatting with readers on social media, or daydreaming about her next story.

She invites readers to get first looks, giveaways, and more by subscribing to her newsletter at: http://elisekova.com/subscribe

Visit her on the web at:
http://elisekova.com/
https://tiktok.com/@elisekova
https://www.instagram.com/elise.kova/
https://www.facebook.com/AuthorEliseKova/

See all of Elise's titles on her webiste:
http://elisekova.com/books/

Or her Amazon page:
http://author.to/EliseKova

Vi's story culminates alongside Vhalla's epic tale of magic, romance, and trumph. Go on Vhalla's journey now in Air Awakens and see how Vi's actions affected Vhalla from her point of view.

THE
AIR AWAKENS
SERIES

A library apprentice... A sorcerer princes... And an unbreakable magic bond. The rare elemental magic that lies in Vhalla Yarl will not only change the Empire's future, but the heart of its Crown Prince. Perfect for readers who want magic and romance!

Series complete!

"I read the full series in a just two days. The worlds was thrilling and the characters endearing... Recommend for fans of Sarah J. Maas and high fantasy"

- Kristen, 5 Star Amazon Review

Find out how Jax became known as
The Crown's Dog in...

THE
GOLDEN GUARD
TRILOGY

Three stories filled with mystery, romance, and adventure. Learn
how the most illustrious fighting force of the Air Awakens world
— the Golden Guard — came to be.

Series complete!

"These books were great! I wish I knew the back story of
these characters before reading the other books. It added a lot
of dimensions to the character interactions, and it leaves me
wanting more!"

- Jessie, 5 Star Amazon Review

ACKNOWLEDGEMENTS

VORTEX VISIONS

THE MAN—In you, lives everything. You are my muse, my support, my inspiration, and the font of my worlds. Never-mind the tangible things you do, such as keeping me alive when I spend too long in the writing cave. Thank you for giving me the love and support that I thought was relegated only to magical princesses in fantasy worlds.

REBECCA—My work wife, my literary other half, without you and the countless hours you invested, this book would not have existed in the most literal sense. I would've never seen the exact point this story needed to begin and would have never written the contents within. Your mark is on these pages alongside mine and I couldn't have asked for a better editorial partner. I can't wait to continue to grow alongside you.

MOM & DAD—Thank you for reading my manuscripts time and again, for buying my books, for your endless support, and for being the best "cruise team" an author and a daughter could ever dream of.

MEREDITH—For all the times I talked to you about this story over a glass of wine… it's finally here! I love you immeasurably, sister.

NICK, AMANDA, & SABRINA—I couldn't have asked for more supportive first readers. Thank you three so very much for all the help you've given me and being so patient through countless rounds of revisions and me talking your ears off about productive things (like story) and the not so productive things (like my paranoia).

HETAL, JERRICA, & EMMALEE—You three were my pinch hitters, the ones who came in when I was worried it was impossible for me to get a fresh opinion. Thank you so much for your initial reads and feedback. I hope you can see, here, how the manuscript was better because of your eyes and thoughts.

KAT, LIZ, & AMBER—Thank you so much for being my final sets of eyes, the last group of guards standing between me and publishing errors.

LUX—Weeks of writing sprints together made this book happen. Every word written, you were there for. You are the writing partner an author dreams about. Supportive, constructive, and always there when I need to sprint. Thank you for your feedback and cheerleading when I needed it most.

KATIE—I hope you know that all the times we talk about story and prose helps me too, immensely. Thank you for reading, giving me your thoughts, and just being the best friend a woman could ask for.

DANIELLE—My dear friend and author sister, you're incredible in every way and have been there for me from such an early point. Every moment I needed to vent, you were there.

MICHELLE—Thank you so much for helping me not only from a story and craft perspective, but also from a business perspective. My career and stories are forever changed by the insights you've given me.

SUSAN—I count my blessings constantly that I get to call you my friend, thank you for helping me personally and professionally time and again.

THE TOWER GUARD—I cannot thank every person in my street team enough. It's because of each of you that I can bring my stories to life. It's because of your help that they get out into the world. For all the ways you've supported me personally, and professionally, thank you. Please know that I see you and all you do and I am forever grateful.

MY ORIGINAL FICTIONPRESS READERS—I don't know if any of you will see this... but if you're someone who was there from the start, I'm so excited to finally share the "second part" to the story I began with you years ago. Thank you for believing in me then, so I could give you this now.

COUNTLESS OTHER AUTHORS, BLOGGERS, AND READERS—I may not call you out by name here (because I can be wretched at remembering names, and acknowledgements can only be so long). But know that I realize how blessed I am to grace your inboxes, your social media timelines, and your shelves. Just because you aren't listed here doesn't mean you aren't important to me—doesn't mean I don't recognize the support you give me. Thank you for letting me be a part of this community.

CRYSTAL CAGED

My Readers — I want to start by acknowledging all of you. Without you, there would be no story, no books, and no world of Air Awakens. Some of you were with me from the start and have seen this world evolve and grow. Or, you may have just joined me with Vortex Chronicles. However long you've been reading my work, thank you. This book, this world, is truly for each and every one of you and it wouldn't have happened without you with me every step of the way.

The Man — From late, sleepless nights, to early starts, you're with me every step of the way. Without your support both professionally and personally I wouldn't be where I am now. Thank you for all the hours you spent with me, talking through story ideas, listening to me as I struggled to find the best narrative path forward, and helping me with your insights. Thank you for pulling me off the kitchen floor when I was down, or pulling me away from my computer when I couldn't take anymore. You are truly my muse and my light.

Rebecca — I asked you to push me, and you delivered. I will never be able to express appropriate gratitude for your patience and help throughout this series. This story evolved so much thanks to you. You challenged me to be better and work harder. I greatly appreciate everything you did to help make this story what it is.

Michelle — You are an incredible friend and colleague in this crazy author career. I appreciate your insights. I love your candor. And I am so inspired by you. Thank you for talking me out of the initial terrible ending I had for this series and pushing me to make something much, much better.(I hope you enjoyed what I decided on!)

Kate — Thank you for your help and support throughout this series. You came in at the eleventh hour and turned things around with a speed I didn't think possible. I appreciate everything you've done for me.

Danielle — You have seen every high and low, good day and bad with this series, and you stuck with me through all of it. I could not have asked for, or dreamed of, a better friend in the publishing world. Thank you for all your cheer-leading, insight, and support along the way.

The Noble Order of Female Fantasy Authors — Ladies, you have become a cornerstone of my day to day survival. You are each unique, incredibly talented, and profoundly supportive. Thank you so much for talking me through the good times and bad, for being there to sprint with, and for being the best friends one could hope for.

Mary and Sarah — I know this manuscript changed a lot from the one you beta read for me. Please know, in part, it was due to your feedback! Thank you for helping me make my work better. I really appreciated all of your insights.

Amanda — From arranging swaps, to general support, you are always there. I don't know how you do it all AND remain such a beautiful soul, but here we are. Thank you for everything. I truly appreciate all you do for me both personally and professionally.

Lux — You're such a lovely person; it has been my supreme delight to sprint with you throughout this series. I hope we can motivate and inspire each other for years to come. I am honored to call you friend.

Devin, Mia, and Veronica — Thank you all for your continued support of me, my work, and my career. Over the past year you have all helped look for ways for me to get my work out into the world. Hopefully, we can do the same with Vortex Chronicles and many more books in the years to come.

The Tower Guard — Last, but certainly not least… To all of my Tower Guard members, you are so essential for me to keep continuing on as an author. Knowing you are in my corner, having you all to laugh and cry with, has really made this career such a profound experience. Thank you for all you've done in helping me get my books out into the world. Here's to the next one!